Fay Sampson was born in Devonport but grew up in the fishing and farming village of Lympstone. She had her first children's novel published in 1975 and since then has had a further eighteen published, as well as two educational books. She has taught adult education classes in writing and visits schools and other groups as 'writer in the community'. She divides her time between Tedburn St Mary and Birmingham, is married and has two grown-up children.

*Daughter of Tintagel*

'A stirring and ingenious recounting of legend' *Liverpool Daily Post*

'Just when you thought every angle had been tackled concerning Arthur and the Matter of Britain, an author comes up with yet another fresh approach. Fay Sampson has brought her characters alive, with feeling and fine skill' *Paperback Inferno*

'A very well written historical novel' *Brumgroup News*

# Daughter of Tintagel

*Comprising*
## Wise Woman's Telling
## White Nun's Telling
## Black Smith's Telling
## Taliesin's Telling
## Herself

Fay Sampson

**HEADLINE**

First published in this omnibus edition in 1992
by HEADLINE BOOK PUBLISHING PLC

This omnibus edition was originally published in five volumes in hardback and paperback: Wise Woman's Telling in 1989 by HEADLINE BOOK PUBLISHING PLC; White Nun's Telling in 1989 by HEADLINE BOOK PUBLISHING PLC; Black Smith's Telling in 1990 by HEADLINE BOOK PUBLISHING PLC; Taliesin's Telling in 1991 by HEADLINE BOOK PUBLISHING PLC; Herself in 1992 by HEADLINE BOOK PUBLISHING PLC

10 9 8 7 6 5 4 3 2 1

ISBN 0 7472 3894 4

Typeset by Medcalf Type Ltd, Bicester, Oxon

Printed and bound in Great Britain by
HarperCollins Manufacturing, Glasgow

HEADLINE BOOK PUBLISHING PLC
Headline House
79 Great Titchfield Street
London W1P 7FN

# Contents

The Convent of the White Nuns

The Sisters

Tintagel Island

Barras Nose

Bossiney Haven

Tintagel Haven

The Mother's Hole

Causeway

Bossiney

The Grave of Gorlois

To Dimiliock

Tintagel

0  5  10
miles

The Western Sea

Camlann

Bodmin Moor

Padstow

R. Camel

Dozmary Pool

Celliwig

R. Fowey

Convent of the White Nuns

Bodmin Moor

Peter McClure 1991

# Author's Note

*In physics, Dark Matter forms an unseen world that is the inverse of the matter we observe. The two were created to exist in equal proportions. Together they hold the universe in balance. But when they come into contact, the result is mutual destruction. Morgan's story is the Dark Matter of Britain.*

The name Tintagel, formerly believed to be Norman, may be much older and Cornish. If so, it should be pronounced with a hard g. One possible meaning is 'the strong place where the two currents meet'.

The Tintagel of legend is a fortress, the birthplace of Arthur and the seat of King Mark of Cornwall. The archaeologists who excavated it believed that in Arthurian times it was in fact a Celtic monastery. Others have challenged this. The headland was certainly occupied in the fifth century, but as yet there is no conclusive evidence of its function.

Legend makes Morgan Le Fay the wife of Urien and the mother of Owain. The historical Urien Rheged and his son Owain flourished in North Britain in the late sixth century, some three generations after the suggested dates for Arthur. Urien's kinsman and neighbour was Gwendoleu, whose bard was Myrddin. Taliesin was Urien's bard; we still have some of his poems. But Taliesin himself became a figure of legend and later poems of a more marvellous nature were attributed to him. I have honoured a centuries-old tradition and telescoped the history of the sixth century to bring them all within the lifetime of Morgan.

I am indebted to a host of sources, translators and commentators. Some of these will be found listed on pages 823–4. But my greatest gratitude is to the late Lucy Paton for her *Studies in the Fairy Mythology of Arthurian Romance* in which she collected with love and learning all the Morgan material. Other scholars have added to and sometimes reinterpreted her work, but not replaced it.

# Wise Woman's Telling

## Book One
## in the sequence
## Daughter of Tintagel

**To Jack**

# Chapter One

It was the worst thing we ever did when we forgot Morgan, that night above all nights. Many's the time I've wept for it since. And that's nothing to the harm that will come of it yet.

And such a night it was. The gale screeching like the Black Hunt across the sky, and the sea howling up at us out of the caves around Bossiney Haven. And the rain! I can feel the cold of it stabbing into my joints to this very day. You'd have thought the Mothers' own waters had broken in the heavens above and they were all three of them screaming in labour.

But I couldn't close the door and get to bed. Not that night. Every door and window had to stand open, never mind the rain, and every knot let loose. There mustn't be anything closed or tied till the baby was safely born.

So I sat in that cruel draught, with my thighs wide open to the night, and holding the lips of my own blood-hole apart, though it had been dry these many years. Easy, easy, I was grunting. I was casting the spells of opening, and at the same time heaving and groaning, just as if I was bringing the child I'd never had into the world.

Morgan wasn't the only one they'd forgotten, my Lady Ygerne and her fine Uther Pendragon, that liked to call himself King of all the Britons. In Gorlois's time she'd have wanted me beside her, where I'd been when her three daughters were born. It was my craft she'd have trusted to bring her and the baby home through it then, never mind the midwife. But Gorlois was dead, and I was out of favour. Maybe King Uther thought I was only good for getting girls.

That's all Morgan was to him, that strutting fool of a man. A little girl. The youngest of Lord Gorlois's brood of daughters. But he should have known better, after what he'd seen. Only nine she might be, but he could hardly pretend she was too young to understand what had happened to them all. Though in fairness none of us guessed what was in her mind even then, though we found out soon, to all our cost.

Nine months they had been forgetting Morgan, King Uther Pendragon and his new queen, Ygerne. Queen before her husband's body was cold in the grave and the worms had hardly begun to nibble his parts. Nine months those two had petted and pawed each other for everyone to see, though not so much lately as they had done at first. Well, not on her side, anyway. But that didn't stop Uther Pendragon from having his pleasure wherever he could find it. And now her time had come, her hour of reckoning for that first night that broke Morgan's heart, and the lamps were burning late in our queen's bower. They were busy now. We could see shadows passing before the light. The baby was pushing to be born.

And all this time that little maid Morgan stood in the doorway with her wet face turned to the storm, and there was nothing I could do to shift her.

'Come away in, my lover,' I begged. 'You'll catch your death of cold, and it will be my back that pays for it with a beating, not yours. Tomorrow will be bad enough as it is, me crippled up with the rheumatism already, and sitting with my feet in a puddle like a leaky boat, without having you ill as well. Come to bed now, there's a good maid, and snuggle under the blankets.'

She never even heard me. I could only see her back. Still, she was. You would have thought she was lifeless, like a storm-struck tree. Hour after hour she'd stood, with her face to the rain and the lights and the bustle. And never a word she spoke or a muscle stirred. But she was living, all right. I could feel a spirit buried inside her that made the rest of the world seem half dead. It made me afraid, I can tell you.

I am an old woman now and I wasn't so young even then, for I had been nurse to Morgan's two sisters that were grown girls, and to their mother before that. Those two were lying there in the darkness under the furs. I could tell Elaine was sleeping because she was snoring like a pig, though before another year had turned she might be sweating and straining with a baby of her own. Pretty and plump and pink she was, and no trouble to any of us. Though not so innocent as she looked, either. She could see further than most. She was always her mother's favourite, and the queen had whispered her what she knew. Mother to daughter. Woman to her own blood. But I had no daughter of my womb. Or son, either.

So it made me cross, hearing her snoring. Young though she was, she could have helped me a little if she'd wanted to, and Margawse too, though that one was newer in the knowledge than Elaine. It was their own mother in pain, wasn't it? But there, they were neither of them wives yet, and it was no work for maids. And they'd no more call than Morgan to help the Pendragon's child into the world.

It was Margawse now who lifted her head. She cried, 'What's the matter? Is something wrong? Has she dropped the baby yet?'

I could smell the excitement strong on her, like a soaked breech-cloth, and I thought, not for the first time either, that it was time she was married and away from that place. The eldest, Elaine, was betrothed already to King Nentres. Uther had seen to that. A handsome queen she'd make. And a wise one too, if you take my meaning. Margawse had come to her womanhood only lately, with no father of her own. And that was a dangerous thing for all of us. I had seen her up against a wall with Uther Pendragon, that day in the treasury. He wasn't the man – for all he called himself a Christian king – to care that he was married to her mother now. He took what he wanted, as we had cause to know. And Margawse was not the maiden to say no – if maiden indeed she was, which I very much doubted.

But what was I to do? Those girls were too headstrong for me. And their mother's head was so turned she couldn't see anyone but the king. Yet they called her a wise woman, Ygerne. And I should know, for it was not her own mother that had the whispering of that one. It's not every peasant woman can claim a queen for her daughter, by the Mothers' blood. They say it was Merlyn brewed the spell that tricked her, and I don't doubt he did, but in a man's world it's the man's story the bards tell. I've often wondered if there was more to it than that. Of course, I wasn't there when she went to the king's fine court, my little Cornish lady. But when she and my Lord Gorlois came galloping home with the king hard on their heels, there was more than a little look of Margawse in her face. She wasn't ill-pleased with herself. And why the king should be so hot after her, when he could have had any lady in Britain for the asking, it's not for me to tell. She never went high in our mysteries. Not as high as me, if I do boast. Still, she did know enough for that. And she wanted to be loved. She wanted a son. Best of all, she wanted a son that might be king.

But she and her daughters had slept in Tintagel on a terrible night, when the spirits were abroad. And in those days Tintagel was a women's place. Merlyn wove his own magic, oh, yes! But it's my belief that under the rock the Mothers were laughing at the lot of us. And true it is that none of us have been the same since that time.

So the night went on, cold-footed as a toad, and Margawse fell back to grumbling.

'I'm freezing. Give me another cover, Gwennol. I'll die soon.'

'You've had every one there is. There's only this old blanket I've got about my shoulders, and I'm not giving you that. I'm as damp as a ditch in February, as it is, and lucky to live till then, sitting here shivering with the door open and the bed-chamber like a bog.'

'Make Morgan come to bed then. Or shut the door and leave her outside.'

She knew I couldn't shut any opening till the baby was born. But she didn't care.

I was past arguing with either of them. I was too damp and cold and tired even to move my jaws. My head was so heavy, I'd have given a month of my life to lay it down and sleep. But I had power to use for a birthing, even for those that didn't want it now. I could still show them. And then, I daren't leave Morgan to watch alone. Only nine years old she was, and there wasn't one of us could bend her to our will. Not even if we had beaten her. Least of all then. Her father was gone and he was the only one that she'd ever let touch her. There was nothing any of us could do for her but wake and watch. And there was no one left to do it but me. Her father was dead, and her mother had forgotten her.

But I'll swear to this. I had never whispered Morgan, not so much as a word. Not then. That was her mother's place. A year before she'd bespoken Elaine, and then Margawse, when Uther Pendragon was coming. But never Morgan. To tell you the truth, my lady was more than a little frightened of Margawse and Morgan, her own daughters. But for all I believed her, I knew there was power in that child already.

4

And when I think how it must have come to her, through no human being, it makes my hair creep sometimes.

A gust of wind slammed the door back against the wall. It blew a stink of wet wool and leather across my face. I shuffled back, trying to get out of the draught. But Morgan never moved, though the gale was dashing rain into her eyes and there was black water swilling about her feet.

An ugly, drenched scrap of a thing she was. As thin and draggled as a black kitten that's just been born. To see her like that you would never have thought she would have grown into a beautiful queen. Margawse now, you couldn't miss her, with her red hair and her skin like buttermilk. Or Elaine, that everyone said was the prettiest of the three, though I never saw much in her myself. But Morgan had always been a strange maid. 'Like a crow in a thunderstorm,' Uther Pendragon said when he first set eyes on her. Yet she had a way with men when she wanted to. The way she used to smile at her father.

And then I caught sight of something fluttering, pale as moths in the darkness, down Morgan's skirt. I peered closer and then I let out a scream. Her little hands were twisting her girdle, tying it tight, knot after knot, over and over. No wonder that baby was slow in coming.

'You little black witch!'

The words were out of my mouth before I knew what I was saying. I tore her crooked fingers from the cord and tugged out those cruel knots till the whole thing fell free. I felt those tight cramps in my belly moving loose and I could breathe deep and strong again. She didn't try to stop me. Just laughed at me with her little white teeth, though never a sound she made.

Well, I daren't take my eyes off her after that, though it made them swim, peering through that murk. I was nearly crying from the fire in my joints and the icy cold in my feet. Then Morgan let out a gasp that was almost a shriek. In spite of my rheumatism I was in that doorway as fast as I could move, never mind the mud squelching under my feet. She clutched at my dress with the bones of her skinny white hands.

'Is it born, Gwennol? Is it here?'

We heard Queen Ygerne cry out louder than the scream of the wind, and there was a thin high wail through the rain and the darkness. He had come. The baby was born alive.

For a moment I forgot Morgan. I am an old woman that never bore a child. Any woman's baby starts a hunger in me, and a queen's baby is more precious than most. And if what I guessed about Ygerne was true, then in a way that child came partly from my doing. Almost my own blood it felt. Then I remembered Morgan. I looked down to see how she was bearing it – and she was gone. I'll swear it was only a moment I forgot her. But I had lost her, like a black cat in the darkness.

Then someone lifted the curtain. I saw the queen's bed, gold in the candlelight. A woman ran out, shouting to us all, 'It's a boy!' And there was Morgan, running towards the light, with her skirt sticking to her knees.

A shadow came between her and the doorway. I can see it now. A man's shadow. You couldn't mistake the shape of big Uther Pendragon, striding into my lady's bedchamber. We saw his shadow huge across the curtain. He was like a giant bending over the bed. Over his wife and son, that should have been the wife and son of Gorlois, Morgan's father. We saw him lift that golden child in his arms before the door slammed shut.

A boy. And Gorlois's little maid was left outside in the dark and the storm. He never even noticed her.

'Morgan!' I cried, though I could hardly hear myself for the wind. I knew it would be no use. She had gone. What hope had I got of catching her, old and stiff as I was, and the rain fit to wash us all out to sea? I knew what she was going to do, poor little scrap, for child she was still, and could still be hurt. She would make her body suffer till it was as bitter as her soul. She'd gone beyond my help now. The darkness had taken her. And we may all suffer for that.

# Chapter Two

She was happy once, in her own way. Though it seems so long ago now that I sometimes wonder if I didn't dream it.

It was only her father she loved. He had the power to swing her off to the Blessed Isles with one hug of his big strong arms about her. And the same power to hurt her. Like a puppy that hasn't got the sense to get out from under its master's feet. She could be sharp with her teeth like a puppy too, but she'd come crawling back as if she was wagging her little tail and begging him to love her again. That was a bitter lesson she had to learn: to make herself be loved and not to love back. There isn't a woman in Britain has learned it better.

It was hunting that her father loved best. So nothing would satisfy Morgan but she must go with him. She was riding into the forest with the hunt almost as soon as she could sit. When other little maids were crawling about the floor playing with dolls, Morgan would be out with the men. I remember the day she came back, her face smeared with blood and her eyes shining like the dew on May-Morning. That was her first kill. I warned her father then.

In those days one of the huntsmen would carry her on his saddle in front of him. Not Gorlois, of course. If she had been a son he might have done. But my lord was too proud a spearman to slow his horse or spoil his aim for the sake of a scrap of a girl-child. It was enough for her that he let her follow him. She would twist her fingers in the horse's mane and crouch down low, as if she was whispering in his ears and urging him on faster.

My lady and Morgan's two sisters, now, they'd ride in the greenwood if the sun was shining. Sidesaddle, like the fine ladies they were — or wanted to be. And the ponies tricked out with bells and baubles that you'd have thought would have frightened every hare and deer for miles around, so loud they jingled. And their gowns and their skirts spread over the horses' rumps so that the light would catch the silken embroidery and the gold. And you can't go dashing under branches and through briars like that without tearing your gay gowns to shreds and messing your pretty hair.

But Morgan, now, she would hunt in any weather. Though if I'd been her mother I wouldn't have let her. But who would listen to old Gwennol? I was just their old nurse, too slow in the joints and too quick with her tongue. By daylight, anyhow. True, I had a name for a powerful skill with charms, but that was no more than women's medicine, or so the men thought. I didn't want Gorlois to know any different. But my lady did, for all her fine airs. She ought to have

7

listened to me then. She'd heeded me once, when she was younger, or she wouldn't be called wise now.

Morgan was eight summers when her father let her hunt on her own pony. I saw them set off that day. She was gripping it between her knees that were as white as two peeled hazel wands, and not much thicker. Riding astride, she was, like a boy, with the skirt of her dress tucked up so high on her thighs it was hardly decent, even for a child so small, with all those men around. But that summer there was never a thought of such a thing in her little mind. Why should there be? It came to her too soon as it was, and from those that should have watched over her to keep her from harm. She'd have worn breeches like a boy then, if I'd have let her. She knew she was all the son her father would ever have. But she was never anything like a boy. She was too fey for that.

I watched them go, with the hounds and the horns and the spears tossing in the sunlight. And my heart was heavy with fear for her. I was twisting my apron between my hands like fishermen's mothers when they stand on the beach, watching the boats fighting their way back to harbour against a gale. But she was laughing, and her father with her. That great, blackbearded spearman and his little black-braided daughter. A giant with a dwarf. Well, they always say giants are stupid. It would be enough for me if he brought her safely back to us.

The hunt turned their backs on the sea and the sunlight, and rode in under those great branches of the oak forest. All their brave colours and bright harness were swallowed up in that old twilight. Hours, they could be lost before anyone caught a sight of them again, except for what lived there. That made me shudder. Gorlois didn't know the half of it. There's places there, old pools and bogs and circles of standing oaks, I wouldn't go near even in daylight without strong spells to guard me. There's times and seasons for places like those, and a right way of coming to them if you want to get away again with your life and your wits. And often as I have been, I'd never have had the courage till I'd drunk that cup that makes me more than old Nurse Gwennol when the moon is up. So I wondered how long it might be before I'd catch a glimpse of them again, up on the clear ridge where the road runs past to Padstow. And it wouldn't be the first time if they came out of that forest fewer than they went in.

We women were left in Bossiney. It was a pleasant enough place — a clutter of houses, a hall big enough for a hundred warriors, and a wall round them. That's all it was then, before the king moved in. Bright sea and sky in front of us, black woods behind. It wasn't that Gorlois didn't have stronger forts in higher places, but what would have been the point in living up there and making ourselves more uncomfortable than we had to? They'd made him Duke of Cornwall, hadn't they? Leader of all their war-hosts. Who had he to fear this side of the Tamar?

But I had plenty to worry about, even if he hadn't. And worse to me than any Saxons.

All day I feared and fretted. Margawse screamed at me for a clumsy idiot when I tugged a tangle of the red hair clean out of her scalp with

8

the comb. I dropped a jug of milk, and trailed my skirt through the fire so we almost had the hall in flames about our ears. And all the time my ears were listening for the horn and my eyes watching for the first horses breaking out of the trees.

Like the little luck-cat she was then, she came back from it alive, and laughing as if she had been in paradise. And her knife still covered in blood.

Her father was mightily pleased with her too. I could see that, and for once I was glad for her. He rode up beside her, his big horse towering over her little pony, and he clapped his hand on her shoulder so hard that she almost fell under the blow.

'Well, Gwennol, what do you think of that? She's galloped all the way across the Alan and up to Caer Delinuth, hunting the biggest boar I've seen in a twelvemonth. And she came in at the last in time to have her knife in his side with all the others, before he'd done squealing. Look, she's got his ear to show you. A boy couldn't have done much better on his first ride.'

He grinned and hugged her to him, and she smiled at him, so happily, it made my heart turn over to watch it. I've never had a child smile at me like that, for all I've nursed so many and broken my heart over one of them. But it's not the same as your own.

I suppose that made me a little sharp.

'Poor lamb! Just look at her. She's almost dead with weariness. We'll have her in bed for a month before she's fit to ride again.'

And I wasn't far from the truth, for she must have driven herself as hard as a grown man. When he took his great hand away from her shoulder, she fairly fell into my arms off her pony, and it was all I could do to hold her upright and set her safely on her feet.

The gown she'd kilted up fell back to her feet, all ripped and splattered with mud as it was. And when she put up her hand she couldn't stop it from shaking now. She picked off the ribbon I'd braided her hair close against her neck with, so she shouldn't hang herself in the forest. She always hated to be bound, and she shook her black hair free.

He saw her then for what she was. A drooping little girl, filthy, tired out, and never as strong in health as any of us would have wished. He knew she could never be the son he wanted. He swore by names I'd never heard him use and didn't think he knew, and he turned his back on her. He flung himself from his horse and strode off to his wife, all splashed with blood as he was. And it wasn't love he'd be pushing himself into her for.

Poor, foolish man. I knew what drove him, while I picked my baby up in my arms. He was praying that Morgan wouldn't be the last child he spawned. And I saw by the look in her eyes as they followed him that she knew what he was thinking too.

9

# Chapter Three

Summers end in killing-time, when the scythe's in the corn and the hare hides herself in the last stand till the reaper throws his sickle at it and there's blood in the stubble.

We drank the harvest home, and those that hadn't got their bellies big at May-time had another go. But we were hardly sober before those whetstones were shrieking again, and it wasn't sickles they were brightening this time. The men were off to war again.

I've never seen a Saxon. Summers come and summers go, like the tides in a cove. You don't expect the world to change. The sea's not going to come pounding in and then refuse to stop. It's not going to come flooding up the coombes and washing into our duns to sweep us all away, is it? There's spring tides and neap tides, full moon and dark. What has been will come again. There's a pattern to everything. Cornwall was like a high ground we'd built on. I couldn't think that those Saxons might just keep marching west and never stop until they crossed the Tamar. Every flood comes to its top and flows back.

Summer after summer it had been going on, the gentry riding out on their brave little horses, all jingling with gold and silver and bronze, and our young lads marching behind them in their breeches and plaids with the pack-horses. They made a gay sight. We never thought they wouldn't come back – most of them, anyway. Mind you, I've seen sights that might have made you wish they hadn't. A face split open by an axe. An arm hacked half off at the elbow and turning green. I couldn't save them all. The Raven must have her share of blood. So the young girls would cling and cry when their sweethearts went. But the older women just twisted their aprons a bit, and sighed, and maybe hung a little something round their man's neck for luck. There's hard work to do without them, but, on the other hand, you can get a sound night's sleep, though it begins to get cold on your own when autumn's putting a frost on the grass.

Of course, it's different if it's a son.

So Gorlois was off again, and laughing as if he was glad to be away from his womenfolk and out of Cornwall. First off it had been Aurelius. He was the one that got his own back on that traitor, Vortigern. But Aurelius was dead, poisoned they say, and now it was his brother Uther that all the Britons were following. To tell you the truth, wise woman I may be, but I never bothered much about where our men were going to fight, or what it might mean for us down here if they won or got beaten. As far as I could see, it was all another kind of hunting and bloody sport to them. They said my own man fell in Kent, when his

10

master was fighting him they called Hengist. I used to tie strong magic round his neck and a hard leather jerkin over his heart. But when his time came round it seems it wasn't enough. I wailed for him when they told me, and cried for him too, in private, in the straw. He was a good man, as husbands go. I've never married since. I didn't need to. I was well provided for, with my lady's babies to bring up, and as for the other, I know those that can bring the thunder in the blood better than any mortal man.

The night's my time. And by day my life was those three girls, and most of all Morgan.

I suppose that's the difference between us and Merlyn. Men off and doing, as if they could change the world by running about. Women staying at home, to hold things as they are. They move in straight lines, while we weave circles. What has been must come again, or so I thought. So I never spoke a spell against the Saxons. It wasn't them I feared.

All the same, I wasn't wise enough to stop our world from changing, though it wasn't a Saxon army that came marching over the Tamar in the end. Of course, I'd heard of Merlyn, even then. Who hadn't? That clever brat that was got by a devil on a nun. The weasel Vortigern, that sold our land for Saxon swords, he meant to make the boy a blood-offering for his stronghold that kept tumbling down. But Merlyn was too sharp for that. 'Dig under the walls and you'll find a pool.' So they did. 'Drain the pool and you'll find two stones.' So they did. 'Break open the stones and you'll find two dragons.' So they did. And the dragons fought, backwards and forwards, till the white one killed the red.

That's power that could make your hair turn white if you think about it too long. It's one thing for the wise, who have the far-sight, to see what's coming. But to make a king and a court and an army, plain men with not a morsel of magic between them, see it too, that's something few druids on earth could do. It drains the strength out of your heart even to imagine holding such a spell. But he was alive to prove he did it, and right-hand counsellor to Uther now. For all that, it was the red dragon he was fighting for.

Morgan darted away from me and ran up to her father's horse.

'Take me with you!' she begged him, as if this was just another hunt they were going on.

'Women don't go to war these days,' he laughed at her.

'Boudicca did! And Mab. And it was Scathach taught Cu Chulainn to be a warrior.'

'Times change. We're Romans now. We're not living in those old stories any more. Would you like to see your pretty mother slashed with battle scars?'

She made a face to show it wasn't her mother she cared for.

'When I'm grown, I'll fight for you. And if you die, I'll hunt the man who kills you, through the length of Britain. They'll make a new story about us that will be sung for a thousand years and more. How Morgan, daughter of Gorlois, avenged his honour.'

Oh, Morgan, Morgan. How could the little mite know how close to her the man that killed him would be?

The men were all laughing at her by now. Well, she was just a skinny, black-haired scrap of a child to shout so bold. Only her father wasn't laughing this time. It never did to speak to Gorlois of dying. He was the bravest man that ever I knew, and I don't doubt he was as foolhardy in battle as the rest of them. But if he fell, he had no son to follow him yet. And not for want of trying. So he glared at her with a face as black as his hair and swore at her to be quiet.

But she'll make good every word she said.

My lady rode a little way beside him to the high road, with the rest of us following along behind as if it was a May-time picnic. Dressed in a clover-coloured gown, she was, with a cloak of gold and black flowing out behind her. As brave and beautiful as the furze and heather that were blazing on the hills. She'd taken mighty good care of the way she looked that day, to make sure he'd hold that sight of her in his mind till he came back again. But Morgan had spoilt it for her, talking of death.

So Ygerne bit her lip and glanced sideways many a time to see from Gorlois's face what kind of mood he might be in now. It was a narrow, tricky road she had to tread, being wife to him. He'd married her for the great beauty that she had, and still had after fifteen years, if you'll believe me. It's the soft Cornish air that kept her pretty cheeks as delicate as the wild roses and curled her hair when there was damp in the wind.

But she'd disappointed him three times now. Two girls she'd given him, and in pretty quick time too. So he'd still had hope the next one would be a boy. Then, nothing. Years they'd waited. Many's the time she'd come to me in tears and begged me to help her. As if I hadn't taught her everything a wife should know, and done a few things in private on my own account that should have quickened any barren cow this side of Bodmin. It worked at last, and mighty proud she was when her belly swelled for the third time. But she wasn't laughing when it came to the birthing. I've never heard a woman scream so. And Ygerne was no coward. I truly thought the child was killing her, and itself as well. But we got it out at last. And it was a girl. Morgan. You wouldn't think a thing so small could have done so much harm. Black as a raven she was, even then, with her hair already grown down to her waist while she was still in the womb.

I laid her beside her mother, who was as white as death. Ygerne asked one question, and I answered her. Then she turned away, and it must have cost her a mighty effort to move her bloody buttocks even that far, after what she'd been through. She wouldn't look at Morgan. She wouldn't touch her. The wet-nurse had her from that moment. And then she was mine.

I didn't believe she'd ever have another child, and nor did she. But the two of us went to lengths I hadn't even dared up to then. I took her to places, women, yes, even men, that Gorlois might have killed her for if he'd known. The old faith is still alive, or you wouldn't be listening to me now. It's more than a bit of harmless medicine, a few charms in a bag, or a poke up the bum under the horse's skirt on May Day. She must have blood.

Ygerne had other ideas too. She went to the saint. To Nectan. As if that white-gowned hermit knew anything about woman's work. Lily-livered folk that call wine blood and bread flesh. Strong voices and soft hearts those Christians have. But it seems he knew a bit more than I gave him credit for, and she came away from his cell with a flea in her ear, duchess or no. She still went beside Gorlois on Sundays after that. She had to. She couldn't very well tell her husband what the saint had said, could she? But she'd a hard job keeping the anger out of her face every time she looked at Nectan. And there'd be times he'd keep his keen blue eyes on her when he preached about witchcraft. He tried looking at me, but I'd pull the hood round my face and stare at the ground or the sky till he'd finished ranting.

Oh, yes. I took their Eucharist with them. We all did. The gentry expected it. They say it was a Roman emperor first had the idea that a crucified man could win the world for them in battle. Well the Romans have gone from Britain now. It seems their fighting Christ couldn't keep the North-gods out of Rome after all. And what have they left behind but monks and nuns without a sword between them? A shepherd's crook, and a bell, and a pen. That's all their weapons now. And maybe they're more dangerous like that. But the men can't see it. Gorlois still rode out to battle against the Saxons under the cross. But who his wife prayed to for his safety was another matter.

So she had to tread carefully. She was his treasure. The most beautiful thing he owned, as long as she could keep her looks. The envy of every lord in Cornwall, and further than that, if they came west to see her. But every time he ploughed her now the seed never sprouted. She knew she'd failed him.

They'd reached the crossroads before she'd plucked up the courage to smile and put her white hand on his bridle, and lean across to kiss him.

'God-speed to your banners, my lord. Let Uther Pendragon know there is high blood beats in Cornwall. Come back to us swiftly with victory and with honour.'

And she hung a charm round his neck, like any good-wife.

She was a brave woman, and a beautiful one. She smiled at him and turned her head so that the cloak blew back from her shoulders and the sun shone behind her through her hair. She wanted to be sure he'd remember her so, and bring him hurrying back to her bed.

He grinned at her then. The wind was blowing over the hills and the white pebbles shone along the road, going east out of Cornwall. There was hard riding and brave adventure and maybe glory at the end of it. There was a light in his eyes that told me his heart was across the Tamar already. He gave her a great bear-hug that swung her clean out of the saddle.

'Never you fear, woman! By Beli and by the Bride of Heaven, those Saxons shall never set foot in Cornwall to steal Gorlois's treasure!'

And he galloped away from her at full speed with never a thought for the lads that were striding out after him on foot.

He never noticed Morgan, holding up her arms to him for a last kiss.

13

# Chapter Four

We were coming to the height of our own killing when they rode back. Samain, I still call it. Fat sheep and sleek cattle for the butcher. They drove them down from the moors with the wool curling on the lambs' backs and the shine of summer on the cows' red rumps. We couldn't keep them all. Not with the grass turning to sour mud in the winter and salt blowing in over us from the sea or snow down on us from the hills. Winter, we were all shut in, folk and beasts. There wasn't room enough for them all in a narrow place. Or food, either. So some must die and others live. Those we kept were the ones that were the best for breeding.

It was a noisy, smelly old time, what with pigs' blood running into barrels and cattle roaring at the knife. And pilchards and mackerel hanging up to dry, all split and skewered, with the seagulls screaming over the buckets of guts.

We kept the feast the old way. We doused every fire to show the summer was dead and gone. Then we scared ourselves silly in the dark. To some like Margawse it was just a game. But Elaine knew better. We still had one of the Old Ones to kindle the new fire on the top of the hill that would light every hearth for another year. It was a good old blaze we made, and then we broke the oatcake, and him that got the burnt bit ran for his life. I daresay we were a bit freer that year, with so many of the gentry away. We didn't mind my lady, somehow. For all her fine clothes, she was not so very different from us.

I can see Morgan's eyes as she crouched beside me, watching it all. Wide and black as two pools in a bog. She didn't need to be told what it was all about.

I could take my girls that night, and not be worried they might come back sprouting. Samain's not like May-time. We huddled close, but I don't need to tell you it wasn't for want of that. We daren't look over our shoulders into the dark for fear of what we might see. It was the night of the dead.

May-time and Samain.

Sometimes I wonder if that's all life is. Breeding and killing. The men to kill. The women to breed.

There's just a handful of us set apart, between the right hand and the left. It's left to us to watch over the heart of things, to keep the world from tearing itself in two.

That lanky saint, Nectan, spent Samain a different way from us. A lamp burning in his chapel all through the night, and him flat on his face, praying for the souls of the dead. And if you'd passed close enough

14

by Tintagel, you'd have heard the white nuns singing psalms.

Gorlois had done his share of killing too. He and his men came back slower, and looking well satisfied with themselves. Like a cat that's eaten a hare and come home to sleep it off.

When all the yelling and the kissing and the boasting had died down, they slept all right. Sprawled out and snoring, as though some fairy-woman had cast a glamour over them to stop their eyes and ears for a year. Like a woman after childbirth, they were. All the struggle and the pain and the fear behind them. They were mighty pleased with what they'd done. We heard that tale sung so many times I was heartily sick of it by Christmas. But Morgan could never have enough of listening. We were coming to the time of the year when we keep the fire blazing high on the hearth at supper-time and the white logs are still glowing at their ends by morning. It was good and warm to be crowded in the hall, with apples and nuts roasting on the hot stones and the ale going round more slowly as our heads began to nod. Morgan would curl up on the floor with her arms round her father's leg. And if the harper fell silent or the men ran out of bawdy stories, she'd dig her pointed chin into his knee and say, loud enough for them all to hear, 'Tell us, Father. Tell us the story of how you saved Britain at Mount Damen.'

And he'd give a great roar of laughter and toss the wine-cup back. But he never said no to the telling of that.

Blaen the harper would touch his fingers over the strings till they began to dance.

Jordan and Britael would leap to their feet on either side of Gorlois's chair. Like two tall schoolboys, they were, hardly more sensible than the day the three of them rode up to Ygerne's father's gate, for Gorlois to court his daughter. And it wasn't long before Jordan tumbled me in the orchard too, though nothing came of that. Well, they were fine warriors, both of them, that could make a man's blood beat faster and a woman blush and a boy's eyes burn bright with talk of battles. It was a fine tale they told.

'The Saxons came marching down from the north.'
'They'd sailed a great army across from the lowlands.'
'Fire flared where they passed.'
'They ruined towns and farms.'
'Octa, Hengist's son, and Eosa rode at their head.'
'Hateful helmets and armour spread over Britain's land.'
'They came down on York, proud city of the Romans.'
'It seemed that no one could save the people.'
'Uther summoned warriors out of all the west.'
'From Cambria and Cornwall and Rheged of the Lakes.'
'They marched across Britain, the Pendragon leading them.'
'The Cross of Christ was on their banners.'
'Gorlois rode at Uther's right hand.'
'A man cunning in battle, skilful and fearless.'
'The ranks of the Britons were few against the hosts of the Saxons.'

'Red blood flowed and brave men fell.'
'Terror came with the white dragon of the pagans.'
'By nightfall we were driven back to Mount Damen.'
'High on the hill we hid amongst rocks and hazel trees.'
'The Saxons dared not follow us in the dark.'
'Like foxes we hid in hollow holes in the earth.'
'Like owls we looked down upon the camp of our enemy.'
'Vast the hordes waiting for us on the plain.'
'They slept in their tents, certain of victory in the morning.'
'Uther summoned his chieftains in the darkness.'
'The noblest warriors of Britain met in counsel.'
'Gorlois of Cornwall spoke words of courage.'
'Gorlois, battle-hardened, gave daring counsel.'
'The chieftains sprang to their feet under the stars.'
'Hope returned to the heart of Uther Pendragon.'

Well, by this time, they were on their feet, swords out. Real swords, with real edges on their blades, mind you. Acting it out and going at it, hammer and tongs. Morgan was ducking her head to keep out of the way of them, and her eyes flashing with the glamour of it, like any boy's.

They were creeping round the hall now, with long, stealthy strides, and making sudden dashes to frighten the women screaming into a corner if they could. Some of them enjoyed that, I can tell you. And you can be sure that Margawse was always just in front of those swords, so that it brought the heart into my mouth. She was a girl that loved danger, when it came from a man.

'The brave band of Britons crept down the hillside.'
'Night and mist were friends to the Pendragon.'
'In silence they drew near to the Saxon sentries.'
'The stars shook with the shouts of men alarmed.'
'Fear ran like fire through the tents of the invader.'
'The Morrigan washed a bloody shroud for them.'
'Men fell in darkness. Brother turned against brother.'
'Octa, that mighty leader, was taken prisoner. Eosa was captured.'
'Gorlois of Cornwall taught Uther the paths of victory.'
'The Britons marched upon York with their banners flying.'
'At the gates, in the sight of all the people, Uther Pendragon spoke.'
'He gave chief honour to Gorlois, Duke of Cornwall.'

Morgan's little eyes were shining by then, and there was colour in her white cheeks for once, almost as high as her mother's.
'The night is a lucky time for Cornwall, then? A time to dare! We take our enemy in their sleep and win the game.'
I heard a little laugh behind my shoulder. It was Elaine.
'And who shall be our enemy in the night-time?'
I didn't take any notice of her, fool that I was.
I was looking at the three of them, towering over Morgan. Jordan,

16

and Gorlois, and Britael. The firelight dancing in their faces. And them laughing and slapping each other on the back as they remembered how they'd won. I saw those three creeping up on a camp in the darkness. Their white teeth grinning in the mist before dawn. Taking their prize.

Gwennol Far-Sight, they call me. I should be ashamed.

Well, there'd been killing enough to last them till another summer. But as for the other . . .

I'd seen Gorlois look at his wife almost before he swung a leg down from his horse. She had a fair, round belly, after bearing three children, and she wore her gowns slender and her girdle pulled tight. But one look, one spark in his eye, and then he could see that was all it was. She hadn't kindled. I've seen that darkness in a man's face many a time, when my husband sat across the fire from me, looking at my barren belly.

# Chapter Five

It was one day when the rain was sheeting down outside and we were all filling in the restless time before supper, cramped up together in the hall and everything stinking of damp. 'I suppose you're Uther Pendragon's best friend now,' laughed Morgan.

She was sitting between her father's thighs and pressing her head back against his kilt.

He jumped up pretty quick when she said that, and kicked her, though he never even noticed.

'Yes, by God and the Blessed Head of Brân! I'm the best friend he has.'

He was striding down the hall, striking his fist into his palm and shouting. But I saw Jordan look at Britael, and the two of them lifted an eyebrow at each other. There's more to this yet, I thought to myself, for all they shout and swagger so loud about their great victory. What's come between Uther and Gorlois, then, if they were so thick as they say at the gates of York?

'But it was because of you he beat the Saxons, wasn't it?' Morgan was on her hands and knees like a black cat. 'You told Uther what to do. You took Octa and Eosa prisoner and freed the North from the hand of our enemies. It was all your doing, wasn't it? If you hadn't led them down the hillside in the dark, the Saxons would have beaten you in the morning and Uther wouldn't be alive and wearing the crown of all the Britons now.'

She was mightily proud of her father then. And had good reason to be, if the tales the bards sang were only half true. He'd saved Uther's skin, and the rest too, and turned the tide for Britain that year. They'd gone rampaging up to the North after that, all the way to the other side of the Wall. And goodness knows what kind of chancy folk or devils they fought with there. And everywhere they went the red dragon had put the white to flight, or so they boasted.

Gorlois grinned. He couldn't help himself. Like Ygerne, he wasn't as young as he used to be. But like her, he didn't look as old as he was. Just a bit of grizzle in his black beard, like an early frost. And his step was spry and firm. For all the battles that he'd fought he hadn't a limp or a scar to spoil his looks. He was a handsome man, and a proud one too. And he liked to be praised. Well, that's what they pay the bards for, isn't it? And why he kept a hundred warriors in meat and ale. 'Gorlois of Cornwall!' they cried when they raised their drinking horns. 'Gorlois the Generous!' 'Gorlois the Gold-giver!' 'Gorlois who saved the North from the sword of Octa!'

18

Well, that was well enough in Cornwall. They were his liege men. But how would a shout like that sound in Dyfed and Gwynedd and Rheged beyond the Wall, and such outlandish places? How did the other chieftains like to hear Gorlois praised above the Pendragon himself? Did Uther's bards sing the same song at the king's court in London as Blaen did here? I bet they didn't. It would have set the Pendragon's teeth on edge, I reckon. No gold ring for the poet who sang a song like that. It's a dangerous thing for any nobleman to be praised above his king. It's shortened many a man's life. What Uther wanted was a man to give him good counsel, but then the sense to keep out of the way and leave the fighting and the glory to him.

But Gorlois couldn't see it. That's all his life had ever been: blood and glory. A woman's blood or a man's. He'd have victory on a bed or a battlefield. Either way, he had to win. He wouldn't care that he was riding into the jaws of death, with his breeches on or off. Maybe he was right. Maybe it was better to live and die the way he did, and not go creeping and careful. He wasn't the man to save his skin and lose his honour. Was he to change because Uther would rather have a soul-friend that had no need of a sword?

All the same, something was heavy on him. We waited for him to come out with it. I know all our heads were up and listening then. I've seen folk like that at haymaking, when you can hear the wind rising in the trees and you know the rain will be on you any moment.

He turned at the door and came striding back and thumped the table. I think he wished it was a man's head.

'I *was* the king's friend!' he said. 'After Mount Damen. He's young yet. He trusted me. I gave the Saxons into the palm of his hand when they could have split and skewered our skulls upon a stake next morning.

'I rode into the north beside him. Gorlois, Duke of Cornwall at Uther's right elbow. We crossed the Wall.

'But there was a snake in the heather. Sliding and slithering into the king's good graces. One of those that slough their skins and shift their shapes.'

I sat forward pretty quick at that, and my heart was thumping faster, for he was getting pretty near to my own business here. I daren't meet his eye. I didn't know how much he knew, but he was sometimes shrewder than I took him for. Besides, I'd half guessed the name he meant. I hadn't thought that one would have come to the surface again so far north. But that was before I knew him. Like an otter, he was, that can swim miles under water, hidden from sight. You never know where he'll rise next. Or like summer lightning, he'll strike at you out of a clear blue sky without any warning.

'I say Vortigern should have killed him when he meant to, prophecy be damned! The fatherless boy! It's plain why his mother would tell a tale like that, isn't it? Either his father was the devil or she's no nun. He talked his way out of that, and he's been talking his way to fortune ever since. Worm-tongue! I'm a plain soldier. I say what needs to be said, and that's the end of it.

'I gave the king good counsel, and it worked. I only say what can be done tomorrow, and I'm proved right or wrong. I don't deal in dreams. I don't try to paint the future.'

All this while Morgan had been staring up at her father's face, like a puppy-dog at her master. But when he started to talk of dreams I saw her eyes wander to the door. The rain had stopped, as it often does just before sunset. The sky was flaming under great purple clouds, like the edge of a creeping fire in the heather that can't be smothered. And I remember all the beads of rain on the ends of the thatch began to glitter. You'd think they were rose-crystals on the trees of fairyland.

'Who is he?' she asked. 'Who is it who can dream a king's future for him?'

'That trickster,' he said, 'that came from no good man's bed. Merlyn, they call him. Emrys Merlyn. Like a jackdaw, he is. You never know where he's going to be popping up next, stealing what doesn't belong to him. And he's no warrior or even a licensed bard. Yet he struts beside the king now as proud as a prince.'

'And will the dreams he weaves for the king really come true?'

Her eyes were wide. But I didn't heed her. It was her father I was watching closely then, and I held my breath to hear him answer. Gorlois was no fool. Not when it came to wars and land and the big affairs of men. It was only the things closest under his nose he couldn't see. Emrys Merlyn was a big enough affair, in all conscience. But I hardly knew if Gorlois counted him as a man.

A chancy, crafty, dangerous creature, he must be.

It's a funny thing. I'd never met him, and never thought I ever would, then. But I'd heard enough. Even to think that name sent a quiver down my spine and set the blood throbbing between my legs. You'd think I was a young girl staring after a man who's never looked her way, but that her body's panting for. We're not so far away in Cornwall that tales don't come our way, and Gorlois could be generous to any passing poet. And lately the songs of Merlyn had begun to grow.

There's many a brave Briton lost his life because of that traitor Vortigern. He thought the Saxons were his friends and called the council of Britain to a peace conference. Fool, that saw the flower of our leaders hacked to death before his eyes. But the fatherless boy he wanted to sacrifice to save his stronghold was cleverer than them. Merlyn slipped out of his grasp, like a tadpole through your fingers. There were some who swore he was a child of hell and others who whispered he was heaven-sent. But what's heaven and hell to the wise like us? Our power is in the earth itself. In springs and stones and under the hollow hills.

For a while after that Merlyn vanished from the tales. He'd hopped out of sight, like a toad in the grass. Some said afterwards he'd fled to the forests beyond the Wall, others that he'd sat on a mountain from which folk come back madmen or magicians. But suddenly here he was again. And now it seems our fairy toadling had turned into a prince, or one that walked pretty close with them. Closer than Duke Gorlois, by the sound of it. Our good lord wouldn't forgive that in a hurry.

He thought he was the one who'd earned the right to have the Pendragon's ear.

I was Gorlois's bondwoman, since the day he married Ygerne. And I've served him loyally, living and dead, down to this hour. For his sake I ought to have hated Merlyn then, even before what happened. Yet, I don't know how it was, but every time I heard the name of Emrys Merlyn spoken it was as though someone had put a finger on that spot between your legs that I needn't tell you of. The one that sends a thrill right through your body. Sometimes religion's like that. I've known those that can kindle lightning in the soul as hot as in the flesh. And sometimes both at once. He was one of those.

So when Morgan asked if Merlyn would dream true I knew the answer, even if Gorlois didn't. It scared me. There are times when I can see the future. And more often than not I wish I hadn't. I've seen a man trapped under the sea, with the fish picking his face away. I've heard an unborn child walled up alive in its dead mother's womb. Weeping comes out of the future louder than laughing. But I haven't made what I see. I'm like Gorlois. I'll pluck and brew, and cast and chant, to bring about what we need for this year. I don't interfere any further than that. I wouldn't know how. But suppose a man or a woman fasted and suffered and prayed hard enough to sweat blood, and went out into the wild places and wrestled with devils till they were nearly driven mad. Wouldn't they come back with powers greater than a mortal witch? A man like that might change the course of the world.

Just for a moment I saw clear. There was something Merlyn wanted from us here in Cornwall. It was only for a heartbeat, but it nearly stopped my heart. But Gorlois was a plain man, a soldier.

'I told Uther we would beat Octa's host at Mount Damen, and come off that hill with our lives and honour. Then I took my good sword in my right hand and made certain that what I'd promised him came true. Well, this trickster Merlyn is a different sort of warrior. We'll see if he can hold his weapons as firm as I hold mine. But I don't doubt he'll use all his craftiness to turn what he says he can see into certainty.'

It was Morgan who dared to ask, 'What *does* Merlyn see for the future?'

But Gorlois just turned his back on her and yelled to the steward to ask if supper wasn't ready yet.

All this time Ygerne had been sewing. She bent her pretty head over the sweet honeysuckle she was embroidering, as though it all meant nothing to her. Swords and sorcery. What was that to Ygerne? The Duchess of Cornwall, safe in her hearth and her hall in Bossiney. She was far away from the glamour of kings and enchanters. I could kick myself now, looking back. I knew better than to believe that on one score, didn't I? She had more ambitions of sorcery than her husband dreamed of. I was as big a fool as him not to have guessed she might have ambitions for the other too.

# Chapter Six

So we came to primrose time. A wet, old winter since Christmas it had been, too, with all the tracks out of the dun running like rivers, and my Lord Gorlois sulky because there'd hardly been one day in seven that was fit for hunting. And all of us coughing and shivering, and the wood too wet to give a good blaze. I feared for Morgan then. I never thought we would bring her through ~~the winter. There was always~~ that feeling on me when I looked at her, as though she was never surely with us.

I've lost many a night's sleep over that child. Aye, and it began right back before she was born. I held her mother's shoulders when she was doubled up with pain. We feared for the child even then. We never thought we would get her to the birthing. And when we did, it seemed as if my lady would die too, with the child still trapped between her legs. And when it was all over, and the blood and the mess cleared away, what had we got to show for it but a scrap of flesh and bone, like a half-picked chicken leg that my lord would have thrown to his hounds?

I sometimes wonder if it would have been better if she had died then. If all that pain and labour wasn't for worse than nothing. But I can't think it. Even if I'd known what was to come, I couldn't have taken the pillow and smothered her, though there are some who say it would have been better if I had. It's funny how it's the ones who give us the most trouble that we love deepest. Take Elaine, now. She was as easy a child as you could wish for. Hardly a tear or a frown we had from her. You could tell she would make a fine mother from the day she was old enough to play babies with her dolls. But I danced at her wedding when she married a king and went to bear him fine sons, and I never shed a tear. But Morgan. Even when they took her away from me, before she was half-grown, I never stopped thinking about her.

But now the wind had changed, and the sea settled like cat-skin, and the sky was as blue as a girl's gown. My lord was restless. He'd been cooped up too long in Bossiney. The wind was drying the tracks and news began to reach us again from outside Cornwall.

I remember that day. It was healing weather. A little mist coming up off the streams at sunrise. Then it was swallowed up in that bright blue sky, as if the heavens themselves had opened their arms and lifted all our chills and tears away from us. For the first time you could feel the sunshine sinking into your bones and doing you good. There are some of the wise have a touch like that, when they lay their hands over your heart.

Gorlois and the men were off at dawn hunting, and Morgan with them. For once I was glad of it. Her legs were growing longer, and mine were getting slower with every year. Sometimes the child would sit for hours, hardly moving. Then she'd be off, as quick as a stream over a waterfall, and how was I to keep up with her, or know what was in her head? Let her father look to her for once, I thought.

Small hope of that. I waved to her when they rode off, but she never turned her face to see. She was too busy trying to keep her pony's head as close behind her father's horse as the men would let her. And him? He couldn't wait for the hounds to give tongue to gallop away at the head of them all. He was so hot to kill whatever might cross his path that I don't think there was a thought in his head about her.

It was always peaceful at Bossiney without the men. We all found some excuse to be out of doors, and outside the walls too, if we could find the chance. The sheep were crooning in the pasture, and the lambs beginning to come. In a few weeks it would be May-time, and summer on the hills. The whole place was like a daisy-flower opening up its petals to the sun.

I busied myself about our sleeping-hut a bit quicker than usual. Elaine's corner wasn't much trouble. Neat and warm and soft as a dormouse's nest. Margawse was the one that made me work. Clothes flung everywhere as she'd rummaged through her chest, sorting out what to flaunt herself in this morning, and the bedclothes all over the floor as if she'd been snatched from her sleep by a gang of Irish pirates. I scolded enough, bending my stiff back to pick everything up, though there was no one around to hear me.

I'd no need to scold Morgan, and I could have wished I had. Her bed-place was straight and tidy as a nun's, or a soldier's. That sometimes made me want to cry. It didn't seem natural. I was not so silly as to think she did it for my sake, to save me work. It felt more like a warning, telling me to keep off. She didn't want even my hands on her things, prying and poking. Not Gwennol's hands, that had reached inside her mother, when the midwife didn't dare, and pulled her into the world.

When that was done, I took a girdle I was plaiting, and sat outside on a bench where I could feel the sun on my face. I looked about for Margawse, but I couldn't see her. Yet I didn't go looking for her. Not then. I was pretty easy in my mind that morning. With most of the men off hunting, and only a handful of slaves about the place, there was little she could get up to. There was a ruddy-faced shepherd boy I'd noticed her sidling off towards lately. But I'd taken care to have a word in his ear and I'd frightened him good and proper with a picture of what evil I'd put on him if he laid a finger on her. I left him shaking so that the poor lad couldn't have got his tool up if Arianrhod herself had come tempting him.

But I'd got used to looking for a whisk of her gay gown round some corner, and I couldn't see her. Or Ygerne and Elaine. They could be in my lady's bower across the way, but why would they sit cooped up indoors on such a sweet morning? I tried to put the thought out of my head, but it wouldn't let me rest. Every time I looked across at

Ygerne's half-open door, it had a still, empty look about it. There wasn't a flicker of movement or a woman's voice from inside.

Presently it got so I had to find out. I unknotted the wools from my waist and went across to look. I didn't need to push the door wide open to know the truth of it. There was no one in the chamber. I went across to the hall, though what would they be doing there at that time of the morning, among all the sweeping and scrubbing after last night's supper? Issey, the steward, must have seen me staring round and asked me what was the matter. But I didn't tell him. I had my pride. He was a decent enough man, but I wasn't going to have a hall full of slaves knowing my lady had taken her two daughters off, without even a word to their nurse about where they were gone. I didn't want them thinking I was too old for my job.

But you can't hide much, living as close as we did. I was taking myself off across the yard, and thinking I was keeping my dignity, when Ewa came past, carrying a bucket of ashes. A cow-faced slave, she was, from up Devon way. She'd never liked me. She grinned at me now, black teeth and all.

'If it's my lady you're looking for, she's long gone. She and her woman Ruan took themselves off just after sunrise. Carrying baskets, to gather the new herbs, they said. She called young Lady Elaine to go with her, and Tual to follow behind to guard them. And then I saw the Lady Margawse go running after them. Funny you not knowing that.'

I could see now why she was smiling so slyly. All the women knew well enough what I was. Not the whole of it by a long way, of course, but enough to make them look up to me more than ever they'd have done if I'd been just those three girls' nurse. They feared me more than a little. And it didn't make them love me, though there's many had reason to be grateful to me, and some for their lives, and their children's. But my lady and her daughters had gone off this morning with their baskets, on what should have been my business before anyone else's. And if I didn't know it, then maybe it was more than Gwennol Far-Sight's legs that were getting stiff and old? Maybe I wasn't the powerful wise woman I used to be, I could see her thinking, plain as if she'd said it out loud.

'There's those that can gather weeds and others that know who to use them on,' I snapped back at her. And gave her a look that sent her hurrying off to the midden with the blood running out of her cheeks.

But it hurt me sorely. Maybe I was getting too soft and slow, drowsing there on the bench when others were busy, and not seeing what was going on under my nose.

I put a shawl round my shoulders and a basket over my arm. I had a good look round to make sure that Ewa wasn't spying and I was off, out of the gates, as fast as I could go.

When I was out of sight of the dun, I stopped to catch my breath. It was a fair, fine day. There were little leverets hopping about in the grass between the hawthorn bushes and red squirrels leaping and shaking gold from the hazel catkins. But I stopped myself smiling at them and shut my eyes. I listened, deep inside. They couldn't hide from me. When I knew where they were, I went into the coombe and up the side of the brook, towards Nectan's waterfall. I didn't need to get that far. Just once I stopped to get my bearings. Then I left the water and began to climb up the steep bank through the trees.

I caught sight of Tual first, sitting on a big mossy stone, with his cudgel on his knees. Then I saw Ruan and Margawse were curled up at his feet. He was telling them some tale from the old wars with the Irish pirates that made them laugh pretty loud and shameless.

He saw me before they did and broke off quick, and they jumped up as though they'd seen a spirit-woman at Samain. Ruan turned her head very sudden, and opened her mouth as if she was going to call out to her mistress. But she thought better of it and laughed at me instead.

It seemed it was a smiling sort of day wherever I went. The sun smiling so sweet and friendly. The faces smiling so sly and secret.

Margawse said,' Have you come all this way looking for us, Gwennol? You shouldn't have worried. Look, you're all out of breath. Mother said she knew what herbs you would want us to pick. Then she took Elaine, and told us not to follow for a while. It seems there's things I'm not old enough to know yet!' And she laughed, so I could have slapped her face.

'We're all right. We've got Tual to look after us.' And that made Ruan laugh as well.

I was too full to answer her. For once it wasn't Margawse I was worried about. Tual was a slave. He won't touch her, though he could foul her thoughts with his stories. I climbed right past the three of them as if they hadn't been there. Ruan called out after me, but even she daren't try and stop me, though she was pretty thick with her mistress these days.

I found Ygerne and Elaine. They were where I had seen them all this time, under a sycamore tree that was making yellow patterns of sunshine on the floor. They must have heard Ruan shout. They were crouched like two startled hares, watching me coming. I didn't say anything. I stood over them with my hands on my hips and stared down at them. I named over the leaves in their baskets and pursed my lips. I knew there was more than that to it. Then I saw it, half hidden under the skirt of Ygerne's kirtle. They hadn't been sharp enough when they heard the warning. I bent to pick it up. A chain of flowers. A dainty thing. Any village maid might have made such a garland to hang round her lover's neck. Until you looked closer and saw what was woven into it. Well, I needn't tell you. They both had blood, and more, under their fingernails. They'd used hooked flowers of course. Those that catch and claw and bind. I held it under my lady's nose, so she had to back away. But still I didn't understand what it was she wanted.

'What's this, then? A spell of summoning? Your man's not at the king's court on the other side of Britain now. Do you need such a chain to bring him back to you from a day's hunting?'

She smiled at me, sweeter than any of the others.

25

'Elaine's new in our ways. There are things she needs to be taught. And after such a cruel winter the forest is full of fallen trees and dangers. The wolves are hungry. There's no harm in us wishing Gorlois's safe return, is there?'

She never thought of Morgan.

I looked her squarely in the face till her eyes fell.

'There are charms for a man's safety. I've filled bags with them by the hundred. And there are spells of binding. Do you think I'm so old and witless I can't tell the difference?'

She always had an answer. 'Summer is coming. Don't you feel it today, Gwennol? Soon Uther Pendragon will be at the wars again, and Gorlois with him. Should I not try to bind him to me, while there is time?'

I saw her put her hand over Elaine's to keep her quiet. The daughter's face was as sweet and smiling as her mother's. But her eyes looked scared. I made up my mind I'd have it out of that girl before the day was over.

It was noon before we got back to the dun, and then I didn't need to be told who that pair had been summoning. There was a horseman in the yard already.

# Chapter Seven

By nightfall the whole dun was in an uproar. That messenger wouldn't tell his news till Gorlois came home. It seems this message was too important for women's ears, even Ygerne's. But we found out pretty quick he came from Uther Pendragon's court up in London. Well, you can imagine the wild stories that went flying round.

'Are they going back to war already? They must be, mustn't they?' says Margawse, gripping me by the wrist as though she'd like to break it.

'Tual says the Saxons have brought a huge army over from the Lowlands to rescue Octa and Eosa.' Elaine's eyes were so big, I didn't know if she was more frightened of the Saxons or of what she'd done.

'They've captured Glastonbury.'

'The Picts have crossed the Wall and they're pouring south.'

I hardly knew where to turn or who to believe. It was too far even for my seeing, and it sounded like fighting men's business, none of mine. Except when Ruan said that about the Isle of Glass. The womb of Britain. That shook me for a while. I've never been so far, though I could take you to other tors, true daughters to that one. But we all know of it, of course, through the Old Ones. And I could feel it then, like a cord that's not yet cut, as if I was a baby feeding on its mother's blood. I'd have known if they'd touched that.

I was watching Ygerne as close as I could through all that flying about and foolishness. She'd got Uther's messenger in the hall and had the fire built up, and she was giving him the best wine in a jewelled horn, just as if he'd been the king himself. And all the time her little white fingers were tap, tap, tapping on the table-top. It didn't do her any good. He knew his job better than to unbutton his lips at the first drink he downed. She had to wait, like the rest of us.

It was still early in the year, and the light was turning purple over the forest before the hunt came home. And then, of course, I had Morgan to wash and get to bed. The poor little mite was so weary she could scarcely hold her eyes open. Still, she half knew there was something going on. She stirred and struggled a bit as I picked her up. Then her head dropped on my shoulder and she let me carry her to our hut. I stripped the muddy clothes off her back and bathed her and salved her scratches. She was so limp and spiritless you'd think she'd been drugged for the Offering, and I don't mean any Christians' Eucharist, either. I chased that idea away pretty quick. I laid her down on her bed, and lifted the black hair away from her little face. She was asleep before I kissed her. A little baby thing she looked on her pillow. And the only still creature in the dun, or so it seemed that night.

I couldn't wait to be off and running across to the hall as fast as I could go. It irked me to be called a wise woman and now to be the last to know the news. I'd have to keep my mouth shut and my ears open, and make believe I knew more than I did. But I needn't have worried. Margawse came flying across the hall as soon as she saw me.

'Gwennol! You'll never guess the news! It's not the Saxons. Just the opposite. King Uther Pendragon is going to wear his crown at a great feast in London. All the lords in every part of Britain who helped him to victory are summoned to his court on Easter Day. And their ladies with them. Think of it, Gwennol! Mother's going to London to meet the king!'

I looked across at Ygerne and nodded. So that was the way of it. She'd been a better pupil than I thought, this daughter who was not of my own blood. She'd got what she wanted, and hadn't even asked my help. Only Elaine's. I watched her now, still smiling over the Pendragon's messenger, like any good housewife with a guest. Well, good luck to her, I thought. It's dull enough for her here in Bossiney, out of the way of all the great happenings. We don't see many kings down here in Cornwall, except him who calls himself King of Dumonia. Of course, I'd been up Exeter way once. His court was a bit grander than our Cornish rounds. They'd built it up with stone the old Romans had left. It must have been a fine city once, before the pillars started tumbling down and the trees grew up through the pavements. But his house wasn't much richer inside than we were used to. That was long before, when Ygerne was newly-married, a slip of a girl as bright and golden as a Lent lily. She turned men's heads wherever she went. Since then, I'd had her children at my knee and stayed at home when they rode off to their kin across the Tamar.

Gorlois was like a dog that's seen a hare. He was mad to go. Anything to be off and doing, meeting with other lords and ladies and playing the great man. I could see him now, his arm round Ygerne's shoulders and fondling her more than I'd seen him do for many a year, except at night when he was drunk and couldn't wait to have her in bed. I knew what he was thinking. Uther could wear his golden crown, to show to all the Britons. But Gorlois had his golden Ygerne, and the king might hunt a long way to find a wife more beautiful than his. She'd be his jewel.

As for his men, there were hands on daggers before they'd hardly started drinking. Gorlois couldn't take a hundred warriors to the feast with him, but he'd want an escort. The Duke of Cornwall's got to look like a noble lord. He fancied himself as a great chieftain now, since that battle. Uther's general. A bigger man, they said, than our king up in Devon. So some could go and some must stay. And who would he choose for the honour, and why? They might have beaten the Saxons for the moment, but there'd be more blood shed in our hall over that victory, long after it was won.

If we thought we'd had excitement enough that evening, it was nothing to what the place was like next morning. All of us were sent flying about, and screaming at each other like birds at mating-time. There were the finest clothes to be looked out and made good, and the jewels and the armour, and the horses to be seen to. And all the food for the journey.

And in the middle of it all, while I was stooping over the well, I heard Elaine's voice behind me. Clear and calm, she sounded, just as if she'd been expecting it.

'Gwennol, you must get out my finest garments as well, and make them ready. I am to go to London with Father and Mother to feast with the king.'

I turned round sudden, and she was smiling down at me, with that same smile on her face she'd had in the woods, only not so scared now. Like a cat that's had the cream and knows you're too late to stop it. That look gave me a queer kind of jolt. It's one thing to whisper a maid and watch her grow into a wise woman, as I had with Ygerne, in place of the daughter I never had. But when your spirit-daughter whispers her own, and the two of them go spell-speaking in secret with never a word to you, you feel as though the world has turned a bit too far. Your star's already gone down into the dark under the earth.

Well, I could see what was in her mother's mind straight away. It was plain to all of us. Elaine was a woman now, with a bloom in her cheeks like the wild rose. And what better chance could there be to marry her off to one of the highest in the land? Though I did think that feast might be a bit like the midsummer horse-fair, with the men sizing up the fillies for breeding and beauty, and their wives knowing it wouldn't be just their sons' pleasure those lords were thinking of. There'd be some sharp bidding and bargaining. A duke's daughter may be bought and sold, the same as a slave. And Elaine was a beauty, or so they told me. I guessed that when that feast was over she wouldn't stay a maiden much longer, and a good price paid, for those that reckon in farms and forts. But when she did come home, and sooner than any of us had looked for, she had a tale to tell that was stranger than any I dreamed of then.

There are some that get what they want through the old knowledge. But there's other ways too, for those that haven't been spoken. We had reckoned without Margawse. Well, I can't be keeping my eyes on them every moment of the day. I had enough to do with helping to get all my lord and lady's gowns washed and mended and trimmed, and Elaine's too. You'd have thought they were going to London for a year, they wanted so much, and we'd be lucky if we could find wagons enough to carry it all.

I heard screaming in the great hall. I put my head inside, and there were Margawse and Elaine, fighting on the floor like two cats. That was a fine to-do, with all the house-slaves standing round and gaping. Some of them were laughing their heads off and the rest were scared out of their skins. But there wasn't one of them that dared lay a hand on those young ladies. Ladies? There was hair and spit and straw flying about in the air and I could see pretty soon there'd be blood too if I wasn't quick.

'Stop them!' I screamed.

Well, those slaves looked at me once, but they wouldn't move. And I hadn't the strength to separate them. Elaine's strong. She may look plump, but there's muscle there under the fat. She'd got Margawse's wrists in a grip and was forcing them away from her face, and kneeing her at the same time for all she was worth. Margawse's eyes were blazing like a smith's forge. She knew well enough she had weapons at her fingertips. But she was so wild she hardly knew where she was hitting, or Elaine's pretty face might have been in rags before then.

I doubled out of that door and yelled for help at the top of my voice. Well, that brought the warriors that were in earshot running. They must have thought the Saxons had found their way to Cornwall at last. The swords were out before they reached me. They soon saw what was what, and that it wasn't fitting for slaves to see what they had seen, in daytime, and not even strong drink to blame it on. Though goodness knows I've seen worse than that at a feast when a fine lady's husband has been given a portion meaner than she thinks he deserves. Anyway, it was Endoder, our horsemaster, and Hedrek, Gorlois's huntsman, that had the separating of them, as if they'd been a pair of their own bitches. They'd put up their swords and dropped the shields they'd grabbed when they saw it wasn't men they had to deal with. But they'd have been glad of them. They took a wound or two, before they had those two under control. If they'd been boys, I think the men would have ducked them in the horse-pond, for all they were Gorlois's children. But they daren't do that to his daughters, even then.

I was gasping as if I'd been in a fight myself.

'You wicked girl! What if you'd scratched your sister now and spoiled her looks, just as she's going to the king's court to find a husband?'

Margawse laughed in my face. I'd handed her the weapon she wanted.

Well, she went straight to her parents, as though she was the one who'd been wronged. I fancy my Lady Ygerne must have heard what was passing. Her bower was not so far from the hall, when all's said and done, and she'd sharper ears than I had. But she wasn't going to interfere, or daren't. But when Gorlois understood how they'd shamed each other, with their skirts up round their bums for half the world to see, he was for whipping the pair of them, never mind who had the right or wrong of it. But Margawse put her hands on her hips and said, 'I want to go to the crown-wearing. And if you don't take me, I'll put such scratches on Elaine's face that no one will marry her, now or ever.'

Well, they threw me out pretty quick, and the rest of us besides. But half the dun heard them shouting at each other. He was furious, for she made him look as if he couldn't manage his own womenfolk. But he knew she meant it. She'd got the upper hand of them all. They could have threatened to banish her or whip her, but she only needed a moment. They couldn't act quick enough to be certain she wouldn't reach her sister before they could stop her.

And besides . . . she might not be fully woman yet, as I knew. But I'd seen her stroking her breasts when I bathed her. It wouldn't be long now. And there were few that saw her that would have guessed she wasn't. She could make every head turn when she walked through a group of men, and she knew it. And it wasn't only heads she stirred, either. There'd be more than a few wet breeches. She couldn't be wed yet, but there'd be plenty would be willing to offer. So she got her way, and I'd more work than ever to do making ready for her, and less time to do it in too.

The moment they told me Margawse was going with them, I knew what would follow. She didn't fight her sisters or run to her mother. There was only ever one person who counted with Morgan. She stood in front of her father, pale as ever I'd seen her, and deadly serious.

'Take me! You must take me with you. You have to,' she said, very low and clear, and looking hard into his eyes.

It twisted my guts to hear her. She was trying to make it sound like an order. But I could tell she was desperate. It was just as if she knew he was going to say no, but was driving herself on to do it just the same. She'd damn herself first in her own heart, but she wouldn't stop till she'd heard him do it to her with his own lips.

Well, of course, he did. How could they have taken her? A little runt like her, who didn't even look the eight years she was. They'd have laughed her out of court, and him with her, parading herself like her lady mother and her sisters. Margawse would get away with it, and brighten plenty of eyes into the bargain, but never Morgan. That was always the way of it. Her father tried to laugh his way out it, of course. That great laugh, that men think will set the world to rights and make women love them again. He put his arms round her to swing and hug her the way she always wanted. But she slapped his face and wriggled out of his clutches. That didn't please his lordship. He was as quick to anger as she was. So they were not good friends when he left for London. But what could she have done if she'd gone with him? He was no more cruel to her than she was to herself.

She ran out of the door. It never crossed her mind to threaten Margawse's trick. She wasn't like that. If she'd wanted to strike her sisters, she'd have done it there and then, without any warning. No matter that it wouldn't have got her what she wanted. It would have been quick and sudden, while the fire was eating her heart. She wouldn't think to wait in the dark, plotting to get her own way. She had a boy's temper, not a woman's wiles. Not then.

# Chapter Eight

I remember the day they left for London, with Morgan still torn between loving her father and hating him. We were all up before dawn and in such a commotion, you'd think the king was coming to us, and not the other way round. Elaine was the calmest. She was ordering the packing of her mother's things, and her own as well, and making a better job of it too, for my lady was as excited as any girl. Margawse was nowhere to be seen, and goodness knows what she might be up to behind the armoury, but she was too big for me and I was too old to go chasing after her, and so I'd told her mother many a time.

Down in the stables they were grooming the horses till you could see your face in their backsides, as if they wouldn't be spattered with mud and sweat by the time they crossed the first ford. I found Morgan down there talking to her father's horse. She was twisting her fingers in his mane as though she wished she could turn into a fly and hide herself away there when he rode off. We must have been the only two in the dun standing still, and not dashing about with our faces all red and bothered. And then Issey, the steward, came running, like a man demented, and calling out that my lady had ordered sweet-meats to be baked for the journey and the honey was all gone, and there wasn't another spare pair of legs to go to the bee-woman and get more, and would I fetch some for the cooks? I burst out laughing in his face. The sun was over the trees already. This was no time to start baking cakes. They should have been on the road and over the hill long before this, and so I told him. But he was as crazed as the rest of them.

'Use your eyes, woman! It will be hours yet before they're ready. Hurry now, before they think of something else to trouble us with.'

Then Gorlois's horse reared up at the shouting and swung Morgan off her feet. She screamed, and dropped down to the ground almost under his hooves. And as bad luck would have it, up came Lord Gorlois behind me, yelling, 'Get that child away from here, you old fool, before she gets trampled to death.'

Well, I can tell when I'm not wanted. I grabbed Morgan with one hand and the empty crock Issey was holding out in the other and took them both off.

I had trouble with Morgan. She tried to snatch her hand away from mine and run back, though her father had marched off out of sight again.

'No, Gwennol! I'm not going! You can't make me. They're going to leave without me and I won't even have said good-bye to him.'

'You great fool,' I told her, sounding like Issey himself. 'Look at them all, running about like a troupe of mummers at Christmas-time. It'll be noon before they're on their way, and they won't leave without your mother's sweet-cakes by the sound of it.'

'They will! They will! You know what she's like. She'll forget she even ordered them. I *won't* go.'

She had the stronger will, but I had more weight. I was fairly dragging her towards the gate, and she had marks on her wrist afterwards to show for it. But I'd lost patience with them all. If I was to be ordered about like a house-slave, I'd do my share of ordering too. Still, I had to calm her, or she'd be darting back like a swift the moment I let go of her.

'Now then, you can see they haven't harnessed the horses yet. And it isn't so far to walk to the bee-woman's. You'll have them in sight when we're on the downs. If they look like leaving, you'll see it soon enough to run and catch them.'

'Are you sure, Gwennol? Are you really, really sure?'

'And your father wouldn't leave without a kiss from you, would he, now?'

She looked at me then, with eyes so dark it was like peering into the night. They told me nothing. But I think it was me saying that that decided her. She was putting him to the test. She must have known he'd fail her.

She darted off ahead of me out of the gate. I picked up my skirts and hurried after her. But I soon slowed down. I couldn't walk very fast, even then. It was quiet up on the cliffs. Just a bit of breeze in the grass and the gulls flashing overhead, and the little spring flowers beginning to come out. It would have done me good to have sat down and rested in the sunshine. Across the bay we could see the white huts of the nunnery on Tintagel Head. Very still and quiet they looked, like birds nesting on a cliff, hatching their young.

It was a queer feeling. You'd have thought we should have been bitter enemies, me and those Christians. That hoarse-voiced beanpole, Nectan, up the coombe, ranting at us for our sins on Sunday. Those clear-faced nuns, busy as bees, growing queens to stock new hives all over Cornwall. And so we were, when we were each about our own business. I can still feel it like a blow to the stomach – the day they overturned the Stone Man of Trigg. I looked for the heavens to open and shiver their cross to splinters, and the unholy hands that raised it. But the gods must have hid their faces from us that day. Next year we watched those white-robed women marching over the bridge to Tintagel Island, with their cross held up in front of them, singing psalms. Yes, and we did more than watch, some of us. I was a young woman then, drawn up with the rest of the wise on the cliffs opposite, hurling slates and screaming curses on them.

The stones didn't reach them, and the wind took our curses away and turned them back on us, it seemed. Gorlois saw to that. He thought himself a proper Roman then, giving those Christian women the land. Never mind that it had been sacred to us long before their time. He wouldn't let us near enough to harm the nuns. Not with our hands, anyway. There's other means. The Romans have gone, and we'll see who lasts longest now, the Latin psalm-singers or us.

Well, they could drive us from the high places under the sky. But most of them didn't know what went on still, in the dark places you all know of. Though there were some even among the nuns that kept the old faith in secret. That made me laugh. And Gorlois never guessed where his own wife went by night when the month came round again. Most of our gods are like any war-lords. They can be beaten. But the Mothers will go on giving birth. You can't stop them.

Gorlois's people followed him to Nectan's chapel, willing or not. And there were some of the gentry who sent their daughters to the nuns to school, to learn to read and write and weave a pretty embroidery. But we weren't idle, either, though we had to be careful and secret the way we went about it.

So you'd think I'd have hated those nuns, looking across at the place that was once ours. But I couldn't somehow. We were like a pair of wrestlers, sizing each other up. The men who ruled us couldn't see what was going on under their noses. But those women did. Not the whole of it, of course, but enough to respect us. We understood each other's ways. And sometimes I envied them, never mind their cold, narrow beds and their meek rules. They were on the winning side now. You could see by the light in their faces.

But the wise women know how to wait.

That morning I could have sat and looked at Tintagel for a long time, and those little white-robed figures going peacefully to and fro. It was so different from the folly we'd left behind us. But Morgan couldn't wait. She was as restless as a butterfly, flitting from one side of the path to the other. She kept getting further ahead and calling back to me to hurry. All the same, I could see she was glad to be out of doors again and feel the wind fresh on her face. I know I was. I couldn't even mind that it was blowing Morgan's hair all any old how, and I'd be half the day combing out the tangles, if I could keep her still long enough. It was enough for me to see her happy for a moment and safely through another winter, though there wasn't a drop of colour in her cheeks, just the tip of her nose red with the wind.

She'd found flowers now, hiding in the moss under the stones, and she was picking a bunch of them for her father. Primroses, mostly, and a few violets. But she couldn't make them into a dainty nosegay as Elaine would have done. She snatched at them too quickly, so that some of them broke off short and others she pulled up by their poor bruised roots. It was all pretty spring above her fist, but underneath you could see the torn stems hanging down.

She was chattering away, as busy as a starling.

'When we get the honey, I'm going to make cakes for Father too. Some he can have for the journey. But I'll make special ones, Easter cakes, that he can give to the king. He'd like that, wouldn't he? The king would be pleased with Father if he gave him Easter cakes, wouldn't he, Gwennol?'

'That's as may be. As like as not you'd run off and forget about them, till they were burnt. The king wouldn't thank your father for offering him a plate of charcoal, would he?'

'I wouldn't! I wouldn't! They'll be the best cakes in the world. And the king will send for the maiden who baked them and offer her his hand in marriage. And I shall be the greatest queen in the land. And when Uther Pendragon is killed in battle, they will bring his body back to me and I shall raise his sword and lead his warriors to victory over the Saxons. And all the people will shout, "Long live Queen Morgan, leader of the Britons!" '

'Get along with you! You couldn't lift King Uther's scabbard, let alone his sword. And if you dance too near the edge of that cliff, you'll end up the seal-king's bride, and a kingdom under the sea.'

Little we guessed then who Uther Pendragon's bride would be within the year.

I was all for staying and chatting at the bee-woman's cottage on Barras Nose. If I was to be treated like a kitchen servant and shouted out of the way, I'd get my own back on them by having a morning's gossip where no one could see me. And the steward could whistle for his honey. But before long Morgan began to tug at my skirt. She was in a hurry to go, and full of the presents she'd planned for her father, the little flowers and the Easter cakes. My heart softened, for I couldn't ever say no to her, though I made sure to scold her for the fidget that she was.

All the same, I couldn't hurry back as fast as she'd have liked me to, with the great crock on my shoulder full of good thick honey now. We came over the cliffs, and the flashing and movement from Bossiney was like a fairground in front of us. Then we dropped into the track that led up beside the stream away from the sea and lost sight of the dun for a while.

It was a hollow way, and soft underfoot. Above our heads the twigs of the hawthorn were bare yet. But the Lent lilies stood as brave as golden war-trumpets. It was very still and quiet, just as if we had stepped into another time and another world. Down there between the hedgebanks we lost the noise of the dun. Morgan looked at me, and I saw the fear in her face. She started to run.

We came out of the hollow road into the sunshine before the gate. And it was a different sight now. The horses were saddled and drawn up in lines, and the slaves holding the pack mules' heads. Even before they saw us, my lord was lifting Lady Ygerne into her chariot. Margawse and Elaine were already sitting up in theirs and smiling. Morgan stopped short with a shudder, like a boat that's struck a rock. She dropped her poor little flowers in the mud. Then she dashed forward through the warriors and flung herself on her father as he settled himself in the saddle. I was left too far behind to hear what she cried at him. Not that I needed to. She hadn't learned then how to trick and act and smile falsely at men. I didn't need to come within sling-shot of her to know what she would be saying. Every line of her body and every twist of her hands was shouting to high heaven. She had her fingers knotted in her father's cloak and her black hair was trailing down his horse's flanks like dried blood. But he flung his arms open and laughed at her, with his teeth white in his beard. Then he tossed her in the air and set her over his horse's neck. By the time I caught up with her, she was hugging and kissing him, though I could tell that underneath she was still angry to think that he might have ridden away without her, while she was still on the downs picking primroses for him.

You couldn't have told her, but it was her own faults in him that made her angry. She always did what she wanted. And when did she ever stop to think of the hurt she was doing to other people? Afterwards she'd give you a laugh and a kiss to make it all right. And where did she get that from but her own father, laughing at the world through his black beard?

Lord Gorlois handed her back to me.

'Bring me a present,' she cried. 'Something splendid from the king's court.'

'What shall it be? A golden goblet, studded with jewels? A cloak trimmed with fur? A wolfhound's puppy?'

'A sword! A magic sword that will kill every enemy!'

He laughed at that, and trotted away from us through the gateway. A fine, proud sight, with his warriors and ladies behind him.

Morgan looked up at me when they had gone past seeing her waving.

'I didn't give him the flowers. He didn't deserve them. He was going away without saying good-bye to me.'

She gathered up the flowers then, what was left of them, for they'd been trampled into the mud till they were pulped and broken. She should have left them there. But she could never let a wound alone. She always had to be testing it to see how much it could hurt. She laid those poor, battered stems across her hand and tried to straighten what petals there were left. I watched her little fingers, stroking and smoothing, as if even then she thought she could heal them. And I wondered, not for the first time either, if perhaps she shouldn't be whispered too, young though she was. No one that knew such things could doubt there was power in the child that she didn't know herself yet. It scared me sometimes. And if she knew the charms of mending she might be a great healer one day, as great as any I'd known.

But all of a sudden I shivered. I cut off the thought short, like the sun going behind a cloud. You can't build walls round a power like that. It goes where the wise woman wills. Left or right. To heal or to harm. I loved the little maid dearly, but I wouldn't trust her with knowledge like that.

So I fell to scolding anyone who was left to listen.

'Yes, and there's me with my arms nearly dropping off, carrying this great crock of honey. And what for, I'd like to know? A slave might just as well have fetched it tomorrow, for all the use it's been. It's not my place to go fetching and carrying like a mule. But your father's like a little boy. He's that excited to be going to see the king, he can't wait. And my lady's not much better, though I don't blame her for that. We see little enough of fine courts and palaces here, and she's beautiful enough to be a queen.'

Young Keby, the stable boy, was coming back from the gate. His cheeks turned red when he saw me and it crossed my mind that it might have had more than a little to do with Margawse disappearing that morning. And maybe that was why he was in such a hurry to turn my thoughts another way.

He burst out laughing. 'Our lord's a lucky man, and he wants the king to know it. But if I had a wife with my lady's breasts, I'd be leaving her at home when I went to the Pendragon's court. I bet she's still good for a tumble in the straw, even if she has got two tall daughters and the little one. And from the tales our lads brought back last year about King Uther, he's not the man to keep his weapon under his cloak when there are pretty women about.'

'Shame on you, Keby Eval's son! We're not all as free with our hands as some I could tell of. That's no way to be speaking of the High King of Britain. My lady's a good woman, and true to her lord, and has been these fifteen years.'

'Don't shout at me. I didn't make the tales. And it's not my hands we're talking about, is it? I'm not the keeper of the High King's weapon. It wasn't me Gorlois swore his oath to, to give the Pendragon whatever service he asked for. You think of that, Gwennol Far-Sight.'

'My lord's a proud man who can take care of his own. And if you want to keep a whole tongue in your head, you'll keep your dirty thoughts to yourself.'

He looked round that empty yard with his insolent grin. There was only me and Morgan.

'Who's left to hear us now but you and me, Gwennol? And don't tell me you hadn't heard the Pendragon's put more than Saxons on their backs all over Britain. I'm only saying what half of Cornwall knows already.'

'Then Cornish folk can know from me that my lady's a pure wife, and always has been. And she's too wise to be having her head turned by a gold crown at her age.'

I don't know why, but I was trembling with anger so that I could hardly hold that stupid crock of honey in my arms. Time I got rid of it, and gave Issey a piece of my mind for putting me to all that trouble for nothing. It wasn't my place to fetch and carry. I looked round for Morgan. She shouldn't have been listening to such talk. But the wind had blown the tangles over her face and I didn't think she'd heard us. I should have known better.

# Chapter Nine

It was a sweet spring, that year – with clouds like young lambs chasing across the sky, and the sea so quiet you could hardly believe how it had been tearing at the cliffs like a pack of wolves all winter. I've often wondered what it must be like to live inland and not to hear the come and go of the waves like blood in the ear.

Our coast looks north, and there's many a tumble of black rock that never sees the sun. But below Bossiney there's one sweet stretch of golden sand when the tide is down. You can sit there in the sun in the middle of the day and watch the green water washing in past the Sisters and a boat or two bobbing out at sea. There's tall old cliffs on either side. From there I couldn't see that stone cross on Tintagel Head, let alone what lay beneath it. When I look back, those are the days it doesn't hurt me to remember, when there was no one to trouble me but Morgan, and I didn't need to be looking up every moment at a warning of what was going to take my baby away.

It was an easy time for us, with our chieftain and his lady away at the court of King Uther Pendragon. And if I was resting my old bones in a bit of sunshine on the beach, mending an old gown for Elaine, who was to worry if Morgan was sometimes out of sight? I was feeling my rheumatism even then, and what would a stiff old body like me be doing scrambling over the rocks of the sea-shore after an eight-year-old that was as nimble as a goat? If it had been Elaine, now, I'd have been worried sick that she'd slip and drown herself in the sea. But not Morgan. She was as sure-footed as a cat. Her sort don't fall. I scolded her often, mind you, but I knew she'd come to no harm. The sea was her playmate.

'Gwennol!' she said, and I nearly fell off the rock with fright, for I hadn't seen her in the shadow of the cliff behind me. She trumpeted with laughter and set me straight again and picked up my sewing from the sand. Then she squatted down in front of me and tipped up her sharp little face.

'Will they come here?' she said. 'My father and the king? If they're out hunting and it starts to get dark, would they ride this way and stay in our dun?'

'Goodness me, my lover! The gods forbid!' I said, and I crossed my fingers for good measure. 'They're miles and miles away. Across the Tamar and a lot further than that. A week's hard riding, or so I've heard tell. And a good thing too, the state we're in. The larder's almost empty and there's hardly a thing growing in the gardens yet but kale. How would we be feasting a king at the back end of winter, with not even a day's notice to brew and bake?'

38

'But they'd bring meat for the feast with them, wouldn't they? A great stag over the horse's back. Or a boar with savage tusks, and their spears red with its blood.'

'And what about your dear mother? Would you have her galloping half across Britain at her age?'

'I wasn't thinking about Mother.'

'I don't need telling that. You're too fond of hankering to run after the men, my handsome. But it's a woman's world you'll have to live in, so you'd better make up your mind to it. I've enough trouble with your sister Margawse that hasn't eyes for anything that doesn't walk in breeches. We'd all sleep a lot sounder in our beds if that one was at school in the nunnery on Tintagel.'

'I'm not like her. Margawse doesn't want to *be* a man.'

She spoke true enough there. To tell you the truth, it wasn't just idleness that kept me in the dun most of the year. Elaine was as happy as a bird to borrow her mother's power over the hall and the kitchen, and see things were well-set and proper. It was Margawse I worried about. I could never see her disappear round some corner or into a dark doorway but I wondered who might be waiting for her there. She'd no pride. Only a red hunger that wouldn't be satisfied. As soon as she was a woman she ought to be married. I thought of May-Eve that was coming. If I could take her with me then . . . That was what she needed. There is a right season for everything. And those that open their blood-hole to the Mother's Son can sleep more easily in their beds on other nights. It wasn't as if she would be the first of her folk to travel that road, for all Ygerne's family were nobles and called themselves Christians now.

Elaine was still a maid. I'd taken good care of that, even after she was spoken. But her mother was a different story. Many's the time she's been into the Mother's Hole with me. She put on a mask and hood, and I blacked her face below so that no one would guess who she was. There's loose tongues among the wise, let me warn you, the same as other women. But there were some that had to know. Well, we have our own lords and ladies by night, as they have theirs by day.

Gorlois never knew the half of it. I told him there were women's times when he must keep out of her chamber. And what I threatened would happen to his parts if he didn't was enough to make any man sweat. He'd curse and shout if his blood was up that night, but he feared me too much to cross her threshold.

So we wrapped a mist round his eyes, the two of us. He may have known there were times and places I had to go where it would have been death for a man to follow me. But I swear he never guessed his own wife went with me. The gatekeeper knew better than to peer under the hoods that went past him. And she wasn't going to tell him. What we do in the Mothers' name we don't call adultery.

There was only one thing that chilled me – if that stringy Nectan should ever make a proper Christian out of Gorlois and tell him our threats were nothing but moonshine compared to his power. Oh, don't mistake me. My power is real enough. I can feel it sometimes, coming up through the soles of my feet out of the good earth. It runs out through my hands into things I touch, like blood from an open cut. But there's one thing can dry it up. A Christian unbeliever. Lucky for me, he never knew that till the day he died. And luckier for his sweet lady's life.

But Morgan was not like her sisters, or her mother. There was a proud spirit in every inch of her. You'd be cutting off pride with every snippet of her finger-nails that curled on the fire. You could see it even in the way she slept, so still and stiff under the furs, while Elaine snored so peaceful and Margawse tossed about. There was always that pride. She would risk anything to get what she wanted, that child. But it wasn't what Margawse wanted. What Morgan dreamed of was to be a queen – or better still, a king.

She sat quiet, looking out to sea. There was a mist starting to rise from the woods in the coombe behind us and the sun was going down over the clifftop for another day. She could sit very still indeed, when she wanted to. I looked down to see what she had been making in the sand. I gave a great start and then hoped she hadn't noticed.

It frightened me. I'd never taught her. But it was there in front of me, or almost. She hadn't the pretty flowers her mother had used. She'd taken living things of the sea, or things that had been living. Empty shells, limpets mostly, and strands of cold wet seaweed, with holdfasts like fingers. But the pattern was the same. It only wanted blood.

'What's that you're doing there?' I asked.

'*You* know! Making a spell,' she said, jumping up with that wicked laugh and hugging me. 'To bring him home to me.'

I kicked that circle into little pieces. I didn't know why it was I had to keep that knowledge from Morgan. I'd never worried when Elaine was whispered. But there was a warning shouting inside me as if the tide was rising. And so it was. The sun had gone from our cove and there was a damp chill in the air. I grabbed her hand and hurried her home.

At dusk they shut the gate of the dun, and though we had nothing but cheese and beer on the table we were sitting late taking our ease when the dogs set up an almighty racket in the yard. Keby went running to the doorway and shouted out. 'Bran's balls, it's my lord and lady! And just look at the horses! You can hardly see them for dust and sweat. They've been ridden fit to break their hearts!'

Well, we were hard on his heels. And what a sight met us. The wild eyes of the horses rolling in the lantern light like night-mares. There were riders leaping down off their horses and shadows of cloaks swooping about like great bats. There were those that shrieked as though they thought the Black Hunt had come to take us. But they were human, all right, and I don't know which of us was more frightened. Gorlois's bodyguards had their swords half-drawn, as if they expected to be attacked at any moment.

We women flew about like hens when a fox gets in among them. And squawking just as loud. The beds weren't aired, and there wasn't a loaf of fresh bread in the place, or a mouthful of stew in the cauldron. And some were dashing to change the rushes on the floor of my lady's chamber, where the puppies had got in and fouled it, and it hadn't seemed worth the trouble of changing them till we knew she was coming home. And now, when I look back at it, I can see we had fouler things than that to worry about.

I was running to and fro like a madwoman, not knowing what to do first. The chariot was empty when I got to it, and the furs all tumbled in the mud. I couldn't find my lady and the girls in the dark and for a terrible time I thought they had been killed or taken by the Saxons. And then I caught up with my lady stumbling towards the hall doorway fit to drop, with Elaine and Margawse holding her by the arms on either side of her.

As soon as I saw their faces, I knew that ours were nothing but children's troubles, slaves' troubles, beside what had happened to them. My Lady Ygerne was weeping and trembling something terrible. Yet for all that, her eyes were bright and you could see she was excited. It struck me suddenly that she was not as much like our little Elaine as I'd been thinking lately. There was something of Margawse in her still, even if she was twice her age. And it's not to be wondered at, for Morgan and Margawse were her blood too.

I didn't like the look of Lord Gorlois. He was angry but he was afraid, too. And that's not a thing I'd ever thought I'd see in him. He was as brave a warrior as you'd find anywhere, our Duke of Cornwall. He couldn't keep still and he had to be shouting and giving orders, though I don't suppose he knew what he was doing half the time. He just had to be on the move. He ordered the gates to be barred again and all the weapons in the dun sharpened and a strong guard to watch through the night. So we all looked at each other, but nobody dared to ask what was the matter.

I caught a glimpse of Morgan's white face as she ran from her bed towards her father. I called out to her, but she wouldn't listen. I could see he had no time for her, but she followed along behind him like a puppy-dog, waiting for him to notice her. I let her go. I had my hands full enough as it was. We took my lady round the waist and helped her to her own bower. She fell to weeping on my shoulder and she was all fluttering and trembling, like a woman when a man strokes her flesh and takes his time about going further. Elaine and Margawse came crowding after us into the bed-chamber. Elaine looked fairly shocked, but Margawse was dying to tell us all about it.

We set her on the bed and shook the cloak from her shoulders. All spattered with mud, it was. I set to brushing her hair, thinking that would calm her. But when we asked her what was the matter, she threw back her head and laughed, and then frightened us more by laughing and weeping at the same time. So Elaine ran to the kitchen for a beaker of hot wine and herbs. When we had quietened her down they told us everything.

# Chapter Ten

Well, you must know by now what happened as well as I do. The bards have sung that lay the length and breadth of Britain. But what was strange was the different ways those three told it.

Margawse was gabbling away as if she couldn't get the words out fast enough. Her red hair was all tumbled over her shoulders and her eyes sparkling like a cat's. I'd seen her wild before, but never as excited as that. You'd think her gown would have split, her breasts were heaving up and down that fast.

'We've been in Fairyland, Gwennol! Such a city! I thought it couldn't be real. White statues on pillars, as if living people had been turned to marble. And such floors in his palace. They'd think shame to put rushes over them. They had pictures in little coloured stones. Can you imagine that, Gwennol? Pictures even on the *floor*! And as warm as summer. You could dance in your bare feet and it was as though the sun had been beating on the tiles, although it was night, in April, inside stone walls.'

Well, there was more of such nonsense. Baths steaming like boiling lakes. Couches of marble. Halls big as our grove in the forest, all under a great tiled roof. Whole streets of such palaces, she said, and the streets themselves paved with giant stones. Temples and churches to foreign gods and goddesses. Market squares. No wooden walls and thatch, you understand, but all made of great blocks of stone, if I was to believe her. Well, I saw Exeter years ago, and that was grand enough for me. But that was a hovel compared to London, if I was to believe her. You couldn't imagine such a thing, could you? I thought her head was turned and her wits were wandering.

Elaine was the one I could get most sense out of, though she was more scared than any of them, poor soul.

'Such crowds of people there were, Gwennol! And I don't just mean common folk, though the streets were thick with them staring at us. But fine lords and ladies from every part of Britain. I didn't think the world could have held so many. And the clothes and the jewels! We were like brown hedgehogs, all covered in dust and mud. But they took us into fine rooms and oh, Gwennol, they had hot baths as big as horseponds, and they washed our hair and oiled our bodies with scent, and we put on our second finest clothes, for we must leave the best ones till the grand feast of the crown-wearing. And then they led us to the great hall for supper and I thought that everyone would titter at us for country bumpkins.'

'The very idea!' I scolded. 'You two young ladies are pretty enough for princesses, and so I've heard say many a time, and you've gowns good enough for any duchess.'

'But they *didn't* laugh, Gwennol. All the heads were turning when we came in. I'm sure I was blushing like a gorse-fire. You know how it is when you feel everyone's looking at you. And they all seemed to have Roman names, like Lucius and Eusebia. And some of them called me Helena!'

Margawse couldn't hold herself in any longer. 'The king, Elaine! Tell her about the king.'

My heart seemed to jump a beat, and then took to hammering like a galloping horse. For what could she mean but that the king himself had looked at them, and which of my two young ladies would it be he'd set his fancy on? And then I remembered what young Keby had said and I turned cold again. It was true it wasn't the first time I'd heard that said about Uther Pendragon. I thought how a king can do pretty much as he pleases, and it's a bold father would say no to him, though it is his own daughters the king would have the maidenhead of. But when all was said and done, he surely wouldn't be ungrateful. A king's a king, and there would be few noblemen who could refuse to wed her for a cause like that, maiden or no maiden, and he'd know there'd likely be jewels and favours to follow for her and hers.

And it crossed my mind just then to hope it might have been Margawse he'd set his fancy on, child though she was, though you'd never have guessed it. For it would be common knowledge if the king took her, and none could shame her after that or know what she might or might not have got up to behind the armoury already. And I'd a shrewd idea the king wouldn't tell, whatever he found out about her, for he'd shame himself to let it be known he was not the first.

But which of those two was it, in truth's name?

'Be quiet, Margawse,' says Elaine. 'I'm getting to that. All in good time.'

'Tell her about the goblet. How the king sent it from the high table.'

Margawse's eyes were shining like two jewels in a goblet themselves, so I made sure now it must be her.

'*Well*,' says Elaine, getting cross because she wouldn't be hurried, 'we were all led to our places at the supper tables. And I could see Father was angry because he thought we should have been on the king's table.'

'And he was saying how he'd fought last year for Uther Pendragon against the Saxons in Elmet, and how he saved York for the Britons. And he was shouting it out loud enough for the king to hear, and people were beginning to look at us for more than our fair faces.'

'I started to be afraid then,' Elaine confessed. 'And I'd been so enjoying it till then. It was like a fairy-tale. Everyone treating us as though we'd always been princesses but never known it. And then I got frightened because of Father shouting, and I thought perhaps we couldn't have been princesses or we would have been up higher, as Father said. And maybe those lords and ladies always treated each other like royalty and there was nothing special in the way they looked at us.'

43

'But there *was*! The king! Go on!'

'Then the feast began, and the pipers started to play, and such food they brought in! Oh, Gwennol, it was all decked out like a May-Day procession with flowers and frills. You'd think it couldn't be real food. But every plate of it was for eating. Then the king signed and the pipers stopped and the chief bard began to sing a love-lay. Oh, it was so sweet! And King Uther Pendragon stood up, with everyone watching him.'

Her cheeks were flushed like roses now, and I began to think I'd been wrong about it being Margawse, and I was all of a flutter. Even Margawse couldn't stop her telling her story now.

'He took his own knife, with the gold handle, from his belt and he kissed the blade. They'd set a swan before him, that seemed to be swimming in a lake of violets. He cut the first slice from the breast. And he laid that portion of honour on a golden platter and whispered to his steward. And everyone watched to see where the plate would be taken. It went past all the under-kings and queens on the high table. Past the benches just below them, with the fine dukes and duchesses, down our side of the hall.'

'And all the heads were turning, and only the king still smiling after the plate had passed people by. You never saw such long faces!'

'But I never thought. I swear I never thought it was coming to us.'

'Oh, Elaine. You ninny! The king's portion? You must have wanted it to be for you!'

'I didn't think of that, I was so busy watching. It came to our table and the steward stopped. It was like a dream. I was so silly. I thought he was going to give it to Father, to make up for not inviting him to sit on the high table.'

'Oh, *Elaine*!'

'And then . . . Gwennol! He put it down in front of . . . Mother!'

I was as stunned as she had been. They were both looking at me, those girls, laughing and frightened at the same time. But I couldn't take it in. I mean, I knew she was still a beautiful woman. But the High King himself!

'The noise, Gwennol! The stamping and the shouting.'

'The men were laughing, and the women were angry. It was wonderful.'

'And Mother went white, and then red, and white again. And then I looked at Father, and I was frightened. He was furious.'

My eyes went to Ygerne then. She was staring across the room as if she was in a trance. There was just this little smile on her lips. When I saw that I could have slapped her face.

'Three times Uther sent her gifts. We'd never guessed. He must have fallen in love with her. The king, Gwennol!'

'The second time he gave her a golden goblet of wine, with a jewel in it. A little dragon brooch of red enamel and silver.'

'He smiled and lifted his drinking horn to her.'

'Then he sent sweetmeats in a casket of silver wire, all decked with lilies.'

'If I had been Father I would have killed him, then and there.'

A small, thin voice like the mew of a cat that's tasted blood. We'd all forgotten Morgan. She was crouched at the foot of the bed, her little white face peering up at us over the furs.

Her voice seemed to wake my lady out of a dream. All this time she'd sat there and never uttered a word. You'd have thought the Sisters had put a spell on her tongue. But when she spoke it hardly made sense.

'I thought it was all a dream. Lost with the Legions. But I have heard the tramp of the emperor's army on the streets. And the lays of the emperor's battles at the feast. And the hymns of the emperor's priest in the church.'

I don't know why, but that put me in a terrible temper. I was shaking with anger.

'And what's wrong with the British tongue, my girl? And the old straight track on the backs of the hills? And a sky-roofed temple to worship our own gods as we've always done?'

But she didn't hear me. And I began to fear she'd tried to spell-speak Uther Pendragon and it had turned back on her. She wouldn't be the first that had happened to. Her eyes were miles away. And was it the past she was looking into or the future?

'I never knew that Britain was so wide or so fair. Day after day we rode. Past forests that seemed to have no beginning or end. Lakes like silver cobwebs in the morning sun. Corn springing green. And still when we lay down at night we were among our own. But the white dragon is cruel. They murdered Aurelius in his bed. And Uther has no wife to bear him sons. If he should fall . . .'

And then that little sharp voice, like claws scratching.

'What did Father do to Uther Pendragon?'

45

# Chapter Eleven

Elaine seemed to be staring into the dark beyond the windows.

'Father sprang to his feet at the third gift, and his hand went towards his knife. Though he couldn't have struck the king in his own hall, could he?'

'I would have done,' cries Morgan.

'And then . . .'

'What? What did he do?'

'Nothing.'

'Tell her about the other man! The man in the archway.'

But Elaine wouldn't say a word more. I looked from one to the other of them. There was a queer look in Elaine's eyes. I've seen it in others. The look of those who can see more than they want to.

It was Margawse who rushed on. There was no stopping her now.

'There was a tall, thin man in one of the archways, on our side of the hall. No one seemed to have noticed him but Father, and then us, when we followed his eyes. He was about the same age as Uther Pendragon. Not too old. Not exactly handsome, because he had a crooked sort of face, but laughing. He was different from every nobleman in the hall. You could see it first in the way he was dressed. A plain white gown. But with a deerskin thrown over it, and the head left on and hanging down over his shoulder. But he wouldn't have been ordinary, even if he'd been wearing a toga or tunic and breeches like everyone else. He even made the king look a bit like a shadow, he was so . . . alive. He was the one who was holding Father from moving or shouting, I'm sure of it. And all he was doing was just crooking his hand a little and pointing a finger at him. And smiling that lop-sided smile. It looked as if Father was in a fit or a trance. I was sure he was going to fall down stiff on the floor at any moment. All we could see doing it was that one finger and his smile. But you felt as if there was a spider's thread between them, and Father was a struggling fly caught fast in it. Then I looked round at King Uther. And he was smiling back at the man. They had the same smile. As if they were brothers.'

'Who . . . was he?' I asked, and my tongue felt dry in my throat.

It was my Lady Ygerne who answered.

'Merlyn! Who else could it be? You guessed that, didn't you, Gwennol? Who here should recognise the Old Ones better than you and I?'

I'm not sure but that didn't give me the biggest shock of the evening, her coming out with it like that, in front of everybody. And I'm not

46

just thinking of Margawse and Morgan, who were too young yet to be hearing about such things. I had the name through Cornwall of a powerful wise woman, and that suited me. And everyone knew I'd shown my lady some little skills of healing. But I'd taken good care they said no more than that about us. There are some names we have that are better not spoken. It's true there were not so many women in that room, but some of them were none of our side, and never would be. And she had spoken out loud a thing which we'd always kept secret, and which should have stayed so.

Emrys Merlyn. I'd known it must have been him, of course. And she'd seen I knew. I was just an old nurse on the cliffs of Cornwall and Merlyn was the king's soul-friend that was known for a great enchanter at the court. And what the two of us might have in common it wasn't for others to know. My mind was in a turmoil now. If I was right, and she had tried a charm to catch the king, she'd have met her match a thousand times over in Merlyn. Even the mighty Pendragons would dance to his tune. And where that dance might lead us now, if Merlyn was pointing his finger at us, I shuddered to think.

All the same . . . Not so old. Not exactly handsome. But laughing. It was not King Uther I hankered to see when they told me all the marvels of his court. I wasn't so old but I wouldn't dearly have loved to come face to face with Emrys Merlyn, just once in my life, though I doubted I'd have the courage to lift my eyes to his, and let him see there what I knew well he would. Well, the world's a stranger place than we have any notion of, and sometimes Fairyland may be closer than we think.

But I was still cross with my lady. If I'd have had my way I'd have sent the others all packing out of the room, and asked her straight out what she meant by it. She's not so old nor so grand that she can't remember me smacking her. But in that dun she was the Lady Ygerne and I was her children's nurse, and what could I say to her with all her waiting-ladies and serving-maids fussing round her?

So I said a bit shortly, 'Well, then. If the king's taken such a fancy to you, what are you doing galloping back here in such a lather before the feast of Easter's over, and acting as though the giants of St Michael's Mount are on your heels with their cudgels?'

The two girls looked at each other then, as if neither of them dared to tell me what came next. So I looked at Ygerne, and her face was red as a horse-shoe from a smith's furnace. But she wouldn't bare her shame to me.

'Is the thing so evil, then, that none of you are going to tell me?'

I might have known it would be Margawse that couldn't keep silent. It was the sort of folly that would put a sparkle in her eyes. What was modesty to her?

'The next day the king did Mother even more honour. We all went to church. And then . . . Oh, Gwennol, he was forever praising her beauty and calling for his bard to make lays for her. He made her walk beside him in the garden and cast petals on the paths in front of her. And when the evening came, he led her with him to the high table, while Father was left with us, halfway down the hall. Afterwards, when there was dancing and singing, we heard . . . Elaine and I heard . . . they were saying on our table . . '

She broke off into giggles. Shameless, she was. As if I hadn't lived long enough in a man's world to guess what was coming next.

'They said . . . everyone was whispering it . . . the king was having a bower prepared, next to his own bed-chamber. And he'd had it filled with flowers, and silks, and perfumes, and silver mirrors. And guess who it was for? Mother!'

Poor silly woman. Couldn't she have seen the way the wind was blowing, long before it got to that? She'd lived long here in Bossiney, with only a handful of Cornish lords and a white-robed priest for company. But she'd feasted in kings' courts too. She wasn't as green as all that.

I looked her straight in the eye.

'And what did you do?' I asked. 'When you found that out?'

'What any loyal wife would do. I told my lord,' she said, with her eyes cast down. Very demure, she looked. 'He was in a terrible rage. He called our people together. He had to keep his voice low, but he was so angry it was as if he was yelling to heaven. He ordered the men to saddle our horses in the dark and bring out our chariot. Of course, Uther's grooms went rushing to tell the king we were going, so Gorlois had them killed, every one, and the guards at the gate too. Even the yard-hounds he killed. So we rode out into the night, like thieves. But Gorlois went back towards the palace with his sword drawn, and Jordan and Britael with him. When we looked round there was a bright light in one of the doorways. Merlyn was standing there. He didn't say anything, Gwennol. He didn't do anything. He just stood and smiled. He has a terrible smile. And Gorlois turned like a man sleepwalking, and came back to us and mounted his horse. When morning broke, we were galloping as hard as we could for the west and Cornwall. And who knows if Uther Pendragon is coming after us now, with half the troops of Britain at his back?' There was a catch in her voice somewhere between sobbing and laughing, so that I couldn't be sure if she was sorry about it.

'Let him cross the Tamar if he dare. He won't rouse Cornishmen to do you wrong. They'll fight for my lord, never you fear,' I told her stoutly.

'Ah, you say that now, Gwennol. But you don't know Uther Pendragon. And he has Merlyn behind him. Uther's not like other men. There is something about him that makes even kings follow him. And love him too. I've seen it in their eyes at court. You don't understand, Gwennol. Even a Cornishman would find it hard to say no to him.'

And a Cornish woman too, I thought to myself. So that's how the land lies. And little you care that good men will have to die for this. And so I told her.

'Lucky for me,' I said, 'that my man is dead, and never gave me sons. There'll be many a woman weeping before this is over.'

But I judged her too hardly. She was right. I hadn't set eyes on Uther

Pendragon — or on his soul-friend, either. It would have taken a stronger woman than her to have refused the glamour of that pair. But for all that, I'll swear she was never unwilling. And what I'll never know is who began that magic. Was it just the little spell she made that called him all the way to Cornwall? Or were there bigger powers than that at work already, to get her to make that boy the bards sing of? Either way, I should have known better than to meddle with them.

That little voice came again.

'Is Merlyn our enemy then?'

I didn't care to answer that. I left the child sitting on the floor, watching us.

We got Ygerne to bed, and her waiting-woman, Ruan, made ready to sleep with her, and by the time I looked round, Margawse had gone. The times I've wished my Lady Ygerne had given me a brood of boys to nurse! I should have been shot of them to their foster-fathers long before this. I went puffing out into the dark to look for her. And sure enough, there she was with some of my lord's young warriors, in the torchlight by the stables, laughing and as excited as her mother. And I don't doubt she was giving them a version of the story a sight more colourful than the one she had told me. I scolded her to bed and left her frightening Elaine with talk of battles coming.

And then there was Morgan to look for. She wasn't in her mother's chamber. I didn't need to go far. I knew I should find her with her father. He, poor man, had drunk himself stupid over the great table in the hall, with the pick of his warriors and house-servants watching by him. And there was Morgan, under the table, curled up asleep beside his feet like a puppy. I got old Sulian, that had seen more battles than any of them, to help me lift her, and she stirred in her sleep and cried out. She seemed heavy for such a skinny little thing, till we swung her clear of the table and a great sword fell out of her hand. It was no magic present from the king's palace. Only Gorlois's own sword that she had been clutching while she slept.

'No, no,' I scolded her gently. 'It will take more than you to save his life now.'

# Chapter Twelve

I don't think any of us got much sleep that night, except my lord, though he never went to bed at all. It was a grey, misty sort of dawn, and chilly, too, for the year was still early. And so quiet. Even the birds seemed as if they were listening. There wasn't a sound from outside, and nobody dared to unbar the gate until my lord gave the order. He slept on, with his head on the table and his beard all wet in the spilled wine.

I huddled close in my shawl as I went to get water for my girls to wash. At least they would die proud and clean. Elaine was shivering and complaining, but then she always did. She wrapped herself in her fur robe and ran away to her mother to find some comfort. I had a fight with Margawse to strip her of her shift.

'Come on, my lass. You'll never make a fine queen with a dirty neck.'

By the time I had towelled her dry, her eyes were sparkling.

'Will there really be a war between the king and Father? Will Uther bring his whole army here to fight us? And all because of Mother?'

'You can wipe that smile off your face. Fighting means dying. And how do you expect your father to stand against King Uther Pendragon and all his fine warriors? If it ends the way I think it will, you'll be laughing on the other side of your face.'

Morgan stripped down to her skinny white body without needing to be told. She didn't smile, and she didn't shiver. You'd have thought the cold had no power over her if you hadn't seen the goose-pimples on her. She washed more carefully than usual, then dressed herself and fastened her girdle tightly. I looked down at her proudly. Even then, she was more of a queen than Margawse. I wondered what would become of her if her father died.

The night had cooled my lady down, and she was frightened now. There are few that can feel romantic in the cold grey of the morning. Now that she was more sensible, I felt kinder towards her. Poor lady, who had thought herself almost ready to be a grandmother. And then to be courted by a king as though she was a handsome young princess. It was enough to turn any woman's head.

And so we all waited for my lord to wake up. Young Keby came by and saw me standing in the door of my lady's bower.

'What did I tell you?' he grinned. 'I said there'd be trouble if he took Lady Ygerne with him to court. I wouldn't mind having it off that one myself, even if she is old enough to be my mother. You can see she knows a trick or two. And Uther Pendragon can spot a good lay when he sees it, by all accounts. I reckon the king'll be standing in that doorway where you are before the week's out, or he's not the man they say he is. How's that for far-sight, Gwennol?'

'You cheeky devil,' I said. 'You want to watch that tongue of yours, or you won't have one much longer. My lady will hear you.'

But it was not her I was worrying about. All the time I was casting my eyes about to see where Morgan might be hiding herself.

'*She'll* be all right. It isn't her throat he'll be cutting, is it? It's the likes of you and me that will catch it in the neck if we stand in his way.'

But he was always a brave lad, Keby, for all he was cheeky. And he was true to his lord and lady to the end.

It was mid-morning when Gorlois walked out of the hall. The men stopped whatever they were doing and looked at each other, wondering who dared speak to him first. But they hadn't made my lord Duke of their war-hosts for nothing, and the morning had made a man of him again. He sent riders to the east to find if there was any news of King Uther coming. And others he sent south and west, to his kinsfolk and his friends, to call them to fight with him for his wife's honour against the king, if need be. And when the messengers had ridden away, the gate was barred again, though it was broad daylight. We couldn't see out unless we climbed on the ramparts, and all we could hear was the honing of swords and the clang of hammer on iron from the smithy-end.

My lady talked a long time to Lord Gorlois. She was no fool, once she'd gathered her wits about her again, now she was away from the glamour of the king's palace. It made me feel better, for it should have taken more than vanity to turn the head of a wise woman, though she was of the lesser sort. But whatever she'd done, she'd have met more than her match in magic there, as my lord was likely to meet his match if it came to a battle.

By and by the sun came out, and we all began to feel a bit safer, with so many men busying themselves for war around us. It was foolish, really. What could they do? But I've seen a sick child stop crying just to hear its mother sing a lullaby, though she can't save its life.

Morgan followed at her father's heels. She was quieter than usual, seemingly listening and thinking. Once she came running back to me, full of questions.

'Is this all because of Mother? Is she as beautiful as that? More beautiful than any woman in Britain? I never wanted to look like her.'

Which was just as well, seeing her hair was as black as a luck-cat's.

'She's beautiful, yes. And I don't mean just what you're supposed to say about any noble's wife. She scarcely looks older than the day she married your father. They say she's the handsomest woman in all Dumonia, that I do know. Though I dare say they're only counting the gentry.'

'And is it so very important to be beautiful? Kings would really go to war because of it? Against their own friends? Father was Uther's friend, wasn't he, last year?'

'King Uther Pendragon would, by all accounts. And he's the only High King we have between us and the Saxons.'

'I used to want to be a king,' she said thoughtfully. 'But perhaps it's more powerful to be a beautiful woman. What do you think, Gwennol? If I was beautiful, would kings go to war because of me?'

I couldn't help laughing, for, much as I loved her, she was a sharp-faced, ugly child. If she had power, it would come from somewhere else.

'Handsome is as handsome does, my fine young lady. And if you want to grow up beautiful, like your sister Elaine, you'd better start drinking up your milk and put some flesh on those sparrow-bones of yours.'

She didn't heed me.

'So my father has the most beautiful woman in all Britain for his wife. Even King Uther Pendragon envies him. You can buy horses and jewels, but you can't buy somebody else's wife. You can only steal her. So Father must fight to guard her. She belongs to us. We won't let the Pendragon take her away from Cornwall.'

That surprised me. It had never struck me that she cared much about her mother till then. All the shine in her eyes was for her father. But she was proud like him. And when she saw her mother was a lady that a king might covet, she began to look at her in a new light.

Ygerne was with my lord, walking the ramparts and arguing about what they should do if the king sent for her. Morgan went back to them. And she stood looking at her mother as though she had never seen her properly before. As a man may look at a mare that he's thinking of buying. And presently I saw her walking behind them. She wasn't dancing about, but copying my lady's steps. And she was twisting her hair in her fingers as though she was thinking of braiding it with pearls as my lady did. Her father looked round then and saw her. He thought she was playing. He grinned through his beard and tossed her up in the air. But Morgan didn't shriek with laughter at him as she used to. She let him put her down. Then she smiled at him like a grown woman, and studied her mother closer than ever.

We hadn't long to wait.

# Chapter Thirteen

I don't know what I expected. The fairy troops of Gwyn, with their silver helmets, galloping out of the mists to snatch us all away. Or the Black Hunt screaming down on us in the darkness on their night-hags, while we lay shivering with our faces turned to the walls. Or those old Romans my granny used to tell of, that stood in squares like human walls, fighting and falling without ever moving a foot.

Not normal human beings anyway. Not like our fighting Cornishmen, grinning through their beards and brandishing their long swords, bragging and showing off like men anywhere. I couldn't square that with what I'd heard of Merlyn.

Well, I did what I could while we waited. Gorlois wouldn't let me leave the dun, and that angered me. I could have helped him more than most, and the gods knew he needed it. It would take more than a strong sword-arm and high courage to save him from this. With Merlyn against us it needed nine times even my strength to build the sort of rampart that had any hope of keeping us safe. And even then I wouldn't have trusted it to hold for long. But he wouldn't budge, and I daren't tell him all I'd planned. I did go so far as to threaten him, but he hardly seemed to notice what I said. I wondered then if it was the beginning of what I'd always feared. That one day he'd slip the bonds I put on him before he married Ygerne. He'd stop believing I had power. I could have shown him then, before it was too late. I could have struck him down. But I held my hand. He had troubles enough coming to him as it was.

So I grumbled away and summoned Ygerne and Elaine and two others that were wise among her women. And do you know, my lady put her fine nose in the air and told me she had more important things to see to. Well, I'd spared Gorlois, but I was sorely tempted to call a curse down on her, there and then.

That left the four of us, and Elaine had been spoken less than a year, though she was a sensible maid and quick to learn. And nowhere for us to go but a grubby lane behind the kitchen, where anyone might chance upon us. The Mothers forgive me, I set Morgan on the corner to give us warning. I built a fire, and we did what we could. A little patterning. A handful of herbs in the flames. A cock killed. But it was poor, thin stuff, and we knew it. All the time I had this sick feeling in my stomach that if this was all the strength we could manage, it might do us more harm than good. But I was like Gorlois. I had to try.

After that, there was nothing but waiting. I don't mind admitting I was almost glad Gorlois hadn't let me go where I meant. It's not much of a wall around Bossiney. It wasn't built for war. But it felt a good deal safer than walking out there on the cliff, with the gulls slipping on the wind over the rocks and nothing but thin air between you and the sea. A cold, lonely place to be caught by what I feared was coming.

And yet. It's a funny thing, but I found my blood was beating faster, like all the rest. And I can't swear it was an unpleasant feeling entirely. I'd lived too much in the old songs and stories. When the world was all battles and magic and high deeds, and things turned upside down for pride or love, and kingdoms lost and won. All of a sudden we found we were living in such a story, and I don't think there was one of us that was wholly sorry, for all the evil that we guessed would come of it. We'd all rather that something happened to us than nothing. So we watched the skyline with our hearts in our mouths. And whether we hoped or dreaded what we might see, it's not for me to say.

But it wasn't much when it came. Three riders, or so it looked. A little after noon next day. They rode lighter than my lord and lady, without chariots. It's a wonder they hadn't overtaken our people on the road. But then, they didn't know the ways into Cornwall. They weren't winging straight homeward, like swans at evening. Or maybe they had reasons for not hurrying. Maybe it suited them to let the birds flock back to Bossiney. It gave them a chance to ride right up to our walls, and look around, see how the land lay and where a strong king's army might do most damage if my lord proved stubborn. Was it the vixen they wanted, or her earth as well? There was one at least that looked long and shrewdly round him before he left us.

They'd ridden hard, but not so fast the horses had foundered. They stood for a while where we had all been looking for them. That little nick where the road comes over the hill from the north-east. We never doubted who they were or why they had come.

They stood so still those first few moments, you might have thought three new pines had sprouted over there on the ridge. They looked hardly human. With the bright air behind them it seemed almost as if you could see through them. Then they moved, and we saw the glint of their armour, and knew then what we had to deal with.

Morgan caught her father's hand.

'Fight them, Father! We will never give in to them as long as we live.'

He just gripped her fingers. I heard her gasp. I don't think he even knew he'd done it.

They started to trot down the hill, and it was so still I could almost swear I heard their harness chiming like bells, though I couldn't have done. You'd think we'd never seen horsemen before. We were all of us on the walls and staring at them as if we couldn't move. Every soul in the dun was there – my lord and his wife and daughters, right down to the smallest slave baby in its mother's arms. Yet there wasn't one voice raised, not even Gorlois's. Just a sort of low murmur, like the sea on shingle under a fog. We were all holding our breath, to see if Uther and all his army were coming over the skyline behind them.

Looking back on it, I don't know why we didn't let her go there and then. We were beaten before we started. But they were high-blooded folk, and I suppose it had to be done the way it was.

We watched them come, and there was just enough dust on the road to hide the horses' legs so that they seemed to be swimming towards us on a brown tide. All this time the cows in the meadow outside the walls went on tearing at the sweet grass. They weren't thinking what might redden it before long. Though our own horses, that we'd picketed inside the dun, began to lift their heads and prick their ears.

Then I gave a great start. There was another rider had come over the hill. It wasn't the whole host of Uther Pendragon, but I don't think it could have shaken me more if it had been. Just one man. There wasn't even a flash of armour on him. As soon as I realised that I knew who it must be. And I couldn't take my eyes off him. He rode alone and slowly on a white horse. And as he drew near, I saw that he was dressed fantastically. A great cloak that seemed to be made of rags, every colour of the rainbow. And his hair white with lime. That made me shiver. I'm not lying when I tell you this: I felt his power, even from where I stood. And something worse than that. I felt sure that power had picked me out, even where I stood packed in amongst all the others. Old Gwennol, the children's nurse. And yet I swear he knew me. My knees were trembling like weak brawn, but I was as drawn to him as a magpie to a silver knife.

I had good reason to fear him, and he let me know it. Halfway to the dun he stopped his horse, at the far edge of our pasture, where the Great Oak grows. He got down and he was a younger man than I'd expected, even after Margawse had told me. He strolled under those huge branches, and he laid his hand on the bark of the trunk as familiarly as you please and tilted his head back to look up at the crown. He lifted his hand in a sort of salute. Even from here I could swear his crooked face was smiling. Well, I'd never in my life dared touch any oak-tree like that, as if we were friends. Never mind that one.

Suddenly I heard noise all around me. I'd only had eyes for one man, but the rest of them had been watching those three in front. Poor, silly fools, as if the danger that threatened us was steel and iron. Men can't see further than a sword and a shield, and most women aren't much better. And all at once the newcomers weren't ghosts or noontime shadows. They were flesh and blood, with men's faces we could see clearly and sweating horses under them. One of them carried a herald's staff.

They were still a good bowshot from the gate when Gorlois leaped down off the wall into the yard, with everybody tumbling down after him. I must have been the last, except for the sentries and a few boys that couldn't take their eyes off a coat of mail. I was always slow. But I was slower that day than I need have been. To tell you the truth, I didn't want to turn away. And it wasn't soldiers I was watching. I'm past bothering with them. Dangerous he may have been, but turning away from him was like being dragged out of a dream into a rough, cold world. And at the same time I was mortally afraid that the gate would open and he'd ride in, and I should have to meet him, eye to eye.

Well, such a to-do there was everywhere, I almost laughed at them when I saw it. Gorlois packed Ygerne and the three girls off into the bower out of sight, and barred the door after them, as if they were mares on heat, which in a way they were. Well, three of them, anyway. Morgan made a fuss, but he wouldn't listen to her. He set warriors with spears everywhere, lined up by the gates and all the way to the hall, and he was shouting for his best mantle and the clasps of silver and garnets, and polishing up his scabbard on the skirt of his own tunic. Pride. The sheer foolish pride of the man, flaunting his jewels and weapons at them, as he'd flaunted his wife at Uther Pendragon. I must have stood gaping like a fool. Next thing I knew I was bundled into the sleeping-hut. They almost threw me on the floor and the door slammed shut behind me. This was to be men's work, seemingly. There wasn't a woman left in sight.

I got to my feet as quick as I could and hobbled back to the window. I couldn't see them open the gates, but they seemed to swing back as if a giant's hand had pushed them. It was so bright over the sea it made me blink my eyes. All the same, even while my sight was dazzled I knew Merlyn hadn't come. I should have felt it in my blood.

Uther's three messengers dropped from their horses. Their legs had that wearisome roll of men who have ridden hard and long. But they were proud and haughty under their dirt, even so. Their leader was a proper lord this time. They told me afterwards his name was Ulfin, he that stood as close friend to Uther as Jordan was to Gorlois. I should have studied that face when I had the chance. I'd be seeing it closer than I wanted to . . . if you could call it seeing. But then, I just watched the fine flash of their cloaks go by me as they walked through our spear-guard into the hall. Then we all had to wait.

After a while I couldn't help myself. I found a stool and clambered up higher on it. I couldn't see much over the stockade even then. But there was a place where the headland reared up above the rest of the cliff. A green mound, caught between the top of the wall and the sky, that I knew was sweet with wild flowers if you could see it closer.

He was there, with a deep blue sky behind him, and the sunlight glistening on his white hair and his coloured ribbons. Sitting on a white horse among the walls of the old people you can still see in the grass. He could have come straight out of Fairyland. But I didn't doubt for one moment he was real, and here in Bossiney now. I think it was the rest of the world I'd have doubted first.

They were carrying wine into the hall now. The best jars too, that they said had come all the way from Palestine. Gorlois would make a fine show of politeness, though there was a dusty answer at the bottom of the cup. We knew what Uther's men had come for, of course. Our Gorlois had insulted him, good and proper, leaving his court without permission and killing his people. He'd ordered him back to London with his lady, on pain of death. We knew what message they'd take back with them, too. Still, a guest's a guest. Gorlois wouldn't have the king say that he hadn't shown them hospitality first.

Our men on guard shuffled their feet and growled as they waited, but the birds in the trees were singing away now as though they hadn't a care in the world.

The king's party came out at last, and walking quicker than before. They looked angry, though I can't think what they had expected. But perhaps it was just a show they had to put on for honour's sake. I often think that so much that happened that year was play-acting. It's always like that with the nobility. Common people like us say what we think, or show it in our faces. Like children.

And that made me gasp all of a sudden and turn my thoughts for the first time that day to Morgan. She was still young enough to wear her heart naked in her face. Even without being told I knew she'd be watching from the window of her mother's bower. I wondered what she'd seen. I let Uther's warriors ride out with their backs to Bossiney and our fate in Gorlois's answer. I hadn't time to look after them. My eyes went straight to the downs.

There was no horseman any more up on that mound of turf above the sea. The place looked as empty then as ever I've seen it. Merlyn had gone.

And you young ones may laugh at this. You think the blood runs cold when you're past fifty. But I tell you this. I never felt such a loss when my own man was gone and I lay alone month after month. It was so bad that moment I had to pull up my skirts and thrust my own finger into my blood-hole to satisfy myself, and never mind who heard me crying. Afterwards, I was ashamed. It had been too small a thing for what I felt.

I couldn't tell you if Morgan saw him or not.

# Chapter Fourteen

I don't know why she did it. It's a thing I can't forgive. She went to Nectan, and not to me. Ygerne, that I'd sung lullabies to in the old tongue before she could speak her mother's name. Ygerne, that I'd taken into the woods showing her leaves and roots even before she knew the power of them. Ygerne, that coaxed me to use a deep charm of mirrors and apples to bring young Gorlois to her door. Ygerne, that I'd whispered into the old way, having no little maid of my own. Did she think I'd failed her, bringing her nothing but daughters?

I chided her to help me build a wall. She just stared at me, with her blue eyes very round.

'They say his parents wore the Roman purple.'

'Rome's gone. Uther Pendragon's flesh and blood. He's king over us only as long as the Britons want him. He can be killed, whatever his father wore.'

'But it wasn't just his father, Gwennol. His *mother* wore purple too.'

And what did she mean by that? I should have seen the way her hopes were turning.

Well, as soon as the gate was opened again she was off. Just her and Ruan, in plain cloaks and hoods. Gorlois was in a fury when he found out. It would be days yet before Uther got his message, like a slap in the face. But he wasn't going to have his prize running loose over the countryside like any milkmaid. He sent Jordan and Britael galloping after her. But they were too late.

It wasn't far from us to the coombe where the saint lived. A sweet, rocky valley, it is, with the river rushing over the stones, cool and green, and the trees and ferns hanging over the water. And then you come on it suddenly. A great hole in the rock, as if a giant had punched his fist through it. And a white spout of water flinging itself down through it into a pool. They knew how to pick their spots, those Christians. He'd made his hut there, and grew his little garden of herbs and kept a few fowls. Just for the eggs. They say he wasn't man enough to kill one.

I'd been there once, when curiosity got the better of me. Just to see what we were up against. I didn't get close. I was still coming through the hazel trees when he heard me. He'd been sitting on a mossy stone out in the water with his long shanks dangling in the stream, and singing to himself or his god. But I hadn't set foot in his clearing before he'd whipped round and was on that bank and snatched up his staff where it was lying in the grass. I thought for a moment he was going to beat me with it. But he just held it at both ends, stretched out like a bar

58

between us. His blue eyes burned and words came out of his mouth. Hard-edged, like steel. Latin, I suppose it was. I couldn't understand it. But I knew what he meant, all right. I don't think he cursed me. I didn't take any pain from it. But I couldn't stir one step forward from where I stood, do what I would. I never tried again.

But it wasn't his staff that stopped Jordan and Britael, so I've heard. It was the sight of my lady, standing among the primroses beside the water, with her hands lifted, praying. Think of that: the wise Ygerne of Cornwall and a bloodless Christian hermit. It made me spit like a cat. What was she, that he'd let her into his holy ground when he'd barred me? I'll tell you what she was. False. For all the power I'd given her, she'd swing from one side to the other where she thought it would do her most good. Though what help she thought she'd get from a childless man like that is more than I can say. And I dare say he thought she was a lamb come back to the fold. She was a wise woman, all right. There was none of us truly knew what was in her mind.

When they'd done their prayers, he put his hands on her head, and she crossed hers over her breast and cast her eyes down very modestly, or so Ruan said. Then she walked over to her husband's men, very meekly. And Britael set her on his horse and led her home. Gorlois raved at her, but she never answered him. Just stood before him with her head bowed down and a little smile on her lips. When he'd blown himself out she said just one thing.

'I have prayed, my lord, for the safety of Britain.'

I could have wished I'd had Gorlois for a son, instead of that one for a daughter.

But she was as false to Nectan as she was to me. Elaine was missing a long time that night, and when she came back she wouldn't meet my eye. It didn't take me long to know what the two of them had been up to behind my back.

I was sick of the lot of them. If they didn't want my help they could seethe in their own cauldron. Why should I burn my fingers plucking them out of the stew? So I stayed where I was. I never called the wise even then. I had messengers as swift as any of Gorlois's. I could have summoned a host that was stronger than his. Our weapons are different but they can shield and kill as surely as metal and wood. I let them lie. Many a time I've grieved over that. I was so angry with Gorlois and Ygerne, I never thought what might happen to Morgan.

Before evening the first of Gorlois's messengers came galloping back, and the news was as cold as the sea-wind that was beginning to rattle the thatch. All next day it was the same tale. It seemed all the chieftains of Cornwall had gone off to that Easter crown-wearing and there was no one left who dared to raise a sword against the Pendragon.

'They'll come back to the west now the feast is done with. My kin will fight for my honour. Blood of my blood. Sword-brothers and father's friends.'

Oh, yes, I thought to myself. Who are you fooling? For which of our chieftains of Cornwall can't count more enemies than friends? Fat cattle stolen. A daughter dishonoured. A son killed in his cups. The gentry know no other way of passing their time but fighting and boasting and raiding. Gorlois had as ready a sword as any of them. And they've long memories in these parts. Our duke couldn't rally heart and hand across the country now. They'd fight for him against the Saxons, but not against Uther. He hadn't Merlyn's glamour round him.

Yet I don't think it even occurred to him to let Ygerne go. Not though this Uther Pendragon claimed to be High King over us all to the Land's End, and Gorlois was only war-lord of Cornwall. I think he knew she fancied Uther. It was that that stuck in his pride. It made him angrier than I'd ever seen him before. He didn't shout and bluster. It was a deep, dark anger, that turned him in on himself. Oh, he'd had fights a-plenty. Cattle-raids, pirates, Saxon wars. But he was always laughing in his beard beforehand as if it were some great sport. And when enough blood was spilt and enough armour dented and enough booty snatched from whoever wasn't quick enough to hide it, both sides would break and ride away. And they'd fill their heads with ale and raise a lament over their dead and in the same breath be planning the next raid.

He wasn't laughing now. He'd fight this battle to the bitter end. He'd see every last one of us dead before he let her go.

But he still had one dagger up his sleeve.

There was a shout from the sentry at the gate, and we all jumped like hares. But Gorlois grinned.

'Let her in,' he cried, and strode across the yard with us crowding after him.

It was no horseman this time, sweating back through bogs and forests to bring us bad news. It was a woman we saw marching in through the gate. Well, three women, to tell the truth, for she'd brought two of her nuns with her. Bryvyth, who'd built her nunnery on Tintagel Head. She had a tall staff in her hand, curled at the top like a shepherd's crook, a white wool gown over a linen smock, and bare feet. She'd cut her hair, and you might think from all I've said that she was a slave. But you'd never have thought that if you'd seen her. Her way's not mine but I can tell those that have power from those that haven't, and she had it. She wouldn't look a man in the face if she could help it, and she kept her head covered for modesty. But she had a way of folding her arms that was as bold as if she'd looked him straight in the eye. She was a big woman, too.

'You sent for me. Is the business so urgent that your man must come yelling at my gate while we're singing in chapel?'

'I've reason enough to rouse the whole of Cornwall.'

'So I hear. And what has Gorlois's quarrel to do with the nuns of Tintagel?'

'It has everything. Uther wants my wife, and he shall not have her. When he hears my answer, there will be an army in Cornwall. I must have a fortress to fight from.'

'The Duke of Cornwall has many strongholds. Did you call me here to tell you which one to pick?'

He moved quickly then, and we thought he was going to strike her. But he caught his hand back.

'Bryvyth Crook-Staff, you may be a woman but you are a learned one, and no fool. There is one place, and one place only, that could hold out against such a war-host: Tintagel.'

We must have all drawn our breath sharply then, like a nest of adders. It was no more than everyone must have thought in their minds many a time. That rocky island, with the sea coming at it on all sides. And just one neck of rock, so high above the waves it made you dizzy, joining it to the land. What chieftain mustn't have envied it for a fortress, these hundreds of years? But if we thought it, it was never spoken. For everyone knew Tintagel was a woman's place. First ours, now theirs. It had a name: the strong place where the two waters meet. There were few standing there that understood the meaning of that, or guessed how it was used. But the men kept away. Why else had those nuns chosen to set their cross there?

'You are thinking that Uther Pendragon would respect sanctuary? A king that would violate a Christian wife?'

'I'm not asking you for sanctuary, woman. I want a fort! A hundred warriors. Three lines of ramparts. Ten men alone might hold that bridge for me against half of Britain.'

She had a temper like his. She raised her staff to him then, like a bar across a door.

'On your knees, godless man! Shame, that you should even think of it. There's one way only Gorlois will come to Tintagel – when he brings his lady wife to me for sanctuary. No warrior passes our wall bearing weapons, nor ever shall. If Uther Pendragon comes, it will be Bryvyth Crook-Staff will meet him on the bridge. But Gorlois, war-lord of Cornwall, will have to fight his bloody battles somewhere else.'

She didn't wait for him to argue. She turned her back and strode out of the gate with her nuns after her. She never once looked back.

Gorlois had a face like thunder. We feared he'd send the guards and have her struck down before she'd reached the downs. But he let her go. There were only a dozen nuns on Tintagel, and a handful of schoolchildren. But whether it was her he was most afraid of, or the place, Gorlois never tried to take it from them by force.

# Chapter Fifteen

Still we sweated. And I soon feared it wasn't only Ygerne that had been spell-struck, up there in London. Gorlois was like a fly trussed in a cobweb. He'd had this one idea, and Bryvyth had thwarted him. Now he didn't seem to know what to do.

That frightened me. It wasn't like him, that was always so quick to leap on his horse and draw a sword. Bossiney's no place for war, but Gorlois had forts enough on the hilltops, above the forests. Chilly, windswept old crags. They weren't the sort of places you'd want to live in, when you could have sweet grazing on the downs and good fishing in the sea. But that's where we should have fled by now. That's what they were built for, in the old times, when it was clan against clan and we hadn't a king over all Dumnonia or a Saxon army to turn our thoughts elsewhere. Gorlois was known for a canny war-lord, but there wasn't the youngest kitchen-maid couldn't see that we should be somewhere else but where we were. And my courage seemed to fall into my boots, for I guessed who'd done this to him, and there'd be worse to come.

His warriors didn't like it one bit either. They buzzed loud enough. I saw Jordan and Britael arguing with him, and old Sulian trying to steady the younger bloods.

'Why doesn't Uther come?' says Margawse. 'What is he doing?'

You'd think she wanted us murdered. She was always impatient, that one, whether it was good or ill coming.

'Let's hope he's changed his mind. Maybe he's put up a doe that will make sweeter hunting than your dear mother,' I told her.

I glanced round at Ygerne as I said it. She tossed a braid over her shoulder and looked away as though she hadn't heard me, so that I couldn't tell if she liked the thought or not.

'He could be in Cornwall by now,' said Tudy. 'Wouldn't he take the high road over the moors to make for the forts? The Pendragon's a man of war. He'd never think we'd be such fools as to stay in Bossiney, like cattle at Samain, waiting to be butchered.'

That struck home. There was a loud growl ran round from near a hundred men. Gorlois had been sitting hunched over the fire, staring into the flames. But when he heard that he straightened up and gazed at Tudy, round-eyed as an owl. But even then we never guessed what was in his mind.

'Maybe he's come to his senses and gone off to fight Picts or Saxons instead of good Cornishmen,' Keby said.

'It's a long march from London,' Sulian tried to warn us. **He was** the oldest warrior Gorlois had, and he'd fought in many a battle against the Saxons. 'And the Pendragon will have an army to muster if he wants to besiege us. Likely enough it will be Pentecost before he crosses the Tamar.'

'Not he,' said Jordan. 'There were warriors enough came with their lords to the feasting to make a fair old war-host. He hadn't got halls big enough to hold us all. There were camp-fires burning in every market-place and tumbledown temple the Romans had left. My lady may have turned his head but Uther's a soldier. He's not so mad with love he wouldn't have the sense to keep those spears about him till he got my lord's answer.'

We came to Sunday. And still we hadn't moved from that round in the meadows, where an army could march right up to our gate, and nothing to stop them. I'd tried what I could to rouse Gorlois with nails and thorns and more besides. But he'd gone beyond my reach by then.

It struck me folk were a sight keener to go to chapel that morning than ever they'd been before. There hadn't been such a crowd gathered round it since the day Nectan came striding up from the beach with his psalm-book on his back and his bell in his hand.

My lady was there inside, of course, fresh as a girl at her first communion. I'd love to know what was hatched between those two, and what they'd prayed for.

The nuns came trooping along from Tintagel Island too, singing as though their God was still in his heaven. They were the only ones that didn't look afraid. What had they to fear from Uther Pendragon? A religion for slaves, my mother used to call it. Nectan feeding us with bread, though he'd hardly a scrap of flesh on his own bones. Big Bryvyth in her housemaid's gown, serving us rich wine from a chalice set with jewels. But they'd caught more than slaves now. I glowered at them from where I stood. Morgan was standing beside me, singing away in her clear voice. I don't think she cared what the words meant, then. Her eyes were fixed on her father. He glared back at those two, and mostly at Bryvyth.

But it was Nectan he collared afterwards, speaking hoarse as though the words choked him.

'When Uther comes, I shall expect you to do your duty as my priest. You cannot wield a sword, but you can call down curses on our enemy.'

I've seen a bull's nostrils widen like Nectan's did then. If I'd been Gorlois I'd have jumped well clear.

'Aye! The prayers of the Lord are more powerful than pagan battle-axes. But do you think I would aim them against a Christian prince?'

'Uther, Christian? A king that turns to a druid for his soul-friend?'

'Emrys Merlyn is the son of a holy virgin. Who are you to slander them both? You who keep a great witch to teach your daughters!'

Gorlois swung round on me then and his eyes went wide. I stood my ground and gave him back look for look. Let him think what he would now. Then he gave a great laugh.

'Old Gwennol! You'd compare her with Merlyn? You haven't met him, man!'

But nothing he could do would shift the saint. There wasn't one of them would give him what he wanted. And when I turned round, there was Morgan, staring at me like a little owl.

The time had seemed long, watching those empty hills. Now, looking back on it, I could have wished it had gone on for ever.

But Uther Pendragon was in more of a hurry than we bargained for. And whether it was just my lady's sweet face, or hot anger because Gorlois of Cornwall had refused to hand over what he wanted, or whether he'd noticed the first grey hairs frosting his beard, it's not for me to say. He was a bold war-lord before, and now he had Merlyn at his elbow. When his heralds came back with Gorlois's dusty answer, I wouldn't mind betting he had his saddlebags packed for war already. Lord Gorlois was known to be a proud man and Uther Pendragon was not a king to sit about waiting for an insult.

We watched Gorlois pace the ramparts, till the stars started to prick through that April sky. He was a dark man in daylight, and he looked darker then. I should have been getting my girls to bed, but none of us wanted to move. It was pretty near like waiting for a sentence of death. I stood outside my lady's bower, with my arms round Morgan. And she was stiller than I was. Stiller than any child her age had a right to be. Watching her father.

He turned his head suddenly and the watchman gave a great cry, so we knew they were coming. Two messengers came galloping in as hard as they could ride. We didn't need to hear them shout.

'Uther has crossed the Exe. He'll be in Cornwall tomorrow!'

That brought Gorlois back to life at last. He came striding down the steps into the dun. The yard was full of our shadows, crowding round him, like a town of ghosts. We held our breath to hear what he would do. We thought we knew the choice. To fight Uther Pendragon and die, or give Ygerne over to him and be shamed. We never guessed the madness that was going through his brain.

He smiled at us, and played with his sword, so that it clinked in his scabbard. It was the only sound in the evening air, except for the sea far off that was like our own breathing.

'I will not stay here,' he said harshly, like a man condemned to die. 'I cannot fight him in the open plain, and he knows it. Nor can I hold this house against him. We shall march to Caer Dimiliock and make a stand there, till enough Cornishmen come to my aid to make a fair battle.'

And not before time, I thought, though it won't save you. Poor fool. Who but your own kin will fight for you now? There's a richer king than you coming, with glamour in his train and the promise of glory after for those who follow him against the Saxons. And what has Gorlois got to offer them now that he's out of favour?

Well, the men burst out cheering, of course. My lady was the only calm one among us. Win or lose, she didn't count on being harmed. She put her hand on his arm and smiled up at him.

'But Uther is on the road already. He may be close behind your scouts. What if he catches us before we reach Caer Dimiliock? Why can we not stay here and defend our own Bossiney?'

Oh yes. I could see the way her mind was shaping. Bossiney's a homely round. It's not one of your high rock forts that will stand months of siege. That wasn't what she wanted. A bitter, wasting war. Growing thin and scrawny like some hermit woman, to fall into Uther's hands when all her looks were gone. She wanted Gorlois to ride out to battle on our cattle pastures. She saw herself standing on the rampart, watching two lords fight it out to the death over her, and she waiting to give herself to whichever of them won, like a prize at a fair. Ygerne the Beautiful. She'd been a virtuous wife, as I account it, but she was too much like Gorlois herself. She'd the same taste as he had for fame and fortune, but it took her a different way. So she turned white like the rest of us when she heard what he was planning.

'You will not ride the same road as me,' he said, barking it out in the voice of a man who knows he is speaking folly but is not to be argued with. 'Dimiliock's strong. It can stand out for many weeks. Maybe Uther Pendragon will grow tired of dashing his head against Cornish granite for what he cannot have. But if I fall, he will find himself cheated of what he came to steal.'

Morgan caught her breath, sudden-like. There wasn't one of us understood him, even then. My lady said, in a strangled kind of voice, 'Then . . . where shall I be?'

We heard the waves far off beating at the foot of the cliffs and I think I was not the only one who saw the height of that drop in my mind and wondered how far Gorlois might go to cheat Uther Pendragon.

'Here!' he cried, and he laughed at last, like the old days, splitting his beard and grinning with his white teeth.

Morgan's was the only laugh that followed his, just as if this was some new game he'd thought of.

'*Here?* You'd leave me here for Uther Pendragon?'

'Three soldiers and a handful of servants. You won't need more. Tudy was right. Here's the one place he'll never dream of finding you. He'll think the place is deserted when he hears I've gone. He's High King of Britain. He'll go where there's a strong fort and a great war-host. You know that man's pride.'

She was terrified now.

'You're mad to leave us to his army!'

'No madder than he is, that thinks he can steal my wife.'

'But he ordered us back to the feast at London. You told him no. You defied him. His troops will burn every village, every dun, every farm, before they reach Caer Dimiliock. What if some of them come here without the king?'

Couldn't he see what she was trying to tell him? It wasn't falling into the Pendragon's hands that she was afraid of. There were those under him who wouldn't stop to ask her name.

He nodded to the warriors behind him. 'I'll leave you a faithful guard. Sulian, Tudy, Coan. They'll know what to do if you're found.'

If they hadn't been grey before those three would have changed colour then. Years now, they'd been too stiff in the elbow to ride to war with the rest. But there was only one stroke he wanted from them this time.

I saw the men's hands drop away from their sword-hilts as if they'd been burned.

My lady gasped at that. She could see that he meant it. The words came rushing out of her.

'And what of your daughters? Would you have them killed too?'

That stopped him. I felt the muscles of Morgan's shoulders tighten under my fingers as we waited. Gorlois went white for a moment. He had no answer to that. He would have died himself and taken her with him if he had to, but not his daughters.

Ygerne seized her moment.

'At least send us somewhere safer than this,' she begged him. 'Let us go to the nuns on Tintagel Island as Bryvyth said. They'd give us sanctuary.'

That touched him on the raw. He swore at her then.

'There's only one way, I'll have you go to Tintagel now. If you hear Gorlois is dead, then shear your hair and take off your gown, and go to Tintagel with my daughters and take your vows as nuns.'

Well, we all looked at each other. We didn't know what to do. I stood clutching my little Morgan's body in front of me for dear life. I'll tell you, I was terrified. If I'd thought him spell-struck before, it was nothing to the madness that had bewitched him now.

But we were only women, and the men had been cooped up long enough. It was Jordan moved first. And then it was like a spark in the straw, and everyone shouting their heads off. It was coming on twilight, but in a moment the slaves were dashing about, emptying the storehouses, though dear knows we had little enough left that was fit to eat after that wet old winter. They were packing it all into panniers and carts. And the war-horses were whinnying as they threw the saddles on.

Ygerne just stood there dumbstruck, with Elaine and Margawse, and watched them bring two chariots out. Three of her women wrapped themselves in cloaks and climbed into them. And Britael lifted a little kitchen-maid into the second one, bundled up so she might have been Morgan.

All Gorlois's warriors mounted and lined up, before and behind, with a train of pack-horses loaded with all the gear they could carry.

I thought Gorlois was gone mad. But at the last he surprised me. He looked me straight in the eye and said, 'If they come near, Gwennol, try all you know. There's more things than morning mist that can deceive the eye, though I fear you've left it too late to gather your brood. Look after my daughters. Fight Merlyn any way you can.'

I hadn't heard his voice so gruff since his hound died. I just stood with my mouth hanging open like a fool. All those years, and maybe he'd guessed more than I thought. Morgan twisted her head back to smile at me, as though she'd always known.

I don't mind telling you, tears stood in my eyes. He was always a brave man. And it was all my doing. When he was just a young lord and whole of heart, I'd pared the apple that had brought him to Ygerne's gate. I put my hands on either side of his face and kissed his head. I felt my power going into his blood then. I couldn't save him. But he wouldn't go into the dark unblessed.

He hugged Morgan strongly to him.

'Be brave, little warrior. Look to the honour of my name.'

It was hard for him to say it. She answered him fiercely.

'Never you fear, Father. Whatever you hear shall make you proud of me.'

She buried her face against his breastplate, and I had to prise her off. But she didn't cry, though she must have known what that parting meant.

He kissed Margawse and Elaine, and whispered to them and fondled their hair. Even Margawse looked pale. And last of all he embraced Ygerne, long and hard. She didn't say a word.

Then he gave the order, and the column started to move. For a long while we heard the tramp of hooves and the creak of carts going past us. When the yard was quiet we scrambled up on the ramparts and watched them go, a host of shadows marching away in the twilight. But they scorned to hide themselves. As dusk turned into night we saw torches spring out and fire flashed red on their spears and armour. All up the hill there were rivers of lights moving. Gorlois's kin were hosting in the dark.

Then our men shut the gate, and we were left in an empty dun.

# Chapter Sixteen

We didn't know if Uther would come on us in the dark, as Gorlois had taught him that night at Mount Damen. We were starting at every sound. There weren't many of us, and we must have looked like a handful of ghosts. My lady and her waiting-woman Ruan, the three girls and myself, young Keby and a couple of kitchen-women. And those grey old warriors, Sulian, Coan and Tudy.

We daren't show a light. The dun was meant to look hollow and deserted. If any nosy folk looked in next morning, then we'd make ourselves out to be a parcel of greybeards and slaves left behind to mind the place, with all the glory and high blood gone somewhere else. But it was better no one saw us at all.

We moved into the great hall, where at least we had straw and water and a little food left. I got the slaves to fetch all the blankets they could find, and we made ourselves ready for weeks of cold hiding. And who could tell what would happen to us after that?

We couldn't use my lady's bower. That was supposed to be empty. But nothing that any of us could say would persuade my lady to dress herself and Gorlois's daughters like common peasant women, still less shear themselves like slaves. She was a brave woman, Ygerne, when all's said and done. She'd meet her death if she had to, but it must be nobly, like a duke's lady, not a kitchen-maid left behind. But I didn't think that dying was as much in her mind as it was in mine just then. And when you come to think of it, she had less need to fear death than the rest of us. There was just those three old men guarding her, and I could see that under their fine mail they were more nervous of what they'd been ordered to do than I was.

No. Ygerne would live, all right. She was what this whole game was about. She was a wise woman who would make shift for herself. When Uther Pendragon came, as come he must, Ygerne would be waiting for him, as beautiful as the day she walked into his feasting-hall and won his heart.

So she changed her dress as well as she could by starlight. She chose it even more carefully than she usually did. She had the decency not to put on her best feast-day robe. The dress she settled on was two years old, and faded with washing, but for all that it was a pretty thing and made her look not more than seventeen years old, and so Lord Gorlois had often told her. Sky-blue it was, by daylight, embroidered with roses and violets, and she tied a girdle of silver about her waist. She still had pearls in her hair. And she dressed her daughters finely too, though she had a tussle with Morgan. That one would rather have gone bare-legged in a coat of mail if anyone had let her. Over it all they put homespun cloaks of dun and russet, such as farmers' wives and daughters wear, with hoods for their jewelled hair. That was for outside only. It was no proper disguise. We all knew that in a twinkling of an eye they could throw them off and show themselves for what they were. Ygerne wouldn't pretend. And it was nothing but that black jealousy of Gorlois that stopped him seeing this was the only safe way.

Yes. There's the rub. Safe. That's the sort of word you and I would think of. I know it was mightily on my mind that long night. But it's not a word that men that are highborn have any use for. They live in some dream of pride and glory, so you'd think they had no fear of death like common folk. And they'd take wives and daughters with them to the grave, like slaughtered hounds, if they had to. A Christian, he called himself, and went to Nectan's chapel, but I hadn't noticed my lord was so very different from the old chiefs that the bards still sing of. I don't think he wished to be. And my lady had always kept one foot, and more, on the old road.

The moon rose late that night. And when it came I minded my lord's last pleading as well as I might. I knew I couldn't keep Uther Pendragon away from us, with Merlyn beside him, but I might yet be able to wrap us round in a Cornish mist so that some things might stay unseen a little while longer. This time I ordered Ygerne to help me and she didn't dare refuse now.

That was the night we whispered Margawse. We needed all the help we could get. But when she was joined to us, it couldn't be done proper. I often wonder if the Mothers were angry with us over that.

But Morgan we never spoke, either of us. Not even then.

I was for lighting a fire under the stars, the way it should have been done. Who would be awake to see us now? But Sulian wouldn't let me. He was a plain-thinking soldier that was more afraid of Uther than of me. So I paid that price for a promise that the men would keep their eyes shut and their backs turned. We sat cross-legged in the yard, under the half moon. I'd put Morgan to bed long ago. But I knew she hadn't stayed there. I could feel her watching us through the dark doorway, like a cat at a mousehole.

I battled against Merlyn that night, as I hadn't dared do before. I should have saved my strength. I had left it too late.

Ygerne's heart wasn't in it. All the time I could see her eyes going over her shoulder, though you couldn't see anything above the ramparts but treetops and stars. She let her cloak fall open, showing her pretty dress, and she put up her hand in the moonlight to touch her hair and her white throat. Even as she chanted the words with me her look was far away. She never wanted to be invisible. It was a poor, weak circle we made, like trying to bind a giant with a daisy-chain.

But then, perhaps she was more sensible than us. How could those four ever hope to hide what they were from the king, with their high bearing and their soft white hands?

When it was done, it was almost daybreak. I stomped up to the ramparts in no good temper. For I knew already it had all been wasted effort, and it had left me tired. I let the sea-breeze blow on my face and I wished I was back in my childhood home in Polzeath and rid of the lot of them.

Then I felt a small, cold hand slipped into mine. Morgan was smiling up at me, as if she was trying to coax me into something.

It made my heart turn over, not for the first time by a long way. For she had a way of smiling, as though you were the only person that mattered in the whole world. And sorry I was for what I had been wishing to her and hers just then.

She squeezed my hand.

'That's not how it should be done, is it, Gwennol? Not like that. Not here.'

And her little lips were still smiling, but her eyes had gone very dark and bright, staring deep into mine.

'Where, Gwennol? Where is the power, really?'

My own eyes went sideways then, though I tried to pull them back. She followed where I looked. And I was pleased to hear her gasp. It wasn't everything she knew, at eight years old. And even then I didn't tell her all of it.

Tintagel Head. That proud stack of rock that was almost an island. Just that one narrow ridge from cliff to cliff that was more dreadful than any drawbridge. The nuns had got it now. It even looked a bit like a fort. There was a ditch and a bank dug in front of the bridge, and they'd put old Padarn there in the porter's lodge. He lived alone, and he was the only man they'd let near them, and then only when there was heavy work to be done. But beyond the causeway it was as peaceful a scene as you could wish to see in an April dawn. The white walls of their little huts scattered about the grass like so many daisies, tucked into the ledges with their backs to the winter storms. The sheep grazing on the hilltop. And the stone cross above it all.

Well, they say they'd carved a cross on it. You couldn't see that from here. Just a shaft of stone pointing at the sky. I needn't tell you what it looked like to me.

So she didn't see my eye go downward. She was gazing like a child spellbound at what she thought I'd shown her. For I didn't give that nunnery more than a glance. My mind was seeing deeper than that. You'll know where I mean. On the beach below those cliffs there's a deep cleft, where a hand has reached inside the bowels of the land and plucked out a hollow way right through the rock. Like a hole between two legs. The sea comes washing in from either side. Even then I thought I could hear the stallions of Manawydan neighing.

I'd left Morgan still staring at the cross of the nunnery with her eyes wide and startled. Well, she wasn't wholly wrong, was she? Those white nuns couldn't have lived where they did, and heard the waves around them, lain in the night alone and still, and not felt something of what went on beneath them. And there were some who did more than that. Though there was the devil to pay later when Bryvyth found out.

So I let Morgan believe what she would that morning. In the end she knew the whole of it, better than anyone.

'Couldn't we go there?' she said, very fierce. 'Can't we go to Tintagel and make magic with them there? Real, powerful magic.'

I shook my head.

'It's too late, my lover. I'm not stirring one foot outside these walls until this is past, and nor will you. We must bide where we are, and use what strength we've got, though it's little enough for what's coming against us.'

'And Father?' she asked. She had a way of piercing straight to the heart of things. 'Does he have those with him who can make magic to keep him? As strong as Merlyn's?'

What could I do but look down at her with the tears beginning to brim in my eyes and hug her close to me. She saw where the real danger lay.

When I lifted my head I thought I could hear a bell on the wind and I pictured those little white figures going to their chapel in the grey dawn light. Well, what if they were? They'd be at their prayers now. I caught myself wondering if they were praying for us.

All the same I wasn't prepared for what I found later that morning. Morgan, with her hands lifted, praying out loud, and not to any god I'd sung to her of. She smiled when she saw my face, and then she looked frightened.

'What's the matter, Gwennol? Why are you looking so angry? Didn't you mean it? Haven't the Christians got the power to save us?'

'Them! No, my girl, they haven't,' I told her pretty short. 'So don't let me catch you looking to them to help you.'

I don't know to this day if I did right. I hadn't the power to save her myself, had I?

At sunrise we shut ourselves in the hall again. There was a ladder to the loft over our heads. Just in case. Elaine was weary and crying, but to Margawse it was all adventure. She'd enjoyed what we'd done last night. It was her first taste of our power, and it had quickened her blood. She was only sorry she couldn't be riding off to Dimiliock now to watch the battle. She hadn't the seeing, like Elaine.

Lady Ygerne sat with Elaine's head on her shoulder. She looked older by daylight. I wouldn't like to tell which way her hopes were turning. Morgan was quiet, too. She was more frightened, now that her father had left her.

71

# Chapter Seventeen

We hadn't much longer to wait. When they came it was sudden, like a flood in February. Keby shouted out to us and we went running to the walls. I could hear our small old guard drawing their swords, grasping at spear and shield. But there was no hope of fighting.

I'd never seen such an army. I thought the hills themselves were moving. It was like the shadow of a great cloud in the east.

'They've taken his bait,' said Coan, very hoarse. 'They're bound for Dimiliock. They're going to pass us by.'

'Don't tempt the gods!' I screamed at him. But it was too late.

We watched the Pendragon's men pouring off the ridge towards us, like a river that has burst its banks, and spreading out over the countryside, in little rivulets. For a while the forest hid them. We could see smoke beginning to go up here and there. Then they were on us. Green and blue, their cloaks were, sweeping in to drown us where we stood. And the light on their weapons and harness flashing like water in the sun.

We weren't waiting out there in the open to see any more and be seen ourselves. We didn't need telling that the only safe place for us was up the ladder into the rafters over the great hall. Lady Ygerne and the three girls went first, with Gorlois's men after them. Their faces were grim and their swords were drawn, and not only for Uther Pendragon's soldiers, I knew.

Now Ruan and the slaves were scuttling up that ladder as fast as they could move. I told them all to go in front of me, for I knew I'd be the slowest. And all the time I was gabbling spells aloud that I'd forgotten I knew.

But when it came my turn to climb that ladder, my stiff old joints clipped at my sinews like the blacksmith's red-hot pincers. Morgan leaned over the hole, and her little white hand was clawing down for mine.

'Come on, Gwennol! Quickly!' she screamed.

There were many things happened that day that I wish I could forget, and can't. But I shall remember that one thing till the day I die. Morgan cried out for me as though she loved me.

But nothing I could do, not even the wet, shaking terror of the Pendragon's men, would get my limbs up those rungs. When they knew it was no good, old Sulian drew the ladder up into the shadows, and their faces disappeared.

That hall seemed bigger than I'd ever remembered it. Too big for me. But I daren't go outside again. So I crept into a corner behind the beer-pots. And then I thought that was the worst place I could have chosen to hide from soldiers, so I crawled away like a rat into another corner and hid myself in the straw. And only then I remembered Keby, that I'd last seen standing on the wall with nothing but an axe in his hand.

We couldn't know till the very last if they would pass us by or not. The coast road runs close by Bossiney. Surely they couldn't have helped but see our dun? I lay with my head pressed to the ground. I could feel my whole body shaking with the tramp of their feet and hear the neigh of their horses. They were coming fast, like hounds that have sighted their quarry. The sound was getting louder, like the tide coming in.

Then it seemed to go quiet and I thought we were saved. Maybe my spell-weaving had been stronger than I'd dared to hope. I lifted my face from that scratching straw. Too quick. There was a shout from outside. Then loud yelling. I dived back under that straw like an old trout under a stone. And there I lay, shivering with fright.

It didn't take them long. They burst through the door. I'd have given anything to be able to see with my ears then. I could hear shouting and banging, but I couldn't make sense of it. There didn't seem so many of them as I would have thought, and more of them inside the hall than out of it, by the sound of it. I could tell when they found the beer, and I thanked my lucky stars I wasn't behind it. Let them drink themselves stupid, I prayed. And I curled myself small like a newborn baby in a cold world.

But they found me. When they pulled the straw off me and rolled me over, they looked like a ring of giants with their backs to the light. Laughing down at me at the thought of what was coming as if I'd been thirty years younger. And they weren't drunk enough for my liking. It only made them rough. I tried to let them take me as easily as I could, for I was an old, used woman and long past the age of bearing, and what did it matter so long as it was over quickly? But I must have been stiff and difficult for all that. It was a long time since I'd had a man between my legs – except in the Mothers' service, and that is something different. Then there's that pulse in the blood that makes us all young maids again, wet inside and out and too eager for stopping, and the one who comes to us then takes us like a king. So they hurt me, and I cried out with the pain. But it was a cruel long time before they had all finished with me.

Someone else came then. A young warrior lord by the look of him, but he wasn't Uther. He was half-drunk as well. He shouted at the men, and they went grumbling out of the hall like whipped curs. But he stopped behind. It wasn't me he wanted. He looked all round and cursed. If he was hoping to find a treasure of weapons still hung on the walls, he could have saved himself the trouble. He might have known that Gorlois wouldn't leave so much as a horseshoe-nail behind for Uther Pendragon to find. So he had me like the rest before he left, since there wasn't anything better.

There wasn't one of them saw the treasure hidden over their heads.

I never had Merlyn's power, and what I'd had felt to be slipping away from me fast, but I couldn't help having a grim sort of smile to myself, even then. That's one spell I'd made stronger than I'd thought.

He strode out of the door, and I heard him call for fire, and I thanked the gods that all our hearths were cold. But one of them must have had a flint. I heard it strike, and then a crackle in the thatch. I thought of my own skin first, even before Morgan's, crouching there as I was in that stale straw with the fire beginning to sparkle in the roof. And anyway, what had any of them done to help me? I'd done my best for them. Those that went up that ladder could get down it fast enough without help from me.

The noise died away. I limped out to the doorway and breathed clean air again. There was a dark cloud of dust up on the ridge going away to the south. It seemed King Uther had taken Gorlois's bait. But his men had left Bossiney burning.

Well, let it burn. There wasn't water enough to put it out. All I wanted was enough to wash myself clean. I'd find some in the well behind the kitchen. I could only go slowly and painfully. There was no one yet to help me.

I pulled myself round the corner of the wall. And it was there I found Keby, hanging over the well with his throat cut like a pig.

A little voice spoke behind me. I might have known Morgan would be quickest down that ladder.

'Is Keby dead? He is, isn't he? And those things they did to you. Was that because of Mother, too?'

I was too sorry for myself to tell her anything but the truth.

# Chapter Eighteen

Bossiney burned. I hadn't the heart to weep for it. Sulian's three and the slaves did what they could to pull off the burning straw from the roofs with rakes and beat out whatever flames they could reach. But for all that, the great hall was a blackened shell, the stables had gone, and the slaves' quarters were nothing but smoke and ruin. They'd managed to save my lady's bower, though there was a great black hole in the roof. They'd all of them worked themselves to death there to salvage what they could. Even my lady and the girls had fought the flames and run through the smoke with whatever armfuls of stuff Uther's men might have missed. All except me, and I could hardly put one foot in front of another. They were all of them black and weary by the time they'd done.

Lady Ygerne pushed back her hair with her sooty hand and said, 'If Uther Pendragon could see me now, I doubt if he'd think I was worth the trouble of finding.'

And her voice trembled, so that I could tell she was near to tears. Poor lady. She hadn't had a mouthful of hot food for a night and a day, and she'd been frightened half out of her wits. But she was as proud as Gorlois, and that's where it hurt her most. She could bear it if her lord died in battle and King Uther took her by force. But what she couldn't bear was for him to come and find her like this, old and tired and dirty.

'There now,' I soothed her. 'We'll wash your pretty face and see if we can find you a clean gown, and there's still a corner to sleep in.'

'I won't stay here.'

'There's nowhere else for us, my handsome. We'll make shift somehow.'

'We can't spend another night waiting for common soldiers to come and burn us in our own thatch like rats,' said my lady.

'They won't come back. Not now they think the place is burned, and only a dead boy and an old used baggage like me inside.'

'And what are we to eat and drink?'

That made me pause a bit. I'd been bleating away at her like a foolish ewe, but I saw she had the better of me now. Sulian and Coan and Tudy had beaten back the flames from the storehouses, but they might as well have saved themselves the trouble. Bossiney was stripped bare: every last grain of corn and joint of salted pork gone. It was little enough Gorlois had left us to eat as it was, marching off with his own men at the thin end of winter with all the provisions they could carry for a siege. They'd even herded our cattle down the road to Dimiliock.

Siege? I couldn't see it, no matter how I tried. A proud man like Gorlois of Cornwall, waiting to die in his hole like a starved shrew, with Uther outside his gates, taunting him for the honour of his wife. A man like that would never stay cooped up for long.

But gone he was, and all our good corn with him, and what little he had left us, Uther's men had stolen.

And there was something worse. There wasn't one of us wanted to lift a bucket from that well, seeing what had fouled it. The men were old soldiers. They'd seen blood before. But even they didn't have the stomach for that.

I didn't care then if I died, so long as I didn't have to move from where I was. All I wanted was somewhere to lay down my head and rest.

'We're to stay here. That was my lord's orders.'

'And how much longer will Duke Gorlois be alive to give anyone orders?'

'Ssh!' I scolded her, for Morgan was listening, with a face like white chalk under the soot. 'We'll face that news if it comes.'

'I won't stay here, like a pig shut in a slaughter-pen. It is not fitting.'

'But where would you go, my lover? You can't reach him now.'

She lifted her chin with that proud look that warned me I was not her nurse any more.

'Where we should always have gone. To the nuns at Tintagel.'

I looked to the warriors for help. They were Gorlois's men, after all, and under his orders. But I could see how it tempted them. They didn't like what they'd been told to do. And whatever Bryvyth said, even three old warriors might make a valiant stand there, defending my lady's honour on Tintagel causeway till the very last. You could watch the thought shaping in their minds.

'But my lord said . . .'

Ygerne looked me straight in the eye.

'Gorlois will not come back, Gwennol.'

I was too weary to argue with her.

I made the slaves get the better of themselves and dip the bucket in the well till they got one that was no worse than pink. You wouldn't have thought a young boy would have so much blood in him. But the Mothers have more. They'll swallow all we give them till we're bled white. But the water will still be bubbling up out of the earth after we're gone.

Ruan chose a dark cloth and washed the soot from their faces. There wasn't one of them dared to ask where the water came from. And after they'd finished, I cleaned my own legs with it. You can wish to die, and yet you go on living.

But none of us cared to drink from that well, though our throats were rasping from the smoke.

The men buried Keby in the meadow. Poor souls. Their old arms were so weary they could hardly lift a spade. But the pigs had been rooting for acorns under the oaks all that wet winter, so the ground was soft. If we lived, my lady would come back and ask Nectan to give him a proper burial. The Church always had them when they were dead.

Then those four wrapped themselves in their cloaks, and put up their hoods to hide their faces. But what was the good? You could no more have hidden who they were than a white mare can hide in a herd of bay and brown horses. Even the way they carried their heads told they were nobly-born. The king would find them out sooner or later. But Ygerne made sure she would choose for herself the place where Uther would see her again.

His men had gone long since. All the same, it was queer and silent on the track. We all felt as naked as babies as we stepped outside that gate. The pasture was empty. There wasn't a body moving on the road. Margawse was quieter than usual. She was looking round her nervously instead of with that bold stare of hers.

The cottages we passed had a dead sort of look. Some of them had their doors wrenched off their hinges and their gardens trampled and every bit of food gone. If they hadn't, the doors were shut, and the smoke-holes were still, as though the hearths below them were cold. They had an unfriendly feel. And with good reason. The bards sing fine songs of the warriors who fall in battle. But there are others the lays don't tell you of. There were common men as well as lords walled up in Dimiliock now who'd never come home again, and women and children who had cause to weep already. If they were inside, peeping at us through the cracks in the door as we passed by, they wouldn't have any reason to love Gorlois's family.

Elaine looked pale and scared, and kept close behind her mother and Sulian. Morgan was the bravest of the three, with her little head held high.

By the time we reached the cliffs, I was so worn out I couldn't look at more than the next step in front of me in the grass. Every time I moved a foot it hurt me. But when I had dragged myself out to the headland I drew a big breath and made myself lift my face to look south.

It was what I'd feared. The sky was filled with a great dust-fog, and I heard men screaming and the clash of weapons. But when I looked round at Sulian and his men I could tell by their faces they hadn't heard anything but the cry of herring-gulls and the splash of the breakers on the rocks beneath us. And they were soldiers that had known more battles than ever I would.

I'd have liked to believe they had the truth of it, and I was just a foolish old woman who'd seen too many horrors for one day. Then I looked at Elaine, and I knew she'd heard it too. It's a bitter burden we carry.

Morgan caught at my hand.

'How far is Dimiliock? Will we be able to see it from Tintagel?'

'No,' I said, to comfort her and myself. 'It's too far for the likes of you to see the fighting. Dimiliock's an hour's hard galloping from here.'

Still so close as that? They seemed to have been gone a lifetime.

'He should have taken me with him. I'm not afraid of the Pendragon. I'd have fought him. Like I fought the fire.'

77

'No, no,' I told her. 'You weren't made to be a warrior. You're forgetting. I thought you'd made up your mind to be a beautiful queen, like your mother.'

She pulled her hand away, sharpish-like. 'Don't dare say that! What made you do it, Gwennol? She's not a queen. Not while Father's alive. And anyway, I don't want to get married now. Not to a king or anyone else.'

And I didn't need to ask what she'd seen that day to make her change her mind.

There's a valley runs down below Tintagel. We came to the head of it, and there was the nunnery, standing against the sky like a fairy fortress. There was the cross on top, and little houses for the nuns all dotted around the sides. Peaceful, that's what it looked, like a farm in the evening when the cattle are coming home. Uther's men hadn't touched it.

They all of them started to hurry when they saw it. But I couldn't have gone any faster if I'd tried. Every step I took was agony, with the raw flesh chafing me as I moved my legs.

Morgan waited for me where the path crossed the stream and began to climb again. She smiled as she held out her hand and pulled me up. But then she was away again up to the next bend, darting backwards and forwards like a squirrel. She was always impatient.

I was far and away the last to reach the top. I couldn't help it. They were all standing there on the edge of the cliff, and I don't flatter myself it was me they were waiting for. An odd, quiet place, it was. Not a soul to be seen. There was a bank in front of us, with a narrow opening, to show that it was holy ground beyond. God's rampart, they called it.

And below it a deep ditch that must have taken days to dig. It made me feel queer looking down into it. But that was nothing to what I knew was waiting for us on the other side.

There was no one about. But for all that, I had a feeling we were being watched.

# Chapter Nineteen

There was no one about, so we started to walk through. But we hadn't taken more than a few steps towards it before old Padarn came out from behind his hut. From the way he was yawning I should say he'd been taking a nap in the sunshine, just as if Uther Pendragon's army wasn't raiding and burning the whole countryside. Well, they'd steered clear of Tintagel. There wasn't a wisp of burning thatch here.

His mouth fell open in a different way when he saw who'd come. Sulian gave him his marching orders.

'Bring your mistress here, fellow. And look sharp about it.'

He didn't need telling twice. He went hobbling away over the bridge as fast as he could go. Poor old man. I don't know what they kept him for. They were a tough lot, those nuns. Half of them were stronger than he was. But then, he was hardly likely to turn any woman's head.

While we waited we couldn't help looking at that neck of stone between us and the island. It wasn't very wide. I could hear the waves pounding on the rocks below, and it seemed to me as if each one that broke was biting a little bit deeper into the sides. I could almost fancy I felt the land shaking beneath me.

Padarn was coming back. A little brown figure he looked on that causeway, like a shrivelled old leaf that the wind might blow away. He was fairly out of breath by the time he got to us.

'You're to go across, my lady. She's waiting for you.'

So Ygerne wasn't the only one who would have her visitors meet her where she chose. I thought our duchess might argue, but to tell you the truth, we'd had enough of standing out there on the open downs. We'd all feel a lot safer on the other side of that bridge.

So we kept our dignity and went on through the gate. Ygerne first, then her daughters, with Ruan and me following. But when it came to Sulian's turn Padarn stuck out his hand.

'I'm sorry, sir,' he said. 'Just the womenfolk unless you give me your weapons. There's no armed men allowed on Tintagel Island.'

Sulian had the sword half out of his scabbard. He had his job to do. But Ygerne turned to him with a sweet smile.

'Put up your sword, Sulian. I shan't need you to defend me here.'

I felt sorry for those grey old warriors. They'd rather have been at Dimiliock, any day. It was a hard task my lord had left them. But they knew their duty. They'd wait by the rampart if she ordered them. They wouldn't budge from it, whoever came. And they were not so old but they wouldn't sell their lives dearly to anyone who tried to pass them.

My lady was walking out on to that high path, so we had to follow her. It made me turn dizzy crossing that, and I wouldn't be the first one, by a long way. You could look down into the sea on both sides, ten times deeper than the deepest well. Green water breaking on black stone. And you could see where lumps of rock had tumbled off and lay smashed on the beach, like bits of broken pot. Up here in the sunshine it might be all peaceful and holy to Christ. But underneath there was something else. A different holiness, where the two streams meet. The Mother's Hole. The nuns should have known they'd never be rid of it entirely.

I wondered then if my lady had more than I guessed in mind when she chose this place. There was power beneath us. I could feel it with every step. What troubled me was what she meant to use it for.

I looked down at Morgan. But for once her little face was hidden under her hood.

There was a nun waiting to meet us on the other side. But she was too small to be Bryvyth. She wore white wool that had never been dyed, the same as they all did, and walked bare-footed. But she greeted us like a lady in her own hall.

'The peace of Christ welcomes you,' she called out to us, 'and the rest of the Spirit upon weary travellers.'

'May your peace return to you,' we answered, as they had taught us.

Peace? Small hope of that, I thought to myself, what with the pain in my guts and the thought of Keby with his blood running away into the well, and Uther Pendragon laying Cornwall waste, all for the sake of my lady's face.

Well, as for her, she held her head so high she might have been visiting another lady in her castle for a feast. 'Lady Ygerne and the three daughters of Gorlois claim sanctuary here from Uther Pendragon.'

That made the little nun gasp.

'Follow me!' she said.

She was off up the path with her skirt flapping, like a startled hare. All over the island we could see white figures turning round or peering out of doorways to get a good look at us.

'That's made a stick to stir the hive,' I muttered to Ruan.

The little nun showed us into the guest-house.

'Wait here,' she said, 'Bryvyth is coming herself.' And she bobbed away backwards out of the door.

I'd never been inside a convent before. Seeing those plain, white nuns, I'd always thought they must live in a poor, bare place. But whatever their own cells were like, when I looked around their guest-house they had tables and benches as finely made as anything we'd had in Bossiney before it was burned. And the curtain that hung by the door was made of wool good enough for a chieftain's cloak.

But I hadn't much time to be nosy. Next thing we knew, there was Bryvyth in the doorway. A big, broad-shouldered woman she was, and she stood on her own threshold like a barn-door. I thought for a moment her knee began to bend when she saw us, as if she was going to bow to Lady Ygerne. But if she had old habits pulling her that way, she got the better of them.

80

'Peace be to all in this house, and the blessed rest of angels this night,' she said.

'And to you also,' we answered.

'And which of you would be the Lady Ygerne?'

They still had their hoods on. But she knew, of course. Hadn't her own hands given the wine to my lady that very Sunday? You couldn't have hidden a fine duchess like Ygerne among a hundred women. And anyway, Bryvyth was looking straight at her when she said it. But she was mistress in her own house, bare feet or not, and she was enjoying it.

My lady drew herself up tall. For all she had come through, she looked as fine and handsome in her homespun cloak as if it had been cloth of gold.

'I am the duchess,' she said. 'My lord Gorlois is fighting with Uther Pendragon at Dimiliock, and I and my daughters have had our hall burnt down about our ears by his soldiers. We claim sanctuary here, with you, for our lives and honour.'

I thought that nun looked at her shrewdly.

'And you're thinking Uther Pendragon would respect my convent, now? What's to stop him going through here like a blacksmith's poker through butter?'

'Uther is a Christian king.'

'A fine sort of Christian, isn't it, that makes war on the husband to steal his wife?'

'He is High King of all the Britons. He is used to having what he wants.'

'For a king so recently made, it's not taken him long to get into the habit. And if you've come from his feast in London, you'll know it's no Christian confessor he keeps company with for his soul-friend.'

There was not much she hadn't heard, that Bryvyth. And she was sharper than Nectan.

'Is it Merlyn you speak of?' my lady asked, and I thought she spoke the name soft and carefully.

'Emrys Merlyn it is. And no friend of the Church.'

I waited for my lady to answer that. When she did she startled me.

'Uther Pendragon carries the cross into battle. Whoever helps him fights for you, Bryvyth Crook-Staff.'

'And if he wins, who will be master on Tintagel tomorrow? My Lord, or Merlyn's?'

'If the Saxons win, there will be no tomorrow for either of you.'

The nun snorted and straightened her shoulders then, like a farmer's wife getting ready to draw a pig.

'Well, they'll not be coming tonight, by the look of it. We'll see what the morning brings. There are clean beds here for the women, if that will suit you. Padern will look to your men in the gatehouse. So I'll see you at supper. We don't get many guests at Tintagel. It's a long time since I had a crack with layfolk that could talk about more than the price of beans.'

She looked across the bridge at the porter's lodge.

'And send word to those men of yours that they can put their swords away and sleep sound tonight. This is a holy place. If Uther Pendragon should come to Tintagel, it's me he will have to reckon with.'

She left us then with a grim smile. The guest-mistress brought warm water and washed our feet, even mine. It was sweet to the touch, that pure spring water. It cleaned more than our skin. And when we drank it cold it tasted better than wine.

The sun was getting low, though we couldn't see it now. A mist was creeping in and the tide was hushed. Presently a bell rang and we could hear the nuns singing in the chapel higher above us. Away in Dimiliock, the first day's fighting would be nearly over. It was a heavy thought that there'd be men dead now that I'd known all their lives. And nothing any of us could do but wait.

They served us a fine supper in their refectory. It opened my eyes, I can tell you. Red wine in glass goblets, just for the gentry, of course. And roast lamb, newly-killed, on fine, glazed dishes. Bryvyth laughed at our faces.

'Yes. We lead a simple life most of the year. But it's our rule to see our pilgrims well-served. Guests are doubly welcome!'

And when I looked at the nuns I could see what she meant. They were sat at tables down the sides, and they were enjoying their feast, I can tell you. Across the bottom of the room were the schoolgirls. Princesses as well as farmers' daughters, so I'd heard. They weren't allowed to talk, but they were staring at us for all they were worth.

The wine loosed Bryvyth's tongue, and she was all evening telling Ygerne about her schooling in Dyfed. Of how she'd travelled Ireland, following him she called Patrick. And of the work of her nuns that were fine potters and weavers and bee-keepers and scribes, and were supposed to busy themselves with everything that was wholesome and beautiful.

Pilgrimage, that's what she called her life. A journey of the soul. Always travelling on to something new.

More than once her eyes went to my face. But she never challenged me. And I was too weary to think it strange for me to be sitting at her table. It was like a dream to us at the end of such a day to be full and warm and at ease, and to feel the arms of the sea guarding us on every side but one. It ended with Elaine asleep with her head on the table, and Morgan creeping into my arms to close her eyes.

We got them to bed at last. The guest-house had three small rooms, opening off a passageway. My lady slept in the far one, with Ruan stretched at her feet. Elaine and Margawse next to them, and I was left with Morgan. We were too tired out and full of food and wine to fear that anyone might come on us in the dark. We didn't trouble ourselves how Coan and Tudy and Sulian might be passing the night on the other side of the bridge.

I shuffled in to put the older girls to bed, and I'd hardly the strength to brush their hair or fold their gowns. We should none of us want rocking that night, after all we'd been through. I'd be gladder than most to close my eyes and put the pain away.

When I got back to Morgan she was standing in her shift at the open

**window,** watching the mist come creeping up over the cliffs and curl in wisps in front of her eyes. She had her back turned to me, and her voice sounded hollow in the fog.

'Where are we? What place is this?'

'Why, maid, you know very well where we've come. To the nunnery at Tintagel, as your mother said.'

After a bit she swung round to me, her eyes black and staring.

'Who are you? Who am I?'

That made me shiver, I can tell you, thinking of some of those charms I had put about us. How did I know what she could see or couldn't see when she looked at me? It made me cross and frightened.

'Hold your tongue now, child, and come to bed. Do you want to ill-wish us all? I'm old Gwennol, and you're little Morgan that's Lord Gorlois's daughter.'

'*Am* I? Am I, old woman?'

I couldn't bear to listen to such nonsense any longer, nor meet the look in her eyes. I rolled over, hunched up tight under my blankets, and tried to wish that long day away. Beneath us I could hear the slow beat of the sea. Like the breath of a living beast, it was, closer than I had ever slept to it before. I knew the tide was rising in the Mother's Hole. And even there in the darkness, with my eyes tight shut, I had a picture of Morgan still, kneeling on her bed in her white shift, staring at me as though she didn't know me.

# Chapter Twenty

I woke suddenly in the night, with that feeling you have when you know there's something wrong. I sat up in bed, and that made me draw my breath sharply. My scars had stiffened while I slept and the crust was splitting. I listened. I couldn't hear a sound now. And somehow that was worse than if I had. I waited, with the skin crawling on my neck, and then I heard it. A scratching on a door, and then a bumping in the passage, and the sound of men's voices, very low.

I'd no thought but that Uther's men were coming to attack us in our beds. Then I heard women whispering. And I thought perhaps they might still be outside the gate and old Padarn had come across the bridge in the dark to warn Lady Ygerne. And what could we do if he had? We'd nowhere left to run.

I clambered out of bed, and I don't mind telling you it made me moan to move. I went to the chamber-door and I must have gasped out loud, for there was a white-clad figure whisking out of the house-door into the night. I made the sign against evil. Then I blinked and came to my senses a bit, for as she vanished over the step I saw the heel of her bare foot and knew it must have been one of Bryvyth's nuns. The little guest-mistress probably. She'd left the outer door open, but I couldn't see far. The moon was up, but so was the mist. The air was white, yet I could hardly see two paces beyond the step. It was a night to trick the eyes. Far below I could just about hear the hiss of the sea. Even that had gone quiet now, as if it was listening.

I put a bar of my own kind on that door, to be sure, mumbling a bit, as you do when you're not really thinking. And I cursed myself for an old fool that had broken a good night's rest for nothing, and got the cold dew on me. Then I turned back, and I had such a shock! It sent the blood out of my face all at once when I saw what I'd done. If my bar had worked, it had shut the good outside and trapped the evil in with us.

Two men were standing on either side of my lady's chamber-door, like sentries. Tall men, cloaked and hooded. They were none of our three old veterans, that we'd left at the gate, for they carried themselves straight and easy, like warriors in the prime of life. I couldn't move for fear, and my tongue stuck in my throat.

I knew they were watching me, though they had shadows for eyes. Then they turned their heads to look at each other and I heard them laugh low.

Well, if I'd been afraid to venture outside my room, first off, it was worse now. I was trembling like a dog in a thunderstorm. I'd have given a year of my life to be back in bed with the covers over my head. But I daren't step past those two men and turn my back on them even if they'd let me by. Then another shape separated itself from the shadows between those soldiers. A woman's, it was.

'Ruan?' I gasped, with my heart in my mouth. It's not often I've been glad to see her, but I couldn't think who else it could be.

It was her, all right, and she giggled to me, with a bright, wicked look in her eyes, that put me in mind of Margawse.

'Ssh!' she whispered. 'What's the matter? Don't you recognise these two? It's Jordan and Britael.'

My lord's two bodyguards, that hardly left his side? I couldn't make sense of it. Or only one way.

'Is he dead, then?'

'No! You ninny, Gwennol! Lord Gorlois is here. He's in my lady's room now.'

'He never is!'

'It's true. He'll be having her in her bed by now.'

'But he's in Caer Dimiliock, with the Pendragon's army round him. How could he get out?'

There was a movement from the middle room behind us, where Elaine and Margawse slept. I heard Elaine cry out.

'No! No!'

And then Margawse hushing her.

'Ssh. Don't disturb the children.' Ruan put her finger to her lips. 'What does it matter how he did it? Let's leave my lord and lady in peace. They'll sleep sweet tonight. If they sleep at all!'

I looked past her. Those two tall guards had never moved, nor lifted the hoods back from their faces. But I could see their white teeth grinning in the shadows.

One of them murmured, 'Goodnight, Gwennol.' It was Jordan's voice, all right.

I breathed a little easier. To tell you the truth, I wanted to believe her. I'd had enough terror to last me a lifetime. I'd known those two since my Ygerne had married Gorlois. A wild-spirited pair they'd been then, like Gorlois himself. That was the sort of hare-brained trick those three would have played, to steal out of a fort under siege, past the very nose of the king himself. Like schoolboys scrumping. And our Cornish orchards grow a rosy apple.

And then the smile slipped from my face. He was Duke of Cornwall, wasn't he? And Ygerne was his own wife. He shouldn't need to steal in to her like a thief in the night.

I shook my head and closed the chamber-door behind me. I couldn't understand a word of it. I'd been so sure we'd never see Lord Gorlois alive again. One Cornish lord against all the hosts of Britain? Besides, I knew his temper. If Gorlois couldn't win, he'd never run away. He'd chosen to take his stand at Caer Dimiliock, and he'd die fighting there. And who could have told him he'd find us in Tintagel?

Tintagel! Gorlois, to beg his way in past Bryvyth?

It wasn't exactly a sound I heard behind me. More like a chill stir in the air, as though someone had unbarred the window. But I knew, even in the darkness, what it was. Morgan was awake and listening.

'What is it? What did she say?'

'Hush, my lover. It's nothing. Go back to sleep.'

'No. Tell me. She said something about Father, didn't she? Is he dead?' She screeched it out at me. 'He is, isn't he? Is that what they've come to say?'

I went to her, and felt for her shoulders in the darkness. She clung to me like a wild thing, and I stroked her hair.

'No my pretty. It's not that.' And then it came out in a rush, to comfort her. 'Your father's alive. He's here. He's come to your mother.'

I should have known better. She was out of my arms, and what chance had I got of holding her?

Then she screamed, outside in the passage. And hurt or not, I was out of that door faster than you'd have thought possible.

I couldn't see her at first. But I saw someone else. In a patch of moonlight, from the door. Not Ruan, this time. Oh, no, not Ruan. The other of those men had moved. Taller than any warrior I'd ever seen, or so he looked then. Standing in a shaft of gossamer light, brighter than mist and thicker than moonshine. With a hood drawn over his face, shadowing it. Then I made out that he had Morgan by the wrists and she was fighting him like a wildcat.

'Let me go! Let me go! I want to see my father!'

Then the hood fell back as he struggled to hold Morgan. I breathed a sigh of relief. I'd been having nightmares with my eyes open for nothing. His face was half-lit in the witchlight, but it was the one I knew: Britael's, that had been my lord's bodyguard these fifteen years, and his friend before that.

'Take your claws out of me, you little screech-owl, or by the hounds of Annwn, I'll put that on you that will bind you stiller than stone from now till morning.'

He had a deep, strong voice, like wind through the standing stones, but this time my knees fairly shook when I heard it. I wasn't a fool. I knew every man in Gorlois's dun. The voice was Britael's, I didn't doubt that. But Britael would never in his life have spoken words like those. I could only think of one man who would.

But Morgan didn't care who he was. She ducked her face to his hand and he let out a yell. And from the bedroom behind her there came another shriek. A woman's cry, that stopped us all in our tracks. To this day I couldn't tell you if it was joy or pain, or both at once. But as long as I live I shall still hear that cry. It was as if the land itself had been entered.

That voice that was Britael's laughed long and loud.

I snatched Morgan to me and covered her ears with my arms. None of us should have heard what we had. Inside my head I could hear my own voice crying out, 'Where are our guards? Sulian! Oh, Mother, where are the guards?' When I listened again there was only the splash of the waves below us, and I knew I hadn't spoken a word. All I saw was what seemed to be Britael's face, smiling at me from the shadows, and the shape like Jordan's grinning at me too. There wasn't a sword in the world could have saved us from those smiles then.

Morgan was flying at him again, but that tall man threw her across the passage, as a wolf might toss a whippet over a stream.

'The little weasel! She bit me. Get her to bed, woman, till tomorrow. And look to it well that she doesn't trouble her mother again.'

I could hear Elaine weeping behind the wall, and Margawse whispering. But I hadn't a thought for either of them.

Morgan was sobbing now.

'Father! Where is Father?'

'Hush, my pretty,' I told her, dragging her back into our chamber. 'Your father is sleeping now. Sound and long. We shall all of us go to join him soon enough.'

# Chapter Twenty-one

Somehow I slept again, and as heavily as if I'd been drugged. When I woke it was full morning. Morgan was sitting at the open window, with the sea-wind slapping the hair across her face like a whiplash. The mist had gone and the breeze was skimming up the crests off the waves like flags.

I looked at the door, and though I knew it was foolishness, I was afraid to step out into that passage. I knew he wasn't there but the terror of it was still on me. You'll think me a silly old fool, crying my eyes out one day because I hadn't met him, and shaking with fear the next because I had. But you haven't known him. I'm not talking about an ordinary man.

Morgan turned her head slowly to look at me, with a strange, cold stare.

'You needn't be afraid. I heard them go.'

And there was a queer thing for her to say, when she'd been so hot to see her father last night. Hadn't she so much as opened the door to see if I was telling her the truth? My mouth fell open, but I didn't know what to say to her. There was a bleak, shut look in her face that I had never seen before. I didn't like it. She'd always worn her heart naked in her eyes.

'See for yourself,' she said, very cool and scornful, not like her tempers or her wheedling smile.

I went to the door, stiff and slowly. But I knew she was right. The passage was empty. There was no sign of any men.

The bell was ringing the nuns to their chapel.

I don't know what I was afraid of finding out, but I didn't go to my lady's room straight off. I stopped at the older girls' door and poked my head in. Elaine was fast asleep, curled up like a plump, round dormouse for comfort. There were tear-marks on her face, and she was sighing in her sleep. But Margawse was sitting up with the covers thrown back and her shift open to her breasts. There was a funny, wild look about her.

'Is he come yet, Gwennol? Has Uther Pendragon found us? We thought we heard voices in the night, but we daren't look. Listen! Isn't that the gallop of horsemen coming?'

'Never you fear, now. It's only the sea on the rocks. You're safe here,' I said, helping her to dress.

It wasn't like Margawse to be frightened. She wasn't the only one. I had a cold feeling that something had happened here that was too late to mend.

I went back to dress myself, and Morgan too. Then I straightened my shoulders and tried to act braver than I felt. Even then I daren't have told you what I feared. I tiptoed to the end of the passage, to my lady's room, and scratched at the door. When I opened it, Ruan was lying at the foot of the bed. Her eyes were open, watching me. She put her fingers to her lips.

Ygerne was asleep, in that narrow convent bed, with her face turned towards me. She hardly looked any older than Elaine. But there were no tears on her cheeks. She was smiling in her sleep. And far be it from me to speak ill of my betters, but when I saw her lying there like that I could have slapped her face. What right had she to look so pink and pretty, when the rest of us were as white as whey?

Whole, she looked, when the rest of us were wounded. Full and satisfied, when her daughters had been robbed. I knew what that look meant well enough.

I went outside to cool my temper in the good sea-wind. It seemed quiet enough in the sunshine, though the waves were roaring on the beach. I could believe Margawse's fancy, that it was like a great troop of horsemen galloping nearer. All over the island I could see the nuns busy at their work. And it seemed to me that their movements were brisker than the day before. I've seen birds darting here and there like that when their nest is threatened. Two were herding the cows out from milking, and some were sitting out of doors, seemingly writing. It was strange to me to see those women with pens in their hands. Their houses were not like the buildings of a dun, all tight together inside a wall. They were scattered about the grass, with their doors open to the sea and the wind, as though those nuns didn't mind being alone with their thoughts. But they were lifting their heads pretty often to look at the bridge.

As I watched, there was a bit of a flurry among them, like wind passing over a field of corn before a storm. I turned just in time to see Bryvyth striding up the path towards the guest-house.

'Bring the Lady Ygerne outside to speak to me!'

A fine, commanding voice she had, that nun.

From inside, I heard Ruan's voice call out.

'My lady is sleeping. Tell her to wait.'

But Bryvyth was not a woman to be kept waiting.

'Lady Ygerne! Come out!' she thundered.

There was a silence. And then Ygerne stood in the doorway, with a white and gold gown we'd rescued from the fire slipped hastily on and her pretty hair unbraided. Her chin was up, but she looked younger than ever.

'Come here!' the nun bellows.

The rest were all creeping up to watch. Bryvyth stood on the path with her nuns gathered behind her, like a stag guarding its does.

'Kneel!'

Ygerne's mouth opened then, and I thought she would say no to that. There was a mighty long moment of awful silence. Then she smiled, and down she went, Gorlois's lady on the muddy grass in her fine gown.

And it was so quiet you could hear the sea sliding down between the stones, like horses whinnying. I've often wondered how much she was laughing at all of us.

The nun wasn't laughing.

'The holy gate of Tintagel was opened last night, after dark. They told me Lord Gorlois had come with two companions, in danger of their lives, to see his wife. For Christian pity I broke our rule. I had the gate unbarred and let them in. Armed men entered this holy island, the Blessed Virgin forgive me! As you value your soul, answer me. Was it your lord who came to you? Did you take him to your bed, here?'

'Yes.' No more than a meek whisper, it was.

'Yet now it is morning and what was done in the darkness is made plain. Uther Pendragon's herald is at our gates. Lord Gorlois is dead. Woman, your husband fell last night at sunset, fighting against the king at Dimiliock. He died of his wounds. And Uther Pendragon has come to claim his wife.'

Well, I'd been watching Ygerne pretty close but it was only a moment I saw it – that flash of lightning in her eyes.

Then I spun round fast enough like all the rest. And what a sight met our eyes! Beyond the causeway was a great troop of horsemen drawn up on the hill facing us. The sun was bright on their weapons and shields and armour and the brave colours of their cloaks. They sat still on their horses with their heads high, waiting as bold as brass, and every so often a horse threw up its neck and whinnied. It wasn't a raiding party this time. There wasn't a sword drawn. He'd won. You could tell even from here there was a grin on all their faces. Oh, no, the Pendragon hadn't come here to fight for Ygerne. He had come to claim what was his own already.

Then Ygerne flashed out at Bryvyth, with her sweet little chin in the air.

'Fool! Look! Can you not see it is Uther Pendragon's spears that keep you Christians safe? Where do you suppose the Church would be if the white dragon comes west?'

'Where it began! Under a tyrant. Did you think the Lamb was a stranger to the knife? The road runs straight from Gethsemane to here.'

Big Bryvyth folded her arms. You'd have thought she wasn't afraid of a Saxon army, or a British one either.

'Go! To your king, and his banners, and his spearmen. Adulteress! Did you imagine we needed your sin to shield *this*?'

Ygerne changed colour then. She went a deep foxglove red. Not just her face, but down her neck and her breast. If she'd been a slug across the path, I think Bryvyth would have looked at her more kindly.

The nun wiped her hands then, as if she'd been gutting mackerel. I've a notion she was enjoying herself now.

'Go!' she thundered. 'Go to that godless man! And never set foot on this holy ground again unless you come with your hair shorn and your clothes rent to do penance for your blasphemy.'

We were dismissed from Tintagel. Tipped off their land. The land that had once been ours. I could feel the earth beginning to burn under the soles of my feet.

There was nothing else Ygerne could do, except keep her dignity. She got to her feet without a word and started down the path. The nuns stepped away into the grass to let her pass, and pulled their skirts aside. That family would never be right with the Church again.

But there was one they forgot. I don't know if the nuns could have healed her even then, but Bryvyth never thought of it. It cost her dearly afterwards. She lost the place that was dearest to her heart, not to the Saxons but through a slip of a girl barely come to womanhood.

I was as bad as the rest.

We'd none of us noticed there was something else between Ygerne and the Pendragon. A tiny black figure out on the bridge of stone. Morgan. Alone on that causeway. Facing a whole army. With the wind tearing her hair backwards like a raven's wing.

# Chapter Twenty-two

Ygerne stopped. It wasn't the drop to the sea she was afraid of, but her own daughter, staring at the Pendragon's army as though she could kill them with her fierce green eyes.

It was a fearsome place, that causeway. No walls on either side, not even a handrail. And the breakers so far below it made you giddy to look, smashing themselves on those rocks, one after the other, till the end of time.

We all seemed to stand there bewitched, nuns, warriors, king, lady, as if she'd put a spell on us. Then I straightened my shoulders. After all, she was my little maid. I'd carried her in my heart these eight years. And likely enough she was the last child that would ever be put in my lap to nurse. If her own mother couldn't go to her across that gulf that separated them – and it was more than sea-wind and gusty air – then I would, who had lived closer to her than her own blood.

There wasn't one of them tried to stop me. I walked past my lady, who was stopped as still as a standing stone, and down to that road of rock. The king was riding slowly down the slope on the other side. I knew it must be him, with his two tall warriors on either side. I wouldn't let myself look at them.

I'd seen Morgan tense. She was as still as a thin-backed stoat, rearing up in the grass when it sees its prey. And near nine years though I'd known her, I'd no notion what she might do next.

I was afeared of them all. That drop to the waves, the king and his soul-friend smiling beside him, that had tricked us, the hundreds of swords in front, and that big nun behind. And most of all, if you'll believe me, that fatherless child no higher than my own chest.

I thought I'd call to her as I stepped out on the bridge. But my tongue was dry, and the wind snatched the breath out of my mouth. The pounding of those waves seemed to crash through my head and drove all the sense away. And yet it felt so quiet where we were. Just the two of us in a world of our own, high up there in the blue air. My old feet shuffling without a sound over the soft turf towards her. Her back was turned to me. All this time she never stirred a muscle. I could only guess what she was going to do. The only bit of her that moved was her black hair streaming out past her shoulders in the wind.

At last I found my voice, when I was hardly an arm's length from her. And very gruff and sudden it must have sounded, fool that I was.

'Come here, my lover. Come to Gwennol. There's nothing you can do will bring your father back to us now.'

I saw her start, just as the stoat jumps in the air. And she was whirling round and flying at me, teeth bared and nails clawing. I stumbled backwards and lost my balance. I heard men's voices shouting and women's screaming, and I don't doubt my own scream was somewhere there amongst all the rest. I saw the blue sky wheeling past me, and then the flash of the sea on the horizon. There was silver, then emerald green, spinning closer underneath me, purple weed, white surf, black rock, and I was falling towards it. Something caught me at last. I felt the jolt through all my bones as I went pitching over the edge. I heard the sound of cloth tearing and I knew I was going again.

Then her hands gripped me hard. She hauled me back from the brink and staggered on to the path with me. I was sobbing and panting like a woman in labour. But Morgan flung her little bony arms around me and buried her head in my breast, weeping fit to break her heart.

We clung to each other, so close you couldn't have separated us. She sobbed, 'I'm sorry, Gwennol! I'm sorry!' And I just stroked her tangled hair and gasped her name, over and over, as though I had lost my wits. And for all the terror of it, I have wished often and often that I could have that morning again. That was the last time Morgan, Lord Gorlois's daughter, hugged me and cried in my arms.

Then she twisted apart from me and turned away. When she faced me again she was a different person. It was as though she had gone from me further than I could ever reach. Her face was hard and cold as stone. I knew then I had lost her for sure.

My fall had broken her spell. On the far side of the bridge the king's voice called, 'Ygerne!' I looked up at Uther Pendragon then for the first time. Tall, he was, and he sat proudly on his horse, for all a little maid had just stopped him in his path. The warrior on his right hand wore his cloak tossed over his shoulder now, and his armour twinkled in the sun. He watched us all with a crooked smile. I didn't swoon over Emrys Merlyn this time. I stood my ground between Tintagel and all the men and faced him back. Even in the morning sunlight, with his hood thrown back, he had still a little of the look of Britael about him. But not enough for me to forgive him what he'd done.

When Ygerne heard Uther Pendragon calling to her, she seemed to come to her senses and remember who she was. She turned her back on those Christian nuns she'd knelt in front of, and lifted her head and smiled at him. Then she walked across that bridge of stone, straight past her daughter Morgan, as though she couldn't see her.

Widowed that very day she may have been. But in her white gown, with her hair loose on her shoulders, she only needed a wreath of flowers round her head, and she would have looked for all the world like a May Queen.

# Chapter Twenty-three

You may think by now that I hated Uther Pendragon. But that was before I knew him.

When my lady went out of Tintagel to go to him, there was nothing the rest of us could do but follow her, though Morgan hung back at the last. We passed the porter's lodge and went through the gate in the rampart, and suddenly Ygerne seemed to move as if she felt she was free. She almost ran to Uther.

And he sat on his horse, like the high king that he was, watching Gorlois's wife come to him, with a great, satisfied smile on his face. And a tall friend on either side of him.

As she passed Merlyn, she turned her face to him for a moment and their eyes met. They smiled at each other. Short and polite, it was, like two swordsmen meeting, searching out each other's strengths and weak points. I stopped short when I saw that and it made me shiver. For wasn't she Ygerne, that I'd nursed on my knee when she was still soiling her napkins? And hadn't I taught her all the wisdom that she knew? But there was a good deal more that I could have told her I'd kept to myself. So, duchess or no, who was she, that she could smile so boldly back at Emrys Merlyn, when I daren't? What had she got more than me, wise as I was, save a pretty face and a womb that could still bleed?

Then Uther sprang down from his horse to greet her as though she was already his queen. But now that she'd got him, she wasn't going to have him seem less than he was, in front of all those people. She sank down on the grass in front of him, with a great billowing curtsy, and bowed her head. She had beautiful hair, had Ygerne, thick and golden, and with her face hidden you couldn't have seen those first wrinkles in the corners of her eyes.

He raised her up, of course. Not daintily, either. It was like a great bear-hug, and they kissed each other as warmly as if they'd been man and wife. I daren't look at Morgan's face.

He had chariots waiting. Very sure of himself was Uther Pendragon. He never doubted that he could take what he wanted, even from the holy house of a nunnery. He lifted Ygerne into one, as if she had been an armful of swansdown. Then he turned to the two older girls and took Elaine by the waist.

She was crying now for her father, and for fear of the soldiers, I don't doubt, and all the sudden terror and strangeness we'd had these two days. He put his arms round her and held her close to him, and he whispered in her ear for a little while. When she lifted her head from his shoulder she smiled up at him and started to dry her eyes.

As for Margawse, I needn't tell you the look that passed between them when his arms reached out to take her. It's not for me to say if that one wept for her father. But she knew very well how tears could put a sparkle in her eyes. He wouldn't be the first she'd flashed her dewdrops at, by a long way. And never a red eyelid or a puffy cheek on her. Not like Elaine, that seemed to be the only soft-hearted one of them, though I've sometimes wondered if she was all she seemed. When he swung Margawse up into the chariot after her sister, they were a mighty long time separating his cloak-pin from the breast of her gown, and there were roses in her cheeks by the time he'd finished.

Then he turned to Morgan, but she twisted her face away from him. And his eyes met mine across her head. Bright brown eyes, he had, and laughing for joy because he'd got what he wanted. And, may the Mothers give me peace, I almost forgave him. I was an old woman, older by far than my lady, and I'd had many men. But that was all it took. One smile from Uther Pendragon. And if he could make me feel like that after all he'd done to me and those I loved, it was time I started thinking less hardly of Ygerne.

But Morgan wouldn't let his hands touch her. She sprang up into the chariot all by herself, and if she could have made those horses rear up and strike their hooves in Uther's face, you could tell by the look in her eyes that she'd have done it.

I'd dearly love to have ridden pillion behind one of the men, the way I was feeling. But you don't expect the gentry to notice things like that. They'd all forgotten me. So they moved off, all those fine riders with their spears held high and their gay cloaks blowing in the wind and the horns sounding, and Ygerne in her chariot at the front. I was left to walk behind. And my parts were still sore.

I looked round for some sign of Sulian and the other two. But I never saw them again after that. Or Jordan and Britael. There'd be more than a few women weeping around Bossiney after that night's work, and many a week before Nectan and his like had finished singing litanies for the dead.

I trudged along the track choked with their dust. Then I heard horse's hooves coming up beside me. A pure white mare. That startled me, as you can guess. What Cornishman would have dared put a leg over her? No ordinary one, anyway. We've been the people of Rhiannon's horse as long as anyone knows. So I didn't need to look further.

Well, it's one thing to be warned, but another thing to build a wall in the time you've got. That tall, lean man was close above me in his skirt of mail and his green mantle with the hood thrown back on his shoulders. A proper warrior he looked this morning. Nothing druid about him now, except for the mare. But for all he was smiling, I could see close up that his face was lined deep, as if he'd seen more blood and heard more screams than a man so young could bear lightly. So I knew he had the seeing too. And I pitied him, whatever he'd done.

He was looking down at me with green-grey eyes that went clean through my head and out the other side. It was not like the way King Uther smiled at a woman. But it set my blood beating like the drums on May-morning, I can tell you.

'Gwennol,' he said, very low and courteous, 'Gwennol Far-Sight, is it? Do you know who I am, this morning?'

That brought me back. I don't know how I dared, but I looked him straight in the face.

'Merlyn, I should call you, sir. This morning.'

'Merlyn, it is. So it seems there is more than one wise woman in Cornwall.'

And what did he mean by that, I wonder? There were many of us in Cornwall, but few higher than me.

'There are some that say so.'

'Then we should be allies, you and I. I serve the king and you the queen.'

'She's not queen yet.' It came out so sharp it might have been Morgan's voice speaking through my lips.

'But will be soon, when Gorlois is buried. And she is still your mistress. By daylight at least.'

'It was Lord Gorlois gave me my meat these fifteen years.'

I saw his hands tighten on the bridle, and I had a hard job not to flinch.

'Then listen, Gwennol Far-Sight. Listen to me well, if you have any love for Gorlois's youngest daughter. That's a wild young hawk you have in your nest. See to it that she keeps her talons away from the king's flock. He's a man that likes to have nothing stand in his way.'

I was too full to speak. I couldn't answer him. Couldn't any of those grinning red dragons understand what they'd done to my little maid? But for all that, when he spoke so grave, I was all of a tremble, and I couldn't look him in the eye any more. He saw too much.

Then all of a sudden he laughed. And before I could let out a gasp, he'd got me by the waist and swung me up on the horse behind him. And I had to cling on tight as we galloped back to the army. Me, Gwennol Far-Sight, on the white mare that should have run free without a bridle, with my arms round the greatest druid in all Britain. The Mothers forgive me, I think I was laughing.

I soon saw that it hadn't taken some others long to forget to cry, either. There was the king on his horse beside Margawse and Elaine's chariot, and teasing and laughing with them both. It was that plump little hen, Elaine, that surprised me. Giving him back jest for jest she was, as if she'd forgotten she'd ever been shy. Forgotten too that he'd just killed her father, and then done worse than that.

I'd never seen Elaine quicken to a man before. It was like seeing her come awake from a long sleep. All her life she'd been one for mothering things, kittens and dolls and such. And here was Uther Pendragon teaching her that if she wanted to be a mother she'd have to learn to be a woman first. And he was a man that taught that very well.

But Morgan was only a child with a flat chest, scowling at him. He hardly looked at her twice. He'd forgotten already how she'd made him check at the bridge. Only Merlyn would remember that. You couldn't fool those eyes. I knew that he'd seen that last change in her face as well as I had. He knew what it meant. There was one at least that would never forget her father . . . or her mother either. And if she lifted the first little finger against the Pendragons for revenge, it would be more than all my wisdom could do to keep her safe.

Well, it seems a great druid can be more of a fool where women are concerned than I thought.

We came in sight of the poor burnt roofs of Bossiney round. They sounded their war-horns again and the horses broke into a trot and Uther's men burst out with a victory-song. Then Merlyn gave a great whoop, and he kicked his heels into the mare and away we went, galloping in great circles around the dun. There was me clinging on to his waist for dear life, and Uther and Ulfin and Merlyn laughing their heads off and all their army with them. Shameless, they were, coming back to Gorlois's home singing like that, as though his women were cows herded in after a cattle-raid.

# Chapter Twenty-four

When Uther saw the state the place was in, he was all for taking Ygerne away at once. To be fair to him, he turned mighty pale when he learned how close his men had come to roasting her alive. Sometimes, afterwards, I'd pass him looking up at that hall-roof with a sick, scared look on his face. And if my guts were twisting worse than usual, I could find myself wishing he'd got what he deserved.

She wouldn't come with him. Not yet. I knew she had her reasons.

First, we had to bury Gorlois. Uther pitched a tent for Ygerne in the Great Meadow, and a snug little bower it made, with couches of lambskin and striped hangings at the door. There were shelters for the rest of us too, and the weather fell warm and blue, so we took no harm of it, in our bodies. I had a feeling that we were cattle put out to grass, in place of the herd we'd lost.

A sore time I had keeping Morgan off her father's body when they brought him home. A child shouldn't have seen it, hacked into bloody rags, with the splinters of bone showing through.

Uther gave Ygerne men, with orders to do whatever she wanted. Then he left us alone with our dead. Nectan came stalking out of the woods when he'd gone. A bit pale and hollow-eyed, but he hadn't been harmed. So many good, red-blooded Cornishmen lay dead, but Uther had left those white Christians alive to bury them.

I'll give Ygerne her due, she did Gorlois proud. Well, the way you put your man in the earth says what he was and that tells who you are. There's a deal of boasting even after death. The number of gentry that come, the size of the feast, the height of the stone.

If she'd had her way, she'd have done it in the old style, in a golden chariot, and full armour, with his sword and his shield and his hound, and much more besides. She knew what was fitting. But Nectan stopped all that.

'We brought nothing into the world, we take nothing from it. He has gone to one who offers riches beyond our dreaming.'

What's this world for? Are we supposed to throw it away like a worn-out clout? Nectan spent long enough sitting in his glade beside the pool, playing his harp to the birds. He seemed to like that. What's his heaven if it's more than the best things on earth? Wine and feasting and song . . . and the women beautiful. Couldn't he feel the life that was in the earth he trod on? Life to death and death to life again. That's how it's always been. The dead are here, among the living. We do well to keep them sweet.

But the Christians buried my lord up on the headland beyond

Tintagel. Bryvyth came striding up, with all her nuns, singing their litany for the dead. She stood across the grave from Ygerne and scowled at her many a time. My lady had made some sort of peace with Nectan, though I don't know how she did it. But never with Bryvyth. That nun had scolded Gorlois often for his wild ways. But I think she'd loved our black-bearded duke in a queer kind of way, or what passes among those white-blooded women for love. But I couldn't forgive her. She'd denied him what he asked her. She'd cost him his life, and what for? Did she think her prayers were stronger than a man's sharp sword? She hadn't even saved his honour. So I wasn't sorry when she got her come-uppance in the end.

It was a fine day for the funeral, and you could see all the way out to sea as far as Lundy. I heard them shovelling earth on to Gorlois's corpse and I stared across the waves at Tintagel. He might have been there now, wielding his sword on the bridge and laughing through his beard at the whole of Uther's army. Then I looked round for Morgan and I could tell she was seeing him too. Bryvyth was her enemy now along with all the rest.

Afterwards that priest buried Keby and the rest with the same words. As if there was no difference between them.

And then Uther came riding back and married Ygerne. And none too soon. I didn't need to wait for her belly to swell to know why she was looking so pleased with herself.

Uther Pendragon was still for taking her away to one of his palaces up east. But she wouldn't go till the child was born. I could have told him why, well enough. She was a beautiful woman, but she wasn't as young and light as she used to be. She wasn't going to appear before all those fine, slender ladies with her waist thickening like a tree-trunk, and too heavy to dance in front of them all. No, she'd wait till she had something better than beauty to show off to them. The king's first son. Gorlois had never given her a boy. Three times she'd waited to bear him a child, and each time it had been a girl. And the last time had been bitterest of all. So she'd use every bit of power I'd taught her now.

Well, he built Bossiney up for her again. He had walls made of fine, planked timber, instead of clay and wattle, and hung doors of carved oak, and put on a new thatch as gold as a buttercup. So in the end it was a handsomer place than it had been before. Then he had the walls painted inside with flowers in all the colours you'd see in a summer meadow. He even had the cheek to ask the nuns of Tintagel to embroider hangings for them, for they were known far and wide for pretty needlewomen. He should have known better. Bryvyth was no more afraid of him than she was of Gorlois. She told him no, and I'll bet she gave him the wrong side of her tongue, too. His cheeks turned purple when he got her answer, and the woman who brought it nearly lost an ear. So my lady and her daughters got out their own needles and set to work themselves, meek as you please. I didn't offer to help. There's things I can see far off, and things I can't see under my own nose, and it was fine work. So I stuck to plain stitching and mending.

Still, for all that, he built a chapel on the end of the hall, which was a thing Gorlois had never done. Nectan came and blessed it when it was finished. But there was another that had got in first.

It was the night after they'd dug the trench for the foundation. Something drew me outside to go and look. I caught him at it. He'd put up a circle, but he wasn't troubling to hold it. I stepped right through it, and hardly felt any hurt.

He was just dropping stones in to cover up what he'd done. But not so many that I couldn't see. He smiled at me like a little boy that you've caught with his fingers in the honey-pot.

'Well, Gwennol. We were here first, weren't we? We'll see which of us will have it at the last.'

There was someone else saw what he'd put there. Morgan had followed me. She never asked me what he was doing, or why. She didn't need to.

As soon as the roof of the hall was up, we all moved in and had a great feast. We were pretty merry that night, I can tell you. I looked up at that clean new thatch that hadn't a trace of smoke. And Ygerne's clean new husband, with the blood washed off his hands. But it was Merlyn I mostly had my eye on. He watched them both. I'd seen what he had put under the walls. He meant that hall to stand and he meant that marriage to stand, too. And he understood what had to be given to pay the price. Yet I had a shrewd idea Bossiney wasn't the place he really wanted, nor Uther neither. Time and again I saw them standing out on the headland, looking across at Tintagel Island. Like a baby hanging from its mother by the cord. Well, let them take it from the nuns if they could. I didn't know which would grieve me most. For men to have it that knew the old way, or women who followed the new. Either way, I'd follow what I knew, if I did have to wait till night fell.

Still, it seemed this marriage was going the way Merlyn wanted. I caught him once, running his hands down Ygerne's body just as if she was a figure he had carved himself. She was enjoying it, till she looked at his face. then she pulled away from him saying, 'You may be a great magician, Emrys Merlyn. But there are some things only a woman can do.'

It wasn't his hands on her parts that displeased her. I could see that. It was his looking at her as if she was something he had tooled. Oh, she was very sure of her power just then.

So she sat smiling to herself and embroidering, while our sweet Cornish spring turned into a hard, hot summer. Then Uther Pendragon rode away to fight the Saxons.

That frightened her. She would have stopped him if she could. Many a time she'd feared that Gorlois might come back and find her old and barren. But as the years went by she hadn't seemed so worried about him getting killed. Now she'd got her new king, it was a different story. She kissed him bravely enough as she buckled his sword about him. But when he was gone, her pretty face crumpled up and she cried in my arms as she hadn't done since long before Gorlois died.

When I looked up, Merlyn was standing in the shadows, laughing at her without making a sound.

'Little fool,' he said. 'Did you think you could keep him? Do you suppose I gave him into your arms for a plaything? We gamble for higher stakes, the Pendragon and I. The survival of Britain.'

'And so do I!' she rounded on him. 'Do you think I want him dead before his son is born?'

'Born to *what*?' he roared. 'A few stones and bogs? The last black lakes and the sea-lochs of the west? The hollow mountains of the dead? All that will be left of Britain if the red dragon fails!'

She turned white, and put her hands on her belly. She knew the danger she was in now. Her face grew thinner as her body thickened. If Uther should fall, there were few of those fine folk outside Cornwall that knew their new queen or cared about her, and none of Gorlois's kin in Cornwall left to love her.

Merlyn left us too before Midsummer. He was one of those that lean more towards the sun than the moon. He'd have his holy place in those stone circles they call the Giants' Dance.

She turned to me then. She begged me to help her weave a strong spell of safety for Uther's return.

I snapped at her, 'If your spells fail, take yourself to your priest and his prayers! It wasn't me you looked to, to bring a king to you. Why should I help you get him back?'

Well, believe it or not, she went. When she was desperate she'd try anything. I never understood what hold that bloodless saint had over her. What power could he use that wasn't forbidden him? Or was it her that used him? But she'd come back from his cell with some of the lines smoothed out of her face, though there were traces of tears on her cheeks too.

And, may the shade of Gorlois give me peace, I softened a little and put what strength I had left to hers. It wasn't just for the sake of Uther's bright, brown eyes, either. The Pendragon was our king now, and her wedded lord. He was all we had.

He came back, in the heat of summer's end, and mightily pleased with himself. The red dragon was driving the white back. Then the drought broke, and from then on it was teeming rain. We were all shut up in Bossiney, waiting for the child to be born. All except Merlyn. Storm or shine, you could no more hold him in one place than you could trap the wind. He'd be in and out, like the sun on a March day. And where he went to, none of them dared to question.

The days grew short and cold, and the wheel-ruts were full of water, and every dog in the place had mud up to its shoulders. You could leave your shoes by the hearth at night, and in the morning they'd still be cold and sodden.

Our world got very small. We couldn't go out, and the mist was so thick you couldn't see the woods beyond the gate. It even drove Morgan home from the cliffs. All summer she'd run wild at the edge of the sea, with her legs growing longer now, so that it was more than I could do to keep pace with her. I'd had to let her go. I'd hoped the sun would heal her wound and the wind wash her mind clean. But too often I'd come up with her and find her kneeling on the very edge of the cliff, staring down at the surf on the rocks as if she wished herself dead. Now winter had come and she was like a cat in a cage. The rain made prisoners of us all. We began to feel as if we were the only people left in the world.

Seeing King Uther pacing up and down the hall I used to wonder how long it might be before he got tired of his new lady. I remembered what they'd told me about his great cities of stone, like London and Winchester, and the houses the Romans had built, with pools of hot water to bathe in. What had we got to offer but a wooden bucket in a poor wooden dun, for all it might be a bit grander now than we'd been used to.

Hours I spent worrying about those fine ladies of Britain, and how Uther might go rutting after them. And I thanked my stars the seas were closed as well as the roads, or I could see he'd have been off. Yet I never saw the danger under my own nose. A blind old fool I must have been, too, and never ought to have been called wise.

My lady – it came hardly to me to say 'the queen' at first – had sent me to the store-house to fetch more wool for spinning. I was coming back past the treasury when I heard the sound of voices inside. A man and a woman. That pulled me up short. There were none, only Uther's trusted guard, that had the right to go in there. Then I shrugged my shoulders and started to move on. What was it to me now what the queen's women did with the king's soldiers? I'd seen many women this year made widow first and mother after, and maybe by the same man. I wasn't standing out in the cold to bother with them.

It was her laugh that warned me. She hardly bothered to smother it. I'd known that laugh for thirteen years. Well, that moved me sharp enough then. Another step, and I'd have flung that door open and caught them both with their breech-clouts down, and praying I'd be in time to stop the worst.

But as I reached for the latch I heard the man's voice, low but clear enough. The blood left my face. Margawse and Uther Pendragon? I'd known she was shameless, but I never thought it had gone that far. Wouldn't she even stop at the man who was now her father?

I was shaking all over, for to tell you the truth, I was more than a little frightened of the Pendragon, for all his flattering ways. I thought of what Merlyn had warned me, how he was a man that liked to have what he wanted. And I tell you, I felt older and more tired then than I'd ever felt before.

Still I couldn't leave it without knowing the worst. I moved very softly to find a knothole to peep through. He'd got her up against the wall, facing me. I got a glimpse of her white thigh, and her skirt up round her waist. I was squinting round to see how far he'd got himself.

Just then, like a small black cat creeping over the mud, Morgan comes sidling up to me. She must have been watching it all from the shadows of the door across the path. She slipped her hand into mine and looked up at me with a small, sweet smile I hadn't seen much lately.

'You can't stop them, Gwennol. I don't want you to. Don't worry. She doesn't love him, you know. And she doesn't love Mother, either. None of us do. Margawse will avenge Father in her own way.'

And that was a chilly thing for a child of nine to say.

Well, I couldn't stop it. But a few more months and I'd have to give that young woman something to stop what might come from it. I still had power enough for that.

I was back in my lady's bower before Uther was. The fire shone red on Ygerne's face, and when he came in his was red too. He smiled down at her and kissed her long and softly, and put his hand on her belly and down between her thighs. A smile from Uther Pendragon is worth rubies from another man.

Then the door swept open with the wind. But it wasn't Margawse this time. Merlyn was with us again in the firelight. Weeks, he'd been gone from us, and nobody ever asked where he went. But he came dancing in now, dressed all in leather, sewn with little bells that rang when he moved, even to the pointed cap on his head. He looked a proper fool. He rubbed his hands and called for hot wine, and he and Uther Pendragon hugged each other, like a couple of schoolboys wrestling. When they parted, Merlyn looked pretty keenly at Ygerne's belly and smiled to himself when he saw how it had swelled. He always had that cunning look on his face as though it had been his own doing, and not Uther's.

Merlyn stayed close by us then. We were coming to the darkest time of the year. My lady was often tired and resting in bed, but Uther Pendragon always had Margawse and Elaine to laugh and flirt with and keep him company. When the rain fell, they used to get out the chequer-board and play the game of the hunt. I sat in the corner, stitching in the firelight and listening to the harper, till my head nodded. What they did when I slept, I shouldn't like to say.

Merlyn sat by the fire with me, watching all of us, or maybe jumping up to show off some trick of his own. I never saw him sleep. I never got used to that. Emrys Merlyn sitting across the hearth from me, as it might have been man and wife. He witched my thoughts, like the rest of them. It wasn't him I should have been thinking of. But what I was worried about was nothing to him. Even he wasn't wise enough to see the harm that was coming of it.

Only Morgan never laughed or played with Uther. She'd rather go to bed early, without light or fire. But often I found her lying awake in the dark.

# Chapter Twenty-five

Midwinter's Eve. In Gorlois's time we used to keep it the proper way. The bonfire should have been stacked on the cliffs and the torch ready to kill the dark and bring the sun to life again, and all of us dancing and drinking around the fire.

But the storm blew and the gale kept us pinned down, like sheep under a hedge. That year I left the kindling of the light to hardier souls than myself. Besides, we had another birth to wait for. Her pains had started. She'd given orders not to let me into her chamber, and that made me angry. But I couldn't help myself. This was my business, before anyone else's. I got my things ready for what had to be done.

We had a bit of cheer in our own hall, but it wasn't like the roof-raising. Our new queen was missing and Uther had a face grey as a snow-cloud. He was striding up and down, up and down all evening, with the drinking-horn in his hand empty as soon as filled. He only stopped to stare at the fine shields and swords he'd hung on our new-painted walls. I dare say he was dreaming of a young hand that might one day hold them. I doubt very much if he was looking at the fine embroideries that Gorlois's daughters had sewed and thinking of their fair hands. He wasn't dreaming of another little maid.

The waiting put him in a sour mood for the dances and bawdy games that we'd always used to chase away the shadows of winter and put fresh heart into the sun. And to tell you the truth, we were a little shy when it came to dancing the hobby-horse in front of him. The Cornish have always been Horse-people, and he was a Dragon-man, and he still felt like a stranger among us. So it wasn't like it should have been.

Then, like a clap of thunder, he rounded on us and sent us all packing off to bed. Margawse started complaining. She ran to him and threw her arms round his neck, kissing him and trying to wheedle another hour of fun. There are few enough feasts for her liking, and she was the only one, bar the hall-servants, that was truly enjoying herself. But he threw her off as if she was nothing to him now. Elaine had the sense to see there was no arguing with him in this mood, and between us we hushed Margawse and led her off to the sleeping-hut. Morgan had got there before us, but she wasn't undressed, and nothing I could do would make her go to bed before that baby was born. So I worked what I could and waited, till I could hardly keep my eyes open, in spite of the draught. And little help I got from Elaine and Margawse.

The child was slow in coming, as though he was her firstborn. But for all it was long, they tell me she had no great pain. And that was a wonder when you think how Morgan nearly killed her, struggling to be born into the light. The Pendragon's child just waited his time.

He came at midnight, as near as I could tell, when the fires were low and the night at its darkest. Hours she had been waiting, Morgan, that was his half-sister, standing there in the wind and the rain, till her hair was plastered to her head like seaweed on the rocks.

And then the curtain flew open and the woman's cry went up that it was a boy, and it was all light. Light in the queen's bedchamber. A great cheer from the hall and logs thrown on the hearth to make a great blaze, so that you'd think they were trying to set fire to the thatch again. And everywhere people running out of doors into the light to hear the news. Boys as young as Keby would have been, and women older than me. Uther went striding off into the queen's bower to claim his own.

Well, there was more cheering when he came back to us, looking like the sun itself, and called for more wine and mead to toast the baby's health. And all the lot of them went crowding into the hall out of the rain, even Ruan that had never left my lady's side since the pains began. She was so proud that night, to see her you'd think she had dropped the baby herself.

All except one.

When Morgan heard that cry, and knew that the Pendragon's child was born, and that it was a boy, she dashed off into the night like a wild thing. I knew then that I had lost her a second time, and the dark she'd gone to now was worse than before. I dragged a cloak over me and stumbled off after her, scolding and shouting her name. It was wasted breath, what with the wind tearing my words away and the water coming over my shoes. She wouldn't have listened, even if she could have heard me calling. But she was my little maid, my last baby. I couldn't cut the cord that bound us together, for all it hurt me.

So there was I, standing out in the storm between the dark where we'd been and the light where the new child was, and, believe you me, my cheeks were wet with more than rain for Gorlois's daughters. Then Margawse went dashing past towards the hall. She'd barely the decency to cover her shift. She wasn't going to be cheated of her wine and merry-making this time. Well, it took them different ways. Morgan wept, that night and many besides. But I dare say Margawse will laugh when she has her revenge. Elaine keeps her own counsel.

I felt sorely tempted then to go after Margawse. I like a drop of hot mead as well as anyone, and I was so chilled with wet and cold I was aching in every joint and bone. And traitor you may think me, but I'd worked hard enough with Ygerne to bring that boy into the world. I had something to celebrate now, after all my trouble.

But there was another thirst on me too. Some of you will understand what I mean. It was a long time since I last held a baby in my arms. And none that were given to me to look after had been boys. I was a lively young woman when I took Ygerne from her wet-nurse. I could race on the beach with any lad, and wrestle too. But she'd never had brothers. Or sons, either. And now at last she had done for King Uther what she never did for Gorlois of Cornwall. She had given him a son, a prince of Britain. And the little babe was there, just behind that curtain, lying on the pillow of her bed.

I scratched softly at the door, but I knew no one could hear me for the wind. So I slipped inside. My lady was lying with her eyes closed and her body under the covers as slim as a girl's again. There was only the midwife left, sitting on a stool beside her. And she was nearly asleep after all her work, with a great jug of mead steaming on the floor by her side.

And there on the bed between them, wrapped in white bands, was that precious baby that we had waited for so long. Fair, he was. Handsome. I never saw a child come out of the womb so perfect. Not a wrinkle on him, nor a red mark anywhere. He lay so peaceful, in a pool of lamplight, with not a thought of what his coming had cost his sisters. His eyes were open, looking up at me.

And for all that I might be bitter towards the king and queen, I lost my heart to their child. He was only a baby, and it wasn't his fault. When I looked down into his little face, there wasn't a thought in my head about Morgan.

# Chapter Twenty-six

Ygerne was looking as pleased with herself as a cat that's found a fat salmon. You could almost hear her purring as she smiled at me. Her hair was brushed out around her on the pillow, like an unbound sheaf of corn. She'd had Ruan bathe and tidy her pretty quickly before the king came, and the lamplight was kind to her. She was beautiful before, it's true, but there was something else glowing through her now. I hadn't seen her as happy as that, not even when she got her pretty Elaine.

Yet I noticed her eyes were a bit anxious, as though she thought it might all be a dream. My hand was reaching out almost by itself, and wanting to stroke that baby's soft cheek, when she caught at my wrist.

'Is he pleased? Gwennol, is the king pleased now?'

I could feel by the tightness of her fingers how much she must have been afraid these nine months. She had taken a high risk. It was like walking over that causeway again. One false step to left or right . . . It might have been a stillbirth, or another girl. But she'd passed the danger, and now her king was waiting on the other side, laughing, with his arms open.

'He's as happy as a boy with his first sword. That is, if he's still sober enough to remember what he's celebrating.'

My eyes strayed to that big jug of mead on the floor. But it was three parts empty already. The midwife saw my look and pulled it closer to her skirts. She wasn't going to share what she'd earned so dearly, though I could see the glint of gold under her other hand too. Uther would have given her something more lasting to remember him by. He'd be a generous lord to anyone who so much as smiled at him that night, now that he'd got what he wanted. He'd even have slapped the shade of Gorlois on the back if my lord had come back to haunt him.

Ygerne had let go of my wrist. She had the baby in the crook of her arm and she drew him close to her side. The two of them stared up at me. Two pairs of round blue eyes, they were. Smiling. Both half-asleep. I could see there was nothing for me here.

I suppose I could have softened towards her a bit. Stroked her forehead, or kissed her cheek, as if she was still my little maid, and asked her to let me hold the baby. But somehow my pride wouldn't let me. I was dying to touch him. But I wouldn't beg him from her. I don't know how to explain it properly, but I felt as if that boy was ours by rights, and she and Uther had stolen him from us.

So I turned on my heel without telling her about Morgan, and went off over to the hall to soothe my hurt and drink the rest of the night away. It was as hot and noisy as a smith's forge. By the time I'd had two cups of ale inside me, the world looked a rosier place. Elaine was there now, still soft-eyed and pink with sleep. As pretty as her mother. But she'd taken the trouble to put on a proper gown, and braid her hair. Uther had his arm round her. His face was red and his drinking-horn was not as steady as it should be, for all he was a strong man who could hold his liquor well. He'd need helping to bed when morning came. I looked round for a flash of red hair and there was Margawse, with her shift unlaced at the neck under her scarlet cloak, flirting with half a dozen of Uther's young warriors.

There was someone else too. Crouched on the stones in the corner of the hearth, as if the cold had got right into his bones. Merlyn. It's a funny thing, but he seemed a different person each time you saw him. He was a man that came and went. You never knew when or how you would see him next.

He was here now, all right. But not looking at all like what I'd expected him to do on such a night. He had an old goatskin pulled round his shoulders, that stank to high heaven, and the rest of his clothes were in rags. A proper beggar, he looked. But what gave me a start was how old he seemed. Older than I'd thought he could have looked, for a man that usually carried himself so tall and moved as if he was going to break out into dancing at any moment. He wasn't dancing now. And it wasn't lime that made his hair look white this time. It was as if that little boy that had just come into the world had drained all the life out of him and left him an old man.

He saw me coming and raised his beaker to me. I wondered then if he had the fever, for his eyes were red and watery. He hardly had the strength to lift his arm.

That cheered me up and put a bit of pride back into me. I felt a bit like Ygerne then, and there must have been a pretty broad grin on my face when I walked up to him.

'Well,' I said. 'You may have brought the stallion to our mare. But there are some things even Emrys Merlyn can't do. It needed woman's wisdom to bring this foal into the world.'

Me, pulling Merlyn's leg, like a milkmaid with a farmhand. I must have been drunk already. He sounded so weary as if it cost him an effort to talk.

'There are many things that Emrys Merlyn cannot do, or the world would not be as it is. And where were you, Gwennol Far-Sight, when this foal was dropped?'

That made me wince. He meant it to.

'I was working my weft, never you fear. I still have power, though I get little thanks for it these days.'

'I told you, Gwennol. We should be allies. Our time is passing. A little space of sunshine before the storm comes. I need your help.'

'Me? Help the Pendragon?'

'Not him. All *this*.'

He stared out then with a wild, flashing sort of look in his eyes, as if the walls weren't there and it wasn't pitch-black night. There was no telling how far he could see across the land.

I couldn't understand what he meant. I was looking round for something else. And what I was hoping to see was a draggled black thing, like a half-starved cat, that might have crept in out of the storm at last for a bit of shelter and comfort. But I hadn't much faith I'd find her here, and I was right. No matter where I looked, there wasn't a sign of Morgan. Still, I worked my way round the crowd thinking she might have slipped into one of the side stalls where Uther's warriors slept, and curled up in the straw. I found more than a few merry couples enjoying themselves but I couldn't find her. Fuddled I might be, but I started to worry where she might have got to on such a night as this. I could curse my way past a closed gate after dark even now, if I had to, though Uther's warriors were not so feared of me as Gorlois's Cornish boys had been. A little maid like Morgan couldn't. But she didn't need to. She was as nimble as a cat. I knew she could be over that rampart in two shakes of a duck's tail. And who was going to stop her in the dark? She could be on the cliffs by now. I pushed that thought away. It was like watching a rat poke its head out of the wall, and then turning your back and trying to pretend to yourself that you haven't seen it.

I needed another beaker of ale. As I pushed my way back round the hall I saw two figures, like giants they were, on the dais. The fire was throwing their shadows high on the wall behind them. Uther was leaning his fist on the high table to hold himself upright, and Merlyn was standing over him now. He was drawn up to his full height again. It struck me then that Merlyn was the taller of the two, though Uther Pendragon was a big man. Merlyn didn't look old now, though his hair was white, and he was the only sober man in the room. He had a clear, singing voice. He kept it low, but I could hear it through all the shouting.

'You made a promise, Uther. On the honour of your father's grave you vowed the boy to me before ever he was conceived. It was a fair bargain. I have fulfilled my part. Now keep yours.'

Uther's fist thumped down on the table. But he wasn't sober enough to keep it steady.

'But he's my son! My only child.' The drink was slurring his speech. He'd be crying soon.

'And therefore most precious and most vulnerable. Our time is shorter than you think. These days are dngerous. I must have the boy. Soon.'

'When?'

But Merlyn looked up and saw me watching. And ill though he'd looked, in three strides he was across the hall like a hawk swooping. He towered over me, and I was mortally afraid. His eyes glittered, and not with firelight either. He gripped my arm like a noose round a hare's neck.

'Gwennol Far-Sight! So it seems your ears pierce the distance as well as your eyes.'

We weren't allies now. We were no milkmaid and farmhand.

'I was only watching out for my young ladies, sir.'

His eyes swung round the hall, and he muttered under his breath, 'Elaine. Margawse.' Then his fingers tightened on my arm, till I fairly yelped. 'And where is Morgan?'

I couldn't meet his eyes.

'It all happened so quick. When the baby was born she went dashing off into the storm like a mad thing. That great fool of a man . . .'

'The baby! The queen's bower? Are you sure she's not there?'

A blacksmith's pincers couldn't have gripped me harder.

'No, sir. It was the first place I looked. There was only the midwife with them. And the little babe was dropping asleep, bless him.'

I didn't tell him it wasn't any thought of Morgan that had taken me there. His hand let go of my arm and he seemed to draw his breath a bit easier. But he wasn't satisfied yet.

'I have business to finish with Uther. Find her, Gwennol. And watch her well these next few days. I warn you, do not forget Morgan. Even for a moment.'

He didn't exactly push me out of the hall. But he looked at me so stern that, I don't know why, I turned and went out into that storm without another word. Merlyn wasn't a man you said no to.

All the same, when I came to, I wasn't best pleased at finding myself the wrong side of that door again. I'd never had that last beaker of ale and it was sheeting down with rain. I looked in our sleeping-hut, but she wasn't there. So I crossed the path to the queen's chamber again, just to make sure.

My heart was beating fast as I opened the door.

They were all three asleep. Ygerne with her face half-buried under her hair. The midwife rolled on the floor, snoring. And that sweet baby tucked up in a wicker cradle all threaded prettily with ribbons of gold.

There was no one to see me now, so I bent my old stiff back and reached out my hands to take him up.

I never heard her coming, but her shadow fell over the basket and made the baby blink. I felt who it was, like a chill in the room when the wind has changed. She was standing close behind me. The water was running out of her hair in rivers, and her dress was black with rain. But she smiled at me sweetly. Oh, very sweetly she smiled!

'Poor Gwennol,' she said. 'Did you think he would be your baby? Did you think they would give him to you when the wet-nurse had finished with him? Were you dreaming of dressing him, and playing with him, and singing him to sleep, as you did with Gorlois's daughters? Don't you know who he is? He's the eldest son of the King of all the Britons. He'll be the greatest prince in the land soon. Fine ladies will feed him gruel. Court bards will sing him lullabies. And the wisest scribes in Christendom will teach him. Did you think they would leave him here in Bossiney with you?'

Oh, she was clever for nine years. Like a hot poker to the eyes it was. Yes, I'd been a foolish old body, dreaming what I had dreamed. And it didn't hurt any the less for knowing she was right. It was the way the child did it. She knew she was all I had left now, but she'd enjoyed bringing tears to my eyes. They'd killed the light of her life, so she'd put out the light for the rest of us.

Her voice woke Ygerne up. She opened her eyes and saw her daughter.

'What is it?' she said, and you could see her move quick to gather the baby close to her. But the pillow was empty. Well, her eyes went wide with fear.

But Morgan laughed and swooped for the cradle. She had the baby in her arms before any of us could stop her. Then she looked up at us with her green eyes, as wide and as innocent as you please.

'What's the matter with you all? What are you staring at? He's my little brother, isn't he?'

She bent her black hair over his face and we thought she was kissing him. Then the baby let out a yell. And when that maid lifted her head, there on his tiny white neck were the red marks of her teeth.

# Chapter Twenty-seven

Those few short days before Christmas I never had an easy moment.
I'd been used to letting Morgan run free. She was a child that needed
to be left on her own. In summer, as long as she didn't wander into
the forest, I'd let her play where she wanted amongst the bramble
brakes or paddle her way through the pools on the beach. Just so
long as she didn't get quite out of my sight. She might seem to be
reckless, but she never came to harm that way. It was Margawse I'd
worried about. Tossing her red hair and flashing her green eyes at
every man in the dun.

But now I had worse than that to fear. I had lost my little Morgan
that I had wept over so many nights when we never thought she would
live to see nine summers. When I looked at her white face now since
the year had turned, it was just as if there was a stranger in the room.
And no child either. Hours she would sit silent, brushing her black
hair till it shone like a chough's wing and cleaning her nails. And where
was my little maid that used to run home to me with her hair tangled
in the wind and her hands full of sea-shells?

And then suddenly I'd look up and she would be gone, like a soul
out of the body. Only her empty stool beside the door. My blood turned
cold each time and the first place I'd run would be my lady's rooms.
Her women would be there, or the wet-nurse, and that sweet boy that
still had no name, and all looking as peaceful as a field of lambs in
spring. And there I'd stand panting in the doorway like a silly old fool,
staring at them. And as like as not, when I got back to our own hut
Morgan would be there, sewing in the light from the doorway. She'd
lift her green eyes and smile at me. But there wasn't any warmth in
her smile now, and no kindness either.

Still, she hadn't learned to be deceitful then, though there were others
who'd deceived her cruelly. Sometimes she would sit scowling over
her work, then jump up suddenly and laugh in my face. She'd be off
like a greyhound, straight to her mother's room for everyone to see.
And all the women would start to their feet and pull their skirts away
from her. They all feared her. The one that was nearest would snatch
up the baby, and Morgan would burst into laughter at their looks. She
enjoyed frightening us. But I wonder now if she hadn't been crying
out to us to stop her.

Hours, I lay awake worrying over her. For who was there to keep
her now from harm? Merlyn had the strength, I didn't doubt that, but
he'd sooner have cursed her than taught her what he knew. I even
thought about the white nuns on Tintagel. Yes, you may stare at me.

112

But they hadn't saved her father, or her mother either. There was only me.

I was sorely tempted then. I knew where there was healing for her hurt. I had led her mother and sisters down that way. But when it came to Morgan, still I drew my hand back. There was this strong feeling on me, as if there was a barrier across the path that I daren't cross. I knew that once I took the first step down that road with her, that way would lead deeper than I wanted to go. Deeper than I'd been myself. And who knows what would come of it? It frightened me. So I held my peace. I don't know if I did right.

Still, I couldn't be watching her all the time. Morgan had hurt me deep, saying what she had about the baby. But it was no more than the truth. He wouldn't be with us long. Who's to blame me if my feet were sometimes straying to that bower when Ygerne's back was turned?

On Christmas Eve, Merlyn, that had been with us since the boy was born, packed his bags to go. It was a strange time to be taking to the road, but that was the way he was. He never said where he was going and we didn't ask. We crowded round him in the yard as they saddled his white mare, and the two of them were dancing about as if they were in a hurry to be gone. The wind had changed. It was blowing from the north now, chasing the rain away and freezing the puddles.

And just as we thought he was ready to ride off, there was a flurry of white in the gateway, like a shower of hail.

Nectan, with his cloak blowing round him. Come to shrive us all before the feast of Christmas. Well, what those Christians call a feast. To tell you the truth, I'd forgotten about their holy day. I had so much else on my mind, good and bad, just then.

We were coming into their time now. It was too raw weather for his bell to gather everyone in the open air. There'd be candles in the chapel and the hall. He'd spread his table with a fair cloth, a book, a chalice and a dish. And he'd make our rafters ring with his hymns. A very different sort of singing from Midwinter's Eve, that would be, though he did it gladly enough. It always surprises me, that folk that live so thinly can sing so heartily as that. Uther's warriors would make a brave sound singing with him.

Then I turned my head, and I saw something that startled me. Merlyn had forgotten the Christians too, or I could tell he'd have gone sooner. It had struck me often that when the chapel bell called us for Sunday or a Christian feast-day, Merlyn always contrived to be somewhere else.

There was a cloud passed over his face when he saw that lean saint coming, and it made me feel queer for a moment. He looked so old. I don't just mean tired and white, like he had after the boy was born. No, worse than that. You'll think me daft but you might have seen such a look if you'd invited the Old Ones to join you at Samain, and the Older Ones had come in their place. The ones our own gods drove under the hollow hills when they took the land.

I thought Nectan checked too at the sight of Merlyn. He crossed himself. I don't think he was afraid. More like a man buckling on his armour. Though I wouldn't have blamed him if he had to screw up his courage. Then he gathered his muscles together and came on. They didn't say anything. Just looked at each other, eye to eye, like two warriors before a battle.

Yes, I thought. That fool of a hermit should have listened when Gorlois warned him.

It didn't last long. I don't think anybody saw it but me. Next moment a smile broke out on Nectan's face, and he turned to Uther.

'Well, your honour? Is your new son keeping healthy this cold weather? I must talk with you about his christening.'

Uther clapped him on the back and laughed.

'All's well with the queen and her son, thank the Lord. Go in and warm yourself by the fire. They're ready for you in the chapel. Give us a moment to bid farewell to Emrys Merlyn.'

The saint thanked him and strode indoors out of the frost.

I had known Merlyn for a man that was very sure of himself. He was like a piper that could make all of us dance to his tune. And he was always quick with a jest or a clever word. But I saw for a moment he didn't know what to do when the saint spoke of the christening. He almost looked as if he was thinking of unpacking his saddle-bags. Then he grinned at us sudden, with that queer one-sided smile of his.

'I don't wait to give my gifts till Christmas Day,' he said.

And I knew then I was right. I don't doubt he had his plans to make for the boy, but we shouldn't see him again until the psalms and the prayers were over.

But he wouldn't let the Pendragons forget him. He reached down into his saddle-bags and drew out something for all of them. Fine, feast-time gifts they were. He gave Margawse a bronze mirror. Beautifully patterned on the back, it was, with leaves and song-birds' heads. I knew she'd be hours admiring her pretty face in it. And for Elaine he had a little case with fine bone needles, and a pair of scissors shaped like a swan's beak, and skeins of coloured silks, that made her turn pink with pleasure. Uther got a set of dice in a silver cup, and Ygerne a golden comb. I didn't see what he handed to her for the baby.

I must have been as daft as the rest of them, pressing round him, hoping for a smile before he said good-bye. His eyes met mine. Grey eyes, he had, like the blade of a fine sword. He looked at me keenly. And when he did smile, I felt the thrust of it deep inside my belly.

'Come here, Gwennol,' he said, and reached into his leather satchel again. 'This is for you.'

Well, I gasped. I'd never expected him to give me anything. A red shawl, it was, that he told me was made of goat's hair. I stood with it over my arm, stroking it, for I'd never had anything of my own so fine and soft, and I could feel the warmth of it already in the cold wind. I know he laughed at my face. Years, I kept that shawl.

When it came to Morgan's turn I was sure she wouldn't be there to see him off. But she was standing a little way off, leaning against the doorpost of our hut, watching us from the shadows that were blue with frost. Merlyn took out a little hunting-knife, with the bone handle carved like a boar, all bristles and tusks. It was a rare piece of craft. He held it out to her.

'For Morgan to stab us all in the heart with,' he said. And the smile never got past his mouth.

Last Christmas Morgan would have loved a present like that more than any pretty thing her sisters had. Wasn't Gorlois the finest huntsman in all Cornwall? And didn't she ride at his heels whenever he would take her? She'd have run straight off with that knife and played that she was the son her father always wanted.

But Gorlois was dead. And this Morgan was a stranger to us. She'd never hunted with Uther.

She said angrily, 'That's a boy's present. I'm a woman now.'

Though she wasn't yet. Not as I understand it, anyhow. Merlyn knew that too. He smiled down at her slowly, and even, I thought, a bit sadly.

'When Morgan, daughter of Gorlois, becomes a woman, then the whole of Britain will have something to fear.'

She looked at him and there was doubt in her face, as if she feared he was laughing at her. She let the knife fall to the ground between them. Then she turned her back and went inside our hut.

'Watch her,' he said to me sharply.

He took my arm then, over that red shawl, and his eyes held mine. 'A little time we must keep him safe, Gwennol. A few more days. And then you may leave the future to me. Watch Morgan.'

I knew what he meant, though I was too choked to answer him.

Then he kicked his heels into the mare's sides and cantered out of the gate with everyone waving and calling after him.

When he was past the oak I turned my eyes away. I was quicker to be rid of him then than I had been that first time. I remembered I had to pick up the knife. It was too fine a thing to be left lying in the mud. But someone else had got there first.

Nectan had come out into the yard again. He was holding the knife out to Morgan. It seems they were the only two in the whole dun who hadn't been caught up in Merlyn's glamour.

'This is yours, I think,' he said. He smiled at her pretty kindly for a childless man. 'It's a good blade. You could whittle a piece of boxwood with it to make an angel for the Christ-child's crib.'

She turned away from him without a word, as she had from Merlyn. He must have felt her watching. He faced slowly round.

'Well,' I said, with a grim sort of smile. 'The son of a holy virgin, is it?'

He had the grace to laugh, though there wasn't much humour in it.

'Yes, Gwennol Far-Sight. You have the better of me there. I was a fool. Too trusting. But we grow wiser. He has run away and I am here. Uther will trust his child to me. And whose side are you on, Gwennol? Will you help me care for the child?'

I smiled at him, as innocent as you please.

'I have always cared for the child, sir. Since the day she was born.'

Fool of a man. He never even noticed.

He held out the knife to me.

'Will you give it to Morgan?'

He had bigger things to think about than that. So he never saw, as I did, that she had turned her head and was staring after him with a sort of hunger in her face.

I'll never forgive him for that. She'd seen he wasn't afraid of Merlyn. She might have turned to him then.

Yes! Don't hiss at me. I'd rather he had taken her for his Church, if it had made her happy.

But it was only the boy that mattered to any of them.

Merlyn had gone. Those that cared to told Nectan their sins. Then we sang their hymns, and made ready for another child's coming.

When it was done I went back to the sleeping-hut. Morgan was there. She was holding Margawse's mirror and smiling at her own reflection as she touched her hair. That gave me a start. Just for a moment she looked like a small, dark copy of her mother. Then she heard me coming and put the mirror down. She picked up Elaine's sewing-case and began to play with the scissors. I heard her draw her breath sharp. When I looked down, one of those dainty blades had pierced her finger, drawing blood.

But the hunting-knife lay on the chest beside her bed where I had left it. She never touched it.

# Chapter Twenty-eight

We kept that Christmas as we never had before. And it was the first of many days' feasting. Uther was as pleased with himself as a dog with two tails, and both of them wagging fit to bust. He carried the baby round the hall for everyone to say how handsome he was and how like his father. Tiny though that mite was, he dandled him on his knee through the mummers' play and the horse's dance and all the sword-swinging in the hall. He couldn't be done with showing him off to the world. I never saw a man tempt the gods so, not even Gorlois, and he was proud enough. In the end I couldn't stand it. I snatched the child off him and took him back to his mother. Let Uther show off his daughters now.

Well, as soon as he'd finished toasting his son he gave it out that he meant to marry Margawse off like Elaine to a king up north, beyond the Wall. They'd be betrothed just as soon as spring came and ships could sail north again to seal the bargain. I think he knew as well as I did we'd need to be quick about it. Margawse had come to her womanhood these last few days.

I didn't grieve over her when I heard the news. There never was a girl I'd be gladder to see wed. I'd had enough of her light-headed ways. Though it was no liege-man of Uther's she'd be marrying, by the sound of it, but a king that he had need to be better friends with. He'd sell Gorlois's filly off at a fair price, to keep the north at peace. At least I needn't fear her shaming us much longer.

And still the Pendragon's boy had no name. There were some that held that he was safer so. What has no name can't be named, and no one can get power over it. But some of the Christians had a different view of it. They said it was a dangerous time. If a child should die unchristened, their Heaven would have none of it, and it would become a pixie spirit, wandering the moors and leading baptised folk astray. But Nectan wouldn't have it was so. And I could have told them there were worse things than babies loose on the moor at night.

But we had no fears that this child would die before its time. You never saw a healthier baby. Day after day we watched him grow. His little cheeks were pink and full and his eyes bright and clear, and the winter sunlight seemed to catch in his hair. He was a child of the light, that one. Every day he grew stronger, like the sun. Many a time I'd make some excuse for passing the door so I could put my head round the curtain and have a look at him lying in his cradle. And if no one was looking, I'd pick him up and cuddle him, and croon in his ear the songs I used to sing his mother. We had no snow that winter, though it froze hard. But for once I was casting charms to make it long and bitter, with snowdrifts up to the roof. When the spring came, I knew what would happen. They would mount their horses and chariots, and Ygerne would take her son up in her arms, as proud as you please, and they would be gone, out of Cornwall.

Still, no good crying about it till it happened. We would make a great feast for him while he was still ours. So we kept that midwinter season as never before. I must say that Uther Pendragon was a merrier man than ever Gorlois had been, and a richer one too. It was a gay time we had, and Elaine and Margawse looked as merry as their mother, whatever they felt inside.

The boy was to be named on what they call the feast of Epiphany. Nectan had planned it. A double celebration, that would be, for the baptism of the King of Heaven and for King Uther's firstborn son. Uther had sent word to all the lords and ladies in Dumnonia to come to the christening, if the roads would let them. Bossiney had never seen anything like it in all my days. The kitchens were busy baking and brewing and roasting till the steam came out of the thatch so thick and wholesome you could almost taste it. Both hall and chapel were decked with armfuls of holly and ivy. And so many lamps everywhere, you'd think they'd never have found oil and fat enough for them all.

Uther thought he had Nectan dancing to his tune, though I wasn't so sure myself. The saint might seem pretty thick with the king and queen these days, but it was his own battle he was fighting with Merlyn over the boy. They were all the same. They only thought about him. But there was one thing made Uther frown. There was someone he could never wrap round his little finger, for all his bright eyes and golden gifts. Bryvyth had been bidden to the christening, with all the other high lords and ladies round about. She might live plainly, but she was a mighty learned woman, and they treated her just the same as if she'd been a bishop. And now she had sent back word from Tintagel she wouldn't come. Things had been done there that couldn't be mended. And that boy was at the heart of it. Uther and Ygerne made more show of treading the Christian way than ever Gorlois had done. They might fool Nectan, but it did them no good with Bryvyth. The Church was never best friends with the Pendragons.

So we came to Twelfth Night, and the boy was to be named in the morning. And as if I wasn't busy enough already, Margawse went down with the fever. It was nothing more than a winter chill, and she was as strong as a horse. But there was no one but me to nurse her, and she was as cross as a dog that's lost its bone because she was missing the last days of the feast. She couldn't bear to be dull. And how I was supposed to see to her and keep my eyes on Morgan is more than I can tell. I took Elaine aside and told her to watch her little sister closely and see she never left the hall. But you'd need to be as watchful as an owl and as fast as a hawk to keep up with that one. Elaine was no match for her. She put me in mind of a plump house-cat that keeps to the warmth of the fire and doesn't like to get her fur dirty in the mud.

I wished Merlyn had stayed. Bryvyth spoke true enough when she said he was a strange soul-friend for a Christian king. He was as slippery as a trout. I knew the times and the reasons, and I could guess better than most some of the places he went. And Merlyn knew that I knew. Many's the time he got up from the bench and looked at me before he went out of the hall with that quick half-smile in his eyes. And I always felt that if I'd been only a little bit younger he might have pulled me by the hand and whipped me off with him. It's a strange thing to say, but I was never sure whether he and I were friend or foe.

But surely he'd be back for the christening? He'd had a way of talking to Uther almost as if the baby belonged to him.

It fell dark early on the eve of Epiphany. The wind was rising till you could almost feel the earth shaking beneath you where the great waves were flinging themselves against the land. There was no rain with it this time. It would be bright moonlight a bit later on, if only the wind could tear a hole in the clouds. They were pressed thick across the sky now, like a black herd of galloping cattle.

The feasting-hall looked a brave sight across the yard, with all the lamps burning and the fire leaping up the logs. But there'd be no games for me that night. I was left sitting by Margawse's bedside. They sent us food, goose-meat and mead, and a bowl of good broth for Margawse. But it wasn't the same. There's no fun in getting drunk by yourself. I missed the company. It's a hard life we lead at Bossiney, though it was a sight gayer since King Uther was our lord, and mid-winter had always been a time for laughter and a bit of horseplay and plenty to eat and drink. And what's the harm in that, even at my age, if it helps to see us through the dark of winter?

And besides, I couldn't have eyes everywhere. I'd sent Morgan off to the hall with her sister Elaine, both of them with their skin washed and the grease sponged off their best gowns and their hair plaited with silk braids. As quiet and demure as a little queen Morgan looked that night. But by now there wasn't one of us that knew what was going on behind those green eyes. So I wasn't easy.

Supper never seems to take so long when you eat it by yourself. I licked the grease off my fingers and picked my teeth and listened for the harp and the singing and the dancers' pipes. The music seemed to come and go between gusts of wind, like the sea. The mead was making me drowsy, but I could tell well enough when the food was finished and the horseplay began, by the noise. A great roar of singing and stamping. And no court bard's ditty, either, I can tell you. And they shouted louder than ever when it was finished. They'd be lucky if there weren't daggers out before the night was over, with all the wine and mead and beer I'd seen them taking into the hall. And in the morning, they'd all of them be nursing sore heads and walking to chapel like sober gentlefolk to see the baby prince baptised with his new Christian name. And he? He'd be fast asleep now, bless him, and not caring a bit for the noise they were making over his coming.

It didn't surprise me when Elaine came back early. She was never one for rough play and bawdy jokes, and there'd be plenty of that tonight. It would have been enough of a treat for her to serve the wine to Uther's guests at the high table in her mother's place. She was fourteen now. Her breasts were filling out and her cheeks thinning. She'd make a proper queen before long. But I was angry when I saw she hadn't brought Morgan.

'Where's your sister?' I said sharply. 'You haven't left her, have you, when I told you never to take your eyes off her?'

She tossed her head a bit more proudly than she used to. She had more than a little of her mother in her.

'You forget, I had more important things to look to, with so many guests.' Then she laughed and hugged me, like the old times. 'Don't worry, Gwennol. She wanted to stay and watch the sword-dancing. It's all right. Mother's still there with her.'

'And much good that will do,' I muttered.

It wasn't Morgan our queen would have her eyes on. In Gorlois's time she was more delicate. She'd have gone to bed earlier, with the baby so newly-born. But she was bolder now that she was Uther's wife. And who was I to blame her? I'm old enough to be her mother, and I'd sooner have been in the hall with the rest of them than stuck in the bed-chamber. Ygerne had come late to her crown, and she meant to have her fill of it.

Elaine must have known what I was thinking, for she said, 'Go on, Gwennol. Why don't you go and enjoy yourself? Margawse is asleep, and I'll be here if she wakes. And you can watch Morgan for yourself.'

I didn't need telling twice. I've never missed Twelfth Night. I'll sit down to a feast, any time. Old Religion or Christian, it's all the same to me, so long as there's plenty of food and drink and dancing.

As soon as I got to the hall I looked for Morgan. And she had gone from the table. I could feel the panic starting inside me. There was her mother laughing, and the king beside her. I looked everywhere. And then I saw her. Like a little black shadow in the corner by the hearth, behind the harper. Well, let her stay there. If the play got rough, she'd be out of the way of it there.

Oh, it was good to be squashed up on the bench among friends, and the warmth of their bodies better than any fire. There was still drink going round, and some scraps of food left, and I went on stuffing 'til I lost a tooth cracking nuts. They plunged hot iron in the mead, and passed it round fizzing hot. We were all more than a little merry.

Then the dogs began barking outside. All the men leaped up and reached for their swords, because who would be on the road in the dark, when the gates were shut and the yard-dogs loosed and food on the table? But we recognised that voice calling to the dogs through the wind. King Uther laughed.

'All's well,' he said. 'It's only Merlyn, come late to join our feast.'

Merlyn. On the eve of the holy-day of Epiphany? So he'd come back to battle with Nectan for the boy, had he?

The door crashed open, and the wind almost took the platters off the table. Merlyn stood there. He was dressed like a druid, in a white gown with bands of gold across his breast. He had a wreath of holly woven round his cap. But there was no smile on his face now. We just sat there gaping at him like fools. You could see his eyes going round the hall, and I shivered as they went over me. But they came to rest on Ygerne.

'Where is your child?' he roared at her.

And never mind that she had four.

Her hand flew to her mouth. She was as drunk and foolish as the rest of us. She didn't understand what he meant. But I did. Maybe I hadn't had time to drink as much as the rest, or maybe I'd seen more than was good for me. But my eyes went straight to the corner by the fire, and it was empty. Merlyn saw my face.

'And where is Morgan!' Like a river bursting into a house, his voice was.

He was running out of that door before I could get to my feet. He was in the queen's chamber by the time I came panting in. When I pushed past him I was mortally afraid of what I was going to see.

At first I thought the room was empty. Then I saw the wet-nurse, lying in her cot, dead-drunk. And that was all. The cradle was bare. No Morgan. No sign of blood.

# Chapter Twenty-nine

Ygerne let out such a scream, you could have heard it all the way to Land's End. But I'd feared worse than what I saw.

'Thanks be! At least she hasn't killed him.'

I don't think that boy's mother even knew what I meant. Wise woman or no, she'd been so besotted with her fine king she hadn't the wit to see what she was doing to her own daughters.

She was standing there, with her hand to her mouth and her blue eyes staring, crying, 'My baby! Where has my baby gone!'

Merlyn turned on her. I'd never seen him so angry, and it made me quail, I can tell you.

'This is at your door! Vain, foolish woman! I thought we were agreed. I gave you two kings. Was that too much for one woman to hold?'

'Guard your tongue!' King Uther shouted at him. 'It is your queen you speak to.' But there were few of us that had much time for Ygerne that night. 'You, Gwennol! Is this Morgan's work?'

'Who else?' said Merlyn.

'By God! I should have sent the bitch to join her father!'

'Gwennol Far-Sight,' said Merlyn, gripping my wrists and looking into my eyes. 'Where would she take him?'

'Down to the sea,' I said, like a woman in a dream. I never stopped to think how I knew it.

Uther Pendragon was out of the door like a shot. Merlyn snatched up a fur from the bed and threw it round me. Then he gripped me by the elbow and bundled me out into the storm. My lady was left behind in a flood of tears. But there were plenty of folk crowding round to fuss over her.

'Which way?' shouted Merlyn. He had his mouth close to my ear, but I could hardly hear him for the gale.

I couldn't tell him. I had this picture in my mind, like the one thing you remember from a dream after you wake up. But where it was, I'd no notion. One wet rock looks much the same as any other on a stormy night.

So I set off as if I was going down to Bossiney Haven, because that's the nearest way to the beach. I could hardly walk for the wind. I had Uther Pendragon on one side of me and Merlyn on the other, and they were fairly carrying me along. When I looked back there were soldiers with drawn swords behind us. And all for a little girl not ten years old. Some of them had lanterns, though they hardly needed them. There was a queer sort of cloudy moonlight, between dark and light.

We hadn't gone far before I stopped. I couldn't say why, but I knew something was wrong. She hadn't come this way. I felt a power drawing me, and I knew she must have felt it too. I could tell now where she'd gone, all right.

There was a good deal of swearing and grumbling when we turned round. We went stumbling back over stones and potholes. But I made them follow me. I was like a hound that's picked up a fresh scent. Then the moon broke loose and we were up on the downs on the edge of the cliff, making for Tintagel.

Merlyn struck his thigh a great blow. And I could tell he was cursing himself this time for a slow-witted fool.

I'd have been plucked right over the cliff if I hadn't had those two tall men on either side of me, holding on. There was a sort of silver mist all round us, though the moon and stars were bright over our heads. The waves were crashing so hard against the cliffs they were sending the spray right up into our faces.

We were almost running now. Sometimes the wind seemed to push us back like a great flat hand. Other times it would come swirling round so I thought it would pick us up and carry us flying. All the time we were drawing nearer to that holy island.

But she wouldn't be there. It wasn't those white nuns she was running to tonight. She wouldn't cross that causeway a second time. I knew what drew her, though I'd never told her a word about it. She didn't need my teaching.

There was a way down to the beach before you reach that terrible bridge. It was a gully, running with water, and rough walking. The lower we got the wetter it was, with the spray coming down on us like rain. The roar of the waves was so loud it mazed your thoughts. I turned colder inside than out. For how could my Morgan and that precious mite be safe on the rocks in such a storm?

Then we got to the bottom and the cliffs sheltered us a bit from the wind. But we could still hardly hear ourselves speak, for the brook was hurling itself off the ledge in a great waterfall.

We could see the waves breaking on the point, shooting high walls of water up into the air, and the flung spray turning to silver in the moonlight. But the bay was quieter. A great black swell was running in. Like hump-backed serpents coming at us, it looked. It dashed itself against the rocks with a hiss a bit softer than the crashes out on the point. The tide was full in. There wasn't a foot of beach you could put a dry foot on. I knew where Morgan had tried to take him, all right. But the Mother's Hole would be full to the roof with the sea now, and the stone in the middle drowned deep by two currents of water. She couldn't have got further than this.

I'd lost her heart long ago. But when I looked at those black shining walls of water rearing up towards us, I thought I'd lost her poor little body too.

Then we saw her. She was standing on a high pinnacle of rock with the waves pounding all around her. How she got there, dear only knows. We wouldn't have seen her, for the water was as black as the mouth of hell, and Tintagel behind her was dark, as if it had turned its back

123

on us. If there was a glimmer of light anywhere on it, we couldn't have seen it through the spray. Likely those nuns were safe in bed, like the good Christians most of them were. Still, for the first time in my life I found myself wishing that Bryvyth Crook-Staff might be awake and praying for us, up there in the dark. We needed all the power we had between us that night.

Even then we couldn't have seen Morgan with her black hair and her gown dark with wetting. But she had a little white bundle clutched to her chest, and just then the wind blew back her sleeves and showed her two white arms.

I must have drawn my breath sharpish. I heard Merlyn hiss between his teeth, so I knew he'd seen her too. But neither of us dared to utter a word. Merlyn waved his hand at the men behind us to be still, though to tell you the truth, you couldn't have heard an army marching over the stones above those breakers. It was Uther broke the spell. He was always a man that couldn't bear to wait, never mind what it cost afterwards.

He swore a great oath and let go of my arm. And he drew his sword so fast it's a wonder it didn't take the head off my shoulders.

'Morgan!' he roared. 'Give him back to me this instant, or I'll skewer you like a sucking pig.'

My heart was in my mouth when he yelled at her like that. I knew her better than he did. A curse like that might have been all she was waiting for. I truly thought we'd seen the last of those two children then.

But she didn't even seem to have heard him at first. Still and black she was, like a woman carved out of bog-wood. And the ends of the baby's white bands fluttering in the wind like prayer-rags.

'Morgan!' he thundered at her.

The wind dropped just then, so that his voice came echoing back off the cliffs.

She turned her head, and looked over her shoulder towards us.

'If you come one step closer, I'll drop him into the sea.'

My heart fairly broke for her when she said that. I knew what it meant. If she'd really wanted to kill her brother, it would have only taken her a moment. She needn't have carried him all the way through the storm to here. One stab with that hunting-knife Merlyn had given her, and it would have been all over and done with. His little life-blood running away on the bedchamber floor, and the Pendragons punished.

But she hadn't killed him yet. I think she couldn't do it unless they drove her now. How long had she been standing up there on that rock in this wild storm, holding her baby brother in her arms? I knew where she had been trying to take him, all right. But why had she held on to him for so long? Then it came to me that she was like a frightened black kitten trapped on a roof, and mewing for someone to come and help her down. I think there were two souls in her. One of them was wanting to kill the boy for the hurt he had done her in his coming. And the other one was crying out to us to save her from that.

I tried to take a step forward but the wind got up again and pushed me back, like a blow on the chest. I lost sight of the children in the spray. Merlyn held on to my arm and murmured in my ear.

'Speak to her, Gwennol. You are the only one here she loves.'

Yes, Emrys Merlyn asking me for help.

It's gone long past that, I thought, thanks to you. Precious little sign of love she's shown to me or anyone else these last nine months. But I had to try. I loved both those poor children, may Lord Gorlois forgive me for it.

'Come along with me to your bed, my lover. He's only a baby. He hasn't done you any harm.'

But even before the words were out of my mouth, I knew that wasn't true. Even sleeping in her mother's belly, he'd done her and her sisters wrong.

'Uther Pendragon killed my father. And he deceived my mother. And neither of them is sorry for it. But I will make them weep.'

King Uther took a great stride into the water till the waves filled his boots.

'The stinking little crow!' he shouted. 'Give me my son back!'

A king's no better than the rest of the gentry that can't keep their temper. All pride and no sense. King he might be, but any shepherd-boy could have told him it was daft to come at her like that, like a wolf on a ewe-lamb. When she saw him with the water up to his waist she moved so quickly that I thought she was going to throw herself off the rock with the baby still clutched in her arms. I know I screamed.

Then Merlyn flung out his arm with the fingers of his hand spread stiff, and called down from the sky the words of power to bind her.

I'd been a fool to think his strength was going.

I hid my eyes in my hands, but I should have covered my ears. I've said a few spells myself in my time, but I've never heard words like those before, and I hope I never shall as long as I live. None of us there should have heard them spoken aloud. It froze me where I stood like a pillar of granite.

But that power held Morgan before she reached the edge of the rock. Stiff and still she grew, like his own hand pointing at her. Just the moonlight flashing in her eyes like frost.

Then our baby prince started to slip out of her arms. It seemed he was the only one the spell couldn't hold. Very slowly he dropped, like a feather falling in a dream. There wasn't one of us could move a hand to stop him. He fell straight into a pool in the hollow of the rocks. Then we saw a great wave come rolling in from the sea and carry him towards the shore.

Quick as a heron, Merlyn went diving through the swell and gathered him up in his arms, all dripping white in the moonlight. He looked down at the child for a long, still time, as if he'd waited years to hold a baby boy like that. Then he gave a great laugh that they must have heard up in Tintagel convent and tossed the boy into the sky. He caught him again, and as the next wave washed over them both he cried out, 'By the power of the old earth and the older moon and the three dark Mothers.

125

'By the power of the bright face of Ludd and Gwydion and Llew.'

The wind came again, and when it had passed Merlyn laughed long and merry.

'By the power of the Father and his Christ and the Spirit of Wisdom!

'I name you . . . Arthur!'

And that moment the precious mite started crying, so that we knew for sure he was alive.

I don't know why he did it, or if you could call that a Christian baptism. Did he think that Bryvyth was listening, on Tintagel Island? Or did he fear, like me, that our time might be over? I couldn't tell you if the boy was ever brought to a priest.

Then Merlyn looked hard at Uther Pendragon and said, 'You promised. He is mine for the fostering now. Britain shall not hear of this boy again until his day comes, and the land cries out to him for help.'

He came splashing back to the shore, and in three more strides he was gone into the darkness. We had none of us stirred.

I've never set eyes on the boy up to this day.

# Chapter Thirty

I couldn't tell you how long we stood there without moving a muscle. Even the sea had fallen still. All of a sudden it seemed as though the charm had let us go. The waves were slapping on the pebbles again, but lower now. All the men were running about at the water's edge, clattering and shouting, as if the pair of them weren't gone beyond finding. We'd lost them both, and more besides.

And it was only then I thought to look for Morgan. Dear forgive me, if I hadn't forgotten her like those others, for the sake of her little baby brother with a face on him like the sun. I was mortally afraid she'd be gone too, drowned deep under the water at last. But she was still there, standing on that high rock with her arms empty. She hadn't moved. I never saw a creature look so lonely, old or young, as that little maid of nine years old.

Next moment Uther came to his senses and went splashing through the waves out to the rock. She didn't fight him now, not even when he grabbed her round the waist. He carried her back and threw her on the shingle at my feet. She caught at my skirt, but she wasn't clinging to me for love, the way she had that morning on the causeway when her heart broke. She was cold and shivering, but when the moonlight fell on her I saw she wasn't crying. Her little white face was as tight and stern as any warrior's.

She hauled herself up to her feet, and it struck me then that she was getting as tall as I was. She looked into that blowing darkness where Merlyn had gone, and she spoke more coldly than any child you ever heard.

'He thinks now he has power over me. But he is not as wise as he believes. A woman could take his power away from him. And then the turn of Gorlois's daughters will come.'

I tried to put my arms round her, but she was stiff as ice. And I looked the way she had, to where I'd last seen Merlyn's back. You fool of a man, I cursed him. And worse than that. I took you for the wisest man in Britain. You had the power to charm her hurt away, though it was you that began it. But in the end you've no more sense than the king here. All you've done is turn her hate from him to you. And there'll be many will pay dearly for that before it's ended.

She lifted her face to me.

'Gwennol,' she said. And there was a little sob in her voice. 'Where is he? Where has Merlyn taken him?'

'I don't know, my pretty,' I told her. 'Somewhere where we'll never find him till he's a grown man.'

Uther Pendragon was marching back up the gully, without a thought for us. Then he stopped and turned, and he bellowed at us for all the world to hear, even the nuns if they were awake at their prayers.

'Get rid of that little hell-cat, once and for all! Take her to Tintagel tomorrow and shut her in the nunnery! And let me not set eyes on her again till those women have schooled the wickedness out of her black heart, or I swear I'll take off her head with my own sword!'

And so I lost my baby.

They sent Morgan to school with the nuns at Tintagel. Though I could have told Uther Pendragon what else she might learn there, if only he'd taken the trouble to ask me. The air was sweet with the singing of psalms in the daytime. But there was that done in the dark place beneath that you wouldn't find in any Christian gospel. Not that Morgan needed anyone to teach her.

There was a scandal when it was found out. It broke Bryvyth's heart. The white nuns have been swept away from Tintagel now. The men have got it for themselves, as they always wanted. Though in the end it wasn't Gorlois who built his stronghold where the two currents meet.

That was years ago. Gorlois's daughters are grown into three tall queens now. Three handsome, wise women, each married to her king. You know the rest as well as I do. Uther Pendragon is dead, poisoned by his enemies, and Ygerne has taken holy vows.

Those white women weren't the only ones swept away. They're still in Cornwall somewhere, clinging to their rocks like gulls. We're not rid of them yet. But in the east the news is worse. That white dragon Merlyn dreamed of is growing fatter every day. There's many a priest and nun won't see another Easter. And many a brave British boy that's food for the Raven. The whole land's in danger now.

And so they say our little Arthur has come again and found his sword.

Well, there you have it. I've done my story, and now I'll tell you why. Morgan herself is here tonight, waiting outside that door. And she's come calling us to help her right her wrongs. So, my sisters, I'll put it to you. What shall we wise women do about the Pendragon's son?

# White Nun's Telling

## Book Two
### in the sequence
### Daughter of Tintagel

## To Kate

# Chapter One

I hate Morgan. She corrupted me. You will think when you read those words that there is penitence, because I have acknowledged my sin. There is not. Morgan showed me an unholy joy. She has fed a poison into my blood that I am powerless to cleanse. It offered me the means of power, but now it has power over me. I cannot give it up. I do not want to. So I am damned.

Once I loved Morgan. At least, I think that is what women mean by love. I had little to compare it with. For a time I was willingly enslaved by her, though I had been set as her warder. Now I think I have no will. I have lost everything – ambition, hope. I hate her for that.

It was not fair to set me, low-born as I was, to watch a princess. I was always proud. Yet I suffered as with a physical pain because I had so little to be proud of. I was not a slave or a bondwoman, and I carried my head high past those who were. Yet I despised what I was.

My parents were farmers. I came from the red lands of mid-Devon, near the holy forest, Great Nymet. From a sheltered farm among apple trees. Strange that when I think of it now it is always springtime there. The waves of blossom foaming round the thatch, nesting songbirds darting in and out of bushes. The blood comes hot in my cheeks when I remember Maytime, and a pulse starts to beat. I knew so little then.

May Eve always disturbed me. I knew that people drank too much. That boys reeled, tugging at girls, into the grass – the lush, green, wet grass of May – that they came home in the morning, wild and dirtied, singing and dancing behind a garlanded pole propped on a cart. It frightened me. The great horns of the oxen poking out of the wreaths of silver and flowers. That thing on the cart, like a great lance, thrusting fearfully. When it was set up I danced around it with the others, stiffly, resentfully, hating the sweaty feel of boys' hands round mine. On the night before May Day I hid my head under the bed-covers.

Yet when I lived there it was not the blossom-time that filled my mind. It was the mud. The slick, red, Devon mud that covered the roads, the yard, the house, weighing down boots and skirts and soul. The weeping sky. The sodden wool around my shoulders. The stench of cows and pigs. The fetid breath of animals and men crowded together in one too small dirty house. No privacy.

My parents were not ungentle with me, though they thought me strange. Between teasing and scolding they tried to push me in the way of red-faced boys likely to inherit a good farm. They could not understand that I should prefer to be alone.

I chose the quiet of the evening, not the morning loud with bird-song and the sweaty bustle of the day's work already beginning. I would leave the paths, where I might meet curious homecomers, and seek solitude among bramble bushes and whispering elms. I disdained to huddle and shiver against the chill of the wind. I lifted my face, unsmiling, to be cleansed of the soil of my labour. I did not spare my aching body. I forced my feet into an unvarying rhythm, up hill and down. There was no joy in my walking, only the need for distance and quiet. Even then, with the animals bedded and the food cooked and eaten, I could not afford to be idle. My hands must always be spinning or knitting as I walked.

I did not heed my mother's chiding. I did not understand her warnings. Indeed I often doubted that she was my mother. She, round and slow and comfortable. I, tall, bony, furiously sharp of mind. Sometimes I dreamed I was a king's daughter, hidden with rustics in time of great danger, waiting to discover her rightful inheritance.

So I went from the house into the grey evening pastures and never even turned my head to answer her.

I did not dream it would be the daughter of a king who would wreck my inheritance.

I say I had no joy, but I knew peace. When I had passed beyond the reek of the chimney-smoke and the lowing of cattle was too distant to be heard, I felt that other life drop from me like a wet cloak. I was myself at last. Alone with myself, as I would always wish to be.

The day had been wet, but the rain-clouds were breaking. There was a streak of yellow sky at the head of the coombe. The sun had gone down and the evening star was bright behind me. I picked my way through the filthy bog of the cows' hooves and began to climb, lifting my skirts clear of thistles and thorns. There was no sound but my own breath. No company but a hare bounding across my path. I would climb to the top of the ridge that enclosed our narrow, smothering coombe. I was subtly driven to extend the boundaries of my world. Even then it was no satisfaction to stand on the highest point, for I only saw the land that lay beyond, that was still not mine.

Yet it must be done. Our valleys are steep. I clambered up slopes, round boulders, through bushes, seeking open ground.

My first warning was a shower of earth from overhead. Then a frightened bellowing and a man's curse.

I have never been quick to move. It seems as though there is a great gulf between my mind and my body. I stood paralysed by fear, struggling to comprehend what was happening. Dirt pelted me. Then, after the first moments in which I should have run, danger appeared more threateningly. A young red milch-cow was slithering and roaring her way down the slope above me. Her eyes rolled wildly and beneath the mud her hooves were as sharp as axe-blades. Behind her leaped a man, brandishing a stick, his face black with anger. I saw in a glance now what it was. Why else should the two of them be out on the hills after suppertime where only I, Luned, and the hare walked? The cow had wandered out of her keeper's sight and gone astray on the hills at nightfall. And the man had lost his supper and wearied his legs to find her before darkness swallowed them both. Even now she would not go gently home, and the two of them battled against each other in mistrust and haste.

I was in their way. Suddenly understanding my danger I scrabbled aside across the hill. The cow took fright and leapt the opposite way, like a hare, skidding splay-legged on the steep incline. The man yelled louder.

'Don't you break your leg now, you black-eyed fool! Not after all the trouble you've caused me.'

Then he saw me. 'You meddling little varmint! 'twas you startled her.'

It was anger first, backed by the unchecked rush of his body downhill towards me. I knew physical terror. I had feared the cow. That was a sensible fear, born of her weight and motion, her position above me, and the damage her hooves and body might do if I stopped their onrush. From the man I feared all that and more. A personal vindictiveness in his eyes, as if I and not the cow were now to blame. I was the butt of his lost time and effort. I the witness of his masculine ineptitude.

I knew the man. Tewdar of Blacklake, with a wife and seven thin-faced children. And he knew me, starting suddenly in the grey twilight out of the red dazzle of his anger, just as I was turning to run another way.

'Luned, Kevern's daughter! You're a long way from home, maidy.'

I did not turn back to him but stayed, still poised on one foot to run. When I met anyone walking, far less startlingly than this, it was always my first instinct to step aside and avoid them, not to be noticed, not to exchange pleasantries. Even if the other was a near neighbour, or a cousin. I do not say friend. There were none I called such. But what should I say to an angry man, alone and unexpected at nightfall? For once I wished myself back home in the firelight, and my mother opposite with a pile of mending on her knee.

Tewdar was breathing heavily. A smile was beginning to spread across his face. It frightened me more than his shouts, though I could not tell why. I moved before he did. It was not a conscious decision. I ran, like the hare, to escape that smile. The smile pursued me. It was in his voice as he chased me down the hill. Wheedling. Eager. Urgent.

'Luned. Little Luned. Have 'ee lost 'ee sweetheart? Wait. I won't hurt 'ee.'

The shout of a man running to catch a cow now, not to drive on.

I ran. Clutching my skirt. Praying I would not stumble. There was mist gathering in the pasture. I dived towards it like a kingfisher into the stream.

There was silence behind me. My own feet thudding on grass. My breath sobbing with haste. Terror returned. Had he outwitted me? Was he ahead, not behind?

I must have stopped and turned, because I saw him. Close above me. And he knew that I saw him. He pulled up too, and the smile spread to a grin. A man's confidence in his overpowering sex. Before

132

my young gaze, he dropped his breeches and displayed his member, pale in the twilight but all too fleshly and real. Hard, stiff, menacing. Like the fresh-cut May-pole of my nightmares.

Do not mistake me. It was not the first time I had seen a man's penis. How could I help it, living as we did? That sign was all around me in the things of power. In wood and stone and leather. On the White Mare's Teaser. In the May Day dances and the Midwinter foolery. Fearful, grotesque. I had seen the little pricks of my younger brothers. Men pissing against the wall or in the bushes. A glimpse of my father half-naked before I hid my face in the blankets. But never before like this. Never aimed deliberately at me. At Luned, at my very self.

I don't know what he expected in his arrogance. That I would falter and blush and pretend to run again, only to own myself beaten, like the cow, now bellowing disconsolately for company on the hill above us.

I have always thought it an ugly thing. That dangling appendage that seems scarcely part of the rest, leading an existence almost separate from the man. I blessed the neatness of women's bodies. Our parts were decently hidden from view. I did not understand then how women's sex is at the core of our being. So I saw that threatening penis, and noticed that his breeches were hooked around his knees. I ran in earnest.

He was angrier then. It would have gone ill with me if he had caught me. By that time it would have been no fumbling, mumbling roll in the grass. I had denied his power.

But I was young and strong-willed. Unweakened by illness or age or deformity. The few moments it took him to snatch up his breeches were enough for me. Pride lent me wings. I flew across the last fields and into the house, like a mouse cheating the hawk. But pride had been humbled. I did not walk in the dusk after that. I was not truly free before I became a nun.

My body was whole, but my mind was violated. I had seen what I wished I had not. Ever afterwards that sight was seared on my imagination. I could never be rid of it. I was soiled, disgusted, shamed. It seemed to me there was a demon in every man I met that might leap out of its cover at me.

You may think this is why I became a nun. It is not. I did not go to Tintagel fleeing what I feared. I went eagerly seeking a higher good. When you know what I worship now you will not believe that. But I set it down as the truth. I thought only of what I was gaining, nothing of my loss. I was too ignorant for it to be otherwise. No dog-eyed boy had made my heart beat faster. I despised babies. How should I miss what I had never wanted?

In my mind there was a vast distance between that bared phallus on the hillside and the marriage-bed. I made no connexion.

Morgan knew more of the ways of men than I did when she was half my age.

She was eight years old when Uther Pendragon killed her father. That same night he came to the convent of Tintagel and entered her mother.

133

# Chapter Two

Morgan's father was not yet dead when I was baptised. A Christian came to our village, swinging down the road from the east: Ruman. A fleece-white tunic over a whiter gown. Strong sandals on his feet. A stout staff. Simple, you understand, but not poor. Good-quality stuff, made with care. This was no ragged vagrant tramping the roads till the bottom fell out of his shoes. He did not carry himself like a beggar either. He was young and tall, and his head was shaved strangely. The front bared to the crown, and the brown hair at the back growing free and curling. I had only seen slaves with their heads shaved. But this was no slave. It was a strange conjunction.

We had not long to wait. He set up his staff at the cross-ways of our village, and bound another stick across it. He took from the leather satchel on his back a box-wood lyre and began to play, and then to sing.

If we had been curious at first we were more so now. Few can resist a minstrel with a new song. There at broad noon, in the middle of the working day, he drew us round him. The children came first. Not shy, as they were of any overseeing noble, or frightened by a beggar in his dirt and deformity. He smiled at them and they squatted round his feet. The women followed next, wiping their hands on their aprons. The men paused at the doorways of workshops and the edges of fields. They wanted to show their neighbours they had important work that could not be left. But they strolled closer too before the song was finished.

I was like the men, I resisted. My mind was hungrier than the others could know for the sound of new things, for the world beyond the ridge of the coombe, but my pride would not let it be seen. I waited, tying weights to the loom, my back to the sunshine and the man in white singing beside his cross. Only when I seemed the last one left in the shadows did I creep slowly to the back of the crowd.

The song was almost over. He sang now of a golden city on a mountain top. Of a king and his bride. Of rewards and rejoicing. He sang for me. It was the dream of my girlhood. Of a crown, of treasure, of rank, of home-coming. Of right restored.

I did not hear what must come before.

And then he talked to us. I did not know the word for 'preaching' then. To me, it seemed like hard words and difficult thoughts. Yet all the time Ruman smiled on us, like a young mother with her first baby. As though he loved us, though we were all of us strangers to him. I could not understand it. That a man should wear the badge of a slave yet carry himself as sure and easy as the greatest lord who rode in Devon.

134

I wanted to listen. Never have I wanted to hear a man so much. But every sentence he spoke sent my mind racing away down new roads. By the time I had caught it and brought it back to the present he had jumped ahead of me and was telling new wonders. I was dazzled. He told of a wide and marvellous world beyond Britain. He spoke of priests and emperors, of Pharisees and fishing-boats, of dangerous voyages, of desert roads, of cities and armies, of wandering shepherds and a pilgrim cross. How could we understand this? We who never moved from where we were, watching the seasons circle round us monotonously.

He called us to leave our old ways and travel with him on the new. To cut down the dark groves and to build a city of light. There were many who growled with fear and anger that first day. And others who gazed at him with a hungry hope. But more and more his roaming eyes came back to me, as though for once I wore my soul in my face.

I sought him out. Snatching hot loaves from the oven and racing off before my mother could catch me with another task. I knew that Cadwal and his wife had taken him to share bread with them, but they told me he had gone out again, down to the river. To pray, they said. I could not make any sense of that. How could a man worship alone? I do not mean the words we murmured at every turn of life, as we crossed the threshold, as we put fire to wood, as we set milk to separate, as we lay down to sleep. You would not go apart to say those. They were bound into the thread of living. But a true meeting with the gods was done with awe and preparation. All my life I had known and feared holy places. How could I not, living so close to the Great Nymet? It was unthinkable to go there alone, without the protection of priests and priestesses. Without the drums and dancing. Without the tribe bringing gifts and prostrating themselves. Without the proper sacrifices.

I did not know that prayer which is thus sacred and set apart could also be solitary.

I heard him before I saw him. He was chanting indeed. But a low, rapid murmur, as though he talked to himself alone. I parted the hazel stems and watched. He sat cross-legged on the grass beside the stream. Not near the ford or the stepping-stones, but round a bend out of sight of the path, where the water ran swift and deep. The sort of place I might have been drawn to myself, though not to pray. The sound of the nearest waterfall sang beneath the babble of his voice.

There was something in his lap. I felt an instant chill. This must be his thing of power. Something more secret and dangerous than the cross of sticks he had made while he preached to us. Something I should not be seeing. Something I must see.

My steps were light and the grass was soft. I saw two stacks of sheets, like kerchieves of linen, yet stiffer than cloth. Joined at one edge so that they could open like so many doors. Patterned in black. Row after row of signs that I knew at once to be powerful magic. You who read this account will laugh that I had never seen a book before. Stranger yet was that I knew in that first moment of seeing the power of the pen, and hungered after it.

135

He had a feather in his hand, the white plume of a swan. And he was tracing the signs from left to right, line after line, and chanting rapidly aloud at every mark. I did not heed the meaning. It was the act itself which astonished me. I did not know the word for reading.

'Come closer. Sit down. Look and listen.'

Ruman did not turn his head, but there was laughter in his voice. I obeyed.

'So,' he said, seeing my face now, 'you followed me.' And he meant more than my walk through the hazel bushes. I nodded. I did not need to ask. The hunger was in my eyes for him to see.

'Can you read?'

I shook my head, storing the word away like a jewel.

'What is your name?'

'Luned.'

He took a twig and scored some marks in the soft earth between us. He pointed to the first. 'L. For Luned.' And so I understood the signs had sounds. I looked at his L. Two strokes. Straight and plain, like myself. I made the same and raised my eyes to meet his. They were not difficult, these symbols of power. I could master them.

There were several in the village that offered him house-room. He refused them all, with that smile of his. He wove himself a green-roofed hut there among the hazels by the brook where I had found him, with only the fox to guard him and the blackbird's chatter for company. I understood that. Few others did.

He would not stay long. Devon was wide, he said, and the darkness deep. I felt that darkness too, with the forest shadowing us round. The past faith of kings and courts had become a rustic, secret thing. There were not many Druids left. The Romans killed some and stripped others of their power. They overlooked the women. An older growth had sprouted like nettles in a neglected field. I feared those long before I sided with the Church. It would have appalled me if I had seen my future then.

The Christian, Ruman, dazzled me. I begged him to teach me all he knew. He smiled and told me of a village Exeter way where anyone who followed his Christ was welcome. A fortress of work and worship and learning. The wonder of it was that they would take anyone who asked. The sons and daughters of chiefs, nobles, craft-workers – yes, and farmers. Young and old. Even a slave might learn to write Latin. They demanded no payment but work. I could not think why they would not ask gold from the nobility.

There were others I knew who went. Whole families of new Christians. The pious seeking a home safe from old temptations. Some of the highborn sent their sons and daughters to learn, nursing dreams of a lost Roman empire.

But it was not for me. It is pain for me even now to write it. My parents refused. Morgan was bitter because Uther Pendragon sent her to such a school. My bitterness was because schooling was denied me. I was the eldest. I was wanted about the house. I was a girl. I could not be spared. And my parents believed they loved me.

I humbled myself to beg, to weep even. It did no good. All they said was that it was time I was thinking of getting a husband. I was nearly fourteen.

I saw my situation then with horror. All my life I had lived with this dream, that I was someone else. Not Luned, Kevern's daughter. Someone greater, wealthier, more powerful. Free. I had only to wait and my heritage would be revealed.

So I had never simpered and nudged and flashed my eyes at boys, in the way of those other girls. I hardly noticed them. What had they to do with me? I do not condemn them. It was not the young men of my village I turned from personally, it was the lives of the women. I saw the running bowels of their babies, the greasy steam of bacon and cabbage, the skirts thigh-high in mud, the nights of fleas and snores, the same stale gossip year after year. I could not believe this was all life had to offer me.

I saw Ruman as my saviour. I had not realised how close the danger was. I had not allowed myself to imagine marrying.

If I had been humbler-born yet it would have been easier. I could have bedded with whom I would, or not at all; lived where I would, alone if I dared. I would be fourteen soon and no man's property.

But I had not the licence of absolute poverty. My parents owned land. Not much, just enough to imprison me. They would want to see me handfast, before witnesses, bargains made, my future contracted. I was trapped between the freedom of wealth and the carelessness of those who have nothing.

When I understood that I fled to Ruman. Running in the afternoon, when I should have been repairing the hurdles round the pig-pen, and never mind who stared after me.

I thought I would find him alone. There was a path through the hazels now where there had been none before. I must have come crashing along it like a stray heifer.

I pulled up short. There was a man with Ruman on the bank of the river. No common man. A warrior. I do not often start and blush but I did then, suddenly conscious of who and what I was. A young and rustic girl. Alone in a wood.

Warrior-bands sometimes rode past us to the Nymet to ask for victory. They were beings from another world than ours. Noisy, gorgeous. A caste apart. I had never come upon a soldier so close, alone, on foot. And he was all that I had heard of them. Hard, male, vigorously young and well-fed. Sporting his weapons of steel like Tewdar's fleshly one. A menace to my femaleness.

His horse was tethered to a hawthorn tree. Well-groomed. Dapple-grey. With a neck like a bent bow.

Ruman saw me, but the stranger did not. He knelt before the saint with a jingle of chains and a creak of leather.

'Duke Gorlois has summoned the war-hosts of Dumnonia. Ambrosius's brother is raising the red dragon again. We'll make Woden's army lick their own blood from the British soil they came to conquer. So bless me, father, that I may kill many Saxons for you.'

'And for that killing you want me to feed you with your Saviour's blood?'

The man's head flew up then, as though Ruman had challenged him.

'Fair's fair! That's what the Druids and your Church both teach us. Glory for the hero dead or alive. The Isles of the Blest or Heavenly Paradise if we fall. It's all one to me. But you both say I must cleanse my soul before I dirty my sword.'

'Pagan against pagan! The red dragon and the white. Who will cleanse my soul if I give the holy flesh of Christ for that?'

'Uther Pendragon is a Christian king, and Gorlois fights under the sign of Christ. If our lifeblood's not good enough payment for you, take that! It should pay for a curse or two against Britain's enemies!'

He tossed a gold ring at Ruman. The saint stood like stone. The ring rolled away to the edge of the brook.

'My curses joined to Emrys Merlyn's? The lamb of God yoked with the serpent?'

'What's wrong with that? You're both men of power, aren't you? I offer my blood and my sword for Britain. You holy men must fight with prayers and curses. Get on with your work, man, and leave mine to me.'

He knelt and bent his head. It was not shame but Ruman's look that drove me back down the path out of earshot of his confession.

The soldier mumbled his sins and Ruman spoke forgiveness to him. I watched the soldier take the morsel of bread and the holy cup, wiping his long moustache with the back of his hand. Everything about him alarmed me. The lusty way he drank the wine. The leap of his body as he rose from his knees. The sudden neigh of his mare as she pawed the turf with wicked hooves.

He turned then and saw me. I was right to be alarmed. His eyes scanned me slowly from head to toe, undressing me.

'Come here, Luned!'

Only Ruman's voice gave me the courage to run past the warrior to sanctuary. I hated both that man and my own weak self for the fire in my cheeks.

Ruman raised his palm.

'In the name of the Father, and the Son, and the Holy Lifegiver, go in peace. And keep Britain safe.'

'Safe! Duke Gorlois wouldn't thank you for a prayer like that! There's no honour to be got in safety, and no gold either. Or women!'

He laughed at me then, and flung himself into the saddle and galloped away.

Ruman forced a smile to his troubled face.

'Don't look so frightened, child. He is right. The Church needs his kind as well as mine. These are dangerous times.'

Then the smile slipped.

'I sometimes think the Kingdom of God here is as brittle as a film of ice over a running river. But you, Luned? You love Christ truly, don't you? You won't turn back to the Druids when I've gone?'

138

'Never!' I told him vehemently. And then, 'Who is this Gorlois? Is he our king in Dumnonia now?'

'Chief warlord of Devon and Cornwall. No king. He takes the Roman name of Duke. A mighty man of war under the Pendragon. Pray for him, Luned. Rome has left us in his hands.'

I knew nothing of Saxons. I feared Duke Gorlois and his warriors far more. No one warned me Gorlois had a daughter more dangerous than himself.

# Chapter Three

Ruman bent and picked the ring from the brookside. His arm flexed as though he would have hurled it over the water. I must have gasped. He turned and smiled as if in apology.

'You are right. It could put bread into the bellies of the poor.'

And he knotted it into the sleeve of his gown.

'So. Why have you come in such haste? I am not leaving till tomorrow.'

It was like a blow in the face.

'Tomorrow! You are not going away from us so soon? You cannot! You will come back, won't you?'

He shook his head. 'I have told you from the beginning, I am a pilgrim for Christ. I must sow his seed in many fields. Three days from now is Pentecost. I am going back to my village of Christ to keep the festival. Then I must travel on.'

'But what will we do without you? Who will be our priest?'

'Someone will come to offer the bread and wine for you at feast times, as often as may be. I may return myself sometimes. The labourers are few. You must strengthen each other.'

'I cannot bear it here alone!'

'Alone? With eyes like yours? Not for long, I think.'

'That is what I mean!'

I poured out my soul to him then. I did not think he was attending. His eyes kept slipping away down the path that the warrior had ridden. His hand played with the jewel weighing down his sleeve.

'You're not listening to me! What shall I do? I cannot bear to be married to one of those clods. I cannot bear to live my mother's life. Help me!'

'I hear you, child.'

'I am not a child. I am fourteen tomorrow.'

His eyebrows rose then with something of his old smile.

'Fourteen? And a free woman?'

'Yes.'

'Then why are you crying? You do not need your parents' blessing. The law of Britain makes you mistress of your own fate. You can walk over that threshold tomorrow and take the road to the west, and no one can forbid you. How brave are you, Luned? Will you travel that road with me?'

I was not brave. I was afraid and unready. The thought of leaving home, village, familiar people, appalled me, though I had never loved them. I wanted a home to come back to. I wanted glory, not adventure.

But I was desperate. What else could I do? What other means of escape did I have? I was more than Luned of Lower Orchard. I must be more. That was the dream that Ruman held before me.

I wanted to leave with him then, just as I was, without a word of farewell. I feared to tell my father.

Ruman came home with me. It was a bitter parting. I do not suppose my parents have ever understood. They argued that they loved me. I have not seen them since.

We set out next morning. Once it was done I felt inexpressibly happy. The kingdom of God beckoned me. I had only to climb the path to achieve it.

It was no golden citadel. A bank of earth around it with a wattle fence, clusters of thatch, smoke, animals. It looked much like the village I had left.

As we neared the gate a handbell was rung for noon. At once everyone stopped working. Men, women, children stood straight and still and burst into singing. The psalm rose from a hundred throats. Ruman was chanting beside me. Haltingly, I tried to join in. On and on, the melody rose to heaven. I found myself lifted up on waves of song.

The psalm ended. Work began again.

Ruman watched my face. 'A chain of praise. By day and night. In this and every house of God. Throughout this land. Across the world. The song that never dies.'

The world. It was beyond my imagining then. Even the thought of Britain was too big for me. And that was only the beginning. The rest was infinite. Choirs of angels singing round the throne of God into eternity. And I was being offered a part in that choir. The gate of heaven was opening for me.

The reality was different. I slept with a family: Jenna and her husband and their three children. I helped with the cooking. I hoed the fields. I shared their life.

Apart from the psalms, heaven on earth was very like the home I had left. The same dung-spattered beasts to be tended, the same teething babies squalling in the night, the same mouths to feed. Only the praise was different. I watched a woman gathering the little children round her and teaching them their letters. I felt a stab of envy. Even they knew more than I did. At last, as I stirred the porridge beside Jenna, I cried out, 'Where is the school where they teach Latin and Greek and rhetoric and geometry? Where is the library?'

Words I had heard Ruman speak, that I did not even know the meaning of.

Jenna laughed. 'Oh, that! We had some holy men and women that had got book-learning in the monasteries of Gaul and Egypt. But it seems we were too homely here for them. Some of them have gone off to be hermits in the woods and caves. Then there were some scholar-women that went further west, to live as virgins under the rule of Bryvyth in some fortress by the Cornish sea. A place they call Tintagel. But that's not for the likes of you and me. They're mostly noble-born. You won't need to bother with that. Brokan was

141

asking me yesterday if I thought you were good with baking and babies.'

Brokan, a freckled boy with wet lips. Next time I stepped outside I felt that every young man in the village was looking me over consideringly. Ruman had tricked me. I began to despair.

It was Crida who saved me. A short, square woman, with a firm step and a quick mind. She came marching down the road from the east. She was no fool. She travelled with a champion to fight off bandits and carry her across fords, and had a band of nuns with her, and a pair of monks. They had tales to tell of Saxon invasion, of churches burned, of priests and virgins as well as layfolk hacked to death, of the Pendragon battling for the cross and Britain. We hung on her words as if she had been a minstrel from the king's court. But it was not her tales of the wars in the east that filled my dreams.

I had plucked up the courage to go to her hut. I told her of my hopes and their betrayal. I would learn nothing here. I begged her to take me with her on her travels.

She looked me up and down with a short laugh.

'What gifts have you got to offer? Do you know your Bible? Can you read and write? Paint or embroider the marvels of God? Preach the word of Christ before commoners and chieftains?'

'All that is what I *want* to learn! It is why I came!'

'And not to be the handmaid of any earthly lord! You would rather be Mary of Bethany, learning alongside the men, than Martha in the kitchen or the mother of your Saviour and a carpenter's wife? You blush too easily, girl. There's nothing to be ashamed of in having a mind. You are right. You must not stay here. You are not the woman to be a drudge even to a Christian man. Go to Tintagel, to the women's fortress. There are others there like you. I will give you a letter to the abbess. She is a tough shepherdess, is Bryvyth, and needs to be. Heed her well. Take her for your chief, your druid, under Christ. If you obey her, she may help you enter the kingdom you've dreamed of.'

'I will! I will!'

She laid cool hands on my forehead.

'Be warned, Luned. It will not be as easy as you think. We carry our earthly bodies with us on the pilgrim road. Do you know how I spent the night before last? Emptying a bucket for Gwaynten. She had sickness at one end and diarrhoea at the other. It was her monthly time too. Puke, blood and shit all night. It nearly killed her.'

I almost vomited myself.

'You see? And you want to travel with me? You haven't started to learn what it means. Copy Bryvyth. She has the finest mind in Dumnonia and the constitution of a fishwife. Remember, it was Martha the housewife who took our Lord into the stinking tomb of Lazarus to raise the dead. They left Mary the scholar behind on her knees in tears.'

I did not heed that warning.

'I will do anything she says, bear any hardship, if they will only teach me.'

'Why, Luned? Why do you truly want to go to Tintagel so much?'

I looked up at her, startled. Was it not obvious why I should want it? To feel my mind expand like a flower in the sun. To drink in all the wealth of knowledge and enlightenment. To achieve greatness. Had she not wanted this herself? Then I saw the hope earnest in her face as she gazed at me, and I knew what she wanted me to say.

'To serve Christ my Saviour. For the glory of God and the spread of his kingdom on earth.'

And in the moment of saying that, I believed it was true.

I came to Tintagel to deny the flesh, seeking a splendour of the soul.

# Chapter Four

I did not know until I came to Tintagel that I would be afraid of the sea. I had never seen it before.

Crida took me across Devon with her band of nuns. At the banks of the Tamar she left me with a group of pilgrims. She made her champion carry me across the river. I would rather have waded through the cold pluck of the water than have his hot hairy arms about me, than to cling to his back and see the lice crawling in his hair.

But I was near my goal. Where Bryvyth ruled like a bishop over her nuns. Where women could rise to the highest of men's work. Where I should be free at last of churning butter and brewing ale and washing dirty linen. I saw that to move beyond the sphere that men allow to women it was necessary to separate myself from the world of men.

So I crossed the Tamar determined to become one of Bryvyth's nuns. Of my own free will, not sent by my parents. I was a child of fourteen. I would have said I was a woman, the law declared it thus, but I was more innocent than I knew. Many a slave-child knows more than I knew then. I thought I knew what I was giving up. The child's games of making home, the girl's scrying to see whom she will marry. That was no sacrifice at all to me. I wanted more from life than that.

For all that my mind was set on the kingdom of God, I will not pretend that I did not give the world a second look. I came from a poor farming place where we might not see anyone greater than a blacksmith between one festival and another, and my eyes had been opened on this journey. Pride kept me silent, yet I could hardly hold back the gasps of wonder at what I was daily learning of the world. We had passed many forts on the road to the west, crag-built, dominating the spurs and tors. We had stepped off the road for chariots of fine, jewelled ladies. I had lowered my eyes when armoured nobles came riding by, grizzled men too old now for the Pendragon's host. I had met merchant-trains, craftsmen, minstrels. All around me I saw wealth, skill, power.

I had thought in my sleepy valley that the world stayed the same from year to year. But I was wrong. Everywhere I looked there was evidence of trading, fighting, travelling. The world was changing all the time.

But even as I set eyes on the halls of power I had dreamed of, I was already leaving them behind. I was changing too. Our ways were parting. I looked at the noblewomen in their gold and tartan and I did not feel inferior. I had vowed myself to God. I felt pride stiffen my back. Could they read and write? Had they studied astronomy and the

Greek philosophers? With Bryvyth, Crida had promised, I would do all this and more.

I saw a dazzle in the sky before we reached the coast. It seemed to me like a sign, the light of the New Jerusalem changing the air above it. Heaven on earth. The aura of knowledge, beauty, truth. When we came over the ridge and I saw the shining plain of the sea, I did not know what it was. I had said little to my companions on the journey. I am not one to gossip. But my face spoke more than I wished it to. They chuckled at my wonder.

'That's Bossiney down there.' One of them pointed to a wide, thatch-filled round in cattle pastures. A great hall stood out above the rest. 'Duke Gorlois's dun. There'll be nobody there now, though. He's away with the warhost, fighting Saxons with Uther Pendragon.'

Nobody there. Only his wife Ygerne. His three daughters. As though the women of that family were nothing.

Even so I started. I had heard that name: Gorlois, Duke of Cornwall. Ruman had said he held our fate in his hands.

So I came closer to Bossiney's walls with a calculating look. The fence on the bank was freshly repaired. The watchman was ageing but alert, the women servants in good clean gowns. It spoke of wealth and order. I felt no envy. An alien camp, so close to Tintagel and so other than it. A man's place. A warrior's home. Power of a sort to be reckoned with, but no rival to what I dreamed of.

It astonishes me now that I could have walked past those walls and not felt who was within.

My eyes were already seeking ahead. I was afraid to ask, but I knew I must sight it soon. The end of my pilgrimage. I began to hear the sea, more rhythmic than the sound of wind in the trees. I began to hear the grating of shingle. I felt the push of the breeze against my face. I started at the scream and swoop of the gulls. I was afraid of the wild noisiness of this coast, disturbed by experiences I did not understand.

We dipped into a rocky cleft and crossed a stream.

I do not know what I expected. A golden-walled city. A river of crystal. A temple glowing with all the jewels of the rainbow. I was very young, you must understand, ignorant, unlettered still. I had seen a vision.

But not of this. The site was stronger than Ruman's village of saints, more forbidding. A black-sided headland, with a glimpse of the sea swilling at its foot between narrow cliffs. We began to climb. A huge earth bank and ditch above us. A porter's lodge. Beyond, a sense of windy space. Tintagel. A grey-green island hung between sea and sky. Its steep sides scattered with lime-washed cells, clinging to the slopes like the nests of the gulls that flashed above them. And even as the gatekeeper came towards us I saw the path I must tread still to reach my goal.

Nothing had prepared me for that bridge of stone. No one had warned me. Or if they had, they had used words that held no meaning for me until then, coming as I did from that sheltered coombe folded among the gentle hills of Devon.

145

Even now it comes back to me in nightmares. At home I could not climb the damson tree beside the house without vertigo. Now I must walk a path scarce two strides wide, while dizzyingly far below me the sea, like a heaving devil, waited for me. Black rocks below the foam on one side. Sunless shingle lapped by cold green water on the other. Even without that drop the hugeness of the sea would have dismayed me. Its endless movement. The oncoming herd of breakers, each one a separate beast menacing me.

This time the pilgrims roared with laughter when they saw my face. I was not the first to be appalled by it. No doubt they remembered their own fear. How could Tintagel's convent look so small, so quiet, at the end of such a road as this?

Yet this was the path I had chosen. I could not turn back. I followed the nun who summoned me across the bridge. It was a fitting passage. It is hard indeed to enter that holy city by the narrow way.

I do not remember which nun it was who led me. I only remember the agony, the giddiness, the terror of consciousness, the terror of losing consciousness. I never wholly conquered it.

I still fear the sea. Year after year I lay awake, listening to the breakers beating against the cliffs, till I thought the rocks would shatter and we would all go crashing into a cold hell.

So it is not surprising that I loved Bryvyth from the moment that I first saw her. She was a stronghold of a woman, a sure buttress of rock against which the waves of the world and the dark gods would beat and not gain entrance. She had a keener mind than I had ever seen in a woman, and the muscles of an ox.

She made me kneel at her feet. I must have been a pitiful figure, trembling with physical fear and the tension of shyness. She bade me tell her why I had come.

I am not a fluent talker. I find it difficult to bring the deep thoughts of my heart to my lips. Even in daily conversation I sit silent. I hear the other women voicing observations that would never have occurred to me to be worth the effort of words. When I am challenged to say what I think I pick a phrase here and there. It never tells the whole.

She watched me shrewdly while I stammered out some fragments of my hopes. I felt myself pale and then redden under that gaze. When I had done she still looked at me, as I often saw her later staring consideringly at a sickly cow. Then she laid her hands on my head and spoke.

'Welcome, Luned. You have walked a long road from Devon, following your star. But not as far I have travelled. I journeyed from Cymru to Erin, seeking for knowledge, like you. They consecrated me a virgin first, and then made me a scholar. When I had learned all that they could teach me, I set sail with a handful of sisters in a little boat, on a pilgrimage for God. His winds washed us to this cove. There was nothing living here then. Nothing earthly, at least. The Romans had come and gone. They left what was here before them, some caves in the rock, and a black reputation.

'I preached Christ to Gorlois and he gave me this island. I think he

146

fears it. He has the ways of a wild barbarian yet, but his soul is struggling for the light. We drove out the Dark Son and his Mother from here with the might of prayer. Now we wrestle for Gorlois himself, and his family.

'With my bare hands I raised my own cell, as you will do. Next we dug a garden. Saints should live by the sweat of their own backs. Then stone by stone and soul by soul we built this abbey. The oratory first, to praise God. A library for our books, to bear witness to his glory. Then a schoolroom to bring more lambs to his flock. The name of Tintagel is spreading beyond the coasts of Cornwall. They have heard of us as far as Jerusalem.'

She must have seen the flame in my eyes. She chuckled deep in her throat and hugged me.

'Is this what you want, Luned? Is this the hard road you choose to tread?'

'Yes!'

'Glory be! Then I can use a girl with strong muscles like yours. There are too many here that were not bred to lift anything heavier than an embroidery needle, and I need to free all that are old and wise for scribes and teachers. You'd be as welcome to my heart as the first apples of harvest if I could put you to work tomorrow with the cows and the kale.

'What do you say, girl? Will take on my yoke?'

Cows and kale. Did she read my face? Had I escaped being a housewife to a monk to become a drudge for other nuns?

I was too proud to change my mind. I could not trudge back across the length of Dumnonia and admit to my family that I had made a mistake.

I will never forget the bitterness of that first winter. I did the work of slaves. Cleaning the byres that the cows had fouled. Hoeing the endless rows of muddy kale. And the weather was like nothing I had ever known before. Rain driving into the pail as I milked the cows, the everlasting gales hurling the sea into my face when I stepped outside the door of my cell, the icy mud, the broken chilblains on my feet. And always the sea, churning away below me, so that my stomach was tight with fear as I fought my way up the paths to the top of the cliff.

I do not write this so that you should pity me. I made my choice freely. I set it down so that you shall know how great the price I paid for the pearl that Morgan robbed me of.

# Chapter Five

It seems impossible now that I should not remember the first time I saw Morgan. I remember the pride of that first Sabbath morning as a full-vowed nun, singing psalms as I strode with Bryvyth's virgins across the causeway on our way to Nectan's church. Bryvyth was a great warrior-woman for Christ. She was not one to shelter in her fortress. All summer she rode the country in her chariot and sent her nuns trudging the lanes two by two. On feast days and Sabbaths we celebrated the Offering with Nectan's congregation. I must have worshipped with Morgan every Sunday after I had made my final act of obedience.

Well I remember Gorlois and his warriors, home from war, gorgeously jewelled and cloaked. It was hard for me not to blush and shrink with fear from them. I was glad to keep my eyes down. But Ygerne his wife I looked at with contempt. I, Luned, plain-faced as I was, despised the duchess for her beauty. I did not imagine she could be wise as well as fair. I saw their two tall daughters, the white gold and the red. Elaine pleased me, grave and stately. Margawse disturbed me, tossing her fiery hair and flaunting the curves of her body. Will you believe me when I say I did not notice there was a smaller sister?

I had no interest in children. Ambition rose in me as I watched Bryvyth hold the chalice to the lips of Gorlois's warriors. Power was in our hands.

But all that was later. It was a year before I completed my vows. All that time I was shut up in Tintagel, safe behind its bank and causeway. Nectan visited us. I took the bread and wine in our oratory with the schoolchildren.

It did not grieve me. I saw enough of the world even on our island. Old Padarn, who once helped to dig that mighty ditch and now served as porter. Nectan, a saint more gaunt and joyless than Ruman, coming to feed us the sacrament. A stream of pilgrims, honoured guests at Bryvyth's table. A glimpse of traders at the gate or on the rocky wharf below our convent. I kept well clear of them, and left that business to those to whom it was appointed.

On Sabbath Eve I sweated the dirt of my labour away in a bath of steam and heard Bryvyth speak absolution for my sins. Next morning, after milking, I donned a fresh gown and discovered again the sense of cleanliness, dignity, worth, of a day without work. For once I could give myself to the full glory of worship without the feel of a hoe clasped between my palms. I learned the beauty of that day.

The rest was more painful. In the midst of drudgery I had tantalising glimpses of glory. What others called work, to me seemed a foretaste of Paradise. That first week I hurried along the path to the work I had to do, to be out of the wind and the giddying pull of the sea waiting for me at every turn of the cliff. Yet there was one doorway before which I found my steps slowing.

It was the library. My stare probed the open doorway, the shelves stacked with scrolls and books, the opened leaves gleaming palely on the desks. The murmur of words, rhythmic as the waves on the beach. Cigfa and Eira, our two most famous scribes, worked in the best places in the sunny porch, sheltered from the wind. They sat on either side of the doorway, white-gowned, like two guarding angels.

Cigfa, herself nobly-born, looked up suddenly and saw me staring. She said to me, 'Be off to your own work, sister. A calf died to make this one sheet of vellum. We do not want it spattered with cow-dung again.'

I walked on without a word, hot-faced. I, who at home had thought myself superior to the other girls, was here the lowest of creatures.

On the other side of the path I had to pass the schoolroom. I did not linger there. I was afraid to meet the curious stares of the children, so much younger than I was, and so much more wise. Some of them, I had heard, were princes and princesses. Others were farmers' children like myself. I could have envied them. If I had been sent to Tintagel as a child I might not have needed to become a nun. Yet I would not waste time in regret. I had chosen a higher path now. Bryvyth was my star, my lighthouse. I would be like her. I would never marry a man. I would never simper and feign and pretend to know less than I did to flatter a husband's vanity. I vowed that one day I would know as much as any man, yes, and more than most.

Yet that winter was dark and long and empty of joy.

Looking back, I see that I could have used the time differently. I could have begged my sister nuns to teach me what they knew. I could have scratched my letters in the earth with the hoe and chanted the alphabet among the rows of beans. But I was too proud to ask. I have always found it difficult to beg a favour. I could not risk the humiliation of being refused. Bryvyth might have forbidden anyone to teach me. Was it only their own scholars' jealousy that had made Cigfa and Eira chase me from the library door?

So I did the physical labour of a farm-slave. I hated the work. It seemed to me an abuse of the soul. But I was strong and skilled. I did it better than anyone else around me. I was always careful of that. It was a matter of pride and calculation. I wanted Bryvyth to praise me. I strove to earn the right to do what I wanted.

Spring came at last. The sea fell quiet and the sun was warm on my face. Bluebells spread themselves across the slopes. Those nuns that had lighter tasks than mine came each one to the door of her hut and sat on the grass to work as they would do all summer. The classes from the school spread out of doors, chattering like finches, the little children of both sexes, the adolescent girls. I watched the groups go from nun to nun, under the hawk-eye of Rathtyen, singing to the harp, embroidering, chanting Latin, reading the stories of the Bible. It frightened me. They knew so much more than I did. Time was passing.

The porch of the library was open to the sun. In the evening light the nuns would be tidying away their wax tablets, and Cigfa and Eira would be wrapping the precious skins on which the Holy Word blossomed in paint and ink. I watched how lovingly they laid them in the satchels hanging from beams, safe from the teeth of hungry mice. I am not one to gossip on doorsteps. I would not linger to be rebuked again. But I nursed my dream. One day these hands that washed the stinking udders of the cows would lift those books and mark those leaves. It would be mine to lay on the page the glory of the Gospels.

In my brief hours of leisure I sat at the door of my cell looking across the cove to the cliffs of Bossiney. Sometimes I caught the flash of colour and the sparkle of metal. Then the young men would be riding or running in games of war outside the dun. They belonged to another world, a world I had not tasted and believed I never would.

I took my vows. Another winter came and went, and another summer. I served two years' hard labour before Bryvyth called me to her. She took my hands in hers. My nails were broken and my palms calloused and lined with dirt. But they were no harder than her own. She was stronger than any of us. Where the work was heaviest she would be at the side of the nun who did it, singing in a joyful shout against the wind. She had milked the cows with me when there was ice on the bucket. She had a body as hard as any man's, and a keener mind.

'Luned,' she said, 'you have a brave soul. For two years the breath of God has blown hard on you, and your spirit has not been stunted by it like the hawthorn or been uprooted before it like the proud oak. God will not wrestle with his beloved beyond daybreak. It's time for a change, girl. I shall not take you away from your sisters, the cows. They could still teach you a fine lesson in humility and service, if you didn't think yourself too clever to listen to them. But I fancy it won't grieve you too much if I tell you to leave the hoeing of beans to newcomers.

'These hands will soon heal. When the morning's work is done, wash them well and eat, and go to Eira in the library. How would you like to learn to read and write?'

The laughter in her eyes mocked me.

'Oh!' I cried. 'If you only knew!'

'Child, child!' she said. 'Maybe I know more than you'd like me to. And don't think I am doing it to please you. A farmer has many animals. Some are good for wool, others for milk or pulling wagons. An abbess must be a canny farmer. She must set each beast to the work she is fitted for, to the greater glory of God. If I please you today, then praise Christ for it. And if I take it away from you tomorrow and give it to others, then praise him all the louder.'

'I will,' I said, though I had no idea then what she meant.

It was like entering Paradise. The first tasks that Eira gave me were child's play after the hard and heavy work of the farm. The nuns showed me how to mix ink. Just the plain lamp-black, not the glowing colours

Eira and Cigfa used for their title-pages. I learned to smooth wax tablets on slats of wood. I sharpened quills. I learned to read.

It came to me so easily it was as though the alphabet had been asleep in my mind all these years. Soon I was reading from the Scriptures. And learning numbers too on the bead frame. It did not take me long to see that before long I would be quicker at this than my teachers.

But the first blow to my pride came when I tried to scratch my words in the sand. I found a chain of letters was not as simple for my hand to manage as the plain, bold strokes of that L so long ago. The stick wavered and straggled like a bird with a broken wing. It was bitter to me to think that even the youngest child in the school could write a fairer hand than I, but I would not be beaten. Hour after hour I worked at it, even at night, scratching the letters upon the floor of my cell by the gleam of moonlight. In time I became perfect.

I worked hard that next winter, safe indoors, once the cows were milked, in a world of books. Across the path gusts of laughter broke from the school. Few of the nuns who taught there could hold the girls for long in silent obedience. Only Rathtyen, our greatest scholar, who taught Latin. Even I was afraid of her. On our side, in the library, there was a murmuring like bees as each nun mouthed aloud the words she was copying. They complained of the cold, but to me it was like the warmth of heaven.

In the doorway, in the best of the light, Eira and Cigfa wrote their Gospels and Psalters. When it was time to illuminate the capitals, Cigfa tended to fruiting vines and palm trees. Eira favoured furred and scaly creatures. Their vision seemed small to me. I, what would I do when my turn came? Each scribe was free to use her own fancy for the greater glory of God. Should I paint the towers of the golden city? The archangel Michael's sword? The thrones of the saints in heaven? What is the highest to which the spirit can aspire?

That summer Cigfa led me along the seashore. In all my time at Tintagel I never wanted to set foot outside the convent bank. I had not Bryvyth's courage. Other nuns fished from the rocks and even splashed and paddled in the cove. I did not like the sea. I was not playful.

But now, as the year turned to the sun, Cigfa and I went across the bridge, searching out the colours for our inks and paints. When the psalm-singing came to us on the wind our voices would rise to join them from a distant world of green holly. Or we might be scrambling over the rocks gathering lichen. Or on the brink of the waves looking for the skeletons of fish. I learned not to shrink back from the body of a dead gull, but to plunder it for its feathers. I gathered the autumn berries not for food but for their colours. In the mornings the mud clogged my feet as I herded the cows from milking. But when I walked on the beach in the afternoon I was testing the sand for the fineness of its grain and the sharpness of its texture.

Along the beach we passed many cave mouths. Black, dripping caverns, where the sun never penetrated. I was afraid to enter them, dreading always that the sea would rise and trap me. But one cave was stranger than all the rest. It was shunned by all of us. A narrow cleft, under the heart of the convent. A passage not dark like the others. At the far end I glimpsed another sky, another sea. But for all its light it held a horrid fascination I could not explain. I watched the tide rise towards it, until the wash from that other sea came flooding through the tunnel to meet the lapping waves of Tintagel Haven. As I saw each foaming collision I felt as though a wild ocean beyond was coming in to overwhelm us. The other nuns whispered about that cave behind their hands. I did not want to know its secret.

One day we wandered a little further, round one more headland. An old woman was sitting propped against the cliff, dozing. A black-haired child, with her skirt kilted above her knees, was scrambling over the rocks searching the pools, like us. For what? They both looked up, startled, at our approach. The woman hauled herself to her feet, making signs I had wanted to forget with her hands, and muttering hoarsely. Cigfa drew me back by the sleeve till the rocks hid us and we saw Tintagel behind us. The child had just stood on the rock with her legs apart like a boy, laughing soundlessly as we fled.

I am not bold. If I sighted strangers I always turned away at once and carried my search elsewhere. But Cigfa seemed more agitated than I was.

'Gorlois's youngest daughter, Morgan . . . and her nurse,' she told me.

'There are three daughters?' I asked. 'I did not know.'

She looked at me curiously. 'You must have seen her at worship every week.'

'I never noticed her.'

But Morgan was there next Sunday. Her little face was grave, her lips ignoring the words that others sang. Her heart was in her eyes as she gazed at her father.

# Chapter Six

The coming of Uther Pendragon shook the convent. It was like one of those great cliff-falls whose crash loosens foundations and leaves the landscape altered.

We were not innocents. You may think we were cut off from the world's affairs, there in the far south-west of Britain, near the Land's End. But we stood on the highway of the sea. Ships put into our haven, or others along the coast, bringing news from Wales and Ireland, from Gaul and Carthage, from Rome and Constantinople and Holy Jerusalem itself. Bryvyth was shepherdess to a large flock in Cornwall and had the ear of great and low. On the ledges of Tintagel we were part of the mighty commonwealth of the Church.

So we knew of great wars in the east and the north of Britain. How Gorlois had rescued the Pendragon and his army from death and destruction, taken Hengist's son captive and saved the city of York. We heard of Uther's crown-feast in London, and the lust he conceived for Gorlois's lady, Ygerne. Of the family's flight to Cornwall and Uther's command to return. So there it stood. King Uther for his honour must lead a warhost to fetch Ygerne back. Gorlois for his honour must defy him.

It meant war between Britons, here on the quiet cliffs of Cornwall. We looked at each other in alarm but Bryvyth's eyes sparkled and the colour was high in her cheeks. She related to us all this news of Gorlois, half-scolding and half-chuckling, like a mother telling tales about her hot-headed son, hiding her fear behind pride. She was nobly-born. Fighting was in her blood.

When the message came that she was summoned to Bossiney, we were at our prayers. Her head went up like a horse's that hears the hunter's horn. Fast we sang our litanies and psalms. Short was our blessing that day.

'The man has seen sense at last! I could have told him. He must send his wife and daughters here to Tintagel. Where else can love and faith and honour find sanctuary but on this holy island? Gorlois, poor lad, must fight the enemy outside the gates. And may God defend the right. But if he falls and the angels carry him up to glory, then Uther Pendragon shall still not have his wife. It is Bryvyth Crook-Staff herself who will bar the bridge. Even the high king of Britain shall not pass that way.'

The light of battle was in her eyes already, and her nostrils were flaring. I knew in that moment how she saw herself: a warrior-champion, standing alone on that neck of rock, defying the king of the Britons with her staff.

She bade us make ready the guesthouse for Gorlois's womenfolk. The place was always clean and decent. Pilgrims and travellers were many. We lodged them better than a common inn. But Bryvyth would have fresh beds laid, the blankets changed, the curtains beaten, fresh rushes on the floor, good meat butchered. She left us busy.

She took Rathtyen and Cigfa with her. We watched their three white figures dwindling over the cliffs to Bossiney.

She came back with a face like thunder.

'Godless man! Does he think I will give Tintagel over to the sword? Shall warriors yell for blood where the angels have sung? Damn him! May the devil take him before he steals what is ours for a fort!'

'It was Gorlois gave us Tintagel to use for a convent,' said Rathtyen drily.

'And who gave it to Gorlois but the God of Cornwall?'

She swept us into the chapel and we prayed. For a curse on the ungodly, for the safety of Tintagel, for Britain whole and Christian. Power was in her voice and a holy anger, the pain of her gift rejected. She made us wrestle all night, prostrate, against the forces of evil. I leave you to judge how far those prayers were answered.

We heard that Gorlois and his household had ridden out to Dimiliock. Silence fell over the cliffs. We waited, like the rest of Cornwall, for what would break it. I sat in the sunshine among the sea-pinks and bluebells looking across the cliff-tops towards Bossiney. There was no stir of movement, no smoke ascending. It had always given me a shiver of unease to catch a distant sight of Gorlois's young warriors, to hear on a sudden gust of wind a shout or the clash of arms. Power tangible. Now the absence of men sent a chill through me. Tintagel felt suddenly vulnerable.

Then there was smoke in Bossiney, in plenty. A great brown wall of it in the sky, shot through with flames. We all ran out of doors to see it. It was all we saw. Tintagel does not stand high. The mainland cliffs walled us round so that we could glimpse little of what passed inland.

We gathered in fear and apprehension. Bryvyth came late to join us from the top of the island. Tears had furrowed the dust of labour on her cheeks like the tracks of snails. Long and silent she stared across the cove towards Bossiney. I wondered that she should grieve so for an abandoned fort. She had damned it heartily enough when it was tenanted, and everyone in it.

She drove us back into the chapel and we prayed again, more urgently than before. For our good Duke Gorlois and his family, for the overthrow of tyrants, for the peace of Cornwall and the Cornish.

They came like ghosts out of the thinning smoke. I think we feared them more than the Pendragon's army. Five women, three old warriors, and a child. Bryvyth's face was white as she watched the womenfolk cross the bridge, weary and grimed but proud. She said no word to us, but the question was in all our hearts. Where is their warband? Where is Gorlois?

I could eat little that evening, though Bryvyth feasted her strange guests royally. I watched those two women duelling each for her honour, while Gorlois at Dimiliock battled for his life. Bryvyth, lavish in hospitality, brilliant in conversation and telling of tales. The duchess courteous and affable, as though she were not the target of a great king's lust, the cause of war, her husband's death-writ.

I did not envy her, great lady though she was, and beautiful. It was better to be like Bryvyth. I scarcely looked at her daughters. I seem to remember that Elaine was pale and nervous, Margawse hot-cheeked with excitement. When I glanced at Morgan her face was white and her eyes hooded.

I woke in the night. My cell was perched on a sheltering ledge below the oratory. From overhead I heard our warrior-abbess weeping and groaning as though her heart would break. I was drawn to help her. But when I stepped out on to the path a thick moon-silver mist baffled my eyes. Even the sea was silent, misleading me. I waited for my eyes to become accustomed to the tricking light. They did not. One step outside my door and I was lost. I knew the peril of that cliff-path to the chapel. I did not go to Bryvyth.

And yet I prayed, there in my cell. Not for Gorlois or his lady, still less for their daughters, but that this troublesome family might leave us quickly, and I and Tintagel be left to prosper in peace.

I did not know then what we battled with.

I rose early to milk the cows before morning prayers. The sea-fog crept clammily between the walls of our cells. The treacherous silver had darkened to grey. I moved cautiously. Every building loomed like an unfamiliar shadow. I cannot say how I missed my way, but I found myself not at the byre but before the guesthouse.

Then I heard a most shocking sound. Men's laughter. Low, but triumphant. Three unfamiliar figures were coming out of the guesthouse. I met the jingle of mail and weapons in the place of unarmed women. I tried to scream out, but I could not.

I did not learn who they were until the morning. Bryvyth believed it had been Gorlois and his friends. Not otherwise would she have allowed them entrance. It was sorcery. Blurred as they were, the faces they turned on me told yet more lies. It was Uther, Merlyn and Ulfin who trespassed on Tintagel that night. Gorlois's enemies, coming from Ygerne's bedchamber.

He knew I was there. He put his seal upon my mouth when I tried to cry out. Merlyn, that wrecked my life along with Morgan's. Merlyn, that tricked and ruined us all. I know my lips have never spoken true since that day.

Dread chilled me so that I had not even the wit to pray. I heard the feet of those false men going across the causeway. I was keener than Bryvyth to know the presence of witchcraft. I feared it more than she did.

The sun vanquished the fog at last. It was a bright May morning. We saw the truth. Uther Pendragon and his whole warhost filled the skyline beyond our ditch. I was quicker to sense that magic had been among us, but Bryvyth was the first to realise just what sin Uther had done. When the herald told her that Gorlois was dead she saw at once that the duke could not have been in Tintagel that night. She knew who had. Her gate had not opened in the dark to admit a faithful husband but an adulterous king.

If she had been red with rage for Gorlois before, it was a white anger that burned in her against Uther now. It was terrible to behold. She bawled Ygerne out of her chamber and commanded her on to her knees. She drove her in shame off the holy island of Tintagel. I loved her for that. I rejoiced that a nun could be more powerful than the paramour of a king.

There was one short check. A tiny figure standing alone on that windswept bridge with her hair black and streaming, defiant as I had imagined only a mighty woman like Bryvyth could be. Yet ridiculous too. A little girl oppose all the might and magic of the high king of Britain?

Those men had not seen, as I had every Sunday morning, Morgan gazing up at her father as he thundered out the hymns to Christ. Uther was High King of the Britons, but Gorlois was Morgan's high king. Uther had slain Gorlois with his own hand.

The brave gesture ended in bathos and accident. Her old nurse shuffled forward to fetch her out of harm's way. The child turned in a fury and the nurse lost her balance. Before all our eyes the two of them tottered on the brink of that terrible drop. From the two hosts of men and women rose a roaring gasp of anguish. Would Morgan hold Gwennol? Or would Gwennol drag Morgan to her death? The terrible moment passed. Morgan and Gwennol stood clasped in each other's embrace.

Ygerne moved swiftly onward. It was then I realised. She had been the only one of us near enough to have saved Morgan. Yet she had not moved to catch her. She swept past her daughter now without turning her head, straight into the arms of Uther Pendragon, who had killed Morgan's father.

I often wonder why that holy island held Gwennol and Morgan safe. Why did Tintagel not hurl those two on to the rocks that morning, so that the convent and the Pendragons would have parted company then?

If her brother Arthur should struggle thus on the brink of disaster, will he be saved?

# Chapter Seven

The nuns of Tintagel lamented at Gorlois's funeral. They did not sing for Uther's marriage to Ygerne.

After the wedding-feast the Pendragon sent costly gifts to the convent. I thought Bryvyth, grim-faced with anger, would refuse them. She did not. She deemed them a small price for honour lost. To me they were riches unheard of. Plate, jewels, silks, wine, enough for a queen's ransom. I know. I helped to count them.

I had been given a new responsibility in the bookroom, keeping a fair record of the convent accounts. They were not the great Gospels I had dreamed of, but they were not as dull as you might imagine. Tintagel was no mean place. Ships came into our cove from near and far. In summer they might be crewed by swarthy brown men and even black, grinning and calling up to us in a barbarous tongue. Like the other nuns I kept away from the landing-stage. Bryvyth and Nonna our cellarer did business with them. They brought us wine from Gaul. Red glazed tableware from Italy. Books from Africa. We traded with tin and corn, with fine weaving and embroidery. We had farms that flourished. People gave us generous gifts. Our nuns were skilful craftswomen. It did not matter to me that I wore a coarse white robe and went barefoot in summer. The wealth which came to us was lavished on the beauty of our oratory, on hospitality, on education, on the care of the poor. That was a cause of pride to me. Riches should be used so, not for self-indulgence but to win power and fame. I had chosen well.

We knew when the Pendragon's son was born at Bossiney, on Midwinter's Day. We spoke little of it in Tintagel, and not in Bryvyth's hearing. It was not a cause for rejoicing. But the news at Epiphany shocked even us. On the stormy night before his christening, Merlyn stole the boy away. The two of them had disappeared without a trace.

I bent over my figures on a dark day in January and heard a sudden rush of chattering from the schoolroom. Ratlityen was hurrying away up the path, following a younger nun. It was nothing to me, except that I paused to ease the cramped muscles of my hand. I do not have a quick, flowing style. My letters were still slow and painful if I tried to form them perfectly, as I wished.

Then a sister came to summon me to Bryvyth in the guesthouse. I took it for some business of buying and selling. Nonna the cellarer was growing old. Sometimes her memory wandered in the middle of bargaining. I had been called for several times recently to settle the account and see that we were not cheated.

But these were no traders. There were three men-at-arms lined up on the far side of the causeway. They had been forbidden to cross bearing weapons, yet their war-like presence dominated the place even at that distance. Pendragon's men, for sure, all curling moustaches and heavy fur cloaks. There was a hardihood and swagger about them that would not let them huddle in their wraps and shiver. They moved briskly about in the cold wind, stamping their feet.

I turned into the guesthouse with an uneasy look at them. I lived now in a world of women. I had drawn a barrier in my mind deep as the convent ditch. All men were on the other side of it.

Inside the guest-hall stood Bryvyth, girded with a sack covered in blood and slime, so that I knew she had been gutting mackerel. Rathtyen was there, and two others. A small old woman, bent, with knotted hands resting on a stick. She had sharp bright eyes that looked everywhere and turned on me with uncomfortable keenness. And there was a girl, thin and straight, with long black hair and a white face. She was dressed in good cloth, but wore no jewels. She carried her head proudly. Even without the tartan and the gold you would know at once that she came from a noble family. My mind connected. The bare-legged urchin combing the pools on the beach; Ygerne's daughter, defying the Pendragon from the causeway; Morgan. What was she doing back here, in the place of her father's betrayal and her mother's shame?

The girl was scowling, staring in front of her at nothing and nobody, out of eyes that burned with green fire.

'Luned,' said Bryvyth, with heavy emphasis, 'this is the Princess Morgan, third daughter of Gorlois, that was Duke of Cornwall, and the Queen Ygerne. Her stepfather, King Uther Pendragon, is sending her to us to be schooled.'

I must have drawn my breath sharply in astonishment. Yet my curiosity centred on Bryvyth, not the child. It was not like her to be angry yet not to lose her temper. We were all accustomed to the lash of her tongue yet she was reining herself in as she spoke those hated names.

I bowed my head to the unsmiling girl, with courtesy but no servility, as the nuns had taught me. But I did not understand what I was doing here. What had this frowning princess to do with me? What did I care that she was stepdaughter now to the king of all the Britons? We had other princesses at school here, from Dumnonia and beyond. My work was in the library, with the convent accounts. Cigfa was glad to find at last a nun with a head for numbers. She could occupy all her daylit hours with curling script and glowing paints. It was Rathtyen, beside me, who had charge of the schoolroom. And there were homelier nuns, who should have been mothers themselves, to care for the children's bodies. It was not my business.

Bryvyth turned back to the girl, and her voice startled me by its hoarse gentleness.

'Morgan, daughter of Gorlois, you are welcome.'

She clasped the girl in her strong embrace. Morgan did not move. She stood unyielding to the warmth that encircled her. Bryvyth's arms dropped away and she turned briskly towards me.

'This is your foster-mother. Her name is Luned. She will be your soul-friend, closest to you in this family of God. You will sleep in her cell, and spend your leisure in her company, and do everything she commands you in obedience and humility. You will confess your sins to her, and she will show you the road to Christ. You must be a loving daughter to her, and she will tend your body and soul.'

Shocked out of obedience, my voice broke out in protest.

'But, Bryvyth . . .!'

She must have expected it. She rounded on me quickly.

'Hold your tongue now, Luned. I'll speak with you alone.

'Now, child, go with Rathtyen. She will show you how we live and labour here in Tintagel. In your working hours you will be subject to her, as to the other teachers. Profit by it. They have a storehouse of treasures to offer you.'

The girl's face did not move as she looked at us all. She held out her hand to the old woman. Unadorned as she was, she bore herself like a queen. She gripped the knotted fingers, but her voice was steady.

'Don't cry, Gwennol. My day will come. Remember what you promised me.'

The old woman caught her in a fierce hug, while the tears ran down the furrows of her face.

'That wicked man! After all I've suffered for you. He can take your body away from me, my lover, but I shall still have your soul.'

'My soul is my own, Gwennol. Not yours or anyone else's. Never forget that. I will vow it to whom I choose, and when I please. But I shan't forget what you've taught me.'

Did I fancy Bryvyth's face darkened at that? The old nurse sucked in her breath sharply.

'Hush! I'll wait for you, my chick. You'll see. It won't be for long. The king and your mother will be going away to London soon. They won't want to stay in Cornwall . . . now that Merlyn's stolen our Arthur.'

Three nuns, with eyes cast down, listening to a tale of murder and childbirth and magic.

'Uther Pendragon will never set me free as long as he lives. He knows that if I could strike either him or his son, I'd do it.'

Bryvyth said loudly, 'It's time for you to go, Gwennol Far-Sight. And I'll have no talk of killing here. Tintagel is a holy place.'

Gwennol laughed at that, sudden and bitter. 'Oh, yes! Tintagel's a holy place. It always was, long before your sort took it from us. And always will be, after you're dead and gone.'

Bryvyth tensed. I waited for her to thunder back. The words did not come.

Morgan smiled then, for the first time, wide and brilliant. She did not return her nurse's kisses, but she endured them more patiently than Bryvyth's hug. Then she unclasped Gwennol's hands from her shoulders. Their fingers knotted and fell apart.

The old woman sniffed and handed a bag to me.

'A few clothes,' she said. 'And little enough for a fine young lady like her.'

She hobbled away across the bridge, leaning heavily on her stick.

'Come!' Rathtyen ordered the girl.

As Morgan walked to the door she paused and stared up into my eyes, deep pools of mistrust on either side. We were waiting to learn what sort of bridge there might be between us. She followed Rathtyen down the path to the schoolroom, straight-backed. There was nothing boyish or impetuous in her movements now.

Bryvyth snorted, like a horse relieved of its harness.

'Well, Luned? Here's a pretty pickle!'

'But why me? I don't like children. There are many here that should have gone to the sort of monastery where they could have married and had babies. Why didn't you give her to one of those?'

'I know the ones you mean. It is not easy for them to be the brides of Christ. I meant Tintagel to be the roost of eagles, like you and me, but there are some little hens that have found their way on to its cliffs.

'But look you, Luned, you don't know the whole of it. It is told abroad that Merlyn stole the baby Arthur away. No one says why. Morgan, his half-sister, took him first. They found her here, in Tintagel Haven on that night of storm. Do you see that rock down there, below the tideline? She was standing on that, with the boy in her arms, and waves dashing all around them. She meant to kill him. The king's firstborn son. She was lucky to keep her life.

'This whelp of Gorlois's is a heavy burden laid on us. Too heavy for most women here. The Pendragon has charged me that I have her watched day and night, that I never allow her to go beyond these cliffs or be the cause of any more harm to him and his family. You know how I have cursed that man. If I could have said no to him, as I have done often before, I would have. I did not sing at his wedding, and I would not have feasted at his son's christening.

'But how could I refuse this? If Morgan is found anywhere outside this island, his orders are that she is to be taken and killed, as he slew Gorlois her father for opposing him. So what choice do I have? Could I say I wouldn't shelter her, and see her die?'

Oh, Bryvyth, if you had known what this would cost you, you might have hardened your heart!

'Pity her, Luned. This is the daughter of sinful parents, and one who has been much hurt, by the look of her. A soul Christ died to save. Nine years old, and come within a finger's breadth of damnation already. Did you mark Gwennol, the nurse? Morgan's soul needs guarding, even more than her poor body. She will need prayer and constant vigilance. We'll save her by love if we can, by whipping if we must. I see a hard battle and a high reward.

'They tell me she's a clever child, and of a wilful, proud spirit. There are only two nuns in Tintagel to match such a temper. Rathtyen is one, but she has her hands full with the care of a whole school. That leaves you, Luned.'

She clasped my shoulders. It was hard to resist such warmth.

'What do you say, girl? Will you fight this battle for us? Your cleverness and strength of will against this proud little princess? It's no easy road I'm setting you on. You're young yourself, and she's a child that's already old in hating. I'm not easy in my mind, for her or us. I'll pray for you both, day and night. You heard the old hag. If you fail, it's the whole of Tintagel that may be prey to evil. I'm thinking you're the best champion our side has.'

She flattered my vanity. Pride tempted me, as she must have known it would. Yet still I recoiled from the task.

'I have my own work in the library. I cannot be spared from that to mind a child.'

Bryvyth nudged me and smiled slyly. 'It occurs to me, mind, you'd need to give up milking the cows. Would that break your heart, now?'

'You know it wouldn't.'

'Well, we couldn't be having you running off and leaving her alone in the early morning, could we? From now on, you'll not be taking your eyes off Morgan till she's safe in the schoolroom. After that, she's Rathtyen's responsibility until work is over.'

'There's Padarn at the gate.'

'And who's to watch the beach? There are more ways in and out of Tintagel than the high road.'

'If she's so clever, she won't run away if she knows she'll be killed.'

Bryvyth raised her eyebrows. 'I'm thinking I've not made myself entirely clear. It's not her mortal life I'm most worried about. It's her eternal soul. Do not forget Gwennol Far-Sight. She and her kind cursed and spat on us when we marched into Tintagel behind the sign of Christ. Watch over Morgan well, Luned. Keep the devil from her, and shield us from harm. And armour your own soul with mighty prayers.'

She looked at me searchingly. Did she not see how brittle a thing my faith was beside hers? Why did she trust me with the task? She made me kneel at her feet and I felt the warmth of her hands on my head.

'In the name of Saint Michael of the heavenly sword we send this our daughter into the fight for God. May the Father arm her. May Christ go before her. May the flame of the Holy Spirit give her heart courage. And may she lead Gorlois's daughter safe into blessed Paradise at last. Amen.'

'Amen,' I answered.

But I was thinking more of the sharp stone under my knee and the draught from the door cold in the small of my back.

# Chapter Eight

The older girls were coming out of the schoolroom when I went after Morgan. Their heads were turning and they were full of excited chatter. I could not blame them. Fearful things were happening in the world beyond us. Yet only once, at Arthur's conception, had the shock-wave breached Tintagel's bank. The coming of Morgan was an event.

They filled the path, but I stopped and frowned at them till they stepped aside, subduing their noise. I passed them without a smile. What were they to me? And what was I supposed to do with a nine-year-old child?

My cell was almost the last along the lower path, perched under a ledge out of the wind. All I saw from the door was the cold sea and the cliffs of Barras Nose across the cove. Beyond that headland lay Bossiney, and our king and queen. But until now that had meant almost nothing to me, a world apart from mine.

Rathtyen and Morgan were waiting for me at the door of the hut. A space separated them. Neither of them was smiling. Someone had left a pile of clean hay and some woollen coverings.

'I'll leave you with Luned now,' Rathtyen said. 'Attend to her and she will show you how to make your bed.'

The girl stiffened. She became hard as rock. Her mouth a crack in her face. Her eyes cold as slate.

'I am a daughter of the queen of Britain. I do not make my own bed!'

'You'll do what I say. There are girls here that are the true-born daughters of kings, and that doesn't stop them emptying slops. I will have obedience.'

When Rathtyen spoke sharply, nuns that had done no wrong trembled. I felt the knot of fear in my own stomach but Morgan did not move a muscle.

'Pick up that hay!'

'Pick it up yourself.'

No one had ever spoken to Rathtyen like that. Other nuns pleaded and scolded and even slapped the pupils, and still could not get what they wanted. But one grim word from Rathtyen was always enough to quell the bravest heart. I stood frozen, with my arms full of blankets. I looked at Rathtyen to find what would follow, and was shocked by what I saw. She did not know what to do.

'Pick up that hay, or you'll feel the taste of my whip,' she muttered angrily.

'I am the Princess Morgan. You would not dare to lay a finger on me.'

'Princess, is it? Who fathered you? There's no king's blood in you

162

that I've heard about. And no honour from king, or queen either, that sent you to us as a prisoner.'

'You are wrong!' Morgan flashed out. 'I come of royal blood by my mother's line.'

'Your mother has a son now, safe where you'll never find him. What should the Pendragon's queen want with Gorlois's daughter?'

That sealed the hatred between them.

But Morgan spoke true. Rathtyen did not beat her. Did she fear that if it came to a fight, she would not have had the strength to win? I did not meet the older nun's eyes. I dreaded that she would ask me to help her hold the girl down. I shrank from the thought of that physical encounter. My battle must be with her mind.

Instead, the breath hissed through Rathtyen's teeth.

'We'll see who is mistress here.'

She strode up the hillside out of sight, and we knew she had gone straight back to Bryvyth.

The child Morgan seated herself on a rock beside the door and waited. Very still, she was, with her hands locked in her lap. She smiled slightly, like a cat that has been at the cream.

I took an armful of hay.

'Watch me!' I said to salve my pride. 'This is how it is done.'

She did not turn her head.

I made up a bed for her alongside mine in hurried silence. The space between them was hardly wide enough to stand in. My mattress was thin and lightly-covered. I made hers deep and soft. I was almost as afraid of this bitter child as I was of Rathtyen. And Bryvyth had called me strong of will!

A younger nun came hurrying to call Morgan to Bryvyth. I thought she might refuse to go but she walked proudly up the path. I followed her. It was the first unwilling step after Morgan on the long and terrible road of the years to come.

We met Rathtyen on the threshold of Bryvyth's cell. She passed us, scowling. Bryvyth stopped me from entering with a curt word. Rathtyen and I moved away from the door, for decency. Yet we stood, not looking at each other, listening. The grey air was chill. The plumes of angry waves spurted towards us. Between the crash of the breakers I heard Morgan start to argue. But Bryvyth wasted no time on words. There was the crack of birch twigs on bare legs. From Morgan there was no more sound. At least her arguments were stopped. Bryvyth was stronger of heart than we were. Morgan came out in silence with her head held high. Tears flashed dangerously in her eyes, but she would not let them fall.

I moved uncertainly towards her. What did one say to a child like that? What did one say to any child?

She walked straight past me. I thought she was going back to the cell. Then she started to run.

'Morgan! Come back!' I cried.

What use? From the moment I picked up the hay we both knew she was mistress.

163

**Yet I had my orders.** I had no choice but to run after her. I, Luned, before the stares of all the homecoming sisters. It was an affront to my dignity. Even as a child on my parents' farm I had soon outgrown the games that other children played. Here at Tintagel I was amazed to see nuns chasing each other in the meadow and playing ball on the beach. It astonished me that Bryvyth herself could lead our worship in chapel on feast days and then tuck up her skirts and run about the sands like any fisherman's brat. She would even paddle in the waves for the fun of it. I kept to myself, above their sport, with my legs decently covered.

But now I must run pelting over the fields after Morgan, with my gown snatched up in front of me for all to see. I could not guess what she might do.

She turned away from the causeway and made for the top of the island. She dashed across the pasture, startling the cows, straight for the furthest tip of the headland.

'Come back here!' I cried angrily into the wind. But what could I do where Rathtyen had already failed?

She flung herself out on to the very last rock, sheer over the dizzying swing of the sea. I stopped at the foot of the outcrop. A black sickness took me. I could not trust myself out on to that height with only the singing air between me and the breakers below.

I sobbed a prayer, as much for my own sake as the child's.

'Lord, let her not throw herself over!'

Morgan turned slowly. Letting go of the rock, she raised herself upright, staggering a little with the force of the wind. One step backwards and she would have gone to her death. Never have I seen eyes more intense and yet as hard as polished stone. They filled me with dread. She smiled at me. If it had not been for those eyes you might have thought it was an invitation to a friend.

'You are afraid?'

'Of course . . . Get down.'

'Climb up here. Stand beside me.'

'I cannot. Get down at once.'

'Climb!'

I do not know why I should have obeyed her, when every nerve in my body protested against it, when I was the one appointed to keep her from danger, not aid her in it. Was this to be the end already of the fight Bryvyth had promised me? The two of us a foot away from death? I did not take that dangerous step because I had been ordered to stay always at her side. It was not because I cared whether the child herself lived or died. Not even the sting of pride to make me fall with her, because her death would be my failure. I went because that nine-year-old child *compelled* me to obey her.

I tried not to look beyond the grey stone, yellowed with lichen, under my fingers. As I reached up a small hand grabbed me and pulled me suddenly to the top. Too quickly. I felt myself totter and thought we should both have fallen over the edge. I screamed. But when I opened my eyes fearfully we were still swaying on the brink, buffeted by the wind. I clung to Morgan. Her fingers were twisted cold and tight among mine.

'It's dangerous here, isn't it? Do you like danger? Look down!'

I shut my eyes, but she dragged my head round. I caught a glimpse of hell's cauldron. I retched on a mouthful of bitter bile.

'Do you see those stones below? I wonder how long this rock beneath us will stand here. One day it will go crashing down through that space to join the others. Perhaps today, while we're standing on it. Doesn't that make your blood beat faster?'

Her eyes were burning again, too brightly green.

'Let me go,' I pleaded. 'Come home with me.'

She laughed, and tossed away my hand so that I gasped and clutched empty air. 'Bryvyth said you were to look after me. That you were to guard me from harm. You couldn't keep a crow from the corn.'

She jumped lightly on to the grass and watched scornfully as I clambered down beside her. The wind tugging at my gown could not disguise how my limbs shook.

That was the first time I followed Morgan into danger. And she had only been with us one hour.

# Chapter Nine

She tricked us from the very first day.

I marvelled that after the terrifying moments on the rock she came back with me to my cell obediently. As we neared our living quarters I saw Bryvyth at her own door, watching us anxiously. I turned to Morgan. She was walking a little way behind me, her eyes cast down demurely, her head inclined, her hands folded together. One would have thought her a picture of submission. I felt a thrill of triumph. The helpless instant of danger was behind me. I had passed the first test. I had brought her back safely.

Bryvyth smiled at me.

Oh, cunning Morgan! Even then she was scheming to hide the knowledge of my weakness from Bryvyth. She knew already she was stronger than I was, and that Bryvyth would have relieved me from the task if she had guessed. I, who was set to guard her, was already her tool. She knew I would never confess my failure to Bryvyth of my own accord.

I got another nun to help me carry a chest to my cell and stood it at the foot of Morgan's bed.

'Put your clothes away,' I ordered, pointing to the bag Gwennol had left. She raised her eyes to me with a slow, insolent stare. She did not move from the bed where she sat. Should I go back to Bryvyth again and compel her? I knew I would not.

I unpacked her possessions and laid them neatly in the chest. There were not many, for the stepdaughter of a king. A few changes of clothes, not richly decorated. Girdles of wool rather than gold. Clasps of plain silver. A bone comb, but no mirror. My hands found something hard wrapped in cloth at the bottom of the bag. I hesitated. Morgan watched me without expression. I unfolded the cloth.

It was a knife, richer by far than anything else she had brought. The hilt was of polished bone, marvellously fashioned like a boar, with bristles of gold and garnet eyes. But this was no jeweller's toy. When I unsheathed it, the blade was long and wickedly sharp.

Do not mistake me. We all had knives. Even in a convent library it is necessary to sharpen pens. The littlest child carried one in his belt. But not a weapon like this. It was a hunting dagger. It could have slit a bear's throat or butchered a stag.

'What is this?' I asked Morgan, and my voice must have been sharp with worry.

To my surprise she recoiled at the sight of it.

'That! Merlyn gave it to me for a New Year's gift. I did not know it was there. Why did she pack it?'

166

'It was a handsome present. Richer than the one you wear in your girdle.'

'I do not want it. It is a man's weapon. I will not touch it.'

'You will have no need of it here.'

'Or afterwards. Gwennol taught me that. There are other ways. Which do you think is worse – the power to wound, or to have the power to heal and not to use it?'

She was on her feet. Her fingers were gripping my wrist. Then she seemed to realise what she was doing and sat down again.

'I do not want that,' she repeated.

I took the knife to Bryvyth. She raised her eyebrows.

'Why would that trickster Merlyn give the girl a gift like that? Did he want her to put Uther Pendragon out of the way with it and sign her own death-warrant, while he rears the brat Arthur to his own liking? Well, it seems she's too wise a child to play his game.'

She sent the knife back to Bossiney. It was almost nine years before I saw it again.

Supper was over, and it was time for evening prayers. Our oratory was small. In summer we sang our praises out of doors. When we were packed together against the winter cold it was hard to see past the tall nuns to the rows of children. Yet I found Morgan's face. Her eyes were blank. Her lips unmoving. I told myself it was not to be wondered at. Though she came from a Christian family, doubtless the words were strange to her. Then I saw her lips tight as a locked door. I knew she did not want to join her voice to ours. Our hymns were an alien language she would refuse to learn.

Suddenly I saw her eyes flicker sideways. Mine followed them. Bryvyth had turned to watch her. The child's rosy mouth parted on milk-white teeth. With a little smile she began to sing, lips shaping the Latin syllables exactly. Her voice rose pure and sweet among the rest. Bryvyth smiled back at her, warm and encouraging. She had duped us again.

So I closed the door on our first night together with a sense of foreboding. For three years I had slept here in my own cell. Narrow and bare, but a castle to me who had lived with a litter of squalling brothers and sisters crowding my days and nights. It was mine. The four-walled space. The silence. The view was grim from the doorway, the everlasting sea breaking upon the dark cliffs of Barras Nose, but it was a small price to pay for solitude. For the right to live with myself. Mistress of my own mind.

Morgan ended that.

It was already dark. A feeble rushlight made the shadows deeper. Morgan stood very still beside her bed. Clad, as she had come to us, in a dark blue tunic over a saffron gown. A tasselled girdle. Her black hair loosely braided. I sensed for the first time that she was uncertain what to do. I was shivering myself from the midwinter cold and my own unreadiness for this task. No one had explained to me the everyday duties of a foster-mother. But one thing was obvious.

'Take off your gown and hurry into bed, before we both freeze,' I snapped.

Already I half-expected her to disobey me. Why should she heed me, who had now so little confidence in my power to rule her? But her head drooped. She touched the knot of her girdle and fingered the hem of her tunic. Then I understood. Nine years, and she had never been expected to undress herself or brush the tangles from her hair. At three years old my sisters had been learning to do that for themselves.

I waited for her to refuse. It was on the tip of my tongue to scold her. To pay back in scorn some of the hurt to my own dignity. But when I saw her begin to tug at her dress she seemed to shrivel in stature before me and become a tired little girl. Something stayed my bitterness. I am not gentle. I was never gentle with myself. I hate to touch others. My movements of caring are clumsy. Yet I argued with myself that it was too cold to stand and wait. Let me have her in bed and forget the darkness of my own altered future in sleep.

I took away her hands from her girdle. They were very cold. I undid the knot. I lifted the tunic over her head. She stood and let me. I think she counted it defeat and not victory to have me serve her this time. Perhaps her thoughts were not on me at all, but on the old nurse with twisted hands who had done this service for her every night of her life.

Her loosened gown fell to the floor. On her flat chest I saw what had been hidden. From a thong around her neck hung a small leather bag. A jarring memory struck me. I was a country girl. I had seen many such bags before Ruman came. Once my mother had hung one round my own neck. I was more frightened of it than of the evil it was meant to ward off. Neither of us spoke. I knew Gwennol had given it to her. I did not want to know what it contained.

We stood in our shifts, barefooted. Cold in body and heart.

'Raise your hands to heaven,' I ordered. She followed me without argument. It was hard to move in that narrow space without brushing each other.

'Pray: O angel guardian of my right hand, attend thou me this night. Drive thou from me the taint of pollution, encompass thou me till dawn from evil. O kindly angel of my right hand, deliver thou me from the wicked one this night. Deliver thou me this night. Amen.'

She had uttered no sound.

'Repeat the Amen.'

She lowered her hands without a word.

'Say it,' I insisted.

Morgan turned her head to me. Her eyes were lost in the shadowed hollows of her face. She said nothing. And the dread began to grow in me again as I knew she would not.

After that, I did not settle her into bed. I did not heap the covers over her shoulders and tuck her round as her nurse would have done. I got straight into my own bed and blew out the rushlight. Let her freeze if she wanted.

She was a quiet child. She slipped between the covers with hardly a sound. I heard a faint catch of breath from her bed. So close I could have reached out a hand and touched her. I do not know if it was a gasp of cold or a stifled sob.

I could not sleep. That was common with me. Wakefulness had been hateful to me at home, with the snores and grunts of so many bodies close to mine. At Tintagel I had learned to treasure these extra hours. I might not burn a light late at night, yet I could lie awake letting my mind go free, escaping at first the demands of dirty beasts and muddy earth and the chatter of nuns hoeing around me. Now there was more to fill my thoughts. Passages from the Bible to memorise daily. The wonders of science and mathematics from the East. The detailed accounts of our farms and quarries and the convent expenditure. I had dreamed a great future for Tintagel and myself.

Now I saw this liberty threatened by one small child so close beside me, silent but trespassing by her very presence upon the space and largeness of my thoughts. I turned to the wall and tried to close my eyes for sleep.

The sound seemed to come from the walls themselves. At first I took it for the hiss and smack of the waves, dragon-like rearing themselves against our cliffs. Then for the creeping winter wind between grass and stones, snatching at us even in the hollows where we sheltered. At last I knew it was inside the cell with me.

Of course, I thought it was the child. I turned over quickly. It was utterly dark. The whispering was all around us. From the walls, from the roof, from the door. Vicious, insistent. Loud enough for me to understand the words . . . and yet I did not understand them. Like no language I had ever known or heard. Terror gripped me. The gap between our beds was very narrow. It seemed an unbridgeable chasm. I summoned all my courage and strength of will to cross it.

My hand reached out in the darkness. I confess that I was seeking reassurance, not giving it. I was terrified that the voice might not be Morgan's. And more afraid still that it was. I wanted to tell myself that this was a human, mortal child. That whatever assailed us, there were two of us to stand against it, to defend each other from its evil. Evil it was, I did not need to be convinced of that.

My hand met Morgan's wrist. Very slight, she felt. A skinny, nine-years girl. She was lying very still. There was no start of movement when I touched her. Yet I knew she was awake. I had listened for the deep slow breathing of the sleeper, desperate to keep my ears from that other whispering all around us. There was nothing. She was lying on her back. I sensed her face turned to the thatch over our heads. I knew, without seeing, that her eyes were open. She did not seem to feel my hand. There was no response, except that the whispering rose to a gibbering screech so that I clung to her, shutting my eyes, babbling prayers.

'O holy Son of God, blessed Christ, who stilled the storm, defend us . . .'

The voices fell a little, as waves die back after the breaker foams. The gloom lightened a little, or my eyes became accustomed to the night. It frightened me more. I did not know what there was to see, and I did not wish to see it. I shut my eyes, still gripping Morgan. Slowly I felt warmth return to her under my fingers. Felt the bone of her arm solid under my hand. A little sigh escaped her, and her breath fluttered on my face as she turned her head sideways.

169

Suddenly she flung my arm away.

'Gwennol! Gwennol!' she screamed as if in terror. And then, 'Stop her! Don't let her! Don't let her!'

Her arms thrashed wildly. I jumped out of bed. She threw herself upon me. Hands grasping my shoulders, head butting into my breast.

'Where is Arthur? When he is king, who will be queen? I will! I will, won't I?' she cried passionately.

I am the eldest child. I had many brothers and sisters. I know what needs to be done to soothe their frets. The words, the movements. It is a skill. It is not necessary to feel love to quiet a crying child. So I spoke to her, and stroked her, and patted her into a hiccupping silence. I do not remember what I said, or what I may have promised her. It was effective. The whispering in the walls had died too. I put it behind me. I had no wish to question what it might have been. I feared to know the answer.

I took a small revenge. I made her stand with me again between the beds. And the night was colder now than it had been before.

'Father of all, guard our souls. Christ in high heaven, defend us this night. Spirit of comfort, bless our beds, And bring us safe to bright morning, here or in heaven. Amen.'

I heard her say the Amen after me. Quickly, almost desperately. She caught my hand.

'Luned, Luned? Will your God save us both? Can he?'

'Of course he can,' I said. 'If you pray, and fast, and are obedient to your teachers in every way.' And then, recalling Bryvyth, I added virtuously, 'And I will pray and fast with you, Morgan.'

She dropped my hand. 'You? You're more frightened than I am. Why didn't Bryvyth give me someone brave and laughing? And to think that Gwennol was afraid of you! That's silly, isn't it? She thinks their star is setting and the Church's is rising. Where is the power, Luned? What is the strongest thing? Is it Uther Pendragon's sword, or Merlyn's spells, or your Christ on his cross? What are you going to fight them with, Luned?'

'Go back to bed, child. God will defend us.'

'Is your cross a weapon? Will it hurt them?'

'Hush. That is sinful talk. You must make confession for it.'

I tucked her round this time. Awkwardly I bent and smoothed her hair. I almost kissed her, but I did not. I do not know why. I cannot tell you what I meant by it. I did not love her then. I wanted to be rid of her forever. If that had been possible I might have lived my life in peace. The nuns of Tintagel might still be singing on those cliffs, and much evil averted.

It was not my fault. Bryvyth should not have called me to fight this battle as their champion. I had neither the strength nor the humility. I did not love Morgan enough until I was deep in her power.

I dreaded to hear the voices again. I hid my head under the covers and muttered prayers to shut them out. Morgan lay silent now, so that I thought at last she was asleep. My prayers slowed and stopped. There was no sound inside the cell but our own breathing.

Then I screamed aloud as her fingers snatched at my arm.

'I will be queen! I will!' she hissed.

# Chapter Ten

That day was the first of many beatings for Morgan, and there was worse to come.

At first it seemed that nothing I or Rathtyen or Bryvyth could do would change her. She was possessed by a blind anger and a stubborn pride. Over and over again she swore to us that she would be a queen. I did not blame her for that. If I had been born in her place, and suffered what she had suffered at the hands of King Uther, I might have nourished such a dream, to oppose his might.

Ygerne and Uther Pendragon were still in Bossiney, waiting for the spring to come and the roads to the cities to be fit for travel and war to begin again. They were planning the marriage-feasts of Elaine and Margawse at Easter. But no word came from them for Morgan.

I thought that first day that she would have no friends in Tintagel either. You had only to watch her sitting on the bench in the refectory. She had a still intensity that created a space around her, no matter how closely the children's bodies might be crowded. I never knew a child who could sit so still. I watched the other girls' eager questions slowing, dying away before her contemptuous answers. I saw the looks they exchanged. She truly believed that Morgan, daughter of Gorlois and Ygerne, was greater by far than they were, though in blood she was not. Many of them detested her.

But not all. I say she had no friends, and she did not. Yet there were those who followed her. Even some older girls fell under her spell. That sort of pale and quiet girl that follows in the shadow of someone strong and vibrant, seemingly unable to live except through others – Morgan had several such, waiting upon her every whim, hanging on her words, flattering her. Poor as she was, she would give them gifts. A piece of amethyst found on the beach, a curious shell, a choice morsel of food saved from the table. She did not do this to curry their favour. It was not to win their love that she bestowed her largesse – they already worshipped her – but she was her father's daughter. Gorlois had given gold and jewels and horses to his warband, a generous duke, an open-handed leader of men. So would Morgan exercise royalty in this little court. Through gifts she asserted her superiority over them. It was hard to stop.

There were no gifts for Morgan. Unless you count what passed at Imbolc, the festival of the Lady of flocks and herds.

On the first of February I woke early. I had not yet lost the discipline that had driven me out in the winter's half-light to milk the cows and ewes before morning prayers. With Morgan's coming I could lie in bed a little longer, my body rested but my mind uneasy.

Today someone was afoot before me. Morgan was going out of the door, wrapped in her cloak.

'Morgan! Where are you going?'

She did not answer me, contemptuous as ever.

I roused on my elbow, watching her disappear. Why had I called out? Where does anyone go on waking from a night's sleep? She would be back in a moment.

I leaned back on my pillow and closed my eyes. A picture came to me, a fleeting glimpse of Morgan departing into the gloom. The whisk of her gown beneath the hem of her cloak. I knew then why I had been alarmed. Morgan was fully dressed.

I leaped up and threw my own cloak over my shift. Barefoot in the cold mud of the paths, I ran after her. There was not light enough yet to see far. I was too proud to cry out to her. She would not have answered. I must find her myself.

I headed for the causeway. If she thought of escaping it would be that way, while Padarn was asleep.

A sound alerted me. The startled mooing of a cow somewhere above. I spun round and climbed towards the plateau and the farm. Was that someone moving through the steaming byre where the shuffling herd waited for milking? As I hurried after, the cows' muzzles seemed monstrous, leaning out of the murk towards me. Their horns barred my way. Was that a flicker of light at the far end, or a trick of the eyes? A cock crowed piercingly and all the hens on their roosts seemed to come to noisy life in front of me.

On over the cold wet grass. It was growing lighter here, with the wide sea all around me. A grey shadow passed by the pens of sheep and they murmured as if in recognition of her.

She was on the summit now, walking swiftly through the meadow. I could see the tracks of her feet in the dew. She was making straight for the southern edge. The ground dipped and I lost her against the boulders. My heart began to hammer. There is a gap in the rocks there, where a path drops sharply down on to a grass-grown terrace. I feared to follow her that way, as I shun all precipitous places.

But Morgan had paused, staring round her at the paling pasture and the still grey sea. I sped across the meadow to catch her. Then she bent. I thought I would lose her down that cleft in the stones. But she had found something.

At the side of that stair in the rock there is a shelf of slate, overhung by rock, like a natural shrine. I had never investigated it. The sides of Tintagel are riddled with holes, great and small. I kept away from them. Now as I saw Morgan bending over it, I noticed two things that made the hair rise on my scalp.

There were cups cut in the rock. Little circular hollows. I had seen such things before. I was not green. I knew what thy were. And today was Imbolc. The cups had been filled. With milk. With bread. With honey. With egg. I saw Morgan's hands make passes over them. Then she dipped her fingers and ate and drank.

If I had been chilled to find such things on Tintagel, and still in use, that was nothing now. I experienced horror. You who have lived in the sophistication of a Christian court cannot imagine the depth of my dread. I was a country girl. Long before I became a Christian and a nun I knew the meaning of such sacrifices. We made oblations for the coming year. They were not for humans. We did not eat of them ourselves. *We did not eat of them ourselves!*

But Morgan was eating them.

I was too frightened to run and tell Bryvyth at once. I do not know what it was I dreaded to say. Even to this day I am not sure what name to give my fears about Morgan. I must live with her. I must see her, speak to her, touch her daily. How could I bear this if I spoke my fear?

So I kept silent, and that memory was blotted out by what followed the next day.

It was the feast of candles. Our little oratory was aflame with light that dark February day. The rest was holiday. We nuns would have been glad to sit over the fire in our little hall, sewing and listening to some story of the saints or the prophets, but the children were restless. Even on a winter's day the little boys would rather be out of doors, running or hurling a ball, and not a few girls too. Morgan was with them.

That was the other side of her. She, who carried herself so queenly in front of the older girls, would suddenly switch and become a mad thing with the younger children. She would laugh and leap and race like an unbroken filly, calling to them to try and catch her.

They adored her. They saw a magic in her vitality that made them dash after her, crazy with mirth and admiration and reckless of any warning we nuns might shout.

She taxed me greatly. I had risen beyond the mere copying of figures in the library now. Nonna's mind was failing. When merchants came to bargain at the gatehouse, it was I who was called to deal with them. I must be in the storehouse, making lists of what was needed in the kitchens. The guesthouse was always busy with travellers. All our wealth, and the accounting of it, was in my hands.

But when the day's work was over, I could not find the peace and solitude I needed. While daylight lasted I must follow a restless, growing girl over the rocks of Tintagel. Worse still, she tempted the younger ones to follow her. The cliffs are steep, the ledges narrow. The wind comes in sudden gusts. I would have to scurry after them, calling to them to take care, always afraid that one of them would fall. Afraid I might slip myself. Knowing it would not be Morgan who fell. Wishing it might be.

That day she stood very still in a circle of children. The smaller ones watched her. She fascinated them. Then, without warning, her eyes flashed. She dashed away up the path, calling to the little boys and girls to chase her. They screamed with laughter and scrambled in pursuit.

My heart was in my mouth. Morgan cared nothing for her own safety or theirs either.

I panted after them, but she was swifter than I was. I saw her flying across the grass to that gap in the rock on the southern edge. The little ones swarmed after her.

'No! Come back!' I begged in vain in the teeth of the wind.

This time she hardly paused at the ledge. Her white hand slid over the slate, its cups empty now. Then she swung herself down, dropping lightly to the grass below.

She disappeared. The children went tumbling through the cleft after her.

'Where's she gone?'

Their shrill voices floated up to me.

There was a laughing call among the boulders. The boys and girls went pelting across the grassy terrace in search of her.

'Don't run! It's slippery!' I yelled.

They did not heed me. She had escaped them again. They searched around, behind rocks, under the cliffhang, even peering over the edge.

A white hand between the stones betrayed her. A flying lock of black hair.

'Here she is! I've found her!'

Howel shouted with glee. A small round boy with curly brown hair. The son of an under-king from the lower reaches of the Severn. He had found their darling.

Bolder than all the rest, he leaped from a rock over her head to land beside her hiding-place. He bounced breathless on the grass slope below. His tiny leather boots skidded on the muddy turf. He started to slither, to roll. At first he chuckled. Then he shouted, screamed. I saw his body bouncing over the rocks out into the air. Falling. Disappearing.

I am not brave. I rushed back to the convent. Half a dozen nuns, the hardiest, went pelting down to the shore, Bryvyth in the lead. That ledge is on the sterner side of the island. There is no beach there. The water is deep, the rocks cruel. They clambered over the stones, searching, calling, weeping. They did not find him.

Days later fishermen sighted his body, wedged in a cleft of rock under black seawrack. It was monstrously bloated and pale. Beginning to soften into disintegration at a touch.

I did not follow the other nuns. Morgan was white and fierce when I caught up with her. What does one say to one who has caused death, at a moment like that? How do you reproach her?

She did not wait to hear me. She flew at me as though her clawed hands would rake my face.

'Where is he?'

'He is dead,' I said.

'He is not! He is not! Show me his body. Let me touch him. Let me try!'

'The sea has taken him. They cannot find him.'

She wept in earnest then.

'It's your fault! All of you! Why did you build your convent in such a dangerous place? You shouldn't ask little children to come and live here. Uther Pendragon was a beast to send me. I would never have come here of my own free will. Is this a fit place for the daughter of

174

Gorlois, the warlord, the hunter? There are no horses for me to ride. Can I not even run if I want to?'

I do not know if the tears were for herself or the dead boy. They had ceased before the beating began.

Bryvyth laid a greater ban on her then, walking round the convent with her crooked staff, beating the bounds of Morgan's close imprisonment. She must not go beyond this circle. Tintagel is narrow enough, for those who must be alone, but this ward was tighter yet. Cell, schoolroom, chapel, refectory, a little run of grass, well back from the cliff. Morgan watched her, eyes flaring in her white face. Lips silent. None of us knew if she would obey, or how we might compel her. It was a fragile fence and we all knew it. One moment's anger, a second's defiance, and the sea lay half a dozen strides away with all its evil temptation. One could never escape far from it.

Yet she kept within the circle. The word from Rathtyen was that she worked hard in the schoolroom. Stiff and silent, except when she must read aloud or make answers. But clever, beyond the common range of pupils, and diligent and seemingly obedient now.

So in chapel. She sang and prayed. It did not seem a mockery this time. Her lips framed the words eagerly, even passionately, calling upon the name of Christ, her saviour. Bryvyth met my eyes. Neither of us was sure. Could it be she was saved?

Bryvyth had imposed a great fast on me for my failure. Morgan chose to share it, though we would not have placed so heavy a burden on any child. She grew paler than ever, and gaunt with hunger or grief.

I found her one day alone in the oratory. Her hands were stretched out to the dark-eyed Christ Eira had painted on the wall above the altar.

'Teach me!' she was crying to him. 'I know how they hurt you. They whipped you, they imprisoned you, they crucified you. But you were the Healer. You were stronger than death. Show me!'

# Chapter Eleven

Death was no stranger to us. Howel was not the only child who would not return from Tintagel. At Easter we put away our mourning for him.

Great Lent ended in Holy Week. Bryvyth would lift my penance from me. We had all been fasting now. I longed for the coming festival as never before. I felt that when the light of Easter dawned I could present Morgan to Bryvyth as my triumph. A soul snatched from darkness. Evil vanquished. Satan defeated. Like Christ, I had harrowed hell.

The Pendragons had gone from Cornwall. Margawse was to be married to Lot of Lothian, Elaine to Nentres of Garlot. No one sent to invite Morgan to their weddings.

Watching her walking the little round Bryvyth had set her, standing gazing across the cove to the cliffs where she had been used to run with her nurse, seeing the rolling haze of the forest she had hunted with her father, even I was moved with a kind of pity for her. The more because she no longer raged and complained. She did what I told her, not quite meekly but as if it no longer mattered to her, as if her body was a shell and the fierce will had gone somewhere else. She spent more time in the chapel than was natural for so young a child.

There is a ban on me even now that I may not tell you what sins she brought to me as her soul-friend in confession. Yet I marvelled that she should accuse herself of a wickedness greater than we thought she had done. Howel's death had been due to no more than her folly. He was no kin of hers. Why was the boy's loss such a torment to her?

But if she was humble with me, she was proud before the older girls. She watched them riding home for Easter with an escort of servants, or receiving letters and tokens before the feast. There was nothing for her. She bore their taunts with aloof silence.

I thought we were a little alike – the pen trembles now as I write this with the foolishness of it – I thought we were akin in our pride, our estimation of our own worth compared with others', our contempt for weaker souls, our need of solitude. And yet there was this difference between us. I had come to Tintagel willingly. It was here I found my freedom. But Morgan was among us as a prisoner.

I went to Bryvyth on Easter Eve.

'Might we relax her punishment a little?' I suggested. 'She is a different girl now. Grave, obedient. And the children will not follow her so readily, since Howel died.'

'Hm! So she's softened even your heart, has she? Be on your guard still, Luned. You hear her confession. Is she as contrite as she should be?'

176

'More,' I said.

She looked at me keenly. She would have liked to ask me more, but it was forbidden.

Nectan came to visit us that evening. We did not allow him to shrive the girls. Any man, even a bony saint in a white hermit's gown, sends a flurry of excitement through a convent schoolroom. Many and wild the sins they might have invented to spend a little longer alone with him. Enough pleasure for them to kneel with eyes downcast and take the sacrament from his sinewy hands.

As we prepared for the great midnight service, Bryvyth and Nectan talked close together. They summoned Morgan to them. Nectan had known her mother many years. He had been confessor to her father, Gorlois. He served as Uther Pendragon's house-priest when the king was in Cornwall. I do not know what he asked her. Morgan must have charmed him, like her mother before her. Very sweet are the women of that family when they wish to be. In the end, I too fell in love with Morgan, and damned my soul. Bryvyth had a sharper mind than Nectan, but she consented to take his counsel.

On Easter Day Morgan would be released from her close confinement. The narrow island of Tintagel would be her garden outside the tomb, so long as she kept away from the youngest children and conducted herself wisely and responsibly.

That Easter Eve we kept the vigil. All day we had been busy, labouring to make ready a huge bonfire. The sorrow of Good Friday was over. Saturday was like a holiday. The children picked primroses for the chapel. They ran to gather driftwood from the beach and haul it up the difficult path with the nuns' help. We put on stout gloves to cut the prickly furze. We dragged dead branches from the woods at the head of the coombe. We stacked them on the highest part of the island. Morgan smiled a little as she watched.

In the dark of night we gathered the children and shepherded them into the shadowed chapel. There was excitement in our prayers. Anticipation.

Then at midnight the bell was struck joyously. Bryvyth seized Christ's candle and brandished it aloft. As she strode through the chapel, lights sprang from her single flame to all our tapers. We followed her, nuns holding the youngest children by the hand. The river of light flowed up the path to the crown of Tintagel and Bryvyth thrust her flame deep into the heart of the Easter fire. Thus Patrick had blazed the faith through Ireland, and overcome the Druids. But this was a custom unknown to me till I came to Tintagel.

The red light leaped in the faces of women and girls. It caught the wonder in the eyes of children. It threw back the shadows and cast a fiery dawn over the sea. The cry went up from all our throats.

'Christ is risen!'

'He is risen indeed!'

The cliffs rang with the good news.

My eyes flew straight for Morgan. I watched her mouthing the words, without smiling, as though she longed to believe them. The flames

177

leaped in her face, leaving her eyes dark hollows. She looked away from our fire and stared into the gloom beyond the light. On every side in the limitless night the cliffs and hills of Cornwall were dark. The Easter flame leaped to heaven in Tintagel alone. A solitary challenge to the dark. I thought she shuddered.

It was three weeks before our fire was challenged. Easter was followed by the feast of May Day. Of course, nuns though we were, we knew what happened on May Eve. Only a few of us were country-born, but even the nobility in the highest villas and duns of Dumnonia were no stranger to the druids and the May-pole and the dancing mare. They might keep the Roman ways and boast chapels and priests but there was something deep in the soil that had never been rooted out. They also went to the greenwood.

So we prayed the more earnestly in our chapel and went to bed that night determined to close our minds to such thoughts in pure sleep. Tintagel was a fortress beleaguered by more than the sea. In the morning of May we would rise and go to our prayers as usual, though in our hearts we would be remembering a different song.

May Eve was not a time of regret for me. I had always feared it. I was glad to escape from the drums when I came to Tintagel. For once I expected to sleep sounder than most.

But not this year. I woke with a start in the darkness. Morgan was standing in the doorway of my cell. There was a glimmer of moonlight catching her white shift and making black snakes of her hair.

'Come back to bed.'

I spoke sharply, confident by now of my authority. She did not move. I repeated the order. She might not have heard me. With a slow chill I knew that I had lost. That I had never really had authority over her. She had appeared to obey me only because it suited her to do so. I listened to the admission of impotence in my own voice.

Disturbed now, remembering what night this was, I rose shivering and came to stand beside her. There was a silver light over the sea, as though the whole world were reluctant to sleep. And as I turned inland, everywhere I looked pinpricks of light outshone the pale stars. On every hill and headland the fires of Beltaine were blazing. A necklace of gold and rubies beaded the throat of Cornwall.

Morgan's hand gripped mine, warm and small.

For the first time since I came to Tintagel I thought keenly of my home. Of my little brothers and sisters, of the drums and the dancing, of the pairs of animals driven for increase through the flames. Of young couples leaping high for new life. If I had stayed, it might have been the hand of a young man warm over mine instead of the small hard fingers of Morgan. I shivered strangely.

She began to tug at me.

'Come, Luned! Come now!'

'No! Come back to bed. May Eve is not for us. We leave all that behind us when we take our vows as virgins.'

I tried to pull her indoors. I should have been stronger than she was. But her hand slipped through mine and she ran away from me. I had no choice but to follow her over the knife-cold grass to the edge of the cliff. Fire reddened the sky across the cove.

'Look! There is someone still in Bossiney after all! They have lit the fire. Do you see? They have lit it as a sign for me!'

Her hand held mine tighter than ever. I felt her whole body straining, yearning, as though at any moment her fierce spirit might snatch it up and soar into the air towards that beacon across the water like a gull.

'Do you hear it?' she cried passionately. 'The drums and the pipes?'

I listened. I could hear the shrill song of the wind and the endless thud of the waves.

'It is only the sea in the caves beneath us.'

'Listen! Listen!'

She was quiet for a while. Then we both heard a new sound, close at hand. Even Morgan drew back, startled, as though it was not what she was expecting. Holding each other's hand we strained to hear as we peered over our ledge.

There was a glimmer of white between the rocks far below us. A whisper of sound. Spectral laughter floated up. An irrational fear seized me that we had glimpsed what no human eye should see on this night. I tried to drag Morgan back to my cell but she pulled away from me and called out.

'Who is it? Who's there?'

There was a shocked silence. I was near to fainting. There was a sudden scrabbling. A stone tumbled and splashed into the water beneath. I could not move. Then there rose an unearthly wailing, chilling the blood. I clapped my hands over my ears. But Morgan cupped hers to her mouth. Her human voice threw back the same sound. She bent over and listened. When I took my hands away the cliffs were quiet. I could hear only the white wave-caps breaking and see the glimmer of a pool of foam round the rock in the cove.

I heard a strange sound beside me. Morgan was bent double, choking with suppressed laughter.

'Oh, Luned, Luned! Here, in Tintagel, of all places! What kind of holy nunnery is this they have sent me to?'

I could not bear it. I shut my heart and ears to her. I dropped her hand and ran back to the sanctuary of my cell, leaving her alone. Let the voices do with her what they would. I could not, must not, understand the truth of what she was saying.

# Chapter Twelve

'Wake up. Wake up.

'For summer is a-coming today . . .'

My eyes struggled open. It was barely light. Morgan was dancing beside my bed, singing the May Day song. Her feet were bare and her skirt swung above her knees as she whirled.

It was a double shock. That May Day should come in the old way, here in the chaste castle of Tintagel's convent. I almost feared to see the painted horse dancing outside my door. Blood hammered in my head like drums.

And then to see Morgan, who had been so sad and stately these last weeks, gay as a skylark. It had always troubled me beyond reason that women old enough to be my grandmother, and weighed down with cares for most of the year, should hitch up their skirts and skip and cackle songs because the calendar said it was a holiday.

As soon as Morgan saw I was awake she laughed and darted out of the door.

I groaned. For years I had stumbled out of bed before winter sunrise to milk the cows. I thought I had done with that. But now it seemed I could be piskie-led by this black elf at any time of the day or night. Besides this was May-morning, and still almost dark. The hour must be very early.

I dressed quickly and hurried outside. She was nowhere to be seen. A grey sea-mist hung over everything. There was no one about. Even the birds were not stirring yet. I caught my breath. I felt that time had slipped, that between night and day, between winter and summer, we had floated into another place and century. Or into no time at all, beyond this world. Then I saw the dark hump of the chapel on the ledge above. Even now there might be someone at prayer there. We had warrior-nuns who could choose to wrestle all night with the devil at such a time as this. I clung to that thought.

The mist walled me round. The silhouettes of rocks loomed darkly through it, with almost human shapes. I listened for the sound of Morgan singing. But there was nothing now. Even the sea was hushed.

My first thought was that she would have run to the beach, the place I most feared. Even in sunlight I avoided it unless my duties took me there. It was too open to the sea and the mainland. I remembered those whispering shapes in the moonlight and quickly turned my thoughts away. The path down to the beach was silent this morning. And that held its own dread. The sky overhead was clearing. But below, the fog hung in a thick gloom over the cove. I could not nerve myself to enter it alone.

I climbed the short path to the plateau, convincing myself that I could scan more widely from there. And that, to my surprise, was where I came upon her, wandering through the dew-wet pasture as though she searched for something. Nun though I was, I knew what she was looking for. She would not find it. There were no may-trees on Tintagel Head.

I stood and watched her, while the first pink flush of dawn crept over the hills to the east and found its reflection in the western sea. The grey turned to blue. At any moment the bell would ring us to chapel. And still the girl darted about the field, running to every bush and turning away.

I held my breath as she neared those hollows in the rock. But she came back from them also, disappointed.

A sharp pain pierced my heart. I did not put a name to it. I looked around me. The grass at my feet was starred with flowers. I would not otherwise have noticed them. I picked a handful, and sat down to wait for Morgan. My fingers had grown smooth and delicate now I worked with the pen. With my nails I pierced the furry stems of primroses and wove into them the slender threads of stitchwort and violet. The garland lengthened in my lap. Far below me the brightening sea washed with the gentle ease of the new-come summer. One tiny fishing boat was pulling out of the mist from our cove towards Barras Nose. Two specks of people in it. A man rowing. Another hooded figure crouched in the bows. The only living beings beside ourselves. A thought disturbed me. What were fishermen doing out at work on this high festival, before the dance was over and the Horse had blessed the sea for its summer harvest?

A shadow fell across my lap. Morgan was standing beside me, frowning, with empty hands. Kneeling to greet her, I lifted the chain of flowers and laid it on her shining black hair.

'Welcome, Summer,' I said.

Two powerful words that linked me to my mother and grandmother, and to all those other women far back beyond. Passed on by me now to my own foster-daughter.

Her eyes looked straight into mine, brightly green as wet moss on thatch. Long they gazed until I thought they would devour me. Then she smiled, very, very sweetly, as only Morgan can.

'Thank you, Luned. You have crowned me your queen.'

She looked away to the sea beyond the cove, and started.

Then her face split in laughter and she dragged me running after her. In vain I protested. Down over the slippery path and tussocked grass. Past the doors of cells where the nuns might already be waking. Down, down to the very edge of the sea where the ripples curled in creaming foam along the shingle.

Dawn had not come to the deep cove yet. It would be hours before the sun breasted its cliffs. The air had a damp, chill feel. Down here in the mist I could not see the sunrise gilding the sea towards Ireland.

181

This cove held always a shadow of danger for me. Beyond its narrow cliffs the cold waves came rolling in unbroken from the west. Strange ships came sailing into it. Merchants from foreign lands. I could no longer avoid them. Swarthy men who sprang on to the wharf and bargained with me in broken Latin. I had risen too high now to hide in my cell.

A road led down the coombe to this beach, below the high guard of ditch and bank. Here was no dangerous bridge set between us and the world. Anyone might come and go, beyond reach of a shout from the porter's lodge so far above. I always longed to retreat within Tintagel's defences.

Worse than these were the caves, black mouths endlessly sucking in the sea. I had a horror of their slimy darkness. But the one cave that was light I dreaded more than all. Through it I glimpsed another, wilder sea. I always feared the tide would come flooding through this tunnel and take me unawares from behind. I knew the tides obeyed the moon. I was studying the science of the stars. Reading about it in the world of books I understood their movements. But here, on the shore, seeing the slither of seaweed in the foam, I could not reason and calculate. I dreaded the unguessed rising of the tide. I only knew that twice every day, moon after moon, year after year, the sea was eating its way under the roots of the convent.

Morgan picked up a flat slate and skimmed it through the water as I had seen the Cornish sisters do. It was a game I had never learned. I tried. My pebble dropped heavily into the first wave and disappeared. Morgan laughed gaily. Her wrist flashed and the little stones went dancing through the green May-Day sea like laughing porpoises.

But she was restless. She began to clamber over the wet slabs of rocks past the caves.

'Come back!' I pleaded. I was as much afraid for myself as for her.

I lacked the power to stop her, so I must follow. Clumsy and inexperienced where she was confident.

The mist eddied. I rubbed my eyes. There was a flame in the gloom. We had come to the convent wharf, though by a dangerous path. A little fire burned on the stone, with a clean steady heat. There was a basket beside it.

Morgan dropped to her knees with a glad cry and lifted the cloth. My mouth was too dry to speak. Who had left this?

There was not much inside the basket. Two pilchards, wrapped in dock leaves. A loaf of bread.

'Oh, blessings upon her! They have not forgotten me. Wait! There must be something more.'

Her hands began to rummage in the basket. I tried to pull her away.

'Leave it alone. How do we know where this has come from?'

She turned her eyes up to me.

'*I* know who it has come from. *You* know.'

The little boat, pulling away round Barras Nose. Where but from Bossiney? Well, she had had little enough from her people since she came to us. It was a poor present for a king's stepdaughter.

I was too innocent, for all my pride and learning. Nuns humbler by far than I would have read the signs.

Morgan turned the fish over. She was right. There, nestling in the bottom of the basket, was a handful of hawthorn blossom. I even smiled for her, fool that I was. She seized the white flowers and thrust them into her crown. The thorns caught in her dark hair. She laughed at me with a fierce joy.

'There! I *am* a queen! They shall all of them see it now and know my power.'

I curtsied mockingly.

Morgan picked up a fish by the tail and tried to hold it over the fire.

'What are you doing?' I cried, shocked. 'A gift must always be shared. We must take this up to the kitchen.'

Again that sweet smile. The brilliant eyes that seemed to swallow mine.

'Please, Luned! There is only enough for two.'

She laid her hands over mine on the basket. I cannot explain to you the power in Morgan's hands. When they touched you, the world changed. It still does.

From far away I heard a bell chime sweetly. I could not tell if it came from the sky above or from the depths of the sea. I did not heed it.

I do not expect you to understand why I searched the rocks for driftwood. Why I showed her how to spear the fish and set them to cook safely over the raked embers.

Only when the sweet taste of flesh and bread was finished did I come to my senses with a cry of guilt.

'What are we doing here? It must be time for prayers. Hurry! We must not be late!'

She did not scramble to her feet. She looked up at me solemnly, the crown a little crooked now on her tangled hair.

'It is already too late for you, Luned. Far too late.'

From far above the morning hymn broke chanting on the air. Beyond the mist. Above the sea. A song of thankfulness for safe deliverance from the dark night.

I started to run towards it, up the steep path from the wharf to the convent. I staggered into the chapel gasping for breath. It was in vain. The smell of grilling fish had reached Bryvyth before I did.

# Chapter Thirteen

The abbess gave me no chance to confess. This time, I was beaten as well as Morgan. It roused me to fury. No one had ever beaten me before. As a child I had scorned naughtiness. The sting of my mother's tongue was punishment enough for any careless fault.

Out of my pain and indignation I tried to argue.

'I would have confessed to you. I would have done penance. When have I ever not? You gave me no time.'

I, Luned, scribe and steward of the convent, heard the break in my weak woman's voice. I knew the humiliation of tears spurting on to my cheeks. Bryvyth should have seen her rebuke was a wound bitter enough.

But she would not listen. She had a strong arm and a high temper to which she could not often give full rein. She did not spare me, or herself. When the beating was over, she broke the twigs across her knee and flung the pieces from her. Tears stood on her own brown cheeks.

'If I cannot trust even you, who is there left?' she cried. 'Did I make a mistake? Was I wrong to believe the women of the west could live like angels, wielding a flaming sword to guard the gates of paradise? Is it too hard to be as pure as skylarks, soaring ever heavenwards? Must you all go down into sin and idleness and disobedience, even you? Didn't you know it is May Day, when we need to be hammering at the gates of heaven for our immortal salvation? I am thinking it would be better for all of us if I took the child away from you and sent you back to the cows and kale.'

I could have taken the chance she gave me then. I could have been free of Morgan forever. I could have saved my soul. But my pride would not accept the disgrace.

'Give me one more chance,' I pleaded. 'I will not fail you again. Morgan is not lost yet. There is a child's heart there still, that we may reach with patience. For the first time today there was something different in the way she smiled at me. Not wickedly, but as though she was beginning to love me. It was for that smile that I listened to her plea. Not out of weakness, but in the hope that I might reach her soul. Do not throw the chance away when a door is beginning to open between us.'

'Have a care, Luned! She comes of a treacherous mother. The darkness is in her blood. Let it not be you that is beginning to change. Guard your own soul first if you would be tough enough to do battle with her.'

She understood Morgan's ways better than I who had lived with her day and night. I deceived myself, because I wanted the praise of victory. Morgan loves only one, and him she can never have. She uses the love of all others to their destruction. And with each fall her power increases.

At the door Bryvyth grasped my arm. In the urgency of her voice there was pleading now. Not for my actions alone, but for her own, just past. For my understanding, forgiveness even. That was not necessary. Did she not see that I dreamed of being an abbess myself one day? I should be hard, as she was hard. My Lord was the Christ of the desert who did battle with devils. I do not think I would have beaten my nuns. Physical contact is repellent to me. But my tongue would have been harsher than my mother's chiding. A whip and goad to drive the steep, rough road that leads to heaven.

My thoughts were winging to the future, rebuilding that dream out of the wreckage of my present humiliation. I hardly heard Bryvyth's voice.

'Never again, eh, Luned? No more maidens washing in the dew. No more maying. No more fishing for pilchards. No more breakfasting on the beach when you should be in chapel praying. We are fishing for souls here, girl. Never forget that.'

She must have felt the tremor in my arm. Suddenly she swept me to her chest in a great bear-hug. Her own voice was not entirely steady.

'There, girl. Don't cry. It is over. I have forgiven you. Seventy times seven I'd forgive you, if only you'll promise to fight the battle alongside me and not run away.'

And all the time her strong hard hand was stroking my hair, my face was buried against the rough wool of her tunic and I was saying to myself incredulously, 'Then she doesn't know the half of it! She has beaten me till the skin split and the blood came, and she thinks that all I did was weave flowers and eat pilchards with Morgan on the beach. Can it really be that no one has told her what came to our cove? Was it only my eyes that could see those white spirits on the cliff and that fishing-boat pulling out of the mist? Does she still not know that Tintagel has had visitors?'

And, may the devil take me, I dared not tell her. I did not confess. Then, or ever. When the only human strength that could have stood between me and Morgan clasped me to her breast, I closed my lips.

I was afraid to speak. Knowing now that in spite of everything Bryvyth still loved me, still wished me reinstated in her trust, I dared not uncover this further, darker sin. She must not know that someone else had left those gifts for Morgan.

I was more afraid yet of those visitants, seemingly invisible except to me. Had they really only been humans from Bossiney? If not, I had eaten their food. I had put myself under their power. It would be more dangerous still to speak of them.

And most of all, that bright May-morning, I was afraid of Morgan. Not, then, of the harm she might do me. Afraid, rather, of what she might not do. Afraid that the sweet gay smile that for the first time had seemed truly to come out of her heart for me, might never dawn again. I believed I had had a taste of Morgan's love that morning. I wanted more. I live my life now in her service. I have seen her bend that smile on others to enchant them. Morgan has never smiled like that for me again. Yet I cannot forget. I go on serving her, though love has curdled.

So I did not even listen to Bryvyth's warning.

Morgan met me stony-faced. She had not cried after her own beating. She never cried, this child who was not yet ten. I could see she despised me for weeping.

As the world judges, Morgan must count among the losers in life. She had lost father, home, her mother's love, even her life itself was threatened by Uther's ban. But she had this which marked her out from all other victims. She would not believe that she had lost. Long before she had an earthly crown she carried herself like a queen. She would not allow those who had power over her the satisfaction of seeing her cry.

We kept our own holiday on Tintagel. Bryvyth had made a play for the children. Saint George and his white Horse battled with the Dragon, and the saint got the victory. The princesses of Cymru looked unhappy. They are Dragon people. But the Horse-women of Cornwall shouted for the white Mare till the gulls took off into the air, screaming. Rathtyen looked disapproving of both sides. I shared her view. It was too like the old ways for Christian children to dress up in the masks and skins of beasts, and for nuns to beat the drums and play the pipes and cheer the swordplay. Morgan laughed and clapped harder than anyone when the white Mare rode down the Dragon and the saint's sword went through his heart.

The long day ended and we came together in my cell. That night I helped Morgan undress. There was no need for it. Morgan was accustomed now to care for herself. I had the charge of her soul but little thought for her body. I was not Gwennol.

Yet that night, I cannot say how it was, my hands reached for her clothes and drew them over her head. Her hair smelt of violets. Her flesh was warm from the day's sun. My hands lingered. Then I gasped as I touched the wounds on her back. They were as cruel as my own, and she was only a child. She did not speak, or pull away. It was not yet dark. Her face was still, without trace of movement, though her flesh had quivered at my touch.

I would not deceive you, seeming to mean more than I say. I wished to hold her, but I did not.

# Chapter Fourteen

Others stole Morgan from me.

We returned to our work, she to the school, I to the library. I missed her. I could not concentrate. The room that had been a haven of peace now imprisoned me. My desk did not allow me to see across the path. I listened for the sound of children's voices. The murmur of reading and the scratching of pens deafened me.

For months the bell that sounded the end of our labours had chilled me. I must put away the tasks I loved, the ordered world of books and figures, to attend to a violent, unpredictable child. This day it was different. I was like a dog pricking up its ears at its mistress's footsteps. At once I tidied away the abacus, the pens, the tablets. Eira was startled to see me move so quickly. I who was always so calm and dignified.

'What is the matter with you? Is it the flux? Too much fish for breakfast, perhaps?'

Her laughter was not malicious, but other sisters had enjoyed the knowledge that I was fallible, and had fallen from grace.

I did not answer her. I am never ready with repartee. I hardly understood myself the swiftness of my feet as I hurried from the library. I expected to see Morgan ahead of me on the path to our cell.

It was my rule that she should meet me there when the day's work was over. I would question her stiffly about the lessons she had learned. She would answer me easily, even scornfully. She was a clever girl. Already there were times when I learned from her some knowledge that my own late schooling had not yet opened to me. I tried to hide my ignorance from her. I did not wish her to think me less than her teachers. I do not think I deceived her.

Today she was nowhere to be seen ahead of me. I scanned the crowd of boys and girls running to play. Morgan with her raven's-wing hair was always noticeable. She was not with them.

A strange panic took me, such as they say a mother feels for her newborn baby. Had she been taken ill, and no one had told me? Eira was right. People had died after eating tainted food. Fool that I was to have trusted any gift that came from Bossiney!

Or was she well but in trouble, kept in the schoolroom by Rathtyen, to be summoned again to Bryvyth? But I saw Rathtyen climb slowly away from the school. I noted that she moved stiffly as though walking pained her. Well, the damp cliffs of Cornwall are the cause of many aches.

Morgan would be indoors, out of sight. I rushed into my cell. She had not been there. The door had been latched and her bed was still neat from the morning. I could not give a name to my agitation. Two days ago I would have feared only that she might be making more trouble for me. Now my fears were for Morgan herself. I cared.

Deliberately, trying not to be seen to hurry, I traced the twisting paths of the convent. They zigzagged to and fro across the cliff, rising to little terraces with clusters of cells, levelling out to larger buildings like our refectory, dipping to the shore or climbing to the fields on the summit.

I found her at last. Sitting on the doorstep of Fyna's cell. They were talking earnestly. You might have thought it was another lesson.

Fyna was a nun younger than I. She had come to the convent scarcely two years before. She came from the moors of Cornwall, of a druid family. That was not surprising. There were still some in Cornwall guarding their secret scholarship when the Romans left. They watched the power of the Church growing: the learning, the healing, the priesthood. Some of the wise among them made common cause with us and were baptised. It was natural that such a family should send a daughter to Tintagel to get wisdom and to give it.

Already Fyna was a noted herbalist. It was a science that made me uneasy. I was sharp of eye and accurate in matters of detail. I could quickly learn to identify plants for my needs. Rose madder, sphagnum moss, woad, all the plants we used to concoct paints and inks. But I did not enjoy the blending of precisely the right tint, as Eira did. It was enough for me that my ink was smooth and serviceable and I could get directly to my task. Still less did I like to think of brewing medicines, tasting, administering the measured dose. I should have been scrupulous in identification and apportionment of weights, but I would have feared the practice. There is gain, but there is also risk. The heart not merely stimulated but racing to destruction. A sleep too deep ever to waken. The poison that kills not only the disease but the diseased. Morgan knows I dread such work and therefore delights to make me do it now.

Fyna showed no such dread. Her face was smooth as a child's. Pink cheeks and clear blue eyes. Those eyes smiled at me now. Round, innocent. Why should they not be? Where was the harm in what they were doing? If her work in the infirmary was not heavy it was common for Fyna to turn from curing the sick to nursing the youngest children, little ones just taken from their families, home-sick and snivelling. She laughed with them and jogged them on her knee, and they played with the pretty hair that escaped from her veil. But Morgan was not a tearful infant, nor was she sick, unless you count the weals on her back. So I saw the two of them, heads bent together, with a start of anger. I did not recognise it then by the name of jealousy. I called her to me sharply. I did not notice that day if there were leaves and flowers on the step between them. There may have been. There may not.

Morgan came with me meekly. Fyna made no attempt to delay her. She only smiled at me, wider.

It was the first of many meetings. I could not prevent them. What could I have said? She talked with a nun who had taken the same vows as I had. She appeared earnest and attentive. She was not disobedient.

Next week it was Ughella, also recently come. She had taken my place with the cattle. Dark. Yellow-faced. But with a deep, bell-true voice. Already Bryvyth was planning to make her our cantor. She would lead us to glorify God with the beauty of her chanting. I found her singing to Morgan in the cow-byre. It was no hymn I knew, though they broke off before I came close enough to hear the words. Again they greeted me courteously, without resentment.

Another time, frantic with worry, I came upon her at last in the most unlikely place of all. The holy hermit Piala had made her cell in a hole in the rocks on the furthest point of Tintagel's cliffs, facing the wind. She came to the convent only to worship on Sundays. She ate almost nothing. Her body was angular, crippled by penances, her face deep-lined and gaunt, but luminous with the rigour of her rule and the intensity of her devotion. I did not admire her. Do not mistake me. I was punctilious in prayer, from the first thanksgiving when I awoke to the commending of my soul in sleep. I loved the order of the set forms of service, the common words sealing me into the great empire of the Church. But I felt no desire for contemplation. I was not one of those nuns who sat for hours perched on some distant rock, staring out at the sea and sky or stood waist-deep in cold water, praying.

Morgan was crouched outside Piala's cave, asking her questions, like the young Jesus at the feet of Gamaliel.

Once my first resentment was past, I began to understand this change in her. I could see the reason for her hunger for learning. She had no friend. Even her followers had dropped away from her after Howel's death. Tintagel was a close prison for a girl who had such a store of physical and mental energy. I even felt proud of my foster-daughter. I yearned for knowledge myself. No day was too heavy that I did not wish to fill my leisure hours with study. I despised play and gossip and idleness. I rejoiced to think that Morgan was becoming more like me, leaving the silly games of children for the serious company and wisdom of adults. It merely pained me to see her seek this help from others and not from me.

Yet I disguised my hurt humbly till the day I discovered she was going to Blatriad, our cook, and to others like her. Sisters of peasant stock who would never rise above the kitchen or the farm.

'Why?' I burst out. 'Why them? What in heaven's name can women like that teach you?'

Her face was sternly serious.

'Things that otherwise might be forgotten.'

I could not help myself. I had suffered the injury too long.

'Why always others? Why do you never want to learn from me?'

She seemed surprised, innocent, as only those who know how to wound can look.

'You? What could you teach me?'

It was like a slap in the face. Could even fat Blatriad have more to offer than I? I pulled out the book I was studying and thrust it under her nose. The theorems of Euclid.

'There! Has even Rathtyen taught you this? The logical proofs of the geometry of the plane? Listen. I will tell you the first hypotheses. All else flows from them, like a mighty river from a few small springs.'

For a little while she listened, blankly. Then she pushed the book out of my hands and grasped them.

'Where is the power in that? Will it change the world? What is the knowledge you really treasure, Luned?'

'What do you mean? This is the wisdom of the Greeks. The greatest philosophers of the East.'

'Games. Toys for idle minds. *Power*, Luned. Where is power to be found?'

I felt my blood quicken, as it did when they summoned me to bargain with a merchant at the gate, as it would when I tallied the yield of the coming harvest from all our farms and calculated our profit or loss. But how could I tell the child that? I, a nun, vowed to poverty and simplicity.

'Power is in the Word made flesh, in Christ's crucifixion, in his rising from the dead.'

Did I live by that?

What had Piala answered? And what had Blatriad?

From that day I found myself looking into my sisters' faces. I am not one to observe others. When we met together my eyes had been for the cross and the holy altar, or for my book. Nevertheless I came out of the oratory one day after the liturgy. It had been a night of storm but it was now a bright morning. We left the chapel two by two, in the order of our seniority. After Bryvyth came old Blatriad from the kitchen with Rathtyen. Younger nuns like Ughella and Fyna walked behind me. Yet on the path beyond the door this pattern dissolved, changed, reformed into different groupings. It was as if there were cracks running haphazardly through our community, separating some from others. I tried to make sense of it. Hens and eagles? Nobles and peasants? Foolish and wise? I could not determine the pattern.

Bryvyth was waiting for me with that broad, open grin of hers.

'Did you think you heard thunder in the night? They tell me there's another great slab of cliff fallen to the sea. One day we'll wake up and find we've lost the bridge that links us to the world. Do you want to come with me and inspect the damage?'

She knew I had never lost my terror of the heights.

It had been on the tip of my tongue to tell her what Morgan was asking. It was the abbess alone who held our community together, rejoicing in our differences, making them work for wholeness. How would Bryvyth have answered Morgan? But I would have to expose how little Morgan esteemed me, her soul-friend. I shook my head in confusion Bryvyth misunderstood.

She clapped me on the shoulder merrily.

'Why so green-faced, Luned? Are you afraid that next time the rock falls you'll be standing on the wrong side of the crack?'

# Chapter Fifteen

I expected it. I make no excuse of ignorance. I was brought up a country girl. A pagan. I had lived by the hinges of the seasons, though I tried to close my mind to those memories. I knew they would come again at harvest-time, that to them was Lughnasad. I held myself ready. Bryvyth had chosen me for this task. I was determined to fight this battle alone, and win.

I tried to hold them off by prayer. I kept vigil through the night, standing and prostrate. I knew Morgan was watching me.

That last night in July it scarcely grew dark. The sea seemed to hold the light, like a sheen of pearl. As I stared with heavy eyes and aching, lifted arms at the imperceptible paling of the sky, I knew that August had come. The blazing wheel would soon be on us.

There was a movement behind me. Quite slowly and deliberately, Morgan was pulling a tunic over her shift. This was the moment I had been armouring myself for.

'Go back to bed,' I ordered, my voice dry with praying.

She walked towards me. I barred the door with my body.

'I must go now.' Her voice was quiet, almost dutiful.

'I forbid it.'

I felt my blood beating faster. Power was rising in me.

Her hand came up and caught my arm. She tried to twist me aside. I was heavier than she was. We struggled in silence, save for the panting of our breath. I felt degraded, outraged that she had driven me to physical violence. But I was winning. I flung her back on to her bed.

At once I was frightened of what I had done. I backed away. She knelt and stared at me, but when she spoke her voice was almost pleading.

'I cannot help it. She is calling me. I *have* to go to her.'

Morgan was coming at me again. Panic was rising in me. Why did she not scream and shout? If only she would not fix on me that silent intensity, like a sleep-walker.

We sprang at each other. She wrestled savagely. This time I thought I would lose. My body was stronger than hers, but there was a spirit within her driving her to a frenzy. When I hurled her to her knees, we were both scratched and bruised. There was a lock of her hair in my fist. I could not remember pulling at it.

I watched her rise for a third time, unsteady, nursing her arm. In the faint light from the doorway I saw the red weals on her flesh, the mark of my fingers. My stomach twisted with sickness. This was not the fight I had planned.

She came closer. I could smell the sweet childish scent of her, and my own rank sweat. I fought for breath.

Her eyes looked up into mine. Shining, with a hint of tears.

'Go back to bed,' I panted.

'I cannot.'

There was a short step between us. She had not crossed it yet. She went on gazing at me as if she was waiting for something.

A great weariness came over me. How long must I go on fighting her? How much must I hurt her? I was not Bryvyth. I was not made to shout and spank and then hug her to my bosom.

Morgan still looked up at me. Tears started from the corners of her eyes and rolled down her cheeks. I do not know why.

She took my wrist, quite gently, and moved it from the door-frame. Still she stood waiting, as if I had disappointed her in some way. I felt humiliated.

'Let me come with you,' I muttered.

She gave a little sigh. 'You cannot help me.'

Yet she did not stop me. I followed her down the path in the grey silence before dawn. She went quite slowly. Once she stopped and looked up towards the furthest headland.

'I wonder if Piala is at prayer now.'

At the foot of the cliffs there is a natural ledge of rock. It is a good anchorage. Even when the gales sweep up the channel from the west, ships may lie safely there.

We stood without speaking on the wharf. That August morning the grey-green water of the cove was mirror-smooth. Beyond the rocks the waves were hardly moving. It had been a dry summer. There was hardly a wisp of vapour in the cove.

Morgan did not play games this time. She was not laughing.

Time passed slowly. It seemed to me that we had been hours abroad and still there was no colour in the sky. A fairy world. A fairy time.

I rubbed my eyes. The light was strengthening. I saw a single dot on the page of the ocean between the headlands. It might have been the head of a seal, but I knew it was not. I watched it, tense and troubled. With infinite slowness it became a coracle pulling into the cove.

There were two people in it. One of them rowing. A smaller hooded one hunched in the stern. I felt that all this had happened to me before.

'Help me, Luned,' said Morgan faintly.

But when I tugged at her arm I could not move her.

'Come away, quickly!' I urged. 'Let us run and tell Bryvyth.'

We had stayed too long. I had betrayed my trust.

The boat bumped softly against the wharf. An old woman's hand shot out of the fold of her cloak and clutched at the stone. Morgan shivered.

'What's the matter? It's only me, my lover. Come to Gwennol.'

Gwennol. The child's nurse from Bossiney, her arms clasped round Morgan as they parted in the guesthouse.

The woman was small and bent. She moved with difficulty. Why did I suddenly remember that day when the Pendragon's war-host had been ranged along the skyline? Why did I feel that Tintagel had been invaded?

'What have they done to you, my lamb? There's blood on your little face.'

Morgan's hand explored the scratches of our struggle. She stared at the stain on her fingers. But her other hand gripped mine. She had not stirred from where she stood.

I was never brave. But I call Heaven to witness that I used all my courage then. I cried out. 'This is a holy place. Go away and leave the child in peace.'

Throwing Morgan off, I heaved at the boat to push it out to sea.

The old woman caught my wrist, dragging me almost over the edge as the silent rower spun the boat back.

'Oh, yes! It's a holy place, and a holy day, and I'm a holy woman!'

I summoned all my piety and faith. I called on the threefold name of God to save us.

Gwennol heard me out. Then she raised her other hand towards me, her fingers spread and jabbing. I did not understand the words that poured from her, but in the depths of my being I recognised their purpose. They struck my hastily-constructed rampart of prayer a shuddering blow at its foundations. I was not always a Christian. I felt my faith collapsing into darkness.

She grinned and let me go. My wrist burned from the grip of her claws.

'Come here, my sweetheart.'

All this time Morgan had not moved. Then, as I reeled back, it seemed as if she could contain herself no longer. She dashed to the boat and grabbed at Gwennol.

'The baby, Gwennol? What news is there of Arthur?'

'Your little brother? He won't come back. His parents will never see him again, my lamb, don't you fret. Merlyn's got him safe and sound somewhere.'

'Not safe enough from me. Not safe enough from me forever. One day I shall find him. I will! I will!'

'There, there! Your time will come.'

The old crone murmured over her. The weeping stopped. Morgan was her small, proud self again.

'It'll soon be sun-up.'

The boatman's face was creased and brown as an oiled wood-carving. He settled to the oars and the coracle pulled out in widening rings of ripples. The first flush of pink was staining the eastern sky. When the boat had dwindled out of sight Morgan turned to me, mocking now.

'Let us run, Luned! We must not be late for prayers again, must we? It would never do for Bryvyth to catch us with this.'

Her hands were clasping a leather pouch.

# Chapter Sixteen

Morgan sat crosslegged in the bright morning sunshine outside our cell. As I came closer she put her hands over what was in her lap. It was a ritual gesture. She did not prevent me seeing what was in her skirt. A heap of twigs, each one different from the rest. Grey, tawny, knotted, smooth, even the sere stem of a reed. Some I could name easily, others more doubtfully. I did not know then the wisdom they spelt.

Morgan looked me full in the face, challenging me.

'Will you tell Bryvyth?'

For a girl of ten she read the minds of adults all too clearly.

I should have answered firmly 'Yes' and not prevaricated.

I could not disguise my scratches from Bryvyth, or Morgan's either. She looked us all over. Her keen eyes seemed to miss nothing. I was sure that what we had done must be transparent. I even felt relief that my failure would be unclothed without my needing to speak a word.

'Hm! I think the oats in the west field may be ready for cutting. I'll see you there.'

I was about to protest that this was a feast day. A rest from the regulation of the convent farms. Between the hours of liturgy I had a pile of books I wished to study. But there was something in the set of her jaw that kept me silent.

The ripe oats rustled against our skirts. Bryvyth tested the grains between her fingers absentmindedly. I knew that that was not why we were here.

'So Gorlois's kitten is not tamed yet. Is there something you should be telling me?'

As I climbed to the plateau my thoughts had been running around the walls of my mind, like a mouse looking for a hole through which to escape.

'An evil spirit visited her last night. I wrestled mightily against it.'

'And which of you won?'

'I never left her side. She cried to me for help. She held my hand. I called upon the name of the Trinity. At dawn the spirit left her.'

Could she not tell that I was begging her to see how I deceived her, speaking the truth, but not the whole of it? She was too open, too honest, too full of fight herself to understand the deviousness of others.

She threw her arms round me in one of her joyous hugs.

'Ah, Luned, girl! I did right, after all. Sometimes I've wondered if you're too pale and prissy for the fight I've given you. But I saw the mettle in you from the first. You came to us a peasant, but you had never a cowherd's mind. You were pagan-born, but you made a pilgrimage to the city of God. I knew you would not desert this battle until you had won.

'But I must see that hell-cat, Morgan. Gorlois's daughter she may be, rest his soul, but I will not have her wounding her foster-mother.'

We walked down the hill with the sun hot in our faces. Bryvyth was swinging along with her energetic stride. I think she relished the notion of combat.

Bryvyth failed me. She was my abbess. My mother in God. She had the care of my soul. She should have seen my inadequacy, my lying silence. She could have saved me.

Morgan did not betray me. She knew the victory was hers. I was under her power. She bore the birching in silence.

Even then I made one last struggle. I took those sticks from under Morgan's pillow. I feared to touch them. There were marks scored through the bark, stained with sap. They were like no figures or letters I had seen before. I took the wood to the kitchen fire. I even moved a turf aside and the red flame leaped out at me. But at the last I did not have the courage to drop those holy rods into the glowing charcoal. I knew it was my own fingers that would burn. I crept back to our cell, shaking at the thought of my impiety. I wrapped them in the pouch and hid them where I had found them. The scent of their sap clung to my hands long afterwards.

The boat came again to the cove where no strangers should land. To the beach that should be holy, but was too open to the world. Yet it seemed to me that they were not strangers enough to that place. I would have feared them less if they had been truly more of the common world outside. In their own dark way they were holier than I dared to admit to myself.

They came not once but many times. All Hallows Eve. Candlemas. May Day. But to them it was Samain, Imbolc, Beltaine.

I could not bring myself to wrestle bodily with Morgan a second time. It could only have ended one way, and I would have had to explain my scars again to Bryvyth. There must be no evidence against me. I ceased to fight with Morgan. I heard her rise from her bed. I let her go. I tried to pretend to myself that I could not stop her, that I was powerless to move, that the girl had laid a spell of binding on me. Perhaps she had. So I closed my eyes and listened to my foster-daughter slipping away into the half-light.

I feared to follow her. I was not strong enough to battle with those others. I lay defeated, shamed by my cowardice, while the sky lightened towards dawn and her bed beside mine grew cold. She would come tiptoeing back in the grey of morning with her feet wet and her white shift muddied and stop by my bed with a mocking smile. Always her hands were clasping some gift.

After a while my prayers shrivelled into silence. Perhaps the words had never really held a meaning for me. While she was gone, I even slept a little. I wished to close my mind to the truth. I did not want to lie awake and wonder what was being done on the shore.

I came to dread those festivals.

Yet Morgan was outwardly more dutiful than ever in the schoolroom and the chapel. She was getting taller now. I would watch the ranks of the convent schoolgirls where she stood, black-haired, white-faced, growing more beautiful with every month. Singing the words, but staring often out to sea.

For two years I did not confess my failure, through outward pride and inward humiliation. I did not pass the burden back to Bryvyth, who believed in Christ's power to save with her whole heart.

It brought me no thanks from Morgan. She despised me.

Then, one October night, the voices began again. This time it was clearly at Morgan's will. She was sitting up in bed, her fingers plaiting and unplaiting three hairy cords, that Gwennol had given her. She stared not at me but towards me, opened her sweet small mouth and began to chant.

At first it was her voice. Clear and hard. Then as her eyes burned in her head and her fingers flew faster the voice deepened, altered. It was a man, a beast, a baby, then things terrible, shapeless, not of this world or time. I clapped my hands over my ears. I shut my eyes. I sobbed for terror. When the room fell quiet and I dared to look up, she was sitting there. White. Rigid. Eyes fixed ahead as before. But not staring. Blank. No life in them. I nerved myself to touch her hand. She was cold. I panicked then. I shook her, threw my arms round her, hugged her, called, screamed. Then instantly hushed myself, trembling lest anyone should discover her so. I thought she was dead. I feared more that she was not. At last I tore my arms away. I threw myself into my bed and crawled under the blankets. I lay huddled there, curled like an infant, terrified.

When the long night had passed and I rose again with a stale taste in my mouth, Morgan was in her bed sleeping. The colour was back in her cheeks, like a wild rose. The breath eased gently from her lips and the tendrils of her dark hair curled over her neck. She looked very lovely, very young. You would have thought her innocent. There was a sharp contraction deep in my body and I longed to gather her in my arms and hug her again, this time for joy. Instead I shook her by the shoulder.

'It is time for morning prayers.'

Fear drove me to tell Bryvyth now. It was not duty. Not love for Morgan, or for Christ. I feared to be left alone with Morgan on Samain Eve. I spun a tale for Bryvyth. I recalled my past struggle with Morgan, as if it was a thing long done with. I said she had babbled something in her trance to warn me she might try to leave the convent that night. Bryvyth believed me.

On the eve of Samain she came to my cell. She was a big woman, and she looked stronger still, standing in the doorway against the yellow evening sky. My heart yearned towards her, and what she represented. If only I could always lean on her. If only I could rest from struggle and let the strength of those shoulders carry all my burdens. But I could not. She loved me for the strength she believed we shared, not for my weakness. I dared not disillusion her.

196

Together we did an awful thing. We bound Morgan. It took the full strength of both of us to do it. Her screams must have appalled the convent. She had never once cried out through a hundred beatings. But she raged against those ropes as though her heart would break. I was sick with the sound of her bitterness, and Bryvyth scarcely less so.

Neither of us slept. In the hour before dawn Morgan lay rigid. When I spoke to her she gave no sign of hearing. I was afraid to touch her. I was frightened lest the soul had gone out of her body and waking might kill her. She has that dangerous druid power now, and uses it. I was not certain if she had it then.

Bryvyth made me follow her down to the shoreline.

There was a circle of water, like glass, reflecting the cliffs. Beyond, a haze of autumn mist walled us in. It was very still, very quiet. I watched the coracle coming slowly out of the fog. It was so like my memory of the first time, I thought I might be dreaming it. I looked around to see if it was happening in reality or only in my own mind.

I could not see the slopes of Tintagel above us. No one but ourselves would know what passed.

Bryvyth stood on the beach, arms folded across her chest, silent. Her face was grim. It gave no flutter of recognition.

The coracle came on. I watched Gwennol's face now, brown, lined, fixed on Bryvyth's. Morgan was in my cell, bound on her bed. She could not be here. And yet she was. I saw her. The small body of a girl in a white shift, floating in the shallow grey-green water over the shingle. Black hair spreading slowly just beneath the surface, eyes closed, face pale as death, between those two grim women. They did not seem to see her, and yet she lay between them. They faced each other over her gently rocking body and still, drowned face. I watched in horror.

Then Bryvyth spoke. She lifted her hand above her head and made the sign of the cross.

'In the name of the great and glorious Trinity. By the power of the Father who created the thunder. By the strength of Christ who harrowed Hell. By the flame of the Spirit that drives out evil. Be gone forever.'

The boat checked. The rower was straining at the oars, but it would not move across the intervening water. Gwennol was murmuring curses of her own, too low for me to hear her, with a sound like the growling of a cat.

The surface of the cove began to shake. I saw a horrible thing. Morgan's face and form began to splinter and disintegrate. I think I screamed.

'Set one foot on this holy shore again and I'll have Uther Pendragon hound you out of your hole in Bossiney, cut out your tongue so you can cast no more spells, string you up on a sycamore tree till you're half-hanged and burn your body on your own bonfire.'

The mist crawled about us, thickened across the cove, crept round the boat. I could only see Bryvyth now, massive as a boulder, white-gowned against the dark mouth of a cave beyond her. Her fists were clenched.

197

'By the might of St Michael, who cast down the devils from high Heaven. By the fire of Patrick, who confounded the druids at Tara. By the sword of St George, who slew the dragon. Go to him who begat you!'

The waves broke on the stones with a hiss of foam. We could see nothing now but fog. Oars creaked, bumped rock, were still. Bryvyth and I waited, and the sweat was clammy on my face. Ages passed. The sun bored a hole through the mist over our heads. Tintagel Haven was empty again, its water like satin. The two of us were alone on the beach. Bryvyth was trembling.

When I staggered back to my cell, sick and spent, Morgan was still there where I had left her, her eyes closed, her face turned to the wall. I should have been overjoyed, confident that Bryvyth had won the victory. But all I could see was the blood on her wrists and the clenched knuckles of her hands.

# Chapter Seventeen

I undid the ropes. Morgan lay so still while my fingers fumbled with the knots, she might have been a block of wood. Yet her skin was hot where I could not help but brush against it. I was afraid of her vengeance.

I thought too highly of myself. I was nothing to her. I was not even worth a furious word. She darted past me into the open air. I feared she would dash for that terrible beach or even fling herself over the cliff into the sea. But she went skimming like a dark swallow up to the summit and over the meadow.

I ran after her. Nuns gathering before prayers turned their heads to stare. I was humiliated again. I saw the wasted years crumble to ashes. It was like that first day she came. Nothing had been gained.

But I was wrong. I had not guessed where she was going. Her flight ended at the very edge of the headland, the cave of Piala the hermit. When I came close Morgan was gasping out her story between sobs. Piala speaks rarely but she talked with Morgan then. I did not hear her words.

Bryvyth came striding up behind me, panting. We watched the two, girl and woman, prostrate themselves on the damp cliff-edge among the gorse.

'Leave them alone,' Bryvyth said, 'but watch her.'

All day I sat, a chill sentinel. When the chapel bell rang I mouthed the psalms. I was numb with cold. Bryvyth herself brought me food and drink. Morgan took nothing. She and Piala had not moved from their attitude of prayer.

Bryvyth muttered, 'It is not natural for a girl of twelve. It's either a saint or a sorceress we've got on our hands.'

Why did she give Morgan to me?

I was strict with myself. I rose before dawn. I kept the fasts. I was exact in every observance. But I did not lacerate my body as the hermit did. It disturbed me to think of Morgan's white flesh lying there in the wind, pierced by thorns of furze.

Thick cloud shortened the November day. Piala rose at last. I felt the pain as Morgan staggered to her feet.

I thought she would come home with me then. But she began to walk quite slowly along the cliffs. I followed her. For a while she stood, gazing over the bay towards Bossiney. Then she started to clamber down towards the shore, not by any path the feet of nuns had made, but climbing over boulders and slithering down the grass.

Fear was rising in my throat, physical dread of the steep drop beneath me, anxiety as to what she intended. The tide was high. Mounds of dark water heaved over the rocks. Morgan had hitched her skirt up round her hips. In the dying light she was searching frantically. I saw her disappear into the huge mouth of a cave. I heard her cry of triumph.

I met her on the treacherous wet rock outside. There was something in her hands. She did not try to hide it. I forced myself to look. A bundle of herbs and roots, tied with a scarlet thread. And I had thought we had won!

What I did next was rash. I am intelligent but my mind works slowly and with calculation. Any actions I make in haste are usually at fault. I tried to snatch the evil gift from her. She resisted me. We struggled on the slippery rocks. There could only be one end. She had spent her childhood running wild along the shore under the too-indulgent eye of her nurse. I grew dizzy over the smallest height. Stiff, awkward in my physical movements, I slipped, skidded, scraped my knees painfully over the rocks and plunged into deep, cold water.

Morgan did not rush to save me. I was not Gwennol staggering on the edge of the bridge between Tintagel's nuns and Uther's army. She let me fall, and did not stay to see whether I drowned.

I could not swim. Why should I ever have learned such a thing? I gasped and choked on salt water and terror. I clung to the rock, rasping my fingertips as I clawed for a hold. But it seemed the sea wanted me no more than Morgan did. Breakers tore me from my hold, washed me forward, engulfed my despairing head. Then they cast me up, scornfully, on the sloping shingle. I crawled to shore, all the wet weight of my woollen gown bearing me down, and the water running in rivers from my sodden hair.

Morgan had gone.

I staggered back to my cell, avoiding the paths. I hauled myself up grassy slopes hidden from view, with the sick knowledge of the drop growing beneath me. I was sobbing with shame and cold and shock.

Morgan was not in the cell. I was almost witless now, and shivering. Her presence would have terrified me yet her absence chilled me more than my wet clothes. So far was I under her influence, that waif of twelve years old, that I could do nothing but sit huddled on my bed, towelling myself as the twilight deepened and the owls began to call.

She came at last, with a puckish smile on her face. Her hands were cupped around a small clay pot which gave off a sickly steam.

She set it down on the floor and put her arms round me. I trembled at her touch. Her voice was like honey.

'Poor Luned. You're cold and shivering. Sip this. It will warm you.'

I retched at the smell of the brew she was carrying to my lips.

'Drink some. I must know what it does.'

I turned away and clenched my teeth. One does not take that sort of gift from Morgan.

She smiled, her teeth like white pearls in the twilight.

'Silly Luned! What are you frightened of? If you were to die and Uther heard of it, he would have me burned, wouldn't he? Well, never mind. There are two sick cows in the byre, poor things. Better to test its power on one of them.'

She was gone again. Without the ropes I had no power to hold her. The smell of that brew lingered in the room. I shuddered. Two of our best milch-cows were ailing. I had summoned Fyna to dose them. I had even turned to old Blatriad's memory for help. But the beasts still hung their heads in their stalls, nostrils dribbling, coughing mournfully. Cattle are valuable.

When she came back she threw her arms around me and kissed me gaily. I had longed for that for two cold years. But it gave me no pleasure now. It was as if a snake had coiled itself about me.

I woke next morning to find her shaking my shoulder.

'Quick, Luned! Wake up. Do you have a wax tablet? A scrap of parchment? I need to write.'

'Don't be silly. Those things are kept in the library or the schoolroom. I do not have a store of them in my cell.'

She slipped in bed with me. Her arms twined round my neck.

'Please, Luned. I must set it down before I forget.'

I wondered at her insistence. Was it a poem that had come to her suddenly, like the ones that Cigfa scribbled in the margins of her books? Or a dream that had visited her in the night which she must catch?

I felt my body quicken strangely at her urgency. I pushed her away from me with the horror of what I could not name. She made a face and was off again in the dawn light. I hurried after her to the door. Would she steal what she wanted from the library now, as she had the bowl last night from the kitchen? But she was coming back already. Tintagel is rich in flat grey slates. She carried one in her hand. Swiftly she scratched characters on it, a growing list.

I looked over her shoulder. She made no move to conceal her work. It was a catalogue of those things she had used last night. Their names, the quantities, her method of preparation.

She smiled at me wickedly.

'What is the matter, Luned? Do you want to be wise?'

I should have destroyed it. Or taken it to Fyna, to see what she knew of such things. Or told Bryvyth. I did none of those things. I feared to touch that piece of slate, as though the words themselves held the same dangerous power as the things they recorded. Just so, we felt a sense of the holy when we handled our Gospel books reverently. I said nothing.

I feared Bryvyth's censure. Younger nuns were entering the convent. Rosslyn had come into the library after me. Quickly she learned to mix the inks and paints, to prepare the wax tablets. Now she was learning to write a fair hand. In a few years she would be copying Latin and Greek. She would be scraping vellum to cut the pages of her first Psalter. Even the blessed Gospels might be hers to beautify one day.

Not mine. I would never pen the Gospels now. I had made myself too useful. I saw that sisters who could turn a capital letter into a fancy of nature, who could trace the convolutions of a spiral and embroider in silver, who could talk easily of Aristotle and Augustine, could still be daunted by rows of figures and the clicking of the abacus.

I had a gift for such things. I went little to the library now, even for the worldly tasks allotted to me. I must be often in the gatehouse bargaining with the men who came to buy and sell. I, who for shyness had once shunned the company even of women. Or walking about the farm and the drying-ovens and the kitchen, counting what stores we had. Or riding out in a chariot to collect the convent rents. Endlessly fingering the beads of my abacus. Tintagel had made me its Judas. The keeper of their purse. Strangely, I no longer minded or thought of the ambition I had lost. I had seen that this was another road by which to ascend. Wealth is power. No one in the convent understood that better than I. I must make no mistake.

Helpless, I observed the progress of the two sick cows. One of them recovered, but the other worsened, staggering now, and blind. One dark December day I watched it die, vomiting blood. I thought how Morgan had held that bowl to my lips.

I accused her.

'The dun cow is dead.'

She stared at me blankly. Her eyes widened with shock then grew brilliant with tears.

'It was not my fault. I had only enough of the herbs of power to heal one of them. And Uther will never allow me outside to gather more, will he?'

I stood staring at her foolishly, with my mouth hanging open, as I struggled to grasp the altered meaning of what I had seen in the byre.

# Chapter Eighteen

I thought that Bryvyth's defences held. The boat came no more to the cove in the grey time between night and morning. I slept more soundly than ever before. When I woke at daybreak, Morgan was in her bed.

I watched her grow in stature and in learning. Her mind was never idle. She piled up knowledge from anyone who could give it, with an insatiable hunger. Yet she had times of bodily stillness like no other child.

From the outside Tintagel looked a poor, plain place. Small huts. Low roofs. A standing stone marked with the sign of Christ. But inside, our little chapel glowed with beauty. Painted walls and ceiling, gold and silver sparkling on the altar in the candlelight, rich embroidered hangings for the sanctuary. In the school the girls learned fine sewing. Morgan herself was an expert embroideress. Our work was sent far and wide to deck churches and monasteries across the west. We nuns matched the work of monks, but they had little skill at ours.

There was plain sewing too in plenty. Making, mending. When the hardest labour of the day was over the nuns would often gather on summer afternoons, sitting on turf and boulders with their sewing in their laps, while one of them, Rathtyen perhaps, read to us some holy story. Though the younger children ran at liberty, the oldest pupils, those who were now young ladies in their own eyes, would come and sit around us with their own stitching. Morgan was one of those now, diligent, deft, almost silent in company. What did she think as she listened to the stories of prophets and apostles, virgins and martyrs, as her fingers embroidered the monogram of Christ?

When the telling was over there would be a sigh of satisfaction. We knew ourselves to be part of that story. The nuns would sew on in silence, with the breeze whispering in the drying grass and the waves washing against the rocks below us. But the girls would fall to chattering. Sometimes their voices would drop low, and there would be a sudden burst of laughter, quickly hushed. The nuns would frown at them for wantonness. We had all been girls ourselves. Well we knew of talk it is not fit for nuns to hear. We had not forgotten all of that.

Our pupils came from the noblest in the land. Tintagel had a high reputation for the fostering of girls. Morgan was not the only king's daughter. She always claimed the name of princess, for all she hated her stepfather Uther.

This pride did not go uncontested. The other girls would come back from the feasts of Christmas and Easter bursting with tales of great halls full of lords and ladies, of gifts exchanged, of mountains of rich food. Their eyes would turn to Morgan in her simple student's gown, sewing with her eyes downcast, within earshot. They would nudge each other as they looked across at her.

Giggling now, and growing red by turns, they would tell of wild young noblemen who raced each other after the boar, of wrestling and swordplay on the greens outside their fathers' forts, of compliments over the wine-cups and poems sung to the harp.

These girls were destined for marriage soon, perhaps for crowns. And Gorlois's daughter?

'Well, Morgan? Where did you go for the feast of Pentecost? They tell me Uther Pendragon wore his crown in Winchester?'

'Indeed he did, Talwyn, for I was there. Such a hosting of noblemen and women you never saw. I did not notice Morgan.'

'Ah, I was there too. And I saw her sisters. The Queen Elaine with King Nentres and Queen Margawse with King Lot.'

'Is it true that Margawse has four children already? Two boys and two girls?'

'Yes. And another coming by the look of it!'

'And you, Morgan. When will you get married? What handsome young king is Uther Pendragon keeping up his sleeve for you?'

And they burst out laughing.

What could she answer, Morgan, who never left Tintagel, who was not free to run along the beach or gallop on her pony after the stag, who was allowed no sight in all these years of her mother and sisters, who must be kept close, confined, guarded, living in a world of white virgins? Prayer, books, sewing, sleep, that was all her life. Plain convent food. Her parents never sent her gowns or gifts, jewelled girdles, trinkets for her hair. She went dressed sober as a nun, in things of Bryvyth's choosing. Uther had given rich gifts to the convent for keeping her safe. But for Morgan's own use, only the bare essentials. I knew, I kept the tally of the spending.

'Morgan's not going to get married, are you, Morgan? She's going to be a nun.'

'A hermit, like Piala!'

'Morgan, a nun! Holy Mother Morgan!'

The colour darkened in Morgan's face and went again. She made no movement. There was no sudden jerking of her needle. No spot of blood on the white linen to betray her.

'My father says that Uther Pendragon may not be high king much longer. The Saxons will overrun half Britain soon.'

'*My* father would strike dead a man who said that in his hall, however high his name.'

'Well then, why was the crown-wearing not in London this time?'

'The roads are too dangerous in the east.'

'You see? My father says Britain was not like that in Ambrosius's day.'

I watched Morgan's needle pause. The wicked, shiny point sticking up through the cloth. She would endure the insults to herself as unflinchingly as she did blows. But this taunt was to the honour of her family. It was a cruel catch. She hated Uther, and yet the glory of the Pendragon's crown reflected on her.

She said in the low fierce voice I always dreaded, 'Uther Pendragon will not allow the traitors to take one foot more of Britain.'

There was an astonished silence. Then a wave of laughter.

'What do you know about it?'

'When did you last see your royal stepfather?'

'Did a chough tell you that? Or a puffin?'

'No! The mackerel bring her messages down the coast!'

They all laughed so noisily that the nuns tried to hush them.

Then Whecca hissed very low, 'My father says that there are kings in the north who never wanted him for over-king.'

'Yes. His own sons-in-law. Morgan's sisters' lords, Lot and Nentres.'

'I've heard that at the next council they're going to challenge him to put off the crown of Britain.'

'What's left of it!'

'You know what's wrong? Why he keeps losing battles?'

'No. Why?'

'My mother says there's a curse on Uther Pendragon. He married into a family that was too wise. The witches have got him in their claws.'

The stares turned sideways again at Morgan, but not so mockingly. There was a little more fear in their looks now.

'How do you know?'

'Well, it's obvious, isn't it? A good-looking man like him. And what has the Queen Ygerne given him? Nothing. If he falls, there isn't a son to follow him.'

Morgan jumped to her feet then, throwing the linen cloth with the crosses on to the grass.

'There is! There is! How dare you say that? He has a son!'

'What do you mean?'

Their mouths fell open. Had they really not heard the story? Was it a secret to the rest of Britain what Morgan had done? Why she was here?

'He has a son! If Uther falls there will be another Pendragon. A better one. To rule over Britain and drive the Saxons from our shores. My brother . . .' and her breath caught on the name '. . . Arthur!'

A little silence. And then the laughter again, more uncertain now.

'That baby?'

'He died long ago.'

'They say the fairies took him.'

'There was a magician, wasn't there? Merlyn, he was called, or some such name.'

'That was ages ago.'

'He's in the Isles of the Blest now.'

'He isn't! He isn't!' Morgan raged at them. 'Don't say that. Don't you ever dare say that to me again! He's alive. Merlyn has hidden him somewhere. I know he has. You'll see! One day you'll see!'

And she raced away from us.

I followed her. She was not in my cell. I found her at last on the southern ledge where Howel had died. She had flung herself face downward on the earth. Sobbing, with her fists beating the grass.

The gulls swung in the sky. We could see nothing of the convent from here. Only the grave-mounds across the water where her father lay.

I sat beside her, saying nothing. I dared not touch her. I think I prayed then for her, with a rare sincerity. Not for myself, that I might rise higher through victory over her. Not in fear lest I should be brought down by her wickedness. But, simply, on that afternoon, for the girl herself, weeping into the earth as though her heart would break.

Such moments do not last.

She grew quiet, sat up and saw me. At once she was on her feet, tightening her girdle, brushing the evidence of tears from her cheeks. She walked ahead of me, back to the convent.

She stopped by the standing stone, with her eyes fixed on mine as though she swore an oath.

'They are right. Uther must die. He is no fit king. He cannot heal the land. I am his daughter now. They must make me queen of Britain.'

My question was cruel.

'And Arthur?'

Very steadily she answered me, as though this was something she had thought about many tines.

'If he consents, we shall rule together, as equals. Sword and scabbard. The earth in balance. If he opposes me, I shall destroy him.'

# Chapter Nineteen

Bryvyth had set me to play the part of a mother to Morgan. I, that
never had warmth in my heart for children, that had chosen to
come to Tintagel because more than any other place in the world it
offered me the life of a man. I was ill-fitted for my task.

One night I stood as usual, arms raised in prayer. Outside, the autumn
twilight was just beginning to thicken. Morgan was undressing beside
me. The darkness in our cell should have been no hindrance to her.
It was long since she had known the helping hands of her nurse. But
now she dropped her nether garment to her feet and stood feeling
awkwardly under her shift.

'Have you got fleas? Don't scratch yourself. You'll only make it
worse.'

She stood examining her fingers.

'Say your prayers and get to bed,' I urged her. 'You looked pale
at supper. I'll help you cut clean bracken for your mattress tomorrow
and burn the old.'

I was not really tired, and I cared little if she was. It was the quiet
hours ahead I valued, before that deep sleep claimed me. But as she
stood gazing at me out of the dark hollows of her eyes, I felt compelled
to break off my prayers and smile at her. She was sixteen now. She
had left the wild mischief of her childhood behind her. I believed my
patient forbearance had succeeded, where Bryvyth's beatings and
Rathtyen's harsh words had not.

I say I did not love children. I never thought of Morgan as a child,
even from the first. She was always herself.

I cannot think now how I deluded myself. I knew what lay under
the mattress of bracken I talked of lifting. Those secret gifts of
Gwennol's, notes of spiritual counsel from Piala, philosophy from
Rathtyen, country-women's lore from Blatriad. A hoard of knowledge,
holy and unholy, all mixed together in a dangerous ferment.

I believed I had tamed her. And now I was in sight of my reward.
Rathtyen had aged suddenly, as though she was being consumed by
an inner sickness. We had all assumed that she would take Bryvyth's
place when that deep-rooted oak fell at last. Rathtyen was a little the
younger of the two, the grey only just beginning to invade her hair
until just lately, when all of a sudden it turned white and sparse. She
had been straight-backed, ferociously intelligent, naturally quick of
movement, but holding herself in by a stern discipline. She was known
to be holy, fasting more than our rule demanded, learned, yet always
hungry for new books brought from afar, hard of hand and voice

towards the schoolgirls, yet spending her days utterly in their service. Now she could hardly haul herself from cell to schoolroom, though she moved more eagerly to the chapel than anywhere else. The keen light of her eye was dimming and the voice croaked as if the words came with effort.

I knew it weighed down Bryvyth, who had had such faith in her. The abbess's own hair was white now, and the wrinkles deepening in her wind-brown face.

Another successor must be found and trained. And who else was there in all Tintagel with a mind, a rule of life, a gravity to equal mine? Already I had all the affairs of the convent under my control. I had scholarship in plenty, though I did not often frequent the library nowadays. I kept my body strictly disciplined. I was constant in prayer and confession of minor faults. I preached abroad now like Bryvyth herself. My public difficulties with Morgan were things of the past. My private struggles no one knew.

Bryvyth loved me.

I could dream now of esteem far higher than I might have had in the book-room with the mere delight of making beauty. What did Cigfa or Eira know of the world outside Tintagel? I could taste power. I had much to pray for that night, plans to make. The picture of myself for Bryvyth's eyes must be painted exactly right in every detail. I wished Morgan asleep.

Still the girl had not moved.

'Morgan?'

'I . . . I need clean linen.'

I must have been sleepier than I thought. Or more elated at the thought of Rathtyen's decline. I was slow to understand her meaning.

'You haven't taken the flux, have you? Two of the girls are in the infirmary with it. Let us pray it is not the blackwater sickness.'

'No. It isn't that.'

Her voice was subdued, unlike her usual tone of command.

I lowered my arms stiffly and bent to her in the narrow space between our beds. I could see only the glimmer of her shift in the dark now. But my hand found the linen at her feet. It was warm and wet. I sniffed at it reluctantly and the thick, sweet smell of blood told me the truth.

I felt a rush of heat and confusion cover my own body. Believe me, I had never prepared myself for this moment, still less her. I spoke rapidly, reining in my disgust.

'Oh,' I said. 'So you've started with *that* at last, have you? We shall have to find you a binder. I'll let you have one of my own for tonight, and in the morning we must ask Nessa to give you linen of your own. You'll need to wash them yourself, and privately. You're a grown woman now.'

Strange how close we could live to each other and still keep our secrets. Never once had I let her see the evidence of my own blood-time.

I busied myself in the chest at the foot of my bed and found my hands were trembling. This was no fitting task for a half-woman like me. I was chaste, virginal. I had chosen to put away from me all that side of life. I had not wanted it. It irked me even now that I could never free my body from womanhood as I had freed my spirit. I had heard it whispered that hermits who live on bread and water cease to bleed because of their holiness, but I could not bring myself to ask questions about such things.

How many years was it since I had first seen with fear the signs of blood on my own thighs? My mother had taken me into the orchard away from the younger children and told me what little she thought I needed to hear. I know now – oh, to my sorrow I know – how much more she could have told me.

But who was there to tell Morgan even that little? I could not nerve myself to do it. Not there, in Tintagel, in the holy women's stronghold. To speak of men and their bodies, and our secret places. Better to keep to the mathematics of the moons and the necessity of laundering linen.

When I had made her clean and comfortable again she lay down to sleep. But even in bed she was restless. The mattress rustled as she turned. Suddenly she sat up and her voice cried through my waking dreams.

'At last I am a woman in body as well as years! I am truly a woman! Merlyn said that when that happened the whole of Britain would fear me. They can't keep me here now, can they? Uther will have to give me my freedom. It isn't true what the others said, is it? He couldn't make me be a nun. He couldn't force me to be like you, could he, Luned?'

Her desperate words cut at my newly-swelling pride.

'Little a girl like you knows what she is despising. I am what I am here by my own choice. And I shall be greater yet. Go and be a queen like your sisters, if you like. Become the mother of drunken warriors. I have put all that behind me. Jewels and swords are not everything. I shall be more than you. I shall be abbess after Bryvyth. The high priest of my own tribe. I shall counsel kings.'

'Oh, Luned, Luned! What kind of power is that? Aping men. You only want this life because it's what men have. The real power is over men. My mother taught me that. Uther never took her from my father. She captured him. She used *this* to get what she wanted. Margawse told me.'

She grasped my hand and, dragging it across, thrust it down between her legs. I felt the moist, thickening ooze between my fingers and struggled to get free of it.

'Is this where power is, Luned? Is it? Is it?'

I pulled myself away from her grip, sickened and defiled by what I had touched.

'Stop it! I want no part of that. I am a holy virgin.'

In the darkness I could not see where my hands were spreading the blood.

'Holy virgins!' She laughed high and wild. 'Nuns! You can tell me that, here in Tintagel, of all places. Oh, poor, ignorant Luned!'

I tried to close my ears against her and clenched my soiled hands in prayer.

Then her voice dropped, fierce and low. 'No. You are right. They are holy. What is done here is holy. Above and below. It is not of the common world. It is not to be done carelessly, crudely, in a drunken stupor. That is not how I shall use my power.'

I would not answer her. It was terrible to me that a maiden like that, who had lived seven years within the walls of a convent, should lie in the darkness plotting how she would join her body to a man's.

She went on whispering in the dark.

'I do not want to be like Margawse. I think I am too like you, after all. However I use this power, I shall always keep my true self to myself. No man shall ever enter that most secret place of all inside me. Except perhaps one.

'But I must tell Gwennol my gift has come. I promised I would. You needn't have blushed and stammered so, my poor tongue-tied Luned. Gwennol taught me all that before I ever came here. And much more besides. Things you wouldn't ever dream of.'

'You will have no more dealings with Bossiney. You know that boat never comes here now. Bryvyth has exorcised the evil from Tintagel.'

Morgan yelped with laughter.

'That's what you think! I should have gone mad in this place if Gwennol had really left me. She will show me what I must do next.'

'You cannot tell Gwennol. I forbid it. You must not communicate with her.'

Alarm was growing. For myself, not for Morgan. For the precarious castle of my ambition.

She rolled over so that her face came close to mine.

'Must not, Luned? Can't I tell her? You will see. Before long, all Britain shall know I have come to my womanhood.'

210

# Chapter Twenty

I went to Bryvyth in the morning.

'Morgan is a woman now,' I said.

'Is she indeed? And is that a reason to drag me out of doors before the sun is through the fog? Why shouldn't she be? Did you think it never happened to princesses? In law she's been an adult these two years past.'

Yet she folded her arms and hugged herself as if the autumn chill troubled her and walked away from her cell to the edge of the cliff. She stood gazing down, though we could see nothing, only the clouded air darker beneath us. Even the sea was noiseless, as it often was in the early morning.

'You'd think we were a thousand miles away from kings and wars. Not in the thick of the fight. A different king. A different battle. But the wounds cut just as deep. And now there is blood.'

'She says she cannot stay here. Will the king set her free and find her a husband now?'

Lips stiff and difficult, as though these were not my words.

'Uther will not do that, and well you know it, or we'd have been rid of her long ago. And do you know why?'

'Because she tried to kill her baby brother, Uther's son. But that was long years past. She was a little girl then.'

'Was that one ever a little girl? Oh, you don't deceive me as much as you think you do, Luned! She's not like other girls, is she? How could she be, the way her father died, the way the boy Arthur was got?'

'You think Uther fears her still?'

I did not find that strange.

'Uther! At Tintagel we play for higher stakes than crowns and forts. Kings come and go. Morgan must fight an older enemy than him.'

I heard the waves begin to swish beneath me.

'Whom?' I said, my tongue dry.

'It was Uther sent her here, in a fit of rage. But tempers cool. I doubt that man would have had the wit to keep up his guard against her so many years, unadvised. She is kept here by the will of one stronger than the king of the Britons.'

'Who? The Pope? The Emperor in Constantinople? For Morgan?'

She had the sense to laugh.

'Oh, Luned, Luned! You walk about with your eyes downcast, but the eyes of your soul look too high. Do you think I'm afraid of armies of men or bishops' croziers? You're too holy to see the darkness under your nose here, in these very stones. It's Merlyn I'm thinking of.'

211

Merlyn. The fey magician of the tales. Soul-friend to Uther once, when Arthur was got. Now lost with that child.

'You believe he's still alive? And *he* fears Morgan would kill the boy yet?'

She took my hand and pointed where the mist was lightening in the cove. A shadow was growing out of it, a familiar darkness, upward-thrusting.

'Do you see the rock? It was there, Luned. On a night of storm, while we lay here in our beds or stretched in prayer, a little girl stood on that very rock with the waves dashing round her and her baby brother in her arms. How could she not have drowned both of them? But she did not. She held him safe. Think on that, Luned. Think on it very well. Is this what Merlyn fears? Not that Morgan would kill Arthur if once she found him, but that she could not? It is in my mind that he may fear her love more than her hate. And so he works to keep them apart.'

The bell rang suddenly, summoning us to chapel. But Bryvyth, always the first to obey her master's call, did not turn yet.

'Why, Luned? Why did she bring him here to Tintagel Haven?'

'To drown him, I thought.'

'I have said she did not. Why? Why are they all drawn here? The unclean brood: Ygerne, Morgan, Gwennol, Merlyn. Yes! He was here that night when Arthur was begot. The shape-shifter, Merlyn, here, in our Tintagel itself!'

She was striding back to the chapel now, anger evident in every step.

'Are we never to be rid of them, then? Was I wrong? Is the place not clean yet?'

She stopped abruptly. Her eyes were on my face. I never found it easy to have Bryvyth look at me so boldly. I could not meet her gaze.

'Watch Morgan. As you love her and Christ, watch her. This is her dangerous time, when her dreams have power. There is something in these stones yet which is warring for her. We have come to the battle for her soul. But we shall win it, by the grace of Christ and his virgin Mother. We shall win it yet, you and I! Only tell me if you learn something strange, if there is anything you hear which I should know. Sometimes I think I've brought us to another world entirely here. A different time. Especially when the mist walls us round like this. I chose a dangerous place when I carved my cross here on the enemy's heart. Faith can be rash as love. There are nights when it is heavy on me that I may have endangered weaker souls. Is there anything at all you should have told me?'

She was offering me another chance. I should have told her then. I should have fallen on my knees and confessed everything. The gifts hidden on feast-days. The little pile of scratched slates under her mattress. The cow that sickened and the one that lived. The voices in the dark. I knew I needed Bryvyth's help. I needed her joyous strength. I needed the stronghold of her prayers.

But how could I tell her this now? How could I confess that all these years I had concealed the truth from her?

**Rathtyen** was dying.

'No,' I lied. 'I'm just afraid of what she may do if we have to keep her here.'

'Hm! I've been afraid of that ever since she crossed that ditch. But we're winning, aren't we? It was a bitter struggle at first, but it seems you're taming her. I've almost forgotten the feel of a birch in my hand.'

I bowed my face as we entered the chapel. The chance of help had passed. I had elected to fight this battle alone. But fight it I would, this time. And I must win. My abbess should not be ashamed of me.

Bryvyth did not dismiss Uther Pendragon entirely from her hopes. She wrote a letter. The two of us walked the short path to Bossiney. In all my years at Tintagel, in all my roaming the roads with a preaching staff in my hand, in all my rides round the farms gathering wealth for the convent, I had never ventured inside the walls of Uther's dun. I remembered how I had trudged past it as a green girl, on my way from Devon to Tintagel for the first time. It had been Gorlois's dun then, Morgan's home. I had thought its inhabitants had nothing to do with me.

I felt the high tower of the gate diminish me. I was conscious of how low I had been born and where I had come from. This was a royal dun now. But I followed the sweep of Bryvyth's stride into the yard and my pride rose again.

Uther had not been there for years, or Ygerne either. Cornwall held too many uncomfortable ghosts for the pair. The place had a rundown, slipshod air, the thatch ragged, dogs scavenging for scraps, slaves gossiping idlehanded, a few old warriors nodding over a chessboard.

Ulfin, Uther's close friend, had been made lord of Bossiney. The name leaped in my throat, a name from long ago. On the night that changed the course of Tintagel, and of Britain, he had been one of those three. An armed man, dangerous, unholy, in the heart of our convent. He had come in the guise of Jordan, Gorlois's bodyguard, the night that had tricked us and robbed Morgan of so much. Ulfin. Uther. Merlyn.

It was no wonder that Bryvyth's nuns kept their skirts away from Bossiney.

Seven years since, but I remembered him. He looked older now. Older than you would expect for a man who had been a laughing young warrior the morning after that shape-shifting. Had Uther aged so much? And Merlyn too? Was this the price of submitting their faces to magic?

Bryvyth gave him the letter.

'See that it reaches the high king within this moon. I stood security once for his stepdaughter, but not forever. She's a grown woman now. Let the Pendragons look to their own.'

A shadow haunted his face.

'Uther Pendragon has bitterer news than a woman to wrestle with.'

'Are the Saxons getting the upper hand in Britain? Man! Did he think that God would bless his banners after the way he fouled our holy house? Is he such a fool? He looked to other powers than Christ to aid him then. Can they not drive the heathen longships back? Is Merlyn's craft too feeble to rescue Britain?'

'I'm a soldier. I spoke of Uther, not of Merlyn.'

'Pah! Uther? Merlyn? Are they two or one? Can Uther Pendragon ever break free of that soul-friend?'

'You know that Merlyn has not been seen these seven years.'

'Not seen? Or not recognised?'

He had the grace to blush at that.

The old men outside the hall raised their heads listlessly. Men that had won their fame in Ambrosius's time and lost it in Uther's.

An old woman hobbled out of one of the huts and stared at us. I started, and so did she. I saw her hand raised and the fingers spread towards us. She mouthed a string of words we could not hear. Bryvyth saw her too. She did not flinch, as I had. She drew the sign of the cross in front of us like a trusty shield.

'It's you, Gwennol Far-Sight, is it? Still alive to haunt us.'

'So Morgan's blood-time has come, you say?'

I think I gasped. I do not know what I had dimly feared, or how and when I thought Morgan might meet and tell her this. The truth was crueller. There was no need now. I had carried the news to her myself. Morgan had had her way. That thing that is most private to women, that should not be talked about, was no secret now to all Dumnonia. Morgan's womb had bled. The heat burned in my cheeks.

Gwennol nodded. Her bright robin's eyes searched our faces.

'So there's blood in our cup stronger than yours. You can't hold her. My little maid will never be the bride of your Christ.'

She turned and shuffled away.

'Do not blaspheme the Lord!' Bryvyth called after Gwennol. 'If a silver coin is lost, God is the housewife who will sweep the floor until she finds it. She will show it to her friends with great rejoicing.'

The witch disappeared through a doorway as if she had not heard. Bryvyth gripped my arm roughly. 'Be strong! Have faith.'

It was in my mind to say that Gwennol did not speak like one who had faith or hope, but as if she saw the future. I was too well-disciplined to voice my thought aloud.

214

# Chapter Twenty-one

Morgan was clean again. She knew of Bryvyth's letter. The news was whispered among all the girls. There was a bright excitement on her now, as though hope dawned at last. Every morning she brushed her hair till it shone glossy black as a chough's wing, and her green eyes glittered like the sea. As the days of October darkened around us, my own thoughts turned to chilblains and mud and drenching winter gales. But Morgan flowered like an opening rose.

As I watched her beauty blossom, panic clutched my heart. If Uther relented, if Morgan left us, I should never in all my life see her again. Hers would be the courts and the dancing, the silks and jewels, the laughter and loving. I would be left to the grey sea and the grey sky, the cold chapel at dawn, the solitary cell. Seven years I had wrestled for Morgan in my prayers. At last I saw what I was praying for. If the answer were no, she would have to make her life with us. My prayers strengthened tenfold.

Yet even as I prayed for her to take the veil, I watched her and admired.

Answers do not come quickly on long muddy roads. It was full moon again. All day Morgan had been restless. A brisk wind was driving white horses over the grey sea. Gulls were flung sideways on sudden currents of air. Since morning the students had been pent indoors over their tasks. When they were freed the other girls hurried to find shelter by the refectory fire. But Morgan flung a cloak about her and went skimming down the slope straight for the causeway.

I was late in finishing my day's work. I was still at the gatehouse with Padarn the porter. A consignment of flour had arrived from the mill. I must call for sledges to ferry it across to our island storehouse.

I saw her coming and my heart leaped with a warning of danger. I did not need to see the girl's face to know it was Morgan. No one else moved with that swift, decisive energy. No other girl had hair so black and wild and free. As she dashed on to the bridge I shouted out to her in fear to stay on the other side. The wind flung itself across the chasm with a prickle of salt in it. Her cloak billowed suddenly, tugging her sideways with it. She threw out her arms, spinning on the edge. Then she found her balance and came running on. I forgot the grave dignity of a nun and raced down the slope to meet her.

'What are you doing here? It is forbidden for you to cross the bridge. Another handsbreadth and the wind would have dashed you to the rocks What is wrong?'

Fear, anger, concern were tumbling out of my lips. Another day she

215

would have laughed at my incoherence. But today she needed something from me. Her eyes blazed urgently in her face. She grasped my arm.

'Who was it? Who was it came to the gatehouse just now? Is it a message for me? Uther's answer? How long, Luned, how long still before I am free?'

'Uther's messenger!' I looked over my shoulder at the speck of the cart still ambling up the head of the coombe. 'That was nothing but the man from Rawlyn's mill with our good corn ground into twenty sacks of flour.'

'Flour?' She seemed to check and steady herself. She stepped into the gatehouse. Padarn touched his head and bowed. To him she was still Gorlois's daughter. Her fist struck suddenly at the nearest sack and a puff of white dust fogged the air.

'Flour! I wait for freedom, and all that comes is dusty flour. Is there nothing from the Pendragon? Will there never be any hope for me? Will it go on like this forever?'

It was not like Morgan to despair. But winter was coming, the time of the darkness of the soul.

'You need not stay as a prisoner,' I reminded her. 'You could live here by your own free choice. Become a nun.'

'And if I did? Would Bryvyth let me cross this bridge, ever? Could I ride round the villages in my chariot, or walk the lanes preaching, as you do? Would I be free to talk with lords and peasants? Would I be trusted on the wharf when the ships come in?'

'Do you wish to go from us so much?' The words came harsh and painful from my lips.

Her eyes found my face with a sort of wonder.

'Seven years. Have I lived with you so close for seven years and you have to ask me that? If I would want to leave Tintagel, of all places!'

Fool that I was, I could not even tell if that was yes or no. I wanted to believe the holy place was precious to her. And, though the words are ashes on my tongue now, that I was dear to her too. Yet I had enough honesty of mind, even in my fondness, to doubt that what I longed to hear could be so.

I only realised I was clutching her wrist when she tore herself away from me and strode back over the bridge. Morgan was her own prisoner, as much as ours. We could never have held her, determined as she was, if she had truly wanted to run away. How often could she have been gone from my side in the night? How often could she have climbed down to the beach and a secret boat? She had friends outside. But she would not go from us only to hide in a peasant's hovel. She was too proud. That was to exchange one prison for another. We both knew that. She would leave Tintagel as a princess or not at all. Ulfin's men had orders to find her and kill her if her presence was rumoured outside our wall. So she must wait for Uther's mercy still. The loss of Arthur lay between them like an unsheathed sword.

I watched her climb the path, up to the plateau of the island, and set off swiftly along its edge. Tintagel Island is not large. Before I had finished my business in the gatehouse she was coming back again on the southern side. Round and round. A tall impatient figure testing the limits of her gaol.

The moon waned, and the leaves spun from the crooked trees.

We were together when the answer came. Three men in fur cloaks appeared on the opposite cliff. We caught our breath as we watched them halt their horses and stare across at our island. No merchants these. No panniered mules. Fine horses bright with display of bronze harness-trappings. The sheen of autumn sun on curried hides. Thick pelts cast carelessly back from strong tanned arms, showing rich-coloured tunics and wealth of warriors' weapons.

Suddenly I had a feeling that Tintagel was vulnerable. A band of women in white gowns, scholars and dairymaids, unused to war. Our bridge, that had seemed an awful barrier, could yet be crossed. We knew that since the fatal night when Uther came. Nor was the sea a strong moat of defence. It had brought a nearer enemy to our island, as I had cause to know. Where was there for me to retreat now? Even the high fortress of Tintagel could not keep the evil world out.

I feared those men, but Morgan hoped. Beside me, her body was almost bursting out of her gown with a fierce excitement. Red lips open and panting, green eyes brilliant. So slender a human frame to contain so mighty a spirit. So small an island to confine such great ambition.

'At last! It is over! He has sent for me. I shall be free, I shall begin to be a queen.'

I watched them with despair.

Long the horsemen stared and seemed to talk together. It struck me that we were stranger to them than they to us. I began to suspect that they feared us too. By our nuns' simplicity and vulnerability we challenged all they stood for. My pride began to assert itself again.

They turned their horses' heads and trotted for the top of the coombe and the path to the gatehouse. It was then I knew the answer, as they filed past on the far lip of the haven. I had not spent so many years in calculation that I could not count horses. As certainty soared in my soul I glanced swiftly at Morgan to see if she had read the message too.

She was dancing. Laughing, with her head thrown back and her arms spread wide, circling on the short-cropped turf. Had she truly not seen?

They left their weapons, reluctantly, I have no doubt, at Padarn's lodge, and came on foot across our holy causeway. Swaggering more than was necessary, to keep up their pride. Glancing, for all that, at the plunging drop on either side. Laughing with each other to cover an unaccustomed shyness in the presence of nuns. Strange that I, who had ordinarily no interest in my fellow humans, could now read all that at a distance in their bearing. I had become wise on Morgan's behalf.

Bryvyth went to the guesthouse to talk to them. Heavy the load she had carried all these years. She must have wished to be rid of it that day. Her precious city of God, so painfully built here, balanced against the welfare of Gorlois's daughter. Two sacred trusts.

I know I prayed while they were closeted inside. Old habits of joyful praise reasserted themselves. I knew now that High God was on my side. Morgan too, her hands moving ceaselessly in strange patterns, her lips murmuring, moving away from me so that I should not hear what she asked. Morgan a beggar. At what throne? And my soul plunged suddenly to think what I would have to face from her soon.

The men came out of the guesthouse and cast curious looks around. They were not used to a convent. You could see what they would be thinking, and jesting about later. We are here. Here where Uther and Ulfin and Merlyn . . . and Ygerne!

The warriors walked back to the bridge, and Bryvyth stood at the door watching them. I turned to look at Morgan.

The gay dancer had turned to stone. The colour had left her lips. Even her hair seemed to hang on her cheeks like dark seaweed on rock, so heavy that the wind could not stir it.

And yet she lived. I could feel her thought screaming after the men. Bidding them turn.

Bryvyth sent for us both. I feared to rouse Morgan, to touch her. But she came, like a chill spirit beside my living flesh.

Bryvyth's face was dark with anger, though not towards Morgan. She relayed the message from Uther in a sharp, rattling voice.

There would be no freedom for Morgan. And no marriage either. As long as Uther Pendragon lived she would stay a prisoner on Tintagel. Arthur had not been heard of again. Morgan should think herself lucky to keep her life. Outside this island her penalty would be death. Only on this narrow rock could she claim sanctuary still.

The blood had not returned to Morgan's face. It was as if her whole being had frozen over. Only once had she started, when Bryvyth spoke of Arthur. Then no more. This was the depth of the bitterest winter, when not even a trickle of water can be heard underneath the ice.

Bryvyth, that strong abbess, was too ashamed to comfort her, and I too afraid.

Then, with a terrifying suddenness, she broke from us and ran. We caught up with her in the furthest sleeping-chamber of the guesthouse. She was leaning over the empty bed and beating her head against the wall.

'I must live out my life here! In Tintagel! Was that night so little to him? Does he not remember? It was *here*. Here in this very room, this bed. That . . . man lay with my mother, with his sword beside him still wet with my father's blood. Gorlois is not avenged, and every day I live, I must wake and be reminded of them both.'

'The Church bids us forgive those who wrong us. Do you think you are the only woman that loved Gorlois?' The words burst sharp from Bryvyth's tongue.

Morgan did not heed her. Where she had been cold before, a dragon breathed in her now.

'I am of age. I am a noblewoman. I am free. *Free!* He has no right to hold me here against my will. The law of Britain does not allow him so much power over a daughter.'

'The law of Britain lies in a sword now, by the look of it. He'll have a cold wait, if he means to sit there till you or the Pendragon dies.'

Our eyes followed Bryvyth's through the open door behind us. A young horseman was standing on the skyline like a sentinel where our track met the mainland road.

'Is it not enough that nuns are my gaolers? Does he mean to humiliate you too?'

'Uther's men have told me the freedom of Britain hangs trembling on that same sword. And with it, this abbey and every Christian monastery and church in the land.'

'And for your Church's safety, my right must be denied?'

'If freedom was all you wanted, girl, it might have been yours. You could have swallowed your pride. You could have offered your love to the Pendragon, as your mother did. But you wanted power. A crown on your brow and your story honoured and your father revenged. The bards will not sing of you, here in Tintagel. Only we shall remember the wrong that was done here.'

I could not read Morgan's face. She wandered away, resentfully. I followed at a distance as she climbed up to the summit and the standing stone. Her fingers traced the initials of Christ's name cut in the rock. Her hands caressed the granite shaft, stone older than any carving. Her eyes swung round the scope of sea, the cave mouths gaping in the cliffs, the distant roofs of Bossiney. The horseman watching.

I left her. I had work to do. She did not come to supper.

When dusk fell I found her in the chapel. She was gazing about her as if she had never been here before. All around her the faces of saints and prophets stared down from the painted walls, large-eyed. Christ in Judgment watched her from the cove of the roof. She moved among them, studying their expressions, fingering the costly goldwork on the altar. She grasped the four-armed cross so tightly I feared she would break it. Long she looked up into the dusky face of the Virgin Mary.

Then she swung round, gazing past me over the sea. The chapel is not far from the edge of the cliff. The high tide boomed in the hollow caves. I did not dare to speak to her.

At last she broke silence.

'Well, I am a woman now, am I not? Even here I can take my fate in my own hands. She has asked me to make my first vows at the dark of the moon.'

My heart leaped with joy.

'Then make them! Put on the bridal veil and be welcome among us.'

But Morgan's eyes held mine without smiling. Wells of sadness I could not begin to measure.

'If I so choose, it is a high and fearful bridge I shall be crossing.'

'But there is power and glory on the other side!' I cried.

'Is there? Is this my only way?'

She was very pale. Still her eyes gazed at me steadfastly, with a look I had seen in them many times before. As though she meant me to understand more than she said. As though she pleaded for some other answer. I could not tell what she wanted from me.

# Chapter Twenty-two

I blame Bryvyth for what happened. She should have seen how great a danger I was in.

It was All Hallows Eve and the dark of the moon. The night of Samain. It affected us all. It was not just from Christian charity that we doubled our prayers for the peace of the dead. Nuns we might be, but it was our own peace we, the living, prayed for secretly. That night was the threshold of the otherworld. By the old reckoning, the dying of one year before the next is born. A night of darkness when the doors of the hollow hills are open and the dead may return. We had not been Christians long enough in Dumnonia to break the bonds of that belief. No Roman calendar, no candles burning in the chapel, could wipe the darkness from our minds. Even Bryvyth was uneasy at suppertime.

I looked down the long table to where Morgan sat for the last time among her fellow scholars. Her face was white and she could scarcely eat. I did not wonder at that. In the new light of morning those lips would take the bread of the Eucharist from Nectan's hands and Bryvyth would lay the white veil on the tumbling freedom of her black hair. But before then she must keep the night's vigil alone in the chapel, like the new warrior of a mortal lord. This night of all nights. I could not have done it.

I glanced at Bryvyth, troubled. Why had she laid so terrifying a burden on the girl? The abbess met my eye, and I saw a strange sparkle there. Excitement and doubt, as though she knew even then the high stakes she gambled for. She was always a warrior-woman, Bryvyth. When Gorlois had staked his life on his wife's honour, she understood. I knew without saying that Bryvyth would keep this vigil too in her own cell, as I would in mine. But Morgan in the chapel must test her calling alone. It was required.

When the handbell called us to vespers we were more than usually reluctant to leave the bright fire of the refectory and venture the short dark path to the chapel.

That night only Tintagel flared with flame.

As the shadows deepened we filed up the path. Nuns, tall maidens near the end of fostering, the little boys and girls from the schoolroom. All around us the hills and headlands lay in muffled grey. Their lights were going out now, one by one, hearths raked and cooling, lamps extinguished, candles dead. Only in Tintagel the flame still burned. Even the nobles in Bossiney kept the custom, Morgan had told me, half in jest, for old times' sake, half in fear. Samain is not a night for jesting. When you gather in the dark round the unlit pile and the chanting begins, you dare not look over your shoulder. You dare not listen to the noises in the trees. You fear even the touch of your neighbour's hand.

On Tintagel we knew better than to jest about it. We fought to keep back the dark.

A whisper frightened me so that I staggered and lost my balance. Morgan was close behind me.

'Dark! Dark all the way to Bossiney. All the way across Cornwall. And the tide is rising with the dark. Everything dark. The lamps are out. The fires are cold on the hearth. All the light of the world goes out on Samain night. The powers of darkness are running free. The dead return.'

'Not here,' I said stoutly. 'Not in Tintagel. This is a holy place. When every light in Cornwall goes out, the flame of faith will still burn brightly here.'

'Will it?' she said, with a little gasp. '*Will* it?'

We crowded into our sanctuary. Bryvyth stood, hooded, before the altar. One by one we lit our candles from her strong flame. Every one of us had a soul to remember. Morgan walked behind me. I looked round and with a sweet pang I saw that she carried her head higher than mine now.

Rathtyen could no longer leave her bed. Morgan would never leave Tintagel now. The thoughts went round and round my head.

Morgan's face was white as the taper in her hand, her dark hair covered, her look grave and melancholy. I felt an urge to put my arm around her.

I lit a candle for my brother Yestin and said a prayer.

Morgan moved to Bryvyth and lit her little flame.

'I commend into the hands of eternal God the soul of Gorlois, Duke of Cornwall. May he be resting in the peace of the angels this night and forever.'

'And God guard the soul of her who prays for Gorlois.'

The voices murmured on. The candles flowered. The little chapel was a field of blossoms. Out of the leaning shadows above us the dark face of the Virgin stared down. Mark and John. Elijah and Moses. The holy Marys. I followed Morgan's eyes, huge in the hollows of her face, as she turned to one and then another. I begged for their fortitude and sanctity. We sang fervently, as though we never wished our hymns to end. Even the sleepiest child and the weariest ageing nun would rather stay close-packed in the warm ranks of worshippers that night than scatter lonely to a dark dormitory or a solitary cell.

Yet we were women under discipline. Bryvyth blessed us. Before the bonfires blazed and the cruel games began along the headlands the nuns would be lying in their chaste beds. Our candles would go out one by one. But our chapel would never be wholly dark. One brave oil lamp, Christ's holy fire, would still burn on, unquenchable since Tintagel's abbess had lit it. On the kitchen hearth, warm coals still glowed under a shield of turf, waiting for sunrise. We did not need the druids' new fire. We told ourselves that if an unhappy spirit strayed on this island it would find peace and sanctuary. Here there was no gap between one year and the next, this world and the other, no dark abyss into which a benighted human might fall. Had not Christ harrowed Hell for us?

Bryvyth and I were the last to go. We hugged Morgan and left her prostrate on the cold floor before the altar. I added my Amen to the firm armouring of Bryvyth's benediction. What more could I have done?

We stepped into the night. It was fully dark. My thoughts flew to Piala, alone in her cave on that desolate headland, wrestling with devils on such a night as this. I shuddered even to imagine it.

Now I stood sentinel in my cell to begin my own long vigil of prayer through the hours of darkness. I did not mean to sleep that night. Tonight, above all nights, I must watch and pray and guard us both till dawn. I think I knew this must be the last time I would fight for Morgan's soul. Tonight I must suffer and struggle. Tomorrow would see my victory.

The wind began to howl. Sea crashed against the rocks. I had always hated it.

Hours passed. I let my tired arms fall to my sides for a moment and hugged my chilled body.

The whispering started in the stones. Words I had thought I would never hear again.

Morgan!

I groped for her bed. She could not be here, tormenting me. She was in the chapel.

No flesh met my hands, but the stones were laughing all around me.

I plunged for the threshold. Darkness met me. Never, as girl or nun, had I gone out of doors alone on Samain night. Even Christians feed their fires, but bar the doors and windows. The old fear persists.

But the devil was loose, and Morgan was in danger. I could not stay alone. I must find her. I must save her. I must keep Tintagel safe.

With a moan of terror I stepped out into the rushing darkness. You may scorn me for a coward, but I used all my courage then. I was too frightened even to see the edge where the grassy cliff fell sheer to the sea. To my left and above me the chapel should be burning with light. I turned, and with a rush of thankfulness saw its windows lit with a golden glow. Our prayers lived still before Christ's lamp. Then, while I watched, the darkness overtook them.

# Chapter Twenty-three

The blackness was horrible in its sudden finality.

I started to run up the path. I was too wise to misunderstand the meaning of what I had just seen. But my heart fought against accepting the truth. Morgan could not have done this to me! All these years I had struggled with her, taught her, loved her. In the eyes of my superiors she was redeemed. It was no longer a truce, the public price she allowed me, to shut my eyes in private. She had embraced the cross. She would take her vows tomorrow. She was my white lamb. The acceptable gift I would lay in triumph at the feet of the abbess. The purchase of my ambition. It must not be true. Morgan could not have done this to Tintagel.

Somehow I crossed the nightmare space. I staggered blindly up the ledges. In my panic I bumped the walls of cells where other nuns lay sleeping. I was the spectre let loose to trouble their peace.

At the door of the chapel I clutched the lintel to support myself. The smoke of extinguished wicks caught my nostrils.

I still prayed the worst would not be true. I prayed my eyes would clear and with all the blaze of candles out I would find the one small true eternal flame burning undefeated.

I hoped in vain. My daughter in God had committed the final blasphemy.

I must have light! I must rekindle the lamp. Never mind the candles. Let the souls of the dead sleep. But Christ must live again. What death had he suffered at her hands, and mine? Quick! Before Bryvyth found out. Be sensible now. I must run to the one place where there would still be fire and warmth, to the heart of any home that I had so often despised but now I must cling on to for comfort. The kitchen.

I turned to go, and all the spirits of Samain came swooping across the plateau and whirled around me. I heard their laughter shrieking. Sobbing, I covered my face with my hands as I ran. I was afraid of dashing over the cliff. But I was more terrified still to open my eyes and see what might be round me.

Bruised by many falls I stumbled against the kitchen door. Inside, warmth welcomed me. I slammed the door and leaned against the wall, panting with relief. Close darkness stifled me like a blanket. The fire had been smothered well for the night. I groped for the hearth. Why couldn't I find it? Surely there should be one ember glowing through the turves? I tripped over a stool and fell. My hands plunged deep into something warm and soft. Ashes. I scrabbled wildly. It was all around me. The sodden ruin of fire. Trickles of water hissing on hot stones.

Still I would not believe it. There must be one coal left with a spark of life I could coax back to flame.

'Oh, please! Please! Just one!'

Out of the corner something dark sprang on me like a huge cat. I screamed. But Morgan grasped me by the elbows and lifted me, dancing me round. She was shrieking with laughter.

'Oh, Luned, Luned! If only I could have left just light enough to see your face!'

'You wicked girl! You should be praying in the chapel. I must get Bryvyth.'

'Oh no, you won't. You wouldn't dare, would you? Think. What will you tell her? That she has lit Christ's fire on Tintagel and guarded it for twenty years, and you have let it go out?'

'It was not my fault. She must see that. You are possessed. Even Saint Anthony was beset by devils.'

'Why do you need to tell her? You never did before. Wait here and I will bring you back fire enough to roast a bull.'

'Where?' I whispered. 'Where could you get such a flame?'

If only I could put it right before Bryvyth saw. And never mind whose brand it was I borrowed.

She seized me by the wrist. Her hand was strangely hot and smelt of foul wet soot. She dragged me out into the gusting darkness. I tried to break free. I found I could not. For the first time I knew for certain that she was a grown woman and stronger than I, in spirit and in body. She pulled me to the edge of the cliff.

'Look!'

The headlands leaped with fire. The hills were chained with gold. Outside Bossiney the wind spiralled the flames up into the night. I could even see the figures dancing in front of the bonfire.

'Our time has come. *My* time has come. I must join my people.'

And still I did not fully understand.

'No!' I tried to hold her back. 'You must not cross the bridge. Uther's men will kill you, or you'll fall to your death in the dark. If Bryvyth finds out . . .'

I did not believe that anything I said would have force over her. I felt the power growing in her till I seemed nothing but a scrap of bone and flesh gripped by her fingers. I was dead beside her. I had nothing with which I could oppose her. The fount of my prayers had been failing for years. The words I uttered were now the rattling of dry stones in an old streambed. She knew it.

She threw me off, scorning my feebleness. She did not want me.

'Yes, be afraid! It is a more dangerous bridge than yours I am crossing to get this fire. And yet the flame is coming to me.'

She turned abruptly. Her feet started down the path, sliding on loose stones. I could have shouted out. Bryvyth's cell was only a little way beyond us. Even then I was too proud to summon help.

'Come back!'

'Let go. This is not for you.'

I grabbed her sleeve. I could not bear to be left alone.

She dragged me on. I began to realise where she was leading me. The terror of windy spaces was below me. The path was narrow even in daylight, jutting with rock.

'No!' I hissed. 'We can't go down there! Not in the dark!'

She pulled free of me suddenly. I was alone in the howling night with the sea reaching up the cliff walls at me.

I groped blindly for her. I could not see or hear anyone. The path was steeply pitched. I could not tell what was in front of me.

'Fool!' Her voice came from lower down. 'You are on the threshold. Is this what you want? To be left alone on Samain night? What will you do? Run back to Bryvyth now and call her?'

I was lost. I could not tell which way to turn. Tonight of all nights I knew the spirits would blind my eyes and catch my feet. The convent was only just above me, but impossible to reach alone now. I had come to the edge of my abyss.

'Oh, no! Morgan, where are you? Wait for me, Morgan! Don't leave me!'

I stumbled upon her. My hand clutched hers again. I felt her warm breath coming quickly.

'Very well. I will bring you to the fire. The first fire of the year, and the oldest in the world. This is the fire that I will kindle on the cold hearth of Tintagel. I will show Bryvyth which of us is the stronger! I will take the first vows!'

She was hurrying me down the path. I stumbled in panic, where she went swift and sure, almost running with eagerness. The path twisted again and I saw them coming into the cove.

Three wild eyes. Three separate lights soaring and swooping over the black waves. A hooded lantern held by a watcher with reddened hands in each prow. Boats, larger than the coracle. Light swaying uncertainly over a mass of shadowy passengers.

In a sudden release of hope I thought that these ships were coming to fetch her. Morgan would escape from us. I should be free of her at last. Ambition shattered. Love departed. But free. The devils would go away with her. I would wake in my bed tomorrow, alone. At that moment I truly longed for such humiliation.

But I deceived myself. When Morgan of Cornwall went from Tintagel it would be as a queen, not a hunted doe cowering from Uther's hounds. She must cross that bridge with a royal escort waiting. She was Ygerne's daughter.

She swung round to me. I could make out the white blur of her face.

'You see! They have come! I knew they would. They have come for me. Not to lay on a veil but to lift it off.'

What could she mean? And then I drew back from her with a frightened gasp. The fishing boats of Cornwall have other uses. They say that in the night they are constrained to ferry the dead. Trance takes the crew and they row out, following the path of the vanished sun, to blest islands in the west from which their passengers never return. It was what I had always feared. Morgan was going to drown herself and the ferrymen would bear her away. And I? Who had these boats come for? Where was Morgan leading me?

Keels ground on shingle.

She had not waited for me. I was alone to choose between the horror of these strangers in the cove or of the black spirit-filled path treacherous above me.

The lights vanished abruptly under the lee of the rocks. I heard muffled voices now, footsteps on the beach. In spite of my terrors they had a reassuring human sound. Women's voices. Then silence.

Somehow I stumbled out on to the shore. I could not see Morgan. The beach was sheltered from the wind. The sea came heaving towards me over ledges of rock, but the tide was not yet full. I drew my breath and looked around. The women from the boats had vanished. I could see the ships dimly now against the glimmer of the shingle. They were drawn high up above the tidemark. Three boats. Large, black, empty. Then I heard Morgan's voice from between them. She was laughing quietly.

'She has come. This is my night. They are getting ready for me. Do you still wish to follow where I am going?'

She could have forbidden me. I should not have been there. She knew what she was leading me into.

# Chapter Twenty-four

I should have turned back. I should sooner have braved the malignant spirits on the path. Better even to have fallen to my death than to have gone forward into this living hell. But that night I was too afraid to walk alone. I needed some human close to me for comfort. I should not have chosen Morgan.

For a while we stood silent. Then a drum beat three times and was still. Morgan began to move.

Wet stones sliding treacherously underfoot in the unequal starlight. The sudden shock of cold water seeping through the shingle. Trembling, I followed as she climbed over rocks that would still be dry at high tide. Then I checked as though I had stumbled into some foulness. My groping hand had found something soft on the cold stone. Cloth. Rough wool. Glimmering white as Morgan's face. My heart lurched sickeningly. I knew what this was. I drew one out. My fingers explored its familiar shape and texture. A heap of habits like my own. Oh, I had known. Ever since that night-time laughter on the cliff path years ago, I had known. But I had denied the knowledge, even to myself.

In front of me Morgan too laughed harshly as she dropped back on to the shingle.

'Now do you see? I have been well instructed here. Go back, Luned. Run to Bryvyth. Beg her to put a binder on this wound, stop up the hole, so that the blood does not come out for the world of men and nuns to see. This is no place for you, is it?'

She mocked me.

Go back? The lonely beach. The black boats. The towering cliffs in the howling darkness of Samain night. She knew I could not leave her. My tongue was dry. I knew where the drums were beating. I saw where she was bringing me. To the very mouth of what I feared most.

The Mother's Hole.

The words shaped themselves unwelcome in my mind. It was a name I had heard only rarely, and then smothered at once. It was never spoken aloud among the nuns of Tintagel. And yet I think that all of us knew its old name. We gave it no other. Indeed we never talked of it at all. Nuns playing on the beach or scrambling after shellfish would not enter it. I shuddered to think what had been under me all this time. The convent straddled it.

Tell Bryvyth? I think she must always have known. Why else had she chosen Tintagel but for the Mother's Hole? She wanted victory. Like me, she deceived herself. The past is always present with us. She should not have trusted her nuns to be as strong as she was.

All the black prohibitions of my life came leaping out of the cave upon me. That darkness into which I dare not set foot, even in bright sunshine. The unseen sea that I could already hear booming and sucking at the further end where the second mouth opened upon chaos. The thunderous weight of blank black rock towering up to the height of the convent. All poised over one narrow arch of dripping stone. How could I bear to put my fragile human skull under that load? I would have been terrified of that cave even if it had been empty.

But it was not.

A lantern opened suddenly in front of us, dazzling my eyes. I shrieked in fear, and heard my voice shudder away in horror. Something was sitting at the cave mouth. The watcher turned the light from us upon herself.

It was a naked woman. Old. White hair hanging waist-long around a grinning face. Pendulous dugs. Squatting with legs wide apart and her shrivelled hands holding the lips of her genitals gaping open. Her thighs and the mouth of her womb-way were black with blood.

She cackled with laughter as I fled from her. But Morgan, a girl new come to womanhood, stood her ground steadily. I could not bear to watch, and yet I had to. I tore my eyes with difficulty from that sentinel.

The watcher nodded. The girl fell on her knees on the stones. The lantern reddened her shift. Her face was in shadow. She called in a loud voice, shocking in its strength.

'I, Morgan, daughter of Ygerne, beg to be admitted.'

Another light flared, deep in the sounding passage between the two seas. It lit a roof streaked with rose and green. Dimly ruddied figures waited, faceless, shadowed heads turned towards us. A close-packed double file of strangers.

An old woman's voice answered hollowly. 'In the name of the gods your mother named . . . Enter, Daughter!'

Another younger, lighter, followed it. 'In the name of the gods the women name . . . enter, Mother!'

I started. If I had feared the ancient's voice, I had expected and recognised it. This second voice I had recognised, and not expected. Had the crack run as deep as that through the convent?

And then a strong man's voice, more shocking to me than all the others. 'By the name of the god in me. Be entered, Wife!'

'No!' I cried out in fear. Not for Morgan, my foster-daughter, even then. Desperate fear for myself. Fear of that unquiet night outside the cave, and the darkness inside that was not dark enough, and the dark in myself that had followed too far after Morgan and was now too afraid either to go on or to turn back.

But Morgan had waited all her life for this. She walked in. White and tall. Maiden and woman now. And the shift seemed to fall from her shoulders of its own accord.

'No, Morgan!'

It was my last choking cry. I could not protect her. If I had truly loved her, unselfishly, I might have found the strength to throw my arms around her and drag us both away before it was too late. We might not have got beyond the beach, but we would have died together, whole. It did not come to that. I let her go without a struggle. I was not Bryvyth. I was not worth answering. We both knew that. In that one step into the cave she was as far removed from me as the width of oceans and the height of mountains. That last forsaken wail was only for myself.

It was lost in the full-throated greeting from the heart of the cave. No words distinguishable, but a long echoing roar that rolled towards us along the walls of rock. Morgan walked on, between the narrow ranks of waiting women, and men. A third light was lifted before her. She bowed gravely, took a torch and kindled it at this flame. She thrust it down, and another torch came to meet hers. Fire blazed between them. The light leaped on a naked man's body facing her. I covered my eyes.

So many years ago, in a coombe in Devon. I thought I had forgotten. And they called that holy.

The watcher squatted in front of me like an effigy in stone.

Outside the cave I felt utterly abandoned. The whole firm substance of my world had gone, lost in the gulf between one year and the next. This time and no time. The solid cliffs were shadows. The stones water. All around me the inlet was a shifting surface of silver and grey. The tidemark had vanished. There was no setting a limit to the sea. I felt it slide towards me, silent as a hunting lynx. Was it still far out, arching caressingly about the wharf? Or just beyond my feet, waiting, hungry? I am afraid of the sea. I never knew the patterns of high water in the haven. But I remembered Morgan's words.

'The tide is rising with the dark.'

A wave touched my foot. With a moan of terror I backed towards the cave, towards firelight and humans. I, that had always wished to be alone. I, that had embraced the coldness of chastity. I was not strong enough to stand the test.

I had forgotten that terrible sentinel. Suddenly I saw her. She had moved bewilderingly. Now she was perched on the rocks over my head, leering down at me. I checked, paralysed.

'Go on!' she hissed. 'You're late. What are you frightened of? This?' She thrust her legs forward in front of my eyes.

'Nuns bleed like the rest of us, don't you? One week in every moon she strikes us. There's only two things dry that wound, and we all know what they are. There now, my lover! You didn't think it was my own blood, did you? With hair so white as mine? But a man that wasn't one of ours wouldn't think of that, would he? Or a book-learned nun! Lucky it's pig-sticking time!'

Her wrinkled body shook with delight.

Another wave washed over my ankles. I sobbed helplessly. I had no choice. The sea was driving me into the hole.

A hand clutched at my gown, tearing it from me. I clasped my arms around my shivering body.

The fire leaped up and robbed me of my last hope.

If only their bodies had not been naked and human. Men among them. If only their faces had not been masked, and animal. I crouched in the shadows just inside the entrance, shuddering, hands over my eyes. I peeped through my half-open fingers, trying to see only the comfort of light I needed and shut out the rest.

I had retreated before the waves without reckoning. I, who had devoted my years to calculation. But all this while the tide was mounting higher and I saw that I had driven myself deeper into a trap of fear. I wanted to cry out to the reddened figures chanting round their fire to run before we were all submerged. But I could not speak or move. I looked back. Treacherous silver had flooded the beach behind me. I did not know how high it would rise in this cave. I had never stayed in daylight to see. With a whisper of fear I crept on ahead of it, towards the fire.

I heard a shriek, and fell to my knees on the stones. I could not tell if the thing that cried out had been human or animal. Then I saw through my fingers their priest holding in his hands something dark, darkly dripping into a vessel beneath. I saw the rosy flesh of Morgan beside him. I saw her lift the cup to her lips and then to his. I sobbed a little to myself, longing for the warmth of drink, the warmth of fire, the warmth of human company. I, that had been so proud that I needed no such vanities. All around me was cold stone, dripping with wet. I looked fearfully over my shoulder to find the cavemouth corked with waves. I crawled still closer to the fire. I feared the devils outside and the sea more than I feared the living witches. I could not bear to drown alone.

I must close my mind to the vows Morgan was making.

At every lift and crash of the coming waves the ranks of male and female sighed and murmured an invocation. The passage bent now. At the far end of the tunnel I glimpsed past those terrible heads grey stars between the waves. A black wall of water rose. I held my breath. It smashed, and the sea came sliding towards us, washing the sides of the tunnel. I heard it suck and ebb away. The distant stars glimmered once more. It had not touched us yet. The worshippers round the fire held their breath too, then sighed and moaned. As each wave fell their ranks swayed a little closer to each other in the narrow passage.

It was a powerful rhythm. The rise. The breathless pause. The crashing fall. Then the long sobbing sigh. The beating of the heart under the sleeping world. The drums of darkness. Listening, watching, trembling for the fall. I felt the same pulse begin to beat deep in the unconsidered parts of my body. I did not know then what it meant. I swear to you, Bryvyth, I did not know!

Fear was moving strongly in me now. Fear of the slow, devouring approach of those waves. Fear of the creeping silver tide smothering the beach behind me. Terrible fear of the unquiet dead outside. Fear of the urgent shuddering of my body that was perilously close to pleasure. Fear of the more than human creatures in front of me. The witch-fire hissed. I could smell the sweat of bodies close to me.

A wave thundered down. Cold drops splashed my arm. A woman screamed. My hands struck out, desperate to find some reassuring flesh. Then a last boom, filling the cave. The walls shrieked and shrieked again with women's cries. My voice shrill among the rest. A wild groping together. Hands seizing, arms enfolding, heat pressing down. My body in ice-cold water, bedded on stones. Sea-water washing over. Warm flesh above. Sharp pain. Devouring hunger. Gasping, crying. Release of tears and uncontrollable shaking of my body.

Then stabbing cold. Separation. Light taken. A featureless, unaccompanied, anonymous stumbling from the cave jostled by bodies I did not know and did not want to know. Splashing through knee-deep water. Stumbling on a sodden roughness of cloth I knew to be my gown. People clambering into boats. Departing. Some of them shielding torches to kindle other fires. Some, white shadows from whom I turned my face away, climbing the path by which I myself had come. And I left on the beach, soaking, shivering with cold and deeply sore, sobbing my heart out. Not even sense enough to have salvaged one brand to light the kitchen fire.

Morgan had lost her shift, snatched by the undertow where she had dropped it. She did not seem to notice that she was naked. But even she cried a little now.

'There! I'll show them all! I *will* have power. There are ways Uther Pendragon does not think of. That fool knows nothing. But *he* understands. That trickster, Merlyn. He is afraid. That is why he keeps my brother from me. Well, one day he will have to bring him into the open. And I shall be ready for him. By then I shall have grown immensely strong. When Arthur stands in the sun, then Morgan will rise from the dark, and my darkness shall cover his light when we two meet together.'

She pulled me impatiently.

'What are you snivelling for? Do you think I care that you have lost your virginity?'

But I wept for the loss of far more than that.

Then she said, sniffing like a sad child, 'I do not know if I am still a virgin. The priest's thing was made of wood. He hurt me.'

# Chapter Twenty-five

It is easier to maintain belief in the woes of the body than those of the spirit. Weariness. Disgust. Pain. I had no need to fear the Samain spirits now. Evil had done its worst. The wind still shrieked and the sea sucked, but they would not pluck me to my death. I had taken their service. The enemies of my soul would let me live and suffer.

In the first grey streak of dawn I knelt in the kitchen. My shaking hands tried to kindle a spark with stick and stone. If I had prostrated myself before the altar and begged as earnestly for light as I did then before the cold convent hearth, my life might have been different now.

Blatriad found me. Her fat hand flew to her mouth. She was always a fool. She thought she could keep the old ways under the cliff and the convent above remain untouched by them. The smell of simple, wholesome food. The pleasure of sisters trooping in to her supper. Nuns singing hymns while they cooked. Her bread lifted up in the Eucharist.

She had not thought what would happen when the two currents met.

Old dolt that she was, she had not even sense enough to see she must help me cover the traces of that night's work. It was her kitchen, her hearth, her heart that had been violated.

She went running away down the path, with her grey hair flying from beneath her veil.

I let my hands drop. The light was strengthening. It was a still grey morning. The first of November. Grey sea, grey sky, grey chapel. And when I looked round, Bryvyth was standing behind me with a face like thunder.

'*She* has done this? So she has tricked us at the last. Seven years, and she has had her revenge. Wait till I find her!'

'She is asleep in bed.'

'In bed! And you did not run to tell me she had broken her vigil? This morning she should have been the bride of Christ! Did you think you could hide the news from me that we had failed?'

'I watched and prayed through the night. As God is my witness, I wrestled for hours to keep her intention pure.'

'And so did I. And still she has shamed us. Why? Michael fought with the archangels and cast Lucifer out of heaven. George slew the dragon. Christ conquered the grave. Are you telling me the devil is stronger than all these?'

'You do not know. You have not slept with her all these years. The voices in the stones. The spells spoken. It was Samain Eve. We should have bound her. I put my soul at risk to stop her. I ran after her to the chapel when I saw the light go out.'

'*What?*'

If she had a face like a stormcloud before, it was chalk now. She was off, running. I followed wretchedly.

The darkness had been merciful. Now cruel daylight showed the truth of Morgan's work. I stopped, appalled.

Bryvyth was standing in the wreckage of the chapel. The candles overturned. The paintings on the walls scored and scratched. The lamp beside the altar was out.

The abbess covered her face and wept.

'Christ and his holy mother! When the high king had set you . . . *I* set you . . . to watch her day and night. And you let her do *this* and still thought to hide it! Twenty years it is. Twenty years since I kindled this flame on Tintagel. We've suffered poverty, drought, storms fit to wreck a lighthouse, pirates even. But always we kept the flame alive. Never till now has the darkness overcome it. Oh, Blatriad, what are you standing there crying for, you old fool? Give me that flint. Do you think my fingers have forgotten how to kindle a spark?'

With hands that trembled only slightly she lit the lamp and the life sprang again in the black and white eyes of the Virgin and the prophets, coloured their ravaged faces. Tears furrowed her own cheeks unchecked.

She prostrated herself on the stone-flagged floor, and Blatriad and I copied her. Her prayers called down Heaven's wrath on herself, implored Christ's mercy on the rest of us. It was a prayer Blatriad and I dared not echo. Here in the chapel we knew too well how we had merited wrath. We pleaded for mercy.

Bryvyth's mercy was for the soul, not for the body. She drove me before her to her cell and made me kneel.

'Oh, Luned, Luned. What was I doing when I set you to guard Morgan for us? I knew the Pendragon had set us a hard task, but I thought a nun could be wiser than a man of war. I planned a match for Morgan. I thought you two would understand each other. Mind matched with mind. Pride with pride. Ambition with ambition. Oh, yes, girl, we all know which way your heart has been set. Rathtyen is dying, and one day I shall wake up and find myself an old woman without an heir. And who shall I look to for help now? Who is there to rejoice my heart and take up the torch? Tell me that! I thought you were a sapling from my own root. I would have done better to have chosen a different guardian entirely. Someone like Eira, perhaps. Meek. Loving. Armoured with humility. How would Morgan have fought with that?'

Eira, painting these faces on the chapel walls that Morgan had ruined. Eira. A fresh sweet voice thrilling down the tunnel.

'*Enter, Mother!*'

'You know little of the courage of loving, Luned. It is my fault. I saw coldness, and called it strength. I saw discipline, and took it for faith. I trusted you. I deceived myself. Your love for Christ has been a service of the will, not the heart. A matter of pride, that will not let you beg for help. Oh, I know. The blame is mine. I should not have

233

so imperilled your soul, and all Tintagel. My softness and your hardness have lost us Morgan.'

And then she beat me. I doubt if she had ever given such a beating in her life. A lesser woman might have died under it.

Later, in private, she beat herself.

When it was finished, and I lay weeping on the floor, she knelt beside me and gathered me in her arms.

'What do you say, Luned? Shall we go away together? Leave all this behind us? I'll get rid of the hell-cat. I'll tell the Pendragon he must take her back. Gold and lands cannot buy our peace. When she has gone, then you and I will cleanse Tintagel. We'll do penance for this shame. We'll set out on the road of pilgrimage that has no end. Build a coracle. Cast ourselves adrift on the breast of God's ocean. Trust the breath of the Spirit to wash us up where he will. What do you say?'

I could only sob into my arms. She wept for a flame extinguished. I, for another lit. She did not know the half of what had been done. Nor would I tell her.

I dragged myself back to my cell, more dead than alive. Morgan was sitting on the doorstep. She looked more child than woman that morning after. Thin. Pale. Her head bent forward over something between her hands, not straight and proud.

I could have believed it had not happened. The devils of Samain had curdled my dreams. I had ridden the nightmare. But the cloth was chafing the wounds on my back. My thighs were bruised. There was pain with every step I took. My body told me it had been so. Morgan did not look up to meet my eyes.

She had a kitten in her lap I had never seen before. A skinny grey thing. Large pointed ears, small face. Ribs showing through mangy fur and crusted cuts. She was feeding it with the hollow quill of a white gull's feather. There was a bowl beside her.

I stopped, sickened. What fresh devilment was this? What had those night-creatures taught her? What familiar was this? But then she lifted her head and smiled at me without apparent malice.

'Look, Luned! Poor thing. I found him trapped on a ledge of the cliff, mewing as if his heart would break. He has a loud voice for such a little waif. I think a hawk must have dropped him. See the wounds of the claws on his sides, the poor wee soul! Lucky it is my hands he has fallen into. I think I can cure him.'

She held the cut feather to his lips and his pink mouth opened trustingly. She let the golden droplets roll on to his tongue.

I staggered against the doorpost. Black imps danced before my eyes. Morgan jumped up with a cry and held me from falling. Her arm was round my waist. I felt an agony of pain and the joy of her touch.

Then she saw the blood on the back of my habit.

'So that's the way of it. It will be my turn next, I suppose. What did they think, she and Uther? That they could throw down a challenge to Gorlois's child and she not answer it? Well, I have taken the vows of Tintagel, have I not? We have done well, Luned. They begin to fear us.'

She led me to my bed, more gently than I would have expected.

'No work for you today. Let me see your wounds. Ah! This makes it sweeter. I did not guess that Bryvyth loved you so much.'

'I do not understand you,' I groaned.

'To beat you like this. You must have wounded her very deeply. I see now how it was. You were her darling. She let you into her heart. She built no defences against you. And now you have hurt her in her inmost place.'

'It was not I! It was not I who put out the flame. It was not I who defiled the chapel.'

'Oh, Luned. You know it was you.'

Did she mock me then?

'Lie still. I will run to Fyna. I need more ointment for cuts deep as this. We have made a powerful salve. I should like to test its effect.'

Fyna. The round blue eyes of the druid's daughter. Two heads whispering together in a doorway.

A concoction of these two mingling with my open flesh and blood.

Morgan was swiftly back. Her hands were cool and gentle, lifting my clothes from me. The work they did was cruel. I cried out as the sting of the salve bit the bared flesh. But her palms stroked on. Rhythmically, surely. I began to relax my clenched muscles and let my head drop on the pillow. I felt the blessing of her touch flow through my veins. She sang as she worked. On and on. I will not tell you what.

I ceased to fight her. I was in Morgan's hands. She had wounded me sorely. She must make me whole.

Bryvyth sent for Morgan. She did not return to my cell.

I could not move for the rest of the day. They let me lie. The kitten mewed, and crawled on to my bed. We slept together. Next day our wounds were clean and healing.

Bryvyth did not beat Morgan. I think she feared to. Morgan was of age now and a full woman. The high king's stepdaughter. She had not taken the vow of obedience, as I had. Instead Bryvyth sent for Nectan. Morgan did not tell me how the priest chose to wrestle with her.

# Chapter Twenty-six

Next day I rose almost without pain. My scars were crusted, but closing quickly. Whether it was the salve, or the touch of Morgan's hands and the chants she sang that worked most powerfully, I cannot say.

Other wounds were not healed so easily.

They told me there was a pedlar at the gatehouse wishing to do trade with us. That was my business.

It was a clear grey morning, the wind brisk but not cutting yet. I seemed to see each detail on the mainland with a clarity it did not ordinarily have. Trees, houses, cattle. A world I had ignored and shrunk from.

I walked slowly towards the causeway, carrying myself a little more stiffly than usual. I looked with the same unaccustomed sharpness into the faces of every nun I passed. I watched their eyes drop before mine, or their faces turn away. The blood mounted in my cheeks. How much did each one of them know? Whose gowns had I fingered on the rocks? I recalled again that laughter and scuffling on the cliff path one summer night long ago. But it had not been like that! It had not been a matter of giggling for me. It had not! It had not!

I had to cross the causeway. It was a daily penance. All my womanhood had been spent on lofty Tintagel, but I had never lost my fear of those heights and the sea. If I could I would have stayed secure on the island and left that chasm between me and the world. For Morgan the abbey was her prison. For me it was a fortress.

There were two asses standing outside the gatehouse, with a man holding their heads. He looked me up and down. I did not meet his eye. Inside, the pedlar was a big hairy fellow, dressed in leather and canvas against the rain and mud. But he carried no common wares. They should have called him a silversmith. He spread out the goods from his saddlebags on the counting-table to dazzle my eyes. Enamel-studded bowls, silver chains for hanging lamps, bright, embossed dishes. I did not wonder that his servant outside carried a large spiked cudgel.

They say all smiths are men of magic. Certainly his goods had put a spell on me. I thought of the five Books of the Law that Cigfa had almost finished. We should be needing a jewelled cover for such a treasure.

'How long will you be staying in these parts?'

He shot a look at the churl in the doorway behind him. I had not expected to hear them laugh.

'That depends how rich the pickings are. Feast times are often lucky for smiths. Even white nuns have been known to exchange their treasures for ours.'

I had reached out my hand to fondle the twining metalwork. I saw his eyes undress me. Shockingly, I knew what was in his mind. I felt the sweat break out on my neck and between my breasts. His face split into a wide yellow grin and the wave of his onion-stinking breath came towards me. I turned, choking, snatching my hand away from the closeness of his. I turned and heard his servant laughing coarsely. *Who else had been in that hole under the cliff?*

I cannot say what I bought from him that morning, or what I paid. Cigfa would have to wait for her book-cover. If only I could be free of him and his knowing eyes. All day I was like a woman struggling to work in a sweat of fever.

But at night it was worse.

Morgan had been taken from me. Bryvyth had banished her to a cave next to Piala's. It was a punishment, not a penance. Morgan showed no contrition for the scarred faces of the saints. She was sent bread and water, a little butter and milk once a week. No one but the hermit was allowed to speak with her. Bryvyth had written in anger again to Uther Pendragon. Morgan must go.

But I could never be free of her now. Morgan had done two ills that Samain night. She had extinguished a flame that would never be mine to light again. And she had kindled another. A terrible burning down in the nether hole where the waters come and go with the moon. I had known it was there. But I had hidden the knowledge of its purpose.

I dreamed of men. Bodies in the darkness. Thrusting hands. How long would they make me wait and suffer like this? How long before the cave was filled with worshippers and the fire kindled? How long before Morgan led me down again?

She came back to us after a month. Thinner now. Her hair dull. Her face set in defiance.

For the last time she shared my cell.

I lay in bed whimpering, moving my legs in the darkness.

Morgan said crossly, 'Stop it. Let me go to sleep.'

I could not sleep. My fingers fumbled under my shift, feeling for unnamed parts of my body. Rousing a hunger they could not satisfy.

Was Morgan asleep? I lay in the dark, listening to her quiet breathing. And it came to me that she might have the power to ease this hunger if she would. My hand reached out across the gulf between our beds. I touched her side. Gently I turned the blanket back till I could feel warm flesh through her shift. She did not stir. Long I let my hand rest there, aching for her to feel my need and turn to me. She did not answer. I did not dare to tempt her further.

Several times in the agony of that restless night I felt the urge to pass water. I rose and unlatched the door quietly, yet not so silently I did not hope my movements might wake Morgan. I squatted on the chill grass and the liquid burned me as it passed. It did not leave my body satisfied.

The new moon looked through the open door on Morgan's bed. She was like moonlight herself. Black hair. White face. Cold. Single. I felt again her hands caressing the weals on my back. I thought that I would gladly have been wounded every day to have her heal me so. I stood in the doorway till I was cold and weary, waiting for her to lift her head and murmur something so that I might go to her side.

At last, disappointed, I crept back to my own bed. Cold now, as it had never seemed before. I scratched myself and cried a little into my pillow.

I think she knew. Perhaps that was her only kindness to me. Not to give me the terrible joy she keeps for men.

# Chapter Twenty-seven

Next day, on Advent Sunday, Rathtyen died. Her soul slipped quietly away in the late afternoon. It was a holy death. We gathered round her. She put her hand on Muriel's and commended to her the charge of the schoolroom. I watched the young woman's face glow with the rush of gratitude and surprise. She spoke with Cigfa and Eira about the books in the library. She commended earnestly those ones which to her were of greatest value. She listed those which would repay copying and offering to the libraries of other monasteries, what works still needed to be sought from them in return. It was a sorrow to her that we had as yet no complete Bible in the translation of Jerome. She looked to us to mend that in the future. So it went on. Thanking Fyna for easing her pain, Blatriad for the special broths she had prepared, even Senara, newly-released from slavery to be a nun, for the milk and eggs that all of us enjoyed. And me, Luned, for my wise care of the convent, my stewardship of our wealth, my circumspection as I dealt with the world of men and money. I listened dry-eyed, but my heart wept. Rathtyen, whose tone had always been so sharp in the service of truth, flattering us all with her dying energy. So learned and yet so blind to the truth.

Bryvyth was less inhibited than I. She held Rathtyen's head between her hands as the words grew fainter, slower. The tears ran freely down her cheeks for grief and pride and joy.

Then the sun dropped clear of a bank of cloud, and over the western sea came a path of gold. All down this celestial pavement ranks of angels hastened towards us with outstretched arms. They entered the cell. The radiance of their being lit Rathtyen's face with a bright glory. Their wings clouded our sight. Then the cell was grey, as it had not been before, and they had taken her soul. We all saw this.

We bore her body to the chapel and set a vigil.

I waited then for Bryvyth to send for me, for the vowed nuns to be gathered in council in the long room facing the sea which served both as refectory and meetinghouse.

Morgan had not returned to my cell. I saw her walking in the dusk with Bryvyth on the summit, both wrapped in their cloaks as dusk fell with the murk closing over the sea and the nearer headlands. Bryvyth's back was more stooped than I remembered, Morgan tall and swift-moving. Supper passed, a sad, quiet meal. There was no summons for me.

When Rosslyn and I went to the chapel to take our turn in the vigil we found Bryvyth alone in the candlelight. She ordered Rosslyn to leave us. When she turned her head, I saw that the abbess was weeping. She rounded on me without troubling to wipe her cheeks.

'Well? Have you come to confess at last? Down on your face!'

I did not understand her. I was serving the penance she had set me. In all my daily work I was meticulous in obedience. How could she know the impurity of my night-time thoughts? Yet she was clearly angry. I prostrated myself before her.

I acknowledged my little failings. Rathtyen's death had shamed me. I had not been as devoted to study as the dying nun. I had neglected my reading. I had allowed myself to become impatient with a widow-tenant who had not paid the rent she owed us since Samain. Tean and I had struggled so long getting a chariot-wheel out of the mud that we had forgotten to sing the midday psalm. The sight of Nectan's chapel near Bossiney had brought our omission back to us, some time after the sun had passed its wintry zenith.

She heard me out in a grey stillness like that whole sad day itself. It was a short recital. I prided myself on honesty, on clarity of self-examination. But my daily life was disciplined. In the exercise of my monastic duties I offered little occasion for criticism. What I felt at night, who I was at night, in the close cell with Morgan, under her spell, that seemed another life, another time, another person. I could not have found the language to speak of it to Bryvyth. I did not think it either prudent or possible.

When I had finished, I expected to hear her rumbustious scolding, like the slapping of reins on the backs of her chariot-team. I waited for some light penance to be pronounced. Not heavy, but strengthening, like the effort of climbing a hill to see the greater vision from the top. I listened for the words of forgiveness.

Nothing came. Bryvyth stood with arms folded, face impassive, waiting still.

I raised my head, and it seemed that this was a mighty effort, as though a mountain slope lay between myself lying prostrate on the chapel floor at her feet and the abbess towering over me. I would not ordinarily have dared to lift my eyes until I heard forgiveness offered.

She met my look, with grey-blue eyes like the sea she lived so close to and did not fear. Clear, cold without the warmth of friendship in them now. Again that sense of otherworldliness. Where was the Bryvyth I knew? Where was the love that always raised me up, embraced me, set me striding once more on the pilgrim road beside her, as pupil and friend?

At last she spoke. Very cold. Precise. As though Rathtyen, dying in holy poverty, had bequeathed Bryvyth her voice.

'So? Is there no more you wish to tell me?'

Oh, the treacherous delicacy of women's faces. The skin too shallow. The blood too quick. The lips unsteady. She read the confirmation of my guilt.

'What more can there be? What do you want me to say?' Let her think it was only the heat of indignation.

'You have deceived me, Luned. Cruelly. Deliberately. Over seven years. I trusted you with the most difficult and dangerous of all our tasks. I saw you fail often. I blamed the strength of the enemy, and the weakness of my own prayers. Night and day I strove to arm you with God's power. I honoured your courage, your tenacity, your unwillingness to admit defeat and hand the burden to another. When you said you were winning the battle, I believed you. You let me rejoice that we had dragged Gorlois's daughter back from the brink of hell. Till Samain night.'

'You beat me for that. I made my confession. I still do the penance you laid upon me then.'

'I punished you for weakness, negligence, cowardice. For sins of omission. For the foolish pride that would not let you call me to help. You did not tell me of sins fouler than that.'

She waited. I was too frightened to question or argue.

'Today I talked with Morgan. Of what her future with us must be if she will not be a nun. She is of age now, and too old for the schoolroom. Rathtyen is dead, and her cell beside mine is empty. I put it to Morgan that she might have a house of her own, under my eye. I asked if it would grieve her to leave you. She laughed and said it would not. You had been no true soul-friend to her, and no gaoler either. She told me the truth of what you two had done.'

'*What?*' I whispered.

'Yes! She told me how all these years you had allowed her meetings with Gwennol. She confessed the black arts she has learned from that hag. She showed me these!' From her sleeve Bryvyth drew the little store of Morgan's slates that I had feared to read. 'Seven years. And you have connived with her. Studied corruption with her. You were here in the chapel. You stood by while she committed sacrilege. She said you smiled on her blasphemy in the hope of winning her love. Fool! What she wanted from you was your rage. Your shouts. Your hand on her arse. Your hugs!'

I could not speak. Treachery and despair whirled through my brain. Morgan was being taken from me. Morgan despised me. Morgan had accused me falsely. Yet still not of everything. The greatest sin of all had been left unsaid.

'Well? What have you to say for yourself that is not beneath contempt?'

What could I do? I confessed to the lesser sins I had not committed, to hide the knowledge of the greater crime.

She raised me up. I knew her arms around me and I sobbed like a little girl.

'The sin is mine. I should not have trusted you like myself . . . The Father is creating us anew. The Son is crucified for us afresh. The Spirit is cleansing us with wind and fire. God absolves the penitent.'

Bryvyth wept for me and for her own lost hopes. I wept for myself.

Today Rathtyen had died. Today Morgan had stolen my inheritance from me.

Before all the community, gathered in prayer, I falsely acknowledged my fault. There was no beating this time. Even Bryvyth's ready arm had grown weary at last. I think I could have endured that with greater pride than that public recital. I was condemned to return to the cows. It was the most visible humiliation of my penance, though there were many others.

I stumbled from the chapel alone, crying bitterly. Someone caught me in the dark. It was Morgan.

'Well?' she demanded. 'Are you satisfied yet? Do you still wish to keep me here?'

I could not speak. My stomach was heaving.

'What is the matter, Luned? Why are you shaking?'

'It is nothing, ' I moaned through gritted teeth. 'Just the cold wind.' But I could not fight down the retching in my throat. I spun away from her to hide this further degradation.

'You're not being sick, are you?' she said impatiently. Suddenly she threw back her head and laughed outrageously, while I spewed up bread and milk upon the grass.

'Oh, you're not, are you? It couldn't be that! Not my holy Luned, of all people! Oh, that would be the funniest thing in the world. The sweetest revenge I could ever have on Tintagel!'

I did not know what she meant. I swear to you, I did not know.

.

242

# Chapter Twenty-eight

Bryvyth and Morgan. Both I had loved. Both abandoned me.

Morgan, my foster-daughter, was taken from me. She moved into the empty hut beside Bryvyth's. She had no human guardian now to fail her. Her door was barred at night from the outside. Bryvyth battled with her for love, a different love from mine. She was a strong-armed warrior defending her tribe from evil. It was too late. I had already betrayed Tintagel. Morgan had taken her vows. She belonged to the Goddess. Doors could not hold her any more.

Even the kitten deserted me for Morgan.

I slept alone again. I, who had waited years, desperate at times to regain my solitude. And now I cried myself to sleep for loneliness. I did not know what was happening in my own body. Too little my mother told me in the orchard. Too little I had gossiped with other girls. Such things were never spoken of in Tintagel among celibate nuns. Or not where Bryvyth might have heard it. I had not wished to listen. I had thought that only in a nunnery could women get knowledge. I did not know what every slave-girl knows.

I knew my body had altered. The moon no longer brought a tide of blood. I believed simply that my womanhood had been taken away. At one time that would have delighted me. That monthly aspect of my life had been a burden to me, a fouling weakness of a woman's nature, a reminder that I could never be truly like a man. I had clung to that once-heard scrap of conversation that lean, hard hermits fasting and praying beyond the norm were sometimes released from our common curse. It was another reason to aspire to holiness, discipline, abstinence. I had embraced them hopefully.

Now I had what I wanted. My body ceased to bleed. And the loss of it was a sharp grief to me. I knew better than anyone that it could not be a reward for Christian virtue. Therefore it must have come as a punishment for the sin I had committed. The clean male God of Sinai and the fasting Christ of the wilderness had rejected me. Now the Three fertile Mothers from whom the earth teems declared me unpleasing to them. I was unfit for any life, unwelcomed by any god. I would have followed Morgan blindly, greedily, after that first time, despising myself, yet exulting too in that uncleanness. But I saw that way was barred to me also now.

Once more I must be up in the cold winter dark, milking the stinking beasts. I must stagger under the weight of hard-filled buckets. I must muck out the freezing byre, when my body longed for rest and warmth. Often Bryvyth worked alongside me in the dark dawn, whistling hymns and scolding the cows heartily. She blamed herself as well as me. But the friendship between us had cooled. Her trust was lost. There was no talk of making that pilgrimage together now.

A week later, Cigfa was declared the abbess's heir.

When I heard the news, I looked at my rough, cracked hands, that I could not hold steady for the cold. I thought of Cigfa, nobly-born, delicately pricking with compasses the lacing patterns of a new title page.

Yet I was too valuable to be utterly cast aside. When I had finished with the cows, I must still turn to the trade and rents and provisioning of the convent. It gave me no joy now. I saw that there was no honour in it. To deal with foreigners in silver, that other nuns would wash their hands after touching, to take a portion of the crops from surly tenants, to scold the cooks when they were wasteful. I had lost my youthful dream of glory. Who would read what my stylus scratched on the wax tablets? They would never illuminate the monasteries of Europe.

And when at last the weary day was ended and I longed to throw myself on the hay to ease my misery in sleep, I could not. I must spend long hours on my feet in prayer. Bryvyth had commanded it. My body obeyed, but she could not compel my soul. Prayer was dry sawdust in my mouth. It meant nothing to me now. I was mocked by both God and Goddess. When Bryvyth stood in her own cell, as I knew she did, did she feel the unequal burden on her soul?

Many of the girls went home for Christmas. Some of the older ones would not be returning. Husbands awaited them. Ygerne's daughter stayed. A horseman came from Uther. There would be no mercy for Morgan until Arthur was found. Each week a party of warriors rode out from Bossiney to enforce his rule. Morgan must be presented before them, pale, furious. He punished Bryvyth too, making her inflict this indignity on her prisoner.

Once the abbess burst out in anger to me, 'If only she'd repent just once and make a full confession of her sins, I'd throw her out of Tintagel that very same hour and let Uther's swords make an end of it. I'd rejoice to see her die with a pure soul now and give us peace.'

But Morgan had made her choice. She showed no repentance. Uther was right to fear her.

Winter tightened its grip.

Still no blood came. I suffered under the burden of more than spiritual unworthiness. I had thought that this cessation might have brought lightness of body, a greater physical freedom, a freer step. It was not so. I was appalled by the growing heaviness of my body, the slowness of my mind. I could hardly bear that. I, whose sharp quick brain had been the match for any man. I, who could out-figure any trader at the gate, whose mind could grasp the tally before my fingers cast the beads. Why was I now so far removed from what Rathtyen had been, ailing in body but at the last reciting Plato as though the book lay open in her mind? Why was I growing so like fat Blatriad, waddling about her kitchen?

Even Blatriad was luckier than I was. I would have given anything that winter to have worked in the warm, yeast-smelling comfort of the kitchen, to have soothed my aching body before the oven. But it was a luxury beyond reach.

If I had been less strong, my body might have given way under the strain. Even that escape was denied to me. I did not know enough to seek release for myself. What was begun that night in the Mother's Hole must be endured to the end.

I accuse Morgan. She could have helped. I do not doubt she knew enough, even then. Her eyes met mine and mocked me. She knew what was coming, and I did not.

# Chapter Twenty-nine

I dragged my heaviness of soul and body through the summer.

Clever, but ignorant, I woke in my cell one hot morning in August.
Cramps gripped my belly. Believe me, I thought I had the flux. I
stumbled to the latrine, clutching the pain. But no relief came. I crept
back to my cell and lay there moaning, too ill to rise. Senara came to
see why I had not milked the cows, and she went hurrying to fetch
Blatriad from the kitchen. They roused Fyna from her bed. Wise though
they were, they did not guess the reason. My belly was not as huge
as Blatriad's.

They made me a potion. Hot, foul-smelling, strong. They went to
morning prayers and left me in a quiet that held no peace. They nearly
killed me. Time after time I crawled to the latrine. It was there at last
that I dropped the baby.

I thought my body was bursting, that I who had aspired to the highest
of honour and virtue was now a gigantic paunch of foulness. Now I
would split and spill my guts into a stinking hole in the ground. My
rottenness into the earth from which I had come. My blood to the
Mothers. My skin once bloated then left empty as a shrivelled toad.
No spirit left. No freed soul winging into the pale blue sky above me.
No choirs of angels singing triumph as they had for Rathtyen. No Father
opening heavenly arms to receive me. No radiant Christ to greet his
bride. My soul had died long since. It only remained to empty this
distorted body.

But before that, pain. Terror. How could my bowels have spawned
anything so monstrous?

Nuns heard my screams, and then the child's, and came running.

I remember little of it, through that sobbing nightmare. Fyna pulled
the baby from the filth of the hole where I had dropped it. I think
some of the others, more shocked, would have let it drown. Even then,
I hardly understood what had happened. That blackened, bloodied
thing, bawling like a hungry calf. The mess that streaked Fyna's gown.
The round eyes and open mouths of a ring of sisters. What had that
to do with me, slumped on my knees on the earthen floor, spent and
torn?

They took the baby from me. I never saw it again. I do not even
know which kind it was. I could not ask.

'Take her to bed.'

I felt Bryvyth's presence, like the wrath that will end the world.

Some of them helped me to rise. Blood slid down my legs. I do not
remember well. I think Blatriad was with me, and the slave-girl Senara.

Not Cigfa. Oh, no. She stood, white-faced, at a distance. This was not work for her hands.

Back in my cell, they stripped my shift away and washed the blood and slime from me. They dressed me in clean linen and drew the covers over me. They spoke above my head, as though I was a baby myself, in anxious whispers. They let me lie.

I was not dead, though I wished I was. I knew now that I was horrifyingly alive. The blood that I thought had dried in my womb for ever had burst forth into doubled life. How could this be?

I groaned like those who would rip out the past and cannot.

I lay, exhausted, waiting for Bryvyth to come.

There were footsteps at the door. Through the black cloud of self-pity I looked up. Bryvyth must understand. She must see it had been none of my own doing. Not my choice. How could I ever have willed such a terrible thing? I did not know how it had happened to me. I would throw myself upon the generosity of her compassion.

It was not Bryvyth. The white moon of Morgan's face hung over me. Her hair, braided above the ears, and then falling free, brushed my face. It smelt of lavender.

She was a tall young woman now, no longer a schoolgirl. Her breasts standing proud above a slender waist. I smiled for the first time, weakly. I was not alone. Morgan had not deserted me. She had led me to this. I knew, without understanding how, it must spring from that night in the Mother's Hole. You must understand that I had sought in libraries for my knowledge. My parents' farm had never been my school. Yet I did not blame Morgan then. I was glad she had come.

A cold smile twisted her mouth.

'Poor Luned. Didn't you know anything? Could you not calculate the meaning of your own measurements? What was there ever in you to make you so proud? You should have asked me for help. I could have ended it long ago. I know enough for that. You could have done it yourself, even. The knowledge was there, on the slates under my bed.'

'How could I guess? Why didn't you tell me?'

'Because you did not ask. I am a queen. It was for you to be the suppliant at my feet. Well, you are mightily humbled now. You must go begging on your knees.'

'What have I left to beg for? Except death.'

'I will not give you that, though I could do it. Death is not alms to be distributed freely, like bread to the poor. I shall keep that knowledge close, like a sheathed weapon. Knowledge without the will to use it is not yet power. One day perhaps I may see the need and discover the will. But I shall not use it lightly. You are too small an object to deserve it. I have other powers I mean to use for greatness. Gwennol and her sisters have taught me. But I shall soon know more than they. The Mothers themselves are teaching me. My own eyes bring me knowledge. My fingertips speak to me. My nose is a scholar. In years to come the bards will sing of my skill.'

I believed her. I had to trust someone then. I would have believed anything Morgan told me.

'What will happen to me?'

'We must consider,' she said, studying my face as she smoothed my hair aside.

Her eyes were strangely bright. She was like a physician bending over her patient, seeing a new disease with interest, even excitement.

'You'll never be abbess now. That was over already, wasn't it? You can't stay here. You have been too shamed. And you're too proud to crawl back to your parents' farm. So what else is there for you? Would you go out of the gate and sell your body to the first man for the price of a meal? Do not turn your face to the wall, Luned.'

She wanted me to beg from her. She was a prisoner. Under a ban of death. Destitute, save for the meagre allowance to feed her with convent food and clothe her with the simplest gown. But in her own eyes she was already a queen. She had a court, a country, weapons, gifts to give.

I caught her hand. The smooth white hand that had healed my back.

'Help me! You can, can't you?'

'I can and will. Should not a daughter care for her foster-mother? Bryvyth trusted me to you for my salvation. Instead, I have made you mine. I have humbled holy Tintagel. I have been revenged on the Church that betrayed my father and imprisoned me. Uther Pendragon is next. Let us move you closer to the king himself. He killed my father and stole Bossiney from us. It is a royal dun now, under that trickster Ulfin. Go there when you can walk. Ask for Gwennol. Tell her I send you to her for safekeeping, as the first of my women.'

'To Gwennol!'

The old witch from the sea. Bryvyth's mighty exorcism on the shore. The spread fingers pointing. The curse chanted.

'What is the matter? You're not afraid of her, are you?' She snatched her hand from me, her eyes blazing. 'Gwennol loves me? Do you know that? Gwennol loves me! When did you ever risk your life to save me? When did you ever hold me in your arms? If Bryvyth had been my foster-mother, she might have done so. But you? When have you ever loved me more than yourself?'

Her rage passed. We both knew I would not answer.

'Wait for me secretly in Bossiney. Gwennol will teach you. This cannot endure. I shall need my own wise women about me soon. One day I *must* be free, and then I shall meet . . .'

She turned away from me and went to the door. For a while she stood in silence, staring out over the sea. Suddenly laughter rippled from her, shockingly. She ran back to me, merry as a mischievous girl.

'Oh, Luned! You were not clever enough by half. Do you not know Merlyn was the baby of a nun too! She swore his father came to her in the night as an incubus from hell. She was powerless to resist him. Many times he covered her while she lay helpless. And they believed her. The Church took her side. The world calls Merlyn a holy child. Merlyn Son of a nun and a devil. What will your child be, Luned? What have they done with it? Did they call it holy?'

She left me then. Alone with my loss. Everything gone. My pride.

My future. My safe stronghold. Maidenhead. Baby. Even the cell that was my home. All lost to me forever. I did not need Bryvyth to stand over me and tell me that. It was too late to confess now and be forgiven. I had deceived her too many times to be believed. It was her fault. An abbess should be a judge of women. I never asked for such a task. I was not equal to it.

They cast me out from Tintagel, without my baby. They judged I was no fit mother for any child. With my belly empty and my breasts painful with unsucked milk, I took myself to Bossiney, the first of Morgan's people.

# Chapter Thirty

I could not pass Bossiney by this time, that place of men and wealth and war. I had not the strong presence of Bryvyth beside me to give me courage. I had not even the grip of my holy staff in my hand, a familiar friend. They had taken that from me, with my white nun's gown, and given me a dress of homespun brown. I was a woman like any other now. I had no protection.

Bryvyth had done her best.

'What will you do, child? I know a farmer, Govan, up Bodmin way. His wife died last Candlemas. He's a good spread of fields and a load of cattle and pigs. He needs a clever wife to help him manage it all. Will I tell him you're willing?'

I bowed my head and thanked her. I would make my own way. She would get no comfort from me.

There was pain in that last parting from her in the mists of morning. The ready tears ran down Bryvyth's cheeks, though not on mine.

Alone, she stood at the island end of the causeway, the fragile neck that held Tintagel to the land. Knowing my fear, she would have crossed the bridge with me that last time for friendship. I told her no. Briefly I saw her, square shoulders slightly stooped, watching me go. She raised her hand in an uncertain blessing. Too late for that. I did not look back again.

I had wanted to see someone else. My eyes had gone past Bryvyth, searching the ledges and the summit for a tall, vital figure, the fall of raven hair, a fair face turned to seek mine. There were a few others about their tasks in the early hush of morning, glancing sideways to see me depart, pretending in their innocence to ignore me. There was no sight of Morgan. Then I remembered. Bryvyth had set a bar on her door. She had divided us.

That was the only thing that sustained me as I walked the short road from Tintagel towards Bossiney. That this was Morgan's home. Had been Morgan's home, in the days when her father Gorlois hunted this forest and Uther Pendragon beat the Saxons and her mother Ygerne prayed in Nectan's glade for a fourth child. Before Arthur was born.

It was Gwennol's place too. Neither Uther nor Ulfin had found the courage to turn her out. And with that thought the solid walls of earth and wattle ahead began to take on a fairy shimmer. If I was cast out from the city of the angels, what had I come to now?

It was too quiet. A listless small boy switching at flies with a spray of oak leaves. The cattle already lying down in the shade after milking. There was no lean young warrior on the gate with excess of mocking courtesy to make a woman blush. The guard was lame, with a facial scar making one eye peer crookedly.

'I come from Tintagel. I have a message to give.' I had fretted all the way over how to announce myself, how to get past Uther's men to Gorlois's nurse and witch.

'You won't find Ulfin here, or any lord with four whole limbs. It's my guess they won't be back for harvest either. The Saxon dragon's eating up the best blood we've got. But my lady Rozen should be up and about soon, if you want to sit down in the shade and wait.'

Another jolt. I had nerved myself to deal with men. After all, it had been my task for many years, though never with warriors. My reckoning had not extended to noble ladies. I had scorned the embroideresses' workshop. I let them deal with their highborn customers directly. I, plain and scholarly, found such noblewomen oddly disturbing.

'There is no need to trouble my lady. My message is for a woman by the name of Gwennol.'

Be wary. Do not use that name too familiarly. He must not guess that I have been sent by Morgan.

'Gwennol Far-Sight? That's a rum do, now. What business do the nuns of Tintagel want with old Gwennol?'

'I am not a nun.'

'I can see that.' He looked me over shrewdly. 'But you've had your hair shorn under that veil not so long since. What was the trouble? Too cold a life without a man in your bed?'

Was my sin so naked I might have worn the scene embroidered on my dress? I could not hide the truth from the first person I spoke to.

He laughed, not unkindly. 'Cheer up, mistress. I'm a soldier. Or was, till Uther led us into a Saxon ambush. He's had no luck since he killed Gorlois. Well, then. You need keen eyes to stay alive in enemy territory, and there's too much of that in Britain now. And shrewd judgment too to tell friends from traitors. Don't you fret. Hair grows again, at your age. And someone will put the roses back in your cheeks . . . if any men come home this time.'

I saw the reason for his kindness. His wounds had cast him out from his own hope of glory. We were two of a kind, driftwood on the beach, uprooted trees broken off from life before our time.

'Well, you look harmless enough. There's only good comes out of Tintagel. I say it's a pity the Pendragon ever crossed them. He needs all the prayers he can get now. Gwennol sleeps down there, this side of the bakehouse. A hut all to herself, she has, and no children to mind now. Don't let on I said so, but I fancy Ulfin is afraid to cross her. They've none of them been so sure of themselves, since Merlyn went. Maybe she could help you, if you asked, whatever the trouble is. She's good with wounds. My sort, at least.'

So I was walking down the quiet path between the houses towards the woman I feared most, after Morgan.

Gwennol Far-Sight was old now, but she was not abed. There were many in that dun who had a drowsy, frowsty look. After the convent it seemed an ill-disciplined place to me. The best of its youth was gone, and many older warriors had climbed into the saddle again to fill their place. Those who were left without them spent too long in bed and had too little work or reason to do it.

But not this one. The old woman sat on a bench in the sun. She was carding wool. At close-quarters I saw her hands were crooked, yet they moved in a steady rhythm that made the finished work pile up beside her with the ease of practice.

She picked me out before I had left the gate. Her eyes were on me all the time, like a fisherwoman drawing in her catch on a slowly tightening line. Yet I was not to be caught. I had come of my own free will. I could have accepted Bryvyth's offer of a husband.

When we were near enough for our eyes to meet she gave me a slow, sure smile of satisfaction, dark eyes intent as a robin on a worm. There was no surprise. There was nothing I needed to explain.

'So she's sent you ahead of her.'

I dropped my eyes. I was not accustomed to stare others in the face. But the silence made me look up again. The smile had gone. She might have been that bloodstained hag guarding the way to the cave, so grim she looked.

'By rights we should kill you.'

A moth that had fluttered into a spider's web.

'You put your dainty foot in a place where strangers are not allowed. Only those the Old Ones recognise are safe in there. Lowenna's a fool. She shouldn't have let you pass her. She knows every sheep she has by name but she can't tell the difference between one nun and another. But you're clever. You must have known what you saw was only safe for the wise.'

'I did not wish to see it. Morgan brought me there.'

'And you were her keeper?' She spat with laughter. 'The Mothers will have blood for it, dearie.'

'There was blood. I have been punished.'

The soreness was still between my legs with walking. My breasts were hard and hot.

She looked me up and down, knowing everything.

'The Mothers have blessed you, I'd say.'

'It was no blessing. I did not want it. And they have taken my baby away.'

I almost cried then, being torn in two.

'But it was alive, wasn't it? Still is, though you can't see it. Life and death. That's what the Mothers give to those they love. Death for all of us. Birthing for the lucky ones. Maybe Morgan was wise after all to bring you down. I never had a baby. Hundreds of women I've helped fill their bellies. I've charmed the babies out of them too. I've nursed other people's children on my knees, even Ygerne herself, that's queen of Britain now. Morgan was my last. They took her away from me and gave her to you bloodless nuns instead. I never had one of my own.'

'We did not want Morgan.' Faithless Luned, to deny I loved her.

'Nobody ever wanted Morgan. Except Gwennol. But she's grown too big for me. And you want her, now.'

I bore that in silence, transparently red with anger.

'Well, what can you do? I take it you've come looking for work, and food in your belly.'

'I can write a fair hand. I can read Latin and Greek. I can figure and cast the reckoning on the abacus.'

'Can you sew?'

Indignation rose. Had I trained that hard, to be a woman like any other?

'That was not my work.'

She fingered my skirt and her hands moved meaningfully up the inside of my thighs.

'But you're not a white nun now, are you, dearie? You went in to the shadow of death, without protection, and the Mothers blessed you. You're a full woman now.'

Then she let go of me and sat back, wincing. Just an aged serving-woman on a hard bench.

'My Lady Rozen will be tickled pink when she hears you've come from Tintagel. She's always had a fancy for fine embroidery, and there's no one can sew as pretty a stitch as the white nuns. But that abbess Bryvyth of yours has got a long memory. There isn't one thread she's let come to Bossiney since the day Gorlois died. Leastways, not by her knowledge. Though there's more than one thing been done at Tintagel that she doesn't know about, isn't there? You *can* sew, can't you?'

'Of course I can.'

We had all, even the highest of us, taken our share of mending, of sewing plain seams. I had shown Morgan how to take care of her own clothes. I did not deceive Gwennol.

'Well, you're clever enough to learn Latin. So you can figure out how to whip a silver thread. Do you want me to ask her for a place?'

A huge lump in my throat to swallow.

'Please.'

For a moment her head bent, muttering. Her nails snagged her skirt. Then she stretched out her claw for me to help her rise.

She hobbled away to the lady's bower beside the hall. I was too ashamed to stand outside and be stared at. I crept into the darkness of Gwennol's hut and sat down on a stool. Dried herbs hung everywhere, scenting the air as I brushed beneath them. More than a normal woman's rafters would hold. I did not examine them too closely lest I should find that not all the bundles were what they seemed. As indeed they were not. When Gwennol came back she found me weeping from exhaustion and grief.

'My lady will see you. It's a funny thing, but she's torn her gown this very morning, just after you came. So here's your chance to show how clever you mean to be. Let's look at you.'

She wiped my face and then parted my clothes at the neck. Her hands reached in and gripped my breasts. I cried out in pain, as first golden liquid and then white spurted out. She mixed a powder with water and made me drink it.

253

'We'll have to take care you don't get the milk-fever. It's a pity it isn't a wet-nurse my lady needs, instead of a seamstress.'

She settled my clothes again and straightened my veil. I might have been a snivelling child, like so many others.

'There! You're one of us now. We're three of a kind, seemingly. I never had a baby of my own. You've borne yours, and lost it. And Morgan was robbed of her little brother Arthur. Well, the world's turning. Our time is coming round. Let's see if we can't bring one of those pairs together, eh?'

# Chapter Thirty-one

I was a good pupil. I do not mean the embroidery, though I quickly became proficient in that too. Yet fine sewing was a necessary burden laid upon me, the price of food and shelter. There was another school I trained in that excited my soul. I was Gwennol's pupil.

I feared the spirits of the otherworld and Gwennol's powers. That fear was real and proper. It grows greater with the years, not less. Those who do not respect the realm of the Old Ones do not live long or keep their sanity. Yet, like that night in the Hole under Tintagel, the dark thing I feared also aroused me. I felt it first as a tremor of danger in the mind. Soon it became manifest in a kindling of the body. You may think from much that has gone before that I was cold, hardly a woman, walled up against the sensations of the flesh. Under Gwennol's teaching I discovered truths about myself I had not known. That coolness had been my defence against the violence of my own physical being. Gwennol loosed it. When the sacred drink was in me and the drums quickened my blood and the darkness covered me, that other Luned inside me was uncaged.

So some on Tintagel too approached the living God. There were those like Piala who abandoned themselves to Him, who allowed Him to invade and possess them. I had never been one of them. Too late I caught a glimpse of their ecstasy. Morgan had barred that way to me forever.

I had not escaped her. Under the earth, between the waters, I met Morgan again. My mind told me it could not be so. Bryvyth had set a great bar on her door. But when the smoke eddied and the flame turned white flesh to rose and eyes sparkled under masks, she was there. The moon-glimpse of her face, the star-shaft of her body, the shadow of her hair. When we invoked the Maiden, Mother, Hag, she came. It could not have been anyone but Morgan. No one else was in the same perfect form both child and queen.

I am one of her people now. With a sharp clarity of memory I see myself prostrate on the floor of the chapel in Tintagel, repeat my final vows, hear Nectan raise me to my feet, feel Bryvyth place the veil on my shorn head. I felt that thrill of awe again. I crossed another threshold.

You cannot come. This time my dress is on the rocks. My new-given name is spoken at the mouth. The watcher's bloodstained hole beckons me but challenges you. Are you repelled? Or do you wish to come in, through the blood, to the cave where life is given? Our language is not so very far apart, you see, though we horrify you.

I told you what I saw that first time, in ignorance and misconception. Now I understand what is being done. And therefore I may not tell you what I see.

Gwennol saw to it that it was only enacted. There were no more babies to quicken my womb.

By day Lady Rozen exclaimed with delight over the work I did for her. The nuns had schooled me in delicacy and accuracy of stitching. Everything that was done in Tintagel was finely made, for the glory of God the Creator. And I had studied the patterns of the scriptorium under Cigfa. Most of the work I did there was plain scholar's copying, convent accounts. But I had learned early how to plot a lacing band of ornament, to mark a fine capital at the beginning of the chapter. It was not difficult for me to transfer the technique from the written page to a silk border. It needed a methodical mind, a knowledge of geometry, the patience to repeat the same motif time after time without deviation around the hem.

She boasted she had never had such a treasure. She displayed my handiwork for the envy of her friends. Luned's embroidery became a special gift she could bestow on those who pleased her.

It gave me a bleak kind of pleasure. I had fallen far in my own esteem. I was shut out forever from the scriptorium of the abbey, to spend my life working for women whose highest goal was to ornament themselves for the envy of others. Solace came at night. Yet I must endure my days somehow. It was a matter of pride to do the work I despised exactly well.

It was a strange dichotomy. Sober seamstress by daylight. Passionate worshipper at the dark of the moon and the four great festivals.

I needed Gwennol. She alone could show me how I might satisfy my soul now.

She did not like me. We sprang from the same farming stock, but our educations had differed. I spoke the high Latin of Cicero and Virgil, while she knew the coarse vocabulary of the market-place. It was natural to me to write down anything I learned, to list names and quantities and applications. She saw me doing this with rage and horror. She swept my careful records into the fire and stamped out the ashes. Such knowledge should be entrusted to the memories of the wise only, to be sung in a sing-song chant, to be recited in an endless chain. It was not impossible for me to learn by rote. I had got the whole Psalter by heart and much of the theorems of Euclid. But I liked the order of the laced tablets of a codex, the sight of a growing store of knowledge, more valuable than gold, like Morgan's slates.

Gwennol needed me. I was an apt scholar, and she was old. She could not refuse to pass on what she knew to one who would retain it so faithfully. I had little natural skill in this field. I would never have the touch of power in my hands like Morgan. My success came from precise application of techniques studied, as I had learned to embroider a hem without love but with exactitude.

So, yoked unwillingly to each other, Gwennol and I began to work for Morgan's freedom.

Gwennol excused herself. 'She was safer over in Tintagel as long as she was a little maid. I knew Bryvyth would never let those men harm her. But she's a grown woman now. She must have her rights. And Uther Pendragon's got his hands full with those pesky Saxons, and his back turned on Cornwall. There'll be more than a few will rally to her when she's free. There's her sisters' husbands for a start.'

Such talk troubled me. I was a stranger to the world of kings and armies. Ulfin came little to Bossiney with his warriors now and in no good humour, his men few and wounded, the news of Britain bleak. Lady Rozen tried her best to cheer him but he wanted sleep, and brief savage love-making, and then excess of wine.

Young men were needed elsewhere now. Yet week after week a guard still rode to Tintagel to have Morgan paraded before them. Old, lame men, almost too stiff to climb into the saddle. But they were enough. She could not have escaped without Uther's knowledge.

Still, when Ulfin's band came home the sight of an armed warrior disturbed me. I have never known how to speak to such men.

'The Pendragon violated a holy place,' I told Gwennol. 'It is not surprising the land is wounded and laid waste.'

Nun or witch, Tintagel was a sacred centre. The women's navel. You must not be surprised that I still hold Bryvyth and her kind holy. We do well to recognise each other's power.

'Then we must find another ruler for Britain. One that knows how to heal the land,' said Gwennol, and set me to work.

Even now it quickens my blood. We two, and those we trusted, there in the far south-west corner of an island on the edge of the Roman Empire, working to shift the world on its axis. And so we did.

Long and secret were our preparations. Much there was new for me to learn. Much more that was old for Gwennol to remember, that she had never used before, perhaps had never heard before. I do not know. In places that I may not tell you of she sat cross-legged, her eyes closed but her face lifted as though she saw through red-veiled lids things it would sear the sight to look on naked. I fed the fire, dizzy with the scented smoke, put in her hands the things she commanded, sang what she taught me, not always understanding, knowing that to understand too much might rob the runes of power. My mind obedient, rational to begin with, saying that this, and this, and this, are what need to be done. The smoke taking over, the intellect melting, the body dissolving. Life running into water and blood and fire. I barely remained conscious to serve Gwennol.

When it was done, we were older, exhausted, and we had only gathered the means. Now we must make the great application. It must be done in the Hole, at night, at the dark of the moon, with the wisest of the wise. It was with a strange shock that I heard Gwennol summon me. I was not long in the mysteries. I had not known I had served the Old Ones so well.

The great rite of Unbinding began.

# Chapter Thirty-two

The world shifted. That which had been bound began to be loosed. Things which had been hidden came into the light. Such power is not easily controlled. We did not suspect what we had woken.

I was alone. It was not my habit, and is not now, to sit with a flock of other women gossiping more than I work. I have a reputation for superiority. I cannot help that. I cannot disguise I am an educated woman. Better my own thoughts and the memories of my learning than filling my head with trivialities and driving out what I so hardly gained.

So I took my stool to some quiet place to do my sewing. I was not often interrupted. I think the men were afraid of me. I could have found greater peace outside the walls of Bossiney. The cliffs were wide and grassy. There were quiet coves. Gwennol still went to such places if the day was sunny and her rheumatism did not trouble her too much. But I went little out of the gate. We were too close to Tintagel still. I did not want to meet the white sisters on the road, going about their works of charity. It would have pained me too much.

I did not find it difficult to be so confined physically. My mind ranged far.

I had chosen a place on the rampart in the early afternoon. The dun was ill-guarded. The Saxons had drained it of its youth. But we did not expect the enemy to come this far. Those that were left in Dumnonia had little heart for raiding. War was no longer a sport, like hunting.

So I watched them come, and no one gave a shout of warning. I did not call out. It was not my place. But I stopped my sewing and lifted my head to follow their progress, as I thought, unobserved.

A man and a woman, riding finely-caparisoned horses. Behind them, two attendants on smaller ponies.

It was he who caught my eyes and filled my thoughts with wonder and disquiet. He was immensely tall. His robes were dazzling white and he wore a white turban, fastened with a ruby and a purple feather. His skirts spread loose and flowing over his coal-black mount. More startling still, his face and hands were black, gleaming faintly in the sun as though anointed with oil. I had seen such men aboard the ships that came to Tintagel. In later years I had traded with them, tuning the ear of my schoolhouse Latin to the strange jabber of theirs. But I had never seen one like this. A prince. With a great curved scimitar at his side.

I scarcely had eyes for the lady beside him. Except to note that she was as fine as he was, but of an opposite kind, as though his darkness had cast a bright shadow. Gold hair, tumbling in curls out of intricate braids. A fair face, shaded under the most delicate of veils. Clothes of as many colours as a meadow in May. A light green gown richly and colourfully embroidered. A rose-pink tunic, an underskirt all white and gold. Jewels on throat and arms and even on the fine blue leather of her boots. Where he was noble in his simplicity, she was a riot of extravagance.

The boy behind was fair and golden-curled. The girl was black and brilliant-eyed.

As they approached Bossiney the man leaned out his hand and caressed the woman's arm, saying something to her that made a smile flash in his dark face. She threw back her pretty head and laughed ringingly, then took his hand in her white one and played with his fingers as they rode side by side.

Reality dissolved. These were creatures out of fairyland. I sat bewitched. It did not occur to me to make any spells to ward against them. I did not think to warn Gwennol.

I lost sight of them as they circled to the gate. But I turned quickly, eager to see their entrance.

Bossiney had changed. The dusty paths, the mud-smeared walls, the ageing thatch had all taken on the bright shimmer of water. The strangers dismounted and walked in through the guard-post like brilliant fish swimming through their true domain.

Little Cador went running to warn my lady. A flock of women came hurrying out of the bower, my Lady Rozen among them. She advanced to greet the strangers, hastening for eagerness and uncertainty. I could see that she was both anxious and honoured to have such unexpected and noble guests.

I had not moved from the rampart. I could not hear the greetings that passed between them. But the name of Uther Pendragon floated up to me. For a moment confusion overtook my wits. This could not be the treacherous king come back to Cornwall, surely? This courtly Moor? They disappeared into the hall. I saw wine being brought, and cakes. The golden boy and the black-faced girl stood in the doorway, teasing each other with peacock feathers. I felt impelled towards the steps, but I resisted. A nameless fear kept me on my stool on the wall, as if the dun below were indeed a pool in which I did not know how to swim.

The guests emerged into the sunlight. The Moor's arm rested lightly around his lady's waist as she leaned on his shoulder. Beside the fresh gaiety of her robes, the stark white of his, Rozen looked shabby. Even the work of my needle on her gown seemed dull and lifeless. The black man walked across the open space in front of the hall. He carried his head nobly and his limbs had the grace of authority that needs no swagger. His eyes looked keenly on all sides. They found me. He moved towards me, slowly, still chatting courteously to his hostess, his fingertips still laced in those of his lady. His brown eyes never left my face. I made no attempt to run or to protect myself, though my body screamed to me for help. I was a half-fledged bird trapped in its nest by a hawk.

He stopped beneath me, and I saw that his face was not truly black, but dark as old, oiled wood.

'Greetings, Luned,' he said, as though I had known and expected him. He extended his hand.

As I came down the steps, I knew. I did not have the name, but I recognised his power. I had felt that same lure, walking down the path towards Gwennol's hut, that morning of my expulsion. This was stronger yet.

'That is she, as you say,' Rozen answered, and I heard the puzzlement in her voice as I bowed. 'You are honoured, Luned. This is Saranhon Star-Gazer, from the court of Uther Pendragon. And this the Lady Nimue.'

But I knew from the way she tasted the names on her tongue that they were new to her.

'So this is the fair embroideress,' exclaimed the lady.

'She has a gifted hand, it is true.'

'And trained on Tintagel, you say!' Nimue laughed like rippling water. Should I be afraid of her too? Could there be power in anyone so gay and pretty?

But Saranhon drew my eyes back to his and made my flesh tremble merely by smiling at me.

'So you were foster-mother to Morgan, Gorlois's daughter? How is she?'

Fear turned me faint. I had not spoken of that to anyone but Gwennol.

'I am no longer a nun. I have not seen Morgan these two years.'

His hand played with his companion's hair. His face did not change. He went on looking at me. He knew I lied. I knew I had angered him.

I was in the water now. Their element. It was cold about me and I was drowning. Words gasped from me, bubbles breaking on the surface, from desperation.

'She is still a prisoner. Against the law of God and Britain. She is of age to leave her parents' home. She has the right to live freely or to marry whom she chooses. Uther Pendragon denies that right by threat of murder.'

'Insolent!' Rozen cried. 'Do you want to be whipped, to speak so to the king's mage?'

'She speaks only the truth now,' said Saranhon. 'You know it. You and your husband are Morgan's gaolers, are you not? But for seven years this woman was the keeper of Morgan's heart. Her eyes say more than could be seen from Gwent or Winchester. It is well that the Pendragons know their danger. Morgan has not forgotten old grudges, has she?'

'How could she, there, where it happened?'

'Or forgiven?'

'Have the Pendragons ever asked for her forgiveness?'

'Or understood the necessity of that night?'

'Necessity?'

Nimue caught his arm. Someone was coming in through the gateway. A small, squat, humpbacked figure, walking lamely.. Gwennol.

There was a flash in Saranhon's eyes. If he had not been black I think colour might have sprung to his cheeks. He watched her come in silence, as he had watched me.

She was not so frightened by him. She did not stop or hesitate or show surprise. It was as though, even out on the cliffs, she had known they had come, and who they were. I felt some of the sureness go out of Saranhon.

Then he stiffened. The muscles of his face became taut. I heard the breath hiss through his pinched nostrils. Even from where I stood I felt the heat of power radiating from him.

As she neared him Gwennol stumbled slightly. Her eyes glazed over and began to wander. She no longer seemed to know where she was going.

'Be off to your own hut,' scolded Rozen. 'We do not need you here.' She apologised to Saranhon. 'Gwennol Far-Sight. An old pensioner from Gorlois's court. We keep her for pity's sake.'

Nimue laughed. Her hand strayed along Saranhon's spine and fondled his neck. His eyes left Gwennol's. A shiver of delight ran through him and before us all he leaned towards his lady and kissed her rose-pink mouth. Very sure of herself and her lover was Nimue. As I saw his hand encircle her thighs I looked away for modesty.

My eyes fell on Gwennol. A change had come over her, as though a fog had lifted. The eyes bright and dark as never before in the two years I had known her, a brilliance of shock and triumph. Lame though she was she almost flew the last few steps to meet him. With an effort Saranhon tore himself from Nimue's hold. I felt him striving to regain mastery, too late.

Gwennol came so close that when she stopped at last and looked up at him, he had to bend his head to her. Her breath came quickly, as though she had been striding fast. Small dark eyes peering up into his large brown ones.

'Emrys Merlyn,' she said. 'Come back to us after nine years!'

There was a gasp from all of us, and a flash like lightning again across the Moor's face. It was a name known but not often or lightly spoken. A name out of song. A name bitter in the history of Bossiney. The Pendragon's magician. The trickster who had penetrated Tintagel's defences. The druid who had held Arthur in his arms that stormy night and stolen him away into silence. Lady Rozen backed away, doubt in her face. I saw that she was thinking of calling the guards. I do not believe they would have touched him. Nimue grasped at Saranhon's arm, alarm in her eyes.

The Moor laughed.

'Life is long. And the world's course is longer still for a multitude of livings. I have been known under many faces and many names. Still, I should have guessed Gwennol Far-Sight had not lost her power of seeing.'

She spat in the dust.

'I don't change. Not like some I could name.'

Yet for all that, he reached out a hand to her and she put up her own. They clasped each other almost like old friends.

'Leave us,' he ordered Rozen and her retainers. But Gwennol put out a hand and stayed me. Nimue remained too, holding the mage's sleeve and tracing her finger lightly on his arm, making him shudder.

'Gwennol Far-Sight,' he said, when we were alone. 'Since you have uncovered me so quickly let us speak plainly. It seems we cannot escape each other.'

'Hm! I thought you'd escaped us all for near nine years. And when did Emrys Merlyn ever say anything without a double tongue?'

'Be careful, old woman, or your own tongue will shrivel in your throat,' warned Nimue.

Merlyn patted her hand.

'Be easy, my love. Gwennol and I are old allies and old enemies. We understand each other.'

Gwennol looked Nimue up and down.

'Who's this pretty dragonfly you've taken up with? And what's brought the pair of you to Cornwall to trouble us again?'

'This is Nimue. She serves the Lady of the Lake. She is of the wise. And what brought me here you should know better than anyone. You and your sisters.' He looked sideways at me. 'You have shaken the land. You may have done a more dangerous thing than you guessed.'

'You still fear Morgan that much, do you? When she's shut up in a convent? And you've hidden Arthur from her for half her life?'

'And will do till he is a full man. That boy was hardly got. You and your kind shall not rob Britain of her king before his time.'

'You needed our kind nine years ago. You needed the magic of Tintagel to make such a child.'

He started then, though the dark of his cheeks hid the full force of his reaction.

'Life he has, however it was got. And life he shall have. Morgan is older than he is. She has come to her power before he is ready for his. The Saxon wars are bitter. Uther Pendragon may not live out his full tine.'

'And what if he dies tomorrow? Do you think Gorlois's people are going to weep for him? Those few of us he left alive. You wouldn't weep yourself, would you, now that he's fathered the boy you wanted?'

'Britain would be left in danger without a high king.'

'Maybe better off without one, if that's how high kings use their power.'

'The forces of Britain must be led. Inspired! And shall be. I am breeding such a leader as will gladden your eyes as much as any woman's, you lecherous old harridan.'

'A sweet boy, and handy with a sword and spear,' smiled Nimue. 'I am teaching him well.'

I felt Gwennol tremble, standing beside me. I put out my arm to stop her falling. But she was firm again, giving them back thrust for thrust.

'A warrior already? Poor little mite!'

'We need time, Gwennol. He is not yet nine years old.'

Merlyn was pleading now.

'The same age Morgan was when he was got. And for this boy's sake Morgan lost father, mother, freedom. And now she must lose husband, children?'

'Morgan is dangerous. She will destroy even those she loves.'

'Do you still fear the power you took from us? How many Queens have there been in Britain since the Romans came? How many women speak in the Great Council now? Who still honours the Mothers?'

'This is no time for petty jealousy. Be practical, woman. The Saxons! Are you so blind and backward here in Cornwall, you don't know that half the country has already fallen to the enemy?'

'Half of Britain is woman, by my reckoning. There's more than Saxons have conquered and raped and had their will of us. I should know.'

Merlin gazed down at her, between cajoling and despair.

'Is this your doing, then, Gwennol? Will you not let her forgive? Have you taught her to destroy us all? Even Arthur, and Britain?'

'Who said anything about destroying? I'm known through all Cornwall for a great healer. Yes, I've taught Morgan all I know.'

'But how will she use that power, Gwennol? Once given, you cannot set a boundary on it. You know the danger.'

'It wasn't us women that taught her to hate you. You did that yourselves.'

'Then since I am too late to direct her power, I must deny her its use. For the good of us all.'

'That's what men always say. And who is there to curb your power, I'd like to know?'

'None but the gods.'

I do not know what made me turn to see Nimue's face. It shocked me. The lady was staring at Gwennol in wonder. Her eyes were huge and shining with a fierce desire. Then she smiled, gloriously. Her hand stopped its frivolous playing and closed round Merlyn's arm. Her white fingers imprisoned him.

They stayed the night. I thought we were done with them. But in the shadows of our hut Gwennol pressed something cold into my hand and whispered in my ear. Outside the door I looked at what she had given me. Nine years, but I still recognised it. A hunting knife, with a carved ivory handle. Morgan's, once.

Unwillingly I carried it to the gate. Merlyn and Nimue with their attendants were riding out. I held it up to Merlyn.

'Morgan returns your gift. She does not want it.'

He checked his mount. A shadow passed over his face, leaving it older. 'So the new moon has passed. The virgin huntress is a woman now. Well, new phases need new gifts. Then give her this.'

He reached into the saddle-bag of Nimue's mare and handed me a gleaming metal disc.

I gasped with the weight and then the richness of it. A mirror of polished bronze. The handle twined with serpents, the back incised with curling vines and inlaid with red enamel. I turned it over. My reflection met me. With a strange surprise I stared at my own face, as if in water. The stern contours softened, beguiling, almost beautiful.

'For a woman, a woman's weapon.' Merlyn smiled grimly. 'Let us see how Morgan will use it.'

263

# Chapter Thirty-three

It was my hand that gathered what was needed from the forest, my feet that waded in the bogs as I searched with a net for the creatures who lived there. My tongue had joined with my sisters' in the spell. It is a strange feeling, the sudden leap of the heart when you know that what you have done in secret is all at once made manifest in the world. Stars fall from heaven, and it is by your hand.

Uther died.

They say the Saxons poisoned him. They spun some tale about his favourite spring of water, poisoned by enemy spies. Let them believe that. Better they do not understand our power too well. Better they think the Mother's daughters weak and worthless. If they thought we had power, they would take it from us. Only Merlyn knew. And he would not come into the open yet.

Mark came instead. His was a name we knew, but a face we had seldom seen. Little joy the nobles had in feasting each other in those days. Kings and chieftains did not tour the halls with their courts. War had the land squeezed in its fist. Even Dumnonia could not escape the shock. The dark tide was rising ever higher from the east, driving the Britons back into the cliffs and crags. Many the refugees who crowded west, destitute, scarred, bereaved.

We knew that Mark was strengthening his fortress at Caer Dore, that he was a grim warlord, that his warriors trusted, if they did not love, him.

He rode through the gates of Bossiney, a big, black-moustached man with a keen grey eye that saw too much. When Gwennol saw him swing down from his horse she gave a start and her hand flew to her throat.

'I don't need the bards to tell me where he got his blood from. Anyone can see he's kin to Gorlois.'

Rozen hurried out of the hall looking pale and anxious. She had been mistress in Bossiney these many months.

'We have food for your men, and beds in the hall, and songs it would not displease you to listen to. Be welcome here.'

It was a long time since such a warband had visited us. Our own men came seldom home. Harvests were smaller in these times. Young men were taken from the fields to follow their masters and did not return. Noblemen were too busy with war to oversee their farms. Kings small and great taxed us to feast and arm their warriors. But Rozen would not be shamed. Though it emptied our barns she would see Mark nobly entertained.

'Ulfin is still in the east? He has not come home?'

'Not since Uther died.'

'He is a fool. Britain has no high king now, and cannot find one. The petty kings quarrel amongst each other. Lot from beyond the Wall. Gwendoleu in Rheged. Nentres of Garlot. None of them is fit to raise the red dragon. I wouldn't follow any of them. Better to come west and set a guard along the Tamar. Let the Saxons take the soft-bellied lands of the south and the east. So long as they never try to pass into Cornwall.'

'You mean to stay at home and not fight, my lord?'

'I mean to stay, and to fight for what is mine. You have a poor place for a fort here in Bossiney.'

'It was not meant for war. Uther rebuilt it for Ygerne, as a marriage-gift.'

'It is mine now.'

Rozen blenched. 'How so, my lord?'

'Gorlois was killed, and Uther took it from him. Now the Pendragon is dead, and I am Gorlois's kin.'

She did not need his grip on his sword-hilt and the grins of the warriors behind him to finish his thought.

Yet she was a courteous lady. She led him to the noonday meal and entertained him well.

Afterwards they rode out to see the estate. They had scarcely gone beyond the gate when Mark reined his horse.

'What is *that*?'

He stood looking, as though he had never seen it before, at the island of Tintagel. The curled body of a newborn baby, hanging from the womb of Cornwall by a single cord.

'Surely you have heard of it, my lord. They call it Tintagel, where the currents meet. It is a Christian convent.'

'It is a God-given fortress.'

'Alas, my lord. Many men have thought the same. But even you may not have it for war. Long before Uther came, Gorlois gave it to the nuns. They do not hold it by our grace and favour. It is theirs by right. They own farms as well, and get a good store of rents.'

'My kinsman Gorlois was a greater fool than I took him for. It is too good a fortress to be in the hands of women. I want that island. We must make them go.'

'I fear you will be disappointed. Those nuns are weak in body but obstinate in spirit. They will not be shifted. No man bearing weapons is ever allowed to cross their bridge.'

'Once I am king there, no weaponed men but mine will cross it either.'

'But how could you persuade the nuns to give it up to you? You would surely not force holy women?'

Gwennol came forward, leaning heavily on her stick, and caught at Mark's saddle-strap.

'Sir! There's other women besides nuns live on that island. Has my lady told you that your cousin Morgan has been a prisoner there going on ten years?'

Mark spun round on Rozen then with a face like thunder.

'Morgan? Gorlois's daughter? Is she still there? How is this? By whose orders was this done?'

'Uther Pendragon was her stepfather. She was a wild maid that needed schooling. He charged the nuns to guard her soul and body.'

'She's nineteen now,' said Gwennol. 'And still unwed. Neither a nun nor a free woman yet.'

'Bring her here,' Mark commanded Rozen.

So, after all these years, Morgan was led out of Tintagel and stood before us in the hall. It was the first time I had seen her by daylight since I left the convent. I found her presence had not lost its power to shock me. She had grown lovelier even than I remembered. But outwardly cold as ice. Her eyes passed over Gwennol and me with barely a flicker of recognition, ignoring our hunger for her gratitude. She stared levelly at Mark. She would beg no man for her freedom, though her heart was bursting.

'Well, my kinswoman. They tell me you once tried to kill your brother.'

'Do those who accuse me say why Arthur lived?'

'Merlyn prevented you!' Rozen exclaimed. 'When he was here this summer he warned us . . .'

'Merlyn was *here*!'

She did not know. Gwennol had not told her.

Mark looked at Rozen, startled, for confirmation.

'He came to us disguised. He bade us keep it secret.'

Morgan's voice was bitter.

'Merlyn! Always that man between me and the sun.'

Then she darted forward and caught Rozen by the sleeve. She could not help herself. It was like the first spurt of water from a breaking dam.

'Arthur! What did he say of Arthur? Where is he?'

Rozen shook her head. 'He would not speak to me of your brother.'

'That boy is dead,' Mark interrupted.

No one contradicted him.

Mark said slowly, staring at Morgan, 'Ten years. Why did Uther fear her so till he died? And Merlyn still?'

'It was foretold a child of Ygerne's would take the crown of Britain. When the Pendragon lost his son, there were only Gorlois's daughters.'

'Morgan? A woman? Third daughter of Gorlois of Cornwall! My kinsman was a mighty duke. A better warleader than Uther. But he did not come of a line of kings. How could the Council acclaim his daughter?'

It was Gwennol who answered, startling me, from close beside where I stood.

'We have more than one parent. Her mother Ygerne carries the royal blood.'

I saw Mark grip the carved arms of the chair where he sat, two raven heads.

'So! Merlyn fears they might return to the old ways? A queen to lead the chariots. A queen who would kill any man who stood in her way.

A queen, so you women would say, who can heal the wounded land. This is dangerous nonsense. Pendragon was no fool. It is better that my cousin stays with the nuns.'

He nodded to two of his warriors. 'Take her back and set a watch on the island. She gets no visitors. Have her shown to you every seventh day.'

I thought Morgan would have screamed out at that. I saw her heart in her face. Even then I pitied her.

But she said not a word to him. Instead she swung round and stared at Gwennol, white-faced.

'My mother. So it comes back to my mother, every time. She gave me life and she takes it away.'

# Chapter Thirty-four

It was a dull November morning, with the air grey and lifeless. Gwennol sat wrapped in a shawl shivering, though the days were not yet cold. But the blood grows thin in old people. They feel a chill that others do not. She wore that shawl often. It was a fine piece of weaving, soft, silky wool, a shade of autumn red.

Gwennol did not settle the shawl about her shoulders and then forget it. She sat stroking the ends of it where they hung over her shrivelled breasts, as if it had been a living animal.

'Merlyn gave me this. The year that Arthur was born. The same year he gave that knife to Morgan.'

'The one she would not touch?'

'Morgan would never take anything from him.'

Suddenly she rocked herself as if a pain had gripped her. She snatched the shawl from her shoulders, screwed it into a ball and flung it on the floor. She stamped upon it, while I watched in amazement.

'A fire!' she snapped. 'Quick, you fool, light a fire.'

My hands shook with bewilderment as I set sticks on the hearthstone. I ran to borrow a hot coal from the kitchen. Soon the hut was filling with smoke. The flames leaped bright and hungry.

Gwennol could hardly wait for the wood to be well alight. She seized the shawl and rammed it into the fire. The good wool spat and shrivelled, turning black and throwing out clouds that choked us. My own eyes smarted, but tears were pouring down Gwennol's cheeks. She watched the flames consume the last shreds of Merlyn's gift, pushing the stray edges of it into the heart of the fire. When it was reduced to a curled black ball she beat it with a poker until the embers fell apart. Then she poured water on them and rubbed them out, scattering them into nothingness and mumbling all the time.

At last it was over. She wiped her face and straightened herself to calmness. Resolute now, she walked to the door.

Mark was pacing the ramparts. He was a restless man. As many times before, his eyes turned to Tintagel. He was not one who took kindly to being thwarted.

I watched Gwennol cross the yard towards him and climb the steps. He stopped his prowling and waited for her. He even held out his hand to steady her up the last step. Already he looked to Gwennol to tell him what others would not. She had been Gorlois's servant long before she was Uther's.

She talked to him now and he bent his head to listen. Long and earnest was that conversation. I think Mark argued hotly. But ever his head kept turning in the direction of Tintagel. At last they both spat on their hands and clapped them together. A bargain had been struck.

That afternoon I was summoned to the hall with all Mark's household. We who had served in Bossiney many years; his warriors newly come from the wars.

Mark sat in the raven-armed chair again, his hand tapping restlessly on the bird's skull. We waited. Gwennol looked pale and faint. I led her to a stool against the wall. I had my face turned from the door bending over Gwennol when Bryvyth entered.

If it had been a shock of fear and joy to see Morgan appear before us in that hall, it was a blow of shame to me now to be in the same room as the abbess. I would rather have been anywhere than where her eye might fall on me. I never went to church in Bossiney, lest I should meet her there, though Nectan thundered at me for it. I did not know if Bryvyth had forgiven me. I had not forgiven myself. I still have not. Gwennol believed she was following the one true way. I knew the glory I had lost forever. Bryvyth's presence was a warning of hell.

She stood before him unbowed, with Cigfa and Muriel on either side. 'Bryvyth Crook-Staff?' said Mark. 'The abbess of Tintagel?'

'I am. It is ten years since I answered a summons to this hall. But I hear you are Gorlois's kin and no lackey of the Pendragon. Gorlois was always a good friend to Tintagel, until the day he asked too much of me.'

'He gave you Tintagel. You refused to give it back in his utmost need. You cost him his life.'

'The gift was made to God, not to me. I cannot give what is holy to men of war.'

'I will ask you Bryvyth Crook-Staff, once and once only, to give me Tintagel of your own free-will.'

'I may not do that. I am a nun. My will is not my own. And even if it were free, I would still not give the place to you. Tintagel is a holy island and shall remain so while I live.'

Mark stood then and beckoned in my direction. The blood flew to my cheeks. I could not think what he meant. But Gwennol rose unsteadily from the stool beside me and shuffled forward through the watching ranks.

'Well, Gwennol Far-Sight? And what have you to say concerning the nuns of Tintagel?'

Bryvyth started, and made the sign of the cross against evil.

Gwennol spat at her. 'I say that those nuns are not as white as they appear. There's blood in them like other women. And some are wiser. There's things done in secret on Tintagel Island that it would fright even men of war to hear about.'

A ripple ran through the throng that packed the great hall, alarm in women's faces, fear, excitement. We knew, all of us. The wise, the Christians, some who swam in and out with either tide. But we were all women. We knew Tintagel's reputation. Clearly or cloudily, we knew its past and its present. An island of awe. The men were only curious. They knew there was an edge of fear about the place, a name to be careful with. But only the wise among them understood why.

None of us could believe that Gwennol would uncover this.

Mark was a man of war. He had seen some opening in his enemy's defences, some weak place where he might breach and enter.

'Speak out, woman, as you promised. Say what you mean. If it is to my advantage, you shall have the price you asked.'

'I have a witness here who will say to that nun's face what has been done at Tintagel all these years under her cross of Christ.'

And she gripped my arm and hauled me forward into Mark's sight.

There was a gasp that was almost a scream from the wise. I saw hands sign, heard lips cursing.

I was terrified. I shrank from it. Believe me, Bryvyth, it was not done by my own choice. But what else could I say, with Gwennol's finger in my back and Mark's hard eyes on my face? What else could I stammer but the truth?

Under their cruel questions I told them about my baby. I told them I was but one, ignorant and unfortunate, among a host of sisters who worshipped at the Mother's Hole. I gave them names, times, the night paths down which the wise had led me, the gifts we brought back, the spells. Everything, except the mysteries themselves. Even Mark did not demand that of me.

I watched Bryvyth's face turn red as dawn on a morning of storm. I saw the shock in her eyes, the guilt, the grief. She stood bereft of words. Bryvyth, who had always been so ready of tongue. Her gaze fixed on me, wounds on her face deeper than she had ever scored on my back. She had truly not known. She had not so much as guessed, for all my sinning, that I was not alone. Strong-hearted, fired with high ideals, in love with God, she could not believe such double-serving possible. When I had done, she turned on me, dry-eyed, and found her voice at last.

'Curse you. Curse you, that you did not tell me this at the very first. Curse you, that you have spoken of it at all.'

Those were her only words, the last I ever had from Bryvyth.

Mark was a hard man but a fair one.

'You see you are disgraced. You cannot stay on Tintagel. Your nuns have fouled it. The Church would be mocked by everyone if you remained. Yield Tintagel to me. I will pay you compensation. You shall have a valley in the south of Cornwall where no one knows you. Where the wind blows softly, and the apple orchards are sweet. A more fitting place than Tintagel for women's bodies.'

Gwennol forced me to watch them leave Tintagel, a tiny remnant that had kept the faith, singing a litany of lamentation. The rest had gone, expelled as I had been, and many of the children had been taken away. I stood among the wise on the opposite cliff, casting stones and chanting scorn. Bryvyth followed her flock across the causeway last, her head bowed, carrying the cross from the altar on her back. We mocked and spat at her.

In the waters of the Haven, outside the Mother's Hole, foam gathered in an eddy, like spilled sperm.

They had scarcely gone when Mark and his troop of warriors came riding down the coombe and through the outer gate of Tintagel. They gave a great whoop of triumph and galloped their terrified horses across the bridge of rock. Tintagel was in the hands of the men.

I rounded on Gwennol then, and my cowardly anger broke out at last.

'Why? You have given Tintagel over to warriors! The sacred place of women. The convent. The Mother's Hole. You, of all the wise, who should have guarded it with your blood!'

Her face appalled me. It was contorted, staring. The breath rattled in her throat. Her eyes flew upward till they were white and sightless. She fell lifeless at my feet.

We women cried out. But there was another cry from the island. Mark's horsemen were circling the summit, shouting. They wheeled around the standing stone and halted. Someone was still waiting beside it. A lone woman in a green gown. Morgan.

She stood like a queen as the warriors reined in front of her. They raised their swords in a respectful salute. Mark helped her to mount a mare beside him. She had her way. She always wins, in the end. Morgan rode out of Tintagel with a royal escort.

Their horses trotted to where we stood, a frightened, close-packed crowd around Gwennol's body.

Mark called loudly, 'Well, Gwennol Far-Sight. Receive the price you set.'

We stood aside. Morgan sat tall and laughing on the mare. She held a thin grey cat before her on the saddle-bow. I recognised its scars.

The smile slowly left her fair face as we pointed where Gwennol lay, still breathing but the soul fled.

Morgan leaped to the ground and ran to kneel beside her nurse. I found my voice. It was then I understood my love for Morgan had curdled to hate.

'The Mothers have punished her. She betrayed them. For you. As I betrayed the Church. For what good?'

Morgan touched Gwennol's face, and the breathing deepened. The eyelids flickered and closed, as if in natural sleep.

Then Morgan rose. She looked long at her old nurse lying on the turf, smitten by the elf-stroke. She turned her head to watch Bryvyth's bowed form dwindling away along the coombe. Lastly her eyes came back to me, glittering.

'She was the only one who ever truly loved me.'

To this day I do not know which of them she meant.

# Chapter Thirty-five

Ruin. The king of Britain dead. The land overrun. The abbey broken.

Mark set a sterner guard on the Mother's Hole than Bryvyth had. Tintagel had expelled us from her womb into a cold world. We could not return.

Yet Morgan was free.

Gwennol recovered, in part at least. One arm and leg hung useless. One side of her face sagged, slack and dribbling. She would never see Morgan's face again. Not all our spells or Morgan's touch could restore her sight.

'It was Merlyn robbed my eyes of light ten years ago,' she mumbled. 'I've never seen clear since that night when Arthur was got.'

Then she smiled, craftily I thought, in the direction of Morgan. 'We gave him back your knife. He's left you something else, dearie. A gift for a grown woman, he said.'

I handed Morgan the bronze mirror.

She studied the beautiful workmanship of its back. Her fingers traced its patterns, caressed the enamelled bosses. Almost I thought she was turning it over to see herself in the polished face.

Then she laughed and let it drop. It clanged heavily on the floor, denting the perfection of its shape, disrupting the pattern.

'I am not Margawse. I do not choose that way, though they call me Morgan the Fair now. That woman who came with Merlyn? Nimue?'

'He said she was maiden to the Lady of the Lake, whoever she may be. One of the wise, seemingly, though not our sort. And no more a maid than I am, if you ask me.

'Nimue. A name like water. Shifting. Covering. And she hides Arthur.'

'She'll keep him for Merlyn, and train him in her ways. You won't find him, my lamb, until they're ready.'

'They do not understand. Nothing can keep us apart forever. One day Arthur will find me.'

'He'll still have Merlyn to stand between you and him.'

'Will he? Will he, Gwennol Far-Sight? Even great Merlyn has his weakness. A woman could be his undoing. What if Merlyn were to drown in his Nimue's embraces? Who would there be to keep me from Arthur then?'

We did not remain at Bossiney long. Morgan's expression betrayed nothing when she told us she was to be married in the spring.

'Mark has arranged it. Some kinglet nobody knows of in the north.

Urien his name. As far removed from Cornwall as Mark could banish me.'

'So you'll have a crown of sorts at last, my pretty.'

'They tell me Urien is young and clever. There will be time to shape him to my purpose. I shall need Luned's help. I see you have taught her well.'

But the look of contempt she threw me belied her words.

'It's me you'll want, my little maid, for work like that.'

'You will not be coming.'

'You wouldn't go without me! Don't talk so daft. Blinded I may be, but I'm not so crippled I can't ride in a cart. How do you think you could manage without old Gwennol after all these years?'

Morgan gave her old nurse a gentle laugh that wounded deeper than the bitter look she had turned on me.

'You would not wish to die so far from Cornwall, to exchange these cliffs for the gloomy mountains near the Wall, the free-running sea for a land of still lakes. Your task is finished, Gwennol. I do not need you.'

'You can't leave me behind, my sweetheart. Not after what I've suffered for you. All the years I've worked for you. Yes, and wept for you. Keep me with you, my little maid!'

The tears were spurting from her sightless eyes.

'Did you not foresee this, Gwennol Far-Sight?'

Oh, cruel Morgan.

I do not want to remember the look on Gwennol's face. But me she compelled to go with her against my will. She possesses me still. I hate her.

My pen trembles as I write these words, knowing that she will find them.

I sacrificed my soul for her. My hopes, my heart, my womb. I have had nothing in return.

Once I made myself too useful to the convent. That power corrupted me. Now I have made myself too useful to Morgan. I shall never be free of her.

All her life Morgan has planned to be revenged on Arthur.

Even as I pen this accusation I know with despair that you whom I write for will never read my words. Morgan will find these pages first. She will destroy them.

Morgan is the Devourer. She destroys everything she touches. Soon she will destroy me.

Yet Urien loves her. And the people here have another name for her. They call her Morgan the Wise, the Healer.

I cannot understand it.

Morgan must kill Arthur, must she not?

I look down with horror at my own hands, that have served her so long. I think I know how she plans to do it.

# Black Smith's Telling

Book Three
in the sequence
Daughter of Tintagel

To Alison and Arthur

# Chapter One

Of course, we knew whose side she was on the moment we clapped eyes on her. Well, she wasn't exactly making a secret of it, was she? I'm almost as much afraid of Morgan of Tintagel as I am of the Horned One himself, but say what you will, she's never been underhand. Still, coming like that to her own wedding, in a Christian church! You could have blown me down with my own forge-bellows, at the time.

Yes, forge. You've guessed, haven't you? I've seen you staring. I've still got more stubble on my chin than a woman should have. Under this skirt there's something there shouldn't be. And I've enough beer inside me now to tell you how I came to be shamed like this. For shame I call it to wear a woman's dress. Do you want to hear? Morgan cursed me.

I was a smith. Do you know what that means? Smith! A wise man that knows the magic of fire and iron. And no common one, either. A king of the craft. They took me for Lord in all the Forest from the Wall to the Lakes. Gods! It hurts me every time I remember. Morgan finished that. She took my manhood and the best part of my magic with it.

It was here in Carlisle, on a May morning, like today.

I'd walked all the way from Lyvennet to feast at young King Urien's wedding. Carlisle didn't belong to him then. His Rheged was a smaller kingdom than it is now. But he was set on having the bishop and his grand church. Urien's always leaned that way. He gets it from his mother.

Not like Gwendoleu. He was the king here in those days, but he'd precious little patience with the Christians. He favoured the Ravens.

I'd tramped the road the old Romans built, with the dawn at my back, and glad to do it. I'd always had a soft spot for the lad. And I'd reason enough to be asked to his wedding. It was these hands forged the weapon he'd lifted when they'd made him a man this May Day. I wasn't court armourer. I was no man's hireling, not even the king's. But I had the craft. It was a secret handed down in my family. It was always us made the new king's sword. And I'd worked more in that weapon than a good steel blade and a fine-ground edge. My craft went deeper than that. It's served him true since then, too. There's never a sword will get past that guard, except by treachery.

Men, swords. That's a bitter thought, that is. I don't mind telling you it brings tears to my eyes when I think what I used to be, before I met Morgan. Urien's a big man now, and in all these years he's never recognised me for who I was, skulking about the women's quarters of his palace with a veil round my face. Sleeping in his own wife's bedroom, even. I'd give anything now for one look from him, man to man, even if he ran me through with the sword I made for him straight afterwards. If only, before I die, I could be looked up to for a blacksmith at my own forge, the way I was that day!

I was a strong man in those days, and I didn't begrudge tramping a score of miles if there was free food and beer to pledge the groom's health with at the end of it. There were plenty of others on the road besides me. It didn't feel like an evil day, standing there in the sunshine with a great crowd of folk lining the street all the way through town to the big church opposite the palace.

There were the three of them, waiting for her on the church steps. Young Urien, in a gold tunic. Gwendoleu, his cousin, that was king here in Solway, standing as stiff beside him as if he was the boy's own father. And Bishop Curran, decked out in his best feast-day robes as showy as the rest of them.

We were all waiting for our first sight of the bride. You don't need me to tell you what the women round me were chattering about. You can be sure their heads were full of the fine gowns and the silks and the jewels the ladies would be wearing. And had anyone heard what the Princess Morgan was like? Was she pretty? Was she kind? You know the way women prattle . . .

Morgan of Tintagel, kind! That shows how little we knew of her before she came to Rheged. They'd brought her up from the south-west, from Dumnonia. It might as well have been Gaul for all we knew about her. Some were putting it about that she was Uther Pendragon's daughter. But others said, no, it was only the Queen Ygerne's blood in her. Anyway, Uther Pendragon was dead of poison years back, like his brother Ambrosius before him, that some call Kings of all the Britons. And neither of them with a son to follow them. We had kings a-plenty without them and busier raiding each other these days than sending the Saxons packing out of Britain, but no great emperor over the lot of them. Well, it was all the same to me. There was plenty of work for smiths, either way. And it's the common folk who have to pay when you get some big, strong-armed warleader that thinks the bards will sing of him till the world ends if he gets a great army together and goes charging off down south to drive the Saxons back to their ships. And whose taxes go up so he can give his spear-host mead and gold before and after? And who goes hungry when they seize good corn to feed their war-horses on the march? Saxons? I'd never seen a Saxon, and I didn't think I ever should, High King or no High King. So what did it matter to me whose daughter Urien's bride was?

But there was a little cloud of dust coming at the end of the street, beyond the gate, and the women-folk were starting to stand on tiptoe. It was a fine May morning, with the roads dry and all the hawthorn in blossom along the Eden Valley. I'd a sprig of it stuck in my own cap, out of respect for the Lady. I dare say I was staring at that old red arch through which our new queen would come as hard as any of them.

And then we saw her. There was no mistaking which she was, for all the fine lords and ladies round her. And when I looked at her, I thought the streets of Carlisle had disappeared. I might have been in our round that holds the nine stone dancers, at sunrise on the first of summer. I'm telling you, Morgan came to us like no queen on earth we'd ever thought to see. Imagine it. A stark, white gown. Plain as a nun's, I might have said at first sight, except that when she rode closer you could see that it was made of stuff so delicate you could almost see the colour of her flesh through it. Little sandals so fine they might have been made of catskin, that hardly hid her bare feet, and a circle of gold on her black hair stuck with fresh flowers. On a mare as white as the hawthorn blossom. Riding astride.

The May Maiden. Not another jewel, nor a golden tassel, nor a scarf of coloured silk anywhere. Just a green ribbon braided in her hair on one side, and a thread of scarlet on the other. She that had the right to wear six colours at once if she'd chosen, being a king's bride. But she'd cast her lot, and not in secret as plenty of nobles do, crossing themselves for everyone to see and going to church to keep their bishop happy, never mind what they do with us in private. Oh, no! With Morgan it was out in the open, before the whole city, riding up to the door of the bishop's church on her wedding-day. I could have kissed her for that, the proud fool that I was. I took her for my sort of queen. And if she was what she claimed to be that day . . . Well then, she'd know what I was, too.

You should have seen the commotion when she rode through that gate. Like a great wind sweeping down a field of corn. I think every woman's hand flew to her mouth. Some were horror-struck, and some were laughing. And as for the men . . . Well, they were grinning all over their faces. The king's escort that had been sent to fetch her looked pretty grim-faced, I can tell you. So what could we all do but look round at the church door to see how the nobles there would take it?

From where I stood I couldn't see their faces. But there was no doubt which of them took her meaning quickest. I thought the old Bishop Curran was going to throw a fit. He banged his crozier down on the church steps, arguing the toss with Gwendoleu. Then he started off running like a hare. Going home, he was, sooner than give one like her his blessing in his Christian church. But Gwendoleu, that was a big king both sides of the Wall then, and not a man to be crossed, he was too quick for the priest. He gripped Curran by the arm just like an eagle snatching a lamb. What chance had the poor old bishop? He wasn't one of your tough hermits, man or woman, that live on berries and water and think themselves so holy they'll sit in judgment over any king in the land. Our Curran was a town man with a taste for fine robes and palace food. He had to go softly. Where would he be if he crossed Gwendoleu? And the King of Carlisle had planned this match. He knew what he was about – or he thought he did. Our little Urien came of the same royal kin as he did. Great-great-great-grandson to good old King Coel. He saw Urien might be top king in the North himself one day if he had powerful friends to back him. There were many useful men would have bedded him with a daughter or a sister to butter their own bread later on. They'd have their eye on the good farmland in Solway. Tie the lad up quick to some Cornish princess that nobody's ever heard of, that's what Gwendoleu thought. Dumnonia's a mighty long way from Carlisle, and Pendragon's dead and half-forgotten, even if she was his daughter. A stranger from the south, that had no friends. You could see his line of thinking.

As for the bridegroom . . . Well, Morgan had startled us. But we'd a surprise in store for her too. Urien was a grand, well-brought-up lad, and generous to us, like his father before him. But he was hardly old enough to use a razor yet. And when I saw what kind she was I doubted if anyone had told the bride that.

The horses were almost on us by now. They'd strewn flowers and leaves, of course. Still, as the gentry rode by people were starting to cough with the dust and press back a bit. I stood my ground. It meant more to me, you see, than any of those standing there. You may laugh at me now, but I was Smith then. Damn you! Can't you understand? Teilo Smith of Way Bank, where the road runs down from Lyvennet to the Long Lake. Any smith's a man of magic, but I was a cut above all the rest. I was a king myself, in our craft. If she was truly the Lady I took her to be, she would know me for her equal.

She turned my head when she came. I'd never thought of a queen as a woman before. It had been years since we'd had one of our own in Rheged. Those that came visiting were always so dolled up in stiff linen and jewels and furs, you couldn't imagine that underneath there was the sort of flesh that a man's hands might want to get hold of. But this one . . . With the sun shining clear through the white gown, and the shape of her thigh laid along the horse's flank, and her little white foot in its fur sandal hanging down. Black hair tumbling loose over her breasts, and pressing the thin stuff close. Eyes, when I got up my nerve to look at them, a truer green than ever I'd seen. A lady rode beside her, dressed all in green, with hair flaming like red gold and eyes as green as her own. Her sister, Queen Margawse, I found out afterwards. That one was chattering and laughing like a blackbird as they rode. Princess Morgan never answered a word. I could see a smile curving her mouth first, like a cat that's having pleasant dreams. But I told a lie. When she got close, it was her eyes shocked me. I'd never thought I'd see a woman look so sad on her wedding-day.

I thought she was going to ride straight by me. She was so close I could hear the horse's breath and smell the scent of her flowers. But her eyes turned away from her sister's and met mine. There was something quickened in them then. She looked full at me, till she seemed to suck the being out of me into herself, and all my secrets with it. The horse walked on. Her look stayed on me as she turned her head. Then, in front of all those kings and the lords and ladies, she bowed, very gravely. Yes, once, Morgan of Tintagel bowed to me.

That shook me, I can tell you. I don't know what I'd wanted from her. A lift of the eyebrows. A tiny smile. Just something to let me know we shared a secret. But you take your life in your hands when you start to play games with Morgan. I ducked out of that crowd like a fox from his back door, before any of the nobles behind her could have me seized and recognise me. As far as the nobility were concerned, I was a master blacksmith. The best, mind you. They could come to me for the finest edge to their weapons and the soundest harness, and the king's sword. But nothing more. Rheged's supposed to be a Christian kingdom. What I did after sunset, when their gates were barred and they were safe in their halls, and I was the only king that walked abroad, was none of their business. On feast-days when the god's Servant dances in his mask and horns on the green, no one asks his name. I dare say they guessed, but it was never spoken out loud. She scared me properly.

So I was round a corner and never saw her face when she first set eyes on Urien of Rheged, that was to be her husband. But I could imagine it! Like a cat that sees a strange tom at her bowl. Well, Gwendoleu should never have done it, for all he was scared stiff the boy might be after his throne. Urien was only just come man enough to be a warrior, or a bridegroom. It was against the custom to match him with a woman her age. And what about her? Now that I came to think again of her face, it hit me between the eyes. Here's a full-grown woman, well into the prime of life. Not like my daughter Mair that was thirteen, and ripe to be married next year. This Princess Morgan is old enough to be the mother of a whole family already. Where have they been keeping her all these years that such a woman should come riding like a May-Queen to her first husband now? And what sort of power is hers, that let them keep her maiden so long?

That was going to be a rum wedding-night for both of them. Gwendoleu must have been laughing and rubbing his hands, to think how he'd fixed it. The old bishop was so scandalised I bet he drank himself silly at their feast to get over the shock. But for all that, Urien had an older head on his shoulders than you'd think for a lad his age. She could have done worse. Still, those two in bed! The boy wouldn't know what to do with a Maiden like that. Not like the Horny Lord.

I pulled myself up short. No, you're well out of this, Teilo Smith. Forget those green eyes and the white thighs and her signs of power. Forget a queen bowed to you. One step more and you'll be in over your head. When Urien rides back with his new bride to Lyvennet, you keep a safe distance away from them, and pray the Lord of the Forest no one remembers what happened today. Slip home safely to Way Bank, to your own wife and your daughter Mair. You want nothing from a woman like that.

# Chapter Two

I should have run while I had the chance. That was the second mistake I made that day. Only moments, it was, I stopped round the corner from the square to listen. I'd have given a week's beer to see that proud Lady's face when she saw which of those two her groom was. But Gwendoleu would have his way over her as he had with the bishop. A woman her age couldn't afford to say no, could she? Oh, aye, she'd marry Urien. He was a king, when all's said and done. But when it came to it, the folk were all shouting and pushing to get near the church steps, so I never heard what it was she said. They say Urien cried out when he got his first sight of Morgan, but he stood his ground and held out his hand to help her down from her horse, proud as they'd taught him. He's a brave one, that lad. He's got more than he ever bargained for in his marriage-bed.

But it was high time for Teilo Smith to be getting away home and putting his wits together again. It's not every day of your life a queen bows to you. Still, we'd never seen a queen the likes of her before.

So I turned for the hills. But the street behind me wasn't as empty as it had been a moment ago. There was a man standing not a yard away from me. Tall, he was. Muffled up in a cloak and hood of whitish-grey, though it was as fair a May morning as you could wish to see.

There's nothing like having a secret for making you feel guilty. I started back as if he'd been a Saxon with a bloody axe. Then it came to me. I'm not stupid. And who's he, I thought, that watches King Urien's wedding round a corner too? I reckoned I wasn't the only one that had got something to hide. So we looked at each other, steady-like, to see which of us had the most to fear from the other.

He spoke first.

'You know this Cornishwoman?' I could tell he wasn't from round these parts himself.

I could have answered no. It was the truth. I'd never set eyes on her before. But that Cornish princess of his had already told half the world she knew something about me that I'd sooner they didn't know. The Christian nobles have got the power: Urien, Bishop Curran and their sort. What the rest of us do has to be done in the dark now. They'll clap and cheer when we come masked with the horns on the great feast-days. But only those that are sworn to us know what's done before and after. It wasn't a thing I wanted talked of, especially among the Christian gentry. I had my living to earn. There's craft and Craft. Even my own wife knew better than to mention it. It belonged to the dark. And I'd meant to keep it that way.

So I didn't answer him straight off. He brought his hands out from under his cloak and made the signs. That made me gasp a bit. I'd been wondering if he was one of their Christian saints, wrapped up in a pale cloak like that. Now we knew each other for what we were, as that queen had known me. Two of them, in the same day. It was a bit too much for me.

'I've never seen her before in my life!' I said, scared-like.

'So?' He considered that for a bit. 'But you will again, be sure of that. She knows you now. And Morgan does not forget.'

'Ah, but she still doesn't know who I am, does she? I mean, she knows *what* I am. She shouted that loud enough. But that won't tell her my name or where I live, will it?'

'You fool yourself if you think you can hide from Morgan. You were standing among a crowd of Urien's people, from Lyvennet way. And by your hands you are a smith. If I can tell that much, even here in the streets of Carlisle at our first meeting, how long will it take her, living among you in Lyvennet itself? Morgan is high in the ranks of wisdom. Even without those marks the eyes of her soul would seek you out wherever you hid.'

I'd feared that much already.

'What would a queen like her want with me? And will it do me any good?'

'That's a wise question. You do well to be wary of her, Lord of our craft though you may be. Listen, Smith. I need a wise man. And one that is likely to gain the ear of Morgan, Queen of Rheged.'

'Would I be right in thinking you're no friend of hers, wise or not?'

'Say a friend of Britain.'

'What's Britain? I'm a Rheged man. Urien's my king. And she's my queen, or will be in another hour when the bishop's done with them.' We could hear their Latin chanting coming from the church now. 'Do you want to set me against my own king's wife? What's your Britain to me, to take a risk like that?'

He grasped my wrist. Hard fingers, he had, and stronger than he looked. There was more power in him than just the muscle.

'The Cymry! The kinfolk. I from Glevissig by the Severn Channel. You in Rheged. Morgan from Cornwall. And more than us. All the unfree of our blood groaning under the heel of the Saxon's white dragon. One land. One language. Britain.'

'That's too big for me. It's all right for you. You're nobility. I can see that. And so's she. Your sort ride the length and breadth of the land and think no more of it than I did today walking from Lyvennet to Carlisle. But I'm a commoner. Rheged's broad enough for me. You leave me out of this.'

'No ordinary commoner, Smith, and well you know it. You have much power. And Morgan covets the power of others for her own ends. You cannot escape her now she has picked you out. A child of nine years old, she was, when last I saw her. I feared her then. Yet not enough, it seems. I did not think that once she was free she would move this close to us so quickly.'

'Who's we? And close to what?'

There was a crafty look came over his face then, though he kept it in the shadow of his hood. He didn't trust me. But I could tell he wanted something out of me. He stared at me for a fair while. Then those fingers locked round my wrist as hard as any slave-shackle I'd ever hammered.

'Dream bigger, man. No Romans, no Saxons, no Christians. *Our* gods, *our* language, *our* land. One Island of Britain, under the Wise.'

'Yes? You want a lot! You'll never shift the Saxons from down south. And even your Morgan's getting married in a Christian church.'

'Pah! Moonshine. Their day has passed already. Rome's fallen. The Church will be next. Soon we shall drive the Saxons from these shores. The old ways will return.'

When I listened to him I began to feel a thrill that seemed to start in the soles of my feet and run right through my body. I believed him, then.

He thought he'd got me. His eyes fairly sparkled.

'Listen, Smith! I could show you something . . . someone . . . that will gladden the hearts of all Britain before long. But we have come to the threshold of danger too soon. The fruit is not ripe yet. We must have no banshee shaking the orchard. I fear Morgan mor ˋ than anything in the world, or out of it. I must learn what she says, what she plans, what she does. Above all, I must know what she knows. I am asking you to guard this harvest for us, Teilo. Befriend Morgan. Coil yourself near her like a dragon hidden in the grass. If you learn anything at all from her – and I am sure you will – send word to me.'

'That's sounds like dangerous talk. You just said as much yourself. She'd be my earthly queen by day and my Lady by night. You're asking me to be traitor to her twice over. I'd be a fool not to keep my mouth shut, wouldn't I? What's there in this for me?'

That iron bit into my wrist cold as ice now. And yet I thought it burned him. I yelled as if I'd been branded for a runaway slave. That made him smile.

'Yes! It is not what you might gain if you agree: it is what might happen to you if you refuse. You would not wish to displease the god, would you?'

It was only half the sign he made, but it set me shuddering. I'd used that against others, but I'd never thought I'd have it turned on me.

'And if I did? Who is it that wants to know, and where do I send word?'

'My true naming is not for you to know yet. Ask for Silver-Tongue, Gwendoleu's bard.'

That made me laugh. 'Go on! Pull the other one. It's got bells on. Gwendoleu's bard, and not harping at this wedding? A king's poet could earn himself a fortune on a day like this.'

'Idiot! *I*, play for *Morgan*'s wedding! Do you think I'm mad? When she singled you out she said she'd never met before, among a thousand? You spoke wisely when you said that this is a dangerous game we're playing. I should have had no need to feign sickness to Gwendoleu if she had seen me today. Morgan and I must dance different circles for a while longer. And listen, Smith! If you so much as breathe one word to anyone that you have met me here, I'll raise the Wild Hunt and have the soul torn from your body by red-eared dogs, and hounded up every mountain in Rheged and down again, and drowned in the deepest lake and raised to life screaming, every night for a thousand years!'

If any other man in the world had threatened me like that, I'd have struck him to the ground. And not with my fist either. But I'd met more than my match in power here. Those eyes went through me like a cold chisel through red-hot iron. I knew he could do what he meant. So he let me go, and I felt my wrist. A smith's used to scorch-marks. But he'd left a white scar on the flesh like nothing I'd ever seen before, and the blood wouldn't come back into it, no matter how I rubbed it.

'Remember well. One people. The Cymry. One land. Britain. One faith. The Old Way. It only waits for someone who can stop these petty kings tearing each other's throats out and lead us to glory again.'

'All right,' I told him. 'So I don't get much choice, do I? I'm thinking it may be the worst road I ever took that brought me to Carlisle to drink at Urien Rheged's wedding.'

He smiled at me then like a little boy, coaxing-like.

'Dream, Teilo! Drink to bigger things.'

And then, blow me, the street was empty. They'd got me fairly trapped, the two of them. This magician and Morgan. I could see I was between his hammer and her anvil. And I was likely enough to be flattened before they'd finished. Well, look what I've come to. I wasn't wrong, was I? The only thing I wanted then was to be safe home in bed under the blankets and having it off with my wife Annis.

# Chapter Three

It's funny how soon you can forget the sweat of danger when you're tucked up safe in bed. I'd had what I wanted off Annis but I was still wide awake. There were some thoughts I couldn't get my mind off for all I'd been warned. It's not every day a queen looks at a smith as though there were just the two of them in the whole world, even if that man's no ordinary smith, but known for a king in his own way in all the Forest south of the Wall.

So I lay beside my wife and let myself dream about a white thigh under a loose gown, and a crown of hawthorn blossom in blackbird hair. It would smell sweet, that hair. I could feel it, thick and silky in my hand. And then I started to think how I'd run my fingers lower down and there'd be warm flesh under that cool hair. Yes, you might well start and turn pale. I must have been bewitched already, to imagine such a thing, mustn't I? I hadn't the sense I was born with. I should have clung to my own wife then like a drowning man clutching on to an oar for dear life. She was a good woman, Annis. I swear I never meant her any harm. But she had feet as cold as frogs. Always had done. You show me a man that hasn't mounted his wife in the dark and dreamed she was someone else.

I'd known plenty of women's bodies. I had my fill of them when I played the part of the Horny One. All sorts, you wouldn't believe. Well, perhaps you would know. Old and shrivelled, some of them, smelly, but still eager for it. They thought themselves blessed if they had it from me. But there were young ones too. At the time they all seem the same. When the fire and the blood are up, and there's drink and drums, everything that comes under the god's hand is more power to him. Only sometimes there was a clean virgin. That's sweet, that is . . . was. You can't imagine. It makes a man feel like the king of stags and roar aloud. But it wasn't often. Well, it couldn't be, could it? It isn't every silly girl we let join us. They have to be old enough to know what they're swearing to. So there weren't so many of them that were green.

And now this, come among us. Almost asking me for it. It made my heart pound so I hardly dared think about it. To have a fine noblewoman like that under my thighs. All that full, ripe, rich ladylikeness. Me, Teilo Smith. And a bride fit for a king.

She wouldn't be a virgin, of course. A woman her age, that had risen so high in our ways. You couldn't expect it. There's maidens and Maidens. But she'd know her art all the better for it. I rolled my Annis over to stop her snoring, and I lay in the hay on those old planks and

I couldn't help dreaming of the king's bed back in Carlisle. Morgan of Cornwall and our boy-king Urien. And what was she teaching her husband now? It made my flesh creep. He was a brave lad, was Urien. We knew he'd make a fine king, given time. But married to her! And him hardly out of the priests' school-house yet. What kind of a marriage-night are they having, the two of them? She'd no father, by all accounts. It wasn't Uther Pendragon, after all. Someone must have had his knife into her, to have kept her unwed all these years and given her to a beardless boy now. If I was dead, I'd hate to think anyone would do a thing like that to my daughter Mair.

Mair.

I had to turn my thoughts away from that. Whatever I might have imagined in the dark I never dreamed like that about Mair. We'd vowed her as a child, of course. But I'd never taken her into our circle to make her own sacrifice, not though I was the High Chief and she was my only daughter. I don't know what it was that held me back. I just had this feeling that Mair belonged in the morning sunshine. I'd take her to our feasting and dances in the daytime, and she'd squeal with laughter and clap her hands. But I took good care she didn't even guess what her father did by night. I didn't want to think of her under any man, even myself. It wasn't a question of good or bad. There's strength and there's softness in this world. There's dark and there's light. You don't get daisies growing under a yew tree.

So I kept my magic for those that were ripe for it. And here's the joke. D'you know what folk round Way Bank said of me? The Christians, anyway. That Teilo Smith never looked at another woman saving his Annis! That was rich, that was. And I'm laughing away till my eyes smart, and I have to pretend it's the smoke from the fire making me cough. Well, I wouldn't look at them would I? What would I need to for? There were only two sorts of women in the world, as far as I was concerned. Those that had vowed themselves to me, and those that hadn't. And if you know what it's like when that fire is lit and the power is in the blood, you wouldn't care to see them in broad daylight either, for all you can feel some of them making eyes at your back from the smithy door or see them squirming against the doorpost or scratching their skirts when you look at them. There's proper times and places for that.

And then there was the other kind, maids like my Mair, and a few goodwives too. Churchfolk, mostly. Well, they could be as bonny as an April day, but there was nothing in them for me. I wasn't going to waste my power on soil that couldn't grow me anything but trouble. I was a hot man, but it's not just the flesh that needs to be satisfied.

Still, for all that, I lay awake and I seemed to know every bit of that body of mine in the dark. I wasn't a young man, but I'd kept myself well. A smith's a man every woman looks twice at. It's the hard muscle, and the shoulders, and the strong hands that grip the hammer that gets them going. And I'd a fine red colour in my face from the forge. Even the dirt in our skin is a different colour. Black dirt, where an outdoor man's is brown. A smith is no common man. He can turn the head of any woman, high or low.

I was a smith! Curse the first one of you that laughs at me! I was a proper man!

. . . Yes, smile. Pity me. It's easy for you. You've always been women. You don't know what I'm missing.

You'll have to excuse me for a bit . . .

. . . Right. Well. Never till now had I turned a queen's head to mine. And I reckon it must have turned my own head. I lay in bed and hugged the thought of such riches as I'd never even dreamed of. If Morgan came to me, under the moon, what kind of greater king would that make me?

Still, it's one thing to lie wrapped up warm in bed and dream. You think you could conquer the whole world. And then you get up in the morning, and your belly's empty and your feet are cold, and you're only half the size you felt you were last night. That grey bard, Silver-Tongue. He was afraid of Morgan. And by the power of his hands he was the greatest magician that I was ever likely to meet. I'd do well to lie low and tread softly. I'd be a fool to meddle with either of them. Him and his dream of Britain.

So I kicked the boy that minded the forge out of bed and shouted at him to rouse up the fire. All that day long I worked at the anvil and tried not to watch the road that ran past my smithy at Way Bank. A week went by, and we heard our king and queen had come home to their castle at Lyvennet. Well, not much more than a wooden fort, really, up there on the hill, looking down towards the foot of the Long Lake. It wasn't half as grand as this stone palace here that the Romans built. I worked with one eye on the road, and sweating from more than the fire. I was sure Morgan would send word for me, you see. Well, she could hardly come riding up to my door herself, could she? Though even that I wouldn't have put past her, come to think of it, bold as she'd acted on her way to the church.

Urien gave a great feast of his own, the day he brought Morgan back from Carlisle. They said there was meat and ale enough for a whole army. And not just for the nobles, either. He was always generous, was Urien. Annis wanted to go. So did I. But I kept away. I hadn't quite lost my senses, even then.

But the sun went down that day, and a week of sunsets after that, and no word had come for me. I told myself they'd still be celebrating the wedding up in Lyvennet. They'd have feasting and singing and wrestling and racing night and day. When it was over, and all the fine lords and ladies had ridden home in their chariots, then she'd remember Teilo Smith.

A month went by and the meadows were going over to hay, and there was never a sign from her. Just one summer day following another. I couldn't have told you whether I was glad or sorry.

I should have known she wouldn't let me go that easily. It came to me that a woman like her had other ways of sending for me than human servants. As the moon got bigger I could feel her drawing me to her, just like my eyes had drawn hers down to mine on her wedding-day.

So I walked to Morgan's dun at Lyvennet one evening in summer, when my work was done and I'd had my supper. I told myself I was her equal, even if I wasn't noble. I came like a man, with a dog at my heels and a stick in my hand, as I might be taking a stroll to cool the heat of my skin in the evening breeze. I kept my dignity.

I took the way that passes between the two rounds, and I couldn't help thinking how it would be to lead the dancing among the stones with one like her. Then I walked on and came to her dun.

I stopped at the edge of the trees, where the forest's been cut back and the grass runs clean up the hill to the walls. I stood there under the last big oak of the woods, as a stag might stand in the gloaming before he steps out to feed. I wasn't as afraid of her as all that. Not nearly as afraid as I should have been. I put my thought out towards her for the second time. I could feel the blood knocking louder and louder. She wasn't the only one that could send her soul out of her body. Mine would be flying soon.

But nothing happened. I came to myself and I found I'd stepped out into the open, like a fool. I could see the sentries up at the gate were looking my way. But I was only one man, with a stick and a dog, and I kept myself too far away for them to shout at me. I stood and watched the shadow of the walls creep down the hill towards me. Then they shut the gate.

I still didn't move. I just stared at the roofs over the top of the walls. Then I started to see strange things in the twilight. A white face, narrow like a half-moon. Hair glossy as it might have been a new-groomed mare's. Eyes . . . well, you've seen them. As much like the eyes of a black cat as a wolf was like my whippet! So I had my second sight of Morgan. But there was no sound. Her face didn't speak. Only those eyes grew till they filled the sky. I could feel them sucking the soul out of me.

They lit lamps up there in the dun and the stars pricked out. The dog started whining. I waited till the moon rose clear of the roofs and her face faded. She wouldn't come any nearer tonight.

After that, she never moved again in weeks or months. Twice the moon fell dark and my folk were waiting for me in the circle. It made me wild the way they looked at me now. Some of them had been there that day in Carlisle. They knew too much. They'd have been whispering to the others behind my back. Fierce I was to the women those nights. I'd been keeping myself for better things than them. They twisted and yelled. But I wouldn't let them get away from me. She wasn't the only one that had power.

I took to watching the road all day. Many a time I'd carry a piece of work to the door. I'd be filing away and hardly looking at what I was doing. There was always plenty of coming and going past Way Bank. On the road from the north it was a different story. The Painted People were raiding closer these days. Sometimes it was a sorry sight, those that came from that side of the Wall, with whatever they'd managed to snatch up before they ran.

Our road was full of king's men. His steward always knows when there's shearing or harvesting afoot. He'll take his share. Open-handed or not, I reckon we pay several times over for the feasts they give us. But a smith's luckier than most. He gets respect. Likely one of Urien's men would stop off at the smithy for a bit of attention to weapon or harness and I'd have to tally it up on the wall against next quarter-day. But when I looked into their faces for a nod or a lift of the eyebrow or a word whispered, there was never anything but shouts and back-slapping and the sort of jokes you'd expect from king's men anywhere.

So I started to look out for another sort of messenger. We didn't get many ladies riding past Way Bank. But there were still a few, though the roads weren't so safe now as they say they used to be when Ambrosius Pendragon kept the peace. After all, wouldn't that be how Morgan would send for me? The men were Urien's, but the women were hers, and there would be more of them that followed the old craft. So every time I heard chariot wheels coming and dainty bells on the harness, I'd be at the door pretty fast. The neighbours could say what they liked about Teilo Smith and the women now. There were plenty of ladies smiled back at me, but none of them ever stopped, except in the way of business, and then I couldn't get rid of them fast enough, smiles or not. It was never Morgan's women, let alone the queen herself, riding up to my door.

She fought a battle with me that summer. Her weapon was silence. I lost. I was bound to, damn it. Once, she bowed her head to me. Morgan, Queen of Rheged, to Teilo Smith. But only once. And that was because she wanted my power when she saw it. I was right to be afraid.

# Chapter Four

Morgan dragged me to Lyvennet like a slave on the end of a chain. I didn't want to go, not for all the hot dreams I'd had of her. But I couldn't help myself. And anyway, it was Lugh's Day, and there was my account to settle. A good bit of work I'd done for Urien, one way and another. I was a free man, and master of my craft. I didn't work for nothing, not even for a king.

After I'd danced the god on the green, I scrubbed myself clean and put on my best, fair-day clothes. I didn't need Annis to tell me I looked a fine figure of a man. I took a sack, for I expected to come back richer than I went, and off we all set.

It's not far to Lyvennet. I left my wife and daughter outside the walls oohing and aahing over the pedlars' wares and I slipped off in the crowd. I thought I'd walk through the gate as easy as winking. I always had on quarter-day before. It was a man's place, was Lyvennet. Or had been in Urien's father's time. Plenty of ale and horses and weapons. A good place for a smith that knows his craft. And always open house on fair-days. Free drink for everybody, whether they came to pay or be paid.

But I pushed through the crowd round the tumblers that morning and everything had changed. The king's steward had set up his table outside the gate and there was a great mob round him of those that had come to pay and those that had come to get. He had soldiers guarding a great heap of stuff. Urien wasn't mean. I was glad to see there was still free beer and the steward looked pleasant enough. But I looked through the gate and there wasn't a soul inside those walls except those that worked there. I knew then what it meant to have a queen in Rheged again. She'd want no common people inside her dun, only those that served her.

I felt sorry for young Urien then. A grand lad. We all liked him. Maybe he was a thought young to take his father's place. But he'd soon grow, and he'd the makings of a fine man already. There were none of that family we'd have trusted more to be king over us. Poor lad. It wasn't his dun now. That was as plain as the nose on your face. It was no doing of his to keep his people out of his gate on fair-day. He'd have given a beggar a better welcome.

But I'll be honest. It wasn't more than a moment's thought I gave to Urien. It wasn't him I'd come to see, was it? I watched that open gateway like a green lad gazing at his first sweetheart's door. Years and years it had been since there were real ladies in Lyvennet, and every time a bright skirt went swinging past the gate my blood raced with the thought that it might be her. When it came to my turn to be paid, I still couldn't take my eyes off that gateway for fear I should miss the one moment she came. Four fleeces and two bars of iron. It should have been more than that. It was good work I'd done. But I hadn't the wit to drive a bargain that day.

It's a funny thing. Some of you may think it strange, me feeling sorry for Urien, and dreaming of doing what I was with his wife. But it's not like you think. What folk like us do in the circle, to honour the Lord of the Forest, is nothing to do with a man and his wife.

I stuffed my sack full and then I sat on the ground and waited, as if I might be expecting to meet a friend. She'd send for me, all right, in her own good time.

After a bit, I saw there was another table, on the opposite side of the gate. There were women there, and none that I knew, so I wondered I hadn't noticed them before. Fine lady's women too, by the look of their clothes. That set my blood racing. They had a store of bowls and flasks in front of them and so many people crowding round you could hardly see what they were offering. But it didn't take long to work it out from the kind of sorry folk that shuffled up to them and the look on their faces when they came away clutching a bit of this or that they'd been given. It was healing medicine. Given? Half of those that came didn't seem to be handing anything over for it. I stared. I could see charms signed and stuff measured out, but as often as not those ladies were left empty-handed. I wasn't used to Morgan's ways then. They were busy all day, too. There were two of those ladies seemed to be in charge, turn and turn about. One was a tall woman, with a cold, bitter face, dressed in good stuff, but plainly. The other was a merry young lass, all yellow curls and ribbons and embroidery, and a bit plump in the face, as if she hadn't lost her puppy-fat yet. But she knew her job.

When I saw them, I knew for sure they were Morgan's women, though I didn't understand what her game was. And my nails were digging into the palms of my hands expecting any moment the queen herself would come walking out. I watched that gate as a cat watches a hedge-bank. She never came. All day I sat, with never a bite to eat, till the sun went down and they carried their tables inside and shut the gate. And here was a funny thing. The king's steward went in a sight richer than he'd come out that morning, for all the beer that was drunk. But the queen's women had hardly a basketful. Annis and Mair came looking for me then, and scolding me for missing all the fun.

I couldn't understand it. I'd been so sure Morgan would call me in. She wanted me. I knew she wanted my power. All this time, I'd felt her pulling me here.

I suppose there was dancing and more drinking and eating, while the light lasted. I don't remember. Then there was nothing to do but to walk home with them, down the road through the forest in the dark. The rest of the folk from Way Bank were laughing hard enough and staggering about. They made out they had to kick up such a noise to scare wild beasts away, but it wasn't that. I hadn't drunk so much. I sat and sulked in my smithy half the night. I didn't want to go to bed with Annis. Morgan must have known I'd come, all right.

It made me angry. She couldn't be such a very great queen, after all, or she'd never have let herself be married off late like this to a puppy. Somebody must have had power over her till now. Well, if she was too proud to go to her own gate to meet me, then I'd have to find a way to get inside and show her who was master. I wasn't going to be beaten by a woman, not if she was queen twice over. I was a king too, and I'd more cunning than most.

I let a moon go by. Then I went to Lyvennet again. If they wouldn't let honest craftsmen through the gate, I'd find another way to prove I was higher than Morgan. Only to do it, I had to humble myself and dress in rags. I didn't have rags, let me tell you. I was a skilled man. I went dressed in stout leather and good wool. My work could buy the best. And I dressed my wife and daughter fairly too. I had to wait till the whole village was out harvesting and steal old clothes from empty cottages here and there. And then I had to foul and tear them, and rub a pair of old boots across rough stone till it looked as if I'd walked hundreds of miles in them. I rubbed peat in my skin and in my hair and beard, so my own wife wouldn't have known me.

I took a staff in my hand, and bent my shoulders a bit, and I trudged up the road to the queen's dun at Lyvennet as if it was the last city in the world.

I laughed in my dirty beard. They didn't recognise me. Not though Teilo Smith was a well-known man for miles around. Near black, I was, as though I'd been years under hotter suns than we get in Rheged. But I kept my fingers crossed under the rags of my sleeves.

'The King,' I quavered. 'The young King Urien. They tell me the old king's dead and he's to be married. I'm a holy man. I come to bring him a blessing.'

'Married!' Those sentries laughed at me. 'Four moons and more ago. Made king of Rheged in his father's place, and married to a princess from down south, out of Cornwall. Time enough now for her to be getting big in the belly. You're a bit late in the day, old man, if you've come to dance at their wedding!'

'All the way from Jerusalem, I've come. Years and years I've been on pilgrimage. And when I heard the old king was dying I made all the haste I could. I've known young Urien since he was a bairn. And I've brought him a gift. A precious gift. The boy shall have it now. Look at this . . .' I drew a bundle of leather out of my pouch and unwrapped it. 'A piece of the true cross of Christ, from Jerusalem.' And there it was, a piece of charred wood out of my smithy fire. But for all that, I rubbed it with my sleeve and it seemed to shine in my hand as I held it up to the light. 'There's not many that have seen the like of that.'

They drew in their breath sharpish.

'Go on. It's not really, is it?'

'And come all that way to Britain. . .!'

You could see them reaching their hands out to touch it, and then stopping themselves in mid-air. I had to chuckle to myself. I was more used to mysteries. I put it away. I let them feel the leather it was wrapped in. That was enough good luck for them. They made the signs of blessing, touching it with their heads and eyes and lips.

'There's more. I can see the future. Let a man put his hand in mine and I can read it like a monk with a book. Sons, daughters, battles, wealth. It's all written there in the lines. Now if I could see the young king and queen . . .' They looked sharp at each other when I named the queen. That's where it stuck, all right. It was always open house with Urien and his father. They'd have a welcome for any strolling poet or pilgrim. They loved a good story.

'Well,' said one of the guards craftily. 'Let's see how good you are first. Read my palm.'

I'd a hard job not to laugh out loud. Read his palm? Dunant of Lyvennet, whose wife was cousin to my Annis. Five sons and a crippled daughter. A broken leg that still troubled him in the winter. And likely to come into a little land at Woodend since his mother died at haymaking. It was too easy. They must be simple-minded not to know who I was.

But I impressed them. They sent word in to Urien, and pretty soon I was inside that gate.

It wasn't playing games now. It never had been really. After all, I was a holy man, in another fashion. And I could see further into the shadows than ordinary folk. It was just that bit about Jerusalem. Well, I knew they liked that, the lords and ladies. Travellers' tales. Rome's finished. Since old Vortigern brought the Saxons over and the traitors slew our Council, the chiefs that followed have had their hands too full to trouble about going abroad. They say it's the same tale all over the Empire. The whole world's on fire. Those old days won't come back. But our nobles still hanker after Rome and the East.

I'd been in that courtyard many a time before, but it felt different that day. I didn't know if I was welcome.

Urien was over by the kennels. There was a mastiff bitch there with a litter of new puppies. He motioned me to keep back. Then one of the guards went and muttered in his ear and he came and joined me. He'd grown taller, even since that May wedding. Tall and straight and a bit serious about the eyes. Aye, he'd make a king. Fair and blue-eyed to her black and green. They were a handsome pair, and in a few years the difference between them wouldn't show so much. I thought of their wedding-night and of all the nights since. Had he . . .? Well, I suppose he must have, by now. A woman like that would know what to do, and he'd be a good pupil.

I'd guessed right. Of course he wanted to hear all about my pilgrimage. He sat down in the sun and called for ale. I had to make it up. It came easy enough. Oliphants and dragons, and the temples of Rome and one-eyed giants on the road over the Alps. I'd seen them all.

'And the holy mountain of Sinai? Did you see that too? And the river

Jordan where Christ was baptised? And the Church of the Star blessed Helena built at Bethlehem? Gethsemane? Olivet . . .?'

He was getting carried away, and I was in deep water, for it seemed he knew more about such places than I did. But I reckoned neither of us had been there, so how was he to know if the pictures I painted for him weren't exactly true? I hadn't been to school like the bards, but I could have held my own with them for story-telling that day.

When I got out my little bit of blackened wood he touched it thoughtful-like, and I had an idea that he wasn't as easily taken in as those sentries had been. He thanked me courteously though, and gave me a golden buckle for it. That wasn't nearly enough, if it had been what I'd said it was, but a sight more than I deserved, seeing it wasn't. He's no fool, but he's generous. Maybe he thought he'd paid a fair price for a good story.

I read his palm too. I gave him the best future I could see. He'd be a great king. Greater than his father. Greater than Gwendoleu. I nearly said he'd be greater than Ambrosius, but I thought that might be going a bit far. But bards would sing of him as long as there were harps in Britain. Fine sons, good health, long years. And a noble death with his sword still in his hand. I was careful to praise that sword, you can be sure. I'd made it for him, hadn't I? But I praised the king more. You should have heard me. I did him proud.

There was only one thing I've been sorry for afterwards. When I told him he'd make a good death on the battlefield a shiver came over me, so I fear he'll die by treachery, after all.

But all the time the words were tripping off my tongue, my mind was busy. The breath was struggling in my chest like a bird in a net, and I hoped that little crowd of men round me would think it was just from the journey and the talking. Where was she? They'd built a new house in the middle of the dun, with the thatch still yellow. A sunny-house for the women. I could see the flicker of skirts in and out of the doorway. But it was never her. I held her husband's hand in mine and thought how those fingers must have touched her white foot and her thigh and breast. Those breasts, full under black hair. I couldn't hold my own hand steady.

Well, when I'd done with him and got my reward I screwed up my courage and asked,

'And the queen? Will I read her fortune too?'

He looked round quickly at the sunny-house, and I made out then he was scared of her too. I didn't blame him.

'Queen Morgan is busy. I do not think she is in the mood for such stories.'

And what does a queen have to be so busy about? I thought.

I pushed my luck then. It was as if I couldn't help myself, though I saw the danger.

'Is it the true Cross you think will not be to her liking, sir? I have other stories better suited to one like her. Witches, mermaids, sorcerer's spells from Syria. I've seen them all.'

'Morgan was schooled in a Christian nunnery. You presume too far.'

I bowed and scraped to him as best I could, but it was too late. 'The queen sees no one today.'

He turned away. I should never have come. I hadn't seen her, and I'd put myself properly in her power now. She'd know I was here, and why. It was a chill walk back to the gate alone, with every window of her sunny-house like eyes on my back. Morgan was watching me, I knew that. It would take more than peat-stain and rags to hide from her what I was. Even if she had forgotten me once, she'd be sure to remember now.

I got outside that gate and I vowed I'd never go back again. I'd done with that. I had to put her out of my mind. But it wasn't so easy. Way Bank lies much too close to Lyvennet for comfort.

# Chapter Five

'Teilo Smith! So this is the throne-room of your kingdom?'

I caught my thumb on the hot iron and I turned and swore. It was fear made me curse, more than the pain. A fear as if I'd turn round and see death come for me. Months I'd waited to hear a voice I didn't know at the door and see a stranger standing there against the light. Now it had come. It was all I could do to keep a grip on the hammer I'd got in my hand.

I'd made up my mind it would be a woman. But the figure was too tall for that. Hooded and cloaked in red, done up with tassels of fox-tails. But there was a grey gown showing under it. That jolted my memory. I called to mind where I'd heard that voice before. On Morgan's wedding-day, in the streets of Carlisle. I can't tell you how sick I felt at that. Disappointed, and a different sort of fear to the one I'd felt first.

'Oh, it's you, is it?' I said. I had a struggle to keep my voice steady.

He threw back his hood. He had white hair, but he carried himself like a young man. Grey eyes, and laughing at my face.

'I frightened you? That's good. You do well to be afraid. It's that that keeps a wise man's head on his shoulders.'

I could see the boy's ears flapping for all he was worth, so I sent him off to chop firewood. I was mad with this magician. What did he want to come to Way Bank for, just when I'd put the pair of them out of my head? I could keep a secret better than he could, by the look of it. If I'm seen to be dealing with nobility, it should be strictly in the way of business.

'You found out where I live, then.'

'The King of Smiths is not difficult to find. Though it's a rough and icy road to here.'

'I didn't ask you to come.'

'Ah, but in all these months you haven't come to me. And I *did* ask you. If need be, I can be as patient as any man either side of the grave. But some affairs are too urgent. For safety's sake they will not wait.'

'They will, when there's nothing happened.'

'Morgan! Come, man, you must have seen her by now.'

'No.' I turned away. I'd done my best to put all that behind me since harvest-time. The queen didn't want to see me, and I didn't want to meddle with her. Or I tried not to.

'But she must have summoned you up. What else would she mean but that? The way she rode to her wedding. The way she bowed to you in the street. Power, Teilo Smith, power! Morgan needs what you hold. She can't have brought a full circle with her from Cornwall, can she?'

'There's a few new women up there, they say. Nothing like enough. I'd have heard if any of mine had gone over to her.'

'Then certainly she still needs you and yours. This is your territory. The Horned One's country. Her Mare does not run here. She must respect the Stag.'

'She's a funny way of showing it, then.'

I wiped my hands on my apron to give myself time to think and stole a look up at him. He wasn't watching. He was picking away at the wooden frame of the door, pulling splinters off it. He looked like a man with something nagging at his mind. Aye, I thought, there's more here. Maybe the queen needs my help, and maybe she doesn't. But this one hasn't come all the way from Carlisle just to wish me the time of day, either.

'She's not the only one,' I said.

'Eh? What's that?'

'I may wear a sooty face, but I'm no man's fool. What's a fine gentleman like yourself doing here in my smithy? What Queen Morgan wants is anybody's guess. She hasn't told me, anyroad. But it's as plain as the nose on my face that you want something pretty bad. That's twice you've begged for my help now. She hasn't.'

He made a face, half-mournful and half-laughing, like a boy that's been caught with his finger in the cream.

'There, I was right! I knew you for a wise man. But it's not I that need you, Teilo Smith. Remember? The Cymry. Look. Look at this!'

He got me by the shoulders and pushed me out of the door.

'There! Do you see that? Those hills?' He was facing me north. It was one of those pale blue winter skies, with the hills making a line across it, cold and clear. 'There's the Wall running along them from sea to sea. And there –' spinning me round south – 'the Pennines, like the long dragon's back. Once the roads on either side were thronged with warriors, lords and ladies, common men and women, coming and going freely from north to south, from east to west. Once our ships were free to sail the sea. Once there was one law from shore to shore, all the way from Lothian to the Land's End. One country of Britain. One Emperor. Don't you remember?'

'How could I remember? I wasn't born then. And nor were you.'

He started a bit and gave that childish little smile he had.

'No! To be sure. I was dreaming.'

'There have been Saxons in the east as long as I've lived. That's how it's always been as far as folks round here can remember. Uther Pendragon beat them a time or two, but he never drove them out entirely. They say even Ambrosius couldn't do that. It's Saxon land in the south and east, ours in the north and west. And just the hill country between us.'

'The lowland the foreigners hold is ours. The soil of the Cymry. Ambrosius knew it. He drove his sword through the Saxons clear down to London town. We British hold that road still. But in other places the land is being eaten away. The Saxon dragon is growing fatter every year.'

'What's that to me? So long as they stay clear of Rheged. Ambrosius is dead and gone. There'll never be another one like him.'

'Won't there, Smith? Won't there? What if I were to tell you that every road and river shall be ours again? What if the British held this island from the cliffs of Dumnonia and Gwynedd to the eastern sands? What if the Saxons went wading back to their keels for ever? What then?'

He was like a man drunk in the middle of the day, and as foolish.

'Oh, aye? That would make you a bigger man then, wouldn't it, Silver-Tongue? And what do you want me to do? Forge a sword of power for your little lad to fight them off with?'

That shook him. For a man that had such wisdom, he was mighty careless with his secrets. His hand shot out and gripped mine. I felt his strength again, and I remembered a bit late why I'd been afraid before.

'Be careful, Smith! Do not seek to know too much before your time. Secrets are power. And power can break a man. I warned you!'

That angered me, I was no ordinary workman. I had powerful secrets already, as well he knew.

'And who are you to threaten me about power? No true bard, I'll be bound, wherever you've sprung from.'

His eyes went crafty, as a man's will do sometimes when he's in drink.

'Harps have their own magic too. A bard stands high as a druid. I can play both. Gwendoleu will not regret the gold he gives me.'

He dropped my arm.

'And why should I tell you who I am? You've told me nothing yet. My true name is one that Morgan of Cornwall knows too well. Twice seven years, I needed! I pleaded with Uther Pendragon to hold her penned up that long on Tintagel. Even fourteen years is young enough for the task that waits. But Uther was dead too soon and my aim has miscarried. I should not have trusted the Church to guard her. I fear Morgan has learned more in her convent than psalms and needlework. Now she is freed and wise and much too close. I must gain more time.

'I could use you in more than one way, King of Smiths. You are the High Chief over many circles. Your people could make a powerful ring of protection for us against her strength. Or, better still, I could set you to work as Morgan's false friend. Your King to her Queen. Let her join the circle with you, for her own foul purposes. You could tell me all she plots. And you alone, Smith, would know how to break her chain and let its power spill.'

I turned pale at that.

'She'd know I'd done it! You couldn't hide that from the Lady. She'd smell who the traitor was.'

'An earthly king takes his life in his hands when he rides into battle. What kind of king are you, to shrink back now when Britain needs you? War, Teilo Smith, is a dangerous business.'

He turned to the door. And just then, in came my daughter Mair, with ale and sweetmeats.

She blushed. She wasn't used to gentlemen, and you could see this man was nobility, in his foxy cape.

'Mother heard you had company. She's sent in some cakes . . .'

I never saw a man's face change so fast. He put his long hand under her chin and smiled, very wide and warm.

'Oh, excellent!' he said. And he was pressing one of her cakes through her lips and then swallowed the rest himself. 'Delicious. This is one secret you've kept well, Teilo Smith.'

When I saw that greedy shine in his eyes as he touched her I could have slugged him with my hammer, magician or no. I turned and thrust the cold horse-bit back into the fire. I was near to branding him with it. I was shaking with anger. What I did with the women of my own kind was between me and the god. But my daughter Mair was no part of it yet.

She laughed a fair bit and slipped away as soon as she could get free of him. She was a good girl. That bard wasn't long going then. He raised his hand first, as if he was blessing me.

'Wealth you shall have, if that is what you want. There will be spoils in plenty when we ride. The enemy's treasure for those who have helped us. Win me three years, Smith. Only three years.'

# Chapter Six

There's nothing like knowing a secret for having it gnaw away at your insides till you can't think straight about anything else. And all the time there's more questions you wished you'd asked while you had the chance. A king that was going to better even Ambrosius? Top-dog over all the other kings? A lad, and by the sound of it, not yet full-grown? That took some believing. Whose son was he? Not Gwendoleu's, that's certain. And a man has to have more than royal blood to be made high king. He needs a host to shout his name, and war-horses, and forts, and a string of battles to his reputation. That's what the bards mean when they sing of a high king in these parts.

No, the great chiefs that followed the Romans were all dead, and left no new ones to come after them. They said Uther Pendragon was the last man of that house. As for what kings we'd got now, young Urien might still turn out the best of them, to my way of thinking. But that crafty bard Silver-Tongue couldn't mean him. He was Morgan's own husband! Gwendoleu? But he was a grown man, and he was more likely to make his kingdom bigger quarrelling with his own blood than get up a host to fight the Saxons. So who was there up here in the north to make such a stir about? What little prince? And why should he fear Morgan of Cornwall might learn where the lad was hiding and what his magician's real name was?

Fear Morgan? Aye. That's good advice, is that. Don't you forget it. You're well clear of her here. When I was inside her castle walls at Lyvennet I'd dreaded her like a fly caught in a web waiting for the spider. Outside, I'd need to watch out for her sticky thread pulling me in. Curse that magician. Why couldn't they leave me in peace, the pair of them? Curse Morgan . . . Yes. Back at Way Bank I thought it! If she'd been old and ugly. If she hadn't smiled at me like that . . .

The nights were full of her face now. It was like the moon in winter, with her green eyes glowing as she looked down on me. A blacksmith, I was. I'd made do for twenty years on coarser meat. She made me twist and groan in bed. I wanted to have her and run a hundred miles from her at the same time.

It wasn't any better in daylight, either. Every time I stepped outside the smithy door I could feel her staring down from her castle walls, overlooking me. It was his hammer and her anvil closing in. I should have had more sense.

I did it for pride, and I've suffered for that ever since. But it was still a mighty lump of pride I had to swallow before I could do what I did. I'd show her I wouldn't take no for an answer. I was High Chief.

I'd seen how the wind blew. Lyvennet Castle was ruled by a woman now. I'd seen fighting-men looking shiftily over their shoulders. Up in the dun men still bent the knee to Urien, because he was the king. But you can't have two rulers in one kingdom. Very well, then. I could play her game. It was a pity, though. I knew Urien could make us a fine chieftain, given half a chance. He's not so old, even now. She hasn't crushed him. Maybe the bards will sing of him yet.

Still, I'd handled power myself for too long not to have a nose for where it lay. I was used to masking for the god. When I put on his skin I was choosing which power I'd serve. This time I chose the side that was going to win.

I stole women's clothes, patched ones but clean. Not Annis's. I didn't fancy that, somehow. I hid them in a basket while I shaved all the hair off my face. I thought Annis was safely in the dairy-shed for an hour. But she came indoors and found me at it.

'Why, whatever are you doing?' she said.

'Nothing for you women to gossip over,' I muttered. 'It's a vow I've taken.'

She was quiet at that. She'd lived with me long enough to know there was a part of my life that wasn't to be spoken of. She knew better than to ask me questions. She was a good woman, was Annis.

'I only came for a clean jug for the whey.'

She took it down from the shelf and she stood by the fire, nursing it to her breast while she looked at me fondly-like.

'It must be all of twenty-five years since I've seen you without a beard. And you looked a fine lad, even then. Do you remember that day when I was sitting at my mother's loom weaving, and you were leading a horse along the road? And the king's soldiers came by, and your horse reared and bolted. We thought it would break clean through our pigsty. But there was you, hanging on to the creature's bridle for dear life and dragging it back to the road. And I thought to myself then, it might not be such a bad thing to be brought to bed by a lad with shoulders like that.'

She was a good woman, my Annis. Not over-handsome, but comfortable. Another man might have been well content with her. It wasn't my fault if I was born to greater things than her, was it? I meant her no harm.

Still, I was glad I wasn't wearing the woman's gown when she found me . . . Yes. Make your sour faces if you like. I *am* ashamed of wearing this!

She said, 'Well, this won't get the butter churned, will it? And you've work of your own to get on with, I dare say.'

'I've got to go out. The boy can mind the smithy. I'll be back by supper.'

I waited till I got to the forest, and then I dressed in the woman's clothes, with a big hood to hide my face. I stuffed my good leather things inside a hollow tree. That left me an empty basket. I'd seen what it was Morgan's women were giving out on Lugh's Day. And it wasn't always 'Queen Morgan' folk called her now. She was getting to have another title among them. I'd heard them name her 'Morgan the Healer'.

Well, that wasn't so strange. The women of our kind have always been known and valued for that. Of course, Morgan would know such secrets. She could practise the women's art if she had a mind to.

I didn't use that side of the craft myself. I was the Black Smith. I had other ways, with fire and iron and stone. Things I wouldn't tell you of even now. But I'd had to learn that other wisdom, along with all the rest. There's not much the High Chief doesn't know. I had it all in my head. Still, it wasn't easy to fill that basket in the middle of winter, I can tell you. She'd have to respect me for it. She might be a grown woman, but I had ten years over her. And maybe we had things growing in Rheged they'd never heard of down in Cornwall. I could teach her a trick or two. I'd show her. I dug roots out of the hard ground with my knife. I searched about till I found leaves that were still green under pockets of snow. I picked the last shrivelled-up berries the birds hadn't stripped off the stalks. There's not many could have gathered such a rich harvest at that time of year.

When I stepped back on to the road I bent over double. Me, that had always carried myself so straight and strong. I clutched that cloak round me and let the hood fall over my face.

There were fresh men on the gate. They didn't know me. The look in their eyes was the same as those others when I spoke the queen's name.

'Herbs,' I quavered, showing them my basket. 'I'm a wise woman. I bring sweet herbs for Morgan the Healer. Can I see her?'

They looked at each other, none too easy.

'Best send them in,' said one. 'Let her women decide.'

They called a boy to carry the basket into the sunny-house. I stood there waiting in the raw wind, and glad enough of the excuse to be wrapped up close inside the cloak. The blood was fairly hammering in my head. The guards saw me shivering. They offered me a seat in the gateway and gave me a beaker of hot ale. At last a woman came out, carrying my basket. They pointed me out to her. She came towards me. A tall woman, and dressed like a lady. I'd seen her before, on Lugh's Day. I didn't care to look her full in the face, but I stole a glance under the edge of my hood. She was older than Morgan. She had a long, hard face, with deep lines. It looked as if care had put scars on it worse than gashes from a sword.

'Queen Morgan thanks you. Those are dainty weapons that you have forged for her.'

So I was right. She knew who it was that had sent them to her. I should have bolted then.

The woman held out the basket. It was empty, except for a silver button lying in the bottom.

'Doesn't she want to see me?'

'Why? What good would it do? She has your gift and you have hers.'

'The wise should help each other,' I mumbled.

'You? Help Morgan? She had no need of what you brought.'

301

I started to go. My wits were in a muddle. I'd been so sure she was calling me here.

Then the woman caught my arm. And pretty quick she let it drop again. She couldn't stop herself shaking. I could see she had to say something to me and was afraid to ask.

'Old woman,' her words came tumbling out fast now, 'there is something more. There is light and there is dark. There is peace and there is war. There is both dying and rising again. You have filled one side of her basket only. Could you supply the other?'

Her hand flew to her mouth, as though she oughtn't to have let those words escape. But I had her now. I could hardly hold the man's triumph out of my voice and keep it womanish.

'Queen Morgan shall get what she wants. Trust me.'

I saw what it was she expected at last. And I was the man who could give it to her.

# Chapter Seven

King of Smiths I might be, but even I had to wait a while. The Horned
God's a thrusting lad. He can dance a pretty quick step to the pipe.
But behind him there's his Mother, and you can't hurry her. She'll
give life too, but in her own time and seasons. So I had to wait for
spring to come and crack the ground open, as if there was so much
blood and sap inside the earth it would fairly burst apart. Sometimes
I dream that'll happen, and we'll all be swallowed down in her darkness.
Pretty, my Mair used to say it was, when all the little spring flowers
came out. She didn't see the danger.

I'd let my beard grow so I had to shave again. I took my basket into
the forest a second time. Another man might have searched a lifetime
and not found some of those things. For a while I sweated a bit and
wondered if I should have brought one of my own wise women with
me to point the way. Granny Sarran, maybe. But I cursed the thought.
I was the god's Chief Man, and I wouldn't be bested by any woman.

I knew the forest, my part of it, anyroad. But I went deeper into
it that day than I ordinarily cared to. It's an awful place. Black mud
sucks at your boots and all of a sudden it'll grab your leg right up to
the knee. There's huge treetrunks lying across your path, and things
like giants' faces growing out of them. You think they're staring up
at you, till you see that even those faces are dead and rotting apart.
I had to search their crawling innards for what I wanted. The trees
that are living have got lichen and moss, like beards, hanging from
them so long and grey they look as if they're hundreds of years old.
Their fingers are knotted into each other over your head tight so you
can't get a glimpse of the sun to know which way is home. I used my
knife to mark the way with notches on the trunks, but after a bit it
got so deep and dark I could hear every tree I cut scream out to the
rest to warn them I was coming.

For years now, I'd been in charge of our rites. I knew how to make
people afraid. I was the one with the horns. I was the one they bowed
down to. I was afraid myself that day. I'd never felt so small and
helpless in my own forest. Though that was nothing to what was coming. I said
the charms and made the offerings for what I was taking. It didn't help
me much.

But I found what I'd come for. Wolfsbane. Blackblood. The Sleeper,
and all the rest of that crew. Under the lot I laid three caps of the Grey
Lady. If Morgan was what I thought she was, she would know how
rare a thing that was.

I was ready for her now. When I got back safe into the daylight and

washed the mud off myself in the beck I felt pretty pleased with what
I'd got. I didn't go home. I put on the same woman's clothes as before
and I'd a job to shorten my stride to match as I set off to Lyvennet.
All the same, when I came in sight of the walls I wasn't feeling so cocky.

I told the same story at the gate. I knew they'd let me through this
time.

'I've brought some more herbs for the queen. She asked me to fetch
these for her.'

Herbs! A sweet name for the stuff I had in my basket today. Still,
they'd be a certain cure for some things. To end a sickness that wouldn't
heal. To rest a broken heart. To quieten a scolding wife . . . begging
your pardon! Well, there's no sleep sounder than the one they bring,
is there?

It was the same tall woman who came to fetch me. Today the colour
kept coming and going in her face, like a fire that's not sure whether
to take a hold or not.

'Queen Morgan will see you.'

She led me straight across the court to the sunny-house. The blood
was fairly pounding in my chest. I felt that every man in the castle
was looking at me. Not to mention those women.

Once, when I was a lad, I was taken out fishing in a boat on the
lake. I looked down and I could see the stones close below me under
the water. Then I turned away. It was only a few moments, but next
time I looked overboard there was nothing beneath me, just darkness.
Only then, deep down, a giant pike came drifting past. It was bigger
than I was. I felt like that now. It was too late to turn back home.

I stumbled in over the threshold of the sunny-house, following the
woman. I'd never been in such a place before. Fur rugs on the floor.
Pictures of animals and trees and flowers all done in wools and hanging
on the walls. Wood light as honey-wax and carved with birds' heads.
The light from the windows was making bright patches on the floor.
There was a little grey cat sitting in a pool of sunshine on a spotted
deerskin.

The woman made me stand in the light. She moved to one side
between two of the windows. Nobody said anything, and I turned to
look that way.

Morgan was facing me, in the shadow between the windows. My eyes
were so dazzled I had to blink before I could make her out plainly.
She was sitting in a high carved chair like a throne. She had on a robe
of blue so deep I thought at first it was black, with a great silver lune
round her neck. Her hair was loose over her shoulders, like on her
wedding-day. Well, you know she can't bear to be bound. And her
face was white in the shadow, just like the moon I'd been seeing all
those nights.

She looked bigger than I'd remembered her.

The woman who had brought me was standing quietly by her side.
More like a ghost than a flesh-and-blood woman that Luned was. There
was another one of them on Morgan's other side. She was flesh and
blood, all right. The young one I'd seen before. Pretty, and just a bit

on the plump side. Another time I'd have been glad to have one like that among my own circle. But I hardly looked at her then.

Morgan fills any room where she sits. You don't need me to tell you. When she looks at you she draws you right inside herself. And the Mothers forbid you should think that I mean anything ill by that now. Whatever I may have dreamed when I was safe in my own cottage, that was all gone here. It would have been like death if I'd let my thoughts stray even one step in that direction. Catch a mouse dreaming of mating with the owl!

'So, you have come to offer me the other half of wisdom? The universe in balance. Put back your woman's hood, Teilo Smith. Let me see who is king in Rheged.'

I let it fall to my shoulders. The three of them burst into peals of laughter. That fairly shocked me. It was no laughing matter, what I'd been through. Then I saw all of a sudden how I must look to them. From the cheeks upwards I had a face scorched red at the smithy fire. But below, there was new, scraped skin that had barely seen the light of day in fifteen years.

That young one was laughing hardest of the lot. I saw her clearly now. She had bright blue eyes. Impudent, she was. Laughing fit to bust. At me, Teilo Smith.

Morgan held up her hand and they both went silent. She stood up, and I had a bigger shock then. I saw why she'd seemed a big woman, sitting in her chair. Her belly was swelling with child, so huge she must have been near her time. We'd heard the queen was expecting, of course. We were all hoping it would be a boy, and my people had worked a bit more for that than just hope. But somehow I hadn't pictured it. Not Morgan, with her belly sticking out like this, the same as any village woman. I can't explain to you, but that sight shook me so much I nearly cried out loud. You see, to me, she was the young moon, the Maiden. That Lady can always come under the King and still be a virgin. She isn't the Mother. Can you understand that?

My basket was lying on the table where her woman Luned had left it. Morgan lifted the cover off and I saw her give a start. That made me feel pretty pleased with myself. I reckoned she was surprised at some of the things I'd found. She stared down at them for a mighty long time. Then she lifted her eyes to mine, and very wide and brilliant they looked. If it had been anyone else I'd have thought she was scared by what she'd seen.

'Why have you brought me these?' Still staring hard at me.

'Because you asked me to!' I blustered. 'Your woman said I had to fill both sides of your basket.'

She swung round then, and the older woman turned paler still and shook in her shoes.

But Morgan never said anything to her, only looked hard from one to the other of us.

She turned back to the basket and picked out my treasures one by one. I could see her lips moving as she looked at them, but I never heard a word. Last of all she came to that rare toadstool that I call the

Grey Lady. There's few enough folks, even of our sort, that know it, and some that do have worse names for it than that. But I always reckon it's best to be respectful. She stood, twisting and twisting it in her fingers, so I began to wonder if she knew its true power. I've known a man that only licked his fingers after picking it, and he sickened and died horribly before sunset. Someone must have ill-wished him pretty badly to make him do that. He was a wise man. And how would I get up the courage to tell Morgan what she didn't know?

'So this is how you would choose to restore the balance. Why? You could have brought me the metals of the Black Smith's art to match my woman's healing. Why these?'

I must have gasped sharp when she said that, and looked quick at her waiting-women. Morgan smiled a bit.

'We can speak freely in front of these two. They know what you are. They are high in the mysteries. Erith is young, but she is wise beyond her years. And Luned – would you believe that Luned was once a scholar-nun? She might have become abbess in her own convent one day. But the Christians don't like their white nuns to bear babies in the Mothers' service, do they, Luned?'

Her older woman looked back at her with that harrowed face of hers. She had strange eyes. Dull, as if she'd used up all her feelings long since.

'I ask you again,' Morgan said. 'Why these?'

'Power!' I blurted out. It was the first word I thought of. I was a fool to tell her that was in my mind. But what was the use? No one could keep a secret from Morgan.

'You ask for power from me?'

'No! I'm High King in all these parts. I came to share my power with you. I thought you wanted it.'

'You thought I wanted these? You come to offer power to me this way?'

She took the things up one by one and laid them out in front of her.

'Wolfsbane. Bitter on the tongue. A little can stir the dull spirit. More drives it mad. Blackblood, to rot the bowels. The Sleeper, that cools a fever but chills the healthy heart to death. And the Grey Lady, for which there is no cure.'

So she did know.

She motioned to the younger girl. There was a silver casket on the other side of the table. Erith opened the lid and showed me what was inside. The things were shrivelled now, even more than when I'd picked them. But I recognised them. It was those healing herbs I'd gathered for Morgan in the middle of winter. The little grey cat jumped on the table and walked along, sniffing, till Erith snatched it off. I didn't say anything, and nor did Morgan. I couldn't think why she'd kept my gifts all this time if she didn't mean to use them.

'The kindly herbs. But did you know that excess of them can kill as surely as the others? While a little of the darker sort, used with great care, may sometimes save life?'

Of course I knew.

'Wounding and healing. Sword and scabbard. I have them both here

306

under my hand. Perhaps you were right, after all, Smith, to leave your own art behind. I and mine suffered long ago through a wise man's magic. I have borne the pain ever since.' She fell quiet again then. None of us dared to say anything. At last she said, very low, 'Are you teaching me that the cure is not to be sought from the men's side? That we must make it ourselves? That the balance lies . . . *here*?'

She raised her head to me then, and the look in her eyes nearly sent me staggering backwards. I swear to you there was terror in them. She might have been a woman pleading for her son's life. It was only a moment, and she was queen again.

'These things themselves are not power, Smith. While they lie on this table they are knowledge only. Power needs the will to use our knowledge.'

'I am the Black Smith. I've used it. Both sides. When the price matched the need.'

'And what price did you hope Morgan of Cornwall would pay you?'

'Nothing, your honour! Not to you. I brought these for a gift.'

She knew I lied. I'd hoped to fatten my power on hers.

She gathered the herbs up, both sorts, and laid them back in the basket. Without a word spoken Luned brought her water and Morgan rinsed her hands very carefully. Luned wiped that table well too, I can tell you, and washed her own hands in clean water afterwards. 'I did not need your gifts. I have had this knowledge long since. But it seems I lack something, after all. The will to act. The courage to hold both sides alone.'

I straightened my shoulders. So she'd recognised my strength. I could feel the manhood rising in me.

'I'm your man!'

She smiled at that. 'Exactly so. Take back both gifts . . . Smith. Show me how a wise . . . *woman* . . . should understand the use of power. Use these yourself.'

That black, bottomless lake was under me again. I could feel the cold water rocking my boat. The pike was swimming back.

'But . . . but who?' I stammered. 'Who do you want me to use them on?' She stroked the great curve of her belly with her narrow, white hands. 'That is for you to choose. I shall watch where you think a woman's power should fall, and how it is used. And I shall learn from what I see. You may go now.'

They sounded soft enough words, but she gave me no chance to argue. Her voice was like a hand, pushing me out of the fort. I pulled up my hood and turned to go. I was in deep now. Luned was holding out the basket to me, twice as full as it had been before.

'Oh, and Smith!' Morgan called, very sweetly. 'When you come back, wear those same clothes. They suit the lesson you have taught me excellently. We have no need of men's craft, have we, you and I? I shall warn the guards.'

I shuffled out of the door, with their laughs beating about my back. And that young Erith mocking loudest of all.

# Chapter Eight

I must have been mad. Looking back on it now, I must have been bewitched to think I could match myself against Morgan. That's it. It was her doing. She'd put her spell on me, there in her castle. How else do you think a man of my wisdom would have done what I did, and in such a way? I was forced to do it.

My will to her power, that's what I thought it was. And I had that basket full of herbs she'd given back to me.

It's a chill thing to look around the circle of folk you know and say, 'Which one of them shall I kill?'

It had to be right. There's always some who are old and sick. Their lives have got so bad they're a burden to themselves and other folk. It would have been a kindness for me to give the last sleep to one of those. But that was too easy. A woman like Morgan wasn't looking to me for kindness. It needed to be somebody strong, in the full prime of life. Power grows by feeding on blood, not slops. That's why those Christians'll never last.

Come to think of it, there wasn't a cottager in Way Bank she'd care about. What's one peasant more or less to a Lady like her? No. Let's come closer. There must be strong men in Lyvennet. Dunant, who guarded her own gate? Easy enough to swap a drink with him. Aye, there it came again. Too easy by half. She'd want more than that.

Morgan had laughed at me. Me. Smith. The king of smiths. She'd laughed me out of her door in my woman's clothes. Well, I'd show her. Yes, and I'd show that sneaking magician too. Common I might be, but I'd not be their tool. I'd show myself as great in the art as they were. They'd both bow down to me before I'd finished.

You want me to show you how I use power, do you, my lady? Right, then. You'll see. I'll come so close to you it'll make you shiver as if a goose had walked over your grave.

I thought I'd got it then. Kill Urien himself. Aye, I could have done even that if I'd wanted. But I still had sense enough to see that it was a daft idea. If Urien's dead, then Morgan's not Queen of Rheged. She wouldn't thank me for robbing her of her crown, would she?

There was a moment, madder than all the rest, when I thought of killing Morgan herself. And I couldn't stop shaking for the rest of that day, for fear she could read my thoughts, sitting up there in Lyvennet and looking down at my smithy door.

She'd made it a dun where the women ruled. The men were drones now. There hadn't been so much as a cattle-raid since Urien brought her back as his bride. All he'd done was get her with child. It was her

308

women she looked to to feed her. She was like the queen-bee, sitting in her sunny-house, growing fatter and fatter on the power she sucked from them.

A women's castle. And then I had it. Those bright, blue eyes laughing over Morgan's shoulder. Impudent, she'd been. I could feel the smile spread over my own face when I thought about it. I could kill that one and enjoy it. That ought to make Queen Morgan gasp. A young witch, like herself. One step away from her elbow. She'd know better than to treat Teilo Smith with disrespect after that.

Since that second time I'd kept my chin shaved. I hadn't lied to Annis. It *was* a vow I'd taken. The folk in Way Bank might look queerly at my bare face, but there wasn't one of them dared to question me. Only my daughter Mair. She stroked my chin.

'You've shaved it again. There's fresh blood on it. Aren't you going to let it grow again, this time?'

Annis told her sharply, 'Let your dad alone, girl. He has his reasons.'

'I'm sorry, Da. But you look so strange these days. All the folk are saying so. Some of them are frightened to bring work to the smithy like they used to. And you're so often away now.'

'Mair!'

She put her arms round my neck and kissed me. 'It's all right. He doesn't mind. He's my Da, isn't he?'

I put her away from me. I couldn't bide still. I couldn't sleep or work. I'd have to get on with it, now that I knew what I had to do. And what if the boy did stare at me when I told him I'd be gone all day again, and he could smother the fire and take a holiday? Come to that, I'd kill him too if he didn't stop staring at me with those big brown eyes.

When he'd gone, I fetched that basket out and separated the plants, the right-hand from the left. I stewed the juice from the herbs of darkness while the forge was cooling. I wished I'd stuck to my own craft. It felt like women's work. I had to borrow some of Annis's pots and bowls while she was outdoors. Still, it's strange how the old chants come back to you from years ago, even though you've gone up a different road since you learned them. I had to do it right. It's not just the plants you need to make the spell stick. I don't have to tell you that.

When it was brewed, and rightly spoken over, I poured it out into a little flask. Then I stoppered it close with leather and wax. I stowed that away in my pouch, very careful. I didn't know what to do with the bowls. I couldn't hang about to wash them now. I could see Mair was outside the kitchen. If she found me at it, she'd ask questions, even if Annis wouldn't. I pushed the pots in a corner by the fire with a bit of sacking over them. I had the sense to tie the dog up so he wouldn't lick them.

Last of all, I stuffed my woman's disguise into a satchel, and strapped it on my back. I had to take that, even though I hated it. I knew I'd want to run to Lyvennet straight off to boast to the queen the thing was done.

When I stepped outside I had a bit of a shock to find some men of our village near the smithy door. I could tell they were muttering about me. I wondered how much they'd seen. They drew back a bit when they saw me come out. They didn't give me the time of day.

Behind the forge there's a green. My wife was there, and Mair now, with a basket of washing between them. They were spreading the clothes on the bushes to dry. They didn't see me. I had a terrible dryness in my throat. To this day it's a grief to me that I didn't call to them to say goodbye.

It was like a fever. I never stopped to think how I was going to come on Erith. I knew the Mothers would send her to me, just like a lamb to the eagle's claws. It had to happen. It was her name I'd spoken over the flames.

I hid myself at the edge of the wood outside Lyvennet. And it wasn't long before I saw them, Luned and Erith, coming out of the castle with baskets in their hands. They came down the hill towards me. Luned walked slow, but Erith was dancing about like a silly child. I drew back deeper under the hazels and let them go by me. It was *her* doing. She'd sent them out to me. She must have done.

I hadn't thought it would be quite so easy. That should have warned me.

I followed them into the shadow. I didn't need the path. This was my forest. I was at home here in my own kingdom. I was the stag. I could tread among dry leaves and twigs, and you'd never hear me. The women made little enough noise themselves, just a rustle of leaves and the twitter of their talking. I made none behind them.

They slowed down when they came to the spring. The moss is deep there and the mud's black and soft. It's a rare place for toadstools. The two of them bent down and started searching. Morgan had sent them to find something for her. When I saw what they passed over, I guessed what it was.

I could have told them where it grew. But I hid and waited. It was a slow business. Erith had stopped chattering now. I let the space get wider between them. Luned straightened her back and took a long look round. Then her yellow gown flickered away among the trees. That left Erith on her own.

I worked the stopper loose in the flask.

She found the toadstool. I heard her squeal for pleasure. And then I took her from behind. The flask was in my hand, ready. I got one arm round her and pressed her body to my chest. With the other hand I forced the juice into her mouth. One gasp was all it took. She'd gulped it in. Straight off, she tried to spit it back, but it was too late. She wrenched herself round and saw then who it was. Teilo Smith, with his face half-shaved, half-scorched. Lady Erith didn't laugh at me this time. Oh, no. She stared. Wide, blue eyes, with whites clear as a child's. Then the pain burned into her guts and her eyes turned bloodshot. I couldn't hold her body. She screamed horribly and fell kicking on the ground.

Don't look at me like that! I know. You wonder how I could stand by and see it. I tell you, I didn't feel anything then. Not triumph, not pity. Nothing. I just stood, and watched her die.

It was only a short time she lay there, writhing about, but for her it wasn't nearly short enough.

There was a crashing through the wood. Luned came running back. She'd heard the screaming. One look and she saw Erith's black face, and me with the flask in my hand. She stared at me, like Erith had. Then she clapped her hand to her mouth and went haring away out of the forest. Silly woman. She didn't need to be afraid of me. You'd only to look at her face to see that Morgan had broken that one already. Where would have been the point in killing her?

So I was left with the corpse. I'd done what I swore I would. It should have made me feel more of a man.

I pulled out the woman's dress. I could feel myself coming over weak the moment I touched it. I hated the feel of it more every time I had to put it over my head. It's funny how clothes can add something to a man, or take it away. You don't know how it felt. You've always been women in your trailing gowns. It would have been different if I'd gone to her dressed in good smith's leather. I could have answered her then.

# Chapter Nine

I had a feeling the sentries drew back as I came near. They didn't challenge me this time. They passed me through the gate before I spoke. Someone must have warned them I was coming. I wanted to hold my head up high as I crossed the yard. I'd earned the right now. Instead of that, I had to duck it under that floppy hood. It didn't seem to hide me as much as it had before. Men stopped working to watch me shuffle towards the queen's house. There wasn't one of them cracked a joke or called out a bit of bawdiness, like soldiers usually will to a woman. They knew something was wrong when they saw where I was headed.

There was a different girl waiting at the sunny-house door, a little scrap of a maid. She looked scared. She showed me in and shut the door on me as quick as she could.

Inside that room I felt as my whippet might, shut in a cage with some wild beast out of the forest. Morgan was not much sitting on her chair as crouched, like a pole-cat on a branch. You could see her hands gripping the carving till they were white as bones. That stupid Luned was shivering behind her.

'So!' she hissed at me. 'You dared to come and look me in the face. What is this you have done?'

I stood shaking in my shoes. The words wouldn't come out. I know I should have answered her back proudly, as king to her queen. I just couldn't.

'Only what you told me to,' I got out at last.

'You fool!'

That wasn't a word I'd take from anyone. I was a wise man. It got my blood up.

'You challenged me! You gave me my herbs back and asked me to show you how I'd use them. Well, so I have.'

'Fool!' she shouted again in a rage. 'Have you understood nothing? To wound and not to heal? To curse and not to bless? To hate and not to love? Is this your wisdom? I challenged you to use both sides of that basket, Teilo Smith. Both sides!'

I suppose my mouth fell open at that. Did she mean those herbs of healing I'd brought her so proudly, first off? I'd taken those out and left them lying in the smithy. I thought she'd scorned them. I thought she'd passed them over as the sort of soft, soppy stuff any village wise woman uses in her trade. Of course I hadn't used them. They hadn't strength to match the other, had they?

And so I told her.

That shut her up. She stared at me for a long time, and all the fury drained out of her face. Queen though she was, she looked like a little girl that's lost her mother in the crowd.

'Can it really be so? Is this the wisdom you are offering me, King of Smiths? Is this the truth of this world? The dark is stronger than the light?'

I felt a bit uneasy then, with her saying that.

'Of course there has to be both. I know that. There's dying and kindling again. Winter and summer. The world's a round. But one half's tougher than the other. It's only fit for the strong. That's common-sense.'

Morgan had got a grip of herself again. She was leaning forward now and there were two spots of colour starting to burn in her cheeks.

'Tell me,' she said, in that sort of voice that's sweeter and softer than the way she's looking. 'Tell me how the king of smiths used this strength. Show me how you killed Erith.'

It was awkward doing it in those woman's clothes. I'd just as soon not have had to go through it again.

'I brewed the spell in my forge. Then I tracked her down. I took her from behind. Like this. And held her till I'd made her swallow the juice. It only took a moment.'

No more than a whisper from her now. And her green eyes fastened on me all the time. She never blinked. Like an adder.

'Then why did you not break her neck or throttle her, *Witch-King*?'

Suddenly she screamed at me: 'Strength? Is that the way of the wise? Brute force, Teilo Smith! Is that all you meant? Men's methods? Is this the wisdom I asked?'

She broke off with a cry and clutched at her belly. I'd forgotten that. She was so huge I thought it must be twins, though her face was thin enough above it. I feared she was going to drop her baby then. Luned came running to hold her. For a moment the two of them weren't bothered about me. Then Morgan pushed the woman away and drew herself up straight.

'I should have known better than to place my hope in a man of your craft. Any soldier in my castle, any slave in my fields, could have killed Erith more quickly than you did, and more mercifully, if that had been all I wanted. You understand nothing of our art. Nothing! Let me tell you this, Teilo Smith. If Erith had wished to kill you, it would not have been like that. You would have suspected nothing till the pain struck. You would have gone to your grave never knowing whose hand had shaped the spell unless she chose to tell you at the end. I taught her!'

'But that was not what I meant.'

'You comprehend no more of the pattern of magic than Urien's wolfhound. The only power you know about is in your muscles. A common blacksmith! Well, you will go from here. And you will never raise that smith's right arm again.' Her own arm was stretched out pointing at me as she said it. 'Your forge shall go cold, your hammer rusty. For what you have done I am taking away your manhood. When I know that you understand and your eyes are open, then come back to me and beg for mercy. You will get it from no one else. Only come dressed in women's clothes as you are now. I like to see you so. And women's clothes

313

you will wear for the rest of your life. Two sides, Smith! You should have remembered. The universe in balance. Go now . . . Woman.'

She sat down then, panting like a woman who has run a race.

Those words stung me like a hailstorm in the face. Who was she to tell a man of my rank how to act? I felt like I used to as a boy when my mother beat me and I wanted to cry out against her but couldn't find the words. What right had Morgan to speak to me like that? No smith is common! I was as wise as she was, never mind that I wasn't a nobleman in a fine castle. A killing's a killing, isn't it? I'd only used what she dared me to. I could have shown her the other side of the art too, if I'd thought she'd wanted it.

She was holding her belly again and gasping a bit. Luned wanted to run for the midwife, but Morgan wouldn't let her. When the pain had gone again she smiled at me more sweetly than ever she'd done before. It made me shudder.

'Go! I have learned your lesson well. There is dawn, Woman, and there is nightfall. I can indeed use both sides.'

So I found myself outside in the yard, shaking for shame and anger. I was a king. I was Smith. Both men and women feared me. They did what I told them. I danced the god. I didn't dress in women's clothes. I wasn't to be scolded like a naughty boy. What I did with my power was not for her to question. But to get out of her gate I had to bend my shoulders and let that hated woman's gown drag about me, and not raise my eyes beyond my hood to look a man in the face. Well, it would be the last time. I wasn't ever going to come back here to be insulted.

I stopped in the wood as soon as I could and tore the patched thing off my shoulders as though a cat had fouled it. Woman, she'd called me! I wasn't having that. I'd finished with her and her 'two sides'. Aye, and that grey magician with his wild talk of a new king. Let him whistle for his news. I certainly wasn't going to tell him about this. What did I care for the pair of them? I'd let the winter snow cover me naked before I'd drag that dress on again and go shuffling back through her gate. A common smith? I'd show her who's common. I'd call my circle again, folk that showed me proper respect. I'd done what she said, hadn't I? The girl was dead.

Still, it had upset me properly. I couldn't get the feel of her squirming body out of my hands. It was Morgan who made me do it. She laid it on me. It would never have happened if she hadn't taunted me. I'd never have needed to use my power against a girl like that.

So I stood in my man's clothes and I rolled up the dress and made to hurl it in the bog. But something stopped me. Morgan's voice chanting in my head. 'Woman's clothes you will wear for the rest of your life.' It seemed like the strength went out of my arm and my hand dropped slack. Before I knew where I was, I found myself pushing that loathsome thing back into my satchel. I was shivering in the wind, even now I'd got my leather jerkin back.

There's not many cottages to pass on the road through the forest to Way Bank. The last was Granny Sarran's at Woodend. She was a good friend to me. One of my own. It was she that had taught me the use of the darker herbs and where to find them, when I was just a green lad. I'd grown a

314

lot greater than her since then. But all the same, she wasn't the woman to be afraid of me. And that was more than you could say for most of them.

She was in her garden, scratting among the kale. When she heard me coming she straightened her back to look. I gave her good-day. But when she saw who it was, she shook her fist and let out a screech. Then she rushed indoors, and the door banged fast behind her.

I stood and stared. I couldn't understand it. It seemed to me to be a chill thing, like a foreboding.

Hundreds of times I've thought about that day. If only I could have started it over again. If only I hadn't done what I did. If I didn't have to feel that girl struggling in my grip or hear her screaming for death. She must have been near the same age as my daughter, though scores of times older than Mair in knowledge. It hadn't been my idea to kill her.

I could see there was a knot of men outside the smithy. Men of Way Bank, with cudgels in their fists, barring the road.

They'd seen me. They were snarling like a dog at a stranger. But you could tell they were afraid. Look at them shifting from one foot to the other. So I think, if I stand my ground now . . . I've only got to stretch out my finger and speak the words of power.

But what's up with them all?

Then I see women crying, behind them. And I go cold. Oh, holy Mothers! She wouldn't do that would she? Not my own daughter! Not *Mair*!

But here's my sweetheart. Breaking out from between the apple trees. Running in front of the men to throw herself at my feet. Clawing my ankles. Her pretty face all streaked and ugly with tears.

'Why did you do it? Oh, Da, why did you do it? What made you kill her?'

Why should she care about it? She didn't even know Erith.

'I had to do it, Mair. The queen laid it on me. She made me strike her down.'

Mair flung herself away from me with a great scream.

'Then it is true! You did poison her! My own mother and you murdered her! And she always loved you so dearly! And to curse her like *that*. I watched her die. It was horrible. Horrible!'

With her scream there was a stone came flying out of the crowd past my ear. I think it was the boy that threw it. And then they were all running at me with their cudgels up.

The breath seemed caught in my throat. I couldn't get the strength to raise my right arm and point at them. My mind was spinning. I couldn't remember the words of power I ought to shout. Annis? My Annis? Ill-wished like Erith? And they were still coming for me.

I knew then *she*'d done it. Crouched up there in her castle she'd thrown her spell. When Morgan stretched out her hand towards me she'd been willing this.

I ran for my life. Without saying another word I turned my back on Mair and ran. I never told her that I hadn't killed her mother. My only daughter, and I've never seen her since. She left Way Bank. She doesn't know. To this day she still believes I cursed her mother.

# Chapter Ten

I went crashing into the forest like a wild boar when the hounds are
after it. I was a strong man and I'd always looked after myself. But
the blood was knocking in my head and I had pains in my lungs. I
couldn't have told you where I was going. I just knew I had to get
away from there.

I don't reckon they wanted to catch me. They were afraid of me.
And they had the sense to be scared of coming too deep into the forest.
More sense than me. I still ran as if the Black Hunt was after me. I
daren't stop to listen if they were still there.

Somewhere in every forest there's a line. You can't see it. You can
run right over it without even noticing. Then, a few steps later, you
know you've come too far. Miles too far, that's how it seems. You look
back, and you can see that other part of the wood. It's a homely sort
of place, where the sun comes through the branches here and there,
and there are blackberries for picking, and you can herd the pigs to
root for acorns. But where you are it's damp and dark and still, and
even then you feel it's not as still as you wish it was, and the hair starts
to rise on the back of your neck. You want to run back into the sunny
side, but there's something here that didn't want you to come and it's
not sure now it's going to let you go.

I'd been in there, of course, and at night too, for rites I wouldn't
dream of telling you of even now. But not without a full month of
preparing and a strong guard forged about me and my circle. And here
I'd come blundering into the black heart of it without one word of
strengthening, without strong drink, without a drop of blood offered
. . . unless you count . . . Oh, no! Not that! That wouldn't shield me.
I was like a baby naked in a blizzard.

I didn't stop till I fell into a dark stream and hauled myself up the
rocks the other side. I looked round. It was all strange to me. My forest,
my own kingdom, but I didn't recognise it. I was the stag. I'd worn
the god's horns. But when I looked round and saw that old black wood
rotting away and feeding on its own flesh, I knew I wasn't king here
any more. I wasn't even a man. I was sobbing with fright like a baby,
and with good reason. I was starting to see faces of demons and spirits
in the trees. There was a ring of them now. Greyish-white, or green.
They were closing in on me. I knew that if I once looked over my
shoulder, I'd see that horrible purple mouth of Erith coming up behind
me. I tried to run again. It's awful stuff, that leaf-mud, with black
water underneath. In the end I was crawling through it on my belly,
like a whipped dog.

You may wonder why a wise man like me didn't stop and say a few spells to help myself. I had the knowledge, didn't I? I couldn't. I can't find the words to tell you the terror I felt then. It drove everything out of my head, and that black fear came in that wouldn't let me think of anything else. I only had one thing in my mind: She's done this. Morgan's made me kill Erith, and then she's punished me by cursing my Annis and putting the guilt of it on me. She's snatched my power away and left me naked here. Even now, she's coming after me. I'll run till my heart bursts, but I can't escape her. If I die, she'll have my shade.

That was an awful time . . . an awful time . . . Better for your peace of mind that you don't know. There are nights I wake up screaming remembering it. And sometimes I've opened my eyes and found Morgan standing over me, watching. There aren't words to tell you the worst horrors of it.

At times I'd come to, and wonder how long I'd been lost and wandering like that. I might be down by the water, far on from Way Bank, no part I knew. I'd never known the lake was so big or so twisting. It was like a serpent coiling its head into the mountains. More than once there was a great storm whipping up the waves and hurling them on the stones, and I was drenched to the skin. Another time I woke to find myself up in the branch of a tree face to face with a lynx, staring at me with yellow eyes, and all that was keeping it from springing at me was that I was singing to it in a high, cracked voice. I didn't recognise that voice for my own, first off. The most terrible of all was when I'd lost the forest entirely. It was night on the mountain, so high up and sheer I couldn't imagine how I'd got there or how I'd ever get off again. There was snow settling on the scree and an icy cloud dropping lower to wrap me round. I lost sight of the precipice in the dark, but I could hear demons screaming underneath the drop.

I should have died then. I don't know why I'd lived so long, or how. Do you suppose I grubbed in the dirt for acorns and toadstools and raw worms, like a wild pig? I've no recollection of where I slept, or how long I was lost. But when I found myself on the bare mountain with the banshees howling for me . . .

. . . What?

Oh, yes . . . Well, I lived through that winter. That's obvious, isn't it? I had help. And not from where I expected it . . .

I came round, as if I'd woken up from a deep sleep after a fever. I was so weak I couldn't lift my head, and didn't want to. But I wasn't fretted. All the frights and horrors had gone, sweated out of me, you might say, and it had left me weak, but clean. I just lay there resting, looking at the sunlight, and not troubling about anything. And then it came to me that I hadn't seen sunlight for a long time. It didn't touch me where I lay but it looked good and wholesome. I saw I was lying in a cave, quite near the door, and there was a little stretch of grass in front of it. Across the tops of the bushes I got a glimpse of a lake, smaller than the one I knew, and as green as grass. There were hills beyond. Grim, dark mountains that still made me shudder, though I couldn't remember then why.

'Christ is risen! Good morning.'

He had a harsh voice. I don't think he talked much. Not to another human being, anyroad. I turned my eyes a bit. I hadn't the strength to move my head. He wasn't a big man, but he was so lean and bony he looked taller than he was. He had on a cream-coloured gown that was none too clean, and he had an apron of hareskin over it. I wondered at that afterwards, when I found he didn't eat meat. He laughed a bit wild and said he saved what the fox left or the eagle dropped. But that came later.

I felt my skin go stiff when I saw him. I hadn't come on many of his kind in my life before. I'd kept well clear of them. But I knew what he was. What I'd taken Silver-Tongue for, first off. A Christian hermit. Not like your house-priests, that play politics and live like gentry and shut their eyes to half of what goes on. This lot are tougher. There's no half measures with them. Sworn enemies we were, our sort and his. So I'd jumped out of the cauldron into the fire.

Brogan, his name was. When he saw that I'd got my wits back he asked me questions. Who was I? Where had I come from? What was I doing, wandering on the mountain where he'd found me lying blue with the cold in the snow? I suppose he must have carried me all by himself down to his cave. I didn't think of that then. Or who told him he'd find me on the peak.

I wouldn't answer him. I don't know that I could even remember it all myself, straight off. I just wanted to go on lying there, like a newborn baby, and not be bothered.

He wouldn't let me. He made me sit up and drink some herb soup. Soon he had me starting to walk, though my legs were as shaky as a couple of reeds. But not that first day.

It took me some while watching that sunshine before I realised from the little new leaves on the bushes that it was spring. I couldn't believe that. That the winter had passed me by, out here in the hills, and I couldn't remember any of it. Only the snow starting to fall on that bare scree, and the cloud coming down. And the screaming.

That hermit Brogan had saved my life. But he was expecting something in return. I could tell that. All the time he was nursing me back to health I could feel him watching me, biding his time.

He'd make me a bed of bracken out of doors and sit beside me for hours telling me stories about his Christ. I hadn't the strength to curse him. I needed his food. But he wasn't satisfied yet.

'The body is healing,' he said. 'But the soul is still troubled. Repent! Admit me as your soul-friend. Unburden your load to me. I can lead you to him who will lift it from you.'

Well, I couldn't tell him, could I? The death-spell? Poison? He'd never forgive that, would he, a Christian like him? So I put him off with tales of this and that and bided my time. I was getting stronger, but I couldn't shift for myself yet. I didn't think I could bear it if he threw me out on my own now.

He thought he'd got me. He thought I'd taken his bait. He taught me their catechism. It was no trouble to me. Hundreds of chants I've had to get by heart in our own business. I said the words, and crossed my fingers behind my back.

One day he watched me carry a skin of water up from the spring and swing it down from my shoulder. It felt heavier than it would have done once, but I could manage it now.

When he saw that, there was a gleam came in his eye. 'It is almost Pentecost. The body is whole again and your soul is instructed. On Sunday Bishop Curran will receive the catechumens and give them their new robe of white. Will you come down with me and accept baptism?'

So that was his game! I saw the danger I'd walked into, straight off. I was a fool to trust a hermit. They may live wild on prayer and hymn-singing where nobody can see them, except some pious folk who'll climb miles out of the way to get their blessing. But they keep their own feast-days, the same as we do ours. That's when you see them coming down from the hills and out of the woods to the big churches. Those times when the towns are full of converts in white after one of their baptisms. The Christians have their own High Lords. Brogan would have to report to his bishop what he'd been doing. Did he think I'd go trotting off down the mountain beside him so he could boast to all the world he'd converted a pagan? And there I'd stand, the murderer, Teilo Smith!

. . . . Smith! Suddenly it came back to me.

The feel of my hammer in my hand, a smell of oak chips on the forge, my daughter . . .

I nearly brained him then, but he jumped aside. I snarled at him like a dog.

'You little white stoat! You thought you'd tricked me. One word from me and you'd have put a noose round my neck. I should kill you now. How much did she pay you to find me out?'

And more such nonsense. He just stared at me with his great hollow eyes. Then he pulled himself together and shot up his hand.

'In nomine Patris, et Filii, et Spiritus Sancti . . .'

I didn't know what it meant then. I thought he was putting a curse on me. I tried to fend it off with one of my own. But my head was empty. There wasn't a word would come to my tongue. I grabbed up a stick, but I couldn't hit him with it. I started to run and then I stopped at the edge of the bushes and let out a scream.

'My satchel! What have you done with my satchel?'

I didn't know what made me say that. I'd never given it a thought till then. But suddenly it seemed as if it was the most important thing in the world to me. I couldn't go without it.

He said, very harsh and sorrowful, 'Unhappy man! It has been your pillow these many months. It is lying there.'

And so it was. All scuffed and stained, but laid safe inside the cave where I'd slept. Then I began to see the awful truth in front of me. Not the whole by a long way. I might have let him hang me if I had. All these months I'd been out of my wits. Summer and winter, I'd lived like a beast or a madman. And in all that time I'd kept it with me, that satchel of old women's clothes. I'd lost my bearings, my reason, near enough my life, but never that. I shouldn't ever be rid of it.

I had to have it. I snatched it up and made to dash past Brogan. He was in the cave door.

'Kneel! Repent!' he thundered.

He could have stopped me. I've never got my full strength back, even now. But when he saw how I'd made my mind up, he just groaned. He picked up the blanket he'd used to cover me with, and I saw then what it was. A whitish cloak, the same stuff as his gown. His own mantle, that he must have given me in the middle of winter. He ripped it in two with his knife and held out half to me.

'At least take this to remember him who saved you.'

I threw it back at him. I'd keep nothing from him and his kind.

'If you breathe one word to your bishop you've seen me . . .'

But I couldn't remember the words of the curse I'd meant to put on him. My tongue tripped up on it, and I was left staring at him with my mouth gaping open like a fool.

Only then a crafty thought came over me. I was getting my wits together now. I grabbed his torn cloak back and ran.

He shouted after me, 'The peace of the Spirit go with you and give you . . .'

But I couldn't hear the rest of it for the clattering of stones on the path.

I stopped when I got down to the lake. Very dark, it was, cold but sunny. I leaned over a rock to get my breath back, for the run had tired me out.

I thought I was looking down at a water-bogle. A gaunt bag of bones with rags of clothes hanging from its hunched shoulders under the water. Elf-locks of white hair draggled over its neck. And a horrible face dark reddish and blotched above the mouth, and deathly pale below, with a few sprouts of white whiskers on the chin.

I made to cry out, and that creature down in the water opened its own ghastly mouth as if was going to swallow me. I backed away, and I must have kicked a stone. It splashed into that thing's face and the horrid picture broke up in waves and bubbles. The stone fell through it to the bottom. And then I knew I'd been looking at my own reflection. I don't know which was worse: the horror of that goblin thing from under the lake, or the sight of what I'd been turned into. I began to shake till I thought the madness was coming back on me. She'd done this. Morgan. She'd put her mark on me, so I was fixed the way I was the day she cursed me. My beard wouldn't ever grow back again. The forge fire was never going to redden my chin to match my cheeks and nose. The big blacksmith's muscles had shrivelled on my arms. I looked like some hag in the rags of a man's clothes.

And so my face is still. Wait while I unwind the linen. There! You may wonder at it. But nothing will change it now. No matter what I do, the winter's never going to fade the red or the summer burn the white. The full beard won't grow again. I'm caught like this. I'm neither one thing nor the other.

Well, I looked up and my heart gave a sort of leap. There was a dark speck at the far end of the lake, that I took for a boat. Men fishing, most likely. My first thought was that I'd shout to them. Call and ask them to take me home with them. Home. A warm house, a fireside, hot stew. I'd drawn in a great breath and I was waving my hand. And then there was a splash on the water and that speck took off. Only a cormorant, flying off up the beck.

I tell you, I felt so lonely at that I could have wept, till I caught sight of myself in the lake again. Then I knew I couldn't have called, even if it had been men. I saw what they'd see.

Teilo Smith, who'd shaved his face for a vow. Teilo Smith, with his hair white and his leathers in shreds from the thorns, but still the same clothes he'd dressed in the day he killed Morgan's young lady. Teilo Smith, who'd poisoned his wife. Morgan had put her brand on my face like a runaway slave.

I saw I had no home, and never would have now. I'd never dare to brag myself Smith any more. Morgan had robbed me of all I'd ever had: my wife, my daughter, house, forge, kingship, tribe. I'd lost the lot, between one day and the next.

There was only one way I could hide what I had been. I took up that hermit's cloak. It was good, thick stuff, and there was a fair bit of it. I found my knife and cut holes for my arms. I took off what I was wearing. Then I pinned the sides of the other together with thorns to make rough shot at a gown like Brogan's. There was a deep hood on the half he'd thrown me. I hid my face in it as well as I could.

It made me feel queer, looking down in the lake again. I didn't know what I was now. I'd sworn I wouldn't ever wear woman's clothes as Morgan had told me, but I wasn't a real man either. Not as I understood it, anyroad. I screwed up my leather tunic and breeches in my hand. I thought about flinging them in the lake for safety. Only . . . I knew if I did that, it would mean Teilo Smith was finished. I'd never be a proper man again. I stuffed them into the satchel with the woman's gear.

# Chapter Eleven

I'd gone past terror. I didn't feel that any more. But I couldn't bear the dark and loneliness a second time, not though I'd been wandering alone a powerful long time before Brogan found me. It was different now. I'd found my wits again. I started along that lake-shore, weeping like a lost child for pitying myself.

Repent, he'd said, that hermit. Of course I repented! It cut me inside like an open wound. I'd poisoned my wife. My plump and loving Annis. I'd killed her horribly with pride and cunning. Erith? Annis? It had sounded the same to Mair. It had got so they were both one in my mind too. Every time I thought about that day it made me writhe with the agony of it, like a snake on the end of a spear.

I suppose I could have changed my mind. Gone back to that harsh hermit, Brogan. Made a clean breast of it. Begged him to keep me safe. But how could he? Teilo Smith, that had shaved his face for his god. A witch and a poisoner. I'd be a known man for miles around.

I hadn't got a razor, but I hacked off half my hair, so that I was as near bald in front as the saint himself. I didn't look so much like Teilo Smith now, save for that chin.

I daren't stop there. I had no way of knowing how near I might still be to Lyvennet. I had to leave that behind. I had to hide Teilo Smith away as secret as his leathers.

It was going on dark when I started to climb up the hills at the head of the lake. I was mortally afraid of the night.

The gods let me live, though. They'd had their vengeance, and there was more to come. I should have known I wouldn't escape her, no matter what I did. Yet at the time, I thought I'd walked out of a nightmare into fairyland.

I came off the hills just as it was growing first light. I hadn't dared lie down and close my eyes, so I was almost sleep-walking. There wasn't a scrap of colour anywhere yet, the fells black as charcoal, and the sky grey. I caught a glimpse of another little lake below me, like an eye opening, and then the mist rose up, white and thick, so I wondered if I'd dreamed it.

I kept on going down the slope, stumbling a bit for tiredness. I wasn't used to that long hermit's gown either. And all the time the mist was rising up to meet me.

I couldn't hear a thing. There wasn't a bird singing anywhere. And all I could see was that clammy white wall around me. I knew I'd found the soft side of the lake when I felt water slopping over my shoes. I couldn't make out any more than the edge of it, very still, a little space of wet pebbles and a few ripples round a clump of reeds. I drank a few handfuls, and the sound of my splashing seemed too loud in the silence. I was afraid to go on. I found a rock and sat down till I could see where I'd come to.

It was a thrush started to sing first, everything twice. And then I heard cattle lowing, far away and hollow-sounding in the mist. A flock of swans came swimming past me and vanished again. I felt the air was starting to thin. When I looked up the sky was blue over my head. I sat and watched that world come into view, and it was the prettiest place I'd ever seen.

Every lake has its own colour. There's black or silver or a chilly green. This one was red-gold with bits of blue sky flashing in it like jewels. And the hills all round it, not black, grim mountains like I'd seen before, but low and gentle, with tops like little running waves. The mist was clearing all the time, just wisps of it curling up like they might have been lily-flowers. Everything round me was gold. The greeny-gold of the little new leaves on the trees, the red-gold of the old bracken on the fells, and the daffodils were the truest gold of all along that shore. Just for a moment I forgot to think about myself and how I must have been the only ugly thing in all that dale.

I couldn't hear any cattle now, just the birdsong and a few ducks taking off from the water. And that was better than if I had, for a quiet herd means they're contented. But I knew that somewhere near-to there must be a farm. And that dale seemed such a peaceful, pretty place, I suddenly longed to be back with my own kind again. I was still afraid, even dressed in the saint's cloak. But I told myself they'd have to be kindly folk, that lived in a spot like this.

I remembered how Brogan's face was burned nearly black, praying out in the sun and wind all day. So I stooped down and rubbed brown peat into my chin and over my shaved head as well.

There wasn't a path I could see, and I was glad of that. It meant it was some out-of-the-way farm, hidden in this hollow in the hills. I wasn't ready for crowds. I picked my way along the shore, stooping under branches and trying to mind my hood snagging on the twigs. For a while I was too busy to look up ahead.

Then I heard a horse neighing. That quickened something in my blood. I'd been a smith, remember. Bridle-bits, buckles, harness-charms, that was all my work. I looked up quick, and found I'd come almost to the end of that little lake, and just then I tripped over a bolt of wood. I went sprawling, but not into soft black mud this time. There were timbers, sawn logs, lashed together to make a causeway over the marsh where the river came into the lake. A proper road.

I can't say what it meant to me, that first solid, built thing I'd come to since I ran from Way Bank. I could feel the heart racing in my chest. I was back among humans. I didn't count that mad hermit. He was half-wild himself, living in a cave like the beasts.

This road might mean danger, but I couldn't part from it now I'd found it. I turned and followed up the causeway. It felt good and solid under my feet. There was a little wood of willows on either side of it, all yellow with catkins. It stopped me seeing far. Then all of a sudden I was on firm ground and there were stones under me. Not cobbles, mind you. Huge slabs of stone, shaped to fit each other with hammer and chisel. Such a road as the Romans had left behind, between Lyvennet and Carlisle. Here, in this little dale with not a town in sight! That made me feel pretty queer, and I began to wonder if this road was as solid as it seemed or if my wits had turned again. The trees were thinning ahead. I'd be coming out on to a meadow pretty soon.

There were the cows I'd heard, red and white speckled. And horses.

Horses? Dozens of them. That shook me. They were fine horses, too, well-fed and groomed. Fine horses mean fine men. This was no common farm I'd stumbled on. And then I saw it. The house at the top of the meadow. Well, I tell you, till then I'd never seen a house like that outside Carlisle, and half of them are falling down. Two storeys high, it was, and as long as a street, with two arms reaching towards the lake at either end. It had porches on columns, open to the air. And the whole of it of plastered stone. Red tiles on the roof. Not a bit of thatch anywhere, except for some huts at the back. It looked as grand a house as ever the Romans built. Just like the road I was standing on.

I just stood gaping and wondering where I'd come to. Next thing, there was a great shout from the house, and a crowd of lads came racing out with saddles and hunting gear over their arms. There were women laughing behind them too, but I hardly noticed them. Those boys were whooping and yelling, and some of them had hounds on leashes, that were yapping round their legs. Well, that set off the horses. Some of them trotted forward as if they wanted to be saddled, and the rest went dashing off in circles round the meadow. But those lads were smart. Before long they'd harnessed and mounted, except for the ones that were running on foot, and the whole lot of them were coming my way at a fair old pace. I heard a horn blow, and seeing those boys' heads go up I turned to look over my shoulder. There was a red deer standing high up on the fellside. The lads let slip the hounds and the dogs and horses broke into a gallop. The runners were pelting after them as hard as they could go. I just stood like a fool staring at the brave sight they made, with their chequered cloaks flying and the metal flashing on lads and horses. I never thought that they were going to ride me down.

They were almost on me when one golden lad at the front saw me. He yelled, 'Clear the way, you fool!' Then he wheeled his horse round hard left in front of my nose and the whole shock of dogs and horses and hunters went rushing past me up the side of the fell. The hounds belled on the summit and I saw those horsemen against the sunrise. Then they vanished over the top like a fairy-rade.

You look too long at the sun and it scorches your eyes so you can't see the world clear after that, just a dark shadow of what was bright before. I was like that for a long while afterwards. I'd seen that boy, a young man almost. Blue fire in his eyes, like sparks struck from steel. Hair gold with just a touch of the red about it, blown back in the wind, strong limbs the sun had turned the colour of copper, and sitting his chestnut horse as though the two of them had been cast by a master-craftsman out of the same bar of metal. I'd seen warriors, princes, kings. I'd had their horses and weapons in my smithy. There wasn't one looked like that lad. And never mind that he had just shouted at me for a fool.

Well, you've seen him. I'm not surprised so many have fallen in love with him, women and men, and given their bodies for him, one way or the other.

# Chapter Twelve

That lad had dazzled my sight. I didn't even know who he was, then. But the moment he'd gone I saw he'd first set eyes on me too late. If only I could have been dressed as a smith when I met him. If he could have recognised me for what I was!

Not a ragged hermit, in a draggled skirt. White hair, and muscles wasted away. I'd been a blacksmith. I'd served fighting men. I was a great Smith.

I felt such a hurt I didn't think about my own danger, even after I'd lost sight of them. My hands felt empty of tools, as if I'd been robbed. I think I had tears in my eyes. I walked on up that road as if I'd been drunk, or in a dream.

I came to with a nasty shock. There was a sudden rush and I found a sword held to my throat and a spear pointing at my guts and a ring of blades all round me.

I let out such a screech, and they all burst out laughing. One of those guards tipped back my hood and looked me full in the face.

A woman. That shook me properly, you can imagine. There was a score of them. All sizes and ages. Hair braided, wearing tunics and boots and a heap of jewellery and not much else. They meant business. They knew what they were doing with those swords, and some of them had spears and clubs. I stood mighty still, only the blood was hammering in my head so hard I thought it would knock my skull apart. But it seemed I'd startled them too.

'Are you a druid or a Christian saint?'

She wasn't a beauty, that one in front, and not so young as some of the others. Square face, square shoulders. She wouldn't have looked out of place as one of those centurion statues they have here in Carlisle.

I could see their Roman mansion and I was standing on a Roman road. I knew which was the safest answer. The Romans were never any friends of the druids.

'A Christian hermit, lady.'

Though come to think of it, the Romans never put women in fighting gear. That was a British thing. I began to wonder if I'd said the right thing, after all.

'Who sent you to us?'

'Nobody sent me. I came into the hills to seek my god.'

I made the Christian sign. I'd seen Brogan do it often enough.

She looked me up and down. She wasn't satisfied. 'Where have you come from?'

326

I waved my hand back down their lake. I didn't need to lie. I'd no notion where I'd been these last few months.

'I cannot tell you, daughter. I was caught up by the Spirit, lost to all humankind. I can no more tell you where I've come from than where I am now.'

She looked at me shrewdly. 'Even the longest wandering has a beginning.'

Well, I gave a bit of a shudder, as if it wasn't a thing I wanted to remember. 'The east end of the Wall . . . Darkness now . . . Our little family . . .'

It wasn't play-acting that made me catch a sob then, thinking of Mair and Annis. That softened them a bit.

'The Saxons?'

I nodded.

'So you crossed into Rheged to escape them? Urien's kingdom?'

'Morgan's now,' said another of the young ones, pretty sharp.

So they knew. I hadn't run far enough. She'd cast her long shadow, even on this dale.

'And in all of Britain you stumbled upon us. By accident?'

I'd told them a pack of lies. But the one thing that was true they didn't want to believe.

I must have staggered then. I know I had spots before my eyes. I'd walked all night and I hadn't got my full strength back.

Two of them caught me. The rest had lowered their weapons now, but they hadn't sheathed them. They started to lead me to the house. And suddenly it was like a tangle of reins slipping loose. All the others began to fall away from me, joking and sparring with each other, till I found there was just the two lasses leading me pretty firmly by the arm. I heard the shriek of metal behind me, and when I turned my head there were pairs of women spread out all over the field, feet splayed, arms up, going at each other with sword or spear, and skilfully too, from what I could make out. They'd forgotten about me. They were playing at war, if you could call it playing. They laughed pretty loud, but they knew how to use those weapons if they had to.

If I'd been lost before I was fairly bewildered here. I couldn't make sense of anything I'd seen.

The lasses led me through one door and out of another into a courtyard. There was a porch all round it, and a little fountain. They left me sitting on a bench. There were a few servants coming and going along the corridors. Slaves, by the look of them, with their hair shorn and wearing colourless clothes. Too like me, I thought.

One of the men brought me food and drink. Milk that was thick with cream, bread hot from the oven, a handful of sweet dried plums. When he gave them to me I nearly grabbed his hand, just to feel the grip of a proper man again. And then I thought, a slave? I'm no proper man myself now. A bloodless saint. Next thing to a woman. So I mumbled my thanks as though my wits were wandering. Pretty soon he left me quiet and went back to his work.

I could have sat there for hours out of the wind in the sunshine. I was watching the servants going about their jobs. They were not over-hurrying but busy. Everything I could see inside that house was well-found and seemly, and so different to Urien's fort it could have been in another country. But then those girls outside, with tunics up to their thighs and muscles like racehorses.

I was half-asleep when another young lady came tripping along to fetch me. I don't know if she'd been out in the meadow with a sword too. But whether she had or not, she was dressed like a proper maiden now, mostly in white. There was gold embroidery round the hem of her gown and her underskirt was fine and delicate, almost like silk. So was her skin. And then I couldn't stop the thing between my legs from leaping up, and I knew I was getting better. I saw the danger. A bit of food and rest, and Teilo Smith was coming to life again, wanting to jump up out of that satchel where I'd strapped him down. Watch your step, I told myself in a bit of a sweat. You're supposed to be a Christian holy man.

I tried to keep my eyes off her, but the sun from the windows in the corridor was turning all the little hairs on her bare arms to spun gold.

She showed me into a room, a hall, you might call it, almost. There was a lady sitting on a chair at the end in the full sunlight, with a lot more gathered round her. Morgan had faced me in a chair like that. But where Morgan was dark, and sat in shadow, this one was all white and gold. Gold curls tumbling over her shoulders, all prettily braided with flowers made out of gold and coral. A white silk dress, and a gown over it, shining like water, and shifting from blue to green. She had white skin too, just touched with pink and gold like the dog rose. I looked at the ladies round her. I tried to square them with those guards that had stopped me in the meadow. But these might have been fairy women, dressed almost as fine as the one on her gilded chair. Only then one of the older ones lifted her arm and I saw the white scar where her sleeve fell back. That made me shudder. So they were mortal flesh and blood that could be wounded, but not like any mortals I'd ever come across. I didn't know what I'd happened on.

There was a pool in front of the steps to the lady's chair, like a little lake indoors. And there must have been a spring at the bottom of it, because the water was bubbling up so the whole surface was moving, and there were fish darting in and out of the sun and the shadows. All round it there were flowering cresses growing among the stones. Stones! Wherever I looked there were little coloured stones set into pictures and patterns. The floors, the walls, they'd even got them on the ceiling over my head. Pictures of grapes and palms, men hunting and women dancing, dragons, dolphins, and even, yes, I was pretty certain those must be pictures of somebody's gods. Not mine, but I wanted to make the signs to protect myself just in case. Only I couldn't do that, dressed as I was, with all of them watching me. I had to make the Christian sign instead, like Brogan had.

When I took my eyes away that lady was watching me with a curious look.

'I see you are a holy man. Valeria tells me you chanced upon us by accident. You are the first for a long time to find your way here uninvited. None of those who did have returned.'

That made me stiffen, all right. I cursed myself for a fool. There had I been, taking my ease, enjoying her food and drink, and not thinking I might have been eating my last meal.

'You wouldn't kill a saint of God, lady!' I gabbled. 'Not even if you worship a different set of them to mine. It's ill luck on anyone to slay a holy man.'

She looked a bit contemptuous at that.

'Say the Lord's prayer.'

That startled me. Which Lord did she mean? I thought I'd better stay with the one whose dress I'd taken. The fewer lies she caught me in, the better. It wasn't hard. Brogan had made me say it over with him three times a day.

'Kyrie eleison,' she said, looking at me hard as if it was some sort of password.

'Christe eleison,' I answered.

I wasn't going to let her best me, whatever it meant.

'What signifies baptism?'

So she was a Christian, after all. I thanked my stars I'd learned that catechism to keep Brogan sweet. She tried a few more after that, but I was ready for her. All my life I've lived by words of power. Thousands of them I've had to get by heart. It hadn't been hard to stow his sort away in my head along with all the rest. You never know when knowledge will come in handy.

That lady leaned forward and studied me, very thoughtful.

'Who may wear the horns?'

I answered her straight off. She couldn't catch me out, so why were they all laughing?

Too late I saw she had. It was no Christian's catechism that wisdom came from. It was an answer I shouldn't have known, dressed as I was. It was a thing not so many of our own kind should know. I stared back at her, my mouth hung open and the blood burned in my cheeks and then ran cold. I thought I was done for sure then.

But the lady wasn't angry with me. She burst out into a sweet sort of laughter, like little bells. All of a sudden, she jumped up and ran down the steps towards me, skipping round that pretty pool in her gold sandals. She took my hand and rushed me out of the hall, with two of her women running after us. In and out of the sun and shadow we went. Round corners, down steps, till I was out of breath with the hurry and the queerness of it. And her little soft hand held tight round mine and setting my body on fire.

Down over the grass we went. There was a narrow stony beach at the edge of the lake and a boat pulled up out of the water. Her women pushed it out and the lady jumped on board. She beckoned to me to follow her. I couldn't guess what she meant to do with me. Her two maidens got in after us and rowed us away.

There were little islands in that lake, mostly covered in trees. The one we were headed for had a small white building on it, like a sort of temple, with steps going down from it to the water. We landed there and the lady led me inside, making the signs I knew.

It was a plainer sort of place than her great house. Marble pillars holding up a dome for the roof. The walls were mostly white, with a bit of a pattern in blue, but no pictures. Inside the door there was a small room with a stone pool. No plants or fish this time. Just plain, with more steps going down into it. At the far end of the inner room there was a table with two candles standing on it. That was plain too. It wasn't much to look at, but it had a holy feel. The lady gave a sort of breathless little laugh and led me into that sanctuary.

I'd been wrong about the pictures. They were there, all right. Someone had drawn them on the floor with charcoal. A twelve-pointed star. There were twelve signs marked, and a different stone laid at each point. It was like another life coming back to me. I felt her watching me.

She led me right into that circle. I didn't want to go. As I passed through that ring I was even more afraid. I wondered if she'd felt the cold sweat break out on my hand.

She stood and faced me. Eyes as bluey-green as her lake. 'Who are you? Tell me the truth this time? Did he send you?'

I shook my head. I didn't know who she meant.

She signed to one of her maidens. The girl lit a fire in a brazier in the middle of the circle. She set a little cauldron to boil. It wasn't long before the fumes made my head swim. The Lady stood across the flames from me. She was rippling like water in the heat.

'Secret for secret. Name for name. I am Nimue, Guardian of the Lake. I do not play games. By the power of the twelve houses you will reveal what you are.'

I couldn't help myself. She didn't curse or threaten me. And she had a prettier smile than Morgan's. I had to tell her.

'Gillie Kernun – Servant of the Horned One.' Yes! You're right. I hadn't even spoken that to my own daughter. It came out pretty hoarse.

'I thought so. Valeria did well to spare you! It is a strange pair of holy men I have now.'

She picked up one of the stones. Her white arms held it so I could see it through the steam.

'What is this good for?'

I looked at her, pretty startled. That's men's magic. There's only the highest Ladies of our craft are allowed to learn those secrets. Stone-lore, fire-lore, metals. Likewise you women have your own mysteries, with blood and earth. There's very few of us know the whole truth of *that*.

And so I warned her. But she just laughed.

She was coming round the fire to me now. She pressed the thing into my hand. It was a shaft of polished greenstone, that fitted snugly in the palm like a tool. Only you'd never have used a beauty like that for rough work.

I shook my head. Her hand stayed round mine.

'Which would you use to bring thunder?'

'I don't know.'

'I think you do.'

The water in her cauldron was bubbling. I was terrified. I told her.

She clapped her hands. She was like a little girl now, playing a game, for all she'd said she wasn't.

'To make one wealthy?'

Well, why not, now? I might have been drunk.

'To turn someone to stone?'

I should have stuck there. I'd put us both in more than enough danger already. But she stood very close and put her arms round my neck. I was drowning. I had to stop her somehow.

We were in that temple a good long time, and she got out of me more at that first meeting than I'd ever told another woman in my life. It scared me senseless when I thought about it afterwards. But at the time there was something else that was frightening me even more. There was one secret I never told Lady Nimue. I doubted that she'd have kept me alive if she'd guessed.

I'd taken every one of those stones of power in my hands, and I hadn't felt a thing. Just a lump of rock, cold and heavy on my palm. There wasn't any thrill ran through me, like there should have done. Those stones didn't speak to me, the way they always had since I was a boy. I'd known what was wrong the moment I'd stepped through that ring. I'd lost my power.

# Chapter Thirteen

The Lady left me. Her maidens washed the marks from the floor and rowed her back to the shore. It wasn't a big lake, but I felt like a prisoner on that island, watching them go. I saw then something I hadn't noticed, rowing out. Straight across the water, on a little grassy slope, there was another temple just like the one I was standing by. I thought it was some trick of the lake, and it was my own reflection I was looking at. There was a man in white standing beside that one too.

I wondered if I had to sleep there alone, like the hermit I'd said I was. I knew Lady Nimue hadn't finished with me yet. But I wasn't sure how long I'd last. Was I like a cow she'd come to milk daily and feed well between? Or a carcase she'd strip bare of flesh and leave just the dead skin and bones? I watched the light go off the meadows as the sun went down and everyone going indoors for supper. I felt pretty sorry for myself.

Her boat came back, though. They'd sent a slave to fetch me. A dour sort of man. He looked me up and down as if he was a mangy dog.

It wasn't full dark yet, and a warm evening. The windows were open and I could hear music and voices coming from their hall. The man led me past there and round to the back of the house. There were two rooms the like of which I'd never seen before. In the first one we passed there were two slave-girls. They had their dresses down round their waists, scraping the sweat off each other's backs and looking for vermin. They shrieked with laughter when they saw us coming and made to hide their breasts, only not so quick as they could have done, if they'd wanted. It made me go hot in that hermit's gown. I followed the man through a second door.

'You're to put these on when you've washed,' he said, throwing me a bundle of clean clothes. I picked them up. It was stuff much like I was wearing, only better made. Plain creamy wool, white linen. So she was another like Morgan. She'd make me live the lie I'd tried on her. I started to pull them on.

'Aren't you going to bathe first? We're not short of water,' he snapped. I heard him mutter under his breath, 'Filthy fanatic!' Then he must have seen me looking. He made a holy sign. 'Begging your pardon, sir. You're not used to Roman ways. This is the wash-room.'

They had tiles on that floor too. Stone basins, and water running all the time through the place, like a stream in a pipe. The man stood and watched, with that sneer on his face. I wasn't sure what I was meant to do. I had to scrub the black mud off my skin the best I could, but there was plenty of it on the towels afterwards. I got those fresh clothes on and that made me carry myself a bit straighter and prouder, milksop weeds though I thought them.

He was staring at me. I realised too late that I'd washed my chin white. He gave me a sour sort of grin. 'That looks better for my lady. Smells sweeter too, if you don't mind my saying so. You won't be wanting this again, sir?'

He picked up the thing I'd hacked out of Brogan's cloak. I shook my head. It was good stuff spoiled. Then I saw that he'd got my old satchel under his arm. Inside there were my own smith's leather tunic and those woman's clothes Morgan had ill-wished on me. I don't know how it was, but I let out such a screech. I couldn't have screamed louder if I'd been a mother and it was my baby he was snatching away. I grabbed it out of his arms and clutched it to my chest. He backed off quick and gave me a funny look.

'All right, all right, sir. I don't want the smelly things. I was going to burn them.'

But I jabbered at him some more and hugged my satchel tight. I couldn't part from those clothes no matter what happened. Not though I hated what they meant.

He showed me then where I was going to sleep. It was one of a row of rooms at the back of a courtyard. The room was small. Just the one big bed. I wondered who I was sleeping with. I didn't know what I was here. Not noble, nor servant. Not man nor woman. I glared at that long-faced slave till he went away. Then I hid my satchel under a corner of the bed. A girl came with some food.

I found out later who I was sharing that bed with. Bytwini. Her Christian chaplain. The one in white I'd seen across the lake. She had a fine sense of humour, that Lady. He didn't look pleased, though he was polite enough, that first night.

I had to sleep beside him. I had to hear him snoring, the same as Annis snored. That was torment to me. I don't mean his body. We never touched each other. Not that way, anyroad. You can't share a bed on a cold night and not lie close to a man sometimes. But I'd wake in the night thinking I was back at Way Bank, with Annis cuddled up to me and Mair just behind the curtain. And then I'd come fully to and know I was in Nimue's house with a Christian priest lying alongside me, and I'd never see Annis again.

In the morning I had to join in his prayers. I knew he was listening to me.

That day Nimue called me to her in a room full of sunshine. There were cupboards in the walls, with locked doors. When she opened them they were stuffed with books. I didn't think there had been so many written in the world. She showed me one special shelf. There were some rolls on it, yellowed and spotted with damp, and a row of big fat books. Beautiful covers, some of those had, thick, soft leather stamped with gold, or dark wood carved with patterns that seemed as if they'd have meanings, and one or two of the bindings just old and brown, half rotted away. She opened some. The old ones were full of words to the end.

But the new ones half empty, pages cut and ready for writing. I'm no scholar, but it gave me a queer sort of feeling, wondering what they were waiting for.

'Well, Gillie Kernun, will you help me fill my books?'

The room swayed a bit.

'Me, my lady? I can't read or write.' Though I could a little, enough to tally the count of what was owed me and mark a sign for the name. But not a whole book, line after line, like this. 'What could I put in them?'

'Magic!' she said, raising her pretty eyebrows. 'Why else should I keep you alive here?'

I was feeling pretty bad already. I'd thought when I saw this dale I'd found myself rest and safety, and here I was already in deeper than I wanted. When she smiled at me like that, so charming, I could feel the water lapping all around me, like the lake opening its mouth to suck me down.

'Just a bit of stone-lore, lady. Good craftsman's stuff. That's all I know. Not the high magic your ladyship's sort would want.'

It was a lie. For all her pretty looks I was terrified of her, and of her books too. What I knew shouldn't be written down. There isn't a language invented by any scribe that's fit to hold those things and put them on a page for the unwise to pick them up and read them. That's too dangerous. They should be chanted in our secret places, or whispered from father to son and mother to daughter. Years, you have to serve before you're fit to be told some of them. How did I know how deep she'd been taken or who else she might show them to?

'That is not true, Gillie Kernun. You could teach me much more.'

She touched my wrist. I felt a thrill from that, all right.

'Do not be afraid, White-Chin. You are among friends here. There is not one of my maidens that has not taken her vows. The Saxons are growing stronger in the east. And in the west the white Christians are spreading, even without the army of Rome to shield them. I guard the wisdom of Britain, that it be not forgotten.'

But she was standing in this fine house the Romans had built, in her pretty white dress and sandals, with a Latin book in her hand. And she kept a Christian priest. What was I to believe? Well, it didn't matter what I thought, did it? She'd gone too far. She'd shown me what she had and what she wanted. I could say yes, or I could say no, but either way I wouldn't leave her dale alive, that I did know.

'Wisdom is for the wise,' I said. 'I'll share what scraps I have with you, my lady.'

Well, she hugged and kissed me. She was always a great one for that. Then she pulled away from me, laughing like a little girl.

'Is there no strength left in your arms, White-Chin? I cannot tell if I am kissing a man or a saint.'

She'd got me by the short hairs, saying that. I cursed the day I'd put on the hermit's guise. Dressed like that I didn't know who I was, myself. She was near driving me mad, but if she'd taken off her clothes there and then in front of me I don't think I could have kept it up.

After that first evening I ate with the gentry. I was their curiosity.
The holy man out of the wilderness. Those ladies lay on marble couches
strewn with cushions. They ate off silver and drank out of goblets of
green glass. I felt a pig in front of them, scared stiff of dropping things
or using my knife the wrong way. But they hid their smiles behind
their hands.

Bytwini never smiled when he looked my way. He didn't eat much
either. No meat, except on Sundays. Water in his wine. And not a
quarter the bread and cheese I'd put away when I worked in the sweat
of my own forge. I tried to copy him. I don't know why. He was the
only one that didn't know I was a sham. Or did he? I went to bed
hungry.

I had to pray whenever he did. I'd got the words by heart already,
Latin or not. The worst was when he made the Offering on Sunday.
We all went to his white chapel by the lake-shore. Those women were
dressed as modest now as any Roman matron. Servants who hadn't
been baptised yet stood in the anteroom. Dressed as I was, I had to
follow into the church with all the rest. When we knelt in front of him
he picked up the dish of bread.

'If there is any cause why you cannot receive this holy sacrament
of your Saviour's flesh and blood, confess it now. Else you will eat
and drink to your own damnation.'

I didn't flinch. I'd been damned by both sides already, mine and his.

But when he got to me he stopped and looked me hard in the eyes.
'Brother, what is done here when the bread is broken?'

That hermit had cheated me! There must have been secrets they won't
tell you till after you're baptised. I floundered out something, but it
wasn't right.

Bytwini ordered me out of his church, in front of all those ladies.
Even her slaves were welcome where I wasn't. And never mind that
every one of her maidens had taken their vows to someone who wasn't
his god. He still fed them his sacrament. Didn't he know? But I saw
him look pretty angry at Nimue before I went.

Nimue tried to make it up to me. She stroked my cheek next time
she had me alone.

'Power, White-Chin. The Church is power, of another sort. I need
every tool in my hand.'

It was two days before the hunt came back. I'd looked for that troop
of lads the first evening, but nobody seemed to be worried when they
didn't show up.

When they did come home at last there was such a hullabaloo we
all went rushing out to look.

There were cattle pouring into the meadow, with a great brown bull
in front of them that had horns as wide as the branches on a hundred-
year oak. He came roaring and stamping, with his cows after him. But
that wasn't all the noise. Those boys were yelling and hallooing and
blowing their horns, and the dogs were barking fit to make themselves
hoarse. A secret dale! I reckon you could have heard the row from the
top of Helvellyn.

The Lady had come running out before anyone else. That golden-haired lad at the front jumped down from his horse and threw his muddy arms round her neck. 'Well, Nimue? Is this not well done?' And he threw back his head and laughed to make the hills ring, like iron on anvil. You couldn't help but smile with him.

She laughed and kissed him, so I wondered if she might be his mother, though she didn't look old enough.

'Reckless, but brave. Did you lose many men?'

He moved away for her to see. I hadn't bothered with his friends till now. They were a motley lot. Some his age, some a bit older. Short fat ones and tall lanky ones, the way boys are when they're still growing. Fair-skinned, brown, red-freckled, and two as black as charcoal. Only one didn't get down. He was hung over the neck of his mare, so his mantle fell over his face.

'Poor Cathno,' Lady Nimue said. She lifted the cloak and touched his grey face with just the tips of her fingers. 'He comes to me too late.'

Some of the other lads were nursing gashes, too. I had a chilly sort of feeling she might be looking to her new holy man to salve them. I didn't know what to do. I could tell her the herbs. I knew which chants I had to speak. But what use was any of that if the power had gone out of my hands?

The field-slaves were herding those cattle in for milking. By the look of their udders they were good and ready for it. It was small wonder they were bellowing. When I looked round, the Lady's maidens were leading off the wounded and I could see the women were pretty used to this sort of thing. It didn't look as if I'd be needed, after all.

When they'd gone, that Nimue stood with her arm round her golden lad's shoulders and the two of them were looking mighty pleased with themselves. And I don't mean he was pleased with himself and she was just proud of him, mind you. They were both laughing in each other's eyes as though it was as much her doing as his. She played her fingers up his back and through his curls in a way that made me go hot and tight. And him too, from the way he grabbed her to him.

But she wriggled clear and pulled the horn out of his belt. She blew a little haunting call, just four notes. There was a bit of a silence round about, for the beasts were settled now and most of the folk had gone indoors. Then there was a call answered far off on the hills, then another, and another, thin and high, like the horns of Elfland. I spun round to look where they were coming from. They were spaced out all along the hilltop. Little black figures standing up against that gold evening sky. It was too far off to see them plainly. But by the way they were standing, feet apart, heads up, spear in one hand and horn in the other, they looked to me like fighting men. I'd no idea they were there before. So it was more than the women down here guarding this dale.

Nimue touched the horn to her lips and then the boy's, with a bit of a laugh.

'You are not quite ready yet for the spoils of manhood. Be careful, Arthur!'

'But soon will be.'

And the two of them came up the steps with his arm round her waist. Arthur . . . That name meant nothing to me then. But when I saw them together like that I knew I'd stumbled on more than I'd guessed.

The lad himself never even looked my way. I might have been one of the slaves. But as the Lady passed she caught sight of me, left standing all by myself staring at him. She stopped smiling. Her pretty blue eyes looked into mine so keen then I nearly fainted.

# Chapter Fourteen

We feasted in the old British way that night, trestles down the hall
and great cauldrons of meat and drinking-horns. There was only a
marble table and couches for Arthur and Nimue and their pet friends.
That caused some trouble. Pretty soon there was an argument broke
out over who was to be sat at the top. In less time than you could crack
a nut it turned to fighting, and more than half those boys were at it.
They'd all changed into handsome house clothes with as much gold
and jewellery as they could hang on them, and some of them had washed
the mud and blood off themselves pretty carefully and others hadn't.
But there was more blood spilled now, and split noses and black eyes.
The dogs were going mad under the tables, and the servants hopping
out of the way and trying to save the food and drink from going over.

Some of the women jumped up, and for all they were nicely dressed
up for that feast I saw them look at their lady, and their hands went
to their belts as though they were wishing they'd got weapons. If she'd
given them the word I could see they'd have sorted those boys out,
even so. But she put out her hand to stop them and looked at young
Arthur, who hadn't done much up till then save yell at his lads. He
had two stout friends either side of him: Cei, that was the tallest man
in the room and a black brow on him like a raven in a bad temper.
Cei the Fair, they called him! And Bedwyr, that looked as pretty as
a girl, but could run or fight or drink with anyone in that hall till he
was the only one left standing. The three of them looked at each other
and went into the thick of it. Arthur had a tough job of it at first, and
he took some pretty hard knocks himself before he'd got them round
to his way of thinking. Cei didn't bother with arguing: he just walloped
anyone who wouldn't stand still. Bedwyr got their arms behind their
backs and twisted them round so they had to listen.

'Shame on you!' cried Arthur. 'There's a fine feast here going to
waste. Meat we've raided. Grease your knives on that and enjoy it,
before the wine's all spilt. We're blood-brothers, heh? Settle your rank
of honour on the field tomorrow.'

There were some of them still growling, and there'd be more quarrels
to settle now than there had been before the fight. Arthur put his arm
round Dillus, who'd started it all by shouting loudest because he'd been
put lower than Custennin. He took a great gold chain off his own neck
and hung it round Dillus's and kissed him. But he led him back to
the bench and made him sit down in the very same place he'd been
put in before. The rest of them watched pretty tense and the hall went
mighty quiet then, but Dillus only growled something about the

338

morning. The meat was carried on to the table double-quick and Arthur raised his drinking horn. He'd carried it off.

I was nothing. I wasn't a servant. I didn't wait at table, but I wasn't sat with the gentry either, not like Bytwini on the end of Arthur's table. The priest was trying to talk pretty seriously to Arthur, but the lad just clapped him on the shoulder and laughed in his face. I was tucked almost out of sight at a table near the bottom of the hall. I'd seemed pretty important to Lady Nimue these last few days, but she'd no time for me now Arthur had come.

A lad with a raiding party. And I was a smith. I'd managed to keep that quiet from Nimue and her women, weapons or not. But this was different. I gripped my beaker so hard it might have been a bar of hot iron I was bending.

I watched them drinking and feasting. They weren't very old, those boys. Half of them not full-grown men. They couldn't hold much liquor. He'd stopped them fighting. But after a bit there was vomit and cups knocked over and boys sprawled on the table or under it. The Lady sat and smiled at it, chatting away to Arthur and Cei and Bedwyr. Her women did what they could to hold things steady and call the slaves to clean the mess and set things straight.

There was a harper, and a good bit of song and story-telling, and that quieted them, till they cheered him at the end. It was all new to me, the way the gentry lived, Roman or British. I'd never heard harping like that, though I knew some of the stories. He sang about the blessed head of Bran that was carried about, and Queen Rhiannon that was made to go like a horse, and Pwyll that changed places with Arawn, king of faery, and a lot more besides. I remember there was one about how Uther Pendragon beat the Saxons. They liked that. Then he sang a new song telling how Arthur had stolen the brown bull of Crec and brought it home. And those that were still awake roared and stamped at that like the old bull himself.

Well, by that time I'd had my fill of meat and beer like everyone else. I didn't bother now about picking at my food like Bytwini did. That one meal was better than all the feasts I'd had in my life put together.

Still, I was sat pulling the gristle out of my teeth, when I saw another of Arthur's lads pissing before he could get to the door. I felt so sad when I watched him the tears were rolling down my cheeks. And not just for myself this time. For all this fine house and their clothes and jewels, Arthur wasn't the prince of Elfland, the way I thought he might have been when I first saw him. That only happens in songs and tales. This lot were mortal. Boys. Dirty and bloody, with black eyes and grease down their tunics. Not fairy warriors at all. Just boasting and brawling and getting drunk and making themselves sick, as boys will everywhere. That made me weep. I was pretty drunk myself.

It was a brisker sight in the morning. Never mind what sore heads those boys might have had, they were all out on the field before the mist was off the lake. The women were there too, instructing them, and pretty stern teachers they were. They knew their business, though how they had come by it themselves still beats me. It was all strange, that place. I sometimes wonder if I dreamed it.

I looked for those sentries on the hill, but I couldn't see them now. And never did unless the Lady signalled. I had a cold thought then. They must have been there in the heather the night I came. Had I wandered between two of them in the dark? Or did they see me? Why would they let me pass?

I didn't have long to worry about that. Lady Nimue had work for me. Every day she'd take me to the library, or her store-room of herbs, or that temple on the lake. Or we'd just walk out of doors. Wherever it was, she'd make me recite to her some more of what I knew. She was going to milk me of magic till her buckets ran over. Greedy, she was, for power. You could see it in her eyes. If I'd been Smith, if I'd been king in the forest still, I'd have smelt the danger. I'd have been pretty careful how much I spilt to that one. But I wasn't king any more, was I? The god had left me. Morgan had robbed me of that. So what did it matter to me what I told the Lady? That's how I thought then.

This particular morning she took a bundle of things, wrapped up in a cloth, and a little writing tablet and led me into a sort of garden at the back of the house. It had stone walls around it, high, so you couldn't see over. And even here, where it was just grass and trees and flowers, the stones of the wall were all cut and squared, not lumps of rock such as you'd put round a sheepfold. Weeks it must have taken, just to make that garden wall. Even the grass was cut into straight edges or circles, with little walks between. There were marble steps and seats. But it wasn't that that took my breath away first off. When I clapped eyes on them I thought I'd seen the gods. They were like the ones in the oak . . . No. I was forgetting. There's only a few of you have seen them, and there are still some things I'm not speaking of, even now.

Only these weren't wood but stone, all shining in the sun. And gods they should have been, by rights. There was a lady with an owl on her shoulder. And a chap with a club, wearing a lion-skin. There was even, begging the Horned One's pardon, one a bit like our own sort, with hairy legs and little horns coming out of his hair. And lots more besides, that had a fishing-spear, or grapes, or breasts to suckle two babies, so that between them they covered just about everything that needs looking after. I should have fallen down flat on my face and howled for safety. But I didn't, not once I'd pulled myself together and got over the shock. I didn't need to.

They weren't gods, though they had the shapes of them. All my life I'd lived by the things of power, even as a lad. My father was king before me. It wasn't just the great ones in the holy place. We brought little ones of that kind away with us too, Wood, clay. Small enough to slip into your pocket. But you wouldn't. You'd carry them carefully, and you'd set them on a shelf in the house and light candles to them. They were the god too, or a bit of him. They were holy. When you spoke to them you were talking to the god himself. So I don't know how it was I could look face to face at these figures, and some of them bigger than I was, and not feel afeared of them. Something changed that day. I felt like a river was sweeping the firm ground from under my feet. I didn't know where I might be carried next, or if I'd ever fetch up safe again. Only one thing I did know: those things had the shape of power, but that was all. They weren't gods. They were nothing but human beings in fancy dress.

My mind was pretty near reeling, taking in all this. The Lady made me sit down on one of her marble benches and unwrapped her things on the seat between us. I had another start. It wasn't stones this time, or herbs, or dead animals, though there were hundreds yet we hadn't talked about. It was a set of weapons, and no common ones either. I recognised the markings on them. The knife. The spear. The bow. Not so richly jewelled as some I'd seen hanging in her hall. But rarer, for all that. It was a bright day. The metal was polished up and winking, so it dazzled my eyes. And she was bright too, looking up into my face with her little-girl smile.

'Tell me, White-Chin, what do you know of these?'

And she stroked my hand, as though she didn't know she was doing it. Like a little wave lapping.

'I'm just a poor seer. I told you, my lady. Only a handful of stone-lore and fire-lore. A few charms for mending. Well, maybe the odd one for cursing too. These weapons are the high magic. You need a king of the craft for that.'

'Do I, Gillie Kernun? *You* know, don't you? You could tell me their secrets if you wanted to?'

And her little hand went creeping up my arm.

I had to save myself.

341

# Chapter Fifteen

That Nimue was no fool. She made them drive that bull and his cows, those we hadn't eaten, back over the hill and turn them loose in a bog the other side. If those that had lost them came tracking the herd, let them try and get them out of there without being sucked under. There'd be precious few hoofprints to follow over those peat hags, and suppose anyone did come scouting round our side to pick up their tracks again and see where they came from, well, she had those who would make sure they never got back to tell of it.

I don't think Arthur minded losing his bull. He'd got his glory. He'd proved he could do it. He'd led his troop and taken what he wanted, before those he robbed got wind of what they'd lost. Those lads killed everybody in sight of that herd who might have told what they'd seen, or so they bragged. They'd come away with only one man lost and a tale to boast of.

She made him be careful after that, though. Only not as careful as she would have been if she'd been his proper mother. She'd make a warrior of him. They still went raiding, and pretty far from home, from the tales they brought back with them. But now it was just killing and looting stuff they could easily carry. No more cattle raids. And she taught him to cover his tracks, make a big circle, ford rivers, scatter and group again to fox the enemy. There would have been some queer tales told round those parts. This troop that rode up out of Annwn, all young and handsome like the Fair Folk, who took what they pleased and vanished into the hollow hills at daybreak or dived into the bogs and were never seen again.

They were learning their lessons well. There was never a horn blew alarm on the hills. Just once or twice when I was with her, my lady lifted her head quick at a hawk's scream. But it wasn't ever a troop of angry horsemen coming over our skyline. As I said, it was like being in fairyland down there in that dale. And just as dangerous to mortal men.

I stayed too long. They say that humans always do in fairyland. But where else could I go? I had shelter. I was wanted there. Lady Nimue made a fuss of me. She gave me a room of my own to stop Bytwini from ranting at her. You can imagine how queer that felt. I'd never lain by myself before. I don't count that awful time after Morgan cursed me . . . For a long time I was so scared I couldn't sleep. It was a fine grand house in daytime, but I wasn't too sure what might be abroad at night.

We'd got into a kind of pattern. I'd spend an hour or two with my lady every morning. I'd forgotten I even knew so much till she plucked it out of me, like finding thorns long after you've fallen into a bramble-patch. Then the rest of the time was my own. Sometimes I'd hang around the back quarters and help the servants a bit. It felt more wholesome than you might think to be fetching a sack of flour or polishing up a bit of harness. I'd like to have done more of the men's work. But they looked sideways at me in my holy man's gown. They never talked free when I was around. They wouldn't share a joke with me. That hurt, seeing real men that didn't have to hide what they were. And it seemed as if I didn't have to try so hard to hide it now. I looked older than I was with my hair turned white, and I hadn't the muscles I used to. I've never got my full strength back since Morgan blighted me. When I'd outstayed my welcome I'd go off on my own. I could wander anywhere I wanted. I might watch the lads training, and hurt myself some more, aching to get my hands on their harness and body-armour. It never entered their heads what I was, of course. Just a white seer, hanging about the field. They'd have taken more notice of me if I'd been a ghost. There wasn't any of them had a use for me, only Nimue.

The time slipped by, and they brought in the harvest. It was a pretty house, but it was built on poor soil. It put more meat than bread on our table.

I was walking round the lake, taking it easy in the sun, and picking up little feathers the birds had dropped by the water's edge. You never know when you'll have a use for things like that. I'd done the full circle and I was nearly back to where I'd hit on that causeway the first day, when I heard a sound that made me stop. Horse's hooves and a loud old jangling, coming along that old stone road through the wood. Well, you may say, what's a road for, if not for horses to travel? I'll tell you, this road only led to one house and it seemed as if it came out of nowhere. There was nobody came to that house by it and nobody went out on it. When Arthur and his mates went raiding over the moors, they'd take the back way over the fells, any path for them but the one that looked plain and easy. So I stopped where I was, under a holly tree, and I wouldn't have been surprised to see some Roman ghost come riding by.

He was stranger than that. And it wasn't a horse but a black mule that came into sight, hung about with huge panniers that clattered a bit. Full of pans and dishes, poking out at the top. Not over-fancy stuff, but worth a fortune just for the metal in them. I should know. And perched on top of the lot, with his legs stuck out on either side, was the queerest sort of fellow you ever saw. He had a cloth of speckled yellow and black tossed over one shoulder, and a skirt of the same that didn't cover his knees, and the rest was bare, and so thin and scrawny you could see the shapes of gristle and bone under his skin. He didn't need covering for his head. He had hair that spread down over his shoulders as thick and white as a lamb's fleece. My elf-locks were cobwebs to his. You never saw so much hair, and so full and curly on an old man. Old? Well, he was, and he wasn't. He had a face scored

343

with lines as deep as the cracks in a piece of driftwood, that's been left out years for the rain to leach and the sun to dry, and as grey too. You couldn't ever have forgotten if you'd seen that face before. And yet I felt I had.

I thought the sun went in as he passed me. I hadn't moved to hide; I just stood still in the shadow. He didn't look, and the mule went clattering on, only the sound of her hooves changed when she struck the causeway. The pedlar was humming a little song under his breath and he peered ahead pretty eagerly as he got near the meadow. I reckon I must have been the ghost, not him, slipping along after him through the trees. There weren't many left out on the field by that time. The lads whipped round and stared, and some of them went for their weapons, but the women-guard looked up at the hills and then at each other. They signed to the boys to let him pass. But they all stared at him riding up to the house.

Then out of the doorway comes the Lady Nimue herself. And she's running down the steps with her arms stretched wide. She fairly threw herself at that pedlar and his mule, and he hopped off, quick as a frog and hugged her to him. The two of them were dancing each other round, laughing and singing as merry as you please.

The boys seemed to come to then and put up a great shout. 'It's Merlyn!' 'He's back!' 'Merlyn!' And they all came pelting up to greet him.

Well! I felt as if three spears had run me through from different directions. I didn't know which of them was going to be the one that finished me off.

This crazy-looking pedlar was Lord to this Lady and she'd never spoken a word about him all this while.

And then his name. Those boys had shouted it out as careless as if he could have been anybody's uncle. Merlyn. There'd be more than one that had that handle. But I didn't need telling twice which this one was, not here. Merlyn, the high magician the tales tell of. The one we wise talked of in whispers. The one that steered the boat of Uther Pendragon and then vanished. And I had stumbled on his Lady's house by chance. Or had I?

And at the back of all this, one thought colder than all the rest. I remembered now where I'd seen that face before, in a very different disguise. That grey bard in the street of Carlisle. Silver-Tongue. In his foxy red cloak, darkening the door of my smithy and flirting with my daughter. So it had been Merlyn all along, binding me to be a traitor to Morgan for the sake of his secret little king.

# Chapter Sixteen

Merlyn. Morgan and Merlyn. So that's what it was. They'd got me caught properly, hadn't they? They'd driven me from one to the other of them across those mountains, like hounds turning a boar on to the spears. I should have known I hadn't escaped. I should have seen where I'd come to. He'd as good as told me, hadn't he? A boy king to rule over all Britain. To drive the Saxons out and make the land one. All summer I'd watched those lads playing at soldiers, and it had never once crossed my head what that enchanter had said to me. That had happened in another life. The day Morgan cursed me was a black pit in my mind. All that other business had been on the far side of it. I daren't let myself remember back so far. Well, I'd had my eyes opened now, and I could see I was in far worse danger than I'd thought. Merlyn had set me to worm out Morgan's secrets, and instead I had found out his.

Arthur. So this was the lad that had to be kept hidden from Morgan, though Silver-Tongue had never let on why.

You can be sure the first thing I thought of was that I'd cut and run before the magician saw me. I'd got the wood at the back of me, and that old lost road. Then I remembered the men in the bracken, and I went a bit cold and I thought that maybe the only escape I was likely to find would be on the end of a spear.

I didn't have a chance to try for it. I wasn't as well-hidden as I thought I was. Nimue must have seen me over Merlyn's shoulder as they hugged. She broke off then and whispered to one of her women. That one came running over the grass towards me while the Lady took Merlyn indoors. Valeria, it was. That square-faced fighter that had held her blade to my throat the first day. She was a sort of captain among them, so I knew it was serious, what she'd come to say. She hurried me back into the wood a bit, where we couldn't be seen.

'My lady counsels that you use discretion, for your safety and hers. Her visitor does not know of your coming, and it is better that he does not. We do not ordinarily welcome strangers.'

'I could see that for myself,' I told her.

She grinned a bit at that. 'You were lucky. You had something that my lady wants. You bought your life with wisdom.'

'And Merlyn's got more than I have.'

She looked a bit shrewdly at me then. 'You know him?'

I was a fool not to be careful.

'I'm a wise man. Which of us hasn't heard of Merlyn?'

'Yes.'

She still looked at me hard. Then she started leading me through the wood, off the road. We came out by the lake edge. She made me keep back while she slipped out and looked. I saw her wave her arm, and another of them signalled back from the house. Valeria hustled me into a coracle pretty fast and rowed me across to the island. I kept my head hidden close. He might have taken me for Bytwini if he'd seen.

'My lady desires you will stay here. Food will be brought to you. Merlyn sees beneath too many hoods. It is better that you do not cross his path. Do not worry. He never stays long.'

'Don't fret,' I told her. 'I've no more wish to be shrivelled into a toad or turned to a block of stone than she has. I'll keep close till he's gone.'

'Good. And, White-Chin, one thing more. Use no charms or spells while Merlyn is in this dale. A great magician like him could sense it.'

Make magic? I hadn't been able to cast one single spell since the day I killed Erith. I'd talked of magic. Charms, recipes, conjunctions, signs. All that and more. But I hadn't used any of it. I hadn't put the bits together and made them work. I didn't know if Nimue had tried.

So I kept close, in that little white temple looking out over the lake. One thing scared me more than anything. Would Bytwini tell him a stranger had come in the false get-up of a Christian hermit? The priest was no friend of mine. I needn't have worried. I wasn't the only one who'd left the house. I saw Bytwini walking by his own little chapel across the water from me. I found out afterwards he'd never stay in the house when Merlyn was there. He tried what he could to be soul-friend to Arthur, and the lad looked up to him. He taught him reading and writing and a lot more besides. But there were some things in this house he couldn't shut his eyes to.

Merlyn came and went pretty often that autumn. I was never easy. There'd be a lass come running up to me where I was singing chants to Nimue in her library or walking down by the lake, and I'd be hustled off into hiding for days or maybe a couple of weeks. The worst was when he came so sudden they couldn't get me down to the water without him seeing, and then I'd have to lie close in my room till it was dark. That made me sweat, being so near to him, only a few walls away, and wondering what would happen if he discovered me. He has a mighty loud laugh.

I saw him close to, once. It was night, but almost as bright as day, with a big golden moon coming up over the roofs of the stables and washing that courtyard outside my window silver. The sort of night that made me think of Morgan. I heard laughter, and when I looked out there were the two of them, Nimue and Merlyn. They were coming out of that garden, the one I told you about, with the old statues. They looked a bit like a pair of statues themselves in the moonlight, her in her white Roman dress and him in a toga, with wreaths of leaves in their hair. They'd stopped still now, very close together, and he was holding a bunch of grapes over her mouth. When I saw the way his hands were going over her I thought of the look he'd had in his eyes the day he'd fondled my daughter. When I'd dashed the tears off and

I could see straight again, they'd gone. I thought he'd have to feel the curse I sent after his back then. But I didn't care, and nothing came of it. It seemed not even black anger could put the strength back in my spirit.

Still, I was sure I couldn't hide from him for long. I'd lost the cunning to put a mist between us. He'd find me out.

I saw Nimue's game. She was feeding on both of us. She'd gobble up Merlyn's high magic while she had him with her, and leave my crusts for other days. And she wouldn't want him knowing she had another larder. When I realised what she was up to I wondered that Merlyn could be such a fool as to share his wisdom with her. I know he'd an eye, aye and plenty more besides, for a pretty woman. But he was supposed to be the wisest enchanter we'd ever had in Britain, wasn't he? And who was she, to learn what he knew? There's ranks and grades and ceremonies to go through, year upon year, and even then you wouldn't come anywhere near where Merlyn was, by all accounts. I began to wonder then if there mightn't be more to this Lady of the Lake than I'd thought. Maybe she wasn't as young and silly as she liked to act with him. Or maybe she's always been young . . . Always?

Those times were bad for me, sitting alone in that temple, night and day. It was a plain enough place, but it frightened me. Things were coming back now. I knew it wasn't only the moon that looked down on the lake, over the tops of the hills. Once Morgan had watched over me in my forge at Way Bank. She was watching me here. I could feel it now. I was a fool not to see it before. She had driven me here, for a reason. I could still put her out of my mind when the lads were on the field and you'd got the clash of sword on shield and the noise of horses' hooves. But sat there in the silence, and especially in the dark, with the water lapping all round me, that was a different story. I'd get back to my room again when he'd gone and I'd find myself pulling that filthy old satchel out from under the bed. I'd sit nursing it on my knee, like a wise woman with her toad. I'd feel inside it. Smith's leathers and woman's skirts. I wasn't safe from her, not here. I'd shudder then. I could tell for sure now, it was Morgan's doing that had put me in this house. For her good, not mine.

I noticed the lads hadn't been raiding for a while. The place seemed to have gone more grim and serious. They still trained on the meadow, harder than ever. There were men giving them lessons now. Hard, hefty soldiers, with muscles like iron bands and scarred faces, in leather battle-dress and dark-red cloaks. I didn't know where they'd sprung from, unless it was off the hills. And there were more noblemen coming in every week. Older warriors, too. The lads were going on men themselves now. By day they didn't laugh as much when they practised, and they fought sterner. Over the wine at night they'd laugh wilder and fight less.

Arthur had lessons of another sort in Bytwini's chapel now. They'd spend hours there alone, the two of them. And sometimes Bytwini would call the whole lot of them round him and make them sit very quiet on the grass while he talked to them.

But other days it was Nimue's turn. He'd row across and she'd be waiting for him on the steps of that little temple in the lake. She'd take his hand and lead him inside. They'd be in there a mighty long time and they'd come out looking grave. And then as like as not they'd burst out laughing and go racing each other down to the boat as if he couldn't wait to be back in the saddle and she was no older than he was.

I should have seen what all this was leading up to. I'd been Smith. That was my craft. Didn't I forge the sword that made Urien a man? But I walked into it as blind as a hare slipping her head through a noose.

It was Midwinter's dawn. I'd never missed that sunrise. I hadn't got the wise around me, or not my own sort. I've no doubt those women had their ceremony, but they didn't call me to join them. But that year there was a bidding on me stronger than I'd ever felt before at that season. I knew it wasn't right to be doing what I had to do on my own. I was awfully scared. I hadn't made the preparations. I hadn't tried to use my craft in all the time I'd taken that saint's gown. I didn't think I still had the power. And if I hadn't, I'd be putting myself in worse danger. But it had to be done, somehow. Up at the house we'd had a great fire, with feasting and dancing half the night. Arthur had gone off early. Bedwyr said he'd taken himself to the chapel, and nobody was to follow. And then the ladies disappeared. Most of the men had dropped off to sleep before it got morning. I slipped away in the dark and howled a bit to myself that I hadn't got the guise of a big he-stag as I used to do. Yet go I must, no matter how wrongly I was dressed.

It was freezing outside. There was ice cracking under my boots and then I was crunching frost on the grass. It wasn't light and it wasn't dark out there in the open. There was just a bit of a glimmer from the water and then black fells all around with snow on the tops. I couldn't see the island in the middle of the lake, no matter how hard I strained. But I knew it was there, so I kept my eyes on where it should be. I chanted the words and made the passes I had to, to bring the sun back and turn the world right side over again. I couldn't feel it working. It wasn't doing any good. All the same, there must have been others at work besides me. The water was getting paler and there was that island, getting more solid now, black first off, then grey and green, and at last I could make out the little white temple, so I knew it must be coming on day. I kept trying, harder.

There was a mist beginning to smoke up off the lake and the sky above it was turning a cold sort of blue. Then I got a shock. A stone moved on the beach quite close to me. I heard feet walking down to the water's edge. Two men. I couldn't see plainly. Just tall grey shadows in the fog. I stayed stock still as the bushes behind me and shut up. I don't know why, but I daren't move.

The lake looked smooth as brown marble in between the curls of mist. It wasn't deep. You could see weed when you looked down. But I'd lost sight of the rocks between me and the island now. The men had stopped walking. They must be watching, like me. Those wisps of fog seemed as if they were walking on the water. Then I swear they started to dance. White ladies circling in rings, with their hands joined together, and their little bare feet skimming the surface. The light got stronger, and I saw the Lady of the Lake. You won't believe this, but I tell you she was standing straight up out of the water. She had her golden hair loose all around her and her white arm lifted high. She was holding up something and it caught the first of the dawn and brought it down to the lake, like lightning.

A man spoke close beside me. His voice rang deep and strong, as if he'd waited all his life to say these words.

'Well, Arthur, your day has come. Will you go out and take it?'

Merlyn! Standing next to me. And I hadn't had one word of warning.

'By God, I will!'

There was the scrape of a coracle on the shingle and a bit of splashing. Then Arthur settled to the oars. He rowed away, in and out of those dancing women. It wasn't so far. I saw clear enough how he took the bright thing from the Lady's hand where she was holding it to him. Then the sun rose up over the fells in a ball of red fire and all the ice round the lake and the frost on the hills was flashing bright as jewels to dazzle us. There was a shout from the boat. Young Arthur was kneeling up and raising his man's sword high to show us. I could see him laughing.

Red, that lake was, with the sunrise full on it now.

# Chapter Seventeen

With Arthur's shout there was a roar from behind me. I whipped round and there they all were, standing clear above the mist on the porches of the great house. The young warriors and the old ones, the Lady's maidens, house-servants and field-slaves, all waving and cheering to see Arthur made man. And over the top of it all the horns from the sentries up on the hills blew for the kill. That was a brave sight, and a sound to make me pull my back up straight even though I'd got tears standing in my eyes and I was wearing that unmanly gown.

It's always that way with Arthur. I don't know what gift Merlyn gave him at his birthing, but there's that fire in him that makes you feel he carries the sun about with him. You'd follow him anywhere. And, yes, I know some of the things he's done afterwards. That wouldn't have made any difference, if you'd been there. When he smiled at you, you could forgive him anything.

Arthur came rowing back to us with his face fairly flushed and his eyes shining. Merlyn hugged him. The man had got tears running down over his cheeks.

Then out of nowhere Nimue was there with us. She had a thick soft cloak, purple as heather, wrapped close around her, so I couldn't tell if she was wet or no. Her hair was dark with damp, but that might have been the mist. There was a glow about her and she was laughing, a bit breathless. I moved back a bit. She'd scared me before. It came to me now that this one at least might not be a mortal woman.

Well, there was a deal of kissing and hugging between the three of them and all the folk from the house were rushing down to the shore shouting. Nimue raised her hand and they stopped where they were, in a big circle round her. She made Arthur kneel down at her feet, holding his new sword. Then from under her cloak she drew out a sword-belt with a scabbard hanging from it. She held it up high in her left hand to show us all. And with her right she took Arthur's hand and made him lift his sword. They were a strange pair. The sword had a hilt that was as grand as any I'd ever seen. Two gold dragons, with rubies for eyes and tongues of red enamel shooting out of their mouths and licking along the guard. You can be sure I'd an eye for that blade too. It was true and deadly, bluish steel, cold, where the haft was hot gold. But the scabbard in her left hand was a different matter altogether. Plain black wood, old and a bit cracked, bound with leather that was scuffed and worn, and fixed with just a few curls of silver. You'd never think to keep a fine weapon like that in such a shabby case. Yet when she brought her hands close those two slipped together as though they'd been made for each other.

The Lady buckled the sword-belt round Arthur's side. Her maidens handed her the rest of the arms. She set the spear in his right hand and the shield on his other arm, and slipped the dagger into his belt. Then, very serious for her, she kissed him on the forehead.

'Rise, Arthur, who shall be Pendragon. In the strength of the names your father and your mother named, go out and win.'

She raised him up.

'Who follows Arthur?'

The crowd went wild. The men were all shouting at the tops of their voices, 'I!' 'I!' And I reckon I must have been yelling and cheering as loud as any of them.

'See, Arthur, how you can rouse the blood of all Britain. Here's a Christian saint would ride to war behind you!'

I turned my head to find Merlyn himself, laughing at me. I was looking straight into his eyes. Me, Teilo, that had been called Smith, with my nose and cheeks still burned red by the forge and a few poor white bristles sprouting on my chin, standing face to face with the wisest of the wise. But he went on slapping Arthur on the back and laughing and dancing about at the joke of it all. He didn't know me. Arthur was grinning at me too now. He reached into his pouch and tossed me something.

'Here, White-Chin. Say a prayer for me!'

I think his smile meant more to me. I nearly missed what he threw me. It was a coin. Money. Not a thing I had any use for. I rubbed my thumb over it. Old words. Somebody's face. It had the feel of silver.

I stammered out some thanks. I didn't feel like cheering and waving any more. For if Merlyn couldn't recognise me, it meant only one thing. It was what I'd feared all along. There wasn't a drop of magic left in me, and never would be again. I was like those statues in her garden. I might hold the things of magic in my hand. But I'd lost all my power to use them. I didn't count.

I got a look at Nimue. I knew she'd have her heart in her mouth and be waiting for him to strip her secret bare. She'd gone a bit pale, but she was no fool. She turned the talk away from me pretty quickly.

'Tell me, Arthur,' she says, with that pretty little laugh of hers. 'Which do you prize the most? The scabbard or the sword?'

'My sword, of course!' he cries, waving it about in front of her nose. Well, a man would say that, wouldn't he?

She shook her head at him. 'Caliburn is a mighty weapon. As long as it sits in your hand you will win every battle. Yet the scabbard is older far. She who trusted it to my keeping swore that its virtue was worth ten times the sword. It holds the power to heal all wounds. I have kept them till this day and armed you with both, as I was charged to do. Do you in your turn guard them well. Sword and scabbard. I have trained you here to use both the one and the other. Cherish that wisdom, for your own sake and Britain's.'

'Trust me. I have had the fairest of teachers. Thanks, Nimue! There'll be plenty of work for both your beauties now. Old Caliburn has slept in his scabbard far too long. Now I'm a man at last he'll be unsheathed and there'll be rivers of blood for your scabbard to stop!'

She laughed, only not so merry as she usually did.

Well, they moved off to the house and there was such a feast that day as beat all the rest. I hung back by the lake to the last. I could have slipped off with the crowd. It was almost as if I was wanting Merlyn to uncover me. He disappointed me. I don't know what I'd started to hope. That Merlyn could save me from Morgan? Give me back the manhood I'd lost?

But the magician never looked my way again. He walked straight past me with his arm round Nimue, fondling her, and the two of them were smiling in each other's faces as if they'd been the lad's own father and mother. I felt a bit sick then. All right, he hadn't spotted power in me because I'd lost it. But it seemed he couldn't sense an untruth either. And he was Merlyn, wasn't he? The greatest enchanter we ever had in Britain.

You can be the wisest of the wise and still be a great fool.

It hadn't escaped Nimue, either. As they were passing me I saw her eyes go quick to Merlyn's face and I thought she held her breath. And then, when nothing happened, she turned her head and stared back hard at me. There was a nasty sort of doubt in her face I hadn't seen before.

She called me to her chamber next day. It seemed it didn't matter now whether Merlyn saw me or not. He thought no more of me in my white skirts than he did of Bytwini. Well, there on her couch was that sword, Caliburn, and the old black scabbard lying beside it.

'White-Chin,' she said, 'is it true? Can the scabbard really be as powerful as she says? Could this keep someone safe, against more than Saxons?'

You'd have thought she was pleading with me for something.

I had to pick it up. I never wanted to touch it. I knew it would say my hands were dead to magic now. I was right. I didn't get any sort of thrill from it, first off. Then, as I held it, there was a heat began to creep through my fingers and up my arms and spread right through my body till it warmed my heart. I hadn't felt such comfort since . . . Well, I hadn't, ever. It wasn't any magic in me that was speaking; it was the thing itself. Anybody would have felt the same.

She watched my face, and let out a sigh.

'Ah! So you feel it too! I'm glad of that. Our hopes hang on such a slender thread.' A little smile of triumph crept into her face then. 'Arthur cannot win all his victories with Caliburn, though men he can rouse in plenty to fight his battles. But a sheath will still be needed to clothe his blade. In the end, the scabbard will be more powerful than the sword.'

I kept quiet at that. I wasn't sure what she was talking about. It wasn't just the weapons, I knew that much. It came into my head again how Merlyn had feared Morgan, though I'd no notion why. But I wasn't going to name Morgan in this house.

The Lady was still watching my face. But whatever she hoped to get out of me, she didn't press it.

I don't mind admitting I'd been sneaking a look at the sword too. That was more my style, never mind the dress I wore. But she didn't offer to let me have a hold of that.

Those lads didn't stay long with us afterwards. They were all made warriors now, those of them that hadn't got man's weapons up to that day. The Lady's maidens armed them, and very prettily they did it too. Merlyn was hopping about all over the place, ordering stores and pack-mules and picking what servants would follow them. He didn't want many, he said. They'd need to ride quick and light. I thought of that elf-troop that had galloped off in the dawn. Well, there'd be flesh and blood Saxons on the end of their spears this time. I never felt so helpless. I was a blacksmith. I had the secret of armouring. Warriors would need me. I hadn't thought what it was like till then, to be a powerless woman and have to see your own blood ride off to the wars and not know if it would be a hero or a bloody corpse that came home again. When I saw them mustering on the meadow to ride away, Bedwyr with a great horn at his side and Cei shouting the baggage-train into line, and Arthur sitting on his chestnut mare with his head in the air and a shine in his eyes as though he was seeing clear into heaven, and that sword Caliburn already half out of its sheath, well, I couldn't help myself. I didn't even think. I ran forward and gripped hold of his leg.

'Take me with you, sir!' I begged. 'I can do fine work for you. You'll need my craft.'

I'd been Smith. I'd furnish his horses rarely, put a fine edge on his weapons, rebuild his body-harness so no Saxon would dent it. But how could he tell that was what I meant, dressed like I was?

He laughed so hard at me his horse reared up in my face and threw me back.

'There's no need for your sort where we're going, White-Chin! This is men's work. Pray for my army, if you like. But I bear a scabbard that says I can never be harmed and a sword that can vanquish every enemy. I can kill and not be hurt!'

He waved Caliburn. Then Bedwyr blew a great blast on his horn and all the swords flashed out, and the lads cheered and the ladies waved their scarves and clapped and called good luck. And off they trotted, that whole brave troop of horsemen, with Merlyn riding beside his golden boy. They rode out of the dale by the old Roman road this time, off to call the kings of Britain to young Arthur's banner.

It was pretty chill on the field when they'd gone. The ground was all churned to black mud and dirtying the hems of the ladies' dresses, and the lake had gone a dull, stormy sort of red. The women trooped indoors and called for hot wine and pretty soon my Lady was sobbing into her cup and some of her women were fingering their own scars mighty thoughtfully.

After a bit Nimue lifted her head and called me to her across the hall. I was shaking before I got there. I think I knew there was something up. Those sweet blue eyes of hers were wet with the tears she'd been crying for Arthur. But she'd forgotten him. She stared at me as if she hated me.

'Get out! I release you. Go back and tell Morgan she has lost.'

# Chapter Eighteen

I must have stood and gawped. Nimue had known! Near on two years she'd given me a bed and fed me from her table, and all the time she'd known just who I was.

I don't know why she hadn't killed me. It would have been no trouble to her women. And then it came to me that maybe this Lady of the Lake likes power more than is good for her, or her little Arthur either. I'd been useful to her, even without the power in my fingers. And so she'd taken a risk. Morgan's creature here in her camp. Or did she just want to show Morgan which of them had the upper hand?

'I'm no servant of Queen Morgan!' I shouted out. 'She murdered my wife by witchcraft and then put the blame on me.'

'She chose you. No one escapes Morgan that easily. She sent you to spy on us.'

I'd known myself all along that's what it must have been.

However it was, Nimue let out a great sigh. You'd have thought she'd just put down a heavy burden.

'You have lost. You cannot hurt him now. Arthur is a man, with Merlyn beside him. And neither of them guesses how well I have served them. Morgan sent you here for evil, yet here I have bound you. Your side is too late to stop Arthur raising his banner. I have armed him with Caliburn that will win every battle and with the scabbard that heals every hurt, None of you can defeat him. Not Saxons, not Christians, not Morgan.'

My thoughts were in a whirl. Merlyn against Morgan, that's what I'd thought it was. Those were the two I'd feared. And now she was saying the enchanter was nothing. It was the women, Nimue and Morgan against each other, all along. And I'd let her stroke my leg, and put her arms round my neck, and . . . There wasn't a word I could trust myself to say to her.

She raised her head to me, and her voice too. She was pretty drunk.

'Go back to Morgan. Tell Arthur's sister she has failed a second time.'

'His *sister*?'

'You didn't know! She hasn't told you?' She pealed with laughter. 'And Merlyn did not either? No, he wouldn't. Even our little changeling has yet to learn his father's name.'

It was all tumbling back now. Bits I'd picked up on the street in Carlisle. Morgan of Tintagel. The last Pendragon's daughter. No, stepdaughter only, out of Ygerne the Wise. I hadn't bothered with it then. Tales of old Cornwall, dead kings. It was nothing to do with me.

'Then it *was* true, what the songs say? Uther Pendragon had a son, and lost him?'

'It is true. And there will be greater songs sung of that boy yet, now he is found.'

'Let me stay here,' I begged. I believed her. 'Let me serve Arthur. I'll never go back to Morgan.'

'You must. You can serve Arthur best in Morgan's hall. Tell her she deals with a wiser enemy than Merlyn now. Frighten her.'

Well, she had to be drunk, with power as well as wine.

Even so, she must have seen she'd gone too far. She laughed a bit, as if she was flirting with me. 'Woman-talk, you understand. We shall not say so in front of Merlyn, shall we?'

I could promise that. I'd just as soon not speak with Merlyn again as long as I lived. Morgan still less. But I wasn't going to stop and argue the toss. Now Arthur had gone, it would be good enough for me if she'd let me out of that dale alive.

'Go then! Take up again that bag you keep under your bed. The burden Morgan laid on you.'

Was there nothing secret she couldn't winkle out of a man? I felt a bit sorry for Merlyn, after all. High Lord of the wise he might be, but she wasn't human.

It made me pull a sour face. Even then I couldn't bear to think of how I'd come by those clothes, or what they meant and what they'd cost me.

'Put on that other dress. Your passport back to Morgan. Your usefulness here is finished . . . Smith.'

So she'd known that too. From the look she gave, I think she meant to wound me, calling me that. She'd never let me be a proper man. Only near enough to torment me. She could use a sword herself. She'd trained Arthur for war. She knew what mattered to men. Just that once she called me by my man's name. And the sound of that was better to me than if she'd kissed me ten times over. It had been true, once. I hadn't made it up.

Still, I left in that holy man's gown Nimue had made me keep. I'd got the satchel strapped on my back, but I'd made up my mind I wasn't going to wear the clothes Morgan had willed on me ever again. Oh no! I wasn't going back anywhere near Lyvennet.

I was mighty scared when I set off up that old stone road. I didn't know what sort of a world I might find. To tell you the truth, I didn't really know where I'd been. I thought the world might have changed, hundreds of years gone by, like in the old stories you hear of folk coming back after a day in fairyland.

I wish it had. The world hadn't changed enough as far as I was concerned.

I came up over the lip of the hills and looked down the other side. It was going on the end of winter. There were pockets of snow lying by the road, grey where it had started to melt and frozen again. And the leaves that should have been green were all black and sodden with frost. No sun overhead. I got a glimpse of the sea in the distance, grey and cold. I stood looking at that plain below me and I knew Nimue's sentries were watching me. Down there at my feet there were houses. Villages, odd farms, even a town or two. There wasn't enough sun to show them clearly, just huddles of brown thatch in the winter mud. But you could see the smoke creeping out of the roof-holes and hanging in clouds. It made you think of fire, a dog in front of the hearth, hot meat. I'd be a man in a man's world again.

Nobody stopped me and you can bet I was hardly over the pass before I had that white gown off my back, and never mind if the wind did blow raw round me. I opened my satchel. But it was my smith's clothes I pulled out of it. The leather had a bit of a slimy feel to it, being wrapped up so long. There was mildew on it. I shook the things out. Rags. I hadn't remembered just how badly I'd torn them, running through the woods like a wild man when I'd lost my wits. Still, they were all I had left. I had to put them on. I'd never worn rags before, only when I went disguised.

I left the saint's garb behind in the heather, though it was good stuff, clean and warm.

I marched off down the hill. I tried to walk like a man and whistle like a man again. It didn't come easy after all this time. I was sorry I'd never been able to grow a proper beard since that black day. Just these few white whiskers.

They were an unfriendly lot at the first village. The dogs came barking and the children ran indoors when they saw me. A couple of men looked round the corner of a wood pile. They had axes in their hands.

'Who are you? What do you want?'

'I'm a smith,' I said. The word felt pretty dry on my tongue. 'If you've got tools to mend, blades to sharpen, I'm your man.' Smith? I sounded more like a tinker.

'Oh, yes? Let's see your own tools. Got a forge on your back, have you?'

I felt my feet go cold and my heart sink down to meet them. I'd left too much of myself behind at Way Bank. They didn't give me a chance to argue. They set the dogs on me. At the next village they stoned me. Third time round a woman screamed when she saw my queer face. I didn't wait for any more. I turned and ran.

I didn't call myself a smith after that. I bent my back and let the hair hang over my cheeks and took to begging my bread. I'd have done better for that to have stuck to that holy man's gown and not left it behind in the heather. Without it, they might throw me a crust or a turnip, but they'd turn me away afterwards. I was no use to anybody. They wouldn't let me stay. I'd be lucky enough if I could find a hayrick for the night.

I'd no notion where I was going, only that it was south, as far away from Rheged as I could get. There were times when I was so cold and lonely I thought I might just lie down and die. But I didn't dare. I was a murderer. I'd killed my wife, or Erith. It was all mixed up. I was afraid to die before I'd paid the blood-price.

Then it started. Folk coming the other way, pulling carts, or carrying what they could. They had a beaten look, but they were hurrying too. They stared at me, seeing me going the opposite way. One woman called out, 'Are you mad, you old fool? Do you want to march straight on to a Saxon battle-axe?'

There were more of them, after that. Some of them had bloody bandages.

I left the road. I knew which I was frightened of most. It wasn't the heathen in front of me, it was those enchanters behind. I went more carefully. But I carried on. I can't say what I thought would happen. That there'd be just a band of Saxons, and I'd get past somehow and find good British folk again beyond?

I was coming off the hills now. There was a great forest down to the east, and bits of farmland and rivers and lakes. It looked a richer, softer land than what I'd come through. Then I saw smoke. Too much of it. Black and rolling where they'd fired the farms. I thought I heard screaming. I didn't know if it was beasts or Britons. I'd gone too far.

I heard a crashing through the bushes and I made sure my end had come. But it was a ewe came struggling out in the open, bleating as if it was slaughter-time. I saw straight off what was wrong. She hadn't been milked in a good long while and she could hardly walk for the great udder between her legs. Well, we could help each other. I put her teat to my mouth and had a good squirt of warm milk.

I turned back then. Only it wasn't soon enough. I heard voices, and no language I'd ever heard before. A nasty harsh sound, like breaking stones. They were behind me.

I held my breath, and I'd have stopped my blood beating too if I could. I tried to tiptoe round. The ground was getting boggy. There was a clump of silver birches right ahead of me. I had my head turned sideways, listening to those evil voices, so I didn't see him till I almost bumped into him.

He was standing with his breeches down, having a piss. He turned his head towards me. He had a helmet on and he looked more like a statue than a man. He had holes for eyes. But I'd seen something worse. There was an axe at his feet. And not like any wood-chopper you've ever seen. He hadn't even bothered to wipe the blood and mess off it yet. The moment he saw me he made one grab at his breeches and another at his axe. I shot out a foot and kicked it into a pool. Then I was off, with him shouting and the rest of them running and yelling to see what was up. They came after me. I couldn't think at first how they didn't catch me. I wasn't fit. They might have tired themselves with killing and burning and stealing already.

Later on, I knew it wasn't that that spared me. It was Morgan's hand over me. She'd put her mark on me for her own. There isn't anybody but herself she'll let destroy me.

But I didn't know that then. I just ran. I kept on going too, long after I'd lost sight of those Saxon butchers. You don't know how fear can weary a man. I was driven. I couldn't stop and rest. Every time I closed my eyes I'd see the blood on that axe. I'd thought I wanted to die, but now I was fighting to live. I'd lost all sense of where I was going. Even if I struck a road I was too afraid to follow it. When I saw another human being I was sure it was a Saxon.

I wept for Arthur then. For that little lad riding off into the early morning to try and save us all from what I'd seen. Power or not, I sang what charms I knew for him.

I lost count of the forests I crossed. I was half-starved by now. So when I saw another village through the trees I didn't turn and run, but crept up quiet. Then I heard children calling, and it was our own British tongue. I thought that was the sweetest sound I'd ever heard. I stumbled up to the gate and set up my whine.

'In the name of the gods your fathers named, pity. Do not refuse the stranger at your door. Food and drink will bring a blessing on her who gives it.'

A woman came to her door. Quite young, she was, and a kind face. She had a bowl in her hand that was giving off a bit of steam in the cold air. Not much smell. It might be a dish of porridge. She smiled a bit.

'Here, granddad,' she said. 'It's not much, but it will line your stomach for a few more miles. Give me your blessing.' Then her hand flew to her mouth and she dropped the bowl on the ground. She let out a screech.

'It's him! Half-Face! The witch from Way Bank. Poisoner! Wife-killer!'

Well, that brought the ugliest crowd I'd ever seen in my life. From nowhere they came. I'd sooner have been chased by a pack of wolves. Howling and snarling they were too, and hurling whatever they could get their hands on at me.

There's one thing I'll say. Nobody really wants to catch a witch. I'd never have got clear else. I couldn't run fast. I wasn't the man I used to be.

But I knew where I was now, the moment she'd called out what I'd done. I'd come full circle. I was back in Morgan's country. I wasn't Teilo Smith any more, but I still had the marks of Teilo Smith branded on me. Morgan had seen to that. When I thought of all I'd suffered to get away from her and where I'd come to, I sat down and wept. I'd been a fool to think I could ever escape from her. If Arthur wouldn't have me, then Morgan must. I was finished now.

I knew what I had to do. I'd been fighting it two long years. I took out the woman's clothes I'd worn for Morgan and they felt heavy as lead as I laid them down on the ground. They weren't rotten and mildewed like my own leathers. Oh, no. The colours looked as fresh as when I'd stolen them. I dragged them on. I stood there then, holding that handful of smelly rags that had once been Teilo Smith. I thought of stuffing them back in my satchel. Just in case. But Morgan had put an end to that. Like she'd seen my beard would never grow again. I was a marked man for the rest of my life. There was only way I had left to hide my chin: under a woman's veil.

I've made sacrifices in a bog before. They're supposed to cost us. There wasn't ever an offering I made that tore the heart out of me as much as that one did. I never said a chant or made a sign. I just pushed the last of my smith's leather clothes down under the black swamp and watched the water creep back over.

I hadn't noticed just what part of the forest I was in, but I knew it didn't matter. I wasn't a bit surprised when I came out of the trees and found myself standing under the walls of Lyvennet again. Those red banks of stone and earth, the walls of her castle. The buildings looked a bit grander than the way I remembered it. She'd been busy up there.

Three years it had taken her. Three years since the first evening I'd stood here like a man, with my dog at my feet, looking up at her house. But she'd had her way.

I wondered if the guards would remember my dress, if they still had the same orders to let me through. It wouldn't matter. She didn't mean to keep me outside her door this time.

There was just one thing startled me when I stepped out of the wood. I suddenly saw that we'd turned from winter to spring. I hadn't expected that I'd come back to Morgan with violets and bluebells and primroses all up the path. That was a bitter joke.

# Chapter Nineteen

Things had changed more than a bit. I found a rare old bustle going on at Lyvennet. I told them at the gate I wanted to see the queen. I had a bit of difficulty when they asked what name they should tell her.

'Say . . . the Woman with the basket.' I kept my chin tucked well out of sight.

I was glad the gatemen were none of them that knew me. All the same I thought they peered a bit strangely under my hood. It might have been my fancy.

She kept me waiting a long time at the gate, so long that I started to wonder if she'd got my message. The whole dun was in an uproar. Urien's men were going about in a brisker way than I'd seen for a long time. Their gear was polished and they were walking smartly. They were handling their weapons as though they expected they'd be using them before long. There were more servants about than ever I'd seen. Pretty young women. And young warriors, too, casting an eye over Urien's horses and trappings as though they'd seen better. I began to think that Morgan must have visitors.

'What's to do?' I said at last. I didn't want to call attention to myself, but curiosity had got the better of me. 'Who are all these folk?'

'Where have you been, granny? Asleep with the fairies?' they joshed. 'Gwendoleu's called the kings of the north to a council. He's giving a big feast in Carlisle for them and their queens. There's some say he'll try and sweet-talk them into a war. King Lot's ridden down from Din Eidyn to get Urien's ear first.'

'Carlisle's going to take on the Saxons?'

They roared with laughter at that.

'Saxons? Gwendoleu? Not him! It's his own crown he's worried about, and it's a young Briton he fears could take the shine off it. It'll be Cymry and Cymry at each other's throats next, if he has his way. You can bet he won't let that upstart boy steal a march on him and get all the glory. If the lad did beat the Saxons, folk might cry him High King of all Britain.'

'Unless he gets a spear in his throat first,' winked the other.

'What boy would that be?' I croaked, just as if I hadn't felt the hard muscles of his leg under my hand and heard his breath come quick for impatience. I can see the shine in his eyes still, looking up over Nimue's lake to what was coming.

'Looks like the queen's got an answer for you at last,' the gatekeeper said suddenly. There was a young woman crossing the yard to us.

I was almost gone past fear after all that waiting. I just had a dread and a sort of numb hopelessness. Men, war, it couldn't ever be my business now. When the girl let me in, Morgan was not in the sunny-house. Only Luned. She recognised me, all right. She looked scared to see me again. I felt a bit better for that. At least there was somebody who still showed me respect. She didn't speak to me. She was busy packing silken ribbons into a box. But all the time her eyes were watching me. I turned my back on her and stood in front of last night's fire. I poked at the burnt logs with my boot. Somewhere there might be a spark of light left. Only the wood fell away into white ash. The fire in my smithy would be cold these two years now. Or would it? I didn't even know if another man had taken my place and kindled it.

Then the door burst open and the room was full of women. One taller than all the rest, with flaming hair, dressed all in green and gold. And Morgan herself, behind her. Beautiful, she looked, dressed in blue and silver. Radiant, somehow. I'd never thought she could look so young and happy. Then I saw why. She was a mother now. She had a fine boy toddling at her skirts and the loveliest little girl I'd ever seen, saving my Mair. So I'd been right. That huge belly giving her pains the day she cursed me – she'd borne Urien twins. And for all the harm she'd done to me, when I saw her like that, so bright and rosy and womanly, I couldn't help myself. Under that sagging gown my thing rose up to meet her.

Morgan started when she saw me. And that flock of pretty, giggling girls turned my way. Yes! Go on, smile again. Some of you older ones were there, weren't you?

I saw that flash in Morgan's eyes, and I knew that they hadn't warned her. It must have been Luned's doing to let me in.

She changed like a thunderstorm in April. Where she'd been laughing as merry as you please before, she was scowling now.

'So, Woman, you have come back at last! Has it taken you so long to learn my lesson? Put back your hood. White hair befits you. I am glad to see that the time has not been kind to you.'

She stroked her little son's head and took her daughter's hand as she said it. Time hadn't spoiled her. She was queen and the mother of a prince now.

That brought the blood to my face. It was all right for her! But I had been Teilo Smith, in the prime of manhood. Listening to her laughing at me I could feel the muscles withering on my bones. My man's pride, what there was left of it, shrivelled up and collapsed. Those girls tittered behind their hands. But not like Erith. Not so knowingly. There wasn't one of them had half her wisdom.

The red-haired woman spoke, and I knew her now for Morgan's tall sister, Queen Margawse, that had ridden beside her to her wedding in Carlisle.

'That's a sick fancy you have there, Morgan, to want a hag like that about you. She's worse than that stone-faced nun. Why, she almost has a beard! Are you so ugly that you need goblins like these to stand you comparison? Even your cat is scarred for life.'

'It pleases me to see them so marred. They are a sign. We are all hurt and unlovely in some parts. You will excuse us.'

She signed for me to follow her into her inner chamber. Only Luned came with us. It was a smaller room than the other one, and her marriage-bed took up most of it. That grey cat was curled up in the middle of the bedspread. Morgan lay down and stroked it and the sweat broke out on me under the veil. I wouldn't have stood so close as that to such a woman if I'd had the choice. She told me to kneel on the floor, so that I was lower than she was. She rested her eyes a long while on me before she spoke.

'Well, Woman.' She's never called me anything but that. I've never had a proper name from her. 'Have you indeed learned my lesson? What have you come to tell me?'

'My wife is murdered!'

I hadn't known I was going to say that. But it was the only thought I had just then. Seeing Morgan's face in front of me again like that, it was as if the two years I'd been away had disappeared and it was still the same black day she'd cursed me, in this very house. It still stung like a fresh burn. Erith? Annis? They were all one woman in my mind. I could hardly tell now which of them I'd killed.

I swear I didn't mean to keep anything back from her. Nimue. Merlyn. Arthur. I'd forgotten clean about them. Annis is dead. And I'm here dressed like a woman, in her place. That was the only thing I could think just then.

Morgan wasn't mocking now.

'*Erith* was murdered! And even that was not enough brutality for you! Did you need to kill your own wife as well? Why? Could you have supposed that would please me? Two women poisoned instead of one, and neither healed?'

'I!' I must have jumped up then and shouted out in a man's voice, because Luned ran to stop me. '*You* killed her! You cursed me, here in this very castle. You said you'd show me how a wise woman ought to work. And I found Annis bewitched to death!'

Morgan had sprung up on her bed and was kneeling facing me. There was a wild light in her eyes, almost as if she were frightened.

'I did not do that! How could you think it? Are you so cunning you would put your wickedness on me? Do you not know what they call me? I am Morgan the Healer. Why should I want to kill Annis, your wife?'

'Because she *was* my wife. Because I killed your waiting-woman. You had to show me you were stronger than me.'

'Hurt for hurt? Morgan the Wise to prove herself to *you*?'

'How else did she die? You cursed me!'

'I did not! I did not! I did not kill your wife!'

To my horror she started sobbing like a little girl. Luned went to comfort her and both those women looked at me as if they hated me.

'Tell him I did not, Luned! Tell him I did not do it.'

The woman drew her mouth down, very prim and severe.

'It was a stern curse you laid on him, for Erith's death.'

'You think that too? I . . . killed . . . Annis! No! Do not say that! How could my anger poison her without my will?'

'A great wise woman only needs to lift a finger. None of our circle left Cornwall. But Uther died. And you are greater than

Gwennol and all her circle ever were. Hate was enough.'

Morgan shuddered. She'd stopped weeping now. But she rolled over and buried her face and lay still as death. I could have fallen where I stood. I don't know which had shaken me most. That Morgan, for all she made herself out to be such a wise enchantress, hadn't seen till then which of us had killed poor Annis. Or that someone like her could do such a terrible thing without even meaning to. She had so much power in her that the ill wish was enough without even the name spoken or the hand pointed.

It was an uncomfortable time, standing there waiting. She got the better of herself in a bit.

'However that other happened, Erith is dead. And that was your doing. I have gathered many others now. But her place I have kept empty. Now you must fill it . . . Woman.'

I couldn't grasp quite what she meant. Or didn't want to.

'You need to make your circle. And you still haven't found enough of the higher grades to play the chief parts?'

She smiled cruelly then.

'I am Chief Lady now. Erith was our Maiden. Did you think you could play that role? No, that was not what I meant. If the rumours are right . . .' The colour was coming and going in her face now. 'If this boy who has raised his banner is who I think he may be . . . I am the daughter of Uther Pendragon's queen. That has brought me much hurt, and may do me more harm yet, if there are others who remember it too. I shall need a wise woman who can guard my back by day and lie in my room at night.'

It took a few moments for her words to sink in, and when they did, the hairs stood up on my neck.

'Erith was . . .?'

'You'd make *that* thing into your tiring woman!' said Luned.

'Erith is dead. What he has taken away he must restore. You took life but you did not give it. From henceforward you shall be the one who keeps off death. Two sides, Woman. That was my lesson.'

I was going cold and hot by turns. How long before I was discovered for what I was . . . what I had been? In her bedchamber! What if Urien . . .?

Morgan was enjoying herself now. She'd got herself and me reined in. Even the cat was purring.

'Kneel.'

She whispered to Luned. The woman fetched a bowl, a towel and a little ivory razor.

'I shall make you Woman, by my own hand.'

Well, I almost screamed at that. When she picked up that razor I had only one thought in my mind of what she was going to do with it. It was all I had. The only thing I'd got that still had manhood in it. She was going to cut it off.

There was more blood than there should have been. I was shivering so much I couldn't keep still and Luned had to hold me. But it was only my chin that Morgan shaved. Those last poor tufts of hair that would keep growing, where before I'd had a thick bush of beard. She has smooth white hands. She didn't mean to hurt me. But she did.

# Chapter Twenty

They gave me fresh linen to bind my face. I hadn't thought till then how shameful a thing it's reckoned to be a woman, and have to hide so much of yourself from the world.

That other queen, Margawse, she raised her red eyebrows and gave a teasing sort of laugh when Morgan came out of her room, with me trying to hide my stained wimple behind Luned's back.

'Your tiring-woman now, is it? You're surely not taking that thing to Gwendoleu's feast in Carlisle? Why, you will make the Pendragon's daughters the laughing-stock of Britain.'

'I am not Uther Pendragon's child!' Morgan flashed out at her. 'And nor are you. We are daughters of Gorlois of Cornwall, that Uther killed!'

'Still,' said Margawse, smoothing her fine green skirt. 'The Pendragon was a bonny king while he lived, and got a good husband for me. It was better to be on the winning side. So Mother reckoned.'

The colour flew to Morgan's cheeks at that and she breathed pretty fast. 'That false man is dead. There shall be no high king of his sort again to ride roughshod over Britain, grabbing what he wants.'

'They say that if Gwendoleu goes, your Urien could be king over Rheged and Solway joined. He might rule both sides of the Wall from sea to sea, as his forefather Coel did long ago.'

'Those that say that talk dangerously. Urien is little more than a boy yet.'

'It was no boy got these two on you,' smiled Margawse, patting little Owain on the head.

Morgan seized the bairn by the shoulders and made to pull him to her. But Margawse let him go and swung her feet up on to the couch. Morgan was left standing stiff as a she-wolf with her two cubs on either side of her, son and daughter.

'If I thought Urien would grow like Uther I would kill him now with my own hands.'

Margawse pealed with laughter. 'Morgan! Morgan! You never change. Who was it snatched our little brother Arthur? Who was it almost destroyed him in the sea? Who got herself imprisoned in a nunnery till the years had cooled her temper and the Pendragon was dead?'

'I . . . did . . . not . . . kill . . . Arthur.' She seemed to have trouble spitting the words out.

'He might as well have been dead. Our mother has not seen her only son these fourteen years. Well, it seems she may have her chance soon.'

'You think it possible? This Arthur they are talking of could be our brother?'

There was a sly sort of smile on Margawse's face. 'Elaine says he is.'

'Elaine! You have seen her? And she . . .?'

'Yes. I thought that would bring a spark to your eyes. Of the three of us, it is Elaine that has the seeing. Our little Arthur is a man and comes into the light at last. Oh, silly, headstrong Morgan! So all your anger was wasted and your punishment for nothing. Could you not have smiled and tricked and waited your chance, like me?'

'I do not trick!'

'And so you scared our dragonlet away into Merlyn's secret lair. Now he has come out full-grown and with a warband at his back. Well, never mind. I know how to deal with warriors!'

'What do you mean?'

'You know very well what I mean. I can see it in your face. Why not admit it? Poor Morgan. The mother of twins and still a virgin at heart!'

Morgan let go of her children and made to strike her. The red queen's maidens rushed in to shield her, but Margawse put up an arm, quite lazy, and turned the blow away.

'He would rather choose my death than yours, if he's the true son of Uther that bedded Ygerne the same night he widowed her.'

'He shall not fall to you! He shall not!'

'Then which of Gorlois's daughters do you think will make an end of him . . . Elaine?'

And Margawse laughed, as if that would be a great joke. Morgan was prowling the room, with her little girl Morfudd clinging on to her hand though she hardly noticed her.

'I knew he was still alive!'

'You? You said Merlyn was less to be trusted than any man living.'

'I trusted him to keep Arthur safe. Why else was the boy got by high magic? Not for Uther's lust, but for Merlyn's.'

'*Merlyn's?* For Mother!'

'Oh, it was not Ygerne's flesh he desired, but her blood. That old and powerful blood. A wise woman, of a true line of kings. That blood we share. Our mother Ygerne has given Arthur twice the power that Uther ever could.'

'And whoever raises Arthur rules Britain?'

'Unless *we* take that power.'

When Margawse had gone to bed Morgan sent all of her women away but Luned and me. It was worse than I'd dreaded. She put me in Erith's place, oh yes, in every way. Her body-servant. That's been my punishment. Woman, she calls me. I've had to serve her woman's body. Guard it, tend it, wash it, dress it. The time came soon enough when I could have wished she'd taken the knife to my parts after all. Instead of that, she's gelded me another way.

Damn you! I was born a man, with a man's hands, a man's desires. She makes me lift the clothes from her body, and each layer's warmer than the last. She makes me wash her skin and loosen her hair. And all the time she sits unmoved, as if it had been Erith's hands touching her flesh. I don't think she loves her own body, the way Margawse does. Cold as death my hands were that first night, and trembling. She never stirred when I touched her. I hadn't handled as many women as you might think. Only my wife, and what I did for the god. And that's not the same. Then I'd got strong drink inside me, and the drums were beating. I *was* the god. I wasn't for ordinary women.

At home, with the horns stripped off, I'd been a man again. Only then I'd dreamed too high. After Morgan's wedding, that day her green eyes looked straight into mine, I'd dreamed. I'd dance the god for the queen and be a full man for her too, whenever she wanted me, night or day. She's made me live with the corpse of that fancy, ever since.

When we'd finished, she laid herself on the bed, with her little grey cat curled close beside her. Luned and I drew the coverlet over her shoulders. We left her lying in that big bed.

I found out then where I had to sleep – stretched like a dog on the floor at the foot of the bed. I couldn't believe she meant it. I had cushions and blankets enough. It wasn't that. All night I could hear every breath Morgan drew. I could feel when she turned in her sleep. I could smell her. It's a scent like pine-forests, she has.

I couldn't sleep. I lay and shivered like the dog I felt. One thing I dreaded more than anything else: that Urien would come. I've had to endure it often enough since then. They put me outside the door while he's there, but it's not far enough I can't hear.

She spared me that, the first time. The night she heard that Arthur was alive, she slept alone.

# Chapter Twenty-one

Next morning I found myself huddled in a wagon with Luned, guarding Morgan's baggage on the road to Carlisle. You can imagine how that felt, trundling through the gates of Gwendoleu's town with all the crowd staring as we went by, where last time I'd been down there in the street on my own feet and I'd been the one staring at the fine folk riding past me.

When it came to the feast I crouched in the darkest corner of Gwendoleu's hall, trying to hide my woman's gown from the real men. I wasn't sorry then to be at a low table. I kept my head bent over my platter and tucked in my shaved chin, for all that I'd wrapped it up in linen. How long could I go on living like this? An old woman with a razor in her pocket. Frightened every hour of coming face to face with somebody who had known Teilo Smith. And there were plenty of them. Woman? She'd put that name on me. But it was the real women I was most afraid of.

I could hardly eat at that feast. I dreaded the night again.

Gwendoleu was hammering on the high table.

'Emrys! Where is Emrys Silver-Tongue? By God, he's been missing from my table once too often! What dog of a bard is it that's not here to sing when I feast the kings and queens of the North? I'll have his throat when I see him!'

I started at that name, and looked round sharp. I'd clean forgotten Merlyn had been Gwendoleu's bard. But he wasn't there. How could he be, with Morgan in the hall?

Margawse beckoned to her own bard, who jumped forward pretty smartly. Well, who wouldn't? There'd be rich pickings at a great feast like that for a poet who knew how to turn a compliment to kings and queens. It wasn't every day he'd get such a chance. This one was a ladies' man. He strolled that hall, peering into all the queens' faces and praising the beauty that he saw and the fine sons they'd given their lords, or would do soon. And many's the buckle and jewel they tossed him for it. It didn't do much for Gwendoleu's temper, though. He had no sons. And no queen either. She'd died in childbed. So he looked pretty darkly at those that had. He knew what folk were saying about young Urien.

But I couldn't be bothered with kings and queens just then. I had that other name to wrestle with. Emrys Silver-Tongue. Like a shadow in the street the day of Morgan's wedding. I wept then, and didn't care who saw me. The greatest enchanter this land has ever known. Soul-friend to Uther Pendragon in the old days, and young Arthur now.

If only I'd met him just half-an-hour earlier. If only I hadn't lost my head when I saw that witch Morgan. If only I hadn't sent my power out to catch hers. I could have been Arthur's man now, instead of Morgan's woman. Smith to a greater king than Urien, maybe. Only by the time I saw Arthur I wasn't Smith. The lad hadn't recognised what I was. He'd shouted me out of his path. I couldn't mend the past, though I've groaned for what I've lost every night since. It had hung on such a small thing either way, like a sword balanced on an anvil. Just a few heartbeats. And I'd tumbled off on Morgan's side, with the women.

Gwendoleu was thumping the table. 'No more women's songs. Can you not sing of war, man? Are all the bards in Britain gone soft? Is that why there's no red blood in our kings' veins these days? Get Emrys Silver-Tongue!'

One of his men came up and muttered in his ear.

'What's that you say? Silver-Tongue's gone off to join that whelp? How dare he leave my court without permission! That braggart boy Arthur, that thinks he's somebody because he's wet his new sword on a handful of Saxons? And Emrys bids me join them! I'll string that druid's harp with his own guts!'

Morgan was on her feet and was holding her throat.

'Emrys . . . What druid? You called him Silver-Tongue. But . . . Emrys *who*? Is that why I have never heard your bard play at any feast where I have been these past three years? No, he would not risk that! Emrys and Arthur. All this time so close to me. Emrys Merlyn!'

There was a noise ran round the hall at that.

'Merlyn?'

'That druid that stole the Pendragon's son?'

'He was here!'

The messenger nodded. Gwendoleu looked so startled he couldn't speak for a bit. Then he crashed his fist down on the table.

'Imposter! False to one king before, and now to me. He calls the Men of the North to follow Arthur? To take our oath to his puppy? I'll see that chief dead who raises his sword to another banner than mine of Solway! Where's Urien of Rheged gone? Has that wee snake snapped out of his egg too to take the red dragon's side?'

He glared down the table. I think he could hardly see for drink. But Urien was a brave lad, I'll say that for him. He rose in his place and gave Gwendoleu back look for look. Men had their hands on their knives. I think most of the kings hardly knew which side to take.

Our chieftain spoke up like a man. 'Urien of Rheged is here, and loyal kinsman to Gwendoleu. There is no quarrel I know of between Lyvennet and Carlisle.'

'So who is this cub that Merlyn Silver-Tongue leaves my board for? What father does this upstart Arthur boast?'

'Sir,' says the man, 'we've heard only that Merlyn has fostered him these fourteen years. Folk are saying . . . he was fairy-got.'

'Hell's balls! Damnation to you if you take me for an idiot!'

He spoke like a plain, blunt man that doesn't believe in the old ways. But he didn't fool me. Gwendoleu practised more than a bit of magic himself. He had reason to fear it more than most.

Bishop Curran was having a word to steady him. That wouldn't cool his temper. Gwendoleu never had much time for the Church. That was more Urien's style.

Margawse's husband, King Lot, leaned over to have a word in his ear. He was a black-browed man, with a twisted sort of smile. Well, if Gwendoleu had been angry before he was madder now. He let out a screech that had brave men backing off from him. There was no telling which one he might hurl his goblet at.

'The Pendragon's lost son was named Arthur? And now here's an Arthur come, and Merlyn calls the kings of Britain to follow him! Is that what you're saying? Another Pendragon?'

Well, you can guess who he was looking so venomous at, when he said that. Margawse, Lot's wife. She was step-daughter to the old Pendragon, wasn't she? Arthur's half-sister. And then at Morgan too.

'You nest of vipers! You litter of weasels! Have you false women been plotting this all these years behind my back? Did you come here to Carlisle to mock me? You'd like to strip Gwendoleu's power from him and give it to your little brother, wouldn't you? Yes, you'll call your husbands to join Arthur's pack! There'll be rich pickings for the whole family.'

He was coming across the dais to them, none too steady. Lot was on his feet, and Urien too, and it was more than daggers their warriors were reaching for now.

It was the bishop that got in his path and stopped him. Old Curran. I didn't think he had it in him. I'd got him down for a place-server that would mind where his meat came from and who feathered his nest. He got Gwendoleu by the arm, though, and talked soft to him.

'Peace, your majesty, in the name of Christ. Would you dishonour your own hall? These ladies are queens and guests.'

'Queens and witches! Get out!'

Those two gathered up their skirts and swept out of the hall. Margawse laughed at him as she went and picked up a plate of fowl and cakes and carried it off with her. She was bold, that one.

We had to follow, their husbands and all the rest of us. But at the door of the ladies' bower the men went another way from me. I had to pull myself up short not to go on with them.

Margawse settled herself on the cushions while Morgan paced up and down the room. She's fuller than Morgan. Softer-fleshed. She had four big sons already, and daughters too. Both those queens have green eyes, but they're not the same. Morgan's can be like winter ice. But Margawse's are warm and inviting. They tell you it's open house with her. She was licking chicken grease off her fingers.

'So! Merlyn was here in Carlisle these last three years, and you never knew it!'

'I sensed treachery. I could not put a name to what I knew. *You!*'

She whipped round sudden on me. I nearly fainted when I saw what was in her eyes. I just cowered in the corner. She'd have the truth out of me now. I should have told her sooner.

But Margawse hadn't finished.

'What if our little brother can beat the Saxons? What if he does indeed free Britain from the foreigners? What will our husbands do? Is Gwendoleu right? Will they cry Arthur high king over all the Britons?'

Morgan's black hair looked like striking snakes, she whirled about so fast.

'Merlyn must not succeed! There shall not be another Uther in the land!'

'What then? Gorlois's three daughters, to bring his little princeling down? Or do you plan to keep all the fun to yourself?'

She leaned back against the cushions and broke out laughing. A sort of slow, lazy laughter, like a cuckoo in May. She's the only one I've ever met who dares to laugh at Morgan.

'Yes! I can see it in your face. Morgan's power matched against Merlyn's. Spells. Potions. And for what? Not to raise your husband Urien over my Lot and Elaine's Nentres? No. For Morgan's pride. You want the bards to sing you the greatest enchantress of all, even though they may blacken your name and gild the fame of poor dead Arthur afterwards. Oh, Morgan, Morgan! Will you never learn? Did you get nothing but magic from our mother? There are more ways than one of killing a cat. Leave the spells to Merlyn and the blades to Arthur. I tell you again, our power is *here*.'

Margawse stroked her own body. Her hands caressed her gown round her breasts and thighs. I just had to crouch in my corner and moan to myself. She stretched herself out on the cushions and her eyes sparkled.

'What do you say, Morgan? A Saxon sword may save us the task in the next battle. But say it does not? Say they spit the little cub back at us. What then? A contest? Your power against mine to see which of us can bring Arthur down?'

'If I had been born a boy! Gorlois's son. Arthur would not have been needed then. I should have shown Uther's kind what kingship means.'

'But you are not. And Gorlois was not a king. Be what you are, a woman. Do not despise it. Remember Mother. Was it Merlyn's power that brought Uther to Tintagel? Or was it Ygerne's? You should ask Elaine. She was there in the woods helping Mother make the charm that got our brother. And where were you?'

Her laughter filled the room. She had no shame. For herself, or for her mother.

This time Morgan hit her full across the face, before anybody could stop her.

'Ygerne is Arthur's mother! Not mine, since the night she lay with Father's murderer! You know where I was the day she cast the spell. I was hunting with Father. That was the last time we rode together.'

She broke out sobbing. That was a terrible thing to me, to see Morgan in tears, as it might have been my own daughter. I don't know how it was, but it frightened me more than when she was angry. It was as if the world rocked off balance.

Margawse had jumped up quick. There was a great red mark across her face. But she watched her sister crying and just straightened her skirt and smiled.

'You see? You rode with the warriors, but the men couldn't save him. This must be women's work.'

She drew out something from under the cushion.

'I found this in your chest in Lyvennet.'

It was a bronze mirror, rare enough to make me gasp. There were chased settings for red enamel and a fine workmanship of serpents on its handle.

'The Christmas Arthur was born, Merlyn made me the gift of such a mirror. Did he give this to you?'

Morgan barely nodded.

'But it is dented. You have not cared for it well.'

'I want no gift from him.'

Margawse admired herself in the mirror.

'My face looks crooked in it, but I can still tell I am beautiful. So are you, Morgan. Look at yourself! Use what you are!'

'Never! I will not be like you!'

Morgan snatched the mirror off her sister and flung it clear through the window. There was a clang as it hit the paving outside. That hurt me as if it had been my own bones breaking, to treat good workmanship like that. Margawse shrugged and smiled and led her ladies off to bed.

Afterwards I went and fetched that mirror. It was too valuable to be left lying there. But I cried out when I picked it up. It had been dented before, but it was broken now. There were bits of red enamel scattered all over the stones. The polished side had cracked in half a dozen places. You couldn't have found your true self in it any more.

And still I hadn't told her what I knew.

# Chapter Twenty-two

I hadn't fooled her. Morgan got it out of me when Margawse had gone. Every last bit of it. Nimue's house. Merlyn. How they'd schooled Arthur. What I'd told Nimue. What I hadn't told her . . . which wasn't much. Right down to the morning Arthur got his sword. You can be sure she made me tell her every last detail of that. I can see her now, leaning forward with her eyes huge in the candlelight. A magic sword that could beat every enemy he fought. A scabbard that would heal every wound he got.

'So, no man can bring him down. But Nimue has netted Merlyn in her lake.'

She was mighty quiet after that, as if she'd gone deep inside herself. But she wasn't tired. Her face was as bright as if she'd never need to sleep again. It was a long while before she started questioning me again.

She bled me like a leech. It was going on dawn before she'd finished with me.

Next morning the men held their council. But I wouldn't have been allowed in there, even if I had been wearing breeches. That was for the kings and such. Should they join Arthur's banner or shouldn't they? Council! We could hear them yelling at each other right across the yard. When I used to take council with the wise about our own business it had been done grave and seemly, I saw to that. But these lords seem to think he has the best right who can shout loudest and hit hardest. They're bred for war. Even among their own kin there's fighting to see which of them will come out on top. Gwendoleu and Lot had plenty to say by the sound of it. Sometimes the shouting would go a bit quiet and Margawse would look at Morgan with her sly grin. Maybe that was young Urien piping up to say what he thought, but then, maybe it could have been the bishop too. They were all in it.

The two queens took themselves off for a walk round the red walls of Carlisle. We followed after them. Morgan had seen to it I had a sharp knife in my belt. She didn't trust Gwendoleu. There were guards following too. But those sisters wouldn't let any of us so close we could overhear what they were saying with their heads together. It was a bright morning. I remember the water round the town throwing a sort of silver light up into the sky. And Morgan still had a brightness about her too and a spring in her step, for all she'd hardly slept a wink that night.

We hadn't got halfway round before we could see there was a commotion in the street and a whole troop more were riding up to the gate. Margawse grabbed hold of her sister's arm.

'It's Elaine! And Nentres. Back from the south!'

Queens or no, the two of them were practically running back to the palace. The kings came crowding out of the hall to welcome Nentres, and there was a fresh lot of horsemen to set the grooms scurrying and the steward shouting for food and beds. The rest of our young men hauled themselves up smartly and looked down their noses at the newcomers. You could see they'd travelled far and were too dirty and tired to show themselves off as they'd have liked. Yes, and the women were not much better. They took the cloaks off Elaine's maids as if they didn't want to spoil their own dresses with the dust.

I hardly got a look at King Nentres before he was gone with the men. But I had plenty of time to study Queen Elaine. She didn't jump down quick out of her chariot like her sisters would. She was fat, and that's not a thing you often see in highborn ladies. I don't mean curved, like Margawse, so you could dream of putting your arm round her and squeezing soft flesh. No, more like a spider. A big sack of a body a man wouldn't want to touch, let alone squeeze. And where Margawse's face was smooth, and dolled up with creams and paints, Elaine's was sagging into wrinkles, though she wasn't much more than a year older. I'd rather not know what she'd seen or done to age her so. I'd been frightened of Morgan from the start, and I had enough sense to see I'd need to step carefully with Margawse. But right from that first sight I had an idea that Elaine might be the most dangerous of the three.

After that we couldn't hear what was going on in the council hall, there was so much fussing among the women over Elaine. The sisters were peeling off her cloak and hood, and sending for food and wine and water to wash her. I brought the bowl and unlaced her shoes. As I washed the dust away with my big, cracked hands I could feel her watching me. I looked up and met her eyes. Not green, like her sisters'. Grey. That should have been cool and quiet, not so unsettling. But they were wise. And you know there's a world of peril in that word. She didn't say anything to me. She didn't need to. I saw she knew more of my secrets than I'd even told Morgan.

She'd brought her daughter with her. That was a solemn child. She stood behind her mother's chair and never spoke once, but sucked her thumb and watched us all. Morgan and Margawse started to interrupt each other telling how Arthur had won his first scrap against the Saxons. How Merlyn had thrown off his disguise and come out into the open and how nobody had suspected he'd been here all the time. How their kings were in council now arguing over it. Should they throw in their lot with Arthur and help him to glory over the Saxons? Or should they turn their own spears against him before he got too great?

But Elaine had brought news of her own. 'The kings of the south will join his banner.'

'Not Mark of Tintagel?'

'Mark, no. Our cousin keeps to Cornwall. But Cador the Duke, and Geraint and many others. They will march east on Lindsey soon.'

'So far into the enemy's land? Following a child of fourteen?' Morgan put her hand to her throat as though something was choking her.

'We were not children at fourteen. Do not imagine he is.'

'The kings of the south have more to fear than our lords. It is their soft cornlands the Saxons covet.' That was Margawse. You could tell she'd be sorry if Lot didn't go to war.

'But why would they trust a boy, whose sword is hardly baptised, to lead them?'

Elaine pulled off her gloves and handed them to her maid, so all the rings on her fat fingers flashed. 'You forget, this boy is Uther Pendragon's son. Do you recall the morning we first set our eyes on that man? First he struck the blow that killed our father. By night he charmed his way into our mother's bed. Next morning he stood on the hillside opposite Tintagel and laughed as she came over the causeway to be his queen, with Arthur already in her belly. Yet before an hour was out, I was laughing with him too, and so were you, Margawse, even with the tears for Father still wet on our cheeks. They say this boy has the glamour to be another Pendragon.'

'I did not laugh,' said Morgan, very low and fierce.

'No, you did not . . .' Elaine looked at her, thoughtful. 'But if the magic of his smile is not enough, Arthur has other sorcery his father used. It was Merlyn who bewitched Uther and himself and Ulfin, past Tintagel's nuns.'

'He shall not bewitch me.'

'I hear that Arthur does not know that story.'

'That sets our husbands a pretty problem!' Margawse laughed. 'Shall they tell the world that Arthur is the Pendragon's son and claim we are his sisters? Or would that strengthen his cause?'

Morgan hit her fist against her palm. 'Why would Merlyn keep such a secret? Why does he not shout Arthur's blood from the ramparts?'

Luned spoke then. That startled me. She wasn't one to raise her voice. 'Merlyn did not win every round, madam. Uther died by cunning, like his brother, great Ambrosius, before him. Both of them poisoned by witchcraft in their beds, not dying valiantly on the battlefield. We saw to that.'

Margawse gave a little giggle after a bit. 'You mean, maybe he thinks the male line he chose has an unlucky sound? Perhaps he fears to put a shadow into our little Arthur's mind.'

'And other people's.'

'Better a boy from nowhere, until victory is sure. An elfin prince, wielding his magic sword Caliburn. Undefeatable.'

Well, they looked at Morgan queerly when she said that.

'Tell them, Woman.'

So she made me go over it all again. I'd rather she'd done the talking herself. Those queens questioned me mightily about sword and scabbard, you can be sure. Elaine kept her eyes on me for an uncomfortable long while after I'd done. I don't think she trusted which side I was on.

Margawse burst out laughing. 'We could tell them the truth, couldn't we, Elaine? We were there, at Tintagel when he was got. We were there in Bossiney the night Arthur was born. We were there at the feast in London when Uther fell in love with Mother. His Easter crown-wearing, after he'd risen to glory driving the Saxons out of York.'

'Uther did not! He did not!' cried Morgan. 'How could you misremember? Has Merlyn bewitched you too? It was Father's courage that saved York. Without him, Uther Pendragon would have been killed shamefully, like a badger in his hole.'

'And if Uther had died before he saw Ygerne, he would not have killed Father. And Arthur would never have been born,' said Elaine. 'A curious deliverance.'

They were all three pretty quiet at that, looking at each other and drumming their fine jewelled fingers. Elaine has a shrouded sort of face. I couldn't tell what she was thinking. Margawse was hot with excitement. She wanted this war. Her sort don't care what side their lord's on or if he falls or not, so long as it makes their blood run faster. There'll always be another man somewhere. Morgan, though, her face was pale and her eyes dark and staring – that surprised me. Urien was getting to be a fine young chief, but I hadn't thought she was as much in love with him as all that, to mind that he might be going into danger.

Well, horses gallop faster than men can talk. Before our kings had made up their minds what to do, Arthur was outside the walls of Lincoln. Then we got word that Cheldric the German had landed with his fleet and was on his way to raise the siege. The Men of the North wouldn't help Arthur then. They thought his luck was finished. We heard how some Saxon chief had disguised himself as a harper with one half of his face shaved and the other hairy, to make folk laugh, and had danced his way past Arthur's nose till his mates inside hauled him up the walls with the good news that help was coming. Lot and Nentres cheered over their wine-cups. That was one in the eye for that guiser Merlyn, you could see them thinking. Only I saw Urien eyeing the weapons hung on the walls. Poor lad. He'd never fought a proper battle. He'd his name to win yet. I could see he'd have dearly loved to have ridden to Arthur's aid then, only Gwendoleu said no.

Those British lads had to fall back from Lindsey. Morgan started singing the day she heard the news, as happy as a skylark. But tides turn. Arthur caught Cheldric and his Germans in a wood. He hadn't men enough of his own to pen them in. They say Merlyn charmed the trees to help them. His warriors chopped them down till they'd made a wall so thick the Saxons couldn't climb out. They had to buy their lives. It was Arthur's first war. He was scarcely fifteen years old yet, but he set a stern price. Those Saxons had to hand over everything they'd got with them. Gold, silver, weapons, armour, even the clothes off their backs. I've heard he drove them naked into their boats and sent them off across the cold sea to find their way home and never come back to Britain. I wish I'd been there to see it. But he kept hostages, youngsters from noble families, to see they kept their word. He wasn't green.

Well, our queens and their husbands had to move now, one way or the other. Arthur was riding back to the City of the Legions. He was a hero. We harnessed our horses and set out south to meet him. Would that family tag on to his cloak-end, now that he'd proved himself? Or would they cut him down for bragging himself too big? They were still arguing the toss amongst themselves. But they'd got the women with them, so it looked like peace.

When we got close we started to hear the stories.

Arthur was a Christian warlord with an open hand. He'd rescued the churches from the heathen and given a great pile of treasure to every man who fought for him, till he'd none left for himself.

Arthur was a fairy's child, come to save old Britain, and then he'd vanish under the hill till he was needed again.

Arthur was a devil's child, who raped women and stole what he wanted for his wars.

Our kings wouldn't humble themselves to go to his fort straight off. And anyway, it was the women of that family who had the true power. They decided one of those queens should go for them to see how the land lay.

Morgan and Margawse were on their feet at the same time. Elaine never stirred.

'Oh, let me! Let me! I shall die if I don't see him soon!'

You can be sure that redheaded one was keen to do it. Morgan hardly got out more than a whisper.

'I will go.'

But Margawse was the elder, and her husband was a bigger king than Urien in those days. She got her way.

You could see she couldn't wait to set her eyes on Arthur. She dressed herself in her finest green gown, with a yellow and purple mantle round her shoulders. She picked out a fine skewbald horse, white and red, and had a rich saddle put on it. She took her four growing sons behind her for squires, with little spears in their hands. With her red hair strung with jewels and her flesh sweet with perfumes and oils she looked like a fairy herself, riding off to Arthur's feast at the City of the Legions.

Morgan was in a foul temper, like a cat with fleas. She boxed Luned's ears and she cut me to the bone with cruel words for what I had been once and wasn't now. There was a goblin in her and it grew worse as the day went on.

When Margawse's troop was just a cloud of dust on the road, she swung round and hissed at me. 'Go after her! Watch everything she does, and bring word to me of what passes between her and Arthur. Miss nothing.'

Once Merlyn had driven me to Morgan like that. Watch her! See what she does and bring me word. Now Morgan was sending me back to spy on him. I was nothing but a piece of jetsam to them, tossed backwards and forwards between his wind and her tide. I'd find no safe landing-place in that storm.

I had no choice. I got a mule. I was scared, all right. I never wanted to see Merlyn again. I muffled myself in cloak and hood though it was blazing harvest-time. Lugh's feast. I must have looked an ugly shadow following behind those pretty laughing women in their bright dresses.

# Chapter Twenty-three

If I'd felt low before, dressed like a woman, I felt worse still when I saw where I'd come. The whole town of Caerleon was an armed camp. Arthur was no king. He hadn't got a proper palace anywhere yet. Soldiers called out as we passed. You'd think they'd never seen a woman before. You might not believe it, but I felt hotter at some of the things they shouted than those ladies in front of me seemed to. I squeezed up tight to the tail of their procession and got myself passed in through the gate with them. If Margawse saw I was there she didn't try to stop me.

It was one of those summer evenings when it seems as if the day never wants to go to bed. The sun had gone down but it was still light outside. There was a smell of horses and leather, and we had to push our way through a fair old crowd of soldiers to get to Arthur's hall. All of them grinning at Margawse and her troop.

He'd set himself up in one of the Roman fortresses. City of the Legions. He always liked that, did Arthur. The Roman uniform, and the badges, and the toga at night. Latin names: Arcturus, Imperator. Only he was never a Roman really, not underneath. Merlyn and Nimue had seen to that.

It wasn't his palace, but he'd made himself pretty much at home there. He'd set up his headquarters in one of their great stone buildings. The weeds had hardly started to pull it apart yet. Inside the hall there were lights beginning to sparkle and the smell of good roast meat to make you hungry. I could hear men laughing loud, sounding a bit drunk already, though it was early yet. They had music, and not just the one harper by the noise. There was a new name for the bards to praise now, and from all we'd heard Arthur was a generous leader. He'd give gold as fast as he got it, if he was in a good humour. Well, a warlord can, can't he? When his storehouse is empty his men take more from those who can't say no to them.

Still, it was their victory celebration. I couldn't grudge it to them. I'd have been the same. Well, I'd thought Gwendoleu's feast in Carlisle was a noisy affair. But the goings-on in Arthur's hall made that seem like Christian Lent! There was a great roar came out to greet us. Even Margawse checked for a moment.

I could see past her into the lamplight. Men. There's a short word to hurt so much. I recognised more than a few of them from Nimue's house. They'd been boys when I'd watched them ride off, but they were men all right now. Young men. Fighting men. And wild with victory over other men. Arthur was a big general now. He'd got warbands flocking to him. Older men, too. I saw the tales were true. They'd kept some Saxons with them. There was a row of strangers down one side of the hall. Yellow hair in plaits. Sick faces. They were the only ones that weren't stamping and cheering. Those had to be the hostages. Saxons? Those monsters with bloody axes I'd had nightmares about? This lot were just human beings, like you and me. They weren't very old, but then nor were most of them in that hall. Arthur's lads had got their manhood taking those hostages.

And what had I sunk to? Worse than when I'd known them before. A dragging dress, with the hem fouled by the dung of their horses. A white-haired head I hardly dared to lift, wrapped up in linen under my drooping hood. Woman!

I'd been Smith. Good smith's leathers, I'd had. With my own hands I'd sunk them in the bog. If only I'd been wearing them the day I met Arthur. If he could have felt the strength of my shoulder muscles, seen me swing a hammer. As fine a craftsman as ever struck spark from iron. The best. I'd had power in my hands. And what had these hands done to bring me so low? It still makes my insides curl every time I think of it. Fool. Fool! It was my own life I cut short when I grabbed that girl. It was Morgan made me do it!

Still, there was one thing those men didn't have, or not enough of it. Women. There were two girls, one with skin as black as peat, dancing in front of Arthur's table. Beads round their foreheads and hips and ankles, and not a lot else. That was making the men yell and stamp. There were serving-maids, but hardly a lady sitting at table. So it was nothing to the cheer that went up when Margawse swept into the hall. Well, who wouldn't cheer? She had her cloak thrown back from her white shoulders and her red hair falling free, and all her women behind her. These ladies smiled merrily, but I could see they were eyeing those warriors to tell how drunk they might be.

I wasn't a true woman, but I was more coward than those who were. I told myself those fighting-men would hardly cheer at the sight of me. I had to slink after the ladies all the same. Morgan had sent me to do it. I must have looked a queer sort of figure, creeping behind them like that.

I never reached the door. A hand gripped my wrist from behind, tight as an owl on a shrew. It turned me to the last light from the sunset. I was eye to eye with Merlyn. I don't know which of us got the bigger shock. He'd been suspicious, but I wasn't what he'd expected, I could see that. There was fear in both our faces, right enough, catching sight of each other like that. He knew me this time, no doubt about that. Merlyn could see keen as a hawk when he was clear of his little enchantress. He realised too late he should have known me before.

'It was *you*! White-Chin, the holy man!'

Two could play at that game. 'Emrys Silver-Tongue? Gwendoleu's bard, is it? In Arthur's camp?'

'Use your wits, man. Merlyn takes many shapes, and good reason for them. If I fooled Gwendoleu it was for Britain's advantage. But you have worse to answer for. I knew Morgan was too close for safety, but I did not suspect she would place you in Nimue's house to spy. How long were you there?'

'A year, near enough. But I wasn't her spy. Never! I was running from her as hard as I could go.'

He peered into my face, closer than I could bear to meet him. I think he was more puzzled than angry.

'Yes. I know why your smithy was empty. I might have fled to the forest myself if she had done that to me. But a year? At the heart of our secret. And Arthur survived.'

'Damn you and Morgan! I didn't want anything to do with either of you.'

'No? Whatever the truth, I am inclined to believe you think that true. Yet what you want is not what is. You were always marked for Morgan. Still, Arthur did live to take his sword, and now he is riding the road to victory. Two rounds so far to us. Who takes the third? You come from Morgan's camp tonight. You followed her here, even into the heart of Arthur's army.'

I nodded. I'd taken Morgan's service now. That's what he'd pressed me to do three years ago. Though there hadn't been a thought about Merlyn in my head when Morgan shaved me. But that wasn't exactly what he meant, saying it was Morgan I'd followed here. It wasn't her inside the hall. Wise though he was, he could still be fooled by a woman.

Merlyn had come late to the feast, keeping his own time as usual. The moment he'd guessed what was afoot he'd kept his back to the door so he couldn't see what I did: red Margawse, with the candles flaming on her hair as she bent her knee to Arthur. She could do that very prettily. It was half mocking to make them both smile, and half as if she was offering herself to him as a sort of tribute. The Queen of Lothian, come to do him honour. And Arthur was laughing and raising her to her feet. Leading her round to the high table. Sitting her down beside him, making everyone else move out of her way. Raising his drinking-horn to her. Not Morgan. Why should I tell Merlyn that? What had he ever done to help me?

Quick as a flash Merlyn called to one of his stewards. In his own way he was as much of a general as Arthur, though it was different weapons he feared. He still had his own face hidden from the hall.

'See the Pendragon eats and drinks nothing that hasn't been tasted. Warn Cei and Bedwyr to be on their guard. Tell them to have every one of the queen's women watched. Trust none of them.'

He let go of my arm. I rubbed the place a bit. He was strong, was Merlyn, even if he did often go dressed like a poet or a fool.

He grinned a bit at that. 'I'm sorry. But I do not take chances, with false women or real ones. Morgan was once a vicious child. I doubt that a girlhood penned up in Tintagel nunnery has mellowed her. And it seems she has learned as much of magic there as of Christian saintliness. But she is long past a child now. Once she might have struck Arthur down with her knife before all his warband, and never mind if she died for it afterwards herself. Now I fear she has grown more subtle. Even so, I wonder why she has humbled herself to pay Arthur court. Morgan was always proud. I do not like it.'

You could see he felt there was something here he hadn't put his finger on. There was a deal of questions he still needed answering. After all these years he didn't want to tangle with Morgan — for Morgan he thought it was in there — till he'd found out from me how the wind blew. And it was a cold thought to me that even a great man like him was afraid of her. He hadn't saved me from those three queens and I was sure he couldn't now. I was Morgan's creature. So why should I tell him it wasn't Morgan there in the hall? He was a wise man, wasn't he, and a lot more than that? And I'd had my wisdom stolen away from me, that day he got me by the wrist. Let him find the truth out for himself, if he was so clever.

Instead I said, 'Court, is it? That's mighty quick. I hadn't heard that they'd cried him a king yet.'

He didn't like that.

'All the island of Britain shall be his kingdom before I've done. Arthur will prove himself emperor by deed as well as blood. When the kings gather, I shall proclaim the lad Ambrosius's nephew. Pendragon's son. His mother Ygerne was of the old royal house of the West. He has the true blood in his veins. And enough Saxon blood on his spear already to prove his right to any diadem. We'll clear the north of Picts and Scots next, all the barbarians who helped the enemy. There'll be a harvest of heads rolling in the heather. We'll take no hostages there. The Church will crown him. Next summer will see him High King over all the Britons.'

'That'll be nice for you. Uther Pendragon's magician. Then sunk to Gwendoleu's minstrel. You'd be coming back up in the world as soul-friend to King Arthur of all Britain, wouldn't you? But where does that leave me? I was Teilo Smith. King in our craft. I had power. Till the black day I set eyes on you and Morgan of Cornwall. *Look* at me!'

Well, there was some pity in his eyes, but a sort of smugness with it, so I could have hit him.

'Too much power, Teilo. And still you aimed higher. It has broken stronger men than you.'

'Not Emrys Merlyn?'

'I never lost my power. I hid it for a season. No one takes it away from me.'

Oh no? I thought. Not even pretty Nimue, wheedling secrets out of both of us, while she's making a man out of Arthur and women out of us? I didn't say that, but he must have seen the look in my eyes. He shook his head.

'Man, I can see Morgan's made you suffer!'

Well, for the sake of that one word he called me, I gave up arguing and let him lead me off to a private room. He filled me with meat and ale while he questioned me about Morgan. We were there a long while. The daylight went and the stars came out and we could hear plenty of shouting and dancing from the hall. I hadn't talked man to man like that since Morgan took me in. He got far more out of me than

I did from him. I was Morgan's servant. He saw I wasn't strong enough to be trusted.

We'd shared more than a jug or two when there was a sudden knocking at the door. His steward was there.

'Sir! Sir! I think you should come. It's Arthur, sir. He's been a long time out of the hall, with the red-haired queen. We thought no harm, after the victory. We could hardly stop him. The young lords have been so long without the company of their own sort of ladies. All her women seemed in such a pleasant humour, and Lord Bedwyr just laughs and won't let me knock at the chamber door . . .'

'The chamber door? With whom? *What* red-haired queen?' Merlyn flung round on me. 'Who has come here tonight? You told me it was Black Morgan!'

'I said nothing of the sort. It was you who said that.'

'*Not* Morgan? Then who . . .' His face went white. He'd known that family too long not to see what it meant. 'Not *Margawse*?'

I nodded. I enjoyed that. It did me good to see him dumbfounded for once.

'Oh, by all the gods! This is a black day's work you've to answer for.' He buried his face in his hands. 'Tell me the worst. How long have those two been gone?'

The steward was stuttering. 'An . . . an hour, maybe. But the queen left her knife on the table and we tasted their wine. Lord Bedwyr is standing guard at the door. Wouldn't he have heard if there'd been any treachery?'

'Heard? Yes, and laughed to hear it, as I once laughed outside another bedchamber in Tintagel!'

Merlyn tore his hair and rushed out of the room.

The hall had gone quiet. The dancing was finished. Those boy-hostages had vanished. They'd be locked up safe somewhere for the night. There were drunk men sprawled over the tables in a mess of crumbs and beer. Half Margawse's women were still leaning on them, with their arms twined round their necks. Some were rolling in the straw with those who were still half-awake. A few more were sat whispering together in a corner. Margawse's sons were sleeping like babies. Even that sharp-eyed Cei was snoring, with his head on his arms. Merlyn rushed past them, knocking over tables as he ran, and out through a door at the back. I couldn't hear what he cursed at Bedwyr before he broke open the chamber door.

'What's all the fuss about?' the steward asked. 'A sweet lady like that, when the lad's won a great victory? Where's the harm in it? I wish I was a general and set to be emperor, I don't mind telling you, if that's the way all the queens come to pay their war-taxes!'

It had been a long time since I'd found anything to laugh about.

'What's the harm? Well, here's the joke. That queen's his sister! Do you think the Church is going to crown him High King now? Let's see if Merlyn can keep this secret for another fourteen years!'

# Chapter Twenty-four

I'd gone to the City of the Legions as Morgan's spy, but it didn't need me to tell her the news. Margawse couldn't wait to do it herself. She came back rosy as a girl, and skipping like a lamb in spring, for all she was the mother of four sons and a powerful queen. It was the women's tents she went to first. She had to tell Elaine and Morgan before any king. She let her cloak slip off and threw herself down on the grass in front of her sisters, and never mind that her green skirts went riding up over her legs. Those white thighs. Redheads like her have skin like buttermilk. She threw back her head and smiled, very wide.

At first I thought Morgan wasn't going to speak to her. She had her mouth fastened up tight. But she couldn't help herself.

'What was he like? Is it really him? Is it our brother Arthur?'

She looked like a cat ready to spring and as hungry too. You could tell it in the sparkle of her green eyes, the way her body was crouched.

Before Margawse had time to answer, Lot and Urien and Nentres, with their chief lords, came rushing up from the horse-lines to hear her story. Margawse liked that even better. She'd rather have men listen to her than just her two sisters. She turned her smile on them.

'Arthur doesn't want to be a king!'

Lot wasn't going to swallow that. 'Pendragon's son! Battle-chief of the Cymry against the Saxons? And not fancy himself as High King? What else could he want?'

'You forget. He has not been told yet that he is Uther's child. Nor I, Ygerne's! And for the rest the title he fancies is Emperor. The Roman Imperator. Leader of Battles. He is a boy of fifteen. War! That's all he cares about. War and glory. To be a hero in a Roman kilt and make the Cymry sing of him as long as the British tongue has bards.'

'For that he must be High King. How else could such a warleader hold the whole island? He needs thousands of men. Garrisons along the coast, south and east. Legions in the north to keep the Picts beyond the Wall. Fast cavalry to drive back the Irish pirates from the west wherever they land. And then a mighty hosting to purge all Saxons, man, woman and child, from the soft belly of Britain. He needs horses. Corn for men and beasts. Forts. Ships. Gold to pay his warriors and mead to sweeten them. He cannot do all that with a pack of schoolboys galloping about like footloose brigands.'

'Fight, yes. But he does not want to sit in the high chair of a council chamber, to listen for hours to old men wagging their beards at him.

To have to bother with taxes, laws, justice. He says Merlyn must see to all that.'

'Such power would please Merlyn very well,' said Morgan.

As if she'd been standing beside me in Caerleon when he'd spoken to me.

'He shall not have that.'

It's not often Elaine speaks. When she does, heads turn her way and there's a queer sort of quiet.

Lot wasn't finished though. 'Merlyn or Arthur, it's all the same. He must have power to order what he wants from those who have it.'

Margawse blushed like a girl and looked down at her hands. 'Arthur does not need to order. He has other means of getting what he wants.'

I got a quick look at King Lot when she said that. He had a face as black as a thundercloud that's going to ruin a harvest. He must have known what she was. He'd lived with her long enough. Gawain their son was almost as old as Arthur.

'Our brother must be High King,' said Morgan.

'You of all people say that?' marvelled Margawse. 'You wanted him dead!'

'I wished him never to have been born.'

'Ygerne's son, and therefore he must be High King. Uther's son, and therefore a dead king. Is that what you want?' Nentres wasn't a man who said much, either. He wasn't hot and fierce like Lot. But when he spoke other men listened. You got the feeling that once Nentres had weighed a thing up it was as good as decided.

Lot laughed at that, very sharp and bitter. 'So that's your game! I see it now. Crown Arthur Pendragon and then murder him. Then claim his diadem for the Pendragon's sister. And look which of our three queens is the eldest!'

Another man would have struck him for that, brother-in-law or no. But Nentres just smiled. There was a nasty while of silence. You could see them all turning the thought over in their heads.

Urien spoke up for himself. 'I think we should take this adventure Arthur offers. Never mind if anyone's High King at the end of it. Britain is being eaten away by foreign rats. If we do not drive them back now they will soon be in Rheged and Lothian and Dumnonia. The north and west will fall like the south and east. If we do not join our swords to Arthur's now, all Christian Britain will fall under the axe of the pagans. Shall it be said of us that we stood by like cowards?'

The lords had started to cheer him. It was what they'd been hoping to hear. They'd sooner fight the Saxons than their own kind. But there were some queer sort of grins when he finished. They had their bishops and churches. They went to the Offering on Sundays. But they couldn't help but know what sort their queens were. Those women didn't trouble to hide it. It wasn't a thing they were ashamed of.

But he'd said the right thing, that lad. It was what all men want. A sword in their hand at last and a call to battle. Urien got his way. Pretty soon they were off to their own side of the camp. It was men's talk now, battle-talk. Maybe there'd be war of a different sort afterwards, but there'd be plenty of Saxon blood to shed first.

When they'd gone, Margawse lay back on the grass and laughed, very long and merry.

'They would all fight against Arthur if they knew the rest of my story. But instead they will make him their king now!'

For the second time Elaine spoke, under the shade of an awning where she was sitting with her daughter.

'Our mother Ygerne would not match her power against less than the High King of Britain. Neither shall we. What we make, we can also destroy.

'Morgan is less particular where her power strikes. A nun. A blacksmith. A husband still ink-stained from the schoolroom. The King of all Britain might be too high for her! Such a shame. Oh, Morgan! He's a pet of a boy to take with you under the blanket.'

She was heaving and writhing on the turf as if she was doing it again.

You could see Morgan didn't believe it at first. Not though she must have known like the rest of us what her sister was. It came out like a screech.

'No! Margawse! You could not! Say you did not!'

I never thought I'd see Morgan shocked. She'd lived through much in her life already. Her father murdered and her mother seduced, if that's how it was, by the same man. Herself a noted Lady in the Old Religion. She's not a virgin. Oh no, Morgan's not a virgin. I should know. Haven't I had to lie with my head in my arms when Urien comes to bed her? Guarding the door, but close enough to hear them. Him serious. Too scared to speak at first. And her murmuring encouragement to him like a mother. But when he comes on her, panting and crying, then she goes silent. She never gasps or whimpers. You'd think she'd emptied herself before he came. I suppose it's a sort of kindness to him. How could a young man like that have lived if Morgan the Wise had really come to meet him?

But Margawse shocked her.

When she saw Morgan's face, Margawse opened her mouth and laughed. There wasn't any sound at first, then high and shrill. Luned and I grabbed at Morgan's arms. Queen or not, we could hardly hold her.

'You foul-arsed cat! *You!* And Arthur? You whore! A wife and queen. The mother of princes. Arthur's own *sister!*'

'Why not? The gods did it with their sisters. Call it a sacred marriage if it makes you feel better. We both enjoyed it. It was a contest, remember? My way against yours. My power, Morgan. Here! I said I would bring him down, not you, and so I have!'

We couldn't hold Morgan then. She tore herself free of us and hurled herself on Margawse. Those two queens wrestled together, rolling on the ground. We had to drag her off. There was damage done. Margawse had the worst of it, and she fell back gasping. But she was still laughing, with her red hair tumbled over her face.

'Oh, dear, Morgan! Arthur has gentler hands than you. Such a pretty little warrior. You should have felt the down of his beard between my breasts. And smelt the sweetness of his breath as he nibbled my neck.'

Morgan stood and stared at her sister, teasing her. And I got a fright. The tears were rolling down her face. She didn't make another sound. She didn't stir. She might have been turned to wood. But the tears were falling like great drops of blood.

Elaine's voice came out of the shadow then. It sounded as strained as if she'd been a very old woman on her death-bed. She must have reached a cruel long way into the future to see what she did. It cost her.

'Margawse is right. She carries Arthur's ruin in her belly. And wounds worse than that.'

Somehow it didn't seem important then, what the men were deciding in their war-council. The battle that counted had already been somewhere else.

Luned and I led Morgan back to her own tent. She said just three words.

'I have lost.'

She lay on her bed and wept the rest of that day.

# Chapter Twenty-five

Morgan turned home for Rheged. She wouldn't stay and meet Arthur now, not though she'd been so hot to see him before. Back at Lyvennet, she dressed herself in black, with just a circle of gold on her head and not another jewel. For days on end she stood at the gate of her castle from morning to night, handing out medicines to anyone that would take it. There were plenty came. But some of them passed on by when they saw her. She looked so wild.

The men stopped, though.

After that, it was all news of war. Arthur hung those hostage boys. Well, he had to, didn't he? That two-faced Cheldric hadn't gone home at all. He'd doubled his ships about and landed back down at Totnes, in Dumnonia where Morgan comes from. He reaped a grim harvest there, from all accounts. There were men beheaded, women raped, children drowned, beasts slaughtered and farms burned. And where was young Arthur while all this was going on? Up north of the Wall giving the Picts what for, so they'd learn not to attack good British folk while his back was turned fighting Saxons. So he had the length of the whole island to ride when he got the news.

But ride he did. They say that when he went into battle in the end he went berserk. He stormed up the hill at the head of his army with his golden dragon-helmet on his head and crying, 'Christ fight for us! The Mother aid us!' and I'll leave you to guess just who he meant. Well, the Saxons fled, and he left Cador the Keen to finish them off. Cador was Duke in Dumnonia. It was his country. He'd seen the slaughter.

Arthur had left some unfinished business in Pictland. They'd got his friends holed up in Alclud and they'd likely have died if he hadn't got back when he did. I wish I could have been there to see it. I'd have given anything to have heard the clash of steel and know it was the edge I put on their weapons that was shearing through hair and bone. I'd have worked all night to mend their broken spears and patch a shield or breastplate for the next day's fighting. I could have helped Arthur win. He got the victory without me though. He taught the Picts a proper lesson.

They say there's a loch there with sixty islands. Sixty streams flow into it and only one runs out. On every one of those sixty crags there's a fierce eagle that flies into the air and screams when disaster's coming. I bet the skies were pretty noisy when Arthur's lads rode up that glen. They drove the savages out into the water till they clung to the rocks for dear life. Then our British boys built boats and went after them.

There were hundreds of them drowned or starved or the loch monsters got them. He'd have finished the lot just as they'd have finished the mates he'd left behind in Alclud if he hadn't got back in time to save them.

It wasn't warriors stopped him. It was Christian bishops and presbyters, dressed like Lent without their fine robes. A sorry procession of them, come to rescue his enemies from what they deserved. Nuns with their heads black with cinders. Pictish women barefoot, tearing their faces with their own claws. Even little children crying for their daddies, so I've heard.

Well, Arthur was young. He hadn't the stomach to say no to them. He let them keep their menfolk, what was left of them. He reckoned he could call it a victory, so long as those painted barbarians kept to the moors where they belonged and left us British the good lands either side of the Wall. The Church crowed they'd got the better of him, though. They're always the same. He saves their churches for them, yet the moment he acts like a man, they're down on him.

Urien rode with Arthur on that campaign. It made a man of him. He came back taller and harder about the body than when he rode out. And sterner in his face too. He'd dreamed of war. All lads do. But he'd seen what it meant now. He's never turned back from that day. When Arthur's trumpet calls, he's there at the front of our men. I don't wonder that Gwendoleu looked sour at him. His Solway warriors would have liked a chance to grease their swords like that. Lot and Nentres fought with Arthur too. But Gwendoleu stayed at home.

And where was I while the men were fighting? Back in Lyvennet, in a dun full of women. Bit by bit the scorch-marks had flaked off my skin, though I've never quite lost the scars. The muscles I'd been so proud of had turned to soft fat. I still shaved a few white bristles off my chin every day. So there was only one thing left to mark that I was once a proper man.

I still have a man's feelings whimpering under this skirt. Hiding a rusty weapon, you might say. What good does it do me? She might as well have taken it with her razor, and left me in peace.

I was never easy. I still went bent to hide my face from guards and servants. Then there came one day when I tried to raise my head and pain caught me in the back. I knew then I'd always go stooped. I couldn't have swung a hammer after that. When Morgan broke my body, she broke my spirit too. I'll always be a lady's woman now, in a women's dun. Me, that was Teilo Smith.

There was another broken like me: Luned. Solemn as an owl, and nearly as wise too, for all she'd once been a nun. For the rest, Morgan had surrounded herself with pretty girls, as young and gay as ever Erith was. Yes, I mean your sort. Preen yourselves as much as you like. But it was only us two that she let close to her. The rest might have been swallows flitting round a rock that's cold and still. Except sometimes she'd go hunting after the boar and the wind would whip the colour into her cheeks and she'd be laughing like a young girl, till she got back.

Margawse came to visit us. Her belly was getting big now with

Arthur's child. And the eldest sister, Elaine the Fair. It always sends a shudder through me when they call her that.

Morgan had stayed slender and hard, like a young fir-tree. You'd never have thought she'd borne twins. And I had the measure of Red Margawse. Bright as a poppy in a cornfield, and as warm. If she'd been short of men, I think she'd have taken even my poor white head in her lap. She knew my secret. She wasn't above teasing me.

But Elaine was fat and pale, like a spider on a leaf. She never stirred out of doors if she could help it. She didn't ride out hunting with her sisters. You never saw her tapping her feet to the harping and dancing. She'd sit over a fire, everlastingly weaving strands of coloured wool and snipping the fringes with her scissors.

The warhost was back from Pictland. That winter it was Urien's turn to stand Arthur a feast. I'd never seen Morgan so fretful. She was all over the place, scolding the stewards to have everything right, as if they hadn't done it all a hundred times before.

Someone else rode through the gate just before Arthur's lot came in sight. A covered chariot. We'd none of us been told about that. A woman got out and helped another lady down, dressed in plain white. Morgan greeted the lady and kissed her, a little stiffly I thought. I couldn't hear what was said. She led her into the hall. I should have followed them straight away, but I didn't.

It wasn't just Arthur I was looking out for. It was a fine cold day, with just a hint of spring coming. It still hurt me to look down from that hilltop and see Way Bank, just a little cluster of thatch among the apple orchards. I'd worked there once. I'd been a man and a king. I'd had a wife and daughter. I'd been Smith. But Morgan had looked out from here and cursed me.

So I had to stand among women on the walls and watch fighting men ride up the hill. Arthur was at the head of them, dressed like a Roman general in his scarlet cloak. He was bare-headed. No need for his dragon-helmet here. He was among friends, wasn't he? And he had all his grinning warriors behind him.

Urien was waiting in the gate to greet him, all decked out in gold chains and best tunic, and practically the whole household was out in the yard. Only Morgan and her sisters hung back a long while in the hall, so I went in to see what was up. I didn't expect Elaine to stir till she had to, but it wasn't like the other two to hide themselves. Margawse was behind the door. She couldn't stop giggling. I guessed she was a bit embarrassed to face Arthur out in broad daylight now he was a great general and not just a little lad out of nowhere. She'd enjoyed the joke, but she hadn't quite worked out how she was to tell him what had come of it.

Morgan was the strange one. She was the lady of the castle, and she can play the part of a queen better than any I know. She should have been at the gate beside Urien to greet her guest. But I found her sitting there, facing that lady in white, and neither of them saying a word to the other.

We heard the noise from the gate. Morgan threw up her head then and her eyes went wide. I saw her sisters were watching her, to see what she'd do.

'Arthur is here!' said Margawse.

'The son of Uther Pendragon, who killed Father,' Elaine murmured. All three of them looked at that other lady.

Morgan got up, very slowly, and drew herself up tall. She straightened her dress. She didn't seem bothered about the shouting outside. Luned brought her a mirror and she smoothed her hair and touched her face. Very beautiful, she looked, that morning. It was a new gown she had on, yellow and crimson, like trees in autumn. At last she picked up a goblet that had been on the table beside her. She held her other hand out to the lady in white, and the two of them walked out into the light of day. There wasn't a hint of a smile on Morgan's face as she went past us.

I looked at Luned, and she at me. Neither of us had any idea what might be in Morgan's mind. This would be the first time she'd met her brother since that night at Tintagel when Merlyn snatched the baby out of her arms. We followed close after her.

Out in the yard it was a sight to warm the heart of any Briton, man or woman. A huge crowd of young men, warriors now. Sure of themselves, they looked, and bearing their new battle-scars proudly. All dressed up in fine peacetime harness with a load of jewellery. And Arthur at their head, jumping down from his horse beside Urien. I'd hardly have recognised him now. He had a full, curling moustache, and his brow was a bit furrowed and his jawline harder. But grinning like a hound as he saw Morgan coming to greet him. He didn't wait for her to cross the courtyard. He came striding to meet her with his arms held out. She stopped still, with the lady beside her. I couldn't see her face, standing behind her, but Morgan did a thing I hadn't expected. She sank down on one knee before him and said in a quiet voice, but so clear the whole dun could hear her, 'Greetings, Lord Arthur, son of Uther Pendragon and Ygerne.'

That stopped him short, and a sort of buzz ran through the crowd. His eyes flew round to the lords behind him. You could see plain enough nobody had told him where he'd sprung from yet. But he had a quick mind. He wasn't slow to see what it meant.

'Lady! You are telling me I am the High King Uther's son? Can you prove this true? *Where is that devil Merlyn?*'

Morgan signed to the lady with her. That other had a small sweet voice, but loud enough for those nearest to hear.

'You have no need of Merlyn. I bore Uther a son, fifteen years ago last Midwinter. Merlyn stole him away when he was one week old. There are those here who can testify to you I am the Queen Ygerne. My own wise woman's blood tells me I have found my lost child.'

The colour flamed in Arthur's face, and then he embraced his mother, only softer than he usually does with a woman. Still, that little lady was almost swallowed up in his arms. A great shout went up from the nobles crowding round. 'Pendragon! Pendragon! Arthur of Britain!

389

Arthur Pendragon!' And soon the whole army was crying that name.

Whatever the lad had said before about being High King you could see now that the fire was in his blood. He swung round on them all with that great grin he gives everybody, as though he knows they all love him. And they cheered him louder.

But Morgan hadn't finished. He turned to her and she held up her goblet to him.

'Morgan, daughter of Gorlois and Ygerne, offers Arthur her welcome.'

I couldn't see Morgan's face, but I watched his. That great grin faded. The blood rose right up to his forehead, dark red under the gold. He didn't know what to say. As if he'd come face to face with something that had never happened to him before. It seemed a mighty long time to the rest of us that those two looked at each other, as though there was nobody else but them in the whole world.

Then he found his voice, and very deep and husky it sounded.

'Arthur Pendragon gives you his heartfelt thanks . . . Sister!'

Again that pause. He gave her a solemn bow. Like two actors in a play, they were.

Then he reached out his hand to take her cup. Their fingers almost met.

'Stop!'

A figure came hurtling across that courtyard towards them. Like a wildman, it was Merlyn, in a black bearskin with a cudgel in his hand. With a roar that sounded more like a beast than a human he snatched the cup from between them. I thought he was going to dash it to the ground. Then he seemed to recollect himself and looked around. Well, you can bet the warriors are all crowding forward, hands to weapons. Urien's angry and Morgan is back on her feet. Merlyn picks on a page, he couldn't have been more than ten years old. And he holds Morgan's goblet to the boy's lips.

'Drink!'

The lad was terrified. You could see his round eyes over the lip of that goblet. He hadn't a notion what it was all about or why they had lighted on him. He swallowed a mouthful. I daresay it was the first time he'd ever tasted good wine. There was a long grim hush while we waited. Merlyn had put a thought into everybody's head that hadn't been there before. It blackened that day and many since. We saw the blood rush sudden to the boy's cheeks. He gagged a bit, and we thought he was going to fall. Then he gave a hiccup and started to grin at us all, wanting to know if he'd done it right, whatever it was for.

Well, a great roar of laughter went up from all those men. Arthur tossed down the wine. He gave Morgan back her cup, but the magic had gone. He hugged and kissed her, but no more than he'd have done any other lady. It was his mother he smiled at and took her hand. As Morgan led the way into her hall she turned such a look on Merlyn that it made me feel faint. I've never seen so much hatred pass between one human and another.

Merlyn was always a fool about women. She wouldn't have done it with her own hand. That's not how she killed my Annis.

But then again, maybe he did know. I wonder now if Merlyn might not have been cleverer than I took him for.

Arthur had had two surprises, and they weren't done yet. At the door of the hall Margawse was waiting to greet him. Arthur gave a start when he set eyes on her, and burst out into a peal of laughter, quite different from the way he'd checked at Morgan. 'The red-haired Queen of Lothian! We meet again!' he grinned.

'She is also your sister. Margawse, daughter of Gorlois,' says Morgan gravely.

Well, that stopped him laughing, all right. He looked down at Margawse's swollen belly and back at her wicked face. And then round pretty quick for Lot. He backed away from Morgan as if he thought her touch would burn him. He'd gone mighty pale, and his glance was going between those two sisters as if they were kelpies risen out of a lake to eat him.

Morgan smiled, very coolly now. 'And this too is your sister. Elaine, the eldest child of Ygerne and Gorlois.'

I don't think Arthur even noticed Elaine.

Arthur and Morgan. That's how it's always been. Those two. Like sword-dancers, nipping in and out of the blades without ever touching.

# Chapter Twenty-six

Those queens had Arthur trapped before he'd hardly started. What's done can't be undone. Still, it was a brave week's feasting Urien gave him. There was dancing and swordplaying and hunting and hurly, games of war where the men could show off in front of the ladies. Arthur's warriors had a fine time of it, with all Morgan's and Margawse's maids to flatter them. There wasn't one of Urien's men could shift Cei in single combat. And Bedwyr stepped a pretty figure in the reel. But Arthur had no joy at that feast. He flung himself into the hunting and wrestling as if he didn't care if he broke his neck. At table he threw back horn after horn of wine. You'd think he couldn't get drunk quickly enough. I saw his eyes going along the board to Margawse, staring at her body with that sick look in his face.

He'd gaze at Morgan too, often enough, and she would look back at him. Very long and grave they stared into each other's eyes, those two. They were always polite, but you'd think they were each accusing the other. Still, for the rest, I'd never seen Morgan take so much trouble to make herself look beautiful or put herself out so much to please men. From that day she changed. Almost reckless she was. She flirted with all his young warriors and made them welcome, almost as if she'd been Margawse. There was one in particular she'd call to sit near her. A thin stick of a young man, with hair as white as a Saxon. I can't think what she saw in him. Accolon, they called him.

She was sweet to all of them except Arthur. Since that first morning she couldn't manage a smile when she looked at him, though she clapped when he fought, harder than she did for her own husband. He showed her honour too. Well, she was his hostess, and his sister. He wouldn't let her shame him.

Margawse and Elaine were at her to decide what they should do next. But she wouldn't talk to them. It was only her mother Ygerne she'd meet in her room in secret. Not even Luned and I were allowed to know what passed between them. For the rest of the time she kept herself busy with her guests, and laughing merry as a lark, except when her eyes met Arthur's. It's a funny thing, though. She wouldn't let Urien in her bed all that week.

On the last day of the feast she made me do something that seemed odd to me. She gave me a parcel wrapped in a linen cloth.

'Take this to Merlyn. Tell him Morgan the Wise returns his gift. She will not use it.'

It was heavy. I could feel hard metal through the wrappings. A handle of twisted branches fitting snugly to the fingers, and a smooth round plate. I guessed near enough what it was. A lady's mirror. It hadn't been my sort of work. I was for horse-harness, fire-irons, tools. Manly stuff. But I'd been a noted craftsman in those parts. If ladies had something broken that they treasured and there was no gold- or silversmith by, they might bring it to Teilo's smithy at Way Bank and smile at me to make it whole again. I know rare work when I feel it. It woke a kind of hunger in me.

I found Merlyn in his sleeping-stall, though it was broad daylight. I hadn't wanted to go, but I felt a bit better when I saw that magician hunched on his bed with his knees tucked up to his chin and a scowl on his face. He'd spent a deal of time sulking indoors since that first morning. He was getting it good and strong from both sides. Morgan and her sisters had fairly bested him. Margawse could hardly stop herself laughing in his face. And Arthur couldn't look at him without shouting and swearing, for keeping a secret past its time. So I didn't expect I'd be a welcome visitor.

I said my message, just as she told me, and held out the package. He gave a great sort of sigh, so I felt a bit sorry for him. He knew what it was too, and he sat for a long time just looking at it without opening the wrappings. At last he shot me a look full in the eyes, and he could see I was greedy for a sight of it. He untwisted the cloth and I must have given a bit of a gasp, for I remembered now when I'd seen that same mirror before. It had been a beauty once. All coiling serpents on the handle and vines and peacocks engraved on the back-plate, and the other side polished bronze, so you could see your face clear in it. Or should have done. Morgan had broken it. She'd flung it from her so hard when Margawse had taunted her the handle had bent. The plate was so buckled and cracked now the loveliest face in the world would have looked crooked in it. I was a craftsman. I felt as if I'd been damaged myself.

'She will not use it,' I repeated.

'Is that phase over so quickly? Must she go straight from the virgin to the hag? And we lose Britain's summer?'

He pulled a face like a goblin, and his head sank between his shoulders. He had his hand deep in his pocket.

'Then give her this!' I'd never heard him sound so vicious. He was usually a merry sort of man.

He had it ready. He must have foreseen. It was a little silver box decorated with dragons and horses. But I knew that wasn't the real gift. There was something inside it that rattled. I took it to Morgan. I don't know how it was, it was only a small thing, that you could fit in the palm of one hand. But it felt heavy, heavier than you can imagine, so that by the time I got back to Morgan's room I could hardly bear the weight of it.

There was only Luned with her. When I told her Merlyn had sent her another gift Morgan didn't move or say a word. I put it down on her lap, very carefully, so my hands wouldn't touch her. She sat and stared at it for a fair old time. Then, with just the tips of her fingers, she opened the lid. It wasn't much. The sort of present any gentleman might give to a lady. A pair of silver scissors, shaped like the beak of a heron. You'd have thought she'd have done like any other lady would, picked them up and tried them, cut something, even if it was only empty air. But Morgan just sat very still, looking down at them for a long, long while. And then she closed the lid.

# Chapter Twenty-seven

Even fat spiders stir out of their hole when the fly touches the web. Margawse's time came. We were all of us gathered there in her castle at Din Eidyn, north of the Wall. Elaine, Morgan, their women, me. When the red queen's first pains started you can guess what I was afraid of. How far would Morgan push her cruel joke on me? If joke it was. I looked at the curtain hanging in front of Margawse's bedchamber, and Margawse herself holding her hands over the belly where Arthur's child was pushing, and I felt mighty queer. There's some magic even I never pretended to.

I needn't have worried. After a bit the pains came so hard that Margawse cried out. It was Elaine got up from the corner of the fireplace where she'd been sitting. She waved her hand to three of her own women and they helped Margawse in with them through the curtain. Morgan took one step after them, but Elaine drew the curtain in her face. I'd never have thought Morgan would stand for that, not with the fierce high pride she had. Then I saw the look in her eyes. Stricken, I'd call it, as if she'd just had news of a death. But there was nothing said by either of those sisters.

I was left outside, and Morgan and Luned as well. This wasn't their work. They weren't welcome at a childbirth, for all Morgan had the name of a great healer. There was something here I couldn't quite put my finger on. You felt these two still carried something of the convent with them from Tintagel. They'd both borne babies, but that didn't count, somehow. You might have thought they were still virgins.

It was Margawse you'd look to for hot blood and birthing. She could hardly stop sons springing out of her hole. Four fine wee warriors in the making already, and folk hardly bothered to count her daughters.

And Elaine? Well, she was only a year older than Margawse, and she had a wide, soft lap to nurse babies on. But sometimes she'd look older even than a great-grandmother. I had a nasty sort of feeling, catching sight of her eyes then, as if I'd only to lean over just a little bit further and I'd be falling down a bottomless well. Hundreds and hundreds of years, going back into darkness, all those women, generation before generation, back to the very first One. That's what I thought I was seeing when I looked at her. I've seen old stone things like her. Those big hips and breasts. That flat face that sees nothing or everything. I kept away from them. They weren't my magic. They wanted more blood than I knew how to give.

It was going on evening when the women went inside the curtain. May Eve. There were the proper things done in the castle courtyard that night, but we had different magic on our mind. Taking out, not putting in. Even so, it still hurt me not to be dancing the god. When the sun went down there was a queer sort of hush outside. Not a cloud anywhere, and the sky so pale it was almost white. Up on the hilltops I knew the bonfires would be standing ready. May Eve, Beltaine. They kept the feast a fine old way in Margawse's land. The Christian bishops had little say up here. This wasn't Roman country like Rheged. When the stars pricked out we could hear the drums begin to beat.

When we'd worked our own spells, Morgan went to stand in the doorway and breathe the cool air. I noticed her hands kept clenching on her skirt and then she'd have to force herself to open them wide, as women must do for the birthing.

But we had a long time to wait. In the middle of the night we saw the fires leaping up on all the crags around us. Before long Margawse's folk came charging back, banging drums and blowing whistles. They danced into the yard, waving torches and singing 'Summer is come in today!'

I thought the baby was being born then. We heard a great cry from the queen's bedchamber. But when we swung round expecting to see someone bursting through the curtain to tell us, it hung still. We turned back to the yard, and I saw a sight that made me suck in my breath. They were dancing the Horse. I'd been the Stag myself. It cuts me to the quick to see another tribe make magic stronger than mine, anyplace. Still, I'd seen Horses before. Morgan had brought hers from Cornwall. When it swings close to us, with its tall hat on its head and its tarred skirts, that's a thing to make men skip and the women scream. All the same, the people love that Horse. A childless woman won't run so far the black skirt can't cover her, and we all weep when the Horse dies before it rises again.

This was a Horse of a kind I hadn't seen before, and it scared me rigid, with the torchlight flaring on its great bony head. They'd taken a real horse's skull, and if I was you I wouldn't ask how that creature met its end. They'd buried it deep till the worms had picked the flesh from the white bone. Then they'd mounted it on a pole and put two great red eyes of glass in the holes of its skull. That god was nodding high over our heads to the beat of drums and the shriek of pipes.

Morgan bowed to her.

And still Margawse screamed inside that chamber.

Dawn came, and there were more fires as they burned the gorse and drove out the spirits from the dun with rattles and horns. You never heard such a din. Then the young ones brought in the maypole, fresh cut and strung with leaves and flowers. A weapon to open up any woman, that was! But still we waited.

There was the old battle. The King and Queen of Summer and all their people. Both of them young, virgins, they have to be, and dressed in the prettiest coloured clothes all hung with flowers. And then the Queen and King of Winter, all in dull greys and browns, trimmed with fur. They looked hefty fighters, both of them. Under those skirts She was a man, like me. It's the same every May Day. You know what it's like. The Summer fights the Winter, and the Summer wins. Their side have a feast, out of doors in the sunshine, with dancing round the maypole, and the Winter's beaten and those folk have to eat their feast shut up in a dark barn, till their turn comes round again. That's how it's always played. The fight's a real old set-to, mind you. It's expected. The lads enjoy themselves giving knock for knock as hard as they can, and the lasses can lay about them too. But we know who'll win. The Summer has to. If it didn't, if one year we didn't make the magic strong enough . . . It makes my mind go dark to think about what might follow.

Well, that year I thought the worst had happened. The Queen of Winter, in her crown of holly, went driving against the little King of Summer, and down he went, that boy in his white gown and his cloak of green and gold. He must have slipped on the sappy grass. There was a great roar as the Winter folk closed round him. And through it I heard three screams higher than all the rest. Morgan's beside me, crying out in terror. Margawse's, as though she'd been split in two. And Elaine's. I swear that hers was triumph.

A moment after, we forgot the battle outside, because the curtain rattled.

'It is done!' said Elaine's voice.

She was standing there holding a little bundle in her arms. She had such a smile on her face as she showed it to us, and suddenly I saw why they called her Elaine the Fair. She'd been a beautiful young woman not so long since.

I hadn't thought a newborn baby would be that small. It wasn't like either of its parents. Dark red skin, and puckered, with black eyelashes closed on its cheeks. Morgan stroked its face with her finger. She still looked pretty shaken.

'Look on him well and know him,' Elaine said.

'Arthur's son,' says Morgan, very low.

'Ours.'

We didn't get long to look at him. Elaine carried him back inside the curtain to his mother.

Outside, it looked as if they'd sorted the battle out all right. The little King was on his feet again. The Summer folk were cheering him. I couldn't see a sign of the Winter people anywhere.

# Chapter Twenty-eight

'I will take the baby,' said Morgan.

They were all three agreed on that. Margawse had crafted their weapon; now Morgan would guard it. Lot might have his suspicions, but Arthur knew. There were some pretty powerful spells spoken over that boy before those three parted. I put my voice to the rest, though I didn't think it would do the poor little chap much good. Morgan had robbed me of my power.

All those long, jolting miles back to Lyvennet I held the wee fellow on my knee in the chariot. Morgan was never a motherly sort of woman, but she fed that baby from her own breast when he cried. It gave me a queer sort of shiver to see that: Arthur's son sucking from Morgan's teat. She let her hair fall forward like a curtain so we couldn't see her face. It mixed with the baby's black hair till you couldn't tell one from the other. He might have been her own bairn. But when he'd finished sucking her, she'd pass him to one of us.

Luned seemed afraid to touch him, so it was mostly me he fell to.

What's done can't be undone. That didn't stop Merlyn from trying, though.

Arthur was off east with his army that summer, winning more battles and growing a bigger duke all the time. He'd got all the common people cheering for him. They love a battle-hero. It's only when he needs their taxes they start to grumble. We knew he'd be back before the end of summer, and Merlyn with him. They'd have a different score to settle when they got the news from Din Eidyn. They couldn't leave it here. Merlyn had used his craft to get Uther's son. Now Margawse had used hers to make Arthur's. He wouldn't let that rest. He couldn't have that boy grow up to spoil things for Arthur.

I thought Morgan meant to hide the child. Get a couple she trusted to bring him up as their own, till the lad was grown and could learn who his father was. I'd thought of a name or two that I knew for wise folk.

Well, I'd been a workman. Noble by skill, but I'd needed to go craftily. Smile and nod at the gentry, and do what you have to behind their back. That was how I was used to thinking.

I should have known Morgan wasn't like that. She's highborn. Wasn't she the daughter of Gorlois, who went to his death and would have taken his wife with him if he'd had his way, sooner than give Uther Pendragon what he wanted? Our black queen walked the ramparts, nursing that boy in her arms, and looking south almost as if she was willing his father to come.

He made for Din Eidyn first, and I bet Margawse laughed in his face. When we heard he was hunting the child in Lothian, Morgan made her plans. She knew we'd be next. She was ready when he came.

Arthur rode up the hill into Lyvennet with Merlyn beside him and a troop of his warriors behind. They hadn't come for a feast this time. They looked grim. We weren't sure then how much his men had been told about what was up. He'd try to keep the worst secret. I saw the way they fingered their weapons and the shifty air they had as they looked over their shoulders. They weren't sure they'd get much help from honest steel. I reckoned he'd sold them a story about witchcraft. They didn't know how to fight it.

Urien greeted Arthur a sight more stiffly this time and had the grooms look to the horses. He must have half-guessed what was going to happen. He'd been with Arthur in battle. Morgan hadn't. She couldn't have carried through with it if she'd known, could she?

Well, Arthur hadn't taken two steps towards the hall before he heard the noise. It was worse than pig-sticking time. I don't wonder the lad looked startled. He didn't know what it meant, straight off. But Merlyn did. I watched that enchanter's face change. If he'd looked sour before, he was furious now. First Margawse had cheated them, and now Morgan. He stormed into the hall, even if he did push Arthur in front of him for form's sake. He knew what they'd find.

Morgan was facing him on the dais before the high table. She was as white as death, but she had her loveliest smile ready for Arthur. She had stood her women all around the hall. And in the straw in the middle, all swaddled up and yelling and trying to kick, there were babies. Scores of them. May-born, all of them, only a few weeks old. She'd gathered every baby in her land the same age as Arthur's son. Highborn, lowborn, craftswomen's bairns or slaves. Well, May Day babies are supposed to be lucky, aren't they? Their mothers expected to take those children home richer than they went. There were more than a few mites had been brought in who looked newer than they should have been. Morgan had seen them all washed and fed and wrapped in clean linen with the same rich shawl around them, so you couldn't tell one from another.

I sometimes wonder what would have happened if she'd won. Would all those babies have got back to their right mothers? There could have been some queer crossings made that day. Slaves for nobles. Baptised Christians for first-vowed pagans. It's hard to tell them apart when they're that small.

His boy was there with all the rest. Morgan's not a cheat. She had her chin mighty high in the air as she smiled at Arthur.

He didn't bother with polite greetings. 'Get these women out!'

She looked a bit dangerous then, but she didn't stop smiling.

'The women are my witnesses.'

Arthur fairly leaped up on to the dais. I moved in quick, but then I stopped. It was my job to protect her, but I was miles out of my depth here. He got her by the arm. He couldn't bawl at her, though you could see he felt like it. He couldn't tell the whole world what was wrong. She'd got that weapon over him.

I saw Urien come in at the back, with Cei and Bedwyr.

But Arthur had a weapon of his own. He leaned over Morgan. He had his arm round her waist now. He was kissing her mouth.

'Give me my son!' he murmured, so that those others couldn't hear him.

The roses came in her cheeks and her eyes flashed a bit greener.

'It is your sister Margawse who gave you a child, not I!' she whispered.

He drew her closer then and his fingers were stroking the hair on the back of her neck.

'Morgan, Morgan! Why do you hold yourself so stiff? *Which is he?*'

She couldn't speak. He smiled at her very lovingly with his blue eyes, like a little boy that's used to getting what he wants.

'Come on, now. Let us be friends. Where is the harm? Would you keep the son from his father?'

'Your child is safe with me.' She was looking him straight in the eye though she could hardly stand.

Arthur turned to Merlyn for help. I think he hoped the old magician could scry the boy out, like a dowser testing till the hazel-stick jumps. Well, who's to say? Perhaps if he'd kept his head, he could have done. But he couldn't hold still. He strode up and down the hall while Arthur waited. He was hopping over babies, peering into their faces till they screamed, and mad as hell because Morgan was mocking them. There was such a racket from the bairns crying, and the smell they were making in the straw, you couldn't think. I never thought such scraps of flesh could have made such a din. All mouth they seemed. My Mair was such a sweet peaceful baby. We only ever had the one.

Merlyn got back from stamping all round the hall.

'Have you found him?' shouted Arthur.

'How can I tell? All babies look the same to me.'

They say Merlyn was married once, before he went wild in the woods. I couldn't imagine it.

Arthur and Morgan were still locked together and murmuring now like a couple of wasps.

'I am asking you to hand my son to me.'

'You could not recognise your sister. Now it seems you do not know your own child.'

'Bitch!' cried Arthur. And he struck her across the face.

Merlyn snapped his fingers. Before we knew where we were, there was a hall full of armed men. Arthur drew his sword. Morgan gasped and some of the women screamed. Well, Urien yelled and his guards came charging in after Arthur's. They took one look at the Pendragon with Caliburn in his hand, and Morgan with his mark on her cheek, and the blood started to run. It's a funny thing. Folk here are afraid of Morgan, but they love her too in a queer sort of way. She's healed many, when no one else could. They haven't suffered by her as I have. But there weren't enough of them. Arthur's warriors had Urien's men back against the wall in no time. This was work the lads understood. Their teeth were flashing as bright as their blades now. But they weren't expecting what came next.

'Pick up those babies,' Merlyn ordered them.

That shook them. A lot of them were too young to be family men. But some of them were. And the rest had little brothers, sisters. They looked to Arthur for a lead. He nodded his head.

Cei moved first. He was always a hard man.

'Do not, for shame!' Urien cried out. Arthur was his hero, but Morgan was his lady. He didn't wanted to bloody his sword in this quarrel. You could see that.

'Urien, for your honour. You swore loyalty to me!' said Arthur.

'You pledged your love to me,' Morgan came back at him.

Urien looked from one to the other. King of Rheged he might be, but in those days he was still a young warrior, who'd not long proved himself in front of his hero. He was in love with Arthur, like the rest of us, or with his dream of him. Or maybe he feared what would happen to the children.

'Give Arthur what he wants,' he ordered his wife.

'I will not,' she told him. 'My father denied Uther Pendragon. So I defy his son.'

'What have our fathers to do with this? Take up the children,' Arthur told his men. 'Do what Merlyn says.'

I think every women in the hall shrieked then, except Morgan. She went white to the lips but she stood her ground. She must have thought he was trying her, to see how soon she'd break. She couldn't have known he meant to kill all those little babies and still kept silent, could she? Those two gazed so hard at each other it was like that first time in the yard. You'd have thought there was nobody in the hall but them, for all the howling. There wasn't either of them would give in to the other.

'Carry them outside and put them in a wagon,' Arthur said.

He never turned to watch them do it. He only stared at Morgan. And she at him.

Cei took the first one in his arms, and then the rest bent to it. When she saw what was happening, Morgan let out one awful wail, but that was all. Arthur turned his back on her and jumped down off the dais.

The other women shrilled louder and started to fling themselves on the swords. It would have made your stomach turn over to hear them. Some of those babies had been born here in our castle. Half of Arthur's warriors kept them penned in behind a fence of blades. I think they were glad enough to keep their backs turned on what their mates were doing. Merlyn was in charge now. I don't think any of the rest of us believed Arthur would go through with it, not on either side. I knew when they got to Arthur's boy. Morgan's face didn't move a muscle. She wouldn't give him away.

They started to carry the babies out. Morgan called after him then, very hoarse and broken.

'Do not do this, Arthur. For your soul's sake.'

A queer thing, that, for a pagan like her to say.

He didn't turn. He just strode out following Merlyn into the daylight. She came to herself then and screamed such curses after him as should have shrivelled the flesh on his bones. Urien's men couldn't look her in the eye.

Morgan paid those parents the honour-price in gold afterwards. It couldn't stop the keening that day, though. After she'd turned the women out of the hall it seemed mighty quiet, like a death-chamber.

'Follow him,' Morgan ordered me. It was hardly more than a whisper she could get out.

I got a mule and went after them. I had a long ride. Merlyn didn't trust her, even then. They went through Rheged and into Gwendoleu's land, all the way to the Solway, searching out every cottage to see if there were more May babies yet. They piled them all in their wagon, with the mothers howling and weeping after them. They didn't butcher the children there and then. They hadn't got the stomach for it and they wouldn't dishonour good steel. I heard later that Arthur had spun them a yarn about a nightmare he'd had. At a May Day feast his hall took fire and a beam fell out of the roof and pinned him by the legs. It was threatening to burn him to death. He'd woken up screaming and sweating. That crafty Merlyn joined in then and told them what it meant. Or as much of it as he thought fit for them to know. That beam was an enemy born on May Day to bring Arthur to ruin. If they wanted to keep their hope of glory they had to find it and tear it out before the fire took hold.

Gwendoleu didn't try and stop them either. It wasn't love for Arthur with him. I think he'd lived close enough to those three sisters to guess pretty near the truth. Arthur was one Pendragon too many for him already. Another son to that line wouldn't suit him.

They got to the Solway Firth with a wagon full of babies. They seized a boat. I couldn't have stopped them. One humpbacked woman against Merlyn and a war-troop. Even if I'd had my old power, what spells could I have done, if Morgan's own curses hadn't been enough to halt them? I just had to watch.

They were a deal of time loading those poor little bairns into the ship. They took trouble over it. They didn't just throw them in, any old how. They were too softhearted for that. They laid them out in rows and settled them as comfortably as they could, and never mind if it was their last voyage. Near on a hundred of them there were, and quieter now. The little mites had worn themselves out with crying. His men pushed the boat down the mud to the water's edge. Merlyn tapped Arthur's shoulder. He'd got the child. He had to finish it. It was Arthur's hand gave the last push and sent it spinning a bit out into the current.

She's a quiet river, the Esk. She doesn't fret and foam. There was a sort of silver light over the water-meadows. A flock of seagulls started to circle over the boat. Their screams were so loud we couldn't hear any more crying. The boat dwindled down the tideway. I saw the first gull dive and I looked away.

Bedwyr laughed then, just a little light sound. And that broke the charm. All those young men began shouting and joking and slapping each other on the back as if they'd won a famous victory. They'd done the job and they hadn't had to get blood on their swords to shame them. Only Arthur couldn't raise a smile, and Merlyn was still muttering and making signs with his hands. He hadn't lost his power yet, as I had mine. But it was wasted effort in the end. He should have known. Those three sisters had forged their weapon to bring Arthur down. He couldn't alter it. His spells would turn back on him.

I had to go home and tell Morgan. She stared at me with big eyes, like a little girl whose puppy has been taken by wolves.

'Arthur . . . has killed . . . them . . . *all*?'

I nodded.

She gave a great yell of grief and tore her dress and pulled at her hair and clawed her face. And all her women did the same. All over the north there were mothers howling, in Margawse's land, and in Elaine's. He didn't stop at Rheged. None of the kings dared say no to him. He'd stirred up too hot a war with the Saxons. They couldn't break with Arthur now till it was won.

Well, if the women cursed Arthur they cursed Merlyn more. Nobles, slaves, Christians, wise. Men damned him behind his back too. Young men that had lost their firstborn sons. Grandfathers. Uncles. Merlyn was done for from that day. It didn't need Nimue to finish him off. In time they could forgive their hero Arthur, as long as he went on winning battles anyrate. It was easier to blame Merlyn. This wasn't warrior's work, it had the mark of magic on it, you could hear them telling each other.

Only Morgan went to the stone circle. She threw herself down on the ground and wept her heart out and beat the stones.

'I hate Arthur! I hate him!'

Then she knelt up and stared at Luned and me, very still.

'Was it because of me? Did I do this? Morgan the Healer! Must I still destroy everyone I touch?'

Well, what could the pair of us say to her?

# Chapter Twenty-nine

Well, if the Church had been stiff with Arthur before, they really came down on him for that. They called a great synod. Their bishops and abbots, some of them women too, came from all over the land. Those Christian folk think themselves somebody because they can hark back to cities with big names like Rome and Constantinople and Jerusalem. They think it's their empire still. They rate their word above a king's.

Arthur listened to them, though. He had a taste for Rome. He fancied the legions and the emperor's diadem. He followed their religion too.

Those long-faced bishops heaped a penance on him. He walked barefoot from Bath to their oldest church in Glastonbury. He kept vigil and fasted a day and a night there. He gave away every last scrap of gold and jewels he had left to pay the honour-price of those children. Their parents got rich, after all. They had it from both sides. They say he paid for his own son's blood with horses. I wasn't there to see Margawse's face when she got her quittance.

But when all's said and done, I don't reckon Arthur was truly sorry for what he did. He'd had to get rid of the boy, hadn't he? If he was made to do penance to wipe his slate clean, he'd pay the price. He'd got what he wanted. It's a bitter war these two sides are fighting, brother and sisters. We haven't seen the last of it, by a long way.

From the time Arthur took the baby, things changed. It had seemed like a dance before, with those sisters and Arthur, bowing and curtseying as they stepped their reel round him. The pipes were playing a lament now.

But Morgan had other tunes in mind. She called me to join her circle. I tell you, I was as scared then as the first time I'd been summoned as a green lad. I couldn't feel any power still. I knew the danger I might be putting myself in. But Morgan had named me, and I had to go. I joined my hands with the rest. I sang the words. I moved my body with the ring. I couldn't think why she wanted me. I couldn't give her what she needed unless she gave me back my power.

When Arthur had finished his fast, the Church decided he'd settled the score. Dubric, top bishop of the land, laid his hands on his head and forgave him. Well, those Christians need Arthur as much as he needs them, don't they? Their priests are flesh and blood, like their congregations. They bleed the same as their Hung-Up Man when the heathen turn nasty. Arthur's the only one they can look to to save them. And so he did. It was like summertime after that. The whole country was coming to life and flowering again. We had hope at last. We thought we'd found a leader who could throw out the Saxons. Everywhere I went following Urien and Morgan it was the same story. Men with a shine in their eyes, quicker to get a leg across a horse than a woman these days. Little kings forgetting to quarrel with their neighbours because they'd bigger fish to fry now. Brothers, we felt like, wherever we rode. Brothers . . .! I couldn't go. I couldn't fettle one horse for Arthur's cavalry. Morgan and her sisters were on the losing side. I'd sunk with them.

Merlyn never did penance. Even the bishops didn't have the nerve to order that. It told against him, though. Folk forgave Arthur afterwards, with his blue eyes and his golden curls and his magic sword to wave over his head. He and his brave lads galloped the land from end to end. They stirred up blood that had run cold and slow too long. And those that never saw him in the flesh fell in love with him as hard as those that had. They had their dream of him. The young Pendragon, that had only seen sixteen summers, who had hammered both Saxons and Picts.

It left Merlyn stranded, though. It was him folk put the blame on for the children.

But if there's one thing you can guarantee will soften the coldest heart, it's a royal wedding. The whole world loves a lover. That was a stroke of genius on Merlyn's part to turn the tide for Arthur.

There was a fort down in Cornwall, Celliwig, that Arthur was mighty fond of. He still had his army headquarters in the City of the Legions. And he had plenty of business in the north, sweetening men like Gwendoleu and Lot to make sure they kept off the Picts. But it was down in Dumnonia he found her, fostered at Duke Cador the Keen's court: Gwenhyvar. When it came to women, that family always seemed to turn to the south-west. The orchards of Dumnonia grow a rare apple.

It worked, that plan of theirs, Arthur's and Merlyn's. They were canny generals, both of them. As soon as they announced the wedding, the Council of Britain cried him High King. There'd be a double coronation on their marriage-day, for him and her. It was little Gwenhyvar's blood that settled it. That was a famous line of kings she brought with her from the west. Better than any wedding-gift. They needed that if Arthur's sons should ever want to be kings. His own birth was still a bit too cloudy for some folk. There was only Merlyn's word for it, and Ygerne's. And the Church wasn't too happy about either of them. But you couldn't argue with Gwenhyvar's history. She could trace kings back to Roman times, and further.

Morgan, Margawse, Elaine, they all got a summons to his wedding. I didn't think they'd go, not after what he'd done. Morgan looked black when she got the news. She rode out hunting that day and so reckless, by all accounts, it's a wonder she didn't kill herself. Her star was waning fast now. Her twins were growing. She wasn't a soft-faced girl, like Gwenhyvar. She'd lost Arthur's son that she'd nursed at her own breast. There'd been wreckage washed up from that ship. A few little scraps of flesh and bone the gulls had left. Arthur was going to be High King.

But I was wrong. Morgan couldn't have wanted to dance at his wedding, but she did. And where she went I had to follow. I stood behind her in the church at the City of the Legions, and I'd even become enough of an old biddy to feel pleased that I'd got a new blue gown to wear, and a fresh white veil for my head. But then I heard the trumpets sounding for the bride's procession, and I looked round and saw the nobles standing on the church steps – Arthur, the Bishop Dubric, and other kings and priests round them – and I couldn't stop myself thinking of another wedding-procession years ago. Me, standing in a windy street, dressed like a man, to get my first sight of Morgan as a bride. And then Merlyn coming.

This was another city and a different queen. I couldn't get a sight of her with the noblemen crowding round to lift her down from her chariot. Then the trumpets rang out again and the choir burst into singing and all the deacons and presbyters and bishops in their finest cloaks came swinging up the nave in a cloud of incense. Arthur was leading his bride, and every head was turned round to stare. I still remember the shock I had when I first clapped eyes on Gwenhyvar. She was lovely enough. It wasn't that. She didn't have power.

I heard a little catch of breath in front of me, so I knew that Morgan had seen it too. We looked at each other, Morgan, Luned, me. And then across at Margawse and Elaine. There was the same thought in all our faces. I hadn't guessed till then how strong we might still be, those three sisters with their wise women gathered round them, yes, and even me, now she'd let me in. I couldn't think why Merlyn had let Arthur pick this little lass for his queen, blood-line or not. He must have been too sure that we were beaten.

She was . . . pretty. Yes, that's the word for Gwenhyvar. Pretty as any girl I've ever seen, I'll grant her that. All dolled up in sky-blue and stiff cloth of gold and hung thick with jewels. I called to mind how Morgan had looked in her plain white dress with fresh flowers on her head, and her hair falling like a raven's wing round her white neck. She'd been beautiful that day; she still was. And flaming red Margawse. There was fire in those sisters, mountains, oceans, ages of beauty. Gwenhyvar's might last for a few days. She was smiling round at us all as if this was the best day of her life. I even felt a bit sorry for her. She'd got what she wanted. A king that would go down in legend. A lusty lover. Wealth for the taking, if he could go on winning battles. And everybody calling her the most beautiful woman in the land, because she was Arthur's queen now. He led her past Gorlois's three daughters. And there wasn't a flicker of fear in her eyes when she smiled at them. Nobody had told her. She didn't know what she was walking into.

I looked round when they'd passed, and got a start that made me wonder if I was seeing things. Merlyn, dressed up like a lord, slipping in at the back of the congregation, and Nimue flashing her silk and coral beside him. That took the cockiness out of me, and I went a bit cold. It was the first time I'd set eyes on the Lady since she drove me out from her lake. And Emrys Merlyn? In a Christian church?

# Chapter Thirty

It was Arthur's sisters prepared his marriage-bed. They were the highest ladies in the land now. It's a wonder Merlyn didn't think of that. I know what kind of charms they laid between the sheets. I helped them do it. It would be a marvel if that coupling ever bore fruit. After it was ready, Margawse and Elaine and all their ladies went off to join the feast. Morgan wasn't in any hurry. She stood there stroking the place where Arthur was going to lie. It looked as if she was willing something more than we'd done yet. Then she gripped the end of the bed. I could see she was having a struggle with herself over something. Well, in the end she turned on her heel and followed after the rest.

That was a feast and a half! You'll never see a handsomer young couple. Gwenhyvar with that long silver-fair hair, cool as a waterfall, and her cheeks bright with wine and as soft as rose-petals. Hardly old enough to be wedded. And him! He had everything falling in his lap now. When he looked at Gwenhyvar he fairly shone like the sun. He'd been lucky in war, and now it looked as if he'd be lucky in bed too, and both of them with golden crowns on their heads. Everybody was feasting and dancing, and there were so many fresh young lasses about, the men were trying not to make drunken pigs of themselves too early. Even Bishop Dubric was laughing with Cei. It seemed like old wounds were healing at last.

. . . Old wounds were healing. All of a sudden a lump of meat jumped up my throat so I was almost sick with excitement. Back there in Gwenhyvar's bedchamber, when my hands were stroking her sheets, and Arthur's, while my voice was chanting the charm with all the others, I had felt it. Yes, *felt* it! The burning in my hands. Magic flowing down my veins. No, not flowing. I was running ahead too fast. But trickling, anyway. Yes, I could say that. Real power. Nothing like what I'd been used to before. Oh, no. But still power. Like the first green shoot of spring that you see poking up through the snow. It was coming back to me.

It wasn't just the beer putting a flush on my face then and making my eyes sparkle. Years fell off me. And better than that. I could feel myself sitting up straighter, squaring my shoulders, lifting my head more like a man. I looked up the long hall, through the smoke of the fire and the steam of the dishes, and I saw Morgan's face looking at me, like the moon through cloud, with her hair black as night round it. Only it wasn't cold and distant. It swam closer as I stared. And it was a warm woman's face, not a proud queen's. Her mouth curved in a smile then and her eyes shone green, sweet as they'd never been for me before. It was only a moment across that crowded hall, but Morgan smiled at me as though I was a man again.

It was gone almost before I'd seen it. She turned to call out some pretty compliment to Arthur and lift her cup. And somebody reached across my face to grab a hunk of bread.

I sat drunk, or bewitched, trying to take in what had happened. My power was coming back. Morgan had smiled at me.

I could have warned Arthur that night. I could have told Merlyn what those queens were doing. I kept quiet. For the sake of the smile in Morgan's eyes. For the first tingle of power in my blood. Not even for the promise, just the hope, that there might be something more to come.

There was one who didn't need warning, though. When we got back to Gwenhyvar's room, Nimue was there before us, and from the look she gave us I don't doubt she'd been busy undoing a bit of what we'd done.

There was the usual lot of laughing and bawdy jokes when the ladies seized Gwenhyvar and carried her off to her bridal chamber, and we left a lot more horseplay behind us as Arthur made out he was trying to follow her. His mates held him back and they were acting out a fair old set-to. He'd have to wait till he was sent for. I'd dearly have loved to have stayed in that hall with the men and joined in the fun. Down a few more beakers with the rest of them before the queens sent word his bride was ready for him. I hadn't felt so much like a man for years. But it was too soon for that. I still had the disguise of a woman, though I'd hotter blood underneath tonight. I'd have to stick with that side a bit longer.

Only when I saw that smile on Nimue's face I nearly changed my mind. If I could have left the lot of them and run back to my blacksmith's forge then it would have been enough for me. Those women could keep the magic. I'd drop it all. Horns, Smith. Just to be like any common man. But I'd learned my lesson too late. I wonder, if back at the beginning I'd been willing to hand over some of my power to her, whether Morgan might have let me keep what I had. Well, that was long past. I was in with them too deep now.

It was funny, I'd seen so many women in their nightclothes by then it didn't stir me like it might have done, seeing Gwenhyvar lying on fine linen sheets, with that white-gold hair brushed out around her and a loose thin gown embroidered with gold that it wouldn't take a man like Arthur a moment to pull off. There were little lamps, but not too close and not too many, and armfuls of flowers and bundles of corn everywhere you looked, so the air was sweet with the scent of them. Only you wouldn't have slept easily if you'd looked too closely at some of them. She was very young, that little lass. Years younger than Morgan had been on her own wedding night. Probably more of a child than Morgan of Cornwall ever was, if half what Luned told me about her is true. Very pleased with herself, Gwenhyvar looked, lying there in that big bed with all of us fussing round her to make her beautiful. Still, a bit frightened too. And she had reason to be, more than she knew of. It was a dark family she was marrying into. Well, she came from Dumnonia. She should have listened to the bards.

They sent us to fetch him. It was my hands that grabbed Arthur's sleeve and helped to haul him away from the wine-cups. You can be sure he came willingly. He wasn't shy. Arthur was no virgin, as we well knew. Cei and Bedwyr were struggling to keep close, but there was such a press of ladies in the corridor they got separated from him. This was women's business.

But Arthur had to stop when he got to the bedchamber door. All three of his sisters were standing there, barring his way. Morgan, Margawse, Elaine. Flashing their smiles and taunting him, they were, even Elaine. Nimue was there with them too, and some of her maidens. Gwenhyvar hadn't brought enough of her own people with her to put up a struggle. It was his own sisters he'd have to fight his way past to get at her. He had to do it right.

Well, there was a fair old tussle, with him laughing and wrestling the women at the same time and all of us joining in and pretending to haul him back. Some of Arthur's lads came up and took us from behind. It was sweeter armfuls than me they went for. You should have heard the squealing.

Then, all of a sudden, it was over and Arthur was inside the door. He slammed it behind him, and the women hammered on it, but it didn't open, of course. It all went quiet then, and we looked at each other and put our dresses straight. The sisters stopped laughing.

I looked back down the corridor. Merlyn was standing by the corner rubbing his hands. He caught my eye over the rest and he took a step nearer, as though I was one of his own people. I stared him full in the face. I wasn't laughing either now. Merlyn couldn't give me back anything I wanted. It was Morgan who'd broken me. She was the one who would have to make me whole. Merlyn was never a healer.

When I looked back, Nimue was watching both of us.

The men went back then to join the singing in the hall, all except Cei and Bedwyr. Feast or not, those two were wearing swords. But we women stayed and listened. Morgan was leaning against the door as if she was guarding it, only she had her eyes closed. We didn't have long to wait. There was just a little cry, and then a man's laugh. Next thing, there was Arthur in the doorway waving a bloodied sheet on the end of Caliburn. Bedwyr snatched it off him and tore back to the hall with it and we could hear all the men cheering. I looked round for Morgan. She wasn't grinning like the rest. She was pressed against the door where Arthur had been. It was shut fast again now. She was shaking. And Merlyn was back at the end of the corridor. He smiled at her then, a very powerful smile, as if he'd done something very clever.

Well, after that, there was nothing left for the rest of us to do but to go back and join the feast.

I've never seen Morgan drink so much, or dance so wildly. She had the men shouting and clapping her. I caught Margawse looking at Elaine as if the two of them couldn't believe what they were seeing.

I couldn't either. Well, you know what it's like when a feast's nearly over, and the bards have run out of songs and we've all drunk more than we should have done. There's plenty of corners in the straw that'll take two, and it was a warm night for those that would rather be private outside. It was a wedding-feast, after all.

That's when it hits me hardest.

Still, it shook me more than anything else that had happened that night when I saw Morgan get up from the wine-cups and pull Accolon by the hand. That lank-haired youth from Arthur's own warband. She could hardly stagger to the door, but he put his hand round her waist and held her steady. Before they disappeared into the night, she had both her arms round his neck. That scared me properly. I looked round for Luned, but she'd gone off to see to Morgan's children. There was only me. I was her guard-dog. That's what she'd collared me for. As close to her in everything she did as a breastplate. I had to follow.

I turned round at the door. Urien had half-risen off the bench. He wasn't as drunk as some of them. I thought he was starting to come after us. But he just sank back down on his seat and put his head in his hands.

When I got outside I had an awful moment. I feared I'd lost them in the dark. But they couldn't walk straight, either of them. And they weren't troubling to keep quiet. Morgan was singing. She's not one to hide what she's doing under a cloak. They took the path down to the river. There's willow trees there, and long, soft grass.

# Chapter Thirty-one

I watched them do it. And I saw her safe back to bed afterwards. I thought she'd sleep then. But every time I opened my eyes I saw by starlight her long white hands clenched round a knot of the sheet.

I don't know when it was I woke, but it felt like the very deadest part of night, everything so quiet I thought it had snowed, though it was summertime. I don't wonder those old Romans went to so much trouble to heat their palaces in winter. There's something unnatural to me about lying in a house of stone, all straight-sided with every corner squared off. No curves to it. No crumbly clay or ragged ends of thatch. They've used the dead bones of the earth, not the living flesh of her. I felt a chill come over me as I sat up.

Then I saw what it was had roused me. Morgan's little daughter, Morfudd. She was tugging at her mother's hand. I went colder still when I thought that it might have been someone worse beside the bed. I was supposed to be the queen's watchdog.

Morfudd was whispering, 'Mam, come on! Come and see.'

I saw Morgan stand up, and she might have been sleepwalking. She had that slow but driven look about her. Well, of course, I feared worse than that, that it was her spirit I was watching, and I might find her body still lying in her bed. But the sheets were empty behind her, and hardly rumpled. She'd lain very still, no matter what she felt.

Morfudd dragged her over to Elaine's bed. I heard Morgan draw in her breath sharp, and I saw why. Then she was making for the door, quicker now. I had to follow where she led. She picked her way through the room outside. It was full of sleeping women and children. Luned was lying there, beside little Owain. We had to step over them both. Morgan put her finger to her lips and signed to Morfudd she'd got to stay behind. She didn't look back at me, but I'll bet she knew I was there.

The torches had burned out in the corridor, and there wasn't so much starlight. She seemed to know which way to go. There was a long porchway opening on a courtyard, then a dark passage. It led straight back to Gwenhyvar's bedchamber, and Arthur's. She had no weapon in her hand. I remember noticing that.

Suddenly she stopped short and pressed herself into an alcove, deep in the shadow. I did the same, though I'd wrapped myself in a darker robe than hers. Someone was coming away from Arthur's bedroom. There was a last torch still guttering down there. I could just about make the guards out. Some guards! Cei and Bedwyr, slumped asleep against the wall. A little heap of Gwenhyvar's women in the antechamber, with their arms flung across each other. Even Arthur's dog was sprawled out and snoring. And one woman, stepping slowly past them all towards us. Heavy but silent. No tiptoeing maiden, this one. No slender lady. Big, like a mountain. With spreading hips and breasts hanging over her waist. But moving quiet and dainty as a cat. Elaine, for sure. She had her cloak wrapped close about her and she was clutching something in the folds of it to her breasts.

She turned before she reached us, round the porch to the other side of the yard. She'd vanished like a huge moth into the dark.

Morgan stood still so long then, I began to fear she'd turned to stone, like another Roman statue. But then she moved on, and she was hurrying more than before, and not so certain either. Nobody stirred in the anteroom, not even if we touched them. I was mighty scared stepping past Cei and seeing the naked weapon in his hand. At the bedroom door Morgan hesitated a long while. I think she had to force herself to raise the latch and swing it open.

Some of the lamps were still burning softly here. The air was full of the sweet scent of flowers. Arthur and Gwenhyvar had their faces turned to each other, his arm thrown over her breasts and a big grin on his face. They were fast asleep. Close by his other hand was a naked sword, with the scabbard dropped on the skin rug below it.

When Morgan saw that, she gave a start. She stepped up to the bed and she raised that heavy sword as if she couldn't help herself. I didn't know what she meant to do, or how I could stop her. She held it lifted in both hands over the couple. Then she ran her finger along the blade, as if she was testing it. I've done the same thing myself with a weapon hundreds of times. She studied the hilt, and felt the jewels on the guard, and the knots and coils of it. I'd seen Caliburn close up once before, in Nimue's house. I knew it was magic workmanship. But Morgan didn't seem satisfied, somehow. She had it poised in both hands again, as though she was weighing it. She must have felt me watching. There wasn't a flicker of surprise in her face when she turned round and handed me the sword.

I almost dropped it. Caliburn! Arthur's sword, that he'd got his manhood from Nimue with and all his victories since. A man's weapon, that Nimue wouldn't let me touch. But when Morgan offers you something, you don't refuse. I took it from her, and the years fell off me. I was a smith again, and I had the armourer's craft. That sword was heavy, and fine workmanship. A good edge to the blade. The right weight and balance. Handsomely jewelled. But . . . that was all. The old true power I'd felt in my blood that evening didn't quicken to it. This wasn't magic. It couldn't be Caliburn. The same look, but not the same feel. Morgan sighed, just a little gasp of sound. She knew it already.

'I have come too late. She was here before me.'

'What does it mean?' I whispered.

'Hurt.'

She took the false sword back from me. She stood holding it over the marriage-bed where Arthur was lying with Gwenhyvar in his arms.

411

Arthur stirred a bit and rubbed his cheek against Gwenhyvar. I saw that sword shiver.

Only, all of a sudden, there was a loud wail.

'Mammy! No! No! Don't do it!'

It sounded shocking through that palace where everybody was sleeping.

Well, I whipped round as fast as if I'd been stung by a hornet, and there was Morgan's little son, Owain, behind us with his big round eyes and not a stitch on him. Luned came running in after him. When she saw what was going on she looked terrified.

Well, Owain's cry was just like cockcrow, or a hunting-horn. It shattered the spell those sisters had put on everybody. Ladies, sentries, Arthur, Gwenhyvar – they were all awake and shouting or swearing, and there was Morgan with that great sword in her hands standing by Arthur's bed and staring down at Owain.

Then she flung it away from her. It would have hit Gwenhyvar if Arthur hadn't caught it. I'd snatched up Owain and tried to cover his mouth, but it was far too late for that. There were weapons on either side of the door. All that saved us then was the clutter of women rushing this way and that and trying to make out what was happening.

Arthur was kicking off the sheets. Morgan had started for the door. She'd got nothing to protect her. She snatched up the scabbard from the rug and held it out in front of her and shouted one word. The mob in the doorway parted like a cleft stick. We were out of the anteroom and then racing across the courtyard into the dark. There was chaos all round us. Torches flaring up. Men yelling. Women calling out to know what was wrong. And nobody sure what had started it. Except Arthur. We heard him shout, 'Seize Morgan! Merlyn was right! She would have killed me with my own sword on my wedding night!'

We met Urien running to meet us. He hadn't heard Arthur rightly. Not then. I threw Owain to him. This was no night for children. We'd lost one boy already.

There was still one hope. Morgan's own people will die for her. One smile can make them hers for life, never mind the healing. I should know. They had horses ready almost before she gave the order. We leaped astride. There must have been twenty of us, men and women. I don't know how many of the guards got killed before the gates were opened and we were galloping for dear life and the north.

They pressed us hard. Arthur's men were battle-hardened and their horses were trained for speed and strength. They ran us down in an old wet wood, where the trees had fallen hundreds of years since and others had sprung up out of the carcases, and even those were hung with long beards of moss. It was coming on morning, and a mist was creeping up out of the bogs and pools between the boulders. Morgan made us dismount. We turned the horses loose and drove them away. Some of the beasts tried to follow us but they soon backed off in terror when they saw where she was leading us. We went right down into the black bog. Morgan spoke a great charm over us. It turned us to stone. We stood still and lifeless, with our hooded heads rising up out of the mud like rocks. There was black water sucking all round us. Horrible serpents slithering over our legs, but we couldn't move. The mist kept shifting to and fro so we couldn't see anything clear. Then Arthur's troop came splashing and shouting down to the edge of the water. They'd followed our tracks this far. But their horses whinnied in fright once their hooves started to sink.

'How wide is this mere? What lies on the other side?' I heard Cei calling to Urien.

Yes. He was with them. Even her husband was hunting her now.

None of them knew how to follow her. Our horses were scattered all over the wood. We stayed in the water, like kelpies, listening.

They picked out some hoofmarks further up and moved on, searching. When their noise had died we heard a bittern booming. A pair of grey herons landed on the water. Then the mist started fraying. I thought we were done for then. I was sure he would have left a sentry behind, but we were alone.

We caught a few of the horses. The rest of our party we left to follow us on foot. It was a long journey. But not as long by hundreds of miles as the distance that was fixed now between Morgan and Arthur.

We daren't stop even in Rheged. All the way into Lothian Morgan carried Arthur's scabbard held close against her.

# Chapter Thirty-two

Morgan fled to Din Eidyn. Margawse and Elaine joined her there. It was women's business now. Their men didn't know the half of what had been done.

We didn't meet in the palace. What we had now was too secret for that. There was a cave in the hillside, with a spring running outside it and hazel trees hanging over the mouth. Inside there was a great slab of rock cut for a table. It had been well-used. Margawse lit a fire on it.

There were nine of us.

Elaine laid Caliburn down on the stone. We didn't need telling this was the real one. I'd sometimes wondered if Arthur did take it into battle, or if it was just for show. I'd thought maybe just owning it would be enough to get him victory. I was wrong. There was enough of that cold north light to see the stains where the blood had been cleaned off. There were nicks on its edge. That sword that had seen hard service. He'd used it.

Elaine said, 'Our brother has won his last victory.'

Morgan had her head bowed, staring at Arthur's weapon. Then she lifted her eyes slowly and looked hard at her sister.

'You would stop him here? With a line drawn across Britain. The north and west for the Cymry, the south and east to the Saxons.'

'Dumnonia is safe, and so are Rheged, Garlot, Lothian. The road to London is still ours. Why should we care what happens to the rest?'

'Britain must always be a woman divided? Her heart given to one king. Her womb to another.'

'Arthur is already too strong. Merlyn's foster-son! The Church has crowned him with their power as well. And now he has Gwenhyvar's blood.'

Morgan bowed her head again.

Margawse had kept pretty silent for her up till now.

'Well, Morgan? Elaine has brought Caliburn. The greatest talisman Arthur had. Where is your boasting now? What weapon will you raise against Arthur?'

'I have it already.'

Morgan signed to me and I gave her the scabbard I had been holding all this time. Only, at the last moment I didn't want to let go of it. There was such a comfort coming off that blackened wood, even through the thickness of cloth that was wrapped round it. I didn't doubt Nimue had spoken the truth. I don't know where she'd got it from. Caliburn was a marvel, but this had an older look by far.

As if the sword had been meant to serve the scabbard, and not the other way round.

Morgan didn't want to give it up either. I could see it cost her an effort to lay it by the sword.

Those other two queens sucked in their breath. Morgan hadn't told them.

Elaine smiled, a bit coolly. It had taken some of the shine off her deed. And Margawse raised her eyebrows.

'A strange prize for Morgan the Healer! Elaine has taken his power to wound. But you have robbed him of healing.'

She knew that already. She'd wept when she came to next morning and realised what she was holding. She'd flown at me as if it was my fault. But she'd kept it with her, hadn't she?

All this time, Morgan's hand was still on the scabbard as though she couldn't hand it over even yet. Then she opened her fingers and stepped back quick.

'Arthur is no longer a god. The barriers are down. He can be defeated and hurt like any other man.' She was pretty vicious the way she turned on Margawse. 'Well, sister? And what blow will you strike?'

She shouldn't have said that. Margawse flashed back at her.

'How dare you ask that? I showed my weapon before either of you. I opened my womb to Arthur. I bore his son. The baby he killed, who was my vengeance for our father. Elaine was right to strip away his power to wound. And I will never let you give him back his healing.'

Well, that was a shock. I'd always seen Margawse laughing. The whole world was a joke to her, and men the biggest laugh. I hadn't thought till then she could be hurt.

That was a black day for Britain when Arthur took those children. It changed a lot. Though it didn't alter as much as he thought it had at the time. I sometimes wonder what would have happened if he'd handed those sisters the victory. Owned the boy for his son. Their child and his. But he had Caliburn then, and his crown to win. He wasn't going to let himself be defeated, was he? By a pack of women.

It was Elaine caught our eyes then. She was leaning forward over the table. Her hands were gripping it in pain and her breath was coming short like a woman in labour.

'No! Starboard! Starboard! The rock!'

We all looked at each other, scared. You can have lived all your life with the power, used it often enough yourself, and still it *is* power. You never get used to it. You wouldn't last long if you did. It can shake the strongest when it comes unasked and it's naked and screaming in the room with you. Elaine's voice rose into a high screech, like seagulls yelping. It had gone past words now. We heard a baby crying out in terror. It was gulping. Gasping for air. Then a little sob, and silence. None of us dared move. The queen's eyes were squeezed shut on her fat cheeks and her mouth slack and dribbling.

'Get a bowl.' Margawse whispered to two of her women.

One of them fetched a basin of water from the spring. They didn't need to be told what else. Dried herbs from the back of the cave, crumbled to a powder and sprinkled over. The pot boiled quickly over the fire and more stuff was added. I recognised some of it. There was a scum that eddied and sank, and the steam coiled off it. I was breathing heavy fumes and beginning to feel a bit strange myself. Morgan pulled up a stool and lowered her sister to sit on it. Elaine's eyes opened, blue in the creases of fat, and she stared down into the pot. It was a long, long time she looked and said nothing.

Margawse couldn't hold herself in any longer. 'What is it? Tell us! What can you scry?'

'A house by the tideway . . . A rat in a fishing-creel . . . A coracle.'

We waited.

'A stone in a field, that the ravens light on. The bonfire lit for Midsummer Night. People dancing.'

'Yes! Yes!'

'A baby boy at a woman's breast.'

Her head sagged forward. Luned moved quick and took the bowl off the table. Elaine was snoring now. We let her rest. She'd done her part.

'I will find him,' Morgan said quietly. 'Rivers do not flow on for ever. I shall find that stone, that house. The sword was meant to go into its own scabbard.'

She looked at Margawse when she said that, very sadly. It struck me then that those two are more alike than you'd think.

Only Margawse wasn't sad. She'd changed entirely. She seized hold of Caliburn. The jewels were back in her eyes and the gold in her hair. She was laughing again.

'You see? Did I not sheathe Arthur well? The boy's alive! We have him trapped!'

She would have grabbed the scabbard and joined them both together, but Morgan snatched it back.

'No! Not like that! Not by guile and treachery. It was meant to be done openly, freely, by his choice and hers. The sword married to the scabbard and the world made whole.'

Margawse laughed at her bitterly then.

'You still hope that? Poor innocent little Morgan! Still galloping after the men and hoping they'll notice you. You have learned nothing, have you?'

'And you have much to unlearn.'

They were like a pair of swordsmen with their guards locked in each other's, that can't get free. Then Morgan twisted round and signalled to Luned and me it was time to go.

Margawse looked a bit frightened. 'Morgan! If you find my baby . . . you won't tell the world straight away, will you? That he is my son by Arthur? Not yet. If Lot found out . . .'

We all knew her husband had shut his eyes for pride's sake these many years. It hadn't sweetened him. He might still kill her if she gave him the proof.

'I promise you, I shall guard Arthur's child as dearly as if I had mothered him.'

I shan't tell you how those three hid that sword and scabbard. They set a fearsome watch over it.

When it was done, Morgan sent word to Urien she was coming home. She was too proud to run away. All the same, we didn't know what to expect.

Arthur was waiting for her. He had men of war camped outside her walls. She only checked for a few moments when we rode clear of the forest and had our first sight of them.

'Lyvennet has a royal guest, and I not there to do him honour.'

The colour was burning in her cheeks and she kicked her horse on. There was a queer sort of hush as she rode through their camp up to her own gate. The yard was full of warriors staring at us.

I wondered what would happen when she walked into the hall. Would Arthur order his men to seize her, in her own castle? Would her husband stand by and watch?

Arthur was by the fire, facing the door. From the look in his eyes, I fancy he wasn't too sure what to do, himself. If he'd seen one flicker of guilt on her face, he might have got up his nerve and given his men the order. But she wouldn't make it that easy for him. She'd grown up in a hard school. Ten years shut up in a convent, because she'd once stolen him away and might have drowned him, but didn't. What had she done worse now by holding a sword over his marriage-bed and not letting it fall? She walked up that long hall towards him, with her hands held out in greeting, and smiling at him sweeter than ever she'd done when they were supposed to be friends.

'Welcome, brother! Morgan of Rheged is grieved that she was not here to offer you her cup a second time.'

He was so surprised he even let her kiss him. She acted a sight freer with men nowadays. Urien looked grimmer than either of that pair. He'd got his men behind him this time, fully armed. Arthur came to and pushed her away from him. There was hot blood in his cheeks, more than in hers.

'You used sorcery on my guards. You tried to kill me. Your brother and your king!'

'All my life I have suffered that accusation. For a man so threatened, Arthur is very much alive.'

'I am your anointed ruler. The sword that Nimue gave me would not serve your evil purpose and turn to strike me.'

He should have seen the start she gave. It was plain enough to me. She was staring at her brother's thigh. He was wearing it now. That jewelled sword I'd held in my hand that looked like Caliburn and wasn't. And something else had changed. It hung in a magnificent scabbard now. Gold filigree studded with seven kinds of jewels, not a thing of battered wood, bound with cracked silver. I was like a dog with two bones. I didn't know which way to turn. I'd been a smith. That was a scabbard fit for a king. Any man would be proud of it. But I'd felt the power of healing in the other one.

'What is that you wear at your side?' she asked, quite steady.

Arthur patted it. 'My sweetheart, Caliburn. What else?'

'And has Caliburn brought you victory this summer?'

'You know we have not taken the field yet.'

'But I see you no longer wear the scabbard.'

'I have a new one. The glory of Rome may have left this island but we still have craftsmen who know how to arm a king.'

'Where is the old one?'

He shrugged. 'Lost sight of in the mayhem you left behind you. It will have turned up by the time I get back to Caerleon.'

'Do you value so lightly the gifts of the Lady? What does Merlyn say about its loss?'

She couldn't seem to take her eyes off his false weapon.

Arthur cleared his throat. He was looking angry again, and a mite uncomfortable. 'Merlyn has left my court.'

'Left you! When?'

'On my wedding-night, while we feasted.'

'Then, Nimue?'

'They went together, it seems.'

'They thought I threatened you with both sword and sorcery, and they left you? Now I understand!'

'I do not fear your spells! I am a Christian king now. I have better guardians.'

Morgan raised her eyes to her brother. She'd turned pale. 'So Merlyn does not know the scabbard is missing? Or that Caliburn was . . . saved?'

'Merlyn's time is past. He has served his purpose. I had no need of sorcerer's help that night.'

'Ungrateful! When without him, you would not be here?'

'What do you mean? Caliburn was a truer friend. Your own son cried out against you and made you drop it. Even the little children accuse you, sister.'

Well, I thought she'd choke.

'Little children! You dare say that . . . to *me*!'

If he'd been red before, he turned nearly purple then.

'I have served penance for that, haven't I? The parents have had their gold. What else could I do? That May Day child threatened my life and, with it, Britain's safety. It was a necessity.'

'Necessity!' she screamed at him. 'Is that what Merlyn said? The blood that must always be shed? The *necessity* for which my father died and you were got by magic?'

'There was no magic! I am Uther Pendragon's son and a crowned Christian king. Merlyn was my foster-father, but no more than that. All the magic my father needed was a brave sword and a loving heart.'

She fell back a step. It's not often you see Morgan taken by surprise. Even Luned gasped out loud, and she was never one to voice her mind in public.

'Has Merlyn never told you?'

'Told me what? The old story? How my father desired Ygerne? The blood of kings from both sides meeting in me to save this island? How Uther slew Gorlois in fair fight? How he married our mother and gave her the son that your father had denied her? And that is why you sisters hate me!'

Morgan cried out at him.

'Did Merlyn not tell you that the Pendragon tricked our mother? That while my father lay wounded Uther took on his features by sorcery? That three of them charmed their way into Tintagel? Uther, Ulfin and Merlyn? That when she lay in his arms Ygerne believed it was Gorlois who was entering her? That you were falsely got?'

You could see he hadn't heard the full story. Like a smack in the face, it was. All his young man's pride in swords and spears and a handsome body melting away into mist and magic. He looked round to someone for help. His friends were nearly all his age. Cei, Bedwyr, Accolon. How could they tell him the truth?

It was Luned's voice settled it. Clear. Cold. Hard. The only time I heard her raise it in front of men without first being spoken to.

'Ask my Lord Ulfin what was done in Tintagel.'

Yes, the old warrior was there, hiding his face at the back of the crowd. Uther Pendragon's boyhood friend. His skin looked as grey as his hair. He must have been twice the age of those ruddy-faced lads round Arthur. But he looked older even than that. Too much magic. I knew the signs. Aye, I should, shouldn't I? Arthur ordered him to come forward. Pride wouldn't let him have it told in secret.

'You were my father's comrade and bodyguard. You have sworn that same oath to me, his son. *Tell us, on your honour, and my father's, how I was got.*'

Ulfin wasn't enjoying this.

'Sire, we besieged Dimiliock. Gorlois broke out to fight us and Uther struck him down with his own hand. When we saw he could not live long we let his men carry him inside the walls. Then Merlyn put a charm on us. Uther took on the form of Gorlois; Merlyn, Britael; I became Jordan. We passed Tintagel's gate-porter at dead of night, pleading extremity of need. He let us keep our arms. The abbess herself, for friendship of Gorlois, welcomed us in. Merlyn and I brought the king to Ygerne's bed and stood guard outside. In the morning Gorlois was dead and his widow was carrying the Pendragon's son.'

Well, Arthur's face might have been on fire as he looked back to Morgan. Neither of them lowered their eyes. I'll give him that. She smiled a bit.

'You see, brother?'

He swallowed, as if he had a job to speak.

'I did not know. It was not honourably done. You have been wronged.'

Now that might sound like Morgan's victory to you. Only if she'd been a man she'd have known she'd lost him for sure then. He might have forgiven her a sword-wound to the flesh, but she'd hit his pride.

She didn't see it. She held out her hand to him, very grave and sweetly.

'Do you understand now what lies between us that must be healed?'

419

'That is long past. My father, your mother. I was only the baby.'
He'd got that winning smile back on his face again as he put his hand
up towards hers. 'Can you not forgive me, sister? What more do you
want?'

'I think you know.'

'I do not. Why draw this sword over my bed to kill?'

'If I had intended that I should have done it, Gwenhyvar would have
been dead before either of you woke.'

'*Gwenhyvar* dead? *Why?*' He dropped his hand.

She'd given herself away. I felt a lurch in my stomach, as though
the rest of us were water that had run out through a hole in a tub,
and left those two. I'd seen his face.

She laughed and tried to turn it aside.

'Why? To make the Pendragon suffer loss, as Gorlois's daughters
have mourned since that night in Tintagel! What else should I mean?'

But it was too late. I reckon he hardly knew what he was saying.

'I warn you, do not touch Gwenhyvar! By God, I'd turn this sword
against you then.'

'As you turned it on my women here in this hall the day you took
the children?'

'Can you never have done with that?'

'Can you still not see the wound that waits to be healed?'

'Healing is your job. Fighting is mine. Take the scabbard and leave
the sword to me!'

'Did Merlyn teach that?'

'Merlyn is gone, damn you!'

Arthur flung himself out of Lyvennet and back to Gwenhyvar.

# Chapter Thirty-three

Funny how clothes can make a difference to the way you feel. Morgan's always been proud, and she's a beautiful woman. She'd look lovely in a piece of sack. But even your richest jewel takes on more fire in a proper goldsmith's setting. It was still the dark colours she favoured, but the cloth was the best you could buy now. Rich green, like wet moss. Blue as deep as your shadow on a frosty morning. Or a dark strong red. But all thick embroidered. She has an eye for good workmanship. And jewels! She'd come to us dressed simple as a nun in her fresh flowers. But now she'd take all the stones Urien cared to heap on her. It was as if she couldn't have the man she wanted, so she was out to dazzle all the others. Except those moons when we danced barefoot and naked on the earth that made us. Yes, even me now; so she could call me Woman every other hour, but then she knew I wasn't.

It's a thing you may not have expected, but I'd come to take a pride in my own clothes too. We were a queer bodyguard she'd chosen: Luned, thrown out of a convent, a clever nun that was fool enough to bear a baby; and me, chased out of the world of men for fancying myself wiser than Morgan of Tintagel. But we were hers; we were queen's women. She couldn't help our faces, but she wouldn't be shamed by our bodies. We had good gowns, like these, the best stuff, and fine white linen for our heads.

So I wasn't too pleased when she told me to slip off my good striped dress and put on a worn old gown of brown that looked as if somebody had cleaned out the hen-coop in it. Still, I saw the sense of it, and the patched old shoes and the otterskin bag. I took a staff in my hand as if I'd trudged miles. I didn't need to walk, though. We took her chariot. Morgan drove, with Luned sitting beside her. She has a way with horses, with any animal, come to that. She has that little grey cat, with the scars on its side where the hair's never grown back properly, and she'll sit for hours with it on her knee, crooning to it. Have you seen the guard dogs in the yard cringe when she passes? Soft as puppies. They wag their tails and flatten their ears and look up at her, all pleading-like, and she'll stroke their heads and murmur something to every one of them.

I showed her the spot where Arthur had pushed those poor little mites down into the water. There's tales enough told of that now. I'm not surprised folk are afraid of the place. A cold stretch of grass and mud. The wind comes whistling over. In the evening they say you can hear the screaming of babies snatched from their mothers and floating out to their deaths, and feel their little tears falling on you like rain.

She stood alone at the edge of the water for a good while. Then we skirted the marshes and went on downstream, working the south side first. At every farm and shed and hut she stopped the chariot, a good way off, and sent me forward. She knew how I could act the part of a wise woman. The hardest part was seeing the women's faces when I asked.

'I have charms to sell, dearie. Medicine for a year-old baby. Do you have such a one? Give him this cordial every new moon while you're weaning him, and he'll grow up strong and handsome as a prince.'

There were a few that showed interest. Mothers who were carrying their bairns on their arms and showing them off proudly to anyone who'd look. But they weren't afraid. Theirs were too young to be him. It was the other women, the ones that slammed the door in my face and cursed me. Some, mostly the young ones, burst into tears. It had been their first, you see. The men growled at me too, and told me to hold my tongue. I got no payment from them, not so much as a piece of bread.

We came to the sea and stood on the sands watching the white horses come running towards us from Man. Next day we tried the north shore.

I think she knew. I reckon she could have taken us straight to the place if she'd wanted. Perhaps she was afraid the gods were playing games with her. She wanted to find that boy too much. I don't say Elaine could have told her wrong; the seeing's always true, but sometimes it doesn't mean what you think it does. If she was going to lose the child she'd set her heart on a second time, then she'd put off the hour. Or maybe it was like when you've got a plate of mushrooms in front of you, and you keep the biggest and juiciest one till the last.

We knew the stone, as we know every holy marker in all our land, and Gwendoleu's. A round rock in the grass by the firth, all on its own as if it had fallen out of the sky. The Stone of Mabon the Son, of Modron the Mother. It seemed like an omen, that. There was a house nearby, a lonely place. And a shed beside, with a man mending a net, and a coracle pulled up on the turf. I gave him the time of day, though it always chokes me a bit, seeing a craftsman at his trade. I went on to the house and he gave a loud whistle after me. It was a clean sort of place, a few beasts and fowls well cared for and making a crooning chatter as I passed them by. I didn't need to knock at the door. There was a woman sitting under an apple-tree with her back to me, rocking a bit with something on her knee. She looked round and saw a stranger. She couldn't have heard her husband whistle. Her face changed, and she gave a little cry and darted into the house, quick as a startled bird into the bushes. She came out again pulling the front of her dress straight and smiling at me as if nothing had happened.

'Good day, Granny. What can I do for you?'

I said my piece and I thought she caught her breath a bit, though she laughed to cover it.

'I've no child so small, thank God. It's a wonder you come peddling such wares in these parts. Are you a wise woman, and yet don't know what happened here last summer? How many other houses have you asked at?'

She was shrewder than I'd bargained for. Plenty of women had cursed me but nobody else had challenged me straight out. Grief's like an empty belly. It won't let you think about anything but yourself. This woman wasn't grieving.

'Death goes and life comes. You can't stop what will be. There'll be a baby again where there were empty arms last summer.' And I looked her full in the eyes and nodded, so she knew I was on her side and not Arthur's.

She was still careful. 'That's true. Sit down and drink a cup of milk. How much would you want for such a cordial? Could it really keep the child safe . . . if I were to have another . . . against sickness and wizardry?'

'It could. And I have one waiting, with power to shield him even from the king himself.' My eyes never left her face.

I saw her colour. It wasn't guilt. It wasn't even fear. She was angry. She had older children. They'd come looking round the corner to see the visitor. She'd shooed them back to work. They looked well grown and sensible enough to keep her secret. And now she was nursing another woman's baby where her own had sucked. He was her foster-child.

'You think they would come back? Those red ravagers! Were there not enough drowned bairns on the sands to satisfy them?'

'Arthur has done penance for it. That arrow's shot. But you're right. The danger's not past.'

'Folk say it was really Merlyn's doing. He'll have a longer memory than the young one.'

'Arthur's flown south. And Merlyn's gone mighty quiet, so I've heard. He's not been seen in a long while.'

'Good riddance, I'd say!'

I drank the milk, and made her a present of the cordial. We hadn't cheated. It was strong stuff, the best magic we could brew. We wanted the child's safety as much as she did. She held the flask to her chest, but she was looking a bit doubtful now, scared, as if she might have given away more than she should.

'Bless me, Mother,' she said. 'We live in bad times.'

'For you, the good times are just beginning,' I promised.

I brought Morgan to her, wrapped in a great black cloak and hood that hid her finery. That gave the fisherman's wife a shock, when she found who it was. But she was equal to it. Her name was Fencha. The two of them talked, woman to woman. Morgan might be a queen, but she was still Morgan the Healer. Everybody knew that, even in Solway. The woman trusted her, and Morgan trusted Fencha. She had milk enough, and no suckling of her own, or coming either.

She fetched her husband in. I liked the man. He wasn't a talker. He'd found the baby on the sand, and worse things than him they'd had to bury. They'd both been agreed on what she'd done. We'd give them payment. Not gold; that might make the neighbours' tongues wag. Good cloth. A pair of cows. A bigger boat. And the promise of more in return for their caring and silence. Morgan could trust him. Still, she made him turn pale when she warned him what she'd do if he proved her wrong.

Fencha had asked us in, when she found it was a queen she had to deal with, and she'd sat Morgan in the best chair. There was a blanket hanging to hide the bed, and no sign of the boy. When her husband had gone back to his work she still didn't open that curtain. She was a careful woman, Fencha, and he was a quiet baby. In the end, Morgan had to lower her pride and ask,

'May I see him?'

Just for a moment, I thought the woman was going to say no. She seemed to think she had power, even over Morgan. But she beckoned us through the curtain. I noticed, though, she picked the boy up off the bed and held him cradled in her arms, as if he was hers, and not three-quarter's blood to our queen. Morgan's sister's child, by her half-brother.

He wasn't a handsome baby. Too red in the face, and a bit puckered, just as if he was frowning. Straight black hair and dark eyes. He stared up at Morgan with a knowing look. She held out her finger and his little fist gripped round it. The blood rushed to her face and her free hand went quick to her heart. She didn't say anything for a while.

Fencha softened a bit when she saw that and put him in Morgan's arms.

The queen lifted a gold chain from her neck and slipped it over the baby's head. It had a pendant, like a horse's head. She'd brought it from Cornwall. It looked a big heavy thing, lying on his tiny chest. She took a silver phial out of the bag on her girdle and made smears of oil over the boy's brow and eyes and mouth and hands and heart. It left a golden stain on his skin, with just a thread of red in it. I knew why. It hadn't come from any flower or root, but it meant life. Luned and I said what has to be said as she made the five marks.

'You are mine now,' she murmured, very low. 'Your name is Modred.'

# Chapter Thirty-four

War. And for the first time Arthur was beaten. So he wasn't a fairy prince. He was Uther's son. Human, like the rest of us. It wasn't much of a setback. He didn't lose too many men. But the wind changed.

Gwendoleu had never been for him. Merlyn had sung songs in his ears that had kept him sweet for some time after, but that summer he went back to the Ravens. He made a deal with the Saxons. Lot did too. We could guess why. Margawse and Arthur hadn't kept their secret as close as they thought they had. Lot hadn't got proof of it, but he knew. He'd have his revenge.

It cost him his life, and more kings with him. Margawse wailed as if she'd been in love with him all these years, after all. She made her sons swear they'd be revenged.

Urien always stayed loyal to Arthur. It cut a split in that family.

There were others wounded by the end of that summer, fighting Saxons. Urien, that young Accolon that Morgan fancied, and Arthur himself. They'd taken them by ship to Cornwall to be healed.

Morgan had a haunted look when she got the news.

'And not to me?'

'There are nuns near Celliwig that have a name for healing. They came from Tintagel, they say.'

She didn't answer that straight off.

'Is Merlyn with them?' she asked.

'He is not.'

'It is nothing,' said Morgan. 'Merlyn was always a man that walked by himself. In Cornwall he was always in and out of Uther's hall; here at midnight, gone by cockcrow, changing his shape with every season. We are not rid of him yet.'

Yet there was never a man came north to Rheged but she asked, 'Is Arthur healed?' And then, 'Has Merlyn returned?'

And always the answer was no.

The Saxons pushed their border out a good long way that year.

Morgan went to Din Eidyn, though it was an early winter and bitter weather for travelling. I didn't hear the scrap, but she came away with what she went for: Arthur's sword and scabbard. She wouldn't tell any of us what she wanted it for.

'It must be ended,' was all she'd say.

It was warmer going south, but wet roads for riding. We took a boat down the Severn. When we reached salt water we cast about till we could hire a bigger ship. It cost her. It was long past sailing weather. It was the first time I'd gone out to sea, and I thought it

425

would be the last. The cliffs got higher, and the waves were almost as big, in spite of all the spells we made to hold them. We were creeping along the coast from port to port, and as likely as not holed up for days on end till the wind dropped. Most of the time I was scared silly. But Morgan seemed as if she was at home on that sea. Well, she was born by it. It's a grim coast, is Kernow. Narrow harbours like knife-wounds, and too many rocks offshore for my liking. I thought she was bringing us to our deaths.

Luned showed me Tintagel as we sailed past. It was a convent once, but it's a stern fortress now, under King Mark, and better suited to it, to my way of thinking. You could see by their faces that Morgan hadn't forgotten how she'd been kept prisoner there, or Luned how she'd been a learned nun.

It made Luned spiteful. I'd never heard her speak so bold to Morgan. 'Is it your brother's death we are bringing, or your husband's? Which of those would make you a bigger queen?'

'Beware! Do not presume too far. Remember Annis.'

That shut her up.

We landed at Padstow. But we didn't ride straight to Arthur's court. Morgan had other business first. There was an old wise woman, who'd been her nurse, and kept a strong circle. They were a long time talking. There were spells made that night that changed the course of Britain.

Then we took the pack-road south to Celliwig. This wasn't a Roman place. No stone turrets and paved streets here. This was boulders, earth, wood, thatch. I felt more at home.

Morgan rode up to the gatehouse. She'd brought both sword and scabbard with her.

'Tell my brother: Morgan the Healer is here and would see him.'

They ought to have recognised her before she spoke. At a name like that they should have waved her through the gate and shown her proper respect. She was the king's sister and the greatest healer in the land. Her own husband was lying here. They didn't. The sentries crossed their spears in front of us. They didn't trust her. It seemed those two couldn't ever forgive each other for what had been done. A lot of things had changed that year, but not the heart of it. We were left standing out in the cold wind. The first snow-clouds of winter were piling up over the moors too, a nasty yellow-grey. It's a pretty enough place to come hunting in the summer, Celliwig, but it struck mighty desolate that December morning.

It was Cei came to the gate. Arthur's a great one for courtesy, I'll give him that. It was the chief steward of his warriors he sent. Only Cei was never a man for sweet talk. He said what he'd been sent to say, bluntly.

'King Arthur will not see you, lady. You are not welcome at his court. Your husband has proved himself a loyal friend. But you sisters he will not trust or forgive again, ever. He knows now you have taken his sword, and the war has turned against us.'

The colour came to her cheek then. Arthur forgive his sisters, when he'd tried to kill the boy? His sister's son. A bond more sacred than your own child! Well, it *was* his own child, wasn't it? That was the trouble. And will be, till one or the other of them dies. Still, that was rich from him, knowing his family history as well.

I thought I knew her. I thought she'd whip out with some stream of scorn that would blister Arthur's face. Or wheel her horse round in a sudden temper and gallop off from his dun, and never mind who she rode down on her way. But Morgan always surprises you.

She bent over the horse's neck to Cei, and let her breasts hang clear of her cloak. Her black hair tumbled down so her face smiled out at him through it. That touch of pink in her cheeks, and her green eyes sweet and dancing. She made her voice like honey.

'Lord Cei, you are my brother's oldest friend. Arthur lies in great danger, but not from his sisters, though we have been greatly wronged. Let me through that I may bring him healing.'

'He does not need your witches' spells to keep him safe. If magic were needed, there is Nimue.'

'Nimue? They have returned! She and Merlyn!'

'The enchanter, no. The Lady came alone.'

'So long without Merlyn? Battles lost. The king hurt. And she comes back alone?'

'Merlyn was never one to stay pinned down.'

'Friend, you have a traitor in your camp. I must talk with my brother.'

Cei had a soldier's face. Wooden. I think his brain was wooden too.

'I have my orders. You must leave this fort. It would shame the king as well as yourself if we have to remove you by force. But I will do it if you are still here one hour from now.'

I saw her hands tighten on the reins. The horse caught her mood. He threw up his head. She sat up straight and kept her seat while he pranced and side-stepped. I caught the bridle and soothed him down, like a smith needs to often enough.

It cost her some effort to keep her voice soft and winning.

'At least warn him, Cei, as you love him. Tell him not to trust his lady . . .'

'There are only two ladies of consequence here. Queen Gwenhyvar. You would surely not accuse her! And the Lady Nimue, his foster-mother, who trained us all to fight and gave Arthur his sword.'

'Will she heal Arthur now? Both the king and the land?'

'He has the nuns for that. This was war, woman! Warriors bleed. We will avenge that wound a hundred times next year.'

He turned on his heel and strode off across the yard.

She hissed things after him that ought to have made him stumble. But he marched on with his back as stiff as a broom pole. Arthur wouldn't let her in.

She hadn't come all this way for nothing, though. When Morgan gets an idea in her head she won't be thwarted. Next morning I was lying in wait at sunrise when the king's court went out hunting.

I could have done with the stout boots I wore when I was a smith.

427

They give women finer ones in queen's palaces, to make your feet look smaller. I could feel the earth through the soles, frozen hard. I hadn't thought till I heard them coming how I'd get him on his own out of all that troop of lords and ladies and the rest. I needn't have worried. Morgan must have had a word in his horse's ear. She's got the skill. She wouldn't have needed to go near the stables to do that. Just a whisper from outside.

Sure enough, I was listening to the horns and peering out of the bushes to see who was riding up front, when there was bit of a crashing through the holly trees behind me. Accolon, on a black gelding. No one else near him. For all the years I've practised magic it still gives me a shiver when a thing falls out pat, like that.

He had a nasty scar across his neck, and he looked whiter still than before. But he could still sit a horse, and Arthur couldn't.

He didn't seem as surprised as he should have done when he recognised me. I took him to Morgan. The queen was leaning against the trunk of a sycamore. That's a sacred tree in Cornwall. She had wrapped herself in a great cloak of fur, mixed grey and black. There were badger-pelts in amongst it. The hood was over her head in the cold and Morgan's little face looked out from it, white as a snowdrop. She smiled at Accolon. The two of them fell to hugging and kissing like a couple of sweethearts before they're married.

I'm not sure if I should tell you what happened next. I didn't like it, and nor did Luned. He wasn't one of the wise. He wasn't the king it was meant for. He hadn't the right to take it.

She drew the sword out from under her cloak. The true one. Caliburn. In its own black scabbard. She handed it to him very solemn and looked up at his face.

'You know what to do?'

As if it was something they'd already agreed between the pair of them.

He nodded, and raised the scabbard up and kissed it, with her hands still holding it. I could guess how that would feel wholesome against his wound. She let go of it.

'It shall be done by nightfall.'

He hadn't taken three steps across the clearing towards his horse when a shout stopped him.

'Hold there!'

Nimue, on a mulberry roan, with a bright red cloak blowing out around her.

'His sword!' she cried. Then she checked. She'd caught sight of Morgan leaning against the sycamore tree, watching her. Nimue doesn't change colour as easily as Morgan does. It's just that sharp edge on her pretty sparkle that warns you she means danger. 'So it is you! You stole Caliburn from Arthur, and the scabbard with it.'

'Arthur has lost more than that. And not by my doing.'

'And just what would that mean?'

The Lady wasn't so bold now, seeing the four of us round her. She feared Morgan. She tried not to show it, but we could see.

428

'Where is Merlyn? What have you done with him?'

That was a mistake on Morgan's part. Yes, you're right, I did look over my shoulder when I said that. It's not often I'd dare say she hadn't been wise. But she was allowing that Nimue had a deal of power now. The Lady smiled. She has a brilliant smile. There's more of the daffodil about her than the snowdrop.

'I, responsible for the enchanter Merlyn? You sisters could never overcome him yourselves, and yet you believe I have?' You could see she was enjoying that.

It was plain to us that Morgan was having a hard job holding herself in. She'd suffered under Emrys Merlyn, all right. She'd lost her father through him, when she was eight years old. She'd seen her mother charmed away to Uther Pendragon. She'd spent ten years shut up in Tintagel because Merlyn feared her. He'd struck a chasm between her and Arthur. And there'd been nothing she could do to stop him.

And now here was Nimue, taunting her that she'd got power over the greatest sorcerer in the land. The Lady of the Lake. Just a pretty little flirt of a witch, to look at her. Only I knew better.

'Where is Merlyn now?'

'Shall we say he is . . . resting?'

'Where?'

'You do not need to know that.'

'*Where?*'

'U . . . under a rock. I will not tell you which!'

'How did he get there? Why did he go under this . . . *rock*?'

'Of his own free will . . . after I coaxed him. He wearied me with his attentions. He was always such a lascivious old man.'

'You coveted Merlyn's power.'

Nimue shot such a look at me then, it made me shudder. She knew I'd talked.

'I never took from him anything he did not willingly give me. You are too bitter. I offered him love and I got what I asked. You have learned that lesson too late. I am as great an enchanter as you three now. Greater. But you were right in one thing. That power that Merlyn had belongs in a woman's hands. Mine, not yours. I am Nimue, Lady of the Lake. I raised Arthur. I shielded him from you. I armed him with sword and scabbard. He is mine. Not yours, not Merlyn's, not the Church's.'

They were fighting over the lad like dogs over a bone.

'I see it all. You have chained Merlyn with sleep, deep underground, have you not? How long will you keep him prisoner? He *is* your prisoner, isn't he? When will you free him? What price have you set?'

Nimue gave a little pouting smile, but didn't answer.

Morgan stared at her, waiting, and then she screamed. I've never heard anything like it. Worse than when Arthur took Modred. It was such a desperate sound it shook a shower of snow from the trees and sent the crows up cawing into the air.

'You cannot do it! You made the great spell of binding, and you did not learn how to unloose it! Merlyn is trapped for ever, isn't he? There is no one, no one, who could break that now except Merlyn himself, and he is sleeping. Aah! Aah! He will not come back to Arthur ever again!'

'Does that grieve you so much? I should not have thought it.' The Lady sounded a bit sour and a lot less sure of herself.

'Grieve *me*? Did you never think of Arthur? Can you not see what you have done?'

'Arthur will recover. What has Merlyn to do with him now?'

'Do you still not know? Can you not feel? The world in balance. Sword and scabbard. It was always Merlyn and Morgan. Male and female. The left and right. And you have broken that! You thought you could take his place! Nimue, Lady of the Lake, to stand against Morgan. To hold the centre steady and keep Arthur on the pivot from destruction. To know the land whole. Fool! Fool! You deserve worse than death!'

Nimue was scared, all right. She had her hand out of her cloak, pointing at Morgan. Accolon leaped forward. He drew that sword out of its scabbard so fast I swear there were flames shooting out of the serpents' jaws. I don't know what would have happened, but there were two great shouts. Morgan's and Nimue's. He dropped them both in the snow, sword and scabbard. Morgan hadn't buckled the belt on. His horse took off, like a stag leaping over a thicket. Poor old Accolon let out a yell and hung on for dear life. He didn't get far. A branch of an elm tree caught him across the throat and swept him clear off the saddle.

Next moment, Nimue's roan was off the other way. She was a good rider. She leaned down as she galloped and scooped her hand through the snow. Morgan dashed forward to stop her. The pair of them dived for the weapons. I thought the horse's hooves would go clear through Morgan's hand. Then Nimue caught it by the hilt. Caliburn. And she waved her treasure over her head to let us know.

She disappeared in a whirlwind of dead leaves and powdered snow. Morgan leaned back against the tree, clutching the scabbard. She was whiter still and shaking.

'The scabbard is worth ten times the sword. She knew, and yet she chose the sword. Now Arthur has the blade, and I its sheath. And still they have not come together.'

She looked down at what she was holding.

'Empty! The beam begins to slip,' she said. 'What waits at the bottom of the shaft into which we are falling? Tell me, Luned, Woman? If I pull Arthur over to my side at last, what will that mean? Will the end be darkness for us all?'

At last she pushed herself away from the tree and went to Accolon. Too late for any magic to help him. His neck was broken. The tears rolled down her cheek. Then she turned her back on him and walked away.

# Chapter Thirty-five

Arthur got better without his scabbard. The prayers of those nuns must have had some power too. Urien came home as well.

After he got Caliburn back things went better for Arthur. He won Badon, and the line was fixed across Britain between Cymry and Saxon. It's held ever since. No more than that. The land's split in two. Ours and theirs. I thought that might have seen the end of another war, and a truce patched up between brother and sisters. But there was worse coming. Morgan's not beaten easily. She made one last try.

Morgan called her sisters to Rheged. I wish I didn't have to talk about this. It makes me sick remembering it, even now. It could have been me, you see. I wonder it wasn't. There was a moment when I wondered if that was what Morgan meant all along. She'd have her revenge. Morgan the Healer? She'd cursed my Annis, hadn't she? In a fit of fury, just because I'd done for Erith. She never forgets, Morgan. She won't forgive. If I'd been Arthur, I wouldn't have trusted her either.

It was an errand we'd been on many times, Luned and me. There'd been an early frost, but the ground had thawed, and there were still berries and toadstools for the taking. I'd grown to fear the forest. My kingdom once. Where I used to walk respectful, but with the tread of a man who has a right to be there. Where I'd danced with the horns. Where I'd . . . Well, there's been nothing of that since I took the skirt. Not like it used to be. I'm only the Man-Woman now, not the God. Morgan had given a bit of power back to me, but not too much. She's kept the real strength in her own hands. She's got me trapped. A half-thing. The man in the skirt. Only enough magic as is useful to her.

I'd done a sacrilege in this forest. I'd spilt the power. I could see the trees watching me. The twigs were stirring on the ends of their branches as if they were itching to get me. I stuck close to Luned, though I knew she couldn't have helped me. She didn't like that. She was scared of me. I could see she hadn't forgotten Erith either.

But it was the things we'd come for she feared more. The herbs of power. Roots, fruit, fungus. She had a sharp brain. She knew what she was looking for and where to find it. But when she hit upon it, she never looked as if she was pleased to see it, no matter how rare it might be. You could tell she had to force herself to reach out her hand and take hold of it. She always wore gloves. Well, you have to be careful. Still, she needn't have shaken and paled the way she always did.

You can never be sure with Morgan whether she's sent you out to stock her herb-room or if she's planning something special. Often you find the things she asks of you, and then you just dry and powder them or stew them in water and store them away. She keeps far more than Nimue. And she has more knowledge of how to use them. But then, Nimue isn't known for a healer, is she? You don't find a rabble of poor and sick at her gate asking for help. What Nimue wants is the power from them.

There's nothing evil in the plants themselves. Every one of the things in Morgan's store-room could be used for healing, of the body or the spirit. Mind you, it isn't all leaves and berries. There are some things that once had another sort of life, and some of those I've never known called on for good. Still, it's not the things themselves. It's how the wise woman uses them.

So I got a shock when I got back. Morgan called me to her. And it wasn't herbs she wanted from me this time. She had gold and silver and copper laid out on a table. I couldn't believe it. She started coaxing me to try a different sort of magic. My old craft. The sort you do with metal and hammer and fire. She'd have seen the fire in my eyes too, when I heard what she wanted. She smiled very winningly, the way she can when she needs something off you. That should have warned me. I'd seen that smile before, and I've never been a free man since. She wouldn't let me go too far, though. I had to keep my skirt, even then. She'll cripple my manhood for the rest of my life. I'll never be Smith swinging hammer on iron again. Only she had these softer metals she wanted to win things from. She needed me. This wasn't women's magic. And she laid her hand on my arm very sweetly and made me feel more than half a man for a bit.

She wouldn't tell me what it was for. Miles of precious wire she made me get ready, drawing it out with fire and tongs, and every bit of it pulled with a strong spell of holding. I wasn't a whitesmith. It was delicate work. I sweated over it. At the same time the women were getting heaps of silk threads ready, dyed to her own liking. Elaine and Margawse arrived at the end of November for Advent Sunday. Urien's always kept the Christian calendar. Our castle was full of Margawse's big sons fighting all over the place and making a racket. I wondered if Morgan would take Margawse to see her last baby, at the fisherman's house. But that was one secret she kept even from the boy's own mother. He was safe with her.

I'd never seen Morgan look so gay as she did that feast-day. She fairly sparkled. Years fell off her. She was like a little girl that's planning a wonderful surprise for somebody she loves best. For days before, she'd been working beside us. She moved so quickly her hair fell loose and untidy and her mouth was open as if she was out of breath. There were roses in her cheeks and her eyes shone prettier than I'd seen them do for a long time. But there were times between when she'd suddenly change. She couldn't bear to stay indoors then. She'd walk the ramparts in the wind with her fists clenched and her eyes burning and her breath coming short. We daren't go near her.

Luned and I couldn't think what she was up to.

But we soon found out. It was Sunday, after the meal at midday. Elaine had gone to lie down. She was looking old before her time. She'd only had the one daughter, but they said it had robbed her of her strength. I think, myself, it's the seeing did it. She moved herself slow and heavy. I wasn't sorry when she was out of the way. She's a brooding sort of woman that sees too much. I never feel comfortable when she's in the room. But Margawse was there, restless as ever and always nosey about what was going on.

Morgan sent two maids, and they came back with a length of cloth. Beautiful stuff it was, velvet, royal purple. I'd never seen cloth so rich and soft both for feel and colour. I'd no idea she had it. I couldn't guess where she'd got it from or what it had cost her. Luned whispered to me it had come from Venice. I was none the wiser. I've never had book-learning like she had. All I know of the world is Britain, and that's enough for me. We rolled the cloth out in front of Morgan. There was plenty of it.

Margawse gasped for pleasure, and clapped her hands together.

'It's gorgeous, Morgan! What are you going to do with it? Is it for a new gown? Oh, I'm wild with envy! Is there not enough for two of us? I will give you my pair of black chariot-horses, my ruby necklace. You could have had my husband if he was still alive!'

She'd got over Lot. She went off into peals of laughter, running as if she was going to throw her arms round Morgan and wheedle her.

Something stopped her. Morgan wasn't in the mood for games now. She wasn't a little girl any more. We could all see that. She was standing over that rolled-out velvet with her eyelids closed. Her hands were knotted together and her lips whispering. We listened, but none of us could make out what she was saying. I don't know if she was casting a spell or saying a prayer.

Then she sat down in her great carved chair, without speaking to us. She stared at the cloth, spread out before her like a big dark lake. She had a box at her side, where she kept her sewing things. We watched her open it in silence. Even Margawse didn't make a sound. Morgan fingered the things, a bit reluctant, taking her time. It seemed as though she had to make up her mind to something. Thimbles, needles, a teasing brush. All rich stuff. Gold, silver, ivory. At last she found the thing she was looking for.

She took it out and laid it in her lap. A pair of silver scissors. Shaped like a heron, with a beak that could open into two sharp blades and then close on the thread and snap it. I recognised them. I'd brought them to her, years ago: Merlyn's gift. In all the time I'd served her I'd never seen her use them. Queer, seeing them again now he'd gone, like a ghost from beyond. She nursed those scissors, turning them over in her hands, as though she was still having a struggle to decide.

Next moment she was a different woman. She sprang up and threw us a flashing smile.

And away she went, down on her hands and knees before us, with those shiny scissors snapping and ripping into her costly cloth. It made us gasp. She was working so fast. She didn't stop to measure or work out where to turn. But the shears seemed to know their own job. Before our eyes the shape fell into place. A wide full mantle big enough to grace a grown man's shoulders. No king in the land wouldn't laugh to get such a gift.

Then she jumped to her feet and cried out as if Margawse had just put her question.

'There! It is a royal mantle, but neither for you nor for me. This shall be my peace-offering to Arthur. A gift of the heart costly enough to mend the hurt between us, if he will have it so. Is it not splendid cloth? A fitting colour for the Emperor of the Britons? And this is only the start. It shall be more magnificent yet, by far. I shall embroider designs upon it with gold and silver thread. I mean to use every art of needlework they taught me in Tintagel. There will never have been a cloak like this for richness, or for labour of love. I shall line it with silk and crust it with jewels, though it empty Urien's treasury to do it. Arthur thinks I have stolen what was his. Then let him have this for recompense!'

Her voice caught there on a kind of sob, or she might have been laughing.

Next day we started the Advent fast. Morgan's made no secret to the Church of where she stands, but she keeps their seasons too. She's still Urien's queen. It's a strange thing, but while she's in their chapel she mouths the prayers as if she means them, and takes their food. Like a wild filly running with a herd of tame horses. I think she's never entirely forgotten Tintagel.

For a month we all fasted and worked on that cloak. I didn't sew. I've never managed to bend my big fingers round that sort of work. But I had charge of the gold and silver wire, cutting and twisting it in fantastic shapes, so the women could lay them on the border and whip them into place with coloured silks. Morgan made me put a charm in every turn. And the jewels! Rubies, coral, lapis lazuli, amethyst. I'd never had such a hoard of stuff to work with in my life. It was my hand over all of it. That border grew like a serpent, getting fatter every day. It took on the shape of a dragon with ruby eyes, opening its great jaws at the throat. It was a feast for the eyes, when our bellies were empty.

We got to the week before Christmas. Arthur always keeps that feast at Carlisle, and a merry one too. The kings of the north had swung back to him since Lot died, though Gwendoleu mostly sulked in his hillfort upriver. Urien looked likely to get Carlisle off him before long.

Morgan's great cloak was all but finished. There was just the lining of gold silk to stitch into place.

The day before Christmas Eve Morgan went suddenly tired. As though her labour was over and the life had gone out of her. The ladies crowded round their handiwork and they couldn't stop chattering and squealing over it.

'The cost!'

'Its true worth is not in the jewels. Any king can buy gems if he is rich enough. But who else in the world could have offered him art to equal this?'

'Such skill!'

'Such devotion.'

'Such craft.'

434

Morgan sent them away. She went into her bedchamber and Margawse and Elaine went with her. They were a long time murmuring together behind the curtain.

They'd left the mantle spread out in the sunny-room and the light was falling in through the windows and making the jewels sparkle. Luned and I stayed guarding it. Morgan's little grey cat was eyeing it too. I could see he had ideas of making a bed on it, and I went to shoo him away. He growled at me, and kept on prowling round the edges.

Margawse came out of Morgan's room. She swung the curtain open, so we could see Morgan sitting on her bed beside Elaine.

'I'm going for a ride. It's too quiet here for me!'

She went out and called to her ladies, but I don't doubt she'd be hoping for men's company before she got to the stables. She'd been cooped up long enough with a crowd of women.

It wasn't long before Elaine followed. She drew the curtain shut behind her, but not before I'd had a glimpse of Morgan lying down now with her eyes shut.

There was nobody else in the outer room but myself and Luned. Elaine gave orders. There wasn't anything special about the way she spoke them. She might have been telling her steward what to get ready for supper. It was just the things she asked for. We knew them, better than most of the wise in Britain, Luned and me. They were the most powerful things we'd got for Morgan's store-room. The sort she hardly ever used. We must have looked at each other pretty oddly. Elaine didn't threaten or coax us. She speaks slow and soft. I've never heard her raise her voice. But we went and fetched them. When she asks, folk don't argue. Besides, those three had been closeted together long enough. This was Morgan's and Margawse's plan too. I was beginning to understand it now.

She hardly had to tell us what she wanted done. We'd half-guessed already. It was powerful stuff. And the three of us to add our voices over it. But it didn't stop there. I found out then why she hadn't called her own women. It was me she needed. She hadn't brought that smith with her that had copied Caliburn. She got me to do the metalwork, bending the ends of all those little silver wires so they stuck through the cloth on the inside. Like a bush of little thorns, with charms as sharp. It was Luned she gave the job of painting them with what we'd brewed. That was cruel. Even though the nun wore stout leather gloves you could see her hands were shaking. We'd lit the lamps, and the wind off the Pennines was making the flames flicker. It was a wonder she didn't prick herself then and make her own fears come true. It took her a long time.

She was given worse work still after that. All afternoon she sat and sewed the gold silk lining over what we'd done. She had to take the gloves off for that, you see. One little slip would have sent that spell into her own blood. She never stitched so careful.

And all the time we were doing it, Morgan was lying asleep, stiff and straight on her bed as if she was dead.

# Chapter Thirty-six

You can't get back what's once been smashed. But you can hurt yourself with working over it. I couldn't ride to Carlisle now without recalling the last time I'd walked there while I was still Teilo Smith. A sweet May day with the river winking away on my left and the blue sky smiling. And me in my leather tunic with my hands still black from handling iron. You might think I rode prouder now, in a queen's chariot. But I didn't. I'd had everything I wanted before. I stood on my own two feet, and danced on them too. Only I'd been too much of a greedy fool to see it. Well, I'd turned Queen Morgan's head, all right, and I'd got what I asked for. Christmas Eve. Luned and me, riding to King Arthur's court at Carlisle to give him a present from his sister Morgan.

She wasn't invited. Not though she lived so close. She was out of favour now.

You can be sure there was another thing I was thinking of. Morgan would have her revenge. She wouldn't force poison on him, like I'd done with Erith. She didn't need to. She'd kill him with her spell. A love-gift! He'd take it. He couldn't refuse it once he'd seen it. He'd put her cloak round him. He'd die for vanity and greed, like his father Uther should have done when he took Ygerne all those years ago in Cornwall.

Morgan would work her spell from a distance, like she had with Annis. She'd enjoy that. She'd seen us off from the yard as pretty as a girl in love with her first sweetheart. Her cheeks were pink with the cold and you could tell she was excited by the sparkle in her eyes. She lifted up the cloak to us so eager it made Luned cry out for fear. But it was parcelled up well. We'd folded it so you could only see the purple velvet on the outside and a bit of that fabulous embroidery on the hem. There wasn't a bit of her treacherous lining showing nor any of those wicked points of wire sticking through. And now the whole of it was wrapped in a deerskin bag to keep it from harm. And us. It was lying on the seat in front of me, beside the driver. I couldn't take my eyes off it, and nor could Luned. She was shaking, and not just with the cold, though it was raw weather. We both knew we'd need to be out of that palace pretty smart before our High King put on his purple. Morgan couldn't have helped but see the danger she was putting us into.

Margawse had waved us off too. She'd like to have ridden with us, impudent as she was. She didn't care that Arthur hated the sight of her since she'd mothered his son. Just once I'd seen how bitter she was under the surface. Just that once. This morning you'd have thought from the way she laughed she'd have bedded him again if she got the chance. But she hadn't forgiven him.

Elaine doesn't stir out of doors unless she has to. She doesn't smile much either. She stood in the doorway, like a spider poking out of a crack, while Morgan passed that cloak to us. Then she went inside and shut the door behind her.

Morgan caught my hand. It's not a thing she often did, though she's bolder with men now than she was at first.

'Tell Arthur . . . Tell him, while he holds the sword, Morgan keeps the scabbard. Tell him the two were made for each other. If he would sheathe his weapon, I will bring the cover for it.'

She blushed when she said it, very deep and rosy.

'Tell him this mantle is the earnest of my faith. The most precious thing I could devise. Its cost is not in wealth of cloth and jewels, but in the gift of hand and brain and eye that have been spent to make it. Such devotion cannot be bought. Nor can it buy his . . .' She had to break off. There was a word struggling to get to the surface, and a depth of cold and anger it needed to come through. '. . . love,' she whispered.

She stepped back then and waved, and we trotted out of the gate with the horses' breath smoking in the winter air.

Sometimes I've puzzled over that. Could she really have meant it? What would have happened if Arthur had taken what she offered him and given her what she asked him on his side? But no. The magic I put in that metal at the first couldn't have held out against the curse I'd laid on it the second time round. It couldn't have turned out any different.

It was a chill grey morning. The sort that makes the trees look black and the sky dirty. There was a hard frost on the road that made the wheels slip pretty often, but it wasn't so bad we couldn't travel. I'd been hoping we'd find there were snowdrifts or floods across the way and be forced to turn back.

When we got to Carlisle those red walls seemed the only colour in a grim world. They let us through the city gate but stopped us at the king's palace. We said our piece, and they took our present through but made us wait behind. I wasn't sorry. I wanted to be out of there, and the quicker the better. But there were soldiers all round us. Luned hadn't told them all Morgan's message. How could she? That was for Arthur's ears only. Her Woman to his Man. We waited a long time till we saw them come out of the church and in by a different door. Presently Bedwyr came to fetch us. Very gallant he acted to Luned, and even to me, though neither of us were noble ladies. Maybe he was teasing us.

It was warm in the hall they took us into. A grand place, it still seemed to me, with marble couches covered in bright rugs and cushions. A log fire leaping in the hearth but something more than that. The floor itself was warm as we walked over it. Well, you're used to it. I wasn't. There was a throng of lords and ladies gathered round the fire. And they looked glad of it too, after their prayers. Advent's a long fast, and it gives you all the sharper an appetite for Christmas. Bishop Curran was there among them. And Gwenhyvar, of course. She looked small and pale. Her clothes seemed too stiff and grand for such a slip of a girl. Not pregnant either, yet, by the look of her. It was Lady Nimue standing at Arthur's right hand, as if she was his rightful queen and not Gwenhyvar. Arthur himself was in front of the fire dressed in a white wool toga with a border of gold. He was drinking a goblet of hot wine and he looked ready for it.

They'd unwrapped the cloak from the deerskin, but no more. It was lying just as we'd folded it, bound up with a golden cord, in the middle of their fine patterned floor.

'This looks a royal piece of work my sister has sent me.'

'Purple for mourning? Would she keep us in Lent?' asked Curran. 'Gold is the colour for Christmas.'

'Cheer up, man! Purple for empire. The Virgin's pains will soon be ended. The feast of the King is coming!' Arthur waved his goblet at us. 'My apologies, ladies, that I kept you waiting in the cold. You will drink a cup of wine with us to make amends?'

I wouldn't say no to that. I needed courage from somewhere. I could see Luned's hand was shaking. I wanted to kick her for a dangerous fool.

They talked politely while we drank our wine, asking after Prince Owain and Princess Morfudd and the big sons of Margawse. There was one son he didn't think he had to worry about.

'Well!' said Arthur, the moment our cups were empty. 'Will you not show us what my sister has sent?'

Morgan was right. She didn't need to force him. He'd seen enough already to tempt him. He could hardly take his eyes off it.

We couldn't put off the moment then, though Luned tried. She stammered out Morgan's message. I thought Arthur's cheeks might have got a bit redder as he listened. But his eye was still on the mantle. I don't think he properly took in what Morgan had said. And what did it matter anyway? In a little while his sword was going to be sheathed for good.

I undid the cord. Very carefully, you can be sure, and one of us on each side, we spread the mantle out across the floor. I felt I'd never seen it properly myself till then. They have more windows in this Roman hall than we did in Lyvennet. The lords and ladies crowded round it and marvelled over it. And well they might.

It was a cloak fit for an emperor. Rich purple, laced with gold at the throat. The dragon fairly danced around its border, with silver scales and jewels for eyes and spots and claws. I've never ceased to wonder how women in a cold bare convent could learn to embroider so gloriously as that. Where do they get it from? I'd never seen a mantle to touch it for richness. And nor had Arthur.

He swung round to Gwenhyvar, and you could see his man's pride in the grin he gave her. He cut a handsome figure as it was, and he'd dazzle any woman in that, or man either.

'Well, my sweetheart? Will you not think your husband a finer fellow when he is robed in this? It seems I have won my last battle. Badon was nothing to it. Morgan the Wise owns my right at last and offers me the purple.'

He couldn't have heard. He hadn't listened to what she was really offering him. Or what she wanted back.

'Oh, yes, yes!' cries Gwenhyvar. And she claps her hands and jumps up and down. 'Put it on, Arthur. Now! Let us see you in it. You must wear it to the Great Offering on Christmas Day before all the people. Oh, do you think Morgan would make a cloak like this for me too?'

Arthur signed to two boys, and they ran forward to pick it up. I held my breath then, but they had hold of it by the hem. We hadn't tampered with that. It was mighty heavy and it trailed on the floor. Two lords moved to help them lift it up to Arthur's shoulders. Custennin of Cornwall was one and Gereint the other.

'Wait!' cried Nimue.

I'd known she was watching me all along. I'd hoped she'd think the sweat on my face was from the heat of the fire and the wine. I hadn't let my hands shake. I've handled strong magic before now. I've killed with it. But she was wise. She could see things under the surface. She could smell power in the room. She knew something was afoot. I stared her straight in the eye.

She looked from me to Luned. That nun was a fool. She was white and near to fainting. She hardly tried to hide it.

Nimue fastened on her like a weasel with a leveret.

'This mantle comes from Morgan's hand. Your sisters were always treacherous. Gorlois's daughter speaks you fair, but she has never loved you. Why should she want to send you such a gift as this? You, Uther Pendragon's son?'

'Because she is my sister. Because we share the same mother's blood. Merlyn is no longer here to divide us. I am Arthur, and not Uther. It was never me that Morgan truly hated. Why should she not be reconciled to me?'

'Then let us put your sister to the test. We will see how well Morgan loves you.'

To the lords, 'Put the mantle on Morgan's woman first.'

I thought she meant me. I don't know why she didn't. Did she remember holding my hand in her fairy palace by the lake? It was Luned she pointed to.

The nun screamed. 'No! No! It's a man's cloak. It's too fine for me. I'm only a serving-woman. Not even a lady. The cloak is not for me. Not for me!'

She tried to break away but Custennin caught her from behind. They laid the cloak on her. She tried to catch it by the collar and hold it off her. She knows its power, I told myself. That may still save her. If her hands are steady. If her gown is thick enough. If she holds just the purple, and lets it touch, ever so lightly on her shoulders.

But how could her hands be steady, knowing what she knew? She couldn't manage. It was too big and heavy, too weighed down with gold and silver and jewels. It fell over her from her throat down to her feet and the hem sprawled on the floor. She was swamped under all that purple. She didn't speak then. She didn't stir one fingernail. You could tell she was holding her breath, as if standing as still as death could save her from it. I knew it couldn't. I could almost feel the weight of it pressing against her back and her breasts driving the bare points of wire into her flesh.

Arthur's court didn't feel it, though. They don't know yet how the magic was done. They've never learned the secret. Nimue held out her hand to keep them back. I could tell by her breathing she knew how close we'd come. All they could do was wait and watch.

Then Luned screamed again. It wasn't fear this time. It was pain. Her face began to swell. She turned black, like a monster. Her lips went blue. Her eyes were bloodshot, bulging out of her head, and there was a horrible froth foaming through her teeth. She crashed to the floor and writhed there yelling and groaning. Our silver dragon coiled and thrashed around her. I came to my senses then and dashed for the door, while everyone was busy shouting and staring. But half a dozen of the men caught me. They held me so I couldn't clap my hands over my ears. I had the horror of a lifetime to live through again. I didn't want to listen to a woman dying in agony like that a second time, but they made me.

Well, Gwenhyvar wasn't the only one white now. I'd never seen Arthur so angry, and he'd had reason enough before. I was sure he'd kill me too. And it flashed on me then why Morgan had fooled him so easily. I reckon he'd wanted to believe it was true, that she really loved him, that those two could heal the breach between them. He'd wanted to think it had all been Merlyn's fault, and now there was nothing to keep them apart.

Well, if he had, that was all over now. He soon got a grip of himself. Bedwyr had his dagger at my throat, but Arthur ordered him to let me go. I couldn't believe it at first, till I saw what he was going to make me do. I was the one who had to pick Luned up, all twisted round in Morgan's mantle, with that terrible face poking out. I had to carry her by myself. None of them was going to help me. They didn't dare to touch her now. It was a mighty long way across the yard, and the whole palace gone silent as the grave with the shock of it. I could feel the hate. I laid her in the chariot and I wondered that I was still alive myself. A thousand spikes I'd cursed, and not one had pricked me. I brought her body back to Lyvennet.

When Morgan saw the nun's black face she shrieked and tore her hair out. Don't think it was Luned she was wailing for. She'd lost someone a sight dearer than that. I think she might have been happier if he'd been dead.

She threw herself on her knees in front of me and grabbed my hand. Morgan the Wise, kneeling to me!

'Tell me I did not do it! Tell me this was not my work! Who am I, Smith? Who am I? Tell me I am not Morgan the Destroyer!'

I couldn't help her. It had very nearly been Arthur. And those three had all agreed upon it, hadn't they?

# Chapter Thirty-seven

The sword won't ever go into its scabbard now. That day won't come when brother and sister will be one. I don't know if it could ever have happened or what that would have meant. But their chance has gone. They'd stepped a queer sort of dance before but the music's finished now. There's been silence between those families a long while. He wouldn't even let their children come to his court till he'd cooled down. Only Urien. He'd always been loyal.

It was Nimue saved Arthur's life. At least she was wise enough for that. But it set a gap between brother and sister deeper and darker than Merlyn ever drove. It'll never be healed.

Morgan knew it. Next day she took her chariot. There was no one else with us; she made me drive. She let me take a weapon. There was something more precious she kept on her own knee. It was the middle of winter and the snow was lying on the hills. It had been a morning like this when I'd seen Arthur get his sword.

When I saw where we were going, there was a knot went tight in my bowels. We passed Way Bank. There was smoke coming out of my cottage, but the forge was cold. Mair doesn't live there now. I've never heard where she went. We drove by without stopping.

It wasn't far beyond that to the Long Lake. But it still wasn't far enough for Morgan. There was a chapel by the water and the priest was ringing his bell for the Christmas Offering. We carried on all along the shore, deeper into the hills yet. The track started to climb and it got rough going. We tethered the horses and went up on foot. Morgan led the way. She hadn't spoken all morning. There was another higher lake. Just a small one, this time. I never saw a blacker water. I got a glimpse of Helvellyn through a gap in the fells. It brought the ravens screaming in my head again and set me shuddering. We were both of us close to madness that day.

Morgan walked down through the reeds to the edge of the water. She didn't seem to notice the ice cracking and the black mud oozing round her feet or the wind catching her hair and whipping it across her face. She was holding Arthur's scabbard in both hands, just as she'd nursed it to her all through the journey. I was aching to touch it. I knew how she'd be feeling the warmth of it through her palms. It was the only thing she had left now to comfort her. Such an old black battered thing it looked. Arthur never valued it as he had the sword, for all both women had warned him. But it wasn't him that was wounded now.

That's still to come.

She took a long, deep breath. She needed to summon every bit of strength she had to do it. Then she hurled the scabbard away from her. It wasn't a good throw. The thing shot up into the air, then did a crooked twist and dropped not far off us. It didn't matter. That little black lake was deep past seeing.

I saw the splash where it fell. I tried to keep my eyes on it. But it didn't sink slowly. We couldn't watch it fade from sight for the last time and say goodbye to it. One moment she had that scabbard in her hand, and then it was gone.

She stood there staring at the ripples. And long after they'd gone I had to rouse her. And still she never spoke a word.

She's only hurt herself. She can't have back what she's thrown away, any more than I can. And there'll be many another hurt before it's done.

The Christmas hymns were ringing out when we got back. She went into the chapel. I stayed outside. When she came out she was a different woman. The way she danced with Urien that night you'd never have guessed how much she'd lost.

But there was another weapon she'd kept hidden.

When Margawse and Elaine had gone home after the New Year, she sent me to the fisherman's hut by Mabon's Stone. Modred was weaned now. I paid Fencha handsomely and I took him back with me.

The boy stood in front of Morgan. She had her twins on either side of her. She looked down at his dark little face for a long time. Then she hugged him to her so fiercely I feared she'd crush him. Modred yelled. Then she came to herself and gave him back to me.

'Guard him as you would my life.'

And to Owain and Morfudd, 'This is your brother.'

Morgan's never met Arthur again, till now. But she's bred his son. All these years she's sat by the fire nursing little Modred on her lap and crooning songs in his ear. Or walked with him on the ramparts at sunset spinning him tales of old battles lost while he looks up at her with his little eyes wide. She's taken him riding under the oak trees, and they've hunted more than deer. She's taught him well.

The king's friends don't come to her hall, though Arthur's let his nephews into his warband since. So how would he know that Morgan's foster-child was born on May Day in a year when all those babies should have died? Urien's kept quiet about it. He's too honest a Christian to think a little chap like Modred could mean anyone harm. She hasn't told him who the boy's mother is, or how he was fathered.

Fourteen now, and he's a handsome lad, for all he was such a scowling baby. Urien's taking him to Arthur's court today.

It's strange: Modred was Margawse's son, but he's growing more like Morgan with every day.

# Taliesin's Telling

## Book Four
## in the sequence
## Daughter of Tintagel

## To Mark

# Chapter One

Well, what would you expect me to say? Lovely, she was. It is written on my soul, that first sight of Morgan the Wise. I, a young lad still, out of the mountains of Powys, fresh from the court of Cynan Garwyn. The prettiest bard in Britain. Farms to my name, a hundred horses trapped with silver, and a hundred purple robes, a hundred armbands of pure gold, and fifty brooches, and a sword to myself in a sheath set with precious gems, just for the look of the thing, you understand.

I exaggerate. But not much. I was worth that. I rode to Rheged with my harp on my back and the world at my feet.

And she? It was like coming home, full circle, as if I'd wandered in a mist, though I'd never set eyes on her and hers before. Or perhaps I had. We have been at the lighting of the stars, she and I.

I came to her from the mountains west of Severn. Slate and granite. Beautiful in the late afternoon. The lakes deep and dark, pregnant with old mysteries. Never mind that she was twice my years and more. Do you grumble about the age of a mountain, when the sunset fires the snow upon its crags? What is age to a woman like Morgan? She would be bewitching for a thousand years.

They tell me she also came from a slate and granite country. Cornwall. I believe them. The stones are in people. The soft, red, crumbling sandstone in the fumbling of the deep-bosomed Devon women. The pure, demure, clean maidens of the Dorset chalk. But Morgan the Wise. Slate and granite. We understand the darker side of life, she and I. The mountains under the rain. The cliffs endlessly baring their breasts to the storm. The Dark Hunt of the Lord of Annwn that hounds you through the nights and days. I was not always Taliesin of the Radiant Brow. I have come a wild dangerous way to fame since I was Little Gwion, though I wear the experience lightly.

Morgan was cold, some would tell you on Arthur's side. Hard. Unforgiving. Others say she burned inside with an unholy passion. But I was Taliesin. Late chief bard of Powys, though I'd been barely acquainted with a razor then. Before that, darling child of the great and terrible Mother Ceridwen, who loved me against her will. The breast of granite was like home to me. I thought I understood her, you see. I was young and clever, and not nearly as wise as I fancied I was.

Pretty pleased I was with myself that day. A lad, fresh out of the hills of Wales, and for all my history, nearly as green as a daffodil leaf about some things, though I'd have knocked you down for saying so, then. For wasn't I Taliesin, the sweet singer? The youngest poet in Britain ever to win the crown of king's chief bard? And the finest. And with the secret knowledge of Ceridwen's cauldron besides, for all they say one of my fathers was a saint. But that's another story.

So I halted at the gate of Urien's castle in Carlisle in my new red tunic and my smart buckskin boots, and my precious harp, Healer, on my back, wrapped soft against the weather. I took more care of that harp than I did of myself. The gift of Cynan of Powys; the prince of cattle-harassers to the prince of poetry. Made my fortune already it had, this harp. And I had the scent of more to come. For wasn't Urien of Rheged higher spoken of than any king in the Island, since Arthur?

Since Arthur. There's a short line to carry such a stress of grief. The High King's not dead, but it was the nightmare every week of my life that the great climax of the tale of Britain had passed and no harper worth the echo of immortality was there to sing that name and send it ringing round the hall of time. Who but me should set the drinking-horns clashing a thousand years from now? Who raise the shout of Arthur that his fame shall not die? Who will tell of his grave and of his passing? Rein in your horses! Wait for me. Taliesin of the Radiant Brow is coming.

Powys first. Now Rheged. And finally?

A fine red castle, Carlisle. Great buildings of stone, and trimly kept. There's wealth here. A smart body of men and horses, by the look of it. And a king over them they respect. Nothing slack and shiftless. If he keeps his bards as handsome as his warriors, I'll do pretty well for myself here. I've seen stone castles in plenty west of the Severn, Caerwent, Carmarthen, Conway. But they were old, tired places, dreaming of lost Rome, and getting weed-grown in the cracks while they slept. I've sung Cynan's praises when he raided them, and got my share of the spoil for my song. But this palace is sharp, new-set. They mean business here in Rheged. And my poet's blood beats out the rhythm of a praise-chant, for such activity spells war. Angles in the east? Cattle raids on neighbours? Who cares? How is a poet to grow rich but out of fighting, when his lord and all his sons ride out to battle and come home laden with loot and yelling of victory? Or not, as the case may be. It's all meat to the bard. I can rhyme you a very pretty elegy.

So I let them lead me to the turret on the wall where the king was taking the air, and I have a spring in my step and my head held high and my chequered yellow cloak thrown back to show them all my finery. For aren't I Taliesin of the Radiant Brow, a very presentable young man, a walking treasure-house of jewels without and songs within that will earn me more gifts yet?

We come out on the rampart, and I am hardly out of breath, and I've readied my brightest smile before I even see them. There's a flash of sky all round me. Light spearing out of dark clouds to blind the eye from spreading mere and sparkling firth.

Urien and Morgan. And it is not warriors and raiding I think of once I see them both, though he's a fine kingly figure, Urien of Rheged, in the prime of life. A little serious, you might say, but who wouldn't be, matched with a queen like that? It is no joking matter. He's a braver man than I am, I can tell you. Morgan has respected him. He is less scarred than most who have lived that close to her.

All that in seconds, and I've turned from him, drawn by a power I haven't felt since I fled Ceridwen. It's a pity really, a generous, open-handed king like that. Triumphant rustler, battle-provoker, tiller-man of the ship of stewardship. But you do not look at any man twice when Morgan the Wise is standing by his side. Like a lone cromlech on a mountain. Like a lone mountain in a plain. And green eyes, like dragon's jewels, burning from the soul of her.

Urien is talking to me, greeting me royally. Chief of battle to chief of song. And it is no more to me than surf on the beach when the moon is full.

Morgan is smiling at me. We face each other, woman and boy – well, not much older I felt that moment – and she smiles at me. Very sure of that smile, she is. Green eyes, softening now, like moss behind a waterfall. Lips curving like the rose. And even as I go weak behind the knees I say to myself: That's a very powerful smile. You've been practising it. Only a moment it's taken you to make me yours. For I have the knowledge, ever since I licked the three drops of inspiration from the cauldron of Ceridwen. I know who she is, and what is happening to me. If she had spread her fingers and spoken the words of power she couldn't have bound me more surely than this.

Not that I'm complaining, mind you. When I feel that smile lick out towards me like flame, consuming my strength, I crumble willingly. She should be a glorious queen. Yet more hungry than happy. I read that in her eyes as the smile fades. Poor lady, so that is the way of it. Too keen a fire for the damp turves that surround you. Begging your pardon, my lord Urien, but I think you take my meaning. You're a plain soldier. A noble chieftain, to be sure, an upright Christian – praised be the name of the Trinity – brave and generous. Only, no magic in those muscled hands. All honest daytime in that face. She calls for moonlight to enhance her flames. And what is a young poet for but to make his lady happy if he can? Let her try me. I will be to her like new-cut ash to burn clean and true on her fire, and she may hold me to her bosom and kindle what sparks she will.

Her lips part now. Urien has finished speaking.

'Welcome to the City of Lugh of the Sunlit Brow, Taliesin.' Her voice wraps me in fur. Astonishingly difficult, it seems, to stand upright. 'You have come to us at a good time. My head is aching. Though your rank is higher now, you will not have forgotten yet the courtesies of a household bard. Your reputation goes before you. Follow me to my chamber and let me test how soft the charms you have to soothe it.'

That takes me back a bit. I have the poetic crown. I'd reckoned myself on the king's side when I was invited here. Chief Bard of Rheged, not the family harper, to sing in the women's room. But Carlisle, it seems, plays by different rules. I'd surrender the crown of all Britain, if Morgan said the word. I bow and smile. Well, I say to myself, you may have the body of a comely consort, but you show the will of a sovereign.

446

You aim for what you want. You don't waste time beating about the covert.

Two chieftains here, then. Both light and darkness. I should tread softly on the sharp-edged bridge between their territories.

I look at King Urien. He appointed me. But he nods assent. He even smiles a little sadly. And, well, I think, you're a generous man. Rest easy, my lord. You'll have your dues of me too, and more besides. I'm not called the finest bard in Britain for nothing.

> Until my life ages,
> And death claims his wages,
> I shall not cease yearning
> Unless I praise Urien.

And so I go after Morgan to her chamber.

# Chapter Two

Black lashes on white cheek, like a magpie's wing. A great queen, and lovely still. I say still, because now I am close to her I can see how the skin of her neck is softly furrowed, like fine leather that begins to lose its oil. She sleeps in the afternoon, her dark hair loose upon the pillow. Let the music fade into a breeze and the voice to a hum, and both fall silent. She does not hear you. She does not need you now.

Is this all? I could have sworn she wanted more of me. I read the hunger in her eyes. But here I sit beside the bed in my new red tunic and my deerskin boots. And if I'd been a virgin before, I'd be one still. She asks more from life, and I am life, am I not? She sleeps. I could reach out my finger now and trace the bones of her face. Stone under moss. But I am afraid to touch her. Not for herself. I think I understand her. She would know I mean no disrespect. The snowflake on the cromlech. The butterfly upon the mountain. No disrespect.

But it is that thing squatting at the foot of the bed, the shape of an old hag. 'Woman' is all the name I've heard it given. Woman! Spent and shrivelled as the skeleton of last year's leaf, watching me with jealous eyes under a wimple that hoods the face more than most, in a castle that seems full of handsome, high-necked women. That's a sour whim of Morgan's to keep a thing so ugly in her bedchamber. Does it crouch and watch like that when the king comes to bed her?

Wait, Morgan stirs. Touch the harp lightly. Take up the song again. The most skilful bard in Britain shall sing your cares away.

No. Not even Taliesin can do that. There is great anguish here. See how she moans under the fine sheets and the heaping wolfskins. Passion and anguish. Taliesin is here; a little comfort. There is only one thing I am good for, besides the song, of course. But I will give it freely, not grudgingly, an acolyte to his goddess.

One word from Morgan. Low, but I recall that she is a queen. The hag shuffles out muttering and the voices of the ladies pause in the room beyond. Nothing that is done here is truly private; be sure of that. They will be discreet, though, these women. I have noted already how swiftly they move to serve her. They are her tribe, not her hirelings. Loyal to her as Urien's warband to him. Best not betray her, Taliesin. She goes a different way to Urien, but the bridge of honour must stand. The curtain falls again, and I see it draped where the old hag sits on the threshold, listening. Well, we both have our duties, she and I.

It is no trouble at all now to be off with the tunic and the boots and the breeches. And never mind the Woman outside. Does Urien know what he's keeping me for? Rest easy, my lord. I pay my dues.

There, it is done, and the tide ebbs for both of us. Here I am. Fine linen sheets, soft chequered wool, wolfskins above me. Naked and warm. And the greatest queen of all lying beside me. For I have lived with enchantresses. Ceridwen's potboy, in a previous life. I've served this brood. I know power when I see it. And Morgan's power is greater than any of them. But she's still a woman, for all that.

Mind you, I could have done without her watchdog, hunched in that fold of the curtain over there. It's stirring, and a face scowls in at me through a slit. The sun shafts on it for an instant and I see what it is now. Oh, ye gods! That's worse than I thought. Especially as he's looking at me as though he'd like to drive a knife through my most sensitive parts. Woman? That was the cruellest joke. Lucky for me Morgan has him under her foot like a crushed beetle. What had he done, to bring him to this? And watch yourself, Taliesin, that you don't end up the same way.

The nightmare has gone, I stroke her shoulder. Her face is buried under the heaping of her still-black hair. You did not think I meant that by the snow on the crags, did you? Autumn is coming, but the frost has barely touched her flesh. I sang of the landscape of the soul. Her muscles are tight, even now. I let my fingers stray among her hair. I am satiated. I could sleep now, or go for a long walk beyond the walls. But I owe her more. I will stay a little. I am not so proud of my own craft that I don't know what it means to be hired. I give value for the gifts I get.

But for all that, I have left her still moaning. It is not that I cannot satisfy, for it was well done. But she is more spirit than body. And that says more than you can ever know, who have not felt the passionate surges sweeping through her. Yet the spirit was somewhere else, more urgent still in its desires. And who is there in the world could satisfy that?

I settle my arm closer about her, and feel her tears warm and wet on my wrist. I leave her grief unspoken. I know my limitations. I am a young man, and good for one thing only. And the harp, of course. And both of those I do superbly well. But that is all.

I dress as before and go back to Urien's tower, and as I pass I try to nod and grin at Woman and those that have a better right to the name, only not too broadly. That would be unwise. Step softly, Taliesin, their eyes follow you.

I am glad to be out in the wind. I find Urien not on the wall but down by the smithy, talking to the armourer over a mailed kilt of leather and silver. He looks at me straightly. He knows, of course. I can tell this pains him. I would not willingly have hurt him; I like the man already. But what choice did I have?

A sharp intake of breath. I've been a fool. This is a king. The penalty for what we've done flashes before me.

But he rests his hand on my shoulder as we move from the furnace.

'Have a care, boy,' he says. 'She can break you as she has broken the others.'

I look up at his face. It strikes me again that, plain soldier though

449

he is, he is a whole man, and kingly. There are few not of her side who could come close to matching her strength.

'But not you?' I ask.

'Morgan,' he says, baring his teeth, 'is not the woman to have married a fool.'

I like him for that grim smile. He's no weak cuckold. I could respect this man. I shall do well here, if I tread lightly.

> Until my life ages,
> And death claims his wages,
> I shall not cease yearning
> Unless I praise Urien.

# Chapter Three

Modred. Morgan's blood. Anyone can see that with half an eye. He pulls up his horse on the racetrack ahead of the rest and swings neatly down. He soothes the sweating beast with a whisper, hands the reins to the ready groom and comes towards me, unhurried but purposeful. He looks pleased with life, but his breathing is steady. You wouldn't think he had just won a race. A young man under control, with deep reserves of power kept hidden, like a salmon that hangs flickering in the current. An arresting face. Darkly handsome. Morgan might have looked like that if Gorlois had ever sired a son. Black Morgan. Black Modred. But there's a difference, as I know before the end of the day.

He greets me courteously, and I see by that smile why everyone finds it so hard to refuse that family. So winning to the world, so bitter to each other. Brown eyes, flecked with green, like tarns in peat. They look deep into me, and seem to like what they find.

'Taliesin of Pure Song!' he smiles. 'Your harp declares you. Welcome to Rheged. The very blackbirds on the trees fell silent for despair the day we heard you were coming to Caer Lugh as Chief of Song. They tell me your bardic crown shines as bright as the Thirteen Treasures of Britain.'

I mumble some nonsense. For a poet, I'm curiously short of words today. My tongue trips and stumbles. I'm blushing like the smith's furnace. His hand on my shoulder now.

'How do things move in Pengwern? What does Cynan Garwyn of Powys plan this summer? Will he raid Brycheiniog or Cornwall?'

A lover of poetry and a soldier too. He is steering me across the courtyard as we talk. Hard to resist, Morgan's brood. I tell him what he wants. He offers me wine, but it is not that that loosens my tongue. I find it important that Modred of Good Counsel should think well of me.

I play a few englynion for him, and he gives me the goblet I have drunk from, rare green glass. He also knows more than a thing or two about harmonies. We stroll beyond the city walls.

'Is it true,' he asks, 'that your mother was an enchantress?'

Ceridwen, the Fair Beloved. And a shudder goes through me as I shape my lips to speak her name. Be careful, boy. Three times that one blessed you. She gave you body, life, and poetry, and all of them against her will. Do not presume that even this far from Lake Tegid she may not come to demand a reckoning, after all.

Still, I tell him. A bard is born to sing, and the inspiration of my awen is upon me. We sit on a boulder by the mere while I tune the harp.

451

I have had many births.
I have been a fierce bull bitterly fighting.
I have been a squirrel that vainly hides.
I have been a spearhead beaten on the anvil.
I have been a roe in an entangled thicket.
And before that? The light shines clear for a moment and I am the child Gwion Bach, set to stir the cauldron of mighty Ceridwen for a year and a day. The herbs seethe and the incantations of the goddess hiss like steam. She is brewing the liquor of inspiration for her son Morvran, the most ill-favoured man in the world, Morvran, brother to Creirwy, one of the three most beautiful women in the Island of Britain. From Ceridwen come ice and sunshine, cursing and blessing. You must understand she loves Creirwy and Morvran equally. The spell is her mother's gift to him. Granted he needs something. He's nothing else to commend him, with hair on him like the bristles of a boar. On the battlefield, there's no enemy dare look at him long enough to strike him.

There are two of us tend the magic, I to stir it, and blind Morda to chop the wood and stoke the fire. It is not for us, this inspiration; an ignorant boy and a sightless slave. But the year's toil has almost spun its hot hard circle and I grow clumsy with weariness. The paddle sticks and jerks. From the throat of the cauldron, three golden, boiling drops arch towards me. A dragon bites the finger of Gwion Bach.

Pain. Well, what would a boy do but suck his finger? I have never been the same since.

She knew, by the bursting of the cauldron. All else inside was poison once the poetry had fled. She knew, by the dying of the horses of Gwyddno Garanhir when the spilt brew had fouled the river. She knew that I had got her blessing and her son had lost it. She could have learned it in the shine of my face.

Terrible, the theft of knowledge. I won a vision, but Morda lost the eye that could not see before she turned her wrath on me and found me missing. She came running, like a storm across the lake. And I must use that precious knowledge now to flee the giver.

Pain. Unmaking. Then the dark hard journey back into being. And always I must do it again. I am driven, hunted, pursued, As a hare I am chased by a greyhound, as a fish by an otter, as a songbird by a hawk. At last I become a grain of wheat trapped under the claw of a black, high-crested hen. I am swallowed, I am consumed. In the inescapable womb of Ceridwen I am made man.

She gives me flesh. I am Ceridwen's son now. I, the little robber, lie between her legs. It's all up with me. I'm a helpless baby, blind with her blood. Now I am washed with herb-scented water. They place me in her arms. The cheated mother looks on the brow of the thief whom she has borne, and loves me. The world is delivered of a miracle.

Not so easy, though, to forgive me. I am a pretty boy, but I am still the usurper of poetry. I robbed her son.

A last death. Sunk in a leather bag in the salt water of the estuary, the day before Beltaine. The cold takes my little breath away, a gasp of song. The river maiden Dubr Dulu hears it. She swims me on her bosom down the lapping tideway and leaves me hanging on the pole of Gwyddno's weir.

May Eve. And Gwyddno Garanhir's prodigal son Elffin finds the crows of ill-luck gathering about his reputation. His father gives him one last chance of fortune: the catch of the blessed weir on this sacred night, a rare inheritance. But it seems the young man is doomed to remain unlucky. The keepers shake their heads in disbelief. The famous trap is empty of salmon for him and there is only a satchel full of . . . me. The Child of the Radiant Brow, the pearl of poetry. Elffin takes me home and fosters me. I have rewarded him richly for that rescue.

I steal a glance sideways to test what effect I'm having. Modred is no fool. But I am startled by what I see. I am aware by the prickling of my hair-roots that I have plucked a chord deep in this man's soul. He is listening to me as though he were Adam and I were singing of his expulsion from Paradise. My song was no mere entertainment. This speaks for him. I summon my awen to do better for him yet. I see new visions.

I have been a prisoner in Caer Pedryvan, four-square, revolving.
I was with Mary Magdalene in the firmament.
I have been enchanted for a year in the foam of water.
I was with my Lord in the highest sphere when Lucifer fell.
That is not what he wants to hear.

'Who was your father?'

That stops me short. I laugh a bit. Fathers?

'They tell me one of them was a saint. You should ask my mothers.'

I get a laugh more bitter than my own for an answer.

Black Morgan. Black Modred. He and I walk back together. He is as generous as his sire . . . if Urien is indeed his father . . . and more than courteous to me now. His hand on my arm is warm. It tells me that we are brothers in some way. Very powerful stuff is poetry. I nearly said it changes things. But that wouldn't be true, would it? It's not like magic. Poetry changes nothing; it uncovers the truth. It points up the pattern of the universe. Beneath the gorgeous trappings of hyperbole, we show you the bonework of reality. We embroider, but we do not reinvent the world. Poetry affirms.

So I suck my thumb of knowledge and nearly choke on a hiccup. His finger-clasp on my arm has grown chill. I see a little of what I have done. I am mischievous Gwion again. My little song has stirred the mud of the deepest lake in the narrowest valley where the sun has never shone. Beneath the attentive smile, under the nobility, Modred is damaged in spirit. I glance sideways and see the way his dark brows meet now over his eyes. I remember this is a warrior of reputation. You'd think twice, aye and thrice, before you crossed Modred in the council-chamber or on the battlefield.

# Chapter Four

We part at the gate. Whatever passion it was I startled, Modred's got it reined in again. He's affable, considerate.

'Our kitchens will need to cook a rare feast this evening to match the banquet of song that you are inviting us to. I am eager for nightfall.'

He grasps my hand and crosses the court, and I see clearly enough where he is going. To the queen's quarters but not, I am sure, for the same purpose she called me. Closeness of another sort, Modred and Morgan. Is she his mother?

Black Modred, Black Morgan. Yes, there's a difference. Now I am under her window again, I can feel her darkness burning, like a lantern behind a shutter, like a smothered fire, like the stars in the darkest night of storm, if you could only tear away the clouds. As Ceridwen, so Morgan holds them both, with difficulty, by great power in her strong person. It is not easily done: the darkness with the light. You may not understand how this should be, those of you who have been brought up by the Church. Arthur and the bishops both use the vocabulary of the battleground. Our side or theirs, Heaven conquers Hell, as though God made the world to run by rules of war. I am a bard. Fighting's my metaphor as much as any spearman. But Christ and the Mothers speak another language, of buried corn, of circling seasons, birth and sacrifice.

Light and darkness. They are two halves of a whole, not good and bad, as you have been taught to understand it. They are two rhythms, created for each other, the voice singing one melody, the harp playing another. Together they weave one song, the penill. Most people, being small, serve principally one. I have been lucky. Made talented in childhood through this last birth, and footloose by my harp, I am free to wander Britain between the two. I am Taliesin, the charmed boy. I am not important in myself, though I wouldn't recommend you to say so to my face – we poets can chant a blasting satire! I am a dragonfly skimming the surface of deep water under the sunshine. I do not swim the deep, cold current of one, or soar in the high heat of the other. I live between the two, caressed by both, a thing without weight. Only my songs matter.

I have been reborn and know more lives than one. Some tell me my father was a white-frocked saint. Others call my mother Ceridwen the Crooked Witch. And I'm still waiting to meet the man who dares to tell me both stories in the same breath . . . Now there's a thought to take to bed with you!

But there have been those that married the hand and voice in full penillion. That could both swim and fly. Merlyn was one, who used magic to charm Uther Pendragon into Ygerne's bed and then set Arthur at the head of Christian Britain. He was a well-shaft deep into the old ways, a gateway to the new. It is not lightly borne. It takes great strength to hold the balance and not be toppled over. But where is Merlyn now?

Walk on, boy. People are staring at you. Do you want them to think their new bard's moonstruck?

Perhaps I am, though.

Morgan? Is there no one in the world who can part that curtain and let out the light in her? Be careful, Taliesin boy. It's early days yet. What is this light that leaps behind her door: the life-giving sunshine or a consuming fire?

But Modred. That's different. The light of courtesy and grace without. Darkness beneath. I have stirred something nasty under his bonfire pile.

Wait! They're coming out again, Morgan and Modred. Their heads are together. She steps with the swift grace of a wild mare on the moors, leading her colt. She walks right past me as if she hasn't noticed me. They pass through the gate, down to the forest, with that false Woman a few steps behind carrying a stick with a heavy head, like a cudgel. What do those two talk of together under the trees, with only the old hag to overhear? I feel astonishingly desolate, for one who's only just met her. There is no place for her harper Taliesin now. She will not teach me what she teaches Modred.

Well, there are plenty of pretty girls in this castle. I shrug my shoulders and look around. You can be sure there are bright eyes looking my way and hoping. If I had seen them first . . . But this day of my coming I only have eyes for my queen. Morgan's is not a face you quickly replace by another. Or a body. Later perhaps. But now . . . Besides, I'm prettier than any of them. I toss my head and smile a bit, and walk by as though I haven't seen them staring.

So I wash and dress in bright court clothes and make ready to sing for my new king at suppertime. The horses are penned for the night and the hall seems full of prancing princes that smell like them of sweat and leather. Urien's here. Only the face I look for before all others is missing. Modred and Morgan are not back, it seems.

A hospitable family this. Hands clasp my shoulder, faces grin. Owain, Pasgen, Rhun, Agravain, Gaheris. Siblings, cousins, foster-brothers. I can no more sort them out tonight than a pack of circling hounds, though I must have their genealogies off pat by tomorrow. Rhiwallawn thrusts a great drinking-horn into my hand, half of an auroch's head piece, bound with silver and mother-of-pearl. The mead's good, too. Gareth's doing a juggling trick with a pair of sharpened daggers. It makes us gasp, and him too when he gets it wrong. True sons of Morgan and Urien, some of these must be, and others not. I watch the fair and square ones, bow-legged, as if they still straddled their horses, sure of sword and sturdy drinkers of mead, outdoor men in a world of spears and dogs. Rhun should be a scholar, by the look of his finely-manicured hands. I suck my thumb and spot the thread of dark Morgan's blood in some, like a fallen hair on a pillow. Owain, now. We know that name, of course, even in Powys. As like to Urien outwardly as one buzzard to the next. But my awen warns me he holds more dangerous power.

There are the women of course. Only I find it hard to look them in the eye since this afternoon. One young lady I shall search for in vain. Morfudd isn't here, Morgan's famed daughter. She is married by this, I'm told, and serving Gwenhyvar at Arthur's court. A pity, though. One of the three most lovable young women of the Isle of Britain, they say. Down, boy.

The young men shout and gesticulate as they wait for the meat to be served. His? Hers? I watch them, and cannot sort out the truth of it. They are already sitting at the board when Morgan enters at last, with Modred following. Urien rises and Modred hands her to her couch and goes to his own place. The high table for him, but a lower seat than most of the young men. Still, he rests his hand on each one as he passes and greets them with a smile and a well-tuned query.

To Gaheris, 'Your horse went lame, I think, or you would have beaten me today. Would you like me to look at his leg? . . . They tell me you've had a book sent from Ireland, Rhun. May I see it tomorrow? . . .'

They answer him soberly. He must be younger than any of them, yet I can see they respect him, and so do I.

It's been a long day, and I'm giddy with travel and strangeness; a long supper, and I am heavy with mead. But my time has come, and all those faces turn to me like daisies opening to the sun. My fingers quiver with anticipation. It has never yet failed. The music rises in me, more urgent than the push of manhood. Believe me, I do not lie. It must out.

I sing first, as I am bound, of the king's fame and feasting, and Urien is as open-handed as I've heard. A horned bull and a cow are no bad beginning. But my praise is colourless yet. I don't know the man and his deeds. He shall have better of me than this in the months to come. So I turn to the tales of Britain and her old glory. I sing of battles past, of days I was too young to see. All the fighting I've known was in my service to Cynan Garwyn. I can hardly praise the wars of the ruler of Pengwern in this hall. The cattle-herds of Rheged graze too close to Powys.

There is a greater name, though. Like the first drum-beat of Beltaine that wakes the dancing horse, like the first rain-drops at the end of drought, like the step of a sweetheart outside the door. Arthur. And the fists beat on the table and the throats roar out his name. And I know it's reality. This is Arthur's family.

We are all his family. Arthur. An incantation like the name of a god. A charm, a legend, and he is not even dead. Arthur. I have never seen him yet. He never came to hold his court in Pengwern. I could not follow the men of Powys to his muster. It is the stale verses of older bards that I must recite. And fear grows in me, like one who sees a wound that will not close, that I may have drunk those drops from the cauldron of inspiration in vain. I can weave the praise of Cynan and Urien, but it is not enough. The harp grieves with the weight of mightier songs unsung. For I am Taliesin, the marvellous bard of Britain. When will Arthur lead us again? Where is the matter of the great song I was born to sing?

My hands move on unbidden, my voice chants. My mind's somewhere else.

After Badon. Truce. The roads are free. In the north and west the people prosper. Forget the lost lowlands of the south and east, numb your heart to the thought that they were half of Britain. Blind your eyes to the women of the Cymry that have borne Saxon children.

After Badon. The Saxons settled in the east, an understanding. Our warriors do not fight across the wall of hills. Our Christians do not march to save Saxon souls. The foreigners keep what they hold. And so do we.

A crippled peace. And where is Arthur now, that turned the tide and made us feel that we, the Cymry, were children of the dragon? The High King of all the Britons is almost forgotten. He has no territory of his own, who unites many. Who needs a general when there is no war? His kinsmen hunt the forests of the north. West, his boyhood friends have turned their spears on neighbours' cattle. Where are the battles of legend, the high glory, the warriors triumphant over the white-faced enemy? Where is the matter for the bards of Britain? Could it be that Taliesin was born too late?

Terrible thought. Drown it with the auroch's horn.

The mead goes round. It's someone else's turn to sing. Morgan looks up and smiles at me.

My sweet lady, there is a gentler side to my art. I can coax airs in the night to charm queens to bed. But they are too delicate to be sung in this hall. It might give rise to misunderstanding. Well, no, that's not my problem. If the world heard those songs, it might understand some things rather too well.

Urien knows already. And still he both loves and fears her. But that's not to say he'd want his grandson's grandchildren to hear these lays. And my poems will still be singing when the world is old. Rest the harp, Taliesin. He lifts his drinking-horn to you.

Tread circumspectly.

The domestic bard has had his turn. It is time to be on your feet again, boy. Pick up the harp once more and sing of the stag that Owain killed on the mountain, of the gold that Urien scatters with a ready hand, of the dun cattle in the pens of Erechwydd. The songs that live are those we earn our bread by. Those of the heart die when the singer dies.

> Until my life ages,
> And death claims his wages,
> I shall not cease yearning
> Unless I praise Urien.

# Chapter Five

I've hardly learned my way round the castle when the summons comes. Arthur will lead a spear-host beyond the Clyde. The troublesome Picts, worrying the heels of good Britons? The wave-bandit Irish, raiding for slaves and gold? The hunt for a famous boar? What do I care? What do any of us care? He rides again, the king of my dreams, and the young men are called to follow him.

They're wild with joy as they rush for their saddles. Owain and Pasgen, sons of Urien's blood, Agravain and Gaheris, sister's sons to Morgan. I have all their pedigrees versified now, except Modred, who calls Morgan 'Mother', and yet . . . I can see nothing of Urien in him, and I'm afraid to ask. I think I see the possibilities. Rhun won't ride with them. He wears a plain gown like a scholar monk. He'd sooner spend his time at the Abbey of the White House beyond the Firth.

Not Urien either. I seek him out. The wind is blowing my hair across my eyes. It cuts sharper in Rheged than I'm used to.

'Will you not ride with Arthur, my lord?'

His hand twists in the mane of the bay horse he's fondling. He's not so old; Arthur's his senior. You can see that he aches to be saddled with his sons. But he shakes his head.

'No. I am King of Rheged. I must fight for the land I hold, or for the Island's safety.'

'But Arthur's campaign!'

'Some fishing village in Strathclyde that pirates have looted? A hill in Lothian where the Painted People have placed their sign? Some high-handed chieftain who's kept his tribute back? I rode with Arthur once. We were both young then. We waded in blood on the beaches of Lindsey when the worm-ships came. We patrolled the high backbone of Britain in the mist and the rain. We stopped the Saxon right hand troubling our Cymric left. I fought at Badon. Those wars are over. The Island of the Mighty? A stew of quarrelling tribes. Dumnonia and Dorset, Gwynedd and Gwent, Elmet and Rheged. I steal their bulls, they take mine if they can. What should I care for the losses of Custennin, or Mark, or Rhydderch? I guard what I have. Lyvennet, Solway, Catterick. What's Britain now?'

I stare at him as if the gale had snatched my breath away.

What is Britain? No kingdom, then, but a dream, and beyond the Pennines a great amputation that aches still when the wind blows from the east? Only a dream, this Britain that we love. Only a dream, a vision that mocks our fractious history. I am a poet! I live by dreams. Britain is a country dreamed by Arthur when the night was blackest and the

458

sun of Rome had set. Yes, Arthur is a man, they say, though strangely got. Arthur the warrior will die. But Arthur the dreamer will live on. As long as he sleeps under some British hill, so long that enchantment will endure. Britain, beyond all common sense, a kingdom of the heart.

'You will let me ride with your sons? I have brought my own horses. I'll stay out of serious trouble. I will sing of how Owain and Pasgen fought gloriously for Arthur . . .'

'You will sing of Urien Rheged guarding Carlisle.'

He shakes my arm then to make me laugh. 'Cheer up, lad! How about a cattle-raid against the borders of Powys? Would you back old Urien against Cynan's cowherds?'

I know he jests. There'll be no cattle-rustling till the young men come home. The tide of history is ebbing round me. I'm a young poet in an ageing king's court.

We wave the warband farewell, the women, children, cripples, veterans, Taliesin.

The yards are still. Spare horses start and throw their heads up when the buzzard screams. They're left at home, imagining, like me. Keen blood knocks on the doors of the heart in vain. My footsteps echo in empty passageways.

And Morgan? I learn that there are rhythms, seasons. I have my place in them. I am not always needed.

I get to know the women well. Too well, at times. Only one resists all my advances. Tegau Goldbreast, fresh and sweet as a jug of cream. But I'm a stalking cat that's smacked for trying to mount her table to come at her. Such soft blue eyes, such unintentioned promise in the curving of her side. And yet, nothing more. I think she teases, but she does not. Her candid face smiles serious reproof. A Christian maiden, in Morgan's bedchamber? Nearer to her than any, except that Woman. She's neither dark, nor damaged, a walking miracle of grace. I may dance with her at night, but that is all. Poor recompense for what I'm denied.

So, each in our own way, we wait.

The harvest is in now, and Morgan has overseen the severing of the last sheaf. There is a nip in the air in the early morning, and often a knot of folk round the kilns where the corn is drying. We stop to warm ourselves as we pass, a good place for gossip.

I pass through the back of the hall, enjoying a bit of bread and honey, and Morgan's there, dressed for riding. Her horses are tacked and ready before the mist has lifted. She names some of her people. Her eye rests on me and I feel an unreasonable terror thrill through me. Because she wants me? Because she might not want me? I guess where she's going. Somewhere like old Caer Wenloe, dark fortress of Gwendoleu that ruled over the Solway before Urien got it. Certainly some secret place that never knew the hand of Rome. I have been with her before. I know what they will do. She names someone else. I am released for today. I am never sure, as she cannot be sure of me. I am too changeable. I hymn the praise of the Trinity in Urien's hall; I know the secrets of Ceridwen. She uses me sometimes, but she does not trust me. She is wise.

I see whom she's chosen to ride with her. Not Tegau Goldbreast. So I'm right. This must be the Mothers' business then. Morgan is curiously tender to the conscience of Christians. I've heard she was schooled in a convent. She never forces Tegau, though she compels others. Me, sometimes. She stands beside Urien in his chapel on feastdays, though she leaves before the sacrament.

Now she rides north with a dozen women and a trusted escort, though they're hardly needed. Morgan the Healer has little to fear from anyone. I am a free man till suppertime.

An ordinary day in autumn. The bracken brown and the apples ripening red.

And then he comes, without warning. Beyond my wildest expectations, Arthur the King, to the court of Morgan of Rheged, and I am there. And when he comes it is all gold and rubies, and the shouting of the hoarsest voice seems like larksong.

They are a noisy lot, too, the crowd of men at his back. You can tell they come fresh from battle. Hard, eager warriors, thighs gripping the horses' flanks, hands firm on bridle and sword. Eyes flashing on all they see. You can tell they have ridden to death and back again, and all the world seems dearer to them now.

And the Pendragon, laughing at the head of them. The High King himself. All through my childhood they have sung me to sleep with tales of Arthur, his battles, and his feasting, and his hunts. Giants slain, great boars pursued, treasures snatched. But not, oh not, the songs I could have made myself. And now he is here before me. Like a golden oak tree firm in a gale. Like a river falling straight and roaring. Like an eagle above its prey. A mighty warrior. A king above kings. And the width of his smile gathers me in with all the others. My hands ache for my harp. How long must I wait till supper? I shall sing him such a praise-song as has never been made before. Arthur must remember Taliesin.

Urien's eyes are brighter blue than I have ever seen them. He's a proud man today. He and Arthur hug each other like schoolboys. I feel the High King's not been in Carlisle for a long while.

Owain and his brothers fall on their father with great shouts and armclasps. I'm scanning the ranks of faces behind Arthur. These are the names out of legend. Gawain, Cei, Bedwyr! I am longing to compose an englyn for each one of them, but I have not come face to face with their particular genius yet. It is hard to contain my impatience and not get drunk with their fame. Oh, why didn't I ride with Owain, to see their long-legged, corn-fed horses in the onrush of battle? These heroes are Arthur's comrades, known and loved, daring in war, faithful when the shields hang quiet. Other quests have scattered the allies of Badon long since. These few stay loyal even before his horn sounds.

In the middle of all this row one quiet man stands closer to the king than all the others, like a son at his father's shoulder, modestly laughing. Arthur takes his hand and joins it to Urien's with a flourish. 'So, brother, since this young man claims no other father, take back your foster-son safe and sound. Look, not a mark on him, though he's presented me with a score of heads. You have taught him well. By the Trinity, I wish that Gwenhyvar had given me a son of my own so brave, so canny, and such good company.'

Urien and Morgan's foster-son? The only one of the litter I never dared ask about. So that's all it is. I don't mind telling you I'd supposed something more scandalous. Too highly-coloured an imagination, Taliesin, that's your trouble. All the same, a grown man and still at the court of his foster-parents? That's odd. Whose is he really, then? It seems his history may be closer to mine than I thought. I kept a prudent silence about my own mother. And the old thought won't so away. I guess what Morgan is doing now at the raven-haunts of Caer Wenloe, or some apple-grove of the Liddel, or a sacred well. I know how we worship the Mothers.

The men are all jesting about each other's deeds and boasting of their own, except Modred. All tongues speak well of Modred.

Word flies fast. Carlisle is being inundated. It seems as if all the housebound elders of Rheged are coming galloping up to greet him. But the smile is fading from Arthur's lips. He scans the thronging courtyard. We all guess whom he's looking for. Urien's face is darkening at this imagined slight. She should have been here long before this. The High King of Britain! Half the nobility of Rheged in her courtyard. And where is Morgan? There are new arrivals every minute, dust-clouds on every road. The Queen of Rheged does not come.

The king's own sister. Queen of half the North. Already the horses are being led to the stables and the cup of the hospitality of Rheged has not yet been offered. If I had been Arthur's sister, I would have run to him with a spilling goblet of red wine. I would have seized him by the hand and taken him to the softest bed. With my own hands I would have drawn off his muddied boots, unlatched his armour, dressed him in a gorgeous mantle. But Morgan does not appear. I watch Arthur's eyes searching in vain for her.

'The men of the North are quick with their welcome, Urien Rheged. But your women insult me still, it seems.'

'The Queen did not know of your coming today.'

'Morgan the Wise? Is there anything she does not know?'

Here comes Tegau Goldbreast hurrying, kneeling to the royal guest, offering up a brimming horn of welcome, a plate of bread and salt. A little late, and the wine trickles over his fingers. She is flushed with more than haste. But it is gracefully done. Her skirt sweeps the stones and pearls gleam in her bowed hair as bright as those that stud the rim of the drinking-horn.

Her voice is soft. 'In the name of my mistress, I give you Queen Morgan's welcome. She rode with her ladies today to a holy place above the Liddel. There is a spring, sacred from ancient times to those of her persuasion. Not a day has passed but your sister has prayed to some god for your safety, and her sons', as we do to the Trinity. She bid me tell you if you ever came in her absence, that her poor house stands ready to be made rich by your entrance.'

Arthur smiles like daybreak then at this pretty speech, and more at the pretty face. He drinks from the horn and passes it to Cei behind him. Tegau gets a far warmer kiss than she'd have permitted from any other man. There's jesting all round me. With cheers a warm-faced warrior is pushed forward to help her to her feet. Her eyes are bright for him above her companionable blushes. Caradawc Strong-Arm's a luckier man than I am, by the look of it. She leads the way. Modred himself attends the king to the best guest-chamber. On the threshold of the palace Arthur turns and lifts his eyes to the haze of hills beyond the Firth. His smile has vanished again. He looks like a child bereft of his toy.

And I? The moment he's gone I have forgotten Morgan. Am I in good voice? Will the harp be in tune? What shall I wear? What should I sing? Sweet angels and all the goddesses of Britain, what must I sing?

# Chapter Six

I'm sitting in the windowseat overlooking the courtyard and trying over a hundred airs on the harp, none of them right, when I see her come. I do not realise at first it is Morgan. Her head droops like her horse's. Her dress is soiled. The women are spent too, the guard respectful, sober.

But when I see it is the queen I do not stop to wonder where they have been, what they have done. Better not enquire too deeply. I have news that must come before everything. The yard is as busy as a feast-day, but she doesn't seem to have noticed. I am not sure if I should yell it from the window or dash for the door. Too late. Someone is coming across the yard to greet her, limping a little; he's taken a leg-wound. Owain. She's dismounted now, swaying a little as she lets go of her horse, looking at her eldest son striding towards her. She puts her hand to her eyes as if to clear a mist. Then his arms are wide and she's enfolded in them.

I'm perched like a wren on a windowledge, watching them. This must be the moment when he tells her who is here. I see her start, step back. Her look flies to the walls of the guest-chambers. She starts to hasten for that door. Then I see her stop, falter with indecision.

Indecision. Morgan? That all-wise queen whose every gesture strikes with the sharp edge of authority.

My heart aches with a sudden tenderness for her, and just the merest touch of self-congratulation; the young and vigorous shoot for the flower that has bloomed past fullness. She is tired, her hair dishevelled, her skirt dusty. Take twenty years away and it would not matter. She could laugh off her careless disarray, the sweet tangle of the wayside briar rose. But the years are more unforgiving now. Arthur is here in her court, sudden, unexpected, after long absence. And she is not as she would like him to behold her.

She's taken charge of the situation, hurrying towards her own rooms, calling to bring the servants running to her and send them flying again in all directions, as if her stewards hadn't begun to prepare the feast hours before this. The doorway takes her from my sight.

I stand at a crossroads of the passageways. Urien's rooms or Morgan's? I haven't been bidden to either. But I cannot wait for evening. I cannot be left sitting on the margin of this day's events. I seem to feel the heat of Arthur from the men's side. So what takes my feet down the corridor that leads to Morgan's chamber? What do I think she wants me for now?

The shadows fox my eyes after the sunlight. A man is coming

unevenly towards me, along the corridor trodden mostly by women. I recognise the limp again. Owain returning from his mother's room.

He checks at me, as I did at him, and peers in my face.

'Taliesin! Do you think my mother has time for harpers now, when Arthur the king is waiting for her appearance?'

'I didn't know . . . I thought perhaps she would want . . .' Not she. I'm the one that wants to be noticed. Arthur's her brother. Do not forget your faithful Taliesin.

He takes my arm, not gently, and steers me back the way I've come.

'Listen, lad. You don't know the board. The stakes in this game are too high for you. We have had other smart young players before you. One bard got more from my father than a cup of gold.'

'Urien Rheged's a generous man!'

'Generous with his sword, when his honour's threatened. Have you heard of Tristvard?'

'No.'

'He won more from my mother than the rules allowed. My father killed him.'

Blood stops. It's more than shadows darkening my eyes. The air's terribly cold in this passage.

'Urien killed a *bard*! Because he and your mother . . .? But Morgan! What did she do then?'

Owain laughs, harsh as a crow.

'She would have slain Urien for it, with the same bloody sword. My sister Morfudd stopped her. Since then, my parents have come to an understanding. She agrees not to taint his honour. He allows her the rites of her kind, so she causes no scandal.'

I remember the smile on Urien's face. *'Morgan is not the woman to have married a fool.'*

And I thought that smile spoke sympathy!

Do not grow up, Taliesin, do not grow up. The rules of this game are stricter than you thought. Only a child is excused.

> I shall not cease yearning
> Unless I praise Urien.
>
> I shall not cease yearning . . .

The words rattle in my head like loose teeth.

Morgan walks into the hall well before suppertime. I'm there already, nervous as a bird with nestlings. And when I see her, even I, Taliesin, gasp in wonder. I thought by now I knew every strand of her hair, every hollow of her flesh. But she is lovelier tonight than I have ever dreamed. Gold embroidered on purple. The finest jewels she possesses braided in her hair. I think her face has been delicately tinted to glow in the lamplight, a bloom of perfection, as though the years were running backwards. Hours, you might have thought her women would have needed to prepare her like this. But it goes deeper than that. Jewels can make a woman look hard. It is more than bathing in scented oils and milk that has softened her so. Her radiance comes from within.

I stand at Urien's elbow, bewitched, watching her come up the long hall towards us. We're all the same. Small hope that I, smart as I am, can catch anyone's eye this evening, with every man and woman gaudy as a kingfisher. But my time will come. Only I can enchant their ears.

Morgan signs to the steward and the horn is sounded. All faces are turned to the door now, all the household readied.

There's a shout from the threshold, 'Peace, my lords and ladies! Welcome Arthur, High King of all the Britons!'

He knows how to make an entrance. He stands four-square, feet widely planted, hands on hips to throw back the cloth-of-gold mantle and show off the sturdy strength of his figure, head tilted, laughing, and the torchlight from the doorway making golden flames of his hair.

Morgan moves. They are advancing to meet each other in the middle of the hall, their hands outstretched across the years that have separated them. Her reverence is queenly. Her jewelled head is bowed, her skirts sweep the floor. In no way does this diminish her dignity. In silence he raises her up and holds her by both hands.

Long they stand silent, looking into each other's faces, her white fingers hidden within his greater grasp. Too long for a brother with a sister.

At last her voice thrills. 'I am grieved beyond measure that my brother the king should honour my hall with his presence after all these years and another woman than I should offer him her cup.'

'A welcome as rich as this was worth waiting for, lady.' His eyes caress her body. The next words come oddly harsh. 'That purple gown becomes you. Did you fashion the embroidery on it with your own hands?'

Their fingers part suddenly. She stares at him, and the sudden swing of her black hair covers the anger flashing in her eyes. Urien comes forward to take Arthur by the arm and lead him to the highest seat. He must understand more than I do. Modred is quick to attend Morgan. And I, that thought I had conned a thousand scrolls of knowledge in my incarnations, from the court of the fair goddess Arianrhod to great Alexander, am busy shelving fresh sheets that no one ever showed me.

We've eaten well. It is time to pick up the harp. Now, more than any night in my life, the melody must ring true. I touch the first string, and the magic of my voice falls over them all. The drunken laughter hushes. The knives are still. I feel the power in my song binding them all.

I sing first of Christ in glory riding on the clouds. Then I rejoice at Arthur's coming to our feast. They are good songs, for a beginning. They please him, and he throws me a golden belt snatched, who knows, from the loins of some dying Saxon or Pict. The gold is nothing to me – well, nothing much – beside his smile. But I search his face for something more. Can he hear the great song inside me that is waiting to be born? Does he sense that I was created to hymn his highest deed?

The lesser bards are buzzing now. Tonight there is strong red wine to ease my throat. I gulp a long, cool cup and feel it turn my skin to fire. Someone is looking at me along the table. Modred. His eyes are shining too.

There is dancing tonight. Morgan grows rosy again as Arthur swings her down the line. Look, they're laughing together. All's well, surely?

She sits by the fire now, and Healer and I must play again. Music without words this time, expertly fingered. Arthur stands between us, horn in hand, leaning over her shoulder and murmuring to her. Only I can hear, beneath my playing, what he says.

'So it is true? You keep the old ways still.'

'My husband is a Christian lord. Rheged is Urien's kingdom.'

'Then, if the High King wanted wisdom, he must apply to its queen.'

She does not start, but her utter stillness speaks more than if she had.

'Arthur of Britain has his own wise woman.'

'The Lady of the Lake? Pah! Nimue and I fell out long ago. She thought because she had raised me, she could rule me, as she does everyone else. But the High King has grown beyond his nursemaid. She wanted to share power with Bishop Bytwini as my soul-friend, but there is room on the throne he worships for only one. There was a rare old row. She left in a temper.'

'And the Christian Church is not enough for Arthur now?'

He leans closer. 'The bishops speak to me of heaven. That is not what I want to hear. It is this world that is slipping away from me too fast.'

She lifts her face to stare at him. In wonder? Disbelief?

'What do you want? You would ask me to turn back time for you? To do still what we have not yet done?'

He raises his horn to her. His look is deadly serious, no flattery, no accusation now.

'Who else should help me, if not my wise sister?'

Did my fingers falter? The spell's not working. Cei roars with laughter at a jest of Owain's. The magic thread has snapped. Arthur looks round and finds his hosts too close for prudence.

The warband are shouting for more manly music, and I am only too glad to answer them. Now I make the shields on the walls ring with chants that have more to do with warriors than wooing. They roar applause.

Morgan's forgotten. This is the life for me. The circling wine jug. The wild tales of battle. The fair and laughing women. Oh, to be a bard in Arthur's court! To transmute his story into song. To ride beside him – all right, behind him! – into battle and come back singing of victory. To know on my death-bed that all the verses I have made are echoing for ever down the years!

But when I draw breath again and look round the hall, I feel in my soul one thing is still missing. One name that was always coupled with Arthur's in the songs of his boyhood. How old would that face look if we could see it now? A map of wrinkles. A magic chart of lines that speaks him wiser even than his years. Who knows of Merlyn the Enchanter now? His loss gapes like a side missing from the figure that is joined tonight in Morgan's hall. Arthur, the noblest king of all the

Britons. Morgan, the most potent of wise queens. Taliesin, the sweetest bard that ever sang. If Merlyn came, the square would be complete.

A shiver runs through me. Once upon a time, Merlyn himself sang in this very hall. He went disguised as Gwendoleu's bard, before Urien came here.

So I sing a new song. I sing of Merlyn, who was the greatest chief of magic among all the wise, who led the victorious Pendragon to Ygerne's bed, who put an enchanted sword in Arthur's hand and guided him on the path to victory. Who sleeps – well, who knows where? In some forest where the nightingale keeps watch? Under a secret stone? What might happen if that magic re-awoke? Could we snatch the Island of the Mighty from our foes, like the fabled spoils from the fairy fortress of Annwn? Will the morning never break that brings great Merlyn back to us?

The notes curl plaintively among the rafters. There, I say to myself, that should bring tears to their eyes. But what's the matter with them? Why is Tegau hiding her eyes behind her hands? Why are Arthur's warriors grinning like schoolboys when their teacher trips? What have I said? What's so funny about Merlyn? It's worse than that. The men of Morgan's branch are frowning blackly. Arthur looks angry. And when I turn for help to my lord and lady I find the sky has turned to thunder in Morgan's face.

I see it now, ass that I've been! All this time I've been singing of Arthur's coming, and I never thought what it meant. When Merlyn enchanted Uther Pendragon to Ygerne's chamber, it was Morgan's father that had to be killed, Morgan's mother who was appropriated.

I've made a fool of myself again. It seems they taught me all the wrong things in Powys.

But Urien is a Christian king, and courteous. He gives me a dagger to add to Arthur's belt and cover my confusion. He is always generous.

> Until my life ages,
> And death claims his wages,
> I shall not cease yearning
> Unless I praise Urien.

# Chapter Seven

There's no room in Morgan's bed tonight, even for so slight a lad as Taliesin. I have angered her. The spectre of a red-eyed wolf has reared its grinning mouth above her hearth, and at my summoning. Merlyn. And I'd thought it was a name of benediction. Still, to be honest, she wouldn't have been interested in me even if I hadn't crossed her. Not on such a night. She had decked herself like the Queen of Araby for Arthur, not for me.

After Owain's warning I find it a relief. Carlisle is too full of the presence of Pendragon and his men.

But the morning is a new day, the mist creeping up from the river and the promise of sunshine beyond.

They are all astir for the hunting, those men that have come with Arthur, and plenty of our ladies with them. It's what I wanted to believe, that life, that zest. All their lives these men have been fighting. They could never sit still in Celliwig or Caerleon. The great battles are over, but there is always some other quest. It has thinned their ranks. Harrying, hunting through the hills, friends dying, maimed. You'd think they'd begin to tire of the sight of blood by now, the older ones at least. But these are Arthur's warband. They have lived another summer. They are alive, whole, most of them, anyway, and reckless with the joy of it. Why should I want them to stop living before their brief lives end? What would I sing of, if they were not as they are? He draws the young men by the magic of his name. The older ones lost their hearts to him long ago. He does not need Merlyn to bewitch them. Like me, they hope to live in legends still untold.

At first, we are all a little heavy-headed, and the beer tastes sour and the chill clutches at our bowels. But we are men. We are alive, aren't we? We laugh and jest all the louder to shout down the goblins on our shoulders. Soon it will be Samain, Winter's Eve. But not yet.

Men, goblins. In the damp before sunrise I cannot hold off the black invaders of last night. I come on Arthur's warriors crowding about the stables, and even in the mist some shapes stand out from the rest, harder-edged. Arthur's sisters' sons. In all the knotted web of kinship, no bond should be more sacred to a man than that. They are many. I name them over to myself. Great Gawain himself, Agravain, Gaheris, Gareth. And from Morgan's body, Owain, Pasgen, Rhiwallawn, Rhun. Sons of Arthur's sisters. No, half-sisters. One mother, Ygerne, that bore three girls and then Arthur, but not to the same man. His father, Uther; theirs, Gorlois. The slayer and the slain. The spoil, their mother.

My heart shivers in the dawn as I recall how Morgan looked when I sang of Merlyn, who brought it about.

And now my bard's training brings names strumming through memory. Young Arthur felled Saxons and Angles: Flame-Bearer, Blood-Axe, Raven-Hold. But other names come softer on the tongue and bitterer to the taste. British names, kings that opposed Arthur in that dawn. There were Cymric spears levelled against the upstart boy. Gwendoleu, here in Solway. Lot of Lothian and Nentres of Garlot, kings who married Morgan's elder sisters. So that's the current I cannot help but feel. There has been treachery here in the North. Urien Rheged? No, never Urien. Urien was always true to Arthur. The bards sing him brave and constant to his High King. So where does Morgan stand? Merlyn is not loved here, that's plain. Is Arthur?

I have seen her gaze locked in his.

I should have turned my eyes to other faces than hers. What might I have read then in the looks of these sisters' sons? For a bard, I've been curiously careless about their genealogy. These are Gorlois's grandsons. How have they been bred? Whose warriors are they really, Arthur's, or their mothers'? How dearly do they love this royal uncle they have sworn to serve?

No! You're a too-wise fool, Taliesin. You see riddles where there are none. Tintagel's an old grief, long buried. Look, Gawain is nearly as old as Arthur. A lifetime's loyalty there, for all his father fell fighting the young Pendragon. And these others are Urien's sons as much as Morgan's. They've risked their life's blood for their uncle already this summer. The sun's up and the mist is fleeing. You're a silly boy and no true bard. You play 'Blerwm, blerwm', upon your lips, and make the world a nonsense-song.

They've looked out a hunting-pony for me to ride. It's not the sober cob that carried me sedately from Powys, with rounded sides and feet like platters. I wish it was. Surely Urien knows I'm no horseman. I'm a horse-owner, yes. I have droves of them, farms, serfs, back in Powys. They make a handsome form of wealth. I don't have to ride them.

I study this grey mare from a respectful distance. A nasty-looking brute. Lively. I don't like the way she rolls her eye at me. I'm a bard, not one of these wild men of Arthur's that ride as if they grew from the saddle.

But here is Morgan among us. She's not dressed for hunting, that's plain. She is dark today, her jewels gone. Black-robed, black-hooded, gold bands crossed upon her chest like a druid priestess. Why? Morgan does nothing without calculation. All eyes fly to her and the racket hushes. I see the hope in Arthur's face. He is not hungry for her body today. Can she offer him something else?

She carries a silver cup of wine, gently steaming. She walks through the press of men and beasts to the centre. The hounds wag their tails. Even the horses stand still for her, though she has said no word. She stops before Arthur's roan and pours the first drops of wine upon the earth, moving her left hand and pronouncing the age-old words. There is a murmur all round. Christians like Urien sit stiff-lipped, others mutter the response. I am one of them. The hunt's a dangerous game. And Arthur? His lips move soundlessly. He watches her intently.

She holds the cup up to him now to drink to his own success. His eyes cannot leave hers as he takes it, and all that I thought I understood last night is not enough. The new day turns dark and the apples fall from the trees like blood.

I have seen fear in Arthur's eyes.

He turns. Bedwyr puts out a hand as if to taste the wine for him first. An insult, surely, in his sister's house! But Arthur's look falls on me, and he gives a curious grin. And I, fool that I am, blush like a girl. It's not ugly doubt after all. He's giving me the first sip as a mark of high favour for my songs.

There is an odd stillness. Arthur's men watching us, Urien's people grimly silent. I was right, the first time. I sense the tension of mistrust. Why are they all looking at this cup and then at Morgan?

There are black flies before my face. I'm going to fall. The king's taster! Why me?

Indignantly I turn to Morgan's face and find its features still, her deep eyes unreadable. Poison? Would she do that to me? To Taliesin? But no, she's not the one who is holding out the cup to me. It's Arthur. I am a trifle to him, Morgan's bard. His golden belt last night has paid for all my songs. He owes me nothing. All the magic of my singing, all the splendour of my praises, cannot buy one more hour of life from him. God, what a waste of talent!

I reach my hand to take the cup. The wine smells spiced. Time crawls as in a dream. From the anger all around me I feel I am reliving an old scene. In some past life of mine? No. The pain's here. A festering wound reopening. It is they who are remembering, not I. The silver's warm from his grasp. My stomach heaves.

Then Arthur snatches the cup back from me, spattering the ground, his horse, my tunic in a mad baptism. With a roar of laughter he drains the wine to the last drop and tosses the empty goblet for me to catch.

'If that is your price! See how well I will trust my beloved sister!'

But she is angered.

'Do you still doubt what I have to offer? Can you not forget? Will you never believe I have done you no harm?'

'No harm? I recall a woman dreadfully dying here, in a poisoned cloak you made for me.'

'That was not my doing.'

'It was not her death you intended, certainly.'

'I am Morgan the Healer!'

'Yes! It was you who stole my scabbard of healing from me. You keep it yet.'

A stillness seizes her. I am a bard. I know the power of a dramatic pause. But the line that follows is not the true revelation. Something has been left unspoken here.

'You kept the sword that wounds.'

'I am the king!'

'And I am . . .?'

470

'I have drunk your cup today. What more do you want from me?' That steady gaze for answer.

Colour dark as the wine rises in Arthur's face. Gawain snatches the hunting-horn hung on his belt by a golden chain. He blows wild notes that set the hounds belling and the huntsmen running to whip them in and bring back order. But blood is up, the horses tossing their heads, the riders impatient. Old griefs and old revenge ebb, leaving those two in an island of animosity and spilled wine.

Modred is ordering the stewards to hand round drink to all the rest. They toss it down with shouting and laughter. The hunt's moving off.

I'm at the tail of the field. The sun shines out, but I'm still cold. There is more here than I knew. Was he right to trust her? What does she want from him, and what has she taken already?

Fly higher, little dragonfly, the water is too deep beneath you.

# Chapter Eight

But now the hunt is on. I'm afraid of horses. In Morgan's circle they worship mares. But in Powys we danced the dragon, and nobody ever asked me to ride one of those. Give me my own two feet on the ground every time, and my harp strapped to my back. I wouldn't bring her here, my precious Healer. I wouldn't risk the fine maplewood cracked on the ground and crushed under cutting hooves. So why do I hazard the brittle bones of Taliesin, the fragile fingers that should pluck the harp? I must be mad. I wince even to think about what a fall could cost.

Still, I'm a poet, with a soul tuned to glory, a warrior on the frontier of song. I am too young, too talented, too bold to spend my life harping of high halls and apple orchards and contented kine. I was thrice-born for something greater than that. Today I am close to Arthur. Even I can catch the wonder of it, though I'm near to screaming and I'm slipping off the mare.

Three notes on the horn. The third strikes deep and low. I know what that means. The hounds have put up a boar. Just my luck. No tall magnificent stag today. A short-legged, snuffling, small-eyed, mean, vicious, snaggle-toothed, devil of a wild he-pig. Begging your pardon! Best not say that here. Don't even think it. A pig's a sacred animal. The ivoried divinity, the favoured flesh, the burrowing guide to the mysteries of the underworld. Little pig, be favourable to us. Sweet pig, lead a charmed path through the dangers of your forest. Holy pig, sacrifice yourself upon our spears. Can I look him in the face on the high table, with the apple trapped between his tusks?

The pounding hooves on the rotting floor of the forest. The beech sprays stabbing for our faces as we duck beneath them. The gleaming backsides of the horses flying before me. Is this how it is to ride into battle? Do the Saxons lurk in ambush like the White-Handed Wraith of the Birch whose touch they say brings madness? Do the Angles rear as straight and unyielding across the path as black-tipped ash trees?

And Arthur away in front of us all, like a god on horseback. No one of his men can outride him, or none of them dares to. He is one with his steed. I have been with Morgan at the dances in the forest where the bodies of men and women sprout monstrous heads of beasts. But Arthur turns the old world upside down. He is the chief in majesty, his tribe's splendour, the head and shoulders of a man knit to the polished quarters of a horse.

Modred rides just behind him, the constant guard for Arthur's back. He is a better horseman than I thought for one so young. Less reckless than Owain and Gawain, cleverer. I think he whispers to his horse as

Morgan would. He scans the bushes on either side. A touch too upright, though, with his hand ready on his spear. He'd better watch his eyes under that holly.

But the pace quickens as the hounds give tongue. They've seen him. I can't spare a look for anyone else now. I'm jolted to death. The mare is slippery with foam and sweat. I'm sliding off. Forget the reins. She doesn't seem to understand them, anyway. Hands knotted deep in the mane. Clinging on. Pray to Rhiannon, Mother of Foals, this brute can steer a safer course than I can. Tree-trunks rushing past. I shall fall off. Help me, somebody, please! They're out of sight. Oh, wait for me!

Terrible dilemma. I'm frightened to death of going faster, and scared out of my wits that I'll be left behind. I know what my body's telling me. Perhaps I could fall off, after all. Brave the wrath we have stirred in the battered forest behind me and limp home to Morgan. But even my weak blood is up. Ahead is Arthur, and the vanishing dream of my boyhood.

The distant horn keens on the wind. I was born too late. I shall never ride with him against the Saxons. I shall never witness him turn the tide back, like a cliff against the sea, like a strong gate under a siege. It's only a tale. But better than nothing is the wild boar, and Arthur's spear in its side, and I, Taliesin, there to see the bright blood. Then they will go, to Celliwig, Caerleon, Camelot. For me, it will be back to the hall of the stately women of the North, to courtly Urien, and danger-loving Owain. But not, oh not, the dream I could have sung.

I mustn't give up. I shall be paying for this for a week. With a backbone jarred and bruised, and my legs aching from the desperate grip on this slimy beast. But on, on. There is a press of warriors ahead, dismounted, broad backs bent over, arms raised. Men shouting. Someone leaps aside with a curse and there's a roar of laughter.

My knees slacken. I tumble to the ground. Scrambling through mud on hands and knees, I see between their planted legs the hounds whipped off the prostrate boar bathed in gore. Arthur is smiling broadly. Morgan's forgotten. I have come too late. He's made his peace with the morning.

There's blood on Bedwyr's thigh. Torn cloth, ripped flesh, white bone. There seems to be a terrible pain in my own chest too. And all that way to ride back again. If I turn my head I know the mare will be grinning at me with yellow teeth.

I stagger upright, clutching a hazel stem. Arthur sees me and laughs aloud. He cuts off the boar's ear and gives it to me for a keepsake. This time it's a great honour. The prize will come spoiled to Morgan's table with a cropped head.

'No gold or silver here, bard! But a purse to hold what you have.'

I gasp my thanks and clutch my trophy. I want to believe he does this to apologise for scaring me and not to slight Morgan. I have it still. But two hours ago I could believe he would have watched me die.

I've bought that keepsake dearly. The twisted horsehair of the mane has cut my fingers. They'll be sore on the harp-strings tonight, no matter how I suck them. But I was there. I was there when Arthur killed the Great Striped Boar in the Forest of Rheged. Well, almost there.

I was right about the sore fingers. And I don't know whether it's going to be more painful standing up or sitting down. I'm so weary and aching I could sleep for a week and never mind the feast. But I am the watcher who may not sleep. I am the bard above all bards. I have balanced a million angels on the point of this well-trimmed fingernail. And what is a bard good for, if he cannot charm the huntsmen till the stars pale and the heavy heads fall sleeping on crooked arms, and the women droop and sigh? King Urien's still half-awake. Sing on, Taliesin. Safe now. Like a skylark between earth and heaven. So small, no one can see it, but its music fills the world. Sing on, and live.

> Until my life ages,
> And death claims his wages,
> I shall not cease yearning
> Unless I praise Urien.

He's asleep now. And Arthur sleeps. The king of all the Britons is dead to the world. Lay down the harp. Relax the tortured fingers. He cannot hear you.

# Chapter Nine

Morgan sleeps little these nights. Go to her now, but softly. She is drawing you. She hungers for your youth. The dangerous magic Arthur asks of her she has never turned upon herself. The Mothers' rites she uses respect both waxing and waning. They will not stay the hurrying years or hold still for her the hope of what she's not yet had. Yet she feeds on me. I age a century each time, but see her softened, rosy, lovelier . . . and still unsatisfied.

Move carefully from the hall. Above all, do not disturb Owain.

Tonight I'm not in the mood. The base of my spine's been hammered so that I walk as if I had two wooden legs, and still it hurts. But the harp knows its duty. It tugs me to Morgan's chamber like a questing hound. My eyelids droop and I stumble against walls. Lucky my feet could find this way even in my sleep. They almost do.

I start suddenly alert. Is someone there, in the passage that leads to Arthur's chamber? Have I been seen? No. All's still again. Only the draught on a guttering torch.

Morgan has been waiting for me. I can see by the restless way she turns from the window with the moon on half her face. She's been to bed before this, I think; the sheet's thrown back. But now she stands with a great green gown flung over her night-shift and her hair brushed loose. I see something else too. There'll be nothing wanted from me here tonight but music. I can tell by the women she has chosen to keep watch with her. Women? That Woman-who-is-not, squatting on the floor, sour because I have kept him from his sleep. The other, fair as he is ugly. Too fair, her bloom untouched, untouchably chaste, Tegau. Oh that a Christian maid, for maid she is, I do not doubt, should grow such breasts, such lips, such eyes. She is handfast to Caradawc Strong-Arm; they'll be married soon. There are others who sigh for that as I do. So young, and yet already a legend for constancy. Nothing for you there, boy, and you have weightier tasks. No need to swoon when her lids swoop down over those blue eyes and lift to flash you an April smile. Your May Day will never dawn with that one.

Aches or not, I think with a pucker of disappointment that I have come here only to give and not to get. For now I'm in her presence it sweeps over me that Morgan can be generous to men when she chooses. Superbly woman, as though one tide was rising to meet another, a second flood that threatens death and brings instead a re-creation. Shattering, and making new; exhausting, healing. I know now that Urien and I are not the only ones. Vain Taliesin. How could we two have contained her? Is she offering her womb to the gods, or punishing . . . someone?

But I am wrong again. Morgan can always surprise you. She sees the pain it costs me to sit, and the heaviness of the harp, and the pout I make as I shift on the stool at the end of my song. She ruffles my hair, as though I were just a little chap that had hardly learned to walk. Even Tegau smiles to see her so motherly. I want to catch Morgan's hand and hold it to my tired forehead, but I restrain myself.

'So you tried to ride with Arthur, and he has hurt you.'

'He gave me a token. The boar's ear.'

'Arthur is careless with gifts. He has left much behind him that he does not recognise.' Her voice is soft as cat's fur. Her hand strokes my head, not sensuously, but with another purpose. I feel myself relax.

'Woman,' she nods, 'the salve for aching joints.'

I am lying on Morgan's bed. The virgin Tegau helps undress me. There's irony. I allow myself to smile at my humiliation. Why not? Very skilled, these women. It is luxury to be in their hands. Even the big square paws of Woman, that should wield something less delicate, are no strangers to healing magic.

The ointment is cold at first, so that I laugh and jump. Then the warmth creeps into the muscles and the glow spreads and it is Morgan singing over me, and not I to her. What if Urien found us now? Well, no harm. No harm, much good, to me at least. I am rocking like a baby in a cradle, like a ship on a gentle sea, as though this bed could carry me to Paradise. Tonight, Paradise is not ecstasy but sleep without pain.

'What's in this salve?' I murmur.

'Primrose and wormwood,' she croons, 'bruised and boiled in butter. Mixed with old lard and yellow wax, and the suet from a he-goat and a sheep.'

'It must be the he-goat's fat that's making me randy,' I smile.

Just words. None of that seems important now. I know it's not the wormwood or the primrose making me whole, but the touch of Morgan's hands, the constant application of her spirit that will leave me rested and her tired. The bitter and sweet of her that is my healing . . . All our healings . . . All our deaths . . .

Tegau touches me on the shoulder. I start awake. The room is dark, save for one candle. I am alone in Morgan's bed. The queen kneels with her back to us. Praying? I dress and stumble from the room, and almost forget the harp. I feel sleepy but well, and I have paid her poorly. Outside the door I almost trip over Woman, settling to sleep across the threshold. For the first time I am caught by a warmth of friendship towards him. Whatever he did, he has accepted her bitter punishment. He guards her well, though I think it brings him little joy.

I follow him next day, Woman, walking slowly as though his skirts are hung with lead and he's forgotten how to stride. I know where he'll be going. A place I've been aware of for months, and kept away from. I've had enough of that kind of bewitchment. Morgan's high ceremonies are more than sufficient. I was once potboy to the cauldron of Ceridwen, and it nearly cost me my life; now I'd rather sing golden hymns to the Trinity in the hall of Urien. Well, I can tune my voice to tell of magic or miracles. I use neither of them. I carry my own enchantment with me. It is not for nothing that my harp is called Healer.

I feel the touch of darkness on my skin as I step through the shadows into the little court. No Romans built this. They're a public people. Big squares, long open porches, rooms in regular rows, that's them. Everything predictable, orderly, no space for secrets in those barrack-room minds. This court is native work. Built? It feels more as if it had grown. A mould on a cast-off army boot. A toadstool sprouting from a block of crumbling masonry. Wattle, clay, thatch, turning their backs on prying eyes. A farmyard sound of clucking hens. A pen of black sheep. I pass a rainwater-barrel and glance in, expecting to see a placid mirror reflecting the sky and my own handsome face, and find its surface alive with eels.

Morgan's Woman has disappeared into one of the huts. I hear a squeal and wince. I've a delicate stomach. I wonder if he saw me coming and is doing it to spite me.

He comes out carrying a small brass cauldron in one fist and a live hare by the other. Long legs scrabbling against the air, long ears twisting as he fights, and screaming nonstop. A hare's a magical animal. He can't save himself, though. Woman sets the cauldron down in the centre of the court and takes a hatchet from his belt. He fixes his eyes on me and not on the hare as he says the words that need to be said. It makes my own neck feel uncomfortably tender. Just a flick of his gaze from mine, a practised jerk of the wrist and the head is off and the dark blood drumming into the pot. I watch him bleed and then skin the beast and remove the organs, wrapping each piece in dock leaves and setting it aside. When it is all done, he puts the parts back in the store-house, and shuts the door. All this time he's muttered plenty to the gods, but not a word to me.

Now he faces me. 'Well, bard? Are you still so green you need lessons in drawing a hare?'

'It's a lesson in courtesy I need to be practising. I've come to say thank you. I've hardly an ache or a bruise to trouble me this morning.'

Smile, Taliesin. Speak fair. Soft words open more doors than heavy blows.

'Why hang around me? It was Morgan's doing.'

'Morgan's my mistress. I give her the service of song I am bound to, and she in turn provides the care which is my entitlement. Thanks to her are but the gilt ink on that contract. You owed me nothing, so I am in your debt.'

'You might have been, if my service was freely given.'

'You're not a slave.'

He shoots such a bitter look at me then I take a step back.

'Slave? No! Worse than that. Woman!'

'Does all the court here know that you are not?'

'Who bothers to look at a whiskery crone? And if they do, who's going to question Morgan?'

'Was this her doing?' What I mean is, 'Why?'

'Yes, boy. You're scared you'll end up the same way, aren't you? Even though you're in and out of her bed like a flea.'

I wait. Silence is a powerful invitation to a lonely man.

'I was Smith. Teilo Smith of Way Bank. A great lord of magic. Near as high as her ladyship herself, though she would never allow it. I planned to set my power alongside hers. Not over her, mind you. A sort of partnership, I thought. She wouldn't have it. Look what she's brought me to!'

'So her power was greater than yours, after all?'

'She got her come-uppance, though, didn't she? There's others can shut doors in people's faces, besides her. He didn't need magic, either.'

This time he waits. I raise my eyebrows.

'Arthur?'

'Aye. That's the one. That's all she ever cared about. The rest of you are nothing.'

I know, but still I wince.

'But he's her . . . brother.'

He laughs, scornful of my sensibility. 'What's that, among kings and queens like them? But it's more than bedding him she wants. We're talking about his kind of power now. She wouldn't want to be his little plaything, like Gwenhyvar. She's the same as I was, though she'd curse me to the black deeps of Uffern if she heard me saying so. She thought the two of them could join hands. Brother to sister. His sword, her sheath. The right and the left hand of Britain, you might say. Noon and night. He wouldn't have it, though. He's a man, isn't he? He thought he'd keep the whole of it to himself.'

'And so he has, hasn't he? Arthur's the High King, and Morgan's just Queen of Rheged.'

He spits and grins with black-gapped gums. 'High King of what, though? Britain? He's only got the half of it, hasn't he? He's kept the sword, but she took his scabbard from him. I haven't gone twenty years in a woman's skirt and not learned something from her. She could have given him all he dreamed of, but he couldn't see it. He wouldn't pay her price. Or not till now, when he sees his time is running out.'

'It's not too late to mend? They're a proud pair.'

He whistles knowingly. 'You're thinking she might still be a dangerous loser. Aye. You're right. Lightning like hers must come to earth somewhere. There's more than love between them. Best keep your head down when those two are around.'

The cup in my hand. The muttering round me. A tale of past treachery.

'There was something about a purple cloak.'

'You heard that, did you? Well, there was once another here like me. A different sort of half-woman. She'd been a nun. Morgan sewed a cloak for Arthur. You never saw such a mantle. I should know. It was my hands helped to work the magic in it. We brought it to him, that nun and I. Only Arthur made the woman try it on in front of him. Here, in Carlisle. It did her horribly to death.'

'And that was Morgan's doing? Her gift to murder Arthur?'

'He believes it was.'

'Don't you?'

'I'm not telling what I know to every chatterbox.'

What about me? Which one of them will it be more dangerous to believe?

'Arthur's a sacred king. He must be well-protected.'

'Swords! Any smith could tell you there needs to be more to them than a fine-ground blade. Arthur's never had time for magic, more fool him. He's lost two soul-friends that had a deal of power. Merlyn first, and now Nimue, by the sound of it.'

'Would that have been an even match? The Lady of the Lake against Morgan?'

I can see I am giving him pleasure. I've rewarded him for his trouble more richly than I thought. To talk man with man. To know secrets that even wise Taliesin, pearl of bards, child of the cauldron of inspiration of Ceridwen, did not guess. That's a rare treat indeed.

'It might have been, if it had been one to one, and not one against three. And now Nimue's left him, has she? Seen off by the bishops!'

'He has their power of prayer to keep him.'

Woman would give no more answer to that than grin at me and wipe his bloody hands on his apron.

# Chapter Ten

And I thought I knew it all when I came to Rheged, fool that I was. Sucking the thumb of knowledge, I, Taliesin, the marvellous boy. And I couldn't even see the questions I should have been asking.

Teilo knew. Oh, yes, he must have known, crouched like a surly dog at Morgan's feet all these years. But he wouldn't help me to the knowledge I most needed. Knowledge is power. He hugged that secret close under his apron. He hated me. To be fair, if I'd been him, I'd have hated pretty Taliesin, too.

So they all left me, innocent as a newborn lamb, to my first meeting with Margawse.

Arthur has gone. He stood for the last time beside the gateway, his great sword Caliburn strapped ostentatiously to his side. Morgan was cold.

'A safe journey, and the peace of your years be on you when you reach home.'

'There is more life in me yet, whether you help me or not!'

'I could have given you more of life than you imagine. But you yourself will not let go and trust.'

The king's hand flew to his sword-hilt. You'd think it was he who was protecting the weapon, not the other way round.

'You have taken enough from me already. You shall not have this.'

'Cling to your man's power then, like your father before you. See if that can restore your waning fire. It is yourself you have robbed.'

So he hasn't got what he came for. Proud, these two, unyielding, righteous. They hurt themselves.

He leaves, and she will not stop him, back to Camelot and Gwenhyvar, and the winter court. Once all the young stallions of Britain must have been jostling for a place in his paddock. As Arthur's warband they would win their fame, impress their women, inspire the bards. Even in peacetime, his would be the feasts, the hunts, the games not to be missed. Now only Gawain and the older men ride with him. The younger ones choose to stay with us and hope for another war.

Hard on his heels, Morgan's sister comes.

She rides into the castle like autumn on the hills, all flame and fruit, bringing her sons' wives behind her and a train of comely lasses. Red as bracken is her hair, and never mind the silver. I part her cloak with my eyes and find that the flesh is warm and yielding.

She pouts at first when she hears that Arthur has gone. Then her look swings around appraising the rest of us.

And there am I, gaping like a fish, as pretty a youth as ever rode out of Powys, and very good at two things, only one of which is singing. What chance did I have?

I have a weakness for green-eyed women. But these eyes are different. Morgan's are like the wild cat's, animal, dangerous. And Margawse? All vegetation. Like a wood in a rainy summer, heavy with blossom, perfumed, feeding on the bodies of men. And oh, she can twine her roots round my foundation any time she chooses, for all she must be older than Morgan.

But softly. That's a dangerous thought. I have been in Morgan's bed, burned by her ice, opening under her moon. And could the same Taliesin lie in the poppied noonday of her sister?

I have no choice. I went to Morgan willingly, not for myself, though you may not believe that. It was a small service I could do for her I worship. I gave myself to her loneliness and longing. But Margawse. Greedy Margawse. She has no shame. She doesn't need me. But she devours every man in sight.

So I find myself lying on tartan wool in the leaping firelight, watching it make roses on Margawse's creamy skin. And I look at her and laugh, for I know I have made her happy. No tears with Margawse. She laughs easily, from the belly, as though the world were one great joke to her. We laugh, lying together in Morgan's castle, and we laugh.

God, it makes me cold, just to think of it. I see it now. She is the destroyer, more than Morgan. Looking back, I am far more scared now than I had sense to be then. I might have died that very night for what we did. They let me live, those two great queens, only because I seemed a boy. I amused them. And because I did what I did extremely well. But if I had been a man. Like Arthur . . .

'He was even younger than you are,' she says, leaning on her elbow and letting the tip of her finger thrill along my breastbone. 'What did you say your name was? Taliesin? You are a jewel of a boy, a perfect youth. It's a long time since I had a lad like you.'

She rolls away from me and lies smiling at the rafters, arms crossed behind her hair.

'But he was man even then. And what a man! Come fresh from victory. Like the great horned one in the depth of the forest. He thought he had proved his right to all the does of the herd by the shock of his antlers. I shall never feel his like in me again.'

Then she laughs and reaches out to pat my flanks indulgently.

'Never mind, Taliesin. You did very well. You're a clever boy. And after all, what is Arthur now? Husband to Gwenhyvar. Father of one skinny stripling, Anir, though he must have a train of lusty bastards scattered across the country. Gwenhyvar? What good to him is a simpering sweetheart like her? She wasn't worth the horses' sweat that brought her up from Cornwall. No, if he wanted a mate fit for a king like himself, he could have cut a richer gem from Cornish mines than that!'

I lie still, hearing the rhythms of her voice sing on. Feeling sick. It takes a lot to shock me. I am the Puck, the mischievous magic boy, in and out of the bed of queens, and still laughing and living. Yet I am nothing in myself. I am not important. It is only my song that matters.

But, Arthur! The greatest king of the Island of the Mighty. A legend in the hearts of all his people. With his own sister? *This* sister!

And she is still laughing over it, after all these years, her whole yielding body at ease across the bed, fruiting with self-satisfaction.

My stomach heaves as she humps herself over me. Very sure of herself, she is, this red-haired, sun-warm queen.

'It is a pity I am past the age of bearing children. We could have made a sweet infant, you and I. What do you imagine? A green-eyed daughter, that could sing magic, like a Cornish mermaid? Something merrier than Modred, anyway, for all I'm his mother that says so.'

Words without sense. Blood stopped. I do not want to believe what I have heard.

'Modred?' I ask faintly, wanting to be wrong. '*Your* child?'

'The son Arthur got upon me that day. What did you think?'

Modred. The boy without a father. The grave smiling, courteous, thoughtful prince. Bold and bitter in battle, by all accounts, yet as skilful in Morgan's councils as in Urien's stables, charming to commoner and nobleman alike. Her favourite, fostered son. No whiff of scandal about him, only a mystery. And yet I thought I'd guessed. Of course, I had not been sure, seeing he is so unlike Owain and the rest. Only, whose else should he have been, black-browed like her as he is? She wouldn't have been the first wise queen of her sort to have gone into the forest and come back with more than she took. Who his father might have been had showed no more to me than the shadow of the stag under the branches. The god disguised, most likely. Yet *Arthur*? His dawning gold with the sunset red of Margawse to make the dark night of Modred?

I slide out from the bed away from those too-open legs.

'I thought he was Morgan's.'

'Oh, Morgan, Morgan! False aunt and foster-mother! She never told you? She let you think he was hers? A lie as dangerous to Modred as the truth! No. I made him, Taliesin. I forged the weapon that will bring Arthur down when I opened my legs and let Modred into the world. The eldest of us, Elaine, restored him when our hopes seemed lost. And then we put him in Morgan's hand. She was always the man among us. Modred has had two births. When he comes to the third, it is she who will strike the final blow.'

I want to shout her down for saying that. Morgan is the exaltation of womanhood to me. Goddess, virgin. No matter that I have entered her many times. She comes to me always new, like the crescent moon out of the dark of the month. But I see the truth of what she is saying. Margawse is all woman, nothing more. But Morgan uses her womanhood like a warrior who seizes the nearest weapon to her hand. She could have matched Arthur, strength for strength. Instead, she is the converse of his shape, the darkness to his light. She fills the space he cannot. Because he is a man, she is a woman.

Yet it was Margawse with Arthur. She who devours men, laughing at me so sweetly over the blanket. I have found more comfort in

Morgan's tears, more love in her unflinching condemnation. I stumble out of the room.

Margawse's voice follows me. 'Beware, Taliesin. Modred is a trap, set and ready to fall. You are not so small you cannot be caught in its jaws. Stopper up well that quicksilver voice. This is one tale you must not sing yet.'

The hall is full. Urien and Owain. Agravain and Gareth, tall sons of Margawse, and one more that I must now add with difficulty to that list.

Margawse has followed me, still tidying her hair. More radiant than ever.

Supper is over now. Morgan has Modred by the hand. They are smiling at each other. Together they are leading the long dance, like the wild reel they leap the night before battle, the sacred struggle acted to please the Old Ones, the light and darkness at the heart of Britain. Their kin clap and stamp. And who is there now, since Merlyn, to watch over the tents of Arthur?

Urien looks at me long. He knows that I have played him false with his wife. But does he know now I have played his wife false with her sister? Would he forgive me that, if he knew? My hands are unsteady over the strings. Urien says nothing. I have come into great danger today.

> Until my life ages,
> And death claims his wages,
> I shall not cease yearning
> Unless I praise Urien.

# Chapter Eleven

I suppose I must have stared at Modred too long. He noticed. Come to think of it, there isn't much Modred doesn't see. And I don't mean just those things that concern himself. We've all got sharp enough eyes for that. At suppertime when everybody else is full of drink and having a good time, Modred's eyes will be going round the hall. If he sees a serving-man with a bit of a fever and wiping his runny nose on his sleeve, as like as not Modred will get up and have a quiet word with the steward and get the man excused to his bed. I've come across him in the woods, sitting on a tree-stump and chatting to the foresters as easily as if they'd forgotten he was the king's foster-son. I've even, if you'll believe me, seen him take a full bucket from a pregnant slave-girl and carry it across the yard for her, and not demand the price of a kiss and a cuddle at the end of it, either. They tell him things. There's not much going on in Rheged that Modred doesn't know.

He let it pass that evening, though more than once he looked up and caught my eye on his. All the same, he never put a foot wrong in the dance or lost the thread of his conversation. He's a true courtier already. When he came to swing Margawse they smiled at each other, but hardly spoke. I was the one who plucked a wrong note or slopped my wine. And those are two things it's not like nimble Taliesin to do.

Arthur's son, Margawse's child. The one so natural, now I know the truth of it, the other so amazing. Yes, now I come to think of it, there is a kingliness about Modred. He conducts himself like a young man born to rule. He may even be more like a king than Arthur himself was at the same age. I've heard stories about that one that would shock some of you; he was a wild lad. What would Arthur think if he knew that Modred was his own?

Margawse though; that sticks in the gullet. I cannot swallow the lump of incredulity in my throat. If he had been Morgan's now, it would have been different. Surely, surely, he should have been Morgan's son? Incest or not, anyone can see the rightness of it. Two great pillars, evenly raised. Two halves of a universal symmetry. Fling in all the clichés of male and female, sun and moon, day and night, and they are not enough. They speak of greater and less, of borrowed light. They make the one inferior to the other. I sing of strengths rooted in separate soils, growing together to embrace and uphold each other. A marriage and a coronation of equals.

It didn't happen. Modred, who should have been their son, is not. What is he then? The child of treachery. Arthur's theft of the womb

484

of another man's wife. Careful, Taliesin! You've gone that road yourself. Margawse's trick, to cheat both Arthur and Morgan. There's an unpleasant beginning to shape so noble a courtier. All men speak well of Modred. All women too, though there's never a breath of scandal about his name. Margawse has warned me not to spill what I've learned. But I cannot hide my knowledge from Modred.

So next day I'm sitting on the edge of the fishpond shaking a stone out of my boot, and it isn't as much of a shock as it might have been when he speaks just by my elbow, though I didn't hear him coming up behind me.

'Can I tempt you to take a walk with me?' he asks.

Modred's like Morgan. For all his courtesy, when he asks you to do something it is not, properly speaking, an invitation.

I glance at the sky. It's a mild October day, with a blue sky deep enough to set off the brilliant reds and yellows of the trees, and not enough wisps of clouds to threaten a drenching for a few hours.

'Yes,' I say, 'if you'd like the company.'

We walk down the hill to the river and on to the shining sands. The wind blows cooler off the sea and the legs of the cockle-women are purple as they fish in the mud. We wrap our cloaks about us and walk on north round the shore of the Solway Firth, paying a boatman to row us across the River Esk. Modred chats lightly, asking me about the merits of wire or gut for the harpstrings, discussing the treatment for galls on a horse, asking my opinion of rebuilding the fort at Caer Wenloe. I know this was not what he has brought me here for. Once he stops, and stands gazing at a little beach on the opposite shore. A few clumps of sad grey willows on either side, no sign of fishing-boats on it, though it looks a good landing. He stands very still and silent. When I look back from that beach to his face I see to my astonishment there are tears on his cheeks. He sees me staring and gives a brisk laugh and points to a heron gliding over the water.

'He has a long memory, the heron. Let him discover you have a pool of fish and he'll strip it bare, and ever afterwards he will remember. If he finds you think he has forgotten and have restocked it, he will be back to swallow the rest.'

We watch the heron land on the beach and wade in the shallows, dissatisfied.

Presently I see where we are coming to. A huge round boulder that has fallen out of the sky. Well, no other explanation, is there? It stands on its own in those bare fields above the mudflats. Just the one house nearby. Not poor, a decent, clean-looking place. A bit more prosperous than you'd expect for a lone fisherman. Still, I wouldn't care to live so close to that stone.

I am wrong. I often have been, where this family's concerned. They flow like an underground river and come out where you're not expecting. It isn't the stone we are heading for, though it's plain enough that it's a sacred marker. Modred walks up to the cottage and whistles merrily, like a robin. A woman comes almost running round the corner of the house. Getting on in years, she is, but still strong and nimble.

Modred sweeps her into a great hug and kisses her. He's not usually so free with women.

'Let me look at you,' she orders, pushing him back. 'Aye. You get more of a man every time you come. You'll do.'

'A man like my father?'

She frowns in my direction. I'm startled too. How much does each of us know?

'Not too like, I'd say.'

So she holds his secret. It is clear these two are old friends, though she is no noblewoman.

Modred draws a parcel out of the pouch he has slung on his shoulder. He shakes it out. A good wool gown. He has an eye for what will please a woman. A deep plain blue, and embroidered round the hem with crimson flowers. Rich and warm. Not too showy for one like her, but a dress she can be proud of wearing. She colours like a young girl when he holds it up against her with his hands on her shoulders.

'Be sure and let me know when the next grandchild's arrived,' he says. 'I've a silver gift put by ready for the naming-day, whether it's boy or girl.'

'Hush now.' She puts a scolding finger on his lips. 'Let be until it's safely born. Don't let the Fair Folk hear you making so bold with the future. It's bad luck.'

He swings her round with his hand on her waist to face me.

'I've brought you something else. The cleverest bard in Britain. He's come without his harp, but he can sing a pretty poem unaccompanied. You shall be royally entertained, as you deserve. Taliesin, this is my wet-nurse, Fencha. And more than that. Midwife, you might say, to my second birthing. I owe my life to her and her man.'

Again I see that quick, troubled look the woman Fencha shoots at him, as though this was a thing that should not have been spoken. But he squeezes her lovingly and tells me to sing, which I do, I, the Chief Bard of Rheged, there in the apple-yard of a fisherman's cottage, with only the two of them and a few fine-looking cattle to listen to me. All the time my eye is roving over the trim woodwork of the house, the well-kept beasts, the smart stout cart and the harness with bells on it hanging in the shed. It is more than the salmon of the Esk has paid for all this. Besides, I haven't seen her husband. He could be dead by now. It is clear this house stands closely with the palace at Carlisle, though it's a long walk between them.

'Will you come in and break some noonday bread with me?' she asks when I've finished.

I'm about to say 'yes', for it was thirsty walking, even before the song. But Modred puts his hand out and touches her arm.

'Forgive us a little while,' he says, smiling to soften her disappointment. 'Give us bread and cheese and a pitcher of milk to drink. I have a tale of my own to tell to Taliesin, and the Stone is the rightful place to do it. We'll come back for a gossip when it's done. We shall have need of good news of farms and families and festivals to take the taste of bitterness off our tongues.'

'Aye,' she says, the smile leaving her face. 'Your story makes hard hearing.'

'Except that I am alive to tell it. All it contains of happiness has been your doing.'

'It's a pity, then, I cannot have a hand in its ending.'

He doesn't answer that.

# Chapter Twelve

We walk down to the Stone and bow to it. Well, you'd have to, a thing like that. Modred offers some milk and bread and speaks the reverence. He's gone further than I have along Morgan's path. Still, it's me flinches and not him when he puts out his hand and actually touches the thing. Taller than him, it is, and rounded. It could easily have rolled over and crushed him.

'Do you know what they call this?' he asks.

'I can guess. There'll be nothing else like it along this coast. It must be the Mabon Stone, isn't it?'

'Yes,' he says, and lets his hand fall back quick to his side as if the rock has burnt him after all. 'Mabon, the Son. Born of Modron, the Mother. This should have been my Stone.'

A shiver of goosepimples runs all over me as he says that. I know he is right, of course, half of it anyway. It's clear whose son he should have been. Only there is a darkness comes down over my mind when I try to think about the other half of what he is saying. What does that make Morgan, then? I think I know. I think I've always known. And I have lain with her.

'And whose is it instead?' he shouts, whipping round with his hand lifted so sudden I don't know if it's me or the Stone he is going to strike.

'Owain's?' I get it in fast, skipping out of the way at the same time. Well, if Morgan is Modron, it doesn't take much working out, does it?

'Owain!' He slumps down and leans back against the Stone, as if he doesn't care if it has power to hurt him. 'Yes, there's more to Owain Enemy-Reaper than horses and dogs and cattle-raids. Be sure of that! Before Urien, Gwendoleu was king here in Solway. He kept a deadly set of chess. Few there were that could face him across that dangerous board. Gwendoleu of the Chained Ravens, that ate two corpses for their dinner and two for their supper. He left no son, or daughter either, to follow him. Urien got this kingdom after he fell. But Urien's a Christian. It was Owain inherited the chessboard and paints black ravens on his shield.'

'And you would have . . .'

He swings round on me with those dark haunted eyes. 'Do you believe Gwendoleu was a traitor? He made a league with the Angles.'

'To arm the Old against the New? Pagan against Christian?'

Modred stands with the light from the sea in his eyes, staring west. 'Do you not see them? The Irish over the water. The Picts in the North. Angles and Saxons along the eastern shore. The Britons in Strathclyde,

Dyfed, Dumnonia. What if we were to join forces, all of us? Both Christian and pagan. Unite these islands in all their diversity.'

'That's a dangerous dream!' I remind him. 'That's how all our troubles began, isn't it? King Vortigern brought Hengist and Horsa here from Saxony and thought he had done a smart deal to buy their swords. Look what happened! They seized the land for themselves and more of their keels came flooding over to join them. Then they slew our best men of the Council in the Night of the Long Knives. Give the English an inch, and they'll be swarming all over us. They'll want to be masters from Land's End to the Orkney Isles! Arthur wanted to drive the Saxons out of Britain. Would you make peace with them?'

'You know he's my father?'

I nod, cautious.

'Arthur Pendragon lies when he rallies us to fight for Britain. He calls us to defend a country that never was. The Cymry were always at war with each other. It is a Roman province that Arthur is fighting for. And the mind of Rome has always despised the British soul.'

'Still, Arthur's son fights with his father now. Bravely too, if half what I've heard is true. How are we bards to make an honest living if you sheathe your swords and seal a peace between the lot of you?'

'Yes! I have fought for Rome and the Christian Church and Arthur.' There's a world of bitterness in his voice for one so young.

'But Morgan's son would have chosen another way?' Silly question. I should have thought before I spoke.

'Why ask me that?'

'Sorry,' I say. 'Tactless, me.' I sit myself down on the grass, a respectful distance from the Stone and put the bread and cheese between us. Might as well make myself comfortable.

'No, Morgan's not my mother, though I find it difficult to give another queen that name.'

'She's a wonderful woman.' I let the praise hang in the air. Let him take it which way he likes. They are both true.

'Margawse! When she gave birth to me, she expelled more than she knew.'

Wait, Taliesin. Beneath the soft speech, the self-control, the courtesy and honour, there has been a great abscess of anger swelling to bursting. You're a harper, not a surgeon. Let him lance it himself if he chooses.

'When she lay with her brother it was not for love but for revenge. Ever since his birth she had waited for that chance, to trick him as Uther Pendragon tricked her mother, having killed her father first. I am her justice, the vengeance for my grandparents.'

'It's not all bad, though. She enjoyed it, didn't she? And what about Arthur? It takes two to make a child. Wouldn't there have been love and laughter on his side too?'

'Sixteen, and already a general. Hot from his first great victory, they say. It was his own fame he was in love with, not my mother. He dreamed of becoming another Roman Imperator. He wanted power over Britain, and with it, every woman in her. Love? He didn't even ask who she was! Laughter? Not once he knew. I was the burning beam that threatened Arthur's palace. I was the bear fighting his dragon in the sky. I was his Nemesis.

'Do you know what he did when he heard I was born and Margawse had hidden me? He went through those three sisters' lands gathering up all the babies born at Maytime. You saw that beach where the heron was? The local people avoid it. They say it's haunted, and well it should be. A warband stood on that beach, all those great names out of song and story: Arthur, Cei, Bedwyr, Merlyn. They put the babies in a boat and pushed it out to sea. And I, yes, I was one of them. His son, his firstborn. More than that; his sister's son, that we hold dearer to a man than his own wife's child. The boat was wrecked, here, just below where we're sitting. All those little children were drowned, or eaten by gulls. Only one came safe to shore, still living. Fencha's husband, Gavran, discovered me on the sand. He took me home. Fencha put me to her own breast, hid me from strangers and friends alike, kept me till the hunt had died away and Morgan's sister Elaine told her by second-sight where to find me.'

'So now? Which of them will you serve?'

'I do not know. How can I? I was misbegotten. I should have been Morgan's dream. The land made whole through her and Arthur. Instead, I am Merlyn's nightmare.'

I sit silent. You may think I am a chatterer. There are some themes too dark even for my tongue. She makes good cheese, does Fencha, but I've lost my appetite.

'I can see why you told me,' I say presently. 'Funny old world, isn't it? We're two of a kind, really. The selfsame thing happened to me. You, drifting down the Solway to be picked up on the sands. Me, thrown into the water in a satchel and found hanging on a fishing-weir. Cheer up, man. We go back a long way, our sort. Take Moses, now. The myths are full of babies in bulrushes. They can't keep us down, can they? We'll pop up somewhere where we're least expected. We're too valuable to be destroyed, you see. The gods have work for us.'

'What dark god singled me out, and left the rest to die? The crucified Christ's Father? Teutates, who waits for his victims by wells and pools? And for what purpose? No, it is not the same with me. Moses's mother set him adrift in hope that Pharaoh's daughter would find him. Even Ceridwen in her fury fell in love with your face and could not bear to kill you. She gave you one slight chance. Your mothers consigned you to the waters, loving you. It was my father cast me out, in anger. I am not lovable.'

Never has the prince of poetry needed to choose his words more carefully. I am an entertainer, an inspirer, a strengthener. I know all the tricks to make a man feel more highly about himself than the sober prose of truth might suggest. That's what they want to hear. But how to tell this man he is better than he wishes to believe? I cannot flatter Modred. I wish I had my harp in my hands to show him what words cannot.

'Steady, now. Arthur's known for a handy man with a sword. He could have taken that blade to your neck and sent your little head rolling on the floor. All over. Oh, sorry! Too late now. But he was no Herod. He gave you the same chance that Ceridwen gave me. Was there not some pity in his heart too?'

'Fear! He dared not slay his sister's son. That would have brought a curse down on his head. If he did not know that, then Merlyn would surely have told him. The waves he pushed me into washed his own hands clean. He could blame the waters for my death and keep his blade pure.'

'Might he still not have hoped? His son, his firstborn. What if he knew now you had come back from the dead?'

'Merlyn warned my father he must kill me before I destroyed him.'

'Merlyn is gone.'

'And I remain. The seed of treachery. Even if Arthur were to welcome me with open arms, nothing can change that.'

'You have freewill,' I say. 'You could break the circle. You could be reborn.'

'How? When I know my birth has already shaped all our endings.'

'In Christ,' I try, looking up at the Mabon Stone and crossing myself, 'there was a new creation.'

But he is sitting in the shadow of the Stone.

# Chapter Thirteen

Samain's past, and now it is all cheer. We are to go to Lothian to celebrate the New Year with Morgan's sisters. There is even a rumour that Arthur and Gwenhyvar may be there to hold court. Do I observe a flash of jealousy in Morgan's eyes when she hears that news?

'What does he hope to win from Margawse that he could not have had from me? Does he think her price will be easier to pay?'

It's a thrill of another sort runs through me when I think what a fire-feast in Red Margawse's court may be like, with all that family gathered. I polish up my harp and pack my smartest clothes.

'Will he come?' is almost the first question Morgan asks Margawse, as she steps into the fire-warmth of Din Eidyn out of the raw wind.

Margawse gives that flick of her head that makes her hair leap like the flames themselves.

'How do I know? I am not the one with the second sight. Still, you know our brother. Arthur must always get what he wants. You have disappointed him. So he must try a woman with a warmer welcome and see if she can give him what all men long for.'

She enjoys teasing Morgan.

After Christmas, the third sister arrives, Elaine the Fair. You can guess I've been curious about this one, knowing the glories of her younger sisters. The black and the red, and now . . . My tongue's hanging out for a sight of the firstborn of these three queens. Elaine the Fair! Imagination makes wild forays and heaps in my poet's lap treasures of gold and crystal, daffodils and roses, fragrance and light.

Elaine uncloaks in the hall. Pale, mountainous; hooded eyes; grey hair under a discreet caul. I see at once there is nothing here for a lad like me. She is the oldest Mother. I could climb on the hills of those knees and lay my head on the vast field of her bosom. But if I slept there, when and where would I wake?

All day she heaps herself by the fire, and her fat fingers endlessly braid wool, red and black and silver. I do not know what she is weaving, but I find I cannot easily tear my gaze from the spiralling strands.

We are all on edge. Will he come? Through so much wrong and bitterness can they still hack a way towards each other? Can the wounds be closed?

It seems they may, when the gatekeeper gives a great shout and all the dogs break into barking. Morgan and Margawse and all their sons are on their feet. Even Elaine lifts her head to listen; her fingers pause. Only a moment. Then she falls to weaving again, more rapidly, as though the time is short.

Time dulls old wounds, but they can still ache when the wind blows cold. I am there close to the doorway when Margawse greets Arthur. A smile of triumph flashes in her face. Her hands reach out. Then, at the last moment, the fire goes out in her eyes. Too much has happened since the night they lay together. He thinks he's cancelled out that past. Now he wants something more from her.

It's the only time I've seen her cold with a man. And he is stiff to her. He does not easily beg, and he is here as a suitor. Yet both of them I have seen more lusty with the flame of life than all their courts. Hard to believe now, the two of them in bed together. Hard to imagine, Arthur setting out to destroy Margawse's son.

Courtesy is a blessed discipline. There are greetings given, gifts exchanged, thanks rehearsed, drink offered and accepted. Such customs grease difficult joints.

And there behind him is Gwenhyvar. All that I looked for in Elaine and didn't find. Ash blonde and rosy, smiling sweet gratitude at all the nephews of Arthur's family who crowd around her. Gawain was already in attendance. It's clear there's a knot here, some privileged band. These are the queen's knights. There's a surprise! I thought it would only be the power of Arthur's name that drew them. Gwenhyvar? Pretty enough, yet after my first smile of pleasure, nothing more. I can't tell what they see in her from here, I, who have stroked Morgan's flesh, been overpowered by Margawse. Is there some magic in her I'm missing?

There's a young lady with her. Like a magic mirror to Morgan that turns time back. Both darkness and warmth in the same lovable person. Morfudd, twin sister to Owain. Gwenhyvar's woman. Here's joy for all of us.

A pale boy stumbles over the doorstep behind them. I hardly notice him.

I'm a guest in Din Eidyn. My duties are lighter, but there's less chance to impress. Still, I stun them at supper. Gwenhyvar claps as hard as anyone. She looks delighted. I know what she's hoping. Next time around it will not be Arthur that I praise. Let her have what she wants. I shall be a richer man by the end of the evening.

Next day it seems the same. I've sung my best. I down a cup of mead and the hall spins headily. Gwenhyvar is laughing with Agravain and Gaheris. Beside the High Queen someone else is looking at me across the table. I start, like a swordsman that has dropped his shield. I should have noticed this lady before. When did she arrive? How could the ready eye and the wise thumb of Taliesin have passed unnoticing over a woman of such beauty, such warmth? Could the blazing sun of Arthur have so blinded me, the radiant moon of Morgan so bewitched me, that I would not have stopped at this? A young-old face, like a very knowing child, heart-shaped, to stir more than just a man's heart. Hair golden as catkins, that are the first flowering of the hazel nuts of wisdom. And I am made unwise as she takes the jug from the serving-man and leans across the table to fill my cup to the brim.

'Taliesin of Pure Song,' and her voice shivers with laughter on that word 'pure'. 'You have sung of God and man. Can you also turn your lay to a lady's service?'

Queen Gwenhyvar, or herself? And how will this one reward me?

'What lady needs the tongue of Taliesin to tell this hall what all the world can see?'

There are many measures of beauty. A dewdrop caught in a rose. Sunset purple in a sky of thunder. The curl of hair upon a woman's temple. What kind is this? I sense a maze of charms confuse me. My thumb warns that I will see whatever she chooses to show me. A blushing milkmaid met behind the shippen, or a naked priestess with the knife.

'All Britain knows your name, Taliesin Radiant-Brow. Can it be that you have never heard of Nimue, the Lady of the Lake?'

Oh, yes, I've heard.

What is she doing here? Hasn't she fallen out with Arthur?

My eyes scan the high table for help. I read their faces freshly. Gwenhyvar is smiling confidently. Arthur looks defiant. The sisters are like watchful wolfhound bitches, bristling around their jewelled collars.

Nimue's fingers brush the inside of my wrist. The long table dissolves into a running river. The shouting beats like surf. Her blue eyes widen in a smile and I am drowning. I do not know how long has passed.

Silence falls like a rope thrown to rescue me, or like a lash. All heads have turned my way. As I grab the shore of reality I catch Morgan's face, and by her look I see the bank may be as dangerous as the river. Too late to slide my hand away unseen. I daren't look at any of their faces, but I sense Nimue has turned that merry smile on Morgan. Slowly, too slowly, she releases me.

I am on my feet. I clutch the harp for security. Gwenhyvar will have to wait this evening. I will only praise Urien. Nothing else is safe.

I'm not the only one disturbed. A voice booms from close to Arthur. Bishop Cyndeyrn of Penn Ryoned is riding into battle.

'Why is that witch here? You swore, my lord, you would cleanse your court of all such fiendish persons. Will you imperil your immortal soul to entertain that kind of counsellor again?'

Nimue smiles, angelically. Margawse looks dangerous. She knows this insult is meant for the sisters too.

'Is the world so full of wisdom I can afford to slight it?' Arthur asks.

'The Lord of Life is a strong tower enough, our shield and spear, arms for our comfort, word for our wisdom, salve for our sin.'

'Work me a miracle yourself, then!'

Arthur's fist crashes down on the table. Then he stares around. All ears are listening. Even the house-slaves are gaping. What is it that he wants so much? What is it that Arthur still needs? What is it that even the High King lacks? I know, I, that have been born anew so many talented times. I, Taliesin, lapped still in the lusty bloom of youth. I know what drives him so urgently to the wise women, Morgan, Margawse, Nimue, only to watch their smiles turn tenderly on me instead. I have what he lacks, haven't I? Better not make it too obvious, though. I feel for him, this waning daystar, and I am afraid.

Arthur's not the victor of Badon for nothing. He grabs the falling standard. His followers must not doubt him. They must not guess he is beginning to doubt himself. He slips a garnet ring on the bishop's finger with a laugh to cover it.

'A miracle? There! Transmute that into bread for the poor, if you don't want it yourself.'

There's applause for that, and the talk and the music and the storytelling flow around us once more.

But my eyes are open, as though a cloak of invisibility had fallen from the world. I feel much older than my years.

The wounds are not all on one side. Arthur and Gwenhyvar, they seem the perfect couple. He, the great golden king, hero of a string of battles, honoured in legend. She, silver-haired, so blonde you'd be hard put to say whether Time had added a thread or two of his own. She has what all women want – well, nearly all – a handsome, famous, loving husband. Both of them years younger than my Morgan. But the dream will not endure for ever, even for them. He feels the power fading in his veins, a vision uncompleted, a truce, but not a victory, a country half-delivered. Now the most famous band of warriors in the world is drifting away from him, declining, dying. His famous bastard, Llacheu of Great Renown, fearless among warriors, has been slain before him. And what has Gwenhyvar given him?

There he is, far down the table. One son of her own, Anir, just come to warrior's age. Unblooded in battle yet, I should think. Not much to look at. Hair flopping over his face, and at that stage when a boy's limbs seem to grow longer every day, and he can't get the hang of using them without knocking things over. He flushes and apologises, and I don't know whether it's pain or impatience that makes Arthur growl every time he looks at him. Both, most likely. Poor lad. It must be a heavy burden, being Arthur of Britain's only legitimate offspring. Funny that. The Pendragon's left a trail of base-born bastards across the Island, yet just this one runt from Gwenhyvar. You'd have thought there'd have been powerful magic made for such a marriage-bed, not to mention the prayers of the Church to bless their holy union. If Arthur should fail, all the weight of the Cymry's hopes, our expectations of a dream fulfilled, will rest on Anir's hunched shoulders. It's no wonder he's stooped with embarrassment and clumsy.

The harp is magic. It can scar with satire or it can turn a timid man brave. Sing of the warrior's glory on the eve of battle and you armour the heart better than any vest of mail; your song is more stiffening than leather binding on the forearm; you intoxicate more thoroughly than a vat of royal mead. So I sing of young Anir and tomorrow's hunt. I make him blush a deeper red than ever.

# Chapter Fourteen

No space for me in Margawse's bed now. Morgan has reclaimed her property. No space in my black queen's either, not in another queen's capital, with Arthur here. I know the rules. That's a relief. I've enough on my plate as it is. At eighteen, I'm beginning to feel like an old man. Well, all right, not all the time. Margawse keeps plenty of lively lasses around Din Eidyn. Still, I'm more careful than I used to be. Urien likes to keep a name for a Christian household, on his side at least, and it's not just his free way with gold that makes me want to stand well in Urien's eyes. There's only one king I'd rather have for my patron.

But tonight I'm terrified of Nimue. At bedtime I'm genuinely glad to play the virtuous Christian and scuttle away from any further closeness that might wet me with her waves. Self-preservation. It's not just fear; I've enough difficulties for a prudent man to handle already. Doesn't do me any good though, does it, this chaste circumspection?

To be an enchantress is not a matter of concocting the correct ingredients in a cauldron, like a housewife cooking a stew. It is more than scanning the heavens to trace the wished-for movements of the stars; a ship's pilot venturing by night does that much. Little can be achieved merely by the pupil's faithful recitation of the runes. High magic is the application of colossal will. That is why even I, Taliesin, famed throughout Britain, am straw to both Morgan and Nimue.

So what's the good? Shore up the bank of a brimming river in one place, and it is bound to break through where you're not expecting it.

I thought I'd escaped when I woke and found myself alone in my own cold bed, just the snoring of men around me in the straw. Too much strong wine, though. I'll have to get up.

Only the ghost of grey light, and bitterly cold. I pull on my shoes and skip outside to relieve myself, whistling to scare off any unpleasant shadows. Quick, now; back inside before my nest in the blankets gets chilled. I'm shivering already.

I've turned and taken a step in the starlight, and there she is, waiting between me and the inner door, Nimue, bright and flickering, like the reflections thrown by water on a wall. Is this a woman or illusion? In this half-light she seems to carry a glow around her, like phosphorescence on a marsh. I find myself turning Christian now in earnest. She brought up Arthur, and he paints a cross upon his shield, but the bishop is right. She's a dangerous lady.

'St Michael and all the archangels, defend me!

'I acknowledge my guilt and my sin is ever before me.

'If thou, O God, shouldst mark iniquities, who could stand it?'

I've been a bad boy. Hell waits for me at the end of the corridor, with smiles and ringlets. I ought to run, and cannot.

'Do not be afraid, Taliesin. I have no quarrel with Urien's bard.'

That's true; I'm Urien's bard, not Morgan's, officially at least. Hang on to that.

'King Urien likes his household to behave honourably. So goodnight, lady. Let me pass.'

Deliver me from the tempter. Shield me, my lord!

'King Arthur only lives for honour.'

She leans towards me, but beneath the softness I sense a tougher fibre now. She means to coax something different from me this time. I feel reprieved but wary. Her voice twines round me like the stems of water-lilies.

'You know that Morgan cannot give him what he wants.'

'What's that?'

I know what Morgan wants. And she would give it back a thousand times over. But what does Arthur want from Morgan? What is honour? Youth renewed? The strength to lead us back to war and fight the final battle? Could she work that?

Nimue shakes her head impatiently. I think she'd like to shake me too. Strange that a woman should seem to promise such wooing in the evening and the wind change so suddenly at midnight.

'Morgan has only one thing Arthur lacks.' She hesitates. Should she hand me the advantage of shared knowledge? Morgan could have it out of me in a moment. 'Well, it's no secret. She stole the scabbard for Arthur's sword. She, or her sisters, keep it still.'

'For Caliburn?'

The sword of old magic. I have seen it on Arthur's thigh, the talisman that got him all his victories.

'I armed him at his manhood with both sword and sheath, as I was charged to. She who entrusted them to me taught that the healing scabbard was worth ten times the sword, and so I warned him. When Arthur was young he would not believe that. Better a sword to slaughter Saxons and win him a shining name in song, better to die on the battlefield if that would win him enduring fame. What did he care for closing wounds? When Morgan stole them both, he begged me above all else to get back the sword, and so I did.'

I see it all now.

'And Arthur has survived beyond his wars? Now age is catching up with him. Could the scabbard really renew him? Make him young again?'

That glint of anger ripples across her waters. Then calm steadies the surface once more.

'He does not understand what he is asking her. Think, Taliesin, think what that would mean. Why is a scabbard offered but to sheathe the sword? Imagine Arthur and Morgan, reconciled. She holds the scabbard, he the sword. They both mean power. She will not let it go, will she? To have it, he must take her too. She is Morgan the Wise.

Tenfold, her power of enchantment would smother his. Do you think that he would ever draw that sword again? Where is Arthur the warrior then? Think, Taliesin, Chief of Bards.'

I smell the nearness of Nimue's perfume, but it's not my body she's disturbing now. My poet's soul exclaims in pain at this threatened violation.

'But Arthur's the High King, our battle-leader! Victor against the Saxons. War's what he lives for. It's all the reason we made him what he is.'

'You understand! I saw in your face you were a wise boy. Where is the place for poets in a pallid peace? You must sing, Taliesin, must you not? A thousand years from now your songs will still be ringing. Make your greatest song for Arthur! He must be more than a mention in the margin of history. You too have power. You feel it, don't you? It is the bards who shall recreate him, not the scabbard, so that for all ages he shall be known as the greatest king that ever was. He must fight again. His finest battles are yet to be. Turn him from Morgan. She offers him nothing but obscurity.'

Her white hand's rising to me and the floor is rippling.

'Praise Arthur! When men speak of kingship, let the very word mean him. Shut your ears to Morgan's wiles. She was always jealous. Chant your great song for Arthur, and you and he will live on to eternity. Scorn Morgan's ways.'

Oh, excellent tempter. She lures me with my life's ambition. Easy then to say, yes. Immortality for me as well as him. I nearly said I'd give my right arm for it, but what's the use of a one-armed harper? And a bonus payment in this life, by the way she's smiling now, her lilies opening. Still, there's more to life than lust. That's just my sideline.

'You said yourself I'm Urien's bard, and Morgan is Urien's queen. Can't I serve both of them? Arthur and Morgan.'

'And let them come together? You know what follows. The bold warriors will not shout, nor the bright spears shake. The warhorses will not gallop long-legged into battle. The light of pride will grow dim in women's eyes. Are not the greatest tales sparkling with the clash of conflict, ruddy with blood spilt, loud with the cry of good victorious and evil slaughtered?'

'Yes,' I admit. 'Brave battle makes the best song.'

That, and the rain on the graves of heroes, and women weeping.

'Then sing it,' her whisper coaxes me. 'Sing how Arthur triumphed over his enemies. Make it come true once more.'

She lets me go, like a trout down a river. Her hand has not even touched my flesh. She has raped me another way.

# Chapter Fifteen

Forgive me, Morgan. I'm not so green I can't see where Nimue's own interest lies. Yet the sense of what she has said rings true in my head as a bishop's bell.

I sing of Arthur. I excel myself. Even as my fingers work their magic I can see the spell's gone home for one at least. Candlelight catches the pale face of Anir, his chin thrust forward, his elbows in the slops of wine, soup down his tunic. His eyes are shining with the glory of the father I hold up before him. The enchantment's strong. For the first time he dreams he might be such a young man.

Snow falls, and melts a little, then freezes again. Even in this weather there are lambs being born, small signs of hope. Come thaw or ice, there is hunting, either on horseback or on foot. These men are like giants with magic boots. They can run up mountains as fast as my fingers can skip a scale on the harp, and still be boasting and swaggering at the end of the day, the young ones, anyway. I fancy Arthur lowers himself a bit more carefully on to his couch. Gwenhyvar strokes his hair. Then she turns away, and there's a circle of young men round her. Owain, Rhiwallawn, Pasgen, Agravain, Gaheris, Gareth . . . and Modred. The flower of her retinue. The pride of his pack. In that shift of light I have seen that Arthur and his sisters are ageing. Their children are full-grown now. Well, Anir almost.

Modred is unacknowledged. Arthur thinks he has settled that score. Hush! That's a dark tale to set folk whispering in corners. Sing instead of Lindsey and Badon and the beaten heathen, and a king to surpass all kings. When the last verse ends we're all safe, sitting by the fire roasting apples.

Gwenhyvar is not so unchaste as to flirt with her escort. She rewards them with a pretty, queenly smile and gives them each a green scarf to wear for her.

It is Arthur who lures them. When he calls for the hounds there's not one of the pack would refuse to follow him. Nimue herself can draw a skilful bow. Urien teases me, and I venture my valuable person on the ice and rocks a couple of times. We chase the stag over the bare cold hills. No kill. It doesn't improve my playing. Where does Margawse draw her fire from in a country like this?

But today I have seen Morgan, Margawse and Elaine with their heads together, looking my way. I will go hunting again, I decide. I need the exercise. A slim handsome young bard gets more valuable gifts than a lazy minstrel who has let himself run to fat. No, I deceive you. I have looked in Elaine's face. I need fresher air to blow away dark thoughts. For once, I prefer pain.

It is too treacherous for horses, and little chance of picking up a scent on the frozen ground, but there are tracks in the snow that a man can follow almost as fast as a dog. Some men, anyway. Not me. Not young Anir, either. He's slithering over the stones beside me trying to catch up with them.

I grin at him in fellowship. I'll make a praise-song for him tonight. 'Don't wait for me!' I say.

I hop along in the rear, happy to be out of doors under a blue sky, and watch the spray of snow at their heels turn into gems every colour of a jewel chest.

Against all expectations the hounds put up a hare. You should just hear the row! You'd think he was a stag of seven tines. The dogs are floundering about and slipping all over the place. The men let out a yell and fan across the mountainside. They're going pell-mell to head the poor beast off whichever way he turns. There are bows levelled and spears raised. All for a scrap of brown fur and a pair of long ears and two bulging eyes.

Arthur's in the middle of the front rank, as ever, laughing and running as hard as the young men. I see my great golden king so full of speed and strength. I think he cannot die. This moment hangs outside of history. The sunlight and the spears. I fix it in my mind. My song shall be my spear, to pin this day to earth and hold it. No! I shiver as my foot goes through the ice into black bog. That's not the metaphor, to kill this day like a trapped hare, or to let it escape up the mountain scree. A song should hold life. Beyond the grave these men shall live, because of me.

Something has dimmed the bright day. The sun still shines, but there is a chill blueness on the snow. The shouts have altered. Why are the men standing on the ridge to my left, looking down? A horn checks the hounds. Baffled, they bark their indignation, and come to a noisy, jostling halt. The hare bolts on for freedom, zigzagging still up over untouched snow towards the peak. The other huntsmen are turning now, stumbling in drifts, skidding on icy rocks to see what's up. I pick my way more prudently through the stiff, scratching heather to where that row of black sentinels stoops against the skyline. Someone's starting to climb down. Gawain. The others yell caution to him.

Only at the last moment can we who have straggled up late see over the edge. The ground falls in a corrie with bare sunless walls. A gravelled hollow, an icy tarn, a few white rocks. One splash of colour sprawls with twisted neck among the stones. A dark green tunic embroidered with crimson. A red and black cloak. Even from here we know those colours: Anir.

Others are clambering down after Gawain, risking their lives at speed for a prince already beyond anyone's help. It doesn't need the shake of Gawain's head to tell us that. But his gesture breaks the stunned silence and all the men are keening now. One voice bursts out above

500

all the rest like the roar of a stag. Fury and grief. Inconsolable rage at the theft of hope.

Anir has made his final stumble, gone clumsily wrongfooted to his death, not gloriously on an enemy's spear or a boar's tusk. Vainly outstretching himself to please his father, he has disappointed Arthur for the last time.

You can read the consternation in their faces. Not for a comrade dead. Men fall in battle or the hunt. It's common enough. But for the death of a dream. The last Pendragon. He hadn't been much of a future, Anir. But he was all they had. After Arthur, what? There are great men beside him; Cei, Bedwyr, Urien. But they are all within a year or two of Arthur. Among the younger generation, who could lift up such a sword as his?

Take the boy up gently in a hammock of cloak and spears. They will carry him home by the low road while we wind sadly down the hill with the chastened hounds. Modred and Bedwyr support Arthur. There are tears on all our cheeks.

Still, I am a bard, and my mind's already inspired with the rhymes of the lament I must be making this night. Rest now, young Anir. Never shall grief for a prince be sung like yours. While the ship of the dead carries you to the islands of Paradise, my harp shall mourn you with an immortal magic. Your grave, and Taliesin's awen, will be remembered.

It's a pity it couldn't have been something bigger than a hare.

It's worse going downhill over the ice. Madness, to go hunting on such a day. Would he have held back if he'd known? The king, with his spear restless in his hand and the Saxons quiet. Is that what Nimue feared? Would I have wanted him to sit at home? Is not this the Arthur we all cheer for, the mad, bold, boyish chieftain of our dreams? Death-dealing Caliburn, made mortal flesh.

I am last as usual. I see the tableau from far off. The sad procession, the women hurrying out of doors, the hunting-party closing in. I run the last furlong to catch up. This is high tragedy, not to be missed. Lucky they have strewn this highway with straw and grit.

Arthur's voice carries in the clear air, sonorous with grief and accusation. It is Margawse he's addressing.

'This is your doing! Vengeful witch! Have you not done me enough harm already?'

'My doing! Did I call out the hounds with the ice hard on every loch? Did I charge up the braes and make every man of the court follow me, whether he would or no? Did I make a fool of myself to prove the man was still a boy, and force your boy to prove himself a man? Arthur Pendragon should look nearer home for his son's executioner.'

Hands are on daggers then, spears raised. Comrades are turning on each other, Arthur's folk, against Margawse's.

Nimue speaks; very white she is. Her pointing finger finds Morgan. 'You! You call yourself the Healer. Can you do nothing for him?'

No flash of triumph in Morgan's face, though Nimue owns that she herself is powerless. She wrings her hands and shakes her head, and seems to struggle for speech. 'You come to me too late. All that I have, all that I know, I would freely have given. I cannot restore his broken neck, or call back the soul you left behind in the glen. What is done must stand.'

'The scabbard!' shouts Arthur. 'You have Caliburn's scabbard. If ever I needed healing, it is now. Restore it! Use it yourselves! I will give you anything you ask in return. You can have the sword itself, if that will save him.'

Does he really mean that?

The blood is dark in Morgan's cheeks and brow and neck. She stands immobile. The whole court is hushed now, waiting for her response.

'I cannot.' Only a whisper, like ice cracking.

'For God's sake, do not deny me!'

'I cannot give you back the scabbard.'

'You hate me that much? The lad lies broken at your feet, and you refuse?'

She shakes her head through a slow eternity of regret.

'When you sent my woman Luned back to me dead, wrapped in the cloak I made for you, my hope was finished. I knew the sword would never come to meet the scabbard. I saw that you and I would never be reconciled. I drowned the scabbard.'

'You did what!'

'It came from the waters. To the waters it has returned. To her who made it.'

'Where? Where did you do this? For God's sake, tell me how far I must go to get it back!'

'You cannot. Her hand has taken it deeper than restitution. Neither of us can ever have it again. I have ritually destroyed that healing.'

'It was not yours. You had no right!'

'No. No right. No right to father's life, or mother's honour. No right to liberty. No right to love. When I, the Healer, destroyed the scabbard, I sacrificed the only power I ever held. I waited for you with empty hands. Since you would not accept equality of strength with me, I offered you the sharing of my powerlessness. And still you kept the sword.'

'They were both mine. Given to me at my manhood. Mine, not yours. I am the king!'

'Exactly. And I am nothing. How could this nothing help you?'

'I offered you the sword today!'

'It was too late.'

'You have killed my son.'

She bows her head in silence.

Elaine moves forward, very slow, and gathers up poor Anir in her arms. He isn't a big lad, but for all her size she must be stronger than she looks to lift him like that, as effortlessly as if he was a baby.

She smiles on him lovingly and rocks him gently. 'Sleep, little one. Fair women will attend your wounds and wine-cups await you. The harps of the Summer Land shall soothe your slumber. In the morning, all shall be well.' Her soft lips kiss his cold brow.

Arthur glares at her, but finds no words.

There is a disturbance in the crowd. A little late, Gwenhyvar comes tumbling through, hair dishevelled, and throws herself on Anir's body. Her mother's keening splits the sky and all the women wail louder with her. Elaine stands motionless as Gwenhyvar sinks in a graceful heap on the cobbles, weeping. Then she walks slowly towards the hall bearing her burden, leaving Modred to kneel and comfort the queen.

Morgan watches this. Her eyes return to Arthur's.

'Yet what if I were indeed to restore your son to you?'

He starts. A gleam of hope is overshadowed by doubt. He backs away, and crosses himself.

'The boy is beyond help. You said so.'

'But how if I gave you a son back from the dead? I brought both sword and scabbard to your gate at Celliwig once, and you turned me away. I sent you a precious cloak and you put it on another. What would you do if I offered you your son again?'

Modred, raising Gwenhyvar, watches intently.

Arthur shouts, 'Murderess! A stolen sword! A poisoned cloak! Everything you promise me is tainted, woman!'

'No. You would not accept him, would you?'

She sighs and nods to her women.

'Prepare a sleeping draught for Gwenhyvar. And, Taliesin, warm your hands at the fire and tune your harp. It is your healing the High Queen will need as much as mine.'

I look to Arthur for permission, but he is stalking off indoors. It is Modred and Gareth who help Gwenhyvar to her chamber.

On the dais in the hall Elaine is laying the boy out on his bier.

# Chapter Sixteen

They have taken Anir's body south, a cold departing. Miserable for me, to see the miles lengthening between Taliesin and the High King. No invitation for me now to sing at Arthur's court.

'I suppose that's the end of it,' I say to Woman. 'He won't want to see his sisters after this.'

'You, a learned bard! You can't see further than a blind kitten, can you?' He snorts contempt. 'They're like the seasons, those four. Spring, summer, autumn, winter, and then spring again. They'll come round. He can't escape them.'

'Do you think it was Margawse's doing?'

Her land, her mountain. Was it her hare? After all, he tried to kill *her* son.

Woman looks at me craftily under his veil. It's been long since he stood upright or gazed directly at another man.

'Who's to say which way the wind blows? Did you know her first husband, Lot, fell fighting Arthur's folk? She swore her sons to vengeance, though it wasn't Pendragon himself that killed him. Well, look at them now. Swarming around him like wasps on a ripe plum.'

I'm not sure what he's trying to tell me. That Margawse would make peace with Arthur? Or something darker?

'Can't he trust his own nephews?' Alarm now. I find Arthur's safety touches me too closely for comfort. Nimue's shaft has taken root.

'It would be a wise man who knew which side that lot are on. Margawse has never played the faithful wife, or widow afterwards. She's had other husbands since, and more that weren't. None of them lasted long.' He grins. He knows where I've been. I think the whole court knows.

Turn it off with a laugh, boy. 'I'm not surprised. It would take a mighty log to outlast her flame.'

'She'd better watch out it's not her that feels the edge of the axe, then. It's more than the women of this family that are dangerous. Avenge their father? They might well do that. They think their mother shames them. If I was her, and warm in bed, I'd want a great gold torque round my pretty white throat, just in case.'

The wind blows terribly cold in Din Eidyn.

The court of Lothian is in mourning, no heart for hunting. I'm not sorry. I'd rather stay snug by the fire and polish up a new lament on the harp. A Chief Bard is his own man, once he has fulfilled his duties. This weather I'd sooner be Gwion Bach tending the flames than bold Taliesin braving the burn.

What's up with the queens, though? Why are Morgan and Margawse coming into the hall cloaked, furred and booted, a glinting adventure in their eyes? Who is the stranger with them, this massive mound of wraps and capes? Elaine the Fair, who never rides or walks abroad, who seldom stirs from the side of the fire! Dressed for travel, in this bitter cold?

The queens' eyes scan the faces turned to them. They name their escort. This time I suck my thumb and try to hide my face. No chance. Morgan's voice orders, 'Taliesin.'

I could protest. I'm Urien's bard, not hers. Even the king has no right to compel me outside my terms of contract. Idle words. We both know I won't waste breath on them.

Woman, her surly watchdog, is named of course. Not Tegau, though. Sweet, true, brave Tegau, that guards her Christian faith like a clear candle. Morgan respects that. I'm a Christian too, aren't I? When Urien's around, anyway. But Morgan knows there's too much of the blood of Ceridwen in me. I'm helpless before her.

Stark January. There isn't cloak and hood thick enough to keep out this cold. And the ruts are frozen into hard ridges under my boots. I slip and slide and worry about breaking my wrist. Hard climbing now. We follow a path up a bare, grim glen where the burn is frozen almost into stillness. At last I hear it sing. It chimes pure chords as it drops into a pool from stone to ice. These rocks are streaked with red. We enter the cave with care, for the stones are slippery. Reluctantly I help Elaine puff and heave herself up over the ledge. I know the signs inside, the stone table, the objects the women are setting out.

'Be thou my soul's shelter, thou my high tower!

'Forgive us our trespasses.

'Deliver me from the tempter.'

The Christian half of me babbles. I am not brave enough. Tegau is a more valiant warrior than I.

At least there should be a fire.

After all, there's nothing terrible done. What's the harm in offering a token to the god of the territory at the beginning of the year? Corn, wine, a kid roasted with herbs. Just a modest dinner with a few friends.

That's not all we've come for. I didn't think it would be.

They stand, we stand, our fingertips upon the table. The knot is made, and hallowed.

'He will keep Caliburn now.' Morgan makes this a truth heavy with grief.

'You destroyed the scabbard without our consent.' Margawse's accusation.

Too slow, the third voice. We wait. All our eyes go to her, Elaine. She does not speak, but her plump hands fumble for a while in the heavy folds of her clothes. Something snakes into the winter light. She spreads it on the tabletop. I have seen it before, this woollen plait of red and black and white. All week she has sat and woven its strands, even while Arthur was watching her. It is braided now through a black and ancient leather, silver-clasped. I see what it is now. An old, old belt, frail with hard use, made newly bright and serviceable. A harness to hang on a warrior's hip. A strap to span his shoulder. The rings and clips that would hold a scabbard secure. A sword-belt.

'Too late, isn't it?'

'It is little enough. But it is well I have kept it. It is all the power Morgan has left us. It will have to serve.'

'For what?'

'Why now? Why did you not say you had this sooner? This is the bond that would have held them both together!'

'What is the use of showing the belt now we have lost both sword and scabbard?' Margawse cries bitterly.

The younger sisters storm at her. Elaine, impassive, waits for their understanding.

'The line that measures out and cries "Enough"?'

'A last rope thrown to save a drowning man?'

'A noose to hang him?'

I should have stayed at home.

# Chapter Seventeen

Their magic knot binds surer than I thought. The buckle tightens, though it seems at first as if I've slipped through the clasp.

Arthur will ride his frontier forts. Nimue, and my songs, have done their work. There's a new restlessness on him, by all accounts. Well, what is a king without warfare, without red blood on the sword, and playing football with heads, and speckled horses spattered with the rush of combat? What is a king if he cannot give gifts? Where is he to get the heaping gold, the corn-fed steeds, the rich-furred mantles, if they're not snatched from the palefaced Saxons, as they seize treasures from us? It's a brisk form of trading. You do not ask the bellowing cattle where they were bred, how many borders they've been driven over, how many times. I finger a brooch of gold and garnets on my tunic and wonder what British, Saxon, Irish, Pictish breasts have warmed its cool metal curlicues before it nestled here. On second thoughts, I wish I hadn't imagined that. Tremors of terror thrill through me. I see yet one more pair of hands rip it from this anchoring cloth. The nest grows cold, Taliesin is . . .

No! Back to Arthur, boy. Picture him in the summer dawn when the first long light comes striding down the hills. He and all his warriors of legend stand high as bardic imagination on the moors. There is a line marked in both British and Saxon minds. The rules are understood. Those ramparts of the border forts, where our High King stands higher still, are not there to repel flesh and steel, but to hold off the advance of ambitious thoughts. There must be fighting, now and then, of course. If there were not, we might wonder if we still needed a High King. But not so much as to upset the truce.

You are right, Nimue. It is not enough. What is a poet without warfare?

This time, it's different. He calls the older men to ride with him. Cador, Nentres, Urien. It is the youngest that he leaves behind to guard Gwenhyvar, against the custom. We understand his message. King Arthur is not finished yet. He is a king without a son because he needs no son. Age, like the Saxons, cannot encroach upon him.

I wonder if Urien of Rheged will decline the call. But now obedience and temptation march side by side. There is little enough of youth left to any of them, and he's still in love with Arthur. They will show their sons the meaning of valour.

This time he's going to take me! I shall have my chance, I shall see Arthur in the glory of battle. No matter what petty skirmish comes my way, my bardic craft can raise it to the realm of high adventure. My voice will be authentic. I was there!

My eyes are shining like Urien's.

'My lord! You will not be sorry. Nimue charged me to sing for Arthur, to rouse him to war. There will be deeds done this summer that shall ring round the world and set the seas shaking on the farthest shores. Your fame will— '

'Nimue?' he interrupts me. 'This campaign is Nimue's doing? She asked your help?'

I flush with indignation. 'What else are we for, the druids, bards, the learned men and women? We are your inspiration. The Christian priests will thunder their psalms over the army too. You live by our poems and our prayers.'

'He banished Nimue once, for being too ambitious. Better that she had stayed by her lake.'

Too free with my tongue, wasn't I? In the morning, Urien's changed his mind. He will not take me. I plead. I remind him of Anir. What if this campaign is his last? What if Arthur's Llamrei were to put her hoof down a foxhole and the High King end his days with a broken head in the heather? Worse, what if this is the year when the settled pattern breaks, when the turgid blood of the British rises like the ninth wave and the last battle sweeps across the strand of history, and I not there to sing of it?

Urien's mouth sets in a tighter line.

'You agreed with me to be Chief Bard to Rheged. Is that not enough fame?'

Even a fair-minded Christian king is not above jealousy, it seems. Do not fear, my lord. The fights of Catraeth, the hall at Lyvennet, the pastures of Erechwydd, the courage of Urien, and the grave of Owain, all these shall live in song, because of Taliesin.

Until my life ages . . .

You know the rest by now.

Only, can't you see I was born for something more than this? Already the short spring day is dying. The light is reddening on the frontier forts.

I am left with the women.

Someone else is discontented with her lot. Gwenhyvar is fair, and Gwenhyvar is chaste, and Gwenhyvar is rather bored. Again she waits alone in Camelot. Well, not alone. Arthur has left her well guarded, rather too well, you might say, this time. Young lords that might have been raising the mead-horn on the eve of adventure, bearing the ash-shaft in battle, goading steaming horses into combat, must now confine themselves to rustic sports while their fathers earn praise as warriors.

In spite of them, the queen craves feminine company. She must hold her court. What is the use of this bevy of young gallants attending her if there are no older ladies to see and envy? She is young yet; and beautiful, isn't she? She could be Margawse's daughter.

They come, obedient to her royal summons, Elaine, Margawse, Morgan, and their households. Reluctant and curious. Does she have no fear of them now? What liquid has Nimue dropped in her ear that makes Gwenhyvar so sure of her own strength? It's been a long time since the three were invited to Camelot. A private enmity, a public loyalty. Arthur is still High King, and they are his sisters. Statecraft decrees he needs their kingdoms' support. Their family honour demands they must not diminish his. Where is the space for love, humanity, the meeting of hearts? These are not common folk. They are the prisoners of their position.

I ride with Morgan, across blue passes, down long green leafy lanes that lead us south, over ringing highroads the Romans left, along the old straight ridgeways that were the spines of a now fleshless past.

We come by the last high track to Somerset, and on our right a maze of meres and marshes tricks the eye with a net of shimmering light, level and liquid to the far-off Severn Channel. Or not quite level. No, not at all. Look, there emerging in the midst under a noonday moon Leviathan rises, a dragon of an island. Beyond its low ridged back a head rears proud and sudden to butt the sky. From miles around it draws the eye and holds it, a great eruption in that watery wilderness.

Morgan reins in her horse abruptly. I do not need her to tell me this is a fairy fortress. The evidence is plain.

'Ynys Witrin.'

The Glass Island. Glastonbury.

Nothing more to say, is there? Its presence follows us, though we turn our heads and move on. It's a powerful place, even at this distance.

'There is an abbey there,' says Tegau presently, looking over her shoulder. 'They have a holy thorn, sprung from the staff of Joseph of Arimathea. They even say the Lord Jesus was here as a child. And that the vessel that caught his blood . . .'

Morgan snorts, not too unlike her horse.

I believe Tegau. I could believe anything of that island.

Ahead of us is high Camelot at last. Against the bright sky its palisades stand silhouetted. Clean stonework flashes on its mighty banks. An old fort rebuilt by Arthur for new wars; a lonely, warlike place to leave a queen all summer.

When we come under its shadow, Morgan looks up. I cannot read her face. I think she does not wish to be here. She doubts the reason for this summons. Is Gwenhyvar as shallow as we have supposed?

A stream winds about the base of the fort through woodland. We climb, under the eye of sentries. Then, halfway up, the wind takes word of who we are and everything changes. Someone is running to meet us. Gareth. Morgan's own daughter Morfudd is close behind him, merry with greeting. We're inside the walls and the grim hard shell cracks open to reveal a sweet kernel of welcome. Gwenhyvar herself is kissing Morgan. You'd think there was common cause on the distaff side.

What a kingly hall! I haven't seen anything to touch it outside Roman cities. He'd like to have built this in masonry, Artorius Imperator. But the plastered wattle becomes Morgan better. Tonight the fire will leap on these painted walls and birds will croon to us from the thatch and we will gather in a circle and tell old stories.

Elaine was here before us, and now Margawse arrives. Agravain and Gaheris embrace her, though not too warmly. Her sons have a prickly northern sense of dignity. I remember Teilo's warning. If I were her, I'd tread carefully with Gwenhyvar's young men. They've a great capacity for hurting each other, this family.

A kingly hall, but a queen's court. There are games and riding and picnics and picking flowers. If Gwenhyvar still grieves for Anir, she covers it well. She teases Arthur's nephews more like a sister than an aunt. Sometimes we row in coracles on the river. 'We could make an expedition to Glastonbury,' says Gwenhyvar. My thumbs are pricking with anticipation, but we do not go.

There's less wine drunk at Gwenhyvar's table. My head is clearer than I'm used to. It makes me oddly uncertain about my actions. The women have retired already. I stroll down the lane that separates the guest-chambers from the royal rooms. I settle my harp in its bag on my shoulder for reassurance. I'm not sure if I'll be wanted tonight.

It is not quite dark, but I see or hear no movement till a man speaks.

'Where are you going, Taliesin?'

Modred? Here, in the shadow between Morgan's house and Gwenhyvar's.

Don't stop walking. A check means guilt. Your harp is the passport. Just Taliesin, going about his job. Thank your stars it's not Owain. He was thought man enough to be away with Arthur.

Modred is barring my way. Not ostentatiously. I hear his hand loosen the knife in its sheath and let it go again. No more than a hint. He stands at ease, motionless, a man fulfilling his duty.

'You think I come too late?'

'Too late for what?'

'To bring Morgan sweet rest.'

'Morgan of Tintagel? You come nineteen years too late for that.'

Nineteen years. There's a nice calculation. The lifetime of both of us. I don't feel like arguing. These men are jealous of their ladies' honour. Still, I thought Modred understood.

I shrug and turn for my own stall in the men's quarters. An early night and plenty of room without the warband. I shan't have to pick my way over a fuddle of drunken warriors.

When I reach the corner, Modred hasn't moved. His shadow still stands at the crossroads between Urien's and Arthur's queen.

# Chapter Eighteen

Next day it's gone clean out of my head. Arthur's back, and half his army! Some lords will have gone home to find their ladies have flown the coop. His warband trot their horses through the hollow twisting way up the big hill, while we look down on them and cheer. Tegau has gone bright red. She's screaming as loud as any of them. Caradawc Strong-Arm's there, and all her virginal water has turned to wifely wine. Oh, unassailable, true Tegau Goldbreast. They'll be married this month.

The standards nod. The high horns cry out to us. The warriors have decked themselves with more jewellery than they went away with. They've found somebody foolish enough to fight with them. That will please him. Kill another calf and count the wine jars. There'll be a rare old feast tonight. Is the harp feeling up to it? It's been singing softer songs lately.

They are nearer now. It's not only the living faces that are lifted to us. There are heads swinging from the horses' necks. That must be a chieftain or two, gracing Arthur's harness. But not too many. Mustn't upset the diplomatic balance. It wasn't Badon, but it will have to do.

They're grinning at the thought of clean clothes, warm baths, good food. And now women! Our ladies waving on the walls don't cheer as loud as the roar of the warriors once they've seen who's waiting for them.

Women? There's a shock, as if I had looked at my own reflection in water and seen a stranger peering over my shoulder. I thought we were the female party welcoming back our fighting men. That's not the whole truth, though. So the tales are true. Arthur has women with him, on his side. Not many, a small tight band of warriors. They're muscled enough, but definitely not men. In kilted tunics, chequered cloaks thrown over the shoulder, braided hair, as rich in ornament of gold and bronze as any man. But weaponed, proud of themselves, defiant, and not without scars by the look of it. The men leave a respectful – resentful? – space between them.

And leading them, in a wicker chariot, with a golden breastplate that moulds itself over her flowing robes, Nimue. She grasps a silvery spear and looks up, smiling triumph.

The world is full of dangerous reverses. Be careful, Taliesin. The Lady of the Lake, that smiles so sweetly from a field of waterlilies, can be the angry storm that races down the loch. Remember Merlyn. Morgan is not the only woman with power.

Arthur dismounts. He's seen his sisters waiting to welcome him. This was clearly not by his knowledge. He glares at Gwenhyvar.

'Is a man not safe in his own home? Do they rob me of my son and come to devour Camelot as well?'

511

'They came to honour me as queen. May I not brighten Camelot in your absence?'

'You'd hold a court without me? Are you growing so high and mighty, madam?'

'Great victors need great courts to celebrate their homecoming.'

'Victory? A handful of heads and a lame horse!'

Then he bursts out laughing and hugs them all strongly, sisters included. He's in a good temper. It's gone well. I see his golden beard caught in the tide of Morgan's black hair flowing over his shoulder. I catch their laughing faces. I think I shall never understand them.

Nimue's the only one who sulks at the sight of reconciliation. I grab hold of Owain.

'Is it true? Did she really fight? Did she use that weapon?'

'She stood in her chariot on a hill and she shook her spear. She cursed our enemies and howled on us to slaughter them.' He grins like a hound. 'Once it was monks and bishops who did that for him. Nimue's better at it.'

Morgan laughs merrier now Arthur's come.

At supper I sing my poor thin songs of battles I have not seen. I mourn the fall of heroes I cannot remember meeting. They'd have to be heroes, wouldn't they, since they died? I make it sound as though this was the high summer in the fortunes of Britain. Some of the silver they have taken comes my way. I'm a rich man already. Does nobody but me hear the poverty in my songs, see the lays that swell in me like a pregnant woman past her time? Taliesin, in Camelot, at Arthur's board – and nothing much to sing about.

The very next day they're off hunting. There's a lust in these men to kill, and in me to tell of it. They need the fame I give them, I need the deeds they do. And not a few women ride with them under the leafy oaks. Morgan, who's lost ten years at least in the fresh wind that blows in with Arthur. Margawse, Nimue. Not Elaine, of course, or Gwenhyvar.

Now, in the spring weather of Somerset, I don't need to be bullied. I'll risk horses and horns and branches and breaks to be at Arthur's heels while I can. For a week the sun shines as never before, and our days are full of sport and the nights of pleasure. Tegau Goldbreast is wed to Caradawc Strong-Arm amid great celebration. The women smile and the men sigh.

Only a week. Tomorrow they ride back to the border. The hounds of age are after Arthur. He dare not stop running.

Hope, Taliesin. His recklessness could provoke the last great conflict yet.

Our final hunt is over. The stag is trussed, and the merriment has faded. I find myself riding back by the mere with Morgan. Our mounts pace softly under the trees. We are neither of us as hard as those we have hunted with.

'Taliesin?'

For once, her voice does not command; it pleads. Be the more careful, boy. Wait, listen.

'You are a light lad. You find a welcome in many rooms. Would you get something for me?'

'What can Taliesin bring you, that my queen herself could not command?'

'Something of Arthur's.'

'What, my lady?'

'It does not matter. Only . . . not spoils of war, a treasure made by craftsmen only for him to bestow again as a gift. Some possession more personal to him. A thing that is truly his, and no other's.'

'Whom shall I ask for this? Arthur himself, or Gwenhyvar?'

She laughs then, and her eyes dance like emeralds in the flickering leaf-light. Very appealing, that smile.

'You need not beg from either of them. You wanted to ride with Urien on this raiding-party. Now I appoint you Morgan's reaver!'

'I'd ask you why, except that I know you wouldn't tell me.'

'Suck your thumb of knowledge and see if it gives you inspiration.'

We joke. We both know this is no laughing matter. Morgan asks nothing lightly from anyone, nor do they refuse her.

Serious, then. Taliesin's to be a thief again. Oh, dear, I remember Gwion Bach, and what it cost last time. Shake that thought off. But I do not play my best this last evening.

I sit down and take the horn of wine they pass me. Everyone seems to be smiling but me. Me and Morgan. Her eyes have gone dark now, like the shadows under a yew tree. Perhaps she too can feel that the day is turning too far. I have arrived too late and she has delayed too long. So little chance remains to both of us. Our dreams must be delivered soon. Her eyes beseech me to remember what she asked.

I force a smile for her. Haven't I seen her laughing, held on Arthur's breast? The men are home and safe, most of them. Everyone's merry. Pity about Anir, but the men are toasting Gwenhyvar. The corn is springing. There's meat on the spits for the poets of Christendom. All's well.

All's well? I'm sorry, Morgan. Nimue looks radiant. She is the one who will goad Arthur to war.

The High King will be late to bed. The men are carousing. Tomorrow the long road east, damp tents, deserted forts, uncertain food. Tonight they will fill themselves to the brim with good meat and mead. The women go earlier to bed, hoping for something else before their heroes are felled by drink.

A lesser talent than me is Chief Bard in Camelot. I leave him twanging. I have other duties.

It is growing late, and half of us are in our chambers. Well, I'm in Morgan's, as it happens. She has come to that age when women flush and thirst and cannot sleep. For a young man I've learned a good deal about the needs of women. I am the hand that strums softly while the castle sleeps, the voice that murmurs poems at the wakeful midnight. It's not a Chief Bard's job. But nobody can charm the restless pillow of my queen more tenderly than I can. I have been discreet. No sentinel challenged me this time. Besides, all the corners of Camelot have been full of sweet laughter and hushings these seven nights.

Her ladies are gathered round. The younger ones are yawning. Such sweet soft faces need their sleep. At last she sends them away, all except

Tegau and Woman. Tegau looks soulful. She is wakeful for someone else, this three-days' bride. Beside her blossom we make a poor pair, Woman and I. The one too manly for a dame, the other too maidenish a man to be a battle-poet.

But now Morgan has a task for me behind the enemy lines. Her hand grasps my wrist, hot and dry. She is thirsty for something more than I can give her.

I feel how fragile the bond that ties Arthur to her. It has been a sunlit week. A sudden storm could separate them for ever. Like her, I know a desolate ache for something to remember Arthur by. For me, one last heroic deed; for her, this keepsake. I nod. Trust Taliesin.

The air is sweet outside. There's still deep-throated singing from the hall. The Pendragon sleeps in a fine house opposite this one, when he's finished drinking, that is; the royal chambers. I tiptoe across the path in the April gloaming, fearful I'll set the guard dogs baying for my throat and bring the warhost running. Does Morgan realise what I'm risking for her?

The lamps are all out but one. Pray that Gwenhyvar and all her ladies are asleep by now. Push the door gently. Close darkness inside. Stupid to come like a thief in the middle of the night.

When else should a thief come?

Taliesin's a thief. And what he is stealing he does not understand.

Cold feet now. Cold in my stomach, too. I'm backing out. Not that I'd say no to Morgan, mind you. I wouldn't dare. But better ways than this, better times, better light.

Too late. Someone's awake! No maiden, either. The hiss of steel, the fumble of an urgent hand and then a sure grip on my wrist. The edge of the blade to my throat. He sees me better than I see him.

'Your name, and business in the queen's house in the middle of the night? And if the name you speak fails to match your face when I get you outside, I'll separate your head from your heart by the same distance.'

'Taliesin,' I squeak.

I feel him check. The warlike certainty's gone out of his grip.

'Taliesin? In Gwenhyvar's rooms?' He speaks louder and less guardedly. I know the voice for Gareth's.

'Silly me! Got the wrong door in the dark, haven't I?'

'That mistake could have cost you your life.' But he lowers the blade. Still, he's not satisfied. 'You didn't think to cheat my aunt Morgan with Arthur's queen, did you?'

Not, would I cheat Arthur, you notice, though the king's his uncle too. Very devious, this kindred.

'Not me! I've a tricky enough boat to row, as it is.'

He chuckles a bit.

'Look over your shoulder, then, and watch where you're steering. The queen's not so lonely she needs the likes of you.'

'Don't worry,' I promise him. 'It wasn't her I was after.'

I back out, trembling like a dog in a thunderstorm.

Gwenhyvar is fair, and Gwenhyvar is chaste, and Gwenhyvar is closely guarded.

# Chapter Nineteen

Arthur's gone again, like a dust storm through our camp. Does he feel, as Morgan does, that the days are oddly short, though the year is moving towards May Day?

It's beautiful weather, and the whole court rides out to cheer them on their way. The women are brightly dressed. They've threaded their hair with ribbons and jewels, to fix a picture of themselves in their menfolk's memories. Tegau's eyes are bright but brave. The young men of Gwenhyvar's guard are showing off before their older relatives. Their pride is hurt because Arthur is denying their manhood. They do not need to spare their own horses; they will be stabled back in Camelot all too soon. They prance and race, circle and gallop round the pacing column of warriors and war-gear.

I let them go, watching them for a while from the ramparts. I haven't the heart for this outing. I'm no horseman. Arthur is leaving us.

Besides, I have other plans. This is a better time for thieving, broad daylight, plenty of people about. People? You thought they'd all of them ridden out with Arthur? Servants. As invisible to the nobility as common flies, that are only noticed when they settle where they shouldn't. But in the life before this I was Gwion Bach. I've sweated over cauldrons too.

Give them a good day and smile at them, then, as you cross the yard. Put a spring in your step and hold your head high. Don't sneak this time. Walk like a man who knows where he's going and has every right. To Arthur's chambers. Whistle a bit. It's a lovely morning. No more difficult, this, than the spell you lay on the host after supper's over, to make them believe tales that will suit your fortune.

Open the door and step inside. Easier in daylight. No warrior with a drawn dagger, this time. No one at all. Not even a slave with an armful of rushes. Makes me feel guilty again, somehow, this emptiness. No harm, though, is there? I know Morgan loves her brother. I have felt myself transformed inside her. I hear the name she cannot help but cry.

No difficulty this morning, knowing which way to turn. A great bear carved on the right, leaping dolphins painted on the left. I listen for a murmur of voices behind Gwenhyvar's door. Nothing. Too nice a day. Her serving-women will have found themselves work outside to enjoy the sunshine. Right, then. Here goes.

A kingly room. The bed's big. Nothing to cramp his style here. Rich hangings to keep out the draughts. Painted wood and cunning carvings. The great hall itself is not more colourfully decorated than this. Scarlet and gold seem to be his favourites.

It's a shame it's not royally kept, though. The bed's unmade. There are dirty clothes in a heap on the floor. Great Arthur should be better served than this. If I were Gwenhyvar, I'd drill a smarter army to attend my king. Still, such untidiness suits my purpose. I look around, judiciously. What should I choose for Morgan? I try not to hurry, though I don't want to linger. It must be done right. This is important to her. She does not easily beg.

I walk to the middle of the room and turn, considering. And then I see it. My heart gives a great bound as if I had peered through the branches of the forest and seen the face of a wolf, not a yard away from me. It is lying on the coffer at the foot of the bed, beside me, a magnificent sword. A name leaps to my mind and fills me with amazement. It can't be, can it? Arthur's great weapon, Caliburn? No sword in all the world to match that. This hilt is heavy with gems. I search for the pair of fire-breathing dragons and find them, and yet . . . I marvel that a soldier could grasp this handily in earnest battle. Jewels are not the true worth of Caliburn. All Britain knows it is his talisman of victory. Would he leave it behind when he rode to war?

The scabbard is richly crusted too, but the poet in me plucks a note of sadness. The true cover for Caliburn is long since lost. Teilo has told me. Ancient black and silver, it was, not much to look at, but wonderful to touch, precious with healing. On a black day, Morgan drowned that scabbard, ritually casting it into a bottomless lake. He thinks she killed herself that day. I will not believe it. I am too young to bury hope. I have seen them laughing.

Caliburn survives alone, dangerously unmatched, the killing tool. They both came to us from the water. The first has already gone home. The sword must follow one day. Not yet! Not yet! With all Taliesin's great song still unsung.

I cannot take this sword for Morgan. I'm not that daft. All the same . . . my hands close round the sparkling hilt and find the metal cold, the gems sharp. Puzzled, I try to draw its unhandy weight.

'No, boy. That isn't Caliburn. She took that once before. She will not get the chance again. It nearly cost Britain his life the first time.'

Guilt floods my cheeks. Gwenhyvar! Back so soon, and alone? She halts in the doorway, her face flushed with distress and streaked with tears. Parting has been too much for her, it seems. Still, though she's not a tall woman she stands straight and imperious now, as if she's forgotten already what she was weeping for.

I try to smile. 'I didn't think it could be.'

She looks at me, considering. I am Taliesin, the finest bard that has ever sung in Camelot, and a limber young lad for a lady. I see she knows that. But she wants only half of what I can offer. I have sung her praises. I will have gold, horses, fine tunics from her, land, even. But I am Morgan's. She does not trust me. I read all that in her face.

What do I care? Why should I want skimmed milk? I, that have tasted wine and blood?

'Didn't you know Arthur had two great swords? Caliburn, his weapon of war, that Nimue armed him with when he came to manhood, and this, the sword of Britain's government, put in his hand by Bishop Dubric at his coronation, on his most sacred oath to guard her peace.'

She takes the regal sword away from me. I'm not sorry. It was a heavy thing to hold.

'I didn't know. Too young for his coronation, me.'

Tactless, that. It was her coronation too. I watch her face change, and I'm trying to cobble together some compliment to cover myself. But she smiles suddenly, and there's a gleam in her eyes as if she's thought of a sudden purpose.

'Wait there, bard!'

She darts across to her own room. I hear the lid of a chest thrown back, the sounds of search. Gwenhyvar returns. In her hands she bears something reverently. At first I think it might be a distaff, but it holds no thread. A shaft of polished greenstone, weighty, valuable. The top is carved into the semblance of birds' heads, fourfold, looking all ways with garnet eyes. From its lower tip three human heads gaze upwards.

'Do you know what this is? Do the bards sing of this?'

I shake my head.

'I did not think so. It is the queen's sceptre,' she explains. 'My staff of office, given to me when Arthur received his sword, in a separate coronation, in another church, before the witness of women.'

Curious. Morgan never told me of that. No, not curious. Morgan speaks very little of Gwenhyvar.

She lays her sceptre beside his sword, and we both stand looking at them. I'm not sure what she's trying to tell me.

'I always thought Arthur got his real power from Merlyn.'

'Merlyn?' Her laugh is light and yet so scornful. 'The bards praise him, don't they? No. It was Nimue who gave him the arms of war, and the Church that entrusted Arthur with this sword of peace. The Lady of the Lake was wiser than Merlyn. Drop by drop she drained him of his secrets, and in the end he told her one too many. Where is Merlyn now? Mad, lost, buried in the forest? They went into the woods together, and Nimue came back alone, laughing at her own cleverness. Since then, she has sought to be the watcher over Arthur, the spirit that wakes when he sleeps, his shadow in the sun. Very powerful is the Lady of the Lake, but he will not trust her. There was only ever one woman in the world who could be to Arthur what Merlyn was.'

There is pain in her face. I have misjudged her, thinking her a shallow, pretty toy, but she is a hurt wife. She sees too much. Arthur and Morgan . . . And I shiver. I see through her eyes this is too dangerous a love for him. We must protect him, she and I.

And because I am sorry for her, I say without thinking whose service I am here on, 'Beware of Modred.'

'Modred? *Modred?*'

Her colour deepens and her eyes widen. Shock? Disbelief? Fascination? I should have known the moment of deep understanding between us had passed. I am back in the shallows of her mind. She thinks I am warning of danger to herself, not Arthur. Her world is once more as narrow as this bedchamber, and made for the same purpose, though a moment ago she was holding a queen's sceptre in her hand.

She crosses quickly to the window and stands looking out, gripping the frame. A vole, held by a stoat, would not have had a more single thought. Sickened, I turn to go. Have I been a traitor? To which side?

Something white, lying on the floor beside the bed. A shirt of Arthur's. Someone should have washed it. The mud of the hunt cakes it, a deep, red-brown, the colour of dried blood. It smells of his sweat.

Behind Gwenhyvar's back I gather it up. This of Arthur's for his sister-queen. Strange that she needs to seek such a keepsake after all these years. Can he really have given her nothing at all?

I push it under my tunic and I'm crossing the outer threshold when I bump into Modred. My turn to colour. Why did it have to be him? Well, somebody would have to be detailed to escort the queen home early, wouldn't they? Modred is always the willing courtier.

He asks sharply, 'Where were you?'

'Talking to Gwenhyvar,' I stammer. 'But I've done her no harm.' They know my reputation.

'With Gwenhyvar? And no harm?' And he throws back his head and laughs coarsely.

I tremble to the soles of my shoes. I have never heard Modred laugh loud and lewd like that. He's always a courteous, quiet-smiling man.

Then he is gone, in through the door of the royal chambers where I have left the sword of kingship.

Walk on, Taliesin. Don't look round.

Gwenhyvar is fair, Gwenhyvar is chaste, and Gwenhyvar is waiting by the window.

# Chapter Twenty

I've put that shirt in Morgan's hands. I don't know if I've done right. She stared at it hungrily, but she didn't cover it in kisses, or me either.

The sisters are impatient to be home now. In Garlot and Lothian and Rheged the corn is sprouting. It will soon be May Day. There is work of more than one sort to be done for the success of herds and crops. While the men campaign, the women must oversee the growth.

Does Gwenhyvar ride her farms as Arthur rides his forts? Hard to imagine. The High King's not like other chieftains. The whole island's his estate. He's a pack-leader, not a sheepdog; a sacred symbol, not a working farmer. Morgan is rooted in the land, Urien's land, Rheged. The fishing banks of the Solway, the pleasant pastures of Erechwydd, the high fort of Lyvennet, and the moors all the way to Catraeth that overlook the Angles. She feeds the earth with what the gods demand. She is the steward of the soil. She heals Urien's people. She keeps their king safe and whole.

And Gwenhyvar? From Caerleon to Camelot or Celliwig, what is she but Arthur's camp-follower? Can her sceptre keep him, or Britain, from harm?

She rides a little way with us to set us on the road. I see her now, her dappled mare standing at the edge of the trees, her skirts spread wide over the horse's flanks, medallions and bells winking on the coloured harness, smiling a little disappointedly. Smiling, because she knows she looks prettier so; sad to see us go. She fears these sisters, but she fears desertion more. It has been a lonely thing to be Arthur's queen.

I raise my hand and crinkle my eyes in a special smile to tell her I understand. No chance of a last song for her; the harp's packed in its bag. The daughters of Gorlois will not wait; there's a long road north for us. So I turn and see her figure dwindling, surrounded by her bright ladies like butterflies. We're leaving Tegau behind with her, wife of Caradawc now. A semicircle of horsemen guard Gwenhyvar. Their hands are lifted too. Half of them are our men. Agravain, Gareth, Modred.

Oh, salt-tide brother of mine, by the water that bore us both, will you guard your unknowing stepmother well for Arthur?

From the midland country the sisters go their separate ways. A few weeks pass. The feast of Beltaine is celebrated and over. Morgan moves contentedly amongst corn and herds. If she was a cat, she'd purr. The calves and lambs look strong. The increase is good.

519

And then it comes, like a flaming arrow in a sleeping camp. Gwenhyvar is taken.

News, rumour, argument, speculation! We're all milling about the exercise yard. We've forgotten the niceties of noble and commoner. He's rich, who seems to have more of the truth. So we grab each other and shout and question. Morgan comes, sweeping across the sward in a gown of green and gold. She looks angry and I think I know why. Where were the men who should have guarded Arthur's queen? They stand too close in blood to her. This touches her honour. Owain, her eldest, is not among them. He rode with Urien and Arthur. Rhun, the clerk, has remained to administer Carlisle. He stands behind her now in his long scholar's gown, tall, frowning, concerned. But the younger ones, Pasgen and Rhiwallawn, her nephews . . . her foster-son, Modred.

Morgan has no reason to love Gwenhyvar.

No! She's as upset as anyone, that's plain to see. She is not feigning, surely? Urien's priest leads us to pray for the High Queen in Carlisle's church, and Morgan is there. In Urien's absence, she takes his place. She knows the rules.

I picture Gwenhyvar, that vulnerable wife, standing in the disorder of Arthur's departure. Am I upset for her, or do I feel the burden of a fine romantic story coming on? Still, no use in a ballad without a satisfying ending. Somebody will have to rescue Gwenhyvar first.

Owain himself arrives. He and his men are haggard and weary. They have scoured the route from Camelot to Carlisle for news of Gwenhyvar. They arrive empty-handed.

Arthur has summoned them all, the women of his blood. I wonder what he wants, but Morgan believes she knows. She is not afraid, as I am. It is not the suspicion that Arthur's wrath may be turned on his sister that makes me nervous. It is my own suspicions. I do not want to part the bracken and see an adder's nest. Her eyes sparkle and she throws back her head and asks Owain, 'Can Nimue not find his queen for him? Does he fall back once more on our wisdom which he has so often scorned?'

'The Lady of the Lake is not far-seeing.'

We all know who in his family has the sight: Elaine.

So it's pack up our bags and trek all the way south again, is it? And I thought I'd done with horses. The harp weighs heavy on my back. There'll be few presents for a poet till Gwenhyvar's found.

I'm wrong again. It's sailing weather now. We skim the shores of Dyfed and come in on the vast tides of the Severn Channel.

Camelot looms, darker already to me without its graceful lady. Four ramparts to pass through, up the steep hill. A narrow cutting, the great oak doors. Our footsteps echo solemnly in the shadowed passage under the great gate-tower. Arthur's not here to meet us.

It is Morgan's daughter again, lovely winning Morfudd, stricken now, who comes running to clasp her mother, with Tegau behind her. There has been no word of Gwenhyvar. The men are out beating the countryside far and wide.

The story pours out. They have told it many times before.

'It was May Morning, so we were all of us up before dawn and dressed in green to go maying.'

'It was Gwenhyvar's wish. She chose ten of us ladies to attend her.'

'And as many warriors, with Gareth leading them.'

'It was grey and misty beside the river, but we thought no harm. This is Arthur's country, his stronghold.'

'We were spread out among the hawthorn trees, gathering flowers and boughs for the festival.'

'We did nothing shameful in our maying. Gwenhyvar is a Christian. She shuns the darker rites, but she likes to keep up any pretty custom.'

Only pretty custom, Tegau! The naked girls in the dew? The maypole? Steady. This is no time for teasing, boy.

'The men had their spears and they were watching the forest. We had not come for hunting, but we all felt it was that dawn stillness when deer might step out from the trees.'

'Then Gwenhyvar called to them, so they put down their spears and she filled their arms with the may-boughs we had gathered.'

'That's when they fell on us in a rush, like a storm of hail.'

'Riders, masked and helmeted.'

'Twenty at least. We never expected it, so near to Arthur's own fortress.'

'In a moment the blackest among them had snatched the queen on to his own horse and galloped away. We heard her shrieking. There was nothing we could do.'

'Our men fought desperately to reach their horses, but it was already too late.'

'The devils escaped, taking their wounded with them, even their dead. Not so much as a riderless horse was left to tell who they might have been.'

'Gareth is sorely wounded.'

Gareth, holding a dagger to my throat in the dark. Gwenhyvar is well guarded? Not closely enough. Poor lad! He'll carry the family's disgrace for this.

Nimue is here, icily furious. You can see whom she blames, no matter that Arthur's sisters were hundreds of miles away.

Could she be right?

Arthur comes back before nightfall, raging like a hound denied food. When brother and sister greet this time there's no laughing embrace. Still, he kisses her. Whatever dark thoughts he has, he needs her wisdom now.

Margawse is the next to arrive. She's come a long way in haste, but she's gleeful, and barely bothers to hide it. There's more bitterness than you'd think feeding her flame. She'd better be careful. Gareth's her youngest son – youngest, that is, of those she acknowledges; Modred's history is still a secret from the world. Arthur is looking for traitors, anything to earth the thunderbolt of his rage, though it shatters what it strikes. I hope Gareth's wound is deep enough to swallow suspicion.

Elaine takes her time. She never hurries. For me, I wouldn't mind if she dawdled so long she never got here. But she comes. Arthur stands by the heap of stones from the old pagan temple he has plundered to face his bulwarks. It has cost him something to ask his three sisters help him find Gwenhyvar. Bishop Bytwini pronounces it a punishment for backsliding from the promises he made to Christ, but Arthur daren't believe him. He's lost. He prays with Tegau and Urien and the rest of us Christians for his wife's safety. Then, like a child, he runs back to his Mothers. I know how he feels.

That evening I watch Elaine take that old black swordbelt from her travelling-bag, and pass it to Morgan. The new colours of her weaving glow clear in the dusk. Morgan looks at it for a long while, and then nods her head.

After all, it seems Elaine can tell Arthur nothing.

522

# Chapter Twenty-one

I should have known. It's back to the saddle for me, isn't it? We're all summoned for this hunt, any man who's fit enough to get a leg across a saddle. At least they've found me a sweeter-tempered grey. The ladies are ordered to stay within the walls. Their lords won't risk being shamed by another rape. We leave them to their own kind of search. Not Nimue and her band, of course; they've gone already, more feared than feared for. Are those Lake-women hunting Gwenhyvar's captors now with their sharp spears? Or have they gone to work a more private magic?

I ride with Modred. There's a strange bond between us. We're two of a kind, rejected, dangerous. The descendants of Jacob, who stole Esau's birthright. Gifted with more than we were meant to have.

We are winnowing the woods, flailing the fields, combing the coasts. We search for a silver pin in the great tapestry of Britain. What wouldn't I give to be sitting in the women's rooms strumming a tune, while the needles flicker and the coloured threads dart in and out of the weave like birds through foliage?

Dappled leaves, throwing their hatched shadows on uneven ground. Enough to dazzle the eye and give me a headache. My mind reels as I wonder at the number of trees in Britain. And every oak is a possible hiding place. We stand on the long ridges above the trees and the mist floats up from the valleys so that each line of hills becomes an island and there are fairylands hidden from sight under white waves. We ask. Everywhere we go, we ask. And it seems to me that the people's faces have a shuttered look. What was open and gossipy before has become secretive. I do not trust their smiles. I think that no one will ever find Gwenhyvar.

She is Creiddylad, maiden of most majesty, snatched by the king of deathless Annwn, Gwyn ap Nudd. And Arthur is Gwythyr, demanding her back to the lord of daylight as his right. On the top of Glastonbury Tor they fight for her, every May Day until the end of time.

I've lost count of how many times we've turned down some river valley till we meet the sea, how often we've climbed a cliff path to ride on the short starred turf, how many cottagers we've hailed with the same question, how many heads have shaken. Modred has wheeled me round so many times I haven't the least idea where we are. We could be at the farthest west of the land where ogres and mermaids live, or half a day's ride from Camelot. I'm losing interest. This ride's a dream, or it would be if it weren't so uncomfortable. I've left my harp at home. I'm even carrying sword and shield. I, Taliesin, like a butchering knight! Will we come back to find that Camelot is dead, her king long gone, only the wind wandering over the fallen ramparts, and my harp cracked and the strings rusted? My voice is cracked and rusty with the dust. We bump along. I'll never complain of being given a hard stool to sit on after this nag. If I can ever sit down again!

Modred is harder. Day after day he hunts Gwenhyvar with a sober, intent look on his face.

That's good news, isn't it? It ought to silence one suspicion.

'One of our family must find her. Arthur believes that we have cheated him.'

Well, is he right? I wouldn't dare say that out loud, of course. I look sideways at Modred under my eyelashes, and he catches the question. He gives me a grin, so sudden and charming that I see for an instant his father in him.

'And if I had? What good would it do me, riding the round of Dumnonia with you, instead of enjoying her? Unless I did it from spite.'

Silly wasn't it? And besides, she's his stepmother, as he well knows.

For days it rains, and the low clouds shroud all landmarks. We have come to a low, wet land. Then the sun pulls up a fog that makes a witching world between the puddles under our feet and the blue sky overhead. No birds sing. No little warblers and thrushes, anyway. Big bitterns boom, tall herons spear the pools, the curlews' cry circles mournfully in the mist. We've lost the friendly hares and squirrels of the woods. Slick, nameless creatures dart across our path and plop and dive into unseen water. The horses start and shudder. We dismounted long ago. We have to feel our way. I think we've lost the road. The water's come through my boots and when my horse tugs back on his bridle I think he's right. The hooves suck out of the saturated ground and leave fresh lakes behind us. It would be hard to turn round and go back.

'Do you know the way?' I ask, and my voice sounds more lost and dismal than I want it to.

I cannot hear what he answers. It might be the whoop of a swan. But there is a way. Sometimes when the mere seems wettest all about us I find under my feet the slippery corrugations of bound timbers. I wonder where it's going. Modred's some way ahead. He seems to be hurrying. His horse trusts him more than mine does me. I envy the bond these warriors have with their steeds that will carry them even into death. Then I remember that Morgan speaks with animals too. I recall I have been a toad, I have been a wren, I have been a roebuck on the mountain. Past lives. Forgotten languages. As a drover, I'm a failure.

The blue is going out of the sky. The shimmering whiteness of water that was all around us closes into a dull, dark circle. The fog has roofed us over. The reeds seem to stand taller, but they make no sound. Modred's a shadow on the wall of vapour. Then he's gone.

'Modred!' I cry. Only a startled clucking and the beat of wings.

'Modred!' Silence. The fog begins to drip.

Terrible panic pounding in my chest. We've been paddling in this marsh for an hour or more, and all I've done is slop my way behind Modred. He's the man of action, prince, hunter. My genius is to record deeds, not to do them. I wasn't responsible. I only followed in his footsteps.

Now there are no steps but mine, no road unless I find it. Even as we stand still I feel myself begin to sink. The horse has suddenly become a friend, but he's as terrified as I am. I hug his neck for warmth and I find I'm nearly crying.

'Help! Modred!' He'll turn back soon. He'll come and save me.

A dark, damp, desolate dereliction. Where was he leading me, anyway? Go back, or on? Where's on, in the winding way that bends from bulrush clump to island of osiers, finds stone for seven steps, then wood in water? Every foot an act of faith, each pace a prayer.

'Holy Jesus, by thy road of sorrows, Gracious Father, creator out of water, Spirit of all our wisdom, get me home!'

One step at a time, and then another. Terror that I shall never find a third. Stooped like a hunchback, smelling the stench of rotting vegetation, peering. Is the fog thickening or the light fading? Bring back the sun! But this is a world without heaven. Is Hell like this, cold, clammy, featureless, without other human life? A fiery furnace would be almost welcome, even the shrieking of tortured fellow human beings. It would be easier if I didn't have to tow this recalcitrant bag of bones behind me. Sorry, old friend! Treacherous thought. Suppose I let go of the bridle? Saved myself. Every time I look round to tug him after me I lose sight of the way I was going.

No. An unhelpful horse is better than nobody. The thought of utter loneliness appals me. I'm weeping now.

Hope's sliding away with every stumble in the mud. It leaves in its place a kind of reckless abandon. As well drown now in this half-light as later, in the dark. Right, then. Splish, splosh, thump, stamp. There's causeway, and sand, and peat, and stone, and . . . Aah! No! I'm up to my neck in foul water.

Humbled, I fumble for firm foothold, shivering with shock, chastened and chilled. I've lost the track; I've lost the horse; I've only my life, and that will leak away by morning. Where is the grave of Taliesin? A mystery.

On hands and knees now, the Chief Bard of Urien Rheged, whimpering like a baby.

And then the steady splash of oars.

# Chapter Twenty-two

Never there where the action is, am I? Chief Bard to Britain? Maybe this is Ceridwen's revenge, that I should have the soul of poetry and lack the opportunity. Modred could have sung the story, but Modred is modest and discreet. If it had been Gawain, now, we'd never have heard the last of it, and a bit more ornament every time he told it. No, Modred may be storming fortresses single-handed, but no bard is by to celebrate his deeds. And where is Taliesin?

I'll tell you where. In a dark, damp, stinking, shuttered shed, in the middle of a marsh, only fit for frogs. A prisoner! I, Chief Bard of Rheged, that have made odes to Arthur. On a quest to deliver the fair queen Gwenhyvar. Bearing a sword and shield, on a hardy horse, but ready to pipe a praise-song too at the first opportunity. There's justice for you!

I don't hammer on the door or try too hard to break my bonds. I'm frightened. These are the Little People, aren't they? Black, straight-cropped hair, a darker skin. They move in a quick, secret way like hunted animals. They don't carry themselves upright and brag and swagger like good Celtic Britons; and yet perhaps they understand more of Britain than we do, as much at home in her waters as the brown trout, as used to the ways of her woods as the dappled deer. Were we the doom to them that the Saxons seem to us? What would I do if I captured a lone Saxon? What are they going to do to me?

These are the folk that make changelings of our children, that turn milk sour and shoot elf-bolts to cripple old men and women. They are different and dangerous. I can barely make out what they say.

Is it safe to eat what they give me? Or will I be goblin-ridden for the rest of my life, pining for fairy food I can never find again? In the end, I can't help myself. I'm starving. Milk and fish. I mutter a prayer to Saint Peter and wolf it down.

You can't go on being terrified for ever. It's like being in a house full of big spiders. Once the horrid novelty's worn off the nerves decline to jump. I'm bored.

I try my charms on the woman who brings me food. She's middle-aged, with dugs that hang like goatskin water-bags, and a skirt that doesn't seem to cover as much as it should. Older women have never been a problem to me. They usually gobble me up like a tasty sweetmeat. She doesn't understand the signals. Fine words are wasted on her untuned ear. I'm a failure.

I'm alive. But in which world? The door opens briefly as the woman leaves. I have a glimpse of pale, still water. Thick willows crowd low islets, closing us in. The fog has gone, but there is little to see. Four children and a dog run into the water, shattering its stillness. They are oddly silent. I don't hear them shout or laugh. The mirror's broken. The door shuts me in.

I remember a boat. Hardly more than a raft with shallow sides. The small, dark, silent men and women that plucked me from my perilous roost among the reeds, and poled me here. Not talkative, these marsh people. Not friendly either, to feed and dry me and then tie me up. I tried singing to them. I thought that might impress them. But a man came and struck me on the mouth. They are a secret people.

This can't be the Blessed Isles, can it? Where are the fair women, the wine, the feasts and song? Too dingy for heavenly Jerusalem. A pallet of reeds for a crystal throne. A chink in the thatch instead of the radiant Lamb that needs no other sun. A muddy puddle at the door for the River of Life.

It's too uncomfortable to be anything but the world I was born into when Ceridwen's nine months were up and Taliesin shot into the midwife's hands to amaze all creation. I wasn't welcome then; I'm not here. Why are they keeping me a prisoner? Where is Modred?

There was a newt crawling over the planking this morning. I talked to him like a friend. I lie awake in the dark hearing all sorts of rustling slithers and pray that they are nothing worse. I've done a lot of praying lately. I've lost count of the days.

Days? Weeks, rather. Life creeps sluggish and slow, like the last blood leaking from a dead dog. Taliesin's dying. I'm not allowed to sing. I have no audience, no praise, no gifts. No women clap me with bright eyes. No men look at my youth, my talent, my face with envy. I'm wasting away. My skin is pale and puckered from the damp. I've sores where I sleep. The daylight is a stranger to me. I'm half-blind. Why do they bother to keep me alive?

Months. Midsummer passed us long ago. The days are shorter now, and the nights colder. I've a terrible cough. I think I know what I'm kept for now, like a prize boar in a pen. When the year turns, and all our strength is needed to haul back the sun . . . When the harvest is in, and the earth lies waiting to be renewed . . . When the gods are hungry for blood . . .

Urien, Tegau, Bytwini, Saint Michael and all the angels, pray for me! . . . Pray for me, Morgan.

The door crashes open. There's red firelight outside. I've never seen such a glare in all the time I've been here. I hear the Little Folk yelp, an inhuman outcry, shocking even me who has grown used to their careful mutterings. Flames leap in the water.

A dark giant shape bursts through the reddened doorway, casting a swooping shadow as he stoops over me. I think I screamed. I can see the light on the blade, feel it touch my skin. Give me back my slimy solitude, the rats and worms! A heave that sends my bonds cutting into flesh. The knife scrapes wrists raw. A last jerk and I fall back jarringly. I'm not dead; I'm free.

Loosed, anyway. But for what fate? A hand hauls me to my feet.

I stumble after. After all these days my legs have forgotten how to walk. I don't understand what's happening, but what use to argue? We are running now, down to the water's edge. Well, he's running and I'm staggering. He pushes me into a little coracle and we spin away. Not slaughter, then, but escape? There are figures leaping in front of the flames. It's all over in moments. We dodge between the islets, from flickering firelight to blinding darkness. I don't think they are following us. Modred settles to the oars.

Modred! When did I realise that? Well, who else should save me? Who else would have known where to find me? He laughs, low, warm and friendly. 'Welcome back to the land of the living, Taliesin. The dead return!'

I start and look around me. The night is lighter now, the mere is wider. The fire we have left is not the only one. On distant hills around us gold beacons jewel the sky like new-made stars. On lower eminences the bonfires redden the mere and sedge. Dark figures dance before the light and in the lake their shadows circle.

I have escaped from fear and plunged into terror. This is Samain night, when the frail walls of mortality are down! The dead return to us, and all else from beyond the grave. The fiends of Hell. The black hounds from the pit of Offern. Ghouls unimaginable, but not unguessed. The night when every Christian stays barred indoors and keeps a light firmly burning. No threshold of darkness to let in the Devil, no need for a flame rekindled while we have Christ's light, yet stay at home and seal the doors and windows well with prayer.

And where am I on the most dangerous night of the year? Adrift on unhallowed water with all the fires of evil raging round me.

'I'm tired,' says Modred, with a sigh. 'Could you take a turn at the oars? Steer by the bonfire on Glastonbury Tor.'

# Chapter Twenty-three

Not fairyland? Not Hell! The sedges of Somerset. And Tegau said there was a blessed abbey at Glastonbury. Oh, bring me safe to those true men of God and I swear I'll never meddle with magic again.

The abbey's not all there is at Glastonbury, though. It was no monks that built that bonfire on the top of the Tor. As we pull nearer I can see explosions of sparks hurtling into the air. The din of hammering metal echoes over the water. Modred grins.

'Govannon's Smithy. He is shaping a weapon for the King of Annwn.'

Not safe then, here. Not safe in any place tonight. The King of the Otherworld comes back to claim his own. Tonight the monks stretch out in prayer in their little church. Their lifted hands hold back the dark in fragile fortresses of faith. Tomorrow the sun will shine upon their gardens, their cattle will graze the slopes of the Tor. But tonight, fire! The Smith of the gods beats out his monstrous challenge on the iron. Gwyn ap Nudd will rise to claim that sword, so mockingly near to Arthur's Camelot. Dawn will send his crew back into the hollow hill they came from. But that's no comfort. Dawn's far off. This night is theirs. I wonder who's dancing round that fire.

I was tied up a long time. My arms are stiff and weak. I can hardly heave the oars through the dragging water. Besides, it's not open mere. Streams wander through the mud. Reeds lean and part. Sometimes a bigger channel's been cut, straight and shining. Then I've lost it, and I have to bend round islands overhung with trees. And every time I look over my shoulder, that fire leaps through the branches at me and the noise terrifies me. I tell myself it's meant to drive out evil. I don't know which is worse: what's up there at the fire, or down here in the dark. I want to be home in bed; in prison, even.

The oar catches on a root. I struggle feebly with it. Modred is saying something. I feel his strong hands taking over. I shift precariously to take his place. Faster now. I can hear the water whispering along the side. Where did he learn to manage an unhandy craft like this? We're swinging round. The Tor's over my right shoulder now. Modred is threading this marsh like a skilled pilot. I must not ask the questions that are surfacing in my mind like frogs. He rows with a bared sword laid across his knees.

The fireglow is dying. The noise grows distant and sweet as a church bell. We bump the bank. No accident. Modred has found a landing in the darkness. He holds the coracle steady while I stagger out and fumble with the mooring rope.

'Where are we going?' I whisper.

But Modred silences me. We creep forward over yielding ground. Again he stays me with a grip on my arm. He goes on alone with a sword in his hand. I'm left clinging to a clump of bushes. Don't leave me in the dark!

A distant murmur of voices. I listen for a shout or the clash of steel. A long stillness now. No human sound, only the hidden noises of the marsh. Then, quite close to me, a whistle. 'Taliesin!'

I stumble forward, obedient and eager as a dog. Modred wants me.

I see the first pale light is beginning to fade the stars. Thanks be! I am alive, my soul shaken but unscathed. I tell you, I've come a good way nearer to the one true God this night. Only let me see the dawn, and I promise this time . . .

Modred is not alone. A small cloaked figure stands beside him, clinging, crying, a woman's noise. Her face is buried in his shoulder. He holds her gently, stroking her hair. She babbles of fear, distress, desertion.

'There,' he smiles. 'Hush, my sweet lady. I swore that I would return and take you to your king. Look, here's Taliesin come to chaperone us!'

I know already as she turns her face. Gwenhyvar. I feel amazement strike through me. Here, after all this hunt? Found. So many men, so many miles, so many months. Found here, so close to home. So close? But is it? Where have I been? Where has she been? Did we cross some threshold? Is this the unclaimed land between two worlds? Not truly earth or sea. Its water not truly fresh or salt. A time not wholly light or dark. The worlds collide at Samain. Only tonight could we come back to the living. I don't know where we've been.

I reach a daring hand and touch her sleeve. It's real.

Modred has saved us both. I'd like to cling to his hand myself. But Gwenhyvar's tears embarrass me. This is Arthur's High Queen. But she can't let go of Modred.

'Do not desert me. If he should blame me for this . . . No matter what lechery he does himself, it would be the fire for me. Do not allow him, Modred!'

'Be brave, my queen. Let your appearance speak you wholly virtuous. These tears are suffering and relief, not guilt. It is anger that has coloured your cheeks, not stolen pleasure. You are a woman wronged and righteous.'

'Uphold me, then, Modred. Be my witness. I am afraid to return.'

'There will be nothing but joy at your appearance, lady. The time is coming when we must restore to Arthur all that is his.'

He leads us a little way on. A hut, dark, without fire. Astonishingly there's a cart. A patient horse waits in the shafts.

'What happened? How did you find her? How did you find *me*?' He shakes his head. 'Save that for Arthur. I shall make a full account.'

So here we are, the secret son of Arthur, courtliest of warriors, driving a cart like a peasant going to market. And the Queen of Britain, squatting among the straw with the Chief Bard of Rheged. No gilded chariot, this. There's a strong smell of pigs.

I'm jolted about in the back like a sack of turnips. Gwenhyvar is huddled in her cloak. She doesn't look joyful at her rescue. Modred is whistling like a ploughman. A chill strikes up from the ground as morning grows. Faint shades of grey. The fires have gone out with the stars, only on Glastonbury Tor a dull glow of red, like a baleful eye. Yet, that's where we're going. Wheels jolting on the causeway. The bank towers over us. Modred calls to the gatekeeper. We're on hallowed ground. Holy to whom?

No sun yet, to draw up the mist. But the shadows lighten and the world grows clearer. I rub tired eyes. That must be the abbey ahead. Not much to look at: wattle and daub, a few huts, a little church. It looks homely, safe as the hencoop when a fox is on the loose. From their oratory we can hear the sound of singing:

> God my Creator, God the Sustainer,
> Merciful Judge, loving and wonderful,
> Thy hand has protected me
> Through the dark waves.

Day. The monks are coming from their chapel, hollow-eyed and hoarse. It's a long hard night for praying men, the Eve of All Hallows.

Modred and I help Gwenhyvar down. Her dress is staled. Her hair's dishevelled. Her face is streaked with tears, but she tries to smile through them and clings to Modred's hand. Courteously, he disengages himself. Her lips tremble and her wet eyes plead. Well, I'm a bard. What should I think? Would he play Trystan to his king's Essylt? Nephew to aunt? No, it's closer than that, isn't it? But Modred's known for an honourable warrior, sword sworn to Arthur. All men speak well of Modred.

The youngest monks have the nimblest legs. They're crowding round us already. It's early in the day for pilgrim visitors. But before the abbot can reach us and hear our story, their heads are turning.

Others are coming slowly down the path that winds from the Tor past the dew-wet churchyard. Not secret devotees of Gwyn, who melt away in the November shadows. A noblewoman leads them.

There's another shock. *Morgan?* Here, on hallowed ground, All Hallows Day? Impeccably cloaked and gowned, but her eyes are heavy, her head bowed. It is clear she has been awake all night. But where? Involuntarily I twist my head and see the tall Tor towering over us, quiet now, her fires sunk down into her dragon belly. A wisp of smoke steals up into the pale blue air. The warfare's over. Gwyn's sleeping it off. The Church can hold this island in peace for another six months.

Trailing behind her is Teilo. He doesn't look so good. His nose is red. With fire or cold or drink? There are smudges of soot on his face too. I remember that Teilo was once a smith.

The abbot Congar starts too when he sees her. He hurries forward, calling to her.

'An awesome vigil, lady. You have passed the night unharmed, Saint Brigid be praised!'

She smiles and bows her head to get his blessing.

Would Urien's queen mock a Christian abbot? It is not like her.

'Let us trust that your prayers and mine for souls in peril will be answered, Father.'

But now the nearest monks have got wind of Gwenhyvar's name. There's excitement! The news is spreading. I've missed what Modred is telling them. Morgan's face holds me. She's stopped stock-still on the path, visibly startled. She is staring at Gwenhyvar as if she can't believe her eyes, and then at Modred and me.

# Chapter Twenty-four

Gwenhyvar claims the sanctuary of the abbey. She will not go back to Camelot. She begs to be reunited with her husband here, under the benign justice of Abbot Congar's eye. I'm not surprised. Even from Ynys Witrin we can see the distant hillfort of Camelot, a stronghold walled for war, a place for fighting-men. In frontier society wives are treasure, possessions to be prized, stolen or spoiled. Here in Glastonbury, among poor, chaste monks, they are more dangerous but less endangered.

Arthur is sent for. I think of all those horsemen threading the maze of Britain in search of their queen. Some may never return to Camelot from that quest. We must wait.

That morning, Morgan beckons me. We leave the gentle abbey and its guesthouse. She leads me up a long and winding maze. It coils round the slumbering dragon of the Tor, climbing into the dull November sky. I do not want to be here. Why haven't I got the courage to refuse her? Still . . . haven't I seen her bowing for the abbot's blessing? I think I nurse a small vain hope that there is not a great divorce between two forces: Abbey and Tor, brother and sister, Arthur and Morgan. Arthur, spirited away by a wizard, emerging as the champion of Christendom; Morgan, brought up in a convent, nursing the flame of the Old Faith between her hands. The Prince of Peace, armed with a sword; Morgan the Healer, who is also the Destroyer. Their shadows cross and mingle. What am I to believe? I fly for comfort to Urien. Sane, human, true. I want to clasp his warm hands, calloused with harness, heavy with rings. Take me back to you, Urien! Take me back. But Urien's not here, is he? I toil unwillingly to the summit.

Ash on open hearths, sodden with rain. Shelters of withered branches. Chewed bones of joints. I find a tiny bronze head — broken from what ritual vessel? His eyes stare at me redly; I drop it hurriedly. But Morgan picks her way among the detritus of festival as if it was nothing but old ground sand upon the beach. She stands, and I come beside her, looking out over the steely water, dark-twigged trees, to a cold sea.

She has something in her hands. I recognise it. The old belt from Arthur's scabbard again. Laced through the leather, the new braids of Elaine's weaving look dulled already in this lifeless light.

'I can give him what he wants,' she says quietly, 'even now. But if it comes from me, he will not accept it. Perhaps he is right. It might indeed destroy him.'

Does she suspect what I do?

Shamefacedly, I join my intercessions to hers. All right, I know I promised!

Later, I see her walking in the orchard with Modred. The wind bends the branches of the apple trees angrily. Modred comes away smiling.

I wonder how long it will take them to find Gwenhyvar's husband. But he appears, riding hard, the very next day, with a stout warrior-band at his back, stern men, spears set, swords jangling on thighs, shields on shoulders. Morgan stands close beside Gwenhyvar, like a sister.

Gwenhyvar's tense, but I observe her grow in stature as she sees this escort. They have come for her. Their mailed might makes her High Queen again. She draws herself up to face them.

Arthur flings himself from his horse before all the rest. I wait for him to throw his arms wide and embrace her, but his face is dark with doubt and dignity defied. We hold our breath. Then he can't help himself. A great joyful grin dawns over his countenance. Gwenhyvar's lost to sight, crushed against his chain-mail shirt.

Not long, that happiness. He's got to find somebody to blame. He rounds upon Morgan.

'You, here! Is this your evil? Was it not enough to steal scabbard and son from me? Must you rob me of my queen all summer too? Why!'

'As always, you accuse me falsely. I came to this holy island with your knowledge and consent, to work what I could for Gwenhyvar's return. Is this my recompense for success?'

'Release is easy, for those who have held the key.'

She will not drop her eyes.

'Ask Modred.'

There's dangerous. This is what I've been dying to hear. Yes, please, ask Modred! My fingers are itching already. Oh, why is the harp still in Camelot?

He tells it simply, modestly. A plainer tale by far than the one I'd like to listen to, but still full of marvels. How we were lost on the mere and separated. How he was caught and imprisoned and believed me dead. How a maiden restored his sword in secret. How he fought free of his captors. How he barely splashed to safety with his life. How he stumbled on a grim fortress with a moat around it and a lone sentinel in a tower, hard to converse with. How he found a perilous bridge and crossed it. How a grisly gatekeeper repelled him and how Modred, angered, forced his way in and slew the guards. Not one remained alive to tell the tale. How, in a shameful prison, he found Arthur's lady, kept without light, without women, without honour.

A little moan escapes Gwenhyvar, and she moves involuntarily towards her saviour. Pain stabs through all of us. You can see it in Arthur's face. Is his bright jewel cracked?

So he must turn to Gwenhyvar herself for the truth of those dark days. She sobs, remembering. Our cheeks grow warm with rage and shame. The abbot leads her to a private chamber. Arthur follows. What she must tell him is not for us to hear.

It's uncomfortable waiting. Modred leans over the fire, as though he would kick a log. But he holds himself still, watchful. Then he gives a small smile in my direction and his boot stirs the flame.

They come back at last. Arthur's striding ahead of the rest. Morgan's arm is round Gwenhyvar. Abbot Congar is arguing.

'Sire! You do your lady wrong. You must take her back. No one else accuses her. She pleads her innocence. Where are the witnesses that it is other than as she says?'

'I am the king. I will not be mocked. Can a man not do what he wants with his own wife?'

'No, sire, you cannot. You are bound to her by the oaths you swore on your marriage-day.'

'Even if the brute has fouled her?'

'The Queen denies it.'

Arthur has halted. Modred is facing him. He is smiling a little. His voice is level, reasonable.

'Before he died, one of the fiends who guarded her let slip that the foulest deed of all was reserved for Samain Night. It seems I came just in time.'

Arthur is glaring at him. The log crackles in the silence and spits fire. Then there's that huge grin again that turns the storm to sunshine. His hand reaches out to clasp Modred round the shoulders. His cheeks are wet with tears.

'Ah, if only I'd had a son of my own like this! Family may fail me and friends come back with empty hands, but Modred, that has no father, has proved truer than all my kinsmen. And what a wife he has restored to me! Look at her, all of you, and honour Gwenhyvar. True to her king through threats and terror. Chaste as a virgin nun against vile advances.'

We cheer. This is the stuff that legends are made of: our queen abducted, castles assaulted, the lady delivered. But Modred is circumspect and modest, and Gwenhyvar is blushingly reluctant to speak. Nobody asks where Taliesin was, that should have been the one to sing this song. They've more interesting captivities to talk about.

He joins their hands in front of him and kisses both, Gwenhyvar and Modred, her small white paw in his darker grasp. Gwenhyvar colours. Modred smiles gravely. He lowers his eyes. His lips brush her hand. But no more than is fitting.

'Who will lead me where this monster lives? Modred has butchered his men; but Arthur himself must slay their master.'

Modred bows, obediently. 'I will try, my lord.'

'What was the traitor's name?' Arthur demands of Gwenhyvar. 'Where is his den?'

She whispers, 'I do not know, my lord. He came to me foully masked. I saw and heard nothing of who he might be.'

The Abbot Congar is no stranger to the powers of evil.

'There is a name. The local people speak it in whispers: Melwas. King Melwas of the Summer Land they call him, though no such authority has been given him by Church or Council. Likely he is not a man of mortal flesh. They say he has such a fortress as you describe, hidden from human eyes save for one night. From there he rules the Summer Land in secret and spreads his darkness on these marshes. Men disappear. The tale goes that none who have crossed his narrow bridge ever return, and mothers use his name to frighten children with. His brood defile even this blessed island of Ynys Witrin on the holy night the heathen call Samain. No Christian eyes dare look on what is done then, for their soul's sake.'

His look slides round to Morgan with wonder.

Action now. We must hunt the villain. We must excise this evil from Arthur's land. A sternly-armed warband sets out, and I am rattling in leather and mail like the rest of them. I'll be in at the climax this time. The last verse of this tale must be better told than the first.

Rain falls, as Modred leads us down the causeway into that wide, wet world. Difficult this time, the Tor at our back and the whole circle of the mere to choose from. We pick our way uncomfortably. No prints to guide us. The land's awash. The fires are out. The islands loom untenanted. No sign of huts. Paths lead us into mud and disappear. We cast about and find ourselves knee-deep in water. There is no one to ask. Our clothes are saturated and our spirits low. How can you lose such a fortress in the daylight? Not hard the answer: easily, if it was never raised by human hands. Nobody says it, but the thought is in all our hearts. Arthur looks keenly at Modred, but he shakes his head. Grim-faced, he tries another way. I trail behind. Hope of a heroic ending died long ago. We won't find what we're looking for in this meandering marsh. Why was Modred so sure by night, so pixie-led by day? False thought! Rain blots out the Tor, pimples the puddles, turns trackways into tarns. The fires were yesterday. There's no truth here.

Sullenly we stumble back to Glastonbury. Arthur is surly. His eyes still accuse Morgan, though nothing is said. Modred's the only one that comes out of this well.

In private, the king questions me. What can I tell him? I have been imprisoned, like Gwenhyvar, but in a place still more vile. Terrible water-serpents were my companions. Goblins, naked and toothless, brought me foul food. Fierce fires encircled my gloomy gaol. It was only Modred who rescued me.

Arthur's no fool. As I finish, I fear he's going to laugh and toss me a trinket for a hearth-tale well sung. But he sighs and frowns. Difficult to shake off, the dark hordes that haunt us from our childhood. They pursue even a Christian king. Angels and elves, boggarts and demons, people our world, whatever gods we name. He is not satisfied, but he dare not disbelieve.

Why then do I find myself curiously reticent on certain points? The raft that rescued me in twilight on the reeds. Why the Little Folk should keep me unharmed. How Modred found me. Why we were not pursued. That steady steering through the twisting channels, coming to Gwenhyvar's waiting-place like the centre of a maze. The cart, the voices, the half-heard murmurs of Gwenhyvar on Modred's shoulder. Peace, boy! That was a night out of time. Nothing is what it appears on Samain Eve. He saved your life, didn't he?

The queen's honour and the king's run parallel. She is escorted home in triumph and royally housed in Camelot again. Gwenhyvar goes back to her winter king, that was once our prince of summer. Fires leap now where they should, on the hearth of kings. All's well again.

# Chapter Twenty-five

And they call this the Summer Land! We'll be here a long time, by the look of the roads. The whole land's a lake.

Arthur has savage moods now, like a boar that's been robbed of his sow, but even he takes no pleasure in hunting phantoms in the pouring rain. Inactivity grates on him, so we fill the days with board-games and gambling, wrestling and dancing. There's plenty of occupation for a nimble bard.

One question still hangs over us, low as the clouds.

Margawse's lip curls when she sees her brother's wife return. She's sorry now she didn't add her powers to Morgan's. Her sons are out of favour because of Gwenhyvar. Those green eyes linger reflectively on Modred. I force my mind to remember that this too is Margawse's child. It's no good. I can't make the connection. Only Elaine looks well content. She smiles and knits endlessly.

Arthur has started to build a church, here on the hilltop, to give thanks for Gwenhyvar's safe return. Cross-shaped, the latest thing, with a mighty tower in the centre; I've seen the plans. But the rain fills the trenches as fast as they dig them. Leave it for summer. Let's go indoors and play more games.

Let's pretend our honour's untarnished, our guards not tricked, the Prince of Darkness doesn't roam the marshes unchecked. Arthur's High King. The singing's loud and the mead's strong and Arthur can still wrestle Cei to the ground.

As the waters swallow the land, the Lady of the Lake returns to us as she should, in a fine barge, swan-prowed, sailed by silky ropes. I didn't see it myself. It's a muddy walk to the river.

Still, I can watch her now, pausing at the foundations of Arthur's church between the gate and the hall. I note the signs her hands trace over it.

She carries no weapon this time, and she's beautiful even in a dripping cloak, but still smiling as coldly as when I saw her last. Arthur's not too pleased with her, either.

'What kind of counsellor is it who keeps away when there is evil magic to counter? All the wise women of Britain were here except you.'

Her eyes flicker maliciously over Arthur's sisters and then Bishop Bytwini.

'You swore the Church was all the strength you needed. My help was scorned. And then in extremity you run back to the women who have always betrayed you. What could I do for you now, that these

537

cannot? It was for those who stole Gwenhyvar away to restore her to you. As I see they have.'

Arthur's rising out of his seat now. He doesn't trust these sisters either but they're his own blood. Pride wrestles with suspicion. He sinks back in his chair.

'If you believe you have the knowledge, if you can spy the seat of treachery better than they can, put it to the test. Do anything you have to do. But find me the villain.'

Her eyes flick up, alarmed. 'I never claimed to have the seeing. Your whole court knows who has the gift for that.'

All eyes turn to Elaine. Her fingers dart; the wool twists and dances. Save for those hands she sits impassively.

'She can tell me nothing.'

'Cannot, or dare not.'

Then Elaine moves, thrusting her needlework into Margawse's hands. She rises, ponderously, to her feet. Why does the least action of this woman carry a meaning greater than it appears, making us hush and watch her?

'A contest? You and I, to see whose net can catch the bird of truth.'

Nimue is afraid. Not all of Merlyn's spell-books could give that clarity of sight to one not born to it. She finds an unlikely ally. Bishop Bytwini upbraids his king.

'Sir! You swore to leave that way behind you at your baptism. How often must I warn you? Have no dealings with these witches.'

No dealings with witches, in a family like his! But Arthur is ready for him. 'Did not King Saul go to the witch at Endor and raise the prophet Samuel to show him the truth?'

'He did, my lord. But—'

'Am I forbidden what Israel's king is allowed?'

'You may ask what you will in the name of the Trinity, my lord. All else is devilish.'

Elaine smiles. 'Ask in whatever name you choose.'

'She mocks you,' Nimue counters. 'It was I brought you up to know both Christ and the Mothers. I put power in your right hand and your left. Bytwini's own hands have given me the holy sacrament, when he was nothing but your household chaplain.'

'And I have worked a heavy penance for it afterwards!'

Whom can Arthur trust? The marsh is here, even in Camelot. Bring us back to summer drought, and hard ground!

He chews his lip. I feel for him. Hard to shake off, the custom of centuries. He'll go to penance, make a good communion. But he must know the name.

So evening comes, and the hall is made ready, the circle drawn and a brazier lit. Arthur sits in a great chair, with Gwenhyvar beside him, holding her hand. She is pale and troubled. Well, what lady wouldn't be, after what she's suffered? Elaine lowers herself, to sit cross-legged within the circle. Nimue faces her. There is a set of ivory pieces before each of them, carved with the sacred alphabet. Morgan, Margawse and their women stand outside the circle, close-ranked, insulted. Packed round the walls are all the nobility of Arthur's court. His kinsmen, greying knights like Bedwyr, Bishop Bytwini, Tegau, lovely Morfudd. All tense and uneasy. In a game like this, you never know how the dice may fall. A pulse jumps in my throat. Elaine knows I was in the marsh a long time without witnesses. Does Nimue?

Arthur calls on the bishop to pray for truth in the name of the holy Trinity. Nimue listens, with a little smile of contempt. A long Amen rumbles around the room.

The test begins. Nimue casts a spray of willow on the flames, Elaine a sprig of gorse. At the first names Nimue conjures, the bishop stalks out of the room. Arthur turns his head uneasily to watch him go. He is in too deep. He wants the culprit too much.

The dice roll.

Smoke thickens. Elaine's voice deepens. We watch entranced. The pieces shift upon the floor, first one side, then the other. Patterns emerge, waver, break and re-form. Lines are lengthening, needles pointing. All of us feel the pressure to shift position, to break, to run. Will it be I? Will it be I? Arthur is leaning forward, peering down, like a hawk about to stoop.

Elaine's eyes are closed. She cannot see how the pieces move under her hand. A name mutters through her lips. In the same instant Nimue, wide-eyed, cries out to us.

'Modred defiled her.'

'. . . It was Morgan's doing!'

'No!' Two voices shriek in protest. Gwenhyvar's and Morgan's. The spell's broken. The smoke is clearing. Elaine slumps, asleep. Nimue looks worn out, a woman once pretty, now faded and spent, half sitting, half lying on the floor.

No one heeds them. Two names are ringing in our ears, and a third word: 'Defiled'. Arthur is on his feet, furious.

Then Morgan flies to her sister, scattering the circle, her nails raked to strike the unconscious face. 'You cheat! You cheat!'

No man dares stop her. It is Margawse who grips her wrists and wrestles her into silence.

Hot blood, darker than foxglove, suffuses Gwenhyvar's face, her neck, her ears. Sweat glistens on her brow. Her hands are clutching Arthur's shoulders.

'She lies! This is evil, my king. You should not have meddled in unholy ways. Modred it was who came and rescued me. Should I not have known if it had been the same hands that snatched me from my friends? The same shape that towered over me in the night? The same voice that promised me dishonour or death? Never was it Modred! Never!'

Doubt clouds the king's face. The whole hall's in an uproar. Only Modred stands unmoved. His face is pale and calm. His hand avoids his sword, hangs lightly by his side, though weapons are out all round him. Arthur is moving like an angry breaker to overwhelm his sister.

'You have deceived me again!'

Morgan has stopped before him, deathly pale.

'I will not waste breath to excuse myself, though I am falsely accused. You would never believe me, though Nimuë knows she has no power of seeing. But this, more serious by far, you must believe. Modred it never could have been that fouled your queen. Modred, of all men, you have no need to fear. Listen to me, Arthur! Elaine is ageing. Her memory is dim and her powers are failing. If she had truly been the wise woman she once was, she could never have made so great a mistake. Not Modred. Never Modred!'

She holds her hand out to her foster-son, this work of half her life. Slowly, his eyes on hers, he comes and takes it in his own, steady where hers is shaking. She leads him closer to Arthur's throne. In her face is an intensity of joy, a task fulfilled. She lays his hand in Arthur's.

'Brother, I give you your own son.'

# Chapter Twenty-six

There's matter for a song, for you. Can't complain now, can I?

Arthur's uncertain. He's sired enough boys up and down the kingdom, but whose is this?

It's Margawse's turn to cause an upset. Not like her to be the last of the three in coming forward. She's blushing like a maid, too, and laughing a bit to cover it. She falls on her knees before Arthur.

'Once, my brother, I bore you a son. You thought him dead in infancy.' Not laughter that makes her voice shake here. 'You did not know the Mothers had kept him from harm, loved him, brought him up to a noble manhood. Morgan has told you the truth.'

It's Morgan's turn again. She draws from the breast of her gown that buckled belt. How long has she nursed it there? I shiver to imagine the warmth in the leather as she slips it round Arthur's neck and then round Modred's sword-arm, binding them together in a loving clasp. It is very prettily done.

'I cannot give you back your scabbard. I buckle this to you instead.'

Arthur's nonplussed. He stands, Modred's hand locked to his. His eyes search Morgan's, looking for treachery, and seem to find none. Then he starts to smile, the sharing of a rare delight.

The threads draw together, the last knot twisting to its seal. I see how much these two have wanted to be reconciled to each other. Was it all for this? Uther's lust for Ygerne, the killing of Gorlois, Merlyn's theft of Arthur, Morgan's banishment, Margawse's incest, the babies drowned. All the sad shocks of history for this one night, a blazing fire on the hearth in Camelot, and a family now standing in front of it, the flames leaping on Arthur's grin, and Morgan's cheeks, and Modred's hand. You would have thought there should have been a simpler way to arrive at this point. Not so much pain.

He stoops and kisses her. The whole hall sighs. Silence for a few heartbeats, between the lightning and the thunderclap. Then Gwenhyvar screams. Well, why not? Certainly she's not Modred's mother.

Modred himself? He gives that rare, grave smile that has made the whole world honour him. It's too much for Arthur. A son, of noble blood, with a royal mother. Tears burst from his eyes, he throws his bear-arms wide and crushes Modred to him.

'Son, forgive me!'

Now there's consternation! Margawse's other offspring look furious. Whatever old tales they may have heard, it's clear they've never known who Modred was. The youngest of the litter, and Arthur's son? And for the rest of the court: the king and his own sister!

'Get that fool of a bishop back! What am I to do? I was a lad then that did not know his own family. I was young. I tried to drown an act of folly.'

Bytwini's here.

'Sire, you served penance for that sin long years ago. The past is paid for. The boy's alive. Once Abraham mistook the Lord's intention and sired Ishmael. But God is merciful. He made that boy heir, not to the Promised Land itself, but to a great fortune. Praise God who has brought you a blessing out of evil.'

Well, there's a cheer to set the roof-posts rocking!

Nobody but me notices that Morgan is still staring at Gwenhyvar. At the queen's scream, her own hands have flown to her face. I see in her half-hidden eyes the horror dawning. Between cupped hands she cries, 'No, Arthur! No!'

Too late, now, isn't it? How could he hear her in all this cheering? They're all flocking round.

'Welcome, lad!'

Cei and Bedwyr are clapping Modred on the shoulder, congratulating him. Tegau is kissing him.

Slowly Morgan turns, walking as if in a dream. She pauses where the Lady of the Lake still writhes, neglected on the floor. Nimue starts back from her. But Morgan's hand reaches down and pulls her to her feet.

'I should ask your pardon, Lady. You see more truly than you know.'

Bitter the anguish in that admission. And then she flees.

In all the rejoicing, there's one word Arthur can't shake off. His turn to look to Gwenhyvar now. Joy's replaced by dark suspicion, jealous rage, as swift as a March storm. Defiled?

Not defiled by Modred, though. He can't believe that now, can he? Not when he's been given the son he's longed for, noble, brave, as clever with the harp as good with hounds, as wise in judgment as deadly with the sword, and most of all, of royal blood, on his mother's side as well as his father's. Ygerne of Dumnonia's line, twice over. Pity about the incest, of course. Still, it looks as if the penance he'd done will serve for that, as well as for infanticide on a grand scale. I've a feeling the rules for kings aren't the same as for the rest of us. Easy to forgive Arthur. He has a famous smile.

But Gwenhyvar can see the other side of his coin. She's running for protection. Where? To Nimue. I wish I could hear what story she's sobbing on the Lady's shoulder!

Elaine's lids are lifting. Women guide her stooping, sleep-ridden, to slump on a bench beside the fire. Does she know what she's said?

Nimue's voice strives for authority.

'Morgan the Faithless has as good as admitted her guilt to me. You do not need me to tell her past treacheries. Remember her lover Accolon, to whom she gave your stolen sword, who would have killed you with it if I had not stopped it. Be certain this was some creature of hers that held your queen captive to spite you and sow the seed of mistrust between you and your wife.'

That's not the name he wants to hear, either. But Morgan's gone. The spell is broken. He glares at Nimue and then at Margawse. She's no friend of his, who tempted him into one dishonour, and then another. At Elaine, who has blackened both Gwenhyvar's name and Modred's. No doubt whose version he's going to believe, is there?

You were wrong, Morgan. Arthur has accepted your gift at last.

He holds out a generous hand to Gwenhyvar and she takes it shyly. She still looks sick and agitated. Of course, that's not surprising, is it? Modred's not her son. Poor Anir's dead less than a year, and here's a replacement. I hope that's all that's the matter with her: a mother's jealousy. You've a dirty mind, Taliesin. This is the stuff of high romance. Still, she stares at Modred, fastens on Modred with eyes wide and helpless as a doe that has seen a fox enter her form.

Modred has not once looked in her direction. He has found his father. His arm is round Arthur. Modred is no longer the rejected child. He is tender with this grey-haired king as a mother with her infant. There are tears in quite a lot of eyes, mine included. Romantic, me, after all. Advent fast or not, we're going to lay on the biggest feast of the year tonight. The prodigal father is embraced by his son.

Morgan is back for the feast. Does nobody but me remark that she has a haunted look? It seems Arthur's in a mood to forgive anyone tonight. All the same, I notice he's pushed Margawse down the table. He'd rather pull the curtain over that side of it. Morgan's a different matter. She's given him his dearest desire. He wears the swordbelt she gave him over his heart, like a trophy, though Modred's unclasped now. Nimue's warning is soon disregarded, drowned deep as Merlyn's nightmare of a traitor son. Modred is seated between Arthur and Gwenhyvar. A happy family party.

Supper is over and I entertain them royally, while they sit around the fire. No need to sing of battles now.

Arthur's magnanimous. He takes Morgan's hand in his. So very thin and white it looks. So vulnerable.

'Sister!' I have never heard such warmth in the Pendragon's voice. Nimue hisses. I do not need to look at Gwenhyvar. I can imagine the hurt.

Arthur is a big man. He grows greater still, looking down on Morgan. And she is all woman before him, her head slightly bent. I grieve for Urien Rheged. We all feel the thrill that carries from her fingers held by his, along her singing nerves, to the heart.

'You have wronged me greatly before this, but today you have given me great joy. The time has come to lay our enmity to rest. For all the occasions I have spurned what you offered, I ask absolution. And all your old treachery to me I now forgive. Let Modred be the symbol of our union. After pain, hope. After bitterness, love. In place of denial, faith.' His other hand is on Modred's shoulder, holding them both to him.

'Symbol for symbol, emblem of oath. I have the belt. I lay my sword before you two.'

Caliburn, gorgeous and warlike. Two dragon-heads rear from the hilt, red-tongued, eager for battle, his royal weapon. He lifts his hand and holds it out to her. The blade is bare between them.

'You tell me you have destroyed the scabbard. We cannot call that back. But what if I now disarm myself? Let you and I give up our warring powers. Shall we make Modred our heir and give him Caliburn, and go down into a happy old age?

I turn for help and find that Nimue is furious. Modred is smiling. Gwenhyvar's . . . astonished?

And I? I feel the bottom falling out of my world. Arthur is giving up his sword. I am too late.

But Morgan is ageing before my eyes. Her cheeks fall in; the warmth has left her face. Her eyes are bottomless lakes.

'No!' she says, pushing the sword aside so swiftly that it cuts her hand. 'No! No!'

She drags the belt off him. The ancient leather snaps.

The tears are flowing down her face. The whole hall looks, aghast. They think she hates him still. Am I the only one that hears her grief, screaming like a harpstring on the point of breaking? The words are torn from her, as though she would say anything but this.

'Do not trust Modred!'

Arthur has snatched Caliburn back. For a moment I think he will strike off her head.

The sword slips back into its false scabbard. He signals angrily to me. My shaking hands pick up the harp.

I sing of Arthur's wars.

# Chapter Twenty-seven

We can't stay now, can we? Their hands have met for a moment; now the reel has flung them apart. Who will be partnering whom when the music ends? My last night in Camelot, then, and all that way north to travel at the foulest time of the year.

The ladies have left the hall, but the drinking's still going on. I've had enough to make me queasy.

I step outside, and find the sky is clearing. The air is crisp and the stars high and bright. I blink like a sentimental fool, looking up at beauty, clean, eternal. A waning moon tonight, and the eyes of angels looking down on me. Tear off the roof, smother the fire, put out the torches. See us as we really are in this cold blue light. Not paragons of chivalry, not potent witches. Men, women, muddled, loving, hurting. Foul before God, but all He has. Surely He must love us? There's no one else.

I wander towards the rampart. Cold tightens the flushed skin of my face. Careful, now! You nearly fell into that hole. What's this, then? The foundation-trench of Arthur's church, half-filled with water, a muddy ditch with a multitude of stars. He's abandoned it until the summer. Gratitude for Gwenhyvar's return is cooling now. Will it ever be built?

Time you were in bed. You can't carry the burden of this turbulent family on your shoulders. But I am Taliesin. My original country is the region of the summer stars. I was with my Lord in the highest sphere on the fall of Lucifer to the depths of Hell. I have borne a banner before Alexander. Yes. But what did you do for any of them? Princes fell and princes won. You sang about it. Let the banner of song for Arthur and Morgan be richly woven. But they must make their own story.

Bed now for me. Which way in the dark? You've made that mistake before. No, I'm forgetting, it wasn't a mistake, was it, Gwenhyvar's house? Poor Gareth, he got it hot and strong the day he lost her. She'll be well guarded tonight. Or will she?

I know that whistle under the breath, the little cheerful tune. I've heard it, jolting in a cart out of a tricksy marsh, with will-o'-the-wisps dancing beside the path. Stars, weep now. Taliesin, you could stop this. One shout would rouse the guards.

Modred, my almost-brother. Modred, my soul-friend. Two babies abandoned, two princes found. The prince of poetry and now the premier prince of Britain. Is this the man who will make this Island one? Is he the hero who will lead the final battle? The son of Arthur, Modred? Have I found my great song, after all?

She won't open to him, will she? Not now she knows. Her husband's son, her stepson-nephew? Look how sickened she was in the hall.

Such a merry little tune he breathes, so confident. And the window opens, the shutter swings, revealing the darkness that waits within. Modred's leg is over the sill. Close the casement now. Shut out the stars. Modred is in, and Arthur's out.

I turn, skin prickling, as I have done sometimes and found a cat staring at me from the corner of the room. There's something pale in that doorway. A woman's face. Not Morgan, not Margawse, not Elaine. Nimue is watching this. Like me, she sees the truth. We hold the axe that could topple Arthur's palace or fell the traitor, that could cleave Arthur from Morgan for ever, the ruination or the salvation of Britain.

Our world's unmade. What shall I do? Tell Morgan? Warn Arthur? But Morgan's heart has cracked already with the knowledge of what she has bred, and Arthur will not allow himself to believe it.

The old king must die; the new one takes his place. And in his youthful mating the land revives. That's how it goes, isn't it? Perhaps . . . Shame on you, Taliesin. Arthur keeps a Christian kingdom. You swore to put all that behind you, didn't you? Keep your eye on the stars; don't look in the ditch.

It's too late at night for theology. I've got a headache.

The viper is snugly in Arthur's tent. Nimue knows. Hang on to that. Nimue is Arthur's guardian, and she knows.

Next morning, the king's like an old dog in love with a young master. He's almost fawning for a pat on the head from Modred. Nimue, Margawse, Morgan have given him what he wanted: a sword, a kingdom and a son. But he can't forgive the women. They have shamed him with this accusation of a double incest. It cuts too deep across old wounds.

The family's splitting. Gawain and Owain will be true to Arthur. Agravain takes the women's side. Gareth and Gaheris are wavering. Urien clasps Arthur warmly. His duty calls him back to Rheged. His love for Morgan, his loyalty to Arthur, are both unquestioned.

Home to Carlisle then, turn my back on Camelot. Never be Arthur's Chief Bard now, will I? There was a time when I thought he might make me an offer. The greatest king we ever had in Britain, but a little lacking in judgment on the matter of music.

Goodbye, Modred. I can't help the lump in my throat as I grasp him by the hand for the last time. Only I wish he wasn't standing beside Gwenhyvar like a son with his mother. I can't look her in the eye now. Well, good luck, boy. You haven't had much till now. Not too late to sweeten the soul, is it? Only, don't wound him to the heart. He is the heart of all of us, Arthur Pendragon.

Arthur and Morgan won't touch as they say farewell. There's too much pride.

Too stormy for ships, and miserable riding even on a Roman road. We're splashed to the shoulders. Sometimes a weary horse will founder, but we buy another and press on. The ground is hardening as we move north and there's an edge to the wind.

I'm caught wrong-footed again. At Chester, Morgan bids farewell to Urien. Not home, then? I look to Urien for advice. I'd rather be back in Carlisle, hot bathwater, thick walls, than wandering west in winter into unwelcome adventure. But Urien nods. I know what that means. Always in the queen's escort, me, never one of the men.

We come to the shores of the Menai strait on the coast of Gwynedd. A large, low island. Mon. So that's it, is it? The womb of wisdom. Once the greatest college of secret knowledge in all Europe. The last calamitous stand of the druids against Rome. I know the story: furious seers massed on the beaches armed with both sword of steel and staff of magic, black-clad women tearing their hair and shrieking imprecations, young boys and maidens, ready to die rather than see their sacred past, their spiritual future, trampled into ignominy under the boot of history. Just for a moment, even the legions faltered. Only a moment, before the end, and all their cherished weave of wisdom went down into oblivion, drowned deep as their gifts to the gods in the innermost lake.

All? Not quite. Some guardians returned. In caves and forest groves, at wells and cromlechs, some strive to bind the salvaged strands together. Morgan has come to keep faith with her mothers, and to ask something in return.

We are given welcome, in great simplicity, but with respect. The women are given a house apart, with many windows opening on the stars.

More women arrive. Women? I am ashamed of what I was expecting: old hags risen out of peat bogs, mermaids with blue skin combing their hair, kelpies with mares' faces? These are fresh girls, maidens every one of them, difficult to come by in the service of magic. Vowed virgins nowadays are mostly Christian. Those that have chosen to serve the other way are soon initiated. But the guardians of Mon have brought her what she asked for, nine pure May-Maidens, wise and whole.

Morgan will not even touch the work herself, though she directs it. I've never seen her so dedicated, so intense. The guards and I may not set foot inside their sky-lit house. For this, even Teilo doesn't get the name of Woman. We hear the girls singing at night as they weave.

A gown, white and silver as a shaft of moonlight. No dewhung spider's web on April morning shone with such sweet purity. It is finished, flawless, fairy-light.

Is this magic, or madness, in Morgan's mind?

'A gift most fitting for Tegau Goldbreast, Caradawc's wife, purest of virgins and now most constant of wives.' She entrusts it to one of the maidens with a challenge. 'Take this to Arthur's court, and give her this message. Make it known that every lady may try this gown, but only she who is true to her husband will the gown fit. It will shame an adulteress with a skirt above her knees. And this for Caradawc Strong-Arm,' laughing crazily now. 'A drinking-horn and a side of bacon! This one will spill the drink of a man not true to his wife, and a mouthful of the other will choke the philanderer.'

'She's out of her mind!' groans Teilo. 'He'll never allow Gwenhyvar to take that test from her. Morgan sent him a purple cloak once that had death stitched in every fold. Does she think he'd let his queen try that gown on, with her spells woven thick in it?'

Morgan's merry as a girl in love, though her eyes are as bright as a woman with fever.

'He is a warrior. He must accept my challenge. Gwenhyvar will be shamed if he refuses.'

'He will take nothing from you.'

'He has taken Modred!'

A cry of agony. All his life she has reared the boy for this. Yet it cannot be how she meant it.

Arthur and Gwenhyvar will celebrate Easter at Caerleon.

# Chapter Twenty-eight

So home to Carlisle and wait. Grey skies in Rheged, bitter cold. Nothing to do but harp by the fire and sport on the wolfskinned bed, is there? We both need cheering up. Only I never get the thong of my breeches undone. I'm not even asked to her chamber.

'No, Taliesin. I am not for you now.'

What's up? What have I done wrong? I must have looked as indignant as a pup that's had a bone snatched off him by the bitch.

'I am Urien's queen.'

'Oh, yes? Since when did that trouble you? And what am I? Only Chief Bard. Only the prince of poets. A mere nobody. The snowflake on the cromlech. The butterfly upon the mountain. I know, I know. Don't tell me.'

She strokes my hair and smiles fondly. How close must I stand to that perfumed breast?

'If you had truly been a prince I would never have allowed you to enter my chamber to stir my cauldron, Gwion Bach. You helped me make our mysteries. You have served me well.'

She's changed. She doesn't give me my quittance in gold, I'll give her that. She presses her lips upon my head. I know what it means. Very final, that kiss. This is a new Morgan.

A cloak of chastity has fallen on her too. The red blood has stopped running. Only Urien may come to her bed now, while she waits. I know her fire still burns; I feel it. But she must be worthy. The white mantle of Tegau Goldbreast will prove Gwenhyvar a whore and the sisters true. Arthur will cast out his adulterous queen soon.

How can Morgan the Wise so delude herself? I weep in my solitary bed, not for myself but for her.

His answer comes. It is Teilo who carries it unwillingly to her, a parcel like the one she sent to Caerleon, the same size, the same weight, the very wrapping. Her maiden-messenger speaks softly.

'King Arthur has commanded Tegau to reject your gift, Caradawc Strong-Arm to send back the horn and flitch.'

There is a letter.

'I want no magic meddling in my Christian court. I do not trust you. You sow dissension. Your gifts are curses that distort the truth they promise. Take back your mischief.'

But Modred was the most mischievous gift of all, and he is firm in Arthur's love, dearer than his wife now, dear as his sword, dear as his honour.

Morgan will not believe it. She stares at the unwrapped gown, the purity of white fouled with his black suspicion, the incontestable proof of magic thrown back in her face. We wait for her to rage, to weep. She calls for her workbox, very calmly, takes out a pair of scissors, heron-shaped. Suddenly, the storm is on her. She seizes, slashes, snaps. The scissors wreak a ragged devastation. The spell's in shreds. All purity, all faithfulness, all loving trust lie heaped in ruins round her. She won't stop there. There's something else.

The belt of Arthur's Caliburn. The last narrow binding that should link sword to scabbard. The colours that newly-furbished it are bloodstained now. She hacks at it savagely, forcing her fingers to drive the blades through the leather till the marks stand out as livid bruises on her hands. Black leather, white linen, both destroyed. Modred's unmade. I know, seeing the scattered pieces, even before she sweeps them up and casts them on the fire with curses.

I play my softest songs to soothe her. I am David to her furious Saul. It's very affecting. I'm weeping hard myself, but it won't put out the stench of that fire.

Nothing but the sword left now, is there?

I see her beauty start to age.

Since she spurned his offer, Arthur will no longer admit to growing old. While Caliburn's in his hand he's still the king. Don't slay me yet, he cries to us. There's still a deal of strength in me to nourish the land. He takes his sword and honour and army to Armorica, to fight for his cousin Howel. Modred he leaves behind as regent. Morgan was right. He must accept her challenge to Gwenhyvar's reputation. Caliburn he takes to war. The sword of government he trusts to his son. He leaves Britain with Modred. He leaves his wife with Modred.

Is this what Morgan wanted? Modred in Arthur's trust, Modred in Arthur's bed, Modred in Arthur's wife. She has tended this foster-son. She has fed him her pain. Is this how she imagined the fruit would taste? The bridge, that should have joined her side to Arthur's, becomes the inroad of treachery. This is her doing. All her life culminates in this. She has tried to warn Arthur. She has failed.

She stands dumbfounded at this outcome.

I wait for her to summon the wise, to work strong magic, to turn the supernatural universe upside down and shake some goodness out of it.

Nothing. She seems as helpless as the rest of us, haggard and haunted.

We wait for news. I listen for the cries of crows to call disaster.

The campaign is going well. Arthur has covered himself in glory. He's killed a giant.

Arthur's besieged. They won't be back for some time.

Cei is killed.

Gwenhyvar is divorcing Arthur.

# Chapter Twenty-nine

Gwenhyvar! Soft-spoken bride to great Arthur, the decorative lady at his side, the sweetly smiling hostess to his warband. I didn't think she had such audacity in her.

Gwenhyvar divorces the king? We've underrated her.

That's roused some swans' nests up and down the country, I can tell you! Morgan is stung from her lethargy into sudden vigour. She's speechless with fury. I watch admiringly, the flinging jet-black hair, her cheeks like firelit windows in the snow. Eyes? Terrible the thrusts of them. And she is only one. Is this happening across the Island? Red Margawse, grey Elaine. Are passions rearing, muscles tensing, anger hardening in Lothian and Garlot and further still?

Gwenhyvar's accusing the king, and she's called a council! What's Modred doing? He's Arthur's regent. If she's not Arthur's wife, she's not the High Queen, is she?

She summons the Church and aristocracy to attend her at a great congress in York. All the noble ladies of Britain are specially bidden to appear.

They'd like to refuse, fling the summons back in her face. But curiosity rages like a forest fire. The kinswomen of Arthur must be there to hear this.

There'll be men too. Arthur has not left the country undefended. Urien rides with us, grim-faced. Always courteous to women, Urien, but there's no question of allowing this. Divorce Arthur? This goes beyond all chivalry. He must oppose her.

York's overflowing. You'd think it was a festal crown-wearing, except that Arthur's missing, and his famous warband. He's taken the young men this time. The flower of the Cymry are falling on foreign soil while Gwenhyvar stabs him from behind.

We crowd into a fine, stone palace with painted walls. I could be there on the floor with princes and dukes. The aristocrat of artists, me, the Chief Bard of Rheged; the harp ranks high as the sword. But I'm not very tall. I slip into a gallery above and crane over, the better to recount the scene. Packed here too with avid watchers; I hope these beams will bear us.

The bishops are gathered at the front of the chamber, croziers in hand, like a gang of shepherds watching out for the wolf. Abbots and abbesses from monastic cities, startling in white among secular riches. On the other side kings: Nentres, Urien, Mark of Cornwall, and still more queens, fiercely resplendent in their court dress. Gwenhyvar's call has roused two dragons, the white of the Church and the red of Britain's noble blood.

They're a terrifying sight, even from up here.

She can't succeed, can she? Why would any woman want to renounce Arthur Pendragon?

It's a pity there aren't more men here. Most of our young colts and our sturdy stallions are in Armorica with Arthur. What's left are old stale hacks. Sorry, I don't mean Urien, of course! Men like Cador the Duke, Gwenhyvar's own foster-father, and grey-faced Ulfin that once helped Uther Pendragon break into Tintagel. There are young toughs left in Britain, of course, guarding the Pennines, the Wall, the coasts. They can't all desert their duty, even though the kingdom is rotting at its centre. Those who can, have ridden in overnight from posts nearby. Agravain, son of Margawse, and a handful like him. Edgy, excited, alarmed, doubtful. Laughing too loudly and flashing their battle-torques.

But the noble women have come in their full splendour. From Gwynedd and Gwent, Clyde and Calchvynydd, from Elmet and Erechwydd. All their married lives their men have gone to war, whether it was Saxons or a neighbour's cattle herd they had their eyes on. When the lords canter off over the hills in the early morning, it is the women who tend the land through the long day. When our boys come home to nurse their knocks and fettle their war-gear, the pattern of seedtime and harvest, of calving and shearing, does not detain them long. We pretend that power is with the men; these ladies carry their stewardship tactfully. Gwenhyvar has broken the code.

The hall's a riot of noise, but the hush that falls as Gwenhyvar enters is like nothing that's ever greeted her before. She's still High Queen. She's wearing her golden crown and a purple robe that surrounds her with royalty. In her hand she carries that greenstone sceptre. The crowds lean to see her coming and then sway back. She walks through their ranks, slow and stately, with a sober retinue following. She does not incline her head to left or right. She doesn't smile. I think she's nervous. I'm not surprised.

Modred is just a pace behind her. Why doesn't he assert his right as regent? His eyes are modestly downcast. Then from time to time he raises them and flashes that rare swift smile at a man here, a lady there, and they nod back to him. Modred has many friends. He's a diplomatic man. Where others of that family are quick with their swords and make enemies, Modred has always offered an open hand, a listening ear, good counsel.

The churchmen part abruptly, sweeping their skirts away from Gwenhyvar more widely than courtesy allows. She ascends the dais, takes her seat in one royal chair, with another empty beside her. Modred stands behind her. Odd that he doesn't occupy Arthur's seat.

When the heralds have silenced us, Gwenhyvar stands to state her grievance. Her voice is small but clear.

'Ladies and lords, I come before you as High Queen, of equal majesty with Arthur . . . No, hear me out!

'Remember this. When Merlyn brought me from Cornwall to marry the Pendragon, it was not just for my beauty or for the hope of sons, though I had both. He chose me out of all Britain for my royal blood, for that most ancient line of the kings of the West. Arthur claims to be the son of Uther Pendragon, and I believed that true. But he came to us out of a childhood shrouded in mystery. Only Merlyn knew the truth of it, and Merlyn is with us no more. My birth is known; my childhood with Cador my foster-father was openly seen. I am no stranger to royalty.

'Then, and only then, was Arthur cried High King. It was my betrothal that legitimated him.'

'Vain woman!' Bishop Bytwini cries. 'What has that to do with repudiating Arthur?'

'The form of our coronation was agreed between Merlyn and the Church. Two separate celebrations, in different churches, one for Arthur before the men, one to crown Gwenhyvar before the women. Is that not so?'

The bishops nod, warily. There's a throb of assent from all the older ladies. Morgan and her sisters must have been there. Before my time, of course.

'In one church Archbishop Dubric of blessed memory placed the crown on Arthur's head and set in his hand the sword of the Island's government, while in the other you, Bishop Bytwini, in the same instant, by the ringing of the bell, gave me this sceptre and pronounced me Queen, not as his consort, not passing on a secondary glory, but in my own right, through my own bloodline, an independent coronation.'

Well, that's set poor Bytwini chattering like an indignant magpie.

'Madam! You distort events beyond all sense and decency! How can the woman be an equal to her lord? It was for convenience and modesty we separated you. One church could not contain so great a gathering of lords and ladies. Many had had to be shut out from your marriage ceremony. It was Dubric's consecration that was pre-eminent. His hand conveyed the true sovereignty of Britain. What I performed on you was the insubstantial mirror of your husband's crowning.'

'The same oil from Galilee. The very gold of our crowns from the same mine in Wales. Are your hands not flesh and blood, as Dubric's were? Are you not both true bishops in the line of Peter? Did you not say when you placed this sceptre in my hand you were giving me the power to rule?'

'A pretty rite for ladies. The dignity due to a loyal wife. How could you think that made you equal to Arthur? You are a woman!'

'And the women are my witnesses. Is not this true?'

A hesitation. Names pass through all our minds, the wheels of mighty chariots: Rigantona, Cartimandua, Boudicca. It's not been so long since, after all, and from the women, like a summer thunder, because they do not know where this may lead, a thrill of confirmation.

'Aye!'

'Then hear this.' Her voice shakes, but she steadies it. She's been well rehearsed. 'The High Queen Gwenhyvar accuses Arthur. Since that day I have played the part of a Christian wife. Obedient, self-effacing, faithful . . .'

I can't be the only one to gasp a protest, can I!

'I have neither used nor abused the power placed in my hand with this sceptre. Yet it is sovereignty, and it is rightly mine. My dignity is Britain's. Arthur has shamed my honour, and so yours. The royal seed that should have fertilised your High Queen has been wasted on other wombs.'

She looks hard at Margawse when she says that.

'He was neither our king nor your husband then,' Margawse cries out.

'And you were neither his first nor his last whore!'

That's foolish, Gwenhyvar. It wasn't in your text, was it? Oh, yes, he's hurt her. Still, she needs the sisters' support.

The Bishop tries to calm them down. 'The Church does not condone that sin. But men are frail. The foolishness of youth . . . Our Saviour teaches forgiveness, seventy times seven.'

'Would Arthur have forgiven me one single act of adultery?' One single act? Those wide blue eyes!

'Christ stopped a stoning for that very cause . . . But a woman's case is different. Your wombs are holy. We must know who is the father of our children. Besides, you do not have a man's desires.'

You can feel the prickle in the air, like unspent lightning. There are more ladies than lords in this hall.

Gwenhyvar's not one for histrionics. She's been nerving herself for a long time to say this. She won't be shifted from her complaint.

'No king may commit adultery against a sovereign queen.'

Oh sweetly grim, that pale frail face, that quiet voice, those periwinkle eyes. Gwenhyvar's going up in my estimation. I could be interested. Down boy, she's spoken for twice over.

Modred is listening to this like a patient shadow.

It's Abbot Congar's turn. 'Let old sins lie, your majesty. The blood of all of us runs slower now. Why shame great Arthur and yourself with this?'

'Not slow enough, my lord Abbot. It seems fresh rains can still stir up a foul flood. I bring sworn testimony. Not tavern-maids on long campaigns, not Saxon captives, not too-hospitable daughters of distant lords. The ladies of my own court, in my own house, this very year, while I lay waiting in my marriage-bed.'

Bytwini's brusque. 'We cannot hear this now. The king is not present to defend himself.'

'What possibility of defence is there, when those of my subjects he has compelled cry out against him? Which of you has Arthur made to lie with him?'

Her women have clustered beside the dais. At her appeal a field of hands, like slowly-sprouting flax, climbs skywards, some shy with shame, some spiky with indignation. So it's not only on the battlefield Arthur's been trying to relive his boyhood! Bytwini's blushing. It's not the thing itself – he knows about sin – but that she should speak about it openly. We all know it happens.

'You hypocrite! Answer for yourself. Adulteress!'

Morgan's voice shocks us with shrill accusation. Even Modred starts. But Gwenhyvar has not yet done. She holds the high estates of Britain in her power now. Princes of land, of art and intellect are listening to her. She feels the intoxication of an audience. She almost smiles.

'Yes, Morgan the Faithless, one woman defied him. Despite his threats to bind her silent she unfolded the tale to me, showed me her bruises, washed my feet with the tears of her wrath, to her great honour and his shame.'

Gwenhyvar's hand reaches out to the group of her ladies below. My cheeks grow hot with indignation. I fear who this must be. Does Arthur's lust run as red as that? Would he touch even Tegau Goldbreast?

Someone is separating from the throng, rosy with womanly warmth, bowing her head in injured confirmation. It's not Tegau. Oh, ye gods! Morfudd, maiden most lovable, twin to Owain the Raven, Morgan's own daughter.

I seem to hear a scream that makes the door-posts tremble. The painted frescoes scatter in whirling dust. The world is tumbling. Steady, Taliesin. No one else has heard it but you. Morgan hasn't spoken. Nobody sees the universe has shattered.

# Chapter Thirty

I tear my eyes away from the flayed face of hope.

'We cannot judge this without the Pendragon.'

'Go to a convent if you're not content.'

Those men are Arthur's friends.

'A potent king may fructify us all,' a woman's voice dissents, while others hiss her.

'Potent!' Over the stiff skirt of court dress, Gwenhyvar's hands angle accusingly across her womb. 'One son in eighteen years, and he is dead. And now, nothing. Your king will not return from Armorica. His fighting arm is failing, like his wasted seed. He cannot give me an heir.'

That troubles them.

She says he's been too much of a lad, and yet he's past it. Well, inconsistency was never a stranger to political rhetoric.

'What need have I of further proof? Our royal marriage contract has been betrayed. If Arthur had caught me in adultery, he would have had me pulled to pieces between two horses. Yet now I bear the punishment of barrenness for his deeds.'

You could speak, Taliesin. Her women know! Why does Tegau stay silent?

'I, the High Queen of Britain, put Arthur away from me for this just cause. Your former king has left this land for wars that will not profit you. He leaves the Island without a father, husband, son. He may be dead already. I, Gwenhyvar, shall rule you myself, and with a truer service.'

That makes us gasp, the men louder than their women. That's not how we understood this divorce. We thought we were witnessing her abdication.

Bytwini tries to stop her. 'Madam you have no right! The High King was anointed. No one, not even I, can take away the grace that God has given him.'

'Your release will not be necessary. Arthur himself has passed his authority to another.'

The curtain sways and parts behind her. A fair lady robed in rippling gold and blue is flowing across the dais towards us. On her upraised hands she bears a splendid sword, more brilliant than Caliburn, no weapon of war. But all our eyes are fixed in incredulity on the lily-face above it. *The Lady of the Lake!* Arthur's soul-friend, Merlyn's successor. Taking Gwenhyvar's side?

The wind has changed upon the mere. Boats stagger in sudden danger. Where's the shore?

556

Nimue offers this sword, not to Gwenhyvar the High Queen, but to Modred the regent. My hands have held that priceless weapon, the symbol of Arthur's sovereignty, given into his grasp on the day of his coronation. Modred of Good Counsel kneels, as one who understands the worth of what he takes and his own unworthiness. His lips touch the blade, his fingers balance the hilt and tip.

'A precious trust. I was endowed with this power by Arthur, to use for Britain's good, without condition. That power, by this sword, on his own authority, I now surrender to its proper lady. My love and loyalty I pledge to Gwenhyvar, sole sovereign of the Isle of Britain. I call all men and women who love her name to serve her likewise.'

Bowing before her, darkly handsome, knightly virtuous, youthfully honourable.

Urien's weapon's half out and many others. The hall is loud with protest. But other lords are cheering. Modred's been working hard. They like his style.

The Chief Bishop rages. 'This Council cannot annul your marriage. It does not have that power. Only the Holy Father in Rome can do that.'

'Rome's gone,' smiles Nimue. 'Even Arthur could not restore it. The Church of Britain stands alone, with you at its head. Come, Bytwini, let you and I be allies.'

'Allies! While you debase the holy law of matrimony, raise women over men, deny all natural order.'

There's a whiteclad abbess or two that bridles at that. They have their own high ladies, this British Church.

Nimue persists, 'I am for Britain, not for Rome. I serve her children. It is to them that I appeal. How do you say? Will you have Gwenhyvar the High Queen over you?'

'No!' cries the Church, and 'No!' shout Urien, Ulfin and a stout rearguard like them. But Cador is Gwenhyvar's foster-father; he's torn. Mark of Cornwall has suffered bitter taunts since Trystan stole his queen Essylt; he has no love for Arthur's court. And the ladies of Britain? They are tasting the savour of an old power long lost.

The cries rise ragged, like the first waves breaching a sea wall. Then the bulwarks tumble and the flood is on us.

'Aye! Gwenhyvar!'

'Gwenhyvar of Britain!'

The nobility is bending its knees in homage.

One voice is momentously silent; though Margawse and Elaine have affirmed Modred's act, Morgan stands staring like a woman possessed. Nimue and Gwenhyvar have noticed. They watch. All hangs on this. Morfudd takes Morgan's hand, appealing to her. Her wise green eyes stare up into her mother's outraged face. As dangerous as Owain, this one.

The dark of the moon. A generation's gone. The king's eyes turn to the rising crescent of her daughter.

Modred, still kneeling, smiles.

One word, torn from the roots of Morgan's being.

'Aye.'

I see her sway. I want to rush and hold her, but I can't move for the cheering press of bodies around me. Nimue's smile flashes, a fierce triumphant culmination of a lifetime's hope.

'The nobility of Britain has affirmed it! I show you Gwenhyvar the High Queen!'

This time the roar of cheering must crack the walls of York.

The bishops, abbots and abbesses are sweeping out. An equal pain in Urien's eyes. His hero and his daughter. He hesitates. His loves are tearing him apart. Then, 'Never!' he cries, and struggles to reach Modred.

Gwenhyvar's blushing, both regal and modest in her bearing. The silver braids tumble over Modred's bowed black hair as she bends to receive the symbol he offers her. She holds both sword and sceptre up to us. She faces us sweetly.

'I rule alone now, because I must. But this sword is a heavy burden for one woman. The land has wilted enough under a feeble grasp. You need a younger king.'

That's clever, Gwenhyvar. You've touched a deep nerve there. The Year-King's run his path and reached the dangerous springtime of another Beltaine. She kisses Modred, chastely, and motions him to rise. His arm supports her trembling majesty. It's been a long ordeal.

Now cries are ringing with delight. An old religion, new romance. The gash is closing over already. New skin is forming.

Arthur, what battlefields, what beds, what pains, what pleasures, have kept you from this wife and son it seems you never knew? Why have you left us to this moment?

Morgan tears her eyes from Morfudd to gaze at Modred. What has she taught him all these years, walking together in the forest shadow? Was it of this? He turns to look at her again and bows respect.

The tears start to fall, silently, agonisingly, from Morgan's eyes. Oh, lad, you don't know the half of what's been done. You haven't seen the belt, that should have held both sword and scabbard, shredded and smoking on her fire.

Nimue's exultant. She thinks these are the tears of defeat on Morgan's face.

She does not know that Modred is already destroyed.

# Chapter Thirty-one

I struggle down the stairs and push through the crowds. I can't find Morgan. Urien is arguing with Modred.

'You took service with Arthur, before he knew who you were, as I did in my youth. You let him comb your hair and shave your face. We pledged him our swords and hearts. Mine will never turn against him, though all the world betrays him.'

'It was not Arthur himself who took your loyalty; it was the Pendragon, the figure of Britain.'

I catch the pain of memory in Urien's face. Modred is wrong. Urien loves Arthur the man, more than he loves his dark-souled foster-son. Urien, who has helped to raise him with his own boisterous boys, knows that behind the smile there is more about Modred that he will never understand.

'I will not break my oath to my anointed king.'

'We are the soul of Britain now, Gwenhyvar and I. Your oath has passed to us.'

'I should kill you with my own hand, here.'

There's a guard around Modred already, but the young man sinks to his knees, very winningly for one who's the most powerful prince in Britain now. His neck is bared.

'No harm shall come to you in this court for those rash words, my foster-father. I give you safe conduct. I make one appeal: that you bless me for the last time before we give you leave to depart from us. If we ever meet on the battlefield, you are free to kill me if you can. I release you from all our bonds.'

Few could resist such grace. Urien swallows down the memory of twenty years: the boy he taught to hunt, to shoot, to rob, to kill, all the wild education of a nobleman. He spins on his heel, so violently his swinging sword must have bruised his own thigh, and strides out of York. No farewell, to either of them, son or Morgan.

Only to me he flings a savage order.

'Get to Armorica as fast as you can. Find Arthur somehow and warn him of their treason.'

Me? I'm Chief Bard of Rheged, not a merman swimming the sea singing of doom. Too late. He's gone.

I turn, and there is Morgan. The tears have dried; her face is hard as granite. Very calm she seems, her hand quite steady. She's holding out a letter.

'Put this in his hand from me. But tell him the truth yourself, Taliesin, as only you know how. Tell Arthur he has lost everything.'

I think I know what she means.

So here I am, sitting on a cross-channel boat twanging my harp, like Trystan drifting to Ireland with a hole in his head. I never fancied myself as Essyllt's romantic lover; I have been wounded in a different place. I have loved song more than woman, though I serve both well. One I've lost already. Britain is dwindling on my horizon. Farewell, Morgan, lovelier than all the women of the world, more loving too, all that passion walled up in a too-strong heart like a closed furnace. Its outside has warmed me generously. I'm lucky to have escaped without a scorchmark. If her door should open, we may all be consumed.

Armorica is over our bows. Brittany, they are calling it now, since so many of our people fled there escaping the Saxons. A shore of song, like Powys and Dumnonia, a country of castles and dragons and giants, a land of legend. The legend of Arthur. Will you come again to us, great king, out of Europe, back to your true home, to the stirring sound of pipes and drums and the voices of noblewomen in the window-seats as they pluck poems from the lyre? Will the very peasants remember your deeds and the stones carry your name? Arthur, my song is still waiting, like a child unborn. Arthur, the news is bad. The battle that is coming is not the one I dreamed of singing.

Land at the harbour. Few folk about. The wind whips over the white sand. It might be the Cornwall I sailed from, save that this beach faces north, that the speech is stranger. My own, and not my own, like the batter-cakes we both make on the griddle. Light as lace they are here. Fairyland. Must I be the one to wake him from it?

I stumble on news. They've broken out of the siege. The enemy's routed. There's a camp around Howel's fortress with a good deal of roistering going on. Like schoolboys let out on holiday, they are. Grey warriors, remnants of Arthur's half-forgotten warband, and green boys, they're all brothers. They've slaughtered giants, they've revenged ravished maidens, they've put the world of chivalry to rights. Give him Morgan's letter.

I cannot watch him read it. Gone in the turning of a day. Queen, crown, son. Present, past and future. Love derided, honour smirched, hope snatched back. Great Arthur is a man destitute. Sing, Taliesin. That's all you're good for. Sing of a king who bestrides a hall like a warrior his horse. Of Gawain the golden knight bearing his sword before him. Of Modred with a battleaxe hacking at the timbers below. Of Gwenhyvar pulling the roof off with her own hands. Of the fall of many brave men. And Arthur, in all this ruin? He snatches his sword from fallen Gawain. He smites off Modred's head. His faithless queen he cuts to pieces and casts her down into a black pit. The tears are running down my nose. I face the window while I sing. This is not the song I meant. Where is comfort now? Where is glory, pride?

I see a wondrous lioness coming over the downs. I watch her break into a bounding run. Now she seizes the king by the waist and bears him straight into the sea. The waves drive them on. Fierce and gentle, that lioness. Strong and stealthy. Terrible and trustworthy. There is an island of peace beyond all storms.

'I will not believe her!' Arthur grates his teeth in a rage. 'She slanders my queen. She blackens my son. She dishonours the very crown of Britain. Morgan was always the destroyer.'

That stops me in my tracks. Tragedy's one thing. But how can you draw tears for a story that's not believed? Well, not credited in public, anyway. I see his drawn face in the morning. I catch his white fists on the drinking horn at breakfast. Too much beer too early in the day. Too foul a temper. Which of them is he grieving for? Gwenhyvar the fair, who must not have played him false? Or Morgan the dark, whose truth he can never accept? Or neither of them? A man's world, Arthur's. Is it Modred his son, dearer than either of them, found, and now horribly lost?

But now he must believe. More news comes from Bishop Bytwini. Gwenhyvar has married Modred, though Bytwini refused to perform the ceremony. Soon he'll be crowned. Arthur can deny the prince of poets, the truth-telling bard on whom his hope of glory hangs. He dare not disbelieve the Church.

War. Not games with giants. Britain is the maiden ravished now, by her own son, by his own son. I hear the screech of weapons on the honing-stone, the hammer of rivets in mail, the creak of leather sails on masts. Do you think my heart is merry because the great battle is finally coming? For all my lightness of the past, do not despise me that much. Believe that this is not the song I wished to sing.

Where can I turn for a foothold in all this mire? Where is faith, where is constancy now? Where is honour?

> Until my life ages,
> And death claims his wages,
> I shall not cease yearning
> Unless I praise Urien.

I'm off, before the fleet is ready. I am going home. Home! Is this how the landscape of the heart looks after an earthquake? We are invading our own country. Arthur of the Britons must attack Britain itself. Modred will take the crown with Gwenhyvar. Modred has married Gwenhyvar. Modred is lying in Arthur's bed. The young king has come like springtime. The old king must die. He knows it.

But he will not accept it. Nothing from Morgan's hand. Not love, not death, not truth. Did they know, when they gave him back his son, what they were doing, Morgan, Margawse, Elaine? Have they borne, found and reared Modred only for this? Is this their vengeance? Arthur believes it is. Devastating the rage, the shock, the wound. Can they never be done, Arthur and Morgan, hurting each other?

The harp is silent on the voyage back. I cannot tune the strings against the seagulls' screams. It sits dumb on my knee. My heart is empty of poetry. This cannot be happening to us. Modred my comrade, my almost-brother. Arthur my king. Morgan, Morgan, what have you done to all of us? What have we done to you? An invisible tide creeps through the timbers, rises, chills me, chokes me. My song is drowned.

# Chapter Thirty-two

Dry land again. I stand disconsolate on the quay. Pick up my bags.
I'm flying north, like a lost child to its mother, a kitten snatched from
its home. I belong to Morgan, to the slate and granite, to the hills of
the west, to the rain of the tears of shattered constancy. She will need
me, won't she?

I belong to Urien. I cannot serve them both.

But what's this? I've been expecting turmoil, revolution. Modred
the tyrant holding on for both queen and crown by the might of the
sword. Civil war, rebellion, cousin slaughtering cousin, the land
trampled. But that's not the truth. Everywhere on the road I meet the
smiles of summer. Gwenhyvar is queen. Modred is Gwenhyvar's
husband. Soon Modred will be crowned king. Most men speak well
of Modred, the women too. It's true, they love him!

A lot's been happening.

'He's made an alliance with the Angles.'

'He's calling a council with the Picts.'

'He's offering to treat with the Irish.'

'I left a sister in Saxon hands over by the Wash. I may see her children
at last.'

'My son was taken hostage by the Picts. Another raid and they'd
have cut his throat.'

'Three times our home's been burned by pirates.'

There's a great hunger for peace. Not for the tense truce of mailed
men, not for heroes standing sentinel on the skyline, for watchers by
the beacons peering out to sea, for armed suspicion on the Wall. One
Britain, open roads, kin reunited. Who will make her laws? The
common people shrug their shoulders. Just let us sow the seed and
leave us alone to hoe and harvest. They've forgotten Hengist and his
greedy axe-men. It's Arthur's troops they call the Red Ravagers.

There's gratitude for you! Wasn't Arthur the gift of Merlyn in our
darkest hour? Arthur, their hero with the enchanted sword? It was
Arthur who stopped the Saxons, wasn't it? And they'd rather have
Modred! I've told you, very winning that family can be when they put
their mind to it. Modred and Gwenhyvar rule not by force but with
the people's consent.

But not from all the nobles, Arthur's generation. War's their god.
No day worth living that's not greased with blood. Modred's a careful
man; he can handle the sword too. He's taken a hostage from every
hostile fortress, just to make sure.

It's a shock to the system. I am a heroic bard. How can I earn my immortality without battles? I'll hardly have enough songs left to make a living. Do you want me to go fasting like a monk to keep this peace? Peace! No fear of that, is there? I've brought the tread of battle stalking at my heels. You and your newmade friends must fight now, Modred, whether you want to or not. You must gird yourself for the war to end all wars, the new order to replace the old, the son against the father, the allied hues of nations opposing the red dragon.

Morgan, Morgan, is this what you want? Modred against Arthur? Can't you stop it?

I'm not safe here. The storm is close behind me. I'm in Gwenhyvar's country and I'm Urien's bard. I run for shelter.

I'm not the only fugitive. But I don't meet him where I might have expected. I've slept at Christian monasteries on the way, where I could hear of them. Decent places for guests, they have, and the food's good. They're pleased to see you, especially on a fast day. Gives them an excuse, you see, to eat like normal men and women. But they are not so many that you can find one every night.

As I move north the ways of Rome and Constantinople are slipping behind me like a cloak from my shoulders. The land of Urien, guardian of Rome's Wall, is still far off. I take to inns and ale-houses. The news is muddled here, with smoke and beer. I listen more than I tell. Will they believe me if I say that Arthur's coming? They think he's besieged or dead in Brittany. Tell Urien first.

A face listening in the corner, like me. Old, this one, ravaged with desperation and indignant wrath. He's attended by younger men plainly dressed, their faces pale mirrors of his own. Clerical gentlemen, these; I know that studious look. The old one's face leaps into focus, like a missing tile restored to a mosaic. I see the whole. Bytwini, chief archbishop of the land, skulking in a common inn. He sees me start and knows me too. Taliesin, Chief Bard to Christian Urien Rheged. Wry our grins across the firelight. Better than crying, anyway. He stretches and strolls to the door as if to take the air. I follow him.

There's a scent of lavender and rosemary outside as our skirts brush the herb patch. The air's grey, not fully dark. The hills brood, featureless.

'They will crown him!' he spits into the cabbages. 'The pagan son of incestuous parents, anointed with holy oil. But not by me.'

'Wasn't it to avoid this conflagration that young Arthur tried to douse the firebrand once?' I remind him. 'You churchmen gave him a heavy penance for that, I'm told.'

His grin flashes white, like an owl's swoop. 'Dreams! And only the witch-king Merlyn to interpret them. It was Merlyn he feared more than the saints, and after Merlyn that slippery Lady of the Lake. There was another way than killing. There is always another way.'

'What way is that, if our fate is written in the stars?'

'To change the enemy's heart. Christ always offers us a choice. To let the fire of love consume the rotten timbers of his sin and build a new and wholesome palace for them both.'

'Accept Modred as his son? He's done that, man. Look what happened!'

'Too late.' He shook his head. 'The child had formed the man. The boy that never knew his father turns on the father for denying his son.'

'*You* pity Modred?' That's stopped me in my tracks.

'Pity!' He fairly shouts at me. 'No! I condemn Modred. In the name of the Father and the Son and the Holy Ghost, I curse him. He has usurped the kingdom, made an adulterous marriage, reduced Christ's representative in Britain to a fugitive like our Lord from Herod. Can you believe the fiend Nimue threatens me with death because I will not crown him? I, that anointed Arthur's wife with these very hands! I, pity Modred? But that's not to say I don't understand him.'

'What would you say,' I murmur, 'if I were to tell you I have talked with Arthur, that I left him on the coast of Brittany not a week ago, that he is embarking an army to regain the crown?'

Bytwini grips my arm. Even in the twilight I can see his eyes glitter. 'Arthur is still alive and free! Is it so? Our prayers are answered! Arthur will come again to deliver Britain!'

New Britain, saved by ageing Arthur? The Christians came with the legions. It is young Modred that summons an older authority. Funny, that. He was Urien's foster-son, schooled in priests' Latin, growing up in the court of Christian Rheged. But he is the one who can turn back the centuries for us. Nimue has found her opportunity, a young man standing in the shadow of Mabon's Stone. Mabon, Son of Modron the Mother.

I totter then. The scent of herbs is heady in the evening air. Morgan, those who blacken your name have never known the power of your healing touch. But we do well to be afraid of you. You are also Morgan the Destroyer.

Bytwini is shaking my arm. He's a younger man already. Hope is setting his agile mind racing, planning, scheming. 'When you see Arthur again tell him he will find Bytwini at Glastonbury. Tell him the Church is for him. Modred, Gwenhyvar and all their crew we have execrated. Bid him in the name of Christ to cleanse the land and the Church will curse these heathen as they flee.'

Another way than killing, did he say? Not this time. He pities Modred, but he cannot forgive him. The Saxons have savaged Christian Britain too sorely for that. As far as he's concerned, Modred's adultery doesn't stop at Gwenhyvar's bed.

'Tell Arthur? Sorry, man. I'm off home to Urien. When I see Arthur again, it will be on the field of his last great battle.'

I can't help myself, can I? The song is forming in my head already.

# Chapter Thirty-three

I should have known the joy had left Carlisle. The ramparts are manned and watchful; the city's braced for war. The harp is no ready passport now. Even I, Taliesin Radiant-Brow, suffer the humiliation of being kept waiting at the gate. The captain's sent for; I'm recognised and passed through.

Inside, the fortress feels half-empty, though there are strangers about. Owain's in Brittany with the best of our warband. Urien has been gathering his second team. The men and women I pass in the street stare anxiously and do not give me good-day. King Urien decrees that Rheged opposes Gwenhyvar; they've no choice, have they? But Modred is a Rheged man too. He's talked with them, he understands them, he's helped them. Here, all men and women spoke well of Modred once. They may still in secret.

I'm at the palace already. Rhun is hurrying to meet me, Urien's behind him, the hounds are yapping round my legs. It's not in the absence of warriors that the awful emptiness lies. Where's Morgan? I'm searching for her in vain. She hasn't come home, has she? I see them speaking urgently to me, but I seem to be deaf. I'm gaping at them like a fish through water. Sense penetrates at last.

'She stayed for Modred's marriage?'

I can't believe that. Surely she's given herself more pain than she can bear already? Arthur and Morgan's time has passed, that never truly came. Modred and Gwenhyvar usurp their place.

He shakes his head. I think he'd like to shake me as well, for anger and hurt.

'Fool! She is still my queen. Elaine and Margawse were witnesses, but Morgan of Rheged never. But your own news, man, for heaven's sake! Did you find Arthur? Is he dead? Or so hot besieged in Armorica that there's no help for us?'

'Arthur is on his way.' There's proud news to be bringing, if only the heart did not feel so hollow.

A silence, a sigh of breath released, a great cheer. The news is flying round the palace, through the city. The very hills will be ringing with it soon. Arthur is coming back!

Quick looks flash between Rhun and Urien, Morgan's forgotten. Rhun grasps his father's wrists. 'Modred must march to repel him. You must go to Arthur's aid. Carlisle is safe as long as they are fighting in the south. Leave Rheged to me. For all our sakes, you must not let Modred win.'

Hard that choice, to fight against his foster-son, to take arms for the

565

Pendragon who so wronged Morgan, who laid lustful hands even on Urien's own daughter. Hard, but not long. Urien has always been as much in love with Arthur as with Morgan. The heart decides, and duty finds its reasons. His sword was pledged to Arthur in the budding of their manhood. Loyalty excuses all.

At once he gives the order. The whole household's busy in the yard or the storerooms. The smithy's working like a thunderstorm. A good job Woman isn't here. There's pain for you. A smith denied his hammer and tongs in such extremity. I should feel the same if I were robbed of song. The hall's a barn from which the swallows have fled in autumn. Iron and gold and bronze have been stripped from the walls. Patches of unsmoked wood show like fresh scars. This is the big one. No workaday cattle-rustling, this. They take the finest gear that will bear the shock of war. If Arthur falls, he will go richly attended to his hero's grave. If Modred dies, it must be by no common weapon. The crows of battle will wade through gold as well as blood. Such excitement!

My hour has come. I feel the sudden rush of joy confirm it. You must forgive me! I was born for this. Forget the anguish. Can I leave Urien bardless in such a battle? How can I feel the golden heat of Arthur catching the gorse on the southern downs of Britain and not bear witness to the conflagration? Who wins, who loses? I'm a bard before I'm a man. Tragedy, victory, Briton, Saxon, Christian, pagan, are all the meat of song. Great deeds I must sing, high praise I must make. Blood I must paint, graves I must name, for mead and gold and fame I must praise the valour of warriors. I shall hymn them all, the victors, the fallen. And the greatest bards that follow shall say, Taliesin made this song.

But it's real war. And war means bloodshed. Hard steel, blue blades, red gore. I've never actually taken part in a battle. I sang of Cynan of Powys's exploits from a safe distance, you understand. Now my hour comes, and with it danger. I'll need armour and a shield. Good stout ones, as well as handsome. How could I sing the battle-song of Britain with a spear sticking through my windpipe? And a weapon? Now's my chance to bear the beauty Cynan Garwyn gave me. Just for the look of the thing, you understand. I'm no hairy butcher. But, no, this is serious fighting. We're going to kill each other. I need a serious blade. I've a duty of self preservation, after all. Whoever falls, it mustn't be Taliesin.

Only one man at the still centre of it, cool among all this fever. I find Urien, of all places, outside the walls, sitting on a boulder brooding over a flock of sheep. I do not heed his stillness. I am breathless with the glory of it all. Win or lose, we know how to live and how to die, we the British. We will ride laughing under the hill, fighting and feasting and singing till the darkness falls and time turns over and the world is young for ever. This is my song.

'Lord Urien! What shall I do for arms? And armour. You wouldn't like to see a Saxon spearhead bedded in this snow-white breast of mine, the blood of Taliesin spilt where the breath of poetry once thrilled. Just a little sword, but serviceable. And a shield. Especially the shield.

Nothing too showy, mind you. I wouldn't want to draw attention to myself. That comes later. But let it be stout. You won't forget that, will you? You won't regret them. When your turn comes to die, I'll sing you such a death-song that your name will live for ever.'

He turns from the ewes and lambs and looks at me sternly, as though I were a yapping puppy not yet well trained.

'They will not be needed. There will be no battle for you.'

'But I am Taliesin! I must be there, when all the heroes of Britain are locked in combat, pagan and Christian, west and east, Modred with Arthur. I have to be there to sing of it. I was born for this!'

'I forbid it.'

I read the truth in the grim furrows of his face. Warlord though he is, he does not want this mighty battle, and I confess now that I do. I must be there. I cannot be left behind like the dregs of wine, unwanted, to go flat and stale. I am choked with tears. I have to be simple.

'My lord!' I beg. 'Take me to the battle.'

Urien leans on the low stone wall of the sheep-pen. The din of the men behind us in the citadel is less than the sound of the wind in the gorse. For the third time he refuses me.

'This is a war that should not be remembered. This is a battle that should never have been fought. If Arthur defeats my foster-son, then I am shamed. If Modred kills the High King, it will be my dishonour.'

I sink to my knees at his feet to plead with him.

'But I am a powerful bard! I have the might of mockery. I can chant satires that will blister the enemy's face. I shall call curses that would make a dragon quake. I'll launch an assault of poetry like any druid! You need me!'

'You're well out of it, lad. This war is evil.'

Evil. A word the saints would use; my father perhaps, if I had ever known him. Does Morgan accept the meaning of it? Where is she now?

His hand rests on my shoulder, heavy and warm. He lifts one more gold collar from his neck and lays it round mine. He knows everything. I have not deserved his forgiveness.

I look about me. When the war is over, who will be king here, who queen? What will become of the sheepfolds of Rheged, and the cattle raids across the Wall, the high-roofed halls and the leaping firelight? Will I, Taliesin, be left lordless, to see it prey to brambles and owls for the rest of my life?

> Until my life ages,
> And death claims his wages,
> I shall not cease yearning
> Unless I praise Urien.

'What shall I do?' I whisper.

'Find Morgan, and help her.'

# Chapter Thirty-four

For a moment the guard drops from his eyes.

I'm left bewildered. Help Morgan? Against Arthur? Or does Urien understand more of his queen than I do?

I stare at him wordlessly as he threads his way through the lambs back to the castle. His back is straighter now. He's made his own choice.

I do not wait to see them march away, those ageing warriors who thought they had straddled a battle-horse for the last time, these lads with the bloom of childhood still on their cheeks. I've seen those stars in eyes before. We are the glory, the chivalry of Britain. We will defend Arthur. We will never be forgotten. I think of Modred's forces: the young warriors garrisoning the Island, hard Saxon frontiersmen who have grown up on foreign soil, Picts still smarting under the humiliations Arthur heaped on them. It will be bloody, this war. There will be mothers weeping. The bards will pile more stanzas on their grave-songs. Which of us will exult in victory?

Find Morgan. Where?

York's abandoned. Modred's coronation is done. With Nimue and all their allies he is marching south.

Almost without my knowing, my hands are turning the horse's head that way. The harp on my back and the burden of song in my heart can feel the pull. Well, why not? As likely to find Morgan in the south as the north, aren't I? And I shall be nearer the battle . . .

The boughs of the may-trees lean towards me and scatter their blossom in white tracks. This is her doing. She has made, now she unmakes. She must be there.

Not long before I come on news of armies. The High Queen will wait in Winchester. I couldn't imagine Gwenhyvar standing in a war-chariot, like Nimue.

Urge the horse faster. Morgan is lost. Now Nimue holds the centre. I feel the Island unstable on its base, breaking loose, beginning to rock on a dangerous ocean.

Where's this? Garlot, where the great roads cross, where the hills of the north go down beneath the southern cornfields, where Saxon and Briton are wary neighbours. Once the great throbbing heart of our tribal kingdoms. Now? The twilight country, the uneasy strand between the ebb tide and the flow, the hollow that is the eye of the storm. Awareness penetrates my brain more slowly than it should. Old Nentres is king here, and Elaine queen. I leap as though a bee had stung me. I know already I am right by the pricking of my thumb. Where else should Morgan be but with this eldest, this all-seeing sister?

Knowing is one thing, acting is another. I find at the last I do not want to turn the horse's head aside and seek their capital, but I must. Rather the battlefield, and the warfare of men.

Black Annis Hill. It's not an imposing place, no stone-faced fortress-eyrie. Huge trees crowd it closer than is customary for a defended stronghold, so I know it is under another protection. Come to think of it, those old oaks themselves have a watchful look. I begin to see faces in them. My heart's beating faster than I like. Steady, Taliesin, Rome has been here before you; Britain is a Christian country, under Arthur. Was! An old hunger long denied is opening its jaws to feast on the ravens' leavings. But Gwenhyvar's a Christian queen; and Nimue can hold the balance, can't she?

Low branches shadow the hollow way until I near the summit. Dark ramparts jut against a sky bright without warmth. I tread in ancient footsteps. Crows peck the yellowed skulls staked on the walls. Some jawbones drop in silent screams. Once, Nentres fought against Arthur. Whose heads are these?

A young woman is one gatekeeper, and on the other side a man dwarfed by nature, though his head is bigger than mine and by the look of his powerful arms I wouldn't want to tangle with him.

'Go in, Taliesin Radiant-Brow; you are expected,' she says before I've opened my mouth.

The dwarf says nothing, but leers at my confusion. No, hold on to your wits, boy. The shape of the harp in your satchel is clear for all to see. Still, how did they know I was coming? Elaine the Fair can see more than I can. Ceridwen's clever boy is a blind baby here.

Nentres's house gives a more barbaric welcome than Urien's Carlisle. Rushes on the floor replace mosaics. Carved wooden posts support the roof. The smoke has dimmed those painted heads so their eyes stare darkly at me now. A cauldron dangles on a mighty chain. Pork seethes. No delicacies from Roman kitchens here.

In the dark hall Nentres broods on his couch. An old wound keeps him at home. He has sent his warband to fight for Modred, but he has a strong guard here. Elaine is seated, stitching as always, with her feet almost in the cinders.

I've found my queen. Morgan, standing over the fire, though the summer day's not cold. The face she turns to me is grey as the ashes. I did not remember that she so resembled her eldest sister. I feel like a stranger.

'You are not needed,' she says.

Oh, Morgan, Morgan, what words could hurt Taliesin more than that?

'Urien sent me,' I say, 'to help you.'

There's a small sigh, a little stirring of surprise. The harp nudges my back. I didn't call her Healer for nothing. Give me an hour. I will sing to Morgan. I will close her wounds. I will bring her back to life. It is a strange board-game they play, these two. They partly understand each other. There is a game they call the King's Table, the light side and the dark, the one striving to attain a distant goal, the other to encircle.

Presently Margawse appears, laughing delightedly to see me. I wish she wouldn't. She hastens towards me, tipping back her creamy throat, and I see that even her beguiling face is not unwrinkled.

'So Arthur returns in great anger? Modred has shamed him with this double incest. A true child of mine! We have bred him well. Arthur can overlook his own sin, but not his son's. The weapons are out now. This time he must shaft us with cold steel. How will you like that, sister?'

Morgan reddens like a stormy dawn.

Oh, Margawse, Margawse! Must you foul everything you touch? Was this what Morgan meant? Great Arthur, her brother, shamed by his own son? From the beginning you have soiled him for her. How could she take him cleanly after you, hating and loving him purely as she did? Arthur and Morgan. Because of you their day must end in death. There is no other way. His light will never split her darkness now.

She knows it. Too full to answer Margawse. Too proud. Too hurt.

Margawse is triumphant. 'The end is near. Soon Arthur will be a song that no one sings.'

The words pierce me. I am Taliesin. It is my destiny she strikes out with those words.

Morgan moves too, in a gesture of denial.

'It's no good. It is finished, little sister. You have looked your last on Arthur.'

Elaine does not turn her head. Her voice comes low and sleepy. 'She has not. Morgan will take our brother's hand once more. You will hold Arthur in your arms again, Margawse. Finally, he shall rest in my lap.'

Silence. Nentres stirs, the hounds whine.

'Where?'

'How?'

'There is an island, where red apples drop from the trees, and the ninth wave breaks upon the shore, and Avallach's daughters follow the path of the stars.'

Margawse and Morgan catch each other's eyes. I hear the distant neighing of horses from the stables.

# Chapter Thirty-five

As I turn from Nentres limping across the yard to bid us farewell, I find Morgan coming towards her horse. She carries something white cradled against her breast like a baby. I watch her push it into her saddle-bag and catch the old stale stains on it. I know then what this is she cannot bear to leave behind. That shirt of Arthur's I stole for her in Camelot. She has carried it all this time. And I'd thought her love was dead! Surely that must mean she still has hope?

The wind that brought Arthur's fleet is strengthening. It buffets our faces. Our ears are strained for news of the powerful tide that is sweeping to meet us.

The sisters thread the valley of the Thames. I dare not ask what they will do when they find Arthur.

A rise in our path beside the river. Difficult to see what lies in the dip beyond it. Then our outrider tops the crest and gives a cry. Too late for warning; we're almost on each other. A smaller escort than ours, and in a great hurry. A woman in a chariot. These are tight-strung days. Weapons are levelled on both sides before questions are answered. I've got my own sword out, the jewelled gift of Cynan Garwyn. I've never had to use it till today.

Close enough to launch a spear, close enough to see the woman's face. It's Gwenhyvar.

Fear, astonishment, relief, a careful calculation. I see all these in her face before she speaks.

'My sisters! Praise be!'

'We are the sisters of Arthur Pendragon,' calls Morgan, 'and he is no longer your husband.'

Not finely calculated enough, Gwenhyvar. But she's grown a bigger woman now. She's tasted sovereignty.

'All the women in Britain are sisters to their queen. I am Modred's wife now. But I hesitate to call such beauties by the name of Mothers.'

'It's you deserve that name, by the look of you,' says Margawse.

Oh, yes, strip away the stiff royalty of court dress and we can see she's thickening. It can't be Arthur's child. And she's not a month married to Modred.

'For this, and every child of Britain, I beg your help. Arthur has driven Modred from the coast. I fled to seek Cheldric the Saxon's help. We need more keels from Germany. Then terrible news overtook us. Winchester's fallen! My treacherous guard rebelled. This is all that is loyal. I am flying for my life.'

Morgan's gaze searches her keenly.

'Where is Tegau . . . and Morfudd? They would not desert you.'

Gwenhyvar shakes her head. Her look shows terror of this mother.

'I do not know. I have not seen them since.'

The finches twitter, and the river splashes over stones.

No sound from Morgan. If eyes could scream, hers would.

Morgan would never have abandoned her people.

'Help me,' pleads Gwenhyvar. 'For Modred.'

The sisters question silently and nod. Who knows what decision they affirm?

'You throw yourself on our protection?'

'I am his wife.'

Her independent royalty is soon forgotten. So shallow a root, to withstand such a tempest. Poor Gwenhyvar, kept in the shadow of the mighty oak of Arthur. How could this pale sapling make a sturdy tree?

Their tents are pitched in a clearing by the river. The soldiery withdraws. Gwenhyvar needs a stronger defence than shields can give. Morgan's eyes summon me. I shake my head. Help me, Urien! But it is Urien who has ordered me to help Morgan.

'Let me only play the harp for you,' I beg. 'That's powerful magic enough.' She allows it.

Gwenhyvar's at the centre of the circle. She's shivering. The bishops have cast her out. This is not her rite. But she fears the loss of her life more than the loss of eternity. The women are all around her. Some men, like Teilo, that are called to the craft. They weave, now left, now right, the fires burn, almost without smoke or flame, the chants are circular, repetitive, monotonous, a looping chain. And Gwenhyvar kneels, fair, frightened, vulnerable, her belly swollen with Modred's child. Her hands have no size or strength to cover it. Her eyes stare. But the power of the ritual is strong on her. It confirms her queen yet.

Morgan questions Gwenhyvar's captain. 'Arthur is winning? Modred has fled?'

'Modred has many friends, madam. His fleet has fallen back on Cornwall. More Saxons are coming. Arthur had no one but the warband he brought from Armorica, and they are dying with every battle. Great Gawain himself is dead.'

'Gawain the Golden!' The cry of grief bursts from Margawse's heart. Her eldest, dearest son.

'He was the first of the mighty to fall on the beach on the day they landed. They say that came as near as anything to breaking Arthur's spirit.'

Her sons are killing each other.

'Curse him who caused it!'

The imprecation hovers like a hawk, above whom?

Now the gale swirls us west, taking Gwenhyvar with us. The first town we come on is in high excitement. They've heard the news. Arthur Pendragon is back! Strong citadels fall to him. The natural order returns.

Ride, ride. Is Arthur ahead? Or will we hear the tread of his army on the highway behind us?

We race for Dumnonia that bred these women. Across the levels the island of Glastonbury mocks us with its ambiguous sanctuary. Camelot's no shelter now. We skirt Exeter. Custennin its king stands high in Arthur's favour. Even Cador, Gwenhyvar's foster-father, may find his loyalty straining. Fly further west yet.

Mark is a dark unknown. Once he was Morgan's jailer. But the bonds of blood are strong. The Pendragon killed his kinsman Gorlois, and Mark has suffered Arthur's mockery because of Trystan.

I think we're heading for his fortress on Tintagel. The sisters turn their eyes with a long gaze seaward. The air shimmers either side of this high ridge. It is more than summer heat, flickering in the eye. There's the flash of mail and weapons below us, a field of tents. Modred's army.

Gwenhyvar's almost weeping with relief. 'Restore me to my husband.'

Morgan smiles. 'And which is he?'

At the same moment pain twists Gwenhyvar's face. A gush of water stains her skirt and makes a puddle leaking through the floor of the chariot. Again that look of understanding between the sisters.

'An armed camp is no place to give birth, your majesty.'

'Where else is safe? Help me!'

She is frightened of more than pain, as well she might be.

'Not long now.'

'I want to be with Modred. I am the High Queen.'

'He has no time for you now.'

The wheels are rolling on.

'Conduct me to your king. I command you!'

But the cries of a woman in labour are not regarded.

Gwenhyvar's not the only one who's glimpsed her salvation on the slopes of Camlann. I let the procession jolt past me along the stony track. I have a job to hold my own horse back. He's keen to be after his fellows. Too soon yet for him to get wind of the multitude of warhorses.

I'm deserting Morgan. Yes. I can't help myself. My place is there, beside the river Camel, no matter whose side I am on. Arthur is coming to his last great battle. Forgive me, Urien. I obeyed your orders this far. But I cannot ride past now, can I? The harp is pulling like a mastiff on a leash. If only the horse would stop bucking! I think he's caught the whinnying on the wind.

Morgan has turned her own mount. She's riding back. Her escort wheels and circles silently around me. No fighting or desertion among these men. The loyalty of Morgan's guards is never in question. They fear her, yes, but there is devotion besides. She has been good to them and theirs.

She has been good to me.

I hear myself plead, like Gwenhyvar.

'Let me go. Please! You do not need me. What use would I be to a woman in childbirth? My work is here. My destiny is here. This is the final fight, the great song of my life.'

Her hand cleaves the air in a sign crueller than any knife. It severs hope. Her voice intones.

'If Arthur wins, you must not sing of it. If Arthur dies, you shall not sing of it. That day will be as if it had never dawned.'

Her finger is stretched out towards me. She names her power. I feel the words in my throat whisper into silence like falling leaves. Is this how she punishes treachery? Margawse, Gwenhyvar, Ygerne, what have you done to me?

How can I tell her what she already knows: that I am the greatest bard that ever lived? I am not important in myself. It is my song, the song of Arthur I was born to sing. If I do not tell it, who will remember? The centuries will roll by like empty waves, and men will ask, 'Who was Arthur? Did he ever live?' If the song dies, then Arthur's name dies too.

Oh, Morgan, Morgan, I deserved better of you than this. I loved you truly. How many nights have I held you in my arms and comforted you? I would have surrounded you with flowers, wrapped you in fur, plucked serenades to charm your cares to rest. But you have forgiven nothing at all.

I cannot hold back my tears. I do not try. Let her see that when she kills my song she breaks my heart.

I am a child to her.

My horse carries me on past Camlann after hers.

# Chapter Thirty-six

We leave them behind us, men in the last day of their life. Will those tents be full of wild laughter and singing tonight? Or will silence fall early over the fields where the fate of Britain waits?

Not Tintagel? Gwenhyvar starts as we roll past the road to the sea.

'Mark would protect me. Tintagel's impregnable. Where are you taking me?'

'No fortress is safe from the Pendragon.'

We wheel south now with our backs to the shining estuary of the Camel. Past Celliwig, that happy home, the favourite hunting-lodge of Arthur, nest for young lovers when the world was young and treachery only a word in a tale. Better steer clear of that. Gwenhyvar's wracked by the convulsions of her own body. Who knows what other pain brings a cry to her lips?

Moors hump their shoulders over us. Mist shadows pools. Wild horses start and run. Then the sun breaks and we are in a valley of apples on the banks of the upper Fowey. White huts of wattle, plastered, golden-thatched. A sound of singing and a chiming bell.

Margawse and Elaine look at each other. 'You would take her here?' as Morgan rides up to the gate in the low bank. A portly nun in an ample creamy gown comes hurrying to admit us.

Gwenhyvar has seen what this is.

'You cannot bring me here! The Church has excommunicated me. They are Arthur's friends!'

'These women know how to keep a sinner safe. They will protect your body. You must answer for your own soul.'

'I did not willingly oppose the Church.' Gwenhyvar's not without spirit, even now. 'Was I worse than Arthur? I tried to make the country whole. They cannot reject me.'

'Be sure they will not do that.'

Did Gwenhyvar shudder as she passed the holy threshold? Better she had trembled when Modred first crossed hers.

Another nun comes briskly to the door of the chapel and stands staring, as Morgan advances with her hands held out as if to an old acquaintance.

'Cigfa!'

'You, back?'

The sign that Christians make to ward off evil.

'A cool welcome for one who was your school's most able pupil! You are the abbess now?'

'Co-arb only still. Bryvyth's heir. Great duties and little power.'

'Bryvyth is still alive!'

For the first time in months, I see a flash of joy in Morgan's face, as if

575

a treasure long lost beyond all hope had been restored to her.

'Wait there. I will send for her. Your friend is sick?'

A start. I truly think Morgan has forgotten Gwenhyvar.

'If the labour of women is counted a sickness.'

The nun Cigfa flushes strangely. 'The convent is no place for child-bearing.'

'So my servant Luned discovered when you expelled her.'

'Through your uncleanness the nuns lost their home.'

'I lost mine long before when you became my jailers.'

'For your own good, to save both your body and soul.'

Morgan bows her head slightly, abruptly ending the argument.

Others help Gwenhyvar to the infirmary. For us, the guesthouse. Margawse laughs wildly, though her face is ravaged by weeping for Gawain.

'These are the nuns that Mark threw out of Tintagel? Your teachers and keepers? And you bring Gwenhyvar here to have her child!'

'I know no surer sanctuary. They kept me safe from Uther.'

The tap of a stick outside on the herb-lined path. A slow but purposeful step. Morgan rises, her gaze on the door.

A tall old woman leaning on a staff. Her skin hangs like leather from her craggy bones, but her eyes are keen under the tufted grey brows and a grin splits her face as eager as a young maid's.

'Morgan, girl! By all that's wonderful! Let me look at you.'

I watch in astonishment as Morgan bows her head and makes a reverence like a dutiful student.

'Mother, I did not hope to find you alive.'

The gaunt old face looks at her keenly. 'I wish I could think that your coming means repentance. But you have always spelled trouble to those who love you. What is it this time? They tell me that Arthur is on the warpath and Modred is near.'

'Gwenhyvar's time has come.'

The old abbess nearly drops her staff. 'That's Gwenhyvar! That adulteress, here!'

A nun appears apologetically behind her shoulder.

'Mother Bryvyth, the children are born.'

'Children, did you say?'

'Twin boys.'

Twins. Modred's sons, Arthur's grandchildren.

'Two boys,' I hear Morgan murmur. 'They could not keep the balance, even now.'

The women are hurrying to the infirmary. I'm not invited, but I tiptoe after.

Gwenhyvar is lying in a plain, narrow bed. Two purpled scraps of flesh wrapped in white bands are held up to the abbess. They are frighteningly small. They seem no stronger than the sticks that girls bind with rags to make a doll.

'Bring me water,' orders Bryvyth. 'I'll need to baptise them quickly.'

Elaine has already taken them in her ample arms. Tears spurt from her puckered eyes. These babes are not long for this world. They may not wait for the avenging sword to find them. Is this all they leave behind them,

Modred so chaste, save in this one great matter, Arthur so profligate? Is this how it ends?

'Keep her,' says Morgan, staring down at Gwenhyvar. 'Guard her closely. I do not doubt she intends to make a full repentance. She will be a less able scholar than I was, but she may make a better nun.'

The High Queen's eyes, dreamy and spent, focus suddenly on us in alarm.

'A nun! Is Modred killed? What will happen to me? Say he is not!'

Bryvyth's face blazes. Infirm though she is, the staff lifts in her fist as if she'd like to cuff Gwenhyvar's ears.

'High Queen! And you do not ask what will happen to your country? Your sin has brought us to civil war.'

Morgan's smile stretches, like a cat's. 'Modred waits at Camlann. The battle is not yet. Whatever happens, it will not concern you. If Modred falls, this convent will keep you secure. If Arthur falls, you shall not enjoy his defeat.'

'What do you mean? I am the Queen! I am Modred's wife.'

'You are Arthur's consort,' Bryvyth thunders.

'You cannot keep me against my will.'

'And should not need to.'

'Arthur is coming. Would you rather we handed you over to him?' Morgan asks.

Modred, you have fished in deeper waters than you knew. To these women Gwenhyvar is Arthur's wife, but Arthur is Morgan's . . . what? I will not name the thought that swims beneath the surface of all our minds. Forget the facts. Forget who's in and out of whose bed. The truth is deeper, older than their history. This Gwenhyvar was never his true mate.

'You will not let him have me? Where are my guards?' The High Queen is appealing to the abbess now. The infirmarian soothes her. She should rest. Poor Gwenhyvar, too frail in every way to play the part they load upon her.

The abbess's grin is humourless, compassionate, shrewd, summing her up. 'This is a fragile place. Those that give all to the poor need few locks. But my nuns are discreet. We have fogous, pit-houses, where hermits live, with trapdoors opening to the sky, wind-eyes to God. We could find you a little cell for contemplation. You would not be discovered, I promise you.'

'But if Modred wins . . .?'

The arms fold like bars across her chest.

'I make the offer once, girl. Or you go back to your husband.'

'I was given no choice,' says Morgan softly.

The abbess rounds on her. 'We all have choice! You chose the darkness!'

'It did not seem so to me. I sought both light and dark.'

They challenge each other. Then the abbess's big arms reach wide. The two embrace each other with a strange intensity.

'Will you not repent, girl? It's not too late.'

There's an appeal, the vulnerability of human love in that furrowed face, beyond the duty of Christian correction. This formidable woman is in love with Morgan, like the rest of us.

'I tried to heal,' says Morgan, muffled. 'But there was no healing.'

'There is, in Christ.'

'Tell Arthur that.'

Gwenhyvar is weeping. 'Do not let him find me. He will not forgive me.'

'Do you forgive yourself?'

'I will do penance. Only keep me safe!'

'If you choose, the world shall not hear of you again, or you of it.'

A moment's panic in her eyes, then the lids close. They have taken her babies away. Gwenhyvar sleeps between chaste covers. Now, only now, the abbess's face softens and she bends over her to trace the sign of the cross.

'That one was never strong enough to be the Pendragon's wife.' She turns to the sisters. 'Will you stay the night?'

She bares her heart to the pain of rejection. Morgan shakes her head silently.

One last meal then, before we leave this place of peace. Margawse terrifies me. Even here, among the ordered sanctity of the nuns, even here under Morgan's nose, her eyes flash at me, still bright with the tears she sheds for Gawain. It is as though she knows the flower of all our manhood must be cut down, and the earth cries out in her: 'Renew me, renew me! Plough me, water me, seed me, make me fertile again.' Oh, Margawse, surely your time for that is past. What the sickle will reap tomorrow can never be restored.

Gawain is dead. Bright Gawain that carried the sun in the wild stiff rays of his warrior's hair. Firstborn son of the dark king Lot, a resurrection out of the land of shades. The promise wanes. Darkness at noonday. His strength is gone.

But his mother's blood rages to recreate what is taken, and even here, even now, I feel my new-found virtue begin to weaken to the urgency of her need. My eyes fly fearfully to my queen.

Morgan is quiet and serious among these women. She'd make a better nun than Gwenhyvar, though she denies it. Yes, even I who have been in her bed and deeper still, know I have never truly possessed her. None of us have. She gave what she did not regard, her body. The tool for which it was fashioned has never entered it. The rest of us are nothing. She might be the virgin priestess of the new moon. Now she talks soberly with Bryvyth.

I think I'm drunk, though I've only had two goblets of wine, watching these women play their several games, even on this night. I had forgotten that Morgan reads Latin and Greek, that she knows more of mathematics than the Bishop of Carlisle, that she can discuss the structure of an englyn as well as any harper.

Elaine eats in almost-silence, crumbling bread into her wine. She stares beyond the walls as though they were not there. For once I lean to her, as the only one of them that has understanding. I feel that she at least knows why we are here. Over that hill, Arthur is sharpening his weapons to kill Modred. Modred is preparing to destroy his father Arthur. Death is advancing. Does nobody but Elaine see him? Red Margawse beckons. Black Morgan talks politics. Grey Elaine opens her arms to receive their children.

I'm wrong. She's not the only one.

'Are you well, Mother? I can have food sent to your cell,' the co-arb Cigfa asks sharply.

The old abbess's face has deepened its lines of care. She's an intelligent lady. She doesn't need second-sight to warn her of catastrophe coming.

I make my excuses. Outside the sun is sliding towards evening. How close is Arthur now? I can see nothing but trees around me and the flash of the Fowey. I stand in the convent garden listening. I hear the rustle of a skirt against leaves.

What need has Margawse of tent or bed when the grass is thick and soft under the apple trees? I'm caught on my uneven path up the hill. Is nothing sacred to you, Margawse? Or are all things sacred? All times, all places, even here, this eve? Nothing can come of it, but strife. Your sons are warring with each other. Must you make war between your sisters too?

Her will is stronger than mine.

The dew is falling on a last, still, chilly dusk. Morgan does not want me, but she knows. I try to jest. The wit withers under her gaze. I plead my youthful weakness. I know I've failed her. Men on the vigil of battle do not act so. Do not grow up, Taliesin. Never grow up. That is your only hope to stay alive. But the whole world is ageing, and Taliesin with it. Nothing is as it should be.

The kings are very near us, the old king and the young, the true king and the false. But which is which? The white nuns are back in their chapel, praying earnestly. They work at prayer. Like smiths, like armourers, physicians, warriors, they prepare themselves for battle, apply all their skill. Fortunate the army that has this warband on its side.

They are praying for Arthur. Arthur, begot by treachery in their own convent. Arthur, who has plundered what he wanted from many a churchland, who will never be done quarrelling with their bishops. Yet still they claim him for their own. He will be Arthur, the Christian king. Arthur, the champion of faith and honour. They need each other. He got his crown from them, and where he reigns, the Church has grown and spread.

We've untethered the horses. But at the last Morgan herself slips in at the back of the chapel and lifts her hands. I glimpse the girl behind the woman. She was schooled as one of them. When she comes out I see the woman grown from the girl. They prayed for Arthur, while she wept for Modred.

Time to leave, though no one will tell me where we are going.

Morgan falls to her knees before Bryvyth and bows her head.

'The end is near. Will you bless me, Mother?'

There's a moment's silence. Margawse moves restively, but Elaine is still. The abbess's gnarled hands rest over Morgan's head. Her lips move. Her voice is too low for us to hear what kind of benediction this can be.

We leave Gwenhyvar and Modred's babies behind us.

We are on the road. Like an eddy in a river we are circling north. The wind whips a high colour in Morgan's face. Her eyes are overbright. Margawse looks at her curiously and smiles.

'So, there is no one between you and Arthur, at last.'

'No one but Modred,' says Elaine.

# Chapter Thirty-seven

The armies can't be far off now. I'm not too late. I could break away. I can still be there.

No, I cannot run from Morgan. Not even Arthur himself could do that. She holds me, as she holds all of us, by the almost-offering of herself, the joys she seems to promise. More warmth than the full-blown generosity of Margäwse. More comfort than our final resting-place in the lap of Elaine.

So we all follow the white tracks of Morgan's feet in moonlit meadows. We see her new moon rise and hope turns over like a piece of silver. It will be different this time, It will be new. It will be clean. No matter how many times the frost has charred the blossom. No matter how often the owl has robbed the nest of chicks. This spring the world will be created afresh. This month the new moon's flawless. The Maiden turns towards us. Morgan will embrace Arthur.

Taliesin, you're a fool.

On, then, on a cross-grained nag behind these queens. On to a last camp under the willow trees. The drums in my blood are loud enough to summon armies. Surely I can hear the din of men and horses? Why is she taking me so close if she's tied up my tongue? Why is she bringing me to the brink of such frustration? Take away the stirring song and all I see is sorrow.

A river, black between shelving banks. The winding Camel, threaded with pools. I search the night beyond for beacons, campfires. Nothing. Our horses whicker. Our escort shift uneasily. We are all awake. I am cold to the invitation of Margawse now, though the firelight reddens her skin and kindles green fire in her eyes. Morgan has silenced poetry and chilled warmth. Elaine watches from the doorway of her tent. How many dead men will sleep in those arms tomorrow night? Margawse is starting to keen, for generations of bitterness, for Gorlois her father, Lot her husband, Gawain her son. I mourn for what I may not tell.

Morgan walks away from us into the darkness. The guards lift their heads and stir, but no one follows. I start to rise, then sink back huddled in my cloak. She doesn't want me, does she?

Each in our own way, we nurse our sorrows on the eve of Camlann. Yet no one stops it.

A splash, more than a vole hunting under the river bank. Our men are on their feet, swords drawn. They're glad of action. Like me, they suffer uselessness, more prisoners than Gwenhyvar in a hermit's cell.

'Peace, if peace can be on such a night.' A woman's voice.

A figure, glimmering in the starlight, steps from a coracle. More females follow. I see the starlight wink on the weapons they wear. Nimue, and her warrior women. The bravest men step back a little. The greeting was peace. I think they'd rather it was Bedwyr leading a night-attack.

'I would talk with Morgan.'

'Morgan is the youngest of us.' Margawse rises to her feet. Always that lazy lateness with her that seems not to recognise alarm. 'I am here, and Elaine too. Will we not do to parley with?'

'You! You have done too much already. And we all know what Elaine is waiting for. But Morgan . . . with Morgan there is still possibility.'

I know what she means. Morgan can always surprise me. I think this tragedy's unstoppable, like a ship slowly capsizing. Perhaps it's not.

'Morgan is here.'

That low and lovely voice behind me. Morgan, on the edge of the firelight, that makes black silk out of her hair and leaves her eyes in shadow.

'Will you fight for us?'

'I am Morgan the Healer. It was you gave Arthur his weapons.'

'And you armed Modred.'

A catch of breath.

'You made him a man.'

'I am a woman.'

'You are Morgan the Wise. You must work for him now.'

'Where is the need, if he has the Lady of the Lake? Is your power not enough? You launched this war. You unshipped Gwenhyvar from Arthur.'

'Where is she? She was seen with you.' Nimue's look searches the unlit tents.

'Safe.'

'I do not speak of safety. She is our High Queen!'

'Was.'

'You have not deserted Modred! You have not betrayed us to Arthur? Tell me where Gwenhyvar is.'

Silence.

'Is her child born?'

Silence.

'You have destroyed them!'

'I leave that to frailty or to Arthur's followers.'

'Traitor to your kind! Have you forgotten Arthur's violence on Morfudd, Uther's stealing of Ygerne? Help Gwenhyvar now!'

'Help Nimue, rather! What was Gwenhyvar to you? A plant more pliable than Arthur, to be trained to your liking.'

'I served Arthur faithfully. Look how he rewarded me!'

'You taught and armed him. You gave him sword and scabbard. Yet you destroyed the balance. When you had the choice, it was the sword you saved for Arthur. This war is your doing.'

'It was you destroyed his scabbard!'

'I offered it to him. He would not make the marriage.'

'They were both his. What right had you to anything?'

Elaine and Margawse rise.

'The right to heal?'

'The right to bear?'

'The right to embrace?'

'We know your rites. Of poison, jealousy, possession.'

'I cast my power away, but Arthur keeps the naked sword.'

'So fight against him! Modred is your weapon.'

Silence again.

Elaine breaks it. 'We opposed Merlyn.'

'And you took Merlyn's place.'

I feel even Nimue draw back. She's a known enchantress. But there is something here. Too dangerous for her to use her magic. We mortals tremble, feel our peril standing so close, the limitations of humanity in the presence of these women. And Nimue feels it too, wise though she is.

'You would not reject the child you made? You cannot still love Arthur?'

A stillness follows, deepens. I, who a few moments ago felt the chill of night and strangeness, am aware how a warmth is thickening in the summer night, more than our paltry campfire could throw out. The heat I felt from Margawse magnified a hundredfold, emanating from the moonwalking, virginal, black-and-whiteness of Morgan the Fay. She is promising royalty, union, wonders beyond the stars. Oh, Arthur, why are you not here to feel it with us?

'Tomorrow Arthur Pendragon will surrender his sword to me.'

'There! I told Modred he had nothing to fear!' Nimue gasps a little as she finds her voice. 'I told him you would not change. I told him nothing could undo your hate for Arthur.'

I, Taliesin, am speechless with amazement. Can she really not feel the truth? Can the night so bewitch, so distort, so deceive her senses? Or do we find each in this story what we want to hear? Morgan the wicked witch, Arthur the noble king. Their tragedy is our misunderstanding.

Nimue moves off, still discontented. The high magic she came for has not been made. She has not reclaimed Gwenhyvar and the children. Her oarswomen paddle her away, like swans upon the river.

No one can sleep tonight. I watch the stars turning relentlessly. I hide my face. I, Taliesin the comforter, need solace now.

Do not grow up. That's what you say to save your skin, isn't it? Do not grow up, Taliesin. I'm only a boy still.

Only a boy, unblooded, on the night before Camlann. Only a boy, tied to the apron-strings of my queen, in the camp of women, while Urien is praying before battle. Only a boy, while all the men of Britain are quaffing mead, or testing armour, or stretched asleep in their tents at Camlann. Better if you had been a real man now, and died like them.

Queen Gwenhyvar is no more. But Arthur and Modred will still fight over her, blindly, unstoppably as the circling year.

# Chapter Thirty-eight

I cannot sleep. I steal from the moonless clearing. Someone else is awake besides the sentry. Woman sees the path I am taking and growls a warning. I do not heed him. It's only Taliesin, a truant schoolboy. Nobody important.

I carry my shame and grief along the willowed water. The boughs hang sadly, trailing their fingers in the current. This is the time of night when the soul is lowest. The river beckons.

Is Modred sleeping?

The river is widening into a mere. The sky is lighter; not dawn, the night's glamour doubled in the sheen of water. No mist at midnight, a shadowed clarity.

There's a little beach. I'm walking delicately over star-washed sand. The water leaks cold through the deerskin boots that were new the day I rode out of Rheged. Very smart, I imagined myself to be, the brave little bard of battle. What do I care for damp now? The whole world is cold to me.

What is Arthur imagining?

Strange I'm not tired. The moon is rising now and the mere is lovely as Morgan's face framed in dark tresses. The water's still widening. The camp is far behind. But I can't get lost, can I? The river will guide me back.

I turn to be sure.

The campfire's gone. The lake stretches wide as a sea in both directions.

Don't panic, boy. A trick of the light. Too much imagination.

That's far enough. I'll just go up to that one black rock at the edge of the water and then start back.

Sand clogs my steps. The cold is creeping up my veins. I could turn here.

Wavelets are whispering. Clouds shroud the moon. The stone's ahead.

One black rock in a level land, humped and ancient.

Stand still, Taliesin.

Black rock.

Granite.

Do not breathe, Taliesin.

Rock, the form of a woman.

Morgan.

She is crouched, bent over the waves. Only her hands work, endlessly lifting and twisting, something white.

I cannot move.

583

Do not grow up! Do not grow up, Taliesin! How could you begin to understand? You must not understand what you are seeing!

A man's shirt.

Arthur's.

I know with sickening truth how she has come by it. I, Taliesin, entering Arthur's house, passing Modred. I, Taliesin, in Arthur's bedchamber, jesting with Gwenhyvar. I, Taliesin, with my own hands hiding under my tunic the muddied keepsake of Arthur's hunting.

I gave it to Morgan.

She is washing Arthur's shirt at the edge of the lake. And the water pours out of the breast, dark as blood.

The washer at the ford on the eve of battle.

The Morrigan.

No, Morgan, no! I would give anything not to have seen this. To believe still in love and life.

Not Morgan the Maiden? Not Morgan the Mother. The Morrigan is washing the shroud for the dead.

The moon slides out from a corner of cloud. It is more cruel still. Light touches grizzled hair. Bones poke through withered flesh. How long is it since my hands were stroking her body?

The Crow of Battle.

She is old, she is ugly, beyond bearing. I shudder and shut my eyes as I turn away from her. But I hear her voice croaking a tuneless dirge, like a rusty hinge, while she works. Oh, Morgan, Morgan! You who had Taliesin for your bard!

She must not see me, trapped in the emptiness of these sedges. She must not hear me go. She must not guess what I have learned.

But the buckskin boots are not soft enough on the squelching shore. And every rustling tuft of moss cries out, 'Look at Taliesin running away!'

Her elf-locked head begins to turn. In my ears the wind is shrieking. 'Return to me! Return!'

I'm racing madly now. I fling myself into the arms of the forest. Not kindly, those clawing limbs, but no place is dark enough for me to hide from her, and never mind about wolves. Far better to be eaten by flesh and blood. Better still to be a man at Camlann and die cleanly on the spears of Arthur, or of Modred; it hardly matters which. I will run shieldless to the comfort of that war. No breastplate for the poor soundbox of Taliesin. I want to die and forget what I have seen.

Whom I have served.

# Chapter Thirty-nine

I've lost Morgan; now I'm lost myself. The campfire's gone. And if I stumbled on either of her sisters, Elaine or Margawse, I should be more terrified.

I'm terrified anyway. I cannot find our men, our women, Woman. Did we exist, any of us? Are we a folksong spun when the true tales of heroes have been told over? Am I a figment of someone's else's imagination?

More like a nightmare. Brambles claw my back. I see less than I need to and more than I want to see: the groping fingers of branches aiming for my eyes, the swoop of bats across the moon. The rhythm of my sobbing breath beats under the cruel descant shriek of owls.

I stumble on, too senseless to stop. Another tearing twist at my tunic. I put up a hand to disentangle myself. Truth enters my disordered brain. I've lost her too.

Healer. The harp. As close to me as my own organs. My essential self. We have never been parted since the day my hands closed round her silky frame and my probing fingers plucked the first throbbing response from her. I do not know if I can live without her.

She lies beside the Camel, as lost to me as the land of Lyonnesse that vanished under the waves. I cannot go back.

Slower now. What does it matter if I die?

Night's thinning into grey morning. I'm still alive. There's cruel irony. I, the bard Taliesin, escaped from the Morrigan, am free on the morning of the battle of Camlann. Free, but lost. I've lost my music, lost my heart, lost my awen.

I blunder on. For pity's sake, will no one tell me the way out of this wood?

The wind is rising. The branches clash like swords. The crows are thrown screaming into the air. How can I hear the tumult of battle above them? Where are Morgan's ravens? Where is Camlann?

Silence suddenly, only the crashing of my own progress deafening me now. I stop and listen. Is that how battle sounds? A far-off moaning, like the sea rolling for ever against some desolate shore. Hard to be certain which way.

I feel the loss of the harp on my back. I am too light, too insubstantial without it. No armour either, only a toy of a sword not made for killing. What am I good for to anyone?

Difficult to force a way through the wood, even when I think I know which side the battle's on. Wet bogs, that wait to suck an offering down. Steep-banked ravines that will hardly let me out. Thickets of thorn where narrow deerpaths beckon only to end in tangled bewilderment.

She laughs at me. Out of the fecund earth her eyes are watching this. She weeps for Modred and Arthur, but me she mocks.

Brave men are falling even now. I can imagine it, can't I? The yelling warriors. The noble gold-torqued men. The plunging of gallant horses. The blood and foam that spatter like spray. The standards swaying against the sun. The struggling shadows. The splintering shields. Bared teeth flashing a grin of victory as the blade goes home.

I could make it up, like any competent bard. It wouldn't be the first time, would it? Cynan Garwyn's a hefty fighter. I kept a prudent distance from most of his scraps. What is a bard blessed with inspiration for, if not to paint the plain wood of reality with brilliant gilding?

But today history is ending, and I am choked with a sense of more than mortal struggle. Arthur the brigand; Morgan the Wise. Arthur the righteous king; Morgan the Faithless. All men spoke well of Modred in his lifetime; Modred the traitor. This day mows down the niceties of plus and minus. Legend is born on the field of Camlann. I must be there! I must touch the myth, the mystery, the magic and feel the bardic lightning in my soul. I could become a legend myself.

Will I tell you the truth?

Is this why Morgan cursed me and sends me stumbling in a swamp? Robs me of my harp?

She doesn't trust me.

She is right.

What's that? I glimpse a grey gown through the holly. Desperate for directions I run after it.

'Stop! Wait for me! Help!'

The hooded head turns. It's an old man, but he hitches up his skirt and runs off when he sees me, muttering to himself. He's nimbler than he looks. But I am fitter than he is, and growing angry now. I catch him by the arm and twist him round.

'Spare me, sir! Spare me! I will keep their secret.'

The grey eyes roll madly. He is witless and wandering.

'Where is the battle? Tell me which way to Camlann.'

'He lives! The king lives for ever. With his white mare beside him and a hundred warriors at his back.'

'Which king? The combat, you old fool! Where is the battlefield?'

The eyes go crafty.

'They are all sleeping. Till the horn of doom sounds and the drum rolls.'

I will not believe what he seems to mean. What use is this fool to me? He has lost his senses. I throw him from me and dash on.

Light promises ahead. The sun is out, but it sucks up a fog in the still afternoon.

Too still. Why is this calm along the Camel? Is it over so soon? Sounds come like echoes, broken, long-delayed.

I'm hurrying downhill now. The hazel brakes are thinning. Cows have been here.

I see my shadow in the mist and take it for a stranger.

The jagged, scattered cries frighten me more than the full-throated roar of battle did.

A horse passes, riderless, wild-eyed and nervous. I stumble on, lower, into the thickest of the fog.

A trampled cornfield. Would that those were just sheaves lying ungathered on damp dark ground. Would that only the coulter of peasants' ploughs had furrowed the soil this deeply. Would that clean rain had watered it less thickly.

I am a royal bard, I was bred to sing of war and red slaughter and glorious death. Mead-singer, gold-getter, praiser of princes. But I stand surrounded by a harvest of corpses and I am weeping like a desolate child. All the tears of the poets of Christendom could not wash out these terrible stains of cruelty. Is this the field of honour I have hymned? The headless torso. Is this the glorious defence of all we love? The screaming of the wounded who cannot die. Is this the myth we raise our children on? I slither in the entrails of a disembowelled horse.

How should these wounded know the end for which they are still dying? I must guess the outcome.

Morgan has been here before me.

Daylight is fading, the mist weeps. And the crows gather, fattening, with eager eyes. I try to chase them off, but they are too many, too single-minded. I vomit instead, and they scream raucous laughter.

'Who's there? If you are for Arthur, name yourself. If for Modred, surrender.'

A handful of shadowy horsemen. The weapons they level at me are solid, though. Spears, swords, that have finished off braver men than me. I see the unnamed bloodstains on them. Unnamed, unsung. Is this the end of Taliesin?

'Taliesin?'

I am face to face with Urien Rheged. I fall on my knees and cling to his hand. Oh, the relief! My earthly king. My human, sane and Christian lord. Owain and half a dozen stern warriors behind him. and never mind the cloud of thunder in Rheged's face.

'I forbade you this battle. Why did you disobey me?'

'I was lost. I came too late . . . too soon. I . . .' I'm sick again.

'I charged you to find Morgan. Is this how you serve her?'

I shudder and cannot speak. His face confronts loss and shuts it away.

I feel his hand rest on my shoulder. 'There, boy. It's over. I fear we are all losers now.'

I cannot accept it.

'Arthur is . . . defeated?'

Yet they have no beaten look, these men. There is a sorrowful majesty about them. Still, they do not rejoice. I look at their set, exhausted faces. I think I know the truth before Urien speaks.

'Great Arthur is dead. Bedwyr bore him away from the battle, dreadfully wounded. He could not have lived. We seek his body.'

The warriors behind him keen like women.

I see it must be so. How could it have been otherwise? I have watched the Morrigan washing the blood from his shirt.

'Then . . . Modred is truly our king?'

'Dead also. Killed by his father's hand.' This, unflinching, from his foster-father.

So all is lost. No victor. No right restored. The High King Arthur and courtly Modred, the son of Uther Pendragon and the child of Arthur, that lately found and clasped each other in their arms. Where are the legends of Britain now?

The long dance is done, and the hobby-horse falls dead. This time he will not rise to the tap of the teasing bladder. The summer will not come. The dancers lie where they have dropped. The few of us that are left must limp away into the winter, leaderless.

I'm sorry, Urien. You're a good man, but it's not the same.

The great battle is over, and I am standing among its carnage. But I, Taliesin, will never sing of Camlann.

Morgan and Arthur. We shall not see them ever again. I do not wish to remember this day.

I will remember Morgan the Healer in Rheged. Let me try to recall her queen in Urien's hall. Lovely, she was. Her hair like the raven's wing and her skin soft as honeysuckle . . .

I'm sorry. I cannot sing of her. There are things a man may not look on and live.

I shall never touch Morgan the Wise again.

I will not go back to search the banks of the Camel. They will all be gone. Keep me with you, Urien. I am afraid.

Not hard to find a mount for me, after Camlann. Next day we turn our horses' heads to the north. Urien, Owain, Taliesin. To the open hills and the cold clean winds of Rheged. To the springing lambs and the fattening calves that lift their heads, expectant, for a lighter, quickening step that will never come. To the sober tale of history.

I have a new harp now, the gift of generous Urien. Its notes are true, but they cannot heal. Lift it down from the wall tonight, Taliesin. The world is waiting. I will sing the songs that I am paid to sing.

> Until my life ages,
> And death claims his wages,
> I shall not cease yearning
> Unless I praise Urien.

Why have you done this to us, Morgan? Why?

# Herself

Book Five
in the sequence
Daughter of Tintagel

To Paul, Catherine and Jane

# Prologue

*I make no excuses. It matters less than nothing to me what you think. I know what others have said of me, even young Taliesin, though I was kind to him.*

*I am what I am.*

*I am eternal. I am the shape-shifter. I am Morgan the Fay.*

*Yes, you may recoil. If you have heard of me at all, it will be nothing to my credit. I am the half-sister of good King Arthur and his archenemy, am I not? The wicked witch, the embodiment of evil.*

*And yet . . .*

*Others call me Morgan the Goddess.*

*After the Battle of Camlann a silk-hung ship comes to fetch the mortally wounded king away to Avalon. I am the queen who takes Arthur in my arms for healing.*

*How could you understand?*

*You do not want to live with this ambiguity. Some editing of the story will clearly be necessary.*

# Chapter One

After Camlann. It is over now. All across Britain women are waiting for the heavy step that will bring the news they dread. In eastern halls the Saxons are laughing as they raise their drinking-horns. What need of invasion now, of armies of spears and battle-axes? We have torn the heart out of Britain ourselves and left a hollow bloodstained shell.

A cold dew covers the field. The ravens have flapped their heavy way to rest. The worms begin their work.

The great names are almost all dead. Gawain, Agravain, Gaheris, Gareth, Modred. Margawse's five sons, our younger generation. All your male lusty love of life, all our wise women's worship of the life-giving forces, seeps away with their blood into the earth.

And here in a lonely chapel in Cornwall the king is dying. A wind is rising in the west, beginning to spread the mourning rumour across Britain. The king is maimed. Plague starts to stalk the land.

It is not the fear of death in battle that appals you. That is how Arthur the soldier wished to go, on the field of glory. But the battle of Camlann is a day that should not be remembered. This is a warfare that should never have been fought.

The people of Britain have rejected Arthur. His queen is faithless. This king has killed his son.

The sad survivors search the field. They will find many sightless faces to make them weep. They will not find Arthur.

The druids howl for their dead and their lost opportunity. Britain will not be whole under Arthur or Modred.

The Christian priests are coming with book and bell. They kneel beside the fallen, grave, compassionate, setting some on the road to healing and committing others to heaven. They will not close Arthur's eyes.

The light is gone from Britain. What died on Camlann's field will never rise again.

Have I done this?

Tonight I stand again, as once in childhood we were parted, with the water between us. So small a pool. So great an ocean of misunderstanding.

I watch, as then, through hard-held tears, and you, as then, know nothing of my watching. You are helpless. Others have carried you to this place.

Tonight I am whole and you are wounded. That is not how it seems.

# Chapter Two

*I am the product of many fictions. I have few facts to offer you.
For the year 537 the Welsh Annals record only this:*

'*The Battle of Camlann, in which Arthur and Modred fell.*'

*It makes no judgment, claims no kinship between them, awards neither the
victory. It does not say they fought on different sides. Dead, they are here
accorded an equal honour.*
*The medieval Welsh Triads sound a more bitter note:*

'*Three Dishonoured Men who were in the Island of Britain: The third
and worst was Modred, when Arthur left with him the government of
Britain. He turned against Arthur. And then there took place the Battle
of Camlann between Arthur and Modred. And Arthur slew Modred
and was himself wounded to death.*'

'*Three Harmful Blows of the Island of Britain: The second
Gwenhyvach struck upon Gwenhyvar: and for that cause there took
place afterwards the Action of the Battle of Camlann.*'

'*Three Futile Battles of the Island of Britain: And the third was
the worst: that was Camlann, which was brought about because of a
quarrel between Gwenhyvar and Gwenhyvach.*'

*The bards' voices are heavy with the burden of this old grief. Women are
dishonoured because they provoke this war. Men are dishonoured because
they fight at Camlann. The war-band of Alan White-Ankle is dishonoured
because they turn away from him by night and do not go with him to
Camlann, where he is slain.*

'*Save seven, none returned from Camlann.*'

'*There was a sad battle, provoked by wanton passion, Camlann
through slaughter and pursuit; and fair Gwenhyvar, lively-nurtured,
yellow-haired, brought it about.*'

'*You would go to battle, if you get a chance, to a more just fight
than Camlann.*'

# Chapter Three

Darkness is here. The Battle of Camlann is finished. Arthur is dying.

No, do not weep. Do not shriek and keen. Do not tear at your faces. Stand silently and bear witness.

Far off now the battlefield by that little river. Out of hearing the bloodstained victors who hunt for their grievously wounded king. They will not find him now. His friends have brought him to the brink of the Otherworld.

They have come upon a holy place. A little chapel by a mere in the heart of Cornwall. The Wheel of Fortune has come full circle for him. We are back at our beginning.

His friends are few now. This war has been cruel. Lucan, who struggled to carry him here, is dead before him, killed by the clutch of his king on a wound of his own that he tried to disguise. Only Bedwyr is left tonight.

And a woman, standing unseen in the shadows across the water, watching.

How long have I been there?

Ever since Arthur was born. I have waited a lifetime, always in shadow, always this depth between us.

The wind troubles the trees. The moonlight slips from my goose-white face and finds it again. Will he see one, or three, or nine women under the shifting branches?

Too late to wonder. Blood dances the reel of death in front of Arthur's eyes. He never saw me clearly when the sun shone for him. How could he now?

One thing alone he grasps as though to let it go would be to surrender life itself. Even in darkness he can see it blazing in his soul through the touch of his practised fingers. The first and last reality for him: Caliburn, his sword. A hilt of doubled dragons, golden, tongued with flame. A blue steel blade marked with the runes of victory, its keen edge dulled by bitter blows, its brightness fouled tonight with a blood so dear he dare not name it.

But he has won. How could he not? While he holds Caliburn he cannot be defeated. This is the sword that gave him Mount Badon. This is the blade that turned the Anglo-Saxons back. This is the weapon that held the line for Christian Britain. Here is his immortal fame. Here is his justification for everything else. Hold it tight.

Why then does he groan from more than the agony of his wound? Why is there no one to heal him?

I clench my fists so hard that the blood spurts from my palms and

593

the forbidden tears creep down my cheeks like falling stars. But I will not move.

He holds his power yet, in the darkness and the pain and the smell of blood. He will not let it go. Beyond all reason his failing strength still grips Caliburn with an obstinate hope. He is Arthur. He cannot die.

But he is dying.

And I stand across the lake, clenching my healer's hands, motionless, waiting. For what?

A cloud wanders across the moon and the darkness swallows me, blots out the chapel where Arthur lies, smothers the lake. Will the world have changed when it lifts? How long have we waited for each other to move, we two? How can this water be bridged?

I, the woman, have power too in my empty hands, of another sort. I hold the gift of life.

Will he take it?

Why does he fear my love?

# Chapter Four

*I come from the shores of sunset.*

*In the British Isles the far south-west is always fairyland: Welsh Dyfed with its magic pigs; the kingdom of Meath in Ireland, famed for its sorcerers; Cornwall.*

*The legends are here, at Tintagel, Slaughterbridge, Dozmary Pool. Here our story begins and ends. Arthur and Morgan. He is, perhaps, history. North is masculine hero-country: Cuchulain of Ulster, Maelgwn of Gwynedd. Future historians will claim the soldier Arthur for Hadrian's Wall. No archaeologist will dig for evidence of Morgan the Fay. I am a legend. The west is where I belong.*

*In the very first story that links my name with Arthur's, I reign on the fortunate island of Avalon, in the farthest west of ocean.*

*Some find in Avalon the Island of Apples. Others say it is the country of Avallach, king of the Otherworld, my father.*

# Chapter Five

I did not know that, as a child. I only knew that the sea called me with a powerful voice. When the sun shone I raced down to Bossiney Cove from my parents' fort and felt the long grass whip my legs as if I were a champion mare in sight of the finishing mark. Barefoot over the sand and straight into the waves. Darkly green my skirt now, undulating round my knees like dulse, my toes sinking into fine sharp shells and sand. Far, far behind me the calls of my old nurse Gwennol, and I laughing and splashing spray in the sun. I knew even then that Gwennol's shouts to me were no more than fond cautions. She would squat in the sun, mending our clothes with her still-deft fingers, her wrinkles deepening as she smiled secretly to herself. She must have known the truth. She never truly feared for me when I scrambled on rock-stacks slick with green slime or waded to meet the crashing breakers breast high. No harm would come to me from the sea. Gwennol was a wise woman.

Yet it was Gorlois, Duke of Cornwall, I called Father, and loved him with all the passion of my eight-year-old heart. He was all the fairy king I ever wanted. Strong, as only a war-leader who clashed with his men every day on the practice-ground could be. He was no king, but battle-chief of the western tribes of Dumnonia. Black-haired as a chough's wing, with the flash of red lips below his moustache. Scarcely a strand of grey in that coarse black hair as I reached up to stroke it, though my two sisters, Elaine and Margawse, were growing marriageable. Only I, of the three, was dark like him, a matter for rejoicing. What did I care if my mother Ygerne called me an ugly little crow? Gorlois was dark and proud. And so he should be. So was I. Look at me, twining my arms round the bound leather of his legs.

'You're going to fight for Uther Pendragon? You're going to lead the warriors of Cornwall to beat the Saxons? Take me too! We'll be fiercer than all the men of Devon and Dorset. The Cornish will be more victorious than the armies of Powys and Gwent put together.'

He threw back his great dark head and his white teeth laughed as he snatched me up on to his horse and hugged me strongly.

'Do you not think I can do all that without you?'

'Of course you can!' I cried at the top of my little voice so that all the war-band should hear me. 'You should be King of Britain, not Uther Pendragon. But you'll need this.'

And I slipped my charm over his head.

Gwennol had never taught me, though she was instructing my eldest sister Elaine. I was a knowing child. I saw that Gwennol might teach

596

me too, whether she would or no. She had a reverence for the sacred things, Gwennol Far-Sight. She could not disguise it. I watched her hands hovering, heard her lips whispering, even when she avoided a holy flower or feather or stone. Playful as a puppy, I skipped out of the reach of her rheumaticky legs, through the gorse-bushes on the cliffs, or over the boulders on the beach, and crouched out of the wind, suddenly still. When she had passed, I would slip back to gather what she had seen and left.

How did I know the patterns to make from my secret store? A sense of rightness. The sacred shapes are there to be discovered, as the petals unfold, as the apple is cut, as the snake lies coiled. The words I sang came to me on the wind. I believed them effective.

Now my garland fell over Gorlois's armour. I grieved to see that the primrose flowers were bruised already by my too-eager hands. Never mind. There were darker, more lasting things in that pendant pouch. I heard the hiss of Gwennol's breath behind me.

'What do you think I am? The May King, to send me to fight with flowers?' Half jovial, half angry, my father blustered. A part of him was afraid to be shamed by a girl. But the hand that grabbed for the holy chain faltered. Gorlois claimed himself a Christian, but the old fears remained. Especially with Gwennol watching.

His arm released me and I slid to the ground. His last kiss was for my lovely mother. They were cantering off, three hundred warriors in a cloud of dust and a storm of cheering. It was a brave show; they could not keep that pace all the way to Winchester to join Uther Pendragon's army. But they would ride the last mile in the same way, with their jewellery jingling.

'What shall I bring you back, my little mermaid?' he shouted to me.

'The head of the Saxon chief to swing from the doorpost!' I shrieked back at him.

They were gone, but not so far I could not see him break my garland with his hand and let it blow away in the sea wind. His blood was up now, fear of the unknown crushed in the thunder of hooves and the feel of leather and metal round him. He thought his manhood was all he needed for this war.

I was a girl. I was not the son he wanted. When he turned his back on me I became nothing.

I spun round too, and felt the wind lash my face with a burst of vicious rain. Then I was running, straight for the high cliffs above Bossiney Cove.

'Stop her! She'll be soaked to the skin,' cried my mother Ygerne, shooing my sisters back under the thatch before the rain could spoil their fine clothes and the embroidered ribbons in their hair.

She always dressed herself and us most beautifully for a day of leavetaking. They said that Ygerne of Cornwall was the loveliest woman in Britain. Curling yellow her hair, as ripe corn when the wind ripples over it, and her fair face touched with pink like the wild rose petals in June. Yet even the richest jewel takes added fire in a silversmith's setting, and the ruby wine glows warmer in a golden cup. She made sure that Gorlois would remember her so. Very potent, my mother's spells of binding. She had others too.

Gwennol could not have caught me. Could not, and would not. She puffed and scolded, but she knew the space I needed. She understood what pertains to healing. She always followed me in my storms of temper, but she seldom interfered. Even then, I believe she feared my untaught power.

That morning my mother did not rely on Gwennol, for all her wisdom. It was Ewa she sent running after me. A black-toothed smelly slave, who caught me in her big wet arms and carried me struggling back.

I lay and wept, with the rain hammering on the walls, a rage beyond reason. I had lost the father I adored, twice over. I had lost his presence and lost his heart. He did not love me. He was my Fairy King, and he had shut me out of his Land of Joy. I patterned sharp thorns and pebbles against him. All day I would not speak or eat.

I woke in the night and the wind was still howling. Summer or not, I could hear the waves drum below the cliffs like the warning of Samain Eve. I was sure they were beating for me.

Thick darkness in the sleeping-hut. A mingled sound of breathing. Elaine and Margawse were asleep. Gwennol had gone. I sensed the emptiness even before I reached for the bed where she should have been guarding us. It was still warm, but untenanted. Wrapping myself in what clothes I could reach, I stole from the door into the damp silver of flying storm.

I was not afraid of the roaming yard dogs. One padded over, sniffed my outstretched hand and licked my bare feet. Beasts always recognise me. I blessed him with touch and word. Then 'Stay,' I commanded. He stood like a grey stone, a stray gold star reflected in his eyes as he gazed after me.

Nimble as a cat, I went over the slippery palisade, dropping on to sodden turf. Cold now, my wet skin taut, toes cramped. I welcomed the pain, accepted it into myself. It had no power to stop me. Gwennol's absence had left the prison door of my childhood open. I could escape from the bitterness of my life, where no one wanted me. It was not the first time my nurse had been missing in darkness, pointing a pathway into mystery for me. But tonight I was not curious about her. I was bound for my own final destination and my beginning. I would rejoin the sea.

Such a noble act could not be done just anywhere. Even when my dark-accustomed eyes showed me the scatter and tumult of the sea, still the last step into the void must not be yet. I paused only to cast stones over the edge and curse my father's name again. For Gorlois's rejected daughter, too short a leap would mock my towering anger. Only the highest and most jagged point was fitting. My mother's blood, if not my father's, was royal.

Westward then, towards the cliffs that faced Tintagel headland. Where else more high and holy, more deep and dangerous than that? I staggered up the slope of Barras Nose to be met by the full force of

the wind and a startled shock. There were lights low on the rocks of
Tintagel Cove that was the heart of this sacred place. On the ledges
of the headland opposite, the convent slept in darkness. Below me,
the beach was astir with a secret life. I had been wrong not to be curious
about Gwennol. My childish fury was forgotten in excitement. Or no,
perhaps these were the sea-folk, mermaids and giants and leviathans,
rising from the waves to avenge me against Gorlois and invade his land.
My kin? Strange that I did not fear them, even at the dead of night,
alone.

The moving lights were gone now. Only a ruddy glow lingered and
played on the walls of the deep cavern that wound right through the
cliff under Tintagel convent. I do not remember that Gwennol had ever
told me, and yet I knew well whose this cave was, though not yet why:
the Hole of Her whose name we never spoke. I crouched and peered
down into the darkness and the hint of flame.

The wind was dying, the sea settling, the tide still rising. I did not
move. I held myself as still and sharp as slate. At last the fire was doused
and in the sudden blackness there came cries that bellowed from that
cavern. I felt my bowels, if not my conscious mind, catch their animality
with an answering bound. The core of my body quickened with a
hungry life. My death-wish was forgotten.

Shaken and strangely joyful, I witnessed shadows lurching from the
cleft, splintering the water, men and women, some still clutching each
other in a drunken stagger. Are these my people? I thought. Have they
come for me? I watched them, frightened, fascinated. The thought of
my death had disturbed me less.

I stole along the cliff to the top of the gully path that led up from
the beach, and waited again. A few boats splashed softly away. Some
white robes glimmered up the zigzag path towards the convent. Other
darker-cloaked figures came my way. I recognised two of their shapes,
even beneath the masks of fox and doe. I stalked Gwennol and my
mother home in the darkness. I dimly understood already why Gorlois
might not be my true father.

# Chapter Six

*If Avallach, Lord of Avalon, is my father, then you might say that Geoffrey of Monmouth was my godfather. No writer before him couples my name with Arthur's. His book:* The Life of Merlin. *The year: 1148, or thereabouts. Before this Geoffrey has written his great History of the Kings of Britain. This is an imaginative chronicle that traces the foundation of Britain back to Trojan heroes. There is plenty about good King Arthur in it, the story of his life and deeds from his conception at Tintagel to his death at Camlann. It starts a whole new literary fashion. It makes no mention of me.*

*But now in this second, more fantastical, volume, the legendary bard Taliesin is swapping stories with the enchanter Merlin.*

*He names me Morgen. I am one of nine excellent sisters who rule by a pleasing set of laws on the Fortunate Isle of Apples.*

*I am the eldest, I am the wisest, I am the healer.*

*I know all the arts. I have taught mathematics and astronomy to my sisters. I am beautiful beyond comparison with mortal women, loveliest of all the nine. I can fly through the air to France or Britain. I can change my shape. I am an eminent physician.*

*We are nine, yet we are three, each triads of ourselves. Geoffrey names us: Morgen, Moronoe, Mazoe, Gliten, Glitonea, Gliton, Thiten, Tyronoe, Thitis, correcting a slip of the scribe's pen, since the only copy that survived lists Thitis twice. Our earliest sources are not wholly trustworthy.*

*The Muses are nine, the Fates are three, the Earth is one. Nine maidens fan the fire for the Otherworld Cauldron of Annwn rimmed with pearls, which Arthur once set out to steal from the Fairy Fortress. Three are the Matronae, the Mothers of Europe. We must not be separated from our sister-selves. To the Greeks we are Kore, Demeter, Hecate. To the Hindus, Parvati, Derga, Kali. We are the Three-in-One. We are the Triple Goddess. Within each separate self we hold a triune being: Maiden, Mother, Crone.*

*We sisters wait with all our centuries of wisdom in our hands where the sea-girt land gives its abundance generously in every season. The earth yields for us grain and grapes without wearying labour, and the woods are sweet with the scent of apples. This is the western paradise of the Isles of the Blest.*

*I, Morgen, wait with all honour ready for the ship that is bringing the dying prince from Camlann. Arthur has fought his last battle. The wound is terrible.*

*His friends have summoned to pilot them the wise Barinthus, an ancient sea-god, messenger of the Otherworld, who also gives directions for Saint Brendan's miraculous voyage. He steers the grieving company over the ocean, guided by the starry heavens.*

*We nine receive great Arthur on that far, fair shore chanting our welcome. Take him up lovingly. Do not keen. With me there need be no grief, no mourning, no despair. My chamber is ready for him. Lay him down gently in my own golden bed.*

*My skilled hands search his honourable wound, while his friends hang on my verdict. My answer is all they hoped, what they trusted, why they have brought him so far to me. This cure will not be swift, it will not be easy, but if Arthur will trust himself to me for long enough, I can heal him. If they will leave him in my hands, he shall be made whole.*

*Other legends add that every year Arthur's wound bleeds afresh. Every year, the hurt must be mended again, with the water of the Tigris or the presence of the Grail.*

*. . . Do not be afraid, Arthur. I am here, I am eternal, there will always be healing . . .*

*Note, in this first story I am not Arthur's sister. I am not mortal. I have no husband.*

*I am dependable when all other help has failed. My plans are wise and effective. I am benevolent to those who trust me.*

*Geoffrey puts this first description of me into the mouth of Taliesin, who says he took Arthur to Avalon himself.*

*Geoffrey of Monmouth is notoriously unreliable.*

# Chapter Seven

And yet I grieved for Gorlois's death with a sharp anger. No one else should have robbed me of his love.

It was Merlyn's doing.

I saw how Gwennol trembled when King Uther's magician was mentioned. I saw the hunger in her eyes. Magic is power. When Uther Pendragon fell in love with my mother at his crown-wearing feast in London, Gorlois fled with her back to Cornwall, leaving the king's guards dead. There was consternation in Bossiney. Of course, Uther would have to come after my parents; we all knew that.

Bossiney rang with the blacksmith's hammer and whined with whetstones. The heavy gate was shut on us, even in the day. I was a prisoner. They would not let me run on the sand or swarm over the rocks or ride my pony after my father in the hunt. We were the hunted now. We cowered in our burrow.

'I'll fight them!' I cried, brandishing old Sulian's big sword. 'You beat Octa and all his Saxons at York. You can beat Uther.'

But my father knocked me aside without looking at me, so that I almost fell off the rampart walk.

I saw how my mother was flushed and nervous, and talking earnestly with Gorlois about his plans for defence. And it came to me slowly, like the knowledge that the tide has turned, that she hoped more from her own power than he did from his. At the age of eight I did not understand fully what our power was, but for the first time I, that had kilted my skirt like a boy and loved nothing better than to ride muddied in the hunt, found myself shortening my steps to match Ygerne's and copying the trail of her green and gold embroidered gown and the swing of the amber beads in her braided hair. I caught Gwennol watching us both knowingly.

And then he came. Not Uther. After days of waiting, three riders only crested the ridge. Two I disregarded. They were like any other men in leather kilts and metal breastplates, flashing their gold chains and tossing their curls, as though we hadn't prouder warriors in Cornwall. I was dragged from the palisade and flung into the women's bower with my mother and sisters, like a prize mare and her fillies when the horse-rustlers are abroad. The door was barred before they strode through the yard to give Uther's ultimatum to Gorlois. 'Return at once to the court, and bring Ygerne with you, or the Pendragon's army will be revenged on you.'

Sword-talk.

The greater threat remained outside our walls. I had seen him from the ramparts. Tall, mockingly strange. A rider on a white mare, dressed in a multitude of coloured rags, gaudier than the feathers of any bird that flew in Cornwall. A man who was not afraid of the sacred, who greeted the things of power like an old friend. I saw him reach out his hand and caress the great oak in Bossiney Meadow. Even at that distance I could have sworn I caught his smile.

While the warriors argued – you could not call it a parley – I climbed on a chest and peered towards the sea. Over the palisade I caught a glimpse of clifftop and a man on a white horse, like a standing stone, staring towards the headland of Tintagel.

And still we women fled to Tintagel, against my father's orders.

I remember the gates of Bossiney swinging wide. I remember Bryvyth the Abbess striding through on her bare feet. She was broad and wholesome as a barn, with two quiet nuns in white gowns attending her.

'You sent for me. Is your business so urgent that your man must come yelling at my gate while we're singing in chapel?' she challenged Gorlois.

'I've reason enough to rouse the whole of Cornwall. Uther wants my wife. When he hears my answer, I shall need a better fortress than this to fight from. There is one place, and one place only, that could hold out against such a war-host: Tintagel. Bryvyth Crook-Staff, for friendship's sake, give it back to me for a stronghold.'

'On your knees, godless man. Shame, that you should even think of it. You gave the headland to us for prayer. You shall not have it back for war.'

'You traitress! Would you take sides with the Pendragon against me?'

'I serve no Lord but Christ, and him I'll fight for with all my strength. There's one way only Gorlois will come to Tintagel – when he brings his lady wife to me for sanctuary. No warrior passes our wall bearing weapons, nor ever shall. If Uther Pendragon comes, it will be Bryvyth Crook-Staff herself will meet him on the bridge. But Gorlois, war-lord of Cornwall, will have to fight his bloody battles somewhere else.'

He would have had her thrown out of the dun in a towering rage, but she grasped her staff and turned on her heel and marched back to her convent over the cliffs like a warrior-queen.

I watched her go, and felt the stirring of another power than Gwennol's.

Bereft of friends, like a wounded stag, my father drew his troops inland to Dimiliock to make his last stand. My mother was terrified when she understood his plan.

'You'd leave me *here*?'

'Three soldiers and a handful of servants. You won't need more. Here's the one place he'll never dream of finding you. He'll think the place is deserted when he hears I've gone. He's High King of Britain. He'll go where there's the strongest fort and the greatest war-host. You know that man's pride.'

'You're mad to leave us to his army! You defied him. His troops will burn every dun, every farm, before they reach Caer Dimiliock. What if some of them come here without the king?'

'I'll leave you a faithful guard. Sulian, Tudy, Coan. They'll know what to do if you're found.'

She gasped, and then she screamed at him, 'And what of your daughters? Would you have your men kill them too?'

I could not speak or move. This was my father, who had tossed me in his arms when I was small, who had lifted me on to his horse and laughed to see me strike my heels against its sides, who had taught me swordplay. My eyes were fastened on Sulian's weapon.

Only a week ago I had hefted that sword and sworn to fight the Pendragon. Did my father want me to bare my neck to this same blade to defend my mother's honour?

'At least,' Ygerne begged, 'send us somewhere safer than this. Let us go to the nuns on Tintagel Island as Bryvyth said. They'd give us sanctuary.'

'There's only one way I'll have you go to Tintagel now,' my father roared. 'If you hear that Gorlois is dead, then shear your hair and take off your gown, and go to Tintagel with my daughters and take your vows as nuns.'

He had serving-women swathed in cloaks to resemble Ygerne and Elaine and Margawse and me, and carried them off in chariots with him and his war-host. He left us alone in Bossiney with a tiny bodyguard. His wits had been bewitched.

Gwennol worked what she could. Margawse, my second sister, came rushing up to me, her red hair, black in the twilight, streaming behind her. She grabbed my hands and whirled me round.

'Morgan! Morgan! I'm to be taken into the circle tonight. I'll be the Maiden.'

'You haven't been maiden since cider-making four years ago.'

She gasped and dropped my hands. 'You little vixen-cub! If your eyes get much sharper they'll cut your nose off.'

I was not initiated. Gwennol feared to wake my power, even then. She made the circle without fire that night, with Ygerne and her waiting-woman Ruan and Elaine and Margawse, newly made wise. I was not summoned, but they could not stop me watching from the darkened hall, though Gwennol scowled and muttered in my direction. Elaine was white and frightened, Margawse hot and eager. And my mother Ygerne? She lifted her face to the east and the shaft of the rising moon. The words of protection slipped from her lips while she dreamed of the way by which Uther must come to her.

In the morning I looked east to the road from London and west to Bryvyth's convent. Which was really the way to power? I made my own childish patterns and hummed over them when Gwennol was out of earshot.

Even so, I was frightened when Uther's army passed us by on the road to Dimiliock, and a stray raiding party broke away from the rest towards Bossiney. We fled up the ladder to the store over the rafters. Gwennol was last, save for that poor boy Keby. None of us missed him at the time. Too late we found he had stayed outside with his axe to fight them off singlehanded.

My nurse's gnarled old hands fumbled on the ladder sides. She hoisted her stiff knees up two steps and could get no further.

'Come on, Gwennol! Quickly!' I screamed at her.

'It's no good, my lover. I can't get up so high.'

I would have scrambled down to pull her with all my little strength, but Sulian had me by the waist and flung me into a corner under the drooping thatch. I lay with my face in cobwebs, hearing the panting of frightened people round me and the rustle of rats.

For a time Gwennol muttered and cursed in the hall below us. Then she fell silent, till the door burst open and the men broke in. For a terrifying long while they searched the hall. They did not see us, crouched on the rafters sheltered by the shadow of Gwennol's spell. But they soon found Gwennol.

I heard her cry out, 'Easy, now! For the love of the Mothers, can't you take it steady?' Then she was screeching without words and there were noises of a man like a bull and others cheering. It lasted a long time. There were eight of them.

When it was over, they looted as much of our home as they could carry and fired the thatch. The moment they had ridden off, we had to scurry down the ladder for our lives. I found Gwennol hanging over the well, retching. Keby's body was beside her. They had cut the boy's throat.

They left Bossiney blazing.

And so, weary and shocked and blackened with soot, we took our tattered dignity to Tintagel. Bryvyth gave us sanctuary. It was the first time I crossed that threshold. I felt the power of the place. I truly believe no warriors could have got across that causeway by force of arms. Hundreds of feet above white-topped breakers to the south and the still, shadowed cove to the north, a neck of rock links the mainland to Tintagel Head. Three men with swords could have kept that gateway. Bryvyth alone with her staff would have been a more formidable foe.

Her generous, honest faith was no defence against a devious sorcerer.

She let them in. Uther, Merlyn, Ulfin. At dead of night, in urgent haste, the names they whispered to the porter at the gate were Gorlois, Jordan, Britael. And so they seemed to be.

Except to Gwennol.

I woke and heard voices in the passageway outside. Ruan's, I recognised. One name brayed in my head like a war-horn. I thought I caught another voice, deeper. Terror entered the room. The door closed and Gwennol leaned against it, breathing fast. I sprang up on my bed.

'What is it? What did she say?'

'Hush, my lover. It's nothing. Go back to sleep.'

'No. Tell me. She said something about Father, didn't she? Is he dead? He is, isn't he? Is that what they've come to say?'

I knew, past comforting. I flew across the chilly floor and buried my face in her skirt, clinging wildly, even though she stroked and comforted me.

'No, my pretty. It's not that. They say your father's alive. He's here. He's come to your mother.'

I felt her shudder.

I was out in the passageway in a moment. Two giant shadows stood either side of a shaft of misty moonlight that slanted so as to leave their faces in darkness. A smaller figure stood in the pale light at my mother's door. Her woman Ruan.

I flew at them. Ruan gave a smothered laugh. Gwennol tried to catch me and clutch me back to her side.

'Hush, my lover. Your father doesn't want you now.'

She could not have held me. But as I fought for the door strong hands, that should have belonged to Britael, my father's boyhood friend, gripped my wrists like a vice. I wrestled with him, scratched and bit. He tried to fling me from him. My little head rang as it hit the wall and my brain rang louder with the voice that should have been Britael's, but never could be.

'Take your claws out of me, you little screech-owl, or by the Hounds of Annwn, I'll put that on you that will bind you stiller than stone from now till morning.'

Oh no, not Britael. The words of power. A man whose strength lay not in swords, though he would bestow swords on others. I had met Merlyn.

I sank my teeth into his hand.

In that instant of agony I heard my mother's cry. That sound is screaming in my ears still.

Then Merlyn laughed in my face, a great shout of triumph. And from inside Ygerne's chamber Uther echoed his shout.

So my brother Arthur was made.

In the morning Bryvyth told me that Uther had killed my father.

# Chapter Eight

*This lusty legend proves too much for the Victorian sensibilities of Alfred Lord Tennyson. In 1859 he completes* The Idylls of the King, *twelve books of poetry chronicling the ideal rule of Arthur. There are sins and failings by many at the court of Camelot, but Arthur is always noble. Tennyson cannot allow his stainless king to be fathered by adulterous trickery. He would rather deny the consistent record of the earliest chronicles. So others will always doctor the evidence they find uncomfortable.*

*True, before Arthur can wed Gwenhvar the poet makes the knight Bedivere repeat to her father a sanitised version of the traditional story. He is careful to have Gorlois slain and Ygerne hastily remarried before Uther beds her. King Uther himself dies childless before Arthur is born. The only part that Merlyn plays is to receive the newborn baby at a secret postern-gate and whisk him away for fear of Uther's rivals.*

*But Tennyson himself has invented a different coming for his sovereign.*

*This second tale is told by the Queen of Orkney and Lot's wife, named here as Bellicent. I, Morgan, do not exist for Tennyson. Bellicent is a daughter of Ygerne by Gorlois, and Arthur's loyal sister.*

*This is her story:*

*The place, Tintagel, still. The time, a night of storm. The witnesses, Merlyn and his master Bleys. They spy a dragon-winged ship, poised upon a wave so high it seems to sail in heaven. From stem to stern its sides are bright with shining people. This vision is gone as soon as seen. The two mages drop to the cove and watch the breakers fall, each mightier than the last. The ninth great wave draws half the deep into itself, and full of voices, all aflame it roars upon them. And in the flame is borne a naked babe to drop at Merlyn's feet, who seizes him and cries, 'The King! Here is an heir for Uther!'*

*Thus Tennyson's Arthur comes to earth even more immaculately than the Christ child. A boy born of no human parent, on either side, heaven-sent for our salvation.*

*Yet even Tennyson makes Merlyn riddle:*

> *'Rain, rain, and sun! a rainbow on the lea!*
> *And truth is this to me, and that to thee;*
> *Sun, rain, and sun! and where is he who knows?*
> *From the great deep to the great deep he goes.'*

# Chapter Nine

I know the truth. I was there.

Certainly there was a baby, born of a woman in the usual way. And very certainly it was a boy.

How could I forget that? The exultant cry that cut through the howling of the south-west gale. A man-child! Victory to Merlyn.

Elaine, Margawse, Morgan, all Gorlois's daughters. And now the Mother's curse had broken and Ygerne was delivered of her first son. Look at Uther Pendragon, dancing a jig with Merlyn. Drunk as lords, that Midwinter night, king and sage. The torches flaming and the wine running. Everybody celebrating. No one as drunk as the High Lord of Britain, as drunk as the High Lord of magic. They had got what they wanted.

That cry screamed in my ears like a hare when the weasel is at her throat. I had heard another cry, uttered in triumph but sounding in my childish heart my father's death-knell.

Those long, hard fingers on my arm. Those steely eyes. A more than physical power that transfixed me and would not let me through my mother's chamber door to where they said my father was.

And then that shout, unbearable. A woman's ecstasy.

Nine months before this cry of triumph.

I was skilled at mathematics, even before I went to the nuns' school. Gwennol, who had nursed Ygerne and then her daughters, had taught me to track the stars and seasons. For a wise woman, that counting has one particular end: the regeneration of life.

On the women's side we knew well who the shape-shifters were who had penetrated Tintagel, even before the Pendragon boasted openly of it. But we could count too how short the days between my mother's husbands. We knew how unpredictable are women's wombs.

Uther boasted of victory. How could this male baby be anything but his? Nine months since the Duke was killed. Now Cornwall had suffered its final defeat. He had got the son that Gorlois could never give Ygerne.

Was Merlyn so confident of his own prowess? Did he never wonder?

Arthur came as their Midwinter baby, the turning of the sun at the darkest time of the year, to light the heart of Britain.

He lit my heart.

Full of resentment, I crept, soaked by the storm outside, into the chamber where my mother lay sleeping. The midwife was drunk on the floor. The baby drowsed in his cradle. And Gwennol was stooping over him, murmuring charms.

I raged at the foolish fondness in her face.

I blamed him then for all our wounds, for my father's loss, for Gwennol's rape, for Keby's throat cut by the well, my old home burned. For Uther's coming. I lashed her in my anger.

'Poor Gwennol! Did you think he would be your baby? Did you think they would give him to you when the wet nurse had finished with him? Were you dreaming of dressing him, and playing with him, and singing him to sleep, as you did with Gorlois's daughters? He's the eldest son of the King of all the Britons. Did you think they would leave him here in Bossiney with you?'

I darted to the cradle.

The baby stirred and opened milk-blue eyes.

I had never held an infant in my arms. I was the youngest daughter. I must have seen other babies but I did not notice them. Nothing prepared me for that soft peach-bloom face that looked up at me so innocently and opened almost in a smile. I had no warning of this fire that leaped in that core of my body discovered only once before. I did not expect to fall in love with my brother.

As Ygerne woke, and reached fearfully for her baby, I snatched him up from his cradle, heedless of her cries and his. I bit my lip till the blood ran and then . . . I nipped his neck, with a tiny precise incision.

He gave one cry, no more. I had wounded myself more deeply than him. I left my kiss upon his neck, meaning our blood to mingle. I marked him for mine. I think it did not sink deep enough to reach his heart.

The child was not left with us long enough for his christening. Uther had planned it for Epiphany, the feast of the wise men's gifts. Merlyn had other schemes.

But the magician disappeared himself the night before Christmas. Merlyn served the high magic to win temporal power. Not for him the feast of the poor child in the manger who would be a crucified king. That is the way of the white-robed Christian saints, who are loved by the poor. It is also the wisdom of women like Gwennol who sanctify the ordinary.

Midwinter too is a time for giving gifts. Merlyn should have remembered that.

The flames leaped on logs to keep back the wild winter day. We three sisters stood around our mother's knee while Uther looked on fondly. Elaine was still fair and virginal, with the soft flesh of childhood not quite melted to maidenly slenderness, though she was promised in marriage to Nentres of Garlot already. Margawse flaunted her unbound hair as fiery as the blood that beat between her thighs and would not let her hungry body rest. And I, Morgan, ugly as a moulting crow, born painfully after long waiting, the third girl, a bitter disappointment to my parents.

What should we give him, this tiny golden brother in Ygerne's lap? I stood and stared at my mother's bright green skirt with its ribbons of daffodil-yellow brocade. They had wrapped him in lambswool and swansdown, so that only his wide blue eyes peeped out at us. But his tiny flesh was born of woman, like mine. Strip away the warm cloth on which he rested, and he had known Ygerne's body beneath. He had travelled down the same red road as myself. Why did one entry into the world bring such anguish, and the other so much joy?

Elaine was pink with self-consciousness. This was a solemn moment. She would cuddle him afterwards. She, who had mothered me when our own mother would not even look at me, loved babies, but she shrank from the messy way by which they are got. She was hesitating on the threshold of womanliness. The ceremonies of adulthood still confused her, yet she was not displeased that everyone was looking at her now, admiring her. Everyone? Were all our household ranged around the hall alike to her, Uther's warriors, Ygerne's waiting-ladies, old councillors, children, serving-maids, male slaves? Did she not, unconfessed even to herself, prize more highly the regard of men? She did not seem to. She was vain enough to boast of rivalry in dress with other young women, as though their opinion was the most important thing to her. But I had seen one man stir her. Uther Pendragon had ways that could set any maid blushing. He made no exception for his step-daughters, even in front of Ygerne.

He had tried his charms on me once. But only once.

What was Elaine holding out to the baby? A stone I had never seen before. A crystal pure as herself. Clear, flawless, cool. His little fist closed round it and at once the jewel became a lively pink, warmed by his hand. She kissed his brow.

'Hold it tight, little brother. Keep it safe. In this small stone there are riches, treasure, corn for your horses, and whatever your heart desires to eat and drink. It can draw precious gems and gold to itself, and perhaps a crown. Prize it above all other friends. It is plenty.'

The baby stared solemnly.

Margawse pushed past her, laughing. She could never be serious. Quick as a leaping flame to take Elaine's place and the centre of the stage. Tossing her hair, that was brighter than all the jewels threaded through it. Knowing the firelight from the great hearth warmed her creamy skin. Eyes rolling round all the men, taking her time, creating an audience, flashing that special spark that seemed to kindle anew for each one of them.

Her hands were nursing a cup, warm copper. She was hugging it to her newly swelling breasts. The metal was doubly inflamed. You could imagine it pliant, melting, cradled there. She held it out now, provocatively, above the baby's face. His large blue eyes swam up to it. His hands were bound in the soft wrappings. He was too young to snatch for it.

Mocking, she waved it. A little liquid splashed him red.

'You will drink deep from this, little man. You will intoxicate all the women of Britain. Queens shall fall to you, and maidens pay you their ruby tribute.'

Then she raised the cup to her lips and sipped from it herself, watching him over the rim with her laughing green eyes. I was curious to know what stained her mouth so crimson.

She kissed the baby full on his yielding lips.

'Wealth and women,' my mother laughed, and rose with the baby guarded in her arms. 'A fortunate child!'

She would not look at me. She never looked at me if she could help it. But every other eye in the room was on me as she turned away. I sensed their shrinking back. They saw the truth about us. Ygerne the Wise. Afraid to take the gift of her third daughter.

I seemed to freeze, a waterfall silenced into icicle. My mother at any rate I was certain of. I was her daughter as well as Elaine and Margawse. This boy was my brother as much as theirs. I could play the fairy queen too.

Ygerne must know, as everyone did, that I had loved Gorlois more passionately than either of my sisters. Did she guess that I had cursed him too? She could not have paled and started from his shade more fearfully than she did now from me.

I dropped my gaze from her averted eyes. I willed my mind upon my little kinsman. How near indeed was this my brother? They do well who say a man's closest bond is to his sister's son rather than to his own child. Only our shared maternity is certain.

Did Uther in his man's pride never doubt? Whose daughter was I? Whose son was this in front of me? Frightened, I clutched the gift I had brought. Suppose I had guessed wrong?

Gwennol's hand pushed me in the back. I stumbled forward, angry at this loss of my rehearsed dignity. My small hand gripped my mother's bright green skirt, detaining her. Ygerne turned, looked down, cold, repelling.

'Let go my dress.'

'I have a gift for the baby.'

'He does not want your present.'

She was too frightened to clothe her rebuke with smiles and pass it off to the court as a mother's pretty scolding. For the first time in my life I discovered a great truth that until now I had used without understanding: that I had power over people. I would not need to wait for my apprenticeship of spoken spells and brewed charms. The Goddess was already present in me. The realisation made me strong and joyful.

I loosed my hand and reached up to the baby in my mother's arms. A moment's pause. I concentrated, and then she lowered him unwillingly. My fingers parted the swansdown. With my left hand I laid my present across his heart. The first little hunting spear that Gorlois had given me. The fine blade stabbed my nine-year-old heart with the recollection of autumn forests, galloping ponies, a laughing man. Farewell to childhood innocence.

'I shall never use this again. I must be a woman now. Take it, and see what you can do with it.'

I kissed the spear, but not the child. I was still not sure of him.

I had armed him with his lance. Would he understand how to use it? But Ygerne shrieked as the weapon touched the baby.

'Unlucky gift of a killing blade! Take that in payment! He owes you no blood!'

She tore a pearl from her hair and threw it at me. The skein was snapped, and all the precious drops slipped from their net and tumbled at my feet, glistening like fallen tears among the rushes. I raised my steady eyes to meet her terrified look.

Uther burst into laughter and even hugged me. He was more than satisfied. His son a gold-giver, a womaniser, a mighty warrior. What could the boy be but another Pendragon? I watched and wondered. One half of this infant was Cornish, that much I knew for certain. Half of myself. But more than that? Was this the last secret child of Gorlois? Was he the foal of Cornwall's Horse, or the spawn of the Head Dragon? And which would draw him more surely into my arms again? I could find no clear sign.

He had the spear now. I must wait till he could use it.

Ygerne was wise. Ygerne must know. But Ygerne would always tell the tale that suited her purpose best.

I pestered Gwennol afterwards. But she scolded and pinched my lips with her calloused fingers.

'Hush, my lover. Do you think my little old bit of magic could have been stronger than great Merlyn's?'

The baby was three weeks old. Epiphany was to be his naming-day, when the Church claimed him for her own and my mother's clan received him. Nectan, the saint, would christen him in our chapel. Druid or not, Merlyn would surely be back for that. This child had been his making, more than Uther's. In this sun-gold baby lay the sorcerer's great hope for power once Uther died. I could imagine how he would take him from their Christian hands, how he would hold the infant in his arms, say over him the words we must. He would look on him keenly, feel the beat of his heart, smell his small sweet breath. Not drunk with joy and wine this time, Merlyn would know if Ygerne had cheated him.

And if she had? Would he ever tell Uther?

'Lucky for him the lad's as fair as a corn-dolly,' I overheard one soldier gibe to another. 'Gorlois was raven-black. Else we might have thought the duke had moulted a feather or two before Dimiliock!' And he stuck his fellow in the ribs so they both doubled up with coarse laughter.

'Ah,' said the other, wiping his eye. 'But her Elaine's as fair as a lily, and the queen says she was Gorlois's daughter.'

'Aye, true enough. But she and Uther are two of a kind. Still, she's a wise woman. If it had been another like that black cat Morgan, she could have changed him with her arts to the right sort.'

'Best not to crack that joke in his lordship's earshot. It would break his dam's heart if she lost her precious pup now.'

I stole, like the black cat they thought I was, softly past.

I was old enough to calculate the moons, young enough not to know that wise women do not lie with their husbands on the eve of battle.

On Epiphany Eve all the court was revelling in the hall, even Ygerne, while in the queen's bower the solitary wet nurse was snoring over a jug of ale. I crept, this time unseen, into the dimly lit chamber and leaned over the cradle of my baby brother. He was a beautiful boy.

Tonight, after Camlann, this beauty is marred with blood and sorrow. On that night too, I looked upon him with the same dread and love.

I feared and hoped what might come to me from my brother. And I feared for him.

I took the baby. Loving and hating him as I had done Gorlois. Cherishing and condemning him as I did my own self. It was January, a night of tempest more terrible by far than that summer storm that had once lured me out on to the cliffs alone. But I felt the same powerful call, to the sea, and above all, to Tintagel.

I longed frantically to carry him westward beyond the sunset to my island that very night, clasped in my arms. I struggled against the gale to Tintagel Cove and fought my way through the waves to stand buffeted by the wind on a high rock. Drenched, I turned to the ocean from which I had come. I lifted one hand. My spirit summoned the ship that would carry us both to the Fortunate Isle of Joy. Beyond all reach of hurt we two would play glad games for ever.

It did not come. The breakers showed no pity. And as I shivered and sneezed, even the vision was snatched away. Behind me, shouts rang louder than the gale. Armed men clattered in haste and anger on to the beach. The Pendragon yelled curses and threats across the angry water. Old Gwennol sang pleas to me, harder to resist. High in the chapel of Tintagel convent, candles pricked. Then Merlyn stretched out his hand and acted.

I felt my being stiffen, body and spirit.

My power could not withstand him. I was only nine years old. I let the baby fall. I watched my brother's small pale face sink beneath the swell, helpless. The ninth wave crashed round my shoulders, stunning me, and carried him to Merlyn's feet. I heard one fierce exultant shout.

'By the power of the old earth and the older moon and the three dark Mothers.

'By the power of the bright face of Ludd and Gwydion and Llew.

'By the power of the Father and his Christ and the Spirit of Wisdom! 'I name you . . . Arthur!'

And they were both gone.

A baby was taken from me. A fifteen-year-old youth, on the first step of manhood, appeared from Merlyn's tutelage with his sword in his hand. After an irretrievable interval of silence, which changed the course of Britain, I made Ygerne affirm this was her son and Uther's.

It is probably true.

# Chapter Ten

*I am the fairy godmother.*

*In the mid-twelfth century, Geoffrey of Monmouth tells the world of Arthur in his* History of the Kings of Britain. *It is a tale of battles, thrones and statecraft. His good fairy surfaces later in the* Life of Merlin. *Within twenty years the Jerseyman Wace has turned the chronicle of Arthur into Norman French with his own robust embellishments. Before the century is out the Anglo-Saxon Layamon has seized upon the tale. In his hand the anti-Saxon hero is changed into, ironically, the quintessential Englishman. You might say the conquest of Celtic Britain is complete. Two chapters in Geoffrey have grown into a swashbuckling saga. Wars, jousts, quests, voyages. Good colourful stuff, a boy's own story.*

*Wace does not mention Morgan. But Layamon knows of Argante.*

*He tells how, as soon as Arthur was born, elves took him. They enchanted the child with magic most strong, they gave him might, to be the best of all knights; they gave him another thing, that he should be a rich king; they gave him a third, that he should live long; they gave the prince virtues most good, so that he was most generous of all men alive. And thus the child thrived.*

*At the end, the wounded Arthur believes that*

*'I will fare to Avalon, to the fairest of all maidens, to Argante the queen, an elf most fair, and she shall make my wounds all sound; make me all whole with healing draughts.'*

*Two women come, and take him in their ship.*

*In Brittany they have guarded an ancient tradition well. We are the Margot-la-fées. Not long since, no woman would bear a child without invoking our help. It is not safe for the baby to start upon the road of life without our fairy blessing.*

*While the mother struggles in labour on bed or birthing-stool, there is work of a different sort being done in the room next-door. Lay the table with the best you have of linen, silver, crockery. Serve up a meal that will not dishonour Otherworld queens. Now, is all ready and fair? If you have not displeased us, we Margots will enter your house.*

*In that other room there is blood and pain. Here is peace and seemliness. The child will be born whole and healthy.*

*And we have brought our gifts.*

*We offer this baby a name, a character, and a destiny.*

*It is more than five hundred years since we first gave our blessings to another hero of the French romances, Ogier the Dane.*

*Six fays come to watch over his birthing and weep when his mother dies. They lean over his cradle and caress the baby. They shower on him their gifts of strength, courage, success, beauty, tender susceptibility, so that he shall surpass all knights.*

*Then Morgan comes last.*

*Oh, yes. Are you remembering* The Sleeping Beauty? *Are you waiting for the story to turn on my wicked fairy's curse?*

*I hate to disappoint you.*

*My gift exceeds all the rest. It is myself I bestow on the baby Ogier. His destiny is that he will never die by the hand of man. After a long, hard-fighting life of glory, he shall come home to me, to my island of Avalon. There, in my welcoming arms, his blessing will be fulfilled. I offer him a never-ending youth and unwearied joys as my lord and love.*

*I keep that promise.*

# Chapter Eleven

For that theft of Arthur, I became Uther's prisoner. He feared the darkness in me, calling it devilry. Darkness is for plotting, grief and love. Men go to war by daylight.

Arthur was gone, and Merlyn with him. Uther had served his purpose. The Pendragon was right to be afraid.

The prison he sent me to was Tintagel convent. That high, hard, windswept roost, almost an island, but for one lofty neck of rock that linked it to the land. Leviathan, with all the ocean before it, caught by its tail. The nuns' lime-washed cells speckled the cliffs like a seagulls' colony, but their songs were sweeter. Within their chapel and their library they enclosed pearls of great price. They clung like limpets to the rock, those white-gowned women. No gales could shake them, nor druid curse dislodge them. When they were swept away and armed men took it for a fort in the end, it was because their own faith faltered.

I was an unwilling heiress of their treasure. Furious, rebellious, appalled to be confined within a space whose circumference barely measured a mile. I know; I walked that tiny plateau time after time, counting each stride, hearing the waves battering the rocks beneath, thinking how short a step I would need to end it.

I could not believe it. I, who had galloped with the hunt through the Forest of Trigg, who had urged my exhausted pony after my father to the uplands of Bodmin Moor, whom Gwennol had allowed to run and climb and dream freely on the sandy shore.

I raced for the farthest outcrop of the headland. I might have dashed myself from that height the very first day.

Someone came after me. The nun they had given me for my foster-mother, Luned. A scared and sallow young woman, more fitted to theology and mathematics than the care of a child. Her hands were rough, her muscles sturdy on her thin bones. She was no aristocrat. My royal status cowed her. The High King's step-daughter sharing her cell! And it was whispered that I was the devil's child.

I balanced, leaning on the wind, and taunted her from the outermost shelf of rock. Beneath me the breakers swung, almost too far away to be heard.

I reached out a wicked hand.

'You are afraid?'

'Of course!' Her flash of anger pleased me. 'Get down.'

'Climb up here. Stand beside me,' I ordered her.

'I cannot. Get down at once.'

'Climb.'

I fixed her with my gaze. Slowly, against all the instincts of her fearful flesh, against all the reasoning of her clever mind, I watched her obey. She could have prayed. She could have yelled for Bryvyth. But she did not. I savoured the taste of sovereignty.

I had no power over my own life. I had lost my freedom. But I had gained my first subject.

I used my power cruelly. I dragged her to the very edge and forced her to look over. She retched her stomach up.

I laughed at her. 'Bryvyth said you were to look after me. That you were to guard me from harm. You couldn't keep a crow from the corn.'

But in that moment of peril, leaning out over the windswept ledge, I had seen a sight that shocked and fascinated me. An older nun, gaunt as a scarecrow, perched on the narrowest foothold of rock on the side of the cliff with her hands raised to heaven in prayer and the ocean before her.

That night, in a cell so close that we could scarcely move without touching each other, Luned undressed me. She had no need to do it. I was nine years old. I had been parted from my nurse Gwennol for the first time. But I was a neat and capable child. I could shift for myself.

Her arms went round me as she lifted my gown. Her cool hands brushed my flesh. Her breath quickened. I knew that I had power over her of another sort.

The Abbess Bryvyth was another matter. I loved her for her strength. I envied her rumbustious faith. When I transgressed, which was often in that first year, she beat me with birch-twigs. Afterwards, she would crush me to her in a hug, scolding and laughing. I believe that in secret she flogged herself for my sins too.

The food was plain, my bed was of bracken in the cell I shared with Luned, my unadorned clothes a cause of mockery to my fellow-pupils for a High Queen's daughter. The hours of prayer and study were long, the work delight.

I learned to write in Latin and Greek, scratched on slabs of slate. In time I came to handle heavy volumes lovingly transcribed from Egypt, Carthage, Rome, Jerusalem. I watched my tutor Rathtyen unroll fragile scrolls and saw how her hands caressed pages even of Hebrew. My fingers traced the compass marks of geometric interlace and spiral. My eyes feasted on the colours and gilt of illuminations.

Geometry, philosophy, theology, the science of calendar and stars. Literature, poetry, rhetoric, disputation. Weaving, embroidery, calligraphy, design and painting. All these the sisters taught me.

In time, I sang the liturgy with them.

There was knowledge at Tintagel that the scholar Rathtyen could not teach me, nor Bryvyth either. But there were those who could and did. In her hunger for wisdom, the far-reaching pilgrimage of the soul, Bryvyth had gathered round her all the keen minds of the west. Among them were the daughters of druids, newly baptised. They found the holy life of the Christian nuns not too dissimilar to their mothers' training. They were noted for herbal lore and astronomy and the breeding of animals. Such knowledge is power. Knowledge is dangerous. It should not be left lying where children can find it.

These women had entered the Church. They had not left the older faith. Christ was their Druid. The Mother was holy.

Gwennol committed me to their care. She came to see me, secretly, rowed in a little coracle round the headland in the mists of dawn.

Luned knew. I wanted her to know. I had stood on the threshold in the pale moonshine of May Eve until she woke, wide-eyed and fearful. I waited, seeking her eyes, not knowing what I hoped. If it had been Bryvyth watching over me, she would have yelled and scolded me back to my bed. If I had tried to run, she would have thrown back the blanket, come after me with huge strides, wrapped me in those powerful arms, marched me back to the cell and barred the door. She would have whipped me. She would have fought with every weapon that her strong love could show her to save my soul.

Luned's voice was high with anxiety. 'Where are you going? Come back to bed.'

I scorned to answer. Where was there for me to go but Tintagel Head? I was a prisoner. If I were found beyond that causeway Uther would have me killed.

And still I waited. She was a clever woman. Could she really not guess?

She came and stood beside me. I took her hand and pulled her round to face the mainland. The lights of Beltaine fires blazed all along the coast and on the hills beyond. Out of the darkness, new life was being made.

'Come, Luned! Come now!'

I started to run towards the fires. I could hear the drums quickening the rhythm of my blood. The pipes were calling to me. Gwennol had kindled those flames as a sign for me.

'No! Come back to bed!' she cried. 'May Eve is not for us. We leave all that behind us when we take our vows as virgins.'

I did not heed her. I do not know what I meant to do. You cannot run far on Tintagel. The cliffs are below you on every side.

Then I stopped, startled. There were muffled voices beneath me on the zigzag path that led down to the cove. Hope streaked across my mind with lightning brilliance. Gwennol had come to me!

'Who is it? Who's there?' I shouted.

'Hush.'

There was a shocked silence from below, and then came a wavering banshee wailing that should have chilled the blood. I saw the flicker of white hurrying down to the beach from the nuns' huts. I guessed the truth and burst out laughing.

Very early next day, I was abroad again. I watched a coracle slipping out of the cove into the misty dawn of May Morning. A close-cloaked figure sat crouched in the stern. I did not need to see beneath the hood to know who she would be. Solon rowed it, my father's old slave whom I had known since babyhood, a man weathered and silent as a storm-struck oak-tree. He was wise too.

I was standing forlorn on Tintagel's high meadow. In all the island

I had found no may-blossom to greet the summer. As I watched the boat, even at that distance I read the hunger in Gwennol's look as she turned her hooded head up to search for me. I was her baby, the last Ygerne would ever give her. Little Arthur was gone. He would never be hers to hold. She would not let the nuns have me entirely.

I raised my hand to her. I doubted her eyes could see that far.

Luned came searching for me. I expected a scolding, but to my surprise she crowned me with summer flowers. Her hands were shy and awkward arranging them in my tangled hair.

I smiled for her. 'Thank you, Luned. You have crowned me your queen.'

She tried to fight a little when she saw where I was leading her. 'In the name of the Father and the Son and the Holy Wisdom, do not go there!'

Yet she came after me, down the steep and stony track that wound between huts where nuns still slept. She hated heights. She feared the sea. For all her sharp mind she was physically inept. My chest was aching, like a waterskin overfilled with tears. Luned could not stop me. I might do anything I wanted. She was my foster-mother. My sins were her failure. To protect her own pride, she would not report them to Bryvyth.

I lured her, unwilling, over the rocks to the great shelf of stone alongside deep water where ships could moor. A small fire was burning, its flames beginning to pale in the growing light. Gwennol had left a basket beside it. Under the dock leaves my eager fingers discovered two fish and a handful of herbs. Hidden beneath the last leaves was a sprig of may-blossom. A harmless-seeming gift. But for me, as I snatched the scented flowers to my face, that May Day was the first of many years of lessons in the way of wisdom.

I forced Luned to feed the fire. In vain she protested that the mist was lifting, that day was near, that the chapel bell would soon be calling us to prayer. I made her help me cook the fish and eat it. All it needed was a coaxing smile. The handbell rang out above our heads. The smell of frying fish betrayed us. We were both thrashed. Luned's penance was heavier than mine.

I trod the left-hand path. Nuns smiled at me and gave the sign. I sat on their thresholds, followed them observantly through the shippens, chanted a hundred times a day the charms they sang me. Bryvyth never saw. Her vision, and Rathtyen's, was too high, too wide, too full of sunlight. She was not curious enough about the darkness.

Luned did not dare to betray me. She told no one of Gwennol's visits. I was her charge, a heavy responsibility. Luned was ambitious. Rathtyen, who should have been Bryvyth's heir, was beginning to waste with a sickness that turned her face grey and racked her with pain. The librarian Cigfa was known for her skill with the pen and her scholarship, but Luned, for all her youth, was growing in importance to rival her. She had a head for mathematics above any other nun. She taught me sometimes, but for the most part she was busy ordering the provisions and trade of the convent and overseeing the outlying farms.

We had a reputation. Ships came to our little quay in the cove from as far as Phoenicia and Cyprus. Wealth of tin and corn and fine textiles passed through Luned's hands. She paid for manuscripts and wine and metalwork. Bryvyth trusted her.

Yet I began to find a comfort in the convent's order. The dark-eyed saints painted in splendour on the chapel walls looked down at me with compassion. I felt Christ's wounds more sharply than my own. I loved the chanting.

My childish wild rebellion slowly froze. I had almost lost hope of change. As long as Uther lived I should not win my freedom. I saw my classmates leave, blushing and self-important, to be married to husbands their fathers had chosen for them. I passed the threshold of womanhood, recognising with pride and awe the signs in my body Gwennol had taught me to watch for. Luned had never spoken of such things.

Then Bryvyth sent to Uther, far away in Winchester. She told him I was a woman grown, and no schoolgirl now. Three horsemen came with his answer. I saw the manes of their mounts stream in the wind and their hooves send divots flying from the turf. They spoke of freedom. I ran to meet it.

Luned panted after me. For once she physically restrained me.

'No, Morgan. Wait! Don't you see?'

I tugged and struggled, careless if I was hurting her. I thought she was trying to hold me back because she wanted me with a love more selfish than Bryvyth's. I had tried her sorely. I was endangering her ambition and her soul. Yet still she would not have me leave Tintagel.

We saw the men come out of the guesthouse and Bryvyth with them. She was folding her staff close to her chest, as if to hold herself from striking them with it. They sprang to their horses and rode away. They had brought no spare mount.

With despair I watched them go, from the guesthouse where Uther had come to seize my mother. I saw I should never be free of the sight of it now. Bryvyth summoned me with her. I screamed then, and beat my head on the stones of that prison. I made for the high headland where I had run that very first day. I flung myself weeping on to the flat, bare rock.

A cold hard hand descended on my head. Piala had found me. The hermit who fasted and prayed on the outermost gale-swept ledge. She uttered one word: 'Sister!' The touch was chastely removed. Piala spoke but seldom to anyone.

That day she sat beside me, silent for hours except when the chapel bell chimed thinly and she rasped the words of our communal prayer. She made no attempt to offer other comfort. I learned from her endurance. Later, I witnessed, though I could not share, her ecstasy.

Soon after that day, Bryvyth called me to her, sitting in the sunshine outside her cell.

'You are sixteen now, girl. Womanhood was late coming to you. You will not be free or married while Uther lives. You must make a life for yourself. You are a clever girl. If you took the veil with us you would soon become a great scholar.'

I met her gaze steadily.

'That is not why you want me to take my vows. The only true reason for becoming a nun is the love of Christ.'

She laughed with delight and hugged me. 'I knew I couldn't fool you! You go straight to the heart of the matter every time. Think about it, Morgan. You've had a bitter coming. But if you were to surrender yourself to Christ in Tintagel willingly, it could turn to joy you've never dreamed of.'

I almost did it. I humbled myself for weeks of preparation. At the Feast of All Saints I would take the white veil. I walked to my solitary vigil in the convent chapel on Samain Eve.

Samain. Did some deeper layer of Bryvyth's mind suspect? Why else should she choose that most dangerous, spirit-filled night of the year to try me, when even Christian souls stay safe indoors and jest uneasily around the fire? All pagan fires are out. This is the night of darkness, when the barrier between the Otherworld and us is down. Why must she make me kneel alone through those hours of terror for my final test? Did she need so much to be sure of me?

For a while she prostrated herself on the floor beside me. Then she kissed me, and said a blessing over me, and left the chapel. She did not leave me without light. Candles glowed all around me, making shadows softly furred as moleskin, out of which the faces of Saint Anne and the Holy Marys watched me tenderly. An oil lamp burned on the altar below the Christ Pantocrator with his fingers raised to bless me.

I should have been safe.

Do not think I am the Devil's child. In our theology there is no Devil but the fiend in each one of us. When with my nails splitting I scored the faces of the painted saints, when with stung fingers I pinched out the candle flames, when with a breaking heart I overturned the cross, I was not striking out in blind defiance. I did not attack the Christ to desecrate his name. I loved that bleeding Lord. He bore my wounds.

But I was embracing darkness. I was crying out to the children of light: 'Why do you deny the other half of creation? The un-male, the un-virgin, the Great Mother. Can you not see what you are doing to us? God did not tear the universe in two, to set the right at war against the left. The kingdom of heaven is here, in the sanctified earth as well as the starry heavens, in the blood and the seed and the springing growth. She conceived us in wholeness. She did not give birth to a false dichotomy of Either/Or. Her ancient wisdom embraces Both/And. Let us weep together over our wounds. Let us be joined.'

I fled to the kitchen, and put out the fire there too. We must not be afraid of the dark. We must make it holy also.

No, I deceive myself. All this I understood much later. Just then I raged against my loss of freedom. I had been hurt, I wanted to hurt back. I would wound even those I loved.

There, by the fireless hearth of the kitchen, Luned found me. She must have seen the sudden darkness in the chapel. That night, at least,

621

she showed a kind of courage, to venture out of doors on Samain Night searching for me through her terror.

I had made my decision, on the cold chapel floor in those long night hours. All this time, unknown to Bryvyth, I had been undergoing another preparation. Samain is holy to the Wise.

There is a hole under the heart of Tintagel, as though a sea-serpent had bored its way from the cove to the open sea. It is not quite straight. At its beginning you cannot look forward and see the sky clear at the other end. You must enter in, and trust yourself to the shadows, under the island's enormity of stone. You must stumble on, past the rose and the green and the black dripping rock, to where the passage turns and the pure light flashes and the sea-pools greet you on another shore. You must choose your time carefully. High tide covers both entrances.

The nuns were forbidden it. They never spoke its name.

No human act can make such places sacred. Their fascination is already present in their creation, calling to us in the shape of living stone. If we are wise, we respond to their leading.

Gwennol came there, and others with her, like insects creeping along the burrow of the snake. Nuns from high Tintagel convent, wise women from Bossiney, some men. That Samain Night for the first time I went to meet them in that cave, leaving my gown and shift upon the rocks.

Luned struggled to hold me back, shocked and terrified. She called me defiant, angry, evil. And so, in part, I was. Yet I went loving too. I ached for wholeness. She never knew my heart. My virgin body feared what must be done. My scholar's soul wept for the life it was losing. But most of all, I dreaded that the old faith I was fleeing to might prove only a different side in the same war.

That first time of my offering myself, in the Mothers' Hole, there was darkness and cold, and then a sudden flaming warmth. Flesh surrounded me from which I shrank in revulsion, for all my resolution, and then came pain. The waters rose and met. All fire was quenched. We struggled to regain the shore and our separate selves. There was no ecstasy, only a hard commitment of the will.

I have done better since.

I have tried to keep the balance. I have sought to heal our wound. It has not been easy.

Luned had followed me, unprepared, too scared to turn back alone. She got a baby from that night. They cast her out of Tintagel.

The full truth of what we had done was not revealed till later. Still, I was punished cruelly for my desecration that night. I bore it gladly. I knew by the strength of her anger how much Bryvyth cared. I had hurt her as deeply now as Uther had wounded me.

She banished me to the farthest pinnacle of the headland for a month. I was not left alone, of course. There was the hermit, Piala, roosting in her seaward-facing cleft of the cliff. A gaunt, grave woman. She spoke so little that the words grated strangely in her gravelled throat. Yet she could sing with a wild haunting cry like a buzzard's scream. I listened to psalms and litanies flung across the wind to the endless ocean

622

as she stood with arms upraised, gown tugging like a banner, face lit with the western light.

And she was wise, wise in her silence, wise in her rarely falling word, wise in the even rarer touch of her dry, cold hand. She understood my yearning for a spirit greater than the body's frailty. She could not have known the wound I had submitted to. It would have horrified her. Yet, in the month I spent with her, she healed it.

There are those who say that Tintagel means the 'Stronghold of the Constriction'. Others hold that it is the 'Place Where Two Waters Meet'.

I have known both truths.

# Chapter Twelve

*I am the maiden from the sea.*

*Geoffrey of Monmouth called me Morgen, 'Sea-Born'. Waves beat around my traditional dwelling-places: the Isle of Avalon, Tintagel, Sicily.*

*Where did I surface from?*

*The Irish know a mermaid, Muirgen.* In The Destruction of Eochaid *she is a prisoner. Her tale is tragedy and loss.*

*Once upon a time, in the days of King Eochaid of Ulster, an enchanted well overflows its banks. The flood pours out unstoppably. The terrible inundation sweeps away palace and people, all the sweet harps and the running horses, the courtiers and slaves. It drowns the familiar farms and forests of Ulster beneath a huge sea. Only two creatures escape in the whole country, Eochaid's shape-shifting daughter Liban and her pet dog.*

*For a year they survive in a chamber underwater. When they emerge, there is nothing for those two to see anywhere but a vast loneliness of empty water.*

*Well, she is wise. Since this is the only world left to them, Liban turns herself into a salmon below the waist and makes her dog an otter.*

*Three hundred years the pair of them swim the watery waste, without parents, without companions, without clan.*

*At last the waters drop and form Lough Neagh. The hills rise green again around it and life returns to its shores.*

*Ireland has changed. The Christians have come.*

*Now here's Bevan mac Imle, a monk, sent to Rome by Saint Comgall of Bangor on a mission to Pope Gregory. The pilgrim sailor comes winging over Lough Neagh and hears rising out of the depths a chant like angels.*

*When Perceval, on the Quest of the Holy Grail, reaches the destined Castle and sees the sacred vessel, he fails, out of politeness, to ask the correct question. Because of that, the Maimed King is not healed.*

*Bevan is no Perceval. With the proper curiosity of the scholar, he enquires: 'What can be making such music?'*

*Is this the question that can heal her sorrow?*

*After three hundred years, the fishy princess falls in love at first sight with the holy man. Liban parts the waves to reveal herself and tells her story. Then she bids him keep tryst with her in a year and a day at the lake isle of Ollorba.*

*We shall never know what joys she has prepared for him in her own sphere.*

*On the appointed day men sail across the lake to the island with nets. They catch her. Fergus is the fisherman who hauls the mermaid into his boat.*

*Her faithful dog-otter is left whining behind.*

*Crowds stand on the beach to gape when they bring her ashore. She is a marvel to look at: the face and body of the loveliest of maidens from the waist up, the powerful scaled tail of a salmon below.*

*To be even half a fish disqualifies her from humanity. She is clearly out of her element. They confine her in a vessel of water. The curious flock to stare at her.*

*A freak is a valuable commodity. Three men argue over the ownership of Liban: the monk Bevan who found her, Fergus the fisherman who caught her and Saint Comgall of Bangor himself on behalf of the abbey.*

*They decide that Heaven must settle the matter. At Bangor, the rule is already a perpetual fast, but they make it stricter yet. Strong prayers are made. A revelation is granted.*

*This is their answer: the mermaid to be laid in a chariot yoked to two stags, and then the beasts to be let free to carry her where they will. The wild deer leap away and carry her over hill, through glen, across forest and meadow, until they come to a halt at last in the town of Tec-da-Beoc. The people come running out to see the wonder. The clergy take charge.*

*In Liban, two worlds are caught in a single person. It must not be allowed to continue. She cannot be both magic salmon and mortal woman. She must declare herself either one or the other.*

*They offer her the choice: to be baptised and shortly depart to heaven as a proper Christian, or to live on for another three hundred years in the way of magic.*

*Christian monks wrote down this story. They say – well, wouldn't you expect them to? – that she chooses to end it there and then and do the decent thing. And after all, it can hardly be said that any of them have given her cause to want to stay among them. Saint Comgall himself baptises her. He names her Muirgen, 'Sea-Born'. She dies a holy death soon after.*

*From then on, the people of Tec-da-Beoc worship Liban Muirgen as their own particular saint.*

*Muirgen's true story will have been older still, before it was edited by the Church to render it suitable for a Christian audience. Who can say now who was the human sailor whom Liban charmed in the first telling of it? Or what taboo his fairy lover put on him, which he broke, to make the wild stags gallop her away from him? Or whether in those watery depths Muirgen is singing still?*

*In this story Muirgen is a victim, not the wise ruler of her own island. A man carries her away in a boat, and not she him. You need not waste your pity. This is not how it was.*

# Chapter Thirteen

I was glad when they told me Uther Pendragon was dead. Do not mistake me. By then I cared nothing for the man himself, one way or the other. It was ten years since I had taken his baby son to the sea, only to watch helpless as Merlyn snatched Arthur away from all of us. No, I danced for joy on the sea-pinks of the cliff because soon I would be free at last.

Mark was my kinsman, Gorlois's cousin. The same pride, the same interest of clan-blood united us. He must avenge my shame.

He summoned me to Bossiney.

You cannot know how much I lived in that short chariot-ride that took me from Tintagel convent to the Duke's hall. I would rather have ridden horseback and astride, but instead I had the Abbess Bryvyth sitting beside me as chaperone. Left to herself, she would have stridden the way barefoot with her crooked staff in her hand, proclaiming her poverty with pride. But, big brawny woman though she was, she knew when to play the part of the high lady. Bryvyth had been Gorlois's friend, and I was Gorlois's daughter, riding to reclaim her right, a princess too, by my mother the High Queen Ygerne. Bryvyth was stateswoman as well as abbess. She understood secular symbols as well as the sacred. She knew what belonged to the wounded dignity of my family. And so, this chariot.

So short a road, and half a lifetime of living to catch up. I had forgotten nine-tenths of what I had been denied on the sea-washed rock of Tintagel. Dogs, eager, warm-coated, noisy, casually fouling the street. The small children of peasants, dirty, playful, self-centredly absorbed in their tiny worlds, startled into wide-eyed shock and excitement as our wheels were almost upon them. Woods bright above with the yellow-green scalloped leaves of oak-trees, secret with moss beneath. A freshwater stream. The curious stares of ordinary men and women.

I had lived ten years in that holy fortress. A dizzying neck of rock, a bank and ditch, a stout gate and a porter's lodge, had separated me from the common world. I felt exposed, with all my nerves laid raw. Yet underneath the trepidation I burned with excitement. I was coming back to my world, my inheritance.

Bossiney now. A shock. Uther's Bossiney. Curious how I always remembered it the way it was in my father's time, before it burned.

I made myself cross that hall I had left defiantly at nine years old. As then, I bore myself high-headed, queenly. My heart was thrilling at the sight of my dark-browed cousin. He was so like my father. I held out my hands to him in a cool greeting. My face I kept still. Inside was triumph, festival. I seemed to hear all the sweet birds of Rhiannon singing for me, glad horses neighing, the bells of Cornwall's saints sounding. This was my feast-day!

I did not lower myself to plead for my release. It was unnecessary. Mark was my kinsman. My equal in pride, in blood-tie with the land of Cornwall, in ambition. He pierced beneath the ice I had armoured myself with. He saw through my steady gaze into my leaping heart. He was shrewd enough to calculate the meaning of my eagerness even before I did.

The Pendragon was dead, and Britain was washing apart in fragments. Dumnonia was splitting into east and west. It was not enough for Mark to be war-leader, Duke of Cornwall, as my father had been proud to style himself. Soon he would proclaim himself King west of the Tamar.

And I was Gorlois's last daughter, unmarried, and still in Cornwall. Bossiney had been my father's dun. Tintagel was Gorlois's own gift to the nuns. My sisters had realms of their own now. Elaine ruled with King Nentres in Garlot, the distant deep heartland of Britain, and Margawse was further off still with King Lot in storm-wracked Lothian. Only I was left in the west, a full woman now, with all my father's authority in my eyes, and something more that Mark had not – the royal blood of my mother Ygerne in my veins.

I thought I had found an ally. He saw a rival. Mark was no fool. Those who whisper he wore ass's ears slander him. He was suspicious of claimants to his land and his wife. He was right. All this my mind allows him.

But not my heart. I cannot forgive the avidity of his stretched smile, nor the dark peat-fire of satisfaction that burned in his eyes, nor the power over my life he so clearly felt and enjoyed when he spoke my sentence.

'Pendragon was no fool to keep you close. Take her back to Tintagel and set a watch on the island. See my cousin gets no visitors. Have her shown to you every seventh day.'

Darkness smothered my soul like an eclipse of the rising sun, a day that never dawned. All creation should have been appalled at it. I opened my mouth and thought I screamed. Yet the silence of centuries of solitude seemed to dull the air as though his words had deafened me. I thought a multitude of gulls rose clamouring from the rocks and beat about my head. But no blood flowed, no feathers fell, I heard no sound. They must have taken me away. I remember nothing of the journey back. I was blind to the new-found world he had robbed me of.

Since then I have pitied Mark. We have both been unjustly maligned, I for revealing Gwenhyvar's faithlessness to my brother Arthur, he for accusing his wife Essyllt and his nephew Trystan. We have worked together to uncover their treachery. But that night I cursed him, weeping.

It was Gwennol saved me. She bought my liberty at a terrible price. That little, earthy, ageing woman who had nursed Ygerne and me. A witch clever enough to interest Merlin once. Did she do it for love of her last baby? Or was she the Wise Crone moving her pieces on the

627

sacred board-game? Did she sacrifice the castle of Tintagel to win the freedom of the queen?

As soon as he saw it, Mark coveted Tintagel for a stronghold. What man has not? That impregnable fortress, cliff-girt, with only a single causeway to the land. Gorlois knew more than he did of its old reputation. He feared it so much he gave it to the keeping of the holy women.

Gwennol surrendered Tintagel to Mark as the price of my release. She betrayed the nuns. There were many who had both trodden the chaste discipline of Christ above, striving for glory beyond the stars, and also danced to the hot life-giving rhythm of the Mothers beneath, in the dark where the waters meet. Some followed the drums for fear, some went to find their freedom. Others made a mockery of one and used it for a cloak to cover the other. That is not how I acted. I would have sought the hard joining of our hands across the battle-line; the meeting of truthful eyes, even in anger; the dialogue. The same hands created us. The same heart calls us to her. We need both Father and Mother. In many bodily acts and many languages, souls turn to worship the one light. Some also bless the dark.

I never deceived Bryvyth, though certain of my actions I found it prudent to keep secret from her. If she had discovered this, I would not have denied it. She knew what I held true, and why I would not take her veil. I believe she loved me more for that but never ceased to pray my heart would change. But others she trusted counterfeited.

Gwennol revealed it all to Mark. Like a clear moon pitilessly rising, she let the light fall fully on Tintagel Cove. She savoured her revenge on Bryvyth for setting the cross on the top of the holy island. She made the abbess witness the betrayal of the sanctuary they both loved. I was not there to grieve for them.

First, Mark demanded that Bryvyth surrender the island to him. Bryvyth refused him roundly.

Then Gwennol beckoned her witness, who was hiding her face from Bryvyth at the back of the crowd.

It was Luned she forced to stumble forward and confess the truth publicly. Poor learned, timorous, ambitious Luned, robbed of both veil and baby. She was Gwennol's pupil now. I had sent her to Bossiney. I found her useful later.

Now she was pushed out, shaking, to stand before Mark and his court. There were a number of the wise among both high and low at Bossiney. She must have been very afraid. With Mark's relentless eye fixed on her, she revealed everything. The cave, the masks, the fire, the blood. Her baby.

When the abbess learned of the doubled truth of her beloved Tintagel, her heart broke. She rounded on Luned, with dry-eyed fury.

'Curse you! Curse you, that did not tell me this at the very first. Curse you, that you have spoken of it at all.'

But what better witness could Gwennol have chosen to uncover the dragon-pool under Tintagel's foundations? The convent collapsed. The firm faith of its nuns in Christ had rotted from the core and now the faith of the people in those holy women crumbled.

The nuns that had stayed true to the high ideals of Bryvyth left, singing a bitter litany of exile. Bryvyth went last, stooping under the weight of the cross. The wise jeered at her, as they had mocked when she came.

Difficult, that leavetaking. Bryvyth had reason to rue my coming.

I was left there, by my wish, alone. I stood on the highest point, beside the old standing stone carved now with the signs of Christ. I watched Mark ride in across the causeway with his young warriors. As their hooves touched the island, the horses broke into a gallop. The men were yelling in triumph. Tintagel was theirs. Mark drew rein in front of me, while they circled us. He saluted me mockingly.

'Cousin, I keep my word. What are you waiting for? You are free to go.'

As I rode across the causeway with my escort, I stared with aching heart after the bowed back of Bryvyth going south. Then I turned to find Gwennol.

She never saw my freedom. The Mothers took their revenge. The instant Mark's men touched the island, the old woman was struck senseless to the earth. I leaped from my mare and ran to cradle her in my arms, as long ago she had held me. When she opened her eyes again, she was blind.

Mark has had no joy of Tintagel. He should have feared the power of the Mothers, as Gorlois did. Essyllt betrayed his marriage-bed there, with her lover Trystan.

Still, his ambition had triumphed. I could not remain in Cornwall now Mark wished to be king. We were too alike. Our thoughts matched too well. And the Cornish people loved me. I was Gorlois's daughter returned. I was the romantic prisoner freed. I had come back to them transformed, beautiful and wise as Ygerne.

He got me a husband rapidly. A kinglet, of course, because we were of the same blood and I must not demean him. A Northerner, to send me far away from Cornwall. A Christian, to keep my ancient powers in check.

Urien of Rheged, fourteen years old, just coming to manhood that May. I had already been a full-grown woman for five years.

I rode north with one thought in my head: '*Somewhere in Britain my brother Arthur is alive, and Merlyn is holding him.*'

# Chapter Fourteen

*I am the Washer at the Ford of Barking.*

*In an old Welsh legend, all the hounds for miles around used to gather at night beside that mysterious ford and bark to wake the dead. There was no one brave enough to go down and find the reason, until Urien Rheged came. What he found at the river's edge was a woman washing.*

At the dead of night I had set the dogs howling and raging to chill the heart. If you are a Christian you would call them the Hounds of Hell. Brave, warlike men glanced in the dark towards the shuttered windows and feigned deafness, sleep, nightmare. I was that nightmare.

In the darkness a young man was awake and dressed. A boy on the threshold of the warrior's way. He girded on a weapon of steel, new-made for this night and all his fights to follow by the last of a long line of master smiths to his family. Teilo was a Smith of the old magic who knew how to temper sword and spirit. The lad bore a weapon of flesh too. His mothers had formed it in the womb, both sheath and shaft. He was Urien of Rheged, the boy-king, fatherless now. He came twice armed and doubly virgin to the eve of manhood.

Come, Urien, by the howling of my dogs I summon you. Come, Rheged, your father's war-band watches you knowingly. Come, boy, down the dark wet path that leads from the curled womb of childhood into the world that awaits us all. Your mother's pain expels you. You are slipping from her, terrified, alone.

He had no comfort on this road, of horse or escort. Not all the spells of druids or prayers of saints were made to keep him from this meeting. This was our purpose. Tonight he must cross the threshold. Even his Christian mother prayed for his courage, not his safety.

His steps rang on the road, crunched on the shingle, came to the water's edge, a thought unwillingly. I murmured a word. My hounds whimpered and were still.

The water divided us. I knelt on a stone, insistently washing the nameless weave of obscurity in the cold shock of the stream. I lifted and wrenched. Starlight, death, fame dripped from my hands.

He stood at the brink. Only a little tremble in his voice as he called across.

'Who are you . . . Lady?'

'It is for you to name me, Urien son of Cynvarch.'

'What must I do?'

'What your father did before you, Urien Rheged.'

He splashed across the shallows, the longest passage of his life in those short steps. His shadow fell across me where I lifted my head.

'Show me your face, then.' His breath indrawn fought the reluctant words.

'It is for you to uncover me.'

I stood taller than him now, this lad of fourteen years. Nine unbound tresses clad me from crown to waist. His hands were dry, warm even now. The hair brushed back across my shoulders.

The moon was young, and I was old. Just enough light to show him wrinkles, blackened hairy chin, jutting eyebrows, warts on nose. I brought him the foretaste of reality. I offered no promise for myself or for him. He must take me as I am.

They had bred him well. His hand found mine. Only a second and his hold was firm. The hounds were nudging round our legs. They were herding us towards an opening in the hollow hill. His grip was tighter now on mine as he left the last familiarity of the sky.

Darkness and silence now, beyond the moon's gaze, the way found only by the reaching foot. A passage down into the earth. He had lost one mother, he must enter another. I slipped his hand and moved ahead. He could not feel me now.

They had prepared the entry well. Invisible horrors assaulted him on every side. Shrieks echoed round. Lights leaped on fiery eyes and were instantly smothered. The blackness was more awful now that he had glimpsed something of what it covered.

He could have turned back. How much of this had he been taught, how much did he guess, what did he believe, this Christian child of holy Brychan's daughter? I heard his stifled cry, the swift slap of his boot-soles on the rock. He was following me still. Well, the lad was determined.

Halt here. A huge and hollow hall, in total darkness. We were all hushed, to know what he would do.

Nothing had prepared him for this. I sensed a child's uncertainty. A hand groping and falling back. I was out of reach. Was he meant to act or wait? I must not help him. Leave him awhile to the stillness of his senses. Nothing to see, nothing to hear, nothing to feel, nothing to know.

Presently I heard prayers whispering from his lips. The name of Christ. Young Urien wanted to be a man and a king. He would undergo the rites they set him. He would meet our challenge. But he would never be truly ours. Still, let it be.

We were coming to the unveiling of the mysteries.

The lights began to sparkle, dazzling his astonished eyes. Illumination spread on ranks of men and women, robed, some masked. It flared on rock walls painted with mythical truths. It reached towards the soaring cavern roof too vast to catch the light. Some secrets must always remain covered in darkness. Urien blinked and staggered, as he adjusted his senses. He had not expected to find himself the centre of such a magnificent company. Teeth grinned at him from familiar mouths but the eyes were masked and watchful. Do not distract him. Let him not miss what follows in the haze of scented smoke from pinewood torches. He was already dazed with wonder and faint with fasting.

631

Behind his back I was preparing myself.

And now at the far end of the cavern, the curtains parted. Once, only once for him tonight, the youth carried the bleeding spear across that floor. Once, now, the maiden's hands were bearing the brimming grail of life past Urien's eyes. Would he understand?

'Boy! Speak now what is in your heart.'

Was it a hound or a man that barked at him? Urien son of Cynvarch was boy-king of Rheged, with all his life stretched out before him. He would not leave here without the manhood he had come to get. He asked his question.

'What do this spear and the vessel signify?'

A sigh of satisfaction from the ring of watchers.

'She is waiting for the wound that will make her whole.'

Following their pointing hands the boy turned. I was enthroned on a golden bed, set about its edge with letters of precious stone and hung with rich tapestries. My head was veiled now in white. Apart from that, I did not seem in this moment to be any other than I was when he met me washing at the ford.

And so he came slowly to my bed. His breath quickened and caught as I drew him down. Before them all, he mated with the moon-scarred Crone. The cavern thundered with their shouts of triumph. And when he put back my veil, still shaken, he found neither the Crone nor a blushing Maiden. I had become for him full-breasted Woman, beautiful beyond all expectation, holding out arms of love to welcome him. For Urien the Man I lay revealed as Queen, Wife, Land, Sovereignty, Joy. I had wetted his weapon. The earth was made whole.

*Then Urien seized hold of the woman and had his will of her.*

*She said, 'The blessing of God on the feet that brought you here.'*

*'Why?' he asked.*

*'Because it was my fate to wash here until I should conceive a son by a Christian. And I am the daughter of the King of the Otherworld, the land of Annwn. Come you here at the end of the year and you will get the child.'*

And so, on a May morning, young King Urien of Rheged came to his wedding-day in Carlisle. Scarcely a week new-made as warrior and man, he waited on the steps of the church in his feast-day clothes. Around him stood the bishop, his powerful cousin King Gwendoleu, chieftains, nobles, men of the north. His kin had picked him a stranger for a bride from faraway Cornwall, once Uther Pendragon's stepdaughter, but now a grown woman with few friends. They had chosen me as a princess who would have no power to lend him if he should grow ambitious.

Well, we would see.

As I rode under the Roman gateway, he would have seen a bride in virginal white, with a chaplet of flowers on her head, sitting a white mare astride. I, Morgan of Cornwall, scorned the stiff tissue of royalty, and the gold and the bright colours of an earthly queen. Today I wore May-Maiden white, an older authority. I had braided two ribbons in my hair, of green and red, for vegetation and blood.

There was a ripple of anger through the reception-party, as when the wind shakes the embroidered curtains across a door. They thought I mocked the Church and the northern aristocracy with such a simple gown. Indeed, I challenged both.

Startled but courteously-bred, Urien took a step forward to help his bride from her horse. A serious boy, who did not disgrace his own gorgeous wedding-garment. He raised his youth's eyes to see my unveiled face. The cry that broke from him then shocked the crowded street.

It was not what they thought, when I parted my unbound hair and smiled winningly down at him through nine black tresses. True, May-Maiden though I seemed, I was years older than he was, and proudly pagan. Yet he had known me older far, ancient beyond any imagining. He had taken hold of my hand in the night. He had followed me under the earth. He had entered my womb. I had taught him manhood. I became Woman for him.

I was his Goddess.

*And so Urien Rheged returned at the year's end and the woman of Otherworld Annwn gave him a boy and a girl, Owain his son and Morfudd his daughter.*

We have done well together, Urien and I.

# Chapter Fifteen

Farewell then, Urien. This is a battle you had no heart for. Arthur, the gold-bearded, laughing-eyed, high-hearted, conquering friend of your youth. Modred, your clever, comely, valiant, vulnerable nephew and foster-son. Morgan the Wise, your beloved wife. We have strained the strings of your heart between us.

You cannot watch and wait on the high ridge while Modred's desperate remnant flings itself on Arthur's too-chivalrously equal force and, fighting for their lives, begins to win. Too many names, great rallying cries, are missing: Gawain, Gareth, Cei, gone before this. Those that survive this day will think they have lived too long.

Spur your horse, then, with a grim pitilessness of grief and anger, down the short slope into the thick of the fray. You did not wait for the long horns to summon you. You have disobeyed Arthur. In your heart you know already he will not live to reproach you. How can you have it sung that the King of all the Britons fell at Camlann, and Urien Rheged did not lift his hand to stop it?

Modred is not yours. Modred was never yours. Did you sometimes fear that he might be mine? By Arthur?

I have deceived you. I intended you no harm. I respected you. Forgive me that I could not love you as you deserved.

I have loved only one.

Does that drive the stern fury in your arms, wielding the sword two-handed, forcing the horse to twist between your knees, almost without thinking? Do you rage against the cruelty of the world that sets your sword against your family, my family, against the family of Britain, for our family? Do you blame me?

You will never blame Arthur.

Are you fighting for me? Do you believe somewhere in your loyal, just, loving Christian heart that if dark Modred dies and golden Arthur wins, heaven will triumph over hell, Britain will be restored, I shall be saved?

No, Urien. I am what I am. Not good or evil. My ancient faith takes no account of morality. My metaphor is not the battlefield, right against wrong. I till the harvest-field. Birth, fullness, and death. All are necessary. Accept them. I am both darkness and light. Accept me.

Watching, unseen, I flinch from the shock of steel and the crack of wooden shields, from the almost human scream of wounded horses and the dreadful animal howl of mutilated men. My tears water the pastures of Camlann. Death is required, but not this disharmony. I have no power to stop this stupidity, this pride, this ambition, this self-sacrifice, this patriotism, this heroism. Did I precipitate this?

I stood for truth. Modred was Arthur's son. Gwenhyvar was Modred's lover. Nimue was protecting them. I said so. Others would have winked and kept silent.

You bore the burden of a lifetime's silence, Urien. One fierce and furious argument we had. Do you remember Tristvard? That handsome bard, before young Taliesin came to bring glory to your court and immortalise you.

Poor Tristvard. Not so winningly boyish as Taliesin. Brown, waving hair, a little crooked in one leg but otherwise exceedingly well-made. Deep hazel eyes, laughing and sympathetic. A taste for fine wine and an expert eye at assessing the jeweller's art. Not one half Taliesin's skill in harping, nor a divine poet. But a good conversationalist, pleasant company to while the time away for a wife who had been cheated of her years of girlhood. He was a little older than me. You were too often away at wars and cattle-rustling.

Do not mistake me. This was no seduction. I chose him, not for the pleasures of the flesh, though I will not deny them. Bodies were meant to be enjoyed, not thwarted. But mating is holy, not a careless sport. I was a queen. I was the Goddess. I must be served. There are seasons. There are rites. The joy of the earth must be recreated in me. I did what I must, well, and gladly.

Owain observed it. A child of eight. He chattered of it openly to others. They told you.

You came disguised as Teilo, my Woman who hides his manhood behind a wimple and a female skirt. Not like you to counterfeit. You never saw that Teilo was once the Smith who had forged your manhood's sword. It was a more bitter irony than you intended. So jealousy humiliates us all. So disguised, you received from Tristvard's own lips the message that he would meet me at the sacred ford.

You, of all men, should have understood the meaning of that place. Terrible your wrath. You could not, would not comprehend. You, the son of sainted Brychan's daughter. You, the upright Christian king. You saw only adultery, violation, treason. In your own kingly form you struck off Tristvard's head, there at the water's edge. Then you rode back and threw the bloody sword at my feet.

I was outraged. I did not feel the guilt you heaped upon me. I had no fear that you might kill me too. I snatched up the stained weapon, the sword of justice fouling the patterned Roman tiles. I was the Mothers' priestess. You had attacked her son. I could have slain you for it.

No time for guards to unsheathe weapons or leap across the floor to stop me. Barely space enough for my women to scream. Owain was watching, staring, strangely smiling. Always a dangerous child, though on the surface so like me.

No. A momentary faltering. I had seen the tears of pain in your eyes. Pain for Tristvard our friend, wastefully, needlessly dying this ugly death. Pain for me, for the lost wife of your dreams whom you would never now have. Pain for a young man's hopes dashed against the walls of reality. I saw your innocence lost in your own deed, by your own hand, for your own honour.

In that heartbeat's hesitation my arm slowed. And someone sprang. Another eight-year-old. Light, and lithe, and passionate. Our daughter Morfudd.

She snatched my wrist and clung to it. The blood of Tristvard, clotting on the blade, smeared her cheeks, her hands, her dress, as she wrestled with me.

'No! No! Mother, you mustn't! Father is crying.'

The guards were round us. Not one of them dared to touch me yet. My husband was staring at me. Your eyes seemed hollow, empty, dark blue tunnels into which I could go down and find great rivers of grief, caverns of disappointment, and springing green, even in this shadow, the obstinate living fern of love.

In silence, we embraced. We kissed, in the reek of Tristvard's blood that stained us both. I would not dishonour you again. I would be discreet. You would accept me for what I am. We were the king and queen. I was united with you.

The battle of Camlann has touched you less than most. The Raven's wings have been dark over your life. I have also sheltered you. You will grieve for Arthur. You will search for his body. You will not find him.

You will never see me again. In the morning you will turn your horse's head to the north. You will leave the land of legends and ride for the cold clear winds of reality. Take Taliesin with you.

Go well, Urien.

# Chapter Sixteen

*I cannot be Urien's wife, if I am Arthur's sister.*
  *The Welsh Annals give 537 for the date of Arthur's death at Camlann.*
*It was probably earlier. Urien of Rheged fell about 590.*

> 'A head I bear in my shirt,
> The head of Urien who governed a court in mildness —
> And on his white breast the black raven gluts.
>
> 'A head I bear on my sword:
> Better his being alive than that he should go to the grave;
> He was a castle for old age.
>
> 'A head I bear that supported me,
> Is there anyone known but he welcomed them?
> Woe my hand, gone is he that sustained me.'

*How did we ever come to marry? I was never more than a legend, the fairy
love, and later the sister, of Arthur. You certainly lived, the king of Rheged
in North-West Britain in the last quarter of the sixth century. Urien Wledig,
Chief among the Men of the North.*

*We know you, because of Taliesin. Fortunate indeed that friendship
between the prince of battle and the prince of poets. Twelve precious poems
have survived to us from Taliesin's own lips. They praise you richly.*

> 'He has a warlike demon,
> The king of the baptised world.
> As you plunder, you scatter,
> You make glad the poets of Christendom.
> Arise around your triumphant rustler-lord!
> An unassailable fortress, bounteous, famous,
> The anchor of his kingdom.
> Like a fiery sphere, like a familiar song,
> Like a magnanimous sea is my shining lord.
> He slays, he hangs, he nurtures, he dispenses,
> He kills in the front line.
> Gentility is around him, and a heap of riches.
> Great and unflagging his fury against the enemy,
> Great is his bounty to poets and women,
> There is esteem and welcome in the hall of the men of Rheged,
> Offerings of wine and jubilation.

> *And gold, gold, gold and gift.*
> *I shall not cease yearning,*
> *Unless I praise Urien.'*

*Truly, you are a mighty king, and popular. Your admirers intend to exalt you still higher by uniting you with me. Any hero worth his salt is drawn into the list of Arthur's war-band. My dowry for you, a higher honour: to be not Arthur's comrade only, but his brother-in-law. Only a sister's son ranks closer than this.*

*Owain, your son, is also historical fact. Taliesin sings his elegy. Early, Owain becomes a legend of his own, my son and yours.*

*Early too, our wedding must have been, before the corruption of my character could harm you both.*

*Taliesin honours you, and so do I. You are a creature of your age, as bloody and barbaric in your defence of Christianity as I in my celebration of paganism. A thief of cattle and horses, loving war for itself. You are as gentle in your court as you are grim on the battlefield, as generous with your gifts as you are rapacious in plunder. I do not blame you. Both of us are true to what we know.*

*Unfitting your end for so renowned a warrior.*

*You are white-haired already. Your sons in their northern lands have begun to mock you, throwing the hazel twigs of derision in your face. But the strife of Camlann between brother Britons was long ago. Now the Angles who have lived with us quietly in the North East are massing. Fflamddwyn, the Firebrand of Bernicia marches on Rheged, demands hostages from you and Owain.*

*On a Saturday morning, the Battle of Leven Forest.*

> ' "Have my hostages come?
> Are they ready?"
> Then answered Owain,
> The scourge of the east,
> "They have not come,
> They do not exist,
> They are not ready.
> And the whelp of Coel
> Would be a pathetic warrior
> Before he would pay anybody a hostage." '

*Slaughter then. Fflamddwyn is beaten. The crows get red in the wake of the ageing king.*

*East now, and war against King Theodoric takes you and your victorious allies to the shores of the North Sea. Rhydderch Hen, Gwallawg, Morcant, Urien, kings of the North; Aedan of the Dal Riada Scots and Fiachna of Ulster. Proud chieftains all. This is Morcant's country. And Fiachna seizes Bamborough back from the Bernicians and installs an Irish garrison. In Morcant's citadel.*

*Honour has been wounded.*

*You quarrelling kings all stand at last in the whistling grass of the long*

low strand that fronts the island of Metcaud, which others have called
Lindisfarne. Three days and three nights you besiege Theodoric. Then tragedy
strikes.

> 'Eurdyl will be joyless tonight,
> And multitudes will be so besides.
> At Aber Lleu has Urien been slain.
>
> Decapitated is my lord, his opponents are powerful.
> There is commotion in every region
> In pursuit of Llovan Llawdivro.'

The greatest of warriors is struck down. But how could spear and shield
protect against the sliding blade of treachery? No final battle for you. No
glorious fall under the rush of blood-spattered horses. No English spear to
run you through and let the daylight in.

Yet just as finally, in secrecy and darkness, your white-haired head is
severed from your body.

> 'This frail white corpse will be covered today
> Under earth and nettles:
> Woe my hand, that such a step could have happened to me!
>
> This hearth, will it not be covered over by the ants?
> More accustomed it was to bright torches,
> And harmless festivities.
>
> This hearth, will it not be scratched up by the fowl?
> Want would not approach it
> In the lifetime of Owain and Urien.'

Howl, you winds. Great Urien Rheged is dead. Carry his desecrated body
west on a gore-soaked bier. Who has ordered this? Who hated Urien so much
that they would see the greatest British king dead sooner than the English
one? Who has fed the ravens with this generous mead-giver?

The traitor King Morcant, Urien's closest ally.

Would it surprise you to learn that his name is frequently given as Morgan?

# Chapter Seventeen

Three years after Owain and Morfudd were born, I held another baby in my arms. Difficult to say this, difficult to think it, even.

Arthur's son, Margawse's child.

There! Four words, and it is done.

My brother and my sister were his parents. His father's father, Uther, had killed his mother's father Gorlois. His only grandmother was Ygerne.

Perhaps you will think it was the incest that shocked me, and so it did. I was convent-bred. I had lived with women who had chosen the cool, hard discipline of chastity, though I had seen that shot through with the fire of religious ecstasy. My soul still ached for that high commitment.

By an act of conscious will I had chosen an older, more physical way. I was the Lady. Many a night I danced barefoot and naked. I had held common flesh, made holy by my touch. I had given myself in a sacred union as the Goddess, even if afterwards I had walked away into a vast cold loneliness.

Did Margawse mock the sacred marriage? Or did I rage against her because we were both Gorlois's daughters?

I had seen my father's corpse brought home from Dimiliock. For love of Ygerne, Uther butchered her husband. They brought him home to us. The laughter silenced. The war-like muscles stilled. The blood of his great heart blackened a hundred jagged cuts, as though in a frenzy Uther's men had danced round their fallen enemy, stabbing and slashing in triumph. The poets still sing this romance.

And where was Uther? Merlyn the enchanter used his magic to change the Pendragon's face to Gorlois's, charm him through the shut gate of Tintagel by night, smuggle him into Ygerne's bed. Solely to get this boy, this Arthur. A political act.

How could my red sister hug the flesh of her half-brother, the fruit of our mother's unholy union? How could she open her legs for him?

Merlyn had orphaned the three of us for Arthur.

Margawse knew all this when she took him. Her blood flows redder than mine. She was bred in a rustic court that called itself Christian but still knew earthy, violent ways. No white nuns had schooled her in their gospel of forgiveness or chastity. She would have scorned either. Margawse is female, animal. She did not care how close a kin he was to her. She enjoyed the bodies of men. She wanted vengeance. She chose the most appropriate way.

Merlyn had kept Arthur close hidden till the time of his manhood.

The lad did not even know he was the Pendragon's son, still less that he had sisters.

He came marching into Caerleon with his standards shining and the tall war-horns braying triumph. He was a boy of fifteen, and already he was victorious over the Saxons in Lindsey. All Britain seemed likely to throw itself at his feet. He was strong, he was golden-haired and ruddy-cheeked. His limbs were whole and hard-muscled, his flesh unmarked. He carried a merry charisma about him that had older men jostling each other to swear him their swords and devotion, and he had laughing blue eyes that could turn women confused and rash.

Yet he had enemies, our kings of the north who had never met him and were jealous of his sudden fame. Lot of Lothian, Margawse's husband, Nentres of Garlot, Elaine's, Gwendoleu of Solway. Even young Urien was wary at first, before he saw Arthur.

We three queens made a guarded magic for our own chiefs and this our refound brother. Too soon to say which of them would serve our purpose best. Then we rode with our menfolk to a camp outside Caerleon. We came all of us prepared to make war against Arthur if he proved too proud. Wise women that we were, we obeyed the necessary laws. In all our journey south we sisters did not once lie with our husbands to sap their battle-magic.

Lot and Nentres were haughty: they would not go into Caerleon to do honour to this lucky boy like the soft southern chiefs. Urien was younger. He longed to see Arthur himself. And so did I.

I was not chosen.

It was Margawse we sent, ravishingly dressed, to spy out his camp and assess the man.

Yet, in his youthful arrogance, Arthur never thought it strange that the flame-haired Queen of Lothian, twice his age, magnificent in beauty, consort to hostile Lot, should come to his camp and consent so easily, merrily to share his bed after supper. He would have considered it, if he had stopped to think, merely his right. None of us told him his parentage then. He never asked.

She came back laughing. I dashed to tear her face when she rolled wantonly on the grass boasting about it. Luned and Teilo had to drag me off her.

I fled home to Rheged. I fasted and dressed in black and sat at the gate of Lyvennet giving myself to the healing of any who passed.

Six months later, it fell to me to tell Arthur the truth.

He came as guest to my fortress in Rheged. How can I recall, unshaken, that moment when he walked in through my gate? My brother, my king, my little child. Not sixteen years, but war had already set her brand on him. He was no longer the golden-downed boy of Margawse's sport. This was a man. The Red Ravager. The Bear of Battle. I had my tribute for him ready. I had brought his mother Ygerne, widow of Uther, once High Queen of Britain. A quiet woman in white, hiding her face in her hood. He learned from my lips and hers that he was the Pendragon's son. There in my high courtyard, above the apple orchards.

I met the full force of his joy. His hands reached out for mine. His face was alight with all the new vision of his future. This was all my doing.

I held a cup in my hands. The wine beat on the sides like the surge of my blood. Our eyes engaged.

'Stop!'

Merlyn sprang like a wildman out of the forest of men and dashed my cup aside. Consternation. Fury among my people. Suspicion had been sown. Pride was endangered. It all ended in laughter. Arthur drank my welcome. But the moment of meeting was spoiled.

Round and round the spiral turns, and we are always parted.

Ygerne was my mother too. I could not hide what followed logically from that.

I showed him we had two other sisters. Elaine and Margawse. Even Margawse hung her head and blushed as she met his horrified recognition. But the smile was more wicked as she took her hands from her swelling body to let him see.

He read in our faces that this could not be Lot's.

And so this child. This little dark-eyed baby. Why did I want to scream every time I looked at him?

Because he was Arthur's son, and I was not his mother.

It is out. Many times I have had to remove a buried javelin point from a man's flesh and seen the bright heart-blood come spurting after it. In that swift moment of danger I must stem the tide. That is my work. I am the healer. It was not so easy to staunch my own wound.

I am more a traitor to our family than Margawse was, in my heart. I would have willingly ignored Uther's lust, Merlyn's deception, the Abbess Bryvyth's holy condemnation. And not for revenge. Do you think it strange? When Margawse told me she had lain with Arthur, I had not seen him since that night when I leaned over his cradle and carried him out into the storm. A girl of nine with her infant brother. Why did I shriek like a woman robbed?

Arthur and Morgan. The Lord and the Lady. I think I always knew we were essential to each other. In us the fractured worlds of gender, politics, tribe and faith should have been made whole. He is the warrior. I am the healer. Our conjoined power should have made this baby.

Modred. His small red fist gripped round my finger. His dark eyes on mine, it seemed, so knowingly.

The spiral twisted, and we were back in the same dangerous region, a generation later. Lust, treachery, a vulnerable baby boy.

I could not stop this castle spinning, even though I knew clearly what was coming.

Merlyn could not allow this. He was as arrogant with his magic staff as Arthur with his weapon. This baby would not be permitted to live.

First, there was a more immediate danger. Modred was born in Lothian, on May Day. At the height of the festival King Lot was drunk. I met him striding to his wife's bedchamber. Margawse was generous to him, as well as to others. Four sons he had, Gawain, Agravain, Gaheris, Gareth, and they were truly his. But Lot was a pagan who feared the old taboos. He had ridden to Arthur's camp at Caerleon under a warrior's ban. He had not touched his wife for a month. This son could not be his.

I feared his human anger. Margawse must guard her own life, I took the child.

We rode south in our chariot through a landscape that did not seem like summer, all three of us nursing our loss. Luned, who might have succeeded Bryvyth as abbess at Tintagel. She was now my servant whom I had schooled in another wisdom. Teilo, who had once forged Urien's sword and hammered runes of protection into its blade. He had tried to play the Master Smith over my Ladyship. I had taught him thoroughly to know the left-hand way of power. So he served me now in the dress of Woman. And I myself, feeling the pain of Arthur's baby sucking my half-dried breasts.

I nursed a greater dread of another man's vengeance than Lot's. When I heard that Merlyn was approaching our fortress at Lyvennet, I did not run. I knew what he had done in Lothian. I knew the story of Arthur's dream. His feasting-hall set on fire. How Arthur must tear out the blazing beam before the whole palace was destroyed. Merlyn's interpretation: a child of treachery was born on May Day. Arthur's warriors must seek it out and exterminate it. No baby from that festival time must escape alive.

It was not for the enchanter's face that I searched when Arthur came storming up to the gate at the head of his war-band. This was the father. My paps had fed his son. He could not do this to us.

Yet I was frightened. I knew that, even so young, war had hardened him. I set a woman's trap for him, a woman's lesson. In the great hall of Lyvennet I laid out the holy evidence of my wisdom. A hundred May-time babies, born of female bodies from male seed. A hundred tiny, noisy chicks lifted from their nests, all washed and dressed identically.

'Arthur,' I smiled. 'You are not yet our king, but you have won much for Britain. Your sword has saved the future of these children.'

One boy alone mattered to him. Arthur of Christian Britain could not have, must not have, a son by his sister.

I saw him stop. I saw the fury in his eyes. Those wide, blue, winning eyes that can turn a woman's loins to water, flashing now. I saw how Saxons see him in his battle-madness. I was denying him what he wanted.

'Get these women out.'

I hardly heard him for the noise of crying.

'The women are my witnesses.'

There were men behind him, unwilling to put their hands on weapons. Cei, Bedwyr, Gawain. Younger, less famous faces. Surely they could not, in cold blood, take them all.

Merlyn was sweeping round the hall, picking his hasty way over tiny bodies, peering into wrinkled, squalling, placid, sleeping features. Ygerne would have known at once. Blood would have spoken to blood. Merlyn's magic was too high for this.

Arthur sprang on to the dais. He seized my arm. I knew, we knew, that even Modred's death could be no more than a shadow between us. I felt myself sway to meet his warmth. He sensed his victory. Eyes softened, melting mine. Hands became tender. Arms surrounded, supported, drew me close to him. My head went down upon his shoulder. I had no strength.

His voice caressed my ear. 'Give me my son.'

Oh, Arthur, I would have given you all I had.

With a last resolve I murmured, 'Last year you could not recognise your sister. Now it seems you do not know your own child.'

He struck me, in my own high hall, in front of my people.

I thwarted his pride. He took them all, because I would not give him Modred.

That nightmare claws me still. Warriors gathering those babies up and heaving them into a cart. My women screaming. Spears pinning them to the wall. My own guard bleeding. Urien's face. His hero and his wise wife gazing across the hall at each other's eyes, appalled. But Merlyn's plan for Britain could not be endangered by a single child, or by a hundred. His Arthur must serve the male imperative.

And I, in women's way, would not betray one solitary, treacherously-got baby to save all the rest.

One last wracked plea, 'Do not do this, Arthur, for your soul's sake!'

But Merlyn signalled. Arthur's eyes hardened and he stared back at me as though I was a stranger. They tried to amputate the past. I too believed in Arthur's dream. I understood that Modred would one day betray Arthur. And yet . . . That cart was full of little Modreds, none of them wholly perfect, not one conceived in a union of unspoiled trust. None would be all their parents had hoped for if they grew to adults. Flawed, vulnerable, harmful, particular in their failings, human. As he was.

We all of us need our dream of the ideal King Arthur. Arthur himself could not live with the evidence of his own reality.

I gave one piercing shriek and tore my face, not for Arthur's son, but for all the rest. I sent my Woman, Teilo, after them to bear witness.

They went through Rheged till the cart was full. They came to the banks of the Solway Firth at evening. There was no need to stain their swords with innocent blood. They piled the babies in a boat. They pushed it out into the tideway. Merlyn signed to his chief. Arthur's own hand was the last to leave the stern.

The cold sea took them. The boat scraped rock and foundered. The raucous gulls feasted.

Merlyn should have known better. The truth was inescapable. Just one baby was saved. Modred was fostered in a fisherman's cottage. I sought him out and found him.

# Chapter Eighteen

*I am Modron, the Mother.*

*The Welsh never called me Morgan. That is a masculine name, and usually an ill-omened one. In Wales there is a sinister man called Morgan, who like me is water-born. He lives at the bottom of Lake Glasfryn in the parish of Llangybi. His is the name that mothers use to frighten their children. He knows the naughty ones and he will rise from his gloomy lair and carry them off. They disappear, of course, under the water and are never seen again.*

*Geoffrey's Morgen, you remember, took men away to bliss in Avalon. Oddly enough, though this Morgan is male, the family who own the land around Glasfryn bear on their crest a mermaid.*

*I stole no child. My child was taken from me.*

*There is a tantalising collection of threefold sayings, the Welsh Triads. Each group alludes to three ancient tales. You might call them a catalogue of the fabulous history of Britain. Some of the stories they point to are known to us; others are irretrievably lost.*

*One Triad lists:*

> *'One of the Three Fair Womb-Burdens of the Island of Britain: Owain son of Urien and Morfudd his sister who were carried together in the womb of Modron daughter of Avallach.'*

*Avallach is King of Annwn, the Otherworld.*

*It is a daughter of the King of Annwn who meets Urien Rheged at the Ford of Barking and gives him a son Owain and a daughter Morfudd. In the medieval romances Morgan is queen to Urien and the mother of Owain. So I must be Modron, must I not?*

*All Europe knows me. In Latin I am Matrona. I have dropped my name like a benediction over towns and waters. The River Marne is holy to me. As Modron, I settled in Britain with the legions. My image is often sculptured threefold. I appear as a triad of myself, the Triple Woman, the Mothers.*

*Mother to whom?*

*Where Modron is the Mother, Mabon is her Son. You can find our sacred stones still scattered around Hadrian's Wall. We have no personal name. Modron means Mother. Mabon is Son. That is the essence of our being.*

> *'One of the Three Exalted Prisoners of the Island of Britain: Mabon son of Modron.*

*My child. Son of the Mother.*

*We have a fine collection of old Welsh tales, the Mabinogion. Listen to the oldest one of all, Culhwch and Olwen:*

645

*Arthur's young nephew Culhwch is mad with love for Olwen White-Track the Giant's daughter. And the whole crazy, mythical court is horsed to win her for him. This is the hunt to end all hunts. A preposterous inventory of impossible tasks to prepare the roaring Ysbaddaden for the marriage he does not intend to grant and furnish his daughter's wedding-feast.*

*There are no instruments in the world can dress the Giant's hair, so exceedingly stiff it is, but the razor and comb and shears that are caught between the ears of the enchanted boar Twrch Trwyth, and they may hunt that beast through the length of Britain and Ireland but he will never give them up willingly.*

*There is only one hound in Britain that is fleet enough to chase this boar, and that is Drudwyn, the whelp of Greid.*

*Only one leash in the world is strong enough to hold Drudwyn, and that is the leash of Cors Hundred-Claws.*

*Only one collar in the world can stand the strain of that leash, and that is the collar of Canhastyr Hundred-Hands.*

*And the collar may only be held to the leash by the chain of Cilydd Hundred-Holds.*

*There is not one huntsman in the world may manage that hound save Mabon son of Modron. But where is he to be found?*

*An immemorial grief. I bore a baby son. He was snatched from between me and the wall when he was three nights old. And in all the ages since the dreadful shriek that revealed my loss, I have never known where he was taken or whether he is alive or dead.*

*Of all the many wonders the giant demands, it is Mabon my son that Arthur says must be found first. And the four he sends on that task are Eidoel my nephew, Gwrhyr Interpreter of Tongues, with Cei and Bedwyr.*

*They seek the oldest animal to tell them where Mabon might have been heard of.*

*The first they approach is the Ouzel of Cilgwri, and this is what she says:*

*'I came here as a young bird and found a smith's anvil. No work has been done upon it save by my beak of an evening, and now there is not so much as a nut of metal not worn away. In all that time I have heard nothing of the man you are asking for. But for Arthur's sake I will guide you to one who may know more.'*

*She takes them to the Stag of Rhedynfre. But:*

*'It is not I you need. When I came here I was scarcely more than a fawn, with a single tine on either side of my head. This ground was bare in those days except for a solitary oak-sapling. I have watched it grow into a mighty tree with a hundred branches. I saw it fall. I have lived on while it decayed to a red stump. From that day to this I have heard nothing of Mabon, son of Modron. But I will lead Arthur's men to one older than I.'*

*On then to the Owl of Cwm Cawlwyd. Her eyes are solemn.*

*'I have seen this valley before us filled with forest and laid waste by men. A second wood grew up in place of the first. That too was felled, and this that you see is the third. And as for me, I have flown so many nights that the roots of my wings are no more than stumps. Nevertheless, I have heard nothing of the one you seek. Yet for Arthur's quest I will bring you to one who has lived longer still and flown farther than any of us.'*

*So to the Eagle of Gwernabwy and the same question.*

'When I came here I perched on a pinnacle of stone and pecked the stars each evening. Now the mountain I stood on is only a hand's-breadth in height. And no word has ever come to me of Mabon son of Modron. But I may yet be able to help you. Flying far in search of food I came once to the lake of Llyn Llyw and sank my talons into the back of a mighty salmon. That should have been a feast for many a day. But he proved stronger than I was, and drew me deep down under the water so that I barely escaped with my life. I summoned all the eagles of my clan to return and destroy him. He met us with messages of peace. The Salmon himself came swimming to the surface and begged me to take from his back fifty tridents that were torturing him. For gratitude to me he may be willing to tell you something.'

And so at last to the Salmon of Llyn Llyw, a vast shadow underwater, in the tidal waters of the River Severn. He is ancient beyond believing, the wisest of all the animals. Here they have dipped so deep into the well of time that at last they dredge up the age-long memory of a mystery.

'It is little indeed I know, but what I have heard I will share with you. With every tide that has ever been, I have swum up the Severn. And each day and each night I hear a cry of distress at the bend in the river, under the wall of Caer Loyw at Gloucester. It has wailed and lamented from a damp deep cell at the water's edge almost since the beginning of time, and I have heard no cry to equal it for sadness in all my life. Let two of you ride on my shoulders and you may judge for yourselves who that prisoner may be.'

So Cei and Gwrhyr Interpreter of Tongues ride the Salmon. And when they come beside the wall they hear a lamentation on the far side that would destroy your heart.

Gwrhyr calls, 'What man is that who grieves so sorely in this house of stone?'

'Alas, and never had man a bitterer cause to lament. I am Mabon son of Modron in the cruellest imprisonment that ever was.'

'Can you be ransomed, or must you be freed by fighting?'

'I shall never be got out except by a battle.'

When he receives this news, Arthur summons his war-band. With all but two warriors he assaults the gate of the stronghold. But Cei and Bedwyr go leaping up the current on the back of the Salmon. While the fight is fiercest, Cei breaks through the wall and carries the prisoner out on his back. So Arthur comes home in triumph, bringing Mabon, a free man, amongst his pack.

Mabon rewards them all by hunting the monstrous boar Twrch Trwyth and his seven vicious piglets across Ireland and Wales and into Cornwall. Many of Arthur's best men are slain in that hunt. Spurring his horse into the midst of the Severn, Mabon snatches the razor from the boar's head while another gets the shears. But worse mischief still is done in Cornwall before they take the comb and even then Twrch Trwyth escapes into the sea.

So they shave the Giant for Olwen's wedding, and he must give up his daughter to Culhwch. And then, they cut off his head.

*I, note well, am this Mabon's mother. The story says nothing more of me since that night, unimaginable ages ago, when I lost my baby.*

*To the Welsh, as to the Romans, my principal function is motherhood. Even the bards have no words to tell you how, for longer than it takes a mountain to wear away to dust, I grieved for that theft of my son.*

# Chapter Nineteen

So there you are, Modred, your wrecked humanity crushing the sunless buttercups where you fell. My fosterling. These arms shielded you under my shawl in your babyhood when Arthur was hunting your life to destroy it. They have not enough strength now to lift you from the earth. I must let you lie. Bedwyr and Lucan have carried Arthur from the battlefield in grief and honour. Your corpse everyone has left to the crows.

Your destiny is fulfilled; treachery is triumphant. Who will remember now your valour, your courtesy, your good counsel?

You were called one of Three Royal Knights of Arthur's Court. The bards said:

> *'No king could refuse them on account of their beauty and wisdom in peace. In war no warrior could withstand them, despite the excellence of his arms.'*

Arthur trusted you.
Gwenhyvar could not withstand you.
Nor could I.
The battle-cap on hair black as a Cornish chough's wing is encircled with silver, and silver loops your broken breastplate. Too soft a metal to withstand the thrust of Arthur's lance. You and I always chose silver rather than gold. We were more at home in the moonlight than in the sun. Did we in our deepest being accept the secondary place that others allowed us? Or did we cherish the truths revealed to those who alone have the courage to listen in darkness? That wisdom endures only as long as we shun the lust for gold. Silver blackens, neglected. Who notices the moon when the sun is in the sky?

Arthur's gold could not protect him, either.

So the shadow falls on Morgan and Modred. We are the figures of disloyalty. Our original fame is tarnished. Villainy is all they have left us of our birthright.

> *'Three Dishonoured Men who were in the Island of Britain: The third and the worst was Modred, when Arthur left with him the government of the Island of Britain when he himself went across the sea.'*

Death has not long since passed this way. The blood is still bright where the gash severed your throat and silenced the song that was almost as pure as Taliesin's. Life has gushed out over your breastplate. This flood will darken by nightfall. A dreadful deed by a weapon never made for this. Caliburn has flashed in the sun for the last time. That Lady who lifted it up for us from beneath the lake is weeping now a salt ocean of tears for what her gift has done. With the most famous sword in the world, King Arthur has killed his own son.

Your wounds are terrible. I kneel beside you, lowering my head to the armoured body I may not lift, and I glimpse the last pale light of the sky clear through the lance-hole in your chest. Was ever daylight cursed as this? You never let us see into you so plainly while you lived.

Robbers are creeping on to the battlefield as the shadows lengthen. You need not fear them. You were robbed before you fell. At your conception your mother Margawse robbed you of honour when she twined with the scarce-bearded Arthur in his bed, and never told him that she was his sister. You were the apt reversal of Merlyn's plans. You were her sweet revenge for the death of our father, the honour-price for the seduction of our mother. Her hostage for Arthur's fame, triumph, his place in the heart of every Briton. How could you feel for him? You were not made to be a human child, the fruit of love. You were formed as our tool.

Your father would have robbed you of life, when he knew. When at Merlyn's bidding he cast you out to sea, he feared you would steal from him a golden crown and a golden reputation.

Morgan and Modred. We are the Sea-Born. I named you. I saved and reared you. My wisdom hid you from Arthur's wrath. I have made you what you are.

You were the child of stories. I held Arthur's son on my lap by the fireside, my arm encircling you, your sleepy head against my breast. I crooned songs for you. In dappled sunshine we walked through the forest and made its ancient trees and new-sprung flowers our college. In gales we struggled to the tops of mountains and, laughing, claimed the far-spread lands and oceans for our own. I taught you the speech of beasts.

I thought you listened wisely. Your little, knowing face turned up to mine. Your small warm hand gripped tight around my fingers. Those dark eyes seemed to drink my knowledge deep.

I told how wisdom might still bind up the wounds of warfare. How Gorlois's and Uther's blood had been united. How all the hurt and loss of Ygerne's daughters could be made good through Ygerne's son. How, though despised, I wielded a power of my own to equal Arthur's. I was the Healer.

You saw how deeply I was hurt.

On the eve of manhood you learned that you were the Pendragon's child. Margawse's vindication. Arthur's shame. Merlyn's nightmare. Morgan's hope.

But secrecy had darkened your childhood. Too long for a child to be without a father. Too bitter to learn that yours had willed your death. What breastplate could I have buckled on you to shield you from that? You saw yourself his living doom, who should have been our reconciliation. Arthur had claimed the sunshine; we were left the night. Today at Camlann, Merlyn's worst premonitions have been realised. Twenty-one years late, Arthur has slain his son.

Let me slip that circlet of gold from your head. The colour does not become you.

The victory is elsewhere. Arthur's shame died when you fell. The bards will rob you of your bright renown. Modred the traitor, who destroyed King Arthur's Britain.

There, I have bloodied the wings of my cloak in the thickening tide. Too late to hold your young life in. Our time is over. We, the women of the Arthur story, will bear the blame for this day's work. Vengeful seductresses, false queens, untrustworthy enchantresses. We are the evil to Arthur's virtue. Forgive us, Modred. You deserved better of history than this.

I cannot heal you yet. The blood begins to clot. The chill is claiming your flesh as the sun goes down. The final battle is still to come. I drowned the power of Caliburn's scabbard long ago, that could close all wounds. Now only the naked slaying blade remains. Wait for me, Modred. Arthur is still alive, and armed. And I must steel myself to play the warrior-woman. Can your father bear to cast away his sword to join the scabbard, and in that surrender make us one at last?

Let me close your eyes to a world that held too much pain. See in this sleep the laughing of fair women, the rush of racing horses, the break of spray on ships that will carry you to my Summer Isle. Believe that this, at least, can be true. Do not yearn for this world. It has wronged you too much.

Men mourn for vanished Arthur. His praise-songs will echo down the centuries. Hero-tales will multiply. Women will measure manhood by him.

Where are the laments for Modred?

> Hear me, you stars.
> I sing him resolute and honourable on the battlefield,
> Comely and courteous among women,
> Just in judgment, a gifted artist.
> Generous to poets.
> Swift horses pricked their ears
> To the whisper of his voice,
> Hounds' hearts took courage
> From the touch of his hand,
> The salmon lay still
> Under the stroking of his fingers,
> And blackbirds alighted
> In the clearing where he sat.
> He was a fatherly prince in caring
> For the slave and the servant in his court,
> He, too young to nurse his own firstborn
> Before he died.

He was a peacemaker, gathering round the table
Painted Picts and pale-haired Angles,
He for whom the Britons
Tore themselves apart.

This was Arthur's son. The king's maternal nephew. Blood of father, blood of mother, doubly royal. The courtly prince, gifted beyond his brothers. The ideal Celtic hero. One thing alone this wise, brave warrior-scholar lacked. The blessing of his father and his mother.

I have loved him from the depths of my being. It was not enough. I was not his parent.

# Chapter Twenty

*I have had happier fosterings.*

One is the hero of the thirteenth-century romance *Floriant and Florete*.

*The king of Sicily is murdered by Maragoz, his steward, who then violently lays claim to the queen's hand. She flees the palace, trying to reach shelter in the castle of a faithful retainer. On the way, the pangs of labour overtake her and a boy is born.*

*I am Morgan Sea-Born. I and two other fays have been disporting ourselves at night out in the salt water. We are returning at midnight from our moonlit swim when we discover the fatherless child beside his sleeping mother.*

*I am the fay of destiny. I foretell that he shall become a great knight one day. But now, this baby is in danger. Take him up quickly, then. Bear him away to my own sanctuary on Mongibel, Mount Etna. Here I baptise him Floriant.*

*The boy is well brought up. I have a tutor who teaches him all the arts and the skills of chivalry that a noblewoman's son should know.*

*I cannot keep him. At fifteen years of age he comes to me and begs to know who his father was. I withhold the saddest part of his history from him for a while. I tell him his father was a king, his mother, a king's daughter. Now his heart is set on rejoining that world. I knight him myself.*

*Next day a magic ebony ship sets sail for my brother Arthur's court at Cardigan. I wave farewell. I have hung the boat with wonderful silken tapestries, embroidered with tales of Troy, from where the British ancestors came long ago. He has many marvellous adventures on the way and to crown them all, the lad arrives at court just in time to win a brilliant victory in a tournament. He does me credit. He bears my message commending him to Arthur's service. He is welcomed and honoured.*

*My foster-son has proved himself to be a valiant young man. It is time for the truth. One of my maidens has been following his adventures secretly. Now she delivers a letter to him from me. Here is the whole sad story of his father's murder, the queen's persecution, Floriant's wayside birth. His mother is still not safe. Even as he reads this, the castle of her retainer, which has been her refuge, is being besieged by the treacherous steward Maragoz.*

*Arthur and Floriant set out to rescue her.*

*It is more than Maragoz they have to fight when they reach Sicily. The Emperor of Constantinople is laying claim to the land. Arthur fights bravely but Floriant excels himself. The Emperor is repulsed. The steward is beaten. The queen is freed.*

*But Floriant has taken a very serious wound: he has fallen in love with the Emperor's daughter.*

*Difficult to win her father's consent, of course, but Floriant is a bold young man and the lovers succeed. Floriant marries Florete. He is made King of Palermo.*

*The story takes a familiar turn. The valiant young warrior becomes a staid, inactive husband. People start to criticise him behind their hands. The loyal Florete recalls him to his knightly reputation. Together they leave the court in search of adventure. They head for Britain again, the land of magic and marvels. There the court welcomes the 'Handsome Savages' from a far island.*

*Floriant beats a dragon.*

*But another sultan is besieging Rome. Concern for his kingdom takes Floriant back. He retires to Palermo.*

*Age is beginning to attack him. I see it is time to call him home.*

*Now Floriant sights a white stag on a hunt. It is, of course, an animal from the Otherworld. What hero of romance ever refused to follow that magical beast into the depths of the forest? Or ever failed to lose contact with his followers? The creature leads him up the slopes of Mongibel to a beautiful castle and dashes in through the door. Floriant charges after it.*

*A threshold is crossed.*

*The stag has disappeared. I am there, on my couch, waiting for him to return after all these years. I have not changed. But he has. Gently, I tell him the truth he does not want to hear. He will die if he stays longer on earth. I have sent the stag to fetch him. If he will live with me now, he will never grow old. There are maidens to welcome him, monsters to fight with, like the Sathenas with gigantic ears and the Pellican who devours a girl every day. Plenty of occupation for a hero. Arthur himself will soon be here.*

*Time passes easily in Mongibel, with feasting and singing and hunting and fighting, all a man could desire. The women I offer him are incomparably fair, but still he grieves for an earthly one. I hold council now with the same two fays who found him long ago after our midnight bathe. Shall we let him go? No. We will bring Florete here instead to share his bliss.*

*Floriant is my foster-son, not my lover.*

*I have other expectations.*

*No need to tell you why I feel no jealousy of Florete.*

# Chapter Twenty-one

Modred had disappeared. The sea had taken him. I paid the woman Fencha and her husband well. They were discreet.

Slowly the wheel turned, the Goddess smiled. I dared not own him yet, but in a fisherman's cottage at Mabon's Stone beside the Solway Firth a little baby crooned and suckled. The Son was born. The Mother would watch over him.

Still, I had power.

The Church, as so often in his turbulent youth, laid a heavy penance on Arthur for those babies. This time, he walked barefoot from Bath to Glastonbury. Then Bishop Dubric laid hands on him and forgave him. Merlyn they did not absolve.

So the stage was cleared for Arthur to be acclaimed High King. For that they needed Cornish Gwenhyvar.

Merlyn arranged the marriage. We were Arthur's sisters. We were summoned.

I could not sleep that night. It would break my heart to see my brother married. I could not bear to stay away.

Caerleon, where all of us but I had first met with Arthur. Where Margawse had lain with Arthur. Where Gwenhyvar would marry Arthur soon. A place of bitter memories for me, and the knowledge of worse to come.

And now Merlyn, coming to *us* to ask for help? Uther Pendragon's sorcerer to Gorlois's daughters? There was strangeness here. Something was wrong.

Merlyn. A creature out of our past, haunting our present, shadowing our future. What could he need from us a week before Arthur's wedding?

I watched him coming into the room where we sat, Elaine, Margawse and I, our faces avid with curiosity. An old man bowed down with the weight of the magic he had used. Bent as a shepherd's crook, and almost as thin. His skin hanging loose on almost fleshless limbs. Hair so fine and light and white it floated in the lightest breeze like unhooked spider's webs. He looked at us sideways, as wary as we were.

An old man with young eyes.

I felt the lurch of my heart that told of treachery. And then he smiled.

Merlyn was not so dried by age and not so stiff with enmity to us that his blood could not run faster when he looked at me. I sensed his double desire. I kindle that lightning in the air when men are close to me. He wanted my body for his own. Merlyn was a sorcerer. He needed me also for a higher use.

I felt my power grow.

'Emrys Merlyn does us honour.' Elaine spoke for us.

'The honour is mine, to come into the presence of three great queens who rule large realms of the Island of Britain through their husbands, but hold a greater majesty in their fair persons.'

'You sentenced my son to die,' Margawse accused him.

He shrugged and spread his hands. 'Blood has to be shed for the good of the land. You know that, Margawse.'

Yes, she knew. We all of us knew the laws. Merlyn himself had taught my sisters for nine months, after Uther married Ygerne. A dangerous education. Gwennol our nurse used the caring, nurturing magic of birth and fruition and death. Merlyn had wider visions, ambitions, strategies. The high magic of kingdoms demands a higher price.

He never taught me this. He feared me, even as a child. I got my education in the Christian convent where Uther confined me. There I learned that blood has been shed once only, for the whole world and for all time. I wove the wisdom of Gwennol and the nuns together. It should have been healing enough.

All this time Merlyn's eyes were on me. I felt his urgency.

'You robbed Margawse of her son, and me of my freedom, and all of us of our father. What do you want from us now?' I asked.

'Arthur is your brother.'

'So you tell us.'

'Ygerne confirmed it.'

I bowed my head.

'Yet, in your wisdom, you have gone straight to the nub of the matter. Tongues will wag. They were dangerous times. Uther's son was fostered in secret. Nimue, Lady of the Lake, was a discreet guardian. He survived. That much is victory. He has gained much from Nimue's teaching. That may be gain, if he uses it wisely. But there is always a price. For a king-in-waiting, something was lost.'

'Legitimacy.'

His turn to bow.

'I see we understand each other.'

And now the blood was starting to hammer in my veins. He could not be asking what I thought he meant, surely?

'The nobles may question Arthur's right to royalty. Needlessly, of course. He has generations of purple through Uther Pendragon, and a crimson brighter than that in the blood of Ygerne. But still, the visibility of the thread was broken. He emerged from the mists.'

'The war-lords will hail Arthur as their battle-leader, the Imperator? But they may yet dispute his claim to be our High King?' Margawse was laughing softly. 'Yes, you are right. Even now Lot would trim Arthur's beard before he gets too great, if he could persuade the others to back him.'

Elaine leaned forward, with that slow deliberation that hushed talk and drew all eyes to her.

'But you are marrying him to Gwenhyvar.'

Gwenhyvar the Giant's Daughter. Gwenhyvar, King Leodegran's

child. Young Gwenhyvar of Cornwall, whose mother was cousin to Ygerne and who could bring Arthur as her dowry the most ancient, most sacred bloodline of all. The Kings of the West, who claimed descent through their maternal line from the still more revered Queens of old.

A slight pause, long enough for us to hear the buzzing of a fly upon the window-ledge. Knowledge crackled between the three of us as though we had touched hands before a thunderstorm.

'What is wrong with Gwenhyvar?' asked Margawse innocently.

'Wrong? Wrong with Gwenhyvar!'

'Gwenhyvar is flawed.' Elaine's voice came deep as a man's, startling from her fair, plump face.

'What do you see?' Too quick now, Merlyn, to challenge her.

'What do I see?' Her eyes were dazed now, her voice thick and heavy. 'I see a woman with a sword.'

She shuddered, as if a goose had walked over her grave, and shook herself awake. She looked around at us questioningly. She did not know what she had said.

'A woman with a sword?' Was that my own voice or Merlyn's shriller than Elaine's, trying out the words, testing the possibilities. I shivered too.

I sensed a sexual excitement in Margawse beside me. We were all looking at Merlyn. Had we helped him? Had we frightened him? Had he got what he came for?

He was like a miser with a bag of gold, who hears the thieves approaching and knows that he must trust his hoard to others' keeping. He cannot bear to let it leave his hands, and yet he dare not wait.

What was this flaw in little, royal Gwenhyvar? What was driving Merlyn to us a week before the wedding?

*Legitimacy.*

The word came back to me with the force of trumpets blowing. Merlyn had come from Celliwig in Cornwall. Bedwyr was following from Cornwall bringing Gwenhyvar. Gwenhyvar would not bring Arthur what she promised. Gwenhyvar was flawed.

My power was reaching its height.

'I see you understand.'

'And you ask *us* to help you?'

'Not me. Oh no, my bright and midnight Morgan! Arthur.'

He knew. He had stood in his wildman's garb in the high fort of Lyvennet and seen Arthur open his arms to greet me after fifteen years. He had seen the meeting of our eyes. He had read my heart.

'The woman with the sword. And the sword is in the stone. The High King must draw the weapon from her rock.' Elaine made facts sound like a dream.

'You want us to legitimise Arthur!' Margawse cried out in amazement.

Merlyn bowed very low.

The eyes of the three of us met and locked. So Ygerne had affirmed Uther, though never Gorlois. So we had each authenticated our own chief. His men would hail him as their battle-leader when he raised his sword. But we holy women took the sword into ourselves in the sacred rite. We would release it only for him we had destined to be King.

'You would trust us that far?' Elaine spoke for all our bewilderment.

Merlyn smiled, that dancing childish smile that had enchanted even old Gwennol to think herself a young girl.

'You are Arthur's sisters.'

He lived for schemes of power. He thought we saw the same world he did. With Arthur High King, his sisters the Queens Elaine, Margawse and Morgan would be powerful ladies. Our ritual assent must make Arthur's right unchallengeable. It would also proclaim our own authority. The secret power of our royal blood would be acknowledged publicly, in the world of men and war-hosts. With the lure of temporal power Merlyn baited the trap of magic for us. He partly succeeded.

'Are you not afraid that a second son might come from that rite?' Margawse taunted him.

We saw the flash of anger in his eyes.

'That nightmare is past and over. Even the Church is ready to anoint King Arthur now. Whatever further sons and daughters he gets need not trouble his sleep.'

'No. What Arthur once did, stays done,' Elaine murmured.

A long silence filled the room, as if in a tent enemy battle-commanders pondered the terms of a truce that might or might not secure their boundaries. We mused on wounded honour, larger empires, old bitterness. I struggled to call down wisdom, to hold the balance, to satisfy the Goddess. We saw between us a young man's face, blue, laughing eyes, a joy of muscled body raised on northern hills to race a horse and fling the spear, a baby born in Cornwall, cradled always in the arms of the women of the West.

'Well?' smiled Merlyn.

His eyes were on me. He knew my heart. He was coming to the moment of his greatest victory. Once, he believed, I had tried to destroy the baby Arthur. Now, I must authenticate him king. Uther Pendragon's son. By offering me political power of a sort, he hoped to curb my more dangerous powers for ever. If I am the land, and Arthur mates with me, then I shall be his love and his Goddess for the rest of our lives, never his rival.

We both knew we had come to the moment of decision. I would not hesitate. The ninth great wave that had torn Arthur from my arms in the sea at Tintagel would bring him back to me in the thunderous foam of our meeting.

I opened my mouth to assent.

'We must draw lots,' Elaine's voice came quietly.

A start broke Merlyn's fixed attention. An instant of fear as his eyes left mine. He shrugged it off. 'As the Goddess chooses.'

His gaze was back on my face, intent now, as if he could will the outcome of the lottery. And mine on his, as if I wished he could.

So slow and fumbling, Elaine's plump fingers. She cut three straws. Two short, one long. So childish a game to settle the future of Britain.

Merlyn must hold the straws. I could feel the enchanter summoning power into his sere hand to guide our choices. We closed our eyes and drew in turn. Elaine was the eldest. I was the last. Margawse took the long straw.

Margawse took the long straw.

Margawse took . . . My soul screams to this day. Margawse took what I never had. Twice over! In laughter and fornication after his victory feast. In solemnity and terror before his king-making.

I was there, in the cavern. I was the Grail Maiden. I carried the vessel of abundance past his eyes.

But Margawse was the Stone. The rock of the Island of Britain. Arthur's weapon was in her. She let him draw it out. And the cavern roared with a mighty shout that must have shaken the fortress of Caerleon.

'Arthur the King!'

One voice had cried out in protest before that ceremony. Nimue arguing furiously at our threshold in Caerleon.

'Merlyn! Emrys Merlyn, what are you doing in there with those witches? You do not need them. Gwenhyvar is coming.'

She never guessed. No rumour from Cornwall reached her to make her doubt the truth of Gwenhyvar. She never met Gwenhyvar's sister Gwenhyvach until it was far too late. She feared when she saw Merlyn restoring our authority to us. She never forgave him. I shudder now when I think how she imprisoned him, solitary, powerless, under the spell of his own giving. Merlyn, my adversary, who understood, as I do, how darkness must balance light.

Nimue was never as wise as Merlyn.

And nor was I.

When we made Arthur king, we affirmed Gwenhyvar's right to be queen.

# Chapter Twenty-two

*I become Arthur's sister.*

*I was originally less, and more, than that.*

*In Geoffrey of Monmouth's* Life of Merlin, *I am one of nine sisters on the Island of Avalon, and Arthur is not my brother. I am the most beautiful of all, the senior. I teach my sisters mathematics and astronomy. I am unmarried. I lay Arthur in my own bed.*

*In his other book, the* History of the Kings of Britain, *Geoffrey gives Arthur a single sister.*

*Uther's brother, King Aurelius, lies dying in Winchester. A huge and brilliant star is seen in the sky. A beam of light from it ends in a ball of fire which spreads into the semblance of a dragon. From its mouth shoot two more rays. One lights the Continent; the other crosses the Irish Sea and sparkles into seven smaller shafts. Three times the vision appears and terrifies the country. Merlyn interprets this portent. The dragon is Uther. The ray of light over Gaul and beyond signifies the conquests of his son. The second ray denotes his daughter, whose sons and grandsons shall hold the kingship of Britain.*

*Merlyn is the Pendragon's court magician, and he is sound enough on the subject of men. But he seems to have been distressingly inaccurate in his assessment of women.*

*Uther takes the crown. Arthur is born. He is followed a year later by a sister, Anna. She is the daughter of both Ygerne and Uther Pendragon.*

*Ana is the Irish goddess of war, but that is probably a coincidence.*

*Arthur fulfils his destiny.*

*Anna marries Lot, Duke of Lothian, brother to Urien. She becomes the mother of Gawain and Modred. But Modred seizes the crown only to lose it ignobly. Both sons fall in the civil war. Gawain seems to die childless. Modred's two sons survive him, but are killed by Custennin, the new High King.*

*The sister's bright future turns to tragedy. It would be wise to avoid any relationship with this family.*

*Anna disappears from the later stories.*

*It is Chrétien de Troyes, late twelfth century, who first brings me into this turbulent dynasty. He calls me Arthur's sister. There are two of us: the mother of Gawain, whom he never names, and Morgain.*

*I bestow on my friends and relations great gifts of healing ointment. I am the lover of Guingomar, Lord of Avalon. I have brought the powers of my fairy island with me into the human scene.*

*When the memory is strong of the matrilineal clan, the emphasis is on Gawain's generation. A man, even Arthur, derives reflected glory from the*

*daring exploits of his sister's sons. There are more stories about Gawain's
sisters than about me.*

*As we move to patriarchy and absolute monarchy Arthur and I become
more important.*

*When Robert de Boron writes his Merlin in the early thirteenth century,
Ygerne has acquired three daughters. The eldest, unnamed, marries Lot,
the second, Urien, and there is a third, whose name is Morgain. I am put
to school, where I achieve outstanding success. I am known as Morgue the
Fay.*

*The Huth Merlin follows. Morgain becomes the second daughter, wife
of Urien, mother of the hero Yvain. Morgue the Fay survives as a separate,
husbandless third daughter.*

*By the Vulgate version of the Arthurian romance Ygerne has had two
husbands before Uther and produces five daughters, wives of Lot, Nentres,
Urien and Karadan. Morgain alone seems to remain unmarried.*

*I am sometimes Gorlois's bastard, sometimes Ygerne's.*

*So, for a time, the Otherworld side of me struggles to hold on to my
independent existence against the human female role of wife and mother.
Then I capitulate. Morgain and Morgue are one. I am married off, sometimes
to Lot but most frequently to Urien. Well, I have ceased to be the fairy
mistress of Avalon and an earthly lady requires a husband. Since Arthur
has become my brother he cannot share my bed, can he? Still, the shadow
of my past falls sometimes on my husband Urien, making his kingdom of
Gorre a delectable paradise or a dangerous Otherworld reached only by a
perilous bridge, hard to escape from.*

*The older tradition still surfaces. Arthur does indeed lie with his sister.
Because of the new relationship, that union is shameful now, not joyful.
In it is sown the seed of Arthur's downfall. Modred, who in earlier stories
is called Lot's son, is now the child of Arthur's incest.*

*It is Margawse's bed Arthur is lured to now, not mine. I have lost him.*

# Chapter Twenty-three

Gwenhyvar, the Giant's Daughter. Gwenhyvar, the 'White Phantom'.

Another pain. I must stand in the church at Caerleon and watch her walk demurely past me to marry Arthur. A child scarcely fourteen, as pale as milk, with hair like the bleached fronds of oats. And yet, I admit it, beautiful in a pure sweet way. Such innocent virginity can quicken men's pulses as much as Red Margawse's eager heat.

Yet as she walked past us to the altar I heard the indrawn breath of the wise women ranked around me, Elaine, Margawse, Luned, Teilo, my Man-become-Woman in his new blue gown. Merlyn had chosen Gwenhyvar for Arthur, and Gwenhyvar was not a child of the Wise. We sensed an opportunity.

We underrated her. Gwenhyvar's power was not in spells or ritual. All the enchantment she needed lay in her own shy, sweetly-smiling self. Without high magic, she worked more harm than all the rest of us.

It seemed power fell into her little hands without her willing it. I witnessed the nuptial mass that joined her to my brother. Then we prepared her for a second ceremony at a different altar. Two churches, two processions, two coronations. One for Arthur, in the Church of the martyr Aaron, for Archbishop Dubric to anoint him in front of all the men. The other, in the sister Church of Saint Julian, to crown Gwenhyvar in the presence of all the women.

There were those who thought this was merely a matter of convenience. Neither church was large. Half Britain had come together for this king-making. Arthur needed all the friends he could win. There were many like Lot who had opposed this crowning. The boy could have remained Duke of Battles, War-Leader of Britain, nothing more. He could not afford to offend the dignity of any chieftain by denying him standing-room at his coronation. He needed their total affirmation. There was no space for women.

We saw it differently. Though that was true, there was an older truth. Merlyn had not chosen Gwenhyvar for his Arthur lightly. It was more than the hero's whim for a pretty West-Country face. Merlyn had calculated that the blood of Gwenhyvar ran royal with the inheritance of the old kings of the West. Our blood, through Ygerne, taps that same source. True, Arthur was also Ygerne's son. But our lineage and, it seemed then, Gwenhyvar's, was certain, our upbringing a matter of public knowledge. Arthur's was clouded. He was spirited away from his parents as a baby. Fifteen years later a youth appeared. We had only Merlyn's testimony they were the same, and Ygerne's wise instinct.

But now, this doubt. Might Gwenhyvar also be false?

We royal women felt our hearts quicken as we escorted the bride to this second altar. We knew what was happening here, though she, as yet, might not.

The silver trumpets sounded for her. White doves were carried in front of her and released. She wore a pale blue gown trimmed with snowy ermine and pearls. She seemed the moon-queen to Arthur's sun, his consort, helpmeet, the sweet reflection of his glory. But she meant more than that.

Bishop Bytwini, in white and gold, waited to greet her with her crown in his hands. She knelt, colouring faintly with proper modesty. He marked her forehead with holy oil. A bell sounded distantly from Arthur's church. And in the hush that followed, the golden circle descended on her silver hair. At that same instant, the nave rocked with the shouts of acclaim from all her noblewomen, and across the town came the deeper roar that told us the Church had made her husband king.

'Receive the Staff of Britain. Wield it well.'

Into her hand, that seemed too small to grasp its weight, Bytwini placed an ancient rod of stone. It gleamed grey-green in the candlelight. A network of shadows traced the carving of strange heads, bird-beaked above, human reversed below. An ancient symbol for a Christian queen. We helped her rise. The stiff cloth of her mantle weighed down her shoulders. It was an effort for her to straighten them and turn to face the congregation. She summoned a radiant smile for all the ranks of ladies massed below her.

'Thank you,' she said. 'I will care for the land, as Arthur will care for me.'

So young, and Maiden still. She did not realise her Arthur was High King because he had wedded Gwenhyvar the High Queen.

Now I and my sisters must prepare her marriage-bed.

# Chapter Twenty-four

*I am the wise healer.*

*I do indeed arrive early at Arthur's court, and for a wedding.*

*By 1160, only ten years or so after Geoffrey of Monmouth introduces me in his Life of Merlin, I have crossed the Channel and begun a new career in the French romances. The courtly Chrétien de Troyes is one of the first to welcome me. He calls me Arthur's sister. He makes only three mentions of me, but they are significant.*

*In the story of Erec and Enide the lovers celebrate their splendid wedding. Among the long list of guests, which includes Maheloas, Lord of the Isle of Glass, an island where thunder is not heard, where lightning never strikes nor tempest blows, where neither toad nor snake live, and it is never too hot or too cold, comes Guingomar, Lord of the Isle of Avalon, of whom it is said:*

*'We have heard of the latter that he was Morgan the Fay's lover.'*

*Years later, after unhappy wanderings, Erec and Enide return to Arthur's court. When Erec is discovered to be sorely wounded, the joy of everyone at this reunion is turned to grief. Arthur sends for a precious ointment made for him by Morgan his sister. It is a sure cure. Any wound, or nerve, or joint anointed with it is certain to be healed within a week if the salve is applied once a day. Though Erec declines to wait that long, my ointment gives him immediate relief.*

*The third time Chrétien refers to me is in the tale of* Yvain, *the Knight with the Lion.*

*Yvain is the French equivalent, though the connection is not made here, of my own son Owain.*

*The hero comes to a magic stone. When water is poured on it a violent storm arises and a fearsome knight gallops up to defend it. Yvain fights with him and gives him a mortal wound. He pursues the fleeing knight back to his castle so furiously that he himself is trapped when the portcullis falls and his horse is sliced in two.*

*He is rescued by the damsel Lunette, who gives him a ring of invisibility. She hides him in the castle till the knight dies. Then she persuades her mistress Laudine that the famous Yvain is just the husband she needs to defend her. After a suitable time she produces him.*

*Yvain in turn defends the stone, till Gawain comes and pours the water that invokes the storm. Yvain comes rushing up. After the fight, there is joyful reunion. Yvain is persuaded to return to Arthur's court. The lady Laudine gives her permission, but charges him solemnly to return in a year's time.*

*Of course, he forgets. Too late he recalls his pledge. Already the damsel Lunette is storming into Arthur's camp. She calls him disloyal traitor, liar, deceiver, and tears Laudine's ring from his finger.*

*Yvain, overcome with remorse, runs mad and naked in the forest. A lady and her two damsels pass that way and spy him deep in slumber. One of the girls is despatched for a closer look. She rides up and recognises Yvain with much amazement by the scar on his face. She returns weeping with the news. A plan is formed. They leave him asleep and hasten to their castle to fetch an ointment.*

*This is a priceless gift from Morgan the Wise. It is kept with the respect it deserves, in a box locked inside a case. The lady entrusts it to her damsel with a warning. It is extremely precious. She is not to be lavish with it. Since Yvain's disorder is only in the brain it will be sufficient to rub just a little of the salve on his temples. The girl is ordered to take great care of the remainder.*

*She returns to the forest, leading an excellent palfrey and bearing fine men's clothes. She goes boldly up to the naked madman. But in her eagerness to cure the lost hero she rubs his entire body till the box of ointment is completely empty. Then she hides behind an oak-tree, leaving the clothes in view.*

*Yvain sleeps in the sunshine, and the black despair seeps from his pores and leaves him whole and sane. He wakes to find himself in his right mind, and as naked as ivory. He is ashamed and bewildered at the evidence of his wildman self. He sees the clothes in front of him and blushes that whoever left them may have recognised him in his bestial state. He dresses his unkempt body and tries to rise. He, who once hunted stags barefoot and ate them raw, finds himself suddenly so weak he can hardly stand. The damsel watches.*

*After a tactful interval she rides up, as though she had only just now come that way. Yvain hails her. She makes a pretence of searching through the trees towards the cries until she finds him. He begs a loan of the spare palfrey she is conveniently leading, and she invites him to her lady's castle till he has recovered. The request is not wholly disinterested. They are expecting shortly to be attacked.*

*By now, standing so long under the trees, the girl has had time to think. Her first rash eagerness has cooled. She realises that the lady's box she clutches in her hands is empty. Morgan's ointment is all gone.*

*She is an intelligent girl. The pair of them have to guide their horses across a bridge over a swiftly roaring torrent. It takes only a moment to fling the box away and see it lost among the cataracts. That bridge is known to be perilous. She will say her palfrey stumbled and the box slipped from her grasp and fell as she almost plunged into the gorge herself.*

*The lady is delighted to see Yvain restored. He need not know how he was cured, or that they observed him in his nakedness, witless. Men's dignity is fragile. But she has not forgotten the ointment. She summons the girl aside. In private she requests the return of the box and the rest of the precious cure it should still contain. Now it is time for the damsel to tremble as she tells her falsehood. She is right to be afraid.*

*The lady is seized with grief and fury. She has lost the best and dearest possession she ever owned. Morgan's gift is irreplaceable. She has won a knight to defend her, but he has proved more costly than she bargained.*

*Chrétien is always courteous about women. Note, I am Morgan the Wise. I am the Healer. The gift I give is the most precious thing anyone could possess. I can heal any hurt, of body or spirit. I am still the magic woman who offers love to a lord on the Island of Avalon. But it cannot be Arthur now. I am his sister.*

*So who is this Guingomar, my new lover?*

# Chapter Twenty-five

I have had many men. I am not promiscuous. I serve the Goddess.

I committed a kind of blasphemy when I prepared Gwenhyvar's marriage-bed. This was not how it should have been. We crumbled the herbs of bitterness to a fine green powder in the folds of her sheets. She would never notice the ergot blighting the rye in the corn dollies we had woven so elaborately and hung over her bed. Even the too-sweet oil of the lamps we left softly burning was tainted.

'She is not one of us,' Elaine said. 'She will bring trouble.'

'Her son shall not inherit over mine.'

I had not told even Margawse where her baby was hidden. Men rarely saw the bitterness with which she mourned both the murder of Gorlois and the loss of Modred. She laughed when she took her revenge. Only I knew the pain.

My loss was different. I must watch Arthur come storming down the corridor towards us, laughing and flushed with wine and lust as a man had a right to be on his wedding-night. His mates ran hard on his heels, cheering him on. And I must join the mock-battle, struggle in the arms of excited young men, pretend that I was trying to keep Arthur from his bride's bedroom door. Pretend!

It was over. We were hot and dishevelled. The door slammed and we were all left on the outside. The men panted and grinned and trooped sheepishly off to down more drink. I leaned, breathless and yet scarcely able to breathe through the tightness that was banding my breast, against Arthur's door, against Gwenhyvar's door. Not long to wait. I heard her small glad cry before the door burst open again and Arthur was brandishing the bloodstained sheet of his triumph on the point of his sword.

Bedwyr seized it from him and raced off. I heard the roar of acclaim from the hall.

The door closed behind Arthur again. He never saw me.

Now they slept. And there was nothing left for me but to join the feast.

I too got drunk. How else could I have borne that night? And I was ashamed and afraid of what I had done. I had been bitter at others before. Gorlois, Luned, Uther, Teilo. I wounded them sorely. Today I had desecrated the Mothers' own bed. Had I hurt Arthur as well as Gwenhyvar?

I felt a strong imperative to purge my sin. I had angered the Mothers. What would come of any union I made that night I dreaded to think. Still I must offer myself. I must make restitution. I must mend the weft.

I chose him calculatingly, even in my fuddled despair. Not kingly Urien. I would not foul my own marriage-bed that night. I honoured Urien, though it has been hard for him to understand. We made a better couple than you might think.

Who, then? Accolon. Yes, that was appropriate. A callow youth, a masculine version of Gwenhyvar. The same slim small bones, the straight pale hair, the blue-grey eyes that showed light without depth. He had payed me pretty compliments, excited to find himself at Arthur's court. I could see him sitting at the corner of the table now, looking over his goblet at this famous company, wondering how a young man with no great pretensions as a warrior could rise to greatness here.

Well, stand up then, Morgan. Carefully now. The floor's as unsteady as a ship.

Light up your face with your best smile for him. Advance towards him. Hold out your hand. He pales and backs away, then blushes and edges uncertainly forward to meet you. You have shattered his young blade's poise. He does not know what to do. Arrest him with your eyes. Soften your lips. You have him now. It does not matter what you say. He cannot resist.

'The hall is warm and the noise too loud. It will be sweeter by the river. Will you escort me, sir?'

Breath was indrawn. Heads turned our way. No one challenged me.

I had no need of this man's safeguard. I had another bitter, surly watchdog. Even tonight, even though he knew plainly what I meant to do, Teilo was following me. I had ended his manhood. Yet he would watch over me while I did with another man what I had denied him with all women. My people are more loyal than I deserve.

'Madam, you honour me.'

Accolon was both eager and overawed. In his eyes I read more of ambition than lust. This was Arthur's sister.

One face I must not look at as I left the hall. It might have broken my heart, if that were possible, as I was breaking his. Forgive me, Urien. I did not choose this marriage. I would not willingly shame you on any other night. It is well that you are more drunk than I am, from the cup I held to your lips. In the morning you will not remember this. Tonight the banshees howl. The Mothers must have their dues.

Forgive me too, Accolon. Your sin this evening was only that you resembled Gwenhyvar. It cost you dearly.

# Chapter Twenty-six

*I am the jealous woman.*

*Accolon was not my first.*

*Chrétien de Troyes names Guingomar, Lord of the Isle of Avalon, as the earliest of my lovers to appear in the pages of medieval romance. We get no more than a passing mention.*

*'We have heard that he was Morgan the Fay's lover.'*

*My name weaves through the lays and literature, shifting and changing. Morgen, Morgain, Morgue, Morgan. So does Guingomar's.*

*In the twelfth century, while Geoffrey was writing chronicles and political prophecies and Chrétien romances, the Breton minstrels were singing their lays of love and heroism.*

*In one of these lays we meet Guingamor, a valiant young knight of Brittany. He has never cared anything for the love of women until a fay captures his heart.*

*He meets her, in the traditional way, on a perilous boar-hunt. He finds her irresistible. She leads him away to her beautiful castle where he forgets the mortal world. Three hundred years seem like three days, but at last a longing to return stirs in him. She lets him go, but warns him that the world is dangerous to him now. She tells him the rules of faerie. He must eat nothing while he is away. He disobeys, of course, and this lively, lusty knight, still apparently in the prime of manhood, sees all his strength shrivel until he becomes a feeble old man of incredible age. The fay takes pity on him and sends her messengers to bring him back to the Land of the Ever-Young over the water.*

*This is a common tale.*

*A more skilful of those Breton poets is Marie de France. Naturally, with a name like that to distinguish her from all the other Maries, she lives in England. She writes between 1160 and 1190, a contemporary of Chrétien's. She may be Abbess of Shaftesbury, half sister to King Henry II, but she can tell a good love-story.*

*Her hero is Guigemar, also beloved by women, also scornful of their love. His downfall this time is a stag-hunt. He falls behind the rest and spies a doe with her fawn half-hidden in a thicket. He draws his bow and shoots. The arrow wounds her, but then flies back and pierces him too. The bleeding doe cries out that she is killed. She pronounces her curse on Guigemar, that no medicine, no herb or root will cure his wound until he is healed by her who will suffer greater pain for his love than any other woman.*

*Guigemar sets out to seek the land across the water where he can find*

669

relief. He rides through the forest till he comes at last in sight of the sea. He has been anticipated. A fair ship is waiting anchored. He goes on board. There is no crew, no pilot, no other passengers. All the same, the ship takes off at speed across the high seas.

It takes him to a port with a high tower defended by a wall on every side except the seaward one. Here an old man, the lord of the city, has imprisoned his beautiful young wife out of jealousy. She takes Guigemar into her tower and heals his bleeding wound. Love blossoms rapidly for the hitherto unsusceptible hero. He lives with her secretly until, after a year and a half, her husband discovers the pair together. Guigemar gets off more lightly than the lady, and is ordered to flee in his ship. Eventually she too escapes and the magic ship is waiting to bring her to Brittany. After much difficulty the lovers are reunited.

The fairy mistress and the human woman have separated. The fairy is beginning to sound vindictive. Never mind that the man has mortally hurt her; this is the hero's story, not the fay's. The human woman suffers too.

So on to the next century and the romance of Lancelot. He is called:

*'The best knight in the world.'*

He is a late arrival in our story, as is his foster-mother, the Lady of the Lake. In Geoffrey of Monmouth's history, Modred is Gwenhyvar's lover.

But the French are jealous of the daring literary exploits of the British, especially Gawain. They need a hero from their own side of the Channel to outshine him. Enter Lancelot, from Brittany.

We are passing on from the chronicles of kings and battles to a different kind of story. What was treachery to his sovereign in Modred becomes in Lancelot the new ideal of Courtly Love.

This doctrine assumes that no self-respecting medieval woman can be in love with her own husband. Granted, love is of slight consideration in these aristocratic betrothals. They are about power and possession. My daughter's hand and half the kingdom in return for killing the dragon. The lady needs some compensation. A romantic 'ami' whose heart and body are totally hers. Courtly Love allows her complete autocracy over his actions. She may command him to do anything, however unreasonable. He is inspired to superhuman deeds to satisfy her, and rewarded by, at least, her smile.

It is the love of Lancelot for Gwenhyvar that destroys Arthur, and the whole Round Table with him. But this courtly couple are portrayed as the hero and heroine of high romance. We must not blame them. Somewhere there has to be another villain and a villainess. Modred and Morgan. So the author requires a reason for me to hate Gwenhyvar.

Meet . . . Guiomar.

He is portrayed as a handsome, valiant knight, nephew to the king and queen. Morgan is Arthur's half-sister, lady in waiting to Gwenhyvar. In the first version I am ugly, but in later tellings, though I am dark I am silky-skinned, my body perfectly modelled, my hands elegant and I am merry and clever. I am also the hottest woman in the Island of Britain and the most lustful.

After a brilliant feast at court the guests troop off to bed, but in a small

670

*chamber deep in the palace I am still embroidering a headdress for my sister, Lot's wife. And Guiomar lingers after the rest have retired. We salute each other debonairly and soon he is winding the golden thread for me. We please each other. The needle slips from my hand and we fall to hugging and kissing. When he sees that I am as eager as he is, we move to the bed.*

*We love in secret. There is more passion on my side than on his. One day Gwenhyvar is attracted by the sound of our quarrelling and finds us in a compromising position. To avert shame from the court she warns Guiomar that his life will be in danger if Arthur hears of our liaison. For love of her, he deserts me all too readily.*

*In my distress I flee the court and seek refuge with Merlyn, who adores me. He teaches me great enchantments. I bear Guiomar's son.*

*The author says that Arthur searches for me unceasingly.*

*Later, in the* Livre d'Artus, *I have my revenge on Guiomar. With the art I learned from Merlyn I create the Vale of False Lovers, my Valley of No Return. Deep in the forest, through a wall of air, come men who have proved untrue to their lovers. They do not get out.*

*In a more sadistic version, I punish the woman too. I fasten two lovers in sight of each other, but out of reach. I make my rival believe she is encased in ice from her feet to her girdle, and wrapped in flame from her girdle to her hair.*

*I rage and grieve for Guiomar, my lost love. But he is not the original one. When I cry out in my restless sleep for the man whom Gwenhyvar stole from me, it is a far more famous name.*

*Yes, I am jealous of Gwenhyvar.*

# Chapter Twenty-seven

Gwenhyvar. Well now. You strayed like a slender-legged filly tossing your mane in the sunshine, too near the lair of wolves. No matter that we squabble among ourselves, Arthur, Margawse, Modred, Elaine, Morgan. We are family.

Still, I have found you a place of safety. Abbess Bryvyth is a warrior-woman of God. She lost Tintagel. She did not retreat from Cornwall. She planted her cross by the River Fowey. It is a nice irony. The white nuns, who kept me Uther's prisoner in my girlhood, and freed my mind to possess the circular earth and starry universe, they will guard you. I cannot save your sons. Nothing of Modred will remain. I think he knew it.

You must have been the only one of us who slept soundly last night, the eve of Camlann. The nuns will have seen to that.

Gwenhyvar. I almost called you 'the queen'. But you are not queen now, are you? You never should have been. You were not the right woman. Britain will not see Arthur again in your lifetime. Modred is already dead. Two tiny strips of flesh, twin boys, mewl in their baskets. You never gave Arthur so much, and the one son you bore him died straining for his manhood. And these? My tears flow faster now, for these are Modred's sons. I think the nuns in their quiet convent cannot shield them long.

Cornwall. The blood flows back to the heart. The far south-west. We were all born here. Arthur, you and I. We come home for our final leave-taking. Custennin of Dumnonia will take up Arthur's fallen crown. Modred's sons, Arthur's grandsons, he will not allow to live. Oh, Gwenhyvar, what have you robbed him of?

You have drunk the nuns' soothing draught, and you lie in darkness, your face serene. Younger than I, and fairer in your sleep. You have known more happiness than I did. I have ended that.

You will wake in a narrow hard bed in an anchorite's cell underground, with only a wind-eye for God to see you. Too late you have vowed yourself to chastity and prayer. Too late for everyone but yourself. Tomorrow they will tell you Modred is dead, and you will weep. They will tell you Arthur was carried away and has been seen no more, and you will shudder and fear the future. When Custennin's men come, the Abbess Bryvyth will belabour their ears. They will search the holy place for you, in spite of her. I think they will not find you. But they will find your babies. The convent cannot hide them.

Gwenhyvar, the Giant's Daughter. Gwenhyvar, the White Phantom. I remember you, pale and slight as thistledown, walking up the church aisle to your wedding with Arthur. And we, all the ranked powers of warriors and wise women, turning our heads to stare and get the measure of you.

I heard the triumphant hiss of breath behind me. Teilo, my servant, that had once been Smith. He was a great master of magic before he met me. He should have known. You fooled him. You almost fooled me too.

He thought you had no magic in you.

In part, he was right.

You did not weave and work at enchantment, like Nimue, Lady of the Lake, coaxing the keys to wisdom out of Merlyn, casting her eyes over my store of herbals from the open door, running her fingers seductively even up Teilo's arm. She wanted power. You accepted it as your right.

You were the still, hollow centre of Camelot's world. And into that well flowed all the life and love that made it brilliant: Arthur, Gawain, all Margawse's and my sons, our daughters too, grey warriors from the British Isles that had known your father, young fighting men from beyond the Channel, even from Africa, the bards and pages, and Modred.

I almost said 'my son'. No, Arthur's son. You learned the truth too late. Too late for you; your bed was fouled already. I saw the horror in your eyes when I declared his provenance before the court. I heard you scream. Yet not too late to save Arthur, if you had wished.

That difficult, painful reconciliation with his son. Were his hands softer now in middle age than the hard-riding, fighting youth's that reached out, oh, so reluctantly, no doubt, to lift the baby Modred from the cart? His son, his firstborn prince. A vast litter of screaming May-born infants bagged up in a boat like kittens to be drowned. And Arthur's mistake. The brat that should not have been got upon his sister.

*He did not know.* I scream that at you, Gwenhyvar; he did not know when he got Modred. But you knew, when you got Modred's sons. You knew by then who Modred was. Arthur was ignorant of that second treachery as he reached out those sinning hands to touch and hold his adult son.

You did not warn him, and you did not let Modred go. And still the honour and the love rained down on you to fill your hollow like a limpid pool. So clear, so pure, so transparent is Gwenhyvar. You seemed to will nothing. You merely let it happen.

You were like Olwen White-Track in the old tale, who was also the Giant's Daughter. She sat and smiled, and for her wedding feast impossible quests were undertaken, treasures stolen, countries ravaged, warriors torn to death by savage boars, Arthur's band devastated. She got her husband.

So you walked up the aisle, the meekly blushing bride with lowered lids. So you were crowned. You stole from Arthur the sceptre that we had entrusted you with. You tore the kingdom from him and reigned yourself. You coupled with his son. Your royal blood legitimised Modred's coronation.

And I consented to it.

There was one woman who did not. Gwenhyvach, your half-sister. Little Gwen, a thing to be hidden, a daughter to be ashamed of. Our story is full of the unacknowledged parts of ourselves crying out to be loved.

I will not ask again who was the false Gwenhyvar, and who the true. I can still see the mark of Modred's hand flaming on your cheek, the tears of outrage in your eyes, Gwenhyvach's smile. Only this I knew: if you were not our true queen, sickness would haunt the land, the crops would wither and the cows and ewes bar up their wombs.

The plague is here.

I leave you now, your children born, emptied of queenship, marriage, motherhood. Pale, exhausted, fearful of the spiritual warfare I have sent you to.

You brought us to Camlann, and you find refuge in a nunnery. Where will the rest of Britain shelter from the storm?

# Chapter Twenty-eight

*I am the Wild Huntsman's lover.*

*I am tempted by lesser men, who might have loved me better, as in the thirteenth-century tale,* Li Jus Adan.

*In the French city of Arras it is their custom to entertain Morgan, with her attendant fays, Maglore and Arsile. One evening, the table is richly laid in preparation for our arrival with fair linen, gold and silver. These citizens know what is due to us.*

*We have come prepared to bless the town. Always we fays offer both promise and danger. Arsile and I are laughing, well-pleased with what we find. We deal out riches, love, beauty, success to the two hosts who have provided this for us. Townsfolk raise their goblets to us. We are welcome here.*

*But there has been a small oversight. No knife has been laid for Maglore. Insult! Anger! Fear! For this omission she will deal them pain, famine, poverty, sorrow. We are not to be trifled with or crossed. If you accept our favours you are committing yourselves to our service. You neglect us at your peril.*

*The feast resumes.*

*Who is this at my elbow, breaking in on the merriment? Crokesot, messenger of the fairy king, Hellekin. He brings an entreaty to me from his master, but I am too busy holding court. These humans please me. I, at least, am honoured here.*

*Well now, here is this excellent young man, Robert Soumeillons, offering me his hand and heart. I like him well. I could stay here with him, in this safe, sunny, ordered city among men who adore me. The idea is tempting. I am on the point of saying yes.*

*But someone is insistently interrupting. Crokesot again. What is this message from his fairy lord, that will not wait?*

*Hellekin the Huntsman, they call him, leader of the Furious Chase. A winter king, grey as the storm-clouds that sweep over Europe when the bitter nights outlast the trembling days. You hear the howling of his hounds and hide your faces to the wall as the Wild Hunt goes past. Do not walk out by night, do not let them catch you; you will not come home.*

*Hellekin the Huntsman wants my love.*

*I laugh and say he sighs in vain. I am giving my hand to the human.*

*Crokesot plays on my imagination. How could the fierce fairy soul of Morgan the Fay be satisfied here in the summery city of Arras?*

*Oh, the pull of the wild dangerous Otherworld against the solid comfort of an earthly marriage. Have I still the courage to fly the night sky with my fairy lover? Or the strength to turn my back on Hellekin, the sense to* stay with a human husband? Which will I risk: heartbreak with the Huntsman or disappointment with the predictable Robert?

Young Robert Soumeillons pleads for my constancy. Crokesot and Arsile argue more passionately for Hellekin.

Passion wins. I choose the Storm-King.

The feast is breaking up. A lady comes to beg my help to disgrace a man. I take flight, singing.

Do not trust me. I am dangerous. I will break your heart.

Arthur, the Bretons say, leads the Wild Hunt.

At Cadbury too, there is an old track called King Arthur's Lane. On a rough night the spectral king and his hounds can be heard bearing down on the unwary.

I will embrace the tempest that is coming. I will ride the storm.

# Chapter Twenty-nine

On Arthur's wedding-night I lay, still haunted by my painful imaginings, in a crowded guest-room of his Roman castle. A tiny hand gripped mine warmly. I came back unwillingly to my body. My little daughter Morfudd was leaning over me.

'Ssh!' A childish scolding.

I followed the nod of her head. We were not the only ones awake. A vast grey shadow was sliding across the painted wall into the darkness of the doorway. I did not need Morfudd's hand dragging me across the room to know what she would show me. The bed of my eldest sister, Elaine, was empty.

And I, who had done so much hurt already to Arthur, Urien, Accolon, was filled with fear. Elaine meant our brother harm. I was the Healer. I had vowed these hands to making men and women whole. I had given way to meanness.

With stealthy haste I followed. And Teilo, once again, followed me. Too late we saw her coming from Gwenhyvar's bridal chamber. She was carrying something swathed, enfolded against her breasts. She still moved smoothly, but I thought her feet dragged heavier than before.

Elaine was all the mother of my own blood I had ever known. Ygerne had rejected me, a third daughter, the seal on her failure in a warrior's world. I had sat cradled in my sister's lap, a fierce, wild, ugly child, leaning sleepily on those same fragrant breasts that passed me now.

Lullabies hummed through my head. I found it hard to move. I watched her slipping away into the dusky garden. I have always struggled to understand Elaine. Little spoken of, quieter than any of us, as wise in magic as Ygerne, our mother's favourite. More innocent than I was as a maiden. More gentle a mother than passionate Margawse. Growing more mysterious as she aged. What was she taking away tonight?

A cold draught eddied along the colonnade, stirring the hair round my face. I shook myself awake and forced my feet into urgent movement. I do not have the Sight, as Elaine does. I dreaded what I would find.

Outside the couple's door, sleep lay unnaturally heavily on Gwenhyvar's women, on Cei, stretched with his hand on his dirk across the threshold, even on Arthur's dog. Our shadows passed over them like uneasy dreams. The door yielded lightly.

Some lamps still glowed, too sweetly.

Arthur and Gwenhyvar slept in each other's arms.

No blood, no devastation. That is not Elaine's way. I cannot say which would have been the greater grief.

A sword lay naked on the bed beside Arthur's hand.

Caliburn.

Even on his wedding-night he would not be parted from his true love. The weapon lay, half lapped in the folds of the bearskin coverlet. The scabbard had dropped, unregarded, into the rushes on the floor.

A naked sword, in a bridal bed? Had Arthur been boasting of his bare blade to tease Gwenhyvar?

It lay only a hand's-breadth from Arthur's grasp. But now those victorious hands held softer skin than the golden dragon-scales wrought by the elves of Avalon for Britain's champion. Gwenhyvar was snuggled in his embrace. Gwenhyvar I could not touch. But this I could rob him of.

I picked the weapon up. I almost dropped it with a sense of shock. It was like lifting a corpse. Even as my hands closed round it I felt its falseness. The dragons were there, with tongues of flame. The letters hammered along the blade. This looked like Caliburn. This was not Caliburn. Elaine had taken the sword forged in Avalon for the greatest King of Britain, trusted by those before us to Nimue, the Lady of the Lake, as guardian, given ritually to Arthur at his coming to manhood. With that, he had driven the Saxons to take the first steps back to the long shores. It was his talisman of victory and meant to win our peace. Elaine had left this one in its place.

A poisonous, jealous thought crept through my mind, like a viper, jaggedly patterned. Could my sisters feel about Arthur as I did too? Were they my rivals as well as Gwenhyvar?

Or had Elaine melted into the night serving a deeper purpose?

Arthur stirred in his sleep, and murmured against Gwenhyvar's cheek.

I was a wronged woman; I was a Wise Woman. I held that treacherous counterfeit in my hands and looked down at pretty sleeping Gwenhyvar, that false substitute for Arthur of Britain's true mate. Heart and duty warred, like wild dogs against a disciplined hound.

I lifted that false Caliburn. I cannot say where it might have fallen.

A small voice shocked us both: 'No, Mammy, don't do it!'

Owain, my son, in the room, and Luned, terrified, chasing after him. Those wide accusing childish eyes. The high, clear voice.

Arthur's castle erupted into rage and horror. The door was flung wide back. Cei's knife was in his hand. A babble of women's voices broke like a floodtide above a swirl of shifts.

With all my art I held them, powerless, back from the door. I heard Arthur roar behind me.

'*Morgan!*'

I must not turn and see his blue eyes blazing at me without love. I must not see him shielding pale, shocked Gwenhyvar. I must keep my strength. I threw down that gilded, useless toy that had replaced the Lady's gift, as Gwenhyvar had replaced the true wife of the High King of Britain. Let him snatch it up and keep it if he loved the look of it. It would betray him. I seized the only thing of worth left in the room, Caliburn's scabbard. The Lady's talisman of healing. Gwenhyvar would not know how to use that. Only the true blade and the true sheath must know each other. I would guard this better.

With that protection, I sped through the doors, like a sudden wind on the lake that agitates the surface and is gone. Teilo yelled for horses. He flung Owain aside. This was no time for children. My people were armed and rushing to meet us. Our mounts were ready in moments. We sprang astride and charged the gates. Beyond was night and freedom and a vast cold loneliness outside the walls. I would not be welcome again in Arthur's court.

Arthur pursued me.

My brother and his men ran us down in a wood. Urien was with them. I led my people down into a cold hiding-place. I whispered runes of concealment over us.

We lurked like stones in chilly bog-water. Over our heads the skeleton of a sacrificed horse swayed creaking from a branch, hung with the dark tatters of its hide. It was an awful place. What had happened here, that the Great Queen of Horses had demanded this offering from her people? What had I sacrificed?

The men quartered the muddy shore of the hollow, but their mounts shied back from the creeping ooze and the swinging bones that creaked against the darkness. They passed us by, unrecognised, and the sound of their horses' hooves was lost in the wilderness.

I turned myself to stone. I had stolen Arthur's healing. I have not felt warm since.

# Chapter Thirty

*I am the traitor.*

*In less than a hundred years my character has changed from Geoffrey's healing fay to what it has since become. Before the mid-thirteenth century I am already the vindictive seductress, enemy of Arthur.*

*I harm Arthur, Urien, Accolon.*

*The Huth Merlin tells how Morgan lures all three of them: Arthur my brother, Urien my husband, Accolon my lover.*

*They are out hunting. A great hart appears, as always. The three of them pursue it and are soon separated ten miles from the rest of the pack. They chase him so hard their horses are ridden to death under them. The stag leads them to – where else? – the bank of a river. They come upon the beast in his death throes in the water, with a brachet biting his neck. Arthur the king claims the prize.*

*But the real adventure is only just beginning. A ship comes speeding down the stream and comes to rest lightly on the sandy shore. She is hung with silk, right down to the water's edge. Night is falling, and they step on board. Out of the darkness a hundred torches flame, and here are twelve damsels to greet them on their knees, lead them to a stateroom richly hung, serve them with choice food and wine. Then, a luxurious cabin for each of them, and sound sleep.*

*When the three of them wake, Arthur is in prison, Accolon is sitting beside a strange fountain, and Urien is in bed in Camelot in my arms.*

*Yet I mean him harm too.*

*First, Arthur learns that there is only one way he may win his deliverance from the tower. He must fight in the place of the cowardly lord of this castle to resolve a quarrel. His adversary is the lord's younger brother, but he is badly wounded before the appointed day. I arrange that his role will be played by Accolon.*

*For a year, Arthur has left Caliburn and its scabbard in my safe-keeping. Note how completely my brother trusts me. When he sends me a message requesting his sword for this fight, I supply a counterfeit, which arrives just before he takes the field. I have already despatched my dwarf to Accolon, carrying the true Caliburn.*

*The contest begins. Naturally, neither combatant knows his opponent's real identity. Arthur cannot win. His opponent has the sword that ensures victory. The king has also lost the scabbard that protects him from hurt. He loses much blood. But still he fights so bravely that Accolon is sorely wounded too.*

*It is the Lady of the Lake who rescues Arthur, as she thwarts all my evil plans. When Arthur is at his last gasp, she realises what is happening. She* strikes *Caliburn* from Accolon's hand by magic. Arthur seizes it back.

Now the battle turns. Arthur has Accolon at his mercy. At the point of the stolen sword, the young man confesses everything: his name, my guilty love that has schemed to set us both on the throne, and all my plots against Arthur's life and Urien's.

Accolon is forgiven. The blame is all mine.

His pardon comes too late. Accolon dies of his wounds. Arthur himself now lies in a convent, gravely ill. Yet he is not so weak that he cannot despatch my lover's bloody body to me, for me to see what I have done.

Ignorant yet of Accolon's fate, I believe there is still one more thing I need to do to complete my triumph. In Camelot, I send my maiden for Urien's sword, and carry it to his bedside. As I raise my arms to strike the final blow, Owain our son, warned by this maiden, comes rushing in and grabs my hand. He threatens that if I were not his mother, he would smite me dead. I beg for mercy and secrecy. He grants me forgiveness, on my solemn promise that I will never harm Urien again.

I make no promise for Arthur's safety.

My brother's gruesome present for me arrives at court, with the taunt that he has *Caliburn* again in spite of all my evil. I stare at the corpse of my young lover. I must not show my heart is breaking. I plead with Gwenhyvar to let me leave. In Arthur's absence, she is unwilling to allow me to go, but I prevail.

I will seek out Arthur in his convent now. I will be revenged. The frightened nuns are reluctant to let me see him, but they do not dare to forbid his sister to enter his chamber.

The sword has been separated from its sheath. He sleeps with *Caliburn* naked in his hand, his boyhood love. All I am able to steal from him is the scabbard. When he wakes, weak as he is, and finds it gone, he calls for men to pursue me. He shall not have it back this time. As I flee, I fling the scabbard deep into a lake past all recovery. Arthur is vulnerable now. His end is marked from here. I have, in effect, slain him.

I turn myself, my horses and my followers into blocks of stone, and so escape the hunt. I barricade my castles. It is my turn to taunt him that he cannot touch me. I am a shape-shifter and, but for the Lady of the Lake, I would have done him worse harm.

Arthur threatens me in his turn.

I send a damsel to him with a richly jewelled mantle as an offer of reconciliation. Again the Lady of the Lake interferes. She orders my damsel to put on the mantle herself. The unhappy girl falls dead in front of the king. My mantle burns her to cinders.

I am accursed. Urien, my husband, is exonerated. His loyalty to Arthur is beyond question. I nearly killed him too.

But Owain carries with him a hint of suspicion. He may be too much my son. He is expelled from the court. His cousin Gawain indignantly insists on leaving with him.

Owain is reinstated later. I never am.

# Chapter Thirty-one

Yes, I ritually killed the scabbard. Almost a suicide.

Do you think it strange that I, of all women, should cast away the power of healing?

You do not understand how dangerous that power may be, how close the scabbard marries with the sword. There is only a fine line between new-won life and sudden death. It needs a great exertion to drag the sufferer back from the brink. In one rash movement we may find that we have overplayed our force and stepped too far.

The killing sword may also win us life. Nothing is simple.

I feared the power in our hands.

A sacred cave above Din Eidyn, Lot's stronghold. A spring ran from the entrance, staining the rock red. Inside, a raised slab of stone, as though the gods had made this chapel for us knowingly.

We laid our tributes on it. Elaine the Fair, our lily-maid, now heavy in the body with the change brought by the bearing of a single child, put down the sword as though it were a thing of massive weight.

Even in the shadow, the gold danced. Flesh-hungry dragons strained from the hilt, opening mouths from which red tongues shot out to lick at cold blue steel. The blade was awesome. Few smiths would know the magic of that hammering, the metal softened and bent and hardened, over and over again, growing stronger with each tripling. The ancient tracery scored in its final setting, spelling a simple truth for those who have the wisdom to read it:

TAKE ME UP.

And on the reverse:

CAST ME AWAY.

One question had hammered in my head since I saw Elaine coming from his chamber, smothering it in the folds of her bosom.

'Why?'

Dull her voice. I could not tell if she knew what she said, or if the spirit spoke through her.

'Let him discover he is vulnerable.'

A threat? A fairy wisdom?

I thought Elaine's eyes read the future more clearly than the present. She saw the handsome, blue-eyed youth riding a high-stepping horse through cheering crowds, claiming his right to the heart and body of every woman, sliding that sword so easily into the entrails of Angles, Saxons, Picts.

I saw a boy, shadowed by doubts and plots and rivalry. A casque of fragile bone shielding the source of immense dreams. A little lifespan weighed down with the vast pains and hopes of this mighty Island.

I matched the scabbard along the weapon's length.

A simple case of black leather and wood, much used, but serviceable still. Banded with silver, once patterned with magic, that had worn so smooth its mystery was almost lost to sight. The fingertips might feel, faintly, the uncertain evidence of wisdom. A lining of old red silk so frail the blade had parted its threads. A plain and quiet thing to lie alongside that flamboyant hilt and blade. Unless you knew.

'Where one has gone, the other must follow. They belong to each other.'

I was not sure what we had done. We had not taken kingship from him. That was a different sword. This was his battle-weapon.

Red Margawse shrugged and laughed lightly, 'A High King's wedding is not so common a feast that I would have left it readily. But you two had created such a pother with your plots that it was impossible for me to stay. It will be a long time before we are invited to that court again. That being so, I brought away a keepsake of my own.'

Her creamy fingers twined between the sword and scabbard, knotting them firmly together. A belt. As simple as the sheath. Black leather, soft, supple and scuffed with use. Old silver clasps.

She lifted it carelessly. It raised the scabbard easily. The tension spread across the table to the separated weapon. The knot grew tight around the pommel of the sword. The leather stretched and strained against the weight of gold. The soft edges of the belt began to split and part.

'No!' I shot out a hand involuntarily. 'It is too frail!'

Elaine's larger hand descended over ours and took the belt from both of us. She unhooked it from the sword and from the scabbard, folded it lovingly and tucked it in her breast.

'Leave it with me. I will make it stronger.'

We made strong spells to keep them.

A time of trouble followed. Ravens came swooping from the east and the north croaking their news of disaster: young, spirited men, wearing gold torques, left as bloodless corpses on the field of battle, strong walls breached and sanctuaries desecrated. Books burned and virgins bloodied. Celtic Britain was shrinking.

Arthur was gravely wounded.

I could not shriek or weep when they told me. The skin of my face felt cold. I thought I had died, still standing.

Had I done this?

Screech-owls sounded in the night, bringing back old scenes, as Luned and Teilo watched over me anxiously. In the faces of these two I read the power I had used.

I remembered a little boy, Howel, in the school at Tintagel. I was older than him; he was in love with me. Always he was at my elbow, bringing me gifts, coaxing a smile from me. I was a serious scholar. One day I toiled over a page of Euclid, meticulously copying a triangle and the bisection of angles. The diagram was exact, the theorem clearly written. The scroll would not disgrace our schoolroom library. Howel came, nudging my elbow to show me a tabby kitten. The ruler swivelled. The nib tore the page. My work was wasted.

I jumped up in a towering anger and cursed the child.

Next day I had forgotten it. Released to freedom, I led a wild game of hide-and-seek across the cliffs. I loved both speed and danger. I fled to the southern side, out of sight of the nuns' cells. On the steep grassy slope I darted behind a boulder and crouched, waiting. The children's cries sang overhead, distant as skylarks. Then a breathless, chuckling laughter followed me down. Howel had spied me. I did not see him slip. One sudden cry, short, high and final. He somersaulted past me. The rocks devoured him. The sea washed him away.

I have tried to hold the balance. I have striven with passion and might and obedience to be wise. It has come hardly to me.

Teilo still bears the scars.

He came to me in Rheged, Lord of high magic to my Lady. He was the Smith. I showed him the herbs of healing. He scorned them. I placed beside them the seeds of death. He took away both.

I had another maiden then, younger than Luned. Erith, golden and merry, and respectful of no one, except the Mothers. She was much less of a scholar than Luned, but far more wise. When I sent them to the forest to gather fungus she had teased me laughingly that great Merlyn could make and unmake kings without such simples. It flicked me on the raw. Arthur had vanished. I could not find out where Merlyn was keeping him and we had all lost sight of Merlyn himself. The years were stealing life from me. I was Urien's wife. I was carrying Urien's child. Once more, I lashed her with my tongue.

Teilo took her. By force, in the forest, with those strong Smith's arms. He made her drink the potion he had brewed with the darker herbs. He scorned to use the ones I had given him to bring life back. They carried her home to me, purple, twisted, terrible. Had I caused this?

My curse drove him mad. It wracked me too. Owain and Morfudd were born that night in grief and pain. I never forgot Teilo. That awful tilting of the balance out of true. He fled to a Christian hermit, to Nimue, even to Merlyn. They could not mend him. Three years later I drew him back to me. And only then he told me that the day I cursed him, his wife fell dead of poison and he was blamed for it. Should I have taken a knife and cut these healer's hands from my wrists, that wreak such havoc in the lives of others?

He came back to me disguised as a woman, and Woman he has remained. He chose the way of death to prove his power over me. I have taught him the path of life.

I did not know how great my power to heal and harm. I did not know how much Arthur depended on Caliburn for victory and how far on himself. Bright clouds of magic and prayer swirled round us both, dazzling our sense of what we were and did. We could not see ourselves, or each other, clearly.

Arthur lay at Celliwig, near to death. We sisters held his sword and scabbard.

We were the land. We were the stone. We were Britain's healing.

I went to Elaine in Garlot, Black Annis Hill, and begged the weapon and its sheath from her on my knees.

'For a Daughter of the Ocean you are strangely impatient. How long does it take for a cliff to be eaten away or a new island to be formed?'

'But it is Arthur who is being eaten away. The King. The Lady's champion.'

'Kings come, kings go. The Island remains.'

'It is not the same. It will never be the same if the Saxons advance.'

'The Romans came, even as far as Cornwall. The Island you love is partly their making. Before us, it was different still.'

'Then why Arthur?'

A heavy pause. 'Or one day Modred?'

'Is it only Merlyn's ambition? Against our rivalry?'

'We gave him his sword of kingship. We have not taken that away.'

'You have stolen what alone defends that right.'

'He loves his first sword more than the other. Does he understand yet that Caliburn is the King's servant, not his god?'

'He is young. He may die before he learns that lesson, and Britain will be overrun.'

'And if we give it back?'

'Let us at least take the risk. He is our mother's son.'

And so, with her unwilling authority, I went to Margawse. She was more ready.

'It would be a shame to see the maggots crawling out of the darling flesh of him. Give him his toy.'

She gave me the sword and scabbard from the secret hiding-place in Lothian. The belt was missing.

It was a far, hard journey to Celliwig in Cornwall. And when I arrived, I was not welcome.

Cei turned me away from the gate of the fort rudely. 'He has wise women enough to look after him. The nuns and, if magic were needed, Nimue.'

'They have returned? She and Merlyn!'

'The Lady came alone.'

A quarrel? Some shift of power? Merlyn deserted Uther when Arthur was born. I did not believe it. Arthur had not achieved his destiny yet.

Lean low. Smile. Keep my voice sweet and reasonable. He must understand.

'Friend, you have a traitor in your camp. I must speak with my brother.'

Words stung my face, like hazel twigs thrown for scorn. I struggled to hold the sense of them.

'Be off with you, woman. It would shame the king as well as yourself if we have to remove you by force. But I will do it if you are still here one hour from now, Arthur's sister or not.'

Never a courteous man, Cei, or a wise one.

What wounded dignity kept me from handing the sword and scabbard over, there at the gate?

I summoned Accolon out of the fort secretly. We met in a clearing in the woods that freezing winter morning. I entrusted Caliburn, sheathed, into his hands solemnly, and with it the message Cei would never have delivered.

'Tell Arthur, we found these separated, even on his wedding night. Always, we offer him the weapon in the stone. Always he sees his glory in the naked blade. What we have allowed him to take, he must return. Tell him that truth and joy wait for our meeting.'

He had no time to carry my message. Nimue came galloping through the wood with her red cloak streaming from her shoulders. She saw the weapon in his hands, but whirled on me.

'So it is you! You stole Caliburn from Arthur, and the scabbard with it.'

But Nimue, Lady of the Lake, had stolen from Arthur a truer friend even than that.

'Where is Merlyn? Why is he not with Arthur? What have you done with him?' I challenged her.

The radiance of her smile showed how much she relished the power she had now taken for herself.

'I, responsible for the great enchanter Merlyn? You sisters could never overcome him yourselves, and yet you believe I have?'

'Where is Merlyn now?'

I sensed her falter, and fear sprang across the gap from her to me. '*Where?*'

'U . . . under a great rock . . . of his own free will! . . . He wearied me with his lascivious attentions.'

'You coveted Merlyn's power.'

'You sisters are too bitter. I offered him love and I got what I asked. The power that Merlyn had belongs in a woman's hands, doesn't it?'

And in that one word 'had' I heard the truth.

'How long will you keep him prisoner? He is your prisoner, isn't he?'

Silence, as long as the silence of the grave. It will never be broken. I felt the world slip from its pivot and tumble into the void. The balance of our enchantments was overturned. I must have screamed.

'You cannot do it! You made the great spell of binding, and you did not learn how to unloose it! Merlyn is trapped for ever, isn't he? There is no one, no one, who could break that now except Merlyn himself, and he is sleeping. He will not come back to Arthur ever again!'

The rest was chaos. Nimue stretching out the finger of power to forestall me. Accolon drawing the sword in a flash of dragon's breath. His horse bolting. Both sword and scabbard lying in the snow where they had fallen, one black, one golden, crystals of ice melting around their silhouettes. So near each other. So small a space of snow between them.

Nimue and I dived for them, I darting forward from the sycamore tree where I stood, she swooping low from the saddle of her roan. I swear I meant to give them back to Arthur. But not from Nimue's hands, with Nimue's words.

She snatched up Caliburn exultantly. Brandishing the sword aloft she galloped off, taunting me. I was left clutching the scabbard to my chilled heart. Nimue, of all wise women, knew its ancient power. She was the present Lady of the Lake. She knew how the weapon and sheath both came from Avalon. She understood that the scabbard of healing was worth ten times the sword. In the moment of decision she had let me keep it because she saw it was the sword that Arthur loved.

Arthur had not been able to undo what he had done, and nor could I. I still held the scabbard in my shaking hands.

We found Accolon hanged, caught in the branch of a tree.

# Chapter Thirty-two

*Am I myself the ambivalent Lady of the Lake?*

*Both of us live in magical realms across, or beneath the water.*

*We are both the foster-mother of heroes.*

*We both rescue orphaned princes and whisk them off to safety. We train them in warfare and nobility. We tell them their parentage. We send them back into the world.*

*We heal their madness and their wounds.*

*We are skilled in enchantments.*

*Both of us are pupils of Merlyn. He loves us lustfully and unwisely. I also am accused of imprisoning him in his tomb.*

*We are both benevolent and dangerous.*

*The world cannot live with this ambivalence in one person. It requires that characters identify themselves as evil or good. Especially if they are supernatural. A polarisation, then: the protective Lady of the Lake versus the malignant Morgan.*

It is the Prophecies of Merlin written by a French-speaking Italian in the thirteenth century, which speaks the worst of me.

*Merlyn, my tutor in magic, is attracted to me, but he has another sweetheart, Nimue. Because of her boasting, I have called her a whore. To win her favour back, he praises her and reviles me:*

*Nimue has a more natural gift for enchantment and more subtle art than any woman in the world.*

*I am the child of heat and lust; she, of paradise.*

*I purpose and work evil; she acts well.*

*I kill good knights; she helps them.*

*I am the enemy of orphans; she fosters them.*

*It is true that I work against Lancelot and Gwenhyvar, whom Nimue encourages. Did I destroy Arthur? Might he have survived if he had stayed innocent of their falsity and the good fellowship of the Round Table not torn itself apart over those two?*

*Nimue and I are enemies because of this. Her good against my evil. And yet . . .*

In the Prophecies of Merlin all women are dangerous.

*I wish to get rid of Nimue. When she sets out on a journey, I order fifteen knights across the sea to capture her and I send a message to King Claudas to lay an ambush. She hears of this in time and guards herself, but she is fearful that I will harm Lancelot. Merlyn she does not trust. He is too fond of me, and on friendly terms with Claudas.*

*Merlyn leads her into a cave in the forest, which contains a tomb. Only she can find the way there. For fifteen months they stay together. Then I enter the forest.*

*I am searching for Merlyn. When the Lady of the Lake hears my hunters' horns, she is afraid. If Merlyn helps me, I will kill her fosterlings, Lancelot and his two cousins.*

*Merlyn assures her he will never again leave this cave. She begs to stay with him. He makes this lover's plea: that after his death she will be buried here with him, in the same tomb. Nimue suggests he lie down in it, so that she can test if there is room for two. The moment he is in, she slams down the lid, and fastens it with the magic he himself has taught her. No one may open it now.*

*Now she reveals another motivation. I have taunted her. I told her Merlyn had boasted to me that he took her maidenhood. Too late for him to swear before God that the charge is false. Merlyn is lost to the world.*

*It is all my fault.*

# Chapter Thirty-three

Arthur recovered, even without his scabbard. The hands of the nuns from the River Fowey must have been skilful, and their prayers were strong.

I nursed the scabbard to my heart and an image in my mind. That small cold space of snow between Caliburn and this sheath. The flakes of ice melting around their separated shapes, flowing together, almost meeting. Soft yellowed moss beneath, waiting for the sunlight to turn it springing green.

So narrow a distance. I would make a great leap of love across it. I would show Arthur he need not fear my ambition or my jealousy. I would heap on him a gift of such generosity he must believe I meant him well.

What should it be? Some precious, healing ointment in an alabaster box? A harp so rare and sweet you would think Rhiannon's birds nested among its strings? But Arthur was whole and warlike again, and music did not seem to move him as it did me. What was appropriate from Morgan the Wise to her Arthur the King?

We had given him royalty. In our blood, in Margawse's flesh, in the ritual sword. Let me be overwhelmingly generous then in affirming it. I had offered my womb, and lost. Let me give him my hands, my eyes, my heart. Arthur should have from my fingers a mantle fit for the Emperor of Constantinople himself. A gorgeous thing. A magic thing. An imperial gift. Let me show how I both loved and honoured my brother.

I set to work. I sent for costly velvet, woven on Venetian looms, dyed richest purple. I beggared Urien's treasury for jewels. I laid in coils of gold and silver wire and heaped up basketfuls of bright embroidery silks. I smiled on Teilo. I let him remember he was once a Smith. He was never a silverworker, but his hands were clever. He had the adept's feeling for the soul of metal. He knew the spells of smiths. Under my coaxing he drew out gold and silver almost to the fineness of sewing thread.

I sketched designs on scrolls of parchment. The nuns, Rathtyen, Cigfa and Eira, had taught me well. I knew the mathematical secrets of interlacing, the dimensions of spirals and circles and Arianrhod's Wheel. I let imagination flow in cats and griffins, serpents of resurrection, vines of plenty. And for the Pendragon, one immense, spectacular dragon danced glittering scales around the border and opened its flaming, laughing mouth upon the collar. The lining should be of shimmering gold silk.

I told my sisters of my plan. Margawse was wild with jealousy as she watched me cut the rare, rich cloth. Elaine said little.

All through the fast of Advent I and my women stitched that miraculous cloak. Drops of my own blood darkened the purple from my too eager fingers.

With every twist of the pattern, with every loop of the needle through the cloth, I whispered a spell of turning, binding, meeting.

At last, just before Christmas, the lavish embroidery was finished. Arthur would celebrate the Christian feast in Carlisle, ten miles from Lyvennet. All that remained to sew was the plain gold lining. And then, we would both rejoice.

When I had set the last stitch of silver, I had Luned and Teilo spread the great mantle across the floor under the lightest window. All the women crowded to look and gasp and admire. I had woven my soul into this embroidery. I could only offer it now. I put my needle away. I had my women sweep up the clippings of silk. An immense weariness came over me. For Urien's sake we all fasted through Advent. But Christmas was almost here.

I lay on my bed, hugging the dream of my love-gift which warmed my heart like the healing scabbard. I closed my eyes in deep exhausted sleep.

Elaine woke me, kissing my feverish forehead, almost a maternal touch. She smiled down kindly.

'It is finished, little sister. Luned and Teilo and I have sewn in the lining.'

I felt a sudden, childish pang of disappointment. This should have been entirely my gift, not Margawse's, not Elaine's. All the plans, all the expense, all the months of skilful painstaking labour had been my doing, or that of the people of my court. I did not want to share my heart with either of my sisters.

Still, it was done. That last plain, simple stitching. The mantle lay, spread out as I had left it, but the jewels and precious thread of the dragon winked more secretively now in the winter lamplight.

I stroked the encrusted hem, took a handful of the soft purple cloth. I would have gathered it up, wrapped myself in it, as soon it would wrap Arthur. But Elaine stopped me.

'We must fold it carefully now. It would be a pity to crush it or loosen the jewels.'

She signalled to Luned and Teilo. With a care I had hardly expected, even in such loyal servants, they folded the widespread mantle. Luned's trembling hands seemed unwilling even to touch the embroidery. Teilo tucked the golden lining out of sight more tenderly than a mother with a baby's crib. I called for the softest of deerskin bags, large enough for it to lie easily within. Blushing, a grown woman and Urien's queen, I kissed the last smooth fold before it was wrapped from sight.

Should I have suspected? We are three and we are nine and we are one. Each of us sisters holds within herself a triune being, Maiden, Mother, Crone. We cannot be separated. What is done, even by a part of one of us, belongs to the pattern. Did Elaine bring death? Or was

691

it the malevolent hag within myself that could not forgive Arthur, even yet?

I was the Maiden again that morning, feeling my eyes dance and my cheeks glow as I stood in the frosty yard waving to the chariot that was taking Luned and Teilo to Carlisle with my gift for Arthur. Soon, soon those wheels would come rumbling home, like the drums before a festival. Luned's and Teilo's faces, that looked so tense and fearful now, would be satisfied and smiling. Arthur would reward my messengers generously. The doors of Gwendoleu's Roman castle where my brother kept court would be flung open to welcome me for the Christmas feast. Arthur's arms would be open. The glory and softness of that purple cloak would enfold us both. I was as eager as a village maid daring herself to send a love-token to her first sweetheart.

I did not have the Sight.

The chariot brought all three back to me in the grey, cold afternoon. Teilo, Luned, the mantle. Teilo was trembling so that he could hardly speak. I could not see Luned, till he showed me. Once my people had carried Erith home from the forest like this, after Teilo had killed her with poison. Poor, pale, plain Luned, who had once been one of Bryvyth's white nuns, was wrapped in death in the purple winding-sheet of my extravagant love-gift. Teilo, who certainly blamed me, would yet not allow me to touch even the hem. He turned it back with cautious hands and showed me her face, accusingly. Black, twisted in agony, tongue bitten, bulging eyes. I covered my own face in horror. I could not deny what I had done.

Luned, my tormented foster-mother at Tintagel. Luned, whom I had led against all her pleading to the Mothers' cave. Luned, whom I had robbed of her scholarly ambition and schooled in a more dangerous, earthy wisdom to serve me. The earth would have her body now. But what of her soul?

They called me Morgan the Healer! And yet, let me be honest, it was not Luned I truly shrieked for. It was for my own lost love. This was Nimue's doing. She stopped Arthur as he reached out his hands to take my gift. She made Luned try the mantle on herself. What would have happened if Arthur had trusted me? Would I have killed him? Could all my spells of love have triumphed over Elaine's? The Crone is not the last you see of us. The circle turns, unbroken. Summer, winter, spring.

Winter was here.

On Christmas Day I shunned the feast Urien was celebrating already in Lyvennet. The magnificent mass of the Nativity, the seething cauldrons of meat, the pipes and drums, the clowns, the horseback games.

I took Caliburn's scabbard, with only Teilo for escort. We drove in a chariot, jolting over the frozen ruts. The ancient leather and soft smooth silver were warm against my heart. In a chapel between Lyvennet and the Long Lake the saint's handbell was chiming the Christians thereabouts to the Great Offering. The door was shut. Behind us voices were rising in a sweet litany of praise, hearts were giving voice to prayers of thanksgiving. Beside the lake it was bitterly cold.

Too late to yearn for Bryvyth's strong enfolding arms. I left the candles and the hymns for the wind whining in the bare twigs of birches and the chill blue light on icy scree.

Above the far, overshadowed end of the Long Lake, where the mountains rear around it, there is a smaller tarn, treeless, black, unguessably deep. It was a fitting place. The Lady is One. All the waters are hers. I gave her back her own.

Caliburn can never now find its true mate this side of Faerie. The scabbard has gone before us.

Tonight we must follow.

That Christmas Day I flung it out over the lake. I felt its warmth ripped from my hands as though the skin was tearing from my palms. One swoop like a wounded blackbird's flight. Brief, awkward. The dark surface opened to swallow it. It sank so swiftly. No chance to call our dreams back. The healing power of the sheath, that should have married the killing power of the blade, was mine no more. We could have made that union, Arthur and I. Man and Woman. The earth balanced. Her people free and whole.

I have used only the healing of any wise village woman since then.

The blade remained to Arthur.

There is an enchanted island, set amidst springtime waters. The sword must come to meet the scabbard there.

# Chapter Thirty-four

*I am the loser.*

*I figure in many contests. Since I have now become the wicked enchantress, I cannot be allowed to win.*

*In the Prophecies of Merlin I am derided, a buffoon.*

*In one story, my friend, the great enchantress Sebille, has a lover, Berengar. I steal his son. Sebille pleads with me to return the child. I pretend to agree, but I mutter between my teeth that I will not unless Berengar leaves Sebille for me. The child's nurse, Flor de Lis, overhears our quarrel. She warns Berengar. In the night the two of them take the boy and flee.*

*In the morning, Sebille finds that she has been abandoned. Both lover and child are gone. She accuses me furiously of deceiving her. She calls me names, seizes my hair. I am showing my age. I cannot withstand her onslaught. She drags me across the floor by the hair, then kicks me repeatedly on the mouth and nose. I bellow like a wounded bull, but I am too decrepit to resist her strength. I am left lying half-dead, unconscious. I only revive after three days.*

*I appeal to Bréhus the Pitiless to avenge me. I get no sympathy from that quarter either. He tells me mockingly Sebille will always outwit me. I am abandoned by all my friends and lovers. Humiliated. I can only weep and nurse my bruised and swollen face.*

*It is the third of our trio, the Queen of Northgales, who makes a patched peace. You may tell by her very name how far from the writer's sympathy she stands. Northgales: the land of the North, the land of the Gaels, the sinister unknown. The wars of Arthur the Briton against the invading Saxons have long, long passed. The Saxons themselves have been defeated since. It is the conquering Norman the minstrels sing and the poets write for now, in French. We Gaels of the west and north are natives, savages, impossible to understand, dangerous.*

*The Queen of Northgales will not accept my complaint against Sebille. She forces me to forswear my hope of revenge.*

*There are many stories that link the three of us: Queen Morgan the Fay, Sebille, and the Queen of Northgales. We are, as we were always in our more distinguished beginnings, wise in magic. We are also, as we have lately become, quarrelsome, vindictive, sowers of disunity. The three of us form*

*'a company unequalled in felony.'*

*We receive a challenge from the Lady of Avalon, who is not the same as the Lady of the Lake. Yes, you may well look surprised. Avallach, you remember, was my father. Avalon is the island I ruled in wisdom.*

*I am indeed a loser.*

*The Lady of Avalon is revelling in delight at some magic rings which the maiden Ayglantine has brought her from India. These she is determined to put to their greatest test, against our powers. One ring confers invisibility. With the other, the wearer can persuade anyone to give her whatever she asks.*

*These secrets are not revealed to us, of course.*

*When we hear her challenge, we put our heads together, we witching three. We shall be shamed if we refuse this contest. One of us must bring the overconfident Lady down. Which will it be?*

*I let the others ride on ahead of me.*

*The Queen of Northgales pits her skill in magic against the Indian rings and loses.*

*Sebille goes next. There is more respect shown here, in her name. The clerks who study the classics know the Sibyl's name. She is the figure of prophecy, the wise foreteller. But she comes from our pagan past.*

*She is also cast down.*

*I am not there to see them lose. I ride, reading in my book of enchantment; I arrive for the final round at the last moment and laugh when I find my friends have failed. The Lady of Avalon is smiling. She is tasting triumph. Our eyes and wills engage.*

*Our battle is in an open court before a tall stone tower. The first move is mine.*

*Once, I could fly through the air from the Isle of Avalon to Brest. Now I summon a legion of fiends from hell. I command half of them to take the form of hideous birds and the rest to merge into a devouring dragon. My birds shall lift the Lady out of her own yard and transport her helpless to the top of that tower. She shall feel the earth reject her. She shall feel the beaks of my ravens pluck at her hair. She shall look down into the waiting dragon's mouth. Exultant, I can see her fear.*

*The demons fly to do my bidding. In her extremity one of her hands flies to its twin and twists the first little circle of gold. Rings are always potent. I should have ordered their beaks to pluck her hands away from each other, and ignore her hair. Why are my servants rushing about now here, now there? Why is the ground covered with flaming dragons pursuing mine? Where has the Lady gone?*

*My attempt has failed. The Lady of Avalon returns to visibility.*

*Now I await her turn. The second ring. I should have feared this more. I should have come sooner to see my friends' downfall. I might have been wiser.*

*It is not blood she draws from me. I should have preferred that. I, Morgan the Wise. I, who surpassed the world in mathematics and astronomy. I, whose healing salves King Arthur called upon when the men he loved were bleeding in their last hour. Other stories. Other authors. Here, I am humiliated.*

*Her request rings about my ears. I open my mouth. No sound comes out. Not a donkey's bray, or a sow's snuffle. I gape and flap my lips like a stranded fish. I am out of my element. I, Morgan the Fay, in a house of magic, and nothing to say.*

*The crowd in the Lady's court watch and grin and begin to whoop as I obey her command.*

*My hands unfasten brooches, buckles, laces. No hedge of mist to shield me. No castle revolving to spin me from their eyes. The clothes are falling from me. Why should I mind? I, the Maiden? I, who dance skyclad for the Goddess? I, who have drawn so many men to my nakedness?*

*But the mantle drops to the stones, and the gown, the shift. I am down to skin, like an unclad baby, powerless and bare.*

*No, not a baby. A cry of shame bursts from me. The magic veneer of beauty with which I deceived men's eyes has been stripped from me. The truth is revealed.*

*I am old and ugly. My flesh is wrinkled. My dugs droop low. My stomach scrapes the ground. A devil has taken my clothes up to the high tower. The Lady of Avalon sends fire to burn them. And all around me people are laughing at me so hard they cannot speak.*

*Time was when an older people knew and reverenced the clothing of true worth, when a naked woman was a symbol of most potent might, a sight to stop the irreverent dead and make the believer incline the knee in respect. A woman past menstruation achieved her greatest power when the well of mysterious life no longer leaked from her.*

*Not here. I am among Normans who proclaim their majesty in stone-built towers and not in oak groves. I am under the Roman church that decks its priests in gold and lace and builds cathedrals shutting out God's sky, and scorns the unworldly Celtic hermit close to bliss in the clearing by a waterfall. I am surrounded by knights who buckle themselves in cases of armour and have no notion of the glory of fighting naked, on foot, with only the patterned protection of pinpricks that etch the symbols of the gods on living skin. They have never known that utter simplicity, that openness to the elements. It speaks no power for them.*

*I am bare. I am an object of derision.*

*No man is so reviled in the romances.*

# Chapter Thirty-five

I had not seen Arthur's face for thirteen years. Urien's cousin Gwendoleu fell, and we moved our court to Carlisle. There we held many feasts and horse-races and contests for warriors. Arthur never came. Urien was welcome at Caerleon and Camelot, and our son Owain had sworn his sword to Arthur's command, but I was banned.

I nursed one hope still, Modred.

Modred, my foster-child, but not my son. Red Margawse's cub. And yet he was growing as like to me in looks as an adolescent boy can be to a grown woman. I saw in him my childhood self. He might have been the boy that Gorlois always wanted. Only, he was Arthur's son and Arthur did not want him. He did not even know the boy was alive.

Now I must set Modred on the most dangerous passage he might ever make, to offer his new manhood's service to Arthur. He would ride without weapons, because I wished Arthur to arm him himself. He went bearing no name of father, because his father was not yet ready to bear the truth.

I dressed my gift with pride. White became his night-black hair. I had prepared fine bleached linen and a tunic and breeches of soft, limed-white leather. My hands caressed his swansdown collar in farewell.

Cornwall. A little baby boy wrapped in swansdown. My childish gift of a lance. Arthur would not remember that.

I had persuaded Urien to give our young man a pure white mount. Modred handled the stallion well. He spoke to horses. They understood his voice.

'Well, are you pleased with him?' Urien teased me. 'I do not remember you took so much trouble over Owain's weapon-taking.'

'Modred came to us with nothing,' I said. 'Let him leave us richer.'

What am I saying in this mumming? Am I making a mockery of his impure origin, denying the past: Arthur's lust, Margawse's adultery, Merlyn's revenge, my concealment?

Modred knew it all now. Last night I had taken him up the fellside to where a standing stone looked out over the sea and the inner lakes. I sat crosslegged upon a boulder, the storyteller, and made him listen at my knee to the tale that would end his childhood.

I had been his mother. I had told him many stories. In the dusk his pale face turned up to mine. His dark eyes were pools filling with knowledge. He made no sound.

I told him everything, from the day when Uther set eyes on his grandmother Ygerne at his crown-wearing feast and wanted her.

When it was finished, he took my hand. He was only fourteen. It was the strange thing about Modred that he always behaved to his elders as if he were twice their years. My schooling at Tintagel was hard, but I was never so completely the mistress of my feelings. Would it have been different if I had not let him see me give way to passion? If Modred had followed his own heart?

His touch caressed my fingers. The stars were pricking through the dusk. When darkness fell, the trial of his manhood would begin. But as the light faded from that limitless seaward sky, he was the one who seemed to reassure me.

'An acorn falls into the ground, and from its rottenness springs a miraculous new oak-shoot. I am that shoot. The winter is over. We shall make the spring ours. I promise you.'

He had a winning smile.

Did I believe that: that through Modred we could make a new beginning, turn back the pages of all our lives and find the first leaf clean, no word of black-inked tragedy left to mar it?

Now, on this crisp morning, the men were impatient to go. Modred's hand took mine again, strangely warm out of his snowy sleeve.

'Mother.'

That word that somersaulted my heart. I had cast the spells of opening for his birth. I had rescued him. I had brought him up. I was his guardian, and I must let him go. I was not his mother.

*I am not his mother. I am not his mother.*

But his hand held me more firmly. 'I will not forget you. The lays of the bards at Camelot can never sing on the strings of my heart as truly as the tale you have told me. Your story and mine. Our wrong will be righted. I shall make him love us both. I will pierce him with the weapon of love he hands me himself. It will break through his shield of suspicion and his breastplate of pride. I shall knot you together with hairs plucked from my own head and seal it with blood from my own veins.'

*And so he has.*

I smiled. I was sick at heart, with the emptiness of the days without Arthur's son. I longed to believe that he spoke the truth, that he meant the truth. He was going to his father's court. This was the purpose of all my fostering. But I searched his dark, intelligent eyes and I was not sure how to interpret his speech. I saw myself suddenly in my nephew's face. I saw how others must see me. I could not read his mind. I mistrusted him.

Over and over again I have tried to cross this water. There is a chasm between me and Arthur. If I have seen a sword-bridge I have walked its slicing edge. If the way has been threatened by lions, I have grappled with them. If the only passage has been sunk fathoms deep in monster-haunted waters, I have plunged down. And always I have been repulsed. I bear the scars.

Arthur would never trust me. Not though I had once stood like this, his large hand holding mine with greater warmth than Modred's smaller one did now, his blue eyes burning for me like the flames from coal, his breath loud and unsteady in the sudden silence. I knew he felt the magic thrill between us.

Is that what he feared? My enchantment. The wisdom I never could or dared to use in this my deepest interest. It meant too much. I cared too deeply. I was the Lady. I have bound myself under a stern discipline.

I have asked nothing for myself from the Goddess. I have worked much good for others. I have not bewitched Arthur. Even now the barge of death is nearing, he must come to me as a free man to a free woman.

*What if he will not come?*

I looked into the impenetrable tunnels of Modred's eyes and I could not tell how shallow his pretty words were. I understood why Arthur did not trust me.

I was too wise, too powerful for my brother. Caliburn's scabbard was worth ten times the sword. He thought I kept it still. Would I dare to tell him I had cast it away?

Urien leaned from his horse and kissed me, laughing.

'Have you two done? The day grows stale with standing. Let the lad go. You did not hold on to the hand of my first-born Owain as long as you do to this fatherless foster-son of ours.'

He was a generous man, but I dropped Modred's hand as if a snake had struck me. Owain was Urien's son, and Modred was Arthur's. Urien had been witness when Arthur took those babies, a young man torn cruelly between wife and hero. He must have guessed who this child's father was, though it was never spoken between us. Did he know truly who was the mother?

Modred smiled at both of us, unnervingly at ease on his first day of manhood. He was a handsome boy, in a sober way. Tall and slender-hipped, though a little large in the chest, as if his swelling heart needed more room than most. Yet I could see more of myself than Arthur in him, except for that winning smile.

He wheeled and waved and cantered off bravely beside his foster-father, and a piece of my heart was torn away, like a shoot from a parent tree that may or may not take root in a different garden.

They told me afterwards he carried himself with dignity when Arthur knighted him. But they said my cautious Modred blushed like a girl and dropped to his knees when he met Gwenhyvar. She gave him his man's sword. Her small pale hands held the blade of his weapon as he swore to serve her with it.

# Chapter Thirty-six

*I am the enemy of lovers.*

*In the royal chronicles of Geoffrey, Wace and Layamon, Modred is named as Gwenhyvar's paramour. In the romances, this lover becomes Lancelot. She spurns Modred who brutally tries to force her into a bigamous marriage.*

*Lancelot and Gwenhyvar. He is a French invention. Chrétien de Troyes is responsible for his popularity.*

*One must make allowances for national jealousy and the tenor of the times. Arthurian stories, the Matter of Britain, are all the rage in France. Jongleurs recite dramatically the 'chansons de geste', their heroic epics, to crowded courts, but romances are beginning to bloom for more private reading. Ladies sit in window-seats in the scent of roses and dream of chivalry.*

*King Arthur is British, and his most famous knight, the golden Gawain, is British too. It would be nice for the French to imagine one of their own in that glamorous circle of the Round Table.*

*No sooner thought than done. The well of creativity is a bottomless cauldron to satisfy any desire. In Chrétien's story, The Knight of the Cart, Gwenhyvar is abducted. It is an old theme. But this time British Gawain fails to rescue her. It is the Breton Lancelot who succeeds.*

*His story develops rapidly in other hands.*

*The baby Lancelot is born in Brittany. He is a prince, fleeing with his royal parents from a city betrayed. On the journey, his father dies of heartbreak. A magical lady seizes the boy and before the eyes of his grief-stricken mother she leaps with him into a lake. The poor queen retires to the conventional nunnery.*

*Safe in this Otherworld, the child grows up, handsome, skilled, brave, proud, taught by fays, but ignorant of his origins. At last, reluctantly, the Lady of the Lake gives in to his insistence and admits his approaching manhood. He shall be knighted by none other than King Arthur. They cross the Channel, that barrier of water between reality and magic, and she conducts him to the court. The lad is dressed in white and armed in silver, riding a white horse, and all his train are similarly white-clad. They make a dazzling sight.*

*Lancelot has had a sheltered boyhood. He falls in love at first sight with Arthur's sovereign lady, Gwenhyvar. In a few words of queenly courtesy to this blushing youth she expresses the hope that he will be her 'ami'. Does she mean her friend, or her sweetheart? He makes his momentous interpretation, and all the unwritten pages of romance spring into joyful life like birdsong at dawn. Arthur dubs him knight, but Lancelot contrives that it is from Gwenhyvar that he receives his sword.*

*The centre has shifted. Arthur is no longer the pivot of the story. This* is not the tale of how Britain came into being and found the greatest of her kings. This King Arthur does not fight the Saxons, to hold the dream of a lost Roman Britain against the grim reality of pagan invasion. His wars are now in distant Europe, against the Romans. At home we are being shown a greyer, unromantic overlord. No wonder Gwenhyvar looks for interest elsewhere.

The glamour is with Lancelot. He is the perfect flowering of the medieval ideal of Courtly Love. For Gwenhyvar, he will do anything without question, whether it is to satisfy her smallest, ignoble caprice, or a quest of the uttermost honour. For her smile, he will suffer any humiliation, rise to any height. She sets the goals of knighthood. She is knighthood's reward.

And so elaborating on Chrétien's Knight of the Cart, the thirteenth-century romances weave ever longer tapestries. Lancelot of the Lake, the Prose Lancelot, three massive books out of the six that form the Vulgate Cycle all bear his name. Arthur is dwindling in importance. Gawain is fading. Lancelot is

'the best knight in the world.'

And Morgan the Fay acquires a new role.

I am now the jealous enchantress who loves, not the heroic Arthur, but Lancelot.

Remember Guiomar, who jilted me at Gwenhyvar's command? I have been given a reason to hate her. Hurt and humiliated, and according to one version pregnant, I flee to Merlyn. Besotted with me, he teaches me all his magic. I am an able student.

Note how my status has diminished. Once I was the fairy queen of the Otherworld Island of Avalon, who taught astronomy to her sisters and offered her wise protection to Arthur. Now I am reduced to Merlyn's pupil.

Guiomar is not the only man to reject me for another woman, even before Lancelot arrives.

I will have my revenge. I create my Valley of No Return, the Vale of False Lovers. Its walls are air. Knights ride through the forest and do not realise they have come too far until it is too late. Good women, sometimes, and all baseborn people may pass through the mist as they please, but false knights never.

It is a pretty enough place. Streams flow and flowers bloom. There is a chapel at the entrance for spiritual comfort. Young men and damsels dance and sing. I have provided good food and courteous servants. But these knights are condemned to perpetual dalliance. Their punishment is to be confined where there is no warfare, no quest to be pursued, no giants to slay, where the requirements of courtly love cannot be met. Only a knight who has been stainlessly true to his lady-love can break the spell. So none have escaped me.

Into my hidden web blunders Lancelot. The entry, that has been all too easy for some, I make hard for him. To enter my domain he must grapple with fierce and clawing dragons, cross the inevitable chasm by a narrow plank bridge, topple fearsome knights. He struggles manfully until a ring given to him by his foster-mother, the Lady of the Lake, reveals them all to be nothing but my enchantment.

*On he presses to my castle, through flaming doorways, up staircases, slaying knights with axes. In hot pursuit he chases one of my guards through every room of the palace until he bursts out at last into a beautiful garden. Oblivious to impending disaster, I lie asleep on a luxurious couch in a curtained pavilion. My cowardly defender rushes in and takes refuge under my bed. Too late he disappears from view. Lancelot storms in after him and overturns my couch, tipping me unceremoniously on to the ground. I wake, screaming, to see both men bolting out of my tent again. A little later, Lancelot reappears carrying the knight's head. He proffers it to me, kneeling, with profound apologies for my rude awakening.*

*The freed prisoners now come crowding in to congratulate Lancelot. My defences are down. The spell is breaking all around me. I curse the woman that he must love so faithfully.*

*This is Gwenhyvar's doing again. Guiomar is forgotten. I have been awakened to a new desire. Jealousy and revenge are focused on another man now. I set my will on becoming Lancelot's mistress.*

*I feast him and all the men he has freed. I too have a magic ring. When I place it on Lancelot's finger as he sleeps that night, I cast him into a deeper slumber still and carry him to a prison deep in the forest.*

*We are not done with rings yet, by a long way. On his left hand he wears the gift from the Lady of the Lake which uncovers enchantments; on his right, another, Gwenhyvar's love-token. I have demanded this one from him, as the price of his freedom, but he swears he will never let it go while he still has the finger it encircles. I could slip it from him easily now he is asleep but I am terrified of his wrath when he finds it gone. Yet I must separate him from that ring. I need it to disclose Gwenhyvar's adultery to Arthur.*

*Gwenhyvar is the woman I hate most in the world. She has robbed me of too much.*

*I feast and fête Lancelot. I offer myself to him with all my arts. He does not want me.*

*Yet we both play by certain rules of honour. I agree to release Lancelot to fight at the Dolorous Tower. Afterwards he duly surrenders himself again to be my prisoner. Still I cannot get the ring from him.*

*Well, sleep then, Lancelot. This time I have drugged you with wine. Daring, I ease Gwenhyvar's ring from his finger and carefully slide another in its place. This was Gwenhyvar's gift to me, the twin of his own. But, like human twins, there is a small and subtle difference. Each bears the image of two lovers embracing. On his, they hold a heart between their hands. On mine, their hands are joined. When Lancelot wakes, I wait with palpitating heart to see if he will detect this substitution. Nothing yet. We play at courtesies. Many times in our conversation I draw his attention to his hand. He regards the ring fondly. He has noticed nothing sinister.*

*Now is my opportunity. I despatch a wise damsel, armed with Gwenhyvar's love-token, to Arthur's court. She tells them they will never set eyes on Lancelot again. The queen, overcome with distress, makes for her chamber. My damsel holds her back. She will not tell her story except in Gwenhyvar's hearing.*

*Lancelot, she says, has suffered a great wound at the Dolorous Tower.*

*Repentance has barely saved his life. Henceforward he will go barefoot and in sackcloth, never sleeping more than one night in the same place, renouncing arms of war. Nevermore will he be called 'the best knight in the world'. And for what sin? In my nest of lies I have laid this living egg of truth. Through all these years Lancelot has been betraying his king and his friend, lying with his queen.*

*Here is the proof. The damsel returns Lancelot's ring to Gwenhyvar. It is all over. The queen falls fainting. Then she recovers — both health and good fortune.*

*Arthur will not accept my story. Gwenhyvar's wide-eyed simplicity pleads for them both. Yes, she gave Lancelot her ring. Yes, he has sworn to serve her. But in chastity and honour, as Arthur's loyal friend. So open and innocent her face, Gwenhyvar, who never uses magic, never studied the arts. My face betrays a lifetime of application. Her magic is in her person, not in her deeds. She beguiles everyone. Arthur believes her.*

*In jealous rage I keep Lancelot prisoner, not for hate, but out of passionate love. I make him dream that Gwenhyvar has been unfaithful to him with a younger knight. In this dream, Lancelot draws his sword to kill his rival, but Gwenhyvar stops him. When he wakes he will find the proof this was no dream. I have laid his unsheathed sword beside his hand.*

*So strong my own resolve, I underestimate the depth of a man's despair. He will not eat, and lest he die, I, in my bitterness, am eventually forced, against my will, to let him go. Only this he must promise me: not to go near the queen until the year is ended. Without this hope, he declines into madness in the forest, where the Lady of the Lake finds and heals him.*

*A century earlier, you will recall, it was my ointment that cured Yvain's madness for a lost lady, in a forest.*

*Once more, a maiden of mine lures Lancelot to my castle. I entertain him lavishly, dress him in scarlet, pledge him from silver goblets, bed him in a chamber fit for King Arthur. Only, the windows are iron-barred, overlooking a garden. He is not my prisoner, you understand, merely my honoured, if reluctant, guest.*

*So Lancelot remains confined till Christmas. When the cold eases, he opens the window to look out. A man is painting an ancient history, and over each picture he writes the meaning of the scene. It tells the tale of our Trojan ancestors, and how Aeneas left Troy, and Brutus founded Britain. And it comes into Lancelot's mind that his own exploits ought to be so recorded.*

*He begs the painter for brushes and pigments. Then, on the spacious walls of his chamber, which is no cramped cell, he begins to paint the romance of Lancelot and Gwenhyvar, all his own brave deeds, all her rewards.*

*Unseen by him, I come each night to gaze on him with love. I see from these pictures with pain where his true love lies. Each morning he wakes, and when the sun falls on his paintings he kisses his image of Gwenhyvar.*

*Two fruitless winters pass and it is Easter again. The roses are opening in my garden. I have created this beauty for him. But May undoes us all. One Sunday morning he watches a bloom unfold that seems rosier than all the rest. It speaks to him unbearably of Gwenhyvar. He has to have it, but it is beyond his reach. With superhuman strength he breaks the bars apart to kiss it, press it to his eyes, pluck it, hide it in his bosom. The barriers are overthrown. So Courtly Love makes heroes out of frail, flawed men. Lancelot, fired by Gwenhyvar, is free, in the hush of sunrise.*

*He hurries across the garden, finds an open door, seizes weapons, armour, saddles a horse. Only the porter is awake yet. My man is surprised to see a strange knight hurrying out of my castle at this hour, but whatever he suspects, it is not the truth. Dreadful my grief when I find Lancelot fled.*

*He has left a message at the gate for me. 'Tell your lady Lancelot of the Lake greets her as*

*"the most disloyal woman in the world".'*

*This, from the man who is committing adultery with his king's wife.*

# Chapter Thirty-seven

I sensed the truth, even before that ominous May Day when Gwenhyvar was abducted in the Summer Country.

When Modred came of age I had persuaded Urien to give him Caerwenloe. This is the old haunted fortress north of Carlisle where Gwendoleu's bodyguard made their last stand after their king had fallen to the sword of Rhydderch Hael. Many men became ravens' meat and their bones are there still. They lie uneasy.

Modred was not Urien's blood, and the fact that he was my nephew was a thing never spoken between us. Urien had sons of his own to inherit the vast lands of Rheged. This one place for Modred, then.

Did I ill-wish him?

I had shadowed his boyhood enough with dark tales of our family. One secret alone I had kept till that last evening: that he was the child of Arthur's, unluckily got, who had been launched in the ship of death into the Solway.

What dark thoughts kept the vigil with Modred afterwards through the night that brought him to manhood? What painful resolve had he come to by morning? He rode with Urien to take service at Arthur's court with a smile on his lips and all my teaching in his heart. We none of us understood what Modred thought.

Should I not have told him the truth? Did I believe that the hurt which Arthur's coming had brought me might be made whole by Modred's restoration? Or did I even then seek satisfaction, twisting the spiral back to our beginning?

Did hate weigh heavier than love?

Well, pagan Gwendoleu fell fighting Christian Rhydderch, and now Urien ruled a wider kingdom. At Caerwenloe one mad survivor babbled of old battles under the apple trees and striped pigs rooted where the bodies of warriors were too hastily buried. The ravens are never still over Caerwenloe.

Gwendoleu left another legacy, an ominous chessboard of gold, whose silver pieces move by themselves. This is a dangerous game that sometimes ends with death. Urien would not touch the board. Owain took it. He played it once with Arthur. Bloody, the outcome.

Modred, who should have inherited Britain, had nothing of his own. Give him the deserted halls of Caerwenloe, the fallen beams, the thistles in the courtyard.

Modred was a scholar before Arthur enrolled him as a warrior. He was intelligent. He had artistry. When he came back to us as a young knight from his first border skirmish I took him to Caerwenloe. His eyes flamed. He walked around the walls, his hands caressing the broken breastwork, fingering the splintered timbers, touching the bloodstained earth as if in recognition.

He turned and hugged me, laughing.

'I will make it a place of song and feasting, a ballad to beauty. Its cauldrons shall be filled with bait for the finest harpers, artists and embroideresses. Arthur himself shall envy it. I will build a hall that would not dishonour even Gwenhyvar.'

Two years he took repairing it. He planned it all on parchment before he built. He asked my advice. Many hours we spent together, with our designs spread over the mosaic floor of Carlisle's palace, like children with their toys, like generals before a battle. Did Urien, descendant of King Coel, lord of the old frontier of the Wall, frown just a little to see his rival's stronghold newly fortified? It was a single homestead he had allowed his foster-son, but it carried a dark inheritance. Urien was Christian. Gwendoleu's Ravens had attacked the Cross. He saw our heads bent together over the shaping of a new fortress. Some things we would not alter. Old blackened pillars carved with signs and faces too holy to be destroyed, hollows in the earth, time-honoured hearths. Modred had been taught by monks from the White House, but he was pagan at heart. How would he use what Urien had given him?

It seemed, for gaiety and sport! Who would have thought our solemn black-browed boy could flower into such a hospitable courtier? My sons told me he had become Arthur's favourite, already wise in counsel for one so young, but an entertaining wit and a marvellous horseman. In the sunshine of Arthur's approval he had blossomed.

So would I have done.

How many nights my bed was ready for him, my body perfumed and waiting. I have made something less than the Sacred Marriage with other men. Arthur never came for me.

But now he came to visit us in Rheged for Modred's sake. I had been up in Caerwenloe. It is a potent place. Arthur arrived at my palace in Carlisle before I returned. My home was invaded by fighting men, horses, servants. By my High King.

When I rode through the gates and found my world changed, Owain came limping across the courtyard to meet me.

'Arthur is here.'

And all the trumpets of Britain sounded on the hills.

I wanted to rush to welcome him. Yet I was afraid to meet him. Eighteen years now since we had met face to face, since our hands had touched. Those years would have changed much.

I hurried to my rooms and prepared myself with trembling care.

That evening I stood in my hall with all the beauty that art and nature could bestow. A rich purple gown, precious stones and gold in my hair. Perfumes of Arabia and creams of springtime flowers. Radiance flooded me from within. I felt I must be outshining my jewels.

He was there in the doorway, golden and laughing, as though the years of our separation had crumbled into dust. We walked towards each other. Skin touched. Our hands entwined. I knew that leap like lightning in my body was matched by the conflagration of his. It was a wonder we did not enfold each other there on the floor of the hall in front of all our people, so great was our longing.

'Welcome, Arthur.' I meant a thousand times that. 'I am grieved beyond measure that my brother the king should honour my hall with his presence after all these years and another woman than I should offer him her cup.'

I waited for the first words I would hear from those lips since he had called for his guards to kill me on his wedding-night. That was all past. It was over. Gwenhyvar could not remain between us.

'A welcome as rich as this was worth waiting for, lady.'

His eyes slipped from mine, lingered over my face, seemed to caress my hair, my body. His hand hardened on mine.

'Purple becomes you. Did you fashion the embroidery on it with your own hands?'

My eyes followed his. I had chosen a marvellous purple gown, patterned in gold and silver, stitched with all my artistry, like the mantle I had sent him as a love-gift long ago that did Luned to death. He had forgiven nothing.

I snatched my hand from his.

Had he only come for Modred, then? I saw how fire warmed his eyes when he looked at the young man, even before he knew this was his son. Blood called out to blood, Arthur's to Modred, mine to my brother, against all reason.

Yet he had wanted me.

No, I was wrong. Arthur wanted something from me. Power.

When supper was over, and he stood disturbingly near me above my stool, I watched the firelight playing on his grizzled hair. I was a woman almost past childbearing. He was a king who spent more time in the judgment-seat now than on a warhorse. The wine was beginning to blur old enmities.

We had added a jewel to our treasure that year. Young Taliesin, prince of poets, whose hands were as skilful on a woman's flesh as over his harpstrings. He was enchanting his audience. Under cover of his song, Arthur leaned closer. I heard the urgency in his voice.

'The bishops speak to me too often nowadays of heaven. That is not what I want to hear. The world is slipping away from me too fast.'

I gasped. I feared for the moment the whole hall must have heard it. But I twisted my head and the face that I met told me cruelly that he did not mean what I had hoped. Turn back the years and start afresh? Arthur and Morgan. Young and free. Before Urien, before Gwenhyvar. No, never free to love each other. Merlyn had seen to that.

My royal brother was asking me for renewal of his man's strength. Did he truly believe his sister had such power? That I was what the common people called me, when they found I spent long days alone in the forest, beside the sacred wells? Morgan the Goddess, mistress of the Land of the Ever-Young? I saw hope and ambition in his eyes. This was a man past the prime of manhood. From his marriage he had only one sickly son, Anir. Did he understand the enormity of what he was asking? Was he prepared to pay the cost?

I never cheated him. I worked all night, with Teilo and Taliesin to help me. Teilo went crippled in a woman's gown, because he had tried to deny the truth of half our existence. Taliesin was young, but wiser, a pretty boy, his face unmarked, though he had a fearsome magical birth from the great Mother Ceridwen. Poetry is truth. A bard who sings from the heart, as Taliesin does, carries the light of youth in his eyes, even to old age. He sang while I worked. He may not have known how he helped me.

Next morning when the horsemen gathered in the foggy courtyard for the start of the hunt, I dressed in my priestess's robes, black, gold-banded across my breasts. With all solemnity, I handed the cup I had brewed for Arthur. I would not explain. He must make the hard pilgrimage to understanding alone. I did not give him then the elixir of eternal youth he wanted. I offered my cup of truth.

He nearly failed to take it. Those hard blue eyes, that had learned what it is to take and hold kingship by the sword, met mine and held them. He partly grasped the truth, that this was not what he desired. Was it fear that made him hand the cup to Taliesin, standing by his elbow with a boy's dream in his eyes as he looked up at his hero? Poor Taliesin. That cup was fear to him! Even though he had watched me while I brewed it, how could he know it would not have hurt him?

But Arthur of Britain was never a coward king. At the last moment he snatched my goblet from Taliesin's unsteady hands. The sharp-scented wine splattered his clothes, his horse, the frosty ground as he swung it to his lips and downed the rest.

'If that is your price! See how well I will trust my beloved sister!'

He had got half of what I intended. The rest will come hard to him.

Two days later there was another hunt. Word came to me in Carlisle that Arthur had been taken suddenly ill out on the fells with a fever-chill. They had helped him to Caerwenloe.

I sensed a sudden darkness before me, as though I had ridden to the very brink of a chasm. Arthur had humbled himself to plead with me, and I had refused him. Now he was ill, and not as young as he wished to be, and I was afraid for both of us. I do not have Elaine's Sight of the future, but I sensed the darkness massing over us. Modred must be the bond that would draw us together, though I could not see how.

I must go to him.

I had fast horses saddled. I called for the most skilled of my people, Taliesin the bard, and Teilo the Man turned Woman, and Tegau my Christian maid. Would they think my cup had harmed him? Today I meant only good. We packed healing ointments. We flew to him over the rough wet ground with the rain lancing coldly through our cloaks. Had they welcomed him fittingly?

I rode through the battlements with a lift of satisfaction and pride. Caerwenloe was a fair haven for Modred now, after such early shipwreck. He had furbished it well. The gable-ends were carved with dolphins, the doorposts with vines. For the principal rooms my skilled needlewomen had embroidered hangings that told ancient tales. There were our ancestors: Brutus, who gave his name to Britain, Corineus who founded Cornwall. The battle with the giants Gog and Magog. The ship of Solomon bringing the Grail. There were wonders on every wall, and mysteries. My sisters Elaine and Margawse had exclaimed with rapture when they saw them.

I should make Arthur well. There would be music in these halls again to astound and delight the ear. Taliesin to sing of Arthur's exploits. Old man Llywarch himself should come to lament his lost youth in poems by the fire. Morgan the Wise would be the brilliant hostess at his table. Modred had not been persuaded to take a wife yet.

The servants had done well. There were roaring fires in Caerwenloe, already there was the smell of baking bread and simmering meat. They had laid Arthur in the guest-chamber.

Modred had proved courteous and hospitable. But young men would not stay indoors for the gale or the rain or an infirm king. The hunt was not finished yet. They had their manhood still to prove.

I opened the chamber door and stole to Arthur's bedside. His face was fevered. He lay in a bed deep with heather and goose-down. The curtains were thickly woven. But this hill was high and exposed. The wind sneaked under the door.

Why had Modred let our High King, our Arthur, lie in any room less than the best? Summon the servants.

'Get your master's room ready. Warm linen sheets, heat stones for his feet, bring lamps and braziers. My brother should lie nowhere but in the chamber where the master of Caerwenloe has his broad bed, in the Raven's own nest.'

I expected no question from any of Modred's servants to my commands. These were all my people. I had trained them. I had given them to him for his household. After the first startled glances, the work was swiftly and well done.

Arthur was stirring.

'It is I, Morgan. I am here. Do not be afraid.'

Give him a strengthening draught, hold the cup to his shaking lips. It was not often anyone would see Arthur so unmanned. His hand was hot where mine rested cool against it.

'How do you feel, Arthur? Can you rise? We have better entertainment for you than this.'

In the weakness of illness he was obedient, though not so swift as my slaves. He trusted me blindly. I was Morgan the Healer.

They seated him in a chair, wrapped him closely in wolfskins, held a canopy over him.

'I can walk, damn you! I'm not an old dotard like Llywarch Hen.'

'Hush, brother. Let me decide what is best. I am Morgan the Wise.'

Carry his chair carefully. Shield him from the rain. It is only a few steps across the court.

I walked ahead of him through that old hilltop fort and felt its dark magic stir beneath my feet.

This chamber I had not entered for a year and a half. Modred always slept alone at Caerwenloe, master of his own soul in his own house. I had sewed tapestries for his walls with loving hands. A sound ship sailing. A father fondly holding his son. A brother and sister with hands entwined. I meant it to be a room for blessed dreams.

I eased the door open on my foster-son's sanctuary, blinked back the fondness that blurred my sight. I had helped prepare this room like the nursery of a much-wanted child. The bed was wide and softly sheeted. Its hangings were an enchantment of colour. My feet sank deep in furs. You would not have guessed so chaste and hardy a warrior as Modred would have chosen to furnish a bedchamber so unsoldierly. There were longings in Modred none of us suspected.

Every wall was painted . . . *Painted?* A sudden shock. Where were the embroideries I had stitched so carefully through all those sunlit summer afternoons, those winters of eye-straining lamplight?

Gone. He had illuminated these lime-washed walls with his own hands, with his own dreams, not mine. Look, read his story. Urien's scholar-priests had schooled him to write a fair hand. The captions were written overhead. Here is the baby boy. Here is the broken ship, the drowned bodies of infants. Here is Modred nursed by the fisherman's wife. Here is Urien bringing his foster-son to court. Here is Gwenhyvar presenting Modred with a sword. Here is the River Camel, and the Michaelmas feast at Celliwig in Cornwall. Here is Arthur's war-band hunting, dancing, wrestling, jousting with spears. Here is Queen Gwenhyvar giving the prize to Modred.

Turn the corner to the wall opposite his bed, where the light would fall upon these pictures before he slept and greet him when he woke. There is the white stag with a golden collar in the forest. There is Modred separated from the rest and giving chase. There is his plunge into the river, and on the other side . . . three maidens in white who lead him inside a flowering hedge. So soft the grass, so skilled this painter, so sweet the waiting, rosy flesh that he portrays.

Had this happened? Would it ever? Was it only the same hunger that kept my own unfulfilled body awake? Would they always torment us out of their fullness, Arthur and Gwenhyvar, secure in the receipt of love upon their thrones? Would they always enjoy what we had not?

Too late to turn back. We had crossed the fatal space.

No arguments from Arthur now as he sank into the warm, soft, pillowed bed. What could I do but sprinkle sweet-scented herbs on the brazier, set Teilo and Tegau to watch? Let Taliesin's harp strum soft airs to soothe him. Leave him to sleep and dream.

Why had I brought him here to this most private chamber? Why had I laid bare Modred's soul? The truth must break us, before we know that we need healing. Do not be afraid, brother. Mine are the arms that will hold your fall.

The rain was over, and drops fell slowly from the thatch. The hunters had not yet returned. I glided into the chamber and found Arthur waking. His eyes came round to meet mine, wide, intelligent, yet a mite bewildered.

I sat on the bedside then, and took his hand. Laughed gaily.

'Poor Taliesin's throat is dry. When ballads fail, we have prepared other tales to entertain you in this room. See around you. Whoever Modred of Good Counsel's mother was, she has bequeathed him an artist's hand.'

'You yourself are famed throughout the land as an embroideress.'

'Modred is my foster-son only, though I would that he had been more.'

'Amen.'

Only because that meant his nephew?

I shivered. When and how would I tell him who Modred's father and mother were?

We sat, like man and wife, examining those pictures. Would you believe we smiled and exclaimed with fondness over the cleverness of the lad we both loved? Arthur could read well enough for a soldier. Could he not understand the captions that spelt out his fate? 'Here is Arthur.' 'Here is Gwenhyvar.' 'Here is Modred.' 'Here Modred is making love to Gwenhyvar.'

Did he wonder afterwards if this was all a fevered dream of his, or Modred's? Did these scenes ever happen?

Shut up our lips, shut up our eyes, shut up our hearts. Was his soul crying, as mine did? We would not drain this cup of truth. It would have destroyed us.

And so it has.

Did Modred truly love her?

# Chapter Thirty-eight

*I am the betrayer.*

*The bearer of unwelcome news is rarely rewarded with gratitude.*

*Already by the mid-twelfth century, when my legend first appears, the Lay of the Horn is being sung. I am not yet named as the supplier of this horn of fidelity.*

*It is Pentecost, and a brilliant feast is being held at Arthur's court. A comely youth enters the hall bearing a magic horn. It is richly fashioned from ivory, chased with silver and gold, and hung with bells which ring with the marvellously sweet sound of fairyland. When it is blown, the hearers lose all control of their actions, servers are struck motionless, plates in hand, stewards totter and stumble with unsteady jugs, knives cut the finger and not the loaf. Around the horn the gold and silver inscription runs: 'This message Mangons of Moraine, the Fair, sends you.'*

*The horn has been enchanted by a fay. If a man whose wife has been untrue to him even in thought drinks of it, the wine will splash his breast. The King of Moraine has sent it to Arthur as a friendly gift.*

*Of course, Arthur has to take the challenge. He shouts for wine, but when he drinks, the liquor spills. In fury he seizes a knife and is about to stab the unfortunate Gwenhyvar. Gawain, Cadain and Owain hold him back. The queen, defiant in her distress, offers to prove her innocence by the ordeal of fire. But Arthur has other ideas. Every man of the court must face the same humiliation. They drink, and each one splashes his clothes, while the ladies' faces burn with amazement. Only one husband escapes: Caradoc, whose wife Tegau becomes a legend for constancy.*

*Arthur recovers his good humour and enjoys the joke. He gives Caradoc the meddlesome horn and Cirencester.*

*By the fifteenth century, in the* Fastnachtspiel, *I am the sender. Arthur and Gwenhyvar are planning a feast again, to which all the crowned heads of Europe will be invited. Suddenly Gwenhyvar remembers. They have failed to include Arthur's sister, the queen of Cyprus. Arthur refuses adamantly to have me.*

*I am furious at the insult. I send a maiden to his feast bearing the magic horn which betrays the unfaithful wife to her husband. He is not to know which queen has sent it.*

*Arthur drinks and splashes his breast. He makes to strike Gwenhyvar but Gawain prevents him. Other men are similarly humiliated. Strife breaks out. Only the King of Spain stays clean and smiling. My maiden returns, and I am in high glee at the disunity I have caused.*

*A knight accuses Gawain of disloyalty with the queen. They fight, till*

*Arthur separates them and denounces the evil the horn has brought. Merrymaking resumes.*

*In the romance of* Tristan *and Malory's* Le Morte d'Arthur, *I am again the one who sends this horn to betray Gwenhyvar. Now the woman herself must drink. But my plans, as usual, are foiled.*

*Two knights, Lamorat and Driant, meet the man I have sent to Arthur's court bearing the horn. At first he will not reveal its secret or the name of the sender, but Lamorat unhorses him and makes him confess.*

*This Lamorat spies an opportunity. He has a quarrel with King Mark of Cornwall, who once forced him to continue fighting in a tournament after he was already weary from beating thirty knights. His thirty-first opponent was Trystan, Queen Essylt's lover. It is true, Trystan did not wish to fight him and only did so on Mark's orders, against his code of honour. The fact remains that Lamorat was beaten. The defeat still rankles. Now he sees his chance to be even with both Mark and Trystan. He orders my knight on pain of death to carry the dangerous horn to Mark's court, instead of Arthur's.*

*The queen Essylt is made to drink, in Gwenhyvar's place, and a hundred ladies after her. Only four drink cleanly. Terrified, Essylt protests her innocence and asks for a knight to defend her honour. Mark swears a great oath that his queen shall be burned.*

*The danger is averted. Once more, it ends in laughter and goodwill. It is the barons who rescue her. They say Essylt shall not be burned*

> *'for a horn made by sorcery that came from Morgan the Fay, as false a sorceress and witch as then was living. For that horn did never good but caused strife and debate, and always in her days she had been an enemy to all true lovers.'*

*I shall have to try again.*

*Luck comes my way. This time Trystan himself rides, unaware, to my castle and asks for lodging. We do not at first recognise each other. I entertain him warmly, but in the morning when he wishes to leave he finds he is my prisoner. I treat him well, but I will not release him until I learn who he is. He is reluctant to tell. Our proper names are our true and vulnerable selves. They should not be readily uncovered.*

*At supper my paramour, Huneson, seeing me laughing with Trystan on the other side of me, burns with jealousy.*

*Trystan decides his freedom is worth any risk. He pays my price. When I learn his name, I wish too late I had not promised to release him. But I keep my word, on one condition. I entrust him with a shield. Its field is gules, and on this blush-red ground stands a knight, with one foot on the head of the king and the other on the queen's. Trystan is to carry this shield to the Castle of the Hard Rock, where Arthur has cried a great tournament. There he must acquit himself as valiantly as he can.*

*He asks me the meaning of the strange device. I tell him it is a knight who holds both King Arthur and Queen Gwenhyvar in bondage and servage. His name I will not disclose for the present.*

*I am motivated by my passion for Lancelot. He has scorned me, and so I will betray his adultery to Arthur.*

*Jealous Huneson chases after Trystan to kill him, but gets a mortal wound himself instead.*

It is dangerous to spurn me. It is dangerous to love me.

*Trystan enters the lists and brings down many knights. As he watches, Arthur wonders at the shield. But Gwenhyvar guesses the meaning, and her heart is heavy with dread.*

I have sent a damsel anonymously to the tournament. She secretes herself in a chamber close to Arthur. Hearing him marvelling aloud what this device can mean, she seizes her chance.

'Sir King, wit you well this shield was ordained for you, to warn you of your shame and dishonour, and that belongeth to you and your queen.'

*Then she is gone.*

*Arthur is angry, and demands to be told who she was. No one can enlighten him.*

But Gwenhyvar knows for certain this must be my doing.

*No one has yet beaten Trystan and so been able to demand his name. When it seems that he may escape unknown, Arthur himself takes the field, with my son Owain. They bring Trystan to a halt and insist on knowing at least where he got the shield.*

'Sir,' he said. 'I had it of Queen Morgan the Fay, sister unto King Arthur.'

*But he cannot tell them the meaning of the blazon. Nor will he disclose his name. When Arthur fights him for it, he knocks the king down and after him, Owain. It is Lancelot who pursues him from the field, finally overcomes him, and brings him back to Camelot to be welcomed as Sir Trystan, knight of the fellowship of the Round Table.*

A doubt has been sown, but Arthur's suspicion does not yet rest on Lancelot. When at last I spell out the truth for him, Arthur will not believe me. He thinks I am lying out of spite to all of them.

*Mark's marriage-bed is betrayed by Trystan and Essylt, Arthur's by Lancelot and Gwenhyvar. It is assumed the reader will take the lovers' side. You may sympathise somewhat with noble Arthur, but certainly not with King Fox of Cornwall.*

*Mark also tries to tell the truth. He sends letters revealing it to both Arthur and Gwenhyvar. He too is rejected.*

Later, I send Mark a poisoned lance with which he stabs Trystan.

We Cornish are dark and untrustworthy. We spell danger to Camelot.

# Chapter Thirty-nine

Anir, Gwenhyvar's only child, was dead, a broken body on a hurdle of spears. A hunting accident, some said. The lad had tumbled, wrong-footed, over a cliff. Caliburn is a dangerous blade to carry without its protecting sheath.

Arthur knew that I had destroyed the scabbard now. He cursed me for it. My hands ached empty without that power. Could it have saved Anir? Was I to blame for that loss?

Others blamed Arthur.

And I? I nursed a terrible fear that, after all these years, Arthur did not truly want an heir. Great Arthur, victor of Mount Badon, High King of Britain. Surely this Arthur could not die? I saw the furious energy in his actions. I watched the rivalry in his eyes when young men boasted of their exploits.

I had spent a lifetime making ready this better son for him, his first-born, my little foundling, Modred. He might yet fling the gift back in my face.

Now Owain came galloping north with worse news still. Gwenhyvar had been abducted from Camelot. Horsemen were scouring the countryside for her in vain. Arthur was summoning all the wisest women of Britain to help him find her.

'The bishops will not like that.'

'Arthur has always walked uneasily with those gentlemen, since he tried to steal Saint Padarn's tunic and got the worst of it. They need his sword, but they do not trust him,' my son laughed.

'All the same, do not mock the Church. The land needs wholeness. Male and female, light and dark, the east and west. The join will not be easily made.'

I seemed to see a shadow flooding over the land, sweeping away little silver-haired Gwenhyvar, the white monks and nuns, leaving our darker power unchecked.

'Merlyn!' I wanted to cry. For even the wiles of that great pagan sorcerer, who had done me so much wrong, had served the demands written in creation. He had let the Church use Arthur, for Britain's good.

But Merlyn was gone. Who guided Arthur now? If Nimue fought the Church because she wanted power, then I must challenge her, and strive to hold the balance.

Who had struck this blow at Arthur's pride, at Camelot's peace, at Britain's unity? Who had taken Gwenhyvar, and why?

I obeyed the summons.

The hill to Camelot was steep, the gate dark and strong. My brother was waiting, angry, on the other side. My treacherous heart skipped like a week-old lamb. But disillusionment followed and despair hung cold and heavy on my shoulders as a sodden cloak. Though I was hundreds of miles away blessing the fields in Rheged that May Day, he blamed me for the abduction of his wife. I saw his grizzled hair, the pent-up energy in his stiffening limbs, the baffled fury in his eyes. Beneath my smile, the muscles of my own face ached.

We must embrace. We were the High King of Britain, the Queen of Rheged, royal brother and sister. The court was watching. The stiffness of our faces repelled each other. But in that closeness our bodies pressed and pulsed. When we parted he was rough and I was cold.

'Where is she?'

'You did not seek my blessing or my sisters' to wed Gwenhyvar. Why should you need our help now she has left you?'

'Left me! Damn you, didn't Owain tell you she was snatched from here by fiends of hell? A troop of masked huntsmen who vanished into the mists of dawn, leaving not so much as a drop of their cursed elf-blood behind them. Only her cry for help upon the air and my nephews wounded fighting for her.'

'Poor Gareth. Owain tells me he took a dangerous gash. May I see him? I have some little skill to heal him.'

'You? You stole Caliburn's scabbard! We are all hurt now.'

'I did not speak of enchantment. There are other ways to heal.'

'Gareth. One of Margawse's brood. You knew he would be Gwenhyvar's bodyguard. Will you sisters even wound your own children to damage me?'

'Damage *you*? So that is why you have summoned us out of Lothian, Rheged and Garlot? For yourself. Because Arthur's pride is hurt. Is that all Gwenhyvar's captivity means to you? Is her danger nothing to you for her own sake?'

I saw by the crimson in his face the shot had struck home. And a treacherous tide of delight surged in my own body. Arthur no longer loved Gwenhyvar. Long, long ago that wedding of the golden laughing prince, his sweet and silvery-blonde princess. Creatures of fairytale when I was already old with grief. Gwenhyvar had scarcely changed, as light and shallow now as then. Even the loss of her son had scarcely touched her. With the young men of Arthur's court she seemed still more girl than mother, though always prettily circumspect.

My brother had grown beyond her. Arthur lived a king's life. He had made hard decisions. He had forced his enemies to surrender and then ordered slaughter. He had seen old friends fall defending him. He had leaned on counsellors, only to find them gone. Merlyn the magician, sleeping under a rock. Now even his foster-mother, the Lady of the Lake, had left him. She had swept off indignantly when she quarrelled with the Church. Only Bishop Bytwini, his chaplain since childhood, remained. He stood behind Arthur now, wary of me as always, reproof in his face. He must have berated Arthur strongly for summoning the wise women to this council.

None of them could give Arthur back his son. He believed we could. I bowed courteously to the bishop.

'Peace to you, Father,' since he did not bless me first.

With pain I saw him turn his face aside.

Margawse was there, dangerous with excitement as always. She was angry at Gareth's wound.

Elaine arrived last, slow, ponderous, the fat wrinkles of her face inscrutable. Elaine has the Sight. Elaine could tell us nothing.

A cold summer then, Camelot almost bare of men, the country scoured in vain, the air empty of news, like a day without birdsong.

The men came, and reported failure, and rode off again. Modred had been missing a long time, and Taliesin with him. I feared more than one thing from their absence.

Arthur met me walking along the ramparts, looking over the wilderness of meres towards Glastonbury. For once his eyes begged, rather than challenged, me.

'Morgan . . .' I let my look encourage him. 'If someone has taken her off to spite me, why does he not send a taunt to say so? What does this silence mean?'

I did not want to hurt him, but he must know the truth.

'That Gwenhyvar may be dead. Or that she went with him willingly, and not as a spoil of war.'

I saw his fist ball and grind against the white stone breastwork. Guilt? Rage? Grief? I would not judge him now.

'Can you do nothing? Morgan the Wise, they call you. Some of them whisper, Morgan the Goddess.'

I shook my head in part denial.

'I have told you how I let go the scabbard. I have used no great enchantments since then. Only the ordinary magic of birth and death. Well, let me try. Tomorrow is Samain Eve. You have forbidden any woman to leave the fortress until Gwenhyvar is found. You will have to let me go.'

His eyes darkened. 'Where?' He suspected that I would not tell him.

'Where else but the most powerful spiritual centre in the country?'

Our gaze travelled to that hill rising like a faery fortress across the marsh from Camelot. Old Ynys Witrin, Glastonbury. An ancient, still spirit-haunted Tor, and at its foot, the earliest Christian church in Britain, if you believed the legends.

'The place is doubly holy. This is the threshold of the year. Samain is the night that brings two times together. The barriers are down. From the unseen world spirits come back to feast with the living again.'

'Samain is dangerous. Good Christian folk stay safe indoors.'

'Arthur the soldier has risked a night attack before.'

'I will escort you.'

'No!' Too quick my protest. 'You are not initiated. What I must do is not for you to see.'

I knew how that must sound. Why should my brother trust me, knowing our histories?

But I was right. He was a general used to taking risks. He saw no other opening.

'Go then, if you must. I do not doubt you have protection better than Gareth's sword gave Gwenhyvar.'

Like a bitter, sulky boy. But would he grieve if I too disappeared?

There is a causeway to the island, among willow trees. I crossed, with a few attendants, and paid my respects at the abbey. A simple collection of huts, a church for choir and pilgrims, a guesthouse and farm. The monks dressed simply in white. This place knew more of Jerusalem than Rome. It understood the potency of mysteries better than the power of law. Holiness shone in the monks' faces. Beneath their courtesy I sensed a fear of women. Yet we shared a common language, these mystics and I. They knew very well the Tor was a battleground of spiritual warfare. That was why they were here. Could I persuade them it was a truce I sought? I must speak carefully. There was no gain in offending their Christian sensibilities.

Abbot Congar's face registered alarm. 'You would keep vigil on the Tor itself? On Samain Night! Lady, beware of pride. Are you so armoured for spiritual battle you would risk your soul where even the priests of Christ fear to watch?'

I smiled, meekly. 'I am a woman. I come in great need. For my sister Gwenhyvar I have vowed this penance. The powers of darkness will beat about your door tonight, Father. Me, they may overlook. The Lord will shelter those who trust him on a mission of love.'

This was not subterfuge, though it was circumspection. That night I felt the power stirring in me again. That night I believed the join might yet be made. That night I had indeed come in love.

With some amazement, Congar let me pass. He offered, hesitantly, to send monks to pray with me. I felt his relief when I refused with a smiling shake of my head.

Did he watch us climb the Tor, treading the sacred serpent path that winds around the breast of the hill? He cannot have lived so close under that omphalos, Beltaine and Samain, keeping vigil in his candlelit church, and not have known that others kept their old feast on the highest point.

I was the king's sister. He let me go.

I had been careful to bring both men's and women's magic. This was a great drawing together I must do tonight. For once, I must give power back to Teilo, who, until he crossed me, had been a master Smith. After twenty years in a woman's dress he had come to understand, unwillingly, through great bitterness, more of the balance than he did when he dared to challenge me.

That night, I put hammer and sword in Teilo's hand again, the mirror and comb in mine. Build the fire high, let the iron ring. Let the images dance in the sparks. Sharpen the edge, hammer the drum, scare this evil away. Part the hair, kneel, let the polished bronze reveal the truth.

I was not Elaine. I could not see yet what I had done.

Dawn, exhaustion, the fires paled, and the light of All Saints' Day dawned purely on the watery waste below us. The chants of Christian monks came sweetly on the air. A cart rolled in across the causeway. I had no sense of victory, only foreboding.

A long path down into the safety of the meadow. The monks had been praying for me. Let them think what they would. I must not show indignation or shame. I must hold the balance. Abbot Congar was hurrying to greet me. The dew of morning was wetting the hem of his gown. How must I look to him, after such a night? Relief, concern, a wary courage, courtesy, all these struggled in his face. I murmured meaningless pleasantries to reassure him.

But there was a stir of excitement among the younger monks. I turned my head, and the smile froze on my face. The cart had stopped; the occupants climbed down. Gwenhyvar was standing there, pale-faced under a great dark hooded cloak. Her eyes looked red with weeping. Modred was beside her, with Taliesin.

Six months, our High Queen had been missing. Beltaine to Samain, while the year turned round from summer to winter. The two young men had been gone almost as long, seeking her. Modred was modest, as always, while Gwenhyvar poured out her gratitude to him for rescuing her.

Who was responsible? Gwenhyvar was incoherent. I could not get sense out of her. She was terrified of Arthur's wrath. I did not blame her. One name kept surfacing, like a branch to cling to in a flood. 'Modred freed me.'

Taliesin looked thin and nervous, and pocked with sores. When I questioned him, he babbled of a watery captivity, of foul serpents and the Little People, of unholy fires and dancing, of Modred saving him.

Take Modred then, march him into the abbey orchard. Let the dew-heavy grass wash my penitent's bare feet and the last yellow leaves drift down to crown my hair. In the name of the Goddess I demanded the truth of my foster-son, Arthur's child, who was not my own.

'Why were you gone so long? How did you find her? Why must it be you who brings her back now? Can you not see how it must look? How can this help us?'

Modred listened and smiled at me, gently, courteously, ever-evasive.

'The departed return at Samain. Arthur lost Gwenhyvar. I am bringing her back to him.'

'Who abducted her? Where has he hidden her all this time?'

'The king lost his wife for six months only. His son has been missing for twenty years.'

'He will think we took her. He will accuse me too.'

Still that smile.

How could I shape the words for what I must not believe? I had spied on a young man's dreams painted on his bedroom walls.

'Do you think you can wound Arthur and not damage me?'

'You tell me my mother was Margawse. Had she not more reason than you to harm him?'

Oh, cruel Modred. I spun away from him. He should not see the tears that flooded my eyes, though he must know the cause too well.

Gwenhyvar was Arthur's prized possession. Let it be only that. A jewel stolen from one man's storehouse to another's court and now put back again.

Do not look at Gwenhyvar and see that she is a woman, still young and desirable, though she has had a full-grown son. Do not remember that Ygerne seemed young and desirable to Uther, when she had full-grown daughters.

Weep for yourself; do not weep for Arthur yet.

Arthur came swiftly enough when he heard the news, and I, like a fond sister, must lead the shaking Gwenhyvar into the abbot's private chamber and stand by her while Arthur shouted his questions.

We each nursed our fears. The abbot was troubled. A simple wattle hut with the sign of the cross was no place for a High King's judgment-chamber.

'I cannot tell you who he was. He came always at night and masked. He kept me on straw, and fed me bread and water.'

'It seems to have suited you as well as swan's meat and honey and a bed of goose-down. Taliesin is weak and full of sores, but your flesh is soft and blooming.'

'I was the High Queen! He would have known that Arthur must one day call him to account for how he treated me.'

'Why should that stay him? It was death already for him to have laid hands on you. But I must find him before I can kill him. It is curious how you cannot say one word to help me.'

There was a name which none of us spoke. I knew the fear that made Arthur shout at her. He had seen those pictures too. Modred was waiting with Taliesin in front of the fire in the guest-hall.

Oddly enough, it was Abbot Congar who rescued Gwenhyvar from Arthur. For once I was glad of his war between good and evil, devils and angels.

'Sire, your adversary may be more dark and difficult to find than you know. There is a legend here of shadowy Melwas, Lord of the Summer Country, who lures the unwary traveller across his bridge into a grim fortress from which none returns. The prison your lady speaks of, with its fiendish jailers, has all the horrors of his den. That must be why even your warrior Modred could not come at her until Samain Night, when all such barriers are down.'

Congar himself was a mighty warrior in prayer. He believed in, and respected, the power of those spirits he called his enemy. At Glastonbury, their two worlds stand very close.

'Devils have lain with women, even nuns. My queen must be above suspicion! Lady, you had better retreat to a convent and take yourself to prayer till this is settled.'

'Sire!' the abbot protested. 'The Church will not allow you to put away your wife for no good cause.'

'Good cause? Have I not cause enough to doubt her?'

But as we entered the guest-hall, Modred turned slowly from the fire, with his face warm. He seemed not to have heard their furious argument. One hand reached out to Gwenhyvar, no more than the courtier's gesture to salute his queen. His smile was reassuring.

'Your majesty, I am more glad than I can say that I came in time. Before I slew him, the gatekeeper confessed that on Samain Night their dread king would come and at last enjoy his prize in the sight of all his foul court at this most unholy feast. Forgive me, lady, these words must pain you,' as Gwenhyvar gasped and paled.

But Arthur looked from one to the other. Then he gave a great shout. 'Then it was true? No man or demon has touched her since me!'

'I am still yours,' Gwenhyvar whispered.

Possession. The Queen of Britain. The soul of the land. Still Arthur's. After that, it was all celebration. Modred our hero had broken the curse. Gwenhyvar was saved. Taliesin of the Radiant Brow had been rescued. Honour was salvaged. Banish all fears of flesh-and-blood enemies. There are good people and there are evil. They are not the same. If Modred had brought her back, apparently undamaged, he could not have been the villain who spirited her away, could he?

They searched the marshes. Of course, they did not find Melwas's castle. In a land of mist and magic, what would you expect? The witching night had passed. We were in winter now.

But Arthur still could not let it rest. He was home in Camelot, within man-made walls. He was a human, Christian warrior. Melwas was now too shadowy an opponent. He needed revenge, a culprit here.

He should not have turned back to Nimue, Lady of the Lake, as subtle, shifting, unpredictable as the marsh itself.

She had returned, from whatever ways she had been searching for Gwenhyvar. She and her warrior-women had scorned Camelot's protection. She looked at us sisters, and in her changing face I saw the current of contempt ruffled by a cold wind of apprehension.

Incautiously, Nimue accused us.

'In your extremity you run back to the women who have always betrayed you. What could I do for you now, that these cannot? It was for those who stole Gwenhyvar away to restore her to you. As I see they have.'

Her blue-green eyes flickered over the three of us, Elaine, Margawse, and me. But they came back to steady into stillness on Elaine, the eldest. I am the healer. My hands are potent but blind. Margawse's heat is all for the present moment, generously giving herself. It is Elaine who has the Sight. She should have known the guilty face.

'She can tell me nothing,' Arthur defended his sister.

'Cannot, or dare not.'

When at last Elaine rose in all her massive power from her seat to answer Nimue's taunts, the Lady of the Lake had reason to regret her rashness and quail.

'A contest, then? You and I, to see whose net can catch the bird of truth?'

'You are trying to trick me. I never claimed to have the Seeing!'

But they were both Arthur's wise women. He ordered the trial. Nimue would have run from the challenge but Elaine was on her feet, facing her, an overwhelming presence.

Arthur compelled them to make the test. The hall was prepared. The fires were lit, the sprigs of druid-wood laid to hand, the rune-stones set.

Bishop Bytwini stalked from the room at Elaine's first words. A stillness gripped the court. The scented smoke seemed to carry me far away as though I saw them all from the height of a circling crow. I could watch dispassionately Arthur's frown, Gwenhyvar's pale face, the unnatural calm with which Modred waited. I saw Nimue and Elaine sinking deeper and deeper into trance. Their hands moved alternately the sacred ivory rune-stones that would shape the truth.

The tension was shattered by a harsh gasp.

'Modred defiled her!'

Possessed by her spirits, Elaine would not have known what she had said. But in that same terrible moment of revelation, Nimue gave a ragged scream.

'It was Morgan's doing!'

You must believe I would have given anything for that to be true. Let Nimue accuse me. Let posterity blacken my name for thousands of years. Let them trumpet across the centuries that I was Arthur's enemy. Anything but acknowledge the truth in my sister's words. I would not believe it. Modred was my lifetime's work. I had saved this young man from death. For twenty years I had shielded him, nursed him in my heart, fostered him in my home, reared him only for Arthur.

Only? No. This was Arthur's royally got son, my gift to him. And with that gift, I would pledge our blood to him, and be rewarded with his gratitude and love. In Modred, Ygerne's daughters, Uther's son, should be made one at last. The terrible chasm that Merlyn drove between us, I would bridge. I saw the future ripped from us, hope scattered to the tempest.

'No! No!'

Swords were already out against Modred. The court was in an uproar. Arthur was on his feet, face blackening with rage. The little baby whom the fisherman saved from shipwreck was face to face with death again. Only I could rescue him, as I had shielded him twenty years ago from the wrath of his father.

Tell Arthur only the truth. Elaine was old. Her powers were fading. Her wandering sight was unreliable. Offer him the greatest truth of all, that must triumph over any accusation.

I took my foster-son's hand and led him up to Arthur. The younger man looked steadily at the older's frown. I joined their warriors' hardened palms together.

'Arthur! Modred it never could have been who fouled your queen. Modred, of all men, you have no need to fear. Brother, I give you your own son.'

I felt a great wave rear. A long, hushed moment. I waited for the pain when it would smash and overwhelm us all. Then it exploded harmlessly in spray and sunlight. Arthur was laughing at my news incredulously. Margawse was kneeling before him, blushingly, as she confirmed the truth of my story. His arms were open to receive his son, while the whole court cheered. Modred was smiling.

On the floor behind me, Elaine began to stir out of her trance.

My nerves are tuned to truth, even though my touch is blind. I felt our doom in the moment before Modred slipped my hand to embrace his father. Even before I heard Gwenhyvar scream.

I had handed Arthur a poisoned apple.

# Chapter Forty

*We weep for what we may not have.*

*We are the Morgans of Brittany. Not the gift-bearing Margots. You would call us mermaids. There, you can see us already, can't you? Fabulous females in a magical seascape of coasts and islands. The jade and purple water over silver sand and kelp-strewn rocks. And I who sit, coiled half in and out of the tide that laps so lovingly around my iridescent tail. Golden hair, green eyes. The white hand that endlessly combs the curling locks. Sweet face bent to admire itself in the silver mirror, that looks up through its lashes to smile so winningly. Predatory.*

*And singing to call down the stars and raise up the dead. Such songs, such voices would stir a monks' cemetery. Or so it seems to you who live on land and feel such longing in your bowels when you hear us.*

*We call the fishermen in their sturdy leather craft. We lure the Phoenician galley wine-laden from the East. We entice the warlike pirate ships from human takings.*

*Come, mariner, I am all yours. Take me.*

*The planking splinters on the rocks. The hide is holed. The mast cracks and falls in a ruination of sails. The seaman plunges, not reluctantly, into the sea's embrace, into my arms.*

*Soft limbs twine around the stiff canvas of his smock. My eager lips seek through his beard for his still-gasping mouth. My heart knocks with a violent joy on the ribbed cage of his sinking body.*

*Hold him now. Love him. Enjoy him. He is mine at last. All that I ever wanted. He shall have his heart's desire. Draw him down to palaces of coral beyond mortal dreams. Feed him on rarest crustaceans, from dishes of pearl and gold. Unstop amphoras of red Rhodian wine and let us be merry. Bed him on softest couches of pale green dulse. Let seahorses dance for him and porpoises tumble. I am a virgin. He is my first. Let the ocean rejoice.*

*Rest here our first entwined fall on the floor of sand that the tide lightly strokes. The eyes of the sea-anemones are curious. Sharks smile. Can you still hear me sing through this green wall of water?*

*Open your lidded eyes. Look on me. You have me entirely. Our dreams are manifest. Lift that limp hand. Stroke my blue and silver side, let your fingers stray over delicate scales, fondle the fragile fronds of fins, cradle my breasts. See, I am hanging my hair over your heart. Feel, I am brushing your cheek with my long lashes. Awake for me. I am opening and thirsting for you.*

*Nothing. He does not move. He will not move. They will never move. Ten thousand times I have called my first love down to me. And I am still a virgin. Still untouched. Unloved.*

*They are all cold.*

*Storm now, and an intolerable wailing. Lightning flashes curses. I beat the fists of my rage upon the rocks. It will not rouse him. They lie, white faces, swelling corpses, bleached, picked bones. The sea is salt with torrents of my limitless grief. Why was I made so? Only to chill what I would most inflame?*

*Still I must sing. I must rise to the rocks, take up the mirror and comb. Calm the sea, bring out the moon. I have so much to give. An ocean of unspent love. Why will he never take it?*

*The Morgans weep for men they never meant to destroy.*

# Chapter Forty-one

I bound their hands together with Caliburn's old belt.

Long ago, when Arthur lay wounded at Celliwig, I took the sword and scabbard from their sacred cave in Lothian. I intended a restoration. It led to a fatal separation.

One thing Elaine kept back, not telling me why: the belt that should have held both sheath and weapon together. It was nothing magnificent. Worn black leather with silver clasps, fragile from the hard use of ancient battles, a slender strap on which to hang both Arthur's life and his victory.

Now the sword and scabbard had passed out of our hands, one snatched away forcibly, one surrendered willingly. We still held this link. We had lodged it safely, in the high hill above Margawse's capital at Din Eidyn.

As Modred grew to manhood, Elaine began to weave. Her feet hardly moved from the hearth, her eyes seldom lifted, her hands were always busy. She plaited a new and brilliant band to twine around the old. Three magical colours: white, scarlet, black.

White for the Virgin, purity of spirit, the high ideal, the untouchable huntress.

Red for the Mother, blood and life, generously given, hungrily taken.

Black for the Crone, our inescapable death, and no less bitterly feared though we know the white will be born afresh.

The colours twisted and spiralled; the belt was new-made and strong. It was finished at Camelot, while Gwenhyvar was still missing. Elaine laid it in my hands with that hooded smile.

'Our season is approaching. Arthur has got the sword back, and you have lost us the scabbard. Bind him with this.'

So, in that fateful, irrevocable moment when I joined Modred's hand to Arthur's, I tied that belt to both. The new wrapped round the old. The strong supporting the frail. Modred and Arthur in each other's arms.

Then Gwenhyvar screamed and flew to Nimue. My old enemy was writhing on the floor, still drugged with trance. And the rafters of Arthur's hall seemed to shiver still with the echo of her accusation: '*It was Morgan's doing!*'

Forgive me, Nimue. You saw more truly than you knew.

Forgive me, Merlyn's shade. You warned of the truth when you interpreted Arthur's dream. His hall ablaze on May Day. A burning beam that must be dragged out and destroyed before it ruined the rest.

Not Moses, this, rescued from the Nile to lead his people to their Promised Land.

I had given him Modred.

I did not remain the Virgin. I could not be the Mother. I had become the Crone.

That night I was shown for a few moments all I had lost. After a splendid supper Arthur took my hand. Never had fire warmed my skin with a more welcoming glow. My brother embraced me joyfully. He had discovered his son. In gratitude he was ready to forgive me anything that night. I never felt myself more joyful in powerlessness, more yieldingly woman, more strongly cherished than leaning on my brother's chest in the circle of those mighty arms. Before the whole court Arthur kissed me, as all my life I had dreamed our lips would meet. What did we care whether those who saw it sighed with romance or stiffened in disapproval? For us this flawed world had vanished. Gwenhyvar, Urien, and all the rest were on another shore. Tonight Arthur the King and Morgan the Queen were joining at last in an Isle of Bliss across the ocean. Tonight . . .

Illusion. A land of dreams that could not be.

Arthur took Caliburn from its false sheath and offered it to Modred.

'Symbol for symbol, emblem of oath. I have the belt. I lay my sword before you two. Morgan, let you and I give up our warring powers. Shall we make Modred our heir and give him Caliburn, and go down into a happy old age?'

At last he was giving up his pride, as I had surrendered mine. The scabbard had passed from sight. He was offering the sword of victory to his son.

The terrible reality forced its way through the charmed circle of the arms still enfolding me. Truth shackled me like a woman torn from her man by slavers. Arthur was married to Gwenhyvar. I had reared Modred. Modred had stolen his father's queen.

I was the Healer. There can be no cure that leaves the poison in the wound. I must lance it out. I must cut this foulness away from him, though the knife slipped in my trembling hand and killed me too.

See how I loved you, Arthur. I feared that what I must say now might destroy you. How could these who witnessed it think my bitter flood of tears betokened rage and hate? I howled for both of us.

'No! No! Do not trust Modred!'

Tear from his chest the ancient sword-belt I had just restored to him. See my own grey hair caught in the buckle that should have bound us all together. What's left now? Caliburn, the unsheathed blue blade glinting wickedly in the firelight. Modred was my gift to Arthur, Caliburn his to Modred. But I had spoiled the feast with my accusation. The moment was marred.

He hurled me away from him. The fragile, ancient leather snapped as I clutched the sword-belt in my hands to tear it off him. The new, bright weaving slipped its moorings. Modred smiled.

Arthur snatched Caliburn back, cutting my palms. He must not believe me. It was a matter of man's pride. His queen deceive him?

His son, his new-found heir, betray him? I insulted Arthur the King. Morgan the Wise was always false.

But he would keep his sword.

I lay sleepless all night with that broken sword-belt under my cheek. I was marked next morning. Grey dawn showed me the desolation of reality. I had given Arthur his son and then blackened his name. I had accused Gwenhyvar of adultery, Modred of treason, and both of them of trespass against the taboo of consanguinity. I bore my punishment. I myself had longed for what was doubly forbidden me. I was Arthur's half-sister; I was Urien's wife. It was never possible.

I destroyed that sword-belt, the magic binding made to bring weapon and sheath together. I had cast the scabbard away willingly, offering the sacrifice of my power. That giving away was never matched by Arthur.

I killed the belt in bitterness. I hacked it in pieces, with fingers bruised and reddened by the marks of the scissors. I washed the bloodstains on it with the rain of my tears. I flung the rags on the fire and heard the wet leather hiss, smelt the foul smoke of ruin. Modred was all I had had to give. I had spent my life's work shaping that blood-bond. Now I had destroyed him.

Even in the darkest night we cling to shreds of impossible hope. One thing of Arthur's remained to me. That spring I had asked Taliesin to steal a keepsake for me from Arthur. Perhaps I had more of the Sight than I knew. I should not be close to him ever again after this. I wanted no jewels, traded from one court to another. No goblet looted in war. Something of himself, unregarded, precious only to me.

Taliesin was a sympathetic young lad. He understood. He brought back a shirt of Arthur's, taken from his bedchamber. His eyes sparkled with pride in his own audacity as he handed it over, softened in pity as he saw how I struggled to receive it with dignity.

I wore Arthur's shirt at night next to my skin. It was muddied from hunting, stale with his sweat. I hugged it to me in the secrecy of the night. It was all I should ever have of him around me now. The linen grew warm as a lover's skin and the stiff stains moved against me like calloused fingers. The smell of him stirred my blood. I could not let this go. In my dreams, one day I would yet wash all these stains clean for a wedding garment.

Dreams. By day I watched, with incredulity and fascination, their power grow. Gwenhyvar and Modred. I had done nothing to stop it.

Arthur flung himself off to hunt in Cornwall, leaving Gwenhyvar with Modred for protection. They say he lodged at the hall of Gwenhyvar's bastard half-sister, Gwenhyvach. He came back furious to prove his manhood and his own might.

There is a hill in London, looking out across the River Thames. It is a holy place, and made holier still by what was buried there. The head of Bendigeit Brân, the Blessed One.

Like a child asleep on its mother's lap, like a wounded warrior that lets his horse carry him safely homeward, like swallows that follow their heart to their nesting-grounds, so are we to Bendigeit Brân. He is our peace, he is our safety, he is the heart of Britain. While his miraculous head lived in the earth on the White Hill, hope would always triumph, no enemy would finally overrun us, we would be the Island of the Mighty for all time.

Arthur said, 'It does not seem right to me that the Island should be defended by the strength of anyone but my own.'

He dug up the Blessed Head. The white bleached vessel of great Brân's skull. He set it on a stake in another place for the crows to mock at. He overturned our cauldron of regeneration.

# Chapter Forty-two

*I am the fay who bestows fabulous gifts on the men I love.*

*I give Hector his wonderful horse, Galatée. Alas, this is a love that turns to hate when the Trojan hero flouts me.*

*In Jaufré I give the hero an amazing tent.*

*Jaufré hears me crying for help and runs to my aid. I am standing on the brink of an enchanted spring. My handmaid appears to be struggling for her life in the water. Jaufré leans over to rescue her. I steal up behind him and push him in. Then I leap in after him. I clasp my arms around him and together we sink deep down into a beautiful land beneath the surface.*

*Jaufré survives the experience. He and his friends see coming towards them a baggage train. I announce myself. I am the Fay of Mongibel. He has pleased me well. I am heaping gifts on him as his reward. Greatest of all of these is my tent. It can be folded so small it may be carried in a single cart. When it is opened out for a banquet it spreads for half a league.*

*What is Arthur's Round Table compared with this?*

*I give Julius Caesar a magical horn and a son.*

*Yes, truly, I am his wife. In Auberon Morgan is stolen in infancy by a fairy king. He keeps me for ten years and teaches me all his enchantments. On his deathbed he leaves me his precious ivory horn. If it is blown by one of truthful honour it can summon twenty thousand armed warriors in an instant. Clearly I offer a valuable dowry for the right man. The doting parents of Julius Caesar covet this for him. They persuade him it makes me a highly desirable bride. The marriage is arranged. His own mother, Brunehaut, is a queen in faeryland. She also brings a legacy, an enchanted golden goblet. If an honourable man circles thrice around it and makes the sign of the cross over it, it will be filled with a limitless quantity of wine.*

*Our son, who receives both these gifts, is Auberon, a little fairy king, dwarfish, but otherwise of great beauty. He lives in a dangerous enchanted wood. The ignorant warn Huon of Bordeaux that any traveller who speaks to the dwarf will never come out of the wood again. The truth is the opposite. Anyone who responds when Auberon addresses him will receive a rich reward. The punishment for not returning his courteous greeting is death.*

*Huon discovers this just in time. Auberon gives him Julius Caesar's goblet and my horn.*

*We offer limitless joys. It is not wise to spurn us.*

729

# Chapter Forty-three

I had threatened Arthur's manhood with my accusation. I compelled him to prove that he was still the unchallenged king. The fragile truce between Britons and Saxons could not bear so great a war as his pride needed now.

Unluckily, he found a cause in Brittany big enough to engage a hero-sized army. King Hoel, his uncle, had lost a niece, poor Helen. The girl had been seized and ravished by a barbaric giant who hurled rocks on his attackers from Mont-Saint-Michel. She died in the monster's arms, but Arthur avenged her, smiting the blood-smeared giant through the brain and ending the terror.

Yet over the mountains was a weakened Rome that still demanded tribute, though it could no longer keep its subjects safe. The men of Greater and Lesser Britain would show them who was master now. They would raise their own standards for all to kneel to: old Rome, still older barbarians, upstart Saxons and encroaching Angles. *We are the British, the Cymry, Arthur's people. Fear his sword.*

He did not leave Britain unprotected. Gwenhyvar was already High Queen. He appointed as her war-leader and his regent, Modred.

When they brought the report to me, they told me that Modred had pleaded modestly he was unworthy to rule. 'Let the honour fall to someone more mature, better loved by the people.'

Did he turn his eyes to Gwenhyvar when he said this? Did he mean the sword of government was rightly hers? What need did Britain have of a regent, while she reigned?

Arthur would listen to no argument. 'You are my son. I am putting this sword into your hands, damn you.'

Not Caliburn, you understand, but the Sword from the Stone.

He must have done this to defy me.

I heard the news and in my mind I saw that sword. This weapon of our peace Arthur the Soldier had hardly wanted and had too little regarded. Caliburn had been Nimue's gift to him. This one was ours.

I must not let myself remember how he got it.

And he is leaving this sword of sovereignty with Modred?

Far away in Rheged I felt, as if in my own bones, the great burden Arthur put off when he handed over the royal sword. It had been a weight too heavy for other men to lift, though he had once parted it from Margawse as lightly as a squire grabbing up a weapon for a friend on his way to some war-game. I sensed his youth returning. This is how Arthur of Britain would always choose to live his life, brandishing Caliburn on the battlefield, not sitting as law-giver with this solemn, civil blade before him. My spirit was grieving. Arthur, I had the strength, the wisdom that you scorned for this great task. I could have borne that sword for Britain. Instead, you left me carrying an empty sheath like an unclosed wound.

So Modred was entrusted with the sword of government, and Arthur kept his battle-magic.

But the known pedigree of frail, pale Gwenhyvar was inked with old royal blood. Did it take the wise counsel of Modred to make her understand the power and destiny in her lineage? She was High Queen of Britain. Arthur, whose descent from Uther Pendragon was always uncertain, had taken his sovereignty from her. I witnessed it.

I was there when, in a church filled with women, in token of that Cornish blood, Ygerne's blood, our blood, she was independently crowned. Gwenhyvar was High Queen in her own right.

Even through my heartbreak I had felt that thrill of affirmation, when Bishop Bytwini raised the circle of gold above the altar and turned to us. Gwenhyvar sat enthroned before him, gorgeous in cloth of silver. Fourteen years old, her violet eyes huge in her solemn face. The choirboys hushed. The white nuns lifted their faces. We listened. And on the waiting air Archbishop Dubric's bell chimed from the sister church where Arthur sat.

'Vivat! Vivat Regina!'

And all of us were crowned in womanhood as the circle descended on Gwenhyvar's head. The heavy greenstone sceptre swayed in her little hand.

Now, twenty-one years later, Arthur left Britain in Modred's hands. He was gone a long time. The country prospered. We had a feeling of peace, as when the sun shines warmly on a day in early spring and all the flowers open.

Angles from the Humber came to trade in our markets. The border farms reported less trouble than usual from Pictish raids. Laden donkeys passed us, driven by half-scared people setting out to reunite with kinsfolk left behind in the Saxon east. The long truce of Badon was crumbling to reveal a larger peace.

Then the news stunned us. Gwenhyvar declared herself Queen Regnant. She was repudiating her consort Arthur.

Once more, I was torn in two. I was Arthur's sister. How could I support this? I was a royal woman of the West. How could I argue against it?

Gwenhyvar summoned all the nobles of the Cymry to a high council in York. The women were especially bidden. Such lords as Arthur had left behind to keep the land came too, Urien from Rheged, Cador her foster-father from Cornwall, Taliesin Chief Bard, the bishops. But most of all the women, secular nobility and abbesses.

All round me the great hall in York was loud with commotion, anger, hope, calculated ambition, shock. Our female world was suddenly full of remembered possibilities.

But *Gwenhyvar*?

Nimue came. She who had been Arthur's foster-mother, now turned with the wind to lap a different shore. I stiffened to see her enter, carrying the jewelled symbol of government laid ceremoniously across her palms. She placed it in Modred's hands, as regent. Then Modred, kneeling, delivered the sword of sovereignty up to his High Queen.

Now Gwenhyvar had them both. The greenstone sceptre and the jewelled sword. I saw they were too heavy a burden for her to hold. Soon she must offer the sword back to Modred, as her new consort.

I am the Mothers' daughter. I am all my sisters. But in Her name I had loved men, and a man. My woman's pride lies partly in my power to heal and enable men, ennoble them. My woman's strength should enrich both of us.

Could I help Gwenhyvar depose Arthur? Should I help her tear this sword from him forcibly? My own pride and power I had surrendered long ago, when I sank the scabbard. Blood and love were all that remained to give. I, Arthur's still-loving sister, stood silent while the great 'Aye!' to Gwenhyvar thundered around the walls.

Yet Nimue was there behind them, eternally young, eternally changeable, guardian of Gwenhyvar and Modred now. Her fair face sought out mine, calculating, as she read my soul. She knew they must win me over. They mistrusted me, even in my powerlessness. Merlyn they had disposed of long ago. Me, they still feared.

I should have known that Gwenhyvar would have a second, less noble weapon. This one was forged to hurt. That treacherous blade slid between my ribs, aimed at my heart.

The High Queen burned with an almost maidenly indignation when Bishop Bytwini challenged her.

'You have no right to put away your lawful husband and your king.'

'No right?' Her violet eyes swept round the women of her court, gathering up loyalty, resentment, self-satisfaction, shame.

'I have been left barren for many years. Your king has wasted the seed, that should have fertilised me, on lesser wombs. I will show you the proof. Speak now, my women, which of you has Arthur persuaded or forced to lie with him?'

Was that all his sin? Arthur had been hot-blooded from a boy. But Gwenhyvar was no ordinary wife. To be untrue to the sovereign High Queen is to be an unfaithful husband to Britain. Did she accuse Arthur of that?

I watched the slowly climbing hands. How few stood modestly still. Chaste Christian Tegau, Caradawc's bride, was one. I could not bear this.

'You hypocrite! Answer for yourself. Adulteress!' I screamed at her.

Gwenhyvar was enjoying her power. She almost smiled at me.

'Yes, Morgan the Faithless, one woman defied him, despite his threats to bind her silent. In her anger and distress she unfolded the tale to me, showed me her bruises, washed my feet with the tears of her wrath.'

Gwenhyvar's hand reached down from the dais and took another. She led a tall and softly blushing noblewoman out before me. Young, raven black of hair, slenderly made, her eyes as green as mine.

Arthur had been unfaithful once too often. He had offended against more than his Queen. While his own son was committing adultery with Gwenhyvar, Arthur had assaulted the virtue of . . .

Morfudd, my daughter.

No, do not try to comfort me. Do not tell me he saw in her the mirror of her mother's youth. Those words would seal the tomb on what I knew already. I was old. My womb was dry. Hope had fled. My furrowed face spoke charms of wisdom not of beauty. The enchantment of youth had passed to my daughter, my beautiful, winsome, winning Morfudd. The magic of youth is what Arthur could not bear to let go. With his offering of himself, she had inherited everything. He would never have eyes, or arms, or heart, or bed for Morgan the Wise now. I had lived too long. My time was over. He had forced on my daughter what he had never offered me.

His time was over too! Modred my foster-son would avenge this hurt. I could have forgiven Arthur easily for marrying Gwenhyvar, pretty irrelevance that she seemed at first. But never this cruel severing of present from future hope. This was the final wound that would slay us both.

The cheering had died. The thronged council chamber was hushed. I sensed the heart-rending pain in Urien at my side. In spite of everything, he remained Arthur's man. Nimue was watching me. Her voice whispered like the first trickle of water through a breaking dam.

'Now, Morfudd! Your mother must give her verdict now.'

My daughter was coming towards me. Cheeks warm with remembered injury, her head held proudly high. Green eyes intent on mine. Her hand reached out.

'Mother?'

My eyes on Morfudd's serious face, this all-too-flattering mirror of my own, my wrinkled hand in her smooth young one. My spirit in her flesh. I heard a stranger's voice cracked with unbearable grief affirm the death sentence on all of us:

'Aye! Vivat Gwenhyvar!'

# Chapter Forty-four

*I am the jealous mother of a lovely maiden.*

*The stories twine like water-snakes.*

*My daughter's name is* Pulzella Gaia, *the Merry Maiden, in a fourteenth-century Italian poem of that title. My spell has cast her into serpent shape. Brave Gawain comes riding by from Arthur's court. The beguiling snake begs him to tell her his name. A knight-errant does not readily reveal that, but, ever-susceptible to female charms, Gawain complies. My spell is broken. He has won himself a fairy lover.*

*Pulzella Gaia rewards him generously. She will grant his every wish. There is just one condition — there always is, with a fairy mistress. Gawain must disclose their love to no one, ever.*

*Of course, he does. Gawain is a boaster. He attends a tourney at the court. When all the other knights start proclaiming the beauty and virtue of their ladies, it proves too great a challenge for his pride. He describes the unmatchable charms of his Pulzella Gaia.*

*Once more, I have my daughter in my power. Pulzella Gaia must surrender herself to the spell of her vindictive mother, Morgana the Wise. This time, I imprison her in a tower of my own castle, Pela Orso. Here she is condemned to stand, waist-deep in water, her lovely legs transformed into a fish's tail.*

*To be a mermaid is not an enviable condition. It is a punishment.*

*Gallant Gawain is not the man to accept such a defeat easily. He sets out on a quest. He will find and free his love again. He forces his way into my castle. He lifts my daughter out of the enchanted water.*

*Now it is my turn to suffer the same punishment. He leaves me floundering in her place. Then he and Pulzella Gaia ride merrily off to Camelot.*

*There is a version that makes me more cruel still. There is less of shape-shifting, more of sadism, in this story.*

*A century earlier, in the* Prose Lancelot, *I play no part in it. Gawain arrives at a castle and hears the piercing screams of a woman. He rushes in to find a damsel, naked as a needle, standing in a marble tank up to her waist in boiling water. She pleads with him to lift her out, but for all his efforts he cannot do it. So she must wait in agony till the best knight in the world comes to deliver her. Through her tears she tells him she has not yet suffered enough for a sin she once committed.*

*You will have guessed that Lancelot is now the one destined to be her long-awaited rescuer.*

*By the fifteenth century, Malory — more of him later — has no doubt whose wickedness is at the bottom of this. It is certainly not the maiden's fault.*

*For five years the poor girl has stood boiling in scalding water in the tower of Castle Corbin. In this story too, Gawain fails to release her. Then Lancelot comes. The searing iron doors of my prison unbolt themselves for him. He bravely enters the chamber, hot as any stew, takes the damsel by the hand and pulls her out.*

*She reveals that I, Queen Morgan the Fay, with my crony the Queen of Northgales, are the ones who devised this torture. Our motive, jealousy, because the damsel was called the fairest lady in the land.*

*Unlike Pulzella Gaia, this lady is not my daughter. But that tradition survives, like so many others, in Brittany. A maiden changed into a serpent. A fairy daughter in a prison.*

*The Bretons still tell of the unhappy offspring of a Margot-la-Fée. Her misfortune is to be the most beautiful maiden in the world. On a certain day of the year she is transformed into a snake.*

*Her mother, the Margot-la-Fée, implores a peasant to go to a point in the road which she describes to him. There he will see a snake, which he is to cover with a basin.*

*The peasant obliges. To be doubly sure, he sits on the basin and stays there till evening. At sunset he lifts the cover, and is astonished to find a radiantly beautiful maiden. In a rush of gratitude, not wholly explicable, she offers him a rich reward for her freedom.*

*Am I responsible? Am I the vindictive, ageing queen, envious of the beauty of the next generation? Or am I, as Modron, the grief-stricken mother, seeking help to unspell my child?*

*No doubt you have formed your own opinion.*

# Chapter Forty-five

I was a wise woman, and I had acted in anger. Well, perhaps I am what they call me, Morgan the Fay. It is dangerous for a man to be false to his fairy mistress. Mistress? I was never Arthur's lover though once I believed that was our destiny. I did not consult the Goddess, she who is always tender to wronged women. I had been hurt, and I hit back.

Gwenhyvar and Modred were married, and Modred was crowned High King, though Bishop Bytwini refused to perform the ceremony. He fled to Glastonbury. I also could not bear to witness that. Bitter enough that I had affirmed my rival Gwenhyvar's right. But to see Modred, Arthur's son, wearing the crown of Britain, Arthur's crown? If I acknowledged that, our field was stripped of harvest. My brother's time, and mine, was over.

Pretend it has not happened. Imagine that slender circle on Modred's black hair is false gold and not the true Welsh metal. Which of us can distinguish truth from falsehood?

> '*Three Futile Battles of the Island of Britain: And the third was the worst: that was Camlann, which was brought about because of a quarrel between Gwenhyvar and Gwenhyvach.*'

Little Gwen. Gwenhyvach. She came limping into the court at York, the Loathly Damsel. We Celts are a race proud of our bodies. Tall, white-skinned, hard-muscled and slender from joyful exercise, our hands nimble with harp and needle, our tongues ready with wit and story, our hearts brave for the danger of horseback or swordplay. We are scornful of slowness, ignorance, cowardice, deformity. The Good God Dagda is not a moral giant; he is the god who is good at everything. That is our ideal.

This lady was hunchbacked, and crookedly so. The left shoulder rose to nestle against her ear. She was short and stout, with legs, to judge by her ankles, as thick as logs. Her face was blotched with purple and her mouth hung awry. Her dun hair was straight and lank.

We were most of us there to witness her arrival. Gwenhyvar herself, silver-blonde, Red Margawse, still merry and passionate, I, Morgan, in all my pied beauty of glossy black hair and fair white face, no longer young but handsome still, and our lovely women.

We were not kind. We were a proud, aristocratic court who tittered behind our hands and moved away from ugliness. I had lived closer than most to misfortune. Charitable white nuns were my teachers, and

736

wise women like Gwennol my nurse. I had healed many. I had held the hands of the dying. I had provided gifts of another sort for those whom nature had wronged.

This deformed woman had an uncommon dignity. It held us stilled now and curious, watching her come through our ranks to where Gwenhyvar had half-risen from her seat by the fire, with Modred at her side. Gwenhyvar was gripping the dragon-carved armrests and Modred had turned his face to her in surprise and alarm.

I knew this lady, Gwenhyvach, Little Gwen. So did Gwenhyvar, Big Gwen. All Gwenhyvar's filial love was centred on her foster-father, Cador, Duke of Cornwall, battle-leader of Dumnonia as once my father Gorlois had been, before Uther killed him. But Cador was not the father who gave her royal blood. That was Leodegran, of the old kings of the West. And she claimed her mother's line was older still. By that lineage she had the right to be what she was now, our sovereign Queen, and Modred her royal husband.

And Gwenhyvach, poor twisted Little Gwen? She was known as the daughter of Leodegran's high steward's wife. I say the wife advisedly, because the girl had been richly endowed, in wealth if not in looks. She was indeed a high lady, we allowed her that, the unspoken admission of a strong vein of royalty mingling with a respectable but lesser blood. Leodegran's bastard daughter, half-sister to Gwenhyvar.

Gwenhyvar bristled like a kitchen cat that sees an unwelcome sibling come to share her bowl.

'We bid you welcome to our court, sister, though you come to pay us your homage a little late. All the nobility of Britain was at our marriage and Modred's coronation.'

'So, you are queen in more than name now?'

'I was always queen, from the day I married Arthur. I was crowned as he was.'

'And no doubt you think you should have been High Queen before that?'

'My royal blood was right, from both my parents, but I needed a champion to uphold my rule. I am no Boudicca screaming her wrath in a war-chariot.' She turned very sweetly to Modred, and he smiled with manly warmth and took her hand.

The Lady Gwenhyvach flushed. 'You throw that in my face? You are right. I have no husband to fight for me, while you have two.'

Anger flashed in Gwenhyvar's face, like a flame leaping between two peat-turves and as quickly smothered.

She seemed to soften a little to this travel-stained sister. 'Is this the reason you have given yourself the pain of your long journey to York from Cornwall? Someone has wronged you? You come to my court to ask for a champion?'

Gwenhyvach spat. A shocking act. It told us she knew that we despised her coarse appearance, and she did not care. Only I, who have looked deeper than most into pools of pain, knew how this bitter behaviour was the dam that held back grief.

'Your court! As if old kings of Britain were not as plentiful as dock-seeds, and as rank in their growth. King Leodegran? What was he? My father as well as yours. Does that make me High Queen?'

'You are his bastard.' Gwenhyvar was whispering hollowly now. She must have been gripping Modred's hand. The smile had left his face and he was watching her curiously.

Little Gwen smiled, a horrid transformation of her marred face, as when the sun peers out from beneath a massive storm-cloud and paints the sky with threatening colour.

'So it is said. And you imply she could not be the Sovereign of Britain who had Leodegran's steward's wife for mother and not Leodegran's queen.'

Modred spoke now. 'Her mother's blood was thought more potent than Leodegran's. I pity you, lady. Fathers are treacherous. I should know. You speak aloud now what was only whispered before. You were raised as the steward's daughter, though one Leodegran favoured strangely. The truth of fatherhood is not easily told. Our faith lies in our mothers. Gwenhyvar's dam, Leodegran's queen, was still more royal than he was. She comes of that ancient line that flows in the veins of kings and queens like the mighty Severn that is an artery from the heart of Britain. So Arthur claimed his royalty from the same line through his mother Ygerne, if one could be sure he was her stolen baby. And I, by my mother Margawse, carry the same blood that fits me to wear the crown beside Gwenhyvar.'

'You understand well, young man. You have done half my work for me.'

'Do not listen to her,' Gwenhyvar urged him. 'She was always a mischief-maker. We have offered to give her whatever boon she came to ask, and she has spurned it. Harper! Some music to lighten the gloom. Why could we not have Taliesin with us to make our spirits dance?'

But I had sent Taliesin away to Brittany, to break the news of her betrayal to Arthur.

'Music, is it?' grinned Gwenhyvach, as the first notes graced the air. 'Would you have me sing my lay to the hall? The ballad of Gwenhyvar the Steward's Daughter?'

'Louder!' Gwenhyvar called. 'Are there no pipers handy?'

But Modred moved his hand. Only a gentle gesture, yet the harp stilled. Gwenhyvar was High Queen, but Modred had a deeper authority.

'Come, sister.' How strange that word from this young man to her whom bodily misfortune had aged to the appearance of twice Gwenhyvar's years. 'Sit by us upon this stool. You have ridden far. Some wine, there! Let me take your cloak. Drink with us, and then tell your tale.'

'I have no patience to hear her. Come, love. Escort me to my chamber.' How hard it was for Gwenhyvar to force that smile. How thin and white her lips appeared, stretched over those bared teeth.

'No tale, unless she listens to it.' Gwenhyvach was enjoying herself now. She was seated warm on a stool by the fire. She was the centre of attention. She knew we all love a story, and the stranger the better. As the firelight leaped on the crooked crags of her face we sensed that this might be more unusual than most.

Modred put out a hand and caught his wife's arm. Her difficult smile was wasted on him. He did not turn his face to hers. Gwenhyvach had hooked him.

And now I thought Big Gwen was near to fainting. I moved her chair for her and she sank into it with a fluttering gesture of her hand as though to force aside unwillingly a curtain of spiders' webs. I signed for wine and she drank it unsteadily. Modred looked at her, briefly, and then back to Gwenhyvach.

Gwenhyvach's smile was wide and bitter. 'I am myself one half of my tale. Look at me. No, don't turn your eyes away in embarrassment. Stare all you want. Now look at my other theme, who calls herself the High Queen Gwenhyvar. Very fair, is she not, for one whose husband has left her many times for other women or needless wars, whose only son is dead on the threshold of manhood, whose womb is barren?'

That made Gwenhyvar colour.

'The world has blessed her with a royal upbringing, a mighty king for a husband, and now a bigger throne. Why then has the Goddess cursed her?'

'Cursed Arthur, not . . .' Modred's quick movement silenced his wife.

'Because her fairness masks an ugly truth, while my loathsome exterior is the prickly husk which covers the sweet kernel of virtue wronged. Pluck up white Gwenhyvar, like a mushroom left till evening, and you will find a foulness of slugs and maggots in your hand.'

'It is you who are cursed for a liar! Look at her, and judge where goodness lies.'

'She knows the truth, even while she calls me liar. She knew, from the night the steward I called father summoned two girls of fourteen to his deathbed. Yes, we are both the same age, though you would not think it to look at me. Our lives have been very different. Would I have graced his court as King Leodegran's daughter? Would the High King Arthur have married me?'

She spat again.

'No. Such men are proud. Women are their possessions. Daughters and wives are jewels to be boasted of and displayed. Beauties to outshine other men's treasures. What use was I to an ambitious man? A crooked girl-child. An ugly daughter. A terrible failure for King Leodegran's queen.'

'*You?* The queen's daughter!' It was Margawse who asked, relishing the salacious scandal.

'So Donaut, the king's high steward, confessed to us, dying. Fortuitously, his wife had borne a daughter a few hours earlier than the queen. Fair as a tear-drop on the cheek, his little Gwen. Will it be heartache then for him to exchange this perfect one for the other? Not difficult. His daughter will be raised as a princess and Leodegran's shame will be saved. Who cares what our mothers felt? My royal dam bowed to necessity to retrieve her failure. Her lowlier one was allowed two sweet years as Gwenhyvar's wet nurse, feeding her own child at her breast like a royal guest, while I was passed off to a commoner woman. Well, I do not complain of that. Deformed as I am, it is enough that they kept me alive. Those who knew the truth feared to lay hands on royal blood and snuff out my warped little life. They let me grow, though others have whispered I must be the devil's daughter.'

'And so you are to say what you have said!'

'Why then did Leodegran reward my foster-parents so richly? What was the steward's Little Gwen to him?'

'His natural daughter! All the world guessed that.'

'Or his legitimate and too-unnatural child.'

'Unnatural indeed to spread such lies about our parent who recompensed your mother generously.'

'Do you deny it, who stood with me, one either side of that deathbed, and heard the truth?'

'How could that be? You say Leodegran bought Donaut's silence. Was the price not high enough? Your story falls.'

Gwenhyvach shrugged. Whosever child she was, I sensed a power in this woman I had looked for in Gwenhyvar and never found. It has nothing to do with fathers. It runs in the mother's blood.

There was consternation all around. Nobody knew what to think, or how far it was wise to reveal which they believed. Gwenhyvar was glaring. Little Gwen grinned at the havoc she had made. And Modred stood unsteadily, his eyes on Gwenhyvar his wife.

'You knew that story? Even before you married Arthur? That you were no queen's daughter, and maybe not even a king's. You claimed the throne of Britain. You married me. Now all that founders, like a tower built on a mire!'

He drew his hand back, he, my courteous, gentle Modred, ever chivalrous to women, ever careful in judgment. His movement sliced the air. The blow slapped against Gwenhyvar's cheek with such bitter force we all winced from the sting of it.

'Modred.' I took his arm. 'The truth is clouded.'

He looked from Gwenhyvar to Gwenhyvach with more brilliant tears than hers in his eyes.

'I know what it is to be rejected, unacknowledged, unlovable.'

My voice was as dry as the rustle of an oatfield in a summer drought. 'Will you still fight Arthur for her now?'

'Gwenhyvar was always the means, and not the cause. I fight falsehood. Arthur denied the truth of who I am. But if she is the false queen, my weapons are rotten. I cannot win.'

So young his face. So old the depth of despair in his eyes. My hand on his.

'You think you see the truth, that Gwenhyvar is false. Then give her up. Give Britain up till Arthur dies. Let her not ruin you both. Make peace with your father.'

'I had no father. And when I lose, Arthur will have no son. Which of us will you aid now, Morgan the Wise?'

I looked to Gwenhyvach for help. She grinned more savagely. 'A plague on both their sides! I'll play no High Queen for you. I am too marred.'

Over her head my troubled eyes met Modred's.

'You may be right. I have betrayed the Lady. Arthur was Ygerne's blood before you were Margawse's. Our old king is not dead yet. The battle between you has still to be fought.'

He bowed and walked away from me, a young man without hope. It was over between us.

My daughter Morfudd was comforting the queen.

Who among us could tell which was the false Gwenhyvar and which the true? Elaine would have known, but Elaine was far away in Garlot. Margawse and I left Gwenhyvar's court together and rode south for her fortress on Black Annis Hill.

Too late to withdraw my challenge to Arthur now. The fatal blow had been struck.

Rumour met us on the road that Arthur's fleet was approaching Britain.

# Chapter Forty-six

*I am both beautiful temptress and Loathly Lady.*

*In a fourteenth-century gem of English alliterative poetry, Sir Gawain and the Green Knight, I issue my enigmatic challenge to Arthur's Camelot.*

*The king and queen and their court are young, they are merry, it is the Christmas season.*

*Into their New Year banquet erupts my champion, a giant of a man. But it is not his size alone that startles them. He rides right into their hall very handsomely dressed for the occasion, without armour, and he is fairly formed, with flowing hair and beard. Yet the man is entirely green, from the curls of his head to his stockinged feet. His clothes are all the same hue, rich with green gems and gold. Even the horse he bestrides is grass-green, its mane braided with gold. In one hand he grasps a holly-bough, in the other, a mighty axe.*

*Green is the colour of the supernatural. Always it offers two possibilities: both promise and danger. You do well to be wary of us. But those who prove faithful can win incomparable riches and joy.*

*So the Green Man rides a circle round the hall, staring into all their faces, holding his branch of evergreen and that monstrous helmet-smasher.*

*This is a wonder then, to satisfy even the king, whose custom it is not to sit down to eat until some new adventure is shown him. The court is hushed till Arthur finds his voice and offers his hospitality.*

*The stranger will not stay to eat with them. Nor will he say yet who he is, or where he has come from.*

*When he issues his taunt to the court it causes consternation. He asks for a champion among these beardless boys brave enough to play a game with him. The challenge is this: to seize the Green Man's axe from his hand and then smite off his head with it. He promises to stand quite still. Then that knight is to present himself in a year and day to suffer the return blow.*

*So why does brave Arthur blanch as he meets the stranger's gaze? It is not customary for the king to accept single combat when he has a retinue of knights to fight for him. Why should Gwenhyvar scream and stagger near to fainting? She knows the falsity that stands to be exposed. They both understand the meaning of the challenge. This game is indeed aimed at the sacred head. Arthur's reputation is in question. Only a man whose honour is unstained could survive this test unscathed. Is this why the court is shocked and silent?*

*The Green Knight roars with laughter. Arthur must take the bait. Red-faced with shame and rage he springs to take the axe, come what may. As he hefts it, the giant stands before him, stroking his beard and arranging the neck of his tunic.*

*Gawain saves Arthur.* Gawain his nephew is loyal to both Arthur and Gwenhyvar. He knows the shameful truth, but he has counselled his brothers to silence. Now he steps into this perilous breach and separates Arthur from that moment of reckoning. Gawain says he will not be missed, he is weak and unwise. The court judges differently. In whispered council they speak of foolhardiness. Good men argue of waste and women weep, but he gets his way. Arthur grants permission. Gawain shall take the adventure of the Otherworld. It will be a great loss to Arthur's court if he does not come back.

The Green Man bows his head, laying his long hair over his crown to bare his neck. There is a moment of horror when Gawain, unwillingly, lifts that mighty axe. Will it strike clean for him? The bright blade falls and the hall shrieks as the unlucky head rolls severed across the floor. Now is the time, now is the urgent danger. Here is hope of rescue. Kick the bleeding head from one to another, lose it under the table. Separate it at all costs from the gory green torso still standing upright, spurting blood, before the appalled Gawain. Everybody knows that a sorcerer cannot live again unless his head is reunited with his body.

But the green arms grope and the huge body arches itself over the floor and the hands snatch among the bloodied ankles. He has it by the thick and verdant hair. The head grins.

More macabre still, he does not set it on its wounded neck but tucks it under his arm as he mounts his emerald horse. It speaks to Gawain now, who must carry the burden of Arthur's honour.

'I am the Knight of the Green Chapel. Meet me there on New Year's Day to take your turn.'

They hang the bloodstained axe over the royal dais.

Little merriment now at Arthur's board, though they try to laugh it off. What are they thinking, each of them, as they lower their eyes to plates of untasted food? What is their friend to die for?

Why should they fear that Gawain will fail?

The year rolls by to All Saints' Day, old Samain. Gawain leaves court amid lamentations, riding his good horse Gringolet and bearing the holy Pentangle, the Endless Knot, on his red shield. He does not know the way to the Green Chapel. The weather is bitter. He quests through North Wales, on across the wintry Wirral, into the unknown, alone.

With just one week left in which to offer his life and save his honour, he comes on Christmas Eve out of this icy wilderness to a borderline. Deep in an oakwood he finds a moat of deep water, the sort of boundary you always have to cross between reality and faerie. Beyond, a shimmering white castle rears its turrets and pinnacles above impregnable walls.

The welcome is warm indeed. Ready servants, fine clothes, leaping fires. The genial lord, a man of stupendous size and fiery-red face, offers him hospitality, wine, and a sumptuous bedroom. He is the host, but not the real master of this castle.

Midnight approaches. The company wend their way to chapel. Two ladies enter. Gawain is captivated.

The wife of his host is a radiant beauty, and young. As she leaves the chapel, he strides to squire her. Her snowy breast and throat are bare and *tempting. Her brow is hung with pearls. Her walk is alluring. In this story she has no name. Let mine suffice for both of us.*

*The castle's true mistress walks beside her. She is old. She is short, she is squat, and her buttocks bulge. Within her close-swathed wimple she is ugly of nose, and swarthy of chin, and her black bushy eyebrows meet across her rutted forehead. I am the figure of sovereignty. I take the highest seat in the hall. I rule here.*

*Gawain does not recognise his aunt. And it was not my golden nephew I had hoped to be entertaining by my side this Christmas night. This is not who I intended to face my challenge, not what I designed it for. Still, the message of doubt has been implanted in Camelot. So let us play the game out to its conclusion.*

*Give the lad good cheer, then, and light him to a soft dreamless bed.*

*Three days of feasting, till St John's Day. Gawain makes ready to leave with the other guests.*

*The host detains him. When Gawain protests that only three days remain for him to achieve his quest, the lord is loud with laughter. Gawain's search is over. The Green Chapel lies only two miles from here.*

*There is no need to be on your way in the morning, Gawain. Stay with us. Three more days, then, to live and laugh and forget your fears. But you are weary with your wandering and our merrymaking. You need to renew your strength. Let the men go hunting while you sleep late and rest and enjoy the ladies' company. Only one game we propose to you, since it is festival-time. Each evening, your host will hand over to you what he has taken in the day's chase, and you must pay back to him what you win indoors.*

*So you lie in soft, warm, heedless sleep while outside the lord and his pack go bounding away to hunt the hinds. And you are prey of another sort as the door slips open to admit a lady who bolts it firmly behind her. The curtains lift and the host's wife is sitting on your bed. You feign sleep, but her closeness cannot be ignored. You pretend to wake, and find her smiling over you. The wrapper slips, and rosy flesh shivers deliciously in the morning air. Her arms imprison you. She offers more. How can courtesy refuse the shelter of covers warmed by your body? But nothing else. You fight gallantly with words where no armour stands between your skins. At long last she releases you. You have taken from her no more than one entwined kiss.*

*For the rest of the day, the old lady is as merry with you as the young one. When the host displays his pile of butchered venison, you pay that kiss back to him exactly, to his amusement.*

*The second hunt, and the wild boar springs across the savage mountains, a giant, ghastly, solitary beast. Desperate for life, he backs against a cliff and hurts many hounds before he is driven into the river and falls to the castellan's sword.*

*So desperately you defend your honour before you yield to temptation. This time, when you are offered the boar's head, you give back two warm embraces to her husband, and nothing more.*

*How would Arthur have conducted himself in such a trial?*

*Whose bed is Gwenhyvar in now?*

*Amid the evening revels, the younger lady flirts with you disturbingly. So we come to the last day of the old year, and the final hunt. Tomorrow*

744

*the test. Gawain must offer himself at the Green Chapel to be beheaded.*

*Now the twisting fox is not more subtle than the host's wife to dodge past your defences. But the fox falls to the gallant hounds and loses its skin. And in my castle, Gawain is proof against the urges of the flesh but falls to a more insidious temptation. His hostess offers him a ring. He will not take it. The lady unfastens a girdle from her waist, green silk with a golden hem embroidered simply along its edges. He refuses that too, but she warns him not to despise its plainness. We have woven art of another sort into this embroidery. No hero who wears this girdle can lose his life. Gawain accepts the talisman and puts it away secretly.*

*Will he give this up?*

*Do not condemn him. He is the sun in all our skies, Gawain the Golden. Our lust for life.*

*His host comes striding in, red from cold hunting, striving to make this last dismal eve bright with his laughter. Gawain is quick to meet him and restores to him . . . three kisses only. A rich exchange for a red fox-skin. But is it enough?*

*The last evening passes as merrily as it can under the circumstances.*

*Gawain's prayers are said. New Year's Day dawns, bitterly cold with driving snow. Gawain is armed and ready. At the very last, in this treacherous temptation to dishonour, he does not totally hide the truth. Over all the rest he has strapped the lady's girdle. The green silk stands out bravely against his red surcoat. Nothing is said.*

*Men will hold on to what they have. They must make themselves invincible, at all costs. How could they be expected to submit, naked, to the wounds that others would give them?*

*Gringolet is led out. Gawain takes his shield. Farewells are spoken. A servant of mine is chosen to show him the cheerless path.*

*One last temptation. They have scaled the snowy fells. The horrid place is near. My man warns him to turn aside. This Green Knight is unmerciful. No one rides by his chapel and lives to tell of it, be he knight or clerk. Gawain should take his way homeward. His shame will not be revealed.*

*Brave Gawain will not be persuaded.*

*With no hope now except in lasting honour, he descends a wild ravine. He finds no church there between the towering cliffs, only a grass-grown mound above a foaming river. This barrow has two dark entrances and is hollow within. The Green Chapel is holy to an older deity.*

*The air is hideous with noise. The giant waits on the crags out of sight, grinding his axe. Now he comes whirling round the rocks, vaulting across the torrent, striding through the snow with his four-foot blade.*

*Gawain must stand his turn. His neck is bared. His head is bowed. He glances up as the axe comes whistling from the sky. In spite of all his courage he flinches. The blow stops short. He suffers the Green Knight's reprimand.*

*Now he must be firm as rock. His hands hold frozen earth. His open eyes are fixed on the winter grass through the snow beneath him, small spears of hope. Around his loins the fragile cord of our woman's giving burns with its accusation of weakness and its promise of life.*

*The Green Knight heaves his axe. Once more its fall is stayed. Still Gawain waits, till in a rage he bids the giant have done and strike.*

745

*The axe descends, and its hurtling fall blots out hope. Sharp pain strikes through Gawain's stretched skin and screams, 'She was faithless!'*

*The wheeling earth steadies. Only the stream is rushing in his ears. Gawain leaps away to defend himself. The Green Knight laughs. It is the host.*

*There is blood in the snow. Blood from Gawain's neck. Blood burns in his cheeks too as the host merrily tells him our plot.*

*His name is Bertilak. He has followed my bidding. I am the mistress here. I am Morgan the Fay, Morgan the Goddess. It was I who ordained this challenge to Arthur's court, the Beheading Test, the quest for the Green Chapel, the hunts, the kisses. Gawain has won his life by his good faith and honour. That was the secret of the taunt. Three blows averted for three temptations resisted. Yet he failed to submit to the rules of my game completely. He would not trust his life to my sense of honour. He clung to the magic girdle. His neck will go scarred for ever by this one nick.*

*Well, he understands now what Arthur never has.*

*Still smarting from that one wound, Gawain will not return and meet me face to face. He takes my green girdle back to Camelot and shows it as the badge of his shame. The court adopts it as a decoration of honour.*

*My plot was aimed at Gwenhyvar. It usually is.*

*How does Arthur feel when this tale is sung of Gawain?*

# Chapter Forty-seven

Gawain is dead.

I heard Margawse shriek for the eldest of her four tall sons by King Lot. He was the last of them to die, fighting in Arthur's quarrel with their half-brother Modred. Her cuckoo child, Margawse's youngest son, and Arthur's firstborn, was all she had left now. Must we cut the tangle of our family to shreds before the knot was slipped?

Arthur had landed from Gaul with his hardened war-host. Gawain was slain, staining the beach like a bloody sunset. Winchester fell to its returning king. Gwenhyvar fled.

We met her on the road and gave her our protection. She could not tell me when and how Morfudd was lost.

Now Cornwall had drawn us back for the final battle.

Yesterday Modred stood at bay with the survivors of his allied army, Angles and Saxons, Irish and Picts, on a bluff of cliffs above the River Camel where it goes hurrying through a narrow valley to seek for the western sea under the watch of the happier hall of Celliwig.

And so we sisters came there, riding through the dusk from the convent where we had left Gwenhyvar hidden. We stopped beside the water's edge.

Modred still had Nimue. Oh, yes. The Lady of the Lake, guardian of warriors, friend of lovers. Ambiguous. As fickle as a pool in times of plenty or drought.

We were both opposites and too alike, the Lady of the Lake and Morgan Sea-Born. Both of us served a more ancient Lady. Both of us loved our fosterlings fiercely. Both of us used these men as instruments for our own designs.

Nimue. Look at her now, flying from the battlefield like a swift white water-fowl from the hunter's bow. The moonlight catches the sparkle of golden breastplate and silver helmet. Her spear shafts the stars. She is still beautiful. She will spirit other protegés away. She will teach other young men war.

We Cornish sisters delivered to Arthur the Sword in the Stone, the blessing of the Island of Britain, sovereignty. She gave him Caliburn. He loved that more.

Do not despise her. She has shielded Arthur well. I might have destroyed him before this.

She should not have protected Modred and Gwenhyvar. She set her shield between me and Arthur. No spear could reach him. But she blessed the blade that would take him from the back.

Yet she went in fear of me. So did they all. They knew I had thrown away the scabbard, that came from Avalon. Myself I could not so easily drown. I was born with power in my hands, to heal or cripple.

Am I to blame for Camlann?

Last night . . . Last night! It seems dark ages before this . . . Nimue found our camp. Margawse, Elaine, I, Teilo, Taliesin, our women and guards, kept our various vigils beside the River Camel.

It was the dark before moonrise. I sought a silence by the water. No one followed me.

Over the hills there was the convent, where Bryvyth had set up her cross after Tintagel, where Gwenhyvar lay like an unlucky gambler, stripped of royalty, husband, lover, and now the twins in her womb. All night in their chapel the nuns would be praying for us. I felt that warmth and power like a fire banked under turves. Tears trickled cold on my cheeks. I should like to be there. I should like to leave the rich dress of a queen for a simple white gown. I should like to surrender authority to my High Lord. I should like to feel my face bright with their joy and certainty and not creased by the care of my more ambiguous faith.

I was Morgan the Wise! Some had called me Morgan the Goddess. I must hold the balance of the world.

Arthur, my brother, lay very close. Modred, my foster-son, nearer still. Between them, Camlann would be a battlefield tomorrow. I had brought them together.

I heard a plash more regular than a moorhen's launching. Oars were approaching. Men's voices challenged from our camp, women's replied. Who would come at night, risking the readied spear? War was men's business now, since the Romans trampled their way to victory over Boudicca. This could only be Nimue, the young-old, the ever-returning, abroad with her spear-maidens, in the dark.

I was as suspicious of her as she was of me. We encompass too much. We love too widely. It is always unwise to assume too readily how we will act. Our worlds are not limited by one side or the other. We may be now here, now there. We may abandon you both. You may tear us in two.

Walk softly up the path, then. Listen to their parley.

'Did you know there was plague in the land? Arthur is growing old. The earth cries out to be renewed. You would surely not desert Modred on the eve of his battle, would you?'

'Desert him? We are here, as you see. We lie scarcely a bowshot from his camp, even for an arm like mine.' Margawse's voice teased her lazily.

'Your nearness has endangered many men before now!'

'Gwenhyvar is almost as old as Arthur. Her womb will be dry soon.'

'Gwenhyvar is carrying Modred's child.'

Light, mocking laughter. She did not know it was a double burden.

'Is she not still?' Nimue's voice rose sharply. 'The child is born? Where? Are they both alive?'

Silence. Twin boys. They may live till tomorrow. But after Camlann . . .

'Where is the Queen?'

Gwenhyvar had laid down queenship. The nuns would hide her well. She would take their veil. We sisters knew that. Nimue could not.

'I would speak with Morgan. You have done too much harm already. And we all know what Elaine is waiting for. But Morgan . . .'

'Morgan is here.'

I stepped out from the thickets of gorse, far from the campfire. Let the starlight catch my face, no more. Let her doubt me, as I am doubting myself. Let her grieve for both Arthur and Modred. Let her fear for her wisdom. Let her lay down her magic.

I sensed an awe in her tonight I had not often felt.

'Will you fight for us?'

'I am Morgan the Healer.' Could she hear the bitterness in those words?

'You armed Modred.'

No. I sent him to Arthur's court. Arthur made him a warrior. Gwenhyvar armed him.

'You three kept the Sword in the Stone of Sovereignty. You bestowed it on Arthur. You gave your voice when it passed to Gwenhyvar.'

'You gave him Caliburn.'

'It was you destroyed the scabbard.'

'I cast my power away, but Arthur keeps the naked sword.'

'So fight against him! Modred is your weapon. You would not reject the child you made?'

Visions of making, in Avalon, of a child at Tintagel, of the Lady lifting a sword for us from a lake, of the scabbard sinking, a baby boy in my arms once more.

'*Tomorrow, Arthur Pendragon will surrender his sword to me.*'

How could she understand?

The flash of victory in her face. Elaine had the Sight, Margawse the will, Morgan the power. Nimue believed she had won us.

The starlight tricked the surface of the water.

No one could win this battle.

'There!' she gasped out. 'I told Modred you would never forgive Arthur.'

Oh, Nimue! How could I answer that?

Her warrior-women rowed her away. I could not suffer the thoughtful gaze of Elaine, Margawse's bitter smile. I stooped inside my tent and searched the dark interior of my travelling-bag.

Taliesin lowered his harp, Teilo half-rose. I gestured them to remain still. It was not darkness or solitude I feared, though I was very afraid.

I took the only thing of Arthur's I still possessed, the shirt he had worn for hunting, which Taliesin stole for me.

Even now, more than a year afterwards, it held the warmth, the smell of Arthur. Old mud crumbled to dust among its creviced fibres. Sweat stained its sleeves. A thread of dark blood showed where a bramble had caught his careless arm. It smelt of life and strength and laughter.

I left the campfire far behind. I walked along the river's bank until it widened into a vast mere. There, where the brook flowed out at a stony ford, I knelt with the last living remembrance of my love in my hands. I dipped it in the cold flowing stream. I watched through dazzled tears all its stains and sweat and impurities swill out into the current that would carry them seawards, on into the ocean, and the ultimate west. The linen between my fingers was pure as a wedding-smock now. Nothing of Arthur left but a chill, clean, bloodless garment.

Once long ago, I knelt at a ford and washed. And Urien Rheged came and got me children. Last night I knelt again, washing a man's shirt in the River Camel, and no one came.

# Chapter Forty-eight

*I am Urien's lady.*

*Urien, Urbgen, the City-Born.*

*Early in the thirteenth century the* Didot-Perceval *tells how the princely knight Urbain becomes the defender of a ford.*

*Urbain is the son of the Queen of Blackthorn. He sets out through the forest in search of adventure. On a tempestuous night he spies a lovely woman riding a mule at high speed. He pursues, and she leads him to her secret castle. There she welcomes him in warmly and pledges him her heart and body in return for his promise to remain with her and her maidens. To him, the castle is surpassingly beautiful, but to all other eyes it is invisible. It stands beside a ford.*

*Urbain must defend the crossing and challenge all comers.*

*He fights loyally for his lady for almost a year.*

*Then Perceval comes. The gallant Urbain calls on a damsel to provide this callow intruder with shield and lance. Alas, he falls to the younger knight's borrowed weapon. His year of delight is ended. It is for Perceval now to defend the lady's ford for a twelvemonth.*

*But young Perceval has another quest in mind. He refuses.*

*A terrible crash, a tumult of smoke and shrieks, thick darkness, follow, denoting the destruction of the lady's magic castle. Her voice calls curses down on Perceval. She cries out to Urbain, warning him to flee or lose her love.*

*A flock of black birds swoops down on Perceval, pitilessly striking at his eyes. Urbain, renewed in courage, joins them in the fray.*

*Fighting for his life, Perceval pierces one of the birds through, and as it tumbles to the earth it turns into a beautiful woman, dead at his feet.*

*Before his horrified eyes, her feathered sisters flock to snatch her up and carry her skywards.*

*Urbain, twice a loser, smiles wryly. Young Perceval need not lament his blow. All is well. These black birds are the fay of the ford and her maidens. They are flying the lady's sister to Avalon. There, their mistress will restore her dead to life.*

*Following his lady's command, he then departs, leaving Perceval his horse. Soon afterwards, he himself is taken up with great rejoicing to follow the black birds.*

*The horse disappears too.*

*Morgan the Fay, they say, allows Arthur to return from Avalon in the form of a raven.*

# Chapter Forty-nine

Slaughterbridge. Such an insignificant valley, the upper reaches of the Camel. So small a stream to carry this deep-laden barge of grief. The meadows lie soft and quiet. But walk a little way upstream and the valley darkens, a stern cliff rises on one side, the river runs swift over rocks, old hills close in.

Tragedy lay all around us. To the south stood Caer Dimiliock, where my father Gorlois fell trying to defend Ygerne's honour from the hands of Uther Pendragon. Over that western hill, Tintagel, where in the night of her widowhood my mother waited for her husband's executioner to become Arthur's father. Let us finish it here in Cornwall, where we began, Arthur Pendragon and I.

No, this was not my contest yet. First came the men's fight.

The war-band of Arthur the king came over the Cornish skyline, and found his son.

Modred was camped on the bluff above the Camel, facing him, with his back to the sea. Not far left for him to flee. Beyond this coast ships have carried the heroic dead out to the blessed islands in the farthest west.

Pitch here, then, the ragged remnants of your host, my foster-son, with the door of your tent to the east and your weapons sharpened. No peace is possible. You have stolen Gwenhyvar. You have enjoyed the High Queen of Britain. You have known sovereignty.

The old king was cuckolded and widowed by your bigamous wedding. He has lost his crown, he has lost his son, his dreams are dead. The spring tide of Britain has turned. It will never reach to the same high-water mark again, but he'll bear us all down in the terrible grip of his undertow.

Or will he?

Come. Listen, behind the lamp-lit walls of the grey king's tent. Is not this the Arthur of old, Arthur the soldier, Arthur the Red Ravager?

'Well, what's the news from the scouts? Are that pack the beaten curs we thought?'

Bedwyr was exultant. 'We've got them squeezed in our fist like a bundle of old rags. One twist, and they'll fall to threads! Angles, Saxons, Picts, Irish! They can't even talk the same language, or agree on the same type of warfare.'

You could almost hear the grin on his face in Arthur's words. 'You'd back Rome's discipline, eh? The way of Ambrosius and Constantine, the tradition of the British Emperors, against a stew of pagan tribes.'

'Tribes! Since they ran from Winchester there's barely enough of the rabble to put together a clan. We'll overwhelm them at daybreak.'

Arthur's voice was loud with indignation or wine. 'Does that match with my honour? Would you set wolfhounds on to run down a hare? Shall I have it sung that Arthur the Briton got his kingdom back from a boy in unfair battle?'

A hesitation round the cross-legged chieftains. You sensed their eyes questioning each other.

'Modred's no boy.'

'We've borne some heavy losses, too.'

'Great Gawain is dead.'

'Gaheris. Gareth.'

Beloved names dropped like leaves from trees. Too many more lay unnamed. They were numbered in death only as spears, save to the distant wives and mothers who still named them daily in their prayers, pleading for life long after the crows had feasted. Unnamed, save to their vengeful comrades.

'You are not suggesting you'd meet him in single combat?'

Well, why not? Surely Arthur's cause was just? Modred had taken his queen and country. Arthur was the anointed king. The Church was with him, in the person of his chaplain Bishop Bytwini here in the tent, as well as in their prayers. Arthur's invincible Caliburn still lived in his hand.

Was it a father's fatal fondness that made him draw back from a duel at the ford? Or did this king gone past his summer need the cloak of cohorts to keep off the whistling blast of his New Year son? Did he weaken himself with the frailty of pity or fear? Cover it with pride.

'How many divisions does he have left?'

'He could make up six, at the most.'

'And ours?'

'Say, nine.'

Arthur struck his fist so his armour jingled angrily.

'By God, I will not have the bards sing I crushed my own son like an ant under my boot. He'd be the one they'd keen the laments over, while I bore the calumny. The victory shall be mine on the field, and in the feasting hall! Six divisions against six! I'll bring back sovereignty from this day and my warrior's honour.'

Again that pause. The shadows shifted across the tent wall. Did Bedwyr shrug before he said, 'Well, so be it. There's no harm done. We hold the high ground on the east, where the land slopes smoothly. If Modred leaves his perch on the cliffs to cross the river, our reserve of horse can be down the hillside to stop him in a moment.'

'I forbid it. Let Urien of Rheged hold his Northmen off. He has no stomach to fight against his foster-son. Let Owain keep back too.'

Owain? A treacherous weakness of relief flowed through me. So the son the Mothers allowed me was not to fight against the son who was denied me. Owain's spear would not be the one to kill Modred. Did Arthur mistrust that Rheged's dread Raven-Band might yet turn against him in this final battle? Owain was, after all, son of Morgan the Fay.

There were younger but wiser chiefs, Modred's generation.

'Do not despise your adversary, sir. Modred of Good Counsel is a canny strategist. He'll fight you with his head as well as his heart.'

'He has no heart, that would so betray his father.'

His friends could offer no salve for this pain. Bishop Bytwini was present, a warrior in prayer, to recall him to his duty.

'We must first prevent this battle, if it is possible. The man must repent his sacrilege. This war is a scandal. Briton against Briton.'

'Britain against a mongrel pack of scavengers!'

'The king against his sister's son, sire!'

Ah! That was the wine-jug overturned. The bishop had courage. Fathers have killed their sons in many dynasties, but the tie of sister's son is far more sacred. You worked more than blind revenge when you lay with our brother, Margawse my sister. You made a union at once sinful and sacrosanct. He cannot escape that bond.

'Do you deny my right to take back what that skulking whelp has stolen?'

'The Church anointed you. For all your sins, you have ruled us as a Christian king. You have protected our bodies and our buildings, and we in our turn have armoured you with our prayers. If this battle must come tomorrow, you can count on our loyalty. We will do our duty, assault Heaven with prayers for your victory and curse the enemy who opposes you. But I charge you solemnly to seek peace first. Win your son's soul, if you can, as you value your own.'

'All right! I'll offer to spare the puppy's life. Will that content you? Modred to surrender his arms, hand back the crown, take ship to exile?'

The bitterness of a man who knew no terms would be accepted. This battle could not have been avoided, could it?

'And Gwenhyvar?'

Eyes hidden behind his hands. Fists clenched and tearing.

'Gwenhyvar is not my wife or queen. Gwenhyvar is not my . . . Gwenhyvar is not . . .'

No. If Arthur survives this battle, Gwenhyvar . . . is not.

Poor pale frightened Gwenhyvar in her secret cell above the Fowey. She may lie paler yet.

If Arthur should come whole from Camlann . . .

Hush, my love! In darkness, I hugged my arms around myself for pity.

'A parley, then?'

'Tomorrow morning.'

'Who will carry the message to his camp?'

'Is Idawc out there? He knows the traitor. They were initiated into my war-band on the same May Day.'

# Chapter Fifty

*'Three Fortunate Concealments of the Island of Britain:*

*'The Head of Brân the Blessed, son of Llyr, which was concealed in the White Hill in London, with its face towards France. And as long as it was in the position in which it was put there, no Saxon oppression would ever come to this Island.*

*'And Arthur disclosed the Head of Brân the Blessed from the White Hill, because it did not seem right to him that this Island should be defended by the strength of anyone, but by his own.'*

*'The third of the Three Unfortunate Counsels of the Island of Britain: the three-fold dividing by Arthur of his men with Modred at Camlann.'*

*'Three Futile Battles of the Island of Britain: and the worst was Camlann, which was brought about because of a quarrel between Gwenhyvar and Gwenhyvach.'*

*'There was a sad battle, provoked by wanton passion, Camlann, through slaughter and pursuit; and fair Gwenhyvar, lively nurtured, yellow-haired, brought it about.'*

*The tradition is deeply-rooted, that Camlann was caused by strife among Arthur's women.*
*Whose word should you believe?*

# Chapter Fifty-one

Ask Idawc, the Agitator of Britain, how it came about.

Look at him. The curling moustaches, the yellow hair bound back in a high pony-tail, the clan marks blue on cheeks and arms. Fire in his grey-green eyes and his colour high. No disciplined Roman this.

He was eager to take the message. Arthur was offering to come to the water's edge. The old king would talk to Modred face to face. He would steel himself to look into the dark eyes of his son, who had stolen his queen and people from him. More than the Camel between them now, since they last met. Could Arthur really bring himself to offer peace?

His hand fell heavy on Idawc's wrist. The young man flinched and laughed.

'Your touch strikes cold for a summer night, my lord.'

Arthur's voice croaked a little, like a Cornish chough.

'My heart may be warmer than you think. You know my son. He has been brother-in-arms to you since I shaved the pair of you in Caerleon and you took weapons in my service. I thought no more of him that day than that he was Urien's foundling. I came to love him, before I knew he was my own. But you enjoyed the years I wasted, fighting beside him, drinking wine with him, wenching . . .'

'Wenching? Modred? Never. He's as chaste as a nun!'

That chilled them all. Custennin of Dumnonia coughed to cover the chiefs' embarrassment. Arthur whipped his hand away as if a snake had struck him.

Urien's voice came steady, reasonable as always. A true friend. 'Forgive me, Arthur. When Morgan brought the boy home, I thought no more than that she wanted to save some noblewoman's shame. Yes, I suspected it might be Margawse. But only much later that you . . . Well, I have already cast my die against him, after he handed the sword you trusted him with to Gwenhyvar. I couldn't turn him from his path. A young man will always argue with his foster-father. Better a friend of his own age.

'Idawc, you've been his battle-mate before this treachery. Make him see sense. Smooth down his prickly pride so he comes to this parley in a mood to listen. We'll find a way out for him, with honour. The lad has his life before him. He is Arthur's only son. He can afford to wait.'

'You'd still acknowledge him as heir to the throne after this?' Bedwyr was on his feet. From the time they were boys together in Nimue's house he had run with Arthur. Blind loyalty to his hero was all he knew.

But Urien had reared Modred. 'When Arthur has gone, it will be another world. It seems Modred has made the people of Britain love him, in a short space. It was always so in Rheged. In God's time, if they want him, he may make a good king.'

'The people of Britain love him? Witchcraft! Your wife was behind him.'

I heard the pain in Urien's answer. 'They tell me she stayed away from his coronation.'

Lucan's voice pierced the hubbub, like a second barbed spear entering the boar's throat from the opposite side.

'It is true the young man appears unnaturally favoured at winning love. Have you forgotten Gwenhyvar?'

That growl of anger. Custennin turned it to advantage.

'They are saying that Arthur's queen may not be the true Gwenhyvar.'

Ah, so that tale had reached Arthur's camp, had it? Or had he always suspected, since that month he lodged with Gwenhyvach in Cornwall? Was that why he came back flinging himself into war in Gaul and Gwenhyvar into Modred's hands? Did his man's faith in himself falter, like Modred's, when he doubted his woman?

'If she has proved false to her king and husband now, might she not indeed have been false when she married him? Let her go, Arthur. She was never worth you. Let Modred keep her. If she is not the daughter of Leodegran and his queen, she brought no sovereignty in the blood you shed on your marriage-bed.'

Uneasy stillness. They were only half Roman, these men. Was Uther Pendragon's inheritance alone reason enough to affirm Arthur High King? Would they begin to mistrust the sword we sisters had given him?

'Are you proposing to wed Arthur to Gwenhyvach instead?' Bedwyr was contemptuous; his laugh barked like a buzzard. 'Do you imagine he could go to bed with that crone and wake up in the morning to find a beauty beside him?'

'Men have found joy in stranger marriages than that.' My husband's voice was barely audible. Oh, Urien Rheged, I have wounded you. It has been hard for you to hold Arthur as your king and friend, and Morgan as your wife. You loved us both too well for your own peace.

'Get to their camp,' Bedwyr ordered Idawc, 'before the sun comes up and takes us unprepared.'

Moonlight was clear as day now. The stars barely showed around it. Even this late, scattered camp-fires blazed like dragon's eyes. Sleep would be slow in coming for some, and some would never sleep again. Idawc carried the herald's wand, and the skinned wood gleamed, a pale shoot of life. But brighter sparkled the gold on Idawc's breastplate, the battle-torque with the boar's head at his throat, the studded guard on his forearm. Two spearmen followed him.

He passed out of the old king's camp, into the unlit no-man's-land. This was the most dangerous walk, down into the valley and the rushing ford, that seemed colder and deeper at this hour. Do not blame him if he strutted and jingled his weapons more than was necessary. Better the sentries on Modred's side knew that he was not coming stealthily, as a spy. They heard his horn, and the notes for parley came small and forlorn to ears that were tuned already for the battle-call. They would sleep lightly tonight, these warriors, if they slept at all, with their weapons within reach.

Heraldic staff or not, Modred's sentries in the shadow of the cliff challenged him sharply. Whatever their kings debated, let it be seen that the men on both sides were ready and strung for war. Idawc laughed, a white-toothed grin that bared gums redder than the sap that wept from his alder-rod.

'By Brân! Don't you recognise me? Idawc, son of Mynio, that played hurley with you and Modred, and once gave him a knock on the head that laid him out cold!'

'Idawc the traitor,' the sentry growled.

Swift movement of the two spearmen behind their herald. He stayed them with a quick lift of his hand. They were all tense. It would take only a little spark to start a conflagration. But the rules of parley are strict as the rules for single combat. Honour is everything. He was led up the steep path to Modred's tent.

Can you bear to follow?

The flap lifted and a young man stepped outside. He stood with his back to the moon. The peat-dark eyes did not catch the light of the stars.

I do not want to hear this. I do not want to hear Arthur plead with his son. I do not want to hear the old king beg for the last of his life from the young one. How could great Arthur parley for the return of Britain and his queen?

What price would Modred set?

Modred was beaten.

How could I wish my brother not to plead, but to march on and grind this smouldering ember into ashes?

I had fed Modred at my breast.

'Idawc ap Mynio! Have you come back to taunt me? Or would you change sides again?'

Oh, yes. When they picked Idawc, his spear-brother, for this mission, did those grey-bearded veterans remember the jealous pride of the young?

Idawc, left behind to guard Britain, when his brothers were off winning glory in Gaul. Idawc, fired by the young man's hope in a younger king. Pledging his sword with the dream of becoming Modred's war-leader. Idawc, chafing as the news was of peace, of diplomacy, of Modred swearing treaties with Saxons and Angles and Picts. Idawc, riding the lonely frontier, restless to see the dust of an enemy war-host, for his horn to vibrate with the battle-alarm. What honour for a warrior in the pride of youth, with his fame still to make, in a settled confederation of the Islands of Britain? What praise for the Red Ravager in peace?

Fire in his heart then, when he heard that Arthur's fleet was swooping towards the coast. The fighting king, hero of Mount Badon, was alive still, he was returning in vengeance, he and his glorious war-band were not entombed somewhere in Gaul. Modred? His new crown was a mockery, a girl's chaplet of daisies. Modred's word of government, entrusted him by Arthur, a small boy's wooden toy. Arthur was the man, Arthur was the soldier. Arthur had the fighting sword, Caliburn. Gallop then. Leave Modred's service. Be there on the beach. Pledge Arthur your spear again as you did in that first, proud, face-warming, unforgettable day, when the king declared you and Modred his warriors and his men.

Now Idawc must turn his spear on his companions. Modred, so long his friend and newly his prince, swept in from the north. Arthur's band was trapped on the beach. They must fight for their lives. In the first bloody onslaught, as his foot touched once again his native soil, Gawain fell. Blood spurted from his mouth into the tide-washed sand and his shadow covered it with his collapse. He was gone, in that dangerous no-man's-land between high-water mark and low. You would believe the sun had fallen out of heaven. Arthur threw back his head, careless of shield. Before the charging enemy, he howled to the sky like a mad dog.

Idawc was rushing in front of him. His armour took a javelin aimed at Arthur. His leather-stiffened wrist hurled it back and found his mark. A friend was dead.

Old men were dying around Arthur. The young were here.

'Remember me, sire? I am Idawc! Bless my weapon.'

Had the tide turned again?

Why did Arthur choose this young man to persuade Modred to a truce? Idawc's voice was scornful. 'You assured us Arthur would not return, but you see he has. Your legitimacy fails. He holds the sword.'

'I keep the sword of government. He has only Caliburn.'

'Only! The weapon that won him twelve great battles, that took Mount Badon? Caliburn is all the legitimacy Arthur needs. You're beaten, like a fox trapped in a hole that has no back door. You can lay down your puny sword in disgrace or leap over the cliff at Tintagel. There is no other escape.'

'My father sent you with this message?'

Idawc's tone assumed a mockery of formality. 'King Arthur of Britain greets Modred the traitor. He will meet you tomorrow morning on the banks of the Camel, to set out the terms for your surrender.'

'Just that?'

'Did you expect more? Did you think he would bargain with you for your life? Man, you stole his wife and crown and sold our country to her enemies.'

'I sought to govern in wisdom. My . . . father . . . handed over the sword of regency to me with all solemnity. Gwenhyvar was High Queen. I laid the sword where it always belonged, in her good hands. She chose to end her marriage to her consort. I, of all men, could most believe his infidelity. I married her. I rule beside her now. She is my legitimacy, more than the fighting-sword she gave me.'

'Gwenhyvar! Haven't you heard? They say she's Leodegran's bastard and Gwenhyvach should have been High Queen.'

That bitter wound Modred could not admit, though blood was blinding the eyes that had once discerned so wisely.

'Gwenhyvar is true! She is, and always has been, Britain's royal lady. I defend her right and honour against all who slander her!'

'You defend your own tin-pot crown. Or you would, if your Germanic friends hadn't scurried back east behind their hills at the first glimpse of a real British war-host.'

'Is this herald's talk? Why has he sent you to me? I have heard bards' satires that would raise smaller blisters on a man's face. Does he think Britain's woes can be healed with scorn and bitterness and taunts?'

'Healed? Did you think we had come to Cornwall for healing? Arthur conquered you at Winchester. You have no hope left. Arthur has come to seize back what is his.'

'He cannot do that. He can enjoy the whole of Britain, as I would have done, by the marriage of east and west. If he tries to rape her, the spirit of one or both of them will die. Britain will lose her wholeness. Even the Church of the West would not send saints across the eastern frontier to save a Saxon. Someone must end the bitterness and close the circle. That was my mother Morgan's teaching.'

'Morgan . . . !' His cruel, mocking laughter spoke for all Arthur's men. 'That mischief-maker? You'd fight us to the death for that old bitch? Is that your answer?'

Modred was known the length of Britain for his wise counsel. Yet it cost my foster-son dearly to answer this levelly and with self-control.

'Tell my father I respected his deeds once. But if that is how he speaks, I am determined never to surrender my sword of good government to his sword of war. Let him rip it from my dying hand first. I can see that his army is stronger than ours. But I will not surrender and witness all I have worked for undone. I would rather he killed me.'

'Arthur gave you life, as he gave you that sword you boast of. He will take both back.'

'Does he forget he tried to take my life once before, when I was born? Tonight, I am alive, and I hold the Sword from the Stone my mother gave him. Tell him to remember his grey hairs. His time is over.'

'That is your answer? Meet him at the river then, mid-morning. Your anger should put a good edge on his own weapon.'

'My fighting-weapon will go sheathed to that parley. Be sure that yours are. One naked blade, and I will warn my warriors to storm to my defence and overwhelm Arthur's traitors till the Camel runs with shameful blood.'

'We know the rules of honour as well as you do, boy.'

Idawc turned with a swirl of his green cloak. He was well pleased. Swift the steps that brought him back to the river. The ford was crossed in three leaps and he was in Arthur's tent.

'Well? Will the lad see sense? Is he grateful for the mercy I'm offering him?'

'The traitor will meet you tomorrow morning. But he will yield you nothing. He taunts you that you have outrun your day. He says he has not fled here but drawn you down into the trap of Cornwall. The Mothers will not allow you to slay their Son. He trusts your sister Morgan.'

The shadow of a cup was hurled across the lamplight. Wine splashed the tent-wall.

'Always that accursed name!'

'Parley all you like. She will not let him surrender. You cannot be free of Black Morgan till you have killed Modred.'

# Chapter Fifty-two

*I am the mother of Owain.*

Among the collection of tales in the Mabinogion is the curiously technicoloured thirteenth-century Dream of Rhonabwy.

Our hero sets out on a quest with two companions. On a filthy night they seek shelter in an even filthier homestead. The floor is treacherous. Where there is not a bump there is a hole, and it is so slippery with cow-muck and urine a man can hardly stand. They wade through dung and holly branches that the cows have chewed to seek a refuge on the floor of the main hall. A dusty dais at each end, and a sulky fire on one wall. No hostess to greet them save a snaggle-toothed crone, throwing a lapful of husks on the fire to keep off the cold and filling the place with choking smoke.

Not a civil word can they get out of her. The master of the house comes home, a bald, wizened, red-haired man and a skinny purple-faced little woman with him, carrying sticks. No supper but bread and cheese and a cup of watery milk. No bed but such foul straw, with branches sticking through it, as the oxen have left unchewed, and it is barely covered by a threadbare blanket alive with fleas, a half-empty pillow and a dirty pillowcase.

No bed, that is, save one. Tormented by bites and scratches, Rhonabwy claims for himself the couch he was not offered. At the far end of the hall a yellow ox-hide has been spread alone on the boards of the other dais. Here he betakes himself to sleep, and dreams.

He enters a land which is, and is not, Britain. A familiar plain leads to the Severn. It is peopled with heroes, larger than life, already beyond the grave. Certainly the young man who challenges him, with yellow curling hair and yellow horse, all tricked out in the green of the fir tree and the yellow of the broom-flower, knows already what he has to repent. He is Idawc, the Embroiler of Britain. This is the spirited young envoy who craved too much for battle. He falsified the message of Arthur to Modred. When the king would speak the kindest words he could to his son and nephew, to bring peace to the Island of Britain, then Idawc spoke them the ugliest way he knew and brought about the Battle of Camlann.

He has served seven years' penance at the Blue Stone for that, but he has more wonders to show. He conducts Rhonabwy to a warriors' camp beside the Severn. Here is Arthur the king, with his bishop Bytwini and the son of Cei decked out in black and white. Old names from story come and go across this scene, and as in dreams, these heroes are both here in camp beside the Severn and yet will be found fighting Osla Big-Knife at midday at the battle of Mount Badon.

Now Idawc sets the scene for Arthur and Owain.

*Arthur's servant is called for, a rough, red, ugly man with a bristling moustache. He rides a red horse and carries a handsome pack.*

*Here on the riverbank he spreads out a fair white mantle of ribbed brocaded silk with an apple of red gold at each of its corners. If a man wrapped himself in it he would be invisible. On it, he sets a great golden chair.*

*Arthur seats himself, and says to Owain, son of Urien, standing beside him, 'Owain, will you play gwyddbwyll with me?'*

*My son accepts the challenge.*

*The gwyddbwyll set is laid before them, a silver board with golden pieces. The game is going well for Arthur. A messenger all in gold comes hasting up from a white and red pavilion that bears a red-eyed black serpent. His news is not to Arthur but to Owain.*

*'Lord, is it by your will that the emperor's men are molesting your Ravens?'*

*Owain lifts his eyes. 'Sire, you heard the boy. Call your men off my little Ravens.' He waits for Arthur's move.*

*'Play on.'*

*They start a second game. Another squire in yellow and red comes hot-foot from a yellow pavilion that sports a bright red lion.*

*'Lord, the emperor's young men have started killing your Ravens.'*

*Owain's voice is low and steady. 'Call them off, my uncle.'*

*'Continue the game.'*

*The third round is in progress when a furious lad in green comes at a canter from a spotted yellow pavilion surmounted by a golden eagle. He carries a speckled yellow spear with a newly sharpened head and a conspicuous standard on it. He speaks with rage.*

*'My lord Owain, the most notable of your Ravens have already been slain. Others are so hurt they cannot lift their wings from the ground. How long will you let this continue?'*

*'I ask you once more,' says Owain to his king. 'Call off this slaughter.'*

*Does Arthur's hand hover above the board for a moment?*

*'Our game is not done yet. Your move, lad. See if you can get yourself out of that trap.'*

*Owain's hand reaches obediently to the board, but his head has turned to the lad with the spear. 'Be off with you. And where the battle is thickest, raise our standard. Let God decide.'*

*Still Arthur is winning. The two contestants address their attention to the fourth game. Now fortunes turn. The air is torn with the shrieks of men and the croaks of exultant birds. When the next messenger comes galloping up to the chiefs on the riverbank, riding a parti-coloured horse of dapple grey and red and yellow, he wears a yellow-red leopard on his helmet and his green and red spear is scarlet with the blood of ravens and black with their feathers. His voice trembles.*

*'Sire! Owain's Ravens have turned upon your warriors. They are swooping from the sky and tearing off the men's heads and eyes and ears and arms.'*

*Arthur angrily turns to the younger man.*

*'Stay your Ravens.'*

*Owain lifts his eyebrows.*

*'My move, I think.'*

*The next game zigzags across the squares. Valuable pieces fall and are lifted away. Into this calculating silence a new commotion erupts, screams of agony and caws of triumph. A pale horse is coming, and now there is heavy green armour with a surcoat of yellow on the rider and a flame-tongued yellow-red lion on his golden helm. He bears blood on the new head of his ashen spear.*

'My king, the Ravens are carrying your men up into the air. They are tearing them apart between them and letting the pieces of flesh fall to the ground. If you do not end it, there will be no heroes left to defend the Island of Britain.'

Now it is Arthur's turn to plead, 'Stop them, damn you!'

'Let us play this game to the end,' says Owain, unsmiling.

When the sixth lad comes, on a white and red horse with yellow-speckled armour, himself wearing a black and white cloak with purple fringes and weeping with rage under the image of a griffin on his crystal-studded helm, the king is encircled.

'Great Arthur! It is too late. They are all dead!'

A lift of Owain's hand. His standard is lowered. The glutted birds wheel from the carnage and their shadow passes to leave a bloody peace. In the moment before his final defeat, Arthur snatches the last few pieces from the board and crushes them into powder in his mighty fist.

Horsemen arrive. The Battle of Badon is over, and Osla Big-Knife sues for truce. Bards sing the praises of Arthur. Twenty-four asses appear, loaded with tribute of gold and silver. The bards — a broad hint, this — are rewarded with the asses.

What does it mean?

Does Owain my son once seek revenge against Arthur? Does he take arms against him at Badon? Or at Camlann? Where does all the flower of Britain's manhood fall?

Owain is my child. No matter how he is goaded, no matter how much blood his Ravens shed in revenge, he cannot be allowed to win. Arthur must sweep the board, even though he smashes the golden king, himself, to get the victory.

Save your sympathy. Rhonabwy is waking on the yellow ox-hide. It was only a dream. It is too early to weep for Owain ap Urien yet. Owain is history. We know he dies three-quarters of a century after Arthur fell at Camlann. Taliesin sings his elegy.

> *'In the grave below is*
> *much-sung great renown,*
> *the wings of the dawn*
> *like shining javelins:*
> *for no equal will be found*
> *to a lord of dazzling joy,*
> *enemy-reaper, grasper.'*

So whose were the Ravens which turned against Arthur?

# Chapter Fifty-three

What purpose can there be in talking now?

They are like men who stand on opposite mountain-tops, bellowing at each other across an unbridgeable whirlpool.

There have been bridges over other chasms, painful and perilous. The edge of a sword, a narrow plank beneath the rushing torrent, and the abyss is crossed, the gatekeeper is overpowered, the prison falls, the Lady is restored.

How can that be done now?

The taunts have stung like horse-flies, and the swelling grows, hard and itching.

Modred has fulfilled his destiny, Merlyn's prophecy. This is the flaw in Arthur's life that has finally cracked the finest jewel apart. Few can know how Modred grieves in his shadowed heart that he was made only for this. Should I have kept the truth from him? Yet how could I not have told him? How could he be my love-gift to Arthur, how could I rejoice my brother's heart with the son he lacked, and the lad not knowing whose he was? I bred him up to be a king's son. Should I have guessed he would choose to be the king?

How could I know that every song I sang to the little boy to praise his father Arthur, every tale of his valiant deeds and battles won, all his fame for generosity, honour, justice, would add fresh wounds to the first vital one when Modred learned the truth? This is the Arthur who rejected you. This is the father whose son you are not fit to be. This is the light in which you cannot live. This glory is not for you.

Black night will not draw back its advance because it sees the majesty of the setting sun. Modred will not yield to Arthur.

Still, pity might yet work a miracle. Arthur has won himself fresh renown from the war in Gaul. He has thrown back Modred's attack on the beaches, hounded him out of Winchester, sent those untried allies running back behind the crumbling frontiers of the east and north. He is winning, and success can make a great man magnanimous. He will agree to a truce, send Modred to Brittany, where there are kinsmen to watch him for further treason. Keep him from meddling in Britain with the chancy Saxons and Picts and Cornish. He can still be named Arthur's heir. The youth has diplomatic skills. Fill up the time that remains to the old king with face-saving occupation for the young. This is flesh of his flesh. Arthur would spare himself.

But the Angles and Saxons have crossed the divide that Arthur set after Badon.

Great Gawain and his brothers are dead.

And there is Gwenhyvar.

This is the wound that is slowly killing Arthur. Crowns are often got by the sword and may be won back so. Arthur Pendragon was our Emperor of Battles by that right arm alone, before I made Ygerne reveal that he was Uther's son. He claimed his right to rule as much by spilled Saxon blood as by his mother's. But gentle Gwenhyvar never needed to lift a sword to prove her royalty.

Warfare has taken Arthur away from Gwenhyvar. It cannot bring her back. Arthur may tell himself he does not want her now, that she was always false.

But was she? Is Gwenhyvach lying?

Did Modred force his queen to sin, or was she all too willing?

Arthur's heart aches with unanswered questions.

He cannot let Modred have what was once his.

In bitterness then, father and son walk towards each other, one down the sloping flower-strewn meadows, the other out from the darkness of the cliff.

Neither of them knows that they have both lost her. She, who was once the Sovereignty of Britain, has vowed herself to a solitary bed. She lies hidden from all men's eyes, husbandless now, in the house of religion where I left her. Without her, both these kings are widowers, and dispossessed.

Nimue knows now, standing in her chariot on the height, the sun catching her spear. This will be almost the last you see of her. She gave young Arthur his arms at the dawn of his manhood. She goaded Modred into this doomed battle. When they fall, she will disappear, and surface sometime later to inspire another young hero.

Is it hopeless then? But all humans will hope. These two approaching the ford of the Camel will become legends greater than all other heroes of Britain. This morning, they are both more and less than that. They have the limitations of mortal men, and the possibilities. One at least will not believe the inevitable.

Such a sunny morning for tragedy. The heather is purple on the distant heights of Bodmin Moor. Behind Modred the sky is brilliant with light thrown up from the sea. The little river Camel winks among cresses and bulrushes. Too close a valley this, for mighty armies. There are hundreds of men on Modred's side, a thousand and more on Arthur's. You may find it strange that in these ancient times such a handful of heroes could brand the names of battlefields on history. The warriors watching mistrustfully above Camlann know many of those facing them on the opposite bank. Without visors, the wilder of them unhelmeted, they recognise the men they are about to kill.

Like two lovers naked beneath their outer robes, then, Modred and Arthur come to their tryst. Yet magic has raised a hedge of mist between them. They must not be allowed to see each other truly. A dart of love might fell this ogre of bitterness and change the Dolorous Castle into the Joyous Keep.

They cannot approach each other alone. Each king comes guarded by a prickly mail-clad retinue. Blades have been sharpened for this meeting and hang loosely sheathed. Men, jealous of honour, ambitious for advancement, grieving for fallen friends. Warriors fiercely loyal to their leader, chiefs too proud to admit they may have chosen the wrong man.

This is not the blessed Isle of Apples. The worm is in the core already. The fruit is about to fall.

Do not judge them too harshly. These two men's tangled histories have been a tale of hurt and treachery from their conception. Why should it be different for them today at Camlann? Where were the good fays at their births to bestow a happy ending? I, Margawse, Elaine? Or Nimue? Could we have changed this?

Follow their paths, then, down to opposite banks of the river, through the long bright grass and the sun-warmed stones. Their war-bands watch from the high ground, alert, suspicious, in an uneasy silence. Bedwyr, Lucan, Custennin, Caradawc, Urien, Owain. These aristocratic men have been bred only for warfare. They distrust peace. The horses paw and snuffle, as restless as their riders. You could believe they were as eager for combat, as swift to strike with their hooves, as single-minded.

The slopes below them are bare of men and mounts on either side of the water. Once juicy pastures, from which the herds of cattle have been hurried away. Nothing to see now but tall red sorrel and gaudy buttercups. Yet the lush grass masks a secret, less intelligent animal life.

'King Arthur recognises Modred the Prince.'

'Modred, High King of Britain, gives good day to his father.'

How much the old king yearns to cast aside his dignity, the young one to retain his.

'It's over, boy. You thought I was dead before my time, did you? Your motley army is hacked to pieces. The brave few that are left to you are cornered here. The same host that defeated them at Winchester has come to finish the task. No need to condemn your men to die. We will accept your surrender.'

'Have you forgotten that I am your child? It was not in your dream that I should be given up to you, was it? Arthur's blood will not own himself bested, as Arthur would not.'

'Do you throw that old story back in my face again? I was younger than you are now, the year you were born. For the love of heaven, boy! I am not an ogre. I don't want to cut off your beard to trim my cloak-tail. Lay down your sword and you'll be honourably treated, as befits my son.'

But if we sisters had surrendered him as a baby, it would have cost him his life. And what treatment befits what Modred has done to Arthur?

'You presume a power you no longer have, venerable father. It is the victor who will dictate the terms after today. I am the May-King now. The Queen of Summer has blessed my cause. The Lady of the Lake fights on my side. Your own sister, Morgan the Wise . . .'

'She was always faithless!'

Yes, faithless to save this one surviving son of Arthur. Yes, faithless to bring these two together at last. Yes, faithless to think that I could give my heart to both of them and not be torn in two.

Which will I bless?

'I see my father fears the powers I can name.'

'Puppy! I'll show you how I despise your powers. Do you see King Urien on the heights with all his Northmen? Do you see Owain Enemy-Reaper? Your foster-father and your foster-brother, true men whom your rebellion shames! I have excused them from staining their swords with their household's blood. We will fight you, man for man. Two thirds of my victorious army against your tired tail-enders. And I will take from you the sword that is mine by sunset without loss of my honour.'

'You are old, my father, and your judgment fails you. I do not need mercy. I have my guarantee of victory: Gwenhyvar the High Queen.'

He must affirm her the true Gwenhyvar. Who knows what he believes? How could either of them tell that Modred has already lost her in his turn?

You cannot imagine the pain it costs Arthur to speak.

'That smiling adulteress! She has given neither of us what she promised. Give her up, son. Not to me, but to the fire. She was never worthy of Britain. Let not a mere woman stand between us. There are few enough of our young men left. For her sake, Gawain is dead, and Gareth and Agravain and Gaheris. Only you remain.'

But Owain, my own son, is not dead yet. He names my sister's children only. And doubt rises within me. Would he turn to Margawse, now, and make her his queen?

Blood hammers in my head.

Innocently the butterflies flutter from flower-heads, disclosing the tapestries of their wings. Small lacquered ladybirds climb dizzying grass stems. Ants march through the dusty soil.

High overhead men's voices boom. Summer heat warms their helmets and perhaps their hearts. Will there come a point when the kings have parleyed too long and the high tension of warfare slackens in their nerves and the sun has moved too far to mark the day of Camlann? The waiting armies fidget and begin to mutter. Sunlight dances on gilded trappings and on serviceable steel.

It could soon be over. The long book of Arthur's battles will be closed. The old warriors will hang up their shields, and only the bards will grow rich from the spoils of war. Arthur and Modred will come to a painful, damaged reconciliation. Pride will be patched up. If I could quell the red rage rising in my heart, I could help this healing.

Small fish swim in brown pools, deaf to the voices that call across the river. The bees are busy in the clover; Camlann to them means only honey. Through the sun-bright grass a sleepy adder coils towards a favourite stone.

And Idawc ap Mynio moves his weight from one restless leg to another. The shadow of his heel descends across the adder's path. So small a shift, to bring about annihilation.

Too quick those fangs to strike. Too sharp the pain to be forgiven. Territory has been invaded. Flesh has been violated. His sword is out of its sheath. Sunlight blazes on the blade. The serpent is severed with one blow. And a shout shatters the peace as the signal flashes up to the watching armies. Treachery! War!

The eager hosts descend like thunderclouds. The blood of innocent insects stains the soil, crushed beneath the onrushing hooves.

# Chapter Fifty-four

*The Morrigan. The Irish Raven-goddess of war.*

*Oh yes, if you know anything at all about Celtic mythology this is the one you have been waiting for, isn't it?*

*Morgan, the Morrigan. How avidly you seize upon their similar sounds. It is obvious, isn't it? This must be my true origin, long before the chronicles and romances were written down. This fits the malevolent character of Morgan the Fay.*

*Mor Rigan. The Great Queen.*

*The Goddess is three and she is one.*

*She appears as Ana, Badb, Macha. Or else as Macha, Badb and the Morrigan herself.*

> *'Badb and Macha, rich their store,*
> *Morrigan, confusion and war.'*

*They are ambiguous.*

*Ana. The Mother of Plenty. Twin mountain peaks are her paps. In Britain we know her as the hag Black Annis, who devours children and hangs their skins on an oak tree to dry.*

*Badb, the 'Boiling'. Does she keep the life-giving cauldron? She is more usually the Scald-Crow of Battle. She foretells disaster. She plots the fight. In battle she darkens the sky. She perches upon a stone and exults in the slaughter. When her sister the Morrigan tries to keep the Ulster hero Cuchulainn from his last battle, Badb disguises herself as lovely Niam, the woman Cuchulainn can never refuse. She urges him on to fight.*

*Macha. Daughter of Strangeness, son of Ocean.*

*Two Otherworld horses rise from a lake in front of Cuchulainn. After a brief struggle they submit to his powerful hand. The pair are thereafter devoted to him for life. They are Black Sainglend and the Grey of Macha.*

*Her city is Emain Macha. One story makes her a war-goddess, protectress of Ulster. She forces their enemies to build her fortress.*

*In a different tale, she marries a farmer. Crunniuc is a widower with a household of sons. Macha simply arrives, a beautiful woman walking in off the hills and over the threshold. She makes herself at home and sets his house to rights. At the end of the day she comes to his bed. He's a lucky man. She brings him comfort and wealth.*

*Macha is fleet of foot, she is fertile, she is fearless. She bestows a blessing.*

*The Ulstermen are holding a fair. The world and his wife are there. Crunniuc is going, of course, dressed up in his holiday clothes. But Macha will stay at home. Her belly is swollen with child, and she is near her time.*

*She bids him farewell and warns him not to say anything foolish.*

*At the end of the feast day, the king's own chariot and horses are brought on to the racetrack. They win the prize. All over the field people are exclaiming, 'Nothing in the world is so fast as those horses.'*

*Crunniuc brags, 'My wife is faster.'*

*A king's reputation is at stake. Crunniuc must make good his boast or die.*

*The summons comes to Macha. A great misfortune, the way she is today, but she will save her husband.*

*The labour pains come on her as she enters the fairground. She pleads with the men to wait, in the sacred name of the mothers who bore each one of them. There is no pity for her. The king asks her name. Macha, she tells him, and that name and those of her children will mark a curse upon this place for ever.*

*Now they are straining at the starting mark of the cursus. Macha is matched against the horses harnessed to the king's chariot. The race is on.*

*The track is long, the burden of her womb exceptionally heavy, the pace relentless.*

*Yet, since that is what the men demand of her, Macha exerts herself to the uttermost. These Ulstermen do not feel the anguish she is suffering. For them and their pride, she runs the race, hurling herself in front of the king's chariot at the finishing line, and wins. All horses own Macha their Queen.*

*For these men and their cruelty, her body splits in pain there on the track in front of the staring crowd. Twins are born, a son and a daughter.*

*For these men and their heartlessness, Macha dies. With her last breath she screams a curse on the Ulstermen listening. Four nights and five days, in the hour of their tribe's greatest need, the same pangs of childbirth she has suffered shall fall upon these warriors too, for nine generations.*

*Only Cuchulainn and his descendants are spared.*

*The place is called Emain Macha, the Twins of Macha, from that day.*

*The Morrigan. The Great Queen. The Queen of Ghosts.*

*Women and water are essential, changeable and dangerous. She is a shape-shifter.*

*At Samain the great god Dagda comes to the River Unius. He finds a woman with nine loosened tresses of hair down her back. The Morrigan is washing herself in the river, with one foot on the north bank and one on the south. The two of them fall to conversing. She mates with him. She brings him her magic aid.*

*It is dangerous to refuse her love.*

*She comes to the hero Cuchulainn as a woman of surprising form wrapped in a many-coloured mantle. She has loved him for the record of his deeds and she offers herself with all her goods and cattle. He is too busy with warfare to want a woman.*

*In warfare itself she will be his help, she tells him.*

*'It was not for putting my trust in a woman's aid that I took this job in hand,' he scoffs at her.*

*It will go harder with him if she fights against him.*

*Cuchulainn wakes in the night to hear a terrible cry from the north. He falls out of bed and rushes out of the house just as he is, with his wife chasing after him holding his clothes and weapons.*

770

*Across the plain he races until he catches up with a chariot drawn by a one-legged red horse with the pole passing clean through its body.*

*In the chariot is a woman in red, red herself, even to the eyebrows of her, and a great crimson mantle sweeping the ground behind her. A big ugly man is walking along beside her, wearing a crimson coat and carrying a forked stick on his back. He is driving a cow away.*

*The guardian hero of Ulster won't have that. He challenges the man, 'That cow is not pleased for you to be taking her.'*

*'What is that to you?' the woman replies. 'She doesn't belong to you or yours.'*

*'All the cows of Ulster are mine to keep,' Cuchulainn tells her.*

*He demands their names, but she answers him in riddles. So he leaps on the chariot and sets his feet on her two shoulders and his spear on the parting of her hair. She will tell him only she is a satirist and the cow is her reward for a poem she made. He has been warned, but he still demands to hear that poem.*

*'Get off me then,' and he jumps to stand between the two wheels.*

*It is, of course, a song of insult. A satirist's words can wound a man as sorely as any weapon. Cuchulainn is about to leap on her to avenge his hurt. In that instant, the woman, chariot, man, horse and cow all disappear.*

*And then he spies her, on a branch close by. She has turned into — wouldn't you expect? — a crow.*

*If he had known she was the vengeful Morrigan he would never have let her get away so easily. But still she taunts him. Whatever he had tried to do to her, it would only have brought him ill luck.*

*Now she has his fate in her keeping. The cow she was driving has come from the dreaded Otherworld cave of Cruachan. This cow is going to mate with the Brown Bull of Cuailgne. A calf will be born from the union. Until it is one year old, so long has Cuchulainn left to live. That calf will cause the fatal Cattle Raid of Cuailgne.*

*They taunt each other.*

*In the thick of battle, she'll hinder every movement of the hero. If he fights in the ford she will be an eel around his legs.*

*He will bruise her against the green stone of the ford.*

*She will become a ravening grey wolf, and take the flesh from his right hand as far as his left.*

*He will break her leg with a cast of his sling, and she shall never have help from him.*

*She will turn herself into a magical white heifer with red ears. Fifty pairs of heifers like her, linked together with bronze chains, shall be wading in the same pool of the river. They will stampede into the middle of the combat, bringing confusion, and Cuchulainn's head will be severed that day.*

*He will gouge out her eye with the point of his spear.*

*Yet the night before Cuchulainn's last battle, the Morrigan breaks his chariot in an effort to keep him at home.*

*When he persists in going, his faithful horse, the Grey of Macha, struggles to resist being harnessed to the war-chariot and weeps tears of blood.*

*A female satirist begs him not to go. Thrice fifty queens lament and beat their hands. His foster-mother's cup of milk turns to blood. He passes two beautiful maidens grief-stricken as they wash a bloody garment at the ford.*

*These women would save his life. But there are others.*

*On his way to the battle he meets three crones, each ritually blinded in one eye. They are cooking a dog with spells on spits of rowan. They invite him to eat. There are two 'geis' on him, two sacred prohibitions. To break either is death. He must never pass a cooking hearth without sharing the food. He must never eat the flesh of a dog, his namesake.*

*He tries to refuse the food. The crone who holds it out to him is insulted. Cuchulainn takes the dog's shoulder-blade from her left hand and eats. He is doomed.*

*The battle is bloody. Cuchulainn receives his death-wound.*

*With the last of his strength the hero straps himself to a standing stone. He will die on his feet, with his sword in his hand, facing his enemies. While his heart still beats, there is a crow perched on the top of a stone nearby, lamenting. She will not leave him while he has breath in his body. As Cuchulainn dies, the crow soars into the sky.*

*At his master's death, Black Sainglend gallops from the battlefield and plunges into the lake from which the horses once rose, making it seethe and boil. The Grey of Macha is wounded too. He bids his master farewell and follows his companion under the water.*

*Not till the smaller birds come to perch on the dead hero's shoulders does his enemy Lugaid dare to come forward to cut off his head. As he approaches, the sword falls from the lifeless grasp of Cuchulainn and severs Lugaid's hand with its last stroke.*

*You may ignore these ambiguities in the Morrigan's character. Her reputation is that she is bloody, vindictive, an implacable man-hater.*

*What does it matter if, in the beginning, she was a goddess of fertility and the protectress of warriors?*

*Mor Rigan. The Great Queen. The British Rigantona.*

*Is she Morgan?*

*The scholars still dispute. Some see Celtic mythology at every turn in the Arthurian path. Others are sceptical.*

*They say that by the time my story is written down in Britain, the language has softened. 'Mor Rigan' would mutate into 'Mor Rian'. I should be 'Morien', not 'Morgan'. Our British 'Rigantona' becomes 'Rhiannon', who is also forced to play the role of a horse.*

*Can the Morrigan really have been the pattern for Geoffrey's Morgen in Avalon? The Raven of Battle for his fairy healer?*

*Writers have seized upon the idea with relish.*

*She makes for a more exciting story, doesn't she?*

# Chapter Fifty-five

This is the day of death. We have come to our final flowering. Here is true tragedy, sprung from a central stem, rooted in character, fed by our origins. This is the name that will beat through history like the sound of the solemn drum.

Camlann, Camlann.

Look at them. Nimue galloping in her chariot along the hilltop, brandishing her spear, calling up valour from the army, calling down vengeance from the skies. The sunlight catches her golden breastplate. She is brave and wonderful. This is the Lady who has shielded the lovers. She is a dangerous woman. Changeable Nimue, who once armed Arthur, who protected and advised him when he was green and malleable. He was insufficiently grateful. He chose the Church.

She has not aged. She has turned from Arthur's grey hairs to Modred's black. She feeds on youth.

My ravens are black and hungry. But they will soon be glutted. Then the field will fall silent. It will be over.

Whose guardian will Nimue be next?

But now the men bellow and the horses scream and the weapons hack through armour to flesh.

On the opposite ridge, the Church's phalanx. Christ's white-robed druids lift their cross, like a sword reversed. 'Michael the Archangel, fight for us! Tread the pagan dragon under your heel.'

Does the Goddess who gave us birth also require these deaths?

We sprout and wither. Earth to earth. Life for life.

Arthur is a dangerous champion for the Christian cause. He has been a thief and a brigand in his youth, the Red Ravager. He tried to violate Saint Cadoc's Christian sanctuary; he killed the monk-historian Gildas's brother. But who else was there for them to turn to when the keels were grounding, when the Saxons and Angles were marching, when the Picts swarmed over the Wall, when the Irish came raiding? Priests and nuns fell at the altar, the church steps ran with martyred blood, the first precious centuries of faith and learning guttered like a candle-flame as the door opened on the night. Who could stop it?

Who but the strength, the laughter, the warlike zest, the ready sword of Arthur the soldier, Arthur our leader of battles, Arthur the Briton? It was not a chivalrous Arthur of the banqueting hall, presiding over Round Table and tournament, that they needed. It was a younger, a more ancient, Arthur. Never mind if the people believe he is half a god himself, with tales of his hounding Cat Palug into the sea or the boar Twrch Trywth across half Britain, and all the mighty hunters of legend at his heels. So much the better if these tales of him terrify the enemy.

Today the Church pays her debts.

Modred the pagan made an alliance with the strangers. Arthur the Christian slew them. Nothing is simple.

The rage is in his blood now; it is a fearsome sight. How could he fight this war otherwise?

No fury is visible in Modred's face. His is too vulnerable a soul to be exposed naked to the sun. A young man under an iron control. What wells of bitterness or grief chill his passion? How little have I known him? What is he thinking as he seeks out his father in the thickest of the fight?

What can any of these bawling men think as they heave their weapons in the heat of battle but, 'This is my death approaching. This is the blade that will finish me. This man is my slayer, unless I kill him first.'

Brother against brother. Fosterlings fighting. Father and son. Is this the Matter of Britain? Where is wisdom and justice? Where is chivalrous love?

It is waste; it is folly.

What else could they do?

It is glorious war.

Look down on this battlefield and see the human condition, bitterly acted out, the pattern of nobility fatally flawed; Arthur is brought to this reckoning by one youthful sin.

There is the horse, obedient between his knees. There is the stabbing spear. There is Arthur drawing his sword to finish a man, to smite at splintering shields, to clear a circle round him.

Caliburn cannot be vanquished, can it? Why, then, am I sick with fear? Why am I screaming to them like Nimue? If Arthur cannot be brought down by force of arms, what is there left to dread but treachery? Would I want him to die in his bed, old, crippled and bitter, his sons dead before him, like King Llywarch Hen?

All day they struggle and bleed on the slippery sides of Camel's banks. The sea-mist creeps inland to cover this shame, this sorrow. The sun is dimmed. The shadows of horses gallop to aid the ghosts of warriors locked in death-holds. The blades ring hollowly on jagged shields and the javelins part the air with the whistle of expiring breath. The crows are gathering, silent, watchful, shuffling on the branches of the elm trees, waiting their time.

I wait my time.

No pity in either of them now. Two loves more cruel in their indignation, their disappointment, fuel the sparks that fly from steel. Cover it over. We will witness no quarter, no plea for mercy. Let them finish it here.

And the mist comes.

Nimue's curses and the Christian priests' prayers are lost in the cloud on the hilltops now. What shall we do when the long day ends, and the stars come out and our hope lies mutilated at the water's edge? What will be left of the Island of the Mighty?

And I? Come lower; stand under the trees with us. I kept vigil when

774

Arthur and Modred were born. I must see them die. Margawse, Elaine and I, holding hands here, cold flesh to flesh, feeling the earth of Cornwall under our feet fed with fresh blood, tears on our cheeks like rain, chanting in broken voices, singing the dying home.

They have met. In a stillness of anger too deep for words. The blunted spears thrust. The broken shields are advanced. Their weary horses stagger and sidestep. What weight of sorrow drives their aching muscles on?

Aah!

Arthur's spear has gone in. The merciless shaft revolves, retracts, in a gush of too-bright blood. The old king is not so staled with battle that might have failed his arm. Modred is down. He kneels on the earth like a dutiful son, weeping for pity more than pain. Arthur is unhorsed beside him. The thin grey daylight shows horribly through the gaping javelin-wound. The father could stand and watch his son die. But Caliburn must strike the final stroke, clean to the neck.

Those lips, that once sucked my breast, bubble like a baby's, but too darkly. You would not think Modred's lungs had breath enough for one more blow.

Now Arthur stands, staring down like a man amazed. No grief, no agony of pain, no tears on his face, only a dead-faced wonder. This was his child, and now he has no son. Who has robbed him?

His warrior's body has forgotten the cunning drilled in him since boyhood. His shield hangs useless at his side. And Modred's hilt quivers like a strange protuberance from Arthur's guts.

Blood has choked Modred's mouth. He has no last word for his father. Only that slow and feeble thrust below the rim of breastplate. This is his final statement. His hands leave his sword. His spirit leaves the world. It is over. We are finished.

Caliburn has got Arthur the victory. He will never need it again. There will be pain soon.

Bedwyr and Lucan come, looming like giants out of the fog. Their shout of anguish now is louder than their king's. Arthur hides his fast-clouding eyes on his friend's shoulder.

'Take me away,' he begs. 'Let no one find me thus.'

These men are loyal. Bedwyr knows what must be done. Shriek now, to cover his drawing out of that sword, the humiliating moans of a royal hero hastily strapped and hoisted on his horse. Lucan bites his lips till the blood runs, as he heaves that weight up. He is wounded too. But he will put his king's need first, though it kills him. They lead the horse away slowly into the fog, supporting Arthur. And when we sisters unstop our ears the bird-headed trumpet is sounding the croaking call that ends even the bitterest battle.

The wind is rising. The mist is thinning into merciful dusk. The priests on either side come chanting down the hill to comfort the dying and to claim their dead.

The legends are done.

Who but the bards will inherit this bloodstained field, now Arthur and Modred are lost?

What is there left, that we should call Britain the Island of the Mighty?

# Chapter Fifty-six

*I am a pagan myth. I am a romantic fiction.*

>*'537 The Battle of Camlann, in which Arthur and Modred fell; and there was plague in Britain and Ireland.'*

*This simple, grief-laden statement lies between two others:*

>*'521 Saint Columba is born. The death of Saint Brigid.'*

>*'544 The sleep of Ciaran.'*

   *A voice out of history, of a sort. The Welsh Annals. Not wholly accurate, of course. The dates, at least, are unreliable. But names bulk on the page with the solidity of remembered truth. These men and women lived and died. Their inspiration and their suffering are not a fiction.*
   *Columba and Brigid? Ciaran? An ecclesiastical history, then. Arthur and Modred are numbered between the saints.*
   *The British Church mourns the passing of Arthur. It owns no knowledge of me.*

# Chapter Fifty-seven

Look, here he is. This is Arthur, the king of all the Britons. He has finished his thirteenth great battle. He has won. He has killed his son.

Study him well. Here is the pinnacle of chivalry. This is what kingship means.

Grieve with all of us.

A man larger than common. His broad chest lusty and loving. My head longed to rest there. Now his beard is matted with bright blood that keeps on welling, and the plates of his body-armour are clogged with a red more shocking than rust.

This little sanctuary is shadowed, far from the ravens' wings over Camlann. Even the pool is still, no tide to fret it. We wait for the pulse of Arthur's heart to die away.

One of these three is dead already, Lucan, brave warrior, whose own broken ribs supported the agony of Arthur to this place. Men do that for their king. The lesser bear great suffering so the great may suffer less. Too powerfully Arthur clutched his friend, driving the splintered bone-ends through Lucan's chest to choke his loyal breath with blood.

What of it? Soon they will all be dead. And those that linger the longest while will mourn they did not die at Camlann.

Not Bedwyr, though. Not yet, though half his heart was killed already when Cei fell in France.

Now he crouches, hunkered on the earthen floor. So the bright images show the gods of old, cross-legged and waiting. His hands are empty, but not for long. I have work for him.

'*Bedwyr!*'

The warrior's head rises, and he shivers, as one who hears an owl and fears she may be something else.

'*Bedwyr.*'

That troubled, loving glance at Arthur. But those blue eyes are tight in the self-centred lock of pain. Arthur does not hear me cry. He has never heard me.

Strangeness has hold of Bedwyr. He is leaderless. Better the voice that calls him to terror than this silence. Strong-muscled yet, only a little stiff with middle-age and battle-weariness, his legs unfold and hoist him upright.

He lets tears fall. Arthur is lying a few steps from the altar, his sacrificed blood shed too early. It will not gladden any god. His son's wound burns in his belly. Modred he slew cleanly, but he is dying slowly at this same son's hand.

'*Bedwyr!*' Even this slow death may come too swiftly for what must still be done.

So, like a sleepwalker, Arthur's dearest remaining friend steps from the chapel into misty moonlight, and leaves the dying with only the dead for company.

A shining mere, cupped in the hills. The smallest sign may serve as token for infinity. I stand on the far, seaward side of it, where the brook spills out, and call to him. I must fight to hold back the heart that would surge over oceans, burst into that chapel, seize Arthur in my arms and sob out his salvation. There is an order in the universe. Its ways cannot be broken, or we break ourselves. I have learned the path of healing. I know its toll.

Will the wind carry my voice over the water?

'I bring a message for Arthur Pendragon.'

The heavy dew of summer trembles on the moonlit bulrushes like frost. He sees me, indistinctly, across the shimmering surface.

'Who . . . are you?'

There is more than query in the tremor of his voice.

Is it Nimue, Lady of the Lake, standing in front of the trees at the water's edge, or Morgan, Sea-Born? Or the shape of something Other, that never knew human flesh and blood, come for the Dragon's son? And which of us would be more dangerous to the king now? Their warlike foster-mother, who brought up both these men and taught them arms, who all this time has been sheltering the love of his adulterous queen, a midwife nursing treachery to the inevitable birth of this last battle? Or Arthur's bitter sister, cheated rival, Modred's foster-mother, who hated Arthur for his father Uther's sake, loved him for his own? Nothing is clear, no ground is sure, except this one certainty: Arthur is dying.

I move into the moonlight; let it fall upon my face.

'Morgan the Wise!'

Oh, yes, there's hope. I hear it. I am Morgan, the renowned physician. It is to me men bring their gravest wounded for healing.

He starts to run around the bank towards me, stumbling on the muddy grass. I stop him with one lifted finger. Merlyn would be proud of me.

'Not yet. Oh, I have healing far beyond the stars. My potions are powerful, my hands are sure.'

'Come round to the chapel, then! Quickly, he cannot have long. Morgan the Holy, I beg you. Undo this evil!'

What lies a man will babble in ecstasy or fear. And a woman too, when her barriers are down. I know why he needs me, why he speaks me fair. He believes I caused this war, that I dealt this wound, and so I, more than any other, am the one who can close it.

Let it pass. He is right in one respect. The time is short, and there is so much to teach him.

'There is a price to pay.'

'For the love of heaven, he is your brother!'

Hold back my tears. I would have given Arthur more than he ever dreamed of asking. This is no time for self-justification.

'Power is mine to work with. I cannot command it. The ways of

Wisdom were carved in the first pattern of creation. Those who would wield it must become her humblest servants. Yes, I know how Arthur may be healed. I did not lay down the path.'

'You called me here. What do you want done?'

Bedwyr has never been humble. He is a warrior-aristocrat, chief of Arthur's personal war-band, his *teulu*, his fighting-family. He is a man who takes orders from one king alone. He is touchy, proud, jealous of insult. Look at him trembling now, trying to plead with me, fighting to keep that ready hand away from his sword and not compel the words of mercy from my throat at its battle-dinted edge. Across a watery space I smile at him. I am less sure of myself than he must think. Say rather, I am less sure of Bedwyr's good sense, and fearful far more of Arthur's rebellion. I could lose him yet, and this time it would be for eternity.

'One thing only. My price is small, for immortality.'

'Name it, Lady.'

'Easy to say. Not easy to give. Caliburn.'

A puzzled stop. 'You want his battle-weapon?'

Not the rich jewelled sword of Britain's government? He could understand my seizing that, though we sisters once guarded the native Stone that allowed it to Arthur. I feel his mind racing with bewilderment, suspicion. He would play for time, but time is what Arthur no longer has. I want the fighting sword, his talisman of victory? The sword we sisters once stole, and in so doing nearly cost him his life? Caliburn, forged ages ago in Avalon. Caliburn, whose healing scabbard-mate I, with my own hands, sacrificed to the Goddess in another pool, and bear the wound that cost me upon my heart still?

'Not I. One greater than any of us requires it.'

His mind is too small, too practical, too human-sized, to sense the shape of the truth that stands behind me.

He knows what Nimue would do with Caliburn. The Lady of the Lake in her golden breastplate, riding in her battle-chariot. But Morgan the Wise? Have I some little king-in-waiting, another Accolon, who hopes to win through warfare, with Caliburn, what Modred failed to secure with the symbol of peace?

Abruptly, then, 'And if he lives? What would Arthur the warrior be without his battle-weapon? What good is his life if he surrenders Caliburn?'

I shrug, as though I do not care, as though it is nothing to me that Arthur is slipping from the world, for ever, and from all worlds of faeryland beyond.

The mere between us is wide enough for our voices to call thinly, like the scream of hawks.

'Do you condemn your king to die, and will not ask him?'

A hesitation, his balance swivelling on the ball of his foot. Loving fear wrestles with indignation. Then we hear a groan, wrenching the heart of both of us. The chapel seems to heave against the stars like a wounded bear, grieving with rage and pain and coming loss.

Bedwyr is running back into that mouth of darkness.

And only now Arthur's final battle begins.

# Chapter Fifty-eight

*I can give, and I can take away. I can hurt and I can heal.*

*Take Ogier the Dane.*

*From the twelfth century, our story is told. You may remember, I am the sixth fairy at his cradle. My gift exceeds all the rest. I promise that he shall never die by the hand of man, but that, after a long life of glory, he will come to live in joy in Avalon, as my lord and love.*

*Ogier does indeed become a great hero in France in the service of Charlemagne. He lives a hundred years. The time has come. I arrange for him to be shipwrecked on a lodestone rock, conveniently near my island, which itself lies just this side of Paradise.*

*The entrance must not be made too easy for him. This is a famous warrior. I have lions for him to encounter, King Kapalus for him to fight. He succeeds, of course.*

*What would you expect on such an island but an apple orchard? He eats the fruit and falls into a dangerous sickness. Expecting only death, he turns to face the east and sees a beautiful lady so magnificently attired he takes her for the Virgin Queen of Heaven. I modestly explain his error and reveal my name. I am Morgue the Fay. I have loved Ogier since the day he was born. It is I who have brought him here to enter my bliss.*

*Ogier protests that a man so sick is no fit companion for the fairest of fays and her maidens. That is easily remedied, since I have caused this sickness. A touch of my hand is all that is needed to restore him to perfect health.*

*I do more than that. I put a ring on his finger which restores his youth. I place a crown on his head which makes him forget all the past. I lead him to Avalon where he is greeted by all my maidens with mirth and songs and the best of entertainment. A son, Meurvin, is born to us.*

*Two hundred years pass as though they were twenty. But Christendom is now in danger again. With heavy heart I know the time has come to loose him. I lift the crown from his head, and memory returns. He cannot believe how long he has been in Avalon. His one desire is now to return to France. I urge him not to forget me, and never to speak of the wonders of my island. I give him two gifts: the ring he has worn since his arrival, which preserves his youth, and a magic firebrand. When the wood is entirely consumed by flames, Ogier will die.*

*Thus equipped, he is transported on a cloud back to the world of King Philip I. Much has changed, but Ogier is still a doughty warrior. He vanquishes the foes of Christianity and seeks more adventures, leaving his firebrand for safekeeping with the Abbot of St Faro.*

*King Philip dies. I have ensured that Ogier is still young, handsome and valiant.* The widowed Queen of France now sets her eye on him as her next husband. Alarmed, Ogier remembers me. He rides to the Abbey of St Faro, demands the firebrand, and flings it on the flames. He pulls the ring from his finger and instantly becomes a man three hundred years old. I race to save him. I snatch the brand from the hearth and lift Ogier into my fiery chariot. We vanish from sight.

But others say Ogier is actually on his way to the altar to marry the Queen of France when a maiden in shining white appears, throws her arms around him and snatches him out of the church in a great cloud.

I am the original fairy mistress. I offer joys untold. I would not advise you to be unfaithful to me.

Renoart is less appreciative than Ogier. It nearly costs him his life.

In the Bataille Loquifer I find the hero asleep by the sea. He is exhausted by weeping for his lost son Maillefer. I come flying down to land beside him, with my sister Marrion and another fay. I will have this hero for my love but my jealous sister designs him harm. We lift him, still asleep, ask God's blessing, change his club and hauberk into birds, his helmet into a harp, his sword into a boy, and enchant him away to Avalon. Arthur greets him and introduces me as the beautiful Morgue. Renoart falls passionately in love with me.

But his ardour quickly fades. He sails off to seek his son. Spurned, I persuade a youth Kapalu in the same fleet to sink his ship. Only at the last moment is Renoart saved from a watery grave by softly singing sirens who carry him to shore.

It is dangerous to reject me.

# Chapter Fifty-nine

He cannot do it, can he?

Even now, in his extremity of pain, Caliburn still lies under his hand. Do the dragons on its hilt bite as his curled hand grips them with each spasm? Does their breath burn? He would rather their cruelty should turn on him, to drive out the pain of that other wound, the thrust of his son's sword.

A dreadful double agony. How could he not feel that?

He found it easier, once, to forget this son.

I remember that day, in the high open courtyard of my fort at Lyvennet. We were young then. I watched a golden-bearded general, with a boy's blue eyes, striding across the space to meet me and learn that he was the Pendragon's son and I was his sister. And then I showed him Margawse. I saw the hope in kingship vanish from his eyes, drowned deep in her blushing laughter. This was my sister, and therefore his. And she was big with his child. I understood what we had both lost. I would have gathered him on my shoulder and let him weep.

And so the Wheel of Fortune comes full circle. Merlyn contrives that Uther should trick Ygerne, steal her from Gorlois to get him Arthur. Margawse tricks Arthur, steals him from . . . me? . . . to make Modred. Now Arthur's own son, treacherously got, steals Arthur's queen. The old king must die, tumbling earthwards from his high revolution.

Earth, open your arms. Receive him gently. This is the Hero of Britain.

He cannot bear to die. It is more than physical fear. Who will inspire the war-host after him? For so he understands the call to kingship. Caliburn was always dearer to him than the sword of peace. His other sons are dead before him. Llacheu of Great Renown, his favourite bastard, heroically in battle. Anir, that poor pale stripling Gwenhyvar gave him, gone early to his long home under the cairn trying to imitate Arthur's reckless folly. Then Modred his firstborn returns from the shades of the Otherworld, like a blossom in February, and Arthur welcomes the son he once tried to kill.

Modred the princely, so lately his well-beloved. Too lately loved. Modred is slain. We knew he must kill the baby. He still had his way to make, his kingdom to win, his reputation to guard. To a soldier it was simple. The baby was in the way. The baby must die.

Was I responsible? To this day I shall feel Arthur's hands on my wrists, hear the screaming of babies who do not yet know what they have to weep for, command the iron to armour my heart. He shall not

782

have Modred! I will shut my ears to the howling of the mothers. I will not see the fearful indecision in the eyes of Arthur's young warriors as they seize their tiny enemies. I will not fall into Arthur's arms, though he supports my waist and smiles and coaxes and all my bones have melted to liquid fire.

I enraged him by my defiance. Saxons had surrendered to him. A British woman wounded his pride.

Might I have calmed the sea? I sent Teilo to bear witness for me. I did not follow the children myself to the coast. Could I have made the ebb-tide carry the ship safely in her bosom when all that freight of innocent babes was cast adrift upon the Solway? I stayed at home and, furious as Arthur, I devised a spell so that Modred, son of Arthur, should come sound to shore. I shudder now, remembering that act. Like Arthur, I was too singleminded. I worked magic only for one. I had my will. Modred was rescued by a fisherman. And all the rest were lost.

I wept then for the cruel profligacy of the Mothers who had robbed so many human hearts to leave us only Modred. Now I let the tears fall for my own heartlessness.

Arthur never knew. We were always adversaries. He avoided my court for shame and so he never saw my dark-browed foster-son growing. In secret, I guarded Arthur's child, taught Arthur's child, cherished Arthur's child. Margawse had given him flesh. I shaped his soul. It was never enough. I told him the truth, and kissed him on the forehead, and lost him. It was not my love Modred wanted then, but his lost father's. The son was acknowledged, that love was given, too late. Modred learned that Margawse was his mother, not me. He has followed her road to revenge, coldly where she went warm.

Forgive me, Arthur. My hands are round the sword that stabbed you as surely as Modred's. I reared him for this. I fed him my grief and bitterness.

Now Arthur rages. He will not die for this. He must not die. He groans for the failure of his hopes, the fouling of his love. Do not think it was Modred's neck only he was severing with that stroke; it was Gwenhyvar's too. A bigamous marriage! His wife to his son? Modred crowned! He'll wipe them both out, from the earth, from history, from his heart. He and Britain will live on. He will yet find his true mate.

I wait for his understanding. I am here, Arthur. I have always been here.

The king's clenched eyes open, reluctantly. He has too many pains to fight within. Bedwyr is shadowing the stars.

'Arthur! My lord. Morgan has come.'

There, I knew that would enrage him. A curse, a twist of the broken body that brings back physical pain howling to eclipse the other. A sharp, animal noise. It is mastered quickly. He is still a fighter, this Arthur.

'That faithless whore!'

No, I am the Faithful Whore. I, the Maiden, have given my body generously. Since my king would not admit he wanted it, what worth was it to me? If, opening it, I could feed the earth, if I could coax the sap to rise, the streams to flow, I would offer it freely. Only my supreme gift, the sovereignty of all Britain, I kept for him alone. Instead, he took it from Margawse. She cheated him. The land has never been made whole. Arthur has chosen to win a fractured kingship by another right, the sword. He has lost it so, and all our blood is passing into twilight with him.

'Morgan is the Healer.'

'She would not heal me, even if she could.'

His face turns from the door. He will not see the truth.

'She makes you an offer.'

Now there is stillness, like a blade of steel. The controlled force of Arthur tenses. The warrior, hard beset on every side, spies a tiny weakness in the ring of enemies, and all his manhood sharpens into one death-defying resolve to escape.

'What?'

'She will heal your wound if you will pay her price.'

'Have I not been a generous king? I've emptied a hundred treasure-houses in gifts. I've won fame for granting everyone whatever they asked me, so long as it was not my horse, my weapons, or my wife.' His voice trembles at the last.

Bedwyr kneels. I do not need to see his face. I can tell by the shaking of his shoulders the tears. This man loves Arthur. As we all must.

'Your sister asks that you surrender your sword to her.'

'Caliburn!'

He does not feel now how he grips the hilt, though his palm will bear the mark of it. Fury is what he knows, and it gives him strength. He tries to rise, and the blood spurts on the earthen floor dampening it more menacingly than the night dew. Bedwyr darts to catch, to cradle him, to lay him down.

I can do nothing but wait. I know the promise I offer may be the sentence that kills him. It must be his choice.

'She would still be queen, would she?' he gasps, when he can speak again. 'And with Caliburn? A warrior-queen, like Boudicca! Tell her she's too old.'

'You need not fear that. The people turned to Gwenhyvar, with her sword of government, and it brought them civil war. You came back with Caliburn. You have won the field. You have proved yourself the true king. They will not trust a queen again.'

I offer immortality. They talk of politics.

It is chill in the chapel. Arthur is stiffening before he is dead, to stop the shuddering of his weakened limbs.

'Tell her I will never give up Caliburn. Remind her she is my subject and my sister. Tell her, when her husband Urien put his sword and coronet under my hand, he pledged his wife's obedience too. *Command* her to heal me. I will be generous to her afterwards.'

Oh, little brother, did you play so at kings in Nimue's foster-house? Did you bind laurel leaves upon your golden brow and wave a wooden sword and order your playmates with your high-pitched shout? Has all the tutelage of the sage Merlyn come to this? Is this your notion of kingship? He might as well have left you to be brought up a warrior's whelp in Uther's court. Your mother and your sisters could have taught you more of the deep fitness of things.

Bedwyr is more afraid. He has seen my face by moonlight. Some little part of him has felt the Lady's power beneath the surface of the pool between us. His hand rests gently on the sword-hilt, over Arthur's.

'Arthur . . . sire, . . . your wound is grave. We have come too far in the mist. It is too late now to turn back and try to find the battlefield and the surgeons. This part of Cornwall is desolate. The people have fled us. I have no salves. I have done what I can, but the dressing I have strapped round you will not hold off death till morning.'

'Gawain might have healed me. He had some skill.'

'Gawain is dead.'

'And Morgan the Wise will watch me die.'

'She says the cure is costly.'

'A false surgeon! She would amputate the arm she wants for herself!'

'She speaks as though the sword is not for either of you now. Remember, she gave the scabbard up.'

'*My* scabbard! It was not hers to drown. But for that spite, I should not be bleeding to death now. She stole my healing. And now she wants to beggar me of my might as well. She has made all Britain a wasteland with her plots.'

Did I deal that wound to Modred, who brought us all to this?

'Will you not test her faith, at least?'

'Morgan is always faithless. Tell her no, no, no!'

I feel a cold wind fret the mist. Low waves lap the shore. I cannot keep it from the chapel door. It chills the sweat on Arthur's face. Within the stiff pride of his battledress he shivers. I can do nothing to stop it.

# Chapter Sixty

*I am the figure of evil.*

*We cannot put it off any longer. It is time at last to turn our attention to Sir Thomas Malory. Forget the Welsh legends, the early chronicles, the thirteenth-century romances, the Breton folk-tales. This is the book that really matters. It has become the definitive version.*

*Le Morte d'Arthur, concluded in 1469, two years before Malory's death in Newgate.*

*This is the one that has coloured all subsequent tellings. Malory's portrayal of me has left its indelible mark upon the twentieth century. It is not a pretty picture.*

*He writes a collection of eight epic tales about the court of King Arthur. There is certainly no shortage of material.*

*It is all here, everything the romantic heart could desire. Arthur's birth at Tintagel, the sword in the anvil, the establishment of the Round Table, Excalibur rising from the lake, Lancelot and Gwenhyvar, Trystan and Essylt, the Quest of the Holy Grail, Modred's treachery, Arthur's falling at Camlann, the queens who come to bear him away.*

*William Caxton, the printer, seizes the opportunity of the newly invented printing press. He arranges the tales into twenty-one books, containing the sum of five hundred and seven chapters, and publishes the collected work in 1485. For one so new to the printed word and the publishing trade, he certainly has an eye for a saleable manuscript.*

*Men clad in armour ride bravely into the forest and do battle with any knight they meet, without revealing their name. Foul enemies are slain in the process and sometimes, unfortunately, friends or brothers. Damsels lure knights into perilous castles, wronged ladies are rescued. The vision of the Grail inspires Arthur's knights. The quest is achieved. The Maimed King is healed. Galahad is transported to heaven.*

*But the fellowship of the Round Table has been weakened by the Grail quest, by the loss of Lancelot through banishment, by the death of Gawain and his brothers who oppose Lancelot. When Arthur dies, the romantic lovers remain separated and make a holy end as nun and monk.*

*Morgan le Fay is the villainess of this piece. I am Arthur's lifelong foe. Time and again I plot to bring about his death. I am the enemy of all true lovers and the bane of Arthur's knights.*

*Malory knows the sources. If there is an unpleasant story about me to be found he uses it.*

*Note what he does not choose to say.*

*He never shows me in my original role as healer. Instead he tells the story of the ointment I give to Alexander l'Orphelin, which causes him agony past bearing until he accedes to my will. He writes of my theft of the magic scabbard that prevents Arthur from losing blood. He tells of the mantle I send him which burns the wearer to death.*

*I have changed a great deal since Geoffrey and Chrétien de Troyes.*

*I no longer offer my lovers an island of enchantment and youth and the delights of faerie. Now I trick hapless knights away to my castle and imprison them because they will not give me their love.*

*Even at the end, I do not appear to bear Arthur away to my land of joy. True, I am one of three hooded queens who take the still-living king into their ship. True, Arthur himself believes he is bound for healing in the Vale of Avalon. True, Malory quotes the legend that Arthur is living still.*

*But we queens are dressed in black and shrieking for grief. Next morning Bedwyr arrives at Glastonbury to find a new-made grave. A hermit reports how at midnight ladies arrived bearing a corpse, begged that it be buried there in the chapel, and paid for the lighting of a hundred candles. Malory knows of the famous inscription on the tombstone:*

## HERE LIES ARTHUR, THE ONCE AND FUTURE KING

*I am not suggesting that Malory invents these unflattering tales of me, though he sometimes gives them a twist of his own. But authorship is the art of selection, what to include, what to omit, what words to use. In the choices we make we give our own selves away. Of all the versions of the Arthurian story available to him in the fifteenth century he seems to be drawn in particular to those from the pens of Cistercian monks whose writings betray how much they fear women.*

*In Malory most women are supernaturally malignant or false to their husbands. They bring about the downfall of good knights. Courtly love of a hero for his unattainable mistress is still romantic, but it is no longer the high ideal inspiring gallant action. Women are dangerous to men. One of Arthur's knights even beheads the Lady of the Lake for slaying his mother.*

*Love is most tender between man and man. Arthur himself is made to say:*

*'I am sorrier for my good knights' loss than for the loss of my fair queen; for queens I might have enough.'*

*But I am the queen of evil.*

*Who is this man who has branded his image of me so searingly on the imagination of the twentieth century?*

*It is charged that on the fourth of January 1450 Sir Thomas Malory, with other malefactors, lay in ambush in the woods of Coombe Abbey for the purpose of murdering the Duke of Buckingham.*

*That on the 25th of May of the same year he broke into the house of Hugh Smyth at Monks Kirby and raped his wife Joan.*

*That ten weeks later he raped her again.*

*That the following year he engaged in sweeping cattle raids and twice extorted money by threats.*

*He is arrested and imprisoned by the Sheriff of Warwickshire. Five days later he escapes by swimming the moat, breaks into a Cistercian abbey, and steals money and valuables from the abbot's chests. Next day he repeats the crime with many accomplices, breaks eighteen doors, insults the abbot, steals more money. Months later he is rearrested and ends up in the Tower.*

*In 1454 he is released on bail but still he plots attacks, goes back to jail, seizes swords, daggers and halberds and escapes again.*

*He seems to spend the rest of his life in and out of prison. It is as a prisoner that he ends his story of Arthur with expressions of piety and hopes for release.*

'I pray you all, gentlemen and gentlewomen that readeth this book of Arthur and his knights from the beginning to the ending, pray for me while I am alive, that God send me good deliverance, and when I am dead, I pray you all pray for my soul. For this book was ended the ninth year of the reign of King Edward the Fourth, by Sir Thomas Malory, knight, as Jesu help him for His great might, as he is the servant of Jesu both day and night.'

*A nice try. We must suppose it fails. He is buried at Greyfriars Church near Newgate Jail.*

*This is the man who writes the epic account of the deeds of gallant knights in shining armour. He has influenced all our imaginings.*

*A would-be murderer. A rapist.*

*Should you trust what he tells you about women?*

# Chapter Sixty-one

Keep back among the trees. Bedwyr is coming out. Arthur's answer
will widen this distance between us into a grievous wound. He must
close it before I can mend the lesser one. It will need high courage.

'Lady Morgan?'

Wait a little. The moonlight shimmers uncertainly across the mere.
The air is cloudy. Let him doubt his eyes. This is the hour of faery.
Give him time to fear. Now speak. Make the voice calm, cool. He must
not guess how much this means to me.

'I am still here. I have always been here. I can wait more lifetimes
yet. But Arthur's own hour is almost over. What is his answer?'

'He will not make this bargain for his sword. He calls you faithless,
proud, ambitious.'

Is it faithlessness that has brought me here to keep tryst with Arthur
now he has passed beyond all other help? Is it pride to hold out my
healing hand to the brother who caused me such humiliation? Does
he call it ambition, that I am offering immortal kingship to him?

Say none of this.

'Arthur has chosen his own way, then, and I mine. If he will not
accept my help, let him turn to others. The Christian Church will ask
its own renunciation from him, before it promises bliss.'

'I cannot tell where we are, but there is no priest near, or nun, or
monk. He has no soul-friend but what I am, a plain soldier of Christ.'

'Need the Christian King Arthur fear to die unconfessed? He took
the Great Offering before the battle. Will he not enter Christ's heaven?'

He bites his moustache. 'Why must you talk of death, Lady? This
is Arthur the Emperor! Would you have him live and love, fight and
fall, take the sacrament and give up the ghost like any other lusty hero
among us? He has no generation to carry on his name. There can be
no second Arthur. This is a king like no Briton before or after him.
This is our greatest chieftain, woman, robbed of the realm he saved!
He embraced his son, only to have him steal his crown and stab him
with a mortal wound. Would you see Arthur Pendragon die at Camlann
in a cuckold's brawl and not go out in a blaze of triumph and glory
against the Island's enemies?'

He calls me proud.

'Must not the grave have us all in the end, and after, Paradise?'

'But his name, woman! Arthur's passing must be worthy of the man.'

'His coming had a cloud upon it.'

'Still the jealous sister! Still bitter, after all these years?'

Oh, yes, I have been bitter. For my father Gorlois, for my mother

Ygerne, for my own lost reputation. Yet I could forgive him everything, if he will only cross this perilous bridge.

'Does not the Church teach us that all crowns are nothing before the throne of Heaven, all swords surrendered in the realm of peace, all distinctions of rank lost in the great choir of praise, save for the shining coronets of saints and martyrs?'

'Traitor! Would you make the Pendragon equal in death with the lowest peasant?'

'Even with a slave, in the carpenter's kingdom, so the nuns taught me.'

The rip of his own sword then, half out of its sheath.

'This is Arthur we talk of! The Great Bear of the starry heavens. His like will not come again once he is dead. Can you not understand that? Cure him, woman!'

Not ready, then, to die in faith, and calls me faithless.

'Have Arthur's groans dulled his hearing? I have promised you I can, and will.'

A sigh, that seems to shiver the rushes on the mere. Bedwyr thinks I have played with him, only to demonstrate how much Arthur is in my power.

'Come then. He will reward you richly. Be quick, lady. He has lost much blood and the wound has entered dangerous organs.'

He strides to the water's edge, holding out an eager hand over the waves. The water splashes round his knees. The bank is treacherous. Step swiftly back into the shadow of the trees by the mere's-foot. More wraith than woman now. Stand tall, warning, with lifted hand. He must recognise the authority I carry. Everything hangs on this.

The wind wars with my voice.

'Stop! Not yet. I named the price. You have brought nothing in your hands to pay his passage.'

An angry slap of boots as he struggles to regain the shore.

'You are his sister, curse you! Half the women of Britain would give their hearts' blood to see him live, though it cost them their own lives. But you, who know more of necromancy than any woman alive, must calculate, reckon the length of your brother's years upon an abacus, make him buy the restoration of his right with a hilt of gold and garnets and a blade of thrice-hammered steel! Have you no heart?'

No heart, who held my brother in my arms at one day old, and bit his neck to mix his life-blood with my own? No heart, who wept to see his light, lewd wife betray his bed, and for no goddess but herself? No heart, who tried by every means I could to warn him, though he damned me for it? I could not make him hear me then. Can I now?

'The laws I serve were written in the creation of the earth and stars and waters. I did not make them. I am called Morgan the Wise only because I have searched deep all my life to understand and obey them. I have learned with pain what makes for wholeness. Tell Arthur I know how to work no other way.'

Believe me, Bedwyr! Make him you love believe me. I will not plead.

I have stated our terms. He must surrender it willingly. This is the only gate to life.

'But his weapon! Caliburn? You know what that means to him?'

Oh, yes. I know.

'I know we women gave him two swords, Arthur the Briton. The Sword in the Stone of the land, the sword of kingship, guarded by Uther's step-daughters, the blade in our hollowed flesh. It was handed to him again by the Church at his coronation, a doubled blessing. This sword he entrusted to Modred when he went to fight abroad. This was the sword Modred delivered up to Gwenhyvar, kneeling, and hailed her Queen over all of us. This is the sword of peace Arthur has won back from him today on the bloody field of Camlann.

'But Caliburn is dearer to him than that. Caliburn he never lent to any other man or woman, nor ever would. When we sisters took it from him, he was like a man deranged until Nimue snatched it back for him without the scabbard.'

'That sword is his right.'

'The Sword in the Stone is as old as the Island of Britain. But Caliburn is older far than that. It was forged in Avalon, before countries, before kings and queens, when there was only a man and a woman. It came from the oldest Lady of all. By her authority, Nimue armed Arthur with it in his youth. It has served him truly. By that same authority, she calls it back to her tonight.'

'You stole it once. He will never let you cheat him again.'

'The night Arthur bedded Gwenhyvar, after both of them were crowned, my sisters and I took it into our safekeeping. Yes, it was vengeance. That marriage wounded us all. We would have done better to have taken back the other sword. Arthur never truly wanted to be king; that was Merlyn's doing.

'Caliburn is a weapon, not a symbol. It inflicts real wounds. In his heart Arthur is still that triumphant youth who first flourished it. He is still Arthur the Leader of Battles. It is not his kingship my brother clutches so fiercely to him on his deathbed, is it? It is his warrior's blade.'

'Why not? So we all rose to fame, Arthur and I and the rest, fighting the Saxons.'

'So you will let him end.'

'Like this? Shamefully killed by his own son? With that son's lifeblood staining the blade you ask for? Arthur the prince of honour and glory, sordidly falling victim to a traitor, who stabs him when he has dropped his shield?'

'I can wipe all of that nightmare away. His sins and shame will not be remembered. The bards shall sing him through all ages as the most valiant, just and chivalrous king that ever was. His fellowship of knights shall be renowned. But I must have the weapon first. Or rather, not I, but she who gave it him.'

'And if he did, would you heal him?'

I have waited a lifetime to say this, to have Arthur ask.

'There is no tear so bitter, but I can wipe it from his eye. No flow of blood, but I can staunch it. No ache so deep I cannot cure it with a kiss.'

My voice rings across the wide, dark water. I have not let it tremble. I am offering him hope.

Bedwyr does not trust me. Bedwyr loves his friend and king. His warrior's code wrestles against his breaking heart.

'I will try a second time. Wait!'

Arthur is blood of my blood. He calls me faithless, proud, ambitious. And so is he. It is himself he should most fear now.

# Chapter Sixty-two

*Who is Arthur's Healer?*

In Chrétien de Troyes' *Erec* I am Morgan the Wise, the giver of marvellous ointments, which can cure any wound, of body or spirit. Erec comes back to Arthur's court badly wounded, with his much-abused wife Enid. It is my salve that heals him.

The *Mabinogion* has a remarkably similar story. Enid's husband appears here as Gereint son of Erbin.

Gwenhyvar has risen too late for the hunting, but she will go after the party all the same. There are only two horses left in the stable. She rides, imprudently, with one maiden. But behind her comes a young, auburn-haired, bare-legged knight of princely mien, with a gold-hilted sword on his thigh and a tunic and surcoat of brocaded silk about him, and two low boots of cordwain upon his feet, and over that a mantle of blue-purple, and an apple of gold at each of its corners. He is riding a high-mettled, brisk, lively, young, willow-grey charger of immense size. This apparition is Gereint son of Erbin. She accepts his escort.

They meet a knight on a huge horse, heavily armoured, accompanied by a lady and a dwarf. At Gwenhyvar's command her maiden rides forward to request the knight's name. The dwarf bars her way, and when the maiden persists he strikes her across the face with his whip and draws blood. She flees back weeping and Gereint indignantly takes her place and gets the same treatment. He cannot fight a dwarf, and dressed as he is, he can hardly challenge the fully armoured knight. He retreats.

Naturally, these men are destined to meet again. There is a tournament for a sparrowhawk, to be given to the victor's lady. Three wins, and she will have the right to a hawk every year for life. The knight who has won the sparrowhawk for the last two years is the same whose dwarf injured Gwenhyvar's maiden. He has also wronged Gereint's host. Gereint challenges him. The young man is hard pressed. It is the memory of that old insult that gives Gereint the final strength he needs to fell the knight. He wins both the sparrowhawk and the hand of his host's charming daughter Enid.

He spares his adversary's life. Now back to Gwenhyvar's court comes a sorry sight. A big bowed knight with his head hanging low, exceedingly sad, and broken worthless pieces of armour about him, and the colour of his blood upon them getting the better of their own colour, with a dwarf and a lady riding sadly beside him. This is the erstwhile Knight of the Sparrowhawk, Edern, son of Nudd, sent from the tournament by Gereint to surrender himself to Gwenhyvar's mercy.

And what does Arthur call for to take care of his wounds? Not the ointment of his sister, Morgan the Fay, as in Chrétien's *Erec*. Here, the healer who *is summoned to Edern's bedside is Arthur's Chief Physician, Morgan Tud.*

*A man.*

*My principal power has been taken from me. Or have I, to keep that power, surrendered my gender?*

As with Erec, so Gereint hears from his faithful Enid the whispers that married life is sapping his reputation for knightly valour. He takes his horse and arms. He orders Enid to put on her worst dress and ride ahead of him. He forbids her to speak to him. Time and again she disobeys and saves his life. He makes her suffer greatly on his many adventures. It is Gwalchmei, whom others call Gawain, who brings the wounded knight down at last and takes him against his will to Arthur's camp. Great the distress of the court to see both Gereint and Enid in this wretched state. A tent is pitched for Gereint, and Morgan Tud and his disciples are sent for again.

*When I heal Erec in the French story, he is well enough to ignore my advice that he be treated for a week, and rides on his way next morning. In the* Mabinogion *it takes Morgan Tud a whole month to make Gereint whole.*

*So who is Morgan Tud?*

The histories know of Margodud, whose father built the Castle of Maidens, where I am so often found in the romances, and Morgetiud, who had a son called Owain. Easy to see a confusion of names and attributes.

*Or was there a mischievous Breton demon, Morgan Tuth?*

*Which of us is the original? Or were we always separate people: Arthur's male court physician, Arthur's fairy sister?*

*Which should he call on for healing?*

*Which of us would you trust?*

# Chapter Sixty-three

There is a smell of blood. Here in the smothering, mothering darkness Arthur strains for life. Only I can give it to him.

This is the thickening, clotting blood of kin that sticks us to each other. He yearns to trust me, even now. I am his sister. I am Morgan the Fay, the wisest of the Wise. Above all I am pre-eminent in healing. As Arthur on the battlefield was always victor, so I in the dark struggle with death may win the day.

Well, so he argues. He is Arthur the soldier. War is his metaphor. Death is his enemy. He has not learned to hold out his hand in friendship to the darkness, to go willingly under the earth. That is not his rite.

Hope is not dying, even at this low hour. We are brother and sister. The children of Ygerne will not be beaten. Arthur Pendragon cannot, must not be allowed to die.

Look at him rising on his elbow. Even in the shadows his eyes sparkle with expectation.

'She is still there? What does she say? What will she have in place of Caliburn? Be quick, man!'

Bedwyr kneels, lowers him softly to the floor. Harness-hard hands are gentle now.

'Nothing.'

'Aah!' He sinks back satisfied. 'I knew it! I've seen the lust in her eyes. She will save me, only for myself.'

'She will take nothing except Caliburn.'

'*No!* She cannot mean it! She will take my weapon from me or else let me die?'

'Steady, Arthur! The wound is bleeding fast. I cannot hold it.'

Still he fights me. It is anger more than fear that drives him on. 'Bitch! Fool!'

Yes, I am a woman, and therefore devoid of reason, though I am called a scholar in astronomy. I must be made to see. He rages against my treachery, but that is not what he truly believes. In his own mind he still sees himself as Arthur the golden boy, Arthur of the winning smile, Arthur Pendragon who has broken as many British hearts as Saxon heads and claimed the rights of kingship over every blushing maid who gladdened his eye. How could I, a weak woman, refuse his glamour?

Has he forgotten already that he has lost Gwenhyvar's love?

I will be honest. He is right, in part. I own my weakness. Now Bedwyr is gone I can let the pent tears flow in the too-brilliant moonlight. These are all the treasure Arthur has allowed me.

But pity is not enough to buy his life. Do you think I would not run to that chapel, swifter than the magical horse that carries Queen Rhiannon, if that would save him? Would I not lay my cool hands on his burning wound? Would I not cradle his pain-crazed head on my breast and sing the rhymes of restoration? Harder for me to hold myself back from giving my love than for Arthur to give up what he loves most. We torment ourselves.

It can be done no other way.

Hold fast, my will. I am a gambler staking insignificant gains against the last great throw that will decide all. The Wise revere me as the wisest. I know how the foundations of the world are laid. I have shown him the hard truth. I have offered him the prize all heroes dream of. Will he believe me?

'She is offering you life. It is your only chance.' That break in Bedwyr's voice. Men love great Arthur with the same intensity as women, perhaps more. He has given meaning to manhood. What would the warrior's world, what would Britain be without Arthur? A wasteland. A desert of the heart. Whom should swords serve but him?

'How could I be Arthur Pendragon without Caliburn?'

'We are none of us young. The great battle of Badon was over long ago. We have held the Saxons back to keep half Britain free. We can make do with lesser swords for lesser battles.'

'And lesser men?'

Yes. In his bitterness he understands more than he knows. Now, can he let go?

'What you have done will stand for ever. The name of Arthur cannot be less than you have made it.'

'You would watch me crumble into a living death, like Llywarch Hen?

> *I am old, I am lonely,*
> *I am decrepit and cold,*
> *after my sumptuous bed of honour;*
> *I am wretched, I am bent in three.*

'Would you leave me weaponless, wifeless, sonless? Shall I have to plead with a reluctant people to crawl back to my heel?'

Does he think that Caliburn can win him back Gwenhyvar? Caliburn has murdered Modred. Will he always see in the jewels and the rune-chased blade of this sword the magic and the glamour of his youth? Did Nimue not teach him the wisdom of the circle? Does he imagine Caliburn was his to own? Does he believe it rose from the lake for Arthur the man to possess and not for Arthur of Britain to wield? Even after Camlann?

'You have won this day. The traitors are dead. The land is at peace. Modred's remnant are fled, or have surrendered their swords to Custennin of Dumnonia.'

'Will my war-host hail my successor already, before they have found my body? And what of the greatest traitor of all, *Gwenhyvar*?' This pains him more than his wound.

'Hidden in some convent, they say. She will not trouble your land again. We will find the place. Our men will seek her bastard child out, and destroy it.'

Not child, but children, Bedwyr, as once you sought and found another baby boy. Gwenhyvar I have lodged with Abbess Bryvyth. She, at least, I have protected in her underground cell.

Gwenhyvar is the past. Her twin babies, grandsons of Arthur, are a future that will never come. My time is passing from this world too. I cannot shield Modred's infants, as once I sheltered him.

Arthur groans. For what? For that moment of ecstasy in which his son got new life upon Arthur's wife? For the last of his blood, innocent as blind kittens but damned from the womb to die? For a lonely life, espoused to Caliburn alone, his first, perhaps his only true love? For simple physical pain?

Dream, Arthur. See visions higher than any of these.

I will embrace my brother. I will offer a dream of such joy that a hundred years will pass as one brief day. His sunlit hours shall be glorious with races and fights, his evenings warm with fine wine and stirring song. Then night. Delight of body and touch, ecstasy of spirit and heart, close tender sleep. He shall lie down spent and laughing, he shall rise whole and eager to greet another brilliant morning. He shall have a crowd of beautiful women, in all their variety, to wait on him; he shall have bold men for companions, vigorous sport to make his days merry. There shall be skilful poets and storytellers. The blossom shall hang fresh as foam on the apple-boughs when he wakes at daybreak, and the red fruit fall ripe into his hand when he rides home at sunset. I shall invite an infinite multitude of stars to light our loving.

Just one thing is required. The hilt lies under his hand. One slender key of steel. Two dragon hasps of gold to open the lock of life.

His voice rasps.

'She has stolen everything from me, even Caliburn. She shall not get it a second time.'

797

# Chapter Sixty-four

*I am the wicked witch who promises healing falsely.*

*I tricked Alexander the Orphan.*

*We are in the dangerous territory of Cornwall again. King Mark is the villain. The Saxons are beaten, but now other heathen ships are invading Cornwall. Mark's brother, Boudwin, sends wild fire among their fleet. He kills their crews and Cornwall is saved.*

*It is all over before Mark hears about it. The glory is all Boudwin's. Mark quickly invites him to his castle, bidding him bring Anglides his wife and their infant son Alexander. Supper passes pleasantly. Then Mark reproaches his brother for not inviting him to share in the slaughter. Boudwin protests it was an emergency; there was no time. No time is left him now. Mark plunges a dagger into his heart.*

*Anglides swoons. But she recovers in time to find good sorrowful knights preparing her husband's corpse for burial. She takes his bloodstained shirt and tunic. Essyllt, Mark's queen, sends word to her to flee the castle with her son, lest young Alexander suffer the same fate. Anglides escapes with horse and child and a poor company.*

*Only just in time. Mark is searching the castle himself, sword in hand. Finding them gone, he orders the good knight Sadok to hunt them down. Mark warns him that if he values his life he must bring them back. Sadok catches up with them. But he too grieves for Boudwin. He lets them live, on condition that Anglides avenges this murder. Then he returns and tells Mark that Alexander has been drowned.*

*The boy comes to manhood. He is to be made knight along with twenty aristocratic lads of the neighbourhood. In church, at the solemn mass, Anglides shows him his father's clothes, stiff with old blood. The young man starts and pales. She tells him the truth of his uncle's treachery. The first charge of young Alexander's knighthood is revenge.*

*He jousts with all his knightly companions and overthrows them. One, in spite, runs to Mark and warns him Alexander is alive, and made a warrior now. Mark rushes to Sadok's chamber, brandishing his sword, and charges him with treachery. Sadok defends his honour and his life, slays four strong knights and escapes the castle.*

*Mark turns to means more to be feared than swords. He sends letters to Queen Morgan the Fay and to the Queen of Northgales. He prays us as great sorceresses to set the whole country on fire and engage dangerous knights so that by no means shall Alexander escape us.*

*But when I hear reports of this Alexander the Orphan, I have other ideas for him.*

*The young man sets out to ask the renowned Lancelot to train him for his grim destiny. He seems to have little need of tuition. He loses his way and fights at a tournament where he overthrows King Carados and twenty knights.*

*A damsel brings me news of him. I will see this young knight. I slip away from my friends in secret. Better to start my journey before I have rivals. I pitch my tent by the wayside where I encounter four more knights. They too have fallen to Alexander, who is now defending a castle. A damsel holds it. But her evil neighbour will permit her to marry no one but himself. Already he has killed twenty knights.*

*Alexander fights this monster more wildly than wittily. I arrive in time to witness the combat, along with the damsel for whose sake he is duelling. Naturally, the Orphan wins, and strikes off the evil knight's head. But the toll has been heavy. He has sixteen great wounds, and one in particular seems likely to lead to his death. He cannot stay upright.*

*I have him in my power now. He is laid on a horse-litter and borne into the castle. I search his wounds and smear them with an ointment of my own. Not kind, that salve. He spends the night in agony. In the morning he capitulates. He will do anything I say if I will soothe him. I release him from his pain. I will serve my own purposes now, not Mark's.*

*The damsel of the castle comes to me to ask my help. She would like to wed this young man who has fought so bravely for her. I tell her she shall see my answer presently. Then straight to Alexander's bedside. I forbid this marriage. He makes her a courteous excuse. She takes it philosophically and settles instead for her childhood sweetheart.*

*Then I drug Alexander so that he will feel nothing for three days and nights. He is laid in the horse-litter again. This time the journey is rough and long. We arrive at my castle, the Beautiful Keep, and he is put to bed. I shall keep him carefully. When he wakes, I ask if he would like to be well.*

'Who would be sick, and he might be whole?'

*Here is my condition. He must swear, by his knighthood, never to leave this castle for a year and a day. And with his oath, I restore him to health. At once he regrets his promise.*

*My cousin arrives at the Beautiful Keep. This castle is rightly hers, but I have taken it. She finds Alexander the Orphan low-spirited. He would rather be on his way to seek his revenge on Mark. She warns him he will be kept for the pleasure of Morgan the Fay. At that he swears he would sooner cut off his balls than pleasure me. They plot together. Her uncle will ride against the castle and set fire to it. She herself will help Alexander out by a secret postern. He need not break his oath. He will stay within the walls and keep the site for her for a year and a day. They kiss and pleasure each other. Her plan succeeds. Alexander goes no further than the castle garden.*

*My cousin sends me her triumphant message. I have lost. I disappear from his story. My plot has gone up in smoke.*

*But there is still an enemy lurking in the shadows.*

*Gratitude is not one of Alexander's chief characteristics. He challenges all comers to the Beautiful Keep. Alice the Fair Pilgrim hears of him. She promises her hand to any knight of Arthur's court who can overcome him. Alice is rich as well as beautiful. There is considerable interest. She has hardly pitched her pavilion to watch, when the first contestant arrives. He loses.*

*But the Fair Pilgrim is fickle also. Despite her offer, she falls for the young defender of the Beautiful Keep before she has even seen his face. He lifts his helmet. She removes her wimple. It is love at first sight.*

*Too bad for the lady of the castle, my clever cousin. She laughingly tells Alice how she helped Alexander escape from my toils and from the castle fire. Alice observes, correctly, that he is much beholden to this damsel.*

*Alexander continues to fight all comers, though he has now won Alice the Fair Pilgrim for himself. Then Modred appears.*

*At that moment, Alexander is standing so besotted with love at the sight of his Alice on horseback that he takes no notice. The ungallant Modred humiliates him, leading him helpless on his horse up and down. Alexander has not yet noticed how he is being shamed. My resourceful cousin arms herself. She sets a shield upon her shoulder, grasps a naked sword and mounts a horse. She has more sense than to attack Modred. Instead she strikes Alexander such a blow on the head that sparks fly from his eyes. It does the trick. Alexander returns to his senses and draws his sword. Prudently, the damsel flees to the pavilion and Modred in the opposite direction.*

*Alexander the Orphan and Alice the Fair Pilgrim tease the damsel for the sad stroke she hit him. The three will not be separated. They make for Benwick, Lancelot's country, and live together in great joy.*

*My evil plots have always been thwarted by another woman.*

# Chapter Sixty-five

Bedwyr is on his knees. He is weeping without shame.

'My lord! Arthur! It is our only chance.'

'Would you trust any of my sisters? Am I so weak even in death I must let them take what they want, and leave me nothing? They would steal Caliburn from me and let me die.'

'If you trust Morgan and she proves false, yes, you will die. But if you do not trust Morgan's healing you will still die. Fight, man! Here is an opening; seize it. Will you surrender to your last enemy while there's a chance?'

'Which is my worst enemy, death or that woman?'

'I believe Morgan loves you!'

There, the words are out. What all the world has known yet will write centuries of romances to deny. It wasn't difficult, was it? Three short words. So we might carve them with a knife in bark, trace them in sand, scratch them upon rock. MORGAN LOVES ARTHUR.

Why could I never say it? Why could Arthur never admit this truth? Why this conspiracy on every side to make us mortal enemies?

'Morgan loves me? Is that why she fostered Modred in her family? So his shadow could foul my sunny court of Camelot? So all the bitterness she's taught him would take its revenge upon my wife and queen? My Gwenhyvar opens her legs for Morgan's boy!'

'Women, Arthur! Margawse was Lot's wife and queen when she opened her legs for you, and got Modred.'

Another day he would have struck Bedwyr for that reminder. King Arthur has saved Britain from Saxon conquest. King Arthur can be forgiven. What have Modred and I achieved? But it is long past time for indignation. The ebbing blood has left him weak. Self-pity closes in to gnaw at his pride. He is sobbing now.

'I did heavy penance for that sin. Where's the priest? Am I going to die without the sacrament?'

'No need for that. We started this day with clean swords, clean souls. So we may depart. Be easy.'

'A clean sword? Look at it! Stained with my own son's blood! Oh, Modred, Modred! Say he was still alive, only drenched in blood from this slaughterhouse of Camlann. Say I did not kill my son!'

He writhes, and his hand grips the fouled blade beside him in his agony. If he had left to him but a token of the strength he possessed when he buckled it on this morning, that grip would do him much hurt. Bedwyr takes it like a dangerous toy from a baby, mothers him, weeps over him.

And I can only watch and wait, knowing that with each moment Arthur's heart beats more faintly, and the choice has still not been made.

The whisper comes after long silence.

'Could she heal this?'

My feet have moved a dozen swift paces towards the brink before I check them.

His wound is deep. Was I the mother of this pain? Did I raise Modred to do this? Certainly I meant no good to Gwenhyvar. They called her the Giant's Daughter. She claimed the blood of kings. But she was never wise. In her, Arthur thought he had wedded the sovereignty of Britain. We had given him that. He told her he served his High Queen best when war took him away to fight for freedom. She did not see it so. Too shallow, vain and selfish, she called his destiny desertion. Arthur was holding the high-water mark of British story, of Christian faith, of Roman law against the encroaching waves of Saxon barbarism. And she was bored.

I never meant the son I restored to his arms to serve him so. To steal his queen, usurp his kingdom, win over the fickle love of Britain's people. When I walked through the woods telling the little boy old tales of hate and saw him stab the bramble bush with a rotting stick, I did not imagine him today defying Arthur, sword in hand, running his father through, destroying his love, his life, his dream, bringing him to this sobbing wreck of all he was. Have I done this?

Pain has always bred pain, since that bright Easter Day when Gorlois took my beautiful mother to Uther's feast, and I was left at home in Cornwall, lonely and bitter. I wove a childish spell of anger. Lust, pride, revenge have howled about us ever since.

How can I end it?

I have shown you a path to peace, Arthur, my brother. I sacrificed the healing scabbard, the easy magic of a talisman that makes us falsely proud of our power. I kept only my woman's wisdom, hardly got. I have learned it in a long initiation of humility to her I serve. I use her ways, rooted in the earth, not high sorcery. From that come all the salves I know. It has been enough.

Can you make an equal sacrifice, my brother? Trust what you are? Be only Arthur, warrior, emperor, winning battles by your own effort without the prop of magic? Has Nimue trained and armed you skilfully enough for this, to make you victorious in history as well as in romance?

'Take it,' he pleads through choking tears. 'I never want to see it again.'

A thrill like unspent lightning prickling in the air makes the roots of my hair tingle on my scalp. Can it be this easy, after all? Can all the snarls and tangles of our conjoined lives fall into one looping rope of life, strong, long and surely spun?

Bedwyr is coming down to the shore, the precious gift unsteady in his hands. His is the swift step of a true friend who fears the time is short. He knows this line must be made fast before it can be stretched out towards eternity. Only I can tie the knot. Shut out all doubts. Forget the history of animosity. Hope speeds him on. His eyes are on this harbour. All shipwrecks before this must be ignored.

My heart is hammering faster than his steps. My hands are reaching out across the width of moon-chased water. I would close the gap as nearly as I may. But there is still this mere between us.

'Halt!'

He is on the opposite shore, and Caliburn is in his grasp. He would run to me now around the grassy margin, but I must not let him. If Arthur is too weak to rise, then Bedwyr must do this in his stead.

'I have brought the sword, Lady! Take it. Hurry! He is in the chapel, and weaker than the hour in which he was born.'

Oh, yes, I remember well that hour, the storm, Ygerne's cry. I hated my brother then. Through Arthur's coming, I had lost my beloved father to Uther's sword and my mother to his softer weapon. I was unwanted.

That was before I saw him, a tiny, soft-skinned boy and held him to my heart. Merlyn parted us.

Tonight, let us lay down the cover on that time, and shut the first painful page for ever as I close this final wound.

'I do not want it.'

'We have no time for riddles, Lady. You demanded it.'

'I asked for its abandonment.'

'Do not play cat and mouse with us. Speak plainly!'

'How did it come to him?'

'It was the first morning of his manhood. Midwinter. A mist upon the lake. The night before, the priest Bytwini had given him the sacrament in the chapel. Then Arthur kept the vigil apart while we feasted. Before dawn, he came to meet Merlyn at the lakeside . . . Why do you ask this?'

'Who gave the sword?'

'You have heard the tale told many times.'

'Tell it to me for the last time.'

'For pity's sake! Arthur is alone and dying.'

'And you alone hold in your hands the means by which he may live. How came that sword?'

'He says he saw fays dancing on the water. And in their midst an arm rose from the lake holding up the sword. At Merlyn's bidding, Arthur rowed out and took it. Then Nimue bound his swordbelt on him, and handed him shield and spear and knife. He was armed with the blessing of the Lady of the Lake.'

'But it was not Nimue's gift. She has demanded her reward in blood and slaughter. The hand that offered Caliburn was older far than Nimue. Now she must take it back.'

'Here? In this pool? But it is not the same lake.'

'The earth is one. The waters are one. There is one Lady.'

He has spilled the wind before the final anchorage. He hesitates. One thing to trust this treasure to a sister's keeping. To know, however jealously, it still lies somewhere safe on earth. To dream that there may one day be an Arthur restored to grasp that dragon hilt again, greasing its rune-rich blade with the blood of Britain's enemies. But drown it? Still now, in brilliant moonshine this little lake is black, cold, immeasurably deep, and even shallow wells may hide the entrances to wide realms of faerie. What falls in this will be lost past all recovering. The water sighs amongst stiff reeds and nameless reptiles plop and croak, and the wind troubles the trees. What is once given to the Goddess can never be taken back.

But Bedwyr is the king's man. He accepts orders.

Unwillingly, and with an unsteady arm, he raises the great blade of Caliburn above his shoulder. It seems to both of us a weight too heavy for the boy Arthur to have hacked his way to glory with. I feel relief draining the blood from my heart. We are all weak now, Arthur from wounds, Bedwyr from reluctance, I from this achievement, almost too late, of my life's hope.

The blue blade trembles against the stars, cold as the water. It is not long for the light now. Do not veil your eyes. You must watch it go.

'No! Do not destroy it!'

A mourning bellow, like a cow that fears she is losing her calf. We both spin like eddying leaves and the blade spills the moonlight to fall back at Bedwyr's side.

Arthur's voice laments hollowly inside the chapel.

'If she takes back the sword, then I am done. You hold my manhood in your hands.'

# Chapter Sixty-six

*I am the fay of the volcano.*

*Mongibel. You call it Mount Etna.*

*My original realm was Avalon, the ultimate Otherworld island. Now I am invading territory closer to you.*

*The Normans cede me part of their empire, in Sicily. Morgan lives now in a dazzling white palace high up on Mongibel. It is set in a delightful plain that can be reached only by climbing the roughest slope.*

*Like Avalon, it is a place of joy, an unending paradise. Here I welcome all the heroes: Arthur, Cei, Bedwyr and a host of others. I give them health, youth, sport, feasting, love.*

*Mongibello, 'the Beautiful Mountain'. Etna, 'I Burn'.*

*There are three regions on this mountain. The first is cultivated, an area of luxuriant fertility. The slope is gentle. Vines, olives, fruit, vegetables, corn abound. It supports a grateful people.*

*The second is wooded and wilder. Pine, broom, chestnut, beech and ferns offer welcome shade. The gradient is steeper now. It becomes harder to see the way ahead.*

*You climb out through the trees into the last and highest region. Your reward is . . . desert, a wilderness of lava, ash and snow. Nothing before you but the peaks and abysses of dangerous upheavals. There is no trace of animal life.*

*My volcano is active now, as always. Its lava flow enriches the land below with wonderful fertility.*

*It also kills.*

*There are more than two hundred craters. With each new eruption the face of my mountain changes.*

*Step carefully.*

# Chapter Sixty-seven

Bedwyr and Caliburn have gone from view. Darkness is humped within the chapel. The moon is going, as the clouds sweep in.

The sea is calling me. I have retreated beyond the limit of the trees now, to where the heather arches over the tumbling brook. They will hardly see me here.

I can only wait.

I cannot bear to wait.

And yet I must. I, that as a nimble, reckless child ran and rode and scrambled over rocks. Exulting in the wind and fearless among horses, I chased the flying vision of my father in the hunt. I climbed the cliffs, scornful of Gwennol's warnings or the nun Luned's pleadings. I thought then I should have been a boy. My father would rather have had me so. So would they all: my mother, kinsfolk, tribe. But if I had been Gorlois's son, Uther Pendragon would have killed me to protect his Arthur. I discovered that femaleness meant life. So I began to learn from others – Gwennol, Ygerne, the nuns – slowly and unwillingly, the glory, power and grief of womanhood.

My boyish freedom ended at Dimiliock, where Gorlois retreated to draw Uther Pendragon to him and lure him away, while we women sought fragile sanctuary on Tintagel. Fragile, because I doubted my mother Ygerne wished the high gate of the convent on the cliffs securely barred. A king would soon be outside, calling for her. Fragile, because we did not know how much respect the nuns might have from that barbaric chief who nonetheless claimed the old authority of Rome. Fragile, because Merlyn was on Uther's side.

Men's bodies are fragile too, beneath their armour.

I have been to Dimiliock since. The ground was cleaned of corpses and the fattened crows had returned to their scraggy shape. The wind moaned there, as it does here tonight. It was all that my iron will could do to hold down my fear-crazed body and stop my feet from fleeing. So many unwilling spirits had found their portal to the Otherworld there. How should my slight and tenuous mortality hold on to this present life and not be swept into the ship of souls with all those others? So after Camlann, too many are dead and we survivors seem like blasphemers.

It is time to go. My ship will soon be here. Must it still end in failure? Shall we leave without him?

I yearn to run around the pool in my distress. Almost, I have broken the Lady's stern command. What now if I pressed forward to the chapel door, offered him my covenant in person, challenged him, pleaded with him, face to face?

No!

Wait still, though this is harder than a lifetime's waiting. My brother and I have met face to face too often, only to part in anger. He made his choice. Gwenhyvar was his queen, Nimue was his counsellor, and what he felt for me, and what he sensed in me, could only anger him. We tormented each other with what could never be. Our physical closeness grated upon our spiritual unlikeness, like steel and flint to spark a catastrophic fire.

Yet Gwenhyvar has gone. Nimue is overthrown. I am still here.

Only be patient. I must summon through distance, waiting, fear, his impossible hope. There is no other way. He must come to me.

But will he? What is that murmur of argument from the chapel now? Oh, how can love be strong enough for this, to wait for the final weakness in Arthur, my brother, my king, my dear? Must his proud body break before his stiff spirit bends? I have so much stored up to give him, and he could die with nothing.

'*Caliburn!*'

Nothing?

He clutches Caliburn back to him, his first, perhaps his truest love. They came together the day he got his manhood. All his life, through doubt of his sisters and disillusionment with his wife, through rivalry of chieftains and treachery of son, Caliburn has stayed faithful. He thought the sword had failed him once when he began to lose, but the weapon he wielded was counterfeit. This blade is his fame, this is his authentication. Can he bring himself to let it go; lay down his weapon to win a greater victory?

'*Why, Bedwyr, why this?*'

Do not imagine I cannot understand your cry, Arthur. Believe I feel how great the darkness into which I am inviting you to step. Do not think I cannot hear you whimper on the poor thin bed of bracken Bedwyr has laid for you. This is a dreadful day, a desolate place, a fearsome hour. Be quick! The gate of the garden I am showing you is narrowing to its final closure. Yet if you break through, will you find yourself its lord or my prisoner?

'Tell her to come and show her face. Let me see for myself if there can be any honesty in those eyes.'

'She will not move beyond the far side of the lake. She sets the terms. My lord, you have no time left to parley.'

'*I will not die!*'

'Arthur, my sword-brother. I am no surgeon. But I have seen enough of wounds to tell that this one cannot be closed by ordinary skill. If you will not take Morgan's risk, well then . . . I have been your soul-friend since boyhood, companion at your side in every fight. I can do you one last service. If you want to unburden to me whatever is heavy on your soul tonight, I think I am Christian enough to hear my king's confession and say the prayer that will send you on your path to peace.'

'You traitor, who call yourself my friend! Are you so sick of Arthur Pendragon, like the rest? You'd send me skywards and leave the land of Britain to Custennin?'

'Not I, my lord! If I had any skill to keep your precious life, if I could guard it safe in the hollow of my hand . . .'

'Morgan is a braver warrior than you are. She comes here to fight for my life with all her armoury. She will not let death have me, will she?'

'So I said, my lord. And yet she has asked too high a price for you.'

'Too high a price? What earthly fee can be more valuable than Arthur's life? I say she honours me, to name a treasure beyond all else I have and tell me the gods will be content with nothing less. Have I an equal? Shall I not buy a second lifetime with an honour-price of my own worth?'

'A second half of life without your greatest talisman?'

Oh, cunning love in Bedwyr that has stopped him arguing longer for my side. Arthur the soldier will do battle even in his dying hour with his closest friend. While Bedwyr counselled submission to me, Arthur jealously raged against it. But if Bedwyr now smooths the path to death, then Arthur will grab the last chance of life. The Lady is wise. If I had rushed to kneel in Bedwyr's place, I should have been thus fiercely opposed.

Caliburn was a two-edged gift. It made a hero of the boy, won him that other sword of kingship, kept for us Britons our partial freedom. Now it sticks to his stiffening hand and will not give us peace.

'*Take it.*'

He is giving it up.

Wait for that sword to cry out, with a shout like the stone of truth. There is a hollow in the highest rock of Tintagel, like the print of a foot. They say that when the true king stands there, a cry goes up from the island itself: '*This is the chief! Follow him!*' Will Caliburn scream like that as it leaves his hand: '*Morgan is taking away his power! Stop her!*' Do either of them realise what it means?

How will it feel to meet at last, just our bare, scarred selves, without the magic of the scabbard, without an enchanted sword? Not quite; we are marked for all time by what we have handled. My miracles of healing have restored whole families' lives; his battles have altered the landscape of history. How could we two sit out the rest of our years in the inglenook of normality?

The Pendragon's weapon of war is in Bedwyr's hand now. A shaft of moonlight from the door shows the eagerness in Arthur's face. He is raised on one elbow, a desperate effort. He wants Bedwyr to run with it. He is making his sally. He is dashing out through the postern of hope, leaving the ramparts of doubt and caution behind him. My brother is taking a great risk. Let its outcome be swift, let it be certain, let it be now. He catches a vision of victory.

And so do I. There is so much Arthur would never let me tell him. All depends on his faith now.

Bedwyr is racing towards the water again with the sword.

All creation waits wide-eyed to see this. The full-faced moon looks down into the pool's bright circle. Hares stretch curious necks, old badgers peer. Shadowed deer stand with poised hoof, their antlers still as branches. Even the moths hang motionless on the stems of trees.

Only Bedwyr moves, more carefully now, his steps crunching on stone, soft on wetter earth, down to the water's edge. His hands bear that wonderful blade, resting across them like a baby. And I find I am gazing at its nakedness with all my being. So I felt once, when I saw my hated brother for the first time, and found I loved him. So I felt, joyful beyond all reasonable hope, when I discovered Arthur's son was still alive and reached out my arms to take him.

I will not touch Caliburn. These hands that warm and heal must not be chilled by this stained steel. I know whose blood shadows the cutting edge. That same small baby, rescued from his father's wrath, saved from the sea, cradled at my breast. Modred is dead. His blood was the last that glutted Caliburn, or ever shall.

I have shed Arthur's blood, as though I had wounded him with my own hands. While he kept the scabbard no weapon could weaken him. I ended that. I made him mortal. I caused this mortal wound. Now I shall give him immortality. We will both have cast away the power that bound us to this world.

Scabbard and sword.

We shall be free and joined.

# Chapter Sixty-eight

*I am the Land of Joy.*

*When Hartmann von Aue writes his German version of* Erec *around 1190, he calls me Famurgan.*

*I am a dangerous goddess.*

*From the time when I first begin to display my magic art, I can go round the world in the twinkling of an eye and return at once.*

*I walk the earth, I can silently fly, I can live upon or beneath the wave.*

*As I desire, I transform a man into a bird or animal.*

*I can work wonders.*

*I compel dragons to bring me from the air a contribution for my work, and the fish theirs from the water.*

*The earth bears no herb whose virtue is not known to me as well as his hand to the author.*

*I can raise the dead.*

*And most wonderful of all, the evil spirits called devils are all under my control.*

*Since Sybil died, the earth has produced, you may be sure of this, never a better mistress of magic skill than Famurgan.*

*Some ten years later, another German, Wolfram von Eschenbach, writes his own wonderfully colourful version of the Arthurian story, Parzival. He mocks his predecessors like Hartmann, while telling a rattling good yarn and scattering literary jokes.*

*I have transformed myself in a curious shape-shifting. The fay is here named Terdelaschoye, the 'Land of Joy'. It is her magic mountain that Wolfram calls 'Feimurgan'.*

*In this guise of Terdelaschoye, I cast a spell of love over the fairy ancestor of heroes, Mazadan. I lure him to Feimurgan, and from our union descend Uther Pendragon, Arthur, Gawain, Parzival.*

*Is this witty German, who claims to be a shrewd judge of women, really unable to distinguish between the lady and her land? Or am I another of his jokes?*

*Well, let it stand. In my place, the earth herself has become a living being, opening arms of welcome.*

*And I am his Country of Bliss.*

So small the circle of water that separates us. I almost think his quivering arms beckoned. Had I could fly to him. I would rather save this dragon prince, gift me eternal life, see it triumph till past with his own death breath.

But I must wait.

Men will always remember how carefully Bedwyr nursed him, how sweetly he will give her the name —

'Bedwyr? Do you —' zenith moon reaches the her the —

# Chapter Sixty-nine

The moon is reaching her zenith. The clouds are tearing apart. Have we waited too long?

Darkness lurches from the chapel. I start with fear. Arthur lies slumped in the shadow of the doorway. He clutches Modred's wound. The strength is ebbing fast between his faltering fingers. He has let the talisman of his victory out of his hands.

Youth is gone. Modred is cold.

Do not change your mind! You killed him, Arthur. You could not nurse that stained blade like a second child.

If only I could run to him! I would throw my arms round his bowed shoulders, hold him in my life-giving embrace, kiss his pain-wracked face, his crouched, exhausted chest.

No. Hold agonisedly still. Listen. Will he fetch it back?

His voice bellows with astonishing strength, startling unseen creatures that slop the surface of the mere, making Bedwyr spin round.

'MORGAN!'

Never till now. For the first time, powerless, he cries my name as though he truly desired me. I have known the truth when our eyes have met, when our hands have touched. Yet he could never admit his need of me till now.

Bedwyr is hesitating between us. The moon hovers uncertainly over the swaying Caliburn, paling the dragons, darkening the slick steel blade.

Draw further back yet, following the stream that slips through the low lip of hills behind me, out of sight.

My steely will astonishes me, I will save him yet though it tortures me.

'Where is the trickstress gone? Has she left me to die in the dark in a Cornish bog after all? Give me Caliburn.'

No, Arthur, no!

Bedwyr is running back to help him. He knows that love requires he cast away the sword. Loyalty demands obedience to Arthur. I cannot hear his muttered chiding, though every gasp that Arthur draws is tearing me apart, as though I sucked it through gashes in my own body.

'What can you see, Bedwyr?'

'Only the stars in the water and the dark shore. But she was there a moment ago, a flicker of white in front of the woods.'

'I can see nothing but moonshine and shadows. Is that a phantom? I cannot make her out. She was always shifty.'

I am here, Arthur. I have always been near you. You could never see.

'*Morgan!*' That plaintive cry, broken now.

So small the circle of water that separates us. I almost think my sandals are bewitched. I feel I could fly to him. I would easily leave this clinging ground, part the night air like a javelin, fill him with my own sweet breath.

Yet I must stay.

Bedwyr's voice is urgent. 'Arthur, I beg you! She will not come while you still keep Caliburn. Pay her what she asks. Let me give her the sword.'

No, Bedwyr. Do not give it to me. I never asked that.

But can he really yield?

Silence, like a rope between us. I take the strain. Walk backwards now, beyond the trees, beyond the lake, towards the sea. My face is fading out of their dimmed sight to a last pale blur, like the flutter of an owl's wing. The tension heightens intolerably.

Which of us will prove more faithless?

I have halted by the farthest boundary of this hollow now, where the stream is hurrying westward. Behind me, a solitary pine, and then a limitless darkness arched by stars. A vast possibility. My land of promise. Can he trust me?

That agonised cry.

'Give it to me, Bedwyr! I will do it myself. I must live!'

You will live. Oh, my brother Arthur, you shall live!

He staggers upright with Bedwyr's help, fighting his anguish, slipping in the clotted blood of his own shedding. He leans gasping on the doorpost of the chapel. I am wracked with his pain.

The moonlight is grey on his matted hair.

Caliburn is grasped between his hands now. He leans on it like a pilgrim staff.

'I cannot see her. Will she not come and take it from me?'

Arthur totters out into the open, dragging the weighty weapon. His loyal friend supports him. Desperately halting now, they shuffle down the uneven slope towards the lake. Bedwyr's arms surround him swiftly as Arthur's legs give way. Still he forces himself to struggle on.

They have come to the mere's edge. A gust of wind troubles the water, sending white-capped waves lapping to his feet. We all wait.

'Will she mock me yet? Rob me of victory and leave me to die here?'

'Sire, you have no other hope.'

No hope, except in the plain shroud of a burial beneath the sign of his weaponless Christ. No swords in heaven. He is not ready for that yet.

Caliburn is alive in his hand once more. The dragons of all his victories are half-upraised. Still he jealously grasps their magic.

The moonlight glints on patterned steel. From the skies, the sparkle of ruby, emerald, sapphire stars leap like lightning to catch their images on the hilt of Caliburn.

Now, Arthur, now! Our moon is turning.

It is too difficult. The great weapon sags into the shadow by his side. The golden dragon-guard of Caliburn's glory has not taken wing. We are gambling for the highest stake of all. What if he were to let go and win nothing from me?

'What can you see?' he demands again.

'Only waves breaking on dark water, and the wind bending the trees.'

Terrible dilemma.

'Yet I will live!'

The shining blade swings high over Arthur's head now, urgently brandished at last. Where does he find such strength?

'Is she there now?'

Sweat glistens on his poor pale face between the encrusted blood. Let me kiss it clean!

'The stars confuse my eyes, sire. There is a white shadow on the farther shore. It may be may-blossom.'

'*Morgan!*'

So small a shout for such a victory. There is a moment in our lives that arrives almost without decision, when the arms swing and stop, when the fingers loose their grasp, and the hands open. When the thing is done. We have let go.

So short a vault into eternity. Caliburn's magnificence flashes across the stars. Great Arthur Pendragon's sword is going home. Swift as a lifespan, it reaches its apogee and falls spinning along Arianrhod's Way, on down into darkness. Our eyes are locked on its descent, our heartbeats seem to catch. We await its final plunge into the nether waters.

Our end is written in our beginning. The circle closes. The serpent's mouth swallows its tail. The sword blade sends a white wave leaping, and we see in this moment a white arm strike up from the depth to catch and flourish the hilt. The Lady draws it under. He has done her bidding. She has given Arthur this blade, blessed its warfare, now she calls it home to her. The rugged half of Britain Arthur has saved. Too late to weep for the fertile part we have lost. I, Morgan the Healer, could have taught him the magic of the scabbard.

Let time stand still, while I give him that long sweet lesson.

He is disarmed, and I am empowered at last.

# Chapter Seventy

*I am a mirage.*

*Fata Morgana. An atmospheric phenomenon seen across the Straits of Messina.*

*Yes, I am still to be found in Sicily.*

*By a trick of the Mediterranean light, objects on the opposite coast appear to be supernaturally tall. Towers soar high in the clouds, and are doubled mysteriously underwater. I show you a fisherman's cottage, and you think you have seen a fairy castle.*

*Beware what you are trusting yourself to, Arthur. I may be an illusion.*

*Wait, though. Not all mirages are totally false. The traveller in the desert is maddened by a vision of shimmering water always just beyond reach as he stumbles towards it. Death, not the wished-for oasis, lies that way. Yet others show the near reflections of far-off solid substance.*

*There is no fairy castle over the water, but the pinnacled images of my mirage are grounded in a smaller, homely reality.*

*I am Fata Morgana, giver of visions. I enchant the truth of that distant shore you have not yet reached. By the wonderful extravagance of my promise I fire your desire to seek and find me. Will I disappoint you at your voyage's end?*

*You must take ship and sail out across the strait before you know the answer.*

the world. She is hard to know. I never have known her before, with all other men I have... I will go away from...
Yes, Arthur, for before I go away...
We part we seek the brink, and the shore, while Arthur was once I am I... to let us pass...
...endlessly... shore, are I am over here why she is... She came to me, and by... and over... Welcome to... Arthur is over here... she... I am... why she...

# Chapter Seventy-one

And so we come. Morgan Sea-Born, Margawse the Red, Elaine the Fair. Ranked round us are all the wisest of the Wise. We bring with us, night-hooded and crowned in moon-silver, the shadow behind all our authority, the Lady. Our ship is swan-prowed and hung with golden chains, its sides draped with purple silk that we have marvellously embroidered. And we three stand, black-robed, keening the laments, but our hearts high with joy, our faces beautiful beyond believing, our hands eager to welcome, our eyes immortally young.

And in our wake, the small shores part and waves wash glittering far behind us. A long, moon-bathed river is opening before our prow. Dark-heathered moors give way as the silver brightens past seeing. We sail the river of life.

'What is it, man? My eyes are swimming in a sea of silver. What is happening? What is that shadow swooping on me like a raven?'

'A ship, my lord. I see a long white-painted neck upon its prow, a swan's head circled with gold. There are no oarsmen, but the mast flies a great sail that blots out the stars.'

'The brook was shallow, Bedwyr.'

'This keel is deep.'

The river flowing from this mere broadens beyond imagination over our stern, an endless sea-road. This night is not melancholy, for all our wailing. Heaven dances in the crest of every surge. Arthur and his sisters are coming together.

We are three, and we are one. Elaine, who was once the Lily Maid, and now the Ancient Sybil. Margawse, full-bodied, gloriously mature, Mother and Whore. And I, Morgan, the youngest and the most senior of us, I am both Crone and Virgin tonight. We have been all things to you, Arthur. Kore, Demeter, Hecate. Parvati, Derga, Kali. Take us in the fullness of our diversity. Embrace our wholeness.

'Who sails this ship, Bedwyr? What is this wailing in my ears?'

'Three great Ladies with royal crowns, weeping and holding out their hands to you.'

Three sisters, Arthur's sisters. We are more than this. In other races we have been the three Fates, the three Norns, the three Graces, that can make each man a king and all women queens. We are the fays who croon over cradles, crown heroes in their heyday, gather them to the Fortunate Isles at last. Your warfare is finished, Arthur. Your work is over.

'Morgan is coming, after all! I knew she could not refuse me. She has ointments more precious than the wisdom of all the physicians in the world. She has healed dying men before, when all other hope was lost. She will save my life!'

Yes, Arthur, my brother. I will heal you.

We glide towards the shore, and the mere widens in a vast dark sigh to let us pass.

Three queens are coming. We were royal women before we took our earthly husbands' coronets. Power was born in our blood. We hold authority, over life, over death, over loving, over hating. We come to hail our brother. This is King Arthur. Praise him! This is more than the Imperator, Duke of Battles, clad in Roman leather and steel, rallying Christianised chieftains to defend the Island. He is more than a courageous Celt, victorious against Saxons for a while. More than the myth of an almost-forgotten god, whom no one worships now, leading his preposterous war-band through the wild hunts of folk-tales. We come for King Arthur of Britain. And in our empty hands we hold his immortality. This night we shall give him that lasting life for which he always craved. No dubious battle-site shall confine him to a page of history. No spurious grave shall hold him, crumbling to dust. Our advent this night shall crown him with an unforgettable name. In his departure he shall endure for ever.

The ship slows, and the sail unbidden spills the breeze. Still we glide forward, and a tension grips us now for we are coming into the moment of greatest danger. Is he weakened enough? Is he weaponless, powerless, lost enough to accept the gift that only we can offer? Creep on, my ship, through the soft sibilance of wavelets to the muddied earthly shore and the bloodied man with hope still in his eyes.

'My sight is clouding, Bedwyr. What colour is the sail?'

'Black, my lord.'

Keep courage, Arthur. For letting go of the land you shall have Paradise, the Fortunate Isles, the Realm of the Ever-Young. Palaces of coral and crystal, golden apples on every silver-branched tree. Swift-racing, dappled horses, lovely women, strong, fair-limbed heroes, who once fell gashed with wounds. Feasting and wine and dancing and song, song, song!

'No, Bedwyr, no! Say it is not that dreaded barge of souls!'

Sing, sisters! Call down magic from the moon. Weave harmonies of healing, lullabies of love. Drown out his cries. Faster, my ship. He may slip from us yet in this last foot of water.

'Morgan has betrayed me! The murdering, lying bitch! I asked for life and she has raised the black sail of my death!'

Gently grounding now. A shudder runs through the ship. Reach out my arms.

'Come.'

For you, little brother, there will be the greatest myth of all. Where is the grave of Arthur? A mystery! He is not dead, but sleeping somewhere. In Britain's darkest hour someone will blow the horn and he will leap to his feet with a hundred knights at his side and his white mare Llamrei pawing the ground.

Arthur cannot die. I will not let him.

He is weeping like a baby. Bedwyr is cradling him on his shoulder. Does he understand? My hands touch the stiffening shirt of leather, the chilly arms.

'Brother.'

Sobbing in helpless rage and furious disappointment.

'*Arthur!*'

He has nothing left to fight me with. He has thrown away his wife, son, sword.

'My dearest heart.'

'You have cheated me!'

He is in my arms now, held close to my breast. He shudders like a frightened hound as we lift him lightly into our barge. Be easy, my love.

His head is resting now in Elaine's wide, soft lap as she strokes his temples. Margawse's fragrant hair tumbles over his chest as she kneels by his side. I hug his feet against my heart.

The silver night in the west is ablaze with exultation. The heavens are dancing. The land is going. Over our bows the ocean tosses jewelled manes, and to the far horizon all the stars are singing the great king home.

The breeze is fresh on the tears of my cheeks, scented with may-blossom.

# Chapter Seventy-two

*I am the woman of your fantasies.*

*We need our fictions.*

*I have been given many roles, benevolent, ambiguous, wicked. I am indeed the Shape-Shifter, as my tale is transmuted down the centuries.*

*No, not my tale. Never till now my own story. I am the immortal fay, the faery mistress, the wicked witch. But it is the deeds of the human hero you would rather hear, a myth in which you seek to find yourself. Morgan is required only to serve the author's purpose.*

*It is Arthur's story you want to read, not mine. Or the love-affair of Lancelot and Gwenhyvar. Or the Quest for the Holy Grail.*

*For each telling, I become what you need me to be. Lover, mother, enemy.*

*In a tale of kings and warriors, I am the goddess who invites Arthur to my island of bliss, the hero's just reward.*

*As the story of the Sovereignty of Britain develops, someone must betray King Arthur. After all, he has Caliburn now. He cannot be defeated in fair fight, can he? Very well, I am that traitor, working by treacherous magic to bring his kingdom down. I plot against his life. I steal his scabbard. I cause his death.*

*When the Norman French become jealous of British heroes and their own knight, Lancelot of the Lake, takes the centre stage, I shift my attention from Arthur. In these courtly romances I am now the jealous temptress spurned by Lancelot, wreaking my vengeance on the lovers. I betray them to Arthur. I destroy the fellowship of the Round Table. Arthur loses the knights who could have saved him. I am responsible for the final tragedy.*

*Do more spiritual writers turn to the Quest for the Holy Grail? I play little part in their story. Even Arthur gives place to the saintly Galahad. Safer to shun me. Pagan, female, I am a dangerous, beautiful woman who turns foul and ugly when I take up the devil's arts.*

*Malory fixes the most powerful image of me. I am the vicious villainess. The evidence is there in his sources. It is partly true. But even he suggests at the end it may not be the whole truth.*

*The original fairy tradition lives on, in Brittany, Sicily. I am overwhelmingly generous to men who please me, alluring, autocratic, ambiguous.*

*The Victorians, like Tennyson, prefer to draw a modest veil over me. Uther, Ygerne, Margawse, Modred, Morgan: best not explore our relationships with the noble King Arthur too closely. Between us, blood and semen have mixed more nearly than the prudish might wish to know. Better a baby washed in from the Otherworld with choirs of angels. Better to say that Modred is*

*'my sister's son — no kin of mine',*

and opposes Arthur from pure wickedness. Better not even mention Arthur has other sisters. Merlyn the sorcerer may fall to the wiles of Vivian. Arthur the king must be stainless.

The twentieth-century writers have no such inhibitions. I am, I must be, the bloodthirsty Morrigan. They seize upon this portrayal of my character with gusto. Malory's version is triumphant. I am the vindictive witch, the figure of evil, the arch-enemy. Arthur is always the goodie. Forget the Lives of Saint Cadoc and St Padarn, which paint him as a free-booting, lustful brigand at odds with the Church. Any evidence that points to ambivalence in either of us is rejected.

In countless children's stories, fantasy novels, television romps and second-rate films I am the unthinking stereotype of the satanic. I may appear beautiful but malevolent, or ugly in face and warped in character. I am a terrifying sorceress, but in the end I am ever thwarted, always the baddie, always the loser.

So, in John Boorman's film Excalibur, you see Merlin tempt me to use once too often the magic I wheedled out of him. Before your eyes I shrivel from a sensuous beauty to a hideous old crone, and die. When the ship comes for the wounded Arthur after Camlann, it cannot be I who carries him to Avalon.

So, in Stephen Lawhead's Pendragon Cycle, I become the poison, the viper, the black-clad embodiment of the powers of darkness. I am entirely possessed by evil. Again, I cannot heal Arthur. I am killed before the final battle. Arthur is wholly good. There is no fault in him. This is the Christ-figure.

In Nikolai Tolstoy's The Coming of the King, women are almost invisible. But Morgan is here, the malevolent hag, the Washer at the Ford, the attacking Shape-Shifter. Wholly wicked.

This is the standard picture. What makes these men seize upon this polarity so avidly? Is it so difficult for them to recognise ambivalence? Why do they find it essential to whiten Arthur's or Merlyn's name and blacken mine? Why must they so select or distort the evidence to deify the man and demonise the woman? Does this tell you more about them than about me?

One struggles to admit a tiny ray of truth.

In T.H. White's The Once and Future King, Morgan is queen over the fairies.

'They have no hearts. It is not so much that they wish to do evil, but that if you were to catch one and cut it open, you would find no heart inside. They are cold-blooded, like fish.'

Margawse is boiling a cat:

'She was not a serious witch like her sister Morgan le Fay. She was doing it because the little magics ran in her blood — as they did with all the women of her race.'

When young Arthur finds me, I am in my magical house in a lake of milk. It is made of butter and cheese and tripe and chitterlings. My prisoners

*are lashed to columns of pork. I am stretched on a bed of glorious lard.
At the approach of an iron knife I writhe in agony like a slug before my
castle collapses.*

This is standard stuff. But when Arthur becomes king he observes,

> 'If my father killed the Queen of Orkney's father, then I think she has
> a good reason for wanting her husband to rebel against me.'

To which Merlin replies,

> 'It is only a personal reason. Personal reasons are no excuse for war.'

Even in the more thoughtful treatments of Morgan the trap awaits us all
to vilify Margawse.
The women writers struggle with our sisterhood.
Rosemary Sutcliffe's Sword at Sunset *finds a down-to-earth explanation
for Arthur's success in the introduction of heavy cavalry. Little place for
an enchantress here. But Ygerne is Arthur's unknown sister by Uther
Pendragon. She lures him to become the father of Medraut in revenge for
her mother.*

> 'I saw a woman and a child, a woman and a girl, beside the peat fire
> in this place, the one teaching and the other absorbing that corroding,
> soul-destroying lesson of hate. All at once I saw that what I had taken
> for the ruins of beauty in Ygerne's face was the promise of beauty that
> had been cankered before ever it could come to flowering and for one
> instant pity mingled with the horror that was rising like vomit in my
> throat. What had I let loose? What had my father let loose before me,
> into the world?'

To Mary Stewart, then: The Wicked Day. *In earlier books, I am the
wronged younger daughter, betrothed to Lot of Orkney, but then palmed
off on Urbgen so that Margawse can marry Lot. But now:*

> 'Morgan's natural aptitude for sorcery had already led her to surpass
> the witch of Orkney, with her sex potions and poisonous spells, by almost
> as much as Merlin in his day surpassed them both. And none of it was
> used for good.'

Margawse's motives are personal, mine political. I plot against Urbgen
and Arthur to achieve greater power for myself. So at the end I can be trusted
to tend the wounded Arthur, because

> 'without him she was, and would be, nothing.'

And so at last to Marion Bradley's The Mists of Avalon. *The feminist
version. A novel for the late twentieth century. Here is indeed my story,
not Arthur's. See it fresh through my woman's eyes. It looks very different.
I am the heroine, much misunderstood. Bradley extols my paganism as much*

*as Lawhead curses it. She rails against the Church as passionately as he praises it. Only at the end we sense a partial reconciliation with the nuns, the converse of Malory's with the hooded queens.*

*We are all trapped by the metaphors of warfare, opposing sides, the Either/Or.*

*Morgan is rooted in circularity, in ambiguity. I am Both/And.*

*Well, you may do with me what you will. I am the Shape-Shifter. I can assume whatever form you wish me to take. Each author alters my myth to serve their particular purpose.*

*No doubt Fay Sampson is using me here for her own ends.*

*This will not be the last you hear of me.*

# Epilogue

How could you understand?

He is not your lover.

You do not wail to see his blood staining your dress.

He is not your brother.

You did not hear your father's wife cry out in the treacherous, shape-shifting, face-changing moonlight as Uther Pendragon twined himself upon her.

He was not your king, though in him you find your definition of kingship.

He is not your dead.

Shield him gently as our ship begins to rock. He cannot shrink from me now as my tender hands caress his face. This gold-bearded, white-lipped, blood-crusted face pillowed in the lap of Elaine.

Close his eyes. The blue, fierce, staring, kingly eyes that will scan no more British battlefields.

Margawse weeps as her trembling fingers unlatch the clotted buckles of his armour.

You do not know what you have to thank him for.

You have nothing to forgive him.

Nimue has left him.

He was never Gwenhyvar's, that was not worth a broken fingernail to him.

He has slain Modred.

But first and last and always he was ours.

Sleep, Arthur. My golden bed awaits you. One night will cancel out a lifetime's pain. When you wake, all will be well.

Night arches over us. Caliburn has blazed for the last time between the stars.

This mere is dark. Glide on, my boat. The king is sleeping soundly.

The river is wide. His breath grows faint. Sail swift, my ship.

Dream well, my love. Morgan Sea-Born is singing the lay of healing.

The sky is brightening. The ocean is dancing. Glory is all about us.

Fly on, my ship. Beyond the Island of the Mighty, beyond the western sea, out past the farthest reach of sunset.

In Avalon the sword will meet its scabbard.

Welcome to my bed, Arthur.

# Bibliography

Many of the older sources are available in a variety of editions and translations. I have listed here some of those I used.

*Trioedd Ynys Pridein, The Welsh Triads* edited by Rachel Bromwich. (University of Wales Press)
*Arthurian Romances* by Chrétien de Troyes. (Dent)
*The History of the Kings of Britain* by Geoffrey of Monmouth. (Folio Society)
*Life of Merlin* by Geoffrey of Monmouth. (University of Wales Press)
*The Mabinogion* translated by Lady Charlotte Guest. (Dent)
*The Mabinogion* translated by Gwyn Jones and Thomas Jones. (Dent)
*Arthurian Literature in the Middle Ages* by R. S. Loomis. (O.U.P.)
*Celtic Myth and Arthurian Romance* by R. S. Loomis. (Hashell House)
*Wales and the Arthurian Legend* by R. S. Loomis. (University of Wales Press)
*Le Morte d'Arthur* by Sir Thomas Malory. (Penguin)
*British History and the Welsh Annals* by Nennius. (Phillimore)
*Studies in the Fairy Mythology of Arthurian Romance* by Lucy Paton. (Franklin)
*Taliesin Poems* translated by Meirion Pennar. (Llanerch)
*Four Ancient Books of Wales* translated by W. F. Skene. (Edmonston and Douglas)
*The Vulgate Version of the Arthurian Romances* edited by Oskar Sommer. (Carnegie Institution of Washington)
*Sir Gawain and the Green Knight* translated by Brian Stone. (Penguin)
*The Works of Tennyson.* (Macmillan)
*Arthurian Chronicles* by Wace and Layamon. (Dent)
*The Poems of Taliesin* edited by Ifor Williams. (Dublin Institute for Advanced Studies)

I am grateful to Martin Myhill and his assistants at the University of Exeter Library for helping me to track down numerous articles and dissertations dealing with the figure of Morgan.

The modern novels referred to are:

*The Mists of Avalon* by Marion Bradley. (Michael Joseph/Sphere)
*The Pendragon Cycle* by Stephen Lawhead. (Lion)
*The Merlin Trilogy* by Mary Stewart. (Hodder and Stoughton)
*The Wicked Day* by Mary Stewart. (Hodder and Stoughton)

*Sword at Sunset* by Rosemary Sutcliffe. (Hodder and Stoughton)
*The Coming of the King* by Nikolai Tolstoy. (Bantam/Corgi)
*The Once and Future King* by T. H. White. (HarperCollins Publishers
  Ltd)

My thanks are due to the authors and publishers given above for
permission to quote copyright material from Rachel Bromwich's edition
of *The Welsh Triads* throughout (with some spellings changed), from
Meirion Pennar's translation of the *Taliesin Poems* on pp. 637–8 (lines
drawn from several poems), 764, and from T. H. White's *The Once
and Future King*, Rosemary Sutcliffe's *Sword at Sunset*, and Mary
Stewart's *The Wicked Day* in chapter Seventy-two.